BAMBI

BAMBI

A Life in the Woods

FELIX SALTEN

Illustrated by RICHARD COWDREY

Aladdin

New York   London   Toronto   Sydney   New Delhi

ALADDIN

An imprint of Simon & Schuster Children's Publishing Division
1230 Avenue of the Americas, New York, NY 10020
This Aladdin paperback edition February 2013
Copyright © 1926 by Paul Zsolnay Verlag
Copyright renewed © 1954 by Anna Wyler Salten
English language translation copyright © 1928 by Simon & Schuster, Inc.
English language translation copyright renewed © 1956 by Simon & Schuster, Inc.
Illustrations copyright © 2013 by Richard Cowdrey
All rights reserved, including the right of reproduction
in whole or in part in any form.
ALADDIN is a trademark of Simon & Schuster, Inc., and related logo
is a registered trademark of Simon & Schuster, Inc.
Also available in an Aladdin hardcover edition.
For information about special discounts for bulk purchases,
please contact Simon & Schuster Special Sales at 1-866-506-1949
or business@simonandschuster.com.
Designed by Hilary Zarycky
The text of this book was set in Yana.
Manufactured in the United States of America 0319 OFF
4 6 8 10 9 7 5 3
Library of Congress Control Number 74-124383
ISBN 978-1-4424-6746-0 (hc)
ISBN 978-1-4424-6745-3 (pbk)
ISBN 978-1-4424-8680-5 (eBook)

FOREWORD

Bambi is a delicious book. Delicious not only for children but for those who are no longer so fortunate. For delicacy of perception and essential truth I hardly know any story of animals that can stand beside this life study of a forest deer. Felix Salten is a poet. He feels nature deeply, and he loves animals. I do not, as a rule, like the method which places human words in the mouths of dumb creatures, and it is the triumph of this book that, behind the conversation, one feels the real sensations of the creatures who speak. Clear and illuminating, and in places very moving, it is a little masterpiece.

I read it in galley proof on the way from Paris to Calais, before a channel crossing. As I finished each sheet I handed it to my wife, who read and handed it to my nephew's wife, who read and handed it to my nephew. For three hours the four of us read thus in silent absorption. Those who know what it is to read books in galley proof, and have experienced channel crossings, will realize that few books will stand such a test. *Bambi* is one of them. I particularly recommend it to sportsmen.

John Galsworthy
March 16, 1928

BAMBI

Chapter One

HE CAME INTO THE WORLD IN the middle of the thicket, in one of those little, hidden forest glades which seem to be entirely open but are really screened in on all sides. There was very little room in it, scarcely enough for him and his mother.

He stood there, swaying unsteadily on his thin legs and staring vaguely in front of him with clouded eyes which saw nothing. He hung his head, trembled a great deal, and was still completely stunned.

"What a beautiful child," cried the magpie.

She had flown past, attracted by the deep groans the mother uttered in her labor. The magpie perched on a neighboring branch. "What a beautiful child," she kept repeating. Receiving no answer, she went on talkatively, "How amazing to think that he should be able to get right up and walk! How interesting! I've never seen the like of it before in all my born days. Of course, I'm still young, only a year out of the nest you might say. But I think it's wonderful. A child like that, hardly a minute in this world, and beginning to walk already! I call that remarkable. Really, I find everything you deer do is remarkable. Can he run too?"

"Of course," replied mother softly. "But you must pardon me if I don't talk with you now. I have so much to do, and I still feel a little faint."

"Don't put yourself out on my account," said the magpie. "I have very little time myself. But you don't see a sight like this every day. Think what a care and bother such things mean to us. The children can't stir once they are out of the egg but lie helpless in the

nest and require an attention, an attention, I repeat, of which you simply can't have any comprehension. What a labor it is to feed them, what a trouble to watch them. Just think for a moment what a strain it is to hunt food for the children and to have to be eternally on guard lest something happen to them. They are helpless if you are not with them. Isn't it the truth? And how long it is before they can move, how long it is before they get their feathers and look like anything at all."

"Pardon," replied the mother, "I wasn't listening."

The magpie flew off. "A stupid soul," she thought to herself, "very nice, but stupid."

The mother scarcely noticed that she was gone. She continued zealously washing her newly-born. She washed him with her tongue, fondling and caressing his body in a sort of warm massage.

The slight thing staggered a little. Under the strokes of her tongue, which softly touched him here and there, he drew himself together and stood still. His little red coat, that was still somewhat tousled, bore fine white spots, and on his vague baby face there was still a deep, sleepy expression.

Round about grew hazel bushes, dogwoods, black-thorns and young elders. Tall maples, beeches and oaks wove a green roof over the thicket and from the firm, dark-brown earth sprang fern fronds, wood vetch and sage. Underneath, the leaves of the violets, which had already bloomed, and of the strawberries, which were just beginning, clung to the ground. Through the thick foliage, the early sunlight filtered in a golden web. The whole forest resounded with myriad voices, was penetrated by them in a joyous agitation. The wood thrush rejoiced incessantly, the doves cooed without stopping, the blackbirds whistled, finches warbled, the titmice chirped. Through the midst of these songs the jay flew, uttering its quarrelsome cry, the magpie mocked them, and the pheasants cackled loud and high. At times the shrill exulting of a woodpecker rose above all the other voices. The call of the falcon shrilled, light and piercing, over the treetops, and the hoarse crow chorus was heard continuously.

The little fawn understood not one of the many songs and calls, not a word of the conversations. He did not even listen to them. Nor did he heed any of the odors which blew through the woods. He heard only the soft licking against his coat that washed him and warmed him and kissed him. And he smelled nothing but his mother's body near him. She smelled good to him and, snuggling closer to her, he hunted eagerly around and found nourishment for his life.

While he suckled, the mother continued to caress her little one. "Bambi," she whispered. Every little while she raised her head and, listening, snuffed the wind. Then she kissed her fawn again, reassured and happy.

"Bambi," she repeated. "My little Bambi."

Chapter Two

IN EARLY SUMMER THE TREES STOOD still under the blue sky, held their limbs outstretched and received the direct rays of the sun. On the shrubs and bushes in the undergrowth, the flowers unfolded their red, white and yellow stars. On some the seed pods had begun to appear again. They perched innumerable on the fine tips of the branches, tender and firm and resolute, and seemed like small, clenched fists. Out of the earth came whole troops of flowers, like motley stars, so that the soil of the twilit forest floor shone with a silent, ardent, colorful gladness. Everything smelled of fresh leaves, of blossoms, of moist clods and green wood. When morning broke, or when the sun went down, the whole woods resounded with a thousand voices, and from morning till night, the bees hummed, the wasps droned, and filled the fragrant stillness with their murmur.

These were the earliest days of Bambi's life. He walked behind his mother on a narrow track that ran through the midst of the bushes. How pleasant it was to walk there. The thick foliage stroked his flanks softly and bent supplely aside. The track appeared to be barred and obstructed in a dozen places, and yet they advanced with the greatest ease. There were tracks like this everywhere, running crisscross through the whole woods. His mother knew them all, and if Bambi sometimes stopped before a bush as if it were an impenetrable green wall, she always found where the path went through, without hesitation or searching.

Bambi questioned her. He loved to ask his mother questions. It was the pleasantest thing for him to ask a question and then to hear what answer his mother would give. Bambi was never surprised that question after question should come into his mind continually and without effort. He found it perfectly natural, and it delighted him very much. It was very delightful, too, to wait expectantly till the answer came. If it turned out the way he wanted, he was satisfied. Sometimes, of course, he did not understand, but that was pleasant also because he was kept busy picturing what he had not understood, in his own way. Sometimes he felt very sure that his mother was not giving him a complete answer, was intentionally not telling him all she knew. And at first, that was very pleasant, too. For then there would remain in him such a lively curiosity, such suspicion, mysteriously and joyously flashing through him, such anticipation, that he would become anxious and happy at the same time, and grow silent.

Once he asked, "Whom does this trail belong to, Mother?"

His mother answered, "To us."

Bambi asked again, "To you and me?"

"Yes."

"To us two?"

"Yes."

"Only to us two?"

"No," said his mother, "to us deer."

"What are deer?" Bambi asked, and laughed.

His mother looked at him from head to foot and laughed too. "You are a deer and I am a deer. We're both deer," she said. "Do you understand?"

Bambi sprang into the air for joy. "Yes, I understand," he said. "I'm a little deer and you're a big deer, aren't you?"

His mother nodded and said, "Now you see."

But Bambi grew serious again. "Are there other deer besides you and me?" he asked.

"Certainly," his mother said. "Many of them."

"Where are they?" cried Bambi.

"Here, everywhere."

"But I don't see them."

"You will soon," she said.

"When?" Bambi stood still, wild with curiosity.

"Soon." The mother walked on quietly. Bambi followed her. He kept silent for he was wondering what "soon" might mean. He came to the conclusion that "soon" was certainly not "now." But he wasn't sure at what time "soon" stopped being "soon" and began to be "a along while." Suddenly he asked, "Who made this trail?"

"We," his mother answered.

Bambi was astonished. "We? You and I?"

The mother said, "Well, we . . . we deer."

Bambi asked, "Which deer?"

They walked on. Bambi was in high spirits and felt like leaping off the path, but he stayed close to his mother. Something rustled in front of them, close to the ground. The fern fronds and wood lettuce concealed something that advanced in violent motion. A thread-like little cry shrilled out piteously; then all was still. Only the leaves and the blades of grass shivered back into place. A ferret had caught a mouse. He came slinking by, slid sideways, and prepared to enjoy his meal.

"What was that?" asked Bambi excitedly.

"Nothing," his mother soothed him.

"But," Bambi trembled, "but I saw it."

"Yes, yes," said his mother. "Don't be frightened. The ferret has killed a mouse." But Bambi was dreadfully frightened. A vast, unknown horror clutched at his heart. It was long before he could speak again. Then he asked, "Why did he kill the mouse?"

"Because—" his mother hesitated. "Let us walk faster," she said, as though something had just occurred to her and as though she had forgotten the question. She began to hurry. Bambi sprang after her.

A long pause ensued. They walked on quietly again. Finally Bambi asked anxiously, "Shall we kill a mouse, too, sometime?"

"No," replied his mother.

"Never?" asked Bambi.

"Never," came the answer.

"Why not?" asked Bambi, relieved.

"Because we never kill anything," said his mother simply.

Bambi grew happy again.

Loud cries were coming from a young ash tree

which stood near their path. The mother went along without noticing them, but Bambi stopped inquisitively. Overhead two jays were quarreling about a nest they had plundered.

"Get away, you murderer!" cried one.

"Keep cool, you fool," the other answered, "I'm not afraid of you."

"Look for your own nests," the first one shouted, "or I'll break your head for you." He was beside himself with rage. "What vulgarity!" he chattered. "What vulgarity!"

The other jay had spied Bambi and fluttered down a few branches to shout at him. "What are you gawking at, you freak?" he screamed.

Bambi sprang away, terrified. He reached his mother and walked behind her again, frightened and obedient, thinking she had not noticed his absence.

After a pause he asked, "Mother, what is vulgarity?"

"I don't know," said his mother.

Bambi thought a while; then he began again. "Why were they both so angry with each other, Mother?" he asked.

"They were fighting over food," his mother answered.

"Will we fight over food, too, sometime?" Bambi asked.

"No," said his mother.

Bambi asked, "Why not?"

"Because there is enough for all of us," his mother replied.

Bambi wanted to know something else. "Mother," he began.

"What is it?"

"Will we be angry with each other sometime?" he asked.

"No, child," said his mother, "we don't do such things."

They walked along again. Presently it grew light ahead of them. It grew very bright. The trail ended with the tangle of vines and bushes. A few steps more and they would be in the bright open space that spread out before them. Bambi wanted to bound forward, but his mother had stopped.

"What is it?" he asked impatiently, already delighted.

"It's the meadow," his mother answered.

"What is a meadow?" asked Bambi insistently.

His mother cut him short. "You'll soon find out for yourself," she said. She had become very serious and watchful. She stood motionless, holding her head high and listening intently. She sucked in deep breathfuls of air and looked very severe.

"It's all right," she said at last, "we can go out."

Bambi leaped forward, but his mother barred the way.

"Wait till I call you," she said. Bambi obeyed at once and stood still. "That's right," said his mother, to encourage him, "and now listen to what I am saying to you." Bambi heard how seriously his mother spoke and felt terribly excited.

"Walking on the meadow is not so simple," his mother went on. "It's a difficult and dangerous business. Don't ask me why. You'll find that out later on. Now do exactly as I tell you to. Will you?"

"Yes," Bambi promised.

"Good," said his mother. "I'm going out alone first.

Stay here and wait. And don't take your eyes off me for a minute. If you see me run back here, then turn round and run as fast as you can. I'll catch up with you soon." She grew silent and seemed to be thinking. Then she went on earnestly. "Run away as fast as your legs will carry you. Run even if something should happen . . . even if you should see me fall to the ground. . . . Don't think of me, do you understand? No matter what you see or hear, start running right away and just as fast as you possibly can. Do you promise me to do that?"

"Yes," said Bambi softly. His mother spoke so seriously.

She went on speaking. "Out there if I should call you," she said, "there must be no looking around and no questions, but you must get behind me instantly. Understand that. Run without pausing or stopping to think. If I begin to run, that means for you to run, too, and no stopping until we are back here again. You won't forget, will you?"

"No," said Bambi in a troubled voice.

"Now I'm going ahead," said his mother, and seemed to become calmer.

She walked out. Bambi, who never took his eyes off her, saw how she moved forward with slow, cautious steps. He stood there full of expectancy, full of fear and curiosity. He saw how his mother listened in all directions, saw her shrink together, and shrank together himself, ready to leap back into the thickets. Then his mother grew calm again. She stretched herself. Then she looked around satisfied and called, "Come!"

Bambi bounded out. Joy seized him with such tremendous force that he forgot his worries in a flash. Through the thicket he could see only the green treetops overhead. Once in a while he caught a glimpse of the blue sky.

Now he saw the whole heaven stretching far and wide, and he rejoiced without knowing why. In the forest he had seen only a stray sunbeam now and then, or the tender, dappled light that played through the branches. Suddenly he was standing in the blinding hot sunlight whose boundless power was beaming upon him. He stood in the splendid warmth that made him shut his eyes but which opened his heart.

Bambi was as though bewitched. He was completely

beside himself with pleasure. He was simply wild. He leaped into the air three, four, five times. He had to do it. He felt a terrible desire to leap and jump. He stretched his young limbs joyfully. His breath came deeply and easily. He drank in the air. The sweet smell of the meadow made him so wildly happy that he had to leap into the air.

Bambi was a child. If he had been a human child he would have shouted. But he was a young deer, and deer cannot shout, at least not the way human children do. So he rejoiced with his legs and with his whole body as he flung himself into the air. His mother stood by and was glad. She saw that Bambi was wild. She watched how he bounded into the air and fell again awkwardly, in one spot. She saw how he stared around him, dazed and bewildered, only to leap up over and over again. She understood that Bambi knew only the narrow deer tracks in the forest and how his brief life was used to the limits of the thicket. He did not move from one place because he did not understand how to run freely around the open meadow.

So she stretched out her forefeet and bent laughingly toward Bambi for a moment. Then she was off with one bound, racing around in a circle so that the tall grass stems swished.

Bambi was frightened and stood motionless. Was that a sign for him to run back to the thicket? His mother had said to him, "Don't worry about me no matter what you see or hear. Just run as fast as you can." He was going to turn around and run as she had commanded him to, but his mother came galloping up suddenly. She came up with a wonderful swishing sound and stopped two steps from him. She bent toward him, laughing as she had at first, and cried, "Catch me." And in a flash she was gone.

Bambi was puzzled. What did she mean? Then she came back again running so fast that it made him giddy. She pushed his flank with her nose and said quickly, "Try to catch me," and fled away.

Bambi started after her. He took a few steps. Then his steps became short bounds. He felt as if he were flying without any effort on his part. There was a space under his hoofs, space under his bounding feet, space and still more space. Bambi was beside himself with joy.

The swishing grass sounded wonderful to his ears. It was marvelously soft and as fine as silk where it brushed against him. He ran around in a circle. He turned and flew off in a new circle, turned around again and kept running.

His mother was standing still, getting her breath again. She kept following Bambi with her eyes. He was wild.

Suddenly the race was over. He stopped and came up to his mother, lifting his hoofs elegantly. He looked joyfully at her. Then they strolled contentedly side by side.

Since he had been in the open. Bambi had felt the sky and the sun and the green meadow with his whole body. He took one blinding, giddy glance at the sun, and he felt its rays as they lay warmly on his back.

Presently he began to enjoy the meadow with his eyes also. Its wonders amazed him at every step he took.

You could not see the tiniest speck of earth the way you could in the forest. Blade after blade of grass covered every inch of the ground. It tossed and waved luxuriantly. It bent softly aside under every footstep, only to rise up unharmed again. The broad green meadow was starred with white daisies, with the thick, round red and purple clover blossoms and bright, golden dandelion heads.

"Look, look, Mother!" Bambi exclaimed. "There's a flower flying."

"That's not a flower," said his mother, "that's a butterfly."

Bambi stared at the butterfly, entranced. It had darted lightly from a blade of grass and was fluttering about in its giddy way. Then Bambi saw that there were many butterflies flying in the air above the meadow. They seemed to be in a hurry and yet moved slowly, fluttering up and down in a sort of game that delighted him. They really did look like gay flying flowers that would not stay on their stems but had unfastened themselves in order to dance a little. They looked, too, like flowers that come to rest at sundown but have no fixed places and have to hunt for them, dropping down and vanishing as if they really had settled somewhere, yet always flying up again, a little way at first, then higher and higher, and always searching farther and farther because all the good places have already been taken.

Bambi gazed at them all. He would have loved to see one close by. He wanted to see one face to face but he could not. They flew in and out continually. The air was aflutter with them.

When he looked down at the ground again he was delighted with the thousands of living things he saw stirring under his hoofs. They ran and jumped in all directions. He would see a wild swarm of them, and the next moment they had disappeared in the grass again.

"Who are they, Mother?" he asked.

"Those are ants," his mother answered.

"Look," cried Bambi, "see that piece of grass jumping. Look how high it can jump!"

"That's not grass," his mother explained, "that's a nice grasshopper."

"Why does he jump that way?" asked Bambi.

"Because we're walking here," his mother answered; "he's afraid we'll step on him."

"Oh," said Bambi, turning to the grasshopper, who was sitting on a daisy; "oh," he said again politely, "you don't have to be afraid; we won't hurt you."

"I'm not afraid," the grasshopper replied in a quavering voice; "I was only frightened for a moment when I was talking to my wife."

"Excuse us for disturbing you," said Bambi shyly.

"Not at all," the grasshopper quavered. "Since it's you, it's perfectly all right. But you never know who's coming and you have to be careful."

"This is the first time in my life that I've ever been on the meadow," Bambi explained; "my mother brought me. . . ."

The grasshopper was sitting with his head lowered as though he were going to butt. He put on a serious face and murmured, "That doesn't interest me at all. I haven't time to stand here gossiping with you. I have to be looking for my wife. Hopp!" And he gave a jump.

"Hopp!" said Bambi in surprise at the high jump with which the grasshopper vanished.

Bambi ran to his mother. "Mother, I spoke to him," he cried.

"To whom?" his mother asked.

"To the grasshopper," Bambi said, "I spoke to him. He was very nice to me. And I like him so much. He's so wonderful and green and you can see through his sides. They look like leaves, but you can't see through a leaf."

"Those are his wings," said his mother.

"Oh," Bambi went on, "and his face is so serious and wise. But he was very nice to me anyhow. And how he can jump! 'Hopp!' he said, and he jumped so high I couldn't see him any more."

They walked on. The conversation with the grasshopper had excited Bambi and tired him a little, for it was the first time he had ever spoken to a stranger. He felt hungry and pressed close to his mother to be nursed.

Then he stood quietly and gazed dreamily into space for a little while with a sort of joyous ecstasy that came over him every time he was nursed by his mother. He noticed a bright flower moving in the tangled grasses. Bambi looked more closely at it. No, it wasn't a flower, but a butterfly. Bambi crept closer.

The butterfly hung heavily to a grass stem and fanned its wings slowly.

"Please sit still," Bambi said.

"Why would I sit still? I'm a butterfly," the insect answered in astonishment.

"Oh, please sit still, just for a minute," Bambi pleaded; "I've wanted so much to see you close to. Please?"

"Well," said the butterfly, "for your sake I will, but not for long."

Bambi stood in front of him. "How beautiful you are!" he cried, fascinated. "How wonderfully beautiful, like a flower!"

"What?" cried the butterfly, fanning his wings. "Did you say like a flower? In my circle it's generally supposed that we're handsomer than flowers."

Bambi was embarrassed. "Oh, yes," he stammered, "much handsomer, excuse me, I only meant . . ."

"Whatever you meant is all one to me," the butterfly replied. He arched his thin body affectedly and played with his delicate feelers.

Bambi looked at him, enchanted. "How elegant you are!" he said. "How elegant and fine! And how splendid and white your wings are!"

The butterfly spread his wings wide apart, then raised them till they folded together like an upright sail.

"Oh," cried Bambi, "I know that you are handsomer than the flowers. Besides, you can fly and the flowers can't because they grow on stems, that's why."

The butterfly spread his wings. "It's enough," he said, "that I can fly." He soared so lightly that Bambi could hardly see him or follow his flight. His wings moved gently and gracefully. Then he fluttered into the sunny air.

"I only sat still that long on your account," he said, balancing in the air in front of Bambi. "Now I'm going."

That was how Bambi found the meadow.

Chapter Three

IN THE HEART OF THE FOREST WAS A little glade that belonged to Bambi's mother. It lay only a few steps from the narrow trail where the deer went bounding through the woods. But no one could ever have found it who did not know the little passage leading to it through the thick bushes.

The glade was very narrow, so narrow that there was only room for Bambi and his mother, and so low that when Bambi's mother stood up her head was hidden among the branches. Sprays of hazel, furze and dogwood, woven about each other, intercepted the little bit of sunlight that came through the treetops, so that it never reached the ground. Bambi had come into the world in this glade. It was his mother's and his.

His mother was lying asleep on the ground. Bambi had dozed a little, too. But suddenly he had become wide awake. He got up and looked around.

The shadows were so deep where he was that it was almost dark. From the woods came soft rustlings. Now and again the titmice chirped. Now and again came the clear hammering of the woodpecker or the joyless call of a crow. Everything else was still, far and wide. But the air was sizzling in the midday heat so that you could hear it if you listened closely. And it was stiflingly sweet.

Bambi looked down at his mother and said, "Are you asleep?"

No, his mother was not sleeping. She had awakened the moment Bambi got up.

"What are we going to do now?" Bambi asked.

"Nothing," his mother answered. "We're going to

stay right where we are. Lie down, like a good boy, and go to sleep."

But Bambi had no desire to go to sleep. "Come on," he begged, "let's go to the meadow."

His mother lifted her head. "Go to the meadow," she said, "go to the meadow now?" Her voice was so full of astonishment and terror that Bambi became quite frightened.

"Can't we go to the meadow?" he asked timidly.

"No," his mother answered, and it sounded very final. "No, you can't go now."

"Why?" Bambi perceived that something mysterious was involved. He grew still more frightened, but at the same time he was terribly anxious to know everything. "Why can't we go to the meadow?" he asked.

"You'll find out all about it later when you're bigger," his mother replied.

"But," Bambi insisted, "I'd rather know now."

"Later," his mother repeated. "You're nothing but a baby yet," she went on tenderly, "and we don't talk about such things to children." She had grown quite serious. "Fancy going to the meadow at this time of day. I don't even like to think of it. Why, it's broad daylight."

"But it was broad daylight when we went to the meadow before," Bambi objected.

"That's different," his mother explained; "it was early in the morning."

"Can we only go there early in the morning?" Bambi was very curious.

His mother was patient. "Only in the early morning or late evening," she said, "or at night."

"And never in the daytime, never?"

His mother hesitated. "Well," she said at last, "sometimes a few of us do go there in the daytime.... But those are special occasions.... I can't just explain it to you, you are too young yet.... Some of us do go there.... But we are exposed to the greatest danger."

"What kind of danger?" asked Bambi, all attention.

But his mother did not want to go on with the conversation. "We're in danger, and that's enough for you, my son. You can't understand such things yet."

Bambi thought that he could understand everything except why his mother did not want to tell him the truth. But he kept silent.

"That's what life means for us," his mother went on. "Though we all love the daylight, especially when we're young, we have to lie quiet all day long. We can only roam around from evening till morning. Do you understand?"

"Yes," said Bambi.

"So, my son, we'll have to stay where we are. We're safe here. Now lie down again and go to sleep."

But Bambi didn't want to lie down. "Why are we safe here?" he asked.

"Because all the bushes shield us," his mother answered, "and the twigs snap on the shrubs and the dry twigs crackle and give us warning. And last year's dead leaves lie on the ground and rustle to warn us, and the jays and magpies keep watch so we can tell from a distance if anybody is coming."

"What are last year's leaves?" Bambi asked.

"Come and sit beside me," said his mother, "and I will tell you." Bambi sat down contentedly, nestling close to his mother. And she told him how the trees are not always green, how the sunshine and the pleasant warmth disappear. Then it grows cold, the frost turns the leaves yellow, brown and red, and they fall slowly so that the trees and bushes stretch their bare branches to the sky and look perfectly naked. But the dry leaves lie on the ground, and when a foot stirs them they rustle. Then someone is coming. Oh, how kind last year's dead leaves are! They do their duty so well and are so alert and watchful. Even in midsummer there are a lot of them hidden beneath the undergrowth. And they give warning in advance of every danger.

Bambi pressed close against his mother. It was so cozy to sit there and listen while his mother talked.

When she grew silent he began to think. He thought it was very kind of the good old leaves to keep watch, though they were all dead and frozen and had suffered so much. He wondered just what that danger could be that his mother was always talking about. But too much thought tired him. Round about him it was still. Only the air sizzling in the heat was audible. Then he fell asleep.

Chapter Four

ONE EVENING BAMBI WAS ROAM-
ing about the meadow again with his
mother. He thought that he knew everything there was to see or hear there. But
in reality it appeared that he did not know as much as
he thought.

This time was just like the first. Bambi played tag
with his mother. He ran around in circles, and the open
space, the deep sky, the fresh air intoxicated him so that
he grew perfectly wild. After a while he noticed that

his mother was standing still. He stopped short in the middle of a leap so suddenly that his four legs spread far apart. To get his balance he bounded high into the air and then stood erect. His mother seemed to be talking to someone he couldn't make out through the tall grasses. Bambi toddled up inquisitively.

Two long ears were moving in the tangled grass stems close to his mother. They were grayish brown and prettily marked with black stripes. Bambi stopped, but his mother said, "Come here. This is our friend, the Hare. Come here like a nice boy and let him see you."

Bambi went over. There sat the Hare looking like a very honest creature. At times his long spoonlike ears stood bolt upright. At others they fell back limply as though they had suddenly grown weak. Bambi became somewhat critical as he looked at the whiskers that stood out so stiff and straight on both sides of the Hare's mouth. But he noticed that the Hare had a very mild face and extremely good-natured features and that he cast timid glances at the world from out of his big round eyes. The Hare really did look friendly.

Bambi's passing doubts vanished immediately. But oddly enough, he had lost all the respect he originally felt for the Hare.

"Good evening, young man," the Hare greeted him, with studied politeness.

Bambi merely nodded good evening. He didn't understand why, but he simply nodded. He was very friendly and civil, but a little condescending. He could not help himself. Perhaps he was born that way.

"What a charming young prince," said the Hare to Bambi's mother. He looked at Bambi attentively, raising first one spoonlike ear, then the other, and then both of them, and letting them fall again, suddenly and limply, which didn't please Bambi. The motion of the Hare's ears seemed to say. "He isn't worth bothering with."

Meanwhile the Hare continued to study Bambi with his big round eyes. His nose and his mouth with the handsome whiskers moved incessantly in the same way a man who is trying not to sneeze twitches his nose and lips. Bambi had to laugh.

The Hare laughed quickly, too, but his eyes grew

more thoughtful. "I congratulate you," he said to Bambi's mother. "I sincerely congratulate you on your son. Yes, indeed, he'll make a splendid prince in time. Anyone can see that."

To Bambi's boundless surprise he suddenly sat straight on his hind legs. After he had spied all around with his ears stiffened and his nose constantly twitching, he sat down decently on all fours again. "Now if you good people will excuse me," he said at last, "I have all kinds of things to do tonight. If you'll be so good as to excuse me. . . ." He turned away and hopped off with his ears back so that they touched his shoulders.

"Good evening," Bambi called after him.

His mother smiled. "The good Hare," she said; "he is so suave and prudent. He doesn't have an easy time of it in this world." There was sympathy in her voice.

Bambi strolled about a little and left his mother to her meal. He wanted to meet his friend again and he wanted to make new acquaintances, besides. For without being very clear himself what it was he wanted, he felt a certain expectancy. Suddenly, at a distance, he heard a soft rustling on the meadow, and felt a quick, gentle step tapping the ground. He peered ahead of him. Over on the edge of the woods something was gliding through the grasses. Was it alive? No, there were two things. Bambi cast a quick glance at his mother but she wasn't paying attention to anything and had her head deep in the grass. But the game was going on on the other side of the meadow in a shifting circle exactly as Bambi himself had raced around before. Bambi was so excited that he sprang back as if he wanted to run away. Then his mother noticed him and raised her head.

"What's the matter?" she called.

But Bambi was speechless. He could not find his tongue and only stammered, "Look over there."

His mother looked over. "I see," she said, "that's my sister, and sure enough she has a baby too, now. No, she has two of them." His mother spoke at first out of pure happiness, but she had grown serious. "To think that Ena has two babies," she said, "two of them."

Bambi stood gazing across the meadow. He saw a

creature that looked just like his mother. He hadn't even noticed her before. He saw that the grasses were being shaken in a double circle, but only a pair of reddish backs were visible like thin red streaks.

"Come," his mother said, "we'll go over. They'll be company for you."

Bambi would have run, but as his mother walked slowly, peering to right and to left at every step, he held himself back. Still, he was bursting with excitement and very impatient.

"I thought we would meet Ena sometime," his mother went on to say. "Where can she have been keeping herself? I thought I knew she had one child, that wasn't hard to guess. But two of them! . . ."

At last the others saw them and came to meet them. Bambi had to greet his aunt, but his mind was entirely on the children.

His aunt was very friendly. "Well," she said to him, "this is Gobo and that is Faline. Now you run along and play together."

The children stood stock-still and stared at each

other, Gobo close beside Faline and Bambi in front of him. None of them stirred. They stood and gaped.

"Run along," said Bambi's mother, "you'll soon be friends."

"What a lovely child," Aunt Ena replied. "He is really lovely. So strong, and he stands so well."

"Oh well," said his mother modestly, "we have to be content. But to have two of them, Ena! . . ."

"Oh yes, that's all very well," Ena declared; "you know, dear, I've had children before."

"Bambi is my first," his mother said.

"We'll see," Ena comforted her, "perhaps it will be different with you next time, too."

The children were still standing and staring at each other. No one said a word. Suddenly Faline gave a leap and rushed away. It had become too much for her.

In a moment Bambi darted after her. Gobo followed him. They flew around in a semicircle, they turned tail and fell over each other. Then they chased each other up and down. It was glorious. When they stopped, all topsy-turvy and somewhat breathless, they were already good friends. They began to chatter.

Bambi told them how he talked to the nice grass-hopper and the butterfly.

"Did you ever talk to the goldbug?" asked Faline.

No, Bambi had never talked to the goldbug. He did not even know who he was.

"I've talked to him often," Faline declared, a little pertly.

"The jay insulted me," said Bambi.

"Really," said Gobo astonished, "did the jay treat you like that?" Gobo was very easily astonished and was extremely timid.

"Well," he observed, "the hedgehog stuck me in the nose." But he only mentioned it in passing.

"Who is the hedgehog?" Bambi asked eagerly. It seemed wonderful to him to be there with friends, listening to so many exciting things.

"The hedgehog is a terrible creature," cried Faline, "full of long spines all over his body and very wicked!"

"Do you really think he's wicked?" asked Gobo. "He never hurts anybody."

"Is that so?" answered Faline quickly. "Didn't he stick you?"

"Oh, that was only because I wanted to speak to him," Gobo replied, "and only a little anyhow. It didn't hurt me much."

Bambi turned to Gobo. "Why didn't he want you to talk to him?" he asked.

"He doesn't talk to anybody," Faline interrupted; "even if you just come where he is he rolls himself up so he's nothing but prickles all over. Our mother says he's one of those people who don't want to have anything to do with the world."

"Maybe he's only afraid," Gobo said.

But Faline knew better. "Mother says you shouldn't meddle with such people," she said.

Presently, Bambi began to ask Gobo softly, "Do you know what 'danger' means?"

Then they both grew serious and all three heads drew together. Gobo thought a while. He made a special effort to remember for he saw how curious Bambi was for the answer. "Danger," he whispered, "is something very bad."

"Yes," Bambi declared excitedly, "I know it's something very bad, but what?" All three trembled with fear.

Suddenly Faline cried out loudly and joyfully, "I know what danger is—it's what you run away from." She sprang away. She couldn't bear to stay there any longer and be frightened. In an instant, Bambi and Gobo had bounded after her. They began to play again. They tumbled in the rustling, silky green meadow grass and in a twinkling had forgotten all about the absorbing question. After a while they stopped and stood chattering together as before. They looked toward their mothers. They were standing close together, eating a little and carrying on a quiet conversation.

Aunt Ena raised her head and called the children. "Come, Gobo. Come, Faline. We have to go now."

And Bambi's mother said to him, "Come, it's time to go."

"Wait just a little longer," Faline pleaded eagerly, "just a little while."

"Let's stay a little longer, please," Bambi pleaded, "it's

so nice." And Gobo repeated timidly, "It's so nice, just a little longer." All three spoke at once.

Ena looked at Bambi's mother, "What did I tell you," she said, "they won't want to separate now."

Then something happened that was much more exciting than everything else that happened to Bambi that day. Out of the woods came the sound of hoofs beating the earth. Branches snapped, the boughs rustled, and before Bambi had time to listen, something burst out of the thicket. Someone came crashing and rustling with someone else rushing after him. They tore by like the wind, described a wide circle on the meadow and vanished into the woods again, where they could be heard galloping. Then they came bursting out of the thicket again and suddenly stood still, about twenty paces apart.

Bambi looked at them and did not stir. They looked like his mother and Aunt Ena. But their heads were crowned with gleaming antlers covered with brown beads and bright white prongs. Bambi was completely overcome. He looked from one to the other. One was smaller and his antlers narrower. But the other one was stately and beautiful. He carried his head up and his antlers rose high above it. They flashed from dark to light, adorned with the splendor of many black and brown beads and the gleam of the branching white prongs.

"Oh," cried Faline in admiration. "Oh," Gobo repeated softly. But Bambi said nothing. He was entranced and silent. Then they both moved and, turning away from each other, walked slowly back into the woods in opposite directions. The stately stag passed close to the children and Bambi's mother and Aunt Ena. He passed by in silent splendor, holding his noble head royally high and honoring no one with so much as a glance.

The children did not dare to breathe till he had disappeared into the thicket. They turned to look after the other one, but at that very moment the green door of the forest closed on him.

Faline was the first to break the silence. "Who were they?" she cried. But her pert little voice trembled.

"Who were they?" Gobo repeated in a hardly audible voice. Bambi kept silent.

Aunt Ena said solemnly, "Those were your fathers."

Nothing more was said, and they parted. Aunt Ena led her children into the nearest thicket. It was her trail. Bambi and his mother had to cross the whole meadow to the oak in order to reach their own path. He was silent for a long time before he finally asked, "Didn't they see us?"

His mother understood what he meant and replied, "Of course, they saw all of us."

Bambi was troubled. He felt shy about asking questions, but it was too much for him. "Then why . . ." he began, and stopped.

His mother helped him along. "What is it you want to know, son?" she asked.

"Why didn't they stay with us?"

"They don't ever stay with us," his mother answered, "only at times."

Bambi continued, "But why didn't they speak to us?"

His mother said, "They don't speak to us now; only at time. We have to wait till they come to us. And we have to wait for them to speak to us. They do it whenever they like."

With a troubled heart, Bambi asked, "Will my father speak to me?"

"Of course he will," his mother promised. "When you're grown up he'll speak to you, and you'll have to stay with him sometimes."

Bambi walked silently beside his mother, his whole mind filled with his father's appearance. "How handsome he is!" he thought over and over again. "How handsome he is!"

As though his mother could read his thoughts, she said, "If you live, my son, if you are cunning and don't run into danger, you'll be as strong and handsome as your father is sometime, and you'll have antlers like his, too."

Bambi breathed deeply. His heart swelled with joy and expectancy.

Chapter Five

TIME PASSED, AND BAMBI HAD many adventures and went through many experiences. Every day brought something new. Sometimes he felt quite giddy. He had so incredibly much to learn.

He could listen now, not merely hear, when things happened so close that they struck the ear of their own accord. No, there was really no art in that. He could really listen intelligently now to everything that stirred, no matter how softly. He heard even the tiniest whisper that the wind brought by. For instance, he knew that a pheasant was running through the next bushes. He recognized clearly the soft quick tread that was always stopping. He knew by ear the sound the field mice make when they run to and fro on their little paths. And the patter of the moles when they are in a good humor and chase one another around the elder bushes so that there is just the slightest rustling. He heard the shrill clear call of the falcon, and he knew from its altered, angry tones when a hawk or an eagle approached. The falcon was angry because she was afraid her field would be taken from her. He knew the beat of the wood doves' wings, the beautiful, distant, soaring cries of ducks, and many other things besides.

He knew how to snuff the air now, too. Soon he would do it as well as his mother. He could breathe in the air and at the same time analyze it with his senses. "That's clover and meadow grass," he would think when the wind blew off the fields. "And Friend Hare is out there, too. I can smell him plainly."

Again he would notice through the smell of leaves

and earth, wild leek and wood mustard, that the ferret was passing by. He could tell by putting his nose to the ground and snuffing deeply that the fox was afoot. Or he would know that one of his family was somewhere nearby. It might be Aunt Ena and the children.

By now he was good friends with the night and no longer wanted to run about so much in broad daylight. He was quite willing to lie all day long in the shade of the leafy glade with his mother. He would listen to the air sizzling in the heat and then fall asleep.

From time to time he would wake up, listen and snuff the air to find out how things stood. Everything was as it should be. Only the titmice were chattering a little to each other, the midges, who were hardly ever still, hummed, while the wood doves never ceased declaiming their ecstatic tenderness. What concern was it of his? He would drop off to sleep again.

He liked the night very much now. Everything was alive, everything was in motion. Of course, he had to be cautious at night too, but still he could be less careful. And he could go wherever he wanted to. And everywhere he went he met acquaintances. They too were always less nervous than in the daytime.

At night the woods were solemn and still. There were only a few voices. They sounded loud in the stillness, and they had a different ring from daytime voices, and left a deeper impression.

Bambi liked to see the owl. She had such a wonderful flight, perfectly light and perfectly noiseless. She made as little sound as a butterfly, and yet she was so dreadfully big. She had such striking features, too, so pronounced and so deeply thoughtful. And such wonderful eyes! Bambi admired her firm, quietly courageous glance. He liked to listen when she talked to his mother or to anybody else. He would stand a little to one side, for he was somewhat afraid of the masterful glance that he admired so much. He did not understand most of the clever things she said, but he knew they were clever, and they pleased him and filled him with respect for the owl.

Then the owl would begin to hoot. "Hoaah!–Ha!–Ha!–Haa!–ah!" she would cry. It sounded different from the thrushes' song, or the yellowbirds', different from the friendly notes of the cuckoo, but Bambi loved the owl's cry, for he felt its mysterious earnestness, its unutterable wisdom and strange melancholy.

Then there was the screech owl, a charming little fellow, lively and gay with no end to his inquisitiveness. He was bent on attracting attention. "Oi! yeek! oi! yeek!" he would call in a terrible, high-pitched, piercing voice. It sounded as if he were on the point of death. But he was really in a beaming good humor and was hilariously happy whenever he frightened anybody. "Oi! yeek!" he would cry so dreadfully loud that the forests heard it for a mile around. But afterward he would laugh with a soft chuckle, though you could only hear it if you stood close by.

Bambi discovered that the screech owl was delighted whenever he frightened anyone, or when anybody thought that something dreadful had happened to him. After that, whenever Bambi met him, he never failed to rush up and ask, "What has happened to you?" or to say with a sigh, "Oh, how you frightened me just now!" Then the owl would be delighted.

"Oh, yes," he would say, laughing, "it sounds pretty gruesome." He would puff up his feathers into a grayish-white ball and look extremely handsome.

There were storms, too, once or twice, both in the daytime and at night. The first was in the daytime and Bambi felt himself grow terrified as it became darker and darker in his glade. It seemed to him as if night had covered the sky at midday. When the raging storm broke through the woods so that the trees began to groan aloud, Bambi trembled with terror. And when the lightning flashed and the thunder growled, Bambi was numb with fear and thought the end of the world had come. He ran behind his mother, who had sprung up somewhat disturbed and was walking back and forth in the thicket. He could not think about nor understand anything. The rain fell in raging torrents. Everyone had run to shelter. The woods were empty. But there was no escaping the rain. The pouring water penetrated even the thickest parts of the bushes. Presently the lightning stopped, and the fiery rays ceased to flicker through the treetops. The thunder rolled away. Bambi could hear it in the distance, and soon it stopped altogether. The rain beat more gently. It pattered evenly and steadily around him for another hour. The forest stood breathing deeply in the calm and let the water drain off. No one was afraid to come out any more. That feeling had passed. The rain had washed it away.

Never before had Bambi and his mother gone to the meadow as early as on that evening. It was not even dusk yet. The sun was still high in the sky, the air was extremely fresh, and smelled sweeter than usual, and the woods rang with a thousand voices, for everyone had crept out of his shelter and was running excitedly, telling what had just happened.

Before they went on to the meadow, they passed the great oak that stood near the forest's edge, close to their trail. They always had to pass that beautiful big tree when they went to the meadow.

This time the squirrel was sitting on a branch and greeted them. Bambi was good friends with the squirrel. The first time he met him he took him for a very small deer because of the squirrel's red coat and stared at him in surprise. But Bambi had been very childish at that time and had known nothing at all.

The squirrel pleased him greatly from the first. He was so thoroughly civil, and talkative. And Bambi loved to see how wonderfully he could turn, and climb, and leap, and balance himself. In the middle of a conversation the squirrel would run up and down the smooth tree trunk as though there was nothing to it. Or he would sit upright on a swaying branch, balance himself comfortably with his bushy tail that stuck up so gracefully behind him, display his white chest, hold his little forepaws elegantly in front of him, nod his head this way and that, laugh with his jolly eyes, and, in a twinkling, say a lot of comical and interesting things. Then he would come down again, so swiftly and with such leaps that you expected him to tumble on his head.

He twitched his long tail violently and called to them from overhead, "Good day! Good day! It's so nice of you to come over." Bambi and his mother stopped.

The squirrel ran down the smooth trunk. "Well," he chattered, "did you get through it all right? Of course, I see that everything is first rate. That's the main thing."

He ran up the trunk again like lightning and said, "It's too wet for me down there. Wait, I'm going to look for a better place. I hope you don't mind. Thanks, I knew you wouldn't. And we can talk just as well from here."

He ran back and forth along a straight limb. "It was a bad business," he said, "a monstrous uproar! You wouldn't believe how scared I was. I hunched myself up as still as a mouse in the corner and hardly dared move. That's the worst of it. Having to sit there and not move. And all the time you're hoping nothing will happen. But my tree is wonderful in such cases. There's no denying it, my tree is wonderful! I'll say that for it. I'm satisfied with it. As long as I've had it, I've never wanted any other. But when it cuts loose the way it did today you're sure to get frightened no matter where you are."

The squirrel sat up, balancing himself with his handsome upright tail. He displayed his white chest and pressed both forepaws protestingly against his heart. You believed without his adding anything that he had been excited.

"We're going to the meadow now to dry ourselves off in the sun," Bambi's mother said.

"That's a good idea," cried the squirrel, "you're really so clever. I'm always saying how clever you are." With a bound he sprang onto a higher branch. "You couldn't do anything better than go to the meadow now," he called down. Then he swung with light bounds back and forth through the treetop. "I'm going up where I can get the sunlight," he chattered merrily. "I'm all soaked through. I'm going all the way up." He didn't care whether they were still listening to him or not.

The meadow was full of life. Friend Hare was there and had brought along his family. Aunt Ena was there with her children and a few acquaintances. That day Bambi saw the fathers again. They came slowly out of the forest from opposite directions. There was a third stag too. Each walked slowly in his track, back and forth, along the meadow. They paid no attention to anyone and did not even talk to one another. Bambi looked at them frequently. He was respectful, but full of curiosity.

Then he talked to Faline and Gobo and a few other

children. He wanted to play a while. All agreed and they began running around in a circle. Faline was the gayest of all. She was so fresh and nimble and brimming over with bright ideas. But Gobo was soon tired. He had been terribly frightened by the storm. His heart had hammered loudly and was still pounding. There was something very weak about Gobo, but Bambi liked him because he was so good and willing and always a little sad without letting you know it.

Time passed and Bambi was learning how good the meadow grass tasted, how tender and sweet the leaf buds and the clover were. When he nestled against his mother for comfort it often happened that she pushed him away.

"You aren't a little baby any more," she would say. Sometimes she even said abruptly, "Go away and let me be." It even happened sometimes that his mother got up in the little forest glade, got up in the middle of the day, and went off without noticing whether Bambi was following her or not. At times it seemed, when they were wandering down the familiar paths, as if his mother did not want to notice whether Bambi was behind her or was trailing after.

One day his mother was gone. Bambi did not know how such a thing could be possible, he could not figure it out. But his mother was gone and for the first time Bambi was left alone.

He wandered about, he was troubled, he grew worried and anxious and began to want her terribly. He stood quite sadly, calling her. Nobody answered and nobody came.

He listened and snuffed the air. He could not smell anything. He called again. Softly, pathetically, tearfully, he called "Mother, Mother!" In vain.

Then despair seized him, he could not stand it and started to walk.

He wandered down the trails he knew, stopping and calling. He wandered farther and farther with hesitating steps, frightened and helpless. He was very downcast.

He went on and on and came to trails where he had never been before. He came to places that were strange to him. He no longer knew where he was going.

Then he heard two childish voices like his own, calling, "Mother! Mother!" He stood still and listened. Surely that was Gobo and Faline. It must be they.

He ran quickly toward the voices and soon he saw their little red jackets showing through the leaves. Gobo and Faline were standing side by side under a dogwood tree and calling mournfully, "Mother! Mother!"

They were overjoyed when they heard the rustling in the bushes. But they were disappointed when they saw Bambi. They were a little consoled that he was there, however. And Bambi was glad not to be all alone any more.

"My mother is gone," Bambi said.

"Ours is gone too," Gobo answered plaintively.

They looked at one another and were quite despondent.

"Where can they be?" asked Bambi. He was almost sobbing.

"I don't know," sighed Gobo. His heart was pounding and he felt miserable.

Suddenly Faline said, "I think they may be with our fathers."

Gobo and Bambi looked at her surprised. They were filled with awe. "You mean that they're visiting our fathers?" asked Bambi and trembled. Faline trembled too, but she made a wise face. She acted like a person who knows more than she will let on. Of course she knew nothing, she could not even guess where her idea came from. But when Gobo repeated, "Do you really think so?" she put on a meaningful air and answered mysteriously, "Yes, I think so."

Anyway it was a suggestion that needed to be thought about. But in spite of that Bambi felt no easier. He couldn't even think about it, he was too troubled and too sad.

He went off. He wouldn't stay in one place. Faline and Gobo went along with him for a little way. All three were calling, "Mother, Mother!" Then Gobo and Faline stopped, they did not dare go any farther. Faline said, "Why should we? Mother knows where we are. Let's stay here so she can find us when she comes back."

Bambi went on alone. He wandered through a thicket to a little clearing. In the middle of the clearing Bambi stopped short. He suddenly felt as if he were rooted to the ground and could not move.

On the edge of the clearing, by a tall hazel bush, a creature was standing. Bambi had never seen such a creature before. At the same time the air brought him a scent such as he had never smelled in his life. It was a strange smell, heavy and acrid. It excited him to the point of madness.

Bambi stared at the creature. It stood remarkably erect. It was extremely thin and had a pale face; entirely bare around the nose and the eyes. A kind of dread emanated from that face, a cold terror. That face had a tremendous power over him. It was unbearably painful to look at that face and yet Bambi stood staring fixedly at it.

For a long time the creature stood without moving. Then it stretched out a leg from high up near its face. Bambi had not even noticed that there was one there. But as that terrible leg was reaching out into the air Bambi was swept away by the mere gesture. In a flash he was back into the thicket he came from, and was running away.

In a twinkling his mother was with him again, too. She bounded beside him over shrubs and bushes. They ran side by side as fast as they could. His mother was in the lead. She knew the way and Bambi followed. They ran till they came to their glade.

"Did you see Him?" asked the mother softly.

Bambi could not answer, he had no breath left. He only nodded.

"That was He," said the mother.

And they both shuddered.

Chapter Six

BAMBI WAS OFTEN ALONE NOW. But he was not so troubled about it as he had been the first time. His mother would disappear, and no matter how much he called her she wouldn't come back. Later she would appear unexpectedly and stay with him as before.

One night he was roaming around quite forlorn again. He could not even find Gobo and Faline. The sky had become pale gray and it began to darken so that the treetops seemed like a vault over the bushy

undergrowth. There was a swishing in the bushes, a loud rustling came through the leaves and Bambi's mother dashed out. Someone else raced close behind her. Bambi did not know whether it was Aunt Ena or his father or someone else. But he recognized his mother at once. Though she rushed past him so quickly, he had recognized her voice. She screamed, and it seemed to Bambi as if it were in play, though he thought it sounded a little frightened too.

One day Bambi wandered for hours through the thicket. At last he began to call. He simply couldn't bear to be so utterly alone any more. He felt that pretty soon he'd be perfectly miserable. So he began to call for his mother.

Suddenly one of the fathers was standing in front of him looking sternly down at him. Bambi hadn't heard him coming and was terrified. This stag looked more powerful than the others, taller and prouder. His coat shone with a deeper, richer red, but his face shimmered, silver gray. And tall, black, beaded antlers rose high above his nervous ears.

"What are you crying about?" the old stag asked severely. Bambi trembled in awe and did not dare answer. "Your mother has no time for you now," the old stag went on. Bambi was completely dominated by his masterful voice and at the same time, he admired it. "Can't you stay by yourself? Shame on you!"

Bambi wanted to say that he was perfectly able to stay by himself, that he had often been left alone already, but he could not get it out. He was obedient and he felt terribly ashamed. The stag turned around and was gone. Bambi didn't know where or how, or whether the stag had gone slow or fast. He had simply gone as suddenly as he had come. Bambi strained his ears to listen but he could not catch the sound of a departing footstep or a leaf stirring. So he thought the old stag must be somewhere close by and snuffed the air in all directions. It brought him no scent. Bambi sighed with relief to think he was alone. But he felt a lively desire to see the old stag again and win his approval.

When his mother came back he did not tell her anything of his encounter. He did not call her any more either the next time she disappeared. He thought of the old stag while he wandered around. He wanted very much to meet him. He wanted to say to him, "See, I don't call my mother any more," so the old stag would praise him.

But he told Gobo and Faline the next time they were together on the meadow. They listened attentively and had nothing to relate that could compare with this.

"Weren't you frightened?" asked Gobo excitedly.

Oh well—Bambi confessed he had been frightened. But only a little.

"I should have been terribly frightened," Gobo declared.

Bambi replied, no, he hadn't been very much afraid, because the stag was so handsome.

"That wouldn't have helped me much," Gobo added, "I'd have been too afraid to look at him. When I'm frightened I have streaks before my eyes so that I can't see at all, and my heart beats so fast that I can't breathe."

Faline became very thoughtful after Bambi's story and did not say anything.

But the next time they met, Gobo and Faline bounded up in great haste. They were alone again and so was Bambi. "We have been hunting for you all this time," cried Gobo. "Yes," Faline said importantly, "because now we know who it was you saw." Bambi bounded into the air for curiosity and asked, "Who?"

Faline said solemnly, "It was the old Prince."

"Who told you that?" Bambi demanded.

"Mother," Faline replied.

Bambi was amazed, "Did you tell her the whole story?" They both nodded. "But it was a secret," Bambi cried angrily.

Gobo tried to shield himself at once. "I didn't do it, it was Faline," he said. But Faline cried excitedly, "What do you mean, a secret? I wanted to know who it was. Now we all know and it's much more exciting."

Bambi was burning up with desire to hear all about it and let himself be mollified. Faline told him everything. "The old Prince is the biggest stag in the whole forest. There isn't anybody else that compares with him. Nobody knows how old he is. Nobody can find out where he lives. No one knows his family. Very few have seen him even once. At times he was thought to be dead because he hadn't been seen for so long. Then someone would see him again for a second and so they knew he was still alive. Nobody had ever dared ask him where he had been. He speaks to nobody and no one dares speak to him. He uses trails none of the others ever use. He knows the very depths of the forest. And he does not know such a thing as danger. Other Princes fight one another at times, sometimes in fun or to try each other out, sometimes in earnest. For many years no one has fought with the old stag. And of those who fought with him long ago not one is living. He is the great Prince."

Bambi forgave Gobo and Faline for babbling his secret to their mother. He was even glad to have found out all these important things, but he was glad that Gobo and Faline did not know all about it. They did not know that the great Prince had said, "Can't you stay by yourself? Shame on you!" Now Bambi was very glad that he had not told them about these things. For then

Gobo and Faline would have told that along with the rest, and the whole forest would have gossiped about it.

That night when the moon rose Bambi's mother came back again. He suddenly saw her standing under the great oak at the edge of the meadow looking around for him. He saw her right away and ran to her.

That night Bambi learned something new. His mother was tired and hungry. They did not walk as far as usual. The mother quieted her hunger on the meadow where Bambi too was used to eating most of his meals. Side by side they nibbled at the bushes and, pleasantly ruminating, went farther and farther into the woods.

Presently there was a loud rustling in the bushes. Before Bambi could guess what it was his mother began to cry aloud as she did when she was very terrified or when she was beside herself. "Aoh!" she cried and, giving a bound, stopped and cried, "Aoh! Baoh!" Bambi tried to make out the mighty forms which were drawing near as the rustling grew louder. They were right near now. They resembled Bambi and Bambi's mother, Aunt Ena and all the rest of his family, but they were gigantic and so powerfully built that he stared up at them overcome.

Suddenly Bambi began to bleat, "Aoh! Baoh-baoh!" He hardly knew he was bleating. He couldn't help himself. The procession tramped slowly by. Three, four giant apparitions, one after the other. The last of them was bigger than any of the others. He had a wild mane on his neck and his antlers were treelike. It took Bambi's breath away to see them. He stood and bleated from a heart full of wonder, for he was more weirdly affected than ever before in his life. He was afraid, but in a peculiar way. He felt how pitifully small he was, and even his mother seemed to him to have shrunk. He felt ashamed without understanding why, and at the same time terror shook him. He bleated, "Baoh! b-a-o-h!" He felt better when he bleated that way.

The procession had gone by. There was nothing more to be seen or heard. Even his mother was silent. Only Bambi kept giving short bleats now and then. He still felt the shock.

"Be still," his mother said, "they have gone now."

"Oh, Mother," Bambi whispered, "who was it?"

"Well," said his mother, "they are not so dangerous when all is said and done. Those are your big cousins, the elk—they are strong and they are important, far stronger than we are."

"And aren't they dangerous?" Bambi asked.

"Not as a rule," his mother explained. "Of course, a good many things are said to have happened. This and that is told about them, but I don't know if there is any truth in such gossip or not. They've never done any harm to me or to any one of my acquaintances."

"Why should they do anything to us," asked Bambi, "if they are cousins of ours?" He wanted to feel calm but he kept trembling.

"Oh, they never do anything to us," his mother answered, "but I don't know why, I'm frightened whenever I see them. I don't understand it myself. But it happens that way every time."

Bambi was gradually reassured by her words but he remained thoughtful. Right above him in the branches of an alder, the screech owl was hooting in his blood-curdling way. Bambi was distracted and forgot to act as if he had been frightened. But the screech owl flew by anyhow and asked, "Didn't I frighten you?"

"Of course," Bambi replied, "you always frighten me."

The screech owl chuckled softly. He was pleased. "I hope you don't hold it against me," he said, "it's just my way." He fluffed himself up so that he resembled a ball, sank his bill in his foamy white feathers and put on a terribly wise and serious face. He was satisfied with himself.

Bambi poured out his heart to him. "Do you know," he began slyly, "I've just had a much worse fright."

"Indeed!" said the owl, displeased.

Bambi told him about his encounter with his giant relations.

"Don't talk to me about relations," the owl exclaimed, "I've got relations too. But I only fly around in the day-time so they are all down on me now. No, there isn't much use in relations. If they're bigger than you are, they're no good to you, and if they're smaller they're worth still less. If they're bigger than you, you can't bear them because they're proud, and if they're smaller they can't bear you because you're proud. No, I prefer to have nothing to do with the whole crowd."

"But, I don't even know my relations," Bambi said, laughing shyly, "I never heard of them. I never saw them before today."

"Don't bother about such people," the screech owl advised. "Believe me," and he rolled his eyes significantly, "believe me, it's the best way. Relatives are never as good as friends. Look at us, we're not related in any way but we're good friends and that's much better."

Bambi wanted to say something else but the screech owl went on, "I've had experience with such things. You are still too young but, believe me, I know better. Besides, I don't like to get mixed up in family affairs." He rolled his eyes thoughtfully and looked so impressive with his serious face that Bambi kept a discreet silence.

Chapter Seven

ANOTHER NIGHT PASSED AND morning brought an event.

It was a cloudless morning, dewy and fresh. All the leaves on the trees and the bushes seemed suddenly to smell sweeter. The meadows sent up great clouds of perfume to the treetops.

"Peep!" said the titmice when they awoke. They said it very softly. But since it was still gray dawn they said nothing else for a while. For a time it was perfectly still. Then a crow's hoarse, rasping caw sounded far above in the sky. The crows had awakened and were visiting one another in the treetops. The magpie answered at once, "Shackarakshak! Did you think I was still asleep?" Then a hundred small voices started in very softly here and there. "Peep! peep! tiu!" Sleep and the dark were still in these sounds. And they came from far apart.

Suddenly a blackbird flew to the top of a beech. She perched way up on the topmost twig that stuck up thin against the sky and sat there watching how, far away over the trees, the night-weary, pale-gray heavens were glowing in the distant east and coming to life. Then she commenced to sing.

Her little black body seemed only a tiny dark speck at that distance. She looked like a dead leaf. But she poured out her song in a great flood of rejoicing through the whole forest. And everything began to stir. The finches warbled, the little redthroat and the goldfinch were heard. The doves rushed from place to place with a loud clapping and rustling of wings. The pheasants cackled as though their throats would burst. The noise of their wings, as they flew from their roosts

to the ground, was soft but powerful. They kept uttering their metallic, splintering call with its soft ensuing
chuckle. Far above the falcons cried sharply and joyously, "Yayaya!"

The sun rose.

"Diu diyu!" the yellowbird rejoiced. He flew to
and fro among the branches, and his round, yellow
body flashed in the morning light like a winged ball
of gold.

Bambi walked under the great oak on the meadow.
It sparkled with dew. It smelled of grass and flowers
and moist earth, and whispered of a thousand living
things. Friend Hare was there and seemed to be thinking over something important. A haughty pheasant
strutted slowly by, nibbling at the grass seeds and peering cautiously in all directions. The dark, metallic blue
of his neck gleamed in the sun.

One of the Princes was standing close to Bambi.
Bambi had never seen any of the fathers so close before.
The stag was standing right in front of him next to the
hazel bush and was somewhat hidden by the branches.

Bambi did not move. He wanted the Prince to come out completely, and was wondering whether he dared speak to him. He wanted to ask his mother and looked around for her. But his mother had already gone away and was standing some distance off, beside Aunt Ena. At the same time Gobo and Faline came running out of the woods. Bambi was still thinking it over without stirring. If he went up to his mother and the others now he would have to pass by the Prince. He felt as if he couldn't do it.

"Oh well," he thought, "I don't have to ask my mother first. The old Prince spoke to me and I didn't tell Mother anything about it. I'll say, 'Good morning, Prince.' He can't be offended at that. But if he does get angry, I'll run away fast." Bambi struggled with his resolve, which began to waver again.

Presently the Prince walked out from behind the hazel bush onto the meadow.

"Now," thought Bambi.

Then there was a crash like thunder.

Bambi shrank together and didn't know what had

happened. He saw the Prince leap into the air under his very nose and watched him rush past him into the forest with one great bound.

Bambi looked around in a daze. The thunder still vibrated. He saw how his mother and Aunt Ena, Gobo and Faline fled into the woods. He saw how Friend Hare scurried away like mad. He saw the pheasant running with his neck outstretched. He noticed that the forest grew suddenly still. He started and sprang into the thicket. He had made only a few bounds when he saw the Prince lying on the ground in front of him, motionless. Bambi stopped horrified, not understanding what it meant. The Prince lay bleeding from a great wound in his shoulder. He was dead.

"Don't stop!" a voice beside him commanded. It was his mother, who rushed past him at full gallop. "Run," she cried. "Run as fast as you can!" She did not slow up, but raced ahead, and her command brought Bambi after her. He ran with all his might.

"What is it, Mother?" he asked. "What is it, Mother?"

His mother answered between gasps, "It—was—He!"

Bambi shuddered and they ran on. At last they stopped for lack of breath.

"What did you say? Tell me, what it was you said," a soft voice called down from overhead. Bambi looked up. The squirrel came chattering through the branches.

"I ran the whole way with you," he cried. "It was dreadful."

"Were you there?" asked the mother.

"Of course I was there," the squirrel replied. "I am still trembling in every limb." He sat erect, balancing with his splendid tail, displaying his small white chest, and holding his forepaws protestingly against his body. "I'm beside myself with excitement," he said.

"I'm quite weak from fright myself," said the mother. "I don't understand it. Not one of us saw a thing."

"Is that so?" the squirrel said pettishly. "I saw Him long before."

"So did I," another voice cried. It was the magpie. She flew past and settled on a branch.

"So did I," came a croak from above. It was the jay, who was sitting on an ash.

A couple of crows in the treetops cawed harshly, "We saw Him, too."

They all sat around talking importantly. They were unusually excited and seemed to be full of anger and fear.

"Whom?" Bambi thought. "Whom did they see?"

"I tried my best," the squirrel was saying, pressing his forepaws protestingly against his heart. "I tried my best to warn the poor Prince."

"And I," the jay rasped. "How often did I scream? But he didn't care to hear me."

"He didn't hear me either," the magpie croaked. "I called him at least ten times. I wanted to fly right past him, for, thought I, he hasn't heard me yet; I'll fly to the hazel bush where he's standing. He can't help hearing me there. But at that minute it happened."

"My voice is probably louder than yours, and I warned him as well as I could," the crow said in an impudent tone. "But gentlemen of that stamp pay little attention to the likes of us."

"Much too little, really," the squirrel agreed.

"Well, we did what we could," said the magpie. "We're certainly not to blame when an accident happens."

"Such a handsome Prince," the squirrel lamented. "And in the very prime of life."

"Akh!" croaked the jay. "It would have been better for him if he hadn't been so proud and had paid more attention to us."

"He certainly wasn't proud."

"No more so than the other Princes of his family," the magpie put in.

"Just plain stupid," sneered the jay.

"You're stupid yourself," the crow cried down from overhead. "Don't you talk about stupidity. The whole forest knows how stupid you are."

"I!" replied the jay, stiff with astonishment. "Nobody can accuse me of being stupid. I may be forgetful but I'm certainly not stupid."

"Oh just as you please," said the crow solemnly. "Forget what I said to you, but remember that the Prince did not die because he was proud or stupid, but because no one can escape Him."

"Akh!" croaked the jay. "I don't like that kind of talk." He flew away.

The crow went on. "He has already outwitted many of my family. He kills what He wants. Nothing can help us."

"You have to be on your guard against Him," the magpie broke in.

"You certainly do," said the crow sadly. "Goodbye." He flew off, his family accompanying him.

Bambi looked around. His mother was no longer there.

"What are they talking about now?" thought Bambi. "I can't understand what they are talking about. Who is this 'He' they talk about? That was He, too, that I saw in the bushes, but He didn't kill me."

Bambi thought of the Prince lying in front of him with his bloody, mangled shoulder. He was dead now. Bambi walked along. The forest sang again with a thousand voices, the sun pierced the treetops with its broad rays. There was light everywhere. The leaves began to smell. Far above the falcons called, close at hand a woodpecker hammered as if nothing had happened. Bambi was not happy. He felt himself threatened by something dark. He did not understand how the others could be so carefree and happy while life was so difficult and dangerous. Then the desire seized him to go deeper and deeper into the woods. They lured him into their depths. He wanted to find some hiding place where, shielded on all sides by impenetrable thickets, he could never be seen. He never wanted to go to the meadow again.

Something moved very softly in the bushes. Bambi drew back violently. The old stag was standing in front of him.

Bambi trembled. He wanted to run away, but he controlled himself and remained. The old stag looked at him with his great deep eyes and asked, "Were you out there before?"

"Yes," Bambi said softly. His heart was pounding in his throat.

"Where is your mother?" asked the stag.

Bambi answered still very softly, "I don't know."

The old stag kept gazing at him. "And still you're not calling for her?" he said.

Bambi looked into the noble, iron-gray face, looked at the stag's antlers and suddenly felt full of courage. "I can stay by myself, too," he said.

The old stag considered him for a while; then he asked gently, "Aren't you the little one that was crying for his mother not long ago?"

Bambi was somewhat embarrassed, but his courage held. "Yes, I am," he confessed.

The old stag looked at him in silence and it seemed to Bambi as if those deep eyes gazed still more mildly. "You scolded me then, Prince," he cried excitedly, "because I was afraid of being left alone. Since then I haven't been."

The stag looked at Bambi appraisingly and smiled a very slight, hardly noticeable smile. Bambi noticed it however. "Noble Prince," he asked confidently, "what has happened? I don't understand it. Who is this 'He' they are all talking about?" He stopped, terrified by the dark glance that bade him be silent.

Another pause ensued. The old stag was gazing past Bambi into the distance. Then he said slowly, "Listen, smell and see for yourself. Find out for yourself." He lifted his antlered head still higher. "Farewell," he said; nothing else. Then he vanished.

Bambi stood transfixed and wanted to cry. But that farewell still rang in his ears and sustained him. Farewell, the old stag had said, so he couldn't have been angry.

Bambi felt himself thrill with pride, felt inspired with a deep earnestness. Yes, life was difficult and full of danger. But come what might he would learn to bear it all.

He walked slowly deeper into the forest.

Chapter Eight

THE LEAVES WERE FALLING FROM
the great oak at the meadow's edge. They
were falling from all the trees.

One branch of the oak reached high
above the others and stretched far out over the meadow.
Two leaves clung to its very tip.

"It isn't the way it used to be," said one leaf to the other.

"No," the other leaf answered. "So many of us have
fallen off tonight we're almost the only ones left on our
branch."

"You never know who's going to go next," said the first leaf. "Even when it was warm and the sun shone, a storm or a cloudburst would come sometimes, and many leaves were torn off, though they were still young. You never know who's going to go next."

"The sun seldom shines now," sighed the second leaf, "and when it does it gives no warmth. We must have warmth again."

"Can it be true," said the first leaf, "can it really be true, that others come to take our places when we're gone and after them still others, and more and more?"

"It is really true," whispered the second leaf. "We can't even begin to imagine it, it's beyond our powers."

"It makes me very sad," added the first leaf.

They were silent a while. Then the first leaf said quietly to herself, "Why must we fall? . . ."

The second leaf asked, "What happens to us when we have fallen?"

"We sink down. . . ."

"What is under us?"

The first leaf answered, "I don't know, some say one thing, some another, but nobody knows."

The second leaf asked, "Do we feel anything, do we know anything about ourselves when we're down there?"

The first leaf answered, "Who knows? Not one of all those down there has ever come back to tell us about it."

They were silent again. Then the first leaf said tenderly to the other, "Don't worry so much about it, you're trembling."

"That's nothing," the second leaf answered. "I tremble at the least thing now. I don't feel so sure of my hold as I used to."

"Let's not talk any more about such things," said the first leaf.

The other replied, "No, we'll let be. But—what else shall we talk about?" She was silent, but went on after a little while. "Which of us will go first?"

"There's still plenty of time to worry about that," the other leaf assured her. "Let's remember how beautiful it was, how wonderful, when the sun came out and shone so warmly that we thought we'd burst with life. Do you remember? And the morning dew, and the mild and splendid nights . . ."

"Now the nights are dreadful," the second leaf complained, "and there is no end to them."

"We shouldn't complain," said the first leaf gently. "We've outlived many, many others."

"Have I changed much?" asked the second leaf shyly but determinedly.

"Not in the least," the first leaf assured her. "You only think so because I've got to be so yellow and ugly. But it's different in your case."

"You're fooling me," the second leaf said.

"No, really," the first leaf exclaimed eagerly, "believe me, you're as lovely as the day you were born. Here and there may be a little yellow spot but it's hardly noticeable and only makes you handsomer, believe me."

"Thanks," whispered the second leaf, quite touched. "I don't believe you, not altogether, but I thank you because you're so kind, you've always been so kind to me. I'm just beginning to understand how kind you are."

"Hush," said the other leaf, and kept silent herself for she was too troubled to talk any more.

Then they were both silent. Hours passed.

A moist wind blew, cold and hostile, through the treetops.

"Ah, now," said the second leaf, "I . . ." Then her voice broke off. She was torn from her place and spun down.

Winter had come.

Chapter Nine

BAMBI NOTICED THAT THE WORLD was changed. It was hard for him to get used to this altered world. They had all lived like rich folk and now had fallen upon hard times. For Bambi knew nothing but abundance. He took it for granted that he would always have plenty to eat. He thought he would never need to trouble about food. He believed he would always sleep in the lovely green-leafed glade where no one could see him, and would always go about in his smooth, handsome, glossy red coat.

Now everything was changed without his having noticed the change take place. The process that was ending had seemed only a series of episodes to him. It pleased him to see the milk-white veils of mist steam from the meadow in the morning, or drop suddenly from the gray sky at dawn. They vanished so beautifully in the sunshine. The hoarfrost that covered the meadow with such dazzling whiteness delighted him, too. Sometimes he liked to listen to his big cousins the elk. The whole forest would tremble with their kingly voices. Bambi used to listen and be very much frightened, but his heart would beat high with admiration when he heard them calling. He remembered that the kings had antlers branching like tall, strong trees. And it seemed to him that their voices were as powerful as their antlers. Whenever he heard the deep tones of those voices he would stand motionless. Their deep voices rolled toward him like the mighty moaning of noble, maddened blood whose primal power was giving utterance to longing, rage and pride. Bambi struggled in vain against his fears. They overpowered him whenever he heard those voices, but he was proud to have such noble relatives. At the same time he felt a strange sense of annoyance because they were so unapproachable. It offended and humiliated him without his knowing exactly how or why, even without his being particularly conscious of it.

It was only after the mating season had passed and the thunder of the stags' mighty voices had grown still that Bambi began to notice other things once more. At night when he roamed through the forest or by day as he lay in the glade, he heard the falling leaves whisper among the trees. They fluttered and rustled ceaselessly through the air from all the treetops and branches. A delicate silvery sound was falling constantly to earth. It was wonderful to awaken amidst it, wonderful to fall asleep to this mysterious and melancholy whispering. Soon the leaves lay thick and loose on the ground and when you walked through them they flew about, softly rustling. It was jolly to push them aside with every step, they were piled so high. It made a sound like "Sh! sh!," soft and very clear and silvery. Besides, it was very useful, for Bambi had to be particularly careful these days to hear and smell everything. And with the leaves you could hear everything far off. They rustled at the slightest touch and cried, "Sh! sh!" Nobody could steal through them.

But then the rain came. It poured down from early morning till late at night. Sometimes it rained all night long and into the following day. It would stop for a while and begin again with fresh strength. The air was damp and cold, the whole world seemed full of rain. If you tried to nibble a little meadow grass you got your mouth full of water, or if you tugged the least little bit at a bough a whole torrent of water poured into your eyes and nose. The leaves no longer rustled. They lay pale and soggy on the ground, flattened by the rain, and made no sounds. Bambi discovered for the first time how unpleasant it is to be rained on all day and all night until you are soaked to the skin. There had not even been a frost yet, but he longed for the warm weather and felt it was a sad business to have to run around soaked through.

But when the north wind blew, Bambi found out what cold is. It wasn't much help to nestle close to his mother. Of course at first he thought it was wonderful to lie there and keep one side warm at least. But the north wind raged through the forest all day and all night long. It seemed to be driven to madness by some incomprehensible ice-cold fury, as though it wanted to tear up the forest by its roots or annihilate it somehow. The trees groaned in stubborn resistance, they struggled mightily against the wind's fierce onslaught. You could hear their long-drawn moans, their sighlike creakings, the loud snap when their strong limbs split, the angry cracking when now and again a trunk broke and the vanquished tree seemed to shriek from every wound in its rent and dying body. Nothing else could be heard, for the storm swooped down still more fiercely on the forest, and its roaring drowned all lesser noises.

Then Bambi knew that want and hardship had come. He saw how much the rain and wind had changed the world. There was no longer a leaf on tree or shrub. But all stood there as though violated, their bodies naked for all to see. And they lifted their bare brown limbs to the sky for pity. The grass on the meadow was withered and shortened, as if it had sunk into the earth. Even the glade seemed wretched and bare. Since the leaves had fallen it was no longer possible to lie so well hidden as before. The glade was open on all sides.

One day, as a young magpie flew over the meadow, something cold and white fell in her eye. Then it fell again and again. She felt as if a little veil were drawn across her eye while the small, pale, blinding white flakes danced around her. The magpie hesitated in her flight, fluttered a little, and then soared straight up into the air. In vain. The cold white flakes were everywhere and got into her eyes again. She kept flying straight up, soaring higher.

"Don't put yourself out so much, dearie," a crow who was flying above her in the same direction called down; "don't put yourself out so much. You can't fly high enough to get outside these flakes. This is snow."

"Snow!" cried the magpie in surprise, struggling against the drizzle.

"That's about the size of it," said the crow, "it's winter, and this is snow."

"Excuse me," the magpie replied, "but I only left the nest in May. I don't know anything about winter."

"There are plenty in the same boat," the crow remarked, "but you'll soon find out."

"Well," said the magpie, "if this is snow I guess I'll sit down for a while." She perched on an elder and shook herself. The crow flew awkwardly away.

At first Bambi was delighted with the snow. The air was calm and mild while the white snow stars whirled down and the world looked completely different. It had grown lighter, gayer, Bambi thought, and whenever the sun came out for a little while everything shone and the white covering flashed and sparkled so brightly that it blinded you.

But Bambi soon stopped being pleased with the snow. For it grew harder and harder to find food. He had to paw the snow away with endless labor before he could find one withered little blade of grass. The snow crust cut his legs and he was afraid of cutting his feet.

Gobo had already cut his. Of course Gobo was the kind who couldn't stand anything and was a constant source of trouble to his mother.

The deer were always together now and were much more friendly than before. Ena brought her children constantly. Lately Marena, a half-grown doe, had joined the circle. But old Nettla really contributed most to their entertainment. She was quite a self-sufficient person and had her own ideas about everything. "No," she would say, "I don't bother with children any more. I've had enough of that particular joke."

Faline asked, "What difference does it make, if they're a joke?" And Nettla would act as if she were angry, and say, "They're a bad joke, though, and I've had enough of them."

They got along perfectly together. They would sit side by side gossiping. The young ones had never had a chance to hear so much.

Even one or another of the Princes would join them now. At first things went somewhat stiffly, especially since the children were a little shy. But that soon changed, and they got along very well together. Bambi admired Prince Ronno, who was a stately lord, and he passionately loved the handsome young Karus. They had dropped their horns and Bambi often looked at the two slate-gray round spots that showed smooth and shimmering with many delicate points on the Princes' heads. They looked very noble.

It was terribly interesting whenever one of the Princes talked about Him. Ronno had a thick hide-covered swelling on his left forefoot. He limped on that foot and used to ask sometimes, "Can you really see that I limp?" Everyone would hasten to assure him that there was not the trace of a limp. That was what Ronno wanted. And it really was hardly noticeable.

"Yes," he would go on. "I saved myself from a tight corner that time." And then Ronno would tell how He had surprised him and hurled His fire at him. But it had only struck his leg. It had driven him nearly mad with pain, and no wonder, since the bone was shattered. But Ronno did not lose his head. He was up and away on three legs. He pressed on in spite of his weakness for he saw that he was being pursued. He ran without stopping until night came. Then he gave himself a rest. But he went on the next morning until he felt he was in safety. Then he took care of himself, living alone in hiding, waiting for his wound to heal. At last he came out again and was a hero. He limped, but he thought no one noticed it.

They were often together now for long periods and told many stories. Bambi heard more about Him than ever before. They told how terrible He was to look at. No one could bear to look at His pale face. Bambi knew that already from his own experience. They spoke too about His smell, and again Bambi could have spoken if he had not been too well brought up to mix in his elders' conversation. They said that His smell differed each time in a hundred subtle ways and yet you could tell it in an instant, for it was always exciting, unfathomable, mysterious and terrible.

They told how He used only two legs to walk with and they spoke of the amazing strength of His two hands. Some of them did not know what hands were.

But when it was explained, old Nettla said, "I don't see anything so surprising in that. A squirrel can do everything you tell about just as well, and every little mouse can perform the same wonders." She turned away her head disdainfully.

"Oh no," cried the others, and they gave her to understand that those were *not* the same things at all. But old Nettla was not to be cowed. "What about the falcon?" she exclaimed. "And the buzzard? And the owl? They've got only two legs and when they want to catch something they simply stand on one leg and grab with the other. That's much harder and He certainly can't do that."

Old Nettla was not at all inclined to admire anything connected with Him. She hated Him with all her heart. "He is loathsome!" she said, and she stuck to that. Besides, nobody contradicted her, since nobody liked Him.

But the talk grew more complicated when they told how He had a third hand, not two hands merely, but a third hand.

"That's an old story," Nettla said curtly. "I don't believe it."

"Is that so?" Ronno broke in. "Then what did He shatter my leg with? Can you tell me that?"

Old Nettla answered carelessly, "That's your affair, my dear, He's never shattered any of mine."

Aunt Ena said, "I've seen a good deal in my time, and I think there's something in the story that He has a third hand."

"I agree with you," young Karus said politely. "I have a friend, a crow . . ." He paused, embarrassed for a moment, and looked around at them, one after the other, as though he were afraid of being laughed at. But when he saw that they were listening attentively to him he went on. "This crow is unusually well informed, I must say that. Surprisingly well informed. And she says that He really has three hands, but not always. The third hand is the bad one, the crow says. It isn't attached like the other two, but He carries it hanging over His shoulder. The crow says that she can always tell exactly when He, or anyone like Him, is going to be dangerous. If He comes without the third hand He isn't dangerous."

Old Nettla laughed. "Your crow's a blockhead, my dear Karus," she said. "Tell her so for me. If she were as clever as she thinks she is, she'd know that He's always dangerous, always." But the others had different objections.

Bambi's mother said, "Some of Them aren't dangerous; you can see that at a glance."

"Is that so?" old Nettla asked. "I suppose you stand still till They come up to you and wish you a good day?"

Bambi's mother answered gently. "Of course I don't stand still; I run away."

And Faline broke in with, "You should always run away." Everybody laughed.

But when they talked about the third hand they became serious and fear grew on them gradually. For whatever it might be, a third hand or something else, it was terrible and they did not understand it. They only knew of it from others' stories; few of them had ever seen it for themselves. He would stand still, far off, and never move. You couldn't explain what He did or how it happened, but suddenly there would be a crash like thunder, fire would shoot out and far away from Him you would drop down dying with your breast torn open. They all sat bowed while they talked about Him, as though they felt the presence of some dark, unknown power controlling them.

They listened curiously to the many stories that were always horrible, full of blood and suffering. They listened tirelessly to everything that was said about Him, tales that were certainly invented, all the stories and sayings that had come down from their fathers and great-grandfathers. In each one of them they were unconsciously seeking for some way to propitiate this dark power, or some way to escape it.

"What difference does it make," young Karus asked despondently, "how far away He is when He kills you?"

"Didn't your clever crow explain that to you?" old Nettla mocked.

"No," said Karus with a smile. "She says that she's often seen Him but no one can explain Him."

"Yes, He knocks the crows out of the trees, too, when He wants to," Ronno observed.

"And He brings down the pheasant on the wing," Aunt Ena added.

Bambi's mother said, "He throws His hand at you, my grandmother told me so."

"Is that so?" asked old Nettla. "What is it that bangs so terribly then?"

"That's when He tears His hand off," Bambi's mother explained. "Then the fire flashes and the thunder cracks. He's all fire inside."

"Excuse me," said Ronno. "It's true that He's all fire inside. But that about His hand is wrong. A hand couldn't make such wounds. You can see that for yourself. It's much more likely that it's a tooth He throws at us. A tooth would explain a great many things, you know. You really die from His bite."

"Will He never stop hunting us?" young Karus sighed.

Then Marena spoke, the young half-grown doe. "They say that sometime He'll come to live with us and be as gentle as we are. He'll play with us then and the whole forest will be happy, and we'll be friends with Him."

Old Nettla burst out laughing. "Let Him stay where He is and leave us in peace," she said.

Aunt Ena said reprovingly, "You shouldn't talk that way."

"And why not?" old Nettla replied hotly; "I really don't see why not. Friends with Him! He's murdered us ever since we can remember, every one of us, our sisters, our mothers, our brothers! Ever since we came into the world He's given us no peace, but has killed us wherever we showed our heads. And now we're going to be friends with Him. What nonsense!"

Marena looked at all of them out of her big, calm, shining eyes. "Love is no nonsense," she said. "It has to come."

Old Nettla turned away. "I'm going to look for something to eat," she said, and trotted off.

Chapter Ten

WINTER DRAGGED ON. SOMEtimes it was warmer, but then the snow would fall again and lie deeper and deeper, so that it became impossible to scrape it away. It was worse when the thaws came and the melted snow water froze again in the night. Then there was a thin slippery film of ice. Often it broke in pieces and the sharp splinters cut the deer's tender fetlocks till they bled.

A heavy frost had set in several days before. The

air was purer and rarer than it had ever been, and full of energy. It began to hum in a very fine high tone. It hummed with the cold.

It was silent in the woods, but something horrible happened every day. Once the crows fell upon Friend Hare's small son who was lying sick, and killed him in a cruel way. He could be heard moaning pitifully for a long while. Friend Hare was not at home, and when he heard the sad news he was beside himself with grief.

Another time the squirrel raced about with a great wound in his neck where the ferret had caught him. By a miracle the squirrel had escaped. He could not talk because of the pain, but he ran up and down the branches. Everyone could see him. He ran like mad. From time to time he stopped, sat down, raised his forepaws desperately and clutched his head in terror and agony while the red blood oozed on his white chest. He ran about for an hour, then suddenly crumpled up, fell across a branch, and dropped dead in the snow. A couple of magpies flew down at once to begin their meal.

Another day a fox tore to pieces the strong and handsome pheasant who had enjoyed such general respect and popularity. His death aroused the sympathies of a wide circle who tried to comfort his disconsolate widow.

The fox had dragged the pheasant out of the snow, where he was buried, thinking himself well hidden. No one could have felt safer than the pheasant for it all happened in broad daylight. The terrible hardship that seemed to have no end spread bitterness and brutality. It destroyed all their memories of the past, their faith in each other, and ruined every good custom they had. There was no longer either peace or mercy in the forest.

"It's hard to believe that it will ever be better," Bambi's mother sighed.

Aunt Ena sighed too. "It's hard to believe that it was ever any better," she said.

"And yet," Marena said, looking in front of her, "I always think how beautiful it was before."

"Look," old Nettla said to Aunt Ena, "your little one

is trembling." She pointed to Gobo. "Does he always tremble like that?"

"Yes," Aunt Ena answered gravely, "he's shivered that way for the last few days."

"Well," said old Nettla in her frank way, "I'm glad that I have no more children. If that little one were mine I'd wonder if he'd last out the winter."

The future really didn't look very bright for Gobo. He was weak. He had always been much more delicate than Bambi or Faline and remained smaller than either of them. He was growing worse from day to day. He could not eat even the little food there was. It made his stomach ache. And he was quite exhausted by the cold, and by the horrors around him. He shivered more and more and could hardly stand up. Everyone looked at him sympathetically.

Old Nettla went up to him and nudged him good-naturedly. "Don't be so sad," she said encouragingly, "that's no way for a little prince to act, and besides it's unhealthy." She turned away so that no one could see how moved she was.

Ronno, who had settled himself a little to one side in the snow, suddenly sprang up. "I don't know what it is," he mumbled and gazed around.

Everyone grew watchful. "What is it?" they asked.

"I don't know," Ronno repeated. "But I'm restless. I suddenly felt restless as if something were wrong."

Karus was snuffing the air. "I don't smell anything strange," he declared.

They all stood still, listening and snuffing the air. "It's nothing, there's absolutely nothing to smell," they agreed one after another.

"Nevertheless," Ronno insisted, "you can say what you like, something is wrong."

Marena said, "The crows are calling."

"There they go calling again," Faline added quickly, but the others had already heard them.

"They are flying," said Karus and the others.

Everybody looked up. High above the treetops a flock of crows flapped by. They came from the farthest edge of the forest, the direction from which danger always came, and they were complaining to one another. Apparently something unusual had happened.

"Wasn't I right?" asked Ronno. "You can see that something is happening."

"What shall we do?" Bambi's mother whispered anxiously.

"Let's get away," Aunt Ena urged in alarm.

"Wait," Ronno commanded.

"But the children," Aunt Ena replied, "the children. Gobo can't run."

"Go ahead," Ronno agreed, "go off with your children. I don't think there's any need for it, but I don't blame you for going." He was alert and serious.

"Come, Gobo. Come, Faline. Softly now, go slowly. And keep behind me," Aunt Ena warned them. She slipped away with the children.

Time passed. They stood still, listening and trembling.

"As if we hadn't suffered enough already," old Nettla began. "We still have this to go through. . . ." She was very angry. Bambi looked at her, and he felt that she was thinking of something horrible.

Three or four magpies had already begun to chatter on the side of the thicket from which the crows had come. "Look out! Look out, out, out!" they cried. The deer could not see them, but could hear them calling and warning each other. Sometimes one of them, and sometimes all of them together, would cry, "Look out, out, out!" Then they came nearer. They fluttered in terror from tree to tree, peered back and fluttered away again in fear and alarm.

"Akh!" cried the jays. They screamed their warning loudly.

Suddenly all the deer shrank together at once as though a blow had struck them. Then they stood still snuffing the air.

It was He.

A heavy wave of scent blew past. There was nothing they could do. The scent filled their nostrils, it numbed their senses and made their hearts stop beating.

The magpies were still chattering. The jays were still screaming overhead. In the woods around them everything had sprung to life. The titmice flitted through the branches, like tiny feathered balls, chirping, "Run! Run!"

The blackbirds fled swiftly and darkly above them with long-drawn twittering cries. Through the dark tangle of bare bushes, they saw on the white snow a wild aimless scurrying of smaller, shadowy creatures. These were the pheasants. Then a flash of red streaked by. That was the fox. But no one was afraid of him now. For that fearful scent kept streaming on in a wider wave, sending terror into their hearts and uniting them all in one mad fear, in a single feverish impulse to flee, to save themselves.

That mysterious overpowering scent filled the woods with such strength that they knew that this time He was not alone, but had come with many others, and there would be no end to the killing.

They did not move. They looked at the titmice, whisking away in a sudden flutter, at the blackbirds and the squirrels who dashed from treetop to treetop in mad bounds. They knew that all the little creatures on the ground had nothing to fear. But they understood their flight when they smelled Him, for no forest creature could bear His presence.

Presently Friend Hare hopped up. He hesitated, sat still and then hopped on again.

"What is it?" Karus called after him impatiently.

But Friend Hare only looked around with bewildered eyes and could not even speak. He was completely terrified.

"What's the use of asking?" said Ronno gloomily.

Friend Hare gasped for breath. "We are surrounded," he said in a lifeless voice. "We can't escape on any side. He is everywhere."

At the same instant they heard His voice. Twenty or thirty strong, He cried, "Ho! ho! Ha! ha!" It roared like the sound of winds and storms. He beat on the tree trunks as through they were drums. It was wracking and terrifying. A distant twisting and rending of parted bushes rang out. There was a snapping and cracking of broken boughs.

He was coming.

He was coming into the heart of the thicket.

Then short whistling flutelike trills sounded together with the loud flap of soaring wings. A pheasant rose from under His very feet. The deer heard the wing beats of the pheasant grow fainter as he mounted into the air. There was a loud crash like thunder. Then silence. Then a dull thud on the ground.

"He is dead," said Bambi's mother, trembling.

"The first," Ronno added.

The young doe, Marena, said, "In this very hour many of us are going to die. Perhaps I shall be one of them." No one listened to her, for a mad terror had seized them all.

Bambi tried to think. But His savage noises grew louder and louder and paralyzed Bambi's senses. He heard nothing but those noises. They numbed him while amidst the howling, shouting and crashing he could hear his own heart pounding. He felt nothing but curiosity and did not even realize that he was trembling in every limb. From time to time his mother whispered in his ear, "Stay close to me." She was shouting, but in the uproar it sounded to Bambi as if she were whispering. Her "Stay close to me" encouraged him. It was like a chain holding him. Without it he would have rushed off senselessly, and he heard it at the very moment when his wits were wandering and he wanted to dash away.

He looked around. All sorts of creatures were swarming past, scampering blindly over one another. A pair of weasels ran by like thin snakelike streaks. The eye could scarcely follow them. A ferret listened as though bewitched to every shriek that desperate Friend Hare let out.

A fox was standing in a whole flurry of fluttering pheasants. They paid no attention to him. They ran right under his nose and he paid no attention to them. Motionless, with his head thrust forward, he listened to the onrushing tumult, lifting his pointed ears, and snuffed the air with his nose. Only his tail moved, slowly wagging with his intense concentration.

A pheasant dashed up. He had come from where the danger was worst and was beside himself with fear.

"Don't try to fly," he shouted to the others. "Don't fly, just run! Don't lose your head! Don't try to fly! Just run, run, run!"

He kept repeating the same thing over and over

again as though to encourage himself. But he no longer knew what he was saying.

"Ho! ho! Ha! ha!" came the death cry, from quite near apparently.

"Don't lose your head," screamed the pheasant. And at the same time his voice broke in a whistling gasp and, spreading his wings, he flew up with a loud whir. Bambi watched how he flew straight up, directly between the trees, beating his wings. The dark metallic blue and greenish-brown markings on his body gleamed like gold. His long tail feathers swept proudly behind him. A short crash like thunder sounded sharply. The pheasant suddenly crumpled up in mid-flight. He turned head over tail as though he wanted to catch his claws with his beak, and then dropped violently to earth. He fell among the others and did not move again.

Then everyone lost his senses. They all rushed toward one another. Five or six pheasants rose at one time with a loud whir. "Don't fly," cried the rest and ran. The thunder cracked five or six times and more of the flying birds dropped lifeless to the ground.

"Come," said Bambi's mother. Bambi looked around. Ronno and Karus had already fled. Old Nettla was disappearing. Only Marena was still beside them. Bambi went with his mother, Marena following them timidly. All around them was a roaring and shouting, and the thunder was crashing. Bambi's mother was calm. She trembled quietly, but she kept her wits together.

"Bambi, my child," she said, "keep behind me all the time. We'll have to get out of here and across the open place. But now we'll go slowly."

The din was maddening. The thunder crashed ten, twelve times as He hurled it from His hands.

"Watch out," said Bambi's mother. "Don't run. But when we have to cross the open place, run as fast as you can. And don't forget, Bambi, my child, don't pay any attention to me when we get out there. Even if I fall, don't pay any attention to me, just keep on running. Do you understand, Bambi?"

His mother walked carefully step by step amidst the uproar. The pheasants were running up and down, burying themselves in the snow. Suddenly they would spring out and begin to run again. The whole Hare family was hopping to and fro, squatting down and then hopping again. No one said a word. They were all spent with terror and numbed by the din and thunderclaps.

It grew lighter in front of Bambi and his mother. The clearing showed through the bushes. Behind them the terrifying drumming on the tree trunks came crashing nearer and nearer. The breaking branches snapped. There was a roaring of "Ha, ha! Ho, ho!"

Then Friend Hare and two of his cousins rushed past them across the clearing. Bing! Ping! Bang! roared the thunder. Bambi saw how one hare struck an elder in the middle of his flight and lay with his white belly turned upward. He quivered a little and then was still. Bambi stood petrified. But from behind him came the cry, "Here they are! Run! Run!"

There was a loud clapping of wings suddenly opened. There were gasps, sobs, showers of feathers, flutterings. The pheasants took wing and the whole flock rose almost at one instant. The air was throbbing with repeated thunderclaps and the dull thuds of the fallen and the high, piercing shrieks of those who had escaped.

Bambi heard steps and looked behind him. He was there. He came bursting through the bushes on all sides. He sprang up everywhere, struck about Him, beat the bushes, drummed on the tree trunks and shouted with a fiendish voice.

"Now," said Bambi's mother. "Get away from here. And don't stay too close to me." She was off with a bound that barely skimmed the snow. Bambi rushed out after her. The thunder crashed around them on all sides. It seemed as if the earth would split in half. Bambi saw nothing. He kept running. A growing desire to get away from the tumult and out of reach of that scent which seemed to strangle him, the growing impulse to flee, the longing to save himself were loosed in him at last. He ran. It seemed to him as if he saw his mother hit but he did not know if it was really she or not. He felt a film come over his eyes from fear of the thunder crashing behind him. It had gripped him completely at last. He could think of nothing or see nothing around him. He kept running.

The open space was crossed. Another thicket took him in. The hue and cry still rang behind him. The sharp reports still thundered. And in the branches above him there was a light pattering like the first fall of hail. Then it grew quieter. Bambi kept running.

A dying pheasant, with its neck twisted, lay on the snow, beating feebly with its wings. When he heard Bambi coming he ceased his convulsive movements and whispered: "It's all over with me." Bambi paid no attention to him and ran on.

A tangle of bushes he blundered into forced him to slacken his pace and look for a path. He pawed the ground impatiently with his hoofs. "This way!" called someone with a gasping voice. Bambi obeyed involuntarily and found an opening at once. Someone moved feebly in front of him. It was Friend Hare's wife who had called.

"Can you help me a little?" she said. Bambi looked at her and shuddered. Her hind leg dangled lifelessly in the snow, dyeing it red and melting it with warm, oozing blood. "Can you help me a little?" she repeated.

She spoke as if she were well and whole, almost as if she were happy. "I don't know what can have happened to me," she went on. "There's really no sense to it, but I just can't seem to walk ..."

In the middle of her words she rolled over on her side and died. Bambi was seized with horror again and ran.

"Bambi!"

He stopped with a jolt. A deer was calling him. Again he heard the cry. "Is that you, Bambi?"

Bambi saw Gobo floundering helplessly in the snow. All his strength was gone; he could no longer stand on his feet. He lay there half buried and lifted his head feebly. Bambi went up to him excitedly.

"Where's you mother, Gobo?" he asked, gasping for breath. "Where's Faline?" Bambi spoke quickly and impatiently. Terror still gripped his heart.

"Mother and Faline had to go on," Gobo answered resignedly. He spoke softly, but as seriously and as well as a grown deer. "They had to leave me here. I fell down. You must go on, too, Bambi."

"Get up," cried Bambi. "Get up, Gobo! You've rested long enough. There's not a minute to lose now. Get up and come with me!"

"No, leave me," Gobo answered quietly. "I can't stand up. It's impossible. I'd like to, but I'm too weak."

"What will happen to you?" Bambi persisted.

"I don't know. Probably I'll die," said Gobo simply.

The uproar began again and re-echoed. New crashes of thunder followed. Bambi shrank together. Suddenly a branch snapped. Young Karus pounded swiftly through the snow, galloping ahead of the din.

"Run," he called when he saw Bambi. "Don't stand there if you can run!" He was gone in a flash and his headlong flight carried Bambi along with it. Bambi was hardly aware that he had begun to run again, and only after an interval did he say, "Goodbye, Gobo." But he was already too far away. Gobo could no longer hear him.

He ran till nightfall through the woods that was filled with shouting and thunder. As darkness closed in, it grew quiet. Soon a light wind carried away the horrible scent that spread everywhere. But the excitement remained.

The first friend whom Bambi saw again was Ronno. He was limping more than ever.

"Over in the oak grove the fox has a burning fever from his wound," Ronno said. "I just passed him. He's suffering terribly. He keeps biting the snow and the ground."

"Have you seen my mother?" asked Bambi.

"No," answered Ronno evasively, and walked quickly away.

Later during the night Bambi met old Nettla with Faline. All three were delighted to meet.

"Have you seen my mother?" asked Bambi.

"No," Faline answered. "I don't even know where my own mother is."

"Well," said old Nettla cheerfully. "Here's a nice mess. I was so glad that I didn't have to bother with children any more and now I have to look after two at once. I'm heartily grateful."

Bambi and Faline laughed.

They talked about Gobo. Bambi told how he had found him, and they grew so sad they began to cry. But old Nettla would not have them crying. "Before everything else you have got to get something to eat. I never heard of such a thing. You haven't had a bite to eat this livelong day!"

She led them to places where there were still a few leaves that had not completely withered. Old Nettla was wonderfully gentle. She ate nothing herself, but made Bambi and Faline eat heartily. She pawed away the snow from the grassy spots and ordered them to eat with, "The grass is good here." Or else she would say, "No, wait. We'll find something better farther on." But between whiles she would grumble. "It's perfectly ridiculous the trouble children give you."

Suddenly they saw Aunt Ena coming and rushed toward her. "Aunt Ena," cried Bambi. He had seen her first. Faline was beside herself with joy and bounded around her. "Mother," she cried. But Ena was weeping and nearly dead from exhaustion.

"Gobo is gone," she cried. "I've looked for him. I went

to the little place where he lay when he broke down in the snow ... there was nothing there ... he is gone ... my poor little Gobo. ..."

Old Nettla grumbled. "If you had looked for his tracks it would have been more sensible than crying," she said.

"There weren't any tracks," said Aunt Ena. "But ... His ... tracks were there. He found Gobo."

She was silent. Then Bambi asked despondently, "Aunt Ena, have you seen my mother?"

"No," answered Aunt Ena gently.

Bambi never saw his mother again.

Chapter Eleven

AT LAST THE WILLOWS SHED their catkins. Everything was turning green, but the young leaves on the trees and bushes were still tiny. Glowing with the soft, early morning light they looked fresh and smiling like children who have just awakened from sleep.

Bambi was standing in front of a hazel bush, beating his new antlers against the wood. It was very pleasant to do that. And an absolute necessity besides, since skin and hide still covered his splendid antlers. The skin had to come off, of course, and no sensible creature would ever wait until it split of its own accord. Bambi pounded his antlers till the skin split and long strips of it dangled about his ears. As he pounded on the hazel stems again and again, he felt how much stronger his antlers were than the wood. This feeling shot through him in a rush of power and pride. He beat more fiercely on the hazel bush and tore its bark into long pieces. The white body of the tree showed naked and quickly turned a rusty red in the open air. But Bambi paid no attention to that. He saw the bright wood of the tree flash under his strokes and it heartened him. A whole row of hazel bushes bore traces of his work.

"Well, you are nearly grown now," said a cheerful voice close by.

Bambi tossed his head and looked around him. There sat the squirrel observing him in a friendly way. From overhead came a short, shrill laugh, "Ha! Ha!"

Bambi and the squirrel were both half frightened. But the woodpecker who was clinging to an oak trunk called down, "Excuse me, but I always have to laugh when I see you deer acting like that."

"What is there to laugh at?" asked Bambi politely.

"Oh!" said the woodpecker, "you go at things in such a wrongheaded way. In the first place, you ought to try big trees, for you can't get anything out of those little wisps of hazel stalks."

"What should I get out of them?" Bambi asked.

"Bugs," said the woodpecker with a laugh. "Bugs and grubs. Look, do like this." He drummed on the oak trunk, tack! tack! tack! tack!

The squirrel rushed up and scolded him. "What are you talking about?" he said. "The Prince isn't looking for bugs and grubs."

"Why not?" said the woodpecker in high glee. "They taste fine." He bit a bug in half, swallowed it and began drumming again.

"You don't understand," the squirrel went on scolding. "A noble lord like that has far other, far higher aims. You're only casting reflection on yourself by such talk."

"It's all the same to me," answered the woodpecker. "A fig for higher aims," he cried cheerfully and fluttered away. The squirrel bustled down again.

"Don't you remember me?" he said, putting on a pleased expression.

"Very well," answered Bambi in a friendly way. "Do you live up there?" he asked, pointing to the oak.

The squirrel looked at him good-humoredly.

"You're mixing me up with my grandmother," he said. "I knew you were mixing me up with her. My grandmother used to live up there when you were just a baby, Prince Bambi. She often told me about you. The ferret killed her long ago, last winter, you may remember it."

"Yes," Bambi nodded. "I've heard about it."

"Well, afterward my father settled here," the squirrel went on. He sat erect and held both forepaws politely over his white chest. "But maybe you've got me mixed up with my father, too. Did you know my father?"

"I'm sorry," Bambi replied. "But I never had that pleasure."

"I thought so," the squirrel exclaimed, satisfied. "Father was so surly and so shy. He had nothing to do with anybody."

"Where is he now?" Bambi inquired.

"Oh," said the squirrel, "the owl caught him a month ago. Yes. . . . And now I'm living up there myself. I'm quite content, since I was born up there."

Bambi turned to go.

"Wait," cried the squirrel quickly, "I didn't mean to talk about all that. I wanted to say something quite different."

Bambi stopped. "What is it?" he asked patiently.

"Yes," said the squirrel, "what is it?" He thought a little while and then gave a quick skip and sat erect, balancing with his splendid tail. He looked at Bambi. "Right you are," he chattered on. "Now I know what it was. I wanted to say that your antlers are almost grown now, and that you are going to be a remarkably handsome person."

"Do you really think so?" said Bambi joyfully.

"Remarkably handsome," cried the squirrel, and pressed his forepaws rapturously against his white chest. "So tall, so stately and with such long bright prongs to your antlers. You don't often see the like."

"Really?" Bambi asked. He was so delighted that he immediately began to beat the hazel stems again. He tore off long ribbons of bark.

All the while the squirrel kept on talking. "I must say that very few have antlers like those at your age. It doesn't seem possible. I saw you several times from a distance last summer, and I can hardly believe that you're the same creature, you were such a thin little shaver then."

Bambi suddenly grew silent. "Goodbye," he said hastily. "I have to go now." And he ran off.

He didn't like to be reminded of last summer. He had had a difficult time of it since then. At first, after his mother's disappearance, he had felt quite lost. The long winter was interminable. Spring came hesitatingly and it was late before things began to turn green. Without old Nettla Bambi might not even have pulled through at all, but she looked after him and helped him where she could. In spite of that he was alone a good deal.

He missed Gobo at every turn; poor Gobo, who was dead too, like the rest of them. Bambi thought of him often during that winter, and for the first time he really began to appreciate how good and lovable Gobo had been.

He seldom saw Faline. She stayed with her mother most of the time and seemed to have grown unusually shy. Later when it had finally grown warm Bambi began to feel his old self once more. He flourished his first antler on high and was very proud of it. But bitter disappointment soon followed.

The other bucks chased him whenever they saw him. They drove him away angrily. They would not let him come near them until finally he was afraid to take a step for fear of being caught. He was afraid to show himself anywhere and slunk along hidden trails in a very downcast frame of mind.

As the summer days grew warmer a remarkable restlessness seized him. His heart felt more and more oppressed with a sense of longing that was both pleasant and painful. Whenever he chanced to see Faline or one of her friends, though only at a distance, a rush of incomprehensible excitement crept over him. Often it happened that he recognized her track, or the air he snuffed told him she was near. Then he would feel himself irresistibly drawn toward her. But when he gave way to his desire he always came to grief. Either he met no one and, after wandering around for a long while, had to admit that they were avoiding him, or he ran across one of the bucks, who immediately sprang at him, beat and kicked him and chased him disgracefully away. Ronno and Karus had treated him worst of all. No, that hadn't been a happy time.

And now the squirrel had stupidly reminded him of it. Suddenly he became quite wild and started to run. The titmice and hedge sparrows flitted, frightened, through the bushes as he passed, and asked each other in a fluster. "What was that?" Bambi did not hear them. A couple of magpies chattered nervously, "What happened?" The jay cried angrily, "What is the matter with you?" Bambi paid no attention to him. Overhead the yellowbird sang from tree to tree, "Good morning, I'm ha-appy." Bambi did not answer. The thicket was very bright and shot through with sunbeams. Bambi did not stop to think about such things.

Suddenly there was a loud whir of wings. A whole rainbow of gorgeous colors flashed from under Bambi's very feet and shone so close to his eyes that he stopped, dazzled. It was Jonello, the pheasant. He had flown up in terror, for Bambi had nearly stepped on him. He fled away scolding.

"I never heard of such a thing," he cried in his split, crackling voice. Bambi stood still in astonishment and stared after him.

"It turned out all right this time, but it really was inconsiderate," said a soft, twittering voice close to the ground. It was Jonellina, the pheasant's wife. She was sitting on the ground, hovering over her eggs. "My husband was terribly frightened," she went on in an irritable tone. "And so was I. But I don't dare stir from this spot. I wouldn't stir from this spot no matter what happened. You could step on me and I wouldn't move."

Bambi was a little embarrassed. "I beg your pardon," he stammered, "I didn't mean to do it."

"Oh, not at all," the pheasant's wife replied. "It was nothing so dreadful after all. But my husband and I are so nervous at present. You can understand why. . . ."

Bambi didn't understand why at all and went on. He was quieter now. The forest sang around him. The light grew more radiant and warmer. The leaves on the bushes, the grass underfoot and the moist, steaming earth began to smell more sweetly. Bambi's young strength swelled within him and streamed through all his limbs so that he walked around stiffly with awkward restrained movements like a mechanical thing.

He went up to a low alder shrub and, lifting his feet high, beat on the earth with such savage blows that the dirt flew. His two sharp-pointed hoofs cut the turf that grew there. They scraped away the wood vetch and leeks, the violets and snowbells, till the bare earth was furrowed in front of him. Every blow sounded dully.

Two moles, who were grubbing among the tangled roots of an old sycamore tree, grew anxious and, looking out, saw Bambi.

"That's a ridiculous way to do things," said one mole. "Who ever heard of anybody digging that way?"

The other mole drew down one corner of his mouth

in a scornful sneer. "He doesn't know anything, you can see that right off," he said. "But that's the way it is when people meddle with things they know nothing about."

Suddenly Bambi listened, tossed up his head, listened again, and peered through the leaves. A flash of red showed through the branches. The prongs of an antler gleamed indistinctly. Bambi snorted. Whoever it might be who was circling around him, whether it was Karus or somebody else, didn't matter. "Forward!" thought Bambi as he charged. "I'll show them that I'm not afraid of them," he thought as though suddenly exultant. "I'll show them that they'd better look out for me."

The branches rustled with the fury of his charge, the bushes cracked and broke. Then Bambi saw the other deer right in front of him. He did not recognize him, for everything was swimming before his eyes. He thought of nothing but "Forward!" His antlers lowered, he rushed on All his strength was concentrated in his shoulders. He was ready for the blow. Then he smelled his opponent's hide. But he saw nothing ahead of him but the red wall of his flank. Then the other stag made a very slight turn and Bambi, not meeting the resistance he expected, charged past him into the empty air. He nearly went head over heels. He staggered, pulled himself together and made ready for a fresh onslaught.

Then he recognized the old stag.

Bambi was so astonished that he lost his self-possession. He was ashamed to run away as he would have liked to do. But he was also ashamed to stay there. He didn't move.

"Well?" asked the old stag, quietly and gently. His voice was so frank and yet so commanding it pierced Bambi to the heart. He was silent.

"Well?" the old stag repeated.

"I thought . . ." Bambi stammered, "I thought . . . it was Ronno . . . or . . ." He stopped and risked a shy glance at the old stag. And this glance confused him still more. The old stag stood motionless and powerful. His head had turned completely white by now, and his proud dark eyes glowed in their depths.

"Why don't you charge me . . . ?" the old stag asked.

Bambi looked at him, filled with a wonderful ecstasy, and shaken by a mysterious tremor. He wanted to cry out, "It's because I love you," but he merely answered, "I don't know. . . ."

The old stag looked at him. "It's a long time since I've seen you," he said. "You've grown big and strong."

Bambi did not answer. He trembled with joy. The old stag went on examining him critically. Then he came unexpectedly up to Bambi, who was terribly frightened.

"Act bravely," said the old stag.

He turned around and in the next moment had disappeared. Bambi remained in that place for a long while.

Chapter Twelve

IT WAS SUMMER AND SIZZLING HOT. The same longing he had felt before began to stir again in Bambi. But much more strongly now than then. It seethed in his blood and made him restless. He strayed far afield.

One day he met Faline. He met her quite unexpectedly, for his thoughts were so confused, his senses so clouded by the restless desire that raged within him, that he did not even recognize Faline. She was standing in front of him. Bambi stared at her speechless for a

while. Then he said as though fascinated, "How beautiful you have grown, Faline!"

"So you recognized me again?" Faline replied.

"How could I help recognizing you?" cried Bambi. "Didn't we grow up together?"

Faline sighed. "It's a long time since we've seen each other," she said. Then she added, "People grow to be strangers," but she was already using her gay bantering tone again. They remained together.

"I used to walk on this path with my mother when I was a child," Bambi said after a while.

"It leads to the meadow," said Faline.

"I saw you for the first time on the meadow," said Bambi a little solemnly. "Do you remember?"

"Yes," Faline replied. "Gobo and me." She sighed softly and said, "Poor Gobo...."

Bambi repeated, "Poor Gobo...."

Then they began to talk about old times and asked each other every minute, "Do you remember?" Each saw that the other still remembered everything. And they were both pleased at that.

"Do you remember how we used to play tag on the meadow?" Bambi reminisced.

"Yes, it was like this," said Faline and she was off like an arrow. At first Bambi hung back, somewhat surprised, and then he rushed after her. "Wait! wait!" he cried joyously.

"I can't wait," teased Faline, "I'm in too much of a hurry." And bounding lightly away, she ran in a circle through the grass and bushes. At last Bambi caught up with her and barred the way. Then they stood quietly side by side. They laughed contentedly. Suddenly Faline leaped into the air as though some one had hit her, and bounded off anew. Bambi rushed after her. Faline raced around and around, always managing to elude him.

"Stop!" Bambi panted. "I want to ask you something."

Faline stopped.

"What do you want to ask me?" she inquired curiously.

Bambi was silent.

"Oh, so you're only fooling me," said Faline, and started to turn away.

"No," said Bambi quickly. "Stop! stop! I wanted . . . I wanted to ask you . . . do you love me, Faline? . . ."

She looked at him more curiously than before, and I little guardedly. "I don't know," she said.

"But you must know," Bambi insisted. "I know very well that I love you. I love you terribly, Faline. Tell me, don't you love me?"

"Maybe I do," she answered coyly.

"And will you stay with me?" Bambi demanded passionately.

"If you ask me nicely," Faline said happily.

"Please do, Faline, dear, beautiful, beloved Faline," cried Bambi, beside himself with love. "Do you hear me? I want you with all my heart."

"Then I'll certainly stay with you," said Faline gently, and ran away.

In ecstasy, Bambi darted after her again. Faline fled straight across the meadow, swerved about and vanished into the thicket. But as Bambi swerved to follow her there was a fierce rustling in the bushes and Karus sprang out.

"Halt!" he cried.

Bambi did not hear him. He was too busy with Faline. "Let me pass," he said hurriedly, "I haven't time for you."

"Get out," Karus commanded angrily. "Get away from here this minute or I'll shake you until there's no breath left in your body. I forbid you to follow Faline."

The memory of last summer when he had been so often and miserably hunted awakened in Bambi. Suddenly he became enraged. He did not say a word, but without waiting any longer rushed at Karus with his antlers lowered.

His charge was irresistible and, before he knew what had happened, Karus was lying in the grass. He was up again quicker than a flash, but was no sooner on his feet than a new attack made him stagger.

"Bambi," he cried, "Bam . . ." he tried to cry again, but a third blow, that glanced off his shoulder, nearly choked him with pain.

Karus sprang to one side in order to elude Bambi, who came rushing on again. Suddenly he felt strangely weak. At the same time he realized with a qualm that this was a life and death struggle. Cold terror seized him. He turned to flee from the silent Bambi who came rushing after him. Karus knew that Bambi was furious and would kill him without mercy, and that thought numbed his wits completely. He fled from the path and, with a final effort, burst through the bushes. His one hope was of escape.

All at once Bambi ceased chasing him. Karus did not even notice this in his terror, and kept straight on through the bushes at fast as he could go. Bambi had stopped because he had heard Faline's shrill call. He listened as she called again in distress and fear. Suddenly he faced about and rushed back.

When he reached the meadow he saw Ronno pursuing Faline, who had fled into the thicket.

"Ronno," cried Bambi. He did not even realize that he had called.

Ronno, who could not run very fast because of his lameness, stood still.

"Oh, there's our little Bambi," he said scornfully, "do you want something from me?"

"I do," said Bambi quietly but in a voice which control and overpowering anger had completely altered. "I want you to let Faline alone and to leave here immediately."

"Is that all?" sneered Ronno. "What an insolent gamin you've got to be. I wouldn't have thought it possible."

"Ronno," said Bambi still more softly, "it's for your own sake. If you don't go now you'll be glad to run later, but then you'll never be able to run again."

"Is that so?" cried Ronno in a rage. "Do you dare to talk to me like that? It's because I limp, I suppose. Most people don't even notice it. Or maybe you think I'm afraid of you, too, because Karus was such a pitiful coward. I give you fair warning . . ."

"No, Ronno," Bambi broke in, "I'll do all the warning. Go!" His voice trembled. "I always liked you, Ronno. I always thought you were very clever and respected you because you were older than I am. I tell you once and for all, go. I haven't any patience left."

"It's a pity you have so little patience," Ronno said with a sneer, "A great pity for you, my boy. But be easy,

I'll soon finish you off. You won't have long to wait. Maybe you've forgotten how often I used to chase you."

At the thought of that Bambi had nothing more to say. Nothing could hold him back. Like a wild beast he tore at Ronno, who met him with his head lowered. They charged together with a crash. Ronno stood firm but wondered why Bambi did not blench back. The sudden charge had dazed him, for he had not expected that Bambi would attack him first. Uneasily he felt Bambi's giant strength and saw that he must keep himself well in hand.

He tried to turn a trick as they stood forehead pressed against forehead. He suddenly shifted his weight so that Bambi lost his balance and staggered forward.

Bambi braced with his hind legs and hurled himself on Ronno with redoubled fury before he had time to regain his footing. A prong broke from Ronno's antlers with a loud snap. Ronno thought his forehead was shattered. The sparks danced before his eyes and there was a roaring in his ears. The next moment a terrific blow tore open his shoulder. His breath failed him and he fell to the ground with Bambi standing over him furiously.

"Let me go," Ronno groaned.

Bambi charged blindly at him. His eyes flashed. He seemed to have no thought of mercy.

"Please stop," whined Ronno pitifully. "Don't you know that I'm lame? I was only joking. Spare me. Can't you take a joke?"

Bambi let him alone without a word. Ronno rose wearily. He was bleeding and his legs tottered. He slunk off in silence.

Bambi started for the thicket to look for Faline, but she came out of her own accord. She had been standing at the edge of the woods and had seen it all.

"That was wonderful," she said laughingly. Then she added softly and seriously, "I love you."

They walked on very happily together.

Chapter Thirteen

ONE DAY THEY WENT TO LOOK
for the little clearing in the depth of the
woods where Bambi had last met the old
stag. Bambi told Faline all about the
old stag and grew enthusiastic.

"Maybe we'll meet him again," he said. "I'd like you
to see him."

"It would be nice," said Faline boldly. "I'd really like
to chat with him once myself." But she wasn't telling

the truth for, though she was very inquisitive, she was afraid of the old stag.

The twilight was already dusky gray. Sunset was near.

They walked softly side by side where the leaves hung quivering on the shrubs and bushes and permitted a clear view in all directions. Presently there was a rustling sound near by. They stopped and looked toward it. Then the old stag marched slowly and powerfully through the bushes, into the clearing. In the drab twilight he seemed like a gigantic gray shadow.

Faline uttered an involuntary cry. Bambi controlled himself. He was terrified, too, and a cry stuck in his throat. But Faline's voice sounded so helpless that pity seized him and made him want to comfort her.

"What's the matter?" he whispered solicitously, while his voice quavered, "what's the matter with you? He isn't going to hurt us."

Faline simply shrieked again.

"Don't be so terribly upset, beloved," Bambi pleaded.

"It's ridiculous to be so frightened by him. After all he's one of our own family."

But Faline wouldn't be comforted. She stood stock still, staring at the stag who went along unconcerned. Then she shrieked and shrieked.

"Pull yourself together," Bambi begged. "What will he think of us?"

But Faline was not to be quieted. "He can think what he likes," she cried bleating again. "Ah-oh! Baoh! . . . It's terrible to be so big!"

She bleated again. "Baoh! Leave me," she went on, "I can't help it, I have to bleat. Baoh, baoh, baoh!"

The stag was standing in the little clearing, looking for tidbits in the grass.

Fresh courage came to Bambi, who had one eye on the hysterical Faline, the other on the placid stag. With the encouragement he had given Faline he had conquered his own fears. He began to reproach himself for the pitiful state he was in whenever he saw the old stag, a state of mingled terror and excitement, admiration and submissiveness.

"It's a perfectly absurd," he said with painful decision. "I'm going straight over to tell him who I am."

"Don't," cried Faline. "Don't! Baoh! Something terrible will happen. Baoh!"

"I'm going anyway," answered Bambi.

The stag who was feasting so calmly, not paying
the slightest attention to the weeping Faline, seemed
altogether too haughty to him. He felt offended and
humiliated. "I'm going," he said. "Be quiet. You'll see,
nothing will happen. Wait for me here."

He went, but Faline did not wait. She hadn't the
least desire or courage to do so. She faced about and
ran away crying, for she thought it was the best thing
she could do. Bambi could hear her going farther and
farther away, bleating, "Baoh! Baoh!"

Bambi would gladly have followed her. But that
was no longer possible. He pulled himself together and
went forward.

Through the branches he saw the stag standing in
the clearing, his head close to the ground. Bambi felt his
heart pounding as he stepped out.

The stag immediately lifted his head and looked at him. Then he gazed absently straight ahead again. The way in which the stag gazed into space, as though no one else were there, seemed as haughty to Bambi as the way he had stared at him.

Bambi did not know what to do. He had come with the firm intention of speaking to the stag. He wanted to say, "Good day, I am Bambi. May I ask to know your honorable name also?"

Yes, it had all seemed very easy, but now it appeared that the affair was not so simple. What good were the best of intentions now? Bambi did not want to seem ill-bred, as he would be if he went off without saying a word. But he did not want to seem forward either, and he would be if he began the conversation.

The stag was wonderfully majestic. It delighted Bambi and made him feel humble. He tried in vain to arouse his courage and kept asking himself, "Why do I let him frighten me? Am I not just as good as he is?" But it was no use, Bambi continued to be frightened and felt in his heart of hearts that he really was not as good as the old stag. Far from it. He felt wretched and had to use all his strength to keep himself steady.

The old stag looked at him and thought, "He's handsome, he's really charming, so delicate, so poised, so elegant in his whole bearing. I must not stare at him, though. It really isn't the thing to do. Besides, it might embarrass him." So he stared over Bambi's head into the empty air again.

"What a haughty look," thought Bambi. "It's unbearable, the opinion such people have of themselves."

The stag was thinking, "I'd like to talk to him, he looks so sympathetic. How stupid never to speak to people we don't know." He looked thoughtfully ahead of him.

"I might as well be air," said Bambi to himself. "This fellow acts as though he were the only thing on the face of the earth."

"What should I say to him?" the old stag was wondering. "I'm not used to talking. I'd say something stupid and make myself ridiculous . . . for he's undoubtedly very clever."

Bambi pulled himself together and looked fixedly at the stag. "How splendid he is," he thought despairingly.

"Well, some other time, perhaps," the stag decided and walked off, dissatisfied but majestic.

Bambi remained filled with bitterness.

Chapter Fourteen

THE FOREST SWELTERED UNDER A scorching sun. Since it rose it had driven even the tiniest cloudlet from the sky and shone all alone in the wide blue depths that were pallid now with heat. Over the meadows and the treetops the air quivered in glassy, transparent ripples as it does over a flame. Not a leaf was moving, not a blade of grass. The birds were silent and sat hidden among the shady leaves, never stirring from their places. All the paths and trails in the thicket were empty. Not a creature was abroad. The forest lay as though hurt by the blinding light. The earth and the trees, the bushes, the beasts, breathed in the intense heat with a kind of sluggish satisfaction.

Bambi was asleep.

He had made merry with Faline all night. He had pranced around with her until broad daylight, and in his bliss had even forgotten to eat. But he had grown so tired that he did not feel hungry any more. His eyes fell shut. He lay down where he happened to be standing in the middle of the bushes and fell asleep at once.

The bitter acrid odor that streamed from the sun-warmed juniper, and the penetrating scent of spurge laurel, mounted to his head while he slept and gave him new strength. Suddenly he awoke in a daze. Had Faline called him? Bambi looked around. He remembered seeing Faline as he lay down, standing close beside him near the whitethorn, nibbling the leaves. He had supposed she would remain near him, but she was gone. Apparently she had grown tired of being alone by now and was calling for him to come and look for her.

As Bambi listened he wondered how long he could have slept and how often Faline had called. He wasn't sure. Veils of sleep still clouded his thought.

Then she called again. With a sidewise spring Bambi turned in the direction the sound came from. Then he heard it again. And suddenly he felt perfectly happy. He was wonderfully refreshed, quieted and strengthened, but racked by a terrific appetite.

The call came again clearly, thin as a bird's twittering, tender and full of longing: "Come, come!" it said.

Yes, that was her voice. That was Faline. Bambi rushed away so fast that the dry branches barely crackled as he burst through the bushes and the hot green leaves scarcely rustled.

But he had to stop short in the midst of his course and swerve to one side, for the old stag was standing there, barring his path.

Bambi had no time for anything but love. The old stag was indifferent to him now. He would meet him again somewhere later on. He had no time for old stags now, however noble they might be, He had thoughts for Faline alone. He greeted the stag hastily and tried to hurry by.

"Where are you going?" asked the old stag earnestly.

Bambi was somewhat embarrassed and tried to think of an evasion, but he changed his mind and answered truthfully, "To her."

"Don't go," said the old stag.

For a second a single angry spark flared up in Bambi's mind. Not go to Faline? How could the mean old stag ask that? "I'll simply run off," Bambi thought. And he looked quickly at the old stag. But the deep look that met him in the old stag's eyes held him fast. He quivered with impatience but he did not run away.

"She's calling me," he said in explanation. He said it in a tone which clearly bleated. "Don't keep me talking here."

"No," said the old stag, "she isn't calling."

The call came once again, thin as a bird's twittering, "Come!"

"Listen," Bambi cried excitedly, "there it is again."

"I hear it," said the old stag, nodding.

"Well, goodbye," Bambi flung back hurriedly.

"Stop!" the old stag commanded.

"What do you want?" cried Bambi, beside himself with impatience. "Let me go. I have no time. Please, Faline is calling. . . . You ought to see that. . . ."

"I tell you," the old stag said, "that it isn't she."

Bambi was desperate. "But," he said, "I know her voice."

"Listen to me," the old stag went on.

Again the call came. Bambi felt the ground burning under his feet. "Later," he pleaded, "I'll come right back."

"No," said the old stag sadly, "you'll never come back, never again."

The call came again. "I must go! I must go!" cried Bambi, who was nearly out of his wits.

"Then," the old stag declared in a commanding voice, "we'll go together."

"Quickly," cried Bambi and bounded off.

"No, slowly," commanded the old stag in a voice that forced Bambi to obey. "Stay in back of me. Move one step at a time."

The old stag began to move forward. Bambi followed, sighing with impatience.

"Listen," said the old stag without stopping, "no matter how often that call comes, don't stir from my side. If it's Faline, you'll get to her soon enough. But it isn't Faline. Don't let yourself be tempted. Everything depends now on whether you trust me or not."

Bambi did not dare to resist, and surrendered in silence.

The old stag advanced slowly and Bambi followed him. Oh how cleverly the old stag moved! Not a sound came from under his hoofs. Not a leaf was disturbed. Not a twig snapped. And yet they were gliding through thick bushes, slinking through the ancient tangled thicket. Bambi was amazed and had to admire him in spite of his impatience. He had never dreamed that anybody could move like that.

The call came again and again. The old stag stood still, listening and nodding his head. Bambi stood beside him, shaken with desire, and suffering from restraint. He could not understand it at all.

Several times the old stag stopped, although no call had come, and lifted his head, listening and nodding. Bambi heard nothing. The old stag turned away from the direction of the call and made a detour. Bambi raged inwardly because of it.

The call came again and again. At last they drew nearer to it, then still nearer. At last they were quite near.

The old stag whispered, "No matter what you see, don't move, do you hear? Watch everything I do and act just as I do, cautiously. And don't lose your head."

They went a few steps farther and suddenly that sharp, arresting scent that Bambi knew so well struck them full in the face. He swallowed so much of it that he nearly cried out. He stood as though rooted to the ground. For a moment his heart seemed pounding in his throat. The old stag stood calmly beside him and motioned with his eyes.

He was standing there.

He was standing quite close to them leaning against the trunk of an oak, hidden by hazel bushes. He was calling softly, "Come, come!"

Bambi was completely bewildered. He was so terrified that he began to understand only by degrees that it was He who was imitating Faline's voice. It was He who was calling, "Come, come!"

Cold terror shot through Bambi's body. The idea of flight gripped him and tugged at his heart.

"Be still," whispered the old stag quickly and commandingly as if he meant to forestall any outbreak of fear. Bambi controlled himself with an effort.

The old stag looked at him a little scornfully at first, it seemed to Bambi. He noticed it in spite of the state he was in. But the stag changed at once to a serious and kindly look.

Bambi peered out with blinking eyes to where He was standing, and felt as if he could not bear His horrible presence much longer.

As if he had read his thought, the old stag whispered to him, "Let's go back," and turned about.

They glided away cautiously. The old stag moved with a marvelous zigzag course whose purpose Bambi did not understand. Again he followed with painfully controlled impatience. The longing for Faline had harassed him on the way over; now the impulse to flee was beating through his veins.

But the old stag walked on slowly, stopping and listening. He would begin a new zigzag, then stop again, going very slowly ahead.

By this time they were far from the danger spot. "If he stops again," thought Bambi, "it ought to be all right to speak to him by now, and I'll thank him."

But at that moment the old stag vanished under his very eyes into a thick tangle of dogwood shrubs. Not a leaf stirred, not a twig snapped as the stag slipped away.

Bambi followed and tried to get through as noiselessly and to avoid every sound with as much skill. But he was not so lucky. The leaves swished gently, the boughs bent against his flanks and sprang up again with a loud twang; dry branches broke against his chest with sharp piercing snaps.

"He saved my life," Bambi kept thinking. "What can I say to him?"

But the old stag was nowhere to be seen. Bambi

came out of the bushes. Around him was a sea of yellow, flowering goldenrod. He raised his head and looked around. Not a leaf was moving as far as he could see. He was all alone.

Freed from all control, the impulse to flee suddenly carried him away. The goldenrods parted with a loud swish beneath his bounding hoofs as though under the stroke of a scythe.

After wandering about for a long time he found Faline. He was breathless, tired and happy and deeply stirred.

"Please, beloved," he said, "please don't ever call me again. We'll search until we find each other, but please don't ever call me . . . for I can't resist your voice."

Chapter Fifteen

A FEW DAYS LATER THEY WERE walking carefree together through an oak thicket on the far side of the meadow. They had to cross the meadow in order to reach their old trail where the tall oak stood.

As the bushes grew thinner around them they stopped and peered out. Something red was moving near the oak. Both of them looked at it.

"Who can it be?" whispered Bambi.

"Probably Ronno or Karus," said Faline.

Bambi doubted it. "They don't dare come near me any more," Bambi said, peering sharply ahead. "No," he decided, "that's not Karus or Ronno. It's a stranger."

Faline agreed, surprised, and very curious. "Yes," she said, "it's a stranger. I see it, too, now. How curious!"

They watched him.

"How carelessly he acts," exclaimed Faline.

"Stupid," said Bambi, "really stupid. He acts like a little child, as if there were no danger."

"Let's go over," Faline proposed. Her curiosity was getting the better of her.

"All right," Bambi answered. "Let's go, I want to have a better look at the fellow."

They took a few steps and then Faline stopped. "Suppose he wants to fight you," she said. "He's strong."

"Bah," said Bambi holding his head cocked and putting on a disdainful air, "look at the little antlers he has. Should I be afraid of that? The fellow is fat and sleek enough, but is he strong? I don't think so. Come along."

They went on.

The stranger was busy nibbling meadow grass and

did not notice them until they were a good way across the meadow. Then he ran forward to meet them. He gave joyful playful skips that made a curiously childish impression. Bambi and Faline stopped, surprised, and waited for him. When he was a few steps off he stood still likewise.

After a while he asked, "Don't you know me?"

Bambi had lowered his head prepared for battle. "Do you know us?" he retorted.

The stranger interrupted him. "Bambi," he cried reproachfully, yet confidently.

Bambi was startled to hear his name spoken. The sound of that voice stirred an old memory in his heart. But Faline had rushed toward the stranger.

"Gobo," she cried and became speechless. She stood there silent without moving. She couldn't breathe.

"Faline," said Gobo softly, "Faline, sister, you knew me anyway." He went to her and kissed her mouth. The tears were running down his cheeks. Faline was crying too, and couldn't speak.

"Well, Gobo," Bambi began. His voice trembled and he felt very bewildered. He was deeply moved and very much surprised. "Well, so you're not dead," he said.

Gobo burst out laughing. "You see that I'm not dead," he said; "at least I think you can see that I'm not."

"But what happened that time in the snow?" Bambi persisted.

"Oh then?" Gobo said thoughtfully. "He rescued me then."

"And where have you been all this time?" asked Faline in astonishment.

"With Him," Gobo replied, "I've been with Him all the time."

He grew silent and looked at Faline and at Bambi. Their helpless astonishment delighted him. Then he added, "Yes, my dears, I've seen a lot more than all of you put together in your old forest." He sounded somewhat boastful, but they paid no attention to it. They were still too much absorbed in their great surprise.

"Tell us about it," cried Faline, beside herself with joy.

"Oh," said Gobo with satisfaction, "I could talk all day about it and never reach the end."

"Well then, go ahead and talk," Bambi urged.

Gobo turned to Faline and grew serious. "Is Mother still alive?" he asked timidly and softly.

"Yes," cried Faline gladly. "She's alive but I haven't seen her for a long while."

"I'm going to see her right away," said Gobo with decision. "Are you coming too?"

They all went.

They did not speak another word the whole way. Bambi and Faline felt Gobo's impatient longing to see his mother, so both of them kept silent. Gobo walked ahead hurriedly and did not speak. They let him do as he liked.

Only sometimes when he hurried blindly over a cross trail or when, in a sudden burst of speed, he took the wrong turning, they called gently to him. "This way," Bambi would whisper, or Faline would say, "No, no, we go this way now."

A number of times they had to cross wide clearings. They noticed that Gobo never stopped at the edge of the thicket, never peered around for a moment when he walked into the open, but simply ran out without any precaution. Bambi and Faline exchanged astonished glances whenever this happened, but they never said a word and followed Gobo with some hesitation. They had to wander around sometimes and search high and low.

Gobo recollected his childhood paths at once He was delighted with himself, never realizing that Bambi and Faline were leading him. He looked around at them and called, "How do you like the way I can still find my way around?" They did not say anything, but they exchanged glances again.

Soon afterward they came to a small leafy hollow. "Look," cried Faline and glided in. Gobo followed her and stopped. It was the glade in which they were both born and had lived with their mother as little children. Gobo and Faline looked into each other's eyes. They did not say a word. But Faline kissed her brother gently on the mouth. Then they hurried on.

They walked to and fro for a good hour. The sun shone brighter and brighter through the branches and the forest grew stiller and stiller. It was the time for lying down and resting. But Gobo didn't feel tired. He walked swiftly ahead, breathing deeply with impatience and excitement, and gazed aimlessly about him. He shrank together whenever a weasel slunk through the bushes at his feet. He nearly stepped on the pheasants, and when they scolded him, flying up with a loud flapping of wings, he was terribly frightened. Bambi marveled at the strange, blind way Gobo moved around.

Presently Gobo stopped and turned to them both. "She isn't anywhere here," he cried in despair.

Faline soothed him. "We'll soon find her," she said, deeply moved, "soon, Gobo." She looked at him. He still had that dejected look she knew so well.

"Shall we call her?" she asked smiling. "Shall we call her the way we used to when we were children?"

Bambi went away a few steps. Then he saw Aunt Ena. She had already settled herself to rest and was lying quietly in a nearby hazel bush.

"At last," he said to himself. At the same moment Gobo and Faline came up. All three of them stood together and looked at Ena. She had raised her head quietly and looked sleepily back at them.

Gobo took a few hesitating steps and cried softly, "Mother."

She was on her feet in a flash and stood as though transfixed. Gobo sprang to her quickly. "Mother," he began again. He tried to speak but couldn't utter a word.

His mother looked deep into his eyes. Her rigid body began to move. Wave after wave of trembling broke over her shoulders and down her back.

She did not ask any questions. She did not want any explanation or history. She kissed Gobo slowly on the mouth. She kissed his cheeks and his neck. She bathed him tirelessly in her kisses, as she had when he was born.

Bambi and Faline had gone away.

Chapter Sixteen

THEY WERE ALL STANDING AROUND in the middle of the thicket in a little clearing. Gobo was talking to them.

Even Friend Hare was there. Full of astonishment, he would lift one spoonlike ear, listen attentively, and let it fall back, only to lift it again at once.

The magpie was perched on the lowest branch of a young beech and listened in amazement. The jay was sitting restlessly on an ash opposite and screamed every once in a while in wonder.

A few friendly pheasants had brought their wives and children and were stretching their necks in surprise as they listened. At times they would jerk them in again, turning their heads this way and that in speechless wonder.

The squirrel had scurried up and was gesturing, wild with excitement. At times he would slide to the ground, at times he would run up some tree or other. Or he would balance with his tail erect and display his white chest. Every now and again he tried to interrupt Gobo and say something, but he was always told sternly to keep quiet.

Gobo told how he had lain helpless in the snow waiting to die.

"The dogs found me," he said. "Dogs are terrible. They are certainly the most terrible creatures in the world. Their jaws drip blood and their bark is pitiless and full of anger." He looked all around the circle and continued. "Well, since then I've played with them just as I would with one of you." He was very proud. "I don't need to be afraid of them any more, I'm good friends with them now. Nevertheless, when they begin to grow angry, I have a roaring in my ears and my heart stops beating. But they don't really mean any harm by it and, as I said, I'm a good friend of theirs. But their bark is terribly loud."

"Go on," Faline urged.

Gobo looked at her. "Well," he said, "they would have torn me to pieces, but He came."

Gobo paused. The others hardly breathed.

"Yes," said Gobo, "He came. He called off the dogs and they quieted down at once. He called them again and they crouched motionless at His feet. Then He picked me up. I screamed but He petted me. He held me in His arms. He didn't hurt me. And then He carried me away."

Faline interrupted him. "What does 'carry' mean?" she asked.

Gobo began to explain it in great detail.

"It's very simple," Bambi broke in, "look at what the squirrel does when he takes a nut and carries it off."

The squirrel tried to speak again. "A cousin of mine..."

he began eagerly. But the others cried out at once, "Be still, be still, let Gobo go on."

The squirrel had to keep quiet. He was desperate and, pressing his forepaws against his white chest, he tried to begin a conversation with the magpie. "As I was saying, a cousin of mine . . ." he began. But the magpie simply turned her back on him.

Gobo told of wonders. "Outside it will be cold and the storm is howling. But inside there's not a breath of wind and it's as warm as in summertime," he said.

"Akh!" screamed the jay.

"The rain may be pouring outside so that everything is flooded. But not a drop of it gets inside and you keep dry."

The pheasants craned their necks and twisted their heads.

"Everything outside may be snowed under, but inside I was warm," said Gobo; "I was even hot. They gave me hay to eat and chestnuts, potatoes and turnips, whatever I wanted."

"Hay?" they all cried at once, amazed, incredulous and excited.

"Sweet, new-mown hay," Gobo repeated calmly, and gazed triumphantly around.

The squirrel's voice cut in, "A cousin of mine . . ."

"Keep quiet," cried the others.

"Where does He get hay and all the rest of the things in winter?" asked Faline eagerly.

"He grows them," Gobo answered, "He grows what He wants and keeps what He wants."

Faline went on questioning him: "Weren't you ever afraid, Gobo, when you were with Him?" she asked.

Gobo smiled a very superior smile. "No, dear Faline," he said, "not any more. I got to know that He wouldn't hurt me. Why should I have been afraid? You all think He's wicked. But He isn't wicked. If He loves anybody or if anybody serves Him, He's good to him. Wonderfully good! Nobody in the world can be as kind as He can."

While Gobo was talking that way the old stag suddenly stepped noiselessly from the bushes.

Gobo didn't notice him and went on talking. But

the others saw the old stag and held their breath in awe.

The old stag stood motionless, watching Gobo with deep and serious eyes.

Gobo said, "Not only He, but all His children loved me. His wife and all of them used to pet me and play with me." He broke off suddenly. He had seen the old stag.

A silence followed.

Then the old stag asked in his quiet commanding voice, "What kind of a band is that you have on your neck?"

Everybody looked at it and noticed for the first time the dark strip of braided horsehair around Gobo's neck.

Gobo answered uneasily, "That? Why, that's part of the halter I wore. It's His halter and it's the greatest honor to wear His halter, it's . . ." He grew confused and stammered.

Everyone was silent. The old stag looked at Gobo for a long time, piercingly and sadly.

"You poor thing!" he said softly at last, and turned and was gone.

In the astonished silence that followed, the squirrel began to chatter again. "As I was saying, a cousin of mine stayed with Him, too. He caught him and shut him up, oh, for the longest while, till one day my father . . ."

But nobody was listening to the squirrel. They were all walking away.

Chapter Seventeen

ONE DAY MARENA APPEARED again. She was almost full grown the winter that Gobo disappeared, but she had hardly ever been seen since, for she lived alone, going her own ways.

She had stayed slender and looked quite young. But she was quiet and serious and gentler than any of the others. She had heard from the squirrel and the jay, the magpie and the thrushes and pheasants that Gobo had returned from his wonderful adventures. So she came back to see him.

Gobo's mother was very proud and happy over her visit. Gobo's mother had grown rather proud of her good fortune. She was delighted to hear the whole forest talking about her son. She basked in his glory and wanted everybody to know that her Gobo was the cleverest, ablest and best deer living.

"What do you think of him, Marena?" she exclaimed. "What do you think of our Gobo?" She didn't wait for an answer but went on, "Do you remember how old Nettla said he wasn't worth much because he shivered a little in the cold? Do you remember how she prophesied that he'd be nothing but a care to me?"

"Well," Marena answered, "you've had plenty of worry over Gobo."

"That's all over with now," his mother exclaimed. She wondered how people could still remember such things. "Oh, I'm sorry for poor old Nettla. What a pity that she couldn't live to see what my Gobo's become!"

"Yes, poor old Nettla," said Marena softly, "it's too bad about her."

Gobo liked to hear his mother praise him that way. It pleased him. He stood around and basked as happily in her praises as in the sunshine.

"Even the old Prince came to see Gobo," his mother told Marena. She whispered it as though it were something solemn and mysterious. "He never let anyone so much as get a glimpse of him before, but he came on account of Gobo."

"Why did he call me a poor thing?" Gobo broke in in a discontented tone. "I'd like to know what he meant by that."

"Don't think about it," his mother said to comfort him, "he's old and queer."

But at last Gobo meant to ease his mind. "All day long it keeps running through my head," he said. "Poor thing! I'm not a poor thing. I'm very lucky. I've seen more and been through more than all the rest of you put together. I've seen more of the world and I know more about life than anyone in the forest. What do you think, Marena?"

"Yes," she said, "no one can deny that."

From then on Marena and Gobo were always together.

Chapter Eighteen

BAMBI WENT TO LOOK FOR THE OLD stag. He roamed around all night long. He wandered till the sun rose and dawn found him on unbeaten trails without Faline.

He was still drawn to Faline at times. At times he loved her just as much as ever. Then he liked to roam about with her, to listen to her chatter, to browse with her on the meadow or at the edge of the thicket. But she no longer satisfied him completely.

Before, when he was with Faline, he hardly ever

remembered his meetings with the old stag, and when he did it was only casually. Now he was looking for him and felt an inexplicable desire driving him to find him. He only thought of Faline between whiles. He could always be with her if he wanted to. He did not much care to stay with the others. Gobo or Aunt Ena he avoided when he could.

The words the old stag had let fall about Gobo kept ringing in Bambi's ears. They made a peculiarly deep impression on him. Gobo had affected him strangely from the very first day of his return. Bambi didn't know why, but there was something painful to him in Gobo's bearing. Bambi was ashamed of Gobo without knowing why. And he was afraid for him, again without knowing why. Whenever he was together with this harmless, vain, self-conscious and self-satisfied Gobo, the words kept running through his head, "Poor thing!" He couldn't get rid of them.

But one dark night when Bambi had again delighted the screech owl by assuring him how badly he was frightened, it suddenly occurred to him to ask, "Do you happen to know where the old stag is now?"

The screech owl answered in his cooing voice that he didn't have the least idea in the world. But Bambi perceived that he simply didn't want to tell.

"No," he said, "I don't believe you, you're too clever. You know everything that's happening in the forest. You certainly must know where the old stag is hiding."

The screech owl, who was all fluffed up, smoothed his feathers against his body and made himself small. "Of course I know," he cooed still more softly, "but I oughtn't to tell you, I really oughtn't."

Bambi began to plead. "I won't give you away," he said. "How could I, when I respect you so much?"

The owl became a lovely, soft gray-brown ball again and rolled his big cunning eyes a little as he always did when he felt in a good humor. "So you really do respect me," he asked, "and why, pray?"

Bambi did not hesitate. "Because you're so wise," he said sincerely, "and so good-natured and friendly, besides.

And because you're so clever at frightening people. It's so very clever to frighten people, so very, very clever. I wish I could do it, it would be a great help to me."

The screech owl had sunk his bill into his downy breast and was happy.

"Well," he said, "I know that the old stag would be glad to see you."

"Do you really think so?" cried Bambi while his heart began to beat faster for joy.

"Yes, I'm sure of it," the owl answered. "He'd be glad to see you, and I think I can venture to tell you where he is now."

He laid his feathers close to his body and suddenly grew thin again.

"Do you know the deep ditch where the willows stand?"

Bambi nodded yes.

"Do you know the young oak thicket on the farther side?"

"No," Bambi confessed, "I've never been on the farther side."

"Well, listen carefully then," the owl whispered. "There's an oak thicket on the far side. Go through that. Then there are bushes, hazel and silver poplar, thorn and shadbush. In the midst of them is an old uprooted beech. You'll have to hunt for it. It's not so easy to see it from your height as it is from the air. You'll find him under the trunk. But don't tell him I told you."

"Under the trunk?" said Bambi.

"Yes," the screech owl laughed, "there's a hollow in the ground there. The trunk lies right across it. And he sleeps under the trunk."

"Thank you," said Bambi sincerely. "I don't know if I can find it, but I'm very grateful anyhow." He ran quickly away.

The screech owl flew noiselessly after him and began to hoot right beside him. "Oi, oi!" Bambi shrank together.

"Did I frighten you?" asked the owl.

"Yes," he stammered, and that time he told the truth.

The owl cooed with satisfaction and said, "I only wanted to remind you again. Don't tell him I told you."

"Of course not," Bambi assured him and ran on.

When Bambi reached the ditch the old stag rose before him out of the pitch-black night so noiselessly and suddenly that Bambi drew back in terror.

"I'm no longer where you were going to look for me," said the stag.

Bambi was silent.

"What is it you want?" asked the stag.

"Nothing," Bambi stammered, "nothing, excuse me, nothing at all."

After a while the old stag spoke, and his voice sounded gentle. "This isn't the first time you've been looking for me," he said.

He waited. Bambi did not answer. The old stag went on, "Yesterday you passed close by me twice, and again this morning, very close."

"Why," said Bambi gathering courage, "why did you say that about Gobo?"

"Do you think that I was wrong?"

"No," cried Bambi sorrowfully, "no, I feel that you were right."

The old stag gave a barely perceptible nod and his eyes rested on Bambi more kindly than ever before.

"But why?" Bambi said, "I don't understand it."

"It's enough that you feel it. You will understand it later," the old stag said. "Goodbye."

Chapter Nineteen

EVERYBODY SOON SAW THAT GOBO had habits which seemed strange and suspicious to the rest of them. He slept at night when the others were awake. But in the daytime, when the rest of them were looking for places to sleep in, he was wide awake and went walking. When he felt like it he would even go out of the thicket without any hesitation and stand with perfect peace of mind in the bright sunshine on the meadow.

Bambi found it impossible to keep silent any longer.

"Don't you ever think of the danger?" he asked.

"No," Gobo said simply, "there isn't any for me."

"You forget, my dear Bambi," Gobo's mother broke in, "you forget that He's a friend of Gobo's. Gobo can take chances that the rest of you cannot take." She was very proud.

Bambi did not say anything more.

One day Gobo said to him, "You know, it seems strange to me to eat when and where I like."

Bambi did not understand. "Why is it strange, we all do it," he said.

"Oh, you do," said Gobo superiorly, "but I'm a little different. I'm accustomed to having my food brought to me or to being called when it's ready."

Bambi stared pityingly at Gobo. He looked at Faline and Marena and Aunt Ena. But they were all smiling and admiring Gobo.

"I think it will be hard for you to get accustomed to the winter, Gobo," Faline began; "we don't have hay or turnips or potatoes in the winter time."

"That's true," answered Gobo reflectively, "I hadn't

thought about that yet. I can't even imagine how it would feel. It must be dreadful."

Bambi said quietly, "It isn't dreadful. It's only hard."

"Well," Gobo declared grandly, "if it gets too hard for me I'll simply go back to Him. Why should I go hungry? There's no need for that."

Bambi turned away without a word and walked off.

When Gobo was alone again with Marena he began to talk about Bambi. "He doesn't understand me," he said. "Poor old Bambi thinks I'm still the silly little Gobo that I once was. He can never get used to the fact that I've become something unusual. Danger! . . . What does he mean by danger? He means well enough by me, but danger is something for him and the likes of him, not for me."

Marena agreed with him. She loved him and Gobo loved her and they were both very happy.

"Well," he said to her, "nobody understands me the way you do. But anyhow I can't complain. I'm respected and honored by everybody. But you understand me best of all. When I tell the others how good He is, they listen and they don't think I'm lying, but they stick to their opinion that He's dreadful."

"I've always believed in Him," said Marena dreamily.

"Really?" Gobo replied airily.

"Do you remember the day when they left you lying in the snow?" Marena went on. "I said that day that sometime He'd come to the forest to play with us."

"No," Gobo replied yawning, "I don't remember that."

A few weeks passed, and one morning Bambi and Faline, Gobo and Marena were standing together again in the old familiar hazel thicket. Bambi and Faline were just returning from their wanderings, intending to look for their hiding place, when they met Gobo and Marena. Gobo was about to go out on the meadow.

"Stay with us instead," said Bambi, "the sun will soon be rising and then nobody will go out in the open."

"Nonsense," said Gobo, scornfully, "if nobody else will go, I will."

He went on, Marena following him.

Bambi and Faline had stopped. "Come along," said

Bambi angrily to Faline, "come along. Let him do what he pleases."

They were going on, but suddenly the jay screamed loudly from the far side of the meadow. With a bound Bambi had turned and was running after Gobo. Right by the oak he caught up with him and Marena.

"Did you hear that?" he cried to him.

"What?" asked Gobo, puzzled.

Again the jay screamed on the far side of the meadow.

"Did you hear that?" Bambi repeated.

"No," said Gobo calmly.

"That means danger," Bambi persisted.

A magpie began to chatter loudly and, immediately after her, another and then a third. Then the jay screamed again and far overhead the crows gave warning.

Faline began to plead. "Don't go out there, Gobo! It's dangerous."

Even Marena begged, "Stay here. Stay here today, beloved one. It's dangerous."

Gobo stood there, smiling in his superior way. "Dangerous! dangerous! What has that to do with me?" he asked.

His pressing need gave Bambi an idea. "At least let Marena go first," he said, "so we can find out ..."

He hadn't finished before Marena had slipped out.

All three stood and looked at her. Bambi and Faline breathlessly, Gobo with obvious patience, as if to let the others enjoy their foolish whims.

They saw how Marena walked across the meadow step by step, with hesitant feet, her head up. She peered and snuffed in all directions. Suddenly she turned like a flash with one high bound and, as though a cyclone had struck her, rushed back into the thicket.

"It's He, He," she whispered, her voice choking with terror. She was trembling in every limb. "I, I saw Him," she stammered, "it's He. He's standing over by the alders."

"Come," cried Bambi, "come quickly."

"Come," Faline pleaded. And Marena, who could hardly speak, whispered, "Please come now, Gobo, please."

But Gobo remained unmoved. "Run as much as you like," he said, "I won't stop you. If He's there I want to talk with Him."

Gobo could not be dissuaded.

They stood and watched how he went out. They stayed there, moved by his great confidence, while at the same time a terrible fear for him gripped them.

Gobo was standing boldly on the meadow looking around for the alders. Then he seemed to see them and to have discovered Him. Then the thunder crashed.

Gobo leaped into the air at the report. He suddenly turned around and fled back to the thicket, staggering as he came.

They still stood there, petrified with terror, while he came on. They heard him gasping for breath. And as he did not stop but bounded wildly forward, they turned and surrounded him and all took flight.

But poor Gobo dropped to the ground. Marena stopped close to him, Bambi and Faline a little farther off, ready to flee.

Gobo lay with his bloody entrails oozing from his torn flank. He lifted his head with a feeble twisting motion.

"Marena," he said with an effort, "Marena. . . ." He did not recognize her. His voice failed.

There was a loud careless rustling in the bushes by the meadow. Marena bent her head toward Gobo. "He's coming," she whispered frantically, "Gobo, He's coming! Can't you get up and come with me?"

Gobo lifted his head again feebly with a writhing motion, beat convulsively with his hoofs and then lay still.

With a crackling, snapping and rustling He parted the bushes and stepped out.

Marena saw Him from quite near. She slunk slowly back, disappearing through the nearest bushes, and hastened to Bambi and Faline.

She looked back once again and saw how He was bending over and seizing the wounded deer.

Then they heard Gobo's wailing death shriek.

Chapter Twenty

BAMBI WAS ALONE. HE WALKED beside the water that ran swiftly among the reeds and swamp willows.

He went there more and more often now that he was staying by himself. There were few trails there, and he hardly ever met any of his friends. That was just what he wanted. For his thoughts had grown serious and his heart heavy. He did not know what was happening within him. He did not even think about it. He merely recalled things aimlessly,

and his whole life seemed to have become darker.

He used to stand for hours on the bank. The current, that flowed round a gentle bend there, occupied his entire thought. The cool air from the ripples brought him strange, refreshing, acrid smells that aroused forgetfulness and a sense of trust in him.

Bambi would stand and watch the ducks paddling companionably together. They talked endlessly to one another in a friendly, serious, capable way.

There were a couple of mother ducks, each with a flock of young ones around her. They were constantly teaching their young ones things. And the little ones were always learning them. Sometimes one or the other of the mothers would give a warning. Then the young ducks would dash off in all directions. They would scatter and glide away perfectly noiselessly. Bambi saw how the smallest ones, who could not fly yet, would paddle among the thicket rushes without moving a stem that might betray them by swaying. He would see the small dark bodies creep here and there among the reeds. Then he could see nothing more.

Later one of the mothers would give a short call and in a flash they would all flock around her again. In an instant they would reassemble their flotilla and go on cruising quietly about as before. Bambi marveled anew at it each time. It was a constant source of wonder to him.

After one such alarm, Bambi asked one of the mothers, "What was it? I was looking closely and I didn't see anything."

"It was nothing at all," answered the duck.

Another time one of the children gave the signal, turning like a flash and staring through the reeds. Presently he came out on the bank where Bambi was standing.

"There wasn't anything," the young one replied, shaking its tail feathers in a grown-up way and carefully putting the tips of its wings in place. Then it paddled through the water again.

Nevertheless Bambi had faith in the ducks. He came to the conclusion that they were more watchful than he, that they heard and saw things more quickly. When he stood watching them, that ceaseless tension that he felt within himself at other times relaxed a little.

He liked to talk with the ducks, too. They didn't talk the nonsense that he so often heard from the others. They talked about the broad skies and the wind and about distant fields where they feasted on choice tidbits.

From time to time Bambi saw something that looked like a fiery streak in the air beside the brook. "Srrrri!" the hummingbird would cry softly, darting past like a tiny whirring speck. There was a gleam of green, a glow of red, as he flashed by and was gone. Bambi was thrilled and wanted to see the bright stranger near to. He called to him.

"Don't bother calling him," the sedge hen said to Bambi from among the reed clumps, "don't bother calling. He'll never answer you."

"Where are you?" asked Bambi, peering among the reeds.

But the sedge hen only laughed loudly from an entirely different place, "Here I am. That cranky creature you just called to won't talk to anyone. It's useless to call him."

"He's so handsome," said Bambi.

"But bad," the sedge hen retorted from still another place.

"What makes you think him bad?" Bambi inquired.

The sedge hen answered from an altogether different place, "He doesn't care for anything or anybody. Let anything happen that wants to, he won't speak to anybody and never thanked anybody for speaking to him. He never gives anybody warning when there's danger. He's never said a word to a living soul."

"The poor . . ." said Bambi.

The sedge hen went on talking, and her cheery, piping voice sounded from the far side again. "He probably thinks that people are jealous of his silly markings and doesn't want them to get too good a look at him."

"Certain other people don't let you get a good look at them either," said Bambi.

In a twinkling the sedge hen was standing in front of him. "There's nothing to look at in my case," she said simply. Small and gleaming with water, she stood there in her sleek feathers, her trim figure restless, animated and satisfied. In a flash she was gone again.

"I don't understand how people can stand so long in one spot," she called from the water. And added from the far side, "It's tiresome and dangerous to stay so long in one spot." Then from the other side she cried gaily once or twice. "You have to keep moving," she cried happily, "you've got to keep moving if you want to keep whole and hearty."

A soft rustling in the grass startled Bambi. He looked around. There was a reddish flash among the bushes. It disappeared in the reeds. At the same time a sharp warm smell reached his nostrils. The fox had slunk by.

Bambi wanted to cry out and stamp on the ground as a warning. But the sedges rustled as the fox parted them in quick leaps. The water splashed and a duck screamed desperately. Bambi heard her wings flapping and saw her white body flash through the leaves. He saw how her wings beat the fox's face with sharp blows. Then it grew still.

At the same moment the fox came out of the bushes holding the duck in his jaws. Her neck hung down limply, her wings were still moving, but the fox paid no attention to that. He looked sidewise at Bambi with sneering eyes and crept slowly into the thicket.

Bambi stood motionless.

A few of the old ducks had flown up with a rush of wings and were flying around in helpless fright. The sedge hen was crying warnings from all directions. The titmice chirped excitedly in the bushes. And the young orphaned ducks splashed about the sedge, crying with soft voices.

The hummingbird flew along the bank.

"Please tell us," the young ducks cried, "please tell us, have you seen our mother?"

"Srrri," cried the hummingbird shrilly, and flew past sparkling, "what has she got to do with me?"

Bambi turned and went away. He wandered through a whole sea of goldenrod, passed through a grove of young beeches, crossed through old hazel thickets until he reached the edge of the deep ditch. He roamed around it, hoping to meet the old stag. He had not seen him for a long while, not since Gobo's death.

Then he caught a glimpse of him from afar and ran to meet him. For a while they walked together in silence; then the old stag asked: "Well, do they still talk about him the way they used to?"

Bambi understood that he referred to Gobo and replied, "I don't know. I'm nearly alone now." He hesitated. "But I think of him very often."

"Really," said the old stag, "are you alone now?"

"Yes," said Bambi expectantly, but the old stag remained silent.

They went on. Suddenly the old stag stopped. "Don't you hear anything?" he asked.

Bambi listened. He didn't hear anything.

"Come," cried the old stag and hurried forward. Bambi followed him. The stag stopped again. "Don't you hear anything yet?" he asked.

Then Bambi heard a rustling that he did not understand. It sounded like branches being bent down and repeatedly springing up again. Something was beating the earth dully and irregularly.

Bambi wanted to flee but the old stag cried, "Come

with me," and ran in the direction of the noise. Bambi, at his side, ventured to ask, "Isn't it dangerous?"

"It's terribly dangerous," the old stag answered mysteriously.

Soon they saw branches being pulled and tugged at from below and shaken violently. They went nearer and saw that a little trail ran through the middle of the bushes.

Friend Hare was lying on the ground. He flung himself from side to side and writhed. Then he lay still and writhed again. Each of his motions pulled at the branches over him.

Bambi noticed a dark threadlike leash. It ran right from the branch to Friend Hare and was twisted around his neck.

Friend Hare must have heard someone coming, for he flung himself wildly into the air and fell to the ground. He tried to escape and rolled, jerking and writhing in the grass.

"Lie still," the old stag commanded. Then sympathetically, with a gentle voice that went to Bambi's heart, he repeated in his ear, "Be easy, Friend Hare, it's I. Don't move now. Lie perfectly still."

The Hare lay motionless, flat on the ground. His throttled breath rattled softly in his throat.

The old stag took the branch between his teeth, and twisted it. He bent it down. Then he walked around putting his weight cunningly against it. He held it to the earth with his hoof and snapped it with a single blow of his antlers.

Then he nodded encouragingly to the Hare. "Lie still," he said, "even if I hurt you."

Holding his head on one side, he laid one prong of his antlers close to the Hare's neck, and pressed into the fur behind his ear. He made an effort and nodded. The Hare began to writhe.

The old stag immediately drew back. "Lie still," he commanded, "it's a question of life and death for you." He began over again. The Hare lay still gasping. Bambi stood close by, speechless with amazement.

One of the old stag's antlers, pressing against the Hare's fur, had slipped under the noose. The old stag was almost kneeling and twisted his head as though he were charging. He drove his antlers deeper and deeper under the noose, which gave at last and began to loosen.

The Hare could breathe again and his terror and pain burst from him instantly. "E-e-eh!" he cried bitterly.

The old stag stopped. "Keep quiet!" he cried, reproaching him gently, "keep quiet!" His mouth was close to the Hare's shoulder, his antlers lay with a prong between the spoonlike ears. It looked as if he had spitted the Hare.

"How can you be so stupid as to cry at this time?" he grumbled gently. "Do you want the fox to come? Do you? I thought not. Keep quiet then."

He continued to work away, slowly exerting all his strength. Suddenly the noose broke with a loud snap. The Hare slipped out and was free, without realizing it for a moment. He took a step and sat down again dazed. Then he hopped away, slowly and timidly at first, then faster and faster. Presently he was running with wild leaps.

Bambi looked after him. "Without so much as a thank you," he exclaimed in surprise.

"He's still terrified," said the old stag.

The noose lay on the ground. Bambi touched it gently. It creaked, terrifying Bambi. That was a sound such as he had never heard in the woods.

"He?" asked Bambi softly.

The old stag nodded.

They walked on together in silence. "Take care when you're going along a trail," said the old stag, "test all the branches. Prod them on all sides of you with your antlers. And turn back at once if you hear that creak. And when you've shed your antlers be doubly cautious. I never use trails any more."

Bambi sank into troubled thought.

"He isn't here," he whispered to himself in profound astonishment.

"No, He's not in the forest now," the old stag answered.

"And yet He is here," said Bambi, shaking his head.

The old stag went on and his voice was full of bitterness. "How did your Gobo put it . . . ? Didn't Gobo tell you He is all-powerful and all-good?"

"He was good to Gobo," Bambi whispered.

The old stag stopped. "Do you believe that, Bambi?" he asked sadly. For the first time he had called Bambi by his name.

"I don't know," cried Bambi, hurt, "I don't understand it."

The old stag said slowly, "We must learn to live and be cautious."

Chapter Twenty-One

ONE MORNING BAMBI CAME TO grief.

The pale gray dawn was just creep-ing through the forest. A milky-white mist was rising from the meadow and the stillness that precedes the coming of light was everywhere. The crows were not awake yet, nor the magpies. The jays were asleep.

Bambi had met Faline the night before. She looked sadly at him and was very shy.

"I'm so much alone now," she said gently.

"I'm alone too," Bambi answered with some hesitation.

"Why don't you stay with me any more?" Faline asked sorrowfully, and it hurt him to see the gay and lively Faline so serious and downcast.

"I want to be alone," he replied. And gently as he tried to say it, sounded hard. He felt it himself.

Faline looked at him and asked softly, "Do you love me still?"

"I don't know," Bambi answered in the same tone.

She walked silently away from him, leaving him alone.

He stood under the great oak at the meadow's edge and peered out cautiously, drinking in the pure and odorless morning air. It was moist and fresh from the earth, the dew, the grass and the wet woods. Bambi breathed in great gulps of it. All at once his spirit felt freer than for a long time. He walked happily onto the mist-covered meadow.

Then a sound like thunder crashed.

Bambi felt a fearful blow that made him stagger.

Mad with terror, he sprang back into the thicket and kept running. He did not understand what had happened. He could not grasp a single idea. He could only keep running on and on. Fear gripped his heart so that his breath failed as he rushed blindly on. Then a killing pain shot through him, so that he felt that he could not bear it. He felt something hot running over his left shoulder. It was like a thin, burning thread coming from where the pain shot through him. Bambi had to stop running. He was forced to walk slower. Then he saw that he was limping. He sank down.

It was comfortable just to lie there and rest.

"Up, Bambi! Get up!" The old stag was standing beside him, and nudging his shoulder gently.

Bambi wanted to answer, "I can't," but the old stag repeated, "Up! Up!" And there was such compulsion in his voice and such tenderness that Bambi kept silent. Even the pain that shot through him stopped for a minute.

Then the old stag said hurriedly and anxiously, "Get

up! You must get away, my son." My son! The words seemed to have escaped him. In a flash Bambi was on his feet.

"Good," said the old stag, breathing deeply and speaking emphatically, "come with me now and keep close beside me."

He walked swiftly ahead. Bambi followed him but he felt a burning desire to let himself drop to the ground, to lie still and rest.

The old stag seemed to guess it and talked to him without stopping. "Now you'll have to bear every pain. You can't think of lying down now. You mustn't think of it even for a moment. That's enough to tire you in itself. You must save yourself, do you understand me, Bambi? Save yourself. Or else you are lost. Just remember that He is behind you, do you understand, Bambi? And He will kill you without mercy. Come on. Keep close to me. You'll soon be all right. You must be all right."

Bambi had no strength left to think with. The pain shot through him at every step he took. It took away his breath and his consciousness. The hot trickle, burning his shoulder, seared him like some deep heart-felt trouble.

The old stag made a wide circle. It took a long time. Through his veil of pain and weakness, Bambi was amazed to see that they were passing the great oak again.

The old stag stopped and snuffed the ground. "He's still here," he whispered. "It's He. And that's His dog. Come along. Faster!" They ran.

Suddenly the old stag stopped again. "Look," he said, "that's where you lay on the ground."

Bambi saw the crushed grasses where a wide pool of his own blood was soaking into the earth.

The old stag snuffed warily around the spot. "They were here, He and His dog," he said. "Come along!" He went ahead slowly, snuffing again and again.

Bambi saw the red drops gleaming on the leaves of the bushes and the grass stems. "We passed here before," he thought. But he couldn't speak.

"Aha!" said the old stag and seemed almost joyful, "we're behind them now."

He continued for a while on the same path. Then he doubled unexpectedly and began a new circle. Bambi staggered after him. They came to the oak again but on the opposite side. For the second time they passed the place where Bambi had fallen down. Then the old stag went in still another direction.

"Eat that," he commanded suddenly, stopping and pushing aside the grasses. He pointed to a pair of short dark-green leaves growing close together near the ground.

Bambi obeyed. They tasted terribly bitter and smelled sickeningly.

"How do you feel now?" the stag asked after a while.

"Better," Bambi answered quickly. He was suddenly able to speak again. His senses had cleared and his fatigue grew less.

"Let's move on again," the old stag commanded after another pause. After Bambi had been following him for a long time he said, "At last!" They stopped.

"The bleeding has stopped," said the old stag, "the blood's stopped flowing from your wound. It isn't emptying your veins now. And it can't betray you any more either. It can't show Him and His dog where to find you and kill you."

The old stag looked worried and tired but his voice sounded joyful. "Come along," he went on, "now you can rest."

They reached a wide ditch which Bambi had never crossed. The old stag climbed down and Bambi tried to follow him. But it cost him a great effort to climb the steep slope on the farther side. The pain began to shoot violently through him again. He stumbled, regained his feet, and stumbled again, breathing hard.

"I can't help you," said the old stag, "you'll have to get up yourself." Bambi reached the top. He felt the hot trickle on his shoulder again. He felt his strength ebbing for the second time.

"You're bleeding again," said the old stag. "I thought you would. But it's only a little," he added in a whisper, "and it doesn't make any difference now."

They walked very slowly through a grove of lofty beeches. The ground was soft and level. They walked easily on it. Bambi felt a longing to lie down there, to stretch out and never move his limbs again. He couldn't go any farther. His head ached. There was a humming in his ears. His nerves were quivering, and fever began to rack him. There was a darkness before his eyes. He felt nothing but a desire for rest and detached amazement at finding his life so changed and shattered. He remembered how he had walked whole and uninjured through the woods that morning. It was barely an hour ago, and it seemed to him like some memory out of a distant long-vanished past.

They passed through a scrub oak and dogwood thicket. A huge, hollow beech trunk, thickly entangled with the bushes, lay right in front of them, barring the way.

"Here we are," Bambi heard the old stag saying. He walked along the beech trunk and Bambi walked beside him. He nearly fell into a hollow that lay in front of him.

"Here it is," said the old stag at the moment, "you can lie down here."

Bambi sank down and did not move again.

The hollow was still deeper under the beech trunk and formed a little chamber. The bushes closed thickly across the top so that whoever was within lay hidden.

"You'll be safe here," said the old stag.

Days passed.

Bambi lay on the warm earth with the moldering bark of the fallen tree above him. He felt his pain intensify and then grow less and less until it died away more and more gently.

Sometimes he would creep out and stand swaying weakly on his unsteady legs. He would take a few steps to look for food. He ate plants now that he had never noticed before. Now they appealed to his taste and attracted him by their strange, enticing acrid smell. Everything that he had disdained before and would spit out if it got accidentally into his mouth seemed appetizing to him. He still disliked many of the little leaves and short, coarse shoots, but he ate them anyway, as though he were compelled to, and his wound healed faster. He felt his strength returning.

He was cured, but he didn't leave the hollow yet. He walked around a little at night, but lay quietly on his bed by day. Not until the fever had entirely left his body did Bambi begin to think over all that had happened to him. Then a great terror awoke in him, and a profound tremor passed through his heart. He could not shake himself free of it. He could not get up and run about as before. He lay still and troubled. He felt terrified, ashamed, amazed and troubled by turns. Sometimes he was full of despair, at others of joy.

The old stag was always with him. At first he stayed day and night at Bambi's side. Then he left him alone at times, especially when he saw Bambi deep in thought. But he always kept close at hand.

One night there was thunder and lightning and a downpour of rain, although the sky was clear and the setting sun was streaming down. The blackbirds sang loudly in all the neighboring treetops, the finches warbled, the titmice chirped in the bushes. Among the grasses or from under the bushes, the metallic, throaty cackling of the pheasants sounded at intervals. The woodpecker laughed exultantly and the doves cooed their fervid love.

Bambi crept out of the hollow. Life was beautiful. The old stag was standing there as though he expected Bambi. They sauntered on together.

Chapter Twenty-Two

ONE NIGHT WHEN THE AIR WAS whispering with the autumnal fall of leaves the screech owl shrieked piercingly among the branches. Then he waited.

But Bambi had spied him already through the thinning leaves, and stopped.

The screech owl flew nearer and shrieked louder. Then he waited again. But Bambi did not say anything.

Then the owl could restrain himself no longer. "Aren't you frightened?" he asked, displeased.

"Well," Bambi replied, "a little."

"Is that so?" the screech owl cooed in an offended tone. "Only a little. You used to get terribly frightened. It was really a pleasure to see how frightened you'd get. But for some reason or other you're only a little frightened now." He grew angrier and repeated, "Only a little!"

The screech owl was getting old, and that was why he was so much vainer and so much more sensitive than before.

Bambi wanted to answer, "I wasn't ever frightened before either," but he decided to keep that to himself. He was sorry to see the good old screech owl sitting there so angry. He tried to soothe him. "Maybe it's because I thought of you right away," he said.

"What?" said the screech owl, becoming happy again, "you really did think of me?"

"Yes," Bambi answered with some hesitation, "as soon as I heard you screech. Otherwise, of course, I'd have been as scared as ever."

"Really?" cooed the owl.

Bambi hadn't the heart to deny it. What difference

did it make anyhow? Let the little old child enjoy himself.

"I really did," he assured him, and went on, "I'm so happy, for a thrill goes through me when I hear you so suddenly."

The screech owl fluffed up his feathers into a soft, brownish-gray, downy ball. He was happy. "It's nice of you to think of me," he cooed tenderly, "very nice. We haven't seen each other for a long time."

"A very long time," said Bambi.

"You don't use the old trails any more, do you?" the screech owl inquired.

"No," said Bambi slowly, "I don't use the old trails any more."

"I'm also seeing more of the world than I used to," the screech owl observed boastfully. He didn't mention that he had been driven from his old hereditary haunts by a pitiless younger rival. "You can't stay forever in the same spot," he added. Then he waited for an answer.

But Bambi had gone away. By now he understood almost as well as the old stag how to disappear suddenly and noiselessly.

The screech owl was provoked. "It's a shame . . ." he cooed to himself. He shook his feathers, sank his bill deep into his breast and silently philosophized. "You should never imagine you can be friends with great folks. They can be as nice as pie but when the time comes they haven't a thought for you, and you're left sitting stupidly by yourself as I'm sitting here now. . . ."

Suddenly he dropped to the earth like a stone. He had spied a mouse. It squeaked once in his talons. He tore it to pieces, for he was furious. He crammed the little morsel faster than usual. Then he flew off. "What do all your great folks mean to me?" he asked. "Not a thing." He began to screech so piercingly and cease-lessly that a pair of wood doves whom he passed awoke and fled from their roost with loud wing beats.

The storm swept the woods for several days and tore the last leaves from the branches. Then the trees stood stripped.

Bambi was wandering homeward in the gray dawn in order to sleep in the hollow with the old stag.

A shrill voice called him once or twice in quick succession. He stopped. Then the squirrel scampered down from the branches in a twinkling and sat on the ground in front of him.

"Is it really you?" he shrilled, surprised and delighted. "I recognized you the minute you passed me but I couldn't believe . . ."

"Where did you come from?" asked Bambi.

The merry little face in front of him grew quite troubled. "The oak is gone," he began plaintively, "my beautiful old oak, do you remember it? It was awful. He chopped it down!"

Bambi hung his head sadly. His very soul felt sorry for the wonderful old tree.

"As soon as it happened," the squirrel related, "everybody who lived in the tree fled and watched how He bit through the trunk with a gigantic flashing tooth. The tree groaned aloud when it was wounded. It kept on groaning and the tooth kept gnawing; it was dreadful to hear it. Then the poor beautiful tree fell out on the meadow. Everybody cried."

Bambi was silent.

"Yes," sighed the squirrel, "He can do anything. He's all-powerful." He gazed at Bambi out of his big eyes, and pointed his ears. But Bambi kept silent.

"Then we were all homeless," the squirrel went on. "I don't even know where the others scattered to. I came here. But I won't find another tree like that in a hurry."

"The old oak," said Bambi to himself. "I knew it from the time I was a child."

"Oh well," said the squirrel. "But to think it's really you," he went on delightedly. "Everybody said you must be dead long ago. Of course there were some people now and then who said you were still alive. Once in a while someone said he had seen you. But nobody could find out anything definite. And so I thought it was only gossip," the squirrel gazed at him inquisitively, "since you didn't come back any more."

Bambi could see how curious he was and how he was fishing for an answer.

Bambi kept silent. But a gentle anxious curiosity was stirring in him, too. He wanted to ask about Faline, about Aunt Ena, and Ronno and Karus, about all his childhood companions. But he kept silent.

The squirrel still sat in front of him, studying him. "What antlers!" he cried admiringly. "What antlers! Nobody in the whole forest, except the old Prince, has antlers like that."

Once Bambi would have felt elated and flattered by such praise. But he only said, "Maybe."

The squirrel nodded quickly with his head. "Really," he said, surprised, "you're beginning to get gray."

Bambi wandered on.

The squirrel perceived that the conversation was over and sprang through the bushes. "Good day," he shouted down. "Goodbye. I'm very glad I met you. If I see any of your acquaintances I'll tell them you're still alive. They'll all be glad."

Bambi heard him and again felt that gentle stirring in his heart. But he said nothing. When he was still a child the old stag had taught him that you must live alone. Then and afterward the old stag had revealed much wisdom and many secrets to him. But of all his teachings this had been the most important: you must live alone. If you wanted to preserve yourself, if you understood existence, if you wanted to attain wisdom, you had to live alone.

"But," Bambi had once objected, "we two are always together now."

"Not for very much longer," the old stag had answered quickly. That was a few weeks ago. Now it occurred to Bambi again, and he suddenly remembered how even the old stag's very first words to him had been about singleness. That day when Bambi was still a child calling for his mother, the old stag had come to him and asked him, "Can't you stay by yourself?"

Bambi wandered on.

Chapter Twenty-Three

THE FOREST WAS AGAIN UNDER snow, lying silent beneath its deep white mantle. Only the crows' calls could be heard. Now and then came a magpie's noisy chattering. The soft twittering of the titmice sounded timidly. Then the frost hardened and everything grew still. The air began to hum with the cold.

One morning a dog's baying broke the silence.

It was a continuous hurrying bay that pressed on

quickly through the woods, eager and clear and harrying with loud yelps.

Bambi raised his head in the hollow under the fallen tree and looked at the old stag who was lying beside him.

"That's nothing," said the old stag in answer to Bambi's glance, "nothing that need bother us."

Still they both listened.

They lay in their hollow with the old beech trunk like a sheltering roof above them. The deep snow kept the icy draft from them, and the tangled bushes hid them from curious eyes.

The baying grew nearer. It was angry and panting and relentless. It sounded like the bark of a small hound. It came constantly closer.

Then they heard panting of another kind. They heard a low labored snarling under the angry barking. Bambi grew uneasy, but the old stag quieted him again. "We don't need to worry about it," he said. They lay silent in their warm hollow and peered out.

The footsteps drew nearer and nearer through the branches. The snow dropped from the shaken boughs and clouds of it rose from the earth.

Through the snow and over the roots and branches the fox came springing, crouching and slinking. They were right; a little, short-legged hound was after him.

One of the fox's forelegs was crushed and the fur torn around it. He held his shattered paw in front of him, and blood poured from his wound. He was gasping for breath. His eyes were staring with terror and exertion. He was beside himself with rage and fear. He was desperate and exhausted.

Once in a while he would face around and snarl so that the dog was startled and would fall back a few steps.

Presently the fox sat down on his haunches. He could go no farther. Raising his mangled forepaw pitifully, with his jaws open and his lips drawn back, he snarled at the dog.

But the dog was never silent for a minute. His high, rasping bark only grew fuller and deeper. "Here," he yapped, "here he is! Here! Here! Here!" He was not abusing the fox. He was not even speaking to him, but was urging on someone who was still far behind.

Bambi knew as well as the old stag did that it was He the dog was calling.

The fox knew it too. The blood was streaming down from him and fell from his breast into the snow, making a fiery red spot on the icy white surface, and steaming slowly.

A weakness overcame the fox. His crushed foot sank down helpless, but a burning pain shot through it when it touched the cold snow. He lifted it again with an effort and held it quivering in front of him.

"Let me go," said the fox, beginning to speak, "let me go." He spoke softly and beseechingly. He was quite weak and despondent.

"No! No! No!" the dog howled.

The fox pleaded still more insistently. "We're relations," he pleaded, "we're brothers almost. Let me go home. Let me die with my family at least. We're brothers almost, you and I."

"No! No! No!" the dog raged.

Then the fox rose so that he was sitting perfectly erect. He dropped his handsome pointed muzzle on his bleeding breast, raised his eyes and looked the dog straight in the face. In a completely altered voice, restrained and embittered, he growled, "Aren't you ashamed, you traitor!"

"No! No! No!" yelped the dog.

But the fox went on, "You turncoat, you renegade." His maimed body was taut with contempt and hatred. "You spy," he hissed, "you blackguard, you track us where He could never find us. You betray us, your own relations, me who am almost your brother. And you stand there and aren't ashamed!"

Instantly many other voices sounded loudly round about.

"Traitor!" cried the magpie from the tree.

"Spy!" shrieked the jay.

"Blackguard!" the weasel hissed.

"Renegade!" snarled the ferret.

From every tree and bush came chirpings, peepings, shrill cries, while overhead the crows cawed, "Spy! Spy!" Everyone had rushed up, and from the trees or from safe hiding places on the ground they watched the contest. The fury that had burst from the fox released an embittered anger in them all. And the blood spilled on the snow, that steamed before their eyes, maddened them and made them forget all caution.

The dog stared around him. "Who are you?" he yelped. "What do you want? What do you know about it? What are you talking about? Everything belongs to Him, just as I do. But I, I love Him. I worship Him. I serve Him. Do you think you can oppose Him, poor creatures like you? He's all-powerful. He's above all of you. Everything we have comes from Him. Everything that lives or grows comes from Him." The dog was quivering with exaltation.

"Traitor!" cried the squirrel shrilly.

"Yes, traitor!" hissed the fox. "Nobody is a traitor but you, only you."

The dog was dancing about in a frenzy of devotion. "Only me?" he cried; "you lie. Aren't there many, many others on His side? The horse, the cow, the sheep, the chickens, many, many of you and your kind are on His side and worship Him and serve Him."

"They're rabble!" snarled the fox, full of a boundless contempt.

Then the dog could contain himself no longer and sprang at the fox's throat. Growling, spitting and yelping, they rolled in the snow, a writhing, savagely snapping mass from which fur flew. The snow rose in clouds and was spattered with fine drops of blood. At last the fox could not fight any more. In a few seconds he was lying on his back, his white belly uppermost. He twitched and stiffened and died.

The dog shook him a few times, then let him fall on the trampled snow. He stood beside him, his legs planted, calling in a deep, loud voice, "Here! Here! He's here!"

The others were horrorstruck and fled in all directions.

"Dreadful," said Bambi softly to the old stag in the hollow.

"The most dreadful part of all," the old stag answered, "is that the dogs believe what the hound just said. They believe it, they pass their lives in fear, they hate Him and themselves and yet they'd die for His sake."

Chapter Twenty-Four

THE COLD BROKE, AND THERE WAS a warm spell in the middle of the winter. The earth drank great drafts of the melting snows so that wide stretches of soil were everywhere visible. The blackbirds were not singing yet, but when they flew from the ground where they were hunting worms, or when they fluttered from tree to tree, they uttered a long-drawn joyous whistle that was almost a song. The woodpecker began to chatter now and then. Magpies and crows grew more talkative.

The titmice chirped more cheerily. And the pheasants, swooping down from their roosts, would stand in one spot preening their feathers and uttering their metallic throaty cacklings.

One such morning Bambi was roaming around as usual. In the gray dawn he came to the edge of the hollow. On the farther side where he had lived before something was stirring. Bambi stayed hidden in the thicket and peered across. A deer was wandering slowly to and fro, looking for places where the snow had melted, and cropping whatever grasses had sprung up so early.

Bambi wanted to turn at once and go away, for he recognized Faline. His first impulse was to spring forward and call her. But he stood as though rooted to the spot. He had not seen Faline for a long time. His heart began to beat faster. Faline moved slowly as though she were tired and sad. She resembled her mother now. She looked as old as Aunt Ena, as Bambi noticed with a strangely pained surprise.

Faline lifted her head and gazed across as though she sensed his presence. Again Bambi started forward, but he stopped again, hesitating and unable to stir.

He saw that Faline had grown old and gray.

Gay, pert little Faline, how lovely she used to be," he thought, "and how lively!" His whole youth suddenly flashed before his eyes. The meadow, the trails where he walked with his mother, the happy games with Gobo and Faline, the nice grasshoppers and butterflies, the fight with Karus and Ronno when he had won Faline for his own. He felt happy again, and yet he trembled.

Faline wandered on, her head drooped to the ground, walking slowly, sadly and wearily away. At that moment Bambi loved her with an overpowering, tender melancholy. He wanted to rush through the hollow that separated him from the others. He wanted to overtake her, to talk with her, to talk to her about their youth and about everything that had happened.

He gazed after her as she went off, passing under the bare branches till finally she was lost to sight.

He stood there a long time staring after her.

Then there was a crash like thunder. Bambi shrank

together. It came from where he was standing. Not even from a little way off but right beside him.

Then there was a second thunderclap, and right after that another.

Bambi leaped a little farther into the thicket, then stopped and listened. Everything was still. He glided stealthily homeward.

The old stag was there before him. He had not lain down yet, but was standing beside the fallen beech trunk expectantly.

"Where have you been so long?" he asked, so seriously that Bambi grew silent.

"Did you hear it?" the old stag went on after a pause.

"Yes," Bambi answered, "three times. He must be in the woods."

"Of course," the old stag nodded, and repeated with a peculiar intonation, "He is in the woods and we must go."

"Where?" the word escaped Bambi.

"Where He is now," said the old stag, and his voice was solemn.

Bambi was terrified.

"Don't be frightened," the old stag went on, "come with me and don't be frightened. I'm glad that I can take you and show you the way. . . ." He hesitated and added softly, "Before I go."

Bambi looked wonderingly at the old stag. And suddenly he noticed how aged he looked. His head was completely gray now. His face was perfectly gaunt. The deep light was extinguished in his eyes, and they had a feeble, greenish luster and seemed to be blind.

Bambi and the old stag had not gone far before they caught the first whiff of that acrid smell that sent such dread and terror to their hearts.

Bambi stopped. But the old stag went on directly toward the scent. Bambi followed hesitantly.

The terrifying scent grew stronger and stronger. But the old stag kept on without stopping. The idea of flight sprang up in Bambi's mind and tugged at his heart. It seethed through his mind and body, and nearly swept him away. But he kept a firm grip on himself and stayed close behind the old stag.

Then the horrible scent grew so strong that it drowned out everything else, and it was hardly possible to breathe.

"Here He is," said the old stag, moving to one side.

Through the bare branches, Bambi saw Him lying on the trampled snow a few steps away.

An irresistible burst of terror swept over Bambi and with a sudden bound he started to give in to his impulse to flee.

"Halt!" he heard the old stag calling. Bambi looked around and saw the stag standing calmly where He was lying on the ground. Bambi was amazed and, moved by a sense of obedience, a boundless curiosity and quivering expectancy, he went closer.

"Come near," said the old stag, "don't be afraid."

He was lying with His pale, naked face turned upward, His hat a little to one side on the snow. Bambi, who did not know anything about hats, thought His horrible head was split in two. The poacher's shirt, open at the neck, was pierced where a wound gaped like a small red mouth. Blood was oozing out slowly. Blood was drying on His hair and around His nose. A big pool of it lay on the snow which was melting from the warmth.

"We can stand right beside Him," the old stag began softly, "and it isn't dangerous."

Bambi looked down at the prostrate form whose limbs and skin seemed so mysterious and terrible to him. He gazed at the dead eyes that stared up sightlessly at him. Bambi couldn't understand it all.

"Bambi," the old stag went on, "do you remember what Gobo said and what the dog said, what they all think, do you remember?"

Bambi could not answer.

"Do you see, Bambi," the old stag went on, "do you see how He's lying there dead, like one of us? Listen, Bambi. He isn't all-powerful as they say. Everything that lives and grows doesn't come from Him. He isn't above us. He's just the same as we are. He has the same fears, the same needs, and suffers in the same way. He can be killed like us, and then He lies helpless on the ground like all the rest of us, as you see Him now."

There was a silence.

"Do you understand me, Bambi?" asked the old stag.

"I think so," Bambi said in a whisper.

"Then speak," the old stag commanded.

Bambi was inspired, and said trembling, "There is Another who is over us all, over us and over Him."

"Now I can go," said the old stag.

He turned away, and they wandered side by side for a stretch.

Presently the old stag stopped in front of a tall oak. "Don't follow me any farther, Bambi," he began with a calm voice, "my time is up. Now I have to look for a resting place."

Bambi tried to speak.

"Don't" said the old stag, cutting him short, "don't. In the hour which I am approaching we are all alone. Goodbye, my son. I loved you dearly."

Chapter Twenty-Five

DAWN OF THE SUMMER'S DAY came hot, without a breath of wind or the usual morning chill. The sun seemed to come up faster than usual. It rose swiftly and flashed like a torch with dazzling rays.

The dew on the meadows and bushes was drawn up in an instant. The earth was perfectly dry so that the clods crumbled. The forest had been still from an early hour. Only a woodpecker hammered now and then, or

the doves cooed their tireless, fervid tenderness.

Bambi was standing in a little clearing, forming a narrow glade in the heart of the thicket.

A swarm of midges danced and hummed around his head in the warm sunshine.

There was a low buzzing among the leaves of the hazel bushes near Bambi, and a big may beetle crawled out and flew slowly by. He flew among the midges, up and up, till he reached the treetop where he intended to sleep till evening. His wing covers folded down hard and neatly and his wings vibrated with strength.

The midges divided to let the may beetle pass through and closed behind him again. His dark brown body, over which shone the vibrant glassy shimmer of his whirring wings, flashed for a moment in the sunshine as he disappeared.

"Did you see him?" the midges asked each other.

"That's the old may beetle," some of them hummed.

Others said, "All of his offspring are dead. Only one is still alive. Only one."

"How long will he live?" a number of midges asked.

The others answered, "We don't know. Some of his offspring live a long time. They live forever almost. . . . They see the sun thirty or forty times, we don't know exactly how many. Our lives are long enough, but we see the daylight only once or twice."

"How long has the old beetle been living?" some very small midges asked.

"He has outlived his whole family. He's as old as the hills, as old as the hills. He's seen more and been through more in this world than we can even imagine."

Bambi walked on. "Midge buzzings," he thought, "midge buzzings."

A delicate frightened call came to his ears.

He listened and went closer, perfectly softly, keeping among the thickest bushes, and moving noiselessly as he had long known how to do.

The call came again, more urgent, more plaintively. Fawns' voices were wailing, "Mother! Mother!"

Bambi glided through the bushes and followed the calls.

Two fawns were standing side by side, in their little

red coats, a brother and sister, forsaken and despondent.

"Mother! Mother!" they called.

Before they knew what had happened Bambi was standing in front of them. They stared at him speechlessly.

"Your mother has no time for you now," said Bambi severely.

He looked into the little brother's eyes. "Can't you stay by yourself?" he asked.

The little brother and sister were silent.

Bambi turned and, gliding into the bushes, disappeared before they had come to their senses. He walked along.

"The little fellow pleases me," he thought, "perhaps I'll meet him again when he's larger. . . ."

He walked along. "The little girl is nice too," he thought. "Faline looked like that when she was a fawn."

He went on, and vanished in the forest.

MORE ANIMAL BOOKS FROM AWARD-WINNING AUTHOR

Bill Wallace

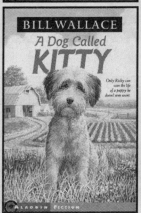

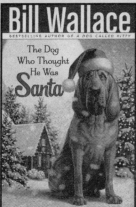

FROM ALADDIN
PUBLISHED BY SIMON & SCHUSTER

If you like horses, you'll love these books:

You and Your Horse

Misty of
Chincoteague

King of the Wind

Justin Morgan
Had a Horse

Take the Reins

Chasing Blue

Behind the Bit

Triple Fault

Best Enemies

Little White Lies

Rival Revenge

Home Sweet Drama

Books by David Darling

Zen Physics (1996)
Soul Search (1995)
Equations of Eternity (1993)
Deep Time (1989)

The Extraterrestrial Encyclopedia

The
Extraterrestrial
Encyclopedia

AN ALPHABETICAL REFERENCE
TO *ALL* LIFE IN THE UNIVERSE

David Darling, Ph.D.

THREE RIVERS PRESS • NEW YORK

Published by Three Rivers Press, New York, New York. Member of the Crown Publishing Group.

Random House, Inc. New York, Toronto, London, Sydney, Auckland
www.randomhouse.com

THREE RIVERS PRESS is a registered trademark and the Three Rivers Press colophon is a trademark of Random House, Inc.

Printed in the United States of America

Design by H. Roberts Design

Library of Congress Cataloging-in-Publication Data

Darling, David J.
    The extraterrestrial encyclopedia: an alphabetical reference to
all life in the universe/David Darling.
        p.   cm.
    ISBN 0-8129-3248-X (pbk.)
    1. Life on other planets Encyclopedias.   I. Title.
QB54.D365   2000
576.8′39′03—dc21   99-38266

10 9 8 7 6 5 4 3 2 1

First Edition

To three of my favorite terrestrials:
Jill, Lori-An, and Jeff

I have chosen that part of Philosophy which is most likely to excite curiosity; for what can more concern us than to know how this world which we inhabit is made; and whether there be any other worlds like it, which are also inhabited as this is?

—Bernard Le Bovier de Fontenelle,
  Conversations on the Plurality of Worlds (1686)

We are on the doorstep to the heavens. We are now on the threshold of establishing: Is life unique to Earth?

—Dan Goldin,
  NASA administrator

How many of those potential heavens and hells are now inhabited, and by what manner of creatures, we have no way of guessing; the very nearest is a million times further away than Mars or Venus, those still remote goals of the next generation. But the barriers of distance are crumbling; one day we shall meet our equals, or our masters, among the stars.

—Arthur C. Clarke,
  2001: A Space Odyssey

Acknowledgments

My thanks for reviewing various portions of the manuscript and providing other assistance go to James Annis (FermiLab), Michael Archer (University of New South Wales), David Black (Lunar and Planetary Institute, Johnson Space Center), Ronald Bracewell (Stanford University), Robert Cesarone (Jet Propulsion Laboratory), Robert Dixon (Ohio State University), Robert Forward (Tethers Unlimited), George Gatewood (University of Pittsburgh), Geoffrey Marcy (San Francisco State University), Philip Morrison (Massachusetts Institute of Technology), Leslie Orgel (Salk Institute), Rachel Street (University of St. Andrews), Jill Tarter (SETI Institute), Steven Vogt (University of California, San Diego), William Welch (University of California, Berkeley), and Alexander Wolszczan (Pennsylvania State University). Additionally, I am indebted to the authors of several reference works that have proved particularly valuable as sources of relevant historical detail. These include *Plurality of Worlds: The Origins of the Extraterrestrial Life Debate from Democritus to Kant* and *The Biological Universe: The Twentieth-Century Extraterrestrial Life Debate and the Limits of Science*, both by Steven J. Dick; *The Extraterrestrial Life Debate, 1750–1900: The Idea of a Plurality of Worlds from Kant to Lowell*, by Michael J. Crowe; *SETI Pioneers: Scientists Talk About Their Search for Extraterrestrial Intelligence*, by David Swift; and *The Encyclopedia of Science Fiction*, edited by John Clute and Peter Nicholls.

Executive editor Philip Turner and editorial assistant Lisa Schneider, production editor Martha Schwartz, and copy editor Lynn Anderson are among those whose meticulous work has been an important factor in the evolution of this book. Lori-An and Jeff Darling, Vera Green, and Marcus Rowland provided valuable assistance with the illustrations. Finally, as always, I am indebted to my agent and friend, Patricia van der Leun, for her enthusiasm and guidance. Although many have contributed to this volume in one way or another, any mistakes or omissions are, of course, my responsibility alone.

Contents

Introduction

There is a feeling among scientists today that we may be on the brink of learning the answer to one of mankind's oldest and most intriguing questions: Are we alone in the Universe? A great deal has been written on this subject over many years and, recently, there has been a flurry of publishing activity following the confirmed discovery of the first planets around other stars. The present book, however, is the first attempt to draw together in encyclopedic form *all* aspects of our age-old quest for extraterrestrial life, from ancient Greek speculation to the results from the latest interplanetary probes. It is intended to serve as an up-to-date reference work—a first port of call—for the interested layperson as well as the student or academic. But more than that, through a comprehensive system of cross-referencing, it is designed to allow the reader to trace the development and interaction of the key themes that have accompanied the debate about life "out there" from ancient times to the present day.

It would be easy to gain the impression that the search for other beings in the Universe is a purely scientific affair. Yet that is simply not the case. While it is true that only science can ultimately settle the question of whether life exists elsewhere or not, up until a few hundred years ago it had virtually nothing relevant to say on the matter, and it is only within living memory that experiment and observation have really begun to come to grips with the problem. The fact is that philosophy, theology, fiction (including hoaxes), the available technology of the time, the prevailing worldview, politics, and other forces in society, *as well as* astronomy and other sciences, have all played important roles in shaping both public and professional opinion on the extraterrestrial issue—and continue to do so today. Using this book as a guide, the reader can explore the long and fascinating history of events, personalities, and conflicting ideas connected with this subject and so come to appreciate more fully the issues surrounding our current search for life and civilizations beyond the Earth. The origin and evolution of life, the possible nature of alien biology and intelligence, the long debate over the plurality of worlds, the fictional representation of extraterrestrials, the theological implications of the discovery of other life (especially sentient life), and the rise and cultural influence of the UFO phenomenon are but a few of the major intellectual threads that intertwine and run through the encyclopedia.

We live in momentous times. The past decade has seen hopes soar within the scientific community that life not only exists elsewhere but exists abundantly throughout the cosmos. The next decade will see those hopes begin to be put to the test and possibly realized. Optimism has grown in the light of a number of extraordinary discoveries. Previously unsuspected, exotic forms of life have been found in all sorts of seemingly hostile environments on Earth—inside rocks more than a mile underground, in highly acidic and saline pools, in boiling, sulfur-rich water issuing from "black smokers" on the ocean bed, and in samples taken from deep below the Antarctic ice sheet. Mounting evidence suggests that some of these "extremophiles" are among the oldest organisms on Earth. If so, it may be that life can take hold wherever there is the slightest opportunity, given a starting brew of simple organic molecules, some water, and an adequate source of energy. The Universe, it turns out, is generous in its provision of all three of these basic ingredients for life as we know it. Every year astronomers add to the catalog of known organic molecules in interstellar space. Even more complex substances have been identified in meteorites and comets, which, it seems, serve as delivery vehicles bringing basic biochemicals to the surface of newborn worlds. Water, too, arrives aboard comets and may survive in the most unlikely places, as evidenced recently by the discovery of ice on the Moon. As for sources of energy, sunlight is but one of a range of options nature can afford. Increasingly, researchers are of the opinion that early terrestrial life may have depended more on energy flowing up from *within* the Earth than on that arriving from outside. Elsewhere in the solar system are other worlds with significant internal sources of heat that from the outside look biologically unpromising. Among these are Europa, the fourth largest moon of Jupiter and now a leading contender to become the first world upon which signs of extraterrestrial life will be found.

And beyond the solar system? Within the last few years, astronomers have demonstrated beyond reasonable doubt that massive planets around other stars are plentiful. Whether Earth-like worlds occur commonly as well has yet to be determined, but since even the moons of large planets are now among the prime targets of astrobiologists, there is every reason to suppose that many potential platforms for life exist throughout the Galaxy.

The search for life "out there" has begun in earnest. In laboratories around the world, molecular biologists are attempting to re-create the steps by which the first primitive organisms appeared; their progress to date appears to support the view that life arises readily and inevitably as a result of self-organizing chemical systems. Other researchers are probing deep underground, under the oceans, and beneath the Antarctic ice for further evidence of life at the extremes. Meanwhile, a growing armada of spacecraft is leaving Earth on missions to fly by, orbit, land on, rove over, penetrate, and return ever-increasing amounts of data and samples from our neighboring worlds. Mars, Europa, Titan, and other prime potential sites of biological and prebiological real estate will be explored in detail during the first decade of the new millennium. With its sights set further afield, the hunt for extrasolar planets is continuing to gather momentum. More sensitive detection methods and larger instruments, both on the ground and in space, will extend the quest to look for terrestrial-type worlds and, within a decade, begin attempts to image these far-off planets and scrutinize their faint light for the signatures of life. On a different front, the search will intensify to detect signals from other intelligent races in the Galaxy. The human race is poised on the brink of its greatest adventure.

How to Use This Book

Entries range from simple definitions of one or two lines to lengthy articles on subjects of central importance or popular interest, and are extensively cross-referenced. Terms that are **boldfaced** have their own entries, as do those preceded by the symbol ➜. Numbers that appear as superscripts in the text are references to books, journal articles, and so on, listed alphabetically by author at the back of the encyclopedia. Although many important historical references are provided, priority has been given to recent primary sources. By looking up these, the reader will find details of earlier papers on the relevant topics. A list of Web sites on subjects dealt with in the encyclopedia is also provided.

Entries are arranged alphabetically according to the first word of the entry name. Thus, for example, "life zone" precedes "lifetime, of civilizations." Acronyms are treated as words, so that "A star" precedes "AAA." Hyphenated words are treated as single words, so that "gamma rays" precedes "gamma-ray burster." If a number appears first in the name of an entry, as in "61 Cygni" or "2001: A Space Odyssey," the entry appears in the position that makes the most common sense. In the case of a numbered star, such as 61 Cygni, this would be under the first letter of its constellation. However, in the case of "2001: A Space Odyssey," or "21-centimeter radiation," it would be under the first letter of the number if spelled out. Where names are also known by their abbreviations or acronyms, the definition generally appears where the name is written out in full. Exceptions are in the case of entries such as "DNA," where the abbreviated form is used almost universally.

Inevitably, in a work of this size and scope, there will be some errors and omissions. I apologize in advance for these, particularly if a researcher feels that his or her work has been neglected or misrepresented, and I hope that readers will contact me, via the publisher or my Web site, with their comments, criticisms, and corrections, so that these may be taken into account in the preparation of a future edition.

Exponential Notation

In the interest of brevity, exponential notation is used in this book to represent large and small numbers. For example, 300,000 is written as 3×10^5, the power of 10 indicating how many places the decimal point has been moved to the left from the original number. Small numbers have negative exponents, indicating how many places the point has been shifted to the left. For example, 0.000,008,53 is written as 8.53×10^{-6}.

Abbreviations

AU	astronomical units	L_S	solar luminosity
c	speed of light	m	meter
cal	calorie	M_e	Earth mass
cm	centimeter	mg	milligram
cm^3	cubic centimeter	MHz	megahertz
d	day	M_J	Jupiter mass
dm^3	cubic decimeter	mm	millimeter
ft.	foot	M_S	solar mass
g	gram	mi.	mile
g	acceleration due to gravity	mi./h	miles per hour
GHz	gigahertz	min	minute
h	hour	mm	millimeter
Hz	hertz	ms	millisecond
in.	inch	nm	nanometer
K	kelvin	R_S	solar radius
kg	kilogram	rev/s	revolutions per second
km	kilometer	sq. in.	square inch
km/h	kilometers per hour	t	metric ton
km/s	kilometers per second	y	year
lb.	pound		

Conversion of Units

1 cm	= 10 mm	= 0.3937 inch
1 m	= 100 cm	= 39.37 inches
1 km	= 1,000 m	= 0.6214 mile
1 kg	= 1,000 g	= 2.2046 lb.
1 t	= 1,000 kg	= 2204.6 lb.
1 light-year	= 9.458 trillion km	= 5.878 trillion miles
1 parsec	= 3.259 light-years	
1 M_S	= 1,047 M_J	= 332,958 M_e
1 M_J	= 318 M_e	

The Extraterrestrial Encyclopedia

A

A for Andromeda

Science fiction novel by Fred **Hoyle** and John Elliot (1962),[288] inspired by seminal developments in **SETI** (→ **Morrison-Cocconi Conjecture**) and the construction of the first giant **radio telescope** at **Jodrell Bank.** Published in the year following Project **Ozma,** it begins with the accidental discovery of an extraterrestrial signal containing a complex message in **binary** (→ **mathematics, as a universal language**)— instructions, as it turns out, for making an immensely powerful computer. A similar theme was explored later by James Gunn in *The Listeners* and Carl **Sagan** in *Contact.*

A star

A bright white star of **spectral type** A, whose spectrum is dominated by **absorption line**s of atomic **hydrogen.** Lines of heavier elements, such as iron, are noticeable at the cooler end of the range. A-type stars on the **main sequence** have a surface temperature of 6,900 to 9,500°C, a luminosity of 7 to 50 L_S, and a mass of 1.5 to 3 M_S. Since their main sequence lifetime is typically only a few hundred million years, it appears they are too short-lived to allow advanced life (or even life at all) to evolve on any worlds that might circle around them. Well-known examples include **Sirius, Vega,** and **Altair.** A-type **supergiant**s, such as **Deneb,** have evolved off the main sequence and have masses up to 16 M_S, a surface temperature of about 9,400°C, and luminosities over 35,000 L_S.

AAA
→ **Absolute Astronomical Accelerometry**

AAO
→ **Anglo-Australian Observatory**

AAT
→ **Anglo-Australian Telescope**

abiogenesis

The development of living organisms from nonliving precursors. Gradual abiogenesis by chemical and biochemical evolution on the surface of the young Earth is the standard model of how terrestrial life arose (→ **life, origin of**), although evidence is accumulating that at least some of the early stages of abiogenesis may have taken place in space. According to a more extreme view, dense clouds of gas and dust in space may serve as the actual birthplace of primitive organisms (→ **life, in space**). By contrast, some advocates of the **panspermia** hypothesis have maintained that there are no compelling reasons to believe that life originally came from nonliving matter. The old theory of instantaneous abiogenesis, known as **spontaneous generation,** was discredited over a period of two centuries by the experimental work of Francesco **Redi,** Lazzaro **Spallanzini,** Cagniard de **La Tour,** Theodor **Schwann,** Louis **Pasteur,** and John **Tyndall.**

abiotic
Nonbiological in origin.

ablation
(1) Removal of the surface layers of a **meteorite** during its passage through the atmosphere. (2) Controlled degradation of the leading surface of a spacecraft during atmospheric reentry or passage through a dusty medium in space, such as the tail of a **comet.**

Absolute Astronomical Accelerometry
A project under development in France that will use the new **spectroscopic** technique of absolute accelerometry to search for **extrasolar planets.** The **Emilie** spectrograph at the **Haute-Provence Observatory** will be dedicated to this task.[128]

absolute magnitude
A measure of the true brightness of an object in space. Specifically, it is the **apparent magnitude** of a star, or other bright object, when seen from a standard distance of 10 parsecs (32.6 light-years). Absolute magnitude is directly related to **luminosity.**

absolute zero
The lowest temperature that is theoretically possible. It defines the zero point on the **kelvin** scale (0 K), equivalent to −273.13°C.

absorption
The capture of **photons** by **atoms, molecules,** or **ions,** which results in a decrease in the intensity of light or other **electromagnetic radiation** as it passes through a substance. Absorption occurs in the atmospheres of stars, planets, and moons and in the **interstellar medium,** giving rise to **absorption lines** or **absorption bands** in a **spectrum.**

absorption band
A series of very closely spaced **absorption lines** resulting from the **absorption** of light by molecules. Bands caused by titanium dioxide and **carbon** compounds occur in the spectra of low-temperature stars (➔ **M stars**), including **red giants.** So-called **diffuse interstellar bands,** possibly due to complex carbon molecules, are observed in the spectra of remote stars.

absorption line
A dark line in a **continuous spectrum** that corresponds to the absorption of light, or some other form of **electromagnetic radiation,** at a well-defined **wavelength.** The pattern of absorption lines in a spectrum is diagnostic of the types of **atoms** and **molecules** present, for example, in the surface layers of a star or the atmosphere of a planet.

absorption nebula
A dark **interstellar cloud** of gas and dust, so opaque that it prevents light from stars or **bright nebulas** from passing through it. Such nebulas appear as "holes" in the sky. They range in size from **globules** a few thousand AU across to sprawling regions of starless darkness such as the **Coalsack.**

abundance, of elements
➔ **elements, biological abundance of; elements, cosmic abundance of; elements, terrestrial abundance of**

accretion
In general, a process of growth by accumulation and adhesion. In the context of the origin of planetary systems (➔ **planetary systems, formation of**), accretion is the process by which small particles collide and stick together to form larger objects in a **protoplanetary disk.** Once a large enough body has formed, its gravitational attraction greatly speeds up the accretion process.

accretion disk
A rotating disk of matter around a star in which **accretion** is taking place. In the case of young stars, accretion disks contain unconsolidated material, such as **cosmic dust** grains, that may subsequently conglomerate into planets and other sizable objects (➔ **planetary systems, formation of**).

acetogens

Autotrophs that use **hydrogen** gas for energy and derive **carbon** for building **organic** molecules from inorganic **carbon dioxide.** They include certain types of **endoliths** found in igneous formations. In these **basalt**ic rocks, the hydrogen is produced by the reaction of oxygen-poor water with iron-bearing minerals. → **extremophiles**

achondrite

A rare type of **stony meteorite** that accounts for about 9 percent of all falls and is composed of rock that has crystallized from a molten state. Achondrites contain a variable amount of calcium and similar elements and usually none of the small rounded inclusions known as **chondrule**s that are typical of **chondrite**s. Most achondrites are chemically similar to **basalt**s and are thought to be the product of melting on **asteroid**s, planets, or moons. Soon after these worlds formed, they were heated from within and partially melted. Although this process is still active on Earth (as evidenced by volcanoes), it ended about 4,400 million years ago on asteroids, 2,900 million years ago on the Moon, and perhaps 1,000 million years ago on Mars. Heating of the primordial mixture of stony minerals, metals, and **sulfides** (of which chondrites are made) produced liquids, the densest of which sank to become planetary or asteroidal cores. Lighter stony minerals rose and solidified to become basaltic rocks, enriched in calcium and aluminum. Subsequent impacts broke off fragments of these once molten surface rocks and hurled them into space. A few then found their way to Earth as achondrites. Although the majority of achondrites found are asteroidal in origin, some are known to have come from the highland regions of the far side of the Moon and from the surface of Mars (→ **SNC meteorites**).

acid

A substance that releases **proton**s (i.e., positively charged **hydrogen ion**s) in solution. Acids have **pH** values ranging from 1 (for a strong acid) to just under 7 (for a very weak acid).

acidic

Having the properties of an **acid**; the opposite of **alkaline.**

acidophiles

Microbes, including certain types of **bacteria** and **archaea,** that thrive in **acidic** environments, such as sulfuric pools, where the **pH** values are in the range 1 to 5. Because high **intracellular** acidity levels would destroy essential molecules, such as **DNA,** acidophiles have evolved the ability to pump **hydrogen ion**s out of their cells at a constantly high rate. The result is a mildly acidic internal pH of about 6.5 compared with a typical external pH of about 2. → **alkaliphiles; extremophiles**

A-class asteroid

A rare type of **asteroid,** reddish in color, with a moderately high **albedo** of 0.13 to 0.35. The **infrared** spectrum of these objects suggests that they are rich in the mineral **olivine.**

activation energy

The minimum energy needed for a specific chemical reaction to take place.

active site

The region on the surface of an **enzyme** to which a specific set of **substrate**s binds. Its properties are determined by the sequences of **amino acids** and the three-dimensional arrangement of the **polypeptide** chains of the enzyme.

Adams, John (1735–1826)

U.S. president with an interest in science who pondered how to reconcile **pluralism** with his Calvinist beliefs. In 1756, he wrote:

> Astronomers will tell us … that not only all the Planets and Satellites in our Solar System, but all the unnumbered Worlds that revolve round the fixt Starrs are inhabited. … If this is the Case all Mankind are no more in comparison of the whole rational Creation of God, than a point to the Orbit of Saturn. Perhaps all these different Ranks of Rational Beings have in greater or less Degree, committed moral Wickedness. If so, I ask a Calvinist, whether he will subscribe to this Alternative, "either God almighty must assume

the respective shapes of all these different Species, and suffer the Penalties of their Crimes, in their Stead, or else all these Being[s] must be consigned to everlasting Perdition?"

Adams almost certainly discussed pluralism with his vice president (later president), Thomas **Jefferson,** and with William **Herschel,** whom he visited in England in 1786. ➔ **Christian doctrine and pluralism**

Adams, Walter Sydney, Jr. (1876–1956)

American astronomer and protégé of George **Hale,** who appointed him to the staff of **Yerkes Observatory** (1901) and then of **Mount Wilson Observatory** (1904). Adams eventually became director of the latter (1923–46) and earned fame through his **spectroscopic** studies of stars and other objects, including the atmospheres of planets. His observations of the Martian atmosphere in the 1920s and 1930s (➔ **Mars, atmosphere of**) showed that Mars was unlikely to support anything but the most primitive kinds of vegetation (➔ **Mars, vegetation on**). Together with Theodore **Dunham,** he demonstrated that **carbon dioxide** was the principal component of the Venusian atmosphere (➔ **Venus, atmosphere of**).

Adamski, George (1891–1965)

"Professor Adamski" to his acolytes though in reality a worker at a hamburger stand on the southern slope of Mount Palomar (home to what was then the world's largest optical telescope), who claimed to have made contact with **flying saucer**s and their occupants. In his bestselling books *Flying Saucers Have Landed* (1953) and *Inside the Spaceships* (1955), he wrote about encounters in the desert nearby with telepathic Venusians. The aliens were here because they were concerned about radiation from atomic explosions, too much of which, they said, would destroy the Earth. Such outlandish tales, though compelling to a lay readership keen for what seemed like inside information about UFOs and sensitized to the issue of atomic weapons, helped further discourage scientists from becoming involved with the UFO controversy. As the historian Steven Dick has pointed out, "Scientists seemed as unwilling to distinguish a poten-

tially credible UFO phenomenon from Adamski's claims as the public was to separate scientific belief in extraterrestrials from UFOs."[152] The increasing vacuum left by science was filled by a variety of individuals and largely amateur organizations that investigated UFOs from the standpoint of favoring the **extraterrestrial hypothesis** (➔ **Keyhoe, Donald; Aerial Phenomena Research Organization; National Investigations Committee on Aerial Phenomena**). The success of Adamski's books also suggests that many people at this time were prepared to entertain the idea that UFOs might have come from other planets *within* the solar system—an indication of the gulf that had opened up between modern astronomical knowledge and some of the quainter, folk notions of space. An *interstellar* origin for putative extraterrestrial spacecraft was at least scientifically feasible. But it had been widely recognized by astronomers since the turn of the century that in the search for intelligence elsewhere, Earth's immediate neighbors looked decidedly unpromising. ➔ **Cold War, linked to UFO reports**

adaptation

(1) A peculiarity of structure, physiology, or behavior that promotes the ability of an organism to survive and reproduce in a given environment. (2) The development of such characteristics by a species over time.

adaptive optics

A technology being developed for use with some of the newest and largest telescopes, including the **Large Binocular Telescope** and **Keck Telescopes,** that allows the image quality of ground-based instruments to rival that of telescopes operating in space. The basis of the technique is to make minute adjustments to the surface shape of a small, very thin mirror placed a short distance in front of the focus. These adjustments have to be made over a timescale of less than one hundredth of a second in order to compensate for distortions in the received light caused by turbulence in the Earth's atmosphere. The result is a level of **resolution** close to the theoretical limit allowed by **diffraction.** Adaptive optics involves a combination of deformable mirror technology, the use of a reference star (which may be natural or artificially produced by a **laser** beam), and high-capacity real-time computation. It is being pioneered at the **Center for Astronomical Adaptive Optics** and will be used extensively, in conjunction with another new technique known as **nulling interferometry,** in the search for **extrasolar planets** and circumstellar **dust disk**s.[14, 15]

adaptive radiation

The evolution of various divergent life-forms from a primitive and unspecialized ancestor. As the original population spreads out from its center of origin to exploit new habitats and food sources, new populations emerge, each adapted to its particular environment. Eventually, these become sufficiently distinct to be recognized as new species.

Addison, Joseph (1672–1719)

English writer and editor whose essays endorsed **pluralism** and, in particular, the principle of **plenitude.** In *The Spectator* of October 25, 1712, having noted the diversity of life on Earth, he writes

[I]t seems very probable from the Analogy of Reason, that if no part of Matter, which we are acquainted with, lies waste and useless, those great Bodies which are at such a Distance from us should not be desart and unpeopled, but rather they should be furnished with Beings adapted to their respective Situations.

adenine

Also known as 6-aminopurine; a **purine** derivative that is one of the five organic **base**s occurring in the **nucleic acid**s of **cells**. In **DNA** it pairs with **thymine** and in **RNA** with **uracil** (➔ **genetic code**). It is also a component of **adenosine triphosphate** (ATP).

adenosine triphosphate (ATP)

The most important carrier of chemical energy in all terrestrial organisms; effectively, the energy currency of cellular **metabolism.** ATP is a **nucleotide** consisting of **adenine, ribose,** and three **phosphate** groups that are linked together by **covalent bond**s. These bonds can undergo **hydrolysis** to yield either a molecule of adenosine diphosphate (ADP) and a phosphate or a molecule of adenosine monophos-

Molecule of ATP.

phate (AMP) and pyrophosphate. In the process, a large amount of energy is made available that can be used for activities such as **chemosynthesis,** locomotion (including muscle contraction in animals), and the active transport of **ion**s and molecules across **cell membrane**s. The reactions bringing about these processes often involve **enzymes** to effect the transfer of the phosphate group to intermediate **substrate**s within the cell. ATP is regenerated by the rephosphorylation of ADP and AMP using the chemical energy obtained from the **oxidation** of food.

Adrastea

The second closest moon of **Jupiter,** moving just one Jovian radius above Jupiter's cloud tops. Adrastea is extremely small and irregular in shape. Like its inner neighbor, **Metis,** it orbits faster than Jupiter spins on its axis, a situation that results in orbital instability and will eventually cause Adrastea to spiral into Jupiter's atmosphere. Adrastea is a **shepherd moon** of Jupiter's main ring and, together with Metis, appears to be the source of the material making up this ring. **→ Jupiter, moons of**

Discovery	1979, by David Jewitt and E. Danielson from *Voyager* data
Mean distance from center of Jupiter	128,400 km (79,800 mi.)
Diameter	25 × 20 × 15 km (16 × 12 × 9 mi.)
Mean density	4.5 g/cm³
Escape velocity	0.014 km/s (50 km/h, 31 mi./h)
Orbital period	0.298 days (7 h 9 min)
Orbital eccentricity	0.000
Orbital inclination	0.00°
Visual albedo	0.05

Advanced Fiber-Optic Échelle Spectrometer (AFOE)

A high-resolution **spectrograph** used with the 1.5-m (60-in.) telescope of the **Whipple Observatory** to perform precise **radial velocity** measurements of stars.[84] An **extrasolar planet** detection program based on the AFOE has been in operation since 1995. It has resulted in the detection of planets around the stars **rho Coronae Borealis**, HD 89744, and a planetary system around **upsilon Andromedae,** and the confirmation of planets around **tau Bootis** and **51 Pegasi.**

aerial

→ antenna

Aerial Phenomena Research Organization (APRO)

An amateur group, founded in 1952 by Jim and Coral Lorenzen, to study the phenomenon of **unidentified flying objects.** Its great ufology rival, a few years later, was the **National Investigations Committee on Aerial Phenomena.**

aerobe

An organism that must have access to **free oxygen** in order to survive.

aerobic

Requiring **free oxygen.**

aerogel

The lightest solid material known, with a density only three times that of air. Its remarkable properties are being exploited on space missions, including some that are of relevance to **astrobiology.** Aerogel was discovered in 1931 by Steven Kistler, a Stanford University researcher, and is sometimes referred to as "frozen smoke" because of its appearance. Although a block of aerogel the size of a person would weigh only 0.5 kg, its internal structure would allow it to support the weight of a small car. Its remarkable thermal insulation properties were employed to keep equipment on the *Sojourner* rover warm during the Martian nights. In addition, it is ideal for capturing microscopic cosmic debris in pristine condition and for this task is being used aboard the *Stardust* probe.

aerolite

→ stony meteorite

aerosol

A suspension of particles in a gas, such as mist in the atmosphere.

AFOE
→ **Advanced Fiber-Optic Échelle Spectrometer**

Agrest, Mates M.

Russian-born ethnologist and mathematician who, in 1959, proposed that certain monuments of past cultures on Earth have resulted from contact with an extraterrestrial race. His writings, together with those of a few other academics, such as the French archaeologist Henri Lhote, provided a platform for the **paleocontact hypothesis,** which was later popularized and sensationalized through the books of Erich von **Däniken** and his emulators.[540]

Agrest, Mikhail M.

Instructor in the Physics and Astronomy Department at the College of Charleston, South Carolina, and son of Mates **Agrest.** Following in his father's tradition of seeking explanations for certain unusual terrestrial events in terms of extraterrestrial intelligence, he interpreted the **Tunguska Phenomenon** as the explosion of an alien spacecraft. This idea was supported by Felix Zigel of the Moscow Institute of Aviation, who suggested that the object had made controlled maneuvers before crashing.

Air Materiel Command (AMC)

That section of the U.S. Army Air Force (later the U.S. Air Force), based at Wright Field (now Wright-Patterson Air Force Base), within which operated the **Technical Intelligence Division** during the height of military interest in "**flying disks**" in the late 1940s and early 1950s.

Air Technical Intelligence Center (ATIC)

Previously known as the **Technical Intelligence Division,** the group within the U.S. Air Force (USAF) responsible for Project **Grudge** and, in its early stages, Project **Blue Book.** It was later renamed the Aerospace Technical Intelligence Center. Blue Book eventually became the responsibility of the U.S. Air Force's Foreign Technology Division as part of a general reorganization.

Aitken, Robert Grant (1864–1951)

American astronomer who eventually became Director at **Lick Observatory** and is best known for his observational work on **binary star**s. His 1910 review of contemporary research on Mars influenced future attitudes toward the possibility of advanced life on that planet (→ **Mars, life on**). Having noted new canal sightings by Percival **Lowell** and others, he commented that at Lick "we do not see canals"—nor, he added, did Eugène **Antoniadi,** Edward **Barnard,** José **Comas Solá,** George **Hale,** and the English observer A. Stanley Williams. Most significantly, he was the first to publicly endorse *both* the work of William **Campbell** (which showed there was little or no water vapor in the Martian atmosphere) and Simon **Newcomb** (which concluded that the canals were an optical illusion). He wrote: "It is difficult to understand how so small [an] amount of water can keep a geometrical canal system on Mars in active operation." Aitken's critique, coming in the same year that Giovanni **Schiaparelli** died, helped finally discredit the canal hypothesis (→ **Mars, canals of**).

In 1911, Aitken argued[4] that the habitability of Venus (→ **Venus, life on**) hinged on the rotation period of that planet:

> If it rotates on its axis once in about 24 hours, we have reason to believe that it is habitable, for the conditions we named as essential to life—air, water in its liquid form and a moderate temperature—are undoubtedly realized. But if its day equals its year, then it must be utterly desolate.

Alais meteorite

A **carbonaceous chondrite** that fell in France on March 15, 1806, and was later examined by Jöns Jakob **Berzelius.** In his published analysis of 1834, Berzelius claimed that, in addition to clay minerals, the meteorite contained complex carbon compounds which he had distilled from a specimen extracted with water. This announcement ushered in the study of **organic** substances that have originated beyond the Earth. → **organic matter, in meteorites**

albedo

A measure of the reflecting power of a nonluminous object, such as a planet or moon. It is expressed as the fraction of total incident energy that is reflected in all directions. Albedo values range from 0, for a perfectly black surface, to 1, for a totally reflective surface. *Visual albedo* refers only to radiation in the visible part of the spectrum. *Geometric albedo* is defined as the ratio between the brightness of an object as seen from the direction of the Sun, and the brightness of a hypothetical white, diffusely reflecting sphere of the same size and at the same distance. Among familiar objects, the Earth has a visual albedo of 0.37, Mercury of 0.11, and Venus of 0.65. From observations of the albedo of a planet or moon, it is possible to make inferences about the nature of its atmosphere (if any) or surface. → **Zöllner, Friedrich**

albedo feature

A marking on the surface of a celestial object in space that is significantly brighter or darker than its surroundings. As in the case of **Syrtis Major** on Mars, it need not necessarily correspond with an actual geological or topographical feature.

alcohols

A family of **organic** compounds derived by substituting one or more of the hydrogen atoms in **hydrocarbon**s by **hydroxyl radicals** (–OH). The simplest alcohols are **methanol** and **ethanol.**

Aldebaran

Alpha Tauri; the nearest **red giant** to the Sun and the fourteenth brightest star in the sky. Recent, though still unconfirmed, observations suggest that Aldebaran may be shifting back and forth in response to a companion with a mass at least eleven times that of Jupiter and an orbital period of 63 days. If this body exists at all, it could be a massive planet or a low-mass **brown dwarf.** → **stars, brightest**

Alembert, Jean Le Rond d' (1717–83)

French scientist who, with Denis **Diderot,** produced the monumental and influential *Encyclopédie* (1751). d'Alembert wrote a number of articles in the encyclopedia which generally

argue in favor of the existence of **extrasolar planets** and life on other worlds but that also point out some of the problems facing **pluralism.** On the question of other planetary systems, he employs a theological argument:

> [I]t is very natural to think that each star…has planets which make their revolutions around it…for why would God have placed all the luminous bodies at such great distances from each other, without their being around them some opaque bodies which receive their light and heat?

Concerning the possibility of life elsewhere in the solar system, he takes a more scientific stance. In the entry "Monde," he notes several reasons to be cautious about unrestrained pluralism:

> 1. One doubts whether some planets, among others the moon, have an atmosphere, and on the supposition that they have not, one does not see how living beings can respire and subsist there. 2. Some planets as Jupiter present changing figures and aspects on their surface…whereas it seems that an inhabited planet ought to be more tranquil. 3. Finally, comets are certainly planets…and it is difficult…to believe that comets may be inhabited.

However, in "Planète," he marshals some astronomical claims, such as La Hire's 1700 report of mountains on Venus, that are more sympathetic to the pluralists' cause:

> Since Saturn, Jupiter and their satellites, Mars, Venus and Mercury are opaque bodies…which are covered by mountains and surrounded by a changing atmosphere, it seems to follow that these planets have lakes, have seas…; in a word, that they are bodies resembling…the earth. Consequently, according to many philosophers, nothing prevents us from believing that the planets are inhabited.

algae

A large, diverse group of simple **photosynthetic** organisms, among the most primitive life-forms known, some of which are **prokary-**

otes and others **eukaryote**s. They occur in aquatic environments or in moist locations on land. The body of an alga may be either **unicellular** or **multicellular** in the form of filaments, ribbons, or plates. So-called blue-green algae are now recognized as being a type of bacteria known as **cyanobacteria.**

Algol

Beta Persei, a **multiple star** system located 114 light-years (35 parsecs) from the sun. Its Arabic name means "Demon Star," apparently a reference to its peculiar behavior. Algol seems to wink slowly, fading for almost 5 hours, reaching a minimum brightness for about 20 minutes, and then gradually returning to its maximum brightness before starting the whole 2.87-day cycle again. Its variability was cited in a 1783 paper by William **Herschel** as evidence of a planet in orbit about the star. However, William **Whewell,** in his attack on **pluralism** in 1853, argued that if the variability were due to an eclipsing companion, this body would have to be much larger than a planet. John **Goodricke** was the first to realize its true nature. Algol is now known to be an **eclipsing binary,** consisting of a larger but fainter **G star** and a smaller but brighter **B star** in orbit around each other. The fast decline in brightness takes place as the G-type component moves in front of and blocks out the light from its brighter partner. The 20-minute minimum corresponds to the period when the B-type star is completely eclipsed. A secondary eclipse takes place when the positions of the stars are reversed, but because the B type is responsible for the bulk of the combined light output and can only blot out a fraction of the larger star's disk, this results in hardly any reduction in brightness. A third, more remote star exists in the Algol system; it has a period of 1.87 years and does not participate in the eclipses.

Algonquin Radio Observatory

A radio observatory located near Lake Traverse, Ontario, and operated jointly by the Institute for Space and Terrestrial Science at York University, Toronto, and the Geodetic Survey Division of the Canada Center for Surveying and Mapping, Ottawa. Its main instrument is a 46-m (150-ft.) fully steerable **radio** **telescope** that has been in operation since 1967 and was used, by Alan Bridle and Paul Feldman in 1974, for the first **SETI** search to be carried out at the 1.35-cm wavelength, emitted by water molecules in space.

ALH 84001

The oldest known **SNC meteorite,** gray green in color, measuring 15 cm by 10 cm by 8 cm (6 in. by 4 in. by 3 in.) and weighing 1.94 kg (4.2 lb.). It was recovered by a team from the **ANSMET** program on December 27, 1984, from the **Allan Hills** region of Antarctica, where it had lain undisturbed since its arrival on Earth about 13,000 years ago. Geological analysis of ALH 84001 has revealed something of its history. It formed originally from molten lava that possibly issued from an ancient Martian volcano, about 4.5 billion years ago. Some 4 billion years ago, it was heated again and deformed by a strong shock, probably resulting from the nearby impact of an **asteroid** or large meteorite. Then, about 3.6 billion years ago, some kind of liquid flowed through the rock and deposited rounded globules of **carbonate** minerals. About 15 million years ago, ALH 84001 is believed to have been hurled from the surface of Mars when an asteroid or **comet** collided obliquely with the planet. Finally, it became the center of a major controversy in 1996, when scientists at the **NASA Johnson Space Center,** led by David S. **McKay,** claimed that they had found inside the meteorite very small fossils and other evidence of Martian biological activity centered around the carbonate deposits. ➜ **Martian "fossils" controversy**

alien

A term often used in place of "extraterrestrial." In the sense that it derives from the Latin *alienus* (belonging to another person or place) this is appropriate. However, since "alien" can also mean "repugnant" or "opposed to," it carries a negative connotation in contrast with the strictly neutral "extraterrestrial." It can also be argued that *any* kind of life or intelligence that is very different from the human variety is alien—whether it occurs on this planet or elsewhere (➜ **dolphins, as a form of alien intelligence**).

Alien

Memorable and influential motion picture (1979), combining aspects of the horror and science fiction genres, in which an ultrapredatory, intelligent extraterrestrial terrorizes the human crew of a merchant spaceship. A direct descendant of H. G. **Wells**'s Martian monsters in *The War of the Worlds,* the repellent creature in *Alien* (designed by H. R. Giger) stands at one extreme of speculation about what life on other worlds might be like and epitomizes the fears of those who have voiced opposition to attempts at interstellar communication (→ **CETI, opposition to**). Sequels to it include *Aliens* (1986), *Alien³* (1992), and *Alien: Resurrection* (1997).

alien abduction

The purported kidnapping, usually for sinister medical or genetic experimentation, of humans by extraterrestrials. The first abduction stories appeared in the wake of revelations of contact with the occupants of flying saucers by writers such as George **Adamski.** As in the much-analyzed case of Betty and Barney Hill, details of the reported abductions were often elicited under hypnosis. Following the publication of John G. Fuller's *The Interrupted Journey* (1966),[211] concerning the Hill incident, the number of claimed cases of alien abduction began to rise steeply. Interest in the subject was further stimulated by the release of *Close Encounters of the Third Kind* (in which the alien kidnappers turn out to be benign). By the 1980s, the abduction scenario, recounted ad nauseam in talk-show interviews and tabloid stories, had taken on a stereotypical pattern, involving a humiliating examination aboard the alien craft, the removal of sperm or ovum samples, and interspecies sexual relations. Abductees generally "recalled" their experiences as a result of hypnotic regression, which, it was claimed, released memories that had been suppressed by a more innocuous recollection. The explosion in alien abduction claims was both accompanied and encouraged by an outpouring of popular literature (for example, by Budd **Hopkins** and Whitley **Strieber**), TV documentaries, and motion pictures sympathetic to the theme. Some plausibility was lent to a phenomenon that might otherwise have been quickly dismissed by the apparent sincerity of many claimees and the establishment of abductee support groups throughout the United States. By the late 1980s, a growing unease had set in with the concept of "recovered memories." Aside from abduction stories unearthed by hypnosis, there was an alarming growth of child sex-abuse claims. After attending therapy sessions, subjects would "remember" having been abused as children, usually by close relatives and involving satanic ritual. Courts had convicted, or awarded civil damages against, a number of "abusers" on the strength of recovered memories alone. Some of the accused had formed their own support groups and were suing therapists, sometimes successfully, for the ruin brought upon them by their grown children. Senior members of the American medical establishment began openly to cast doubt on the whole technique. However, in 1994, the endangered case for alien abduction was given an unexpected boost by the publication of a book by John **Mack,**[371] professor of psychiatry at Harvard, which argued strongly in favor of the view that the abductions were real. Unfortunately for Mack, he was devastatingly criticized by his peers, and his case was further undermined by the revelation that one of the subjects he had described was a journalist on a debunking mission. Although the extraterrestrial option is given short shrift by the scientific community in general, alien abduction as a phenomenon with genuine psychological and possibly geophysical underpinnings has been the subject of a number of serious investigations and conferences.[322, 467, 557] Even if aliens are not to blame, it may be that tales of abduction can shed valuable light on effects such as **false memory syndrome** and **temporal lobe lability.**

alkali

A soluble hydroxide of a metal, such as sodium hydroxide ($NaOH$). In solution, an alkali releases hydroxyl ions, OH^-.

alkaline

Having the properties of an **alkali**; the opposite of **acidic.**

alkaliphiles

Microbes, including some **bacteria** and **archaea,** which thrive in highly **alkaline** environments, such as soda lakes and **carbonate**-rich soils, where the **pH** values range from about 9 to 11. Alkaliphiles maintain a mildly alkaline **intracellular** pH of about 8 amid surroundings of much higher pH by continuously pumping **hydrogen ion**s across their **cell membrane**s into their **cytoplasm.** ➔ **acidophiles; extremophiles**

Allan Hills

A region of Victoria Land, Antarctica, to the west of which large numbers of meteorites have been recovered in recent years, including **ALH 84001.** The meteorites become concentrated on areas of "blue ice" by natural movements of the ice sheet and are easy to find due to the light background and the absence of other rocks.

Allegheny Observatory

The observatory of the University of Pittsburgh, located in Riverview Park, Pennsylvania, 10 miles northeast of the main university campus. For most of the twentieth century, this facility has specialized in astrometric observations and its primary research goal continues to be high-precision **astrometry,** particularly as applied to the detection of **extrasolar planets.** One of its principal researchers, George **Gatewood,** announced in 1996 the preliminary finding of a planetary system around the nearby star **Lalande 21185.** Allegheny's main instruments are the Thaw Memorial 0.76-m (30-in.) refractor, constructed in 1914 and used in the work leading to Gatewood's discovery, and the James E. Keeler 30-in. reflector, built in 1906 and also used for astrometric research. Among the special equipment applied to extrasolar planet detection are the **Multichannel Astrometric Photometer** (MAP) and the more recently developed **Multichannel Astrometric Photometer and Spectrometer** (MAPS).

Allende meteorite

A **carbonaceous chondrite** that fell near the village of Pueblito de Allende in the Mexican state of Chihuahua on February 8, 1969, scattering several tons of material over an area measuring 48 by 7 km. Specimens of the meteorite were found to contain a fine-grained **carbon**-rich matrix studded with many **chondrule**s, both matrix and chondrules consisting predominantly of the mineral **olivine.** Close examination of the chondrules by a team from Case Western Reserve University[237] revealed tiny black markings, up to 10 trillion per square centimeter, that were absent from the matrix and interpreted as evidence of **radiation** damage. Similar structures have turned up in lunar **basalt**s but not in their terrestrial equivalent, which would have been screened from cosmic radiation by the Earth's atmosphere and geomagnetic field. Irradiation of the chondrules, it seems, happened after they had solidified but before the cold **accretion** of matter that took place during the early stages of formation of the solar system, when the parent meteorite came together. ➔ **organic matter, in meteorites**

all-sky survey

A survey that makes no prior assumptions about the most likely directions to search for a particular type of object, whether it be distant galaxies or signals from an extraterrestrial civilization. An all-sky survey attempts to sweep out entire sections of the sky as they appear from a given location. Whereas instruments used in **targeted search**es must be continuously moved to track selected objects, those conducting all-sky surveys operate in what is called *transit mode;* that is, they point in a fixed direction while the Earth rotates underneath them. The majority of current **SETI** projects, such as Project **Argus,** involve all-sky surveys.

Alpha Centauri

The nearest star system to the Sun and a trinary (consisting of three stars). The two bright-

Sun   Alpha Centauri A   Alpha Centauri B   Proxima Centauri

Relative sizes of the Sun and the stars of the Alpha Centauri system.

Distance 4.395 light-years (1.349 parsecs)		
	A	**B**
Spectral type	G2 V	K5 V
Apparent magnitude	0.0	1.38
Absolute magnitude	4.4	5.8
Luminosity (Sun = 1)	1.53	0.44
Mass (Sun = 1)	1.1	0.88

est components, A and B, revolve around each other once every 80 years and are separated by about 25 AU (3.75 billion km, or 2.3 billion miles). Alpha Centauri A is a yellow **G star** similar to the Sun but about 1.5 times as bright; B is a smaller, orange **K star** with about 0.4 of the Sun's luminosity. Both these stars are metal rich and 5 to 6 billion years old. The third member of the system, **Proxima Centauri,** is a **red dwarf,** less than 10,000 times the luminosity of the Sun, which moves in a very wide orbit around the main pair.

Whether or not the Alpha Centauri system contains any planets is undetermined but there has been much speculation about how, if it did, a planet would have to move in order to have the best chance of supporting life.[45, 47, 256] If it circled widely around either A or B, it would not only lie outside the **habitable zone** of either of these stars but be subject to complex gravitational influences that would tend to destabilize its orbit. On the other hand, an even wider path that took a planet around both main stars might be stable but would fall even further outside the habitable zones. The best chance for life (as we know it) might be on a world that circled closely around A or B and enjoyed similar levels of light and warmth to those on Earth. To an inhabitant of such a world, the other star would appear about 1,000 times brighter in the sky than our Moon and be visible for half the year in the daytime and half the year at night. A and B would

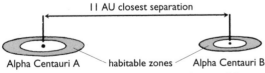

Approximate habitable zones of Alpha Centauri A and B.

make a striking color contrast of orange and yellow, while Proxima would appear as a dim red point of light barely visible without a telescope. → **Orion, Project; stars, nearest; stars, brightest**

Alphonsus

A lunar crater 118 km (73 miles) in diameter that has frequently been associated with **transient lunar phenomena.** In 1958 and 1959, various observers reported seeing reddish clouds in its vicinity, and on November 3, 1958, the Soviet astronomer N. A. Kozyrev, working with the 50-in. reflector at the **Crimean Astrophysical Observatory,** claimed to have obtained a spectrum of the event that suggested a gaseous emission. Assuming that the phenomenon is real, the likeliest explanation is that gases occasionally escape to the surface through fractures in the crust.

Altair

Alpha Aquilae; a conspicuous, white **A star** that is about ten times more luminous than the Sun. Altair is one of the nearer solar neighbors and the twelfth brightest star in the night sky. → **stars, brightest**

Alvarez, Luis Walter (1911–88)

American high-energy physicist at the **University of California, Berkeley,** and Nobel Prize winner (1968) who, together with his son, Walter, and others, championed the idea that the **mass extinction** at the end of the Cretaceous period (→ **Cretaceous-Tertiary Boundary**) was caused by the impact of an **asteroid**—a thesis that has now met with widespread acceptance. In January 1953, Alvarez sat on the **Scientific Advisory Panel on Unidentified Flying Objects.**

Amalthea

The largest of **Jupiter**'s non-Galilean satellites and one of four moons that circle around Jupiter inside the orbit of **Io.** Amalthea is potato-shaped like the Martian moon **Phobos** but ten times bigger. Two large craters stand out on its heavily cratered surface: Pan, 90 km in diameter and 8 km deep, and Gaea, 75 km in diameter and 16 km deep. Two mountains have been identified: Mons Ida and Mons Lyctos.

Discovery	September 9, 1892, by Edward Emerson Barnard
Mean distance from Jupiter	181,300 km (112,680 miles)
Diameter	270 × 168 × 150 km (168 × 104 × 93 miles)
Mean density	1.8 g/cm³
Escape velocity	0.084 km/s (302 km/h, 277 mi./h)
Orbital period	0.498 days (11 hours 57 minutes)
Orbital eccentricity	0.003
Orbital inclination	0.40°
Axial period	0.498 day
Albedo	0.05

Amalthea is dark and the reddest object known in the solar system. Its coloration is probably due to **sulfur** from Io's volcanoes that has spiraled down toward Jupiter and impacted on Amalthea's surface. Bright green patches on the moon's major slopes are of unknown origin. Amalthea is also unusual in that it appears to give out more heat than it receives from the Sun. Tidal stresses could be one possible source of this heat; alternatively, it may arise from electrical currents induced in the moon's core by Jupiter's powerful magnetic field. Material lost from the surface of Amalthea, and also from **Thebe,** appears to make up Jupiter's Gossamer Ring. → **Jupiter, moons of**

Ambartsumian, Viktor Amazaspovich (1908–96)

Georgian-born Armenian astrophysicist and director of the **Byurakan Astrophysical Observatory** whose interests included stellar evolution of stars, planetary nebulas, and radio galaxies. He was the principal organizer of two major conferences on **SETI** at the observatory in 1964 and 1972 (→ **Byurakan SETI conferences**).

AMC
→ **Air Materiel Command**

Ames Research Center
→ **NASA Ames Research Center**

amide bond
The **covalent bond** that forms when an **amine** reacts with a **carboxylic acid.**

amines
Derivatives of **ammonia** (NH_3) in which one or more **hydrogen** atoms are replaced by **organic** groups. Amines are produced by the decomposition of organic matter.

amino acids
The chemical subunits of **polypeptide**s and **proteins,** and therefore one of the fundamental building blocks of life as we know it. They consist of a central **carbon** atom attached to a **carboxyl group** (–COOH), an **amino group** (–NH_2), a hydrogen atom, and a side group (–R), giving the general formula R–CH–NH_2–COOH. Only the side group differs from one amino acid to another.

The manufacture of amino acids represents one of the earliest stages in **prebiotic** molecular evolution and one of the easiest to accomplish in the laboratory. Pioneering work in this field was carried out by Alfonso Herrara in his Laboratory of Plasmogeny in Mexico City, between 1924 and 1942, and by Stanley **Miller** and Harold **Urey** in their famous experiment of 1953 (→ **Miller-Urey Experiment**). Although a good deal of amino acid synthesis must have taken place *in situ* on the young Earth, evidence is growing that a contribution came from "seeding" as a result of cometary and asteroidal collisions (→ **cosmic collisions, biological effects of**). Such impregnation of virgin worlds with ready-made **organic** matter from space, during the early bombardment phase of planetary systems, may occur commonly throughout the universe and serve further to stimulate **prebiotic** chemistry where conditions allow. The discovery of **amino acids, in space** provides powerful support for this idea. However, it is unclear how important this cosmic seeding is compared with planet-grown prebiotic material and whether it could actually prove decisive in the development of life.

Twenty different amino acids are found in the proteins of terrestrial life-forms. All of these, with the exception of **glycine,** the simplest, have an **asymmetric carbon atom** (one that is attached to four different groups) and can therefore exist in distinct mirror-image forms, or **enantiomers.** One of the forms is "left-handed," or **levorotatory,** (L-), while the other is "right-handed," or **dextrorotatory** (D-). Outside the living world, wherever amino acids occur (with the interesting exception of **organic matter, in meteorites**), they consist of equal amounts of the L- and D- forms in what is called a *racemic* mixture. However, terrestrial organisms use L-amino acids exclusively, giving rise to speculation about how this selection was originally made (→ **enantiomers, bias in terrestrial life**).

Although only twenty different amino acids take part in the **chemosynthesis** of terrestrial proteins, more than one hundred naturally occurring amino acids are known. This prompts the question as to whether extraterrestrial life could be built up from a different set of these fundamental organic compounds. To explore this possibility, Andrew Ellington and colleagues at the University of Texas, in 1998, grew a strain of the bacterium *Escherichia coli* that was incapable of manufacturing the essential amino acid tryptophan and therefore had to be supplied with it as a nutrient.[125] The researchers also gave it the related synthetic amino acid fluorotryptophan. Although toxic to earthly creatures, this might conceivably be an essential ingredient of life elsewhere. With 100 percent artificial substitute, the bacteria died within three cell divisions. With 95 percent fluorotryptophan and 5 percent normal tryptophan, however, the *E. coli* survived and slowly grew. After many generations, the bacteria started to divide at a greater rate as if **mutation**s had arisen that were less susceptible to the synthetic chemical's toxic effects. Eventually, the bacteria were able to cope with a diet of 100 percent artificial substitute—growing extremely slowly but nevertheless surviving on this "alien" organic.

Two interesting possibilities are brought a step closer by this work. The first is that life on other worlds might have evolved and adapted to utilize a nonterrestrial mix of amino acids. If so, then any indigenous foodstuffs would have to be analyzed carefully before they were passed as fit for human consumption. Extraterrestrial fruits, for example, containing amino acids of a different type or handedness to those found in our own bodies would either be indigestible or poisonous, a fact often overlooked in the *Star Trek* universe, where crew

THE TWENTY AMINO ACIDS FOUND IN TERRESTRIAL LIFE-FORMS		
Amino Acid	Formula	Number of Atoms
Glycine	$C_2H_5O_2N$	10
L-Alanine	$C_3H_7O_2N$	13
L-Serine	$C_3H_7O_3N$	14
L-Cysteine	$C_3H_7O_2NS$	14
L-Aspartic acid	$C_4H_6O_4N$	15
L-Asparagine	$C_4H_8O_3N_2$	17
L-Threonine	$C_4H_9O_3N$	17
L-Proline	$C_5H_9O_2N$	17
L-Glutamic acid	$C_5H_8O_4N$	18
L-Valine	$C_5H_{11}O_2N$	19
L-Glutamine	$C_5H_{10}O_3N_2$	20
L-Methionine	$C_5H_{11}O_2NS$	20
L-Histidine	$C_6H_9O_2N_3$	20
L-Leucine	$C_6H_{13}O_2N$	22
L-Isoleucine	$C_6H_{13}O_2N$	22
L-Phenylalanine	$C_9H_{11}O_2N$	23
L-Tyrosine	$C_9H_{11}O_3N$	24
L-Lysine	$C_6H_{15}O_2N_2$	25
L-Arginine	$C_6H_{15}O_2N_4$	27
L-Tryptophan	$C_{11}H_{12}O_2N_2$	27

members habitually sample the culinary delights of alien worlds without first checking their biomolecular credentials. The second possibility arising from the Texas study is that microbes from Earth might be encouraged to grow elsewhere in the solar system (for example, on Mars), feeding on what would normally be toxic chemicals in the soil and releasing gases to help in **terraforming** the environment.

amino acids, in meteorites
→ **organic matter, in meteorites**

amino acids, in space
The first detection of an **amino acid** in space was made in 1994, when **glycine** was found in a star-forming region about 1 light-year across within the **molecular cloud** known as **Sagittarius B2**. This discovery adds weight to the idea that some important **prebiotic** chemicals, including amino acids, form on grains of **cosmic dust** and are later deposited on the surface of young planets during impacts with comets and

asteroids (➔ **cosmic collisions, biological effects of**). A long-standing puzzle connected with the origin of life on Earth is why all of the amino acids in terrestrial organisms are "left-handed," or **levorotatory.** One possible answer is that the choice was made not on the Earth's surface but long before the Earth and Sun even formed, by the action of **ultraviolet** light on **interstellar molecules.** Support for this view came with the 1995 discovery of excess left-handed amino acids in the **Murchison meteorite**[135] and the 1998 discovery of **polarized light** in a star-forming region of the **Orion Nebula.** The existence of circular polarized light (in which the plane of polarization continuously changes) in the Orion gas clouds, shown by James Hough of the University of Hertfordshire and colleagues using an instrument attached to the **Anglo-Australian Telescope,**[32] is especially significant. Although the observations were made at **infrared** wavelengths, the team argues that ultraviolet light in the same region, which is obscured by the clouds, should be polarized as well. Ultraviolet light can force chemical reactions to make molecules of mostly one handedness instead of an even split between the two forms: right-handed ultraviolet light destroys right-handed molecules, leaving an excess of left-handed ones, and vice versa. If the solar system formed in a similar environment, claims Hough, a 5 to 10 percent excess in the handedness of molecules—the same as that found in the Murchison meteorite—should result. This might be enough to allow the favored types to gain an upper hand during the early evolution of life on Earth (➔ **enantiomers, bias in terrestrial life**).

amino group (–NH₂)

One of the chemical groups common to all **amino acids,** which in turn are the building blocks of **proteins.** In it, one atom of **nitrogen** is attached by **covalent bonds** to two atoms of **hydrogen,** leaving a lone **valence electron** on the nitrogen that is available for bonding to another atom.

ammonia (NH₃)

A colorless, pungent gas that is highly soluble in water. It occurs in the atmospheres of **gas giants** and as widely scattered molecules in **molecular clouds.** The **nitrogen** atom in ammonia has a spare pair of **valence electrons** with which it can form a bond with an additional hydrogen atom. The resulting ammonium (NH_4^+) ion behaves chemically like an ion of sodium, though the **base** ammonium hydroxide (NH_4OH) is much weaker than its counterpart sodium hydroxide. This makes it more useful for biological reactions, which generally involve only small energy transfers. The fact that ammonia has physical properties similar to those of **water** has led to many suggestions over the past few decades that **ammonia-based life** is a possibility.

Density relative to air 0.59; melting point −77.7°C; boiling point −33.4°C; specific heat (at 20°C) 1.13 cal/g/°C

ammonia-based life

In 1954, J. B. S. **Haldane** suggested that an alternative biochemistry could be conceived in which water was replaced as a **solvent** by liquid **ammonia.**[251] Part of his reasoning was based on the observation that water has a number of ammonia analogues. For example, the ammonia analogue of **methanol,** CH_3OH, is methylamine, CH_3NH_2. Haldane theorized that it might be possible to build up the ammonia-based counterparts of complex substances, such as **proteins** and **nucleic acids,** and then make use of the fact that an entire class of organic compounds, the **peptides,** could exist without change in the ammonia system. The amide molecules, which substitute for the normal **amino acids,** could then undergo **condensation** to form **polypeptides** that would be almost identical in form to those found in terrestrial life-forms. This hypothesis is of particular interest when considering the possibility of biological evolution on ammonia-rich worlds such as **gas giants** and their moons (➔ **Jupiter, life on**).[189, 192] Close examination, however, exposes serious problems with the notion of ammonia as a basis for life. These center principally upon the fact that the **heat of vaporization** of ammonia is only half that of water and its **surface tension** is only one third as much. Consequently, the **hydrogen bonds** that exist between ammonia molecules are much weaker than those in water so that ammonia would be less able to concentrate non-**polar molecule**s through a **hydrophobic** effect. Lacking this ability, it is difficult to see how ammonia could hold **prebiotic** molecules together sufficiently well to allow the formation of a self-reproducing system.

anabiosis

A temporary state of reduced **metabolism** in which metabolic activity is absent or undetectable. → **cryptobiosis**

anabolism

The aspect of **metabolism** that involves building up complex molecules from simpler material, with the absorption and storage of energy. It is the opposite of **catabolism.**

anaerobe

An organism that can survive and grow in the absence or near absence of **free oxygen.** *Facultative* anaerobes can live with or without free oxygen; *obligate* anaerobes are poisoned by it.

anaerobic

Not requiring **free oxygen.**

analogous

Biological structures that have a similar function but a different evolutionary origin, such as the eye of an octopus and the eye of a whale.

analogy, argument from

In the wake of the **Copernican Revolution,** it became common to argue the case for **pluralism** based on analogy between the Earth and the other planets circling the Sun. Since those in favor of pluralism generally assumed that (1) the other worlds of the solar system were similar to the Earth, and (2) God would not have created a lifeless world (→ **teleology**), the conclusion followed that all the solar planets supported life. By the middle of the seventeenth century, analogical reasoning had been extended to others stars that, now considered to be suns in their own right, would have been wasted had they not had their own systems of inhabited planets.

Ananke

The thirteenth closest moon of **Jupiter.** It is one of the group of four outer Jovian moons that exhibit **retrograde** motion and are therefore almost certainly captured **asteroid**s. → **Jupiter, moons of**

Discovery	1951, by Seth Barnes Nicholson
Mean distance from Jupiter	20,700,000 km (12,870,000 mi.)
Diameter	30 km (19 mi.)
Mean density	2.7 g/cm³
Escape velocity	0.018 km/s (65 km/h, 40 mi./h)
Orbital period	−631 days (retrograde)
Orbital eccentricity	0.169
Orbital inclination	147°

Anaxagoras of Clazomenae (c. 500–c. 428 B.C.)

Greek philosopher from Ionia who gave up his wealth to pursue a life of study. At the age of twenty, he moved to Athens and effectively established it as the new center of Greek philosophy. For three decades he helped shape the thoughts of a number of illustrious pupils, including Pericles the statesman, Euripides the playwright, and possibly even Socrates. Anaxagoras's explanations of the Moon's light, eclipses, earthquakes, meteors, rainbows, sound, and wind seem surprisingly modern, and he put forward some provocative ideas that bore on the possibility of extraterrestrial life. He thought, for instance, that the Moon has "a surface in some places lofty, in others hollow" and that a race of humans dwelt there (→ **Moon, life on**). He also postulated that the Sun was a brightly glowing rock "bigger than the Peloponnese" and that the stars were other suns lying at such a distance that they appeared to give out no heat. When he was about thirty-three, a meteorite big enough to fill a wagon landed in broad daylight near the town of Aegospotami. Anaxagoras caused a sensation by claiming it had come from the Sun. To him, there was no difficulty in thinking about the Sun and Moon as sizable *physical* objects rather than as deities. In fact, in place of the traditional pantheon of gods, he argued that there was just a single eternal intelligence, or "Nous," that pervades the cosmos. The Athenian authorities, smarting from a recent military defeat at the hands of the Persians, were in no mood to be subverted from within by such heretical views and arrested Anaxagoras. Charged with impiety, he was sentenced to death. Fortunately, Pericles, the most respected man in Athens, put in a good word for him, and the sentence was commuted to exile. Anaxagoras retired to Lampsacus on the Dardanelles, where he continued teaching for another 20 years. → **ancient philosophy, related to the possibility of extraterrestrial life**

Anaximander of Miletus (c. 610–c. 540 B.C.)

Greek philosopher of the Milesian School, student of **Thales of Miletus,** and possibly the first person to speculate on the existence of other worlds. Anaximander held that the fundamental essence of all things is not a particular substance, like water, but *apeiron,* or the infinite. It seemed reasonable to him, given this boundless creative source extending in all directions, that there might be an indefinite number of worlds existing throughout time, worlds that "are born and perish within an eternal or ageless infinity." The **pluralism** he taught, therefore, was not of a multitude of planets in space but of an endless *temporal* succession. Anaximander also pioneered the notion that the Earth is not flat, suggesting it was cylindrical and that it floated free, unsupported, at the exact center of the Universe, with people living on one of the flat ends. As for the Sun, he said it was as large as the Earth—an audacious theory at that time. → **Anaxagoras of Clazomenae; ancient philosophy, related to the possibility of extraterrestrial life**

Anaximenes of Miletus (c. 585–525 B.C.)

Greek philosopher, student of **Anaximander of Miletus,** who was the first to draw a clear distinction between planets and stars. → **ancient philosophy, related to the possibility of extraterrestrial life**

ancient astronaut hypothesis

→ **paleocontact hypothesis**

ancient philosophy, related to the possibility of extraterrestrial life

The idea that there might be other inhabited worlds dates back thousands of years and has

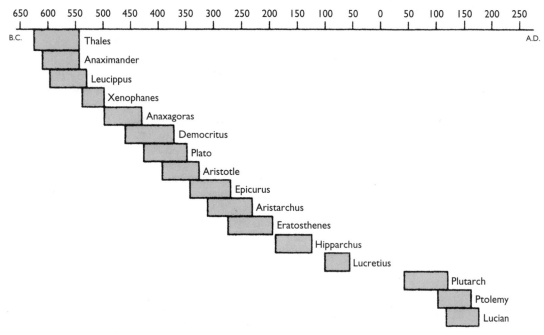

Time chart of ancient philosophers in this book.

roots in both Eastern and Western thought. Doubtless it first took the form of beliefs in gods, goddesses, and other spiritual beings that inhabited realms beyond the Earth. On a more intellectual level, Buddhism taught **pluralism,** as did some of the schools of Greek philosophy. Of the latter, **atomism,** as developed and propagated notably by **Leucippus, Democritus of Abdera, Epicurus,** and **Lucretius,** is the most significant because the concept of multiple worlds and life is implicit in its cosmological scenario. Prominent among other ancient philosophers who speculated about the possibility (or impossibility) of other worlds and life, or who made discoveries relevant to these subjects, were **Thales of Miletus, Anaximander of Miletus, Anaximenes of Miletus, Xenophanes, Anaxagoras of Clazomenae, Plato, Aristotle, Aristarchus of Samos, Eratosthenes of Cyrene, Hipparchus of Nicaea, Plutarch, Ptolemy,** and **Lucian of Samosata.**[150] → **medieval philosophy, related to the possibility of extraterrestrial life**

android

A robot in human form; androids have been a mainstay of science fiction since the 1920s, when they first appeared in Karel Čapek's play *R.U.R.* Their most endearing fictional representative in recent times has been Mr. Data of the television series *Star Trek: The Next Generation.* Conceivably, such creatures will eventually be built as **artificial intelligence,** achieved through the use of powerful, general-purpose **neural network**s encapsulated within a sophisticated, lifelike framework. Androids would be particularly useful for interstellar missions, since their appearance and behavior could be made sufficiently human for them to blend in well with biological crew members. At the same time, their superhuman capabilities would allow them safely to test the waters of potentially hostile environments. An even stranger possibility is that, at some future point, human beings may decide to evolve into androids themselves. Replacing a frail, short-lived biological body with an effectively immortal substitute made of indestructible materials might be an option worth considering for interstellar travelers. Not only would they be better

equipped to deal with otherwise life-threatening emergencies, but they would not have to worry about growing old on potentially long journeys between the stars (→ **interstellar travel**). Whether such a melding of man and machine will ever transpire, it seems certain that high levels of machine intelligence and sophisticated robotics will play a crucial part in our and other races' explorations of the Galaxy.[408] → **cyborg**

Andromeda Galaxy (NGC 224, M 31)

The nearest major **galaxy** to our own and the most remote object normally visible to the naked eye from Earth. It lies at a distance of 2.3 million light-years (700 kiloparsecs), so that we see it now as it was before our species evolved. Andromeda is a **spiral galaxy** similar to our own but about 1.5 times as massive. It is the largest member of the **Local Group.**

Anglo-Australian Observatory (AAO)

A facility housing the **Anglo-Australian Telescope** and the 1.2-m (48-in.) U.K. Schmidt Telescope, at an altitude of 1,150 m on Siding Spring Mountain near Coonabarabran, New South Wales, Australia. Nearby, on the same site, are instruments of the **Mount Stromlo and Siding Spring Observatories.**

Anglo-Australian Planet Search

An extension of the **San Francisco State University Planet Search** program. It uses the **Anglo-Australian Telescope** (AAT) in conjunction with a high-resolution échelle spectrometer to monitor the 150 brightest **sunlike stars** in the Southern Hemisphere by the **radial velocity method.** The AAT Planet Search began in September 1997 and is expected to continue in its initial phase, looking for **extrasolar planets** as small as **Saturn,** until 2002. Beyond this, observations are planned until 2010 aimed at detecting planets of lower mass.

Anglo-Australian Telescope (AAT)

A 3.9-m (153-in.) reflecting telescope located at the **Anglo-Australian Observatory.** It came into operation in 1974 and, among many other tasks, is presently being used in the **Anglo-Australian Planet Search.**

angular momentum

The momentum an object has because of its rotation. A planet's angular momentum in orbit, for example, is obtained by multiplying the planet's mass by its velocity and the radius of its orbit. According to a basic conservation law of physics, the angular momentum of any object in orbit must remain constant at all points in the orbit.

ANI

→ **Astronomical Nulling Interferometer**

animal

An organism belonging to the **kingdom** *Animalia*. Animals are multicellular **heterotrophs** that are generally mobile so that they can seek out food. Specialized sense organs allow them to detect changes in their surroundings, while a nervous system processes information from the senses and enables an appropriate response to be made to environmental stimuli.

ANSMET

→ **Antarctic Search for Meteorites**

Antarctic Dry Valleys

→ **Dry Valleys, Antarctica**

Antarctic Search for Meteorites (ANSMET)

An ongoing search, sponsored by the Polar Programs Office of the U.S. National Science Foundation, that since 1977 has led to the discovery of more than 7,000 **meteorite**s (about three times the number found outside Antarctica), including the famous **ALH 84001.**

antenna

A structure for receiving or transmitting electromagnetic signals.

anthro-, anthropo-

Prefixes meaning "human" or "humanlike."

anthropic principle

The idea that the existence of life, and in particular, our presence as intelligent observers, constrains the nature of the Universe. It was first discussed in 1961 by Princeton physicist Robert Dicke,[154] who argued that for advanced **carbon-**based life to exist, the Universe had to be roughly the age that we find it to be: much younger, and there would not have been time for sufficient interstellar levels of carbon to build up by **nucleosynthesis;** much older, and the "golden" age of **main sequence** stars and stable planetary systems would have drawn to a close. Although not everyone was convinced, in 1973 the concept was given its now-familiar name and raised to greater prominence through the efforts of Cambridge physicist Brandon Carter,[101] encouraged by the eminent pioneer of **quantum mechanics,** John Wheeler. Carter distinguished between two degrees of the hypothesis: the *weak anthropic principle*, which was essentially a generalization of Dicke's idea, and the *strong anthropic principle*, which went much further and claimed that "the Universe . . . must be such as to admit the creation of observers within it at some stage." It was not long before Wheeler found a crucial role for those observers in his *participatory anthropic principle*. Somehow, suggested Wheeler, we play a part in actualizing the world in which we find ourselves. Our observations today, at a quantum level, constrain the Universe so that it had to have evolved in precisely the way that would eventually give rise to us. As for the implications of the anthropic principle for extraterrestrial life, they are controversial. According to one view, if the nature of the Universe is such that it must inevitably give rise to life as we know it, its biogenic powers have presumably been exercised elsewhere and many times over. Curiously, however, two of the most ardent proponents of the anthropic principle, English astronomer John Barrow and American mathematical physicist Frank **Tipler,**[43] have argued that the principle favors the conclusion that we are unique.

anthropogenic

Resulting from or influenced by human activities.

anthropomorphic

Resembling a human being in external appearance.

anthropomorphism

A review of science fiction from **Lucian of Samosata** to *Star Trek* exposes our bias toward anthropomorphism when speculating what forms extraterrestrial intelligence might take. Yet the great diversity of creatures on Earth, sharing as it does a common biochemical heritage, suggests there will be even greater differences between terrestrial life-forms and any organisms that have developed on other worlds. The chances of meeting anything like a Vulcan (➔ **blood, of extraterrestrials**) or a Klingon, for instance, must be incredibly remote. As Loren **Eiseley** put it:[180]

> [N]owhere in all space or on a thousand worlds will there be men to share our loneliness. There may be wisdom; there may be power; somewhere across space great instruments, handled by strange, manipulative organs, may stare vainly at our floating cloud wrack, their owners yearning as we yearn. Nevertheless, in the nature of life and in the principles of evolution we have had our answer. Of men elsewhere, and beyond, there will be none forever.

The particular species that develop on a habitable world are shaped not only by the action of universal physical, chemical, and biological laws but also by chance. Accidents of time and place, including occasional, random impacts with comets and asteroids, alter the course of a planet's biological evolution in ways that are unpredictable and nonrepeatable (➔ **cosmic collisions, biological effects of**). Consequently, even an exact duplicate of the young Earth would not give rise to the same collection of flora and fauna we see around us today. Even more unfamiliar would be the life-forms that would emerge on a world that differed (perhaps only slightly) in its gravity, atmospheric constitution, **rotation period,** size of **orbit,** or type of **host star.**

At the same time, certain biological features might recur routinely from one inhabited world to the next. Structures such as eyes, legs, and wings are so eminently useful, and have evolved independently in so many different guises on Earth (➔ **convergent evolution**), that we might expect to see numerous intriguing variations of them across the Galaxy.

The presumption that intelligent life on other worlds will be approximately human seems, at first sight, to point to a failure of imagination, not to mention a poor understanding of evolutionary theory. Yet fantastic, unearthly creatures have populated our legends since ancient times. It is not that we or our predecessors lacked the capacity to envisage alternative life-forms. Rather, our tendency to populate the cosmos with humanlike beings has, at least over the past few centuries, had religious roots. God, according to the Bible, made man in his own image. Therefore, it has been argued, if God put intelligent, moral beings on other worlds, these creatures would have to be like us, since God is unique.

More recently, both scientists and science fiction writers have broken away from the anthropomorphic paradigm and speculated freely on the ways in which intelligence elsewhere might be encapsulated. Yet in the portrayal of aliens in film and on television, there is the obvious restriction, even allowing for sophisticated makeup techniques, of having to use human actors. Indeed, to account for the embarrassing preponderance of minor human variants in the *Star Trek* universe, including Earthlings, Klingons, Romulans, and Ferengi, it was explained in one episode of *The Next Generation* ("The Chase") that a long-dead humanoid race had tampered with the genetic makeup of life on widely scattered planets in the galaxy so as to give rise to beings that resembled the ancient prototype. Not only was this a neat way to cover up the limitations of facial latex, but it also offered a new slant on the concept of **directed panspermia.** To some extent, modern filmmakers have been given more liberty to indulge their imaginations thanks to electronically controlled models and computer animation. Nevertheless, the general effect of extraterrestrial depictions in movies (which influence far more people than do science fiction novels) has been to instill in the public's mind the idea of a universe awash with creatures not unlike ourselves.

Having said this, there are some scientists who, arguing on evolutionary grounds, have come full circle back to the belief that extraterrestrial intelligence will tend to be anthropomorphic. Frank **Drake,** for example, has argued[575] that:

There are reasons why we are bipedal, why our head is on top, why we have two eyes and why they have to be in the head and close to the brain, and why the mouth has to be close to the eyes.... We don't need five fingers but we do need fingers. We don't need a nose but we do need the mouth and eyes and ears. There would be enough similarities so that if you saw [an intelligent extraterrestrial] in the twilight you would think it is a person.

→ **evolutionary theory and extraterrestrial life**

anticodon
The three-**nucleotide** sequence at the end of a **transfer RNA** molecule that is complementary to, and forms **base pairs** with, an **amino acid**–specifying **codon** in **messenger RNA.**

antiparticles
Counterparts of ordinary subatomic particles that have the same mass and spin but opposite charge. Certain other properties are also reversed, including the magnetic moment. The antiparticles of the **electron, proton,** and **neutron** are the **positron,** antiproton, and antineutron, respectively. The encounter between a particle and its corresponding antiparticle is marked by the spectacular, instantaneous conversion of the mass of both partners into energy in the form of **gamma rays.**

Antoniadi, Eugène Michael (1870–1944)
Greek-born astronomer who spent most of his life in France and became a leading and decisive critic of the canal hypothesis of Mars (→ **Mars, canals of**). Early in his career, Antoniadi worked at Camille **Flammarion**'s observatory at Juvisy and claimed to have seen Martian canals. In 1898, he put forward a geological explanation for some of the markings, while others, he argued, were the boundaries of shaded areas. As late as 1903, he maintained the "incontestable reality" of the canal phenomenon. So great had become his reputation as an observer that by the 1909 **opposition** of Mars he was given access to the largest telescope in Europe, the 83-cm (33-in) refractor at the **Meudon Observatory.** With this instrument, he claimed, he was able to resolve the canals into streaks or borders of darker

regions and concluded, "The geometrical canal network is an optical illusion; and in its place the great refractor shows myriads of marbled and checkered objective fields." Quickly, observers in the United States, including George **Hale,** confirmed Antoniadi's opinion, and worldwide belief in the canal hypothesis went into rapid decline. In his magnum opus, *La Planète Mars* (1930),[19] he presented a state-of-the-art summary of Martian topography and helped set the scene for the modern investigation of the planet.

Antoniadi was also a regular observer of the inner planets, **Mercury** and **Venus,** and his *La Planète Mercure et la rotation des satellites* (Paris, 1934) was the only work on this subject for two decades. In it, he published the most detailed pre–Space Age map of Mercury based on the assumption, first made by Giovanni **Schiaparelli,** that the planet always keeps the same face toward the Sun (→ **Mercury, rotation of**)—an assumption now known to be false. Antoniadi claimed to have seen local obscurations, which he thought were due to material suspended in a thin Mercurian atmosphere.[20]

apastron
The point in any orbit around a star that is furthest from the star. It usually refers to a **companion**'s orbit about the **primary** in a **binary star** system.

aperture
The diameter of the main mirror in a reflecting telescope, the objective lens in a refracting telescope, or the dish of a **radio telescope.** Increasing the aperture of a telescope increases the instrument's sensitivity and **resolving power.**

APEX
→ **Athena Precursor Experiment**

aphelion
The point in the orbit of a planet or other object in the solar system that is furthest from the Sun.

apoapsis
The point in the orbit of a body, such as a planet, moon, comet, or spacecraft, that is furthest from the **primary.**

Apollo asteroid

An **asteroid** whose orbit brings it within the orbit of the Earth. The prototype is Apollo-1862, which was discovered in 1932, when it approached to within about 10 million km of the Earth.

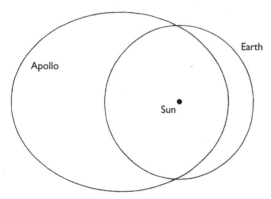

Comparative orbits of the asteroid Apollo and the Earth.

apparent magnitude

The brightness of a star (or other luminous object), measured on a standard **magnitude scale. → absolute magnitude**

APRO

→ **Aerial Phenomena Research Organization**

Aquinas, Thomas (1225–74)

Leading Italian scholastic theologian who defended the teachings of **Aristotle** and argued against **pluralism.** He reasoned that if there were many inhabited worlds, they would have to be either different, in which case they could not all be perfect (thus casting doubt on God's own perfection), or identical, which (considered from God's point of view) would be pointless. → **medieval philosophy, related to the possibility of extraterrestrial life**

Arago, Dominique-François-Jean (1786–1853)

Director of the **Paris Observatory** and secretary of the French Academy of Sciences who, through his lectures and writings, did much to popularize astronomy and support the view that life is common throughout the solar system. In his *Astronomie populaire*, published posthumously, Arago echoed William **Herschel**'s views about life inside the Sun (→ **Sun, life on**):

> [I]f one asked me whether the sun can be inhabited by beings organized in a manner analogous to those which populate our globe, I would not hesitate to make an affirmative response. The existence in the sun of a central dark nucleus enveloped in an opaque atmosphere, far from the luminous atmosphere, offers nothing in opposition to such a concept.

Phrases such as "nothing in opposition to" were a common feature of his and other pluralist writings and tended to mislead since they appeared to suggest a positive conclusion where the evidence was, in fact, neutral. Arago also wrote about the possibility of life on comets, "I do not pretend to draw from these considerations the conclusion that comets are populated by beings of our species. I have presented them here only to render . . . their *habitability* less problematic." On the prospects for finding creatures on the Moon, however, he was more pessimistic. (→ **Moon, life on**)

archaea

Primitive **prokaryote**s that, until recently, were known as archaebacteria and placed in the same **kingdom** (*Monera*) as **eubacteria.** Largely through the work of Carl Woese and his colleagues at the University of Illinois, they are now generally recognized as being genetically and structurally distinct and forming their own **domain,** Archaea. Unlike bacteria, archaea lack **peptidoglycan** in their **cell wall**s. They also have unusual (ether-linked) **lipids** in their **cell membrane**s that are not found in any other group of organisms. The structure and function of the **gene**s in archaea are surprisingly similar to the structure and function of the genes in **eukaryote**s, while those of eubacteria are not. There are major differences, too, in some of the fundamental biochemical processes of **metabolism** between archaea and bacteria. Archaea are currently classified into three groups: Crenarchaeota, Euryarchaeota, and Korarchaeota.

Crenarchaeota include **sulfur**-metabolizing **hyperthermophiles** and **acidophiles.** These are **chemautotrophic anaerobes** that thrive at temperatures from 70°C to 113°C (158°F to 235°F) in regions such as hot sulfur springs, **hydrothermal vents**, and volcanoes. Eury-archaeota include a mix of **methanogens** (all anaerobes), extreme **halophiles** (mostly **aerobes**), and a few sulfur-metabolizing thermophiles. Korarchaeota is a newly recognized group.

Archaea are thought to be among the earliest terrestrial life-forms to have evolved, survivors from a time when the environment on Earth would have been too hostile to allow anything other than **extremophiles** to develop (➔ **Earth, early history of**). At the same time, the features of archaea generally resemble the features of eukaryotes and bacteria more than they do those of each other, suggesting that archaea may lie close to the root of the terrestrial tree of life (➔ **life, origin of**). Korarchaeota, in particular, have been singled out as the closest organisms yet found to the universal ancestor. It may be that archaea and other varieties of extremophiles are commonly the first to colonize young planets and that as time goes by they retreat to regions such as hydrothermal vents and subsurface rocks where primordial environments remain. If so, this offers new hope of finding such primitive life-forms underground on Mars and possibly even Venus, as well as in any hydrothermal regions on the large moons of the outer planets, including **Europa** and **Callisto**. ➔ **ballistic panspermia**

archaebacteria
➔ **archaea**

archaen
A member of the **domain Archaea**.

Archimedes (c. 287–212 B.C.)
One of the most prominent of Greek scientists and mathematicians; born in Syracuse, the son of an astronomer. In his book *The Sand Reckoner* he brought to wider attention the **heliocentric** theory of **Aristarchus of Samos** and played an important role in demystifying the cosmos, estimating that it would take 1 followed by sixty-three zeroes of grains of sand to fill all of space. To him goes the credit of constructing the first known planetarium (based

on the **geocentric** model), a fantastic instrument of brass powered by water, which was eventually shipped to Rome and admired there by Cicero two centuries later. ➔ **ancient philosophy, related to the possibility of extraterrestrial life**

arc-second
An angular measurement. There are 60 arc-seconds in 1 arc-minute, 60 arc-minutes in 1 degree, and 360 degrees in a full circle. One thousandth of an arc-second = 1 milliarc-second.

Arcturus
Alpha Bootis; a brilliant orange **K star** with a luminosity of about 115 L_S and a radius of 28 R_S. ➔ **stars, brightest**

Area 51
A secret military installation on the edge of **Groom Lake,** Nevada. Existence of the base is not publicly acknowledged for security reasons and civilian maps of the region carry no mention of it, only a travel restriction warning. Eyewitness reports from individuals living near the compound testify to unusual aerial activity, including strange craft flying over the mountains and unexplained lights in the night sky. Such sightings are hardly surprising, considering that the U.S. Air Force has for many years test flown some of its most covert vehicles there, including the U-2 spy plane, the B-2 Stealth bomber, and the SR-71 Blackbird. When objects as commonplace as Venus or lozenge-shaped clouds can be taken for **unidentified flying objects,** it should raise few eyebrows that new aircraft with strange appearance, unfamiliar lighting, and extraordinary performance capabilities might be similarly misinterpreted. Some of the latest piloted military hardware can fly at speeds and in ways comparable to those claimed, in early flying saucer books and films, for alien spacecraft in the Earth's atmosphere. There are now something like genuine, intelligently directed UFOs on this planet—and they are human-built. Yet despite the obvious possibilities for misidentification of secret planes with flying saucers, there are those who insist that the Air Force is doing more in the wilderness of the

Nevada desert than test-flying the latest high-performance jets. The claim from some ufologists is that Area 51 also serves as a facility for examining captured extraterrestrial craft and alien corpses. This view was popularized in the film *Independence Day,* the producers of which were requested by the government to take out all references to Area 51. When they refused, the government withdrew its offer to assist with the movie. Such secrecy naturally serves to stoke the fires of speculation. There are obvious reasons for the Department of Defense to keep the Nevada installation out of the public eye if some of the most advanced military hardware in the world is being put through its paces there. On the other hand, the heavy blanket of security enveloping the base allows those who want to put forward more extreme views to do so, secure in the knowledge that it is just about impossible for them to be proved wrong.

Arecibo Message

The first attempt at **CETI;** it consisted of a message beamed toward the star cluster **M 13** on November 16, 1974, by the **Arecibo radio telescope.** The signal, transmitted at 2,380 MHz with a duration of 169 seconds, delivered an effective power of 3 trillion watts, the strongest man-made signal ever sent. A technique first suggested by Frank **Drake** (➔ **Drake's cryptogram**) was used to encode the message, which consisted of a string of 1,679 binary digits, or

numbers 1 to 10, reading right to left

atomic numbers of key biological elements

formulas for sugars and bases in nucleotides of DNA

double helix of DNA; vertical bar indicates number of nucleotides in DNA

human figure, height of human (right), human population (left)

solar system, with Earth displaced upward

Arecibo dish, with diameter

Arecibo message.

bits. An intelligent being striving to decipher the message, it is hoped, would eventually recognize that 1,679 is a multiple of two **prime numbers,** 23 and 73 (➔ **mathematics, as a universal language**). Arranging the bits into 73 rows of 23 characters each and representing a zero by a blank space and a one by a solid space enables a meaningful picture to emerge. The top part of the message establishes that the number system to be used is binary. Under this appear the **atomic numbers** for the main biological elements, **carbon, hydrogen, oxygen, nitrogen,** and **phosphorus,** and the makeup of **DNA.** The rest of the message deals with the appearance, size, and number of human beings, our location within the solar system, and a description of the transmitting telescope. Following the announcement that the transmission had been made, a debate began (which continues to this day) on the wisdom of attempting CETI (➔ **CETI, opposition to**).

On its 25,000-year-long journey, it is likely that the Arecibo Message will be seriously degraded by its interaction with **cosmic dust** in the **interstellar medium.** Moreover, the loss of even a few bits of information would render the signal undecipherable. To address this problem, a much larger message has recently been broadcast that contains data duplicated in such a way that the loss of some parts of the transmission need not result in a total loss of meaning (➔ **Encounter 2001 Message**).

Arecibo Observatory

The facility of the National Astronomy and Ionosphere Center located 19 km (12 miles) south of Arecibo, Puerto Rico. Its principal instrument is the **Arecibo radio telescope.**

Arecibo radio telescope

The largest single-dish **radio telescope** in the world. It came into operation in 1963 and is operated by **Cornell University** for the National Science Foundation. Occupying a large karst sinkhole in the hills south of Arecibo in Puerto Rico, its area of almost 9 hectares is greater than that of all other such instruments in the world combined. The surface of Arecibo's 305-m (1,000-ft.) fixed, spherical dish is made from almost 40,000 perforated aluminum panels, each measuring 1 m by 2 m (3 ft. by 6 ft.), supported by a network of steel cables strung across the underlying depression. Suspended 150 m (450 ft.) above the reflector is a 900-t platform that houses the receiving equipment. Although the telescope is not steerable, some directionality is obtained by moving the feed **antenna** (upgraded in 1996). The immense size and accurate configuration of the dish allow extremely faint signals to be detected. For this reason, it has been used extensively in **SETI** investigations and in the first attempt at **CETI** (➔ **Arecibo Message**). It was also featured in the film *Contact*.

areobiology
The study of possible life-forms on Mars. ➔ **Mars, life on**

areography
The physical study of Mars, named after Ares, the Greek god of war.

Argus, Project
A global **SETI** program that will eventually involve 5,000 small **radio telescope**s worldwide, built and operated by private individuals, mainly radio amateurs and microwave experimenters. The project, an **all-sky survey,** is being coordinated by the **SETI League.** Prototype stations went into operation in 1996, and full-sky coverage is planned for 2001. In Greek mythology, Argus was the all-seeing watchman with a hundred eyes, charged by Hera to guard Io. Not surprisingly, it has proved to be a popular appellation for instruments capable of all-around vision. It was the preliminary name given, in 1971, to an ambitious scheme that eventually grew into Project **Cyclops** but was never realized and the name of another, very different array of antennas under construction at Ohio State University (➔ **Argus radio telescope**). In fiction, too, it has been employed by Arthur C. **Clarke** for his **omnidirectional antenna** in *Imperial Earth*[114] and by Carl **Sagan** in *Contact*.[495]

Argus radio telescope
Not to be confused with the **SETI League**'s project of the same name (➔ **Argus, Project**),

this instrument, to be built at Ohio State University, marks a new approach in **radio telescope** design. Comprising a planar array of sixty-four small, mass-produced **omnidirectional antenna**s capable of "seeing" in all directions of the sky at once, it is scheduled for completion in mid-2000. Argus will operate in the 200-MHz-to-2-GHz frequency range with an **instantaneous bandwidth** of 1.5 MHz. A huge amount of computer power will be marshaled to form a complete sky map within seconds using the digitized signals from the individual antennas. Although initially its sensitivity will be low, Argus will provide an important means of testing the technology of array-based, all-sky-imaging radio telescopes—instruments ideally suited to detecting short-duration or fast-changing sources, possibly including stray or beamed radio signals from extraterrestrial civilizations. Among future instruments that will use this technique on a larger scale are the **One Hectare Telescope** and the **Square Kilometer Array.** Argus will be constructed, with financial support from the **SETI Institute** and the North American Astrophysical Observatory (a nonprofit corporation that receives donations and coordinates the volunteer staff), on the west campus of Ohio State University at the university's Electroscience Laboratory and Radio Observatory. The project director is Robert **Dixon.**

Ariel
The fourth largest and brightest moon of **Uranus.** Long **rift valley**s stretch across Ariel's entire, heavily cratered surface, the floors of

Discovery	1851, by William Lassell
Mean distance from Uranus	191,800 km (119,200 mi.)
Diameter	1,158 km (718 mi.)
Mean density	1.56 g/cm^3
Escape velocity	0.541 km/s (1,948 km/h, 1,210 mi./h)
Orbital period	2.520 days (2 days 12 hrs 29 min)
Orbital eccentricity	0.0034
Orbital inclination	0.31°
Axial period	2.520 days
Visual albedo	0.34

which appear as if they had been smoothed by a fluid. Flows of liquid **ammonia, methane,** or even **carbon monoxide** may have been responsible. ➔ **Uranus, moons of**

Ariosto, Ludovico (1474–1533)

Italian poet who, in 1532, wrote the epic poem *Orlando Furioso*. In it, one of the characters travels to the Moon in the divine chariot that carried the prophet Elijah in a whirlwind to Heaven (➔ **Moon, voyages to**). On his arrival, he finds the Moon well populated by civilized people (➔ **Moon, life on**).

Aristarchus (crater)

A conspicuous lunar crater, 45 km (28 miles) in diameter, surrounded by a system of bright rays, that has been the reported site of **transient lunar phenomena** in the form of reddish glows.

Aristarchus of Samos (c. 320–c. 250 B.C.)

Leading astronomer of classical times who was the first to propose a **heliocentric** scheme for the solar system. He also devised a method of calculating the relative distances of the Moon and the Sun. ➔ **ancient philosophy, related to the possibility of extraterrestrial life**

Aristotle (384–322 B.C.)

Major Greek philosopher, student of **Plato**, and founder of the Lyceum in Athens, who argued vehemently against the pluralistic teachings of **atomism.** "The world must be unique," he wrote. "There cannot be several worlds." He justified this stance on a number of grounds. For example, in his *Metaphysics,* he explains the motion of the planets and stars (around the Earth) as due to the "Prime Mover" acting at the periphery. If there were other Earths, he said, there would have to be a plurality of Prime Movers, an idea he rejected as philosophically and religiously unacceptable. In Aristotle's cosmology, the Earth was located at the center of a nested system of crystalline spheres to which were attached the Moon, Sun, planets, and stars. According to his doctrine of "natural motion and place," the four basic elements of earth, air, fire, and water tended to move to their rightful positions with respect to the Earth: fire moved naturally outward, earth moved naturally inward to the center, while air and water assumed intermediate stations. This fundamental tenet underlay Aristotle's belief in a single *kosmos,* or world system, with the Earth at its focus. If there were more than one world, the elements of fire and earth would have no unique natural place to which to move—for him, a physical and logical contradiction. Aristotle also maintained that there was a clear distinction between the terrestrial and celestial regions. The latter knew neither life nor death, and the bodies within it were composed not of earthly matter but of a fifth element, or "quintessence." It was the innermost sphere, carrying the Moon, he believed, that marked the boundary between the impermanent, "sublunary" realm of the Earth and the unchanging, "superlunary" domain of the heavens. ➔ **ancient philosophy, related to the possibility of extraterrestrial life**

Following its transmission to the West in the twelfth century, Aristotle's doctrine of a one-world, geocentric cosmos was appropriated by the Church and largely upheld as being in keeping with the Christian belief in a special relationship between God and man. However, it did not go unquestioned by medieval theologians, particularly as its insistence that there could be only one world appeared to put constraints on God's power. Between the thirteenth and fourteenth centuries, university scholars, including Jean **Buridan,** William of **Ockham,** and Nicole d'**Oresme,** gradually reformulated the Aristotelian dictum of natural place so that an omnipotent God would at least have had the logical option to create other worlds. Having said this, almost all medieval Scholastics held to the view that God had in reality created only one world. Extraterrestrials were restricted to spiritual beings such as demons, ethereal in their makeup, that, it was supposed, lived in the "middle region" between heaven and Earth. Only following the **Copernican Revolution** and the overthrow of Aristotle's geocentric cosmology could the idea of other worlds and other life made of ordinary matter finally take hold.

Arizona Search for Planets (ASP)

Previously known as the Wyoming Arizona Search for Planets (WASP), a project to search for **extrasolar planets** using the **photometry** (occultation/transit) method.

Arnold, Kenneth (1915–84)

Businessman, part-time deputy sheriff, and accomplished private pilot whose sighting of luminous objects while flying his own Callair plane over the **Cascade Mountains** marked the start of the great **saucer flap of 1947.** Arnold was returning from Chehalis to Yakima, Washington, after a business trip when he heard that a C-46 transport plane belonging to the U.S. Marine Corps had come down near Mount Rainier. In the hope of claiming a $5,000 government reward, he determined to spend an hour or so searching for the wreckage. While he was making a 180-degree turn above the town of Mineral at an altitude of 2,800 m (9,200 ft.), "a tremendously bright flash lit up the surfaces of my aircraft." At 2:59 P.M., he observed "a formation of very bright objects coming from the vicinity of Mount Baker, flying very close to the mountaintops and traveling at tremendous speed." Using the clock on his instrument panel and Mounts Rainier and Adams as markers, and estimating that the formation would pass about 35 km (23

Fortean Picture Library

miles) in front of him, Arnold calculated that the objects were traveling at more than 2,720 km per hour (1,700 miles per hour). Since they appeared to be flying in formation and, therefore, in Arnold's view, were artificial, this speed was astounding. Only later that year would the sound barrier, of about 1,200 km per hour (750 miles per hour), be broken by Chuck Yeager in a jet aircraft. Commented Arnold, "They didn't fly like any aircraft I had seen before. . . . They flew in a definite formation, but erratically . . . like speed boats on rough water or similar to the tail of a Chinese kite . . . they fluttered and sailed, tipping their wings alternately and emitting those very bright blue-white flashes from their surfaces." It was while he was describing his encounter to reporters later the same day that the term "**flying saucer**" was coined.

Arouet, François-Marie
→ **Voltaire**

Arrhenius, Svante August (1859–1927)

Swedish physical chemist and Nobel Prize winner (1903), famous for his work on electrolytes, who was the first to present a detailed scientific hypothesis of **panspermia.** In this, he argued that life arrived on Earth in the form of microscopic **spores** that had been propelled across interstellar space by the **radiation pressure** of starlight. His seminal 1903 paper on the subject[22] was in response to "the failure of repeated attempts made by eminent biologists to discover a single case of spontaneous generation of life."[23] In its fully developed form, Arrhenius's hypothesis reached a wide audience through his book *Worlds in the Making*[24] (1908, first published as *Världarnas utveckling* in Sweden in 1906). Arrhenius was optimistic that, subject to the low temperatures in space, spores would be able to remain viable for very long periods. As for the effect of solar radiation, although Arrhenius was aware of the potentially lethal effect of **ultraviolet** on living cells, he insisted that "All the botanists that I have been able to consult are of the opinion that we can by no means assert with certainty that spores would be killed by the light rays in wandering through infinite space." His support for panspermia tied in with his fundamental belief that "all organisms in the universe are related and the process of evolution is everywhere the same." He thought that life on other worlds might be common, though he opposed Percival **Lowell**'s claims about Martian canals. In *The Destinies of Stars*[25] (1918), he presented a carboniferous swamp version of Venus that remained popular for many years (➔ **Venus, life on**).

artifacts, alien

If intelligent extraterrestrial life exists and has entered the solar system in the past, there is the possibility of finding traces of these visits on Earth, on the surface of our neighboring worlds, or in interplanetary space. Supporters of the **paleocontact hypothesis,** also known as the "ancient astronaut" hypothesis, maintain that such evidence is to hand, although this suggestion is rejected by the majority of scientists. More attention has been paid in orthodox circles to the idea of large-scale **astroengineering** works by highly advanced races, including **Dyson sphere**s, that might be detectable over interstellar distances, and also of sentinel devices (➔ **sentinel hypothesis**) or **Bracewell probe**s sent to search for the presence of intelligent life in the solar system.[209, 634]

artificial gravity

The simulation of the pull of gravity aboard a space station, manned spacecraft, or **space colony** by the steady rotation, at an appropriate angular speed, of part of the structure.

artificial intelligence

Progress in areas such as machine vision, natural language processing, and the construction of **neural network**s suggests that it may be only a matter of time before computers acquire a level of intelligence that is comparable to or greater than our own. Certainly the rate of evolution of technology-based intelligence is many orders of magnitude greater than the biological development of the brain. This suggests that either machines will eventually supersede us, or, more likely perhaps, we shall become part machine ourselves through the addition of powerful neural prostheses. Small steps toward the integration of man and device are already being taken in the form of elec-

tronic implants to provide improved hearing, sight, and mobility. It may even be a universal fact that once life has achieved a certain level of technical sophistication, its subsequent evolution takes place at enormous speed and in directions that we are poorly equipped to imagine (➔ **intelligence, nature of**).

artificial life

Life that has not evolved through the normal slow biological channels. It is generally taken to mean either computer-resident entities that display certain properties, including the ability to evolve and reproduce, that are normally associated with corporeal life-forms or sophisticated robots and **android**s that may someday take their place alongside biological organisms. NASA mission planners are already considering the case for future robot explorers, built along the lines of insects and other relatively simple creatures, that would be adept at investigating unusual environments. The possibility cannot be discounted that some extraterrestrial life may be artificial and perhaps even more sophisticated and more widespread than its biological creators. ➔ **noncorporeal life**

ashen light
➔ **Venus, ashen light of**

Asimov, Isaac (1920–92)

Prolific Russian-born American author of popular science and science fiction. Asimov frequently discussed the likelihood and possible nature of extraterrestrial life in his factual books and articles, notably in *Extraterrestrial Civilizations*[29] (1979), but, with one exception, avoided the topic completely in his novels. Only in *The Gods Themselves*[28] (1972) do such life-forms play a major role and then to the extent that they are "among the most fascinating and believable aliens yet imagined in science fiction."[247]

associations, stellar

Sparsely populated groupings of stars, typically a few tens to a few hundreds of light-years across. They consist mainly of very young stars that have formed in the relatively recent past—a few million or tens of millions of years ago—

from the same large **interstellar cloud.** Their mutual gravitational attraction is insufficient to bind them together permanently, however, and eventually the grouping breaks up and the individual stars go their separate ways. Two distinct varieties of stellar association are recognized: **OB association**s and **T association**s.

asterism

A distinctive pattern of stars in the sky but not including any of the eighty-eight recognized **constellation**s. Examples include the Big Dipper, the Northern Cross, the Square of Pegasus, and **Orion's Belt.**

asteroid

A subplanetary object composed of non-**volatile** material, ranging in size from about 10 m to about 1,000 km across, in orbit around the Sun (or any other star). Asteroids are thought to have formed through the **accretion** of small (roughly meter-sized) objects that were prevented from growing as big as planets by (in our solar system) the influence of Jupiter's gravity. The largest asteroids were internally heated by radioactive decay and so became molten long enough to differentiate into a core, a mantle, and a crust. Subsequent collisions shattered or broke fragments from the original asteroidal bodies, giving rise to the variety of asteroids and meteoroids found in orbit around the Sun today. Although most asteroids are made of rock, some (having come from the cores of large asteroids that broke apart) consist of metal, mainly nickel and iron. A small proportion of the asteroid population may be burned-out **comet**s whose icy constituents have been lost through vaporization; the rest are in their original state. All contain remnant material from the earliest stages of development of the solar system. Asteroids are classified according to their reflectance spectra, which vary considerably and point to differences in composition. Among the main categories are **S-class, C-class, P-class, D-class,** and **M-class.** With a few exceptions, such as the **Apollo asteroid**s and the **Trojan asteroid**s, the chief repository of these objects is the **Main Asteroid Belt** between the orbits of Mars and Jupiter. Past collisions between asteroids and the Earth appear to have played a crucial role in the evolution of life on this planet (➔ **cosmic collisions, biological effects of**). In particular, the impact of an asteroid about 65 million years ago caused a **mass extinction** in which the last of the dinosaurs were wiped out (➔ **Cretaceous-Tertiary Boundary**). The detection and tracking of so-called **Near-Earth Object**s that might collide with the Earth in the future are receiving increasing attention. In addition, a number of space missions to investigate asteroids more closely, including the return of samples, are under way or scheduled over the next few years. These include *NEAR, MUSES-C,* and *Deep Space 1.*

asteroid belt
➔ **Main Asteroid Belt**

asteroids, collisions with
➔ **cosmic collisions, biological effects of**

Astraglossa

An early **radioglyph** scheme for interstellar communication proposed by the British mathematician Lancelot Hogben. He gave details of it in a 1952 lecture to the **British Interplanetary Society** entitled "Astraglossa, or First Step in Celestial Syntax."[274] Hogben suggested that numbers be represented as ordinary pulses (e.g. five pulses for the number 5) and mathematical concepts, such as "plus," "minus," or "equal," each by a distinctive signal—a radioglyph. ➔ **Morrison's radioglyph scheme**

astrobiology

The study of extraterrestrial life, also known as **exobiology** or bioastronomy. It remains, as the evolutionary biologist George Gaylord **Simpson** put it, "a science looking for a subject." Astrobiologists face the problem of having access to biological samples from only one planet. This makes it difficult to know if life elsewhere, assuming it exists, follows the same or a similar pattern. Speculation cannot be confined to **DNA**-based organisms, and there is even the possibility that we may have difficulty in recognizing certain alien species as living entities.[265] ➔ **extraterrestrial life, variety of**

Astrobiology Institute
→ NASA Astrobiology Institute

astrobleme
An eroded impact crater on Earth, of which about 150 are known. Among the largest are the 200-km-wide Sudbury Crater in Ontario, Canada, and the 180-km-wide **Chicxulub Crater,** which extends into the Gulf of Mexico. While some astroblemes are almost 2 billion years old, about 60 percent were formed within the past 200 million years.

astrochemistry
The study of the chemistry of the **interstellar medium** and of celestial bodies. It involves the detection and identification, mainly by **spectroscopy,** of the **atom**s and **molecule**s (both **inorganic** and **organic**) that are present and the ways they interact.

astroengineering
The construction of very large artificial objects in space by technologically advanced beings. Searching for the radiation signatures of such objects, it has been suggested, represents an important alternative strategy in **SETI.** Among those to put forward specific suggestions in this regard are Freeman **Dyson** and Nikolai **Kardashev.**

astrometric observations
→ astrometry

astrometry
The precise measurement of the position of astronomical objects. Astrometrical observation of nearby stars, for example, is one of the techniques used to search for the presence of un-

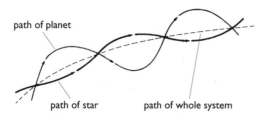

Wobbles in a star's motion produced by an orbiting planet.

seen companions, such as **extrasolar planets,** low-luminosity stars, and **brown dwarf**s.[447] The gravitational influence of the unseen companion causes the path of the primary to wobble slightly, instead of following a smooth trajectory across the sky.[68]

Astronomical Nulling Interferometer (ANI)
Informal name of the apparatus used in conjunction with the **Multiple Mirror Telescope,** at the end of 1997, to carry out the first examination of the environment of a star using the technique of **nulling interferometry.**

astronomical unit (AU)
The mean distance between the Earth and the Sun. 1 AU = 149,597,870 km = 92,955,806 miles = 499 light-seconds. One **light-year** equals 63,240 AU.

asymmetric carbon atom
A **carbon** atom in a **molecule** of an **organic** compound that is attached to four different atoms or groups of atoms. The result of this asymmetry is to allow two spatially distinct but chemically identical arrangements of atoms that are mirror images of each other and known as **enantiomers.**

Atacama Large Millimeter Array (ALMA)
A giant instrument currently in the planning stage designed for observing the Universe at millimeter and submillimeter wavelengths (very short radio waves). It will involve a collaboration between the **European Southern Observatory** (ESO) and the **National Radio Astronomy Observatory** (NRAO), have a total collecting area of 7,000 square m made up of sixty-four linked 12-m (39.4-ft.) antennas, and be located at an altitude of 5,000 m in northern Chile at a site known as Chajnantor. Among the ALMA's numerous uses will be the observation of star-forming regions, **protostar**s, and **protoplanetary disk**s. ALMA will also play an important role in the search for **extrasolar planets** through accurate **astrometry,** and possibly even the direct detection of planets and their atmospheres. Current estimates suggest that construction will start sometime between 2003 and 2008.

Atchley, Dana W., Jr.
Specialist in communications technology and president of Microwave Associates, Inc., a company with expertise in building sophisticated electronics equipment. Upon hearing of preparations for Project **Ozma,** as a result of Otto **Struve**'s publicity for Frank **Drake**'s work, Atchley donated one of the world's first **parametric amplifier**s to the project. He was also an attendee at the seminal **Green Bank conference** on SETI in 1961.

Athena
A package of six instruments to be carried aboard *Mars Surveyor 2003.* It will include (1) Pancam, a panoramic camera with a **resolution** almost four times that of cameras on **Mars Pathfinder;** (2) Mini-TES, or the Mini-Thermal Emission Spectrometer, for observing **infrared** emission from rocks; (3) APXS, or the Alpha-Proton-X-ray Spectrometer, for analysis of chemical composition; (4) the Mössbauer Spectrometer, for determining the composition of iron-bearing minerals; (5) the Microscopic Imager, for close-up examination of samples; and (6) the Mini-Corer and Sample Container. The first four of these instruments also make up the **Athena Precursor Experiment** (**APEX**).

Athena Precursor Experiment (APEX)
A package of instruments to be carried aboard *Mars Surveyor 2001.* These are test versions of four of the six instruments that will make up the **Athena** package aboard *Mars Surveyor 2003.* Three of the APEX instruments are fixed to the *Mars Surveyor 2001 Lander* and one to the roving vehicle to be deployed from it.

ATIC
➔ **Air Technical Intelligence Center**

Atlas
The second of **Saturn**'s moons; it orbits near the outer edge of the A-ring and probably acts as a **shepherd moon** for this ring. ➔ **Saturn, moons of**

Discovery	1980, by R. Terrile
Mean distance from Saturn	137,670 km (85,560 mi.)
Diameter	40 × 30 km (25 × 19 mi.)
Orbital period	0.602 day (14 hours 27 minutes)
Orbital eccentricity	0.000
Orbital inclination	0.00°
Visual albedo	0.9

atmosphere
The gassy envelope that may surround a planet or moon. How much atmosphere a planet can retain depends upon its mass and the distance at which it formed from its host star.

atmosphere (unit)
The standard atmospheric pressure at sea level on Earth. 1 atmosphere = 1.013 **bar**s = 1.03 kg/cm^3 = 14.7 lb./sq.in.

atmospheric pressure
The force per unit area at any point in an **atmosphere** due to the weight of atmospheric gases above it. Atmospheric pressure is measured in **millibar**s (mb), **bar**s, or **atmosphere**s. The standard atmospheric pressure at the surface of the Earth is 1,013 millibars. On Venus the surface pressure is about 90,000 millibars (90 bars), while on Mars it is about 7.5 millibars.

atom
The smallest particle of an **element** that can take part in a chemical reaction. An atom consists of a **nucleus,** containing positively charged **proton**s and uncharged **neutron**s, which is surrounded by much lighter, negatively charged **electron**s. The number of protons is equal to the number of electrons so that, overall, an atom is electrically neutral.

atomic mass
The number of **proton**s and **neutron**s in one **atom** of a particular **isotope** of an **element.** Although all atoms of a given element have the same **atomic number,** their atomic mass can differ depending on the number of neutrons they contain.

atomic number

The number of **proton**s in one **atom** of an **element.** Naturally occurring elements have atomic numbers ranging from 1 (hydrogen) to 92 (uranium).

atomism

The earliest cosmological worldview to espouse **pluralism** and the existence of extraterrestrial life. Developed in Greece in the fourth and fifth centuries B.C. by **Leucippus** and **Democritus of Abdera,** and later by **Epicurus, Metrodorus of Chios,** and **Lucretius,** it taught that the cosmos consists of nothing but identical, indestructible particles (atoms) moving randomly in a void. Starting from the assumption that the Earth had come about by the chance association of atoms, it was a natural step to postulate that other Earths and other life-forms had originated elsewhere in the same way. However, the atomists considered that these other worlds, held to exist both simultaneously and in temporal succession, lay within their own self-contained universes— distinct kosmoi (➔ **cosmos**)—that were entirely separate and inaccessible from our own. It is important to recognize that this was a purely philosophical doctrine that made no appeal to empirical evidence or observation and is therefore completely distinct from post-Copernican notions of other possibly inhabited worlds in the solar system and planets circling around other stars. The atomist doctrine, as expressed in the writings of Lucretius, was eventually rediscovered in medieval Europe, where, once again, it clashed with the one-world system of **Aristotle.** ➔ **ancient philosophy, related to the possibility of extraterrestrial life**

ATP

➔ **adenosine triphosphate**

AU

➔ **astronomical unit**

Auf zwei Planeten

➔ **Lasswitz, Kurd**

aurora

A glow in the **ionosphere** of a planet or moon caused by the interaction between the object's magnetic field and charged particles from the Sun.

Australian National Radio Observatory

A facility located near Parkes, New South Wales, the main instrument of which is the fully steerable 64-m (210-ft.) **Parkes Radio Telescope.**

autocatalysis

A form of **catalysis** in which one of the products of a reaction serves as a catalyst for the reaction. Before the emergence of **protein**-based **enzymes,** which are the principal biological catalysts today, it is believed that a substance, such as **RNA,** may have served as both a replicator and an autocatalyzer in the first terrestrial life-forms.

autocatalytic

The action of **autocatalysis.**

autotrophs

Organisms that are able to synthesize all the complex **organic** molecules they require for life using only simple **inorganic** compounds and an external energy source. They include **plants, algae, archaea,** and some **bacteria.** The chief inorganic sources of **carbon** and **nitrogen** are **carbon dioxide** and nitrates, respectively. Autotrophs can be subdivided into **photoautotrophs** and **chemoautotrophs,** depending upon how they derive the energy for their **metabolism.** Organisms that are not autotrophic are known as **heterotrophs.**

axial period

The time taken for an object to make one complete rotation on its axis. The axial period of a planet is its "day."

axial rotation

The spin of an object around its axis.

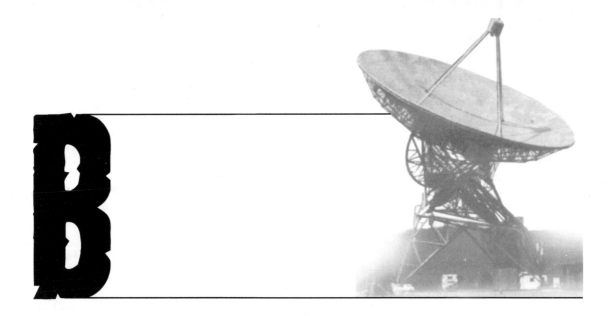

B

B star

A large, luminous, blue-white star of **spectral type** B with a surface temperature of 10,200 to 30,000°C. The spectrum is characterized by **absorption line**s of neutral or singly **ionized** helium, with lines of atomic hydrogen evident, especially at the cooler end of the range. **Main sequence** B stars, examples of which include **Spica** and **Regulus,** have a mass in the range 3 to 20 M_S and a luminosity of 100 to 50,000 L_S. Often they are found together with **O star**s in **OB association**s since, being massive, they are short-lived and therefore do not survive long enough to move far from the place where they were formed. Their brief **main sequence** career, measured in tens of millions of years, probably allows too little time for even the most primitive forms of life to develop on any worlds that circle around them (assuming that life could exist at all in such an environment). B-type **supergiant**s, of which **Rigel** is a familiar example, may be up to twenty-five times as massive and 250,000 times as luminous as the Sun.

back contamination

The accidental delivery to Earth, by sample-return probes or returning crewed missions, of microscopic biological contaminants from other worlds. Such contamination, in the form of alien **virus**es, **bacteria,** or **spores,** to which

terrestrial life would have no immunity, could prove disastrous. For this reason, elaborate preparations were made to quarantine the first *Apollo* astronauts and the lunar samples they brought back (➔ **Lunar Sample Receiving Laboratory**). In the event, upon the return of *Apollo 11,* the agreed-upon quarantine protocols were immediately and seriously breached. The crane aboard the aircraft carrier scheduled to lift the command module out of the sea unopened was found at the last moment to be unsafe. For this reason, and also to prevent the astronauts from becoming seasick, the spacecraft's hatch was opened and the crew were allowed to exit while their craft was still in the open sea. Had there been any lunar **pathogen**s aboard, these would have been released into the atmosphere.

Fortunately, the Moon is, and almost certainly has always been, lifeless. However, in the light of recent findings, the risk of back contamination now seems much more real (though still small) in the case of some other satellites and minor objects in the solar system. Since NASA is planning, or has already launched, missions to collect and return samples from such objects, it has become a matter of urgency to decide how best to handle the samples upon their arrival here. With this concern in mind, NASA requested that a task force of the National Research Council survey the potential for microscopic life-forms existing on moons, **asteroid**s, **comet**s, and **cosmic dust.** The Task Group on Sample Return from Small Solar System Bodies, made up of eleven scientists, including astronomers, biologists, and chemists, and chaired by Leslie **Orgel,** considered the conditions under which known types of life can propagate, including the presence of water and **organic** compounds, the availability of energy sources, suitable temperatures, and protection from **ionizing radiation.** It also took into account conditions under which life can remain dormant (➔ **bacterial spores; suspended animation**) and the possibility that materials containing life-forms could have been transported to objects from elsewhere in the solar system (➔ **ballistic panspermia**). The task group's report,[438] published in 1998, concluded that, of the space objects considered, the greatest potential for harboring microorganisms was offered by the Jovian moons **Europa** and **Ganymede** (although recent findings suggest that **Callisto** should also be included), and that strict containment procedures should be adopted for material brought back from these worlds, along the lines of those recommended in a 1997 Research Council report for samples returned from Mars. In addition, samples from certain types of **asteroid**s, notably the **P-class asteroid**s and **D-class asteroid**s found in the outer parts of the **Main Asteroid Belt,** were deemed to merit strict procedures because so little is known about their origin or composition. The task group also recommended that dust particles collected near Europa, Ganymede, and these asteroids be treated with the same precaution. On the other hand, it was concluded that the Moon, **Io,** new comets, and cosmic dust exposed for long periods to ionizing radiation in space could safely be assumed sterile. The report recommended setting up a database of the conditions under which **extremophiles** had been found living on Earth with a view to setting limits on survivability elsewhere in space and determining the levels needed to sterilize extraterrestrial samples. ➔ **forward contamination**

background noise

An unwanted, randomly fluctuating signal superimposed on the signal from a cosmic radio source.

bacteria

A large group of **unicellular** and simple **multicellular** organisms that lack **chlorophyll** and multiply through cell **fission.** Until recently, all bacteria were grouped into a single **kingdom** of **prokaryote**s, *Monera,* which included both **eubacteria** and **archaebacteria.** Eubacteria are distinguished by having very strong **cell wall**s containing **peptidoglycan.** Archaebacteria lack peptidoglycan in their cell walls, and their **gene**s are more similar to those found in **eukaryote**s than are those of eubacteria. The differences are so great that most biologists now agree that archaebacteria and eubacteria should be assigned to separate kingdoms. In the new taxonomic scheme, eubacteria, including **cyanobacteria,** make up the kingdom Monera, while archaebacteria, redesignated **archaea,** make up the kingdom Archaea (➔ **life, classification of**).

Bacteria are able to survive for long periods under adverse conditions by entering a state of **suspended animation.** When frozen or dried out, they become dormant, shielding themselves with protective chemicals obtained from their environment or, if these are not available, producing their own. In the latter case, as a colony of bacteria begins to freeze or dry out, many of the cells break open, discharging their contents, which include **proteins,** gums, and **sugars,** all of which act as protectants. Providing the colony is sufficiently dense, enough cellular material is released to enable a few bacteria to survive in a dormant state, cocooned, as it were, by the remains of their dead associates. Bacteria have been reported as surviving in this way for 4,800 years in the stonework of Peruvian pyramids, for 11,000 years in the gut of a mastodon preserved in a peat bog in Ohio, and for 18 months on the surface of the Moon (➔ *Surveyor 3*). Such discoveries, though requiring careful verification for the possibility of contamination, encourage the belief that bacteria might be able to travel between worlds in a planetary system (➔ **ballistic panspermia**) or even between stars (➔ **panspermia**). In addition to entering suspended animation, some bacteria can survive indefinitely in the form of **bacterial spores.**

bacterial spores

A highly resistant resting phase displayed by some types of **bacteria.** These **spores** are formed in response to adverse changes in the environment. The original **cell** replicates its genetic material, and one copy of this becomes surrounded by a tough coating. The outer cell then disintegrates, releasing the spore, which is now well protected against a variety of trauma, including extremes of heat and cold, and an absence of nutrients, water, or air. In 1995, Raul Cano and Monica Borucki of California Polytechnic State University in San Luis Obispo reported having recovered and reanimated bacterial spores from the digestive tracts of bees that had been entombed in amber for 25 to 40 million years.[97] Similarly remarkable claims have been made for the temperature resistance of spores. About 1 in 100,000 have been shown to survive brief exposure to the 3,000°C flame of a rocket exhaust, while others have emerged unscathed from a bath in liquid helium at −269°C. These findings are cited as evidence by proponents of **panspermia** that spores might be able to travel for millions of years across interstellar distances yet remain viable.

bacteriophage

Also known as a *phage;* a **virus** that attacks and infects **bacteria.** Bacteriophages make up a diverse group of viruses, some of which have complex structures, including double-stranded **DNA.**

bacteriorhodopsin

The basis of a simple **photosynthetic** system that provides some species of **archaea,** known as *halobacteria,* with chemical energy. Interestingly, it is chemically very similar to the light-sensitive pigment rhodopsin that is found in the vertebrate retina.

Baker, Henry (1698–1774)

Microscopist who advocated both **pluralism** and the notion of the great **chain of being.** He compared the abundance of life seen through the microscope with that which he believed was revealed through the telescope on a cosmic scale.

Baker, Thomas (1656–1740)

Learned antiquarian and fellow of St. John's College, Cambridge, who argued against **pluralism** and its claim that God would not create lifeless worlds. In his *Reflections upon Learning* (1699) he writes:

> [T]here is more Beauty and contrivance in the Structure of the Human Body, than there is in the Glorious Body of the Sun, and more perfection in one Rational immaterial Soul, than in the whole Mass of Matter. ... There cannot then be any absurdity in saying, that all things were created for the sake of this inferior World, and the Inhabitants thereof, and they that have such thoughts of it, seem not to have consider'd, who it was that died to redeem it.

Ball, Robert Stawell (1840–1913)

Irish-born astronomer and mathematician who became astronomer royal of Ireland, professor of astronomy and geometry at Cambridge, and an exceptionally well-known popularizer of his subject through lectures and books. His notions of **astrobiology** were modern in the sense that they were informed by both astronomical observations and Charles **Darwin**'s theory of evolution. In *Story of the Heavens* (1885), he suggests that while life may be common on other worlds it is likely to be very different from the forms we know on Earth:

> Could we obtain a closer view of some of the celestial bodies, we should probably find that they, too, teem with life, but life specially adapted to the environment. Life in forms strange and weird...

The Moon he thought lifeless because of a lack of atmosphere (➔ **Moon, life on**). As for the giant planets, he took the view of Richard **Procter** that these worlds were hot—perhaps too hot for life—because of the outflow of vast quantities of internal heat, but that in time they might cool to be habitable. Toward Mercury and Mars, he was open-minded (➔ **Mercury, life on; Mars, life on**), while on the specific topic of Martian canals he commented in his *In Starry Realms* (1892) "that the 'canals' present problems of a very mysterious nature, which have not yet been solved" (➔ **Mars, canals of**). His speculations extended even to the prospects for **silicon-based life,** a topic he dealt with in his 1894 article "The Possibility of Life in Other Worlds."[38]

ballistic panspermia

With the discovery of **meteorite**s on Earth that almost certainly came from the Moon and Mars, it has become relevant to ask whether **prebiotic** chemicals and even primitive life have been routinely transported between different worlds of this and other planetary systems. The significance of certain features and substances found within the **SNC meteorite, ALH 84001,** remain a matter of debate (➔ **Martian "fossils" controversy**). However, it is clear that if rocks from other worlds have arrived here, then the possibility exists of terrestrial material having been transported elsewhere. As Wallis and Wickramasinghe say in a 1995 paper:[613]

> The mass of escaping ejecta from the presumed 10-km object that caused the 180-km Chicxulub crater...amounted to ~300 Mm³, of which one third may have been rock and 10 percent higher-speed ejecta that could have transited directly to Mars....The survival and replication of microorganisms once they are released at destination would depend on the local conditions that prevail. Although viability on the present-day Martian surface is problematical, Earth-to-Mars transfers of life were feasible during an earlier "wet" phase of the planet, prior to 3.5 billion years ago. The Martian atmosphere was also denser at that epoch...thus serving to decelerate meteorites, as on the present-day Earth. Since the reverse transfer can occur in a similar manner, early life evolution of the two planets may well have been linked.

Exchange of material between the Earth and Mars would have been especially common during the first 800 million years of the solar system's existence, that is, between 4.6 and 3.8 billion years ago (➔ **Earth, early history of**), when major impacts with **asteroid**s and **comet**s were frequent. If simple organisms arose on either world during this time—and there is tentative evidence of terrestrial microbial life dating

back 3.85 billion years—they may have been transferred inside ejected rocks to the neighboring planet and formed a colony on arrival (➔ **cosmic collisions, biological effects of**). There are even plausible reasons to suspect that life may have evolved first on Mars and then, via ballistic panspermia, spread to the Earth (➔ **Mars, life on**).[552] Or, there may have been a regular cross-fertilization of microorganisms between the two worlds. Conceivably, Venus, too, was involved in the transference of life when its surface conditions were more clement than they are today. One consequence of the possibility of such cross-fertilization is that if life, or evidence of past life, were found on Mars, it would not immediately imply independent biological evolution.

Balzac, Honoré de (1799–1850)

French novelist who expounded the ideas of Emanuel **Swedenborg** in several of his works, including *Seraphita* and *Louis Lambert*.

band spectrum

A molecular optical **spectrum** consisting of numerous closely spaced **absorption line**s that occur across a limited range of frequencies.

banded iron formation

➔ **Martian "fossils" controversy**

bandpass

The range of frequencies that can pass through a filter, such as one in an electrical circuit.

bandwidth

The difference between the lowest and highest frequencies of a **frequency** band expressed

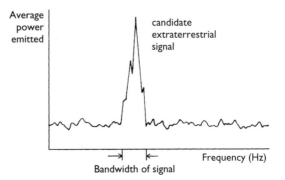

in terms of numbers of cycles per second (hertz).

bar (b)

A unit of pressure, used especially in giving the pressure of a planet's or moon's atmosphere. One bar is approximately the average pressure at sea level on the Earth. 1 bar = 0.987 **atmosphere**s = 1.02 kg/cm^2 = 100 kilopascals = 14.5 lb./sq. in. Atmospheric pressures are often quoted in millibars (mb), or thousandths of a bar.

Barnard, Edward Emerson (1857–1923)

Self-taught American astronomer who worked at the **Lick Observatory** (from 1888) and later at the **Yerkes Observatory** (from 1897), and was considered one of the finest observers of his day. In 1892, he discovered **Amalthea,** a small moon of Jupiter and the last moon to be found without photographic aid. At the turn of the twentieth century, he played a prominent role in denouncing the existence of Martian canals and insisting that they could be broken down into more diffuse detail (➔ **Mars, canals of**). In 1916, he discovered the nearby star that now bears his name (➔ **Barnard's Star**).

Barnard's Star

At a distance of 5.96 light-years (1.83 parsecs), the second nearest star system to the Sun, after the trinary system of **Alpha Centauri.** It lies in the constellation of Ophiuchus and was discovered in 1916 by Edward E. **Barnard.** Being a **red dwarf,** it cannot be seen from Earth without the aid of a powerful telescope. Barnard's Star is approaching us at the unusually high rate of 108 km per second (67 miles per second), so that every century its distance decreases by 0.036 light-year. By A.D. 11,800, at its point of closest approach, it will be just 3.85 light-years (1.18 parsecs) from the Sun. Barnard's Star is also distinguished by having the largest **proper motion** of any star (about 10 **arc-second**s per year). This and its proximity make it an ideal candidate for searches for **extrasolar planets,** since any systematic wobbles in its movement across the sky caused by orbiting worlds would be relatively large. However, no planets have so far been confirmed around Barnard's Star, the claim by

Peter **van der Kamp** of two Jupiter-class worlds having been rejected. It now seems certain that if Barnard's Star does have any planets, they are sub-Jovian in mass. Barnard's Star was chosen as the hypothetical target of Project **Daedalus.** ➔ **stars, nearest**

Barnes, Ernest William (1874–1953)

English theologian, bishop of Birmingham, and accomplished scientist who pondered how to relate Christian doctrine to the possibility of extraterrestrial intelligence (➔ **Christian doctrine and pluralism**). In his Gifford lectures, given in Edinburgh between 1927 and 1929, he expressed the opinion that God created the universe "as a basis for the higher forms of consciousness" and deduced that this purpose is best served by a multiplicity of inhabited worlds. Noting that there appeared to be nothing "exceptional either in mass or in size or in any other way" about our galaxy and endorsing the view that life on Earth originated as a result of natural biochemical processes, he concluded that there are probably billions of planets in the observable universe supporting intelligent life, some of it far in advance of our own. ➔ **Milne, Edward A.**

barophiles

Organisms, both macroscopic and microscopic, that thrive in environments where the pressure is unusually high, for example, deep in the ocean or far underground. Three categories of microbes found in high-pressure environments can be distinguished. *Barotolerant* microbes are found in the ocean to depths of 4 km (about 400 atmospheres) but grow better at 1 atmosphere. *Barophilic* species occur at 5 to 6 km and grow better at high pressure (500 to 600 atmospheres) than low. *Extreme barophiles* live at great depths where the pressure is at least 700 atmospheres and will not grow at all at 1 atmosphere. ➔ **extremophiles**

Barsoom

The local name for Mars in the science fiction novels of Edgar Rice **Burroughs.**

Barthélemy, Jean-Jacques (1716–95)

French abbé who in his multivolume work, *Voyage de jeune Anacharsis en Grèce dans le milieu du quatrième siècle avant l'ère vulgaire* (1788), reminds his readers of the important contributions to the extraterrestrial life debate made by **Democritus of Abdera, Leucippus,** Petron, Pythagoras and his followers, **Xenophanes,** and others, 2,000 years earlier.

barycenter
The center of mass of a system of objects moving under the influence of their mutual gravity.

basalt
A dark, fine-grained rock of volcanic origin. It is the commonest type of lava.

base
A substance that combines with **hydrogen ion**s (H+) when dissolved in water, thereby lowering the hydrogen ion concentration in the solution. Basic (or alkaline) solutions have **pH** values above 7.

base pair
A complementary pair of **nucleotide base**s, consisting of a **purine** and a **pyramidine.**

B-class asteroid
A subcategory of **C-class asteroid**s with an **albedo** in the range of 0.04 to 0.08. Although fairly low, this is at the high end for C-class objects.

beacon, interstellar
A hypothetical **omnidirectional antenna** set up by an extraterrestrial civilization to broadcast its existence and/or other information to fellow technological races in the Galaxy or beyond. The presumption is that such a beacon would transmit some kind of repetitive message. However, the power required would be enormous. Whereas a beamed, unidirectional message from a race at a similar stage of technological development to our own would be easy to detect with conventional **radio telescope**s, even over distances of several hundred light-years, the same amount of power used to operate an interstellar beacon would result in a very feeble signal. Only an immense array of receivers, such as that proposed for Project **Cyclops,** would be capable of detecting the faint transmissions from interstellar beacons of Type I **Kardashev civilizations** outside the immediate solar neighborhood.

Beagle 2
Proposed lander for the **European Space Agency** probe *Mars Express*. An onboard mass spectrometer will be used to search for **organic** material, water, and water-deposited minerals in samples obtained by a robot arm and a "mole" that will crawl across the surface at the rate of 1 cm every 6 seconds and burrow beneath large boulders. Exterior weathering from small rocks will be removed using a modified dentist's drill prior to examination. *Beagle 2* is being developed primarily in Britain by a consortium of university-based researchers and industrial partners.

beamwidth
The angular extent of the beam of a **radio telescope.**

Beattie, James (1735–1803)
Scottish poet, professor of moral philosophy and logic at Aberdeen, and advocate of **pluralism,** who in his *Evidences of the Christian Religion* (1786) replies to those who question that in a universe so large, God should have troubled to redeem the inhabitants of one small planet with the sacrifice of his son. He agrees with Richard **Bentley** that the soul of one good man is worth more than all the material contents of the universe. Moreover, he argues that the redemption of mankind might have extraterrestrial consequences and that

> it is not absurd to imagine, that our fall and recovery may be used to them as an example; and that the divine grace manifested in our redemption may raise their adoration and gratitude into higher raptures and quicken their ardour to inquire … into the dispensions into infinite wisdom.

→ Christian doctrine and pluralism

Beck, Lewis White
American philosopher who is among the few of his profession to consider the possible im-

pact on humanity of extraterrestrial contact (➔ **extraterrestrial intelligence, implications following first contact**). He has argued that popular science and science fiction have so prepared people for the discovery of intelligent alien signals that, if it comes, it will have no great lasting effect on individuals' lives. It might, however, have longer-term consequences since:

> there is no limit to what in coming centuries we might learn about other creatures and, more portentiously, about ourselves. Compared to such advances in knowledge, the Copernican and Darwinian Revolutions and the discovery of the New World would have been but minor preludes.

Becquerel, Paul (1879–1955)

French plant physiologist who, working in the cryogenic laboratory of Heike Kamerlingh Onnes in Leiden, the Netherlands, and inspired by Svante **Arrhenius**'s ideas on **panspermia,** showed that **bacteria** retained their germinating power for as long as two years under extreme cold in a vacuum. He also found, however, that the same strains were quickly killed by **ultraviolet** radiation, thus contributing to the experimental data that cast serious doubt on the panspermia hypothesis.

Beer, Wilhelm (1797–1850)

Berlin banker and brother of the composer Meyerbeer, who set up a private observatory equipped with a 9.5-cm refractor. In collaboration with Johann H. von **Mädler,** he produced, in 1830, the first accurate lunar map (*Mappa selenographica*) and a companion descriptive volume (*Der Mond*), describing the surface features. These showed the Moon to be a world very unlike the Earth and contradicted the pro-**selenite** claims of Franz **Gruithuisen** and William **Herschel** (➔ **Moon, life on**). Beer and Mädler's map remained the best available for several decades and helped persuade most professional astronomers that the Moon is uninhabited. The two also collaborated in the production of the first systematic chart of the surface of Mars.

Belinda

The ninth moon of **Uranus.** ➔ **Uranus, moons of**

Discovery	1986, by *Voyager 2*
Mean distance from Uranus	75,100 km (46,700 mi.)
Diameter	68 km (42 mi.)
Orbital period	0.624 day (14 hours 59 minutes)
Orbital eccentricity	0.000
Orbital inclination	0.03°
Visual albedo	0.07

Bentley, Richard (1662–1742)

English theologian who strove to accommodate the dramatically enlarged cosmos of the late seventeenth century within traditional religious doctrine. Upon this matter he corresponded with Isaac **Newton.** Bentley accepted the evolving consensus among astronomers that "every Fixt Star [is] of the same nature with our Sun; and each may very possibly have Planets about them." Moreover, he saw no theological barrier to these worlds being populated:

> As the Earth was principally designed for the Being and Service and contemplation of Men; why may not all other Planets be created for the like uses, each for their own Inhabitants who have Life and Understanding?

He was adamant, however, that the physical extent of the universe did not diminish the unique relationship between mankind and God, insisting that "the soul of one virtuous man is of greater worth and excellency, than the sun and his planets, and all the stars in the world." ➔ **Christian doctrine and pluralism**

Bergson, Henri-Louis (1859–1941)

French philosopher and writer who popularized the idea of an *élan vital*, or creative force, at the heart of evolution, rather than a deterministic natural selection.[51] Together with Hans Driesch in Germany, he advocated a return to a form of **vitalism** ("neovitalism") that, as Leonard **Troland** put it,[593] asserts that the phenomena of life are not determined by law-abiding forces but by a form of activity the effects of which are unpredictable,... chaotic and beyond the range of science.

Berkeley, George (1685–1753)

Irish philosopher of the idealist school who, in his *Three Dialogues Between Hylas and Philonous* (1713) and *Alciphron; or the Minute Philosopher* (1732) argued for the existence of numerous worlds inhabited by different degrees of intelligence. He countered the anti-Christian objection that there is more bad in the world than good by suggesting that the Earth and its sinners might bear "no greater proportion to the universe of intelligences than a dungeon doth to a kingdom." → **Christian doctrine and pluralism**

Berkner, Lloyd V. (1905–67)

Acting director of the **National Radio Astronomy Observatory** in **Green Bank** and chairman of the National Academy of Science's **Space Science Board** in the 1960s. It was Berkner who gave Frank **Drake** approval to use the facilities at Green Bank to conduct Project **Ozma.** Shortly after, Otto **Struve** took over as Green Bank's director.

Bernal, J(ohn) D(esmond) (1901–71)

Irish physicist who carried out important research into the chemical origin of life and speculated on what general principles might apply to all forms of life in the Universe.[52] He also inquired into the future of mankind and the **colonization of space.** Bernal graduated from Emmanuel College, Cambridge, and began his research career in crystallography under William Bragg at the Davy-Faraday Laboratory in London before returning to Cambridge. In 1937, he was appointed to the Chair of Physics at Birkbeck College, London, where his studies in crystallography led him to examine increasingly complex biological materials and eventually the processes leading to the origin of life. In a 1947 lecture, "The Physical Basis of Life," he suggested that clays may have played a role in concentrating **organic** molecules (→ **clays, role in prebiotic evolution**) and pondered on the nature of life in a cosmic context:

[T]errestrial limitations obviously beg the question of whether there is any more generalized activity that we can call life.... Whether there are some general characteristics which would apply not only to life on this planet with its very special set of physical conditions, but to life of any kind, is an interesting, but so far purely theoretical question.

In a 1952 lecture to the **British Interplanetary Society** (chaired at the time by Arthur C. **Clarke**) he further helped bring the possibility of extraterrestrial life into the province of mainstream biology by arguing that "the biology of the future would not be confined to our own planet, but would take on the character of cosmobiology." Following the discovery of organic substances in the **Orgeuil meteorite,** Bernal suggested[53] that the material might have been due to **contamination** on Earth; otherwise, it must have formed inorganically in space or as the result of living things on the parent body from which the meteorite came. An inorganic origin, as a result of processes in the early solar system, said Bernal, could mean that meteorites had provided the raw materials for the first synthesis of life on Earth (→ **cosmic collisions, biological effects of**). As long ago as 1929, in his remarkably perceptive book *The World, the Flesh, and the Devil,*[54] Bernal discussed the possibility of colonies in space (→ **Bernal Sphere**).

Bernal Sphere

A spherical **space colony** of the type first described in the 1920s by J. D. **Bernal.**[54] As the material and energy needs of the human race grew, Bernal surmised, it would be natural that someday orbiting colonies would be built to harness the Sun's energy and provide extra living space for a burgeoning population. He conceived of self-sufficient globes, 16 km (10 miles) in diameter, each of which would be home to 20,000 to 30,000 inhabitants. Almost half a century later, Gerard K. **O'Neill** based the scheme for his "Island One" space colony on a smaller Bernal sphere, some 500 m in diameter. Rotating twice a minute, it would generate an Earth-normal **artificial gravity** at its equator. One advantage of a sphere is that it has the smallest surface area for a given internal volume, thus minimizing the amount of radiation shielding required. → **Dyson sphere; Tsiolkovskii, Konstantin Eduardovich**

Bernardin de Saint-Pierre, Jacques-Henri (1737–1814)

French proponent of **natural theology** whose *Harmonies de la nature,* published posthumously in 1815, was widely read in both France and England. In it, Bernardin de Saint-Pierre argued for a teleologically uncompromising form of **pluralism:** "Nature has made nothing in vain, and what would be the use of desert globes?" He even claimed that comets are inhabited and that celestial objects have souls.

Berthelot, Pierre-Eugène-Marcelin (1827–1907)

French chemist who, in 1868, analyzed samples of the **Orgueil meteorite** and reported finding in them **hydrocarbon**s of the alkane family "comparable with the oils of petroleum."

Berzelius, Jöns Jakob (1779–1848)

Swedish chemist who analyzed samples from various **meteorite**s, including, in 1834, the **Alais meteorite.** In the latter, he confirmed the finding of chemists Louis Thenard and Louis-Nicolas Vauquelin that **carbon** compounds were present. He then speculated about the origin of these substances and, in particular, whether they offered proof of life on other worlds (→ **panspermia**). Perhaps influenced by his belief that most meteorites came from volcanic eruptions on the Moon, he was skeptical: "The carbonized substance that this earth [i.e., the meteoritic rock] contains . . . would not authorize the conclusion that in its original habitat, this earthy substance was of organic nature."

Bessel, Friedrich Wilhelm (1784–1846)

German astronomer and mathematician, assistant to Johann **Schröter** at Lilienthal, who became director of the Königsberg Observatory in 1810. Bessel was a superb observer and made many important contributions to positional astronomy, including, in 1838, the first direct measurement of a star's distance, that of **61 Cygni,** by trigonometric **parallax.** He ar-

gued against the existence of life on the Moon at a time when several notable compatriots of his, including Karl **Gauss,** Franz **Gruithuisen,** Joseph von **Littrow,** and Wilhelm **Olbers,** were in the pro-**selenite** camp (→ **Moon, life on**). In particular, he noted the sharpness with which stars are occulted by the Moon, indicating the absence of a lunar atmosphere. In a lecture, delivered in 1838, he took the supporters of **pluralism** to task for ignoring the astronomical evidence that our neighboring worlds (with the possible exception of Mars) are not suited to life as we know it:

> The moon is decisively different from the earth in the primary point of an atmosphere; the sun is of an entirely different nature; for Mercury and Venus we have found no basis for assuming a similarity; Mars appears to possess an atmosphere and summer and winter, even snow and ice; . . . Jupiter and Saturn are very dissimilar to the earth in the matter of which they consist.

Beta Life

A term used in the influential *Science of Life*[622] encyclopedia by H. G. **Wells,** Julian Huxley, and G. P. Wells to describe the kind of life that might exist on other worlds. The authors felt that if there were life on Mars, for example, it would be so different that it would have to be considered as something entirely new:

> . . . an analogous thing and not the same thing. It may not be individualized; it may not consist of reproductive individuals. It may simply be mobile and metabolic. It is stretching a point to bring these two processes under one identical expression.

Beta Pictoris

A relatively nearby star (58.7 light-years, or 17.8 parsecs, away) of **spectral type** A5 V that is surrounded by a large dust ring seen almost edge-on. The existence of this circumstellar disk, containing gas and dust at a temperature of about −173°C (−279°F, or 100 K) and extending up to 600 AU (90 billion km, or 56 billion miles) from the star, was first revealed in 1983 by the ***Infrared Astronomy Satellite.*** An image of the disk was obtained in 1984 by Richard Terrile and Bradford Smith using the

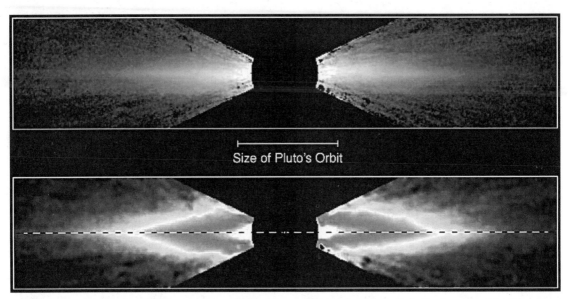

Size of Pluto's Orbit

Detailed image of the circumstellar disk around Beta Pictoris obtained using the 3.6-m telescope of the European Southern Observatory.
European Southern Observatory

2.5-m telescope at **Las Campanas Observatory** equipped with a **charge-coupled device** and a **coronograph.** Speculation followed about whether it might be a **protoplanetary disk.** However, this is almost certainly not the case, since Beta Pictoris is a **main sequence** star with an age of approximately 100 million years. The dust presently in its disk has a lifetime on the order of 100 *thousand* years and therefore must undergo continuous replenishment (→ **regenerated disk**). Although the disk is unlikely to be the site of planet formation today, it may be that existing planets move within it.[604] Support for this idea came with the observation of a gap in the disk of a radius of 10 to 30 AU (1.5 billion to 4.5 billion km). It has been suggested that the dust-free region may have been cleared by a planet of about five Earth masses moving in a near-circular orbit 20 AU (3 billion km) out from the central star.[133, 331] Spectral analysis has revealed redshifted absorption features that some believe are due to comets falling onto the star's outer atmosphere.[55] If this is the case, it is again consistent with the presence of a planetary system since one or more gas giants might be responsible for the infall events. In 1996, using the *Hubble Space Telescope,* a small warp was detected in the disk within 80 AU (12 billion km) that, according to one theory, is due to the gravitational influence of a massive planet orbiting at right angles to the disk. In January 1998 came the announcement of a larger warp further out in the disk, some 11 billion km (7 billion miles) from the star. This might be due to a **brown dwarf** in a wide orbit around Beta Pictoris or the nearby passage of another star. → **planetary systems, formation of; UX Orionis**

BETA, Project

Billion-channel Extraterrestrial Assay; a **SETI** program, conducted by the **Harvard SETI Group,** that began observing in October 1995. Its predecessor, Project **META,** and other searches had found occasional candidate signals that had the expected characteristics of artificial transmissions but did not repeat when later observations were made. This prompted a meeting on "Intermittency in SETI" at the **SETI Institute** in January 1994. As a result, the Harvard group determined that its next search system should incorporate means of (1) rapid and automatic reobservation of candidate events, (2) better discrimination of interference through a simultaneous three-beam configuration, and (3) coverage of the full 1.4-to-1.7-GHz **waterhole** band of frequencies. Project BETA uses the **Harvard-Smithsonian radio telescope** and a 240-million-channel Fourier **spectrometer** to analyze 80 million channels with 0.5-Hz **resolution bandwidth** and 40-MHz **instantaneous bandwidth.** As in the case of META, support for it comes from the **Planetary Society,** NASA, and private foundations.

Betelgeuse

Alpha Orionis; a **red supergiant,** with about 20 times the mass and 800 times the radius of the Sun, so huge that it could easily contain the orbits of Mercury, Venus, Earth, and Mars. It will probably explode as a **supernova** at some point within the next 100,000 years. Even at its relatively remote distance, it normally ranks as the tenth brightest star in the sky. However, its luminosity varies on an irregular basis as its surface pulsates in and out. Betelgeuse is expelling large amounts of material in the form of a vigorous **stellar wind,** some of which has collected as an immense dust cloud. Although astronomers had known of the existence of this cloud for some time, the first image of it was captured in 1998 by astronomers at the **Center for Astronomical Adaptive Optics** using the **Multiple Mirror Telescope** and the technique of **nulling interferometry.**[271] This demonstration of the effectiveness of this technique was an important early milestone in using nulling interferometry to obtain images of **extrasolar planets. →
stars, brightest**

Bianca

The third moon of **Uranus. → Uranus, moons of**

Discovery	1986, by *Voyager 2*
Mean distance from Uranus	59,100 km (36,700 mi.)
Diameter	44 km (27 mi.)
Orbital period	0.435 day (10 hours 26 minutes)
Orbital eccentricity	0.001
Orbital inclination	0.16°
Visual albedo	0.07

Bickerton, Alexander William (1842–1929)

Somewhat eccentric New Zealand astronomer who revived the **catastrophic hypothesis** of the origin of the solar system, first suggested by Georges **Buffon,** by proposing that the planets were produced when the Sun underwent a grazing impact with another star. In 1926, Bickerton exposed the limits of his predictive powers when, commenting on the prospects for space exploration, he wrote, "This foolish idea of shooting at the moon is an example of the absurd length to which vicious specialization will carry scientists working in thought-tight compartments."

Big Ear

The **radio telescope** of **Ohio State University Radio Observatory** that was used in the **Ohio SETI Program,** the longest-running project of its kind carried out to date. It will best be remembered for its detection of the so-called **Wow! signal.** The brainchild of observatory director and founder John **Kraus,** Big Ear was larger than three football fields and of an unusual design that has subsequently been copied at other sites around the world. It consisted of a flat, tiltable reflector 104 m (340 ft.) long by 30 m (100 ft.) high, a fixed standing parabolic reflector 110 m (360 ft.) long by 21 m (70 ft.) high, an aluminum-covered ground plane 110 m (360 ft.) wide by 152 m (500 ft.) long, and two feed horns mounted on a movable assembly. Its sensitivity was equivalent to that of a single circular dish-type radio telescope 53 m (175 ft.) in diameter. Big Ear surveyed the sky by **drift scan.** The flat, tiltable reflector was pointed skyward to pick up cosmic radio waves, which were then bounced over to the parabolic reflector to be focused into a beam. This beam was reflected back across the ground plane to the feed horns. The aluminum layer of the ground plane kept the feeble signals from being absorbed by the ground. After a few days of observing in one position, the tiltable reflector was moved slightly to allow a different section of the sky to be scanned. In 1998, Big Ear was demolished to make way for a golf course. One hundred small pieces of the metal mesh covering the instrument were rescued by members of the **SETI League** and offered in exchange for a minimum $100 donation each, with the proceeds to be divided between the SETI League and the Ohio State University Radio Observatory. The latter is now engaged in construction of the **Argus radio telescope.**

Big Occulting Steerable Satellite (BOSS)

A space mission designed to provide improved **resolution** of closely spaced objects (including **binary stars**) and facilitate the separation of dim objects from nearby bright objects, such as **extrasolar planets** around their host stars. BOSS will function as an artificial moon, occulting (i.e., passing in front of) objects on demand. The mission is being designed by researchers at Case Western Reserve University, Cleveland, Ohio; the **Jet Propulsion Laboratory;** and the California Institute of Technology.

Billingham, John (1930–)

English-born aerospace physician and **SETI** pioneer. Billingham originated the idea for Project **Cyclops** and in 1984 became chief of the Life Sciences Division at **NASA Ames Research Center.** He currently chairs the International Academy of Astronautics SETI Committee and is a senior scientist at the **SETI Institute.** Having obtained an M.A. from Oxford and a medical degree from Guy's Hospital, London, in 1954, he specialized in aviation medicine and physiology for the Royal Air Force in England before coming to the United States in 1963 to take charge of the Environmental Physiology Branch at the **NASA Johnson Space Center.** Three years later, he moved to Ames, becoming chief of the Extraterrestrial Research Division in 1976 and also acting chief of the Program Office for the Search for Extraterrestrial Intelligence—the first person in the United States to head a government unit officially concerned with extraterrestrial intelligence. Beginning in the 1960s, he worked to establish SETI as a legitimate NASA activity, was instrumental in organizing the studies that formed the basis of Project Cyclops, and became codirector of that project with Bernard **Oliver.** His early views on space travel and life in space were influenced by reading H. G. **Wells** and attending meetings of the **British Interplanetary Society,** and later by Carl

Sagan and Iosif **Shklovskii**'s book *Intelligent Life in the Universe.*[57, 58, 59, 60, 575]

binary

A number system in which there are only two different digits. As the scientist-hero of Fred **Hoyle**'s *A for Andromeda* explains:

> It's arithmetic expressed entirely by the figures 0 and 1, instead of the figures 1 to 10, which we normally use and which we call denary. 0 and 1, you see, could be dot and dash.... The binary system is basic; it's based on positive and negative, yes and no... it's universal.

It is generally accepted that binary may prove to be a lingua franca for communication between technological civilizations in the Galaxy. → **mathematics, as a universal language**

binary pulsar

Two **pulsars** in orbit around their mutual center of gravity. The term is also used to describe a system in which a pulsar orbits around any other type of star.

binary star

Two stars in orbit around their common center of mass and held together by their mutual gravitational pull. Surveys have shown that one star in every two or three is a member of a binary or **multiple star** system. The two components of a binary system each move in an elliptical orbit around their common center of gravity. The further apart they are, the more slowly they move. Their **orbital period**s may be measured in tens, hundreds, or even millions of years. The question of whether planets in a binary star system could conceivably support life has been widely discussed. → **binary stars, habitable planets of**

binary stars, habitable planets of

Two key questions arise when considering whether life could evolve in a binary or **multiple star** system. They are: (1) Is it possible for planetary systems to form around such stars, and (2) If it is, can planets orbit so as to provide tolerable surface conditions for biological activity? On the subject of planet formation, it has been suggested that the gravitational disturbance caused by another nearby star might prevent material from settling into a stable **protoplanetary disk.** However, evidence is now to hand of such a disk around one of the stars in a young binary system. Assuming, then, that planets do form, could they support life? Before 1960, it was generally thought not. Then the Chinese-American astronomer Su-Shu **Huang** showed that there existed various special orbits in which a planet could move in a two-star system and enjoy clement, stable temperatures. Basically, there are three possibilities: a wide, roughly circular path around both stars, a figure-eight orbit around both stars, or a small orbit around just one star. The exact circuits required for habitability would depend on details such as the type of stars involved and their separation distance. Due to its proximity to the Sun, the **Alpha Centauri** system has been widely discussed in this regard. In fiction, Brian Aldiss has speculated what effects the climatic swings of a planet circling around a binary star might have on the social structures of its inhabitants. In his *Heliconia* series, he looks at life and culture on a world orbiting in a complex planetary system of a binary star such that its seasons last hundreds of years.[46, 49, 276, 295, 625]

bioastronomy
→ **astrobiology**

biodiversity
The variety and variability among living organisms and the ecological complexes in which they occur.

biogenesis
The production of substances, biological structures, or new organisms by existing life-forms.

biogenic
Produced by living organisms.

bioindicators
→ **biomarkers**

biomarkers
Characteristic chemicals, chemical complexes, **biominerals,** accumulations of **trace elements,**

fractionations of stable **isotopes,** spectral features, and other indicators that provide clues to the presence of extant or past biological activity. Establishing what are reliable biomarkers in extraterrestrial rocks or other samples and in the spectra of **extrasolar planets** and thereby developing a catalog of biosignatures is crucial in the search for life beyond the Earth. → **extraterrestrial life, detection of**

biome
The largest recognized ecological unit. Terrestrial examples include grassland, desert, savanna, temperate and tropical rain forests, and tundra.

biominerals
Minerals formed from the remains, or as a result of the metabolic activity, of long-dead organisms. → **biomarkers**

biopoiesis
The development of living matter from complex **organic** molecules that are self-replicating but nonliving. It is generally assumed to be the process by which terrestrial life came about.

biosensor
A sensor used to obtain information about a life process.

biosphere
That part of a planet or moon in which life can exist. It may include the crust, oceans, and atmosphere.

biospheres, recognition of
One of the central challenges in **astrobiology** is the detection of the signatures of life over interstellar distances. In the case of contemporary terrestrial life, the most distinctive signatures include the high concentration of **free oxygen** (O_2) and **ozone** (O_3) in the atmosphere and the green surface coloration due to **chlorophyll,** all the result of the activity of plants. Similar features in the spectra of **extrasolar planets,** when it becomes possible to observe these, will provide strong evidence of Earth-like biospheres.[336] Less is known about the principal signatures of the terrestrial bio-

sphere prior to about 1 billion years ago (➔ **Earth, early history of**). Further work is needed in this area so that techniques can be developed to search for biospheres akin to that of the primitive Earth. ➔ **Origins Program**

biota
Living organisms of a particular place or period.

bipedalism
The ability to walk permanently upright on two feet—a characteristic that distinguished the early hominids from the apes. The question arises whether *all* intelligent, technological species in the Universe display this characteristic. According to one school of thought, large-brained, land-dwelling life-forms need a vertical posture in order to balance the weight of the head on top of the spinal column. Moreover, the transition to two legs frees the hands for delicate manipulation, which is essential for toolmaking. Contrasting with this is the view that any speculation based on **anthropomorphism** is likely to prove too restrictive when considering the forms that advanced organisms can take on other worlds.

BIS
➔ **British Interplanetary Society**

bit
A **binary** digit, either 0 or 1.

Black Cloud, The
Cosmologist Fred **Hoyle** ranks among a small but influential group of scientists (which also includes Carl **Sagan**) who have written works of "alien" fiction that are extrapolated from their basic scientific beliefs. In his novel *The Black Cloud*[286] (1957), Hoyle describes the arrival near the Earth of a small **interstellar cloud** that can think and move of its own accord. A living organism half a billion years old, as big as the orbit of Venus, and as massive as Jupiter, the Black Cloud has a "brain" that consists of complex networks of molecules that can be increased in number and specialization as the creature desires (➔ **intelligence, nature of**). Once it learns that the third planet of the Sun is inhabited by an intelligent race, it establishes contact and begins to reveal some extraordinary facts about intelligence in the Universe:

> [I]t is most unusual to find animals with technical skills inhabiting planets, which are in the nature of extreme outposts of life.... Living on the surface of a solid body, you are exposed to a strong gravitational force. This greatly limits the size to which your animals can grow and hence limits the scope of your neurological activity. It forces you to possess muscular structures to promote movements, and ... to carry protective armor.... [Y]our very largest animals have been mostly bone and muscle with very little brain.... By and large, one only expects intelligent life to exist in a diffuse gaseous medium.... The second unfavourable factor is your extreme lack of basic chemical foods. For the building of chemical foods on a large scale starlight is necessary. Your planet, however, absorbs only a very minute fraction of the light from the Sun. At the moment, I myself am building basic chemicals at about 10,000,000,000 times the rate at which building is occurring on the whole ... surface of your planet.

The Cloud goes on to discuss the evolution of intelligence, the difficulty of communicating an appreciation of arts and the quality of emotions between beings of different neurological structure, how it feeds and reproduces, and other aspects of life as a giant nebular organism.

Could such an interstellar life-form exist? In his preface, Hoyle writes that "there is very little here that could not conceivably happen." But one of the potential obstacles to off-world life is that the density of matter between the stars is so low that interactions between particles take place far less frequently than on a planet's surface. Consequently, the evolution of interstellar organisms, if it can occur at all, might take thousands or even millions of times longer than that of terrestrial life—a much longer period than the present age of the universe. On the other hand, perhaps our sole experience of evolution on a planetary surface leaves us ill equipped to surmise how biological organization might take place under completely different circumstances. It may even be, as Hoyle and his colleague Chandra Wickramasinghe have proposed, that we are wrong in supposing that life was created on the Earth. In an echo of the Black Cloud theme, they theorize that primitive life-forms may have come together on the surface of grains of **cosmic dust**. → **life, in space**

Black, David C. (1943–)

Chairman of the **Origins** Subcommittee of NASA's Space Science Advisory Committee and past chairman of the Solar System Exploration Subcommittee. He is currently director of the Lunar and Planetary Institute, Johnson Space Center, where he is investigating a number of issues related to the formation of planetary systems and the nature of low-mass companions to stars.

black dwarf

The hypothetical end point of evolution of a **white dwarf** after it has cooled down to the extent that it can no longer shine, even dimly. It is thought that the universe is not yet old enough to harbor any black dwarfs.

black hole

A region of space where the pull of gravity is so strong that nothing, not even light, can escape.

black smoker

A marine **hydrothermal vent** at the crest of an oceanic ridge that produces a dense plume of black, fine-grained, and very hot **sulfide** precipitates. The warm, chemical-rich environments around black smokers have been found to be home to hundreds of new species, including previously unknown types of giant clams, crabs, and pink brotulid fish. One type of organism, a reddish worm known as *Vestimentiferan*, which builds and lives in a tube up to 7.5 m (25 ft.) long, is so different from any other known animal that it has been classified in a phylum of its own. At the base of the food chain are **chemoautrophic archaea** that use chemical energy derived from the breakdown of **hydrogen sulfide** to build **organic** compounds.

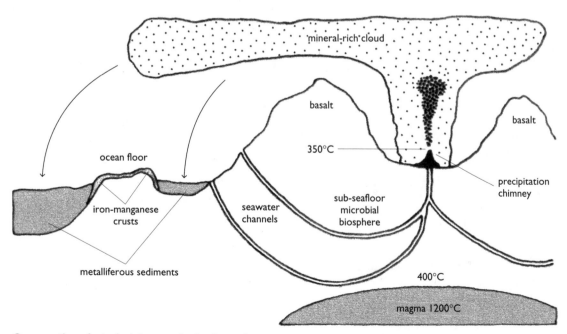

Cross section of a typical deep-sea hydrothermal vent.

Blish, James (1921–75)

American science fiction writer and graduate of Rutgers University (microbiology) and Columbia University (zoology), who imaginatively portrayed extraterrestrials and the consequences of their discovery. In *A Case of Conscience* (1958) he addresses a scenario in which a Jesuit priest and biologist must try to reconcile his beliefs with the discovery of an alien race of intelligent reptiles (➔ **dinosaurs, intelligent**). ➔ **incarnation and redemption**

blood, of extraterrestrials

A favorite theme of science fiction is the diversity of pigmentation that might exist among extraterrestrials due to differences in the color of their blood. *Star Trek*'s Mr. Spock, for example, has a greenish tinge to his skin on account of being a green-blooded Vulcan. The variation in the color of the blood of terrestrial species is due to differences in the metallic component (➔ **prosthetic group**) of the blood from one species to another. Human blood, like that of all mammals and birds, is red because of a cocktail of iron-containing pigments, including hemoglobins (red), myoglobins (red), chlorocruorins (green), and hemerythrins (violet). Horseshoe crabs and certain other organisms, on the other hand, have blood in which the oxygen-carrier is hemocyanin, a copper-containing pigment that is blue. Perhaps Mr. Spock has blood that is similar to that of the humble sea cucumber (Holothurioidea), which is yellow-green and based on vanadium.

Blue Book, Project

The last, and by far the longest, of three studies conducted by the U.S. Air Force into the phenomenon of **unidentified flying objects.** Initially headed by Captain Edward J. **Ruppelt,** it was launched in March 1952 following a wave of sightings, including one by an Air Force pilot over Fort Monmouth, New Jersey, in September 1951. Over the next seventeen years, Blue Book sifted through thousands of reports, but as the Air Force's interest in the phenomenon waned, so did the number of staff working on the project. This often led to potentially interesting cases being inadequately researched and given facile explanations, with the result that proponents of the **extraterrestrial hypothesis** could claim that there was a cover-up in official circles. Meanwhile, Blue Book's astronomical consultant, J. Allen **Hynek,** became increasingly convinced that a genuine and potentially important phenomenon lay behind some of the unresolved UFO reports. Following a wave of sightings in 1965 and a renewal of public interest, the Air Force set up the Ad Hoc Committee to review Project Blue Book in the fall of that year. The committee recommended that research on the problem be strengthened by involving universities. In March 1966, sightings of UFOs in Michigan by more than one hundred witnesses and the failure of Blue Book to come up with a credible explanation for them prompted the House Armed Services Committee to hold an open hearing on UFOs, out of which came a decision to implement the Ad Hoc Committee's recommendation. A tender was put out to academic institutions to sift through the annals of Project Blue Book and come up with some definitive conclusions. Eventually, the contract went to the University of Colorado under the supervision of Edward **Condon.** In January 1969, the **Condon Report** appeared and concluded that any further official UFO investigations would be unjustified. As a result, Project Blue Book was canceled.

blue shift

The displacement of **spectral lines** in the **spectrum** of an object toward shorter wavelengths. If caused by the line-of-sight approach of the object (➔ **Doppler effect**), as is usually the case, this displacement, when measured, allows the velocity of approach to be calculated. ➔ **red shift**

blue supergiant

A massive, luminous star that has exhausted the hydrogen in its core and left the **main sequence.** Blue supergiants, of which **Rigel** is an example, expand and cool to become **red supergiant**s before finally exploding as **supernova**s.

blue-green algae

Photosynthetic organisms now correctly known as **cyanobacteria.**

Blum, Harold F. (1899–   )

Professor of biology at Princeton University who, in his *Time's Arrow and Evolution*[63] (1951), argued that if life exists elsewhere in the Universe,

> it probably has taken quite a different form. And so life as we know may be a very unique thing after all, perhaps a species of some inclusive genus, but nevertheless a quite distinct species.

Pointing out the general tendency of the Universe to become more disorganized with time in accordance with the second law of thermodynamics, he suggested that a system such as life, which runs against this trend, might be rare. Moreover, he adopted what would become the party line among evolutionary biologists in the era of space exploration, contrasting with the position of most astrobiologists, that (1) the appearance of life on Earth might have been due to a series of lucky accidents, and (2) that if it did evolve on other worlds, it would be very unlikely to resemble any terrestrial variety. → **evolutionary theory and extraterrestrial life**

Bode, Johann Elert (1747–1826)

German mathematician and astronomer of Titius-Bode Law fame, who enthusiastically endorsed an extreme form of **pluralism** and **natural theology**. Bode argued in two influential texts on astronomy—his *Anleitung* of 1768 and *Erläuterung* of 1778—that essentially every significant object in space, including the Sun, stars, planets, moons, and comets are inhabited by rational beings (→ **plenitude, principle of**). For him, habitability was "the most important goal of creation" (→ **teleology**). Concerning the key Christian issues of **incarnation and redemption,** he suggested that extraterrestrials everywhere "are ready to recognize the author of their existence and to praise his goodness." As for objections against the habitability of planets too far from or close to the Sun, he replied that varying atmospheric conditions compensate for the different levels of solar radiation in order to make life possible and further noted that "the rational inhabitants, and even the animals, plants, etc. of the other planetary bodies are characterized by forms different from those which occur on our earth." This flexibility was especially important in his argument for life on comets: "Who can conceive what special arrangements of the wise Creator in regard to the climate, zones, dwelling places, sectioning of creatures, natural products, may not be expected for all those on a cometary body?" Concerning the Moon, he cited Johann **Schröter's** reports of changes on the lunar surface that "may indicate natural upheavals and a culture perhaps organized by its inhabitants" (→ **Moon, life on**). Bode was among the earliest advocates of the much wider cosmos with "island universes" (external galaxies) as envisaged by Immanuel **Kant** and William **Herschel.**

Bok globule

→ **globule**

bolide

A **fireball** that produces a sonic boom. Bolides are often associated with **meteorite** falls.

Bolingbroke, Henry St. John (1678–1751)

English Tory statesman who, in his *Philosophical Works,* published posthumously in 1754, argued for the existence of "numberless worlds [which are] habitations of ten thousand millions of intellectual corporeal beings." He supported the notion of the great **chain of being** but suggested that the idea of advanced extraterrestrials being angels or demons had to be abandoned in favor of natural creatures "tempered in a finer clay, cast in nobler moulds, than the human."

Bonnet, Charles (1720–93)

Swiss entomologist and botanist who argued in support of **pluralism,** the great **chain of being,** and **transmigration of souls** in his *Contemplation de la nature* (1764) and *La Palingénésie philosophique* (1769). His writings, translated into German, Italian, and English, continued to exert an influence a century later, when they were revived by Camille **Flammarion,** Pezzani, and others.

Borel, Pierre (c. 1620–71)

Protestant physician and counselor to the French court who, inspired by the atomistic philosophy (➔ **atomism**) of his recently deceased compatriot René **Descartes** and also of **Lucretius,** published *A New Treatise Proving a Multiplicity of Worlds* (1658). Although scientifically naive in parts, it was among the first of a wave of seventeenth-century books enthusiastically endorsing **pluralism** and "aerial navigation" as "the way whereby one can learn the pure truth concerning the plurality of worlds." A like-minded contemporary of his was Savinien **Cyrano de Bergerac.**

Boscovich, Ruggiero Giuseppe (1711–87)

Croatian-born Jesuit scientist, philosopher, and poet who, for much of his life, taught at the Collegium Romanum and the University of Padua. In his *De lunae atmospheraera* (1753), he presented evidence that the Moon has, at best, only a thin atmosphere. Yet for the most part he was a strong supporter of **pluralism.** In his *Philosophiae naturalis theoria* (1758), he speculated without restraint on the possibility of other universes that may occupy different orders of space and time from our own. His position in the pluralist debate contrasts sharply with that of a contemporary theologian in Italy, Giovanni Cadonici.

Bracewell probes

Hypothetical automated spacecraft sent out by advanced technological races with the object of making contact and exchanging information with other intelligent beings in the Galaxy. They are named after Ronald **Bracewell,** who first discussed their possibility in 1960.[72] Bracewell argued that interstellar "messenger probes," as he called them, offered an attractive alternative to the conventional **SETI** approach of listening for extraterrestrial signals and, if successful, engaging in a slow dialogue across many light-years.

As originally conceived, Bracewell probes, powered by high-speed propulsion units for **interstellar travel** and autonomously controlled by computers with a high degree of **artificial intelligence,** would be dispatched toward star systems that had been earmarked as biologically interesting. Upon arrival at a target star, a Bracewell probe would enter a near-circular orbit in the middle of the star's **habitable zone** and in the same plane as its

planetary system. This would ideally place it to make contact with any intelligent, technological residents. Having powered up its instruments, using light harvested from the host star, it would scan for **narrowband** radio transmissions indicative of an artificial origin. If any were found, it would record them, identify their source, and broadcast their contents back unaltered in order to draw attention to itself. This would allow the existence and location of the probe to be established and a subsequent dialogue to be conducted.

The use of messenger probes, Bracewell pointed out, offers a number of advantages over the strategy of searching for interstellar signals and subsequently trying to carry out a remote conversation (➔ **CETI**). A probe *in situ* could deliver a far more powerful signal to target worlds than could a transmitter positioned many light-years away, so that its chance of being noticed would be that much greater. It would also not have to rely on potential recipients continuously monitoring a large number of stars. If necessary, it could bide its time while a species evolved to roughly the stage we are at now (➔ **sentinel hypothesis**). If its ploy of echoing local radio transmissions were not immediately successful, it could try beaming a message of its own across a wider frequency range. Once it had established contact, its other great strength would come into play; that is, the conversation with the contact race could be carried out virtually in real time. Using its onboard intelligence and memory store, the probe could pass on a vast amount of information about its origins and the civilization that had sent it, without the need to wait many years for an exchange of greetings across the interstellar void. If it were large enough, it could even carry artifacts, including gifts, devices, and objets d'art.

Preliminary telescopic searches for Bracewell probes were carried out at **Kitt Peak National Observatory** and **Leuschner Observatory.** Among the sites regarded as most promising for scrutiny are the Earth-Moon **Lagrangian points** and other similar stable orbital regions in the solar system. These locations are analogous to favored radio frequencies in traditional SETI, such as the **21-centimeter line** and the **waterhole.** In 1974, Duncan **Lunan** hypothesized that a Bracewell probe was responsible for long-delay echoes first reported in the 1920s.

Civilizations like ours that have learned how to carry out interplanetary missions may quickly go on to acquire the ability to launch artificially intelligent robot spacecraft to nearby stars at reasonable speeds. Indeed, since Bracewell first suggested the idea of messenger probes, rapid progress has been made in a number of relevant technological fields, including robotics, information storage, and spacecraft propulsion. These developments are bringing closer the time when we may be able to send out Bracewell probes of our own, a subject dealt with fictionally by Michael McCollum in his *LifeProbe*[390] (1983).

More recently, Bracewell has suggested that it would be sufficient merely for a messenger probe to pass *through* a planetary system to achieve its goals (as in the case of Project **Daedalus**). Without the need for retrorockets, such a probe could be made smaller and at much lower cost. Our contribution to the success of attempts by alien races to establish contact in this way might be to construct a sophisticated space watch system, possibly an extension of one designed to search for **Near-Earth Object**s.

Bracewell, Ronald Newbold (1921–)
Australian physicist and electrical engineer, born in Sydney, who designed and developed microwave radar equipment in Australia during and immediately after World War II. From 1954 to 1955, he lectured on radio astronomy at the **University of California, Berkeley.** Since 1955, he has been on the Electrical Engineering Faculty of Stanford University and is now professor emeritus.[575] In his book *The Galactic Club*,[74] he gives an account of how he became involved in speculations about life in space in the post-*Sputnik* era:

I recall discussing the Cocconi-Morrison article [➔ **Morrison-Cocconi Conjecture**] with Stanford colleagues in 1959 and developing a number of ideas.... Looking back...I realize the odd coincidence that in 1954–55, when I was lecturing at Berkeley, two people were there who also became key figures in the new developments.... I believe that my association

with Otto Struve [who had invited Bracewell to come from Australia] and Su-Shu Huang...must have prepared my mind for the subject of life in space. [➔ **Struve, Otto; Huang, Su-Shu**]

Bracewell's name is associated with the robot spacecraft (➔ **Bracewell probes**) he proposed might be sent out by advanced civilizations to establish contact with other races in the Galaxy. In 1978, he showed how an **optical interferometer** consisting of two 1-m telescopes separated by 20 m could be used to search for large **extrasolar planets** by a method now known as **nulling interferometry.**[75] In 1995, he was among two dozen scientists selected by NASA to investigate various approaches to planet searching using interferometers in space (➔ *Space Interferometry Mission*).

Bradbury, Ray(mond) (Douglas) (1920–)
American science fiction writer among whose novels with a strong extraterrestrial theme was *The Martian Chronicles*[76] (1950), originally published in the 1940s as a set of linked magazine stories. As a boy, Bradbury had been one of the millions who had hung on every word of the adventures of John Carter in the Mars books of Edgar Rice **Burroughs.** *Chronicles* is set against a similar Percival **Lowell**–inspired backdrop, but Bradbury explores the nature and psychology of its aliens more seriously.

Brewster, David (1781–1868)
Scottish physicist and elder of the Free Church who was the staunchest opponent of the antipluralist views expressed by William **Whewell.** Brewster was a close friend of Thomas **Chalmers** and shared his views on the ubiquity of life in the universe grounded in **natural theology.** His review of Whewell's *Of the Plurality of Worlds: An Essay* is extraordinarily hostile, containing phrases such as "too ridiculous even for a writer of romance" and "utterly inept and illogical." Brewster's own book, *More Worlds than One: The Creed of the Philosopher and the Hope of the Christian*[80] (1854), which was read even more widely than Whewell's *Essay*, argued for an uncompromising brand of **pluralism** designed to reveal the

cosmic glory of God and his works. He maintained that every star has a planetary system like our own, every planet has life, and even the Sun and Moon are inhabited.

bright nebula
Alternative name for an **emission nebula** or a **reflection nebula.** ➔ **nebula**

brightest stars
➔ **stars, brightest**

British Interplanetary Society (BIS)
An organization of several thousand members formed in 1933 to promote the exploration and utilization of space. In the 1930s, the BIS came up with plans for a manned lunar spacecraft, three decades before *Apollo*. In the late 1970s, it prepared a detailed design for a robot star probe, Project Daedalus, to explore the system of **Barnard's Star.** It publishes the monthly magazine *Spaceflight* and a technical periodical, *Journal of the British Interplanetary Society.*

brown dwarf
A substellar object that may be defined in one of two principal ways: by its mass or by its origin. The former is normally used for practical purposes, since it is easier to measure an object's mass than to establish how it was made. The upper mass of a brown dwarf is that which is just insufficient for normal hydrogen **fusion** to be triggered in the core. Based on theoretical considerations, this is believed to be about

0.084 M_S, or about eighty-four times the mass of Jupiter (M_J). The lower mass limit is somewhat arbitrary, as there is no obvious point of transition between a high-mass planet and a low-mass brown dwarf, but it is generally taken to be about 0.013 M_S or about 13 M_J.[509] Some astronomers argue that a more significant distinction between planets and brown dwarfs is their mode of formation. By this criterion, brown dwarfs are held to form in the same way as stars, as condensations in an interstellar gas cloud. Planets, by contrast, accrete from material in a circumstellar disk (➔ **planetary systems, formation of**).

Brown dwarfs give off substantial amounts of **infrared** radiation as a result of slow gravitational contraction and small-scale **deuterium** fusion. The more massive a brown dwarf, the higher its surface temperature, though a typical value is about 1,000 K. True stars, by contrast, have surface temperatures of 2,500 K or more. The spectroscopically determined presence of lithium (which is eventually consumed by fusion reactions in bona fide stars) and **methane** (which cannot survive at temperatures much over 1,200 K) are strong indicators that an object is a brown dwarf. The first brown dwarf to be confirmed on the basis of a combination of mass determination, spectroscopic studies, and direct imaging was **Gliese 229B.** Half a dozen more are suspected because of their methane spectra. A number of other strong candidates await confirmation (see table below), while some objects, such as

SOME BROWN DWARF CANDIDATES

Host Star	Spectral Type	Distance (light-years)	Mass (Jupiter = 1)	Semimajor Axis (AU)	Period	Eccentricity
HD 110833	K3 V	~56	17	~0.8	270.04 days	0.69
BD-04 782	K5 V	—	21	~0.7	240.92 days	0.28
HD 112758	K0 V	~54	35	~0.35	103.22 days	0.16
HD 98230	F8.5 V	—	37	~0.06	3.8 days	0.00
HD 18445	K2 V	—	39	~0.9	554.17 days	0.54
HD 29587	G2 V	~148	40	~2.5	3.17 years	0.37
Gliese 229	M1 V	19	~40	~40	~200 years	—
HD 140913	G0 V	—	46	~0.54	147.94 days	0.61
HD 283750	K2 V	~54	50	~0.04	1.79 days	0.02
HD 89707	G1 V	~82	54	—	198.25 days	0.95
HD 217580	K4 V	~59	60	~1	454.66 days	0.52

the companion of **HD 114762,** lie close to the borderline between massive planets and low-mass brown dwarfs. Determining the precise mass of companion objects, however, is not easy. The most successful technique currently used to search for invisible companions, including both extrasolar planets and brown dwarfs—the **radial velocity method**—provides only a lower mass limit. To circumvent this problem, Michel **Mayor** and colleagues used a combination of radial velocity measurements and **astrometric observations** by the *Hipparcos* satellite of ten brown dwarf candidates. They concluded that most of the candidates orbit in planes that are nearly at right angles to our line of sight and are therefore much more massive than previously thought. If they are correct, a substantial fraction of suspected brown dwarfs may, in fact, be low-mass stars powered in the conventional way by hydrogen fusion. Mayor's work suggests that there may be relatively few objects in the range 5 to 50 M_S and thus a fairly clear distinction between brown dwarfs and planets. A similar claim was made in July 1998 by Tsevi Mazeh and Dorit Goldberg of Tel Aviv University and David Latham of the **Harvard-Smithsonian Center for Astrophysics.** Other astronomers, however, are not convinced by these analyses and argue that there is more likely to be an unbroken continuum in mass between heavyweight planets and lightweight brown dwarfs. The recently found methane dwarfs, which are free-floating, suggest that brown dwarfs can form in isolation and may outnumber true stars.

The name "brown dwarf" was coined in the 1970s by astronomer Jill **Tarter.** There have been suggestions that these objects could support life (➜ **brown dwarfs, life on**).

brown dwarfs, life on

The possibility that low-mass **brown dwarf**s may contain liquid water suggests that they may also be capable of supporting some kind of life, an idea first put forward by Harlow **Shapley.**[534] Conceivably, organisms might evolve to be able to exploit the deep **infrared** radiation given off by such an object, both for **photosynthesis** and perception, the latter through eyes equipped for infrared vision or

thermal sensors like those of snakes. Wrote Shapley:

> The imagination boggles at the possibilities of self-heating planets that do not depend, as we do, on the inefficient process of getting our warmth through radiation from a hot source, the sun, millions of miles away. What a strange biology might develop in the absence of the violet-to-red radiation!

One problem would be the high gravity—100 times stronger than on Earth. However, considering the ability of ants, for example, to lift around 160 times their own body weight, it is not out of the question that life could evolve under gravitationally extreme conditions (➜ **gravitational life**).

Brown, Harrison (Scott) (1917–86)

Geochemist at the California Institute of Technology who in the 1960s supported the claim, made by Peter **van der Kamp** and others, that extrasolar planets were common. By extending the **luminosity function** to low masses, he concluded[82] that

> planetary systems are far more abundant than we have so far suspected. Virtually every main sequence star should have a planetary system associated with it.

Brown is also among the scientists who have used science fiction to express their more daring speculations. In 1968, he published (with Chloë Zerwick) *The Cassiopeia Affair*,[83] which, like Fred **Hoyle**'s *A for Andromeda* (1962) and James E. Gunn's *The Listeners* (1972), explored the consequences of radio contact with intelligent extraterrestrials.

Bruno, Giordano (1548–1600)

Scholastic philosopher and lapsed Dominican monk who had a dangerous passion for unorthodox cosmological beliefs. In his books, such as *De l'Infinito universo e mondi* (On the Infinite Universe and Worlds), published in 1584, he expounds the doctrine of **pluralism** without restraint:

Innumerable suns exist; innumerable Earths revolve about these suns.... Living beings inhabit these worlds.

Drawing upon such sources as **Lucretius, Nicholas of Cusa,** and Nicolaus **Copernicus,** he went further than any of these and not only populated planets and stars, including all the other worlds of the solar system, but also attributed souls to every object in the heavens and even to the Universe as a whole. Contrary to later popular belief, he was not burned at the stake in Rome principally for his cosmological views but rather for his denial of Christ's divinity. Even so, his fate served, temporarily at least, to limit the speculative inclinations of others.

Büchner, Ludwig (1824–99)

German materialist philosopher who, in his *Kraft und Stoff* (1855), attacked the **teleology** inherent in pluralistic views of the universe based on **natural theology.** He pointed out that there are many examples of phenomena surplus to the requirements of life, such as the Sun "constantly squandering uselessly huge quantities of light and heat in the cold realms of space" and also shining "during those untold of ages of the past in which no creature existed . . . to turn these glorious arrangements to account."

Buffon, Georges-Louis Leclerc, Comte de (1707–88)

Foremost biologist of seventeenth-century France, the opening volume of whose forty-four-volume *Histoire naturelle* (1749–1804) contains his **cometary collision hypothesis** of the origin of the Sun's planetary system. In the 1775 *Supplément,* he argues that terrestrial-type life occurs on every world where the temperature is the same as on present-day Earth. This leads him to compute the times and durations for which the various planets and moons of the solar system have been, are, or will be habitable, based on the assumption that most of their heat is internal rather than derived from the Sun. According to his calculations, Mars is already dead, Earth has 93,291 life-sustaining years left, while Jupiter

has not yet cooled to the point at which life can begin.

Buridan, Jean (c. 1295–1358)

French scholastic philosopher, Oxford contemporary of William of **Ockham,** and rector of the University of Paris who, in commenting on **Aristotle**'s *De Caelo,* argued that

it must be realized that while another world than this is not possible naturally, this is possible simply speaking, since we hold from faith that just as God made this world, so he could have made several worlds.

Buridan was among the university intellectuals struggling to embrace Aristotelian doctrine within the teachings of the Christian Church. To this end, he suggested that God *could,* in principle, have created other worlds in each of which the four classical elements of earth, air, fire, and water would have ordered themselves according to Aristotle's scheme. His ideas were taken further by Ockham and Nicole d'**Oresme.** ➔ **medieval philosophy, related to the possibility of extraterrestrial life**

Burroughs, Edgar Rice (1875–1950)

American popular fiction writer, best remembered as the creator of Tarzan, who also wrote a series of adventure stories set on Mars (known to its natives as "Barsoom"). Published between 1917 and 1948, these ten novels, among the best of which were *A Princess of Mars* (1917), *The Chessmen of Mars* (1922), and *Swords of Mars* (1936), saw hero John Carter encountering a variety of alien-looking but human-acting creatures on a world extrapolated from the Mars of Percival **Lowell.** Though lightweight in content and superficial in their portrayal of alien life and intelligence, they nevertheless had a lasting effect on those who read them in their formative years, including, by their own acknowledgment, Ronald **Bracewell,** Ray **Bradbury,** Arthur C. **Clarke,** and Carl **Sagan.** Moreover, they helped entrench the popular notion, especially in the United States, that Mars was still a place of mystery and possibly the abode of beings more advanced than ourselves. It was, after all, during the time when Burroughs wrote his Martian adventures that *The War of the Worlds* **radio play** triggered such mass panic across America. ➔ **science fiction involving extraterrestrials, 1900–1940**

Burton, Charles E. (1846–82)

Irish astronomer who, in 1880, was among the first to provide observational support for Giovanni **Schiaparelli**'s claims of linear markings on the Martian surface. By May 1882, however, a few months before his death, his confidence in the reality of the canals had waned: "I strongly incline to the opinion expressed by Messrs. Green and Maunder, that they are boundaries of differently tinted districts." ➔ **Mars, canals of**

Bussard, Robert W.

American physicist who, in 1960, while working for the TRW Corporation of Los Angeles, suggested a form of interstellar propulsion based on the principle of the ramjet.[87] ➔ **interstellar travel**

Butler, R. Paul

Astronomer, currently with the Department of Terrestrial Magnetism at the Carnegie Institution, Washington, D.C., who, together with Geoffrey **Marcy** and other colleagues, has been involved with the discovery of well over half the presently known **extrasolar planet**s. He was previously a staff astronomer at the **Anglo-Australian Observatory** (1997–99) engaged in the **Anglo-Australian Planet Search,** a research scientist at San Francisco State University (1993–97) engaged in the **San Francisco State University Planet Search,** and a visiting fellow at the **University of California, Berkeley.**

Byurakan Astrophysical Observatory

A facility of the Armenian Academy of Sciences, founded in 1946 through the efforts of Viktor **Ambartsumian.** Located at an altitude of 1,500 m (5,000 ft.) on Mount Aragatz, 40 km (25 miles) to the north of Yerevan (in sight of Mount Ararat), its main instrument is a 2.6-m (100-in.) reflector.

Byurakan SETI conferences (1964 and 1971)

Two important early meetings on the subject of **SETI** held at the **Byurakan Astrophysical Observatory.** The 1964 Conference on Extraterrestrial Civilizations stemmed from discussions by Iosif **Shklovskii**'s group at the **Sternberg State Astronomical Institute** and was organized by Nikolai **Kardashev.** Held three years after the seminal **Green Bank conference (1961),** it was attended entirely by radio astronomers and had as its aim "to obtain rational technical and linguistic solutions for the problem of communication with extraterrestrial civilizations which are much more advanced than the Earth civilization." The emphasis on (1) communication, and (2) the broadcasting of powerful signals by highly advanced intelligence from great distances (possibly even extragalactic), was in contrast to the greater attention paid in the United States to searching for messages from nearby stars and civilizations more on a par with our own. The Soviet approach was typified by Kardashev's classification scheme for technological races (➔ **Kardashev civilizations**) and Vsevolod **Troitskii**'s interest in the possibility of detecting signals from other galaxies.[589]

The 1971 Byurakan conference was the first international SETI meeting and was sponsored by the Academies of Sciences of both the Soviet Union and the United States. Viktor **Ambartsumian,** Kardashev, Shklovskii, and Troitskii carried out the organization on the Soviet side, while Frank **Drake,** Philip **Morrison,** and Carl **Sagan** performed the same function on the American side. Participants included twenty-eight Soviets, fifteen Americans, and four scientists from other nations. Radio search methods, techniques and consequences of contact, message content, and extraterrestrial astroengineering were among the topics discussed. A tentative conclusion of the conference was that there might be a million technical civilizations in the Galaxy, although it was recognized that the **Drake Equation** gave a subjective rather than an objective probability.[193]

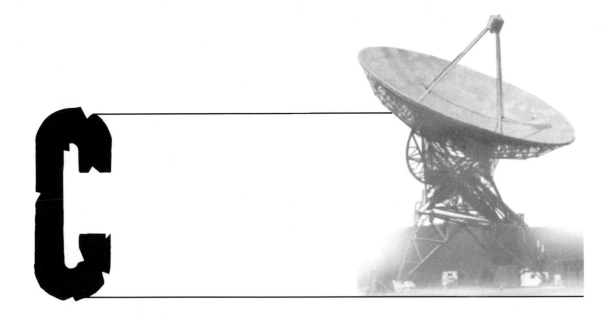

C

CAAO
→ **Center for Astronomical Adaptive Optics**

Cairns-Smith, A. Graham
Scottish chemist who in 1971 proposed a radically new theory of the origin of life on Earth[91] in which the first organisms were derived from clay. In his view, mineral life-forms, evolved from complex **prebiotic** clay crystals, and needing neither a **reducing atmosphere** nor a primordial soup, were the earliest inhabitants of the planet. Subsequently, a "genetic takeover" by **organic** molecules led to the **carbon**-based life that exists today. Many modern ideas concerning the formation of self-replicating molecules now invoke some kind of inorganic scaffolding, often referred to as a "naked gene" or "urgene."

calcium (Ca)
A soft, gray, metallic **element** that tarnishes rapidly on exposure to air. It occurs commonly on Earth (→ **elements, terrestrial abundance of**), in various forms of its **carbonate** ($CaCO_3$), e.g., chalk, limestone, and marble, and its sulfate ($CaSO_4$), e.g., gypsum. It is essential to terrestrial vertebrate life, being the basic constituent of bones and teeth (→ **elements, biological abundance of**).

Atomic number 20; density relative to water 1.55; melting point 840°C; boiling point 1,484°C

caldera
A large volcanic crater formed by the collapse of underground lava reservoirs.

Caliban (97U1)
A small, remote moon of **Uranus** that, together with **Sycorax,** is the faintest and most recently to have been discovered by a ground-based telescope. → **Uranus, moons of**

Discovery	1997 by B. J. Gladman, P. D. Nicolson, J. A. Burns, and J. J. Kavelaars
Mean distance from Uranus	7,165,000 km (4,453,000 mi.)
Diameter	~40 km
Orbital period	579.4 days
Orbital eccentricity	0.082
Orbital inclination	139.2°

Callisto
The second largest moon of **Jupiter** and the third largest in the solar system, after **Ganymede** and **Titan.** Orbiting beyond

Discovery	January 7, 1610, by Galileo Galilei
Mean distance from Jupiter	1,883,000 km (1,170,000 mi.)
Diameter	4,806 km (2,987 mi.)
Equatorial diameter (Earth = 1)	0.377
Mass (Earth = 1)	0.018
Mean density	1.86 g/cm³
Surface gravity (Earth = 1)	0.127
Escape velocity	2.43 km/s (8,743 km/h, 5,437 mi./h)
Orbital period	16.69 days (16 days 16 hours 34 minutes)
Orbital eccentricity	0.007
Orbital inclination	0.51°
Axial period	16.69 days
Albedo	0.17
Surface temperature	168 K
Surface composition	Dirty ice

Jupiter's main radiation belts, Callisto is the outermost of the **Galilean satellites.** It also has the lowest density of the Galilean satellites and probably a very different internal structure.

The interiors of the other three big Jovian moons are thought to be completely differentiated, with clear boundaries between core, mantle, and crust. This is probably due to gravitational squeezing by Jupiter, which helped keep the interior of the inner Galileans molten long enough for heavier materials to settle fully at the greater depths. Being further out, Callisto seems to have arrested early in its development, so that its internal rock is not fully segregated. Measurements by the *Galileo* spacecraft have, however, been interpreted by some researchers as pointing to the existence of a subterranean watery ocean on Callisto, of the kind hypothesized for **Europa** (➜ **Callisto, ocean and possible life on**).

Callisto's surface, the darkest of any of the Galilean moons (yet still twice as bright as our own moon), is the most heavily cratered of any object in the solar system, testifying to an almost complete absence of geological activity over the past 4 billion years. Indeed, Callisto is the only body greater than 1,000 km in diameter that shows no signs of having undergone any significant resurfacing since the end of the early bombardment phase of the solar system about

Galileo image of the Valhalla region of Callisto showing detail as small as 155 m (170 yards) across. A prominent fault scarp and numerous impact craters are visible.
NASA/JPL/Caltech

3.8 billion years ago. Its surface features are dominated by shallow impact craters and rings. Two large features, Valhalla and Asgard, which resemble bull's-eyes, are believed to be the remains of massive impacts. Seven chains of impact craters have been mapped and are thought to have been formed when **comets** were broken up by Jupiter's gravity and collided with Callisto. In February 1999, the discovery was announced, based on measurements taken by *Galileo*'s near-**infrared** mapping **spectrometer,** of **carbon dioxide** ice on Callisto's surface together with a very tenuous atmosphere of carbon dioxide. Since this gas must constantly leak into space under the action of **ultraviolet** rays from the Sun, it must be continuously replenished, possibly by venting of carbon dioxide from the interior. This discovery means that all four Galilean moons are now known to have thin atmospheres.[323]

Callisto, ocean and possible life on

The first indication that **Callisto** might be of astrobiological interest came in October 1998 with the publication of a paper proposing that Callisto, like **Europa,** might have an underground ocean of water and perhaps the basic ingredients for life. This suggestion followed from measurements of Callisto's magnetic field by the *Galileo* spacecraft. Krishnan Khurana of the University of California, Los Angeles, and colleagues found that Callisto's magnetic field fluctuates in time with Jupiter's rotation, suggesting that Jupiter's powerful magnetic field generates electric currents in the moon that, in turn, give rise to the fluctuations. In trying to understand how currents could flow within the body of Callisto, Khurana and colleagues hypothesized the existence of a subterranean ocean of salty water that would effectively act like a giant battery. This idea was given further credence by *Galileo* data, which showed that the electric currents within Callisto flow in different directions at different times.

Whereas Europa is heated internally both by tidal stresses *and* the decay of radioactive elements, Callisto is significantly heated only by the latter. Therefore, the outermost Galilean moon may not be quite as good a prospect in

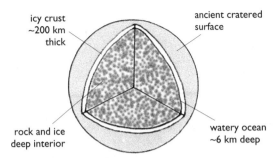

Hypothetical interior of Callisto.

the search for extraterrestrial life as its Jovian neighbor. Nevertheless, it seems certain now that future probes will scrutinize both Europa and Callisto for signs of subsurface water and prebiological or biological activity. One possibility is that if primitive life has evolved on these worlds, it may be similar to the **halophiles** found in highly saline environments on Earth. Plans to investigate the astrobiological potential of the Galilean moons have also been given a boost by the discovery of a large lake deep under the ice of Antarctica (→ **Vostok, Lake**) that may serve as a test bed for instrumentation.

Calvin cycle

The series of dark reactions of **photosynthesis.**

Calvin, Melvin (1911–97)

American biochemist at the **University of California, Berkeley,** who won the Nobel Prize for Chemistry in 1961 for his work on **photosynthesis.** Using carbon 14 as a tracer, Calvin and his team mapped the complete route that carbon takes through a plant. In doing so, he showed that sunlight acts on **chlorophyll** to fuel the manufacture of **organic** compounds, rather than on **carbon dioxide** as had been previously believed. In 1950, Calvin and his associates began pioneering experiments in **prebiotic evolution** by irradiating a solution of carbon dioxide and water vapor with **ionizing radiation** from a cyclotron. Simple organic chemicals, including formic acid and **formaldehyde,** were produced—though not **amino acids** as in the **Miller-Urey Experiment,** carried out three years later. Calvin's work on prebiotic evolution encouraged him to believe that such processes may have occurred elsewhere in the solar system and on many extrasolar worlds. In 1958, Calvin was appointed chairman of **Panel 2 on Extraterrestrial Life,** assembled to consider the problems of contamination by spacecraft. It was his opinion that

> We can assert with some degree of scientific confidence that cellular life as we know it on the surface of the Earth does exist in some millions of other sites in the universe.

During the formative stages of NASA's astrobiology program, Calvin became chairman of the Space Biology Committee, and in 1961 he was among the attendees at the first **SETI** conference, held at **Green Bank** in the aftermath of Project **Ozma.** In January 1960, he and Susan K. Vaughan announced that during their investigation of a sample of the **Murray meteorite,** they had found a number of organic molecules, including one that was chemically similar to **cytosine.** Calvin concluded that

> [A]s to whether or not there were possibly prebiotic forms out on astral bodies other than the earth, seems to be answered, at least tentatively, in the affirmative.

He received a B.S. from Michigan Technological University (1931) and a Ph.D. in chemistry from the University of Minnesota (1935). Following postdoctoral research at the University of Manchester, England, he joined the Chemistry Department at Berkeley in 1937. He was director of the Chemical Biodynamics Division of the Lawrence Berkeley Laboratory (1945–80) and director of UC Berkeley's Laboratory of Chemical Dynamics (1963–80).[93]

Calypso

A small moon of **Saturn.** Calypso and **Telesto** are referred to as the **Tethys** trojans because they move in the same orbit as Tethys, Calypso trailing the large moon by about 60° and

Discovery	1981, by Brad Smith and others from *Voyager 1* data
Mean distance from Saturn	294,700 km (183,200 mi.)
Diameter	34 × 22 × 22 km (21 × 14 × 14 mi.)
Orbital period	1.888 days (1 day 21 hours 19 minutes)
Orbital eccentricity	0.000
Orbital inclination	0.00°
Visual albedo	0.6

Telesto leading by the same angular separation. ➔ **Saturn, moons of**

Cameron, Alastair G. W.

Professor of astronomy at Harvard University and former chairman of the **Space Science Board.** In 1963, while at NASA's Institute for Space Studies, he edited an influential anthology on the subject of interstellar communication.[96] In the introduction, he writes:

> [T]here may be millions of societies more advanced than ourselves in our galaxy alone. If we can now take the next step and communicate with some of these societies, then we can expect to obtain an enormous enrichment of all phases of our sciences and arts. Perhaps we shall also receive valuable lessons in the techniques of stable world government.

Cameron's own research led him to dispute Otto **Struve**'s claim that stars that spin slowly, such as the Sun, do so because they have transferred **angular momentum** to a planetary system. Instead, Cameron proposed that virtually all single stars, irrespective of their rotational speed, have planets, and that loss of angular momentum occurs when young stars eject matter into space in the form of vigorous **stellar wind**s. His research today remains focused on the origin and development of planetary systems.

Campanella, Tommaso (1568–1639)

Italian poet and philosopher who wrote extensively in favor of **pluralism** following the telescopic discoveries of **Galileo.** His *Apologia pro Galileo* was the main source used by John **Wilkins** in *The Discovery of a World in the Moone.*

Campbell, John W(ood), Jr. (1910–71)

American science fiction author and editor with a physics degree from the Massachusetts Institute of Technology (1932) who speculated imaginatively on the physical diversity that extraterrestrials might possess (➔ **extraterrestrial life, variety of**). His acclaimed novella "Who Goes There?" (1938) features a shape-shifting alien, unfrozen after 20 million years, that assumes the forms of its human victims at an Antarctic research station. The story was filmed as *The Thing* (1951), but without the shape shifting, and then in a remake (1982) that was truer to the original plot. Chronologically, "Who Goes There?" stood more or less midway between two other memorable monster-alien tales, *The War of the Worlds* and *Alien.* As the editor of *Astounding Science Fiction,* Campbell was a key figure in the so-called golden age of science fiction, bringing to public attention, through his impressive stable of writers, a menagerie of strange extraterrestrial forms and demanding of his authors a close attention to contemporary astronomical knowledge.

Campbell, William Wallace (1862–1938)

American astronomer at **Lick Observatory** (which he joined in 1891 and of which he served as director from 1901 to 1930) whose **spectroscopic** observations of Mars played a major role in undermining the hypothesis of Martian canals (➔ **Mars, canals of**) and advanced Martian life (➔ **Mars, life on**). Previous studies by William **Huggins** (1867), Jules Janssen (1867), Pietro **Secchi** (1870s), Hermann Vogel (1873), and Edward **Maunder** (1892) had all come out in favor of water vapor in the Martian atmosphere. However, working with "improved spectroscopic apparatus" at Lick in the summer of 1894, Campbell found no trace of water vapor on Mars. Later that year he wrote a paper arguing that Mars might have a much thinner atmosphere than was generally supposed. In support of this view, he cited Robert **Ball**'s 1892 discussion of George

Stoney's kinetic theory of planetary atmospheres, according to which Mars should have lost most of any atmosphere it had once had. He also pointed to the brightness of the polar caps, a fact that was difficult to account for if the reflected sunlight had to pass twice through a relatively dense layer of gases. As to the belief that there were sizable bodies of water on Mars, Campbell noted that Johann **Zöllner**'s measurement of the Martian **albedo** could easily be reconciled with the presence of dark and light regions of dry land. Although Campbell's claims about a thin, dry Martian atmosphere were criticized at the time, they became crucial in the first decade of the twentieth century when combined with the arguments presented by Simon **Newcomb,** Maunder, and others that the canals were illusory. ➔ **Aitken, Robert Grant**

canali

A term first used by Pietro **Secchi** and later adopted by Giovanni **Schiaparelli** and others to describe certain features claimed to have been observed on the surface of **Mars.** *Canali* can be correctly translated from the Italian as either "channels" or "canals." Schiaparelli generally intended and preferred the former and, indeed, often used an alternative description, *fiumi* (rivers) for the same features. Almost inevitably, however, *canali* was usually translated into English as "canals," implying an artificial origin. ➔ **Mars, canals of**

canals, Martian
➔ **Mars, canals of**

cannibalism, interstellar
➔ **CETI, opposition to**

Capella

Alpha Aurigae; a bright yellow **G star.** Close examination reveals it to be a **spectroscopic binary,** composed of two yellow **giant star**s of **spectral type**s G0 and G8, each about thirty times bigger than the Sun, revolving around each other with a **period** of 104 days. ➔ **stars, brightest**

capture area

The total surface area of a telescope or **interferometer** upon which radiation falls.

captured atmosphere

An atmosphere acquired during the **accretion** of a planet and subsequently retained. The atmospheres of **gas giant**s are of this type.

captured rotation

➔ **gravitational lock**

carbohydrate

An **organic** compound consisting of a chain or ring of **carbon** atoms to which **hydrogen** and **oxygen** atoms are attached in the ratio of approximately 2 to 1. The general formula of carbohydrates is $C_x(H_2O)_y$. They include **monosaccharides** and **disaccharides** (both **sugars**), and **polysaccharides** (important varieties of which are **starch, glycogen,** and **cellulose**). They play an essential role in the **metabolism** of all terrestrial organisms and, in the case of cellulose, the structure of **plants.** Fred **Hoyle** and Chandra Wickramasinghe have made the controversial claim that some features of the spectra of **interstellar cloud**s may indicate the presence of carbohydrates in space. If verified, this would have important implications for the origin of life.

carbon (C)

The fourth most common **element** in the universe (➔ **elements, cosmic abundance of**) and the basis of all terrestrial life (➔ **elements, biological abundance of**). Carbon's biological importance stems primarily from its unique ability to (1) link together to form long chains of atoms and (2) form complex molecules with **oxygen** and **nitrogen** that are neither unstable nor too stable to prevent reactions with other molecules. This latter ability, in turn, derives from the fact that oxygen and nitrogen atoms can share more than one electron with a carbon atom. The resulting double or triple bonds are strong enough to hold long molecules together yet, under the right chemical conditions or given the appropriate **enzyme,** can easily be induced to break, leading to further reactions.

The fact that the three most important bio-

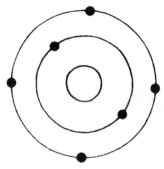

Carbon atom

logical elements, together with **hydrogen,** also happen to be the most common chemically active elements in the universe (helium being inert) is both surprising and remarkable. There appears to be no reason a priori why these elements should be so well suited to producing life as we know it. Indeed, if their chemical properties were somewhat different they would probably be biologically useless—as most elements are except in specific circumstances (for example, iron in hemoglobin). Equally remarkable is the fact that carbon is manufactured inside the core of evolved stars by a process that involves either a fortuitous coincidence or a piece of cosmic tuning. In this process, two **helium** nuclei come together to make a nucleus of beryllium, which then has to capture a further helium nucleus to complete the synthesis of carbon. However, when the astrophysicist Fred **Hoyle** first looked closely at this reaction in the 1950s, he realized that there was a problem. According to what was then known, the capture of a helium nucleus by a beryllium nucleus was far too improbable to account for the observed cosmic abundance of carbon. He reasoned that the only way enough carbon could be made was if there existed a very specific match of nuclear energy levels, or resonance, between helium, beryllium, and carbon under precisely the conditions thought to prevail in the cores of stars at this stage in their evolution. Experiments promptly confirmed Hoyle's deduction—there was indeed a previously unsuspected resonance, very close to the energy value he gave. Crucially, for carbon-based life-forms, there is not a similar resonance at the same energy among carbon, helium, and oxygen. If there were, a large part of the carbon inside stars would quickly be changed into oxygen, and life as we know it would be impossible. These happy coincidences are cited by those who argue in favor of the **anthropic principle,** although Hoyle himself has put forward a more extreme interpretation:

> If you wanted to produce carbon and oxygen in roughly equal quantities by stellar nucleosynthesis, these are the two basic levels you would have to fix, and your fixing would have to be just about where these levels are actually found to be.... A commonsense interpretation of the facts suggests that a superintellect has monkeyed with physics...and that there are no blind forces worth speaking about in nature.

Given the unique ease with which carbon forms long, complex chains and rings, it is difficult (though not impossible) to imagine life with a different chemical basis such as **silicon.**

Atomic number 6; density relative to water 2.25 (graphite), 3.52 (diamond); melting point 3,550°C; boiling point 4,289°C

carbon dioxide (CO$_2$)
A minor component of the Earth's atmosphere (0.03 percent by volume) but one that is essential to life (→ **Earth, atmosphere of**). It is taken in by plants during **photosynthesis** and produced by animal respiration. The building of an organism requires a way of making **organic** molecules from carbon dioxide. This is achieved during the **Calvin cycle** of photosynthesis in green plants. By means of this cycle, plants incorporate carbon dioxide into **sugars,** which form the basis of all the organic molecules synthesized by **cell**s. Carbon dioxide is also an important **greenhouse gas.**

Density (at 0°C) 1.98 g/dm^3; melting point −56.6°C; boiling point −78.5°C

carbon fixation
The conversion of **carbon dioxide** into **organic** compounds during **photosynthesis.** It represents the first stage of the dark reactions of photosynthesis, in which carbon dioxide from the air is combined with ribulose 1,5-biophosphate. → **Calvin cycle**

carbon monoxide (CO)
A colorless, odorless gas.

Density (at 0°C) 1.25 g/dm^3; melting point −199°C; boiling point −191.5°C

carbon star
A **red giant** that has more **carbon** than **oxygen** in its atmosphere. In such a star, the oxygen in the outer layers is combined in the form of **carbon monoxide.** The excess carbon forms grains, which are a component of **cosmic dust.**

carbonaceous chondrite
A rare type of **stony meteorite** that contains large amounts of the magnesium-rich minerals

SOME WELL-KNOWN CARBONACEOUS METEORITES		
Locality	*Date of Fall*	*Mass Recovered (kg)*
Alais, France	March 15, 1806	6
Cold Bokkeveld, South Africa	October 13, 1838	3
Kaba, Hungary	April 15, 1857	3
Orgueil, France	May 14, 1864	12
Nogoya, Argentina	June 30, 1879	4
Mighei, Russia	June 18, 1889	8
Indarch, Russia	April 7, 1891	27
Mokoia, New Zealand	November 26, 1908	4
Haripura, India	January 17, 1921	0.5
Ivuna, Tanzania	December 16, 1938	0.7
Murray, Kentucky, U.S.A.	September 20, 1950	12.6
Allende, Mexico	February 8, 1969	>2,000

olivine and serpentine and a variety of **organic** compounds, including **amino acids.** Although fewer than one hundred carbonaceous chondrites are known, they provide a great deal of information about the origin of the Sun and planets, and even of life itself (➔ **organic matter, in meteorites**).

One of the more outlandish proposals concerning these objects came from Leslie C. Edie of Bellmore, Long Island. In the April 13, 1962, issue of *Science*,[177] he suggested that the long-chain molecules within carbonaceous chondrites might represent encoded information put there by an extraterrestrial civilization. The meteorites were then hurled out into space in the hope that they would eventually be found by another race. (➔ **genome, interstellar transmission of**)

carbonate

A salt of carbonic acid (H_2CO_3) containing the carbonate **ion** (CO_3^{2-}). A common example is calcium carbonate ($CaCO_3$), which occurs as limestone.[41]

carbon-nitrogen cycle

A cycle of six consecutive nuclear reactions resulting in the formation of a **helium nucleus** from four **proton**s. The **carbon** nuclei with which the cycle starts are effectively re-formed at the end and therefore act as a catalyst. This is believed to be the predominant energy-producing mechanism in stars with a core temperature exceeding about 15 million°C.

carboxyl group (–COOH)

A chemical group found in all **carboxylic acids.** It consists of a **carbon** atom joined by **covalent bond**s to two **oxygen** atoms, one of which in turn is covalently bonded to a **hydrogen** atom. One **valence electron** on the carbon is available for bonding to another atom so that the carboxyl group can form part of a larger molecule.

carboxylic acids

Organic compounds that contain one or more **carboxyl group**s. They are generally weak **acid**s. Examples include **amino acids** (the subunits of **proteins**), **nucleic acid**s, and complex **lipids.**

Carme

The fourteenth known moon of **Jupiter.** It is one of the group of four outer Jovian moons that exhibit **retrograde** motion and must therefore be captured asteroids. ➔ **Jupiter, moons of**

Discovery	1938, by Seth Barnes Nicholson
Mean distance from Jupiter	22,350,000 km (13,890,000 mi.)
Diameter	40 km (25 mi.)
Mean density	2.8 g/cm³
Escape velocity	0.025 km/s (90 km/h, 56 mi./h)
Orbital period	−692 days (retrograde)
Orbital eccentricity	0.207
Orbital inclination	163°

carotenoids

Pigments used by plants, in addition to **chlorophyll,** as light-harvesting chemicals in **photosynthesis.** They consist of **hydrocarbon**s made up of **carbon** rings attached to chains with alternating single and double **covalent bond**s. Carotenoids are able to absorb light across a wide **frequency** range.

carrier wave

An electromagnetic wave of a specific **frequency** and **amplitude** that is broadcast by a radio **transmitter** in order to convey information.

Carter, Jimmy (James Earl) (1924–   )

In 1973, while governor of Georgia, Carter reported seeing an **unidentified flying object** that later analysis revealed was almost certainly the planet Venus. His interest in the phenomena continued into his presidential years. In 1977, while he was in office, a call went out from the White House for the establishment of a new agency (never subsequently formed) to take up the investigation of UFOs where the U.S. Air Force had left off six years earlier.

Cascade Mountains

A range extending over 1,120 km (700 mi.) in the northwest United States from northern California through Oregon and Washington to British Columbia. Its highest peaks are Mount Rainier (4,392 m, 14,409 ft.), Mount Adams (1,742 m, 12,277 ft.), Mount Baker (3,285 m,

10,777 ft.), and Mount Hood (3,424 m, 11,233 ft.). The region is tectonically active—a fact spectacularly demonstrated by the 1980 eruption of Mount Saint Helens—and riven by faults. The phenomenon known as **earthlights,** believed to be associated with faults, has been seen close to the location where Kenneth **Arnold** reported the first "**flying saucers**" in 1947, suggesting a possible link.

Cassini, Giovanni Domenico (1625–1712)

Italian-born French astronomer who became professor of astronomy at the University of Bologna in 1650 and later the first director of the **Paris Observatory.** In 1666, he identified one of the polar caps on Mars. He derived the **axial period**s of Jupiter and Mars and discovered four satellites of Saturn and the dark division (now named after him) in Saturn's rings.

Cassini (spacecraft)

A **Saturn** probe, built jointly by **NASA** and the **European Space Agency,** that was launched on October 13, 1997. The 5,650-kg (12,450-lb.) spacecraft will go into orbit around Saturn in June 2004 after a **gravity-assist**ed journey that will take it twice around Venus and once each around the Earth and Jupiter. Upon arrival, *Cassini* will engage in a series of complex orbital maneuvers in order to achieve its major scientific goals, which include observing Saturn's near-polar atmosphere and magnetic field from high inclination orbits, several close flybys of the icy satellites **Mimas, Enceladus, Dione, Rhea,** and **Iapetus,** and multiple flybys of Saturn's large, enigmatic moon **Titan.** The climax of the mission will be the release of the *Huygens* **probe** and its descent into Titan's atmosphere.

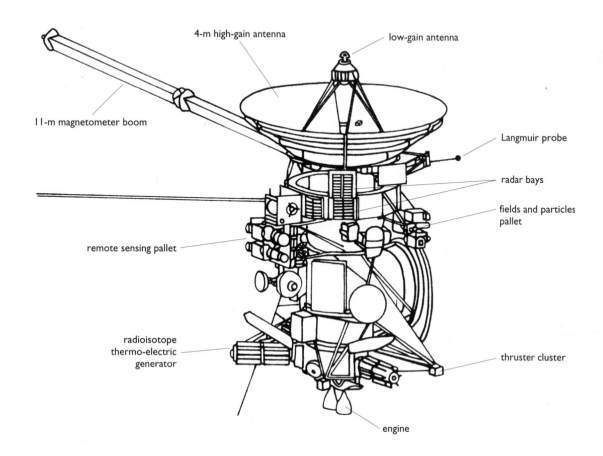

4-m high-gain antenna

low-gain antenna

11-m magnetometer boom

Langmuir probe

radar bays

fields and particles pallet

remote sensing pallet

radioisotope thermo-electric generator

thruster cluster

engine

Castor

Alpha Geminorum; a **multiple star** system with six components. Two binary pairs orbit around the center of mass of the system with a period of about 500 years, while a pair of **red dwarf**s orbit around the center of mass at a distance sixteen times greater than the distance between the main components. ➔ **stars, brightest**

catabolism

That part of **metabolism** concerned with the breakdown of complex substances into simple ones and the consequent release of energy. Its converse is **anabolism.**

catalysis

The action of a **catalyst.**

catalyst

A substance that alters the rate of a chemical reaction but is itself unchanged at the end of the reaction. Biological catalysts are known as **enzyme**s.

catastrophic hypothesis

The now-defunct idea that the planets and smaller bodies of the solar system originated in a violent event involving a collision or near collision between the Sun and another object. On and off, it played an important role in the extraterrestrial life debate from the second half of the eighteenth century to the first half of the twentieth century, since it implied that **extrasolar planets** might be very scarce.

The earliest version of it was the **cometary collision hypothesis** of Georges **Buffon** (1749), but this was largely ignored in favor of the **nebular hypothesis,** proposed by Immanuel **Kant** and Pierre **Laplace.** Theoretical difficulties with the nebular hypothesis, however, led to various revivals of the catastrophic hypothesis. The first of these was due to Alexander **Bickerton** in 1880. Realizing that nothing less than a stellar-sized intruder could have dislodged substantial amounts of solar matter, Bickerton proposed that the Sun had suffered a grazing impact with another star and that this had drawn out a tongue of hot gas from which the planets had subsequently coalesced. He suggested that so-called spiral nebulas (now known to be external galaxies) were products of similar encounters. However, Bickerton's scheme could not explain the large amount of **angular momentum** possessed by the giant outer planets.

Further technical difficulties with the nebular hypothesis at the turn of the twentieth century prompted other suggestions involving stellar encounters. The **Chamberlin-Moulton planetesimal hypothesis** appealed to a remote passage of a second star, while the **Jeans-Jeffreys tidal hypothesis** involved a close passage or (in the version due to Jeffreys) a grazing collision. Throughout the 1920s and 1930s, it was widely accepted that some version of the catastrophic hypothesis held the key to the origin of the solar system and consequently, because close stellar encounters must be very infrequent, that life in the Universe was exceptional. But then fatal cracks began to appear in this scenario. In 1939, Lyman Spitzer argued that hot gas sucked out of the Sun would dissipate into a thin cloud rather than condense to form solid planets. In 1943, Henry **Russell** pointed out that if material had been wrenched out of the Sun with sufficient momentum to explain the large amount of angular momentum possessed by planets such as Jupiter, this material would not have gone into orbit but would have escaped from the Sun's gravitational pull altogether. To address this objection, it was proposed that, before the planets were formed, the Sun might have been a component of a **binary star** system. If the encounter with a third passing star had occurred with the companion star already moving at the distance of the giant planets, any material removed from it would have had the necessary angular momentum from the outset. It was easy to show that such an encounter could also cause the companion to escape from the Sun forever. Later variants on this binary star theme included Fred **Hoyle**'s suggestion that the Sun's companion may have exploded as a **supernova,** throwing out debris from which the planets were made. All such ideas, however, have now been superseded by an updated version of the nebular hypothesis. ➔ **planetary systems, formation of**

CCD
→ **charge-coupled device**

C-class asteroid
A type of dark asteroid, gray in color, with an **albedo** of 0.03 to 0.08, that is common in the outer part of the **Main Asteroid Belt** 2.5 to 3.5 AU from the Sun. The "C" stands for "carbonaceous," as these objects are believed to be similar in composition to **carbonaceous chondrite**s. Subcategories include **B-class asteroid**s, **F-class asteroid**s, and **G-class asteroid**s.

celestial equator
The projection of the Earth's equator onto the **celestial sphere.**

celestial sphere
A huge imaginary sphere centered on the Earth, on which the stars appear to be fixed.

Celestis, Inc.
A Texas company that has made a business out of launching the cremated remains of individuals into space. In April 1997, Celestis sent some of the ashes of **Star Trek** creator Gene Roddenberry, 1960s icon Timothy Leary, and twenty-two other individuals into orbit around the Earth using an Orbital Sciences Corporation Pegasus XL rocket released from a converted L-1011 jumbo jet. Celestis, Inc., is affiliated with the Celestis Foundation, the president of which, Charles Chafer, is also president of the private **CETI** company Encounter 2001.

cell
The fundamental unit of terrestrial life. Cells may exist on their own as independent organisms, as in the case of **bacteria, archaea,** and **protists,** or may form colonies or tissues, as in higher life-forms. Each cell consists of **protein**-rich material that is differentiated into **cytoplasm** and a **nucleus.** Forming a boundary around the cytoplasm is a **cell membrane,** which in **plants** and some microorganisms is in turn surrounded by a **cell wall.** The two main types of cell are **prokaryotic** and **eukaryotic.**

cell membrane
The membrane surrounding the **cytoplasm** of a **cell,** consisting of a **lipid bilayer** with embedded **proteins.** It regulates what enters and leaves the cell, maintains the correct **intracellular pH** level, and provides a means of separating charges so that the cell can, for example, generate the energy-carrying molecule **adenosine triphosphate.** The cell membrane is both a physical and chemical barrier that defines the boundary between the individual and its environment. Its origin is intimately connected with the origin of life as we know it (→ **cell membranes, origin of**).

cell membranes, origin of
Cell membrane formation was a crucial stage in the evolution of terrestrial life. However, whether the first self-replicating life-forms on Earth possessed a membrane or whether they were merely naked strands of **nucleic acid** is as yet undetermined. Even if the earliest organisms did possess a membrane of some sort, it was probably not of their own making. The likelihood is that ready-made receptacles were to hand that they could have used. Such receptacles may form in interstellar space on the surface of **cosmic dust** grains. At least two pieces of evidence support this view: (1) the discovery of what appear to be two-layered **vesicle**s in material extracted from the **Murchison meteorite** (→ **organic matter, in meteorites**); and (2) the synthesis of similar microscopic structures on Earth in experi-

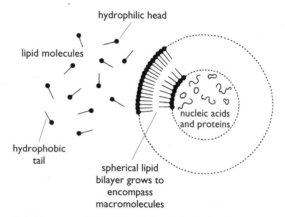

hydrophilic head

lipid molecules

hydrophobic tail

nucleic acids and proteins

spherical lipid bilayer grows to encompass macromolecules

Possible scenario for the origin of the first cells.

ments designed to replicate conditions within **interstellar cloud**s of gas and dust. → **life, origin of**

cell wall

The rigid outermost covering of the **cell**s of **plants, bacteria,** and some **protists.** The cell wall surrounds the **cell membrane.**

cellulose

A **polysaccharide** that is the main constituent of the **cell wall** in all green **plants** and most **bacteria.**

Centaurs

A recently discovered class of object, about 100 to 400 km in diameter, that move around the Sun in elongated orbits in the vicinity of Saturn, Uranus, and Neptune. Centaurs are believed to have an icy composition similar to that of **Jupiter-type comet**s and to have escaped from the **Kuiper Belt.** The first to be discovered were **Chiron,** in 1977, and **Pholus,** in 1992. These two differ markedly in their surface color. Chiron is neutral, reflecting all wavelengths of light equally well, whereas Pholus is dark and very red (→ **red Centaurs**). Possibly the difference in appearance is due to a difference in composition. However, this seems unlikely since the original composition of an object is largely determined by the distance from the Sun (and hence the temperature) at which it formed. Both Chiron and Pholus are thought to have formed in the Kuiper Belt at a temperature of −233 to −223°C (40 to 50 K). More likely, the color difference is due to later events. Pholus's dark red hue is probably due to prolonged bombardment by **cosmic rays** that has led to the formation on its surface of complex **polymers** rich in **carbon** and **nitrogen.** Chiron, on the other hand, may have suffered a collision at some point within the past couple of billion years that has exposed some of the lighter underlying material (just as relatively recent craters on the Moon have bright rays of dust excavated from below). Every 10 to 100 million years, a close encounter with a giant planet ejects a Centaur into interstellar space or diverts it into the inner solar system, where it may subsequently collide with one of the terrestrial worlds.

Center for Astronomical Adaptive Optics (CAAO)

A facility of **Steward Observatory** that is itself within the Department of Astronomy of the University of Arizona. The mission of the CAAO is to develop state-of-the-art **adaptive optics** systems for imaging and spectrometry at near-**infrared** wavelengths. These systems will form an integral part of the various large telescopes under development by Steward Observatory, including the 6.5-m conversion of the **Multiple Mirror Telescope,** the **Large Binocular Telescope,** and the Southern Hemisphere **Magellan Telescopes.** An important technique being developed at the CAAO is **nulling interferometry,** which will be applied to the direct imaging of **extrasolar planets** and circumstellar **dust disk**s.

Center for UFO Studies (CUFOS)

A Chicago-based organization founded in 1973 by J. Allen **Hynek** for the scientific investigation of reports of **unidentified flying objects.**

cephalopod intelligence

In a sense, a form of alien intelligence on this planet. In 1947, funds from the Marshall Plan—the U.S. program to help rebuild Europe after the Second World War—were allocated to researchers at Naples Zoological Station in Italy to study the brain of the octopus. The results of this work, it was hoped, might help U.S. Air Force engineers design better computers. To this day, however, cephalopod brains remain a mystery (→ **intelligence, nature of**). Although unusually large, they seem to work along fundamentally different lines from those of primates like ourselves. Much processing in the cephalopod nervous system appears to be done in ganglia distributed around the body. Part of the reason for this is that these creatures communicate via fast-changing patterns of body color for which a distributed processing network is essential.

cephalopods

Intelligent marine predators equipped with a complex, efficient nervous system (→ **cephalopod intelligence**). More than six hundred species of these advanced mollusks are known, including octopuses, squids, nautiluses, and extinct ammonites. The cephalopod eye, with its well-developed retina comparable to that of vertebrates, provides a remarkable example of **convergent evolution.** All cephalopods are capable of swimming by jet propulsion.

Cerro Tololo Inter-American Observatory (CTIO)

An observatory located 55 km (34 miles) southeast of La Serena, Chile, at an altitude of 2,215 m and operated by the U.S. Association of Universities for Research in Astronomy. Its main instrument is the 4-m Blanco Telescope, opened in 1976, and a Southern Hemisphere twin to the 4-m instrument at the **Kitt Peak National Observatory.** On the same site are four other telescopes of smaller aperture. The 8-m Gemini South Telescope (➔ **Gemini Telescopes**) is under construction on a peak 10 km to the southeast.

Cerulli, Vicenzo (1859–1927)

Italian astronomer who was among the earliest to argue that the Martian "canals" were an illusion created by the eye's tendency to link discrete points and produce the appearance of lines (➔ **Mars, canals of**). In this view, he was opposed by Giovanni **Schiaparelli** but supported by José **Comas Solá,** Eugène **Antoniadi,** and others.

cetaceans

Whales, dolphins, and porpoises. These aquatic mammals have long been noted for their intelligent and sometimes apparently compassionate behavior (➔ **dolphins, as a form of alien intelligence**). More recently, it has become clear that they produce an extraordinary variety of complex vocalizations across a wide frequency range, which in addition to uses such as echolocation and mating rituals, may serve as a sophisticated form of communication (➔ **humpback whales, songs of**). ➔ **cephalopods**

CETEX

➔ **Committee on the Exploration of Extraterrestrial Space**

CETI

Communication with Extraterrestrial Intelligence. Unlike **SETI,** which is a passive, listening pursuit, CETI attempts to initiate a dialogue with intelligent extraterrestrials. It does this by actively sending out coded signals at specific **target stars,** star clusters, or galaxies. The earliest attempt at CETI was the **Arecibo Message,** devised by Frank **Drake** and beamed toward the great **globular cluster M13** in Hercules. On March 14, 1999, a far more elaborate message was sent out from a radio telescope in Ukraine as part of a CETI program sponsored by a Houston company, Encounter 2001 (➔ **Encounter 2001 Message**). The company also plans to send hair samples and personal messages from sponsors into space (➔ **Encounter 2001, The Millennial Voyage**). Information affixed to the starbound *Pioneer* (➔ *Pioneer* **plaque**) and *Voyager* (➔ *Voyager* **interstellar record**) spacecraft represent another form of attempted communication with alien intelligence. Over the years, a number of prominent scientists and other individuals have voiced their concern at the possible consequences of humans advertising their existence to civilizations of unknown disposition who may have technologies vastly superior to our own (➔ **CETI, opposition to**).[492]

CETI, opposition to

The pros and cons of attempting to notify the Galaxy of our existence have been debated since the dispatch of the **Arecibo Message** in 1974. In the wake of this transmission, U.S. diplomat Michael Michaud suggested that the message had repercussions that went beyond science into the realm of politics. He proposed a public discussion of the possible benefits and risks of establishing contact. More strident was the protest by Martin **Ryle,** the British astronomer royal, who argued that "any creatures out there [may be] malevolent or hungry." He requested that the **International Astronomical Union** approve a resolution condemning such attempts at **CETI.** However, in a letter to Ryle, **SETI** pioneer Frank **Drake** pointed out that:

> It's too late to worry about giving ourselves away. The deed is done. And repeated daily with

every television transmission, every military radar signal, every spacecraft command.... I think that hostile tribes bent on war, be they terrestrial or extraterrestrial, destroy themselves with their own weapons, before they have any notion of how to attempt interstellar travel.

The argument thus quickly and inevitably became entwined with a debate about the likely nature of intelligent extraterrestrials (➔ **extraterrestrial intelligence, character of**), those in support of CETI favoring the view that high intelligence will generally be benign, while those in opposition warning of dire consequences, including potential invasions and even cannibalism, if our whereabouts became widely known. In the latter camp is Michael Archer, professor of biology at the University of South Wales, who believes that the phonograph records attached to each *Voyager* probe could effectively serve as giant dinner invitations proclaiming "Come to Earth, we have lots of nice, exotic things to eat." At the other extreme, Carl **Sagan** and William Newman proposed that there may exist a "Codex Galactica" to educate young societies, such as our own, in appropriate forms of behavior. As for the dangers of humankind literally falling prey to an alien race, Sagan pointed out that advanced extraterrestrial carnivores would almost certainly find our particular combination of **amino acids** unpalatable. Moreover, it would hardly be cost-effective in energy terms to cross interstellar distances merely to find something to eat, when synthesizing food locally on a large scale could be done with a fraction of that energy.

CfA
➔ **Harvard-Smithsonian Center for Astrophysics**

chain of being, great
A doctrine expounded by John **Locke** and others, according to which there is a complete continuum of existence from the lowest life-forms to human beings to extraterrestrial creatures with intellectual and sensory powers far greater than our own. Some saw this full spectrum of life as a necessary manifestation of God's omnipotence, and it was often extended to include degrees of spiritual advancement. For example, it was commonly believed that other planets might be the home of angels or similar creatures that had progressed further along the road to divinity. In some cases, this belief was linked to that of the **transmigration of souls.** The great chain of being was one of a number of philosophical or theological arguments put forward from the seventeenth century onward in support of **pluralism.**

Chalmers, Thomas (1780–1847)
Scottish Presbyterian minister and powerful evangelical orator, well versed in science and philosophy, who had a significant impact on the debate about **pluralism** in the nineteenth century. Following an invitation by David **Brewster** to contribute to the *Edinburgh Encyclopedia*, Chalmers began to explore the relationship between Christianity and extraterrestrial life (➔ **Christian doctrine and pluralism**). This formed the subject of seven influential sermons he delivered in Glasgow in 1815 and that were published in 1817 as *A Series of Discourses on the Christian Revelation Viewed in Connection with the Modern Astronomy*. In Britain and America, the sermons sold by the tens of thousands, editions continuing to appear in the United States until 1860 and in the United Kingdom as late as the 1870s. Chalmers wrote, "[T]here are other worlds, which roll afar; the light of other suns shines upon them." These extrasolar planets, he urged, "must be the mansions of life and intelligence." Chalmers saw the abundance of life in the universe as a reflection of God's generosity and power (➔ **plenitude, principle of**). To the question of how God could care for the Earth in a universe teeming with worlds and life, Chalmers replied with his **microscope argument.** Concerning the redemption, he suggested that just as Christ's redemptive action has extended over time on Earth, so it may extend over the vastness of space. The Earth, he proposed, might be "the actual theatre of a keen and ambitious contest amongst the upper orders of creation" (a theme later taken up by C. S. **Lewis** and others in science fiction). His command of contemporary astronomical knowledge made his evangelical pronouncements all the more persuasive, and the effect of his sermons was to

help convince many that pluralism could indeed be reconciled with Christianity.

Chamberlin, Thomas Chrowder (1843–1928)

American astronomer at the University of Chicago who, together with Forest **Moulton,** developed a new version of the **catastrophic hypothesis** about the origin of the planets (➔ **Chamberlin-Moulton planetesimal hypothesis**).

Chamberlin-Moulton planetesimal hypothesis

A **catastrophic hypothesis** proposed by Thomas **Chamberlin** and Forest **Moulton** in 1905, in which the planets of the solar system are seen to arise from an encounter between the Sun and another star. In this scenario, the gravity of the passing star tears a succession of bolts from the solar surface. Bolts coming from the side nearer the star are thrown out to distances comparable with those of the giant planets, while those from the far side of the Sun are ejected less violently to the distances of the terrestrial planets. From the inner remains of these bolts the initial cores of the planets formed, while the outer parts expanded and cooled into a huge swarm of solid particles spread out in a disk rotating about the Sun in a plane determined by the motion of the passing star. The cores gradually grew into planets by gathering in the **planetesimals,** most of the growth taking place in the outer parts of the solar system, where material was more plentiful. Eventually it became clear that, like other variants of the encounter idea, not enough **angular momentum** could be conveyed to the ejected material to explain the state of the solar system as it exists today.

Champollion

Also known as *Deep Space 4;* the fourth mission in NASA's **New Millennium Program.** Its goal was to have landed scientific instruments on the **nucleus** of a **comet** and demonstrated technologies for collecting extraterrestrial samples for return to Earth (➔ **comet sample return probe**s). However, in June 1999, budget constraints led to the project's cancellation.

Chandrasekhar Limit

The theoretical upper limit to the mass of **white dwarf** stars—approximately 1.4 M_S. Above this mass, a white dwarf would not be able to stabilize itself against further collapse due to its own gravity and would become either a **neutron star** or a **black hole.** At or below the Chandrasekhar Limit, a white dwarf can balance the compressional force of gravity with a quantum effect known as **degenerate electron pressure.** ➔ **stars, evolution of**

chaotic inflationary theory

A contemporary cosmological theory that posits that the Universe grew out of a quantum fluctuation in a preexisting region of **space-time** and that other universes could do the same from regions within our universe today. A new universe, or "babyverse," that formed by this budding process would have its own set of physical laws, material particles, and possibly life—entirely unlike anything with which we are familiar.

charge-coupled device (CCD)

An electronic imaging device widely used in astronomical applications. It consists of an array of small picture elements, or pixels, made from semiconducting silicon. When **photon**s fall onto this array, they release electrons that can be counted and used to build up a picture of varying light intensity that can be stored on a computer or viewed on a monitor.

Charon

The only known moon of **Pluto.** Unlike its primary, the surface of which is covered in

Discovery	1978, by James Walter Christy at U.S. Naval Observatory
Mean distance from Pluto	19,600 km (12,180 mi.)
Diameter	1,186 km (737 mi.)
Mean density	1.3 g/cm³
Escape velocity	0.61 km/s (2,196 km/h, 1,365 mi./h)
Orbital period	6.39 days (6 days 9 hours)
Orbital eccentricity	0.000
Orbital inclination	98.80°
Axial period	6.39 days
Albedo	0.5
Surface temperature	~–240°C (–400°F)

methane ice, Charon appears to have a coating of water ice. This observation, together with the possibility that Charon is subject to significant **tidal heating** as a result of Pluto's gravity, has led to the suggestion that there may be a subice liquid ocean of water on the moon that could harbor microbial life. Charon is due to be observed at close range by the *Pluto-Kuiper Express* in about 2014.

chemoautotrophs

Autotrophic microorganisms, including many varieties of **archaea** and **bacteria,** that are able to synthesize all of the **organic** compounds they need from **inorganic** raw materials in the absence of sunlight. The energy required for **chemosynthesis** is derived from special methods of **respiration** involving the **oxidation** of various inorganic materials such as **hydrogen sulfide, ammonia,** and iron-bearing compounds.

chemosynthesis

The manufacture of complex substances from simpler chemical building blocks within living organisms.

Chicxulub Crater

A 180-km-wide submerged impact crater straddling the northwest coastline of the Yucatán Peninsula in Mexico. The environmental effects that accompanied its formation are thought to have been responsible for the **mass extinction** at the end of the Cretaceous era, 65 million years ago, in which the last of the dinosaurs disappeared (➜ **Cretaceous-Tertiary Boundary**).

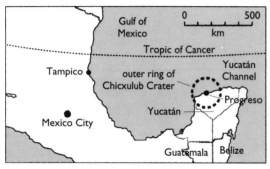

Location of the Chicxulub Crater.

Childhood's End

Science fiction novel[109] (1953) by Arthur C. **Clarke** in which benevolent aliens with the appearance of devils arrive on Earth and establish peace and a world government. Despite their enormously superior knowledge and technology, however, these "Overlords" are far less advanced than the "Overmind," a communal consciousness that is poised to absorb the youngest members of the human race (➜ **noncorporeal life**). The Overlords, who are incapable of making this dramatic evolutionary jump themselves, serve merely as midwives for other species that are in the throes of undergoing the transition from individual corporeal to collective noncorporeal form.

chirality

The existence of distinct right- and left-handed forms of a molecule, known as **enantiomers,** due to the molecule containing an **asymmetric carbon atom.** Most biological substances, including **amino acids** and **sugars,** display this property.

Chiron

An object, about 200 to 300 km in diameter, in orbit between Uranus and Saturn, that was discovered in 1977 by American astronomer Charles Thomas Kowal. At first, the nature of Chiron was unclear. However, it has now been classified as a **Centaur,** a large, cometlike body that has been displaced from the **Kuiper Belt** into an orbit that takes it no closer to the Sun than the **gas giant**s. Owing to its remoteness, Chiron never develops a tail like that of a true comet, although it does lose some volatile material around **perihelion** that forms a fuzzy **coma.**

chlorine (Cl)

A greenish-yellow, gaseous element.

Atomic number 17; density 1.6 g/dm^3; melting point −101.0°C; boiling point −34.6°C

chlorophyll

The green pigment involved in **photosynthesis.** It consists of a **porphyrin** ring in the center of which is an **ion** of magnesium. Chlorophyll *a* is the primary photosynthetic pigment in all

Molecule of chlorophyll *a*.

organisms that release oxygen (i.e., all **plants** and **algae,** including **cyanobacteria**), while chlorophyll *b, c,* and *d* and bacteriochlorophyll act as accessory or alternative pigments to type *a* in certain organisms. Interestingly, although the Sun radiates most strongly in the yellow region of the spectrum, chlorophyll absorbs most strongly in the red and blue regions, so that it appears far from ideal for the job it does. However, it may be that, in selecting this molecule, nature achieved the best compromise. The biochemist George **Wald** has said:[610]

> Chlorophyll…possesses a triple combination of capacities: a high receptivity to light, an inertness of structure permitting it to store the energy and relay it to other molecules, and a reactive site equipping it to transfer hydrogen in the critical reaction that ultimately binds hydrogen to carbon in the reduction of carbon dioxide. I would suppose that these properties singled out the chlorophyll [molecules] for use by organisms in photosynthesis in spite of their disadvantageous absorption spectrum.

The fact that chlorophyll was selected for such a crucial biological task on a planet where its absorption spectrum does not closely match the host star's emission at different frequencies suggests that it may be a universal molecule for this role.

chloroplasts
Structures found within the **cell**s of green **plants** and **eukaryotic algae** that contain the membranes, pigments (➔ **chlorophyll**), and **enzymes** necessary for **photosynthesis.**

chondrite
A type of **stony meteorite** that (usually) contains **chondrule**s. Almost all chondrites also contain iron and nickel, as well as some stony minerals and **sulfides.** From their texture and their mixture of stone, metal, and sulfides, which would separate on melting, it is clear that chondrites have not melted since their formation. Indeed, they are believed to be composed of **primitive material,** unaltered since the formation of the planets about 4,550 million years ago. This is confirmed by the observation that, **hydrogen** and **helium** aside, the relative abundance of elements in them closely matches that of the Sun. A rare category of chondrites, important in the study of the origin of life, is the **carbonaceous chondrite**s.

chondrule
A near-spherical aggregate of coarse crystals about 1 mm across formed by the rapid cooling and solidification of a melt at about 1,400°C. Chondrules are found in a variety of **stony meteorite**s known as **chondrite**s but solidified before they became incorporated.

Christian doctrine and pluralism
At the heart of Western religious debate about the possible existence of life on other worlds are the key issues of the supposed special relationship between man and God, the **incarnation and redemption.** Early Christian scholars, having embraced the one-world, **geocentric** cosmology of **Aristotle,** generally rejected **pluralism.** This continued to be the case following the introduction into the West of many previously unavailable classical writings in the thirteenth century. However, debate did broaden at this time, and there were several suggestions that while God had actually created only one world, it was in his power to have produced many. **Nicholas of Cusa** was exceptional, as a high-ranking cleric, in speculating freely upon the possibility of multiple life-bearing worlds, including an inhabited Sun and Moon. William **Vorilong** was among the first to comment on how this doctrine might be compatible with a belief in Christ's sacrifice and

redemption (➔ **medieval philosophy, related to the possibility of extraterrestrial life**). Following the **Copernican Revolution,** the debate over the theological implications of pluralism intensified. The dawning realization that the Earth was an ordinary planet and that the Sun was just one of many stars, each perhaps with its own retinue of worlds, forced philosophers, theologians, and scientists to confront the possibility that life, including intelligent life, might be common in the Universe. Some continued to reject this view, arguing that Christ's atonement and God's relationship with man were unique and that there could therefore be only one inhabited world. Others employed a variety of arguments designed to show that Christianity and pluralism could comfortably coexist (➔ **plenitude, principle of; chain of being, great; microscope argument**). These efforts to enlarge the Christian cosmos resulted in the rise of **natural theology** and the doctrine of the **transmigration of souls,** which reached its most extreme form in the pronouncements of Emanuel **Swedenborg.** The debate climaxed in the middle of the nineteenth century, following publication of an antipluralist essay by William **Whewell.** Thereafter, theological and scientific arguments related to the possibility of extraterrestrial life became increasingly decoupled if not entirely divorced (➔ **SETI, religious dimensions of**).

chromosome
The **organelle** responsible for the physical transmission of hereditary information from one generation to the next. In **bacteria** and **archaea,** the chromosome consists of a single naked ring of **DNA.** In **eukaryote**s, each chromosome consists of a single linear DNA molecule composed of many **gene**s.

chromosphere
The lower level of a star's atmosphere, lying between the **photosphere** and the **corona.**

Chryse Planitia
A relatively smooth, circular plain, possibly an ancient impact basin, in the north equatorial region of Mars, 1,600 km (1,000 miles) across and 2.5 km (1.5 miles) below the average planetary surface. It appears to have suffered water erosion in the past (➔ **Mars, water on**) and was chosen as the site of the *Viking 1* landing in 1976.

Chyba, Christopher
Consulting professor in the Department of Geological and Environmental Sciences at Stanford University and holder of the Carl Sagan Chair for the Study of Life in the Universe at the **SETI Institute.** He also chairs the Science Definition Team for the *Europa Orbiter.* Much of Chyba's current research lies in **astrobiology,** including the investigation of a putative ocean on **Europa** from an orbiting spacecraft, water and **organic** molecules on Mars both past and present (➔ **Mars, water on; Mars, life on**), and the environment of the prebiotic Earth (➔ **Earth, early history of**). He earned a Ph.D. at **Cornell University** under the supervision of Carl **Sagan** and was featured in *Time* magazine's December 1994 cover story, "50 for the Future."

CHZ
➔ **continuously habitable zone**

circumstellar disk
A broad ring of material orbiting around a star that may be either a **protoplanetary disk** or a **regenerated disk.**

City and the Stars, The
An expanded version of Arthur C. **Clarke**'s first science fiction novel[110] (1956). Heavily influenced by Olaf **Stapledon**'s cosmic visions, it tells of an inhabitant of the utopian but totally insular Earth city of Diaspar who escapes to travel the Galaxy. He thereby learns of man's past encounters with galactic civilizations leading to a vast experiment: the creation of a noncorporeal intelligence (➔ **noncorporeal life**). Clarke was to echo this theme of human destiny lying among the stars in some of his other well-known works, including *Childhood's End* and *2001: A Space Odyssey.*

civilizations, extraterrestrial
➔ **Kardashev civilizations**

Clark, Alvan (1804–87)
Famous American optician whose company was responsible for the manufacture of the

giant objective lenses used in many of the world's leading **refracting telescope**s, including those at the **Yerkes Observatory** (40 in.), the **Lick Observatory** (36 in.), Pulkova Observatory (30 in.), **U.S. Naval Observatory** (26 in.), and the **Lowell Observatory** (24 in.). These instruments were used extensively for planetary studies in the late nineteenth and early twentieth centuries.

Clarke, Arthur C(harles) (1917–)

British author (resident in Sri Lanka since 1956) of science fiction and popular science who worked on the development of radar during World War II, originated the concept of communications satellites in the October 1945 issue of *Wireless World,* and earned a first-class degree in physics and mathematics from Kings College, London (1948). His nonfiction books of the early 1950s, including *The Exploration of Space* (1951), brought him fame as an enthusiastic advocate of space travel, although he had begun writing science fiction two decades earlier, influenced most significantly by Olaf **Stapledon**'s *Last and First Men.* Informed by his science and engineering background and suffused with his liberal optimism about man's destiny among the stars, Clarke's writings combine meticulous technical authenticity with an almost mystical vision of the future. The notion that mankind's further evolution is inextricably bound up with extraterrestrial contact is recurrent throughout his work. In *Childhood's End*[109] (1953), *The City and the Stars*[110] (1956), and *2001: A Space Odyssey*[111] (1968) and its sequels, Clarke employs highly advanced aliens as agents of human transformation, while in *Rendezvous with Rama*[113] (1973) and its sequels, he explores the idea of first contact with an outside intelligence in the form of a robotic alien ship that temporarily enters orbit around the Sun (➔ **Bracewell probe**). Several prognostications made by Clarke in his novels have subsequently been borne out in fact, including the possibility of life on **Europa** and the existence of a moon around **Pluto.** Among his scientific contemporaries who used fiction to speculate about the nature of alien life and intelligence and the consequences of human-alien contact were Hal **Clement** in the United States and Fred **Hoyle** in Britain.

classical Jovians

Planets that, like Jupiter, are massive and orbit their **host star**s in a nearly circular orbit at a distance of several AU. **Extrasolar planets** fitting this description include the companions of **47 Ursae Majoris, Rho**[1] **Cancri** A, and, if confirmed, **Lalande 21185.**

clathrate

A form of compound in which one component is combined with another by the caging of one kind of molecule by the structure of another. Cometary nuclei may contain ice in the form of clathrate hydrates.

clay, role in prebiotic evolution

J. B. S. **Haldane** and, more recently, A. Graham **Cairns-Smith** have been among those to promote the idea that clay minerals may have played a vital role in the manufacture of large **prebiotic** molecules, their lattice structures acting as templates for the organization of organic matter into **polymers.** ➔ **life, origin of**

Clement, Hal (1922–)

American science fiction writer (real name Harry Clement Stubbs) and college physics teacher with degrees in astronomy and chemistry who speculated in detail about the intelligent life-forms that might evolve on a world of extremely high gravity (➔ **gravitational life**). His books *Mission of Gravity*[121] (1954), *Close to Critical* (1964), and *Starlight* (1971) explore the biology and physics of a giant, rapidly spinning planet, Mesklin, whose effective gravity varies from 3 times (at the equator) to 700 times (at the pole) that of the Earth. Robert **Forward** presents an even more extreme scenario for gravitational life in *Dragon's Egg* and *Starquake.*

Clementine

A lunar probe built by the U.S. Naval Research Laboratory and launched by NASA on January 25, 1994, for the Department of Defense. *Clementine* was a small probe designed to map most of the Moon's surface at a number of resolutions and wavelengths from **infrared** to **ultraviolet.** Its most important discovery was that of ice under the surface of craters at the lunar poles (➔ **Moon, water on**), later confirmed by *Lunar Prospector.*

close encounters

Three of the six categories of **unidentified flying object** in the classification scheme devised by J. Allen **Hynek.** A *close encounter of the first kind* (CEI) is any UFO reported to have been within about 500 ft. of the witness. A *close encounter of the second kind* (CEII) is a UFO that leaves markings on the ground, causes burns or paralysis, frightens animals, or interferes with engines or TV or radio reception. A *close encounter of the third kind* (CEIII) includes a purported sighting of the occupants of a UFO. To these categories, ufologists have added two others: a *close encounter of the fourth kind* (CEIV) is one in which a person reports having been abducted (➔ **alien abduction**), while a *close encounter of the fifth kind* (CEV) is one in which it is claimed that communication takes place between a human and an alien.

Close Encounters of the Third Kind

Motion picture directed by Steven **Spielberg** and released in 1977.[559] The technical adviser was J. Allen **Hynek,** astronomical consultant with Project **Blue Book,** who made a cameo appearance. Interesting parallels between the film and John Bunyan's *Pilgrim's Progress* have been drawn by English-born physicist Paul Davies:[138]

> Spielberg's aliens…appeared in a halo of bright light and possessed a serene, other-worldly quality reminiscent of biblical encounters with angels. Much of the imagery…was Bunyanesque, especially near the final scene when the alien mothercraft appears in the sky, awesome, brilliantly illuminated and suggestive of [the] Celestial City. Throughout the story the aliens set the agenda, and privileged humans were drawn psychically and with religious, pilgrim-like fervor towards the all-important encounter after many trials, tribulations and doubts.

The release of *Close Encounters* coincided with a new wave of UFO sightings and public interest that filtered up through official circles. This culminated in a debate by the UN General Assembly special political committee, in which there was a call by Grenada's delegate (unsuccessful, as it turned out) for an international agency to study the phenomenon. ➔ **SETI, religious dimensions of**

cluster

A relatively close grouping of stars. There are two distinct types: **open cluster**s and **globular cluster**s.

coacervate

A spherical aggregation of **lipid** molecules making up a **colloid**al inclusion that is held together by **hydrophobic** forces. Coacervates measure 1 to 100 micrometers across, possess osmotic (➔ **osmosis**) properties, and form spontaneously from certain weak **organic** solutions. Their name derives from the Latin *coacervare,* meaning "to assemble together or cluster." It was suggested by Aleksandr **Oparin** that coacervates may have played a significant role in the evolution of **cell**s.

In water, organic chemicals do not necessarily remain uniformly dispersed but may separate out into layers or droplets. If the droplets that form contain a colloid rich in organic compounds and are surrounded by a tight skin of water molecules, they are known as coacervates. These structures were first investigated by H. G. Bungenburg de **Jong** in 1932. A wide variety of solutions can give rise to them; for example, coacervates form spontaneously when a **protein,** such as gelatin, reacts with gum arabic. They are interesting not only in that they provide a locally segregated environment but also in that their boundaries allow the selective adsorption of simple organic molecules from the surrounding medium. In Oparin's view, this amounts to an elementary form of **metabolism.** J. D. **Bernal** commented that they are "the nearest we can come to cells without introducing any biological—or at any rate any living biological—substance." However, the lack of any mechanism by which coacervates can reproduce leaves them far short of being living systems.

Coalsack

The finest visual example of an **absorption nebula** in space. It lies at a distance of about 530 light-years (160 parsecs) in the constellation of Crux Australis, the Southern Cross, where it appears as a gaping hole in the Milky Way.

Cocconi, Giuseppe (1914–)

Retired director of the proton synchrotron at CERN (the Conseil Européen pour la Recherche Nucléaire, now renamed Organisation Européene pour la Recherche Nucléaire), the European particle physics laboratory, near Geneva, Switzerland. Together with **Cornell University** colleague Philip **Morrison,** he was responsible, in 1959, for the seminal paper on the subject of **SETI** (➔ **Morrison-Cocconi Conjecture**). Cocconi obtained a doctorate in physics from the University of Milan (1937) before becoming physics professor there in 1942. Subsequently, he taught at the University of Catania in Italy until 1947, when he was invited to join the staff at Cornell. He returned to Europe as a senior physicist at CERN in 1962 and played no further significant part in SETI work. He recalled in an interview with sociologist David Swift[575] how the idea for his SETI proposals with Morrison came about. He had been in conversation with his wife, Vanna, also a physicist at Cornell, the evening before:

> We were thinking that a narrow burst of gamma-radiation could be a signal that can travel far and straight in galactic space and be peculiar enough to be recognized. And that was the triggering. Next day, I went to see Phil Morrison and discussed the possibility of extraterrestrial communication.

A few days later, Cocconi realized that the newly completed **radio telescope** at **Jodrell Bank** would be just powerful enough to transmit a detectable signal to the nearest star. He therefore wrote to Bernard **Lovell** at Jodrell Bank requesting that the instrument be used in a search for extraterrestrial signals but was turned down.

codon

The basic unit of the **genetic code.** It consists of a **nucleotide** triplet in **DNA** or **messenger RNA** that codes for a specific **amino acid.** As there are sixty-four possible codons but only twenty amino acids in terrestrial organisms, some amino acids have more than one codon (known as "degenerative codons"). There are also "stop" codons, which serve to terminate a **translation.**

coenzyme

An **organic** non-**protein** that plays an essential part in some reactions catalyzed by **enzyme**s. Coenzymes often serve as a temporary carrier of an intermediate product of the reaction.

coevolution

The simultaneous long-term evolutionary adjustment of two or more groups of organisms caused by the selection pressures that each exerts on the other. It is commonly observed in symbiotic associations. For example, many insect-pollinated plants have evolved flowers with a color and shape that make them attractive to particular insects, while these insects have evolved specialized mouthparts and sense organs for finding and extracting nectar from these plants.

cofactor

One or more non-**protein** components required by an **enzyme** in order to function. Some cofactors are metal **ion**s, such as ions of iron, zinc, or copper, or simple **organic** molecules. When the cofactor consists of a complex molecule, it is known as a **prosthetic group,** an example of which is heme in hemoglobin. Prosthetic groups are always tightly bound to their parent enzyme. Cofactors that are not tightly bound are referred to as **coenzyme**s.

Cold Bokkeveld meteorite

A **carbonaceous chondrite** that fell in many pieces (the largest recovered weighing 3 kg) near the Cold Bokkeveld Mountains, in Cape Province, South Africa, on October 13, 1838. From a sample of it, Friedrich **Wöhler** extracted an oil "with a strong bituminous odor." Having also extracted **organic** material from the **Kaba meteorite,** he concluded that these substances had a biological origin. Only later was it realized that carbon compounds could be created in space by inorganic processes. In 1951–52, G. Mueller at University College,

London, found chemicals resembling **hydrocarbon**s in the Cold Bokkeveld stone, a discovery referred to by Melvin **Calvin** and Susan K. Vaughan in their work on the biological significance of **organic matter, in meteorites.**

Cold War, linked to UFO reports

Anxiety and actual aerial activity related to the Cold War between the United States and the Soviet Union contributed significantly to the saucer flap of the late 1940s (➔ **saucer flap of 1947**). In May 1945, Germany had surrendered; three months later, Japan was A-bombed into submission. Yet despite its military success and new superpower status, America felt more insecure than ever. Already it had been attacked once out of the blue, by the Japanese at Pearl Harbor. Now there was the rising menace of communism and the fear that a Red tidal wave would steadily and relentlessly engulf the free countries of the world. At the end of the war, the United States alone had atomic weapons, but it was only a matter of time before the Soviets, too, would be as lethally equipped.

On March 4, 1947, less than four months before Kenneth **Arnold**'s seminal sighting of a "**flying saucer,**" the Soviets rejected a U.S. plan for atomic energy control. Eight days later, President Truman made clear his policy, the Truman Doctrine, that America should support any country that was trying to resist external threats to its freedom. Rapid military buildup on both sides of the Iron Curtain became a grim inevitability. Although America was strong, it would have to become much stronger and more vigilant. It would have to stockpile weapons, build up its defenses, and use its ingenuity to evolve ever more powerful forms of deterrent in a desperate attempt to stay one step ahead of the Soviets. And all the time, every minute of every day, it would have to scan the skies to watch for the moment when the enemy might stir and choose to unleash its weapons on the American homeland.

Nervousness and suspicion stemming from the Communist threat began to spread among the general public and seep into the national consciousness. But these negative feelings were accompanied, strangely, by a great sense of optimism and confidence about what new technological breakthroughs might bring in other areas. The launch of the first artificial satellite and the dawn of the Space Age lay only 10 years away in 1947. The possibilities of space travel and of finding life on other planets were being discussed widely from a practical standpoint for the first time. And America had suddenly taken a giant leap forward in this direction with the capture of scores of V-2 missiles at the end of the war and the decision of the chief German rocket designer, Werner von Braun, to bring his expertise to the United States. Those sleek shapes on the launch pads, it was clear, could be utilized for two very different ends: to reduce enemy cities to rubble or to take the human race on the first few steps of its journey to the stars. Even as the threat of nuclear Armageddon loomed and the Cold War went into deep freeze, people began to feel exhilarated by the prospect of exploring the new frontier of space. It made for a heady brew of conflicting emotions that would boil over in the saucer frenzy of 1947. (➔ **space missions, linked to UFO reports**)

Speculation as to what might lie behind the sudden outbreak of mysterious sightings abounded. Were they hoaxes or mistaken identifications of familiar objects? Or was the explanation more sinister: that the skies over America were being visited by foreign devices—from Moscow or Mars? At the start of the saucer scare, the U.S. military appears to have been as confused and nervous as was the public at large. It initiated the first of a series of investigations into the phenomenon, principally to determine if there was a significant threat to national security (➔ **Sign, Project**).

In September 1949, the news that everyone had feared came: the Soviet Union had exploded its first atomic bomb. It was time to raise the stakes. The following January, President Truman ordered the development of the hydrogen (fusion) bomb, a terrifying escalation of the arms race. Even as humans contemplated their first sorties to the edge of space, it appeared as if the world was poised on the brink of nuclear catastrophe. On June 25, 1950, Soviet-backed North Korea invaded its southern neighbor. Two days later, Truman ordered American troops to intervene, and the Korean War began.

In many science fiction films of the early fifties (➔ *Invaders from Mars*), the extraterrestrial invaders were a scantily veiled substitute for the Communist threat. And 1950 saw another alien-Communist parallel come to the surface. In making his allegation of fifty-seven "card-carrying Communists" in the U.S. government, Senator Joseph McCarthy exploited the same fears and anxieties of the American people as *Amazing*'s Raymond **Palmer** had done several years earlier. The Men in Black had been joined in the Congress by Reds masquerading as true blue patriots. Two years later, the Republicans were in power and the fanatical McCarthy was in charge of the investigation into "un-American activities." If the public had been jittery before, it was now driven to the verge of paranoia, thanks to McCarthy's increasingly vociferous and hysterical claims. The Communists, he insisted, were no longer just out there biding their time, mustering their forces; they had managed to infiltrate American society at all levels. No one, it seemed, could be trusted anymore. Neighbors, workmates, even family members, despite every appearance of innocence, could secretly be operating for the other side. Again, science fiction served to both reflect and magnify a prevalent fear: that the ordinary-looking people standing next to you might not be what they seemed (➔ *Invasion of the Body Snatchers*). Military interest in flying saucers quickly declined after the initial saucer flap, to be revived temporarily in 1952 following the "**Washington Invasion.**" That same year, a much lengthier but lower-key study of UFOs began under the auspices of Project **Blue Book.** Meanwhile, the Cold War intensified, mistrust on the part of both sides deepened, and the world stared, as never before, down the barrel of a thermonuclear gun.

On August 20, 1953, Moscow announced the explosion of the first Soviet H-bomb. Three weeks earlier, the Korean War had ended in stalemate with 30,000 dead American troops. Back home, anti-Communist sentiment had never been higher, and McCarthyism was at its peak. With suspicion rife that the Reds had tunneled their way into the very machinery of government and public life, it was not hard for ordinary people to be convinced, by conspiracy theories, about aliens. Rumors initiated by the saucer faithful began to intensify that the government and the military knew more about UFOs than they were prepared to admit. The public was hungry for anything that looked remotely like inside information on the subject of flying saucers, and some fanatics (➔ **Keyhoe, Donald**) and charlatans (➔ **Adamski, George**), no doubt seeing the commercial possibilities, were happy to oblige—even if it meant peddling fake photos and stories that were manufactured from beginning to end. In addition, there was a subtle shift of public attitude in some quarters toward UFOs in the mid- to late fifties, a change of sentiment augured and perhaps partly inspired by the film **The Day the Earth Stood Still.** What if the aliens were not, after all, malevolent? What if they were actually here to warn us—capitalists and Communists alike—of the dangers of meddling with forces over which we had no control? Central to the claim of early saucer contactees, such as Adamski, was that the UFO inhabitants were both benign and wiser than ourselves. Far from wanting to take over our planet, they wished to help us, to forewarn us of what might happen unless we could defuse the nuclear time bomb that had been set ticking. So, although the contactees may have been myth mongering on a grand scale, they were also reflecting a mood of the times. They voiced what many people badly wanted to believe: first, that flying saucers existed and, second, that the creatures inside them offered a solution to the most pressing problem facing the world in the 1950s: the very real and imminent possibility of nuclear devastation. ➔ **Roswell Incident; Mantell, Thomas F.; science fiction involving extraterrestrials, in films and on television**

collisions, with asteroids and comets
➔ **cosmic collisions, biological effects of**

colloid

Also known as the dispersed phase; a substance or substances that comprise the suspended particles in a **colloidal dispersion.** Of special interest to studies of the origin of life are the colloidal entities known as **coacervate**s.

colloidal dispersion

An intimate mixture in which small particles are permanently dispersed throughout a **solvent.** Milk, for example, is a colloidal dispersion of fats, **proteins,** and milk sugar in water. The suspended particles are intermediate in size between visible particles and individual **molecule**s.

colonization, of space

→ **space colony; interstellar colonization; terraforming**

Columbus Optical SETI Observatory (COSETI)

A small observatory located in Bexley, near Columbus, Ohio, that uses a 25-cm (10-in.) telescope to search for extraterrestrial **laser** signals (→ **optical SETI**). Its director is Stuart A. Kingsley.

coma

The gaseous envelope that is seen to develop around the **nucleus** of a **comet** as it approaches the Sun.

Comas Solá, José (1868–1937)

Spanish astronomer whose observations of Mars played a part in discrediting the canal hypothesis (→ **Mars, canals of**). Shortly after the **opposition** of 1909, he wrote, "The marvelous legend of the canals of Mars has disappeared . . . after this memorable opposition."

comet

An object composed of **primitive material,** including ice, rock, and **organic** compounds, that formed during the earliest stages of the solar system, more than 4.5 billion years ago. The solid part, or *nucleus,* of a comet is typically no larger than a few kilometers across and contains icy chunks and frozen gases with fragments of embedded rock and dust. At its center, the nucleus may have a small rocky core. **Long-period comet**s and **Halley-type comet**s are thought to have originated in the

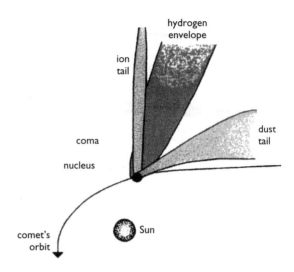

Oort Cloud at the limit of the Sun's gravitational domain. On the other hand, **Jupiter-type comet**s, which are a category of **short-period comet,** appear to have come from the **Kuiper Belt** beyond the orbit of Neptune. As a comet moves toward the Sun, solar energy vaporizes various ices on the comet's surface and causes the released gases to glow. From vents on the sun-warmed side, gas and dust escape in fountains and form a tenuous atmosphere, the *coma,* typically a few hundred thousand kilometers in diameter. Closer to the Sun, solar radiation and the **solar wind** blow material from the coma into a glowing *tail,* millions of kilometers long, that is often split into a straight tail of **ionized** gas and a curved tail of dust.

During the ancient bombardment phase of the Earth around 4 billion years ago, comets are thought to have contributed significant amounts of water (→ **oceans, origin of**) and possibly the first organic molecules that led to the start of **prebiotic evolution** (→ **life, origin of**). The same may have happened on other worlds within the solar system and may be a key factor in establishing the conditions necessary for life on planets elsewhere. Subsequent collisions between the Earth and both comets and **asteroid**s may have been a major factor behind **mass extinction**s and evolutionary surges (→ **punctuated equilibrium**), such as that which led to the appearance of man (→ **cosmic collisions, biological effects of**).

A variety of **carbon**-based molecules have been detected in cometary material, though it remains uncertain how elaborate the organic chemistry of comets may be. Some researchers, notably Fred **Hoyle** and Chandra Wickramasinghe, have argued[293] that life itself may have been seeded on Earth through cometary collisions and that even now **pathogen**s regularly rain down on our planet as the Earth sweeps through dusty comet tails, giving rise to global epidemics (→ **epidemics, from space**). Although these ideas have received scant support from the scientific community at large, it is becoming increasingly apparent that comets have influenced the development of terrestrial life and may even have helped to instigate it.[583] Their further investigation from space, following the success of a number of probes to **Halley's Comet,** including *Giotto,* is therefore a matter of priority. Among the comet missions currently in progress or scheduled for launch (though threatened by budget cuts) are *Deep Space 1* (possibly to Comet Wilson-Harrington or Comet Borrelly), *Stardust* (to Comet Wild 2), *CONTOUR* (to Comets Encke, Schwassman-Wachmann 3, and d'Arrest), and *Rosetta* (to Comet Wirtanen).

comet sample return probe
A spacecraft designed to capture material from the tail, **coma,** or **nucleus** of a comet and return it to Earth for laboratory analysis. Several such missions are under way or planned for the near future, including *Stardust.*

cometary collision hypothesis
Proposed in 1749 by Georges Louis Leclerc de **Buffon,** the idea that a comet struck the Sun and broke off fragments that formed the planets. This was the first version of the **cataclysmic hypothesis** of the origin of the solar system. Buffon mistakenly assumed that comets can be approximately as large as stars. The impact, he assumed, was off center, so that not only were the planets thrown out into their orbits but they (together with the Sun) were set spinning on their axes, some so rapidly that they threw off additional material from which their moons were made. A decade later, Immanuel **Kant** put forward the earliest form of the rival **nebular hypothesis.**

comets, collisions with
→ **cosmic collisions, biological effects of**

comets, organic matter in
→ **organic matter, in comets**

commensal
In biological parlance, two entities existing together but at the expense of each other.

Committee 14 on Exobiology
The result of the merger in August 1960 between the East and West Coast groups (**EASTEX** and **WESTEX**) of the **Space Science Board**'s **Panel on Extraterrestrial Life.** At the same time as this merger, **Panel 2 on Extraterrestrial Life** was dissolved to allow the Space Science Board to be the sole representative in bioastronautics for the National Academy of Sciences. Committee 14 was chaired by Joshua **Lederberg.**

Committee on Contamination by Extraterrestrial Exploration
Set up in 1958 by the International Council of Scientific Unions (ICSU) to evaluate the issue of possible contamination by spacecraft, first raised by Joshua **Lederberg,** and develop recommendations about quarantine procedures. The standards proposed by the committee were adopted by the ICSU in October 1958.[145, 148] → **back contamination; forward contamination**

Committee on Planetary and Lunar Exploration
A panel of scientists from various U.S. universities, chaired by John A. Wood of the **Harvard-Smithsonian Center for Astrophysics,** which advises the **Space Science Board** on issues related to the exploration of the solar system. It is currently engaged in two projects: (1) reviewing the status of knowledge about **Europa** in the light of the *Galileo* mission with a view to recommending a strategy for further exploration of this moon, and (2) reviewing the technology available for exploring the atmosphere and surfaces of solar system objects.

Committee on the Exploration of Extraterrestrial Space (CETEX)
A committee convened by the Council of Space Research (COSPAR), part of the International Council of Scientific Unions (ICSU), to make further recommendations concerning the issue of **contamination** by spacecraft. In 1959, it produced two reports.[197, 478]

communication, with the Moon and planets
Speculation about the possible existence of intelligent life on the Moon (➔ **Moon, life on**) and nearby planets (➔ **Mars, life on; Venus, life on**) led to numerous proposals for ways of communicating with any inhabitants there might be on these worlds. Various methods of visual signaling were suggested in the nineteenth century, including those of Karl **Gauss** (1822), Joseph von **Littrow** (1842), and Charles **Cros** (1869). In the 1890s, during the height of the canal controversy (➔ **Mars, canals of**), interest was focused on communicating with advanced Martians (➔ **Galton, Francis; Pickering, William Henry**). This interest was intensified by the announcement of the **Guzman Prize** and by reports of lights on the surface of Mars (➔ **Mars, changes on**), which were taken by some to be efforts by the inhabitants to send signals to Earth (although in *The War of the Worlds,* H. G. **Wells** offered a more disturbing alternative). The dawn of the twentieth century saw the first attempts and conjectures concerning radio communication with the planets, by Nikola **Tesla** (1901), David **Todd** (1909), and Guglielmo **Marconi** (1919).[300] These would pave the way for efforts to detect and transmit *interstellar* radio signals several decades later (➔ **SETI**).

companion
An object that may be a star, a **brown dwarf,** or a planet, that is in orbit around a brighter star. In a **binary star** system, it is the fainter of the two components. A companion may be detected directly (i.e., visually) or indirectly (➔ **companion, unseen**).

companion, unseen
An object such as a planet that is in orbit around a visible star, the presence of which can only be inferred by an indirect technique. ➔ **extrasolar planets, detection of**

competitive exclusion
Also known as Gause's principle after the Russian biologist G. F. Gause, the notion that two species cannot indefinitely occupy the same ecological **niche.** The one that is more efficient in taking advantage of available resources will exclude the other.

COMPLEX
➔ **Committee on Planetary and Lunar Exploration**

condensation (reaction)
A chemical change in which two or more molecules react with the elimination of water, or some other simple substance. It is the basic process by which subunits, such as **amino acids** or **monosaccharides,** join together to form biochemical **polymers.**

Condon, Edward Uhler (1902–74)
Princeton physicist and past director of the U.S. Bureau of Standards, who chaired the committee, set up at the request of the U.S. Air Force in 1966, to assess the evidence on **unidentified flying objects** gathered by Project **Blue Book.**

Condon Report
The final 1,465-page document arising from the study headed by Edward **Condon** into the phenomenon of **unidentified flying objects** based primarily on data collected by Project **Blue Book.** It was delivered to the U.S. Air Force in November 1968 and released in January 1969. In it, Condon wrote:

> Our general conclusion is that nothing has come from the study of UFOs in the past 21 years that has added to scientific knowledge. Careful consideration of the record as it is available to us leads us to conclude that further extensive study of UFOs probably cannot be justified.

The report attracted widespread criticism, not least from some parts of the scientific community, which felt that whether or not the **extraterrestrial hypothesis** was valid, the Condon study had been too quick to dismiss certain well-documented UFO cases for which there was no obvious explanation. The American Institute for Aeronautics and Astronautics (AIAA) had formed a subcommittee on UFOs in 1967 that, following the release of the Condon Report, issued its first public statement:

> The Committee has made a careful examination of the present state of the UFO issue and has concluded that the controversy cannot be resolved without further study in a quantitative scientific manner and that it deserves the attention of the engineering and scientific community.

In December 1969, at its annual meeting in Boston, the American Association for the Advancement of Science (AAAS) held a symposium, organized by a committee including Carl **Sagan,** Philip **Morrison,** and Thornton Page, to allow a more open and thorough airing of scientific views than it was felt the Condon Report had achieved.

conic sections

A family of curves to which the circle, **ellipse, parabola,** and **hyperbola** belong. It includes all the possible paths of a point that moves so that its distance from a fixed point (the focus)

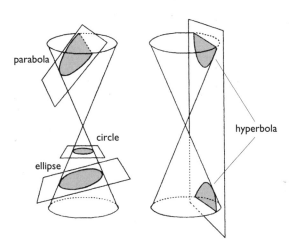

is a constant fraction of its distance from a fixed line (the directrix). This fraction is known as the **eccentricity.** Conic sections are so named because they can be obtained by slicing through a right circular cone at various different angles.

conjugation

The temporary union of **unicellular** organisms, during which genetic material is transferred between the two cells. In **prokaryotes, plasmid**s transfer copies of bacterial **gene**s from one bacterium to another. **Gene transfer** as a means of plasmid movement was discovered by Joshua **Lederberg** and Edward Tatum in 1947.

constellation

A grouping of stars in the night sky that forms a recognizable pattern. The stars making up a constellation are not actually bound together in close association but just happen to lie in roughly the same direction as seen from the observer's viewpoint. For example, the five brightest stars in the constellation of Cygnus the Swan (making up an arrangement also known as the Northern Cross) are approximately 74, 270, 410, 750, and 1,600 light-years from the Sun. Moreover, the dimmest of the quintet, Gienah (Epsilon Cygni), lies nearest to the Sun, while the brightest, **Deneb** (Alpha Cygni), is the most remote. Were these two stars to exchange places, Deneb, which is intrinsically one of the most luminous stars visible to the naked eye, would outshine Venus in our night sky.

Any future travelers to the stars will quickly grow accustomed to the changing shape of constellations as they cross the interstellar voids. The first groupings to become noticeably distorted from their familiar forms will be those made up largely of nearby stars, such as Cassiopeia (three of the brightest members of which are less than 100 light-years from the Sun) and the Big Dipper (with four stars less than 100 light-years away). By contrast, none of the prominent stars in Orion is less than 300 light-years distant, and several are 1,000 to 2,000 light-years from the Sun. Only a very lengthy interstellar voyage would suffice to seriously disturb the Great Hunter's well-known outline.

Contact

Science fiction novel (1985) by Carl **Sagan** that portrays, with technical authenticity, the sequence of events that might follow the receipt of an interstellar message. Some of the characters are loosely based on actual members of the **SETI** community, while the **wormhole** transport system employed later in the novel was investigated theoretically by the physicist Kip Thorne and his colleagues at the California Institute of Technology.[495]

contact, with extraterrestrial intelligence

→ **extraterrestrial intelligence, implications following first contact; extraterrestrial intelligence, procedures following first contact**

contamination

The release onto the Earth or another world of nonindigenous organisms or organic matter that could (a) have catastrophic consequences for any native life or (b) compromise the scientific findings of biological experiments. The urgent need to address the issues of both **back contamination** and **forward contamination** at the dawn of the Space Age was first pointed out forcibly by Joshua **Lederberg** in 1957. Following his advice, the National Academy of Sciences urged the International Council of Scientific Unions (ICSU) to evaluate the problem, which it did through the **Committee on Contamination by Extraterrestrial Exploration** and the **Committee on the Exploration of Extraterrestrial Space.** The National Academy of Sciences pursued its own investigation of the contamination issue through its **EASTEX** and **WESTEX** panels. More recently, with the imminent prospect of multiple sample-return probes and the suggestion that there might be life in the outer solar system, new recommendations have been made by a task force of the National Research Council on how to handle extraterrestrial material.

continuous spectrum

A **spectrum** in which all **wavelength**s between certain limits are present. White light, for example, can be dispersed by a prism to give a continuous spectrum in the optical region from red to violet. Dark **absorption lines** crossing a continuous spectrum are caused by the absorption of radiation at specific wavelengths.

continuously habitable zone

A region of space around a star where a planet can sustain liquid water at its surface, for at least part of its local year, considered over a long enough period for sophisticated life to emerge.

CONTOUR (Comet Nucleus Tour)

A **Discovery Program** mission to take images and comparative spectral maps of the nuclei of at least three **comet**s and analyze the dust flowing from them. Scheduled for launch in July 2002, *CONTOUR* will fly past Comet Encke at a distance of about 100 km (60 miles) in November 2003 before moving on to similar encounters with Comet Schwassmann-Wachmann 3 in June 2006 and Comet d'Arrest in August 2008.

convection

(1) Fluid circulation driven by large temperature gradients. (2) The transfer of heat by this circulation.

Convection and Rotation of Stars (COROT)

A French space mission, scheduled for launch at the end of 2002, one of the objects of which will be to search for **extrasolar planets** by **photometry.** It will use a 30-cm telescope equipped with **charge-coupled devices** (CCDs) to monitor the **light curve**s of selected stars for evidence of unseen companions.

convergent evolution

The independent development of similar structures or capabilities in organisms that are not directly related. Examples include the eyes of **cephalopods** and mammals and the ability to fly of certain insects, birds, bats, and teleost fish. The frequency with which convergent evolution has occurred on Earth supports the idea that certain basic anatomical structures and physiological mechanisms might be common among life-forms throughout the Universe.

Copernican Revolution

The dramatic and far-reaching change from a **geocentric** to a **heliocentric** worldview prompted by the work of Nicolaus **Coperni-cus.** It enabled the true status of the Earth, as an ordinary planet, to be realized and marked the beginning of the end for the belief that there was a fundamental division between the nature of things terrestrial and extraterrestrial. As Bishop John **Wilkins**[626] noted, classical philosophers had asked

> of what kind of matter that should be, of which the heavens are framed, whether or no of any fifth substance distinct from the four elements, as Aristotle holds, and with him some of the late Schoolmen, whose subtill brains could not be content to attribute to those vast glorious bodies, but common materials, and therefore they themselves had rather take pains to prefer them some extraordinary nature.

But in the wake of Copernicus, wrote Wilkins, it was apparent

> that the heavens do not consist of any such pure matter which can privilege them from the like change and corruption as these inferior bodies are liable unto.

This breakdown of the Aristotelian dichotomy between terrestrial space and the region beyond also saw the demise of the medieval belief in the physicality of demons and other such semimaterial extraterrestrials. The way was now open to the idea that there might be other worlds like the Earth and other creatures on those worlds that might resemble ourselves. As demons and their ilk retreated to the realm of the purely spiritual, so post-Copernican intellectuals began to ponder the possibility of alien life-forms made of flesh and blood.

At first, the new **heliocentric** scheme was resisted, but not, as Arthur **Lovejoy**[359] has pointed out, because it demoted the Earth:

> It has often been pointed out that the older picture of the world in space was peculiarly fitted to give man a high sense of his own importance and dignity.... Man occupied, we are told, the central place in the universe, and round the planet of his habitation all the vast, unpeopled spheres obsequiously revolved. But the actual tendency of the geocentric system was, for the medieval mind, precisely the opposite. For the center of the world was not a position of honor; it was rather the place furthest removed from the Empyrean, the bottom of creation...the geocentric cosmography served rather for man's humiliation than for his exaltation.... Copernicanism was opposed partly on the ground that it assigned too dignified and lofty a position to his dwelling place.

Those who were among the first to voice support and provide further evidence for the Copernican system, including Galileo **Galilei,** were not generally inclined to say much about its implications for extraterrestrial life, though Giordano **Bruno** was an early exception. Instead, it was left for others of a more speculative nature, such as Wilkins and Francis **Godwin,** to begin to people the newfound worlds. Yet when post-Copernican **pluralism** did take root, it was not in response to hard astronomical data (for there was still virtually none of this relevant to astrobiology) but rather to an appeal to **teleology** and reasoning by analogy. In Lovejoy's words:

> The more important features of this new conception of the world, then, owed little to any new hypotheses based upon the sort of observational grounds which we should nowadays call "scientific." They were chiefly derivative from philosophical and theological premises. They were, in short, manifest corollaries of the principle of plenitude.

The most fundamental tenet of those who advocated the plurality of worlds in the wake of Copernicus was that *God (or nature) makes nothing in vain.* If there were other planets, they must be inhabited. Otherwise, why would they exist? (→ **plenitude, principle of**).

Copernicus, Nicolaus (1473–1543)

Polish astronomer (born Mikołaj Kopernik) who in his *De revolutionibus orbium coelestium* (On the Revolution of the Celestial Sphere) challenged the **geocentric** worldview of **Aristotle,** accepted by the Church and by most intellectuals in Europe at that time, by arguing that the Earth and other planets orbit around the Sun. Prudently, Copernicus himself was not inclined to explore the ramifications of his new scheme. But his demotion of the Earth to a mere satellite of the Sun encouraged others, such as Giordano **Bruno,** to speculate that there might be many Earth-like worlds bearing life in the universe. ➔ **Copernican Revolution;** Johannes **Kepler**

Coralie

A high-precision **échelle spectrograph** developed through a collaboration between the **Haute-Provence Observatory** and **La Silla Observatory.** It is attached to the **Leonard Euler Telescope,** and the two instruments together form a dedicated, automated system for searching for large **extrasolar planets** in the southern hemisphere. Essentially an enhanced version of **Elodie,** Coralie has superior spectral resolution, a more efficient light detector, and improved instrumental control, including on-line data reduction and analysis. Coralie can measure the **radial velocity** of a star to a precision better than 7 miles per second (25 km per hour)—about the speed of a fast human runner. While in its commissioning phase in 1998, it was used in the detection of a planet in orbit around **Gliese 86.**

Cordelia

The innermost moon of **Uranus.** Cordelia acts as the **shepherd moon** of Uranus's epsilon ring. ➔ **Uranus, moons of**

Discovery	1986, by *Voyager 2*
Mean distance from Uranus	49,200 km (30,600 mi.)
Diameter	26 km (16 mi.)
Orbital period	0.335 days (8 hours 2 minutes)
Orbital eccentricity	0.140
Orbital inclination	0.00°
Visual albedo	0.07

Cornell University

An institution that has traditionally been at the leading edge of both **SETI** and planetary science. Many SETI pioneers have studied or taught there. Charles **Seeger** enrolled in the school of engineering in 1939 and founded the Cornell Radio Astronomy Project in 1946. In the same year, Philip **Morrison** joined the physics faculty, to be followed in 1947 by Guiseppe **Cocconi.** Also in 1947, Freeman **Dyson** arrived at Cornell, becoming a professor in 1951. Frank **Drake** obtained a bachelor's degree there before returning as professor of astronomy in 1964 and becoming head of the **National Astronomy and Ionosphere Center** in 1971. Among other prominent figures who graduated from or taught at Cornell were Carl **Sagan,** Jill **Tarter,** Christopher **Chyba,** Thomas **Gold,** and, perhaps most influentially in the early stages, Otto **Struve.**

corona

The uppermost portion of a star's atmosphere, characterized by low density and high temperatures (over 1 million°C).

coronograph

A special telescope that blocks the light from the visible disk of a star so that the fainter surroundings can be seen.

COROT

➔ *Convection and Rotation of Stars*

COSETI

➔ **Columbus Optical SETI Observatory**

cosmic abundance

➔ **elements, cosmic abundance of**

cosmic background radiation

Diffuse **microwave radiation** that arrives with almost uniform intensity from all directions in space. This cosmic "hiss" is believed to be the much-cooled remnant of the fireball in which the Universe began.

cosmic catastrophes, biological effects of

Violent events in the Universe, both local and remote, may have profound consequences for life. In some cases, they may prevent life from becoming established at all, while in others, they may significantly affect the course of a planet's biological evolution. Among the cosmic phenomena that astronomers have identified as being of potential biological importance are:

1. Large-scale stellar **flares**
2. Nearby **supernova** explosions
3. **Gamma-ray bursters**
4. Impacts by **asteroids** or **comets** (➔ **cosmic collisions, biological effects of**)

cosmic coincidences
➔ **anthropic principle; carbon**

cosmic collisions, biological effects of
An inevitable corollary of the birth of planetary systems is the formation of numerous smaller objects, including **asteroids** and **comets**, and the collision between some of these bodies and larger, possibly life-bearing worlds. Thus any comprehensive model of the origin and evolution of life must factor in the possible consequences of such collisions. During the early, intense bombardment phase of a new solar system, numerous large-scale impacts may preclude the development of life or force it to take place well below the surface of a planet, where there is some protection (➔ **Earth, early history of**). Impacts may also result in the transference of **prebiotic** or biological material between worlds (➔ **ballistic panspermia**). Later in the course of a planet's development, occasional collisions with objects at least several kilometers across may dramati-

Artist's impression of the impact theorized to have caused the last great mass extinction 65 million years ago. NASA/JPL/Caltech

cally influence the course of biological evolution by wiping out many species or entire genera (➔ **mass extinction**s) but, at the same time, providing the opportunity for other categories of organisms to flourish. Such appears to have been the case at the **Cretaceous-Tertiary Boundary,** when, apparently in the wake of an asteroid impact, the mammals and ultimately humankind filled the ecological void left by the demise of the dinosaurs and their kin.

cosmic dust

Microscopic grains of matter that occur in space. They play an important role in the origin of planetary systems (➔ **planetary systems, formation of**) and possibly even that of life itself. The composition, size, and other properties of dust particles vary from one location to another. Grains in dense **interstellar cloud**s, for example, are larger than those in the general **interstellar medium,** while larger particles still are found in circumstellar **dust disk**s.

Most of the dust in interstellar space comes from stars that have moved off the **main sequence** and entered the **red giant** phase of their evolution (➔ **stars, evolution of**). These stars have extended atmospheres rich in **silicon, oxygen,** and **carbon**—elements that were manufactured in the stellar core but that have been dredged to the surface by convection currents. Depending on its life history, a red giant may have surface layers that are rich in either carbon or oxygen. A **carbon star** gives rise to a dense pall of carbon particles in the form of **graphite** flakes or amorphous lumps, each measuring about 0.01 micron across. In the case of an oxygen-rich star, the oxygen atoms react with silicon and any metal atoms in the star's atmosphere to form **silicate** grains roughly 1 micron across. As the grains are blown away from the star by **radiation pressure** and their temperature falls, they begin acquiring additional atoms of **hydrogen,** oxygen, carbon, **nitrogen,** and **sulfur** that have also escaped from the parent star. These ac-

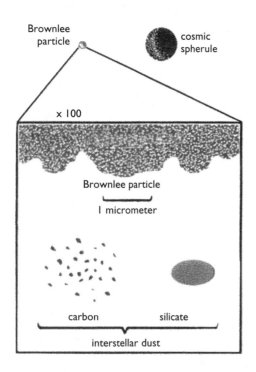
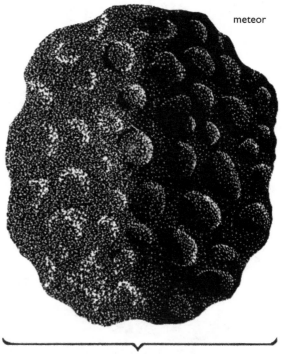

Comparison between interstellar dust, comprised of carbon and silicate particles, and larger particles including meteors, cosmic spherules, and Brownlee particles that occur in the solar system.
New Scientist

creted materials build up into icy mantles of water ice and solid **ammonia, methane,** and **carbon dioxide.** Through a variety of chemical "sticking" processes, other substances may then be added to the mantle ices, including small molecules such as **carbon monoxide** (CO) and **hydrogen sulfide** (H_2S). Bombardment by **ultraviolet** radiation from local hot stars or more remote stars triggers reactions between the different chemical species on a grain's surface and leads to the formation of simple **organic** substances.

Dust grains that have drifted into the general interstellar medium find their way into denser clouds and eventually into **molecular cloud**s where the density is sufficiently high for more complex organic synthesis to take place (➔ **interstellar molecules**). How far up the scale of **prebiotic** synthesis such interstellar cookery can lead has yet to be determined, but it certainly extends as far as the simplest of **amino acids.** According to Fred **Hoyle** and Chandra Wickramasinghe, it extends as far as life itself, with the largest of dust grains being none other than living bacteria. Although this extreme theory has few supporters, mainstream science has gradually come around to the view that organically laced debris from space may have been an important means by which life was able to originate on Earth so early (➔ **Earth, early history of**).

cosmic radio background
➔ **cosmic background radiation**

cosmic rays
Charged particles, mostly **proton**s but also including nuclei of heavier **element**s, that travel through space at velocities close to that of light. Storms on the surface of the Sun are known to produce cosmic rays, as are **supernova**s, but other more powerful sources are thought to exist.

cosmic year
Alternative name for a **galactic year.**

cosmology
The study of the universe considered as a single entity.

cosmos
A term used synonymously with "universe." The *kosmos* of the ancient Greeks and Christian Middle Ages consisted of the Earth at the center of a series of concentric, revolving spheres to which the Moon, Sun, planets, and stars were fixed. In the scheme of **Aristotle** and **Ptolemy,** which prevailed until the **Copernican Revolution,** only one *kosmos* was allowed with nothing beyond. According to the school of **atomism,** however, there were many *kosmoi*, distinct and separate from our own, each with a world, possibly inhabited, at its heart.

covalent bond
A chemical bond formed when two **atom**s share a pair of **valence electron**s. Unlike **ionic bond**s, covalent bonds connect specific atoms and so give rise to true, discrete **molecule**s.

Coyne, George V. (1933–)
Director of the Vatican Observatory and a Jesuit priest who is involved in the search for **protoplanetary disks** around young stars. Concerning the effect on Christian doctrine of the possibility of alien life, Coyne has expressed the opinion that salvation does not require God's incarnation (➔ **incarnation and redemption**). His belief is that if alien beings have sinned, God is free to choose to save them in some manner other than by becoming incarnate in alien flesh. ➔ **Christian doctrine and pluralism**

Crab Nebula (NGC 1952, M 1)
The remains of a **supernova** that was recorded by Chinese astronomers as a "guest star" on July 4, 1054. So bright was the explosion that the object could be seen in broad daylight for three weeks. The Crab Nebula is about 6,500 light-years (2,000 parsecs) from the Sun and has now expanded to a diameter of about 13 light-years (4 parsecs). It contains about 1 M_S of material in a characteristic crablike shape. At the center of the Crab is the core of the star that gave rise to it—a **neutron star** spinning at 30 revolutions per second. This was the first **pulsar** ever detected and remains only one of two pulsars to be observed optically, though it can also be seen at radio, infrared, X-ray, and gamma-ray wavelengths.

crater

(1) A bowl-shaped structure formed by the impact of a **meteoroid** or **asteroid.** (2) A depression around the opening of a volcano.

Cressida

The fourth known moon of **Uranus.** → **Uranus, moons of**

Discovery	1986, by *Voyager 2*
Mean distance from Uranus	61,780 km (38,400 mi.)
Diameter	62 km (39 mi.)
Orbital period	0.464 day (11 hours 8 minutes)
Orbital eccentricity	0.000
Orbital inclination	0.04°
Visual albedo	0.07

Cretaceous-Tertiary (K-T) Boundary

The end of the Cretaceous era about 65 million years ago, marked by a **mass extinction** in which the last of the dinosaurs (as well as the ammonites and many other species) died out. When Luis **Alvarez** first proposed that this had been brought about by the collision between the Earth and an asteroid (→ **cosmic collisions, biological effects of**), many paleontologists were skeptical. Among the counterarguments was that there had been a gradual decline in many types of fauna and flora throughout the Cretaceous—the number of genera of dinosaurs, for example, having fallen from thirty to seven during this era. However, Alvarez and others were able to support the impact theory by their discovery of a thin layer of material at various points around the globe that is so highly enriched with elements such as iridium and osmium that it could have come only from an extraterrestrial source. The K-T Boundary is now generally believed to have been precipitated by the impact of a 10-km-wide **asteroid** that created the **Chicxulub Crater.**

Crick, Francis Harry Compton (1916–   )

British molecular biologist now at the Salk Institute, California, who in 1962 won a Nobel Prize for his part in the elucidation of the structure of **DNA.** He was led by his belief that the chances of life originating on Earth were very low to argue the case for **panspermia** and, in particular, a radical form of this hypothesis known as **directed panspermia.** More recently, Crick has been involved with examining the possibility that **RNA** was the first replicator molecule on Earth during an early biological era known as the "**RNA world.**"

Crimean Astrophysical Observatory

A leading center for astrophysical research in Russia, located at Simeis in south Crimea, between Sevastapol and Yalta, and operated by the Russian Academy of Sciences. Its principal instruments are a 2.6-m (102-in.) optical telescope, a 22-m (72-ft.) **radio telescope** used for observations in the millimeter-wave region, and a solar telescope.

Cromie, Robert (1856–1907)

Irish author of *A Plunge Through Space*[134] (1890), which passed through many editions and laid the foundation for its author's fame as one of the pioneers of the interplanetary novel. After a flight, using antigravity, to Mars, the explorers come upon a utopian civilization.

Cros, Charles (1842–88)

French inventor and polymath who in 1869 proposed a method of sending signals to either Mars or Venus. It involved focusing the rays from one or more electric lights by parabolic mirrors. Periodic flashing of light from the mirrors would, he suggested, send the equivalent of a Morse code message. If the signals received a response, he said, "It will be a moment of joy and pride. The eternal isolation of the spheres is vanquished." Flashes reported by Charles Messier, Johann **Schröter,** and Warren Harding on planets such as Venus, he suggested, might be attempts by the inhabitants to communicate with us. By 1870, his ideas had spread to Italy and England. → **communication, with the Moon and planets**

crust

The outermost, solid layer of a planet or moon, generally consisting of low-density rock, various ices, or a mixture of the two.

cryobiology

The study of biological activity at low temperatures.

cryobot

A long, pencil-shaped probe with a heated tip that can melt its way down through a thick layer of ice and deploy equipment for returning data from any watery environment that may lie below. Such devices will be used to explore Lake **Vostok** and eventually the subice ocean hypothesized to exist on **Europa.** Having penetrated through to the bottom of the ice crust, cryobots on these missions will release two principal devices for operating at interfaces where life might be expected to occur: an *ice-water interface station,* which will monitor conditions at the top of the watery sea, and a *sediment exploration station,* which will descend to the seafloor. The latter will also release a **hydrobot** that will rise like a bubble to the top of the subice sea, taking measurements and searching for signs of life as it goes.

cryophiles

Organisms that thrive at low temperatures.

cryptobiosis

A reversible state in which an animal's **metabolism** has come to a standstill.

CTA-102

A powerful celestial source of radio waves, cataloged in the early 1960s by the California Institute of Technology, and proposed, in 1963, by Nikolai S. **Kardashev** in the scientifically conservative *Astronomical Journal* of the USSR as evidence of a Type II or Type III **Kardashev civilization.** A worldwide sensation followed a TASS agency announcement that Gennady Sholomitskii of the **Sternberg State Astronomical Institute,** following up Kardashev's idea, had found CTA-102 to be the beacon of a "supercivilization."[541] Shortly after, observations from **Palomar Observatory** identified CTA-102 with a **quasar.** → **SETI, false alarms in**

CTIO

→ **Cerro Tololo Inter-American Observatory**

CUFOS

→ **Center for UFO Studies**

CW Leonis

In the **infrared** region of the spectrum, the second brightest star in the sky (after the Sun). CW Leonis is a **carbon**-rich **red giant** in the process of shedding material from its outer layers at a speed of 9 to 24 km per second (6 to 15 miles per second). Over a period of 10,000 to 30,000 years, this mass loss will result in a **planetary nebula** about 1 light-year across.

cyanobacteria

A group of **photosynthetic bacteria** that contain **chlorophyll** and other light-harvesting pigments. Cyanobacteria, which are still active today, appeared on Earth at least 3 billion years ago and played a crucial role in changing the terrestrial environment by releasing oxygen into the atmosphere. They were previously but inappropriately known as blue-green algae.

cyborg

Contraction of "cybernetic organism," a human-machine hybrid. In the strictest sense, anyone with a medical implant (such as an artificial pacemaker or cochlear implant) or prosthesis (even including contact lenses or a walking stick), falls into this category. But the term is usually reserved for speculative creatures that might exist in the future on Earth or already elsewhere. The concept of a human-cybernetic synergy was popularized in David Rorvik's *As Man Becomes Machine* (1971).

Cyclops, Project

An ambitious scheme proposed in the early 1970s but never implemented to deploy a vast array of steerable radio dishes in an attempt to eavesdrop on the radio transmissions from extraterrestrial civilizations. It had its origins in 1970 with a suggestion by John **Billingham,** then head of the Biotechnology Division at **NASA Ames Research Center,** to Ames director Hans Mark that NASA should carry out a small-scale study of ways and means in **SETI.** The optimistic conclusions of this initial investigation prompted a more ambitious "design study of a

Artist's concept of the Cyclops system at ground level, showing the central control and processing building.
NASA/Ames Research Center

system for detecting extraterrestrial intelligent life" conducted in 1971 as part of a summer faculty fellowship program in engineering systems at Stanford University (an annual event jointly sponsored by Stanford, NASA, and Ames). Participants included Billingham and Charles **Seeger,** but the central figure proved to be Bernard **Oliver,** who originated the bold concept of a phased array of one thousand 100-m antennas covering a total area some 10 km

Artist's concept of the Cyclops array from above.
NASA/Ames Research Center

across. This giant multicomponent instrument would search the sky in the **waterhole** frequency band with sufficient sensitivity to be able to detect the stray radio emissions of a race at a similar level of technological development to that of humankind, over distances of several hundred light-years. Of course, Cyclops would also have been capable of detecting intentionally beamed messages over colossal, even intergalactic, distances. But in its ability to pick up the domestic radio "noise" of a civilization that, like our own, is not engaged in strenuous full-time efforts at interstellar communication, it would have been unique. Being a phased array, it could have been built incrementally and operated at whatever capacity was available. If no signals were detected with a small "orchard," more dishes could have been added to boost the sensitivity until the full configuration was in place. The total (1971) price tag of $6 billion to $10 billion proved too daunting, however, and the proposal was rejected—although NASA did begin work on a much less ambitious SETI program a decade later (➔ **High Resolution Microwave Survey**).[57]

16 Cygni

A Sun-like star around which has been found a planet with a mass about 1.5 times that of Jupiter in an extraordinarily elongated orbit.

Host Star	
Distance	70.5 light-years (21.6 parsecs)
Spectral type	G1.5 V
Apparent magnitude	6.2
Temperature	5,430°C (5,700 K)
Luminosity	1.33 L_s
Mass	1.00 M_s
Planet	
Mass (Jupiter = 1)	1.52
Semimajor axis	1.7 AU (255 million km, 158 million mi.)
Orbital period	804 days
Eccentricity	0.67
Discovery	1997, by Geoffrey Marcy, Paul Butler, William Cochran, and Artie Hatzes, San Francisco State University Planet Search
Method of discovery	Radial velocity

The planet's distance from the primary varies between less than the Venus-to-Sun distance and more than the Mars-to-Sun distance.[262] ➔ **extrasolar planets**

61 Cygni

A **binary star** system consisting of two **K star**s that is one of the Sun's nearest stellar neighbors. It was the first to have its distance accurately determined (by Friedrich **Bessel** in 1838) by trigonometric **parallax.** 61 Cygni has a period of 720 years, with one of the components itself a binary with a period of 5 years. It was the host of Hal **Clement**'s fictional fast-rotating planet, Mesklin, in *Mission of Gravity.* ➔ **stars, nearest**

Cyrano de Bergerac, Savinien de (1619–55)

French author and prolific duelist (most of the duels being fought on account of his extraordi-

Engraving of Cyrano's hero, Gonsales, on a planetary excursion powered by evaporating dew (c. 1680).

narily large nose). His enthusiasm for **pluralism** is evident in his *Histoire comique des états et empires de la Lune et du Soleil* (A Comical History of the States and Empires of the Sun and the Moon), published posthumously in 1656. This inventive fantasy sees the reappearance of Francis **Godwin**'s Domingo Gonsales and probably helped inspire Jonathan **Swift**'s *Gulliver's Travels* and **Voltaire**'s *Micromégas.* It also introduced several novel ideas for aerial and space propulsion, notably the rocket and (as Arthur C. **Clarke** has pointed out) the ramjet.

Cytherean

(1) Pertaining to Venus (e.g., Cytherean meteorology). (2) A hypothetical inhabitant of Venus. In mythology, Cythera is the Ionian island upon which the goddess Venus first set foot.

cytochromes

Respiratory pigments found widely in **aerobic** organisms. They consists of **proteins** with an iron **prosthetic group** similar to that of hemoglobin. The **oxidation** of cytochromes by molecular **oxygen** and their subsequent **reduction** in the **cell** is the principal route by which atmospheric oxygen enters into cellular **metabolism.**

cytoplasm

The jellylike matrix that surrounds the **nucleus** of a **cell** and is bounded by the **cell membrane.** It contains the **organelle**s of the cell as well as the **sugars, amino acids,** and **proteins** that the cell uses for growth and reproduction. Cytoplasm was formerly referred to as protoplasm.

cytosine

A **pyramidine** that is one of five organic **base**s found in the **nucleic acid**s of **cell**s. In both **DNA** and **RNA** it pairs with **guanine.** Controversy surrounds its **prebiotic** origin together with that of **uracil.** In 1999, Robert **Shapiro** pointed out[532] that

> [n]o reactions have been described thus far that would produce cytosine, even in a specialized local setting, at a rate sufficient to compensate for the decomposition.

This claim is opposed, however, by Stanley **Miller** and his colleagues, who believe that cytosine and uracil could have been formed efficiently on the young Earth in chemically concentrated environments around the edges of lagoons.[484]

Daedalus, Project

The first full-scale study for an interstellar spacecraft, conducted from 1973 to 1978 by a group of scientists and engineers of the **British Interplanetary Society.** Daedalus called for an unmanned probe to be accelerated to about 12 percent of the **speed of light** by a series of nuclear **fusion** explosions and sent on a 50-year mission to **Barnard's Star.** The large amounts of helium 3 fuel required, it was suggested, could be mined from Jupiter's atmosphere. → **interstellar travel**

Däniken, Erich von (1935–)

Swiss author of several best-selling books, beginning with *Erinnerungen an die Zukunft* (1968, translated in 1969 as *Chariots of the Gods?*), which promote the **paleocontact hypothesis.** Although the underlying thesis of past extraterrestrial visitation is not implausible, the evidence that he and others have assembled to support their case is suspect (often simply false and manufactured) and undisciplined. Nevertheless, von Däniken's works have sold in the millions and testify to the genuine desire of many ordinary people to believe in intelligent life beyond the Earth. Just as George **Adamski**'s popular, and also purportedly nonfictional, books answered a need of millions to believe in the **extraterrestrial hypothesis** during a time when nuclear war seemed imminent (→ **Cold War, linked to UFO reports**), so von Däniken, more than a decade later, was able temporarily to fill a spiritual vacuum with his tales of ancient astronauts and God-like wisdom from the stars. → **SETI, religious dimensions of**

dark matter

Matter of an undetermined nature believed to exist in very large quantities throughout the Universe. Its existence has been inferred from the anomalous rotation of galaxies (including our own) and the motion of galaxies through galaxy clusters, which cannot be explained on the basis of known luminous matter. In fact, it seems as if about 90 percent of the total mass of the Universe may consist of dark matter.

dark nebula

Alternative name for an **absorption nebula.**

Darwin

A proposal for a European space-based interferometer that would operate in the **infrared** part of the spectrum (→ **Infrared Space Interferometer**). Its principal aims would be to search for Earth-like planets around nearby stars and then look for a signature of life, such as the presence of **ozone** in the atmosphere[335] (→ **extraterrestrial life, detection of**).

Darwin, Charles Robert (1809–82)

British naturalist who revolutionized biology with his theory of evolution through natural selection. He also speculated, in a letter to the botanist Joseph Hooker (1871), on the possibility of a chemical origin for life:

> It is often said that all the conditions for the first production of a living organism are present, which could ever have been present. But if (and Oh! what a big if!) we could conceive in some warm little pond, with all sorts of ammonia and phosphoric salts, light, heat, electricity, etc., present, that a protein compound was chemically formed ready to undergo still more complex changes, at the present day such matter would be instantly devoured or absorbed, which would not have been the case before living creatures were formed.

Recognizing, however, that the science of his time was not yet ready for such a concept, he added:

> It is mere rubbish thinking at present of the origin of life; one might as well think of the origin of matter.

→ **evolutionary theory and extraterrestrial life**

Davy, Humphry (1778–1829)

Brilliant experimental chemist and president of the Royal Society whose widely read book *Consolations in Travel, or The Last Days of a Philosopher* revealed some extraordinary personal beliefs concerning extraterrestrial life. Published posthumously, *Consolations in Travel* recounts a vision, based partly upon dreams, in which Davy describes a universe full of every conceivable kind of life and in which souls migrate from one world to another as they acquire knowledge (→ **transmigration of souls**). It presents a philosophy akin to that of Emanuel **Swedenborg** and so impressed Camille **Flammarion** that he arranged for it to be translated and published in France (1868).

Day the Earth Stood Still, The

Classic, intelligent science fiction film released in 1952 (→ **science fiction involving extraterrestrials, in films and on television**). In it, radars pick up a fast-moving object in the atmosphere. A flying saucer sets down in Washington, D.C., and is immediately surrounded by the military—the heavy-handed response to the arrival of all interplanetary travelers since *The War of the Worlds* **radio play** in 1938. A man-alien emerges holding a device that, unfortunately for him, looks indistinguishable from a Buck Rogers ray gun. Encircled by tanks and other artillery, he then makes the awesomely crass mistake of pressing a button on the gadget (a gift, it turns out, intended for the president). Cue a nervous young soldier to open fire. Cue Gort, a giant ponderous robot, to emerge menacingly from the saucer, vaporize a few of the heavy artillery pieces, and carry his injured companion back into the spaceship. The man-alien's mission, it transpires, is to try to make world leaders see sense and abandon their nuclear brinkmanship before it is too late. But when he fails, he reveals that the Earth will effectively be put under house arrest until it is mature enough to join the wider community of spacefaring worlds. As a final twist, the robot emerges as the real master—an indestructible interstellar police officer built to keep the galactic peace. Barely had the film been released when it seemed it might come true. In July 1952, unidentified blips were reported to have appeared on radar screens around Washington, D.C. (→ **"Washington Invasion"**). → **Cold War, linked to UFO reports**

daylight disk

One of the six categories of **unidentified flying objects** in the classification scheme devised by J. Allen **Hynek** in the 1950s. It is defined as an aerial object seen at a distance during the daytime that does not appear to correspond with any known natural or artificial phenomenon.

D-class asteroid

A category of asteroids with very low **albedo** (in the range 0.02 to 0.05). Their strong reddish coloration at long wavelengths suggests the presence of **organic** material. D-class objects are rare in the **Main Asteroid Belt** but increasingly common at distances of more than 3.3 AU from the Sun.

De Concilio, Januarius (1836–98)

Catholic priest and professor who argued for the ubiquity of extraterrestrial life on theological grounds. In an 1884 article, he wrote:

> [A]s there is an immense distance between the highest intellect of mankind and that of the lowest pure spiritual substances, the cosmological law of affinity demands that there should be some intermediate species to soften down the immense contrast.

These intermediate species, he suggests, are the inhabitants of other worlds. Life, in his view, *must* exist everywhere since a sterile planet would be a waste of God's powers. On the difficult question of Christ's **incarnation and redemption,** he asserts that although it happened only once, on Earth, its effect must extend to all other "species of incorporated intelligences [which] may have fallen, and very likely did fall." ➔ **Christian doctrine and pluralism**

debris disk
➔ **regenerated disk**

Declaration of Principles (Concerning Activities Following the Detection of Extraterrestrial Intelligence)

A document drafted in 1989 by a special subcommittee of the **SETI** Committee of the International Academy of Astronautics that sets out principles to be followed for researchers and others in the event that an unequivocal signal is detected from an extraterrestrial race. The principles are:

1. Any individual, public and private research institute, or governmental agency that believes it has detected a signal from extraterrestrial intelligence, should seek to verify that the most plausible explanation for the evidence is the existence of extraterrestrial intelligence rather than some other natural phenomenon or anthropogenic phenomenon before making any public announcement. If the evidence cannot be confirmed as indicating the existence of extraterrestrial intelligence, the discoverer may disseminate the information as appropriate to the discovery of any unknown phenomenon.

2. Prior to making a public announcement that evidence of extraterrestrial intelligence has been detected, the discoverer should promptly inform all other observers or research organizations that are parties to this declaration, so that those other parties may seek to confirm the discovery by independent observations at other sites and so that a network can be established to enable continuous monitoring of the signal or phenomenon. Parties to this declaration should not make any public announcement of this information until it is determined whether this information is or is not credible evidence of the existence of extraterrestrial intelligence. The discoverer should inform his/her or its relevant national authorities.

3. After concluding that the discovery appears credible evidence of extraterrestrial intelligence, and after informing other parties to this declaration, the discoverer should inform observers throughout the world through the Central Bureau for Astronomical Telegrams of the International Astronomical Union, and should inform the Secretary General of the United Nations in accordance with Article XI of the Treaty on Principles Governing the Activities of States in the Exploration and Use of Outer Space, Including the Moon and Other Bodies. Because of their demonstrated interest in and expertise concerning the question of the existence of extraterrestrial intelligence, the discoverers should simultaneously inform the following international institutions of the discovery and should provide them with all pertinent data and recorded information concerning the evidence: the International Telecommunications Union, the Committee on Space Research of the International Council of Scientific Unions, the International Astronautical Federation, the International Academy of Astronautics, the International Institute of Space Law, Commission 51 of the International Astronomical Union and Commission J of the International Radio Science Union.

4. A confirmed detection of extraterrestrial intelligence should be disseminated promptly, openly, and widely through scientific channels and public media, observing the procedures of this declaration. The discoverer should have the privilege of making the first public announcement.

5. All data necessary for confirmation of the detection should be made available to the international scientific community through publications, meetings, conferences, and other appropriate means.

6. The discovery should be confirmed and monitored and any data bearing on the evidence of extraterrestrial intelligence should be recorded and stored permanently to the greatest extent feasible and practicable, in a form that will make it available for further analysis and interpretation. These recordings should be made available to the international institutions listed above and to members of the scientific community for further objective analysis and interpretation.

7. If the evidence of detection is in the form of electromagnetic signals, the parties to this declaration should seek international agreement to protect the appropriate frequencies by exercising procedures available through the International Telecommunications Union. Immediate notice should be sent to the Secretary General of the International Telecommunications Union in Geneva, who may include a request to minimize transmissions on the relevant frequencies in the Weekly Circular. The Secretariat, in conjunction with advice of the Union's Administrative Council, should explore the feasibility and utility of convening an Extraordinary Administrative Radio Conference to deal with the matter, subject to the opinions of the member Administrations of the International Telecommunications Union.

8. No response to a signal or other evidence of extraterrestrial intelligence should be sent until appropriate internal consultations have taken place. The procedures for such consultations will be the subject of a separate agreement, declaration or arrangement.

9. The SETI Committee of the International Academy of Astronautics, in coordination with Commission 51 of the International Astronomical Union, will conduct a continuing review of the procedures for the detection of extraterrestrial intelligence and subsequent handling of the data. Should credible evidence of extraterrestrial intelligence be discovered, an international committee of scientists and other experts should be established to serve as a focal point for continuing analysis of all observational evidence collected in the aftermath of the discovery, and also to provide advice on the release of information to the public. The committee should be constituted from representatives of each of the international institutions listed above and such other members as the committee may deem necessary. To facilitate the convocation of such a committee at some unknown time in the future, the SETI Committee of the International Academy of Astronautics should initiate and maintain a current list of willing representatives from each of the international institutions listed above, as well as other individuals with relevant skills, and should make that list continuously available through the Secretariat of the International Academy of Astronautics. The International Academy of Astronautics will act as the Depository for this declaration and will annually provide a current list of parties to all the parties of the declaration.

declination

The angular distance of a celestial body north (positive) or south (negative) of the **celestial equator.** It is one of two coordinates commonly used to define the position of an object in the sky, the other being **right ascension.**

Deep Space 1 (DS1)

The first mission in NASA's **New Millennium Program.** *Deep Space 1* is an experimental probe designed to test twelve advanced spacecraft and science instrument technologies that may subsequently be used on missions in the twenty-first century. Launched in October 1998, *DS1* is powered by a solar electric (xenon ion) propulsion system and is capable of autonomous navigational maneuvers. Its flyby of asteroid 1992KD on July 29, 1999, and possibly of two comets (Wilson-Harrington and Borrelly) in an extended mission lasting until 2001, will help test a miniaturized instrument known as the Integrated Camera and Imaging Spectrometer.

Deep Space 2 (DS2)
→ *Mars Microprobe Mission*

Deep Space 3 (DS3)
→ **New Millennium Interferometer**

Deep Space 4 (DS4)
→ *Champollion*

degenerate electron pressure
The pressure produced by closely packed **electron**s as a result of the **Pauli exclusion principle.** It is what supports **white dwarf**s against further gravitational collapse.

degenerate matter
Matter in which all the available quantum energy states allowed by the **Pauli exclusion principle** have been occupied. Degenerate matter occurs, for example, in stars that have collapsed under their own gravitational pull following the exhaustion of their usable nuclear **fusion** energy reserves. → **neutron star; white dwarf**

degenerate neutron pressure
The pressure produced by closely packed **neutron**s as a result of the **Pauli exclusion principle.** It is what supports **neutron stars** against further gravitational collapse.

degenerate star
A star, such as a **white dwarf** or **neutron star** that is composed of **degenerate matter.**

Deimos
The smaller of the two diminutive moons of **Mars.** Like its sister satellite, **Phobos,** Deimos appears to be a **C-class asteroid** that was captured in the remote past by the Martian gravitational field. However, it displays none of the grooves and crater chains found on Phobos, while many of its craters are less distinct, probably because of infilling by crater ejecta that may lie tens of meters thick on the surface. The larger craters, such as Voltaire and Swift, named after their literary connections (→ **Swift, Jonathan, and the moons of Mars**),

measure only about 2 km across. → **Mars, moons of**

Discovery	August 10, 1877, by Asaph Hall
Mean distance from center of Mars	23,400 km (14,540 mi.)
Diameter	10 × 12 × 16 km (6 × 7 × 10 mi.)
Mean density	1.7 g/cm³
Escape velocity	0.0057 km/s (20 km/h, 13 mi./h)
Orbital period	30.2 hours (1 day 6 hours 21 minutes)
Orbital eccentricity	0.0028
Orbital inclination	1.10°
Axial period	30.2 hours
Albedo	0.07

Democritus of Abdera (c. 470–400 B.C.)
Greek philosopher who developed the ideas of **atomism,** originally put forward by **Leucippus.** In the hands of **Epicurus** and **Lucretius,** atomistic philosophy was popularized and used to argue for the existence of extraterrestrial life. Democritus was the first to claim that the Milky Way is made up of stars. → **ancient philosophy, related to the possibility of extraterrestrial life**

denaturation
The breakdown of the normal structure of a **protein** or **nucleic acid** due to changes in temperature, **pH** level, or concentration of **ions** in the solution in which the protein occurs. Denaturation usually renders a protein biologically inactive.

Deneb
Alpha Cygni; an extremely luminous **A star,** roughly 70,000 times brighter than the Sun. It ranks nineteenth in the list of brightest stars as seen from Earth even though it is among the most remote stars visible to the naked eye. → **stars, brightest**

Denning, William Frederick (1848–1931)
English amateur astronomer who became a leading observer of meteors and discovered several comets. In an 1886 article in *Nature,* he reported observations of Mars that substanti-

ated Giovanni **Schiaparelli**'s claims as to the existence of *canali*. ➔ **Mars, canals of**

density
The ratio of the mass of a substance or object to its volume.

density wave
In a **spiral galaxy,** a wave, similar to a sound wave, that propagates through the **interstellar medium** of the disk in a spiral pattern. Such passing waves are thought to help trigger the collapse of **interstellar cloud**s to form bright new stars. The light from these stars, in turn, gives rise to the visible phenomena of the spiral arms. Spiral density waves are believed to be generated by resonances in the gravitational interaction of the stars of a galaxy as they move in their orbits. On a much smaller scale, spiral density waves may play an influential role in the early evolution of planetary systems (➔ **eccentric Jovians**).

deoxyribonucleic acid
➔ **DNA**

deoxyribose
A ring-structured **pentose** sugar derived from **ribose.** It is the sugar found in **DNA.**

Derham, William (1657–1735)
Anglican clergyman and disciple of Isaac **Newton** whose widely read *Astro-Theology: or, A Demonstration of the Being and Attributes of God* (1715) promotes **pluralism** by arguing that God would not have created habitable worlds without them actually being inhabited. Derham avoids, however, discussing the possible nature of extraterrestrials, pointing his readers instead to the speculations of Christiaan **Huygens** in his *Cosmotheoros.*

Descartes, René (1596–1650)
Immensely influential French philosopher and mathematician, often referred to as "the father of modern philosophy." He proposed a revised form of **atomism** and so helped pave the way for the expansion of **pluralism** to include the planetary systems of other stars. In Descartes's cosmological worldview, not only are atoms the fundamental essence of nature, but they form vortices analogous to the solar system around every star. For religious reasons, Descartes avoided speculating on whether or not these vortices would give rise to inhabited extrasolar worlds. His reluctance to enter the pluralist debate is evident in a letter he wrote to his compatriot Pierre Chanut:

> I do not see at all that the mystery of the Incarnation, and all the other advantages that God has brought man obstruct him from having brought forth an infinity of other very great advantages for an infinity of other creatures. And although I do not infer from this that there would be intelligent creatures in the stars or elsewhere, I also do not see that there would be any reason by which to prove that there were not.

Others who followed him, however, and accepted his vortex theory, such as Pierre **Borel** and Bernard Le Bovier de **Fontenelle,** were not so restrained in drawing far-reaching conclusions about the ubiquity of extraterrestrial life.

Desdemona
The fifth known moon of **Uranus.** ➔ **Uranus, moons of**

Discovery	1986, by *Voyager 2*
Mean distance from Uranus	62,800 km (39,000 mi.)
Diameter	58 km (36 mi.)
Orbital period	0.474 days (11 hours 23 minutes)
Orbital eccentricity	0.000
Orbital inclination	0.16°
Visual albedo	0.07

Despina
The third known moon of **Neptune.** Irregular in shape, it orbits just 27,700 km (17,200 miles) above the cloud tops of its primary. Like the five other inner moons discovered during *Voyager 2*'s 1989 flyby of Neptune, Despina is among the darkest objects known. ➔ **Neptune, moons of**

Discovery	1989, by *Voyager 2*
Mean distance from Neptune	52,400 km (32,600 mi.)
Diameter	148 km (92 mi.)
Orbital period	0.335 days (8 hours 2 minutes)
Orbital eccentricity	0.0001
Orbital inclination	0.07°
Visual albedo	0.06

detection of life
➔ **extraterrestrial life, detection of**

deuterium
An **isotope** of **hydrogen** in which the **nucleus** contains one **proton** and one **neutron.** The abundance of deuterium in natural hydrogen is about 0.015 percent.

dextrorotatory
Rotating the plane of vibration of **polarized light** to the right, as seen by an observer looking directly toward the oncoming light.

Dick, Thomas (1774–1857)
Scottish theologian and philosopher who made important contributions to the **pluralism** debate.

Diderot, Denis (1713–84)
French writer and philosopher who was chief editor of the *Encyclopédie,* a major work of the Age of Enlightenment that included many references to **pluralism.**

diffraction
The spreading or bending of waves as they pass through an opening or around the edge of an obstacle. Due to diffraction, a telescope can never form a perfect image. A pointlike source, for example, will be seen as a small disk surrounded by a series of rings; a thin line on a planet will become widened into a band that decreases in intensity on both sides. The only way to overcome the limitations of diffraction is to use a telescope of larger **aperture.**

diffraction grating
A device used to disperse light into a **spectrum** (➔ **dispersion**). It consists of a number of narrow, closely spaced lines (typically several thousand per cm), ruled either on glass to form a *transmission grating* or on metal to form a *reflection grating.*

diffuse interstellar bands (DIBs)
Broad **absorption band**s that occur between wavelengths of 440 to 685 nm in the spectra of distant stars and are due to the absorption of light by material in the **interstellar medium.** More than one hundred DIBs are known, and a variety of complex molecules have been suggested, though not conclusively identified, as their cause.[268]

diffuse nebula
Alternative name for an **H II region.**

Digges, Thomas (c. 1546–95)
English mathematician and astronomer who was the first to promote in Britain the **heliocentric** view of the solar system due to Nicolaus **Copernicus.** He was also a pioneer of the enlarged, stellar universe, maintaining that the stars, instead of being fixed to a crystalline sphere, were other suns lying at great distances. However, although he helped pave the way for others, such as Christiaan **Huygens,** to contemplate the possibility of extrasolar planets and life, he continued to regard the Sun as special and centrally located in the Universe. It has been suggested that Digges may have met Giordano **Bruno** during the latter's stay in England and derived some of his ideas from the Italian.

dinosaurs, intelligent
What would have happened if the asteroid that supposedly hit the Earth at the end of the Cretaceous period (➔ **Cretaceous-Tertiary Boundary**) 65 million years ago had missed? One possibility is that the dinosaurs would not have become extinct, advanced mammals would subsequently not have appeared, and some of the descendants of dinosaurs might have evolved to become intelligent in our place. In 1981, paleontologist Dale Russell, curator of vertebrate fossils at the National Museums of Canada, in Ottawa, proposed such a scenario based on extrapolations from *Stenonychosaurus,* a 11-m, 40-kg carnivorous dinosaur with perhaps the intelligence of an opossum.

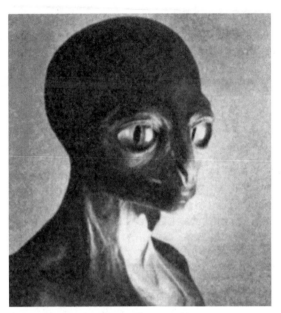

A hypothetical intelligent dinosauroid.
National Museums of Canada

Had the dinosaurs survived, argued Russell, and a species such as *Stenonychosaurus* grown smarter, it would eventually have needed to stand upright to balance its heavy head. A shoulder structure would have evolved to allow the "dinosauroid" to throw objects. Projecting how other characteristics of this species might have developed, he came up with a model of a large-brained, reptilian biped with enormous eyes, three-fingered hands, an absence of external genitalia (typical of reptiles), and a navel (since a placenta is found in some modern reptiles and may have been needed to enable the birth of young with big braincases). Fictionally, Harry Harrison has explored the consequences of saurian intelligence in his *West of Eden* series.

Dione

The fourth largest moon of **Saturn** and possibly the densest after **Titan.** Its core probably makes up about one third of its total mass, although like **Tethys** and **Rhea** it is composed primarily of water ice. The surface includes heavily cratered terrain, moderately cratered plains, lightly cratered plains, and bright, wispy material. The heavily cratered regions feature craters of all diameters up to and exceeding 100 km (60 miles), whereas the plains areas tend to have craters no larger than about 30 km across. Contrary to what might be expected of a satellite in **gravitational lock,** it is the trailing hemisphere of Dione on which the majority of intense cratering exists. This suggests that, during the early period of heavy bombardment in the solar system, Dione was tidally locked to Saturn in the opposite direction to which it now spins. Subsequent major collisions with any objects large enough to cause craters more than about 35 km (21 miles) in diameter, of which there are many on Dione, would have been capable of altering the rate and direction of the moon's rotation. The likelihood is that Dione has been tidally locked in its current state for several billion years, judging by the average albedo of the leading and trailing hemispheres. The albedo decreases from the leading to the trailing hemisphere since the former has suffered a higher rate of micrometeorite impacts. Streaks of bright material that interlace a dark portion of the surface are of uncertain origin but may be fractures associated with faults through which water has upwelled. → **Saturn, moons of**

Discovery	1684, by Giovanni Cassini
Mean distance from Saturn	377,500 km (115,400 mi.)
Diameter	1,120 km (696 mi.)
Mean density	1.4 g/cm³
Escape velocity	0.1 km/s (360 km/h, 224 mi./h)
Orbital period	2.74 days (2 days 17 hours 46 minutes)
Orbital eccentricity	0.002
Orbital inclination	0.02°
Axial period	2.74 days
Visual albedo	0.6

diploid
Having two sets of **chromosome**s.

direct imaging
→ **imaging, of extrasolar planets**

direct (rotation)
In the solar system, **axial rotation** or **orbital rotation** that is in a counterclockwise direction

when viewed from the Sun's north pole of the primary; the opposite of **retrograde.**

directed panspermia

The idea that life might have been intentionally spread throughout space and seeded on the surface of other worlds by a guiding intelligence. A detailed version of this hypothesis was put forward in 1973 by the molecular biologists Francis **Crick** (codiscoverer of the structure of **DNA**) and Leslie **Orgel.**[132] The chances of microorganisms being passively transported from world to world across interstellar distances, they felt, were small. The probability of successful seeding would be greatly increased, they pointed out, if the fertilization had been carried out deliberately by an existing technological civilization. Their argument depended first upon demonstrating that it was possible for an advanced extraterrestrial civilization to have developed in the Galaxy before life first appeared on Earth. This they were able to do (➔ **extraterrestrial civilizations, ancient**). As for the means of dispensation:

> The spaceship would carry large samples of a number of microorganisms, each having different but simple nutritional requirements, for example, blue-green algae, which could grow on CO_2 and water in "sunlight." A payload of 1000 kg might be made up of 10 samples each containing 10^{16} microorganisms, or 100 samples of 10^{15} microorganisms.

Crick and Orgel further suggested that directed panspermia might help resolve one or two anomalies in the biochemistry of life-forms on Earth. One of these was the puzzling dependence of biological systems on molybdenum. Many **enzymes,** for example, require this metal to act as a **cofactor.** Such a situation would be easier to understand if molybdenum were relatively abundant on Earth (➔ **elements, terrestrial abundance of**). However, its abundance is only 0.02 percent compared with 0.2 percent and 3.16 percent, respectively, for the metals chromium and nickel, which are chemically similar to molybdenum. Crick and Orgel commented:

> If it could be shown that the elements represented in terrestrial living organisms correlate with those abundant in some types of star—molybdenum stars, for example—we might look more sympathetically on "infective" theories.

A second example they give concerns the **genetic code:**

> Several orthodox explanations of the universality of the code can be suggested, but none is generally accepted to be completely convincing. It is a little surprising that organisms with somewhat different codes do not coexist. The universality of the code follows naturally from an "infective" theory of the origin of life. Life on Earth would represent a clone derived from a single set of organisms.

There might be a variety of reasons why an advanced civilization would wish to intentionally initiate life elsewhere: as an experiment in **astrobiology** using an entire world as a laboratory; to prepare a planet for subsequent colonization (➔ **terraforming**); or to disseminate the genetic material of the donor world to ensure its survival in the event of a global catastrophe (➔ **extraterrestrial civilizations, hazards to**).

directional antenna

An **antenna** that radiates or receives **radio waves** in a narrow beam.

directivity

The ratio of the maximum sensitivity of an **antenna** to its average sensitivity. It varies directly as the effective **aperture** of the antenna and inversely as the square of the **wavelength.**

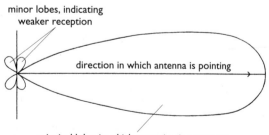

minor lobes, indicating weaker reception

direction in which antenna is pointing

principal lobe, in which reception is strongest

disaccharides

A group of **sugars,** the **molecule**s of which are derived by the **condensation** of two **monosaccharide** molecules. Upon **hydrolysis,** disaccharides yield the corresponding monosaccharides.

Discovery Program

A recently implemented NASA program of small probes that operates under the rubric "faster, better, cheaper." The first four missions to be launched—*Near Earth Asteroid Rendezvous, Mars Pathfinder, Lunar Prospector,* and *Stardust*—all have some astrobiological interest. The basic requirement of the Discovery Program is that a mission should take less than 3 years to complete in order to take advantage of the latest technology.

disk, galactic
→ **galactic disk**

disk star

A star that lies within the **galactic disk** of a **spiral galaxy** such as our own. So-called *thin disk* stars, such as the Sun or **Alpha Centauri,** lie at a typical distance of about 1,000 light-years from the galactic midplane. *Thick disk* stars, on the other hand, such as **Lalande 21185,** tend to have higher velocities out of the galactic plane and lie at an average distance of about 3,500 light-years from the midplane. Beyond the limits of the Galaxy's thick disk is the **galactic halo.**

dispersion

The splitting apart of a beam of light of mixed wavelengths, by refraction, into its component wavelengths. It may be achieved by a prism or a **diffraction grating.**

diurnal

Daily; active during the day; denoting an event that happens once every 24 hours.

divergent evolution
→ **adaptive radiation**

Dixon, Robert S. (1939–   )

Assistant director of the **Ohio State University Radio Observatory** and director of its **SETI** program, which currently includes the design and construction of the revolutionary **Argus radio telescope.** It was Dixon who first suggested to John **Kraus,** director of the university's radio observatory, the idea of using the **Big Ear** telescope (now demolished) to look for intelligent extraterrestrial signals. This led to the **Ohio SETI Program,** which began in 1973 and went on to become the longest-running SETI project so far attempted. Dixon is also the chief research engineer at Ohio State's University Office of the Chief Information Officer, where he develops Internet-based audio and video services, and wireless computer networks. He obtained B.S. and M.S. degrees in electrical engineering from the University of Wisconsin, and a Ph.D. in electrical engineering and radio astronomy from Ohio State.[156, 157]

DNA (deoxyribonucleic acid)

The genetic material of most terrestrial organisms and one of two principal types of **nucleic acid**s found in living **cell**s (the other being **RNA**). DNA is a stable **macromolecule** consisting (usually) of two strands running in opposite directions. These strands twist around each other in the form of a double helix and are built up from components known as **nucleotide**s. There are ten nucleotides per turn in the double helix (1 turn = 3.4 nm). Each nucleotide consists of a sugar (**deoxyribose**)-**phosphate** section attached to one of four organic **base**s: two **purines, guanine** and **thymine,** and two **pyramidines, adenine** and **cytosine.** The bases on opposite strands project toward each other like the rungs of a twisted ladder. Complementary base pairing is highly specific: thymine always pairs with adenine (via two **hydrogen bond**s), and cytosine always pairs with guanine (via three hydrogen bonds). This specificity is a direct consequence of the shapes of the bases and is fundamental to terrestrial life since it underlies all aspects of inheritance and **gene** expression including DNA replication, DNA repair, **transcription,** RNA splicing, and **translation.**

The sequence of bases along the length of a DNA strand varies from species to species and from individual to individual, and determines the organism's development (→ **genetic code**)

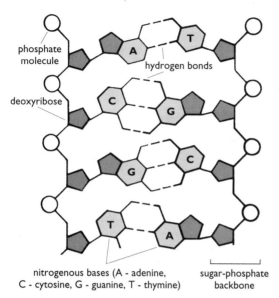

phosphate molecule

hydrogen bonds

deoxyribose

nitrogenous bases (A - adenine,
C - cytosine, G - guanine, T - thymine)

sugar-phosphate
backbone

Part of a DNA molecule.

species tend to harbor a large pool of genes, which allows them to survive and adapt effectively in the event of environmental change. He concurred with George Gaylord **Simpson** that a rerun of history would not re-create human beings and that while natural selection might lead to many other forms of life and intelligence elsewhere in space, it would be unlikely to fashion a duplicate of humanity (➔ **anthropomorphism**). He wrote:[158]

> Natural scientists have been loath, for at least a century, to assume that there is anything radically unique or special about the planet Earth or about the human species. This is an understandable reaction against the traditional view that Earth, and indeed the whole universe, was created specifically for man. The reaction may have gone too far. It is possible that there is, after all, something unique about man and the planet he inhabits.

➔ **extraterrestrial intelligence, forms of; extraterrestrial life, variety of**

dolphins, as a form of alien intelligence

The controversial neurophysiologist John C. **Lilly** has argued[349] that dolphins represent a nonhuman form of intelligence on this planet with which we might learn to communicate. If he is right, the fact that intelligence has evolved at least twice on Earth increases the chances that it might be common elsewhere. Additionally, our efforts to understand the complex language of dolphins may help prepare us for the problems we may face when attempting to communicate with an extraterrestrial race. Lilly's claims for dolphin intelligence are supported by the remarkable learning skills and playful, inventive behavior of these animals. In recent years, researchers have observed bottlenose dolphins and beluga whales in captivity creating underwater rings and helices of air for their own amusement. A particularly strong "ring culture" has developed at Sea Life Park Hawaii, where the tradition is passed down from experienced adults to novices. Researchers Ken Marten, Karim Shariff, Suchi Psarakos, and Don J. White describe[382] how dolphins also draw humans into their play:

by controlling **protein** synthesis. Although double-stranded DNA forms the genetic material for most terrestrial organisms, **bacteriophage**s and **virus**es may use single-stranded DNA, single-stranded RNA, or double-stranded RNA.

That DNA might be able to survive for hundreds of thousands of years in the vacuum of space is suggested by the results of research announced in 1998 by Evan Williams and his colleagues at the **University of California, Berkeley.**[514] The Berkeley group concluded that double-stranded DNA could maintain its structure in a vacuum for as long as 35 years at room temperature, and perhaps almost indefinitely in the very low temperatures of space.

Dobzhansky, Theodosius (1900–75)

Russian-born American geneticist and zoologist who emigrated to the United States in 1927 and joined Thomas Hunt Morgan's group at Columbia University. The following year, he moved with Morgan to the California Institute of Technology and became a professor there in 1936. Dobzhansky's studies in population genetics served as a basis for his explanation of how the evolution of races and species could have come about through adaptation. His key discovery was that successful

> [O]ne day during a period of intense ring making, Tinkerbell repeatedly blew a ring and then came to the lab window where one of us (Psarakos) was videotaping, as if to include her in the activity. Once, we blew soap bubbles inside the lab in front of the dolphins' window, and within a few minutes one of the dolphins joined in by blowing simple, rising doughnut rings near the lab window. The real surprise came when the dolphin swam away… and made several fluke vortex rings—so different from what we each blew at the window.

Lacking hands with opposable fingers and thumb or alternative manipulative append-ages, dolphins are physically incapable of de-veloping tools. Nevertheless, their behavior speaks of a creative, self-aware mind at work. They may serve as an indication that high in-telligence is not always, or even often, accom-panied by a significant level of technology (→ **intelligence, nature of**). Yet to what extent the absence of delphian technology represents a fundamental limit to how closely we can hope to comprehend the thoughts of this fellow cerebral species is unclear.[492] (ch. 24) → **cetaceans**

domain
A new taxonomic group above the level of **kingdom,** first proposed by Carl **Woese** and his colleagues in 1990.[628] In Woese's scheme, terrestrial life-forms fall into three domains: Archaea, Bacteria, and Eucarya. → **life, classi-fication of**

"Doomsday" asteroid
→ **cosmic collisions, biological effects of**

Doppler effect
The phenomenon whereby the **wavelength**s of light or other radiation coming from a lumi-nous object are changed when the object is in relative motion toward or away from the ob-server. → **Doppler shift**

Doppler shift
The change in position of **spectral lines** due to the **Doppler effect.** If an object is approach-ing, its light is compressed and any lines in its spectrum appear at shorter wavelengths than if the object were at rest (→ **blue shift**). If the object is receding, the opposite effect occurs and the spectral lines are shifted toward the longer-wavelength, or red, end of the spec-trum (→ **red shift**).

Doppler spectroscopy
→ **radial velocity method**

Douglass, Andrew Ellicott (1867–1962)
Graduate of Trinity College in Hartford, Con-necticut, and assistant to William **Pickering** at Harvard's Arequipa Station who in 1894 scouted several sites in Arizona for Percival **Lowell**'s new observatory, including the one that was eventually chosen in Flagstaff (→ **Lowell Observatory**). He subsequently served as a junior of Pickering and Lowell at Flagstaff and, to begin with, supported their views on the Martian canals (→ **Mars, canals of**). How-ever, when Lowell fell ill in 1897, Douglass took over as acting director and began experi-menting with artificial planet disks. His results led him to question some of Lowell's asser-tions, including his claim that he had seen faint shadings and cusp caps on Venus. For this heresy, he was dismissed from his post. He then went on to found the **Steward Observa-tory.**

Doyle, Arthur Conan (1859–1930)
Scottish physician and author, best known for his Sherlock Holmes stories, who occasionally wrote fiction about unusual forms of life. In "When the World Screamed" (1929) he envi-sions the Earth as a gigantic living organism (→ **planets, as living beings**). The notion of a refugium on a dramatic scale is the subject of his novel *The Lost World* (1912), while "The Horror of the Heights" takes as its (now obsolete) theme the idea of strange organisms inhabiting the upper atmosphere.

Dragon's Egg
Science fiction novel[200] (1980) by Robert L. **Forward,** based on an idea first suggested by Frank **Drake,** that describes a thriving commu-nity of intelligent beings living on the surface of a **neutron star** (→ **neutron star, life on**). The extraordinarily high gravity, 67 billion times that of Earth, means that everything, includ-ing the life-forms, is made of tightly packed

nuclear matter. The dominant creatures on Dragon's Egg are "cheela," which are similar in intelligence and biological complexity to humans. As Forward explains:[202]

> This implies that they contain the same number of nuclei, so it is not surprising that on Earth their mass is about the same as human beings—70 kilograms. Their bodies consist of complex molecules of bare nuclei. The cheela are flat, flexible creatures about 50 millimeters in diameter and 0.5 millimeters high. They have a density of about 7 million grams per cubic centimeter, the density of the crust of the neutron star.... Cheela cannot breathe or talk because the "atmosphere" of Dragon's Egg is only a few micrometers thick (around the "toes" of the cheela). The cheela communicate by strumming the crust with their lower surface, or "tread," to produce directed vibrations in the neutron star's crust.

Forward builds a detailed, scientifically informed picture of the anatomy, environment, culture, and technology of his hypothetical condensed-matter sentients and explores the difficulties that the cheela and our own species would face in making contact. Among these are that the inhabitants of the Dragon's Egg live their lives a million times faster than human beings, so that

> Talking to these beings would be difficult. Their biology depends upon the strong nuclear force instead of the electromagnetic force. Nuclear reactions happen much faster than chemical reactions, because the nuclear force is much stronger.... With a time difference of a million to one, a second to a human—the time it takes to say "Hello"—would be the equivalent of a week to a star creature. It would hear "He..." on Sunday and "...lo" on the following Saturday.

Forward took his speculations further in the 1985 sequel, *Starquake*.[201]

Drake Equation

A formula devised by Frank **Drake** and used as a focal point for discussion at the **Green Bank conference** in November 1961. Intended to provide a way of estimating the number of ex-

traterrestrial civilizations in the Galaxy that currently have the ability to engage in interstellar communication (➔ **extraterrestrial intelligence, likelihood of**), it is written as

$$N = R_* \times f_p \times n_e \times f_l \times f_i \times f_c \times L$$

Symbol	Meaning
N	Present number of extraterrestrial races capable of interstellar communication
R_*	Mean rate of star formation, averaged over the lifetime of the Galaxy
f_p	Fraction of stars that have planets
n_e	Average number of planets in a planetary system suitable for life
f_l	Fraction of suitable planets on which life actually develops
f_i	Fraction of life-bearing planets on which intelligent life develops
f_c	Fraction of intelligence-bearing planets on which the capacity for interstellar communication develops
L	Average lifetime of a technological civilization

Unfortunately, of the seven factors that appear on the right side of the Drake Equation, only one (R_*) can be estimated at present with any degree of confidence. Current and near-future research on **extrasolar planets** will gradually reduce the uncertainties in three other factors, f_p, n_e, and f_l. However, the values of the remaining three factors, which relate to the evolution of extraterrestrial intelligence and technology, are likely to remain a matter of pure speculation for a very long time, unless contact is made with a more advanced civilization that could convey this knowledge immediately.

Despite the enormous uncertainties involved in using the Drake Equation, which can result in a value of N from less than one to more than a billion, it is at least interesting and instructive to consider each of the factors involved. Aside from Factor 1, the values suggested below are simply the author's own "best guesses."

Factor 1: R_* (the mean rate of star formation)
To a first approximation, this is simply the total

number of stars in the Galaxy (about 400 billion) divided by the age of the Galaxy (about 10 billion years). That is, $R_* \simeq 40$ stars per year.

Factor 2: f_p (the fraction of stars that have planets)   Until recently, this was a matter of pure conjecture since there had been no confirmation of the existence of any planets beyond the solar system. Improved methods of detection, however, have led to a flurry of discoveries of extrasolar planets (➔ **extrasolar planets, detection of**) and of what appear to be **protoplanetary disk**s. This has raised the expectation that planetary systems may be the rule rather than the exception. A conservative estimate might be that one half of all stars in the Galaxy are accompanied by planets. That is, $f_p \simeq 0.5$.

Factor 3: n_e (the average number of planets in a planetary system that are suitable for life)   Here there is considerable uncertainty. It is still not known what constitutes a "typical" planetary system and, in particular, how common it is to have **Earth-class planet**s orbiting within the **habitable zone** of a host star. Nor is it clear how adaptable life can be to different environments (➔ **extraterrestrial life, variety of**). The discovery of life on **Europa,** for example, would increase the number of opportunities for life to have evolved elsewhere. Unless for some reason the solar system is significantly atypical, it might be reasonable to assume that in every two planetary systems there is at least one world capable of sustaining life. That is, $n_e \simeq 0.5$.

Factor 4: f_l (the fraction of suitable planets on which life actually develops)   Again, we are hampered by having knowledge, at present, of only one inhabited world. It may be that some crucial step in the evolution of life is extremely improbable, in which case, even if an environment is biologically clement, life is unlikely to appear. The scientific consensus, however, is presently shifting toward the opposite conclusion; namely, that unless conditions preclude the possibility of life altogether, life is likely to evolve. This view is supported by the discoveries of **organic** material in space (➔ **interstellar molecules**), meteorites (➔ **organic matter, in meteorites**), and comets; of water (both liquid

and frozen) on worlds other than the Earth; and, most significantly, of **extremophiles,** which thrive in what, to other organisms, would be extraordinarily hostile environments. The present consensus of astrobiologists suggests that $f_l \simeq 1$.

Factor 5: f_i (the fraction of life-bearing worlds on which intelligent life develops)   How often does life in general serve as a precursor to intelligence on a par with or greater than our own? When this issue was raised at the Green Bank conference, John Lilly's claim that intelligence has arisen not once but twice on this planet (➔ **dolphins, as a form of alien intelligence**) encouraged the attendees to adopt a value for f_i of 1. As Carl **Sagan** put it:[540]

> [T]he adaptive value of intelligence…is so great—at least until technical civilizations are developed—that if it is genetically feasible, natural selection seems likely to bring it forth.

Further evidence for this is the evolution of "brainy" dinosaurs, which, had they not become extinct (➔ **Cretaceous-Tertiary Boundary**), might conceivably have become the dominant form of intelligence on Earth (➔ **dinosaurs, intelligent**). However, it is also possible that some planetary environments, while allowing the emergence of primitive organisms, pose obstacles to higher forms of life. Bearing all these factors in mind, a reasonable estimate might be that $f_i \simeq 0.1$.

Factor 6: f_c (the fraction of intelligence-bearing worlds on which the capacity for interstellar communication develops)   If the example of dolphins is used to argue the case that emergence of intelligence is common, it must also, in fairness, be used to moderate any estimates of how frequently intelligent life develops the capability for communication over interstellar distances. The existence of large brains, and apparently intelligent behavior, the case of dolphins reveals, is no guarantee of the development of a significant level of technology. For this to happen, a species must possess a high degree of manipulative ability—which, for humans, means having dexterous hands instead of flippers. Perhaps it is a general rule that wherever aquatic (or aerial?) intelligence emerges (➔ **cetaceans; cephalopods**), it is nontechnological in nature (➔ **intelligence, nature of**). Intelligence plus technology may occur only among land dwellers. As in the case of the previous factor, it might be appropriate to adopt a conservative value of $f_c \simeq 0.1$.

Factor 7: L (the average lifetime of a technological civilization) Of all the factors in the Drake Equation, this is the least well understood and potentially the most decisive. Various arguments have been brought to bear on the question of how long a typical civilization can be expected to survive, once it has developed the minimum capability to send and receive messages over interstellar distances (➔ **extraterrestrial civilizations, lifetime of**). Estimates vary between about 100 years, assuming pessimistically that races tend to self-destruct at about the technological level humans have reached today (➔ **extraterrestrial civilizations, hazards to**) and several billion years, assuming that once a technological civilization arises it survives as long as its host star. Yet this is only one of the issues involved in assessing a likely value for *L*, and it is probably not the most significant.

Although in Drake's original formulation, *L* is taken to be the total lifetime of a technological civilization and *N*, therefore, the number of civilizations capable of interstellar communication, what is really of concern in assessing the likelihood of success by contemporary SETI programs is the time span over which a civilization is likely to be trying to communicate over interstellar distances *by the kind of technology with which we are familiar today* (that is, principally the transmission and reception of radio waves). The important point, which is often overlooked, is that these two quantities may be different by many orders of magnitude. From human experience, it is apparent that once a certain threshold of technological sophistication has been reached, as happened during and immediately after the Industrial Revolution, subsequent progress can be very rapid indeed and its direction virtually unpredictable. Only an average human lifetime separates the first mechanically powered human flight by the Wright brothers from the launch

of the first spacecraft to the outer planets. Less than a lifetime separates the first, room-filling programmable computers, such as ENIAC, from present-day laptop computers of vastly greater processing power. The history and pace of technological development suggest that it is unreasonable to suppose that the best means of communication available in one century will necessarily be the best available in the next. What the next breakthrough will be, beyond light-speed, electromagnetic communication, is impossible to say. Perhaps it will involve sending messages outside of normal **space-time** through microscopic, artificially constructed **wormhole**s or exploiting one of the more esoteric consequences of nonlocality in **quantum mechanics** or using faster-than-light particles (➔ **tachyon**) or some other means, such as Philip **Morrison**'s **"Q" waves.** But it strains credibility to imagine that in the remote (and perhaps not-so-remote) future we shall still be reliant upon radio transmissions and their like for long-range signaling. In the same way, it is unreasonable to suppose that a civilization with a technology significantly in advance of our own will be broadcasting messages that are detectable by any of our present-day instruments. A generous estimate might be that there is a 500-year window during which a technological civilization employs current terrestrial-type methods for communicating over interstellar distances. On either side of that window, it is not likely that we would be aware of the other civilization's presence, just as a dog is unaware of the plethora of electromagnetic signals that surround it on our own planet. Whether or not extraterrestrial technological civilizations survive typically for a thousand years or 10 billion years is not the factor that determines how many races we can hope to make contact with. Providing that civilizations typically survive for the few hundred years until they achieve the next quantum jump in communications, this supplies the only value of *L* that is relevant in the context of our current communications capability. Given these considerations, then, it might be reasonable to assume that $L \simeq 500$ years (with apologies to Walter Sullivan, who dedicated his book ***We Are Not Alone*** to "those everywhere who seek to make 'L' a large number").

Inserting these values into the Drake Equation gives

$$N = 40 \times 0.5 \times 0.5 \times 1 \times 0.1 \times 0.1 \times 500 = 50$$

That is, if these estimates are valid, there are roughly fifty civilizations in the entire Galaxy that are likely to be engaged in trying to communicate using the means presently available to us on Earth. Assuming, as we have, a 500-year "radio window," and given the fact that humans have had the ability to receive and broadcast interstellar messages for about 50 years, this suggests that there are about five radio-capable civilizations that are marginally behind us in their technology and about forty-five that are somewhat more advanced yet not sufficiently advanced to have progressed beyond our "earshot." Fifty "radio-stage" civilizations equates to one for roughly every 8 billion stars. Since the nearest such civilization would probably lie well over 1,000 light-years away, it would not be possible to exchange even a single greeting before one or both of the parties had transcended the proposed 500-year radio window.

The ideas discussed here afford one possible explanation of the negative results produced by **SETI** programs to date. It may be that high intelligence and undreamed-of technology are common in the Galaxy but that we simply lack the means, at present, to detect their presence.[324] → **extraterrestrial intelligence, more advanced than we**

Drake, Frank Donald (1930–)

American radio astronomer, professor of astronomy and astrophysics at the University of California, Santa Cruz, and **SETI** pioneer.[575] In 1960, at the **National Radio Astronomy Observatory** at **Green Bank,** he conducted Project **Ozma,** the first systematic search for intelligent signals originating outside the solar system. He devised the **Drake Equation,** was involved in sending the **Arecibo Message** (→ **Drake's cryptogram**), and, in collaboration with Carl **Sagan,** engaged in the first systematic U.S. attempt to detect Type II **Kardashev civilizations** using the **Arecibo radio telescope.** Also with Sagan and others, he was instrumental in persuading NASA to affix the

Pioneer **plaque** and the *Voyager* **record** to the first deep space probes. He has speculated about the nature of extraterrestrial life and intelligence (→ **extraterrestrial life, variety of**), including the possibility that life could exist on a neutron star (→ **neutron star, life on**). Drake received a B.S. in physics from Cornell University (1952) and, after serving in the U.S. Navy, a Ph.D. in astronomy from Harvard. For the next five years he worked at Green Bank; then, after a year as chief of the Lunar and Planetary Sciences Section at the **Jet Propulsion Laboratory,** he joined the faculty of Cornell (1964), where he was professor and director of the **National Astronomy and Ionosphere Center** (which includes the Arecibo telescope). In 1984, he became dean of natural sciences at UC, Santa Cruz. Drake has presided over the **International Astronomical Union**'s Commission on Bioastronomy and chaired the SETI Advisory Committee of NASA's Office of Aeronautics and Space Technology. He is president of the Astronomical Society of the Pacific and of the **SETI Institute** and a founder and director of the **Extrasolar Planetary Foundation.** Among his nontechnical published works are *Intelligent Life in Space*[163] (1962) and, with Dava Sobel, the autobiographical *Is Anyone Out There?*[165] (1993).

Drake's cryptogram

A coded message devised by Frank **Drake** and sent to a number of scientists to gauge the difficulty in deciphering artificial extraterrestrial signals. The message, consisting of a string of 1,271 ones and zeros (or **bits**), was sent to all of the participants following the **Green Bank**

```
1111000010100100001100100000010000010
1001000001100101100111100000110000110
0000000010000100001000100010101010001
0000000000000100010000000010011
0000000000000000010011011010110101
0000000000000000010010001110101010
0000000010101010100000000111010101
1101011000000100000000000000100000
0000000100100111110000011101000010
1100001110000010000000010000000010
0000011110000010110001011101000000
1100101111101011111000100111100100000
0000001111010000011000111111110000010
0000110000011000100001100000001100010
1001000111100101111
```

The sequence of binary digits in Drakes's cryptogram

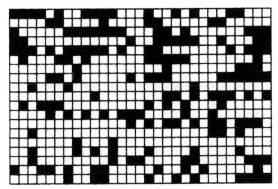

An incorrect deciphering of the cryptogram as an array of 29 columns and 19 rows.

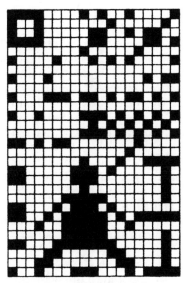

The correct deciphering of the cryptogram as an array of 19 columns and 29 rows.

miliar, to some extent, with the workings of Drake's mind, some idea emerges of the problems to be faced in interstellar communication. → **lost languages; radioglyph**

drift scan

A method of conducting sky surveys, including some **SETI** programs, that involves a **radio telescope** remaining stationary and allowing the rotation of the Earth to sweep its beam in a narrow circular path across the sky each day.

Dry Valleys, Antarctica

A small, ice-free region at the edge of the Antarctic continent that is among the coldest, driest places on Earth. Since it most closely resembles the surface of Mars, it has become the scene of intense activity by scientists testing life-science equipment bound for the Martian

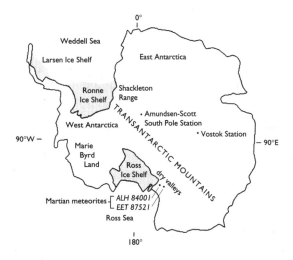

surface. The mats of hardy **cyanobacteria** found inhabiting what, at first, appear to be the completely sterile Dry Valleys offer hope that a similar resilient ecosystem might exist on the Red Planet. They are also helping researchers to design instruments with perhaps the best chance of success in the search for nearby extraterrestrial life.[281]

du Prel, Carl (1839–99)

Popular German philosophical writer whose influential *Die Planetenbewohner und die Nebularhypothese* (The Inhabitants of the Planets

conference in November 1961. The key was to recognize that 1,271 is the product of two **prime numbers**, 31 and 41, so that the information is intended to be displayed on a grid of 31 bits by 41. There are two possibilities: 41 lines of 31 bits each, or 31 lines of 41 bits each. The first possibility yields nothing of significance, but the second gives a meaningful picture. Only one of the recipients, Bernard **Oliver,** was able to decode the message. Given that all the scientists involved were of the same species, spoke the same language, and were fa-

and the Nebular Hypothesis, 1880)[166] drew a close (and fallacious) analogy between cosmic and biologic evolution. Du Prel argued that the same process of Darwinian natural selection that had acted on terrestrial organisms had also operated on the planets of the solar system, so that those most advantageously placed during their formation period actually survived. From this du Prel concluded that "all planets that have cooled down are habitable and therefore inhabited." Life, he conjectured, had reached a more advanced stage on some worlds so that what man had achieved through technology, nature had accomplished elsewhere organically—for example, through the evolution of extra senses.

Dunham, Theodore

American astronomer at the **Mount Wilson Observatory** who, together with Walter **Adams,** carried out **spectroscopic** observations of the planets. These helped confirm that the atmosphere of Venus is composed primarily of **carbon dioxide** (➔ **Venus, atmosphere of**) and that **methane** and **ammonia** are predominant in the outer atmosphere of Jupiter and Saturn.

dust

➔ **cosmic dust**

dust disk

A disk of material rich in grains of **cosmic dust** and possibly larger objects that is in orbit around a star. Dust disks include **protoplanetary disk**s and **regenerated disk**s.

dust lane

A dark swathe of obscuring **cosmic dust** seen against the starry background of the **Milky Way Galaxy** or the disks of other **spiral galaxies.**

dwarf bacteria

Bacteria, also known as "ultramicrobacteria," that have shrunk to less than a thousandth of their normal volume because they have used up virtually all their internal reserves. These emaciated microbes are commonly found at great depths under the Earth's surface (➔ **endoliths**), where nutrients are scarce. In their reduced state, dwarf bacteria have an extremely low metabolic rate and may divide only once every century or so, compared with a normal reproduction time measured in minutes, hours, or days. The discovery of such extremely small organisms that are able to survive without light on a starvation diet appears to increase the chance of finding primitive life elsewhere in the solar system and beyond.

dwarf galaxy

A small, dim **galaxy,** generally of irregular or elliptical type, that is intermediate in size between a conventional galaxy and a **globular cluster.**

dwarf star

A term used, oddly enough, to describe any star that is of normal size for its mass. The Sun, for example, is classified as a yellow dwarf. In general, dwarf stars lie on the **main sequence** and are in the process of converting **hydrogen** to **helium** by nuclear **fusion** in their cores. An exception to this is **white dwarf**s, small stars that have reached the end of their evolution.

Dyson civilization

A race that has managed to harness the bulk of the radiated output of its **host star** by constructing a **Dyson sphere.** It would therefore qualify as a Type II **Kardashev civilization.** ➔ **Dyson, Freeman John**

Dyson, Freeman John (1923–)

English-born theoretical physicist, president of the Space Sciences Institute, and professor emeritus at the Institute for Advanced Studies, Princeton, who has proposed several novel ideas in the field of **SETI.** Dyson has speculated how advanced civilizations might be able to travel between stars (➔ **interstellar travel**),[172] continue to survive in the far future of the universe, and capture the bulk of the radiative output of their **host stars** (➔ **Dyson sphere**). As one of the characters in Larry Niven's **Ringworld** explains:

> Dyson was one of the ancient natural philosophers, pre-Belt, almost pre-atomic. He pointed out that civilization is limited by the energy available to it. The way for the human

race to use all the energy within its reach, he said, is to build a spherical shell around the Sun and trap every ray of sunlight.

Dyson argued that the most reasonable strategy in SETI is to assume that (as in the case of the human race) extraterrestrial civilizations are not actively trying to communicate, and that our best chance of finding them is to look for by-products of their technological activity, such as "leaks," especially in the **infrared** part of the spectrum. He has also suggested looking for the radiation "skid marks" of alien starships as they decelerate from high speeds. An advocate of the colonization of space, Dyson has acknowledged the source of much of his inspiration:[575]

> There's an aspect of things which I find amusing: the flow back and forth between science and science fiction, which has been an important part of my life. I started out reading science fiction and then became a scientist, and that set the slant on my scientific work. I like to make connections between life and cosmology and astronomy. Science fiction raises all these interesting possibilities and has had some influence on science in the last 25 years—not only in the area of SETI, but also in other ways.

Dyson recalls H. G. **Wells**'s *First Men in the Moon* and Olaf **Stapledon**'s *Last and First Men* and *Star Maker* as being especially influential. He obtained a B.A. in mathematics from Cambridge University (1945) and was a fellow at Trinity College from 1946 to 1949. In 1947 he went to **Cornell University** on a Commonwealth Fellowship and joined the faculty there as a physics professor in 1951. He moved to Princeton two years later. Among his nontechnical and autobiographical works are *Disturbing the Universe*[173] (1979), *Origins of Life*[174] (1986), and *Infinite in All Directions*[175] (1988).

Dyson sphere

An immense artificial structure proposed by Freeman **Dyson** in 1959[169, 171] for the purpose of intercepting vast amounts of solar energy. Dyson calculated that if mankind's current Malthusian (exponential) growth rate in energy consumption were to continue, the human race would reach a crisis point within the next two to three millennia (➔ **Malthus, Thomas Robert**). At this point, all the nonrenewable sources, such as fossil and nuclear fuels, would be exhausted, and even renewable sources exploited on a planetwide scale would be unable to cope with further demand. The problem is that the Earth intercepts less than one billionth of the total radiant output of the Sun. To provide for future growth, the human race will need to capture much more of the Sun's light. It could do this with a Dyson sphere: a spherical shell 2 to 3 m thick, centered on the Sun and rotating around it at about the orbital distance of the Earth (see Note 1 below). The material for building the sphere, Dyson suggested, could come from disassembling the planet Jupiter and utilizing the minerals and metals from its deep interior. Dyson acknowledged that the inspiration for his scheme came from Olaf **Stapledon**'s *Star Maker:*

> As the eons advanced, hundreds of thousands of worlds were constructed, all of this type, but gradually increasing in size and complexity. Many a star without natural planets came to be surrounded by concentric rings of artificial worlds. In some cases the inner rings contained scores, the outer rings thousands of globes adapted to life at some particular distance from the Sun.

Stapledon, in turn, may have borrowed the idea from J. D. **Bernal,** who also influenced Dyson directly.

Following the publication of Dyson's proposal, several letters appeared in *Science* pointing out that a *solid* circumstellar sphere would be subject to intolerably high stresses. Dyson replied that what he actually envisaged was a loose collection of more than 100,000 objects traveling on independent orbits in a shell about 1 million km thick. Dyson's intended (fragmented) arrangement may be referred to as a Type I Dyson sphere and a solid shell as a Type II. It is the latter, in fact, that subsequently received the most publicity through a number of science fiction stories woven around the theme, including Robert Silverberg's *Across a Billion Years* (1969), Bob Shaw's *Orbitsville* (1975), and Frederik Pohl and Jack Williamson's *Wall Around a Star* (1983). A Type II Dyson sphere also features in the ***Star Trek: The Next Generation*** episode "Relics." In order to produce the **artificial gravity** to allow such a structure to be habitable on its inner surface, the sphere would have to rotate. But the required rate of rotation (see Note 2) would set up such extreme stresses in the shell (tending to deform it into an oblate spheroid) that no known material would be able to withstand them. Even if the structural integrity of the shell were not compromised, only the equatorial regions would be suitable for permanent habitation, for two reasons: the air of the inner biosphere would tend to collect at the equator, and it would only be there that the maximum level of artificial gravity would be achieved. The "pull" would decrease as the distance from the equator increased, until it became zero at the poles. Additionally, a Type II sphere would be unstable since even the slightest collision, say with an asteroid or comet, would cause the structure to drift off course and eventually collide with the Sun.

A Type I Dyson sphere, on the other hand, appears to be such an inevitable and achievable piece of **astroengineering** that we might expect not only the human race eventually to build one but other civilizations more advanced than our own already to have theirs in place. Dyson pointed this out and suggested how such structures would appear over interstellar distances. A Dyson sphere would absorb most of the visible and shorter wavelength radiation from its host star and reemit a portion of it in the form of **infrared** radiation.[507] Its infrared output, in fact, would be similar to that of a **protostar**. The artificial nature of the object might be revealed in other ways. Said Dyson, "One would look in particular for irregular light variations due to starlight shining through chinks in the curtain, and for stray electromagnetic fields and radio noise produced by large-scale electrical operations." Several searches have been carried out.[306]

A third type of Dyson sphere—a Dyson "bubble"—has been proposed in which the shell would be complete, very thin, and nonrotating. It would consist of statites, or stationary solar sails, which would reflect light onto collectors for use in external habitats. The entire mass of the structure would be approximately that of the Moon or a large asteroid. ➔ **ringworld**

Notes

1. The surface area of a sphere of radius r is $4\pi r^2$. The area of a circle of radius r is πr^2. The interior surface area of a Dyson sphere with a radius of 150 million km (the Earth-to-Sun distance) is $4 \times 3.14 \times (150 \times 10^6)^2$ or 2.83×10^{17} km^2 (283,000 trillion km^2). The cross-sectional area of a sphere the size of Earth (equatorial radius 6,378 km) is $3.14 \times (6.38 \times 10^3)^2$ or 1.28×10^8 km^2 (128 million km^2). Hence, the amount of solar radiation captured is greater in the case of the Dyson sphere by a factor of $(2.83 \times 10^{17})/(1.28 \times 10^8)$ or 2.2 billion. The interior surface area of the Dyson sphere exceeds the total surface area of Earth by a factor of just over half a billion.

2. To produce Earth-normal gravity at the equator of a Dyson sphere, the sphere would have to rotate so that its angular acceleration matched the acceleration due to gravity at Earth's surface (approximately 9.8 m/s^2). Angular acceleration is given by v^2/r, where v is the tangential velocity and r the distance to the center of rotation. Therefore, we require

$$v^2/r = 9.8$$
$$\text{or } v = \sqrt{9.8\,r}$$
Since $r = 150$ million km, this gives
$$v = \sqrt{((9.8 \times 150 \times 10^6)/1{,}000)} \text{ km/s}$$
$$\text{or } v = 1{,}212 \text{ km/s}$$

early-type

Descriptive of hot, luminous stars of **spectral type** O, B, or A. Such stars were originally thought to be at an earlier stage in their evolution than *late-type* objects, such as the Sun. However, it is now known that their high temperature is an outcome of their high mass. Early-type stars are not considered good candidates in the search for inhabited extrasolar worlds because of their short lifetimes on the **main sequence.** → **stars, lifetimes of**

Earth

The third planet of the solar system and the only world in space on which it is certain there is life. Liquid water covers 71 percent of its surface to an average depth of 3,900 m and played a crucial role in the origin and evolution of terrestrial organisms. Volcanism and impact cratering are also in evidence, although the dominant geological process is erosion and deposition by water or ice.

Distance from Sun:	
Mean	149.6 million km
	(93.0 million mi., 1.00 AU)
Minimum	147.0 million km
	(91.4 million mi., 0.98 AU)
Maximum	152.2 million km
	(94.6 million mi., 1.02 AU)
Equatorial diameter	12,756 km
	(7,928 million mi.)
Mean density	5.52 g/cm³
Escape velocity	11.18 km/s
	(40,248 km/h, 25,014 mi./h)
Orbital period	365.26 days
Orbital eccentricity	0.017
Orbital inclination	0° (by definition)
Axial period	23.93 hours
Axial inclination	23.4°
Number of moons	1
Atmospheric composition	78% nitrogen, 21% oxygen, 0.9% argon
Maximum temp. (day)	50°C (122°F)
Minimum temp. (night)	−70°C (−94°F)
Mean temperature	15°C (59°F)
Albedo	0.36

Earth, atmosphere of

The sea-level composition is approximately 78 percent **nitrogen,** 21 percent **oxygen,** 0.9 percent argon, and 0.04 percent **carbon dioxide,** with variable small amounts of water vapor and pollutants such as **sulfur dioxide** and **carbon monoxide.** Variations in temperature define the various layers of the atmosphere, which include, in ascending order, the troposphere, stratosphere, mesosphere, thermosphere, and exosphere. The troposphere extends to a height of about 8 km at the poles and 18 km near the equator, and accounts for three quarters of the atmospheric mass. At the top of the troposphere, where the temperature falls to −60°C, is the tropopause and, above this, the stratosphere. Temperatures within the stratosphere, where there is no vertical air movement, are at first steady and then rise to about 0°C at an altitude of about 50 km. The heating within the stratosphere comes from the absorption of **ultraviolet** radiation from the Sun by **ozone** molecules. Beyond the stratosphere is the mesosphere, in which the temperature once again falls since ozone is less plentiful. At the top of the mesosphere, at a height of about 85 km, the temperature is −90°C. Above lies the thermosphere in which oxygen and nitrogen absorb solar ultraviolet causing the temperature to rise to about 1,300°C at a height of 500 km. The heating effect of this high temperature, however, is negligible since the density at such altitudes is only one million millionth that at sea level. "Shooting stars" (trails of incinerating meteors) and auroras are produced in this region. Finally, beyond the thermosphere is the exosphere, which contains the Van Allen radiation belts, extends into the Earth's magnetosphere, and merges with the near vacuum of interplanetary space. The earliest terrestrial atmosphere probably formed from the vaporization of volatile materials in the outer layers of the Earth's crust and was gradually altered by a number of factors, including the later presence of life, until it acquired its present composition (➔ **Earth, early history of**).

Earth, early history of

The Earth was formed about 4.55 billion years ago through the **accretion** of small particles within the **protoplanetary disk** that surrounded the infant Sun. Its primordial atmosphere probably consisted of a mildly **reducing atmosphere** of **carbon monoxide, carbon dioxide, nitrogen,** water vapor, and a small amount of **hydrogen,** derived from volatile matter that permeated the outer layers of the planet. Heat released by the breakdown of short-lived radioactive elements led to further massive **outgassing** of these substances. What little free hydrogen there was soon escaped into space, allowing the formation of an **ozone** layer that subsequently protected the surface against the Sun's **ultraviolet** radiation. However, conditions for the evolution of life were hardly clement during the first few hundred million years after the Earth's formation. In that early period, from about 4.55 to 3.8 billion years ago, the Earth is thought to have been struck repeatedly by objects measuring 100 km or more across and traveling at around 30 km per second. Each such impact would have seared the surface at temperatures of up to 3,000°C, stripping away any atmosphere, boiling away any oceans, and rendering life impossible down to a depth of about 1 km below the surface. Recent discoveries of **extremophiles** in deep subsurface rocks and high-temperature environments, however, suggest that once life appeared it might have survived the traumas of bombardment by retreating deep underground.

Earth grazer

An **asteroid** or **comet** whose orbit occasionally brings it close to the Earth.

Earth, oceans of

➔ **oceans, origin of**

Earth-class planet

A planet having a mass 0.5 to 10 times that of the Earth (M_e) and a radius 0.8 to 2.2 times that of the Earth. Planets more massive than 10 M_e have enough gravity to attract a large **hydrogen-helium** atmosphere and so become **gas giant**s. Those less massive than 0.5 M_e are likely to lose any potentially life-supporting atmosphere because of low gravity and a lack of the **plate tectonics** needed to recycle **carbon dioxide** back into the atmosphere.

Earth-crossing asteroid

➔ **Earth grazer**

earthlights

It was the eccentric American collector of anomalous material Charles Fort who compiled the first catalog of reports of mysterious lights in the sky, long before anyone had thought to equate such manifestations with alien spacecraft. In fact, for all his many bizarre ideas, Fort had a literally down-to-earth view of what the luminous phenomena might be. He called them "earthlights" and noted a possible geographical connection between them and regions prone to earthquakes and tremors.

In 1954, F. Lagarde matched the centers of activity in a French wave of **unidentified flying objects** to the location of geological faults. Two decades later, Canadian researchers Michael **Persinger** and G. Lafreniere found a similar pattern of correlation between UFO reports and sites of tectonic disturbance in North America. At Hessdalen, southeast of Trondheim in Norway, geologist Erling Strang has been monitoring earthlights since the early 1980s, tying the visual phenomena to local variations in the Earth's magnetic field. Strang has found that a typical apparition is matched by a 1,000-fold increase in magnetometer readings.

The most violent tectonic events on Earth happen where oceanic crustal plates and continental plates meet. One such place is in the northwest of the United States, where a plate under the Pacific Ocean is diving below the continental United States. This movement has lifted up the **Cascade Mountains,** a chain of volcanoes, whose ability to burst spectacularly into life was demonstrated most recently by the Mount St. Helens eruption. The Cascade peaks are linked by fault lines, and it was over these very mountains that Kenneth **Arnold** saw the objects that were destined to become the archetypal "**flying saucers.**"

From every continent come reports of a similar nature. In West Africa, balls of light seen gliding over the surface of water are called *aku*—the devil. In Malaysia, aerial lights known as *penangau* are believed to be the phantom heads of women who died in childbirth. And in the northwest Australian outback, so-called *min-min* lights have a sacred significance to the Aborigines. That earthlights exist is virtually beyond doubt. That they are linked in some way to tectonic activity and to sudden surges in ambient magnetic field strength is on the way to becoming firmly established. But what remains unknown is the mechanism by which the lights are created and sustained. In some cases, earthlights have been seen to persist for up to 2 hours. Whatever is behind the phenomenon, it is certainly not a sudden, momentary electrical discharge like that of a lightning strike.

Laboratory studies have offered a few tantalizing clues. In 1981, at the request of Michael Persinger, Brian Brady of the U.S. Bureau of Mines carried out an experiment in Denver in which a granite core was crushed in darkened conditions and filmed in slow motion. Afterward, the researchers observed lights on the film, flitting out from the decaying core and moving around the chamber of the rock crusher. These were only tiny, transient events, however. Great slabs of rock grinding against each other on either side of a fault would release vastly more energy. What is not clear is how the energy source generating the earthlights could be maintained and directed for long periods. One problem is that the Earth is a good conductor and allows any local buildup of charge to leak rapidly away. This makes it difficult to explain how the charge around an active fault could remain in place long enough to drive a lengthy UFO display on the surface or in the sky above.

Some preliminary ideas have been put forward. According to John Derr of the U.S. Geological Survey,[146, 147] the presence of water in the rocks may be crucial. Heat produced by tectonic movement, he argues, creates sheaths of steam, which coat the edges of the fault. These sheaths serve to insulate the buildup of charge at the center of the fault from the conducting rocks further out. Eventually, enough charge accumulates for it to burst out into the atmosphere and give rise to a visible display. This model, however, falls short of explaining either the duration or the peculiar behavior of earthlights. ➔ **Marfa Lights; Egryn Lights**

earthquake lights
➔ **earthlights**

EASTEX

The East Coast group of the **Panel on Extraterrestrial Life,** chaired by Salvador Luria and also including Bruce Billings, Dean Cowie, Richard Davies, George Derbyshire, Paul Doty, Herbert Freeman, Thomas **Gold,** H. Keffer Hartline, Martin Kamen, Cyris Levinthal, Stanley **Miller,** E. F. MacNichol, Bruno Rossi, W. R. Sistron, John W. Townsend, Wolf **Vishniac,** Fred Whipple, and Richard S. Young. It held its first meeting on December 19–20, 1958, at the Massachusetts Institute of Technology and produced a final report circulated as SSB (Space Science Board)-93. EASTEX was merged with **WESTEX** into **Committee 14 on Exobiology** in August 1960.

eccentric Jovians

Extrasolar planets with a mass similar to or greater than that of Jupiter that move around their **host star**s in highly elongated orbits. They include the planetary companions of **70 Virginis, 16 Cygni** B, and possibly **HD 114762,** which range in mass from 1.74 to 10 times that of Jupiter and in orbital **eccentricity** from about 0.25 to 0.68. The discovery of these objects, together with that of another unexpected class of extrasolar planets, the **epistellar Jovians,** has prompted a revision of contemporary theories about how planets are formed (➜ **planetary systems, formation of**).[298] According to one new hypothesis, the gravitational forces exerted by **protoplanets** on the material of the surrounding **protoplanetary disk** create alternating spiral **density wave**s, like those that, on a much larger scale, give rise to the arms of a **spiral galaxy.** These waves then act back on the forming planets, pushing them out of their circular orbits into ones of higher eccentricity. A second hypothesis assumes that in some cases a young planetary system starts out with several "superplanets," each one at least as massive as Jupiter. The powerful gravitational interactions between these giant worlds causes them to be thrown around, so that they may end up in highly eccentric orbits, some of them lying close to the central star, others much farther out. An interesting prediction of this model, which can be tested, is that a system containing one eccentric Jovian close to the host star should contain at least one more massive planet, probably lying much further out. ➜ **classical Jovians**

eccentricity

A parameter that describes the shape of an orbit or any curve that is a **conic section.** An

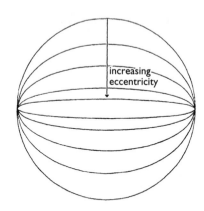

almost circular orbit has an eccentricity close to zero. The more elongated the orbit, the higher the eccentricity, up to a maximum value, for a closed orbit, of 1. As a guide, the orbital eccentricity of most of the planets in the solar system is less than 0.1 (0.017 in the case of Earth), although that of Mercury and Pluto exceeds 0.2.

échelle grating

A **diffraction grating** in which the grooves are quite widely spaced and have a zigzag or step-like cross-sectional profile. The light to be dispersed is made to fall on the grating at right angles to the faces of the grooves. This has the effect of producing a series of overlapping spectra with a high degree of resolution. A second, low-dispersion grating, or a prism arranged perpendicular to the échelle, serves to separate out the overlapping spectra.

échelle spectrograph

A **spectrograph** in which an **échelle grating** is used to disperse the incident light into a **spectrum.**

E-class asteroid

A rare category of **asteroid,** spectrally similar to **M-class asteroid**s and **P-class asteroid**s but of higher **albedo** (in the range of 0.25 to 0.60).

eclipsing binary

A **binary star** system in which the components periodically pass in front of each other as seen from Earth. When this happens, the total light received from the system is reduced. Exactly how the light varies depends on the nature of the component stars and their separation. →
Algol

ecliptic

The plane of the Earth's orbit extended to meet the **celestial sphere** so that it also coincides with the annual path of the Sun across the sky. The orbits of the planets, with the exception of Pluto, lie close to the ecliptic.

ecosphere

An alternative name for the **habitable zone** around a star.

ecosystem

A complex interacting system, involving many interconnected feedback loops, that includes both organisms and their nonliving environment.

ectotherms

Cold-blooded animals, such as reptiles, fish, and amphibians, whose body temperature is regulated by their behavior or surroundings.

Edelson, Robert E.

Head of the **SETI** office at the **Jet Propulsion Laboratory** in the late 1970s.[176]

Edgeworth-Kuiper Disk

→ **Kuiper Belt**

Egryn Lights

Unusual lights seen near the Welsh village of Egryn in the winter of 1904 that may offer a clue as to the nature of some reports of **unidentified flying objects.** According to one eyewitness, "Between us and the hills, apparently two miles away, there suddenly flashed forth an enormous luminous star with intensely brilliant white light and emitting from its whole circumference dazzling sparkles." Another said, "[It was] poised in mid-air, a mass of fire of every conceivable color spreading on all sides and descending into a rainbow shower to the surface of the mountain." Even more spectacular

events were seen in the vicinity of some ancient megalithic remains in the neighborhood. From the ground, several multicolored columns of light sprang, 2 to 3 m high. One of these appeared to flutter as if there were some internal instability, and then started to produce spheres of light that slowly rose up its length before exploding at the top. It has been suggested that the people who once lived in these parts, more than 3,000 years ago, may have witnessed something similar, and, interpreting it as a supernatural event, built stone edifices to mark the locations where the lights had appeared. It is at least an intriguing possibility that these and certain other prehistoric monuments were purposely erected close to where unusual, energetic events took place on the planet. This in turn provides at least a plausible basis for the seemingly outlandish claims of a link between the flight paths of UFOs, energy currents flowing in the Earth, and the arcane knowledge of lost civilizations.

Drawing on reports from December 1904 to March 1905 of the lights near Egryn and also those seen several kilometers to the north and south, writer and independent researcher Paul Devereux plotted on a large-scale map the exact location of each sighting. He then sought the advice of professional geologists, who pointed out the existence of a major, deep-seated fault, the Mochras Fault, running north to south between the coastal towns of Harlech and Barmouth and passing almost directly under the village of Egryn. When Devereux compared the places where the earthlights had been observed with the path of the fault, he found a striking correlation: the reported sightings were strung out like beads on a thread. Checking the geological records, Devereux learned that the area had been subject to tremors immediately around and after the occurrence of the lights, culminating in a minor earthquake under the southern Welsh town of Swansea in 1906.[149] Similar seismic activity in the **Cascade Mountains** may have been responsible for the "**flying saucers**" seen by Kenneth **Arnold** in 1947. → **earthlights**

Ehman, Jerry

Professor at Ohio State University who in August 1977, while checking through data from the **SETI** project being carried out at the **Ohio State University Radio Observatory,** came across the now-famous **Wow! signal.**

Eigen, Manfred (1927–)

Nobel Prize–winning chemist who has conducted numerous experiments in **prebiotic** evolution to understand the process by which different species of **RNA** compete and evolve. Like Ilya **Prigogine** and Stuart **Kauffman,** he is a prominent supporter of the application of **complexity theory** to origin of life studies.

Einstein ring

An effect associated with a **gravitational lens.** It occurs when light from a background source is spread out into a ring by the gravity of an intervening object along the same line of sight.

Eiseley, Loren Corey (1907–77)

Holder of the chair of anthropology at the University of Pennsylvania and lyrical science writer who echoed a view, expressed earlier by Alfred Russel **Wallace** and William **Matthew,** that extraterrestrial life must be morphologically diverse:[180]

> Every creature alive is the product of a unique history. The statistical probability of its precise reduplication on another planet is so small as to be meaningless.

Elara

The twelfth known moon of **Jupiter.** → **Jupiter, moons of**

Discovery	1905, by Charles Perrine
Mean distance from Saturn	11,743,000 km (7,298,000 mi)
Diameter	76 km (47 mi.)
Mean density	3.3 g/cm³
Escape velocity	0.0522 km/s (188 km/h, 117 mi./h)
Orbital period	259.65 days (259 days 16 hours)
Orbital eccentricity	0.207
Orbital inclination	24.77°
Axial period	0.5 days
Visual albedo	0.03

electromagnetic radiation

Radiation, consisting of vibrating electric and magnetic fields, that propagates at the speed of light (300,000 km per second in a vacuum). → **electromagnetic spectrum**

electromagnetic spectrum

The entire range of **electromagnetic radiation** from the longest **wavelength**s (lowest frequencies) of 1,000 m or more to the shortest wavelengths (highest frequencies) of about 10^{-15} m. It includes **radio waves, microwave radiation, infrared, visible light, ultraviolet, X rays,** and **gamma rays.**

electron

A negatively charged subatomic particle with a mass equal to 1/1,837 that of a **proton.** Electrons occur in the outer parts of atoms, in orbitals corresponding to definite fixed energies. When an electron in an atom jumps from one particular orbital to another, it gives rise to the emission or absorption of **electromagnetic radiation** at a specific characteristic **wavelength.**

element

A substance consisting entirely of **atom**s of the same variety. There are ninety-two naturally occurring elements, the most cosmically abundant of which are the two lightest, **hydrogen and helium** (→ **elements, cosmic abundance of**). Heavier elements are manufactured in the interior of stars before being returned to the **interstellar medium** by mass loss from **red giant**s and other phenomena such as **supernova**s. Subsequent generations of stars and their planets form from this heavy element enriched material. It is a remarkable and sobering thought that most of the atoms of which we and our world are composed were forged in the multimillion-degree interior of long-dead suns.

elements, biological abundance of

In all terrestrial organisms, **carbon, hydrogen, oxygen,** and **nitrogen** are the primary constituents, making up 96.3 percent of the body weight of human beings and a similarly large proportion of all other organisms on Earth. Several factors contribute to their predomi-

THE ELECTROMAGNETIC SPECTRUM

Band	Objects Comparable in Size to the Wavelength	Frequency	Wavelength
RADIO WAVES		3 kHz (10^3 Hz)	100 km (10^5 m)
Long radio waves		30 kHz (10^4 Hz)	10 km (10^4 m)
AM		300 kHz (10^5 Hz)	1 km (10^3 m)
Short waves	football field	3 MHz (10^6 Hz)	100 m (10^2 m)
FM and TV	human	30 MHz (10^7 Hz)	10 m (10^1 m)
		300 MHz (10^8 Hz)	1 m (10^0 m)
Radar		3 GHz (10^9 Hz)	10 cm (10^{-1} m)
S-band			
X-band			
Microwaves	sand grain	30 GHz (10^{10} Hz)	1 cm (10^{-2} m)
		300 GHz (10^{11} Hz)	1 mm (10^{-3} m)
INFRARED RADIATION	bacterium	3×10^{12} Hz	100 μm (10^{-4} m)
		3×10^{13} Hz	10 μm (10^{-5} m)
VISIBLE LIGHT	virus	3×10^{14} Hz	1 μm (10^{-6} m)
ULTRAVIOLET RADIATION	macromolecule	3×10^{15} Hz	100 nm (10^{-7} m)
		3×10^{16} Hz	10 nm (10^{-8} m)
		3×10^{17} Hz	1 nm (10^{-9} m)
X RAYS	atom	3×10^{18} Hz	100 pm (10^{-10} m)
		3×10^{19} Hz	10 pm (10^{-11} m)
		3×10^{20} Hz	1 pm (10^{-12} m)
		3×10^{21} Hz	100 fm (10^{-13} m)
GAMMA RAYS	nucleus	3×10^{22} Hz	10 fm (10^{-14} m)
		3×10^{23} Hz	1 fm (10^{-15} m)
		3×10^{24} Hz	0.1 fm (10^{-16} m)

nance: (1) They can combine with one another through **covalent bond**s to form **molecule**s. (2) These bonds can be broken at temperatures compatible with life, so that the atoms can be rearranged into an enormous variety of other molecules. (3) Carbon is exceptional in its ability to form the basis of **macromolecules**. (4) **Water,** which is composed of oxygen and hydrogen atoms, plays a central role in the biochemistry of terrestrial life. About 90 percent of the atoms (75 percent by weight) in terrestrial organisms are oxygen and hydrogen. (5) Among the simpler molecules formed by the four main biological elements are water vapor and gases that are soluble in water. As water vapor in the Earth's primordial atmosphere condensed and fell as rain, it brought the other dissolved substances into the early oceans. Subsequently, according to the consensus view, the interaction of small molecules led to more complex substances and eventually to life itself (➔ **life, origin of**). Interestingly, the four principal biological elements are also the four most common chemically active elements in the universe (➔ **elements, cosmic abundance of**), **helium** and neon being inert. In contrast, only oxygen is highly abundant in both terrestrial organisms and the Earth's crust (➔ **elements, terrestrial abundance of; trace element**).

DISTRIBUTION OF ELEMENTS IN THE HUMAN BODY BY WEIGHT

Element	Atomic Number	Percentage	Role
Oxygen	8	65.0	Cellular respiration; component of water
Carbon	6	18.5	Basis of organic molecules
Hydrogen	1	9.5	Component of water and most organic molecules; electron carrier
Nitrogen	7	3.3	Component of all proteins and nucleic acids
Calcium	20	1.5	Component of bones and teeth; triggers muscle contraction
Phosphorus	15	1.0	Component of nucleic acids; important in energy transfer
Potassium	19	0.4	Main positive ion inside cells; important in nerve function
Sulfur	16	0.3	Component of most proteins
Sodium	11	0.2	Main positive ion outside cells; important in nerve function
Chlorine	17	0.2	Main negative ion outside cells
Magnesium	12	0.1	Essential component of many energy-transferring enzymes
Iron	26	Trace	Essential component of hemoglobin in the blood
Copper	29	Trace	Component of many enzymes
Molybdenum	42	Trace	Component of many enzymes
Zinc	30	Trace	Component of some enzymes
Iodine	53	Trace	Component of thyroid hormone

elements, cosmic abundance of

In the universe as a whole, **hydrogen** is by far the commonest element followed by **helium** and more distantly by heavier elements such as **oxygen** and **carbon.** Locally, the proportion of heavy elements varies from one star system to another and is an influential factor in the formation of planets. (→ **planetary systems, formation of**)

elements, terrestrial abundance of

The proportion of **elements** within the Earth changes dramatically with depth, heavier elements, notably **iron** and nickel, having sunk to the center of the planet during its early stages of formation. The table below ranks the elements according to their preponderance in the lithosphere, which includes the crust and the upper part of the mantle.

COSMIC ABUNDANCE OF ELEMENTS

Element	Number of Atoms per 10,000,000 Atoms of Hydrogen
Hydrogen	10,000,000
Helium	1,400,000
Oxygen	6,800
Carbon	3,000
Neon	2,800
Nitrogen	910
Magnesium	290
Silicon	250
Sulfur	95
Iron	80
Argon	42
Aluminum	19
Sodium	17
Calcium	17
All other elements	50

DISTRIBUTION OF ELEMENTS IN THE EARTH'S CRUST (BY WEIGHT)

Element	Atomic Number	Percentage by Weight	Element	Atomic Number	Percentage by Weight
Oxygen	8	46.60	Chlorine	17	0.05
Silicon	14	27.72	Carbon	6	0.03
Aluminum	13	8.13	Rubidium	37	0.03
Iron	26	5.00	Vanadium	23	0.01
Calcium	20	3.63	Chromium	24	0.01
Sodium	11	2.83	Copper	29	0.01
Potassium	19	2.59	Nitrogen	7	0.005
Magnesium	12	2.09	Boron	5	Trace
Titanium	22	0.44	Cobalt	27	Trace
Hydrogen	1	0.14	Zinc	30	Trace
Phosphorus	15	0.12	Selenium	34	Trace
Manganese	25	0.10	Molybdenum	42	Trace
Fluorine	9	0.08	Tin	50	Trace
Sulfur	16	0.05	Iodine	53	Trace

ellipse

The path followed by one object that is gravitationally bound to another, for example, by one of the stars in a **binary star** system or a planet going around the Sun. An ellipse is a **conic section** and is mathematically defined as the locus of a point which moves so that the sum of its distances from two fixed points, known as "loci," is constant.

elliptical galaxy

A **galaxy** in which the stars are arranged in an ellipsoidal or spheroidal volume of space. Unlike spiral galaxies, ellipticals have no **galactic disk** or **spiral arm**s and relatively little interstellar material. They may account for about 80 percent of all the galaxies in space. The majority of them are dwarf galaxies. But among their ranks are also the most massive galaxies known: the giant ellipticals, containing upward of a trillion stars. It used to be thought that ellipticals were the oldest galaxies, but more recent studies, including computer simulations, suggest that they have formed from collisions and mergers between spiral galaxies. So-called starburst galaxies appear to show this process in action.

Elodie

A high-resolution **échelle spectrograph** in operation at the **Haute-Provence Observatory** and used in the detection of the first extrasolar planet, **51 Pegasi b.** It is fed by a fiber-optic bundle from the Cassegrain focus of the observatory's 1.93-m telescope. An improved version of Elodie, known as **Coralie,** is in operation in the Southern Hemisphere.

Emilie

A **spectrograph** specifically designed for use in the **Absolute Astronomical Accelerometry** project at the **Haute-Provence Observatory.** It will operate at the Coudé focus of the observatory's 1.52-m reflector.

emission line

A bright line in the **spectrum** of a luminous object caused by the emission of light at a particular wavelength.

emission nebula

A cloud of interstellar gas that is caused to glow by the **ionizing radiation** of one or more nearby, hot stars. The main categories of emission nebulas are **H II region**s, **planetary nebula**s, and **supernova remnant**s.

enantiomers

Molecules that are optical isomers, or mirror images, of each other. Enantiomers can be distinguished by the direction in which they rotate the plane of polarization of **polarized**

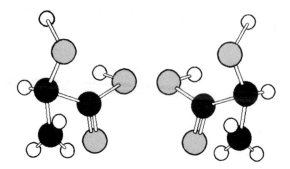

Enantiomers of the two forms of lactic acid. Carbon atoms are shown in black, oxygen atoms in gray, and hydrogen atoms in white.

light and are referred to, therefore, as being **dextrorotatory** (D-) or **levorotatory** (L-). ➔ **enantiomers, bias in terrestrial life**

enantiomers, bias in terrestrial life

All organisms on Earth use **amino acids** and **sugars** in only one of the two possible mirror-image forms (➔ **enantiomers**): the amino acids are all left-handed (L-), and the sugars are all right-handed (D-). This has prompted theorists to speculate on how such a bias came about. One possibility is that the **inorganic** molecules that provided a substrate on which **prebiotic** chemicals assembled in pools on the young Earth were themselves of a particular handedness (➔ **silicon-based life**). Another theory is that the choice was initially made in space, by the action of circular **polarized light,** before the solar system even took shape (➔ **amino acids, in space**). Research published in 1998 by Keno Soai and his colleagues at the Science University of Tokyo[537] supports the view that once an enantiomer imbalance of even a few percent had arisen, it would be amplified by subsequent chemical reactions. Soai's team examined a mixture of compounds containing a slight excess of one enantiomer of the amino acid leucine. The components of the solution reacted to give a substance known as pyrimidyl alkanol, also with a slight excess of one enantiomer. This molecule, however, then acted to catalyze its own formation (➔ **autocatalysis**), so that quickly almost all the pyrimidyl alkanol in the solution was of the same handedness. Although pyrimidyl alkanol is not itself relevant to prebiological development, its autocatalyzing behavior shows how a minor enantiomer imbalance could quickly give rise to the bias found in living systems. The fact that a choice was made has proved vital, because **proteins** (which are made from amino acids) can fold consistently only if made entirely of one form or another, but not both. ➔ **life, origin of**

Enceladus

The eighth moon of **Saturn** and the most reflective object known in the solar system. It is also the most geologically evolved member of Saturn's retinue and displays a young surface with at least five distinct types of terrain. Even the most heavily cratered areas of Enceladus are much more lightly pockmarked than the other icy satellites, while some regions are crater-free down to a resolution of 2 km (1.2 miles), indicating that the surface has undergone major change during the last 1 billion years. On either edge of the ridged plains, a series of truncated craters indicates that melting of the surface occurred after the end of the intense bombardment phase. Linear markings in the southern hemisphere are rectilinear fault lines associated with movement of the crust. Other, curved lines appear to be a complex system of ridges similar to the grooved terrain on **Ganymede.** All of this suggests that Enceladus may have an interior that is kept in a liquid state by **tidal heating** due to the gravitational effects of Saturn and the large neighboring moons **Tethys** and **Dione.** Because Enceladus reflects almost 100 percent of incident sunlight, its surface temperature is only −201°C (−330°F). ➔ **Saturn, moons of**

Discovery	1789, by William Herschel
Mean distance from Saturn	238,100 km (147,980 mi.)
Diameter	500 km (311 mi.)
Mean density	1.24 g/cm³
Escape velocity	0.2 km/s (720 km/h, 447 mi./h)
Orbital period	1.376 days (1 day 9 hours 1 minute)
Orbital eccentricity	0.065
Orbital inclination	0.02°
Axial period	1.376 days
Visual albedo	0.99

encounter hypothesis
→ catastrophic hypothesis

Encounter 2001 Message

An attempt at **CETI** a quarter century after the seminal **Arecibo Message** was broadcast to a giant star cluster in Hercules. This new signal, designed by Yvan Dutil and Stephane Dumas at the Defence Research Establishment Valcartier near Quebec City, was sponsored by the Houston-based company Encounter 2001 and transmitted on March 14, 1999, from a **radio telescope** in Ukraine. Whereas the Arecibo Message was made up of only 1,679 **bits** of information, the loss of any one of which on its long journey might make the message unintelligible, the Encounter 2001 Message consists of 300,000 bits, with built-in redundancy so that even if some bits are lost to noise en route, any recipient should stand a good chance of making sense of the contents. The first part of the message is a greeting, based on what are presumed to be universal mathematical and physical laws (→ **mathematics, as a universal language**), to tell anyone tuning in who we are and that we would like a reply. Later, the company broadcast the names and addresses of two thousand people who signed up at its Web site and paid a fee. Additional transmissions are scheduled for 2000 and 2001. → **Celestis, Inc.; Encounter 2001, The Millennial Voyage**

Encounter 2001, The Millennial Voyage

A small spacecraft to be sent on a trajectory out of the solar system that will carry writings, drawings, photos, and DNA samples (in the form of human hair) from people around the world who have paid a fee to **Celestis, Inc,** the company organizing the mission. The spacecraft is scheduled for launch by an Ariane 5 rocket in 2001.

endoliths

Organisms that live inside rock, or the tiny pores between interlocking mineral grains. Thousands of different species are known, including representatives of **bacteria, archaea,** and **fungi.** Endoliths have been found inhabiting the Earth's crust at depths up to nearly 3 km (2 miles).[317] Many are **autotrophs** that manufacture their own **organic** compounds from **inorganic** chemicals in the rock. Other varieties of endolith feed on the organics produced by the autotrophs, giving rise to microscopic underground communities known as SLiMEs (Subsurface Lithotrophic Microscopic Environments). The extreme depth at which endoliths can exist has yet to be established. The main problem that organisms face at increasing depth is not so much the very high pressure but the rising temperature. **Hyperthermophiles** are known that thrive in the vicinity of **black smokers** at a temperature of more than 110°C. For oceanic crust, where the temperature rises about 15°C per kilometer of depth, a tolerance of 110°C would allow microbial life to extend down to about 7 km below the seafloor. For a continental crust, where the temperature rise is faster, a 110°C threshold would allow life to continue at depths of up to 4 km.

In 1998, evidence was also found of "rock-eating" microbes at depths of about 1.5 km (~1 mile) beneath the ocean floor.[195] A team from Oregon State University found minute tracks in core samples of basalt obtained from under the Pacific, Atlantic, and Indian Oceans by the Ocean Drilling Program. In every case where a track was examined closely, it was found to contain **DNA.** One theory is that the organisms that create such trails seek micronutrients from the rock in the form of iron, potassium, or sulfur. They appear either to consume the rock or to excrete some kind of acid that dissolves it.

The discovery of endoliths and the varied and innovative means by which they acquire nutrients and energy brings closer the prospect that life arises frequently in the Universe. Wherever there is internal heat, the presence of underground water, and a supply of inorganic chemical nutrients, as, for example, there may be on Mars, the large moons of the gas giants, and even comets, subsurface life may exist.[10, 208]

endosymbiosis
→ endosymbiotic theory

endosymbiotic theory

A theory first proposed by Lynn **Margulis** and now widely accepted that **eukaryotic cells** evolved from a symbiosis between different species of **prokaryote**s. Larger species, it is suggested, engulfed smaller ones, which continued to live and function within the larger host cell, eventually losing all possibility of independence. Two **organelle**s believed to have entered larger cells in this way are **mitochondria** and **chloroplasts.**

energy-based life
→ **noncorporeal life**

enzymes
Biochemical **catalyst**s, the majority of which are **globular proteins,** although some, known as **ribozymes,** are composed of **RNA.** About one thousand different varieties are found in the human body. Enzymes facilitate key processes in the biochemistry of organisms that, otherwise, would take place too slowly for the maintenance of life. Enzymes speed up

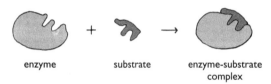

| enzyme | substrate | enzyme-substrate complex |

Simplified view of an enzyme binding to its substrate.

chemical reactions of **substrate**s by lowering the **activation energy.** They have complex **tertiary structure**s that are held in shape by weak chemical bonds between the **polypeptide** chains. Each enzyme has a specific surface configuration with one or more clefts known as "active sites" to which only certain substrates can bind. Each enzyme is highly specific to the reaction it catalyzes, as the substrate must fit precisely into the active site. If the active site loses its unique shape, it can no longer provide a point of attachment for its substrate and the enzyme is said to be "denatured." This can happen if the enzyme is subjected to temperatures or **pH** levels outside the narrow range in which it normally operates. Many enzymes require the assistance of certain accessory substances, known as **cofactor**s and **coenzyme**s, to function properly.

Epicurus (341–270 B.C.)
Greek philosopher who was born on the Ionian island of Samos. Eventually, he moved to Athens, where he opened a school of philosophy in a garden that he had bought and laid out for the purpose. He developed further the doctrine of **atomism,** as expounded by **Leucippus** and **Democritus of Abdera,** including the idea that life exists elsewhere in the universe. In his *Letter to Herodotus,* he writes:

> [T]here are infinite worlds both like and unlike this world of ours...we must believe that in all worlds there are living creatures and plants and other things we see in this world.

Everything, he believed, could be explained in terms of natural causes. As for the gods, he taught that they existed only in the spaces between worlds, and had no interest at all in human affairs. → **Lucretius; ancient philosophy, related to the possibility of extraterrestrial life**

epidemics, from space
A highly controversial suggestion, by Fred **Hoyle** and Chandra Wickramasinghe, that **virus**es carried by **comet**s, and released from their tails, are the cause of mass outbreaks of influenza and other viral diseases on Earth.[289] Although the great majority of scientists are dismissive of this idea, it was lent some credence by the detection in 1987 of a **polymer**ic form of the organic molecule **formaldehyde** in the dust from **Halley's Comet** by the *Giotto* probe. Christopher **Chyba** and Carl **Sagan** of **Cornell University** commented at the time that the observations "strongly suggest the presence of complex organic grains or organic-coated grains." There remains, however, an immense gulf between the growing recognition that some types of basic organic chemical syntheses do take place in space and acceptance of the idea that the evolution of primitive life-forms takes place on **cosmic dust** grains as proposed by Hoyle and Wickramasinghe. → **life, in space; panspermia**

Epimetheus
The fifth (equal) moon of **Saturn;** Epimetheus shares the same orbit as **Janus.** Normally sep-

Discovery	1980, by R. Walker et al. using *Voyager I* data
Mean distance from Saturn	151,420 km (94,110 mi.)
Diameter	144 × 108 × 98 km (89 × 67 × 61 mi.)
Mean density	0.7 g/cm³
Escape velocity	0.032 km/s (115 km/h, 72 mi./h)
Orbital period	0.694 day (16 hours 39 minutes)
Orbital eccentricity	0.009
Orbital inclination	0.34°
Axial period	0.694 day
Visual albedo	0.8

arated by about 50 km, every 4 years these two satellites approach each other, exchange a small amount of momentum, and swap places. It is possible that they formed from the breakup of a single parent object. The surface of Epimetheus reveals a number of valleys, grooves, and ridges, and extensive cratering, with several craters more than 30 km (19 miles) in diameter. **→ Saturn, moons of**

epistellar Jovians

Extrasolar planets, similar in mass to Jupiter, with remarkably small, circular orbits around their **host star**s and **orbital period**s of less than 10 days. They are also referred to as "hot Jupiters" or "51-Pegasi-type planets." The discovery of this class of planet was unpredicted and has compelled theorists to reconsider and refine their models of planet formation (**→ planetary systems, formation of**). The prototype epistellar Jovian is the 0.44-Jupiter-mass (M_J) planet detected around **51 Pegasi,** with an orbital radius of less than one eighth of Mercury's distance from the Sun. Some presently known examples are listed below.

Name	Mass (M_J)	Orbital Radius (AU)	Period (days)
HD 75289	0.42	0.046	3.51
51 Pegasi	0.47	0.050	4.23
HD 187123	0.52	0.042	3.10
upsilon Andromedae	0.68	0.057	4.61
HD 217107	1.28	0.040	7.11
tau Bootis	3.87	0.046	3.31

The surface temperatures of these worlds are believed to range from about 1,000 to 1,700°C (1,800 to 3,100°F). Although it is conceivable that they are enormous balls of rock and metal, it seems much more likely that they are **gas giant**s, similar in composition to Jupiter. Calculations show that even at such high temperatures, the large gravitational pull of these planets would allow them to retain a massive hydrogen atmosphere with ease. The main difficulty for astronomers lies in explaining not how epistellar Jovians can survive in such small orbits but how they came to be there in the first place. Conventional theory suggests that giant planets should be able to form only in the cooler outskirts of a **protoplanetary disk.** In an effort to accommodate the new findings, astronomers Douglas N. C. Lin and Peter Bodenheimer of the University of California, Santa Cruz, and Derek C. Richardson of the University of Washington have extended the standard model by suggesting that a young **protoplanet** condensing out of a protoplanetary disk will carve a groove in the disk, separating it into two sections.[350] They theorize that the inner disk will lose energy through friction, causing the disk material and protoplanet to spiral in toward the central star. As the protoplanet draws nearer, it will cause the surface of the star to bulge. The rapid rotation rate of the young star, however, means that this bulge will tend to move ahead of the planet, tugging it forward and tending to whip it into a larger orbit. According to this model, an epistellar Jovian moves in a small, stable orbit, subject to two equal and opposing forces—the drag of the inner protoplanetary disk and the young rotating star's forward tug.

For a planet in such a small orbit, there is a significant probability (about 5 to 10 percent) that it will **transit** in front of its primary as seen from Earth and therefore be detectable by **photometry.** This is highly significant because data obtained from photometric observations of a transit will allow a direct measurement of the mean density of the planet and therefore its nature to be established. **→ eccentric Jovians; classical Jovians**

epsilon Eridani

One of the nearest, reasonably Sun-like stars, with about three quarters the mass of the Sun

Distance	10.50 light-years (3.22 parsecs)
Spectral type	K4 V
Apparent magnitude	3.7
Absolute magnitude	6.2
Luminosity (Sun = 1)	0.3

and with one third the luminosity. It has been the target of intense scrutiny by **SETI** projects, including the first, Project **Ozma.** It is now clear why these searches could not have been successful: epsilon Eridani is a young star, with an age of 500 million years to 1 billion years. Intelligence could not have developed in so short a time, even given the availability of a suitable planet. In September 1998, however, came news that the epsilon Eridani system may be like the solar system in other ways. Observations at submillimeter (very short radio) wavelengths showed that it is surrounded by a ring of dust at about the same distance as that of the **Kuiper Belt** from the Sun.[236] A bright region in the ring might be caused by particles trapped around a young planet, while a partially evacuated region nearer the star might indicate the presence of other unseen worlds. The density of dust in the Eridanian system is about 1,000 times that found in the solar system today, but roughly what it would have been like in the solar system about 4 billion years ago—about 600 million years after the Earth and other planets formed, toward the end of the period of heavy bombardment. This discovery adds to the growing body of evidence that planetary systems around other stars are the rule rather than the exception. Moreover, epsilon Eridani provides a window into what conditions may have been like in the neighborhood of the Sun at a time when life was first beginning to emerge on the young Earth. → **stars, nearest**

epsilon Indi
→ **stars, nearest**

Eratosthenes of Cyrene (c. 276–c. 194 b.c.)
Greek astronomer and mathematician who made the first reasonably accurate calculation of the Earth's circumference, obtaining a value of about 46,000 km. → **ancient philosophy, related to the possibility of extraterrestrial life**

EROS (Expérience pour la Recherche d'Objets Sombres)
A French program to detect and study dark objects in the Galaxy, including **brown dwarf**s and **MACHOs,** through their gravitational **microlensing** effects on stars in the **Large Magellanic Cloud.** It employs the Schmidt camera and a **charge-coupled device** at the **European Southern Observatory.**

eruptive variable
A star whose brightness increases sharply and unpredictably as a result of some highly energetic event. Among the types of eruptive variables are dwarf novas, **flare star**s, **novas**, and **supernova**s.

ESA
→ **European Space Agency**

escape velocity
The minimum velocity an object, such as a rocket or **rogue planet,** must have in order to escape completely from the gravitational influence of another body, such as a planet or star, without being given any extra impetus. It can be calculated by taking the square root of $(2Gm/r)$ where r is the distance from the center of the gravitating body of mass m and G is the gravitational constant. This is equal, but in the opposite direction to the velocity it would have acquired if it had been accelerated from rest, starting an infinite distance away. The escape velocity of the Earth is about 11 km per second (7 miles per second). If the body's velocity is less than the escape velocity, it is said to be gravitationally bound.

ESO
→ **European Southern Observatory**

ESO Coudé Échelle Spectrometer
An instrument attached to the 1.4-m telescope at **La Silla Observatory** that is being used to search for **extrasolar planets** by the **radial velocity method.** It was successful in detecting **HR 810,** a planet in one of the most Earth-like orbits so far found.

ET
Abbreviation for "extraterrestrial."

E.T. The Extra-Terrestrial

Motion picture (1982) directed by Steven **Spielberg,** in which a benign, lovable alien (a botanist on a research expedition) is stranded on Earth following the hurried departure of his spacecraft. The contrast between, on the one hand, creatures such as E.T. and those featured in **Close Encounters of the Third Kind,** and, on the other, the malignant invaders in the **Alien** series and *Independence Day* could hardly be more stark.

ETH

→ **extraterrestrial hypothesis**

ethane (C_2H_6)

The second member of the alkane series of **hydrocarbon**s; a colorless, odorless gas.

Melting point −183°C; boiling point 78.5°C

ethanol (C_2H_5OH)

Also known as ethyl alcohol.

Density relative to water (at 0°C) 0.61, boiling point 78.5°C

ethene (C_2H_4)

The first member of the alkene family of **hydrocarbon**s.

Melting point −169°C; boiling point −103°C

ETI

Abbreviation for "extraterrestrial intelligence."

eubacteria

In the five-**kingdom** system of taxonomy, one of the two main orders of true **bacteria** (the other being archaebacteria). They lack **photosynthetic** pigments and have very strong **cell wall**s that are generally spherical or rod-shaped. Motile eubacteria possess a flagellum for locomotion.

eukaryote

An organism composed of **eukaryotic cell**s. **Animal**s, **plants, fungi,** and **protists** are all eukaryotes. → **prokaryote**

eukaryotic

Pertaining to a **eukaryote** or a **eukaryotic cell.**

eukaryotic cell

A cell characterized by membrane-bounded **organelle**s, most notably the **nucleus.**

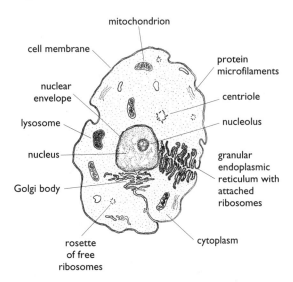

Europa

The smallest of the four **Galilean satellites** (slightly smaller than our own Moon) and the

Discovery	January 7, 1610, by Galileo Galilei
Mean distance from Jupiter	670,900 km (417,000 mi.)
Diameter	3,138 km (1,961 mi.)
Equatorial diameter (Earth = 1)	0.246
Mass (Earth = 1)	0.00812
Mean density	3.01 g/cm³
Surface gravity (Earth = 1)	0.135
Escape velocity	2.02 km/s (7,272 km/h, 4,520 mi./h)
Orbital period	3.551 days (3 days 13 hours 13 minutes)
Orbital eccentricity	0.009
Orbital inclination	0.047°
Axial period	3.551 days
Albedo	0.64
Surface temperature	−162°C (−260°F)
Surface composition	Water ice
Atmosphere	Tenuous oxygen

second nearest to **Jupiter** after **Io**. Europa's surface is remarkably smooth and flat, with no differences in relief of more than a few hundred meters. The surface composition of water ice results in an **albedo** almost seven times that of the Moon. Two types of terrain are in evidence. The first is mottled reddish brown or gray and covered mainly by small hills. Linear ridges in these regions are thought to be the frozen remnants of cryovolcanic activity where liquid or partially frozen water has erupted onto the Europan surface and instantly frozen. The second type of terrain consists of smooth plains, crisscrossed by large numbers of cracks, both curved and straight, some extending for thousands of kilometers. The fracture patterns closely resemble those seen in the broken ice pack in the Earth's Arctic and Antarctic Oceans. From these surface clues, and the fact that Europa is heated internally by both **tidal force**s and radioactive decay, scientists have hypothesized that a subsurface ocean of liquid water might exist on the moon (➔ **Europa, ocean on**) and that, if this is the case, life of some sort may have evolved in it (➔ **Europa, life on**). Few craters are in evidence, especially larger ones, suggesting that the surface has been resurfaced within the past few million years. Europa, like Io, is suspected of having an iron-sulfur core.

Observations with the ***Hubble Space Telescope*** in 1994 revealed the presence of a tenuous atmosphere of **oxygen** molecules, with a

A 34-km by 42-km (21-mile by 26-mile) area of Europa imaged by Galileo. Visible are crustal plates of ice, up to 13 km (8 miles) across, which have been broken apart and "rafted" into new positions.
NASA/JPL/Caltech

pressure barely one hundred billionth that of the Earth. In the words of one of the researchers who made the discovery, "If all the oxygen on Europa were compressed to the surface pressure of Earth's atmosphere, it would fill only about a dozen Houston Astrodomes." The oxygen is nonbiological in origin. Europa's icy surface is exposed to sunlight and is impacted by dust and charged particles trapped within Jupiter's intense magnetic field. Together these processes cause the frozen water ice to produce vapor as well as gaseous fragments of water molecules. After the gas molecules are produced, they undergo a series of chemical reactions that ultimately form molecular hydrogen and oxygen. The relatively lightweight hydrogen gas escapes into space, while the heavier oxygen molecules accumulate to form an atmo-

sphere that may extend 200 km (125 miles) above the surface. Since the oxygen gas slowly leaks into space, it is clear that it must be replenished continuously. In September 1999, the discovery was announced, based on infrared data from *Galileo,* of frozen sulfuric acid on Europa. This may originate from inside the moon or from volcanoes on neighboring Io. Either way, the implications for the possibility of Europan life are ambiguous. While sulfuric acid is an unpleasant chemical for humans, many bacteria on Earth prosper in sulfur- and acid-rich environments. → **Jupiter, moons of**

Europa, future probes of

In light of the extraordinary findings of the *Galileo* probe and the success of its extended investigation, the *Galileo* **Europa Mission,** a

Artist's impression of a future cryobot-hydrobot mission to explore the ocean that is theorized to exist on Europa.
NASA/JPL/Caltech

number of future missions are being planned or evaluated to find out more about **Europa** and, in particular, whether it has a subsurface ocean of liquid water and, possibly, even life. The first of these will be the *Europa Orbiter,* which could be launched as early as 2003 and serve as a precursor to other, more ambitious projects for which proposals are being considered, including:

Europa Ice Clipper: a flyby mission to obtain samples of Europa using an impact sampling method. As the *Clipper* approaches the moon, it would release a 10-kg hollow copper sphere on an impact trajectory. The spacecraft would then divert to fly through the plume of surface material thrown out by the collision of the sphere.

Europa Ocean Explorer (Icepick): a mission to soft land on Europa and explore what lies beneath its icy crust with **cryobot**s and **hydrobot**s. Some of the techniques and instrumentation required by this project are being developed as part of NASA's **Europa Vostok Initiative.**

Europa, life on

Together with **Mars, Callisto,** and **Titan, Europa** is considered one of the most biologically interesting worlds in the solar system. There are two main reasons for this: (1) the possible presence of a subsurface ocean of liquid water, which could provide a medium and **solvent** for life (➔ **Europa, ocean on**) and (2) the possible presence of undersea volcanic vents. On Earth, in recent years, a profusion of previously unsuspected life-forms has been found at great ocean depths, thriving, in the absence of both light and oxygen, on chemical nutrients upwelling through **hydrothermal vent**s from the interior of the planet. Indeed, many scientists now speculate that terrestrial life may actually have evolved under such conditions (➔ **life, origin of**). Europan life, too, may have arisen in this way. Following the *Galileo* **Europa Mission,** which has supplied valuable new data on Europa, other spacecraft to this intriguing moon are under study (➔ **Europa, future probes of**). The possibility of life on Europa has been explored in some depth fictionally by Arthur C. **Clarke** in the three sequels to his *2001: A Space Odyssey: 2010,*[116] *2061,*[117] and *3001.*[118]

Europa, ocean on

Great interest surrounds the possibility that an ocean of liquid water might exist between 1 km and a few tens of kilometers beneath the icy surface of **Europa.** The history of this idea appears to extend back to a 1971 theoretical paper[347] in which the author, John S. Lewis, argues that "the Galilean satellites of Jupiter and the large satellites of Saturn, Uranus, and Neptune very likely have extensively melted interiors." Speculation about a subice ocean and hypothetical Europan life (➔ **Europa, life on**) stepped up following *Voyager 2*'s close encounter with Europa in 1979,[481, 486] while by the time the *Galileo* spacecraft arrived at Jupiter in 1995, the ocean model was well established as a plausible hypothesis. What the new probe found only strengthened its case. High-resolution images provided clear evidence of near-surface melting and the movements of large blocks of icy crust similar to those of icebergs or ice rafts on Earth.[394] *Galileo*'s cameras also revealed very few impact craters—a sure sign that **resurfacing** has taken place in geologically recent times, no more than 30 million years ago. Various sources of heat have been discussed by planetary astronomers over the years as the means by which Europa's ice shelf might be kept molten from below, but the principal mechanisms are now thought to be tidal distortions caused by the shifting gravitational pulls of Jupiter and the other large Jovian moons and the internal decay of radioactive elements. Similar **tidal heating** may have created an ocean on **Callisto,** drives volcanoes on **Io,** and may give rise to water geysers on Europa, though none have yet been observed.

Europa Orbiter

A follow-up mission to *Galileo* that will probe **Europa**'s surface with a radar sounder in an attempt to determine the thickness of the ice and locate any ice-water interface. Other instruments will include an imaging device capable of resolving surface detail as small as 100 m and an altimeter for accurately measuring the topography and movements of the surface in response to tidal stresses. The orbiter, which could be launched in 2003, will serve as a precursor of other projects that will sample the Europan surface and, eventually, penetrate the top layers of ice to discover exactly what lies underneath (**→ Europa, future probes of**).

Europa Vostok Initiative
A NASA program of investigation of Lake **Vostok** that has the ultimate goal of developing instrumented probes to explore the subice oceans thought to exist on Jupiter's moons **Europa** and **Callisto.** Important preliminary data have been obtained from the **Lo'ihi Underwater Volcanic Vent Mission Probe.**

European Southern Observatory (ESO)
An organization founded in 1962 and involving eight European nations that operates a major observatory in the Southern Hemisphere at La Silla, near La Serena in Chile. **→ La Silla Observatory**

European Space Agency (ESA)
An international organization of thirteen member countries (Austria, Belgium, Denmark, France, Germany, Ireland, Italy, Netherlands, Norway, Spain, Sweden, Switzerland, and the United Kingdom) for cooperation in space research and technology.

evolution
A change in the **gene** pool of a population over time.

evolutionary theory and extraterrestrial life
Although earlier naturalists had realized that living things must have changed during the history of life on Earth, it was Jean-Baptiste de **Lamarck** who first developed an evolutionary philosophy based on the key idea of **adaptation.** His theory of the "inheritance of acquired characteristics" remained popular in France for most of the nineteenth century and influenced the speculations of Camille **Flammarion** and J. H. **Rosny** concerning extraterrestrial life. Elsewhere, however, Lamarckism was called into question, undermined by the experiments of August **Weismann** in Germany and superseded by Charles **Darwin**'s theory of evolution by **natural selection.** According to Darwinism, the traits favored by natural selection vary in different environments and cause the genetic change in populations of organisms over generations. This view had an especially powerful effect on scientific thinking in

Victorian Britain, where it was championed by Thomas **Huxley** and the sociologist Herbert **Spencer** and used by H. G. **Wells** as the basis of his essays and stories about possible alien life-forms. In time, Darwinian ideas would transform and unify biology, helping it to become a modern, autonomous science, but in themselves they could not make biology into a *universal* science akin to Newtonian physics. Whereas the movements of the Moon and planets could be readily observed and therefore used as the basis for a generalization of the theory of gravity beyond the Earth, no data on extraterrestrial organisms were available from which the biologist could establish some cosmic principles of life. Consequently, there was no way of predicting if, on other Earth-like worlds, life would appear as a matter of course and, if it did, how far its development would progress and in what directions.

For the most part, biologists in the first half of the twentieth century steered clear of questions about extraterrestrial life, having problems enough trying to understand how life had started here (**→ life, origin of**). The tendency among those biologists, such as W. D. **Matthew,** who did venture an opinion, was to argue that since life appeared to have originated on Earth only once or at most a few times over the course of many millions of years, and then as the result of an incredibly unlikely chain of chemical reactions, the chance of it happening elsewhere was very low and perhaps even zero. Astronomers, on the other hand, except during the 1920s and 1930s, when the **catastrophic hypothesis** was resurgent, tended to assume that the vast number of stars and presumed accompanying planets virtually guaranteed that life was abundant, whatever the details of its origin. Greater interest and urgency were added to this debate in the 1950s by the results of laboratory work in **prebiotic** synthesis, including the **Miller-Urey Experiment,** and the imminent start of planetary exploration and proposals to search for life on Mars and other neighboring worlds. The laboratory creation of the basic chemical building blocks of life as well as structures that resembled **cell membrane**s encouraged researchers involved in origin of life studies and in the nascent field of **astrobiology** to express optimism that the emergence and evolution of life is essentially deterministic—an inevitable consequence given certain starting conditions. This optimism was dented somewhat by the failure of the *Viking* spacecraft to find incontrovertible evidence of life on Mars and, more seriously, by the failure to synthesize in the lab more complex prebiotic chemicals, including **proteins** and **nucleic acids.** Jacques **Monod,** Francis **Crick,** Fred **Hoyle,** Norman **Horowitz,** and Ernst Mayr were among those who spoke out against the consensus view of astrobiologists. More recently, the pendulum has swung again in favor of the idea that a "life principle" may operate in the Universe tending to produce increasingly complex organic systems from simple beginnings wherever conditions remotely allow it.

There was also, and continues to be, disagreement over how different extraterrestrial life is likely to be from the varieties found on Earth (→ **extraterrestrial life, variety of**). Again, the dispute centers on the relative importance attributed to factors of chance and "contingency," on the one hand, and necessity and determinism, on the other. How far up the ladder of life would significant differences begin to appear between the life-forms that have evolved on one world and those that have evolved elsewhere? The commonality in space of basic organic chemicals such as **amino acids** suggests that they and the larger units into which they polymerize, including **proteins,** may be general ingredients of life throughout the Universe. The phenomenon of **convergence** also argues in favor of cosmic similarities between life-forms. Set against this, however, is the vast morphological diversity of organisms on Earth and the major, unpredictable effects that random cosmic events such as asteroid impacts may have on the course of evolution (→ **cosmic collisions, biological effects of**). These factors suggest that, over all of space and time, life must be almost unimaginably diverse.

ExNPS
→ **Exploration of Neighboring Planetary Systems**

exobiology
A term introduced in 1960 by Joshua **Lederberg** "to distinguish this aspect of space biology—the evolution of life beyond our own planet." It is synonymous with **astrobiology** and bioastronomy.

exon
A section of **DNA** in a **eukaryotic** cell that is both translated (→ **translation**) and transcribed (→ **transcription**) into a **protein.** → **intron**

exoplanets
→ **extrasolar planets**

exosphere
(1) The outermost layer of a planetary atmosphere that merges with the interplanetary medium (→ **Earth, atmosphere of**). (2) The highly tenuous atmosphere that is the only atmosphere possessed by some planets (such as **Mercury**) and moons (such as the **Galilean satellites**).

Exploration of Neighboring Planetary Systems (ExNPS)
One of the key elements of NASA's **Origins Program.** It is intended to be a long-term program of scientific investigation and technological development with the goal of detecting and probing Earth-like planets around nearby stars. Responsibility for identifying a specific plan for ExNPS has been assigned to the **Jet Propulsion Laboratory.**

EXPORT
→ **Extra-solar Planet Observational Research Team**

extinction, biological
The failure of a taxonomic group to produce direct descendants, causing its global disappearance at a given point in time.

extinction, interstellar
The reduction in intensity of light as it passes through the **interstellar medium** due to absorption and scattering by **cosmic dust.** The effect is more pronounced for shorter (bluer) wavelengths, so that starlight seen over great distances, especially looking along the disk of the Galaxy, appears reddened.

Extrasolar Planetary Foundation

A nonprofit scientific organization, founded in 1998 to support "the detection and study of the planetary systems of other stars, especially those which may contain planets habitable by intelligent life." Among its founders and directors are George **Gatewood** (chairman) and Frank **Drake.**

Extra-solar Planet Observational Research Team (EXPORT)

A consortium of European astronomers employing the telescopes on La Palma and Tenerife to study **extrasolar planets** and the formation and evolution of **protoplanetary disks.** EXPORT's work is intended, in part, to serve as a ground-based precursor of the **European Space Agency**'s *Infrared Space Interferometer* (IRSI).

extrasolar planets

Worlds in orbit around stars other than the Sun. The great majority of extrasolar planets detected at the time of writing (**→ extrasolar planets, detection of**), with the exception of the **pulsar planets,** have small orbital radii

CONFIRMED EXTRASOLAR PLANETS

Host Star	Distance (light-years)	Mass (Jupiter = 1)	Orbital Radius* (AU)	Period (days)	Eccentricity
Gliese 876	15.38	2.1	0.21	60.9	0.27
Gliese 86	35	3.6	0.11	15.8	0.05
rho¹ Cancri A	41	0.84	0.11	14.6	0.05
upsilon Andromedae:	44				
b		0.71	0.059	4.62	0.03
c		2.11	0.83	241	0.18
d		4.61	2.5	1267	0.41
47 Ursae Majoris	46	2.39	2.1	1108	0.03
tau Bootis	49	3.87	0.046	3.31	0.02
51 Pegasi	50	0.47	0.05	4.23	0.02
HR 810	51	2.26	0.93	320	0.16
rho Coronae Borealis	55	1.13	0.25	39.7	0.03
14 Herculis	55	3.3	2.5	1619	0.35
70 Virginis	59	6.6	0.43	117	0.40
HD 192263	65	0.76	0.15	23.9	0.22
HD 195019	65	3.43	0.14	18.3	0.05
HD 210277	69	1.28	1.15	437	0.45
16 Cygni B	72	1.52	0.6–2.7	804	0.67
HD 134987	82	1.58	0.78	260	0.25
HD 114762	91	11	0.34	84.0	0.33
HD 75289	95	0.42	0.046	3.51	0.05
HD 10697	98	6.59	2.0	1083	0.12
HD 130322	98	1.08	0.088	10.7	0.05
HD 37124	108	1.04	0.585	155	0.19
HD 168443	108	8.13	0.303	58.1	0.52
HD 217107	121	1.28	0.074	7.11	0.14
HD 12661	121	2.83	0.79	265	0.33
HD 89744	130	7.2	0.88	256	0.70
HD 222582	137	5.4	1.35	576	0.71
HD 187123	153	0.52	0.042	3.1	0.03
HD 209458	153	0.63	0.045	3.52	0.02
HD 177830	186	1.28	1.00	391	0.43

* Values listed are of the **semimajor axis.**

and masses similar to or greater than that of Jupiter. This apparent bias arises simply because high-mass objects in compact orbits produce comparatively large effects on their **host stars** that put them within reach of the methods, and the sensitivity of those methods, that are currently available. At the same time, the existence of giant planets in sub-Mercurian orbits (→ **epistellar Jovians**) and in highly elongated orbits (→ **eccentric Jovians**) has come as a surprise and forced theorists to revise their understanding of how young planetary systems evolve (→ **planetary systems, formation of**). The challenge now is to develop more sensitive techniques capable of finding **Earth-class planets**, especially those in orbit within the **habitable zone**s of their host stars. These are potentially the most important worlds in the search for life, although, as in the case of **Europa** and **Callisto**, large moons of giant planets may also prove to be biologically interesting.

The discovery of (1) extrasolar planets around roughly one in twenty of the **target stars** searched (remembering that many lower-mass worlds around these stars almost certainly await detection), (2) a planetary system in the case of **upsilon Andromedae**, and (3) **circumstellar disk**s around stars of widely differing **spectral type**s, has led to heightened optimism that planetary systems are common throughout the Universe. However, some researchers have urged caution. In 1997, Guillermo Gonzalez of the University of Washington, Seattle, and his colleagues pointed out[229] that almost all of the stars around which planets have been detected to date are richer in **heavy element**s than is the Sun (→ **heavy element concentration, related to the occurrence of planets**). The relative scarcity of such stars might also imply strict limits on the numbers of planetary systems. Moreover, argued Gonzalez, the phenomenon of **inward orbital migration,** which might account for the presence of giant planets in orbits close to their host stars, would tend to scatter any terrestrial planets that had formed between the migrating planet and the star, resulting in a dearth of Earth-like worlds and, therefore, advanced life.[228] The next decade should see a clarification of such issues.

The table below lists the extrasolar planets confirmed as of March 2000, in order of dis-

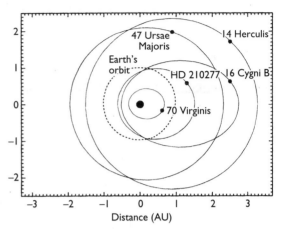

Comparison of the orbits of some extrasolar planets.

tance of their host stars from the Sun. See individual entries for further information on each object. A separate table is provided for pulsar planets.[61, 69, 108, 136, 224, 253, 373]

extrasolar planets, detection of

The distances to other stars and the faintness and low mass of planets in comparison to their host stars make the detection of extrasolar worlds difficult. Direct imaging may be possible in the near future through **nulling interferometry,** although it may already have been achieved by conventional means in the unusual case of **TMR-1C.** In addition, a variety of indirect detection techniques are available, some of which have already achieved positive results. A planet orbiting a distant star can make its presence known by causing small, regular variations in the line-of-sight velocity (→ **radial velocity method**) or position (→ **astrometry**) of its host star, by slightly dimming the light from its host star if it happens to pass in front of it (→ **photometry**), by contributing to a **gravitational lens** effect (→ **microlensing**), or, if the host star is a **pulsar,** by altering the period of the pulsar's cyclic pulses. Several dozen searches for extrasolar planets are in progress or under development using these various techniques (→ **extrasolar planets, searches for**).

extrasolar planets, searches for

Refer to individual entries for details.

Program	Method	Location
Absolute Astronomical Accelerometry	Radial velocity	Ground
Advanced Fiber-Optic Échelle Spectrometer (AFOE)	Radial velocity	Ground
Anglo-Australian Planet Search program	Radial velocity	Ground
Arizona Search for Planets (ASP)	Transit	Ground
Astronomical Nulling Interferometer (ANI)	Imaging	Ground
Atacama Large Millimeter Array (ALMA)	Imaging/astrometry	Ground
Big Occulting Steerable Satellite	Occultation	Space
Convection and Rotation of Stars (COROT)	Photometry	Space
Coralie/Leonard Euler Telescope	Radial velocity	Ground
Elodie	Radial velocity	Ground
ESO Coudé Echelle Spectrometer	Radial velocity	Ground
Extra-solar Planet Observational Research Team (EXPORT)	Spectroscopy/transit	Ground
Full-sky Astrometric Mapping Explorer (FAME)	Astrometry	Space
Global Astrometric Interferometer for Astrophysics (GAIA)	Astrometry	Space
High Accuracy Radial Velocity Planetary Search (HARPS)	Radial velocity	Ground
Hobby-Eberly Telescope (HET)	Radial velocity	Ground
Infrared Space Interferometer/Darwin	Imaging/spectroscopy	Space
Kepler Mission	Transit	Space
Large Binocular Telescope (LBT)	Imaging	Ground
McDonald Observatory	Radial velocity	Ground
Microlensing Observations in Astrophysics (MOA)	Microlensing	Ground
Microlensing Planet Search (MPS)	Microlensing	Ground
Mid-Infrared Large-well Imager (MIRLIN)	Imaging	Ground
Multichannel Astrometric Photometer (MAP)	Astrometry	Ground
Multichannel Astrometric Photometer and Spectrometer (MAPS)	Astrometry	Ground
Next Generation Space Telescope (NGST)	Imaging	Space
Palomar Testbed Interferometer	Astrometry	Ground
Planet Imager	Imaging	Space
Probing Lensing Anomalies Network (PLANET)	Microlensing	Ground
Pennsylvania State Pulsar Group	Pulsar timing	Ground
San Francisco State University Planet Search	Radial velocity	Ground
Single Telescope Extrasolar Planet Survey (STEPS)	Astrometry	Ground
Space Interferometry Mission (SIM)	Astrometry	Space
Stellar Astrophysics and Research on Exoplanets (STARE)	Transit	Ground
Terrestrial Planet Finder (TPF)	Imaging/astrometry	Space
Transits of Extrasolar Planets (TEP) networks	Transit	Ground
University of St. Andrews Planet Search (UstAPS)	Microlensing	Ground
Very Large Telescope	Astrometry/imaging	Ground
Vulcan Camera Project	Transit	Ground

extraterrestrial

(1) (adjective) Originating or existing beyond the Earth. (2) (noun) A life-form that originated outside our world.

extraterrestrial civilizations, ancient

Based purely on a consideration of the time scales involved, the possibility exists that our **Galaxy** is home to one or more extremely old

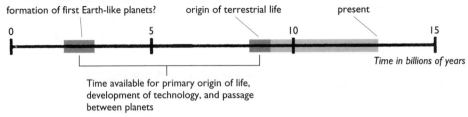

formation of first Earth-like planets? origin of terrestrial life   present

0   5   10   15

Time in billions of years

Time available for primary origin of life,
development of technology, and passage
between planets

A time line of cosmic evolution as envisaged by Crick and Orgel.

intelligent races. The age of the Galaxy, as estimated from the age of its oldest member stars contained within **globular clusters**, is thought to be about 12 to 15 billion years. However, at its inception, the Galaxy would have contained none of the **heavy elements**, including **carbon** and **oxygen,** needed to form the basis of life. Such elements are manufactured only inside stars, by **nucleosynthesis,** and are subsequently disseminated throughout galactic space by mass loss from **red giants** or when massive stars explode as **supernovas**. The first life-forms in the Galaxy, therefore, could have begun to emerge only following the demise of the first generation of stars and the subsequent reconstitution of heavy-element-enriched **interstellar clouds** into new stars and planetary systems. This would have been about 2 billion years after the Galaxy's formation. Assuming the passage of another 5 billion years, as in the case of the solar system, between the formation of a star and the emergence of an intelligent race on one of its planets, it is possible that advanced civilizations were present in the Galaxy 7 billion years after it was formed. If such civilizations did actually emerge, and if they have survived to the present day, then they must now be 5 to 8 billion years ahead of us in their development. Considering the rate at which our own technology is currently progressing, it is very difficult for us to project what such an ancient and advanced species might have achieved. It is possible that at some point it established a **galactic empire** and that it rose through the various stages of **Kardashev civilizations.** However, such developments, though extraordinary by present human standards, might take only millions rather than billions of years. A civilization so ancient might well have evolved by now beyond even the most ambi-

tious **astroengineering** schemes that we can imagine. Moreover, its most significant accomplishments might not necessarily have been technological at all (➔ **extraterrestrial intelligence, more advanced than we**). ➔ **directed panspermia**

extraterrestrial civilizations, hazards to
Whatever species exist on other worlds, they must inevitably, as terrestrial life-forms do, face a variety of threats to their existence. These threats may come in the form of competition with or predation by other species, gradual adverse changes in the environment (for example, due to the onset of an ice age), or a sudden cataclysm, such as the impact of an asteroid or comet, a massive stellar flare, or the eruption of a nearby **gamma-ray burster,** that is capable of causing a **mass extinction** or even a complete planetary sterilization (➔ **cosmic catastrophes, biological effects of**). In addition to these natural dangers, many more of a self-inflicted nature may confront an intelligent race (and its fellow species) once it has achieved a substantial level of technology. Among these are the very hazards that humanity presently faces:

1. Large-scale nuclear or biological war
2. Global epidemics of lethal disease resulting from
   a. the emergence of antibiotic-resistant **pathogens**
   b. **back contamination**
3. Environmental disasters stemming from a combination of industrial pollution, overpopulation, and destruction of natural habitat, including
   a. global warming due to a gradual elevation in the level of **greenhouse gases**
   b. disintegration of the **ozone** layer

4. Unforeseen side effects of new technologies, such as genetic engineering

As Iosif **Shklovskii** and Carl **Sagan**[540] have pointed out:

> We can imagine two extreme alternatives...: (a) a technical civilization destroys itself soon after reaching the [interstellar] communicative phase (...less than 10^2 years); or (b) a technical civilization learns to live with itself soon after the communicative phase. If it survives more than 10^2 years, it will be unlikely to destroy itself afterwards. In the latter case, its lifetime may be measured on a stellar evolutionary timescale (...much greater than 10^8 years).

Since we cannot even predict the near-term fate of our own species, we are in no position to say whether advanced civilizations tend to survive for long periods or whether they self-destruct soon after acquiring the means to communicate over interstellar distances. Furthermore, even if technological races, on the whole, manage to overcome the problems they create, it is not clear how often natural disasters tend to purge a world of its life and intelligence. There are some indications, for example, that the Sun is an unusually placid star and also that in the past gamma-ray bursters were much more common and may have periodically sterilized galaxies of their life before intelligent beings could develop the means of interstellar communication and travel.

extraterrestrial civilizations, lifetime of

One of the reasons put forward to explain the fact that we have yet to find evidence of other intelligent races in space (➔ **Fermi Paradox**) is that technological civilizations have a relatively short lifetime. For one reason or another, it is hypothesized, they are destroyed, possibly through ecological catastrophe or nuclear war (➔ **extraterrestrial civilizations, hazards to**). The problems currently besetting humankind in this regard may, the supposition goes, always occur and always prove insuperable. At the other extreme of speculation is the suggestion that a majority of extraterrestrial civilizations survive and continue to evolve indefinitely. If this is the case, we might expect that there are intelligent races in the Galaxy that are both much older (➔ **extraterrestrial civilizations, ancient**) and further ahead of us (➔ **extraterrestrial intelligence, more advanced than we**).

extraterrestrial civilizations, types of
➔ **Kardashev civilizations**

extraterrestrial hypothesis (ETH)

The belief that at least some **unidentified flying objects** are extraterrestrial spacecraft. It was first expressed following the 1896–97 wave of "mystery airships," which itself followed quickly on the heels of Percival **Lowell**'s claims about an advanced civilization on Mars. Although secret experimental aircraft controlled by individuals or governments was the most popular explanation, the idea that the "airships" came from beyond the Earth was not without its supporters. The extraterrestrial hypothesis became more popular and sustained, however, following the UFO wave that began with Kenneth **Arnold**'s sighting of "**flying saucer**s" in 1947. In both cases, the extraterrestrial explanation was not immediately sought by the public but was encouraged by speculation in the media.

extraterrestrial intelligence, character of

Science fiction has envisaged the possibility of everything from kind, wise, and even cute extraterrestrials, such as *E.T.*, to utterly malicious, scheming monsters, like H. R. Giger's *Alien*. On balance, ever since H. G. **Wells** unleashed his marauding Martians (➔ *The War of the Worlds*, **novel**), the fictional creatures from "out there" have tended to be of the usurping, death-ray variety—not surprisingly, since this makes for a more compelling plot. But if we do encounter other intelligences among the stars, will they in reality prove to be friendly or hostile?

A poll conducted for the **Planetary Society** by the Marist Institute in 1998 suggested that 86 percent of Americans who think there is life on other planets believe it will be friendly (➔ **opinion polls, about extraterrestrials**). Similar optimism has been expressed by many scientists who have figured prominently in the search for extraterrestrial life, including Frank **Drake,** Philip **Morrison,** Carl **Sagan,** and Ronald **Bracewell.** An argument in favor of alien beneficence is that any race that has managed to survive the kind of global crises currently facing humanity (and that presumably confront all technological species at some stage in their development) is likely to have resolved the sources of conflict we still have on Earth (➔ **extraterrestrial civilizations, hazards to**). Morrison, for instance, doubted that advanced societies "crush out any competitive form of intelligence, especially when there is clearly no danger." Similarly, Arthur C. **Clarke** has stated that

> As our own species is in the process of proving, one cannot have superior science and inferior morals. The combination is unstable and self-destroying.

However, there can be no assurance on this point. After all, human beings appear to have made very little progress, over the past two millennia or so, toward eliminating or controlling their aggressive tendencies. And there is no reason to suppose that we shall change much in this respect over the next few centuries, during which time we may well develop the means of reaching the stars in a realistic timescale. Those who are pessimistic about the general nature of extraterrestrials argue that Darwinism and its fundamental tenet, "survival of the fittest," virtually guarantee that any advanced species will be potentially dangerous. Michael Archer, professor of biology at the University of New South Wales, Australia, has put it this way:[21]

> Any creature we contact will also have had to claw its way up the evolutionary ladder and will be every bit as nasty as we are. It will likely be an extremely adaptable, extremely aggressive super-predator.

In a similar vein, medical anthropologist Melvin Korner has written that

> Evolution predicts the existence of selfishness, arrogance and violence on other planets even more surely than it predicts intelligence. If they could get to Earth, extraterrestrials would do to

us what we have done to lesser animals for centuries.

In 1964, Freeman **Dyson** considered the two polar extremes to which intelligence might evolve:[170]

> Intelligence may indeed be a benign influence, creating isolated groups of philosopher-kings far apart in the heavens and enabling them to share at leisure their accumulated wisdom.... [On the other hand,] intelligence may be a cancer of purposeless technological exploitation, sweeping across a galaxy as irresistibly as it has swept across our own planet...the technological cancer could spread over a whole galaxy in a few million years, a time very short compared with the life of a planet.... Our business as scientists is to search the universe and find out what is there. What is there may conform to our moral sense or it may not.... It is just as unscientific to impute to remote intelligences wisdom and serenity as it is to impute to them irrational and murderous impulses. We must be prepared for either possibility and conduct our searches accordingly.

Perhaps the most reasonable assumption in the absence of any data is that, just as in our own case, the potential for good and evil will exist in every intelligent extraterrestrial race. Civilization is unthinkable without some measure of compassion, yet how could a species that had emerged successfully after several billion years of live-and-let-die biological competition not also possess a ruthless streak? The question is surely not whether any advanced race we may meet among the stars is capable of aggression—it certainly will be unless it has genetically or otherwise altered itself to be purely pacific—but whether it has learned to override its more basic instincts. A further point to bear in mind is the variation in character that can exist between individuals *within* a species. Will the first representative of an alien race that we encounter be a Gandhi or a Hitler? Fears about what consequences might follow from making contact with a superior species, malevolent or benign, have led to calls from some leading scientists to avoid attempts at **CETI** (➔ **CETI, opposition to**).[33]

extraterrestrial intelligence, forms of

In speculating about the guises that intelligence may assume elsewhere, it is worth remembering the diversity of intelligence that exists even on Earth, both within and between species. This broad terrestrial spectrum strongly suggests that among organisms that have evolved on other worlds and adapted to different environments and perhaps with a different biochemical basis, there may be an even richer variety of intelligent forms, just as extraterrestrial life in general is likely to prove surprising and novel to us (➔ **extraterrestrial life, variety of**). However, some aspects of intelligence may not be so different from one planet to another. All creatures are subject to the same physical rules and, as Carl **Sagan** points out in *The Dragons of Eden:*[494]

> Natural selection has served as a kind of intellectual sieve, producing brains and intelligences increasingly competent to deal with the laws of nature.... [T]he same evolutionary winnowing must have occurred on other worlds that have evolved intelligent beings.... I think we will find that much of their biology, psychology, sociology and politics will seem to us stunningly exotic and deeply mysterious. But I suspect we will have little difficulty in understanding each other on the simpler aspects of astronomy, physics, chemistry and perhaps mathematics.

That a common appreciation of physical science and mathematics (➔ **mathematics, as a universal language**) will exist among intelligent races is a fundamental assumption of those engaged in **SETI**. Yet we already known of species that appear highly intelligent and have an intuitive understanding of complex physics (➔ **dolphins, as a form of alien intelligence**) but that are completely nontechnological. Furthermore, it may well be the case that outside a certain technological "window," intelligent species are incapable of or not interested in establishing contact (➔ **Drake Equation; extraterrestrial intelligence, more advanced than we**).

The biological evolution of intelligence is slow, although as in the 5-million-year development of modern humans from an ape ancestor, it may undergo comparatively rapid spurts. By contrast, it is likely that technology can dramatically enhance intelligence over almost insignificant timescales. The human race now appears to be on the brink of this development with the first practical applications of brain-computer links. Once such connections are perfected and become freely available, it is difficult to predict what levels of intelligence a man-machine symbiosis might achieve.

The idea that sentient machines might be the ultimate product of life's evolution has long existed in fiction. The Greek god Hephaistos is described in the *Iliad* as having artificial women of gold to help him around the house. A bronze giant, Talos, was supposed to guard the shores around Crete. And in his witty satire *Erewhon* (1872), Samuel Butler suggested that machines are evolving faster than people because people tend and develop them. More recently, following the dawn of electronic computers, writers such as Arthur C. **Clarke** and Isaac **Asimov** have explored futures in which machines, both benign and malignant, partly take over human affairs. In view of the rapid progress made in computer technology and robotics over the past couple of decades, it no longer seems far-fetched that artificial intelligence may one day far exceed that of humans. Developments such as the Internet and prototype brain-computer links suggest that some form of part-human, part-machine life-form might emerge in the not-so-distant future. Fictional explorations of such possibilities are commonplace—for example, Mr. Data and the Borg in *Star Trek*. As time goes on, and we see the pace of our own technological development far outstripping that of biological evolution, the conclusion becomes compelling that if advanced extraterrestrial intelligence exists, at least some of it may be partly artificial.[77]

extraterrestrial intelligence, implications following first contact

Fictional portrayals of the first direct contact between an extraterrestrial civilization and our own have conditioned us to expect one of two extreme situations: the aliens will be either ruthlessly aggressive (biological selection having made them, like our own species, into the ultimate survivors) or utterly benign, peaceful, and wise (sociological selection having led them to renounce war as a prerequisite of self-preservation). Compare, for example, the disturbing *Alien* series of movies with *E.T. The Extra-Terrestrial* or *Close Encounters of the Third Kind*. A similar bifurcation of opinion is evident among scientists who have considered the possible consequences of contact. Ben R. Finney, professor of anthropology at the University of Hawaii, has examined various proposed scenarios and divides them into two main categories: "paranoid" and "pronoid." Those of the paranoid persuasion tend to argue against attempts at **CETI** (→ **CETI, opposition to**). Inescapably, however, our viewpoints are anthropocentric and our speculations about the possible temperament of other intelligent species based on projections of the duality in our own nature—the good and the evil that are inherent, inseparable components of the human psyche (→ **extraterrestrial intelligence, character of**).

One thing seems certain. If there are other spacefaring, star-to-star-communicating races in the Galaxy, we must be technologically primitive in comparison with the great majority of them (→ **extraterrestrial intelligence, more advanced than we**). A major concern, then, is what might follow from first contact with creatures who, whatever their nature, possess knowledge and power far in excess of our own. Examples from human history seem to offer a cautionary note: exploration has gone hand in hand with exploitation, colonization with conflict and subjugation. In almost every case, the more technologically advanced interloper has eventually imposed its ways and assimilated or emasculated the weaker party, intentionally or otherwise. Even if this were not to happen, it is uncertain how the human race would react to the discovery that it was, in cosmic terms, so backward. An optimist might argue that we would relish the prospect of rapid growth and would quickly learn from our older, wiser mentors, as children do from adults. A pessimist might insist that we would be crushed to learn that, despite all our efforts, others had vastly surpassed us. Concerns such as these were raised in a study carried out for NASA by the Brookings Institution at the dawn of the space era (→ **NASA-Brookings Study**)

and have also been expressed by several prominent scientists, including Nobel laureates Martin **Ryle** and George **Wald.** Others, such as Carl **Sagan,** William Newman, and Arthur C. **Clarke** have defended the view that mature civilizations in the Galaxy would recognize the risks of first contact to younger races and would avoid revealing too much about themselves or their knowledge until the time was right.[60, 70, 105, 153, 257]

extraterrestrial intelligence, likelihood of

Frank **Drake,** one of the early pioneers of **SETI,** devised a formula—the so-called **Drake Equation**—to help assess the number of other races in the Galaxy that might be attempting to communicate with other stars at any given time. This formula, however, can produce either a very high number or a number close to zero, depending on the initial assumptions made.[590, 633]

extraterrestrial intelligence, more advanced than we

If other intelligent races exist in space, the chances are high that some of them will prove to be much more scientifically and technologically advanced than we are. The astonishingly rapid progress made, for instance, in the development of computers over the past few decades shows what dramatic strides can be achieved by a technologically ambitious race in a relatively short period of time. Given another century or so, humankind may have acquired capabilities in genetic engineering, nanotechnology, life prolongation, **artificial intelligence,** space propulsion, and other fields that at present we can barely imagine. As Arthur C. **Clarke** once wrote, "Any sufficiently advanced technology is indistinguishable from magic."

What would an alien race that was a thousand, or a million, years ahead of us be like? Would it have evolved so far in ways we cannot yet conceive that we would be as unaware of its presence and activities as ants are of human beings? One of the arguments sometimes put forward against the existence of advanced extraterrestrials is that if they were present we would have picked up signals from them by now. However, beings that are significantly ahead of us might lie beyond our communications horizon; that is, we may simply not have the means to tap into their conversations. A communications horizon of only 1,000 years might render us oblivious to 99.9 percent of the intelligent technological races in the Galaxy (→ **Drake Equation**). Another argument is that advanced intelligence would leave clear visible signs of its existence, for example, large-scale engineering projects in the Galaxy (→ **astroengineering**) that would be the equivalent of bridges, highways, and skyscrapers on Earth or, alternatively, a profusion of self-replicating spacecraft (→ **von Neumann probes**). But this, again, assumes too much and is based on a parochial extrapolation from our own present-day capabilities. For all we know, very advanced stellar and galactic engineering projects have the appearance of natural celestial objects, so that we may be looking straight at them without realizing their true nature. Or perhaps, more likely, the devices of highly evolved species are not dramatic and obvious but are subtle and discreet so that they are simply undetectable from afar. It may be, for example, that instead of great starships, the most advanced races employ elevator-sized cubicles to "beam" themselves instantaneously to any point in the cosmos. Science fiction writers once envisioned future computers the size of planets. But in fact, computers have shrunk in size and may soon be so small and adaptable that they will blend unnoticed into our environment.

Nor can we be sure of the general direction that other intelligent species might take in their development. We tend to measure progress and advancement on a scientific and technological scale—by the sophistication of our inventions and our knowledge of the physical universe. Yet there are and have been societies on Earth that have not given such high priority to the pursuit of rational understanding or the development of technology. In cultures that place more value on intuition, the direct experience of nature, spiritual fulfillment, and transcendental modes of awareness, a remarkably different view of the world seems to prevail. It may be that we shall encounter in the future alien races whose technological ac-

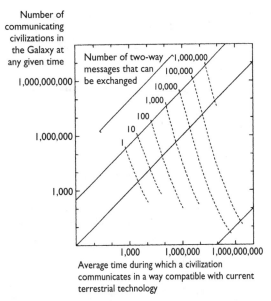

The relationship between the average lifetime of a communicating civilization and the number of civilizations in our galaxy.
Tobias Owen

complishments are relatively modest but who have explored to depths beyond our comprehension the nature and potentialities of consciousness. It is difficult to come to terms with the possibility that despite all our achievements we may still, comparatively speaking, be close to the bottom of the ladder of development.

There is also a difficulty for Western religions with the concept of aliens who may be more spiritually advanced than ourselves. This problem stems from a common assumption, made by many theologians, that God works through a historical process. As E. W. **Barnes** put it, "If God only realizes Himself within an evolutionary process, then elsewhere He has reached a splendor and fullness of existence to which Earth's evolutionary advance can add nothing."

The notion of a kind of cosmic spiritual ladder, on which we may be close to the bottom rung, provokes speculation about where our race, and others in the universe, may eventually be heading. This question has been addressed in science fiction by Olaf **Stapledon** in

Star Maker,[563] Arthur C. **Clarke** in *Childhood's End,*[109] Isaac **Asimov** in *The Gods Themselves,*[28] and others. Both Stapledon and Clarke, for example, envisage a future union of individual sentient minds into a single "Overmind" (to use Clarke's term). A similar prediction of the emergence of a single cosmic superbeing (essentially a conscious universe) stems from extreme speculation based on the **anthropic principle.**

extraterrestrial intelligence, procedures following first contact

The extraordinary importance of the discovery of signals from another civilization in space has led scientists, engineers, lawyers, politicians, and others around the world to debate what course of action should be taken in the event of an unequivocal detection. Campaigning in the late 1960s by Rudolph Pešek of the Czech Academy of Sciences led the International Academy of Astronautics to set up a **SETI** Committee with Pešek as its first chairman. This met for the first time at the Academy's Vienna Congress in 1971 and has held two sessions at every annual congress since. Over time, the practice emerged of devoting one of the sessions to the science and technology of SETI and the other to the international, societal, political, legal, and media aspects of the search for, and the consequences of discovery of, intelligent extraterrestrial life. Two issues, in particular, have demanded special attention: (1) the protocols to be followed by researchers following a confirmed detection and (2) how and if to respond to the signaling civilization. A subcommittee was established to address these. In 1989, it produced a document called "**Declaration of Principles (Concerning Activities Following the Detection of Extraterrestrial Intelligence**)," which was subsequently endorsed by a number of international astronomical organizations, including the **International Astronomical Union.** More recently, in another document titled "A Decision Process for Examining the Possibility of Sending Communications to Extraterrestrial Civilizations," the subcommittee has put forward recommendations on the issue of response that have been similarly endorsed.

extraterrestrial life, detection of

Astrobiologists are now on the threshold of the search for life on many other worlds, both within the solar system and beyond. One of their immediate objectives is, therefore, to identify the means by which extraterrestrial life can be detected and recognized. Where life exists or has existed beyond the Earth, its presence may be disclosed in a variety of ways. Most obviously, if it is large, it may be identified visually at close range by the cameras of a spacecraft. However, with the possible exception of macroscopic marine life in the putative subsurface oceans on Jupiter's large moons, this is an unlikely scenario for the foreseeable future. Instead, astrobiologists must rely upon more subtle methods that involve looking for key "signatures," or **biomarkers,** of life. These may consist of chemical traces or microscopic fossils in extraterrestrial rocks or other samples that have been brought to Earth or, alternatively, collected for examination *in situ,* as in the case of the *Viking* landers. The difficulty researchers face in establishing whether certain substances or structures are biogenic or not, even when samples are available for detailed laboratory analysis on Earth, has been amply demonstrated by the recent and ongoing **Martian "fossils" controversy.** Many chemicals, including **amino acids** and **polycyclic aromatic hydrocarbons,** can be produced easily both inorganically and as a result of metabolic processes in living things, so that other clues must be sought to establish their exact provenance. In the case of amino acids, a biogenic origin would be indicated by a heavy bias toward either the left-handed or right-handed forms of the molecules (although the possibility of terrestrial contamination would, as always, need to be ruled out). The presence of **sulfides** may also point to life, but in this case it would be important to use other evidence to estimate the temperature at which the sulfides had formed. In a hot environment, sulfides form readily enough by simple inorganic reactions, but at low temperatures the only known way in which they can come about is through **enzyme**-assisted metabolic activity. One of the current goals of astrobiologists is to compile a catalog of such possible signatures of life, much of the data for which will have to come from studying life in its varied forms on Earth and the evolution of biochemical pathways that yield preservable records.[458]

As space probes over the coming decade return ever-increasing amounts of data and samples pertinent to the search for life in the solar system, a new generation of telescopes will focus on the dim light reaching us from planets circling around other stars. Advanced spaceborne **optical interferometer**s, such as the *Terrestrial Planet Finder, Darwin,* and the *Planet Imager,* will be capable not only of detecting extrasolar worlds and imaging their disks but of analyzing the spectra of light reflected from their atmospheres and surfaces. On Earth, life has produced easily detectable atmospheric and surface changes, including high concentrations of molecular **oxygen** and **ozone** in the atmosphere and a distinctive spectral feature due to **chlorophyll** on the ground. The signatures of these substances in the spectra of **extrasolar planets** would represent powerful, and almost incontrovertible, evidence for at least advanced plant life on a global scale. Yet 1 billion years ago, the Earth itself might have appeared sterile to any remote alien observers who used only these criteria in their search for life. Recognizing the likelihood that much of the life in the Universe will be at the lower end of the evolutionary scale, astrobiologists must strive to understand better the atmospheric and surface spectral signatures of the Earth as they were between about 1 and 4 billion years ago, when microbes were the loftiest organisms on this planet. At the other extreme, it may be that if we knew where and how to look, we would find startling proof of very advanced life, including civilizations far ahead of us in their technological accomplishments (➔ **extraterrestrial civilizations, more advanced than we**). Some attempts have already been made to pick up messages from such beings (➔ **SETI**) or to detect other signs of their presence (➔ **Dyson sphere; Bracewell probe; Kardashev civilizations**).

extraterrestrial life, likelihood of

Two arguments that appeal purely to statistics and arrive at opposite conclusions are often brought to bear on this issue. According to the first, life on Earth has come about through such a long and unlikely sequence of events that there is virtually no chance of it having been repeated elsewhere. The opposing statistical claim is that stars are so incredibly numerous (around 400 billion in our galaxy alone), and planets possibly even more so, that life elsewhere must be commonplace. In fact, although superficially appealing, both these claims are weak. The first is based on the misconception that Darwinian evolution is akin to rolling a die many times and fortuitously achieving one predesignated outcome. The second, in its failure to consider the many factors that might influence the development and survival of life, is too naive to carry much weight. It is characteristic of problems concerning which there is a lack of observational or experimental data that solutions can be proposed that are completely contradictory. This is true, for example, of all major problems in philosophy and religion. The fact that *no* claim concerning the nature or likelihood of extraterrestrial life can yet be refuted indicates that astrobiology is still an embryonic science that is in the process of making the transition from a branch of philosophy to an empirical endeavor. No one yet knows if extraterrestrial life exists. Developments and discoveries within the past few years have shifted the consensus of scientific opinion to the view that life, at least in its simplest forms, may be quite common. However, there will be no certainty on that point until the first traces of organisms on other worlds are found. ➔ **evolutionary theory and extraterrestrial life**

extraterrestrial life, variety of

Two schools of thought exist on the question of what life (assuming there is any) on other worlds will be like. These fall under the headings of "divergionism" and "convergionism," or, to use Harold **Blum**'s terminology, "opportunism" and "determinism." In reality, the truth may well lie somewhere between these extremes. Divergionism stresses the unpredictable and nonrepeatable aspects of evolution that generate novelty and therefore might tend to lead to a spectacularly wide range of organisms across the Universe. Convergionism, on the other hand, argues that while life will inevitably exhibit some differences from one world to another, natural selection will tend to come up with the same optimum designs, reflected in similar biological structures and processes, wherever living things develop. Both these points of view can cite evidence based on observations of life-forms on our own planet.

In favor of divergionism is the astonishing biodiversity found on Earth. Bearing in mind the remarkable differences between, say, hummingbirds and oak trees or whales and bacteria, all of which have a common heritage, it is difficult to set limits on what richness of form might occur among extraterrestrial species.[155] Even a replay of terrestrial evolution would almost certainly lead to substantially different end products, a claim first put forcibly by Alfred Russel **Wallace** and echoed many times since. Conceivably, for instance, an evolutionary rerun would fail to give rise to the land vertebrates at all. Even if it did, the probability of a repeat at the same pivotal point in Earth's history of the cataclysm that ended the dinosaur dynasty and, as a consequence, allowed higher forms of mammalian life, including ourselves, to fill the vacated niches, would be low indeed. This incident alone is enough to suggest that random cosmic events, especially asteroidal or cometary collisions, can have profound and totally unpredictable effects on the course of a planet's biological development.

Given the serendipitous nature of **mutation**s and major external influences, divergionists would argue that even if life is constrained to having essentially just one biochemical basis, evolution, in its blind exploration of all biological options, will generate across the vastness of space and time every conceivable, viable type of organism. Still greater diversity could be anticipated if life can arise from a variety of different molecular building blocks. An important factor in this is where the first few chemical steps leading to life tend to take place. If **prebiotic** synthesis happens almost exclusively on the surface of suitable worlds, it is more likely that wide home-grown variations in biochemical development will occur than if the organic starter kit arrives from the communal resources of

space. That at least some prebiotic chemicals are seeded on infant worlds by asteroid and comet impacts now seems very likely, suggesting that certain fundamental subunits of life such as **amino acid**s, which have been found in **interstellar cloud**s, may be common biological currency. Yet at what stage up the ladder of prebiotic synthesis major variations between worlds become apparent is not clear. Some biologists believe that wherever life occurs it will use at least some of the same molecules, such as **sugars,** and therefore will have some similar biosynthetic pathways, such as the citric acid cycle used to burn sugar and yield energy. Certainly, on an extrasolar planet, the chance of anything like the same **gene** combinations that underpin contemporary terrestrial life emerging must be vanishingly small. But whether genes themselves, **DNA,** and **proteins** lie routinely at the heart of life throughout the Galaxy has yet to be established. The greater the possible biochemical diversity of organisms, the more scope for divergionism to envisage novel forms of cosmic life, including perhaps creatures so different from anything we know that we might not recognize them as being alive. Our very definition of life might need to be reexamined (➜ **life, nature of**).

Convergionism, on the other hand, while acknowledging that chance and circumstances play a part in shaping how life evolves, places greater emphasis on the fact that natural selection is subject to universal laws. Therefore the same motifs will tend to recur in subtly different guises as evolution keeps discovering the same best solutions to survival in different environments on different worlds. At the level of gross anatomy, for example, it would be surprising if certain features, such as legs, wings, fins, eyes, and ears, or their near equivalents, did not evolve independently in many different locations in space. The phenomenon of **convergent evolution** on Earth suggests that this is true. On the other hand, there is the danger of **anthropomorphism,** and we need to consider carefully the bold attempts by both scientists and science fiction writers, over the past century, to explore the outer limits of what life elsewhere might be like. H. G. **Wells** offered an early vision of something disturbingly alien with his Martians and **selenite**s, while his

Victorian contemporary Arthur Conan **Doyle** raised the prospect of a single planetwide organism in *The Day the Earth Screamed*—a concept given some scientific credibility by the **Gaia Hypothesis.** Wildly unanthropomorphic aliens go back at least as far as the Lensmen novels of E. E. "Doc" Smith in the 1930s and Olaf **Stapledon**'s *Star Maker* of 1934, even earlier if one includes the now-neglected late-nineteenth-century writings of J. H. **Rosny.** Biologists have mused on whether life could have an entirely different chemical basis: **silicon,** perhaps, instead of **carbon** (➔ **silicon-based life**) or **ammonia** in place of water (➔ **ammonia-based life**). Some scientists have speculated further. Fred **Hoyle** described an intelligent nebula in *The Black Cloud,* while Frank **Drake,** an early pioneer of SETI, wondered if life might evolve on a **neutron star** (➔ **neutron star, life on**), an idea taken further and cast into fictional form by the aerospace engineer Robert **Forward.**[13, 455] ➔ **intelligence, nature of; extraterrestrial intelligence, more advanced than we**

extremophiles

Organisms that thrive in what, for most terrestrial life-forms, are intolerably hostile environments.[244] The majority of known extremophiles are varieties of **archaea** and **bacteria.** They are classified, according to the conditions in which they exist, as **thermophiles, hyperthermophiles, psychrophiles, halophiles, acidophiles, alkaliphiles, barophiles,** and **endoliths.** These categories are not mutually exclusive, so that, for example, some endoliths are also thermophiles.

The discovery of extremophiles points out the extraordinary adaptability of primitive life-forms and further raises the prospect of finding at least microbial life elsewhere in the solar system and beyond.[525] There is also growing support for the idea that extremophiles were among the earliest living things on Earth (➔ **life, origin of**).

Chemoautotrophs, which obtain their energy from the **oxidation** of **inorganic** chemicals, might be particularly suited to alien environments. *Thiobacillus,* for example, makes a living by **oxidizing sulfur** to sulfuric acid, while other types oxidize hydrogen to water or nitrites to nitrates. *Ferrobacillus* is especially interesting because the energy won from oxidizing ferrous iron to ferric is very small, so that this organism must have evolved some ingenious way of boosting its low-grade energy input to the high levels needed to make essential chemicals such as **adenosine triphosphate.**

Certain species can tolerate wide extremes of acidity and alkalinity. *Thiobacillus* will grow in solutions containing 3 percent sulfuric acid, while other types of bacteria have been found in the saturated brine of the Great Salt Lake in Utah and in an icy pool in Antarctica containing 33 percent calcium chloride.

Some bacteria have survived enormous pressures up to 10 t per square centimeter, while low pressures appear to pose no threat to them at all, providing that liquid water is present. However, although bacteria have been found growing in the radioactive cooling ponds where fuel cans from nuclear reactors are stored, they are not tolerant of highly **ionizing radiation.** For this reason alone, the notion of **panspermia** is not easy to uphold.

extrinsic variable

A **variable star,** the light fluctuations of which are not due to changes in the star itself but to an external effect as in an **eclipsing binary.**

F star

A white or yellowish-white star of **spectral type** F whose spectrum shows strong **absorption lines** of **ionized** calcium that are more prominent than the hydrogen lines. Moderately strong lines due to iron and other heavier elements are also in evidence. **Main sequence** F stars, of which **Procyon** is an example, have a surface temperature of 5,800 to 6,900°C, a mass of 1.2 to 1.6 M_S, and a luminosity of two to six L_S. Relatively nearby, **late-type** members of this category are generally included in the list of **target stars** for **extrasolar planet** searches and targeted **SETI** programs. F-type **supergiant**s, of which Polaris (the Pole Star) is an example, have a mass up to 12 M_S and a luminosity up to 32,000 L_S.

"face," on Mars

The dream of finding traces of an advanced civilization on **Mars** has been a long time a-dying and is far from dead in the minds of some romantics, even today. Among the many photographs taken in 1976 by the *Viking* orbiters are two of a region known as Cydonia, at latitude 40° north, that include a feature reminiscent of a human face, roughly 2.5 km (1.6 miles) long, 2 km (1.2 miles) wide and up to 940 m (2,600 ft. high). Science fiction writers have long employed the theme of artifacts being placed at strategic sites in the solar system by an alien race in order that someday, when our species had the technological know-how, it would uncover these relics and perhaps go on to make contact with their creators (→ **sentinel hypothesis**). The film and novel *2001: A Space Odyssey*,[111] with its enigmatic black monoliths, put this idea firmly on the map of possible future scenarios. And for some believers it seemed that with the discovery of the "face" on Mars, that speculation had become fact—a quarter century ahead of schedule.

The "face" was first noticed in July 1976 by NASA personnel and promptly dismissed as a "trick of light and shadow" when shown to journalists at a press conference at the Jet Propulsion Laboratory in Pasadena, California. Three years later, computer engineers Vincent DiPietro and Gregory Molenaar, under contract at NASA's Goddard Space Flight Center, took a fresh interest in Viking frame 35A72, which had been filed away under the label "Head," and a second frame, 70A13, on which DiPietro found another image of the "face," under different lighting conditions, taken 35 days after the first. Also on frame 70A13, the attention of the two researchers was drawn to what appeared to be a five-sided pyramid, about 800 m high and 3 km long, located 16 km from the "face." The images on both frames were processed by DiPietro and Molenaar using a new software technique they had devised. Their conclusion: the "face" and the "pyramid" were hard to reconcile with any naturally formed objects.

In mainstream scientific circles, DiPietro and Molenaar's published findings were largely ignored. However, former NASA consultant Richard Hoagland, who played a part in designing the interstellar plaque mounted on *Pioneer 10* (but whose unorthodox views had increasingly distanced him from most planetary scientists), was intrigued. To the southwest of the "face" he pointed out "a remarkably rectilinear arrangement of massive structures interspersed with several smaller pyramids" that, provocatively, he named "the City." In his book *The Monuments of Mars*, he builds a thesis as imaginative, as ingenious, and ultimately as insubstantial as that of Percival **Lowell** a century earlier.

In 1988, Mark Carlotto, another computer specialist, processed the *Viking* images using a method called "shape from shadowing." From an analysis of the shadows cast by the "face" in the two *Viking* pictures he came up with a 3-D reconstruction of its profile. He then processed this to find out how the "face" would appear from different directions and with the sunlight falling on it from various angles. There are many examples of rock formations on Earth that look like human heads, but only from certain directions. In the case of the Martian "face," Carlotto concluded that it continues to look like a face from whichever direction it is viewed. Moreover, he claimed that "[the image enhancement] indicates that a second eye socket may be present on the right, shadowed side of the Face; fine structure in the mouth suggests that teeth are apparent."[99]

A number of best-selling pseudoscientific books and many articles have been written that make much of the significance of the "face." Even the loss of the *Mars Observer* spacecraft in August 1993 was attributed by some believers to a cover-up to hide the discovery of Martian life! Unfortunately, the arrival of the *Mars Global Surveyor* (MGS) probe brought unwelcome news for those seeking confirmation of an alien edifice. Commenting on a high-resolution picture of the "face" taken by MGS in April 1998, Ron Baalke of JPL said, "It's just an ordinary-looking hill. With no shadows there are no facial features at all." Not surprisingly, fans of the "face" have repudiated the findings and published their own processed versions of the MGS images. In doing so, they have continued a tradition—a quest for a mythical Mars. It took a single-minded researcher and articulate communicator, Percival Lowell, to give the theory of canals credibility in the public mind. His nearest equivalent today is the small band of amateur investigators who still hope to discern, at the limits of resolution and beyond, hints of intelligent design.

false alarms, in SETI
→ SETI, false alarms in

false memory syndrome
The recollection of seemingly real events, often under therapy, that never in fact happened. In the 1980s, following an explosion in reported cases of **alien abduction** and childhood abuse, most notably in the United States, psychologists began to investigate possible neurological sources of the many claims. A consensus has since emerged that human memory is surprisingly prone to confusing whether an event actually occurred or the individual merely heard about it. In particular, psychologists have found that it is easy under laboratory conditions to induce people to remember events that never actually took place. In one study, Stephen Ceci of Cornell University and his colleagues asked young children whether each of five events had ever happened to them. Four of the events were real, while the fifth was fictitious: getting a finger caught in a mousetrap and having to go to a hospital. Almost all the children correctly remembered the true events, but more than a third also gradually became convinced that the mousetrap incident was also real. By the final week, some children "remembered" elaborate details and continued to insist they were true even after their parents and researchers told them otherwise. Taken together, such laboratory studies strongly suggest that false memories, including many reported recollections of alien

abduction, can inadvertently be planted by therapists.

FAME
→ **Full-sky Astrometric Mapping Explorer**

faster-than-light particle
→ **tachyon**

fatty acids
Organic acids consisting of long **hydrocarbon** chains that terminate in a **carboxyl group** (–COOH). Many fatty acids occur in living things as components of **lipids.**

Faye, Hervé-Auguste-Étienne-Albans (1814–1902)
Leading French astronomer and professor at the École Polytechnique who, at a time when **pluralism** was popular among the intelligentsia in France, argued that extraterrestrial life might be quite uncommon. Habitable planets would be unlikely, he thought, around stars that were small, variable, or tightly packed in clusters. Within the solar system, he suggested that the requisite climatic, atmospheric, chemical, and geological conditions necessary for life occurred only on Earth and possibly on Mars and Venus. Furthermore, adopting a modified version of the **nebular hypothesis,** Faye considered the formation of planetary systems like our own to be a rare event.

F-class asteroid
A subcategory of **C-class asteroid**s, with an **albedo** of 0.03 to 0.07, the spectrum of which shows little or no **absorption** of **ultraviolet** light.

Fermi, Enrico (1901–54)
Italian-American physicist and Nobel Prize winner (1938) whose theoretical ideas were used in the development of the atomic bomb. During a luncheon with colleagues in Los Alamos in the summer of 1950, he posed what has become known as the **Fermi Paradox.**

Fermi Paradox
Physicist Enrico **Fermi** asked, "If there are extraterrestrials, where are they?" The fact that no convincing evidence had been found of extraterrestrial activity in or near the solar system suggested to him that there were no intelligent extraterrestrial societies in the Galaxy. "If they existed," he said, "they would be here." The same point, also known as the Space Travel Argument, was subsequently raised more forcefully and visibly in 1966 by Freeman **Dyson,**[171] in 1975 in two articles by Michael Hart[258] in the United States, and David Viewing[605] in Britain, as well as by others. Straightforward calculations showed that a technological race capable of **interstellar travel** at (a modest) one tenth the **speed of light** ought to be able to colonize the entire Galaxy within a period of 1 to 10 million years. Given that credible strategies for achieving human **space colonies, interstellar colonization,** and interstellar travel were already being discussed, the Galaxy-wide spread of advanced spacefaring civilizations seemed readily achievable. Therefore, if such civilizations existed, why had they not come to the solar system? To advocates of the **extraterrestrial hypothesis** of **unidentified flying objects** or the **paleocontact hypothesis,** the answer was simple: intelligent beings from the stars *had* arrived. Yet the continuing lack of hard evidence to support these claims, together with the availability, in most cases, of more mundane explanations, led the scientific community to consider other possibilities. Two camps emerged. In one were those who accepted Fermi's conclusion that the absence of extraterrestrial artifacts in the solar system implied an absence of extraterrestrial intelligence throughout the Galaxy. According to this view, **SETI** was a pointless exercise—"a waste of time and money," as Hart put it. A particularly extreme anti-SETI stance was taken by Frank **Tipler** (→ **Tipler's Argument**). In the opposing camp were those who favored the existence of advanced civilizations elsewhere in the Galaxy and who sought, therefore, to circumvent the Fermi Paradox. Various explanations have been put forward, including that extraterrestrials are:

1. Interested in us but do not want us (yet) to be aware of their presence (→ **sentinel hypothesis; zoo hypothesis**)

2. Not interested in us because they are by nature xenophobic or not curious (➜ **intelligence, nature of**)
3. Not interested in us because they are so much further ahead of us (➜ **extraterrestrial civilizations, more advanced than we**)
4. Prone to annihilation before they achieve a significant level of interstellar colonization, because they
   a. Self-destruct
   b. Are destroyed by external effects, such as
      i. The collision of an asteroid or comet with their home world
      ii. A galaxywide sterilization phenomenon, e.g., a **gamma-ray burster**
      iii. Cultural or technological stagnation (➜ **extraterrestrial civilization, hazards to**)
5. Capable only of interplanetary or limited interstellar travel because of fundamental physical, biological, or economic restraints (➜ **interstellar travel**)

Fermi-Hart Paradox
➜ **Fermi Paradox**

FGK stars
Stars belonging to **spectral type**s F, G, or K. Being most similar to the Sun (type G2), these are considered the most likely to be capable of supporting life on worlds that circle around them within their **habitable zone**s. They are therefore the types generally selected in SETI programs that employ a **targeted search.**

fibrous proteins
Proteins that play structural roles in organisms. They include keratin in hair, actin and myosin in muscles, and collagen, the most abundant protein in a vertebrate body.

final causes, doctrine of
➜ **teleology**

fireball
A particularly bright **meteor** (**apparent magnitude** greater than −3) and a phenomenon that may explain some reports of **unidentified flying objects.** Fireballs are often followed by **meteorite** falls.

first contact
The moment at which two intelligent, communicative species, such as humankind and an extraterrestrial race, first encounter each other, either physically or via remote signaling. ➜ **extraterrestrial intelligence, implications following first contact; extraterrestrial intelligence, procedures following first contact**

First Men in the Moon
H. G. **Wells**'s 1901 romance about a trip to the Moon (➜ **Moon, voyages to**) in which two explorers find a flourishing underground lunar civilization of which the head (literally) is the giant-brained "Grand Lunar" (➜ **Moon, life on**).

fission (cellular)
A form of asexual reproduction occurring in **bacteria, archaea,** and certain other **unicellular** organisms such as diatoms and protozoans. The parent **cell** duplicates its circular **DNA** and divides to produce two identical daughter cells.

fission (nuclear)
The splitting of an atomic **nucleus** into smaller fragments with the release of energy.

Flammarion, Camille (1842–1925)
French astronomer and author of more than seventy books who did more to encourage public interest in the subject than anyone else of his day, although many of his scientific and philosophical arguments were eccentric. He set up his own observatory at Juvisy. His first book, *La Pluralité des mondes habités* (The Plurality of Inhabited Worlds), originally published in 1862, secured his reputation as both a great popularizer and a leading advocate of extreme **pluralism.** By 1882, it had gone through thirty-three editions, and it continued to be translated and reprinted well into the twentieth century.

Flammarion's passionate belief in life on other worlds was nurtured by his readings of previous pluralist authors such as Bernard de

Fontenelle, Savinien **Cyrano de Bergerac,** Christiaan **Huygens,** Joseph **Lalande,** and David **Brewster.** He and another French writer, J. H. **Rosny,** were the first to popularize the notion of beings that were genuinely alien and not merely minor variants on humans and other terrestrial forms. In his *Real and Imaginary Worlds* (1864) and *Lumen* (1887), he describes a range of exotic species, including sentient plants that combine the processes of digestion and respiration. This belief in extraterrestrial life Flammarion combined with a religious conviction derived not from the Catholic faith in which he had been raised, but from the writings of Jean **Reynaud** and their emphasis upon the **transmigration of souls.** Man he considered to be a "citizen of the sky" and other worlds "studios of human work, schools where the expanding soul progressively learns and develops, assimilating gradually the knowledge to which its aspirations tend, approaching thus evermore the end of its destiny." His linking of pluralism with transmigration, though an old idea, helps explain why these doctrines are often found together in writings from the closing decades of the nineteenth century.

Flammarion's best-selling work, his epic *Astronomie populaire* (1880), translated as *Popular Astronomy* (1894), is filled with speculation about extraterrestrial life. An entire chapter is taken up in arguing the case for lunar life (➔ **Moon, life on**), while Mars he considers "an earth almost similar to ours [with] water, air . . . showers, brooks, fountains. . . . This is certainly a place little different from that which we inhabit." In 1892, he speculated further on the fourth planet in his *La Planète Mars et ses conditions d'habitabilité,* though in prose less florid than in his earlier work. Concerning the canals (➔ **Mars, canals of**), he is open-minded, suggesting that "they may be due to superficial fissures produced by geological forces or perhaps even to the rectification of old rivers by the inhabitants for the purpose of the general distribution of water." As to Martian life, he concludes that "the actual habitation of Mars by a race superior to our own is in our opinion very probable" (➔ **Mars, life on**).

Flammarion's fertile imagination moves from romantic science to scientific romance in his *Récits de l'infini* (1872) and *La Fin du monde* (1893). The former includes several tales that describe the reincarnation of a spirit on other worlds in various alien forms, while the latter has been seen as a precursor of Olaf **Stapledon**'s *Last and First Men.*

flare

An explosion in the **chromosphere** and **corona** of a star that results in the ejection into space of a burst of charged particles and radiation, especially **X rays.** Minor flares occur regularly on the **Sun** and give rise to **aurora**s when they reach the Earth. Once or twice a decade, much larger solar flares known as "coronal mass ejections" release enough energy to disrupt electricity supplies and communications satellites. One such outburst in 1989 brought down the power grid in northern Quebec. However, even solar activity of this magnitude is mild by normal stellar standards. From studying records of other lone stars in the Galaxy of comparable size, brightness, age, and composition to the Sun, astronomers have found that about once a century, most Sun-like stars are prone to eject "superflares," with about 10,000 times more energy than the event that caused the Canadian blackout. A solar superflare would be enough to melt large floodplains on the icy satellites of Jupiter and Saturn and instantly destroy about half of the Earth's **ozone** layer. Although it would not wipe out life on Earth, it might have serious short-term consequences for the food chain at high latitudes (where the ozone depletion would be greatest) and result in elevated levels of **ionizing radiation** over the whole planet with mutagenic and possibly long-term evolutionary effects. If the Sun is indeed unusual in its stability and hospitality toward life, this could have important implications for the frequency with which life and intelligence emerge on other worlds. ➔ **extraterrestrial civilizations, hazards to**

flare star

A **red dwarf** that displays sudden and unpredictable changes in light output lasting for a few minutes. The flares are believed to occur in the star's chromosphere and to be similar in nature to solar flares but much more energetic.

The nearest star to the Sun, **Proxima Centauri,** is a flare star, as is one of the components of the nearby **binary star** system Luyten 726-8, also known as UV Ceti. Indeed, flare stars are sometimes referred to as UV Ceti stars.

flux density

The energy in a beam of radiation passing through a unit area at right angles to the beam in unit time. In radio astronomy, flux density is measured in **jansky**s (Jy).

flying disk

An alternative description, commonly used between 1947 and 1952, for the phenomenon also known as "**flying saucer**s." It appears to have been the preferred term in military circles until it was superseded by "**unidentified flying object**" at the start of Project **Blue Book.**

flying saucer

A term coined following the reported sighting by Kenneth **Arnold** on June 24, 1947, of nine luminous objects in the sky over Washington State. Arnold, a businessman and part-time deputy sheriff, was piloting a private plane when he saw unusual lights heading south from the direction of Mount Baker toward Mount Rainier at what he estimated was a supersonic speed. In describing to reporters later how the objects moved, he said that they hugged the contours and appeared to undulate "like a saucer skipping over water." By the time the story appeared in print, his words had been distorted to the phrase "flying saucer." Arnold's sighting, and the great publicity it received, triggered the great **saucer flap of 1947.** Various theories have been put forward to account for the incident, including an especially plausible one that involves the little-understood phenomenon of **earthlights.** ➔ **Cold War, linked to UFO reports; Technical Intelligence Division**

Follow-Up Detection Device (FUDD)

A stand-alone subsystem of the **Targeted Search System** used in Project **Phoenix** and previously in the targeted portion of NASA's **High Resolution Microwave Survey.** It consists of a box of electronics that intensively analyzes, at high resolution and sensitivity, any candidate signal that is picked up, while the telescopes involved in the search continue with their next set of observations. Identical FUDDs at the main antenna site and a remote antenna site enable a signal to be confirmed as extraterrestrial in origin.

Fomalhaut

Alpha Piscis Austrini, a nearby **A star.** In 1983, observations by the *Infrared Astronomy Satellite* revealed that Fomalhaut, like **Vega** and **Beta Pictoris,** is surrounded by a **dust disk.** This may be material left over from the formation of a planetary system (➔ **planetary systems, formation of**) or, more likely, a **regenerated disk.** Recent measurements have shown the disk to have a radius of about 175 AU (26 billion km, or 16 billion miles). ➔ **stars, brightest**

Fontenelle, Bernard Le Bovier de (1657–1757)

French man of letters and satirist who enthusiastically endorsed the atomistic philosophy of René **Descartes** and used it to argue for the ubiquity of life throughout the solar system and the existence of inhabited planets around other stars. He was a central figure in promoting **pluralism** in the late seventeenth century, not because of any great scientific reputation, but because of his literary style, which was accessible to the layperson, elegant, and compelling. Voltaire considered him "the most universal genius that the age of Louis XIV has produced," and he could reasonably be called the first successful science popularizer. Like many who followed him, he discovered that extravagant claims about extraterrestrial life sold well. His *Entretiens sur la pluralité des mondes* (Conversations on the Plurality of Worlds),[198] first published in 1686, was eventually translated into every major European language and influenced the thinking of generations to come. Its message unfolds in the form of witty after-dinner conversations between the author and a fictitious marchioness, in the gardens of her château. Of the inhabitants of Saturn, the author declares in typically expansive style that they live miserably...the sun seems to them but a little pale star, whose light and heat cannot but be very weak at so great a distance. They say Greenland is a perfect bagnio, in comparison of this planet.

Yet such descriptions are tongue in cheek, and Fontenelle has his marchioness point out the dangers of drawing conclusions in a scientific vacuum:

You know all is very well without knowing how it is so; which is a great deal of ignorance, founded upon a very little knowledge.

Beyond the florid passages that attracted such a wide readership and helped *Entretiens* become the first astronomical best-seller, Fontenelle makes serious philosophical points. His support for pluralism, for example, is grounded in five main arguments, not original to him:

(1) the similarities of the planets to the earth which is inhabited; (2) the impossibility of imagining any other use for which they were made; (3) the fecundity and magnificence of nature; (4) the consideration she seems to show for the needs of their inhabitants as having given moons to planets distant from the sun, and more moons to those more remote; and (5) that which is very important—all which can be said on one side and nothing on the other.

As to the status of man in the Universe, Fontenelle is ambiguous. On the one hand, he presents a post-Copernican case for the Earth's occupying a privileged position in the solar system:

We alone can recognize that we, in a company of fourteen worlds, revolve around the sun.... We alone can establish truths about the motions and properties of the planets. If the Creator had not wished us to do this, he would not have given us such a convenient observatory.

But when it comes to the wider cosmos, with its innumerable stars and planets, he argues both for and against anthropocentrism. As the chivalrous scientist, he proclaims:

When the Heavens were a little blue Arch, stuck with Stars, methought the Universe was too straight and close...but now it is enlarg'd...I begin to breathe with more freedom, and think the Universe to be incomparably more magnificent than it was before.

However, his marchioness replies:

You have made the Universe too large...that I know not where I am....Is every Star the centre of a Vortex, as big as ours? Is that vast space which comprehends our Sun and Planets, but an inconsiderable part of the Universe?...I protest it is dreadful.

"foo fighters"

Mysterious aerial lights seen by aircrew on both sides in World War II, especially after 1943, and during the Korean War. Their name derives from the cartoon character Smokey Stover, whose catchphrase was "Where there's foo there's fire." Many reports were made of balls of light, varying in color and in size from several centimeters to about 2 m across, moving in close pursuit of warplanes. A common assumption among Allied pilots was that they were some form of enemy invention such as reconnaissance drones. However, when enemy aircrew were interrogated, it became clear that both German and Japanese fliers had encountered the same phenomenon. As the minutes of the secret meetings of the **Scientific Advisory Panel on Unidentified Flying Objects** in 1953 noted, "[T]heir exact cause or nature was never defined." The minutes also reveal that both the panel's chairman, H. P. Robertson of the California Institute of Technology, and another panel member, Luis W. **Alvarez** of the University of California, "had been concerned in the investigation of these phenomena, but David T. Griggs (professor of geophysics at the University of California at Los Angeles) is believed to be the most knowledgeable person on this subject. It was their feeling that these phenomena are not beyond the domain of present . . . physical science."[399] The same view was later espoused by Donald H. **Menzel** and Ernest H. Taves,[397, 399] who suggested that foo fighters were light reflections from tiny ice crystals formed by supercold air eddying around battle damage on the aircraft. Another possibility is that they were akin to ball lightning. The significant point is that, like the "**Los Angeles Air Raid**" and Kenneth **Arnold**'s sighting, foo fighters were not considered as an aspect of a single phenomenon until hindsight included them in the UFO canon. As the Robertson Panel in 1953 concluded, "If the term 'flying saucers' had been popular in 1943–1945, these objects would have been so labeled."

Forbidden Planet

Released in 1956, this was one of the most sophisticated of the pre–Space Age sci-fi films. In it, a human crew journeys to the stars in a spacecraft indistinguishable from a flying saucer and encounters the still working artifacts of a long-dead civilization, the Krell. The plot was loosely based on Shakespeare's play *The Tempest.* → **science fiction involving extraterrestrials, in films and on television**

formaldehyde
→ **methanal**

forward contamination

The accidental contamination of other worlds with microbes, such as **virus**es or **bacteria,** brought from Earth. Since 1967, a policy of **planetary protection** has been in place in order to control contamination of planets by terrestrial microbes and organic constituents during planetary missions. That such contamination is at least possible was demonstrated by the apparent survival for many months on the Moon of *Streptococci* bacteria on *Surveyor 3.* The risk is that on a planet or moon that was not sterile, the release of terrestrial microorganisms, to which the indigenous life-forms would have no immunity, could prove devastating. This risk is particularly great where crewed missions are involved. The ship, air, and occupants of the first human mission to Mars, for example, will inevitably release a microbial menagerie into the Martian environ-

ment. Thomas **Gold** hypothesized that it might even be possible to seed life accidentally on a previously virgin world in this way (→ **"garbage theory," of the origin of life**). Fred **Hoyle** and Chandra Wickramasinghe, in a modern version of **panspermia,** have suggested that life originated on Earth from **prebiotic** chemicals and possibly even microbes delivered on meteorites or the dust from comets (→ **life, in space**) and furthermore that such "contamination" continues today, giving rise to epidemics (→ **epidemics, from space**). The theme of life from one world being unable to resist infection by "alien" microbes has been employed in fiction. In ***The War of the Worlds,*** H. G. **Wells** eventually kills off his Martian invaders with earthly bugs. Michael Crichton's *The Andromeda Strain* (1964) envisages the genetic alteration of terrestrial microbes by **ionizing radiation** high in the atmosphere and their return to Earth as deadly mutants.[214, 280, 415, 491, 497] → **back contamination**

Forward, Robert L(ull) (1932–)

Consulting scientist, future technologist, and author of science and science fiction who has speculated about unusual forms of extraterrestrial life and proposed several novel interstellar propulsion systems. The author of ***Dragon's Egg***[200] (1980) and *Starquake*[201] (1985), about life on a **neutron star** (→ **gravitational life**), he has explored the idea of using antiproton annihilation[203] and **laser** sails for **interstellar travel.** Together with Robert P. Hoyt, he has also developed the concept of using space tethers for powering orbital and interplanetary missions. Forward obtained a B.S. in physics from the University of Maryland (1954), an M.S. in applied physics from the University of California, Los Angeles (1955), and a Ph.D. in gravitational physics from the University of Maryland (1965). From 1956 to 1987, he worked at Hughes Aircraft Company Corporate Research Laboratories in Malibu, California, and since 1962 he has also run his own consulting company devoted to investigating new energy sources and propulsion concepts.

"fossils," Martian
→ **Martian "fossils" controversy**

Fourier analysis
Breaking a complex signal into an ensemble of sine wave components.

Fox, Sidney W. (1912–98)
American biochemist who has figured prominently over the past few decades in laboratory studies concerning the origin of life (→ **life, origin of**). Fox received a doctorate from the California Institute of Technology (1940), served on the faculty of Iowa State University (1943–55), and was director and professor of the Oceanographic Institute of Florida State University (1955–61). At the behest of NASA, Fox held the position of director of the Institute of Bioscience at Florida State (1961–64) before moving to the University of Miami to become director and professor of its Institute of Molecular and Cellular Evolution (1964–89). In 1989, he became distinguished research professor in the Department of Plant Biology at Southern Illinois University and since 1993 has been distinguished research scientist in the Department of Marine Sciences at the University of Southern Alabama. Fox is best known for his seminal experiments in the synthesis of **thermal proteins** (previously known as "proteinoids") from **amino acids** that he carried out in the 1960s and for his demonstration that these proteins, when placed in water, spontaneously self-organize into structures, known as **microspheres,** that resemble primitive cells. On three occasions he has been invited to the Vatican to explain the results of his work to the pope. His most recent experiments have sought to demonstrate that the cell-like structures he has created in the laboratory also act as protonerve cells.[205]

Fred Lawrence Whipple Observatory
→ **Whipple (Fred Lawrence) Observatory**

free oxygen
Oxygen in its molecular forms, O_2 (normal, diatomic oxygen) or O_3 (**ozone**), uncombined with other elements. Free oxygen is a requirement of all **aerobic** organisms, and its copious presence in a planetary atmosphere is diagnostic of the presence of life.

frequency
The number of waves passing a fixed point in 1 second. Frequency is measured in **hertz** (Hz), **kilohertz** (kHz), or **megahertz** (MHz).

frequency bandwidth
→ **bandwidth**

Full-sky Astrometric Mapping Explorer (FAME)
A space telescope designed to measure, with high precision, the positions, distances, and motions of about 40 million stars within 6,500 light-years (2,000 parsecs) of the Sun. Among other uses, it will provide a rich database for detecting large **extrasolar planets** and planetary systems in our part of the Milky Way Galaxy. FAME, which will be developed by a group at the **U.S. Naval Observatory,** was chosen by NASA as a medium-class *Explorer* (MIDEX) mission to be launched in 2003 and 2004.

fungi
Eukaryotic, usually **multicellular,** nonmotile, **heterotroph**ic organisms. Fungi digest their food externally, rather than ingesting it, and reproduce by **spores.**

fusion (nuclear)
The joining together of two light nuclei at high temperatures to form a heavier **nucleus** with the release of a large amount of energy. **Main sequence** stars produce light and heat through the fusion of **hydrogen** into **helium** in their cores. In **red giant**s, successively heavier nuclei fuse, at higher temperatures, to form elements such as **carbon, oxygen,** and **silicon** (→ **stars, evolution of**), which are the basis of Earth-like planets and life.

G

G star

A yellow star, of **spectral type** G, whose spectrum contains many **absorption line**s of neutral and **ionized** metals, together with some molecular **absorption band**s. **Main sequence** G stars, of which the **Sun** and **Alpha Centauri** A are examples, have a surface temperature in the range 5,000 to 5,800°C and a mass of 0.8 to 1.1 M_S. They are the prime targets of searches for **extrasolar planets** and targeted **SETI** programs. G-type **giant star**s, such as **Capella,** are slightly cooler but more luminous than their main sequence counterparts, while G-type **supergiant**s have a mass of 10 to 12 M_S and a luminosity of 10,000 to 300,000 L_S.

GAIA

→ **Global Astrometric Interferometer for Astrophysics**

Gaia Hypothesis

The idea that life on Earth controls the physical and chemical conditions of the environment. Named after the Greek Earth goddess Gaea, it was originally formulated by James **Lovelock** and Lynn **Margulis** in the late 1960s and early 1970s and has attracted both critics and supporters in large numbers. Different forms of it have been proposed, varying from "weak" to "strong." Weak Gaian models assert

simply that the **biota** have a substantial influence over certain aspects of the **abiotic** world, such as the temperature and composition of the atmosphere. Or they may go further and argue that just as the biota influence their abiotic environment, so the environment influences the evolution of the biota by exerting Darwinian selection pressures. The version put forward by Lovelock and Margulis is strong in that it depicts terrestrial life as influencing the abiotic world by a series of negative feedback loops in a way that is fundamentally stabilizing. As Lovelock puts it in *The Ages of Gaia:*

> The Gaia hypothesis says that the temperature, oxidation state, acidity, and certain aspects of the rocks and water are kept constant, and that this homeostasis is maintained by active feedback processes operated automatically and unconsciously by the biota.

The oceans, the atmosphere, and all biological material on Earth are thus portrayed as integral components of a vast self-regulating system. Not only that, but life, in the original concept of Gaia, is seen as regulating the environment so as to maintain suitable planetary conditions *for the good of life itself.* In the opinion of Lovelock and Margulis:[364]

[T]he Earth's atmosphere is more than merely anomalous; it appears to be a contrivance specifically constituted for a set of purposes…it is unlikely that chance alone accounts for the fact that temperature, pH and the presence of compounds of nutrient elements have been, for immense periods, just those optimal for surface life. Rather… energy is expended by the biota to actively maintain these optima.

According to the Gaia Hypothesis, individual life-forms on this planet exhibit the sort of cooperative action in regulating the chemical composition of the atmosphere and the amount of **ultraviolet** radiation that can pass through it (**➔ Earth, atmosphere of**), the surface temperature of Earth and its water content, and other key factors expected from a single organism.[363] This gives rise to the notion of **planets as living beings.**

galactic bulge
The ellipsoidal region at the heart of a **spiral galaxy.** Deep within the central bulge lies the **galactic nucleus.**

Galactic Club
A term coined by Ronald **Bracewell**[74] to describe a Galaxy-wide community of advanced technological races. Our prospects for membership in such a club, should it exist, may depend on our ability to solve our present environmental, political, and sociological problems, as well as our capacity to reach a certain level of proficiency in interstellar communication or transport. Bracewell proposed that we may be under surveillance by races interested in our progress.
➔ Bracewell probes; sentinel hypothesis

galactic disk
The flattened component of a **spiral galaxy** in which, together with many ordinary stars such as the Sun (**➔ disk star**), lie the biggest and brightest of stars: the **O star**s and **B star**s. The disk is also home to large tracts of interstellar material from which new stars are continually being made.

galactic empire
The idea, well explored by science fiction writers, that our galaxy is effectively governed by one or more ancient, highly advanced civilizations. That a galactic empire might exist has also been the subject of serious scientific speculation, despite the fact that we have so far not encountered any signs of a major alien presence among the stars. In fact, there are several valid reasons why we might not be aware of a technologically superior race in our midst (**➔ extraterrestrial intelligence, more advanced than we**). There is the possibility, too, that if a Galaxy-wide empire does not exist now, it may do so in the future if mankind is able to establish efficient, faster-than-light modes of interstellar communication and transport.

galactic halo
A large, relatively dust-free, spherical region surrounding a **spiral galaxy,** such as our own. The inner, visible part of the halo, which has roughly the same diameter as the **galactic disk,** is occupied by **Population II** objects, including **globular cluster**s and old, individual stars. Beyond this is a much more extensive region containing large amounts of **dark matter,** the presence of which is revealed by its gravitational effect on the galaxy's rotation. The nature of galactic dark matter is still undetermined but the most popular theory, supported by some recent observations, is that the extended halo is home to vast numbers of small, unseen bodies known as **MACHOs.**

galactic nucleus
The central part of a **galaxy.** Galactic nuclei are small and bright and may, in the case of larger galaxies, harbor supermassive **black hole**s. The energy generated by such objects as they draw in surrounding matter is considered, by many astronomers, to be responsible for the high luminosity of **quasar**s and other manifestations of active galactic nuclei.

galactic year
The Sun's period of rotation around the center of the Galaxy, equal to about 225 million years.

Galatea
The fourth known moon of **Neptune.** Like the five other inner moons discovered during the 1989 flyby of *Voyager 2,* Galatea is among the darkest objects in the solar system. **➔ Neptune, moons of**

Discovery	1989, by *Voyager 2*
Mean distance from Neptune	61,900 km (38,500 mi.)
Diameter	158 km (98 mi.)
Orbital period	0.429 day (10 hours 18 minutes)
Orbital eccentricity	0.0001
Orbital inclination	0.05°
Visual albedo	0.06

galaxy

A large collection of stars held together by mutual gravitational attraction. Galaxies occur in a great range of shapes and sizes, the main categories being ellipticals, spirals, and irregulars. Their masses range from about 100,000 to about 3 trillion M_S in the case of the largest ellipticals.

Galaxy

The galaxy in which we live. It is a **spiral galaxy** containing 200 to 400 billion stars and spanning about 100,000 light-years (30,000 parsecs).

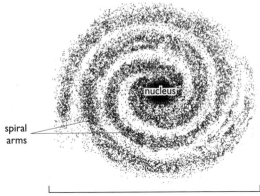

spiral arms

nucleus

100,000 light-years

Plan view.

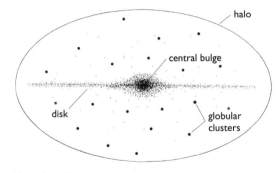

halo

central bulge

disk

globular clusters

Elevation view.

Galilean satellites

The four largest moons of **Jupiter,** discovered by Galileo **Galilei.** In order of increasing distance from the primary, they are **Io, Europa, Ganymede,** and **Callisto.**

Galilei, Galileo (1564–1642)

Great Italian astronomer and physicist who, among his many achievements, was the first to make and publish systematic telescopic observations of the Moon, planets, and stars. In his *Siderius nuncius* (Starry Messenger), he noted that the Moon was "not unlike the face of the Earth," that its dark regions might be seas and its bright parts land, and that "the Moon has its own atmosphere." Although within a few years he came to doubt these conclusions, they were given wide credence by others (→ **Moon, life on**). In particular, they immediately led to the first piece of speculation about extraterrestrial life based on instrument-derived data. Johannes **Kepler** wrote to Galileo with the suggestion that one of the large features he had seen on the lunar surface might have been excavated by intelligent inhabitants who "make their homes in numerous caves hewn out of that circular embankment." Galileo would not be drawn on this except to say that if there were lunar life it would be "extremely diverse and beyond all our imaginings." He also discovered the four large ("Galilean") moons of Jupiter and the phases of Venus. His defense of the Copernican system in *Dialogue on the Two Chief World Systems* brought severe censure from the Church, and he was forced to recant before, at the age of sixty-nine, being sentenced to life imprisonment (commuted to house arrest).

Galileo Europa Mission (GEM)

The *Galileo* spacecraft was originally scheduled to end its investigations of **Jupiter** and its environs on December 7, 1997. However, following funding approval by NASA and the U.S. Congress, the mission was extended for a further two years through the end of 1999. The first part of the extended mission, lasting more than a year, was devoted to searching for further evidence of a subsurface watery ocean on **Europa.** During eight orbits of Jupiter, *Galileo* made close approaches to Europa of

200 to 3,600 km, enabling a camera resolution of down to 6 m. Following the Europa Campaign ("Ice") was scheduled the Perijove Reduction/Jupiter Water Study ("Water") and the **Io** Campaign ("Fire").

Galileo (spacecraft)

The first spacecraft to conduct long-term observations of **Jupiter** and its moons from orbit and the first to deploy an instrumented probe to investigate Jupiter's atmosphere *in situ*. *Galileo*'s six-year journey to the largest planet in the solar system involved two **gravity assists** from Earth and one from Venus. Failure of the craft's high-gain antenna meant that all communications had to be conducted at a much

Launch	October 18, 1989
Arrival at Jupiter	December 7, 1995
Mass:	
Orbiter	2,223 kg (2.15 t)
Descent probe	339 kg (746 lb.)
Instruments:	
Orbiter	10
Descent probe	6

lower data rate using the low-gain antenna. Nevertheless, the mission was a triumph. During its 57 minutes of active life in Jupiter's atmosphere, the descent probe managed to spring some surprises for researchers, including the unexpected lack of water in the Jovian cloud tops. *Galileo*'s 2-year primary mission involved studying the planet's atmosphere, magnetosphere, and satellite system (**→ Jupiter, moons of**), encountering one moon during each orbit, and returning a steady stream of images and other data. Following the completion of the primary mission in December 1997, *Galileo* began a two-year extended mission known as the *Galileo* **Europa Mission.**[505]

Galton, Francis (1822–1911)

English statistician and meteorologist who, in a letter to the London *Times,* published on August 6, 1892, proposed using a combination of mirrors to reflect sunlight toward Mars in order that it might be detected by any Martian astronomers with the aid of telescopes. This

was similar to an earlier idea put forward by Charles **Cros** in France. It stimulated a lively debate in England on (1) the likelihood of there being intelligent life on Mars and other neighboring worlds (including the Moon), and (2) the merits of trying to send signals. One of those who opposed the scheme was Richard **Hutton. → communication, with the Moon and planets**

gamma rays

The most energetic and shortest-wavelength type of **electromagnetic radiation.** Gamma rays lie beyond **X rays** and have wavelengths less than about 0.1 nm.

gamma-ray burster

An astronomical source of an intense, short burst of **gamma rays** and **X rays.** Incredibly, for a brief time, a gamma-ray burster (GRB) may produce as much energy as the rest of the Universe put together. So violent is this phenomenon that it has been put forward as an explanation of why no traces have yet been found of advanced extraterrestrial civilizations.

GRBs were discovered by chance in mid-1967 by several of the Vela military satellites designed to monitor compliance with the Nuclear Test Ban Treaty, though the data on them was only made available to scientists without security clearances some 6 years later. More recent observations have shown that bursts, which typically last a few seconds to a few tens of seconds, occur about twice a day, at random locations across the sky. In 1997, the Italian-Dutch BeppoSAX satellite, using a narrow-field X-ray camera, was able to pinpoint the position of some GRBs precisely enough for their afterglows to be later identified optically. The first optical **spectrum** of a GRB, obtained at the **Keck Observatory,** showed that the object lay about halfway to the edge of the observable universe, so that for the burst to have appeared as bright as it did its energy output must have been enormous. For a few seconds, the burster gave out more than a million times more energy than an entire galaxy such as the Milky Way. On January 23, 1999, a burster was imaged for the first time while it was actually in progress. Detectors aboard NASA's orbiting

Compton Gamma Ray Observatory picked up and identified the location of the event, and 22 seconds later the Robotic Optical Transient Search Experiment (ROTSE) in Los Alamos, New Mexico, took images of the patch of sky from which the emission came. The source was so bright optically that it could easily have been seen through an amateur telescope, yet a spectrum taken using the Keck II telescope on the following night revealed its distance to be an astonishing 9 billion light-years.

A number of theories have been put forward to explain transient emissions on this scale, including the merger of two **neutron stars**, two **black holes**, or a neutron star and a black hole, or the explosion of a hypothetical type of **supernova** known as a hypernova. Although uncertainty remains about the exact mechanism involved, it is clear that the effects of so powerful a burst of high-energy radiation could be devastating for any nearby inhabited planets. James Annis, an astrophysicist at Fermilab near Chicago, has speculated that such events could sterilize entire galaxies, wiping out life-forms before they had the chance to evolve to the stage of interstellar travel.[17] "If one went off in the Galactic center," he wrote, "we here two-thirds of the way out of the Galactic disk would be exposed over a few seconds to a wave of powerful gamma rays." It would be enough, according to Annis, to exterminate every species on Earth. Even the hemisphere shielded by the planet's mass from immediate exposure would not escape, he claimed, since there would be lethal indirect effects such as the demolition of the entire protective **ozone** layer.

The rate of GRBs in the universe today appears to be about one burst per galaxy per several hundred million years. However, Annis points out that theories of GRBs suggest that the rate was much higher in the past, with galaxies suffering one sterilizing event every few million years, thus preventing life from progressing beyond even the most primitive stage. If this view is correct, then there are likely to be no ancient civilizations anywhere in space and it is only now, with the GRB rate at a more modest level, that species have a chance to develop to the spacefaring stage. According to Annis, "It may be that intelligent life has re-cently sprouted up at many places in the Galaxy and that at least a few groups are busily engaged in spreading." **→ extraterrestrial civilizations, hazards to**

Ganymede

The largest moon in the solar system, Ganymede is bigger than Mercury and three quarters the size of Mars. It has a magnetic field, discovered by the *Galileo* spacecraft, which strongly suggests it has a metallic core. Around this is a mantle of ice and **silicates,** overlain by a thick crust of water ice. The surface of Ganymede testifies to a complex geological history that has given rise to two types of terrain. About 40 percent of the surface is covered by dark, highly cratered regions that are evidently the remains of the original crust. The other 60 percent is light, grooved landscape that forms intricate patterns. This younger terrain may be due to tensional faulting or the release of water from beneath the surface. Groove ridges as high as 700 m (2,000 ft.) have been observed stretching for thousands of kilometers. **→ Jupiter, moons of**

Discovery	January 11, 1610, by Galileo Galilei
Mean distance from Jupiter	1,070,000 km (665,000 mi.)
Diameter	5,262 km (3,270 mi.)
Equatorial diameter (Earth = 1)	0.413
Mass (Earth = 1)	0.0248
Mean density	1.94 g/cm³
Surface gravity (Earth = 1)	0.145
Escape velocity	2.74 km/s (9,864 km/h, 6,131 mi./h)
Orbital period	7.155 days (7 days 3 hours 43 minutes)
Orbital eccentricity	0.002
Orbital inclination	0.20°
Axial period	7.155 days
Albedo	0.42
Surface temperature	−156°C (−249°F)
Surface composition	Dirty ice

"garbage theory," of the origin of life

Possibly the least appealing idea about how life began on Earth. Thomas **Gold** of **Cornell University** suggested[220] that biological contaminants accidentally left behind by interstellar survey parties could introduce life to a previously sterile or **prebiotic** world. He envisaged a group of extraterrestrial visitors having a picnic somewhere on the young Earth. What if they dropped a few crumbs of food and from the microbes in those crumbs we eventually evolved? → **forward contamination**

gas giant

A term invented by the science fiction writer James Blish to describe a large, massive planet, the bulk of which is composed of light substances, principally **hydrogen, helium, methane,** and **ammonia,** in their gaseous or liquid state. The four gas giants of the solar system are, in order of increasing distance from the Sun, **Jupiter, Saturn, Uranus,** and **Neptune.** The majority of **extrasolar planets** discovered so far are thought to be of this type. Gas giants are also referred to as Jovians, or Jupiter-type planets.

Gatewood, George G. (1940–)

Professor of astronomy at the University of Pittsburgh, director of the **Allegheny Observatory** since 1977, and chairman of the **Extrasolar Planetary Foundation.** Gatewood specializes in high-precision **astrometry** aimed at detecting **extrasolar planets** around nearby stars. He designed and built the **Multichannel Astrometric Photometer,** which was used in the discovery (yet to be confirmed) of a planetary system around **Lalande 21185.**

Gauss, Karl Friedrich (1777–1855)

Foremost German mathematician of his generation and director of the Göttingen Observatory. The story has often been repeated that Gauss proposed a method of signaling to either the Moon or Mars (→ **communication, with the Moon and planets**). In one version of this, he is supposed to have suggested that lanes of forest be planted in Siberia in the form of a huge right-angle triangle with squares on each side (as in Euclid's demonstration of Pythagoras's theorem) as a means of revealing our presence to any inhabitants of the Moon. There is no direct evidence that he ever did this. However, he was a believer in **pluralism** and, following his invention of a heliotrope (a device for signaling in which a mirror reflects sunlight), he commented on the possibility of using it to contact lunarians. In a letter to Wilhelm **Olbers** in 1822, he wrote:

> With 100 separate mirrors, each of 16 square feet … one would be able to send good heliotrope-light to the moon.…This would be a discovery even greater than that of America, if we could get in touch with our neighbors on the moon.

Gauss also remarked, in a letter to Alexander von Humboldt (1854), on the antipluralist views of William **Whewell,** "[I]t would . . . be very precipitous to deny without elaborate argumentation all inhabitants to the moon" (→ **Moon, life on**).

G-class asteroid

A subcategory of **C-class asteroid**s with an **albedo** in the range 0.05 to 0.09 and a spectrum of which shows strong **absorption** of **ultraviolet** light. The largest asteroid in the solar system, Ceres, is of this type.

GEM

→ *Galileo* **Europa Mission**

Geminga

The second most powerful source of high-energy **gamma rays** in the sky. Discovered in 1972 in the constellation of Gemini, Geminga is the closest known **pulsar** to the Earth and the only known pulsar that is radio-quiet. It has been identified optically with an extremely dim blue star, one hundred millionth the brightness of anything visible to the naked eye. High-precision timing of Geminga, achieved by combining observations made by the *COS-B* satellite in the late 1970s and observations by the Energetic Gamma Ray Experiment Telescope (EGRET) aboard the Compton Gamma Ray Observatory, has indicated that the pulsar may have a companion planet (→ **pulsar planets**). However, the variations in the pulsar's period may also be due to **pulsar-timing noise,**

Pulsar	
Distance	512 light-years (157 parsecs)
Period	0.237 second
Planet (To Be Confirmed)	
Mass (Earth = 1)	5.1
Semimajor axis	3.3 AU
Orbital period	5.1 years
Eccentricity	0.0(4)

and further observations are needed to discriminate between these two possibilities.[388]

Gemini Telescopes
Two identical 8.1-m (26-ft.) telescopes for optical and near-infrared observations being built and operated jointly by the United States, the United Kingdom, Canada, Brazil, Chile, and Argentina. Gemini North, at an altitude of 4,200 m on Mauna Kea, Hawaii, was dedicated in June 1999; Gemini South, due for completion in 2000, is at an altitude of 2,515 m on Cerro Pachón, Chile.

gene
The basic unit of heredity. A gene consists of a long sequence of **DNA nucleotide**s that occupy a specific position (locus) on a **chromosome.** Genes can carry the code for synthesizing **proteins** and **RNA** molecules and also regulate the **transcription** of RNA sequences.

gene transfer
The transfer of one **chromosome** or **genome** segment to another chromosome or genome. Gene transfer occurs in both **prokaryote**s and **eukaryote**s. There are three routes for the entry of **DNA: transformation, transduction,** and **conjugation.**

general theory of relativity
Intellectual creation of Albert Einstein that describes gravitational forces in terms of the curvature of **space-time** caused by the presence of mass. The basic idea of the general theory is that frames of reference undergoing acceleration and frames of reference in gravitational fields are equivalent. Among its predictions are that time runs more slowly in strong gravi-

tational fields and that there exist **gravitational lens**ing and **gravitational waves. → special theory of relativity**

genetic code
The means by which the genetic information in **DNA** is used to control the manufacture of specific **proteins** in **cell**s. The code consists of a series of triplets (→ **codon**s) of bases in DNA, from which is transcribed (→ **transcription**) a complimentary sequence of codons in **messenger RNA** (mRNA). The sequence of these codons determines the sequence of **amino**

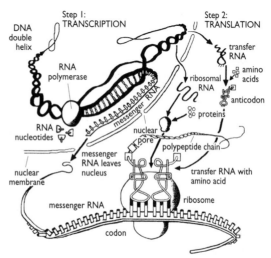

The fundamental steps involved from reading the genetic code to synthesizing proteins.

acids that go into making a particular protein. Using all the triplet combinations of the four bases in DNA and mRNA gives sixty-four different possible codes.

Geneva Extrasolar Planet Search Programs
A variety of observational programs run by Michel **Mayor,** Didier **Queloz,** and others, at Geneva Observatory, which has resulted in the discovery of several **extrasolar planets,** including those around **51 Pegasi, 14 Herculis, Gliese 876, Gliese 86,** and **HD 75289.** Among the current programs that originated at Geneva are the extrasolar planet search at the **Haute-Provence Observatory,** its Southern Hemisphere counterpart centered on the **Leonard Euler Telescope,** and the M-dwarf

(→ **red dwarf**) programs. Future projects will involve the UV-Visual Échelle Spectrograph (UVES) and the **High Accuracy Radial Velocity Planetary Search (HARPS).**

genome

The complete genetic description, or **gene** sequence, of an individual organism.

genome, interstellar transmission of

The possibility of sending to the stars the instructions needed to clone an individual has been dealt with both in fiction, such as Fred **Hoyle** and John Elliott's *A for Andromeda,*[288] and scientific debate. Among those who have speculated about transmitting **genome**s across interstellar distances is John Rather, of the Kaman Aerospace Corporation, who advocated the use of **laser** light as a carrier. In the case of a highly advanced species, he said, "it is even possible that they may have developed from organic bodies to some state, such as self-replicating electronic bodies, that are much more versatile than organic matter." Such beings might then transport themselves over large distances by laser beam. "There are definite possibilities," suggested Rather, "for achieving data rates sufficient to transmit large numbers of the alien species."

genotype

The total set of **gene**s present in the **cell**s of an organism. → **phenotype**

geocentric

Earth-centered, as in the cosmological worldview expounded by **Aristotle.**

"germination," of Martian canals

A phenomenon first noted by Giovanni **Schiaparelli** in 1879. In observing the canal he had named Nilus, stretching between Lunae Lacus and Ceraunius, he saw "two tracks regular, uniform in appearance, and exactly parallel." By 1882, he had charted as many as twenty germinations. Observers such as Henri **Perrotin,** William **Pickering,** and Percival **Lowell** provided confirmation, though by the early 1890s the consensus was growing that the germinations could be explained as an optical or psychological effect. → **Mars, canals of**

GHz

→ gigahertz

giant molecular cloud
→ **molecular cloud**

giant star

A star whose surface layers have expanded and cooled following the exhaustion of its core hydrogen reserves. In this post–**main sequence** state the star has a diameter of five to twenty-five times that of the Sun and a luminosity of a few tens to a few hundreds of times that of the Sun. Nearby giants include **Aldebaran, Arcturus,** and **Capella.** → **supergiant**s

gigahertz (GHz)

One billion **hertz** (cycles per second).

Giotto (ESA Halley Probe)

A **European Space Agency** probe that encountered **Halley's Comet** in March 1986. Images were obtained of the comet's **nucleus** and measurements made of Halley's composition. The spacecraft was struck by a small particle 2 seconds and 605 km (376 miles) before closest approach that knocked its communications antenna out of alignment with Earth. Further impacts also destroyed the probe's camera. However, communications were reestablished after the encounter, and *Giotto* subsequently went on to an encounter with Comet 26P/Grigg-Skjellerup in 1992.

Gliese 86

A nearby **binary star** system in the southern constellation of Eridanus, in which has been found an **extrasolar planet** of the **epistellar Jovian** type. The separation of the two stars is about 10 AU (1.5 billion km) or about 100 times that between the planet and the star it revolves around. The planet's **host star** is a bright, rather cool dwarf, somewhat less massive and luminous than the Sun, just at the limit of naked-eye visibility. Contrary to most stars with known planetary companions, Gliese 86 contains less metals than the Sun, by a factor of two. The observed characteristics of the planet together with the binary nature of Gliese 86 support the idea that planetary systems may form in ways other than the standard agglomeration scheme (→ **planetary systems, formation of**).

Host Star	
Distance	35 light-years (10.7 parsecs)
Spectral type	K0 V
Temperature	4,980°C (5,250 K)
Mass	0.79 M_S
Luminosity	0.4 L_S
Apparent magnitude	6.12
Planet	
Mass	3.6 M_J
Semimajor axis	0.11 AU (16.5 million km, 10.2 million mi.)
Orbital period	15.83 days
Eccentricity	0.045
Inferred surface temp.	380°C (730°F)
Discovery	1998, by Michel Mayor et al., using 1.2-m telescope at La Silla Observatory
Method of discovery	Radial velocity

Gliese 229B

The first confirmed **brown dwarf.** It is in orbit around the nearby **red dwarf** Gliese 229 in the constellation of Lepus. Gliese 229B was discovered in 1994 by a team of astronomers from Caltech and Johns Hopkins University using the 60-in. reflector at **Palomar Observatory** equipped with an **adaptive optics coronograph,** an image-sharpening device developed at Johns Hopkins. Further imaging was performed using the *Hubble Space Telescope,* and an **infrared** spectrum was obtained using the Palomar 200-in. telescope. This spectrum showed strong **absorption line**s due to **methane,** strikingly similar to those found in

Host Star	
Distance	21.8 light-years (6.7 parsecs)
Spectral type	M1 V
Absolute magnitude	8.14
Brown Dwarf	
Mass	20–50 M_J
Semimajor axis	~44 AU (6.6 billion km, 4.1 billion mi.)
Orbital period	~40 years
Discovery	1995, Caltech/Johns Hopkins team at Palomar Observatory
Method of discovery	Infrared imaging

the spectrum of Jupiter's atmosphere.[511] Since methane can exist only at temperatures less than 1,200 K and the coolest stars have a surface temperature of 1,800 K, this is conclusive evidence that Gliese 229B is not a star. There remains, however, a possibility that it may be a very massive planet. The decisive factor is how GL 229B formed. If it condensed, like a star, from an **interstellar cloud,** it is certainly a brown dwarf. On the other hand, if it grew by **accretion** in a **circumstellar disk,** then some astronomers would argue that it is a large planet. If the former is the case, then it is likely to have a much more elongated orbit (like that of most binary stars) than if it were planetary in nature. This determination may take a number of years, however, since GL 229B is in a wide orbit around its primary, similar in size to the orbit of Pluto around the Sun.[8, 242, 386, 435, 436]

Gliese 614
→ **14 Herculis**

Gliese 876

A **red dwarf** around which has been found a planet with about twice the mass of Jupiter. This is the closest known **extrasolar planet**

Host Star	
Distance	15.38 light-years (4.72 parsecs)
Spectral type	M4 V
Mass	0.32 M_S
Luminosity	0.016 L_S
Apparent magnitude	10.17
Planet	
Mass	2.1 M_J
Semimajor axis	0.21 AU (32 million km, 20 million mi.)
Orbital period	60.85 days
Eccentricity	0.27
Discovery	1998, independently by Delfosse et al. at Haute-Provence Observatory and Geoffrey Marcy et al. at San Francisco State University Planet Search
Method of discovery	Radial velocity

and the first to be detected and confirmed in orbit around a dwarf star. Although Gliese 876b is considerably closer to its primary than Mercury is to the Sun, it has an estimated surface temperature of only −75°C due to the red dwarf's low **luminosity.** The high mass of Gliese 876b suggests that it is a **gas giant** and therefore probably unsuitable, in any case, to terrestrial-type life. Any large moons that it might have, however, might offer more clement conditions for life as we know it. The relatively high **eccentricity** of the planet's orbit provides another reminder that our own solar system is not necessarily representative of planetary systems as a whole.[144, 377]

Gliese Nearby Star Catalogue
An inventory of all the known stars lying within 80 light-years (25 parsecs) of the Sun. It was first published in 1969 and was updated by Gliese and Jahreiss in 1991.

Global Astrometric Interferometer for Astrophysics (GAIA)
A proposal for an advanced space astrometry mission to build on the work started by *Hipparcos.* It has been recommended within the context of the **European Space Agency**'s Horizon 2000 Plus plan for long-term space science. *GAIA* would measure the distance and velocity of more than a billion stars in the Galaxy to an accuracy two to three orders of magnitude greater than that possible with *Hipparcos.* More specifically, with respect to astrobiology, it would rigorously scrutinize some 200,000 stars within 650 light-years (200 parsecs) of the Sun for the presence of Jupiter-mass planetary companions.

Global Microlensing Alert Network (GMAN)
An early-warning service operated in cooperation with the **MACHO Project.**

globular cluster
A spherically symmetric grouping of about 100,000 to 1 million old stars, measuring several hundred light-years across. Most globular clusters are found in **galactic halos** and consist of **Population II** stars. More than one hundred

are known in the halo of our own galaxy. One of the nearest, **M13,** was the target for an early attempt at **CETI,** though whether planets exist within globular clusters is still a matter of debate.[545]

globular proteins
Proteins that consist of long chains of **amino acids** folded up into complex shapes. An important category of globular proteins is **enzymes.**

globule
A compact, dark, round pocket of gas and dust embedded within a much larger **interstellar cloud.** Globules are the smallest and most regular features of the **interstellar medium** and are believed to be gravitationally unstable objects that are collapsing to form **protostar**s. Having no internal heat source, they are, surprisingly, among the coldest known naturally occurring phenomena with a temperature only a few degrees above absolute zero. Typical globules have masses of 20 to 100 M_S and measure 1 to 2 light-years across.

glucose
A **hexose** sugar and the most common simple sugar. It is important in animal **respiration** and other processes in organisms.

glycerol (C_3H_8O)
A sweet-tasting **alcohol** that can react with **fatty acids** to form fats. Each fat molecule consists of a molecule of glycerol combined with three molecules of fatty acids.

glycine (NH_2CH_2COOH)
The simplest **amino acid.**

glycogen
The chief **carbohydrate** used to store energy in animals. It is a **polysaccharide** consisting of a long, highly branched chain of **glucose** molecules.

glycosidic bond
The chemical bond by which **glucose** molecules join together to form **polysaccharides,** such as **starch** and **glycogen.** It is formed by a

condensation reaction and involves an **oxygen** atom becoming attached by a **covalent bond** to a **carbon** atom in each of two glucose molecules.

GMAN
→ **Global Microlensing Alert Network**

Godwin, Francis (1562–1633)
Bishop of Hereford and author of what is arguably the first science fiction story to be written in the English language. In *The Man in the Moone*,[460] published posthumously in 1638, Godwin conveys his astronaut, Domingo Gonsales, to the Moon in a chariot towed by trained geese (→ **Moon, voyages to**). (Gonsales had intended a less ambitious flight but discovers that the geese are in the habit of migrating a little further than ornithologists had supposed!) In keeping with both popular and scientific opinion of his day, Godwin accepted the notion that air filled the space between worlds and that the Moon was inhabited by intelligent human beings (→ **Moon, life on**). → **Wilkins, John; Cyrano de Bergerac, Savinien.**

Gold, Thomas (1920–   )
Austrian-born American professor emeritus of astronomy at **Cornell University,** founder and director of Cornell's Center for Radiophysics and Space Research, and onetime member of the **EASTEX** committee. He was the first to understand the **pulsar** phenomenon in terms of fast-spinning **neutron star**s. Among his many other original and frequently unorthodox ideas have been the **"garbage theory" of the origin of life** and the highly controversial notion that petroleum deposits formed nonbiologically at great depths. This would explain, Gold believes, the surprisingly high concentration of helium found in petroleum since as the liquid rose to the surface it would collect helium from the many kilometers of rocks through which it percolated. A few kilometers underground, as Gold sees it, the upwelling petroleum acts as a nutrient for deep-dwelling microorganisms that are the source of the biological molecules found in crude oil. In a recent book,[221] Gold argues that a number of planets, moons, and even asteroids in the solar system probably have internal **hydrocarbon** reserves, which could provide an energy source for subterranean microbes. **Titan,** in particular, which has **methane** and **ethane** in its atmosphere, he considers a promising place to look for subsurface life.

"Goldilocks"
Nickname of a planet discovered around the star **70 Virginis** because it may have surface conditions that are "just right" to allow the formation of liquid water—the single most important ingredient of life on our planet.

Goodricke, John (1764–86)
Dutch-born English amateur astronomer who was the first to realize that **Algol** is an **eclipsing binary** rather than an intrinsically variable star.

Gore, John Ellard (1845–1910)
Irish science popularizer and astronomer who, like Richard **Procter,** at the end of the nineteenth century argued in favor of the universality of planetary systems on the grounds that stars without planets would serve no purpose. In his review of Gore's *The Worlds of Space*,[232] under the title "The Living Things That May Be," H. G. **Wells** criticized the author for failing to speculate widely enough on the possible forms that extraterrestrials might take and suggested the possibility of **silicon-based life.**

Goudsmit, Samuel Abraham (1902–78)
Dutch-American physicist at the Brookhaven National Laboratory who, together with George Uhlenbeck, first proposed, in 1925, that subatomic particles have the property of spin. He was among the distinguished group of scientists which comprised the 1952 **Scientific Advisory Panel on Unidentified Flying Objects.**

Gould Belt
A local collection of stars and clouds of gas and dust that appears to be a spur connected to the lower edge of the **Orion Arm** of the Galaxy. It is about 700 light-years (230 parsecs) wide and 70 light-years (23 parsecs) thick. The Sun lies approximately 40 light-years (12 parsecs)

north of the belt's equatorial plane and about 325 light-years (100 parsecs) from its center.

Gould, Stephen Jay (1941–)

Harvard paleontologist, well known for his prolific popular writings and his formulation with Niles Eldridge of the theory of **punctuated equilibrium,** who has considered how evolutionary theory impacts on the likelihood and possible nature of extraterrestrial intelligence (**→ evolutionary theory and extraterrestrial life**). In his 1989 book *Wonderful Life,*[235] he argues against the repeatability of species and of humanoids in particular (**→ anthropomorphism**), pointing out the

> staggeringly improbable series of events, sensible enough in retrospect and subject to rigorous explanation, but utterly unpredictable and quite unrepeatable.... Wind back the tape of life to the early days of the Burgess shale; let it play again from an identical starting point, and the chance becomes vanishingly small that anything like human intelligence would grace the replay.

At the same time, he is quick to assert that while the contingency inherent in evolution suggests a lack of humanlike beings elsewhere, it does not, as some evolutionists such as George Gaylord **Simpson** and Ernest Mayr have claimed, imply a lack of extraterrestrial intelligence in general:

> When we use "evolutionary theory" to deny categorically the possibility of extraterrestrial intelligence, we commit the classic fallacy of substituting specifics (*individual* repeatability of humanoids) for classes (the probability that evolution elsewhere might produce a creature in the *general* class of intelligent beings). I can present a good argument from "evolutionary theory" against the repetition of anything like a human body elsewhere; I cannot extend it to the general proposition that intelligence in some form might pervade the universe.

Gould refers to the phenomenon of **convergent evolution** as evidence that intelligence in other forms may have arisen elsewhere.[234] Indeed, Gould is one of four evolutionists (the others being Tom Eisner of Cornell, David Raup of the University of Chicago, and Edward O. Wilson of Harvard) who have signed a pro-**SETI** petition in the belief that some finite chance exists of finding intelligence beyond the Earth. **→ extraterrestrial intelligence, forms of; extraterrestrial life, variety of**

graphite

An allotrope, or particular crystalline form, of **carbon.** It is a major component of **cosmic dust.**

gravitational collapse

The process by which material is drawn together as a result of its mutual gravitational attraction. Each particle of the infalling mass is accelerated toward the center of collapse and so gains kinetic energy that is generally manifested as pressure. Once this pressure has reached a certain level, it halts any further collapse; the stabilized object can then dispose of excess energy by radiating it into space. Gravitational collapse is the essential precursor of the formation of stars from **interstellar cloud**s and is also the dominant process in the closing stages of stellar evolution, when **white dwarf**s, **neutron star**s, and **black hole**s form.

gravitational lens

A phenomenon, predicted by Einstein's **general theory of relativity** and first discussed by Einstein in 1936, that occurs when the gravitational field of an object bends and focuses the light (and other radiation) from a more distant object lying along the same line of sight. When the distorted image of the background source is very small (on the order of a microarcsecond) or is formed locally within our own galaxy, the effect is referred to as **microlensing** and can be used as a sensitive method of searching for **extrasolar planets.** The type of image produced by a gravitational lens depends on the precise geometry of the alignment, the spatial features of the background source, and the strength and shape of the gravitational field around the lensing object. This means that if the lensing object happens to be a star and its planetary system, details about the orbiting planets can be worked out from observations of how the lens affects the light of a background star during alignment.

gravitational life

Hypothetical life that has evolved under and adapted to conditions of extreme gravity, either very high or very low. The prodigious strength-to-mass ratio of some terrestrial organisms (the rhinoceros beetle, for example, can manipulate objects of up to 850 times its own body mass) suggests that even complex mobile creatures might occur on worlds where the surface gravity is significantly higher than Earth's, providing that other basic biological requirements are not compromised. However, some scientists and science fiction writers have speculated on the prospects of life in places where the gravitational pull is far beyond the normal planetary range. Hal **Clement**'s *Mission of Gravity* and its sequels consider the nature of life on a world where the gravity pull varies between twice and seven hundred times that on Earth. Even more extraordinary are the conditions facing organisms that reside on the surface of a **neutron star,** as described by Frank **Drake** and Robert **Forward** (→ **neutron star, life on**). At the opposite extreme, in *The Black Cloud,* Fred **Hoyle** considers how freedom from planetary gravity in interstellar space might allow intelligence to evolve to a much higher order.

gravitational lock

Also known as "captured rotation," the tying of the **orbital period** of a planet or moon to its **axial period** through a tidal effect caused by the gravitational pull of the primary. The gravitational lock experienced by the Moon, for example, explains why it always keeps the same face directed toward the Earth. Likewise, the five inner satellites of Jupiter complete one orbit for every axial rotation. Mercury is locked in a 3-to-2 resonance with the Sun, so that it completes three orbits of the Sun (each lasting 88 days) in the time it takes to spin twice on its axis (→ **Mercury, rotation of**). The opportunity for life to evolve on planets around **red dwarf** stars may be compromised by this phenomenon. So small is the **habitable zone** around a red dwarf that any planets within this zone may be forced into a 1-to-1 lock, thus preventing the kind of climatic variations, such as wetting and drying, that may have been conducive to early biological development on

Earth. It may be possible, however, to envisage alternative pathways leading to life that do not require a day-night cycle.

gravitational microlensing

→ **microlensing**

gravitational waves

Vibrations in the fabric of **space-time** that travel at the **speed of light** and are predicted by Einstein's **general theory of relativity.** The most intense gravitational waves, resulting from large masses undergoing high accelerations, are expected to be produced when stars collapse or matter falls into a **black hole.** Although they have yet to be detected, evidence for their existence has come from observations of the only known **binary star** in which both components are **neutron star**s. A gradual minuscule increase in the orbital period of this system can be accounted for exactly if energy is being lost by gravitational waves at the rate predicted by general relativity.

gravity

One of the four fundamental forces in nature. It operates between all objects in the universe that have mass.

gravity assist

Also known as the "slingshot effect." This is an important spaceflight technique already used successfully on a number of interplanetary missions, including *Voyager,* the *Galileo* mission, and the *Cassini* mission, whereby the gravitational field of a planet is used to increase the speed and alter the course of a spacecraft without the need to expend fuel. The inbound flight path is carefully chosen so that the spacecraft will be whipped around the assisting body, being both accelerated and deflected on a hyperbolic trajectory. At first sight, it may seem as if something has been gained for nothing. However, the additional speed of the spacecraft has been won at the expense of the planet, which, as a result of the encounter, slows imperceptibly in its orbit and, as a result, moves fractionally closer to the Sun.

great chain of being

→ **chain of being, great**

Great Red Spot

A mobile, reddish, oval feature in the atmosphere of **Jupiter,** approximately 48,000 km (30,000 miles) long and 11,000 km (7,000 miles) wide. It has been studied for over a century and may have been first seen as much as 300 years ago. Its color varies from pale pink to brick red and may be due to the condensation of **phosphorus** at the cloud tops or to contamination by **organic** molecules such as nitriles produced by electrical storms in Jupiter's atmosphere.

Green Bank

The location in West Virginia of one of the major observing facilities of the **National Radio Astronomy Observatory.** It was here that Frank **Drake** used the 26-m (85-ft.) Howard E. Tatel **radio telescope** in Project **Ozma.** Further **SETI** programs, using the 91-m (140-ft.) dish at Green Bank were led by Gerrit Verschuur (1972), Benjamin **Zuckerman,** and Patrick Palmer (1972 and onward), and David **Black,** Jill **Tarter,** and colleagues (1977). The largest and most recent instrument to be built here was the **Green Bank Telescope.**

Green Bank conference (1961)

An informal, private gathering convened by the **Space Science Board** at **Green Bank,** West Virginia, in November 1961, on the subject of "Intelligent Extraterrestrial Life." Following the publication of Giuseppe **Cocconi** and Philip **Morrison**'s seminal paper on **SETI** and

High resolution image of the Great Red Spot taken by *Galileo.*
NASA/JPL/Caltech

Frank **Drake**'s pioneering Project **Ozma,** the aim was, in the words of the conference organizer, J. P. T. Pearman,

> to examine, in the light of present knowledge, the prospects for the existence of other societies in the galaxy with whom communications might be possible; to attempt an estimate of their number; to consider some of the technical problems involved in the establishment of communication; and to examine ways in which our understanding of the problem might be improved.

In addition to Pearman, the attendees were Dana **Atchley,** Melvin **Calvin,** Giuseppe Cocconi, Frank Drake, Su-Shu **Huang,** John **Lilly,** Philip Morrison, Bernard **Oliver,** Carl **Sagan,** and Otto **Struve.** The group whimsically constituted itself "The Order of the Dolphin" because of Lilly's work on dolphin communication (➔ **dolphins, as a form of alien intelligence**). Subsequently, Calvin had buttons made showing a dolphin emblem from an ancient Greek coin and sent one to each participant. During the conference, Calvin was awarded the Nobel Prize for Chemistry, an event anticipated by Pearman, who had smuggled in three celebratory bottles of champagne. Drake presented the now-famous **Drake Equation** in an effort to formulate mathematically the conference's central problem. During each session, a different factor of the equation was discussed.

Green Bank Telescope

A fully steerable **radio telescope** with an elliptical dish measuring 100 by 110 m (154 by 169 ft.), completed in 1998 at **Green Bank.**

Green, Nathaniel E.

British amateur astronomer and professional portrait artist who was among the first to suggest that Giovanni **Schiaparelli**'s *canali* on Mars were illusory. Based on his own observations, Green suggested, in 1878, that the linear markings described by the Italian were a product of drawing technique or that "the atmospheric vibrations have a tendency to cause a series of points in a line to appear connected together."[238] The optical illusion theory was later taken up by Edward **Maunder,** Simon

Newcomb, Eugène **Antoniadi,** and others. ➔ **Mars, canals of**

greenhouse effect

The process in which **greenhouse gases** in the atmosphere of a planet or moon transmit radiant energy from the **host star** but are opaque to the longer wavelengths of **infrared** radiation, or heat, which reradiate from the surface. This results in an elevation of the surface temperature. The Earth, for example, is about 35°C warmer overall than it would be without any greenhouse contribution, while the **runaway greenhouse effect** on Venus pushes up the surface temperature by as much as 500°C.

greenhouse gases

Gases, such as **carbon dioxide, methane,** and water vapor, that can play a significant part in elevating the temperature of a planet or moon through the **greenhouse effect.**

Greg, Percy (1836–1889)

English poet, novelist, and historian who wrote a number of science fiction tales, including *Across the Zodiac: The Story of a Wrecked Record*[240] (1880). This was possibly the first story to involve a powered spaceship (the craft in Jules **Verne**'s early Moon yarn having being shot out of a huge cannon). Greg describes a propulsion system based on "apergy"—an antigravity force. Arriving on a Lowellian Mars, the protagonist finds a race of technically advanced humanoids, one of whom he marries (qualifying the book perhaps for another sci-fi first) though it all ends unhappily when his Martian bride is killed.

Griffith, George (1857–1906)

Prolific author, traveler, and adventurer, described by Sam Moskowitz as "undeniably the most popular science fiction writer in England between 1893 and 1895 . . . it is entirely conceivable that Griffith's science fiction outsold that of Wells." His work, however, was overshadowed by that of H. G. **Wells** and was never influential in the United States because of the author's anti-American views. George Chetwynd Griffith-Jones portrayed a fully inhabited solar system in his *Stories of Other Worlds,* serialized in *Pearson's Magazine* from

**"The bones crumbled instantly to white powder."
Illustration by Stanley Wood for Griffith's "A Visit to the Moon."**

January to June 1900 and published in book form as *A Honeymoon in Space* (1901). Like Wells, he sets his extraterrestrial yarn explicitly in the context of Darwinian evolution. On their postnuptial tour of the Moon and planets, the eccentric earl of Redgrave and his young American wife discover that each world illustrates the effect of biological evolution according to the stage each has reached in its development. Jupiter is still primordial and volcanic, while Saturn, further along its life cycle, harbors giant reptiles and humanoids living in caves and trees. Following other Victorian writers of science fiction and romance, including Percy **Greg,** Robert **Cromie,** Gustavus **Pope,** and Wells, Griffith describes, on some of his worlds, civilizations that have surpassed our own technologically and intellectually but then degenerated in one way or another. On the Moon, the Redgraves find a race that has passed its peak and fallen into barbarous decay, while on Mars there are "purely intellectual beings" who, having regressed culturally, are now merely "cold" and

"calculating" (much as Wells describes his Martian invaders in *The War of the Worlds*). Yet not all is doom and gloom, and Griffith offers other evolutionary endpoints for intelligence. On Venus, life has matured spiritually rather than materially in an environment free from sin (a theological theme that would be taken up in greater earnest by C. S. **Lewis**). On the other hand, "superhuman intelligence" on Jupiter's moon Ganymede has managed to transcend the degrading Darwinian struggle for survival and attain a state in which high rationality and culture are combined.

Groom Lake
A dry lake bed located about 145 km (90 miles) north of Las Vegas. On the edge of Groom Lake is a high-security military research installation, part of the Tactical Fighter Weapons Center, that is known to ufologists worldwide as the infamous **Area 51.**

Groombridge 34
→ **stars, nearest**

Grudge, Project
The second investigation into the problem of "**flying disks**" (or UFOs, as they were soon to become known) carried out by the U.S. Air Force following the yearlong Project **Sign.** Unlike its predecessor, Grudge was dismissive of the **extraterrestrial hypothesis** and sought instead to explain away sightings in terms of natural phenomena (such as the planet Venus) or illusions. To this end, it appointed an astronomical consultant, J. Allen **Hynek.** However, Grudge's attempts to demystify all the claimed aerial activity had the opposite effect to that intended. Supporters of the extraterrestrial hypothesis began to ask why, if the Air Force regarded UFOs as easily explicable, it had shown so much interest in them? In 1950, Donald **Keyhoe** began making accusations of a cover-up. Ironically, at the end of the same year, Grudge had been wound down to such an extent that the investigation team consisted of a single junior officer. The Air Force's interest in UFOs was briefly revived by a new wave of sightings in 1951–52, following which Grudge gave way to Project **Blue Book.**

Gruithuisen, Franz von Paula (1774–1852)

German physician turned astronomer, among the most prolific of his age in terms of published output, and professor of astronomy at the University of Munich from 1826, who argued energetically in favor of advanced life on the Moon and inner planets (→ **Moon, life on**). On the subject of a lunar civilization he supported Johann **Schröter**'s similarly exuberant claims and wrote such papers as "Discovery of Many Distinct Traces of Lunar Inhabitants, Especially of One of Their Colossal Buildings" (1824), claiming that he had seen roads, cities, and a star-shaped "temple." Such extraordinary inferences, from what otherwise may have been sound telescopic observations, made him the object of ridicule by fellow astronomers, even those who appeared generally sympathetic to the idea of lunar life, such as Karl **Gauss,** Joseph von **Littrow,** and Wilhelm **Olbers.** Gruithuisen's overactive imagination also led him to suggest that the "ashen light" of Venus (→ **Venus, ashen light of**) was due to "festivals of fire given by the Venusians . . . celebrated either to correspond to changes in government or to religious periods."

guanine

A **purine base;** one of five organic bases found in the **nucleic acid**s of **cell**s. It pairs with **cytosine** in both **DNA** and **RNA.**

Gulliver (Viking experiment)

→ *Viking* **labeled release (LR) experiment**

Gulliver's Travels

→ **Swift, Jonathan, and the moons of Mars**

Guzman Prize

A prize of 100,000 francs, announced by Camille **Flammarion** in 1891, to "the person of whatever nation who will find the means within the next ten years of communicating with a star (planet or otherwise) and of receiving a response." It was bequeathed by a French widow, Clara Goguet Guzman, an admirer of Flammarion's writings, in honor of her son Pierre Guzman. → **communication, with the Moon and planets**

H I region

An **interstellar cloud** composed primarily of atomic **hydrogen.**

H II region

A part of space where the **hydrogen** in the **interstellar medium** is in an **ionized** rather than a neutral state. Generally, these are regions where **OB stars** are pouring large amounts of **ultraviolet** radiation into the surrounding cloud from which they were recently formed. The ultraviolet light strips **electron**s away from hydrogen atoms by the process known as photoionization. Then, as the electrons recombine with protons (hydrogen nuclei), they emit a characteristic series of **emission line**s as they cascade down through the energy levels of the atom. The visible radiation in these lines imparts to H II regions their beautiful colored glows.

habitable zone (HZ)

An imaginary spherical shell surrounding a star throughout which the surface temperatures of any planets present might be conducive to the origin and development of life as we know it. Also referred to as the "ecosphere."

The single most crucial factor to the evolution of terrestrial life has been the ready availability of liquid **water.** Not only does water serve as the **solvent** for biochemical reactions, but it also furnishes the **hydrogen** upon which living matter depends. Water will remain liquid under a pressure of 1 bar (terrestrial sea-level pressure) between 0°C and 100°C. Even on Earth, however, geographical, seasonal, and diurnal variations can cause the temperature to fall well below freezing (as low as −70°C in Antarctica), yet life can survive under these conditions. At the other end of the scale, although most terrestrial organisms cannot endure temperatures consistently above 45°C, **hyperthermophiles** have been found thriving around **hydrothermal vent**s at 113°C.

It is reasonable to assume that if the Earth had been marginally closer or further from the Sun, life of some kind would still have evolved on it. But the limits of the Sun's HZ are not easy to fix. The discovery of primitive life, or fossils, on **Mars** would extend the HZ of the Sun out to at least 225 million km (140 million miles). On the other hand, the absence of Martian biology would not rule out the possibility that if the Earth, with its greater mass able to retain a denser atmosphere, had orbited at the distance of Mars it would have been capable of nurturing life. Indeed, Mars itself enjoyed warmer, wetter conditions in the past under which primitive organisms may have evolved. Much further from the Sun are the **gas giants** and their large moons, at first sight inhospitable to life. Yet the effect of **tidal heating** on these worlds, resulting possibly, in the case of **Europa** and **Callisto,** in the existence of large amounts of subsurface liquid water, makes them biologically interesting.[480] Were life to be discovered on one of Jupiter's moons, the outer margin of the Sun's HZ would be pushed out to almost 800 million km (500 million miles). Its inner margin is somewhat easier to define. **Venus** is approximately terrestrial in size, mass, and composition, but its proximity to the Sun has prevented its development from following an Earth-like course. On our own planet, temperatures were low enough for most of the water vapor released in large quantities from primordial volcanoes or colliding **comet**s to condense and form oceans of water (➔ **oceans, origin of**). These oceans subsequently mopped up the bulk of the **carbon dioxide** also produced by volcanic activity. On Venus, however, it was too hot from the outset for the water vapor to condense. As a result, the massive amounts of carbon dioxide pumped into the primitive Venusian atmosphere remained there and served to bring about a **runaway greenhouse effect.** The already uncomfortably high surface temperature soared to around 460°C, at which point any kind of complex biochemistry along terrestrial lines was ruled out. Based on present knowledge, therefore, and until more is known about conditions on worlds such as Europa (and possibly **Titan**), we can reasonably put the extent of the Sun's HZ for an Earth-sized planet at 120 million to 240 million km (75 million to 150 million miles)—that is, 0.8 to 1.6 times the radius of the Earth's orbit.

Regarding other stars, the size and location of the HZ depend on the nature of the star in question.[259, 313] In general, hot, luminous stars—those of spectral types "earlier" than that of the Sun (G3–G9, F, A, B, and O)—will have wide HZs, the inner margins of which are located relatively far out. For example, to enjoy terrestrial temperatures around **Sirius** (twenty-six times more luminous than the Sun), an Earth-sized planet would have to orbit at about the distance of Jupiter from the Sun. By contrast, if the Sun were replaced by Epsilon Indi,

which has only about one tenth the Sun's luminosity, the Earth would need to be in a Mercurian orbit to receive its present level of warmth. The situation becomes even more extreme in the case of a **red dwarf,** such as **Barnard's Star** (about one two thousandth as luminous as the Sun), the HZ of which would extend only between about 750,000 and 2 million km (0.02 to 0.06 AU). Even if planets exist so close to their parent star (as now seems likely following the discovery of **epistellar Jovians**) the development of life might be made problematic by a **gravitational lock.**

By contrast, the HZ of a highly luminous star would in principle be very wide, its inner margin beginning perhaps several hundred million kilometers out and stretching to a distance of a billion kilometers or more. However, this promising scenario is spoiled by the fact that massive, bright stars are much more short-lived than their smaller, dimmer cousins. In the case of the giant **O star**s and **B star**s, these very massive objects race through their life cycles in only a few tens of millions of years—too quickly to allow even primitive life-forms to emerge. Given the rate of evolution of life on Earth, it is possible that microorganisms might have time to develop on worlds around **A star**s (➔ **stars, lifetimes of**). But in the search for extraterrestrial intelligence, the HZs around **F star**s and later must be considered the most likely places to look (➔ **Sun-like stars; target stars**). Among **extrasolar planets** discovered to date, only one, the companion of **70 Virginis,** appears to move within its star's HZ. It is, however, an extremely massive planet with an orbit of high **eccentricity,** both of which factors argue against it supporting a terrestrial-type ecosystem.

Of course, it might be that life can develop along very varied lines. If it could be based on **ammonia** as a solvent, instead of water, this would allow it to thrive at low temperatures. Then again, it may be that life is possible in the atmospheres of Jupiter-like planets. Such novel biological forms would extend the HZs of stars beyond those considered.[161] The idea of galactic HZs, and of preferred regions within the Galaxy to search for intelligent life, has also been discussed.[35]

Note

If all of the complicating factors discussed above are ignored and the habitable zone is defined simply as the distance from a star where the effective temperature is in the range 0–100°C, it is straightforward to calculate the radii of the HZ's inner and outer bounds. The relevant formula is:

$$L = 4\pi r^2 \sigma T^4$$

where L is the star's luminosity, r is the distance from the center of the star, σ is the Stefan-Boltzmann constant (= 5.67×10^{-8} W m^{-2}K^{-4}), and T is the effective temperature (in Kelvin). For the Sun, this yields a range for the HZ of 0.7 to 1.5 AU. The HZ range for other stars can then be calculated easily since, from the above formula:

$$L_{star}/L_{Sun} = r_{star}^2/r_{Sun}^2$$

In the case of **Vega**, $L_{star}/L_{Sun} = 53$, which gives a range for HZ of 5.1 to 10.9 AU. In the case of

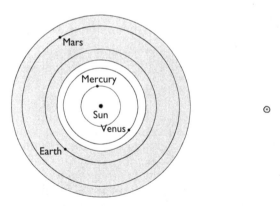

Comparison of the estimated habitable zones around the Sun and a typical red dwarf.

Kapteyn's Star, $L_{star}/L_{Sun} = 0.004$ and the corresponding HZ range is 0.044 to 0.095 AU.

Haldane, J(ohn) B(urdon) S(anderson) (1892–1964)

British-born biochemist (later a citizen of India) who, in a 1929 essay,[250] speculated about the chemical origin of life on Earth. Haldane proposed that **carbon dioxide,** together with **ammonia** and water vapor, made up the bulk of the Earth's primitive atmosphere (➔ **Earth, early history of**). His reasoning was that coal came from plants, which, in turn, obtain their **carbon** from carbon dioxide in the air; therefore, before life came into being, all the carbon now in coal must have existed as carbon dioxide. Much of the **nitrogen** now in the atmosphere, he argued, would have been combined as nitride salts in the Earth's crust. Water acting on these nitrides would have released ammonia, giving rise to a **reducing atmosphere.** Before there were plants to give off oxygen, Haldane pointed out, this gas would have been absent from the atmosphere. Therefore, there would have been no protective layer of **ozone** to block **ultraviolet** radiation from the Sun. Citing experiments carried out two years earlier by E. C. C. Baly and his colleagues at Liverpool, Haldane concluded that the effect of this energetic radiation on the primitive carbon dioxide–ammonia–water vapor atmosphere would be to give rise to simple **organic** chemicals, including, probably, **amino acids.** These organic compounds would accumulate in the Earth's oceans until they "reached the consistency of hot, dilute soup." Further chemical synthesis would take place, ultimately giving rise to the first primitive organisms, which would then feed on the rich organic nutrients around them. ➔ **Oparin-Haldane Theory**

Haldane also wrote on the possibility of **silicon-based life.** His semifictional essay "The Last Judgement" in *Possible Worlds*[249] (1927) provided some of the basis for Olaf **Stapledon**'s extrapolation of the future of mankind in *Last and First Men,* while "On Being the Right Size" (also from *Possible Worlds*) discusses some of the factors that may constrain the size and morphology of extraterrestrials.

Hale, George Ellery (1868–1938)

American astrophysicist, director of **Yerkes Observatory** (1897–1904), who moved to **Mount Wilson Observatory** in 1904 and thereafter initiated construction of some of the world's largest telescopes, including the 2.5-m (100-in.) Hooker telescope. The 5-m (200-in.) instrument at **Palomar Observatory,** commissioned ten years after his death, was named in his honor. Although not outspoken on the subject of extraterrestrial life, he did play a role in discrediting the hypothesis of the Martian canals (➔ **Mars, canals of**). In January 1910, he wrote to Eugène **Antoniadi:**[18]

> In spite of the very fine seeing on certain occasions, which required a power of 800 to show the smallest details with an aperture of 44 inches, no trace of narrow straight lines, or geometrical structure, was observed.... I am thus inclined to agree with you in your opinion (which coincides with that of Newcomb) that the so-called "canals" of Schiaparelli are made up of small irregular regions.

Hall, Asaph (1829–1907)

American astronomer who in 1877 at the **U.S. Naval Observatory** discovered the two small Martian moons, **Phobos** and **Deimos.** He apparently entertained the notion of intelligent life on Mars at this time, for in his discovery paper he writes about how the moons would appear to "Martian astronomers" (➔ **Mars, life on**).

Halley's Comet

The most famous **short-period comet.** It orbits the Sun once every 76 years and has been observed regularly for more than 2,200 years. Upon its return to the inner solar system in 1986, it was met by a small flotilla of spacecraft, including *Giotto,* which sent back images of Halley's potato-shaped **nucleus,** measuring 16 by 8 km (10 by 5 miles). The nucleus is dark, reflecting only 4 percent of the sunlight falling on it, and rotates once every 3.7 days. On the sunward side, temperatures were observed to reach 77°C (350 K), which, in the zero pressure of space, is enough to turn ice into vapor. Measurements by *Giotto*'s mass spectrometer indicated a composition for Halley of 45 percent water ice, 28 percent stony minerals, and 27 percent **organic** material.

Halley-type comet

A recently distinguished subcategory of **short-period comet**s. Also known as intermediate-period comets, Halley-type comets have periods of 20 to 200 years and are believed to originate in the **Oort Cloud.**

halo, galactic
➔ **galactic halo**

halophiles

Microbes, including **bacteria** and **archaea,** that live, grow, and multiply in highly saline environments. Extreme halophiles, all of which are archaea, inhabit water that is up to ten times more saline than ordinary seawater (approximately 30 percent salt content) including that found in the Great Salt Lake in Utah, Owens Lake in California, the Dead Sea, and saltines. They are mostly **aerobic,** have specialized **cell wall**s, and incorporate pigmentation in the form of **bacteriorhodopsin,** for photosynthesis, and **carotenoids,** for **ultraviolet** protection. The suggestion that Jupiter's moon **Callisto** may have an underground saline ocean (➔ **Callisto, ocean and possible life on**) raises the possibility that primitive life-forms similar to terrestrial halophiles might be found there, as well as on the neighboring moon, **Europa.** ➔ **extremophiles**

handedness
➔ **chirality**

haploid

Descriptive of a **nucleus, cell,** or organism that has only a single set of unpaired **chromosome**s, i.e., half the number of chromosomes found in **diploid** cells. Reproductive cells, together with some animals, **protists, fungi,** and certain stages in the life cycle of plants, are haploid. The **fusion** of two haploid cells restores the normal (diploid) number.

HARPS
➔ **High Accuracy Radial Velocity Planetary Search**

Harvard College Observatory

Founded in 1839 and located in Harvard, Massachusetts. The observatory carries out a broad program of research in astronomy and astrophysics and includes among its instruments the 0.38-m (15-in.) "Great Refractor," installed in 1847, which for 20 years was the largest telescope in the United States. In 1973, the Harvard College Observatory became part of the **Harvard-Smithsonian Center for Astrophysics.**

Harvard SETI Group

Researchers at Harvard University have been actively involved with **SETI** since the late 1970s. The first high-resolution Harvard search took place in 1978 at Arecibo (➔ **Harvard-Arecibo off-line SETI**). This was followed by **"Suitcase SETI"** (1981–82), Project **Sentinel** (1983–85), Project **META** (1985–94), and Project **BETA** (1995–   ).

Harvard-Arecibo off-line SETI

A **SETI** project conducted by Harvard researchers in 1978, using the **Arecibo radio telescope,** that targeted two hundred candidate stars. The search was centered on the **21-centimeter line** of neutral hydrogen and examined 1-kHz **instantaneous bandwidth** segments with a **resolution bandwidth** of 0.015 Hz (the highest resolution and sensitivity ever achieved in SETI). The tiny bandwidth of 1 kHz meant that a transmitting civilization would have had to precompensate the carrier beacon for its motion relative to the Sun—an unlikely but not unfeasible scenario.[283] Analysis of the data took place off-line by long Fourier transforms. A follow-up search at Arecibo was carried out by the Harvard group in 1982 using **"Suitcase SETI."** ➔ **Harvard SETI group**

Harvard-Smithsonian Center for Astrophysics (CfA)

A joint collaboration between the **Smithsonian Astrophysical Observatory** and the **Harvard College Observatory,** located in Cambridge, Massachusetts. The center's research mission is to study the origin, evolution, and ultimate fate of the Universe and includes searches for **extrasolar planets** and **circumstellar disk**s. In 1999, it independently announced the discovery of the two outer planets in the **Upsilon Andromedae** system. Among the facilities operated by the center are the **Multiple Mirror Telescope** (MMT) and the Fred Lawrence **Whipple Observatory.**

Harvard-Smithsonian radio telescope

A 26-m (84-ft.) fully steerable **radio telescope** located at the Harvard-Smithsonian Agassiz station in Harvard, Massachusetts. It is used in Project **BETA** and was earlier used in Project **META.**

Hat Creek Observatory

A **radio telescope** observatory near Mount Lassen in northern California, founded in 1960 and operated by the Radio Astronomy Laboratory of the **University of California, Berkeley.** It is currently the site of a ten-telescope array known as the BIMA (Berkeley-Illinois-Maryland Association) Array and may become the site of the **One Hectare Telescope** for use in **SETI.**

Haute-Provence Observatory (Observatoire de Haute-Provence)

A French national facility established in 1937 and operated by the Centre National de la Recherche Scientifique (CNRS). It is built on a plateau 645 m (2,100 ft.) above sea level at Saint-Michel in southern France, about 95 km (60 miles) north of Marseilles. Among its instruments are reflecting telescopes with apertures of 1.93 m (76 in.), 1.52 m (60 in.), 1.2 m (47 in.), and 80 cm (36 in.), and a 60/90-cm (24/36-in.) Schmidt camera. Attached to the 1.93-m telescope is the **Elodie** spectrograph used to search for **extrasolar planets.**

HD

The designation of an object in the Henry Draper Catalogue.

HD 10697

A star with a recently discovered **extrasolar planet.**

Host Star	
Distance	97.8 light-years (30 parsecs)
Spectral type	G5 IV
Apparent magnitude	6.29
Planet	
Mass	6.59 M_J
Semimajor axis	2.0 AU (300 million km, 186 million mi.)
Orbital period	1083 days
Eccentricity	0.12
Discovery	1999, San Francisco State University Planet Search
Method of discovery	Radial velocity

HD 37124

A star with a recently discovered **extrasolar planet.**

Host Star	
Distance	107.5 light-years (33 parsecs)
Spectral type	G4 IV-V
Apparent magnitude	7.68
Planet	
Mass	1.04 M_J
Semimajor axis	0.585 AU (87.8 million km, 54.5 million mi.)
Orbital period	155 days
Eccentricity	0.19
Discovery	1999, San Francisco State University Planet Search
Method of discovery	Radial velocity

HD 75289

A star similar to the Sun but somewhat brighter in the constellation of Vela. Around it has been found an **epistellar Jovian,** the sixth in order of discovery, with a mass only 1.4 times that of Saturn. HD 75289 appears to be similar in age to the Sun, although, as in the case of most other stars with known giant planets, its metal content is about twice the solar composition. → **extrasolar planets**

Host Star	
Distance	94.3 light-years (28.9 parsecs)
Spectral type	G0 V
Apparent magnitude	6.35
Temperature	5,700°C (5,970 K)
Luminosity	1.99 L_S
Mass	1.05 M_S
Planet	
Mass	0.42 M_J
Semimajor axis	0.046 AU (6.9 million km, 11 million mi.)
Orbital period	3.51 days
Eccentricity	0.053
Discovery	1999, by Michel Mayor et al., Coralie, at Leonard Euler Telescope
Method of discovery	Radial velocity

HD 114762

A Sun-like star with an unseen companion, first reported in 1989 and described by its discoverers as "probably a **brown dwarf,** maybe even a giant planet."[330] The existence of this companion has since been confirmed, though its nature remains controversial.[124, 252] It lies close to the upper mass limit for **extrasolar planets** and the lower mass limit for brown dwarfs. If it proves to be planetary in nature, the high **eccentricity** of its orbit would place it in the category known as **eccentric Jovians**.

Host Star	
Distance	91.3 light-years (28 parsecs)
Spectral type	F9 V
Apparent magnitude	7.3
Planet	
Mass	11 M_J
Semimajor axis	0.34 AU (45 million km, 28 million mi.)
Orbital period	84.0 days
Eccentricity	0.33
Discovery	1989, by David Latham et al. at Harvard-Smithsonian Center for Astrophysics
Method of discovery	Radial velocity

HD 130322

A star with a recently discovered **extrasolar planet**.

Host Star	
Distance	97.8 light-years (30 parsecs)
Spectral type	K0 III
Apparent magnitude	8.04
Planet	
Mass	1.08 M_J
Semimajor axis	0.088 AU (13.2 million km, 8.2 million mi.)
Orbital period	10.72 days
Eccentricity	0.048
Discovery	1999, Geneva Observatory
Method of discovery	Radial velocity

HD 134987

A star with a recently discovered **extrasolar planet**.

Host Star	
Distance	81.5 light-years (25 parsecs)
Spectral type	G5 V
Apparent magnitude	6.45
Planet	
Mass	1.58 M_J
Semimajor axis	0.78 AU (117 million km, 73 million mi.)
Orbital period	260 days
Eccentricity	0.25
Discovery	1999, San Francisco State University Planet Search
Method of discovery	Radial velocity

HD 168443

A Sun-like star around which has been found a high-mass **extrasolar planet** in a small orbit of very high **eccentricity**.[378]

Host Star	
Distance	~108 light-years (~33 parsecs)
Spectral type	G5 V
Apparent magnitude	6.92
Temperature	5,160°C (5,430 K)
Luminosity	2.1 L_S
Mass	0.95 M_S
Planet	
Mass	8.13 M_J
Semimajor axis	0.303 AU (41.6 million km, 25.8 million mi.)
Orbital period	58.1 days
Eccentricity	0.52
Discovery	1998, by Geoffrey Marcy, Paul Butler, Steven Vogt, Debra Fischer, and M. Liu at Lick and Keck Observatories
Method of discovery	Radial velocity

HD 177830

A star with a recently discovered **extrasolar planet.**

Host Star	
Distance	186 light-years (59 parsecs)
Spectral type	K0
Apparent magnitude	7.18
Planet	
Mass	1.28 M$_J$
Semimajor axis	1.00 AU (150 million km, 93 million mi.)
Orbital period	391 days
Eccentricity	0.43
Discovery	1999, San Francisco State University Planet Search
Method of discovery	Radial velocity

HD 187123

A star almost identical to the Sun,[231] in the constellation of Cygnus, around which has been discovered a planet with at least half the mass of Jupiter. At one ninth the average separation distance of Mercury from the Sun, HD 187123b orbits more closely to its host star than any other planet yet discovered.[89] → **extrasolar planets**

Host Star	
Distance	153 light-years (47 parsecs)
Spectral type	G5 V
Apparent magnitude	7.79
Temperature	5,560°C (5,830 K)
Luminosity	1.35 L$_S$
Mass	1.0 M$_S$
Planet	
Mass	0.52 M$_J$
Semimajor axis	0.042 AU (6.3 million km, 3.9 million mi.)
Orbital period	3.10 days
Eccentricity	0.03
Discovery	1998, by Paul Butler, Geoffrey Marcy, Steven Vogt, and Kevin Apps at Keck Observatory
Method of discovery	Radial velocity

HD 192263

A star with a recently discovered **extrasolar planet.**

Host Star	
Distance	64.9 light-years (19.9 parsecs)
Spectral type	K2 V
Apparent magnitude	8.1
Planet	
Mass	0.76 M$_J$
Semimajor axis	0.15 AU (22.5 million km, 14 million mi.)
Orbital period	23.87 days
Eccentricity	0.03
Discovery	1999, Geneva Observatory
Method of discovery	Radial velocity

HD 195019

A Sun-like star around which has been found a three-Jupiter-mass **extrasolar planet** of the **epistellar Jovian** type. Spectroscopic measurements of the host suggest that it has a "quiet" **chromosphere** (an important factor in its suitability to support nearby life) and a metal content that is somewhat greater than that of the Sun.[194]

Host Star	
Distance	65 light-years (20 parsecs)
Spectral type	G3 IV–V
Apparent magnitude	6.91
Temperature	5,330°C (5,700 K)
Luminosity	2.35 L$_S$
Mass	0.98 M$_S$
Planet	
Mass	3.43 M$_J$
Semimajor axis	0.14 AU (21 million km, 13 million mi.)
Orbital period	18.3 days
Eccentricity	0.05
Discovery	1998, by Geoffrey Marcy, Paul Butler, Steven Vogt, and Debra Fischer at Lick and Keck Observatories
Method of discovery	Radial velocity

HD 209458

A star with a recently found **extrasolar planet.** Calculations by the planet's discoverers, Geoffrey **Marcy** and colleagues, indicated that it had its orbital plane edge-on to the Earth so that it might be seen to transit the star. This was confirmed by Greg Henry of Tennesse State University, using an automatic telescope in southern Arizona, who confirmed a 1.7 percent drop in the star's brightness as the planet made its passage across the stellar disk. The amount of dimming of the star's light gave the first-ever accurate measure of the size and density of an extrasolar world.

Host Star	
Distance	153 light-years (47 parsecs)
Spectral type	G0 V
Apparent magnitude	7.65
Planet	
Mass	0.63 M_J
Radius	1.27 R_J
Surface gravity (Earth = 1)	0.99
Semimajor axis	0.045 AU (6.8 million km, 4.2 million mi.)
Orbital period	3.52 days
Eccentricity	0.02
Discovery	1999, San Francisco State University Planet Search
Method of discovery	Radial velocity

HD 210277

A star slightly larger than the Sun[231] in the constellation of Aquarius, around which has been discovered a planet similar in mass to Jupiter. This is the first **extrasolar planet** to be found whose average distance from its **host star** is nearly the same as that of the Earth from the Sun. However, its orbit is so elongated that its separation from HD 210277 varies between less than the Venus-to-Sun distance and more than the Mars-to-Sun distance. As a result, the planet must be subject to extreme seasonal changes in temperature.

Host Star	
Distance	69 light-years (~21 parsecs)
Spectral type	G0 V
Apparent magnitude	6.63
Temperature	5,300 °C (5,570 K)
Luminosity	0.93 L_S
Mass	0.92 M_S
Planet	
Mass	1.28 M_J
Semimajor axis	1.15 AU (172 million km, 107 million mi.)
Orbital period	437 days
Eccentricity	0.45
Discovery	1998, by Geoffrey Marcy, Paul Butler, Steven Vogt, Debra Fischer, and M. Liu at Keck Observatory
Method of discovery	Radial velocity

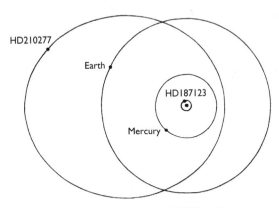

Comparison of the orbits of HD 210277 and HD 187123 with those of Earth and Mercury.

HD 217107

A Sun-like star around which has been found an **extrasolar planet** slightly more massive than Jupiter in an extraordinarily small orbit of significant eccentricity.[194]

Host Star	
Distance	64.2 light-years (19.7 parsecs)
Spectral type	G7V
Apparent magnitude	6.16
Temperature	5,090°C (5,360 K)
Luminosity	1.32 L$_S$
Mass	0.96 M$_S$
Planet	
Mass (Jupiter = 1)	1.28
Semimajor axis	0.074 AU (11.1 million km, 6.9 million mi.)
Orbital period	7.11 days
Eccentricity	0.14
Discovery	1998, by Debra Fischer, Geoffrey Marcy, Paul Butler, Steven Vogt, and Kevin Apps at Lick and Keck Observatories
Method of discovery	Radial velocity

HD 222582

A star with a recently discovered **extrasolar planet.**

Host Star	
Distance	137 light-years (42 parsecs)
Spectral type	G5
Apparent magnitude	7.70
Planet	
Mass	5.4 M$_J$
Semimajor axis	1.35 AU (202 million km, 126 million mi.)
Orbital period	576 days
Eccentricity	0.71
Discovery	1999, San Francisco State University Planet Search
Method of discovery	Radial velocity

heat capacity

The amount of heat needed to raise the temperature of a substance (or object) through 1°C. It is measured in calories per g-°C. The high heat capacity of **water** is one of the factors that makes it such an effective solvent in biological systems. → **heat of vaporization**

heat of vaporization

The amount of energy needed to change a liquid into a vapor once it has reached its boiling point. Together with **heat capacity,** it is an important property in determining how effectively a **solvent** can regulate the internal temperature of an organism. The fact that **water** has both a high heat of vaporization and a high heat capacity makes it ideal in this respect, and is one of the reasons it is so essential to life as we know it.

heavy element

In astronomical terms, any element heavier than **helium.** Astronomers also refer to such elements as "metals" (although many, such as carbon, are not). Heavy elements, which are essential for the formation of planetary systems (→ **heavy element concentration, related to the occurrence of planets**) and the evolution of life, are formed only by **nucleosynthesis** inside stars.

heavy element concentration, related to the occurrence of planets

In the absence of **heavy elements,** it appears impossible that planets or life can form (→ **planetary systems, formation of**). But more particularly it has turned out that of the host stars of known **extrasolar planets,** the great majority have an above-average heavy element content. Several, indeed, boast the highest known concentration of such elements in our region of the Galaxy, with up to three times the level found in the Sun. This bias has inspired theorists to examine the possible consequences for planet formation and for the frequency with which planets occur in the Galaxy. Some astronomers, such as Guillermo Gonzalez and his colleagues,[228] have suggested that there may be the equivalent of a **habitable zone** in the Galaxy, within which stars must lie in order to be able to acquire planetary systems. This narrow band located roughly halfway out in the **galactic disk** would harbor material with sufficient heavy element content to enable the condensation of planets in **circumstellar disks** but not so high as to produce large amounts of debris, which would shatter newly formed worlds or lead to planets being thrown around by mutual interactions. Other researchers, including Douglas Lin, have argued that there is such a wide variation of heavy element concentration within our own solar system that minor variations in heavy element enrichment elsewhere may not be such an important factor in planet formation. Rather, according to this idea, the high level of these elements in stars known to have planets may be a consequence of one or two planets having fallen into their primaries and consequently enriched the star's surface layers. Stellar ingestion of large numbers of comets and asteroids could have the same effect.

heavy water (HDO or D_2O)
Water containing a substantial proportion of **deuterium** atoms.

Hegel, Georg Wilhelm Friedrich (1770–1831)
German philosopher whose anthropocentric philosophy, in which he held that the Earth is the best of all possible worlds, led him to oppose **pluralism.**

Helene
A small moon of **Saturn,** known as a **Dione** trojan because it has the same orbit as its larger companion, preceding it by 60°. ➔ **Saturn, moons of**

Discovery	1980, by Pierre Laques and Jean Lecacheux
Mean distance from Saturn	378,000 km (234,900 mi.)
Diameter	36 × 32 × 30 km (22 × 20 × 19 mi.)
Orbital period	2.737 days (2 days 17 hours 41 minutes)
Orbital eccentricity	0.005
Orbital inclination	0.2°
Visual albedo	0.7

heliocentric
Sun-centered, as in the cosmological worldview expounded by Nicolaus **Copernicus.**

heliopause
The boundary of the **heliosphere,** where the pressure at the outer part of the heliosphere equals that of the surrounding **interstellar medium** (ISM). It is believed to lie 100 to 150 AU from the Sun in the direction in which the Sun is moving, but much further out downstream. Additionally, the heliopause distance probably fluctuates in response to changes in ISM and **solar wind** conditions. The thickness of the heliopause is unknown but could be tens of astronomical units. Upstream of the heliopause, in the ISM, theory suggests the existence of a bow shock where the incoming interstellar wind first reacts to its impending collision with the Sun's magnetosphere. Downstream from the Sun is thought to be a long, turbulent tail. The extent to which interstellar matter penetrates inside the heliopause is open to question but may be partially determined by the first **interstellar probes.**

heliosphere
The region of space, surrounding the Sun, which is inflated by the **solar wind** and within

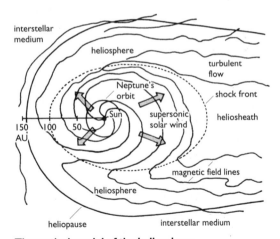

Theoretical model of the heliosphere.
Originally presented at the 1983 AAS/AIA Astrodynamics Conference held August 22–25, 1983, Lake Placid, New York, and originally published in the AAS publication *Astrodynamics 1983,* American Astronautical Society (AAS), AAS Microfiche Series, vol. 45, paper no. AAS 83-308, "Prospects for *Voyager* Extra-Planetary and Interstellar Mission" by Robert J. Cesarone, Andrey B. Sergeyevsky, and Stuart J. Kerridge (JPL). Reprinted with permission of the AAS: American Astronautical Society Publications Office, P. O. Box 28130, San Diego, CA 92198.

which the Sun exerts a magnetic influence. Despite its name, the heliosphere is almost certainly greatly elongated due to the movement of the Sun with respect to the **interstellar medium.** It is bounded by the **heliopause.** Data returned by *Pioneer 10, Voyager 1,* and *Voyager 2* (contact with *Pioneer 11* has been lost), as these probes head for interstellar space, will help further characterize the heliosphere.

helium (He)

A chemically inert **element** that is the second most abundant element in the universe. It occurs commonly in stars and in the atmospheres of **gas giant**s. ➔ **elements, cosmic abundance of**

Atomic number 2; density 0.18 g/dm³; melting point −269.7°C; boiling point −268.9°C

Hellas

Physicist Philip **Morrison** estimated that what we know about the civilization of ancient Greece amounts to somewhat under 10 billion **bit**s of information—a quantity he therefore suggested be called a "Hellas." The communication of cultural information between stars, he proposed, can be conveniently discussed in terms of this unit. For example, the amount of information we would need to convey to an extraterrestrial race in order to give a comprehensive picture of our own culture would be on the order of 100 Hellades.

Helmholtz, Hermann von (1821–94)

The leading German physicist of his day and an early advocate of the idea of **panspermia.** In a public lecture delivered in 1871 he said:

Who can say whether the comets and meteors…may not scatter germs of life wherever a new world has reached the stage in which it is a suitable dwelling place for organic beings? We might, perhaps, consider such life to be allied to ours, at least in germ, however different the form it might assume in adapting to its new dwelling place.

Criticizing this hypothesis, which was put forward independently in the same year by William **Thomson** (Lord Kelvin), Friedrich **Zöllner** argued that **meteorite**s reach such high temperature on falling through the Earth's atmosphere that any organisms contained within them would be incinerated. In reply, Helmholtz pointed out that the interior of a meteorite would remain cool during its passage through the air and that, in any case, organisms on the surface might be thrown free before the temperature became intolerable. ➔ **Arrhenius, Svante August; ballistic panspermia**

Henry Draper Catalogue

A catalogue of 225,300 stars down to an **apparent magnitude** of 8, compiled at **Harvard College Observatory** and published in 1918 through 1924.

14 Herculis

An orange-yellow **K star.** Its abundance of **heavy element**s is greater than that of the Sun and the discovery that it has a massive planet lends support to the idea that such large worlds tend to form in heavy-element-enriched environments.[231] The planetary companion of 14 Herculis has a mass about three times that of Jupiter and moves in an eccentric orbit about its host star with a period of 4.4 years. This puts it in the category of **classical Jovians** along with the companion of **47 Ursae Majoris,** which it most closely resembles. ➔ **extrasolar planets**

Host Star	
Distance	55 light-years (17 parsecs)
Spectral type	K0 V
Mass	0.79 M_S
Apparent magnitude	6.67
Temperature	4,830°C (5,100 K)
Luminosity	0.75 L_S
Planet	
Mass	3.3 M_J
Semimajor axis	2.5 AU (380 million km, 230 million mi.)
Orbital period	1,619 days
Eccentricity	0.35
Discovery	1998, by Michel Mayor et al. at Haute-Provence Observatory
Method of discovery	Radial velocity

Herschel, (Frederick) William (1738–1822)

Hanoverian-born British astronomer to George III and one of the greatest of observers, who effectively founded stellar astronomy and, in 1781, discovered Uranus. By counting stars in different parts of the sky, he concluded in 1785 that the Sun is near the center of a flat system of stars roughly five times wider than it is thick. At first, he agreed with Thomas **Wright** that nebulas might be external galaxies, but later he changed his mind when he failed to resolve them telescopically into stars. Despite his astronomical credentials, in matters of astrobiology his contributions were less impressive. Swimming against the tide of professional opinion, he insisted that the habitability of the Moon was an "almost absolute certainty" (**➔ Moon, life on**) and, in common with Isaac **Newton** before him, was convinced that there were intelligent beings, which he called "solarions," living *inside* the Sun, which he believed to be a large planet with a cool, temperate interior (**➔ Sun, life on**). Sunspots he took to be apertures in the Sun's bright outer shell through which we could see inside and the solarions could peek out at the stars. His observations of Mars in the 1780s led him to surmise that the bright areas at the poles were ice caps, the dark patches were seas, and the lighter, yellowish areas were dry land. The inhabitants, he concluded, "probably enjoy a situation in many respects similar to ours" (**➔ Mars, life on**). His work was continued by his son (**➔ Herschel, John Frederick William**).

Herschel, John Frederick William (1792–1871)

British astronomer who continued the work of his famous father [**➔ Herschel, (Frederick) William**] on binary stars, star clusters, and nebulas. In 1832 he took a large telescope to the Cape of Good Hope and, for the next six years, carried out the first systematic observation of the sky in the Southern Hemisphere. It was during this time that the great **"Moon Hoax"** was perpetrated.

hertz (Hz)

Unit of **frequency.** One hertz is a frequency of one cycle per second. 1,000 Hz = 1 kilohertz (kHz); 1,000,000 Hz = 1 megahertz (MHz).

Hertzsprung-Russell diagram

A graph that, for any collection of stars, shows the relationship between **spectral type** and **luminosity.** It was first plotted by Henry Norris **Russell** in 1913 but was discussed independently by Ejnar Hertzsprung at about the same time.

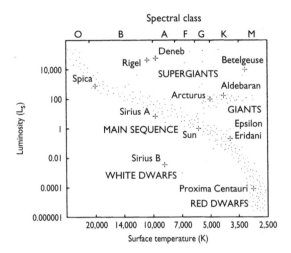

HET

➔ Hobby-Eberly Telescope

heterotrophs

Organisms that, unlike **autotrophs,** cannot derive energy directly from light or from **inorganic** chemicals, and so must feed on other life-forms. They obtain chemical energy by breaking down the **organic** molecules they consume. Heterotrophs include **animals, fungi,** and some types of **bacteria.**

Hevelius, Johannes (1611–87)

German lunar cartographer who, in his *Selenographia* (1647), drew seas on the Moon (**➔ Moon, water on**). He also championed the existence of lunar inhabitants, which he called "selenites" (**➔ Moon, life on**). **➔ Riccioli, Giovanni Battista**

hexose

A **monosaccharide,** or simple **sugar,** containing six **carbon** atoms in the molecule. Examples include **glucose,** fructose, and galactose.

High Accuracy Radial Velocity Planetary Search (HARPS)

A program to detect **extrasolar planets** by the **radial velocity method** using the 3.6-m (11.8-ft.) ESO telescope at the **La Silla Observatory.** When operational, the detection equipment will be capable of radial velocity measurements accurate to about 1 m per second for a slowly rotating star.

High Resolution Échelle Spectrometer (HIRES)

A large instrument, designed by Steven **Vogt** and attached to the Keck I telescope (➔ **Keck Telescopes**), that breaks up incoming light into its component colors and measures the precise intensity of each of thousands of color channels. Operating in the 0.3-to-1.1-micron wavelength range, it is 10 to 100 times more sensitive than any comparable system and has been used in the detection of a number of **extrasolar planets** as part of the **San Francisco State University Planet Search** program.

High Resolution Microwave Survey (HRMS)

A NASA **SETI** project to search for microwave signals coming from an extraterrestrial intelligence. It consisted of two elements, an **all-sky survey** and a **targeted search.** The former, conducted by the **Jet Propulsion Laboratory,** was to observe the entire sky over the 1-to-10-GHz frequency range, plus spot bands up to 25 GHz. This was to explore the possibility that there might be civilizations transmitting strong signals, possibly as **interstellar beacon**s. The Targeted Search, conducted by the **Ames Research Center,** was a high-sensitivity search, in the 1-to-3-GHz range, to look for weak signals originating near **Sun-like stars** within a distance of 100 light-years (30 parsecs). A 10-million–fold increase in capability over the sum of all previous searches was anticipated through the use of high-performance data processing equipment known as the **Multi-Channel Spectrum Analyzer** (MCSA).

The HRMS began its observational phase on October 12, 1992, at the NASA Goldstone Deep Space Communications Complex (All-Sky Survey) and the **Arecibo Observatory** (Targeted Search). In a coordinated program, the Arecibo antenna was pointed at the star

Gliese 615.1A and the Goldstone antenna began to scan a small area of the sky that included the position of the target star. During the following year, the All-Sky Survey team continued observations at Goldstone on a part-time basis while continuing to build the operational system with sixteen times the capability. The Targeted Search team returned from Arecibo after the scheduled 2-month observing session and disassembled the system for upgrades and expansion. In October 1993, the U.S. Congress voted to discontinue financial support for NASA's SETI program and HTMS was canceled. Subsequently, however, the Targeted Search portion of HTMS was rescued through the intervention of the **SETI Institute** and was relaunched as Project **Phoenix.**[151]

Himalia

The tenth known moon of **Jupiter.** ➔ **Jupiter, moons of**

Discovery	1904, by Charles Dillon Perrine
Mean distance from Jupiter	11,470,000 km (7,130,000 mi.)
Diameter	186 km (116 mi.)
Mean density	2.8 g/cm³
Escape velocity	0.117 km/s (421 km/h, 262 mi./h)
Orbital period	250.57 days (250 days 14 hours)
Orbital eccentricity	0.158
Orbital inclination	27.63°
Axial period	0.4 days
Visual albedo	0.03

Hipparchus of Nicaea (c. 190–c. 125 B.C.)

Greek astronomer and mathematician, considered the true founder of his science, who compiled a catalog of the positions and relative brightnesses of more than one thousand stars.

Hipparcos

A **European Space Agency** satellite, launched in 1989 and designed to carry out **astrometric** surveys to an unprecedented degree of accuracy. Its name is an acronym for High Precision Parallax Collecting Satellite and was chosen for its (somewhat strained) similarity to that of the Greek astronomer **Hipparchus.** Although due to a faulty launch, *Hipparcos* ended up in a highly elliptical orbit instead of the intended geosynchronous one, its mission was eventually a triumph and resulted in two catalogs: the *Hipparcos* catalog of 118,000 stars with positions, **parallax**es, and **proper motion**s measured to an unprecedented accuracy of 2 milli**arcsecond**s and the Tycho catalog of more than a million stars with measurements of somewhat lower accuracy. It has been indirectly useful to those involved in the investigation of **extrasolar planets,** since it has enabled the distance (and therefore the true brightness) of the host stars of newly discovered planets to be known to greater accuracy. However, a second-generation astrometric mission, such as the *Global Astrometric Interferometer for Astrophysics* (*GAIA*), will be needed to make a serious contribution to our knowledge of the occurrence and distribution of planetary systems by this means.

HIRES
➔ **High Resolution Échelle Spectrometer**

hive intelligence
A decentralized, multicomponent mind, or appearance of mind, such as that displayed by social insects on Earth, notably ants, termites, and some species of bees. The hive centers and functions around the queen, who alone produces new individuals, each of which is a slave to the needs and demands of the community. Indeed, the individual in such a "superorganism" is akin to a single cell in the body of a conventional animal and quickly dies if it becomes separated from the rest. The cohesion and complex cooperative behavior of the hive are made possible by a tight communications, command, and control system that, in the case of social insects, is based upon the rapid transmission of pheromones. So efficient and purposeful is a colony of ants that much has been written, particularly by science fiction authors, about the possibility of hive intelligence as the organizing principle in some extraterrestrial societies. This idea was taken up by H. G. **Wells** in *First Men in the Moon* (1901) and has been explored many times since. In general, the prospect of a hivelike human community has been regarded as repugnant and the ultimate nightmare that might result from totali-

tarianism. Cold War–era films such as *Invaders from Mars* (1953) and *Invasion of the Body Snatchers* (1956) drew a close parallel between the alien hive and the suppression of individualism under Communist regimes. This negative portrayal has continued with the Borg in *Star Trek* and their attempts to assimilate other sentient species into the "collective," although curiously it is the Federation—a cosmic extension of the United States—that tends, in the end, to do most of the absorption of other cultures. A different perspective on the loss of individuality and emergence of a group mind is offered by writers such as Olaf **Stapledon** in *Star Maker* and Arthur C. **Clarke** in *Childhood's End,* who foresee mankind's eventual melding with some form of broader extraterrestrial consciousness as a triumph of transcendent evolution.[122, p. 573]

Hobby-Eberly Telescope (HET)
A 9-m (29.5-ft.) telescope under construction at the **McDonald Observatory.** Among its uses will be **radial velocity** measurements of nearby stars in the search for **extrasolar planets.**

Hoerner, Sebastian von
German radio astronomer who worked at **Green Bank** with Frank **Drake** and later at the Astronomisches Rechen-Institut (Astronomical Calculation Institute) in Heidelberg. He was active in the 1960s in discussions about **SETI,** the number of advanced civilizations in the Galaxy, and the feasibility of **interstellar travel.** In a 1961 paper,[606] he discussed various factors that might affect the longevity of technological races and what this in turn would mean for the chances of success of SETI programs. He was not generally optimistic about the long-term survival prospects of machine-using species, noting that science and technology on Earth were often driven by

> the fight for supremacy and by the desire for an easy life…. [These forces] tend to destroy if they are not controlled in time: the first one leads to total destruction and the second one leads to biological or mental degeneration.

The latter view he shared with Ronald **Bracewell.** He also considered the possibility that a species might lose interest in material progress or be completely wiped out. In Hoerner's opinion, it was feasible that a succession of technological species might rise and fall in the lifetime of a planet, each new emergence taking hundreds of millions of years. His calculations showed that if the average longevity of an advanced race is 6,500 years and each habitable planet produces an average of four technological species, perhaps one in every 3 million stars might support a race capable of interstellar communication. The mean distance between such worlds would be about 1,000 light-years. Von Hoerner was among those, including John **Pierce** and Edward **Purcell,** who regarded interstellar travel as an unlikely proposition. Even assuming that spacecraft could be accelerated to almost the speed of light, at which point relativistic **time dilation** would come into play, von Hoerner argued that it would never be acceptable for travelers to cross a thousand light-years or more to reach another inhabited planet, only to return home and find that many centuries had passed by.[607]

homeotherm

An organism, such as a mammal or bird, capable of maintaining a stable body temperature independent of the environmental temperature.

hominid

Any primate in the human family, Hominidae. *Homo sapiens* is the only living representative. *Australopithecus* is an extinct genus.

hominoid

The collective term for **hominid**s and apes. Together with monkeys, hominoids constitute the anthropoid primates.

Hopkins, Budd

New York artist turned hypnotherapist whose best-selling books *Missing Time* (1981) and *Intruders* (1987) were built around interviews with hypnotized subjects who claimed to have suffered **alien abduction.** In one case, that of Linda Cortile, the victim was purportedly removed from her twelfth-floor Manhattan apartment. Through his popular and credulous writings and lectures, Hopkins played a significant role in consolidating the mythology of abduction and sinister extraterrestrial eugenics programs and connecting it with that of an official government cover-up.

Horowitz, Norman Harold (1915–)

American biochemist at the California Institute of Technology who, in the mid-1940s, used the **Oparin-Haldane Theory** as the basis for his own theory of biochemical synthesis.[277] In doing so, he helped bring to greater prominence the idea of the chemical evolution of life. However, he was not optimistic about the prospects of finding extraterrestrial life, citing the absence of a theory to explain the origin of **nucleic acid**s and **proteins.** Later, he was the principal investigator on the *Viking* pyrolytic release experiment. Believing, after the mission, that *Viking* had ruled out the possibility of Martian life, he drew the sweeping conclusion that "[s]ince Mars offered by far the most promising habitat for extraterrestrial life in the solar system, it is now virtually certain that the earth is the only life-bearing planet in our region of the galaxy."[280, 281]

Horowitz, Paul (1942–)

Harvard physics professor and electronics specialist who, since the mid-1970s, has been closely involved with **SETI.** He has played a leading role in the design and implementation of Project **META** and its successor, Project **BETA.** Horowitz obtained a bachelor's degree (1965) and doctorate (1970) at Harvard before becoming a professor there in 1974.

host star

The star around which a particular planet, **brown dwarf,** or lesser object revolves. Also known as the *central star* or *primary.*

"hot Jupiter"

→ epistellar Jovians

Hoyle, Fred(erick) (1915–)

Eminent and maverick English astrophysicist who carried out wartime work on radar, alongside Hermann Bondi and Thomas **Gold** (his future "steady-state universe" collaborators), before being appointed Plumian professor of astronomy and experimental philosophy at Cambridge in 1958. In addition to carrying out much important work in cosmology and **nucleosynthesis,** Hoyle was an early supporter of the modern view that **extrasolar planets** and life are ubiquitous. In his standard text *Frontiers of Astronomy,*[285] (1955) he writes:

> [W]e may expect planetary systems to have developed around the majority of stars.... Living creatures must it seems be rather common.

Then, in a more caustically humorous vein (attacking Cold War follies):

> This is a pity, because the supporters of various ideologies after attempting to impress the superior merits of their views on each other (through the aid of fusion bombardment and other massive activities), could proceed to impress themselves on the rest of the Milky Way. Not only this, but the opportunity for tax-collectors would be enormous. With taxes levied on say 250,000,000,000,000,000,000 individuals...it would be possible to whack up the defence programme for the Milky Way to something like reasonable proportions.

Hoyle has made a career out of challenging orthodoxy. However, far more remarkable and contentious than any of his earlier work have been his more recent claims about the origin of life. In association with Chandra Wickramasinghe, he began, in the 1970s, to develop the notion that complex **organic** materials and even primitive microorganisms evolve in interstellar space (➔ **life, in space**). Much criticism and derision was initially directed at this hypothesis; yet, while some aspects of it continue to appear implausible to many, other aspects, including the idea that comets serve as delivery vehicles for **prebiotic** chemicals, have come to be accepted.

Even in *Frontiers,* Hoyle's future thesis about the origin of life in space was beginning to take shape:

> The physical and chemical requirements must...have been far more favorable for the building of complex molecules *before* the Earth was aggregated....The Earth intercepts only a tiny fraction of the ultra-violet light emitted by the Sun....The energy source was therefore much greater before the planets were aggregated....Another point in favour of a pre-planetary origin of life appears when we consider in a little more detail how the complex molecules were built up. This requires the addition together of many smaller molecules.... If the molecules were dissolved in the sea, for instance, the chance of enough of the right kinds of molecules coming together would be negligible....Bernal has called attention to the necessity for solving this problem of association, and has suggested that favourable conditions would probably occur if the molecules were coated as a film on the surface of a solid particle. Such a condition would undoubtedly best be satisfied...while the planetary material was still distributed as a swarm of small bodies....There is no suggestion that animals and plants as we know them originated in interplanetary space. But the vital steps on which life is based may have occurred there.

Almost contemporaneously with this firm scientific proposal of life's off-world origin, Hoyle allowed his fertile imagination full rein in his first science fiction novel, ***The Black Cloud*** (1957), in which an intelligent interstellar cloud arrives in the solar system (➔ **extraterrestrial intelligence, forms of**). In a later "alien" story, *A for Andromeda,* and its sequel, he turned to some of the possible consequences of **SETI.**

HR 810

Also known as Iota Horologii, a star with a recently discovered **extrasolar planet** that moves in the most Earth-like orbit yet found.

Host Star	
Distance	50.5 light-years (15.5 parsecs)
Spectral type	G0 V
Apparent magnitude	5.4
Planet	
Mass	2.26 M_J
Semimajor axis	0.93 AU (140 million km, 86 million mi.)

Orbital period	320 days
Eccentricity	0.16
Discovery	1999, ESO Coudé Échelle
	Spectrometer, La Silla
Method of discovery	Radial velocity

HR 4796A

A 10-million-year-old star lying at a distance of 220 light-years (68 parsecs) around which has been found a nearly edge-on **dust disk.** The discovery was announced independently, in April 1998, by one group led by Ray Jayawardhana from the **Harvard-Smithsonian Center for Astrophysics** and Charles Telesco of the University of Florida using the **Cerro Tololo Inter-American Observatory,** and another by David Koerner of the University of Pennsylvania using the **Keck** (II) **Telescope** in conjunction with **MIRLIN.** HR 4796A's disk, the inner edge of which lies about 50 AU from the star, is especially interesting because it is just the right age to contain planets in the final stages of accretion (➔ **planetary systems, formation of; protoplanetary disk**). Indeed, it is thought that the empty region between the disk and star has probably been swept clear by a collection of newly formed planets similar to the infant solar system. HR 4796A appears to be a missing link between disks around very young stars (➔ **T Tauri star**) and those around more mature stars such as **Vega** and **Beta Pictoris.**

H-R diagram
➔ **Hertzsprung-Russell diagram**

HRMS
➔ **High Resolution Microwave Survey**

HST
➔ *Hubble Space Telescope*

IHT
➔ **One Hectare Telescope**

Huang, Su-Shu (1915–)
Chinese-American astronomer who, in the late 1950s and early 1960s, was among the first to carry out detailed analyses of the types of stars that might be capable of nurturing life, especially advanced life, on planets circling around them.[294, 295, 296] He drew attention to the variety of **habitable zone**s that might be found

around stars of different size and **spectral type** and made other contributions in the early years of **SETI.** He suggested that it would be difficult for any technological race, in the face of continually negative results, to sustain interest either in searching for or beaming out interstellar signals over long periods of time. For this reason, he thought that a powerful system capable of "eavesdropping" on stray communications (➔ **Cyclops, Project**) would have the best chance of success. Huang came to the United States in 1947 on a fellowship granted by the Chinese Nationalist government, earned a Ph.D. in astrophysics at the University of Chicago under Otto **Struve,** and in 1950 moved, at the same time as Struve, to the **University of California, Berkeley.** Eight years later he joined **NASA.**

Hubble Space Telescope (HST)
An orbiting observatory built and operated jointly by **NASA** and the **European Space Agency** that is equipped with a main mirror 2.4 m (94.5 in.) in diameter. Science operations are conducted from the Space Telescope Science Institute (STScI) in Baltimore, Maryland. Following upgrades and repairs since its launch on April 25, 1990, the main science instruments attached to the telescope are the Faint Object Camera (FOC), the Wide-Field and Planetary Camera 2 (WFPC-2), the Near Infrared Camera and Multi-Object Spectrometer (NICMOS), and the Space Telescope Imaging Spectrograph (STIS). With its high resolution, the *HST* is proving to be a powerful tool in the investigation of **circumstellar disk**s around young stars in which new planets may be in the process of formation. It may also have been the first instrument to image an **extrasolar planet,** in the unusual case of the object known as **TMR-1C.** *HST* is expected to remain operational until about 2010, by which time the *Next Generation Space Telescope* (*NGST*) should be in use.

Huggins, William (1824–1910)
English amateur astronomer who worked from his private observatory in Tulse Hill, London, became president of the Royal Society (1900–05), and was a pioneer of astronomical **spectroscopy.** He and his colleague William

Allen Miller were the first to analyze the composition of bright stars. In announcing their first results in 1864, Huggins expressed the view that their discoveries provided

an experimental basis on which a conclusion, hitherto but a pure speculation, may rest—viz. that at least the brighter stars are, like our sun, upholding and energising centres of systems of worlds adapted to the abode of living beings.

While this was an overstatement encouraged by theological belief, stellar spectroscopy would come to play an increasingly prominent role in the debate over the existence of habitable **extrasolar planets,** as would Huggins's discovery that some nebulas were composed of gas rather than stars and his early investigations of the nature of planetary atmospheres. In 1865, he established that the Moon possessed, at best, a negligible atmosphere by observing the spectrum of a star while it underwent an **occultation** by the Moon and noting that light of all wavelengths was simultaneously cut off.

humpback whales, songs of

Although all toothed whales and dolphins generate a wide variety of vocalizations, the most extraordinary range and complexity of sounds are produced by the humpback whales. The mournful calls of these **cetaceans** can be heard for hours at a stretch in the winter breeding grounds of the Caribbean and Hawaii. Elaborate phrases, each a slightly different length, are repeated over and over again. Within one season, all humpbacks from the same area sing broadly the same song, which evolves over time. Part of a song may change rapidly for several months and then remain unchanged while other parts are modified. After about eight years, an entirely new song appears. How much information the whales exchange via their calls is still unknown, but there have been some intriguing suggestions. In 1999, John Buck and Ryuji Suzuki of the University of Massachusetts, Dartmouth, claimed they had found evidence of a hierarchical grammar like that of human language in the humpbacks' songs; other researchers, however, remain skeptical.

Hutton, Richard Holt (1826–97)

English essayist and editor who, writing anonymously in *The Spectator,* argued against the proposal made by Francis **Galton** that an attempt be made to send signals to Mars (**→ communication, with the Moon and planets**). He thought it unlikely that intelligent Martians exist or that, if they do, they have the same faculties as we or have reached the same level of development. Moreover, he argued, if communication were achieved, it would be detrimental to humankind because it would be yet another sign of our insignificance in the cosmos. We shall be ready to interact with other beings, he believed, only

when we shall have mastered the tendency to regard our own insignificance as an excuse for treating our wills as impotent because they are not omnipotent, and our reason as all but imbecile because it is not omniscient.

His concerns auger some of those expressed more recently about **SETI** (**→ extraterrestrial intelligence, implications following first contact**).

Huxley, Thomas Henry (1825–95)

English biologist who became the foremost expounder of Darwinism of his time and a pioneer of the modern idea that life evolved from nonliving matter. His Edinburgh lecture "On the Physical Basis of Life" in 1868 can be seen as the starting point of the scientific debate about the chemical origin of life and the final denunciation of **vitalism.** Pointing out that **protoplasm** (which he considered to be the fundamental substance of life) was made principally from the elements carbon, hydrogen, oxygen, and nitrogen, which were combined into water, carbonic acid, and nitrogen compounds, he said:

These new compounds, like the elementary bodies of which they are composed, are lifeless. But when they are brought together, under certain conditions, they give rise to the still more complex body, protoplasm, and this protoplasm exhibits the phenomenon of life. I see no break in this series of steps in molecular complication.

His line of reasoning was soon taken up by John **Tyndall** and others. Huxley's tutelage of H. G. **Wells** played a significant part in the young writer's preoccupation with aspects and extrapolations of evolutionary theory in his early science fiction novels, including *The War of the Worlds.* → **evolutionary theory and extraterrestrial life**

Huygens, Christiaan (1629–95)

Dutch physicist and astronomer who discovered **Titan** in 1655 and determined that Saturn has rings. He also figured in one of the great unsung moments in planetary exploration when at 7:00 P.M. on November 28, 1659, he sketched a feature—a dark triangular patch—on the surface of Mars that he had just seen through his modest telescope. Eventually, it came to be known as **Syrtis Major,** the "Great Marsh," and for many years it was presumed to be some kind of watery body. The significance of its sighting lay in the fact that whereas the large bright and dark areas on the Moon had been visible for all to see from prehistoric times and Galileo **Galilei** had telescopically discovered the **Great Red Spot** on Jupiter (an atmospheric feature), Syrtis Major was the first *permanent* marking to be glimpsed on the surface of another planet. Huygens quickly used his discovery to demonstrate that the Martian day—the time it takes Mars to spin around once on its axis—is similar in length to our own.

He was deeply involved, too, in speculation about the existence of extraterrestrial life, a subject that dominates his *Cosmotheoros, or New Conjectures Concerning the Planetary Worlds, Their Inhabitants and Productions,* published posthumously in 1698. Huygens employs the same five arguments in favor of **pluralism** as Bernard de **Fontenelle** had done in his hugely popular work but reveals (not surprisingly) a greater command of late-seventeenth-century astronomical data. The evidence he marshals against life on the Moon is pertinent and almost decisive (→ **Moon, life on**). However, he is less surefooted when it comes to making inferences about the planets. He notes the excessive solar heat received by the inner planets and the deficiency suffered by those lying beyond the Earth's orbit but fails to explain how the supposed inhabitants of these worlds cope with the temperature extremes to which they are subject. Again, he notes the spots seen telescopically on Jupiter but then rashly assumes that these are clouds of water vapor and therefore evidence of habitability. Concerning the possibility of extrasolar worlds and life, he writes:

> Why then shall we not ... conclude that our Star has no better attendance than the others? So that what we allow'd the Planets, upon the account of our enjoying it, we must likewise grant to all those Planets that surround that prodigious number of Suns. They must have their plants and animals, nay and their rational creatures too, and those as great admirers, and as diligent observers of the heavens as ourselves.

He makes some creditable estimates of stellar distances based on a consideration of how far away the Sun would have to be to appear as bright as Sirius and then uses these estimates to account for the failure to detect extrasolar worlds.

Huygens probe

The **European Space Agency** (ESA) component of the **NASA** *Cassini* mission to **Saturn** and its environs. The *Huygens* probe, named in honor of the Dutch scientist Christiaan **Huygens,** will be released by the *Cassini* orbiter in November 2004 and enter the atmosphere of **Titan** three weeks later. At first, the 2.7-m- (8.9-ft.-) diameter probe will use its heat shield to decelerate. Then, at an altitude of about 175 km (110 miles), its main parachute will deploy, followed 15 minutes later by a smaller drogue chute. Throughout the remainder of its 140-km (90-mile) descent, *Huygens* will take measurements of the temperature, pressure, density, and energy balance in Titan's atmosphere and relay this information to the orbiter. It will also send back images, including the first clear views of Titan's surface. After the probe mission is completed, *Cassini* will turn its

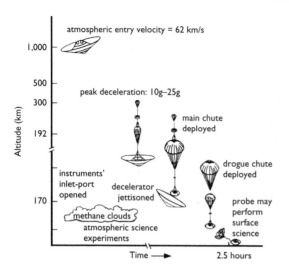

atmospheric entry velocity = 62 km/s

1,000

500

300

peak deceleration: 10g–25g

main chute deployed

192

Altitude (km)

drogue chute deployed

instruments' inlet-port opened

decelerator jettisoned

170

probe may perform surface science

methane clouds

atmospheric science experiments

Time →

2.5 hours

Sequence of events during descent of the *Huygens* probe.
NASA/JPL/Caltech

high-gain antenna toward the Earth and begin transmitting its recorded data.

hydrobot

A remote-controlled submarine of the type that is expected to be deployed eventually on **Europa** (→ **Europa, future probes of**). Hydrobots will be released into the subsurface liquid ocean that may exist on Europa, where they will image their surroundings, take a variety of measurements of their physical and chemical environment, and search for possible forms of life.

hydrocarbon

A general term for any **organic** compound that contains only **carbon** and **hydrogen.** Hydrocarbons are classed as *aliphatic* (based on straight or branched carbon chains) or *aromatic* (based on benzene rings).

hydrogen

The most abundant **element** in the universe (→ **elements, cosmic abundance of**) and one of the most important to life as we know it. Hydrogen atoms are the simplest and least massive of all, normally consisting of one **proton** and one **electron.** Two other **isotopes** of hydrogen exist: **deuterium,** or "heavy hydrogen," with a **nucleus** containing one **neutron** and one proton, and radioactive tritium with a nucleus containing two neutrons and one proton. Hydrogen makes up the bulk of most stars and **gas giant** planets. In space, it may exist in atomic (→ **H I region**), ionized (→ **H II region**), or molecular form (→ **molecular cloud**). The presence of atomic hydrogen in space can be mapped by observations of the **21-centimeter line.**

Atomic number 1; density 0.09 g/dm^3; melting point 259.1°C; boiling point −252.9°C

hydrogen bond

A weak chemical force that can operate both within and between certain types of **molecule**s. A hydrogen bond results when a **hydrogen** atom that is attached to another atom by a **covalent bond** is also attracted to a neighboring electronegative atom (such as **oxygen** or **nitrogen**), either in the same molecule or in a separate molecule. Although only about 10 percent as strong as covalent bonds, hydrogen bonds are crucial to life as we know it. They are responsible for many of the unique properties of **water,** for the **tertiary structure** of **proteins,** and for the interaction between **purines** and **pyrimidines** that contributes to the stability of the **DNA** double helix.

hydrogen cyanide (HCN)

A colorless liquid or gas at normal Earth temperatures that is central in the **prebiotic** synthesis of **amino acids.** The fact that it occurs abundantly in **comet**s has fueled speculation that cometary collisions may have played a significant role in supplying some of the raw materials for prebiotic evolution.[385]

Density relative to water (at 22°C) 0.70; melting point −14°C; boiling point 26°C

hydrogen ion

A **hydrogen atom** that has lost or gained an **electron** and in consequence has a charge.

The positive hydrogen ion (H+), having lost its only electron, consists of just a **proton.**

hydrogen peroxide (H₂O₂)

A highly **oxidizing** compound of **hydrogen** and **oxygen.** It has been claimed by some (➔ **Oyama's hypothesis, about the active nature of the Martian soil**) that the presence of this substance on the Martian surface would explain the results of the *Viking* biological experiments. While this has yet to be proven, hydrogen peroxide is known to form constantly on the surface of **Europa** as a result of the bombardment of charged particles moving in Jupiter's powerful magnetic field.

hydrogen sulfide (H₂S)

A gas that is well known for its odor of rotten eggs.

Density relative to water (liquid) 1.54; melting point −85.5°C; boiling point −60.7°C

hydrolysis

The reverse of a **condensation** reaction. A water molecule is added to the point in a **polymer** where two subunits are joined, causing the polymer to split apart at that point.

hydrophilic

Having an affinity for water.

hydrophobic

Lacking an affinity for water.

hydrothermal vent

An opening in the ocean floor out of which hot, mineral-rich water erupts. Following the discovery of a plethora of new species, including many previously unknown types of microbial **extremophile**s in the vicinity of **black smoker**s, deep-sea vents have been touted as sites where the origin of life may have taken place (➔ **life, origin of**), not only on this world but elsewhere, including possibly **Mars** and **Europa.**[64] To test this theory, Koichiro Matsuno and colleagues at the University of Tokyo built an artificial vent in which water is heated to 110 to 350°C (230 to 662°F) in one chamber, pressurized to 200 atmospheres, and

cooled to near freezing in another. The water then returns to the heating chamber, in the same way that sea water cycles through the circulation system of a natural vent. The Japanese researchers added **glycine,** the simplest **amino acid,** to the system and found later that **peptides** had formed. When they added copper, a **trace element** commonly found in the water from natural vents, they observed that the peptides grew still longer.[299]

hydroxyl radical (–OH)

A single **hydrogen** atom and a single **oxygen** atom bound together. It occurs commonly in space and was the first **interstellar molecule** to be found (in 1963). The characteristic **emission line** from interstellar OH, at 1,662 MHz, marks the upper frequency limit of the **waterhole.**

Hynek, J. Allen (1910–86)

Astronomy professor at Ohio State University who went on to become associate director of the **Smithsonian Astrophysical Observatory** (1956), and chairman of the Astronomy Department at Northwestern University (1960). He is best remembered, however, for his involvement with research into **unidentified flying objects.** This began in 1949, when he was invited by the U.S. Air Force to become the astronomical consultant to Project **Grudge,** based at nearby Wright Field (later Wright-Patterson Air Force Base), outside Dayton. He continued in this position with the subsequent and much longer Project **Blue Book,** gradually shifting over the years from a position of extreme skepticism to one in which he believed that UFOs represent "an aspect or domain of the natural world not yet explored by science." In 1973, four years after the cancellation of Project Blue Book, Hynek founded the **Center for UFO Studies** (CUFOS), based in Chicago.[297]

hyperbola

A curve formed by the intersection of a cone with a plane that cuts both branches of the cone (➔ **conic sections**). Everywhere on a given hyperbola the difference between two fixed points, known as the *foci,* remains constant.

hyperbolic orbit

An open orbit in the shape of a **hyperbola,** the **eccentricity** of which is greater than 1. A hyperbolic orbit is followed by an object which escapes from the gravitational field of a larger body.

hyperbolic velocity

A velocity that exceeds the **escape velocity** of a celestial body, such as a star. It allows an object, such as a spacecraft or **rogue planet,** to break free of the gravitational attraction of the larger body by following an open, **hyperbolic orbit.**

hypergravity

The condition experienced in an intense gravitational field.

Hyperion

One of the smaller and more remote moons of **Saturn.** Hyperion's highly irregular shape may have resulted from an ancient collision in which part of the moon was blasted away. Its elongated orbit exposes it to varying gravitational forces from Saturn that alter the rate at which the moon spins from one orbit to the next. Hyperion has a reddish surface that closely matches in color the dark material on **Iapetus.** ➔ **Saturn, moons of**

Discovery	1848, by William Cranch Bond
Mean distance from Saturn	1,483,000 km (922,000 mi.)
Diameter	400 × 250 × 240 km (250 × 160 × 150 mi.)
Mean density	1.4 g/cm³
Escape velocity	0.107 km/s (385 km/h, 239 mi./h)
Orbital period	21.3 days (21 days 7 hours)
Orbital eccentricity	0.104
Orbital inclination	0.43
Axial period	Chaotic
Visual albedo	0.3

hyperthermophiles

Microbes that reproduce and grow at very high temperatures, in the range of 60 to 113°C (140 to 235°F). The first to be identified, *Sulfolobus acidocaldarius,* which is both a hyperthermophile and an **acidophile,** was found in the late 1960s in a hot, acidic spring in Yellowstone National Park, Wyoming. Since then, more than fifty hyperthermophiles have been isolated. The majority are **archaea,** although some **cyanobacteria** and **anaerobic photosynthetic bacteria** grow well at 70 to 75°C (158 to 167°F). The most heat-resistant of all known hyperthermophiles are the anaerobic archaea, including members of the genera *Pyrolobus, Pyrodictium,* and *Pyrococcus.* For example, *Pyrolobus fumarii* grows on the walls of marine **hydrothermal vents** ("smokers"). It multiplies best at about 105°C (221°F), can reproduce at up to 113°C (235°F), and stops growing in "cooler" environments below 90°C (194°F). Another hyperthermophile that lives in deep-sea vents, *Methanopyrus,* is of special interest because of its ancient genetic makeup. Analysis of its genes suggests that it may have been among the earliest organisms on Earth. Further study of it may help shed light on how the first **cell**s survived (➔ **life, origin of**).

The upper temperature limit of terrestrial life has yet to be determined. But, although the search is on for "superhyperthermophiles," it would be surprising to find microbes thriving at 150°C (302°F) or more. At this temperature, current understanding suggests that no biological strategy could prevent the breakdown of chemical bonds that hold **DNA** and other vital molecules together. ➔ **extremophiles**

Hz

➔ **hertz**

HZ

➔ **habitable zone**

Iapetus

The next-to-outermost moon of **Saturn,** remarkable in that its brightness changes by a factor of *seven* as it moves around its orbit. This has prompted the suggestion that the brightness variations might be artificial. For example, Donald Goldsmith and Tobias Owen in *The Search for Life in the Universe*[226] (1980) wrote:

> This unusual moon is the only object in the Solar System which we might seriously regard as an alien signpost—a natural object deliberately modified by an advanced civilization to attract our attention.

By coincidence, Iapetus is the site of the "Star Gate" in Arthur C. **Clarke**'s *2001: A Space Odyssey.*[111]

Whereas the leading hemisphere of the moon is dark with a slight reddish color, the trailing hemisphere is bright. It may be that the dark surface is composed of matter either that was swept up by Iapetus as it moved in its orbit or that welled out of the moon's interior. Then again, the red covering may consist of the same complex **organic** chemicals that are found in primitive meteorites. However, there are no bright-rimmed craters on the dark hemisphere, which suggests that, if the dark

coating is thin, it must be constantly being laid down since, otherwise, bright material would be visible that had been excavated by impacts. One possibility is that the dark material came from the surface of the outermost satellite, **Phoebe,** as a result of micrometeorite impacts and was then swept up by Iapetus. The fact that only the leading hemisphere of Iapetus is dark supports this idea. However, Phoebe has a slightly different color to the low-**albedo** side of its inner neighbor. Moreover, the dark material on Iapetus seems to be concentrated on the floors of craters, as if it had an internal origin. Conceivably, since Iapetus originated so far from Saturn, it may have formed with

Discovery	1671, by Giovanni Cassini
Mean distance from Saturn	3,560,000 km (2,213,000 mi.)
Diameter	1,460 km (907 mi.)
Mean density	1.21 g/cm³
Escape velocity	0.586 km/s (2,110 km/h, 1,311 mi./h)
Orbital period	79.33 days (79 days 8 hours)
Orbital eccentricity	0.028
Orbital inclination	14.72°
Axial period	79.33 days
Visual albedo	0.05 to 0.5

methane ice or **ammonia** ice in its interior. The dark material could then be explained in terms of eruptions of methane. This hypothesis is supported by the appearance of a dark ring of material, about 100 km (60 miles) in diameter, that straddles the border between the leading and trailing hemispheres. Similar rings were formed on the Earth's moon and on Mars when dark volcanic material flowed into impact craters and filled around the central peak. ➔ **Saturn, moons of**

IAU
➔ **International Astronomical Union**

ice
A term used by planetary scientists to refer to a variety of **volatile** substances, including **water, methane,** and **ammonia,** when in their solid state.

ice dwarf
An object that is larger than the nucleus of a normal **comet** and icier than an **asteroid.** Ice dwarfs measure up to several hundred kilometers across and populate the **Oort Cloud** and **Kuiper Belt** in large numbers.

ice volcanism
The eruption of molten ice or gas-driven solid fragments from the surface of a planet or moon.

ice-water interface station
➔ **cryobot**

imaging, of extrasolar planets
New techniques, such as **nulling interferometry** and the use of **adaptive optics coronograph**s, are now being developed to the stage where they are capable of directly imaging **extrasolar planets.** Already, nulling interferometry has given astronomers their first glimpse of a dust cloud around **Betelgeuse,** while an adaptive optics coronograph at the Palomar 1.5-m (4.9-ft.) telescope has enabled the first unambiguous identification of a **brown dwarf,** in the case of **Gliese 229B.** Direct imaging will become an increasingly important method for studying extrasolar planets. Firstly, unlike the **radial velocity method,** which is highly successful for discovering planets in orbits close to their host stars, imaging allows systems with larger separations (similar to those in the solar system) to be probed. Secondly, once objects have been resolved by direct imaging, it will be possible to examine their spectral features in detail and search for signs of life (➔ **extraterrestrial life, detection of**). A variety of projects to image both Jupiter-like and Earth-like extrasolar worlds are under development or planned for the future (➔ **extrasolar planets, detection of**).

impact crater
A **crater** formed on a surface by the collision of a projectile.

impactor
An object that strikes the surface of a celestial body.

incarnation and redemption
A concern of theologians for centuries has been that the discovery of intelligent life on other worlds might have serious implications for Christian doctrines, especially those of the incarnation and redemption. In recent times this problem has been addressed, among others, by Edward A. **Milne** and E. L. **Mascall.** ➔ **Christian doctrine and pluralism**

inclination
When referring to a planet's orbit, the angle between the plane of the orbit and the **ecliptic.** When referring to a moon's orbit, the angle between the plane of the orbit and the plane of the primary's equator.

incubation period
The time during which an infectious disease develops, from the point when the infecting organism enters the body until the appearance of the first symptoms. This can be as short as a few hours for cholera or as long as a decade in the case of leprosy. One of the problems in establishing quarantine protocols to minimize the risk of **back contamination** is the uncertainty about what relationship might exist between an alien **pathogen** and a terrestrial host.

infrared

That part of the **electromagnetic spectrum** extending between the regions of visible light and **microwave radiation,** with **wavelength**s between 0.75 and 1,000 microns.

Infrared Astronomy Satellite (IRAS)

A joint U.S., British, and Dutch spacecraft launched by NASA on January 25, 1983. It mapped 95 percent of the sky at **infrared** wavelengths using a main telescope with an aperture of 57 cm (23 in.). Among many new discoveries, it found **dust disk**s encircling several stars, including **Beta Pictoris** and **Vega.**

Infrared Space Interferometer (IRSI)

A Cornerstone Mission in the **European Space Agency**'s Horizon Plus initiative, one of the principal goals of which will be to search for and characterize Earth-like **extrasolar planets.** Among the leading proposed designs is *Darwin.* Final selection of the Interferometer Cornerstone will be made in about 2000 for launch in the period 2009–2017.

Infrared Space Observatory (ISO)

An orbiting **infrared** telescope launched by the **European Space Agency** on November 17, 1995. Its instruments include a camera, an imaging **photopolarimeter,** and two **spectrometer**s, designed to make observations at **wavelength**s between 2.5 and 200 microns.

inorganic

Denoting the chemical **element**s and their compounds, other than the compounds of **carbon.** The **oxides** and **sulfides** of carbon and the metallic carbides, however, are generally considered inorganic. → **organic**

instantaneous bandwidth

The widest contiguous **frequency** range across which a **radio telescope** and its associated receiving equipment can make observations at any given time.

integration time

The interval over which measurements from a **radio telescope** are taken from any one direction within the **instantaneous bandwidth.** Longer integration times allow more averaging in order to filter out **background noise** and boost the **signal-to-noise ratio.**

intelligence, nature of

Like life and beauty, intelligence is a surprisingly difficult quality to define. However, just as the search for extraterrestrial life demands careful consideration of what life is and therefore what "signatures" should be sought in the effort to reveal its presence (→ **extraterrestrial life, detection of**), so the quest for intelligence beyond the Earth calls for a close examination of the nature of intelligence. The scale of this problem is made clear by the fact that we have trouble in defining and quantifying intelligence even within our own species. So-called intelligence tests tend to measure only a very narrow band of mathematical, verbal, and visuospatial skills. Creativity, intuition, imagination, artistry, and many other abilities must be taken into account in any true multidimensional view of what intelligence means. Clearly, there are different ways in which high degrees of intelligence can be manifested. It may be hard to decide who was the greater scientific genius, Newton or Einstein, but it is probably meaningless to try to calibrate the relative intelligence of, for example, Einstein, Shakespeare, Gandhi, and Bach. Moving beyond *Homo sapiens* to some of our fellow terrestrial species, the difficulties in assessing the presence and level of intelligence are compounded. Whatever we take intelligence to mean, it evidently forms a continuum. An amoeba is not intelligent by our standards, yet it has intelligence to a limited degree. A snake, by anyone's measure, is more intelligent than an amoeba, and a dog brighter than a snake. Brain-to-body-mass ratio and neural complexity are obviously important correlates of intelligence. Thus we find that **cetaceans** and **cephalopods,** which have big, complex nervous systems, display apparently intelligent behavior. Yet these creatures live and communicate in such nonhuman ways that we begin to see in them the possible diversity that intelligence may take in extraterrestrial environments. There is the possibility, too, of significant levels of intelligence based not on large, single brains but on a more distributed processing arrangement, such as exists in some insect colonies (→ **hive intelligence**) and perhaps even in entire ecosystems (→ **Gaia Hypothesis**). Finally, intelligence is almost certainly not exclusive to organic systems. It may be that within a few decades **artificial intelligence** will rival or exceed our own. → **extraterrestrial intelligence, character**

Intelligent Life in the Universe

A groundbreaking and influential book on the subjects of **SETI** and **astrobiology,** first published in 1966.[540] Coauthored by Iosif **Shklovskii** and Carl **Sagan,** it is a highly extended and revised version of Shklovskii's *Vselennaia, zhizn, razum* (Universe, Life, Mind), published in Moscow in 1962. → *We Are Not Alone; Search for Life in the Universe, The*

interference pattern

The pattern of "peaks" and "troughs" that results when two or more waves that have traveled slightly different paths from the same source are brought together. This basic principle is exploited by astronomical **interferometer**s as a way of increasing **resolving power.**

interferometer

An instrument consisting of linked telescopes that collects the **electromagnetic radiation** arriving from a celestial object along two or more different paths and combines the results to form an **interference pattern.** It enables details of the source to be resolved that would be missing from the images obtained from telescopes working independently. **Radio interferometer**s, such as the **Very Large Array,** have been in use for several decades. More recently, technological advances have made possible the construction of **optical interferometer**s. Several of these are now being developed and designed, both on the ground (→ **Keck Telescopes; Large Binocular Telescope**) and in space (→ *Darwin; Space Interferometry Mission; Terrestrial Planet Finder; Planet Imager*).

International Astronomical Union (IAU)

The world coordinating body for astronomical research, founded in 1920.

interplanetary communication
→ **communication, with the Moon and planets**

interplanetary magnetic field (IMF)

The magnetic field carried with the **solar wind.**

interstellar beacon
→ **beacon, interstellar**

interstellar cloud

A local concentration of gas and dust between the stars. Although space is never completely empty (→ **interstellar medium**), matter in the form of **atom**s, **molecule**s, and **cosmic dust** particles is clumped together more densely in interstellar clouds. These are of two main types: **molecular cloud**s and **H I region**s.

interstellar colonization

Given the innate human tendency to explore and expand—"to boldly go"—it seems reasonable to suppose that, over the coming millennia, our race will set up colonies elsewhere in space, first on other worlds in the solar system, and later on the planets of other stars.[159] If there are other technological civilizations in the Galaxy, some of them are presumably older and more advanced than ourselves and will have started their interstellar colonization earlier. Even assuming that the light-speed barrier is ultimately unassailable (an unlikely scenario), it should still be possible, given the will, to settle the entire Milky Way system within 10 million years. The fact that no substantive evidence of the activities of alien colonizers has yet been found has suggested to some that such beings do not exist and that we may be alone in the Galaxy (→ **Fermi Paradox**).

interstellar communication
→ **SETI**

interstellar distances

A simple model helps give some idea of the extraordinary emptiness of interstellar space and the great gulfs that exist even between neighboring stars. Think of the Sun as a ball as wide as the dot over this "i." Earth would then be a microscopic speck about 2 cm away and Nep-

TRAVEL TIMES TO PROXIMA CENTAURI			
Form of Transport	Speed (km per second)	Distance traveled in 1 year (km)	Time to Proxima Centauri (years)
Foot	0.0013	42,000	1,000,000,000
Car	0.026	830,000	50,000,000
Boeing 727	0.26	8,800,000	5,000,000
Voyager 1	17	510,000,000	76,000
Light beam	300,000	9,460,000,000,000	4.28

tune a barely visible speck just 60 cm from the Sun. On this scale, the nearest star, **Proxima Centauri,** would be another tiny speck 1 km in the distance. Alternatively, consider a hollow ball the size of Earth. A dozen oranges scattered at random within that immense volume would approximate the scale of the stars and the spaces between them in the vicinity of the Sun. To appreciate the problem that the vast interstellar spaces present to future star travelers, the table above shows how long it would take using various forms of transport to travel the distance from the Sun to Proxima Centauri: 4.28 light-years (1.31 parsecs), or approximately 40 trillion km (25 trillion miles). ➔ **interstellar travel**

interstellar dust
➔ **cosmic dust**

interstellar erosion
Although the erosive effects of traveling between stars may be significant for future high-speed interstellar spacecraft, they are anticipated to be negligible for the relatively slow-moving present-day vehicles (➔ **interstellar probes**) that are leaving the solar system. This is relevant when considering the future prospects of the *Pioneer* **plaque**s and *Voyager* **interstellar record**s. Most of the degradation that these externally mounted messages will suffer has probably already occurred during their departure from the comparatively dusty

environs of our own planetary system. In interstellar space, where the average density of particles is about one trillionth the density of the best vacuum that can be produced on Earth, the wear and tear on spacecraft is expected to be very much less.

interstellar medium (ISM)
The material that exists between the stars, which, in our own galaxy, consists of about 99 percent gas and 1 percent **cosmic dust** grains. It is strongly concentrated in the **galactic disk,** with an average density of about one particle per cubic centimeter but a much greater local density, of 10 billion particles per cubic centimeter, in prestellar clouds known as **globule**s. The gas of the ISM is mostly hydrogen in an ionized (➔ **hydrogen ion**), neutral, or molecular (➔ **molecular cloud**s) state. However, in the formation of **terrestrial planet**s and the evolution of life, the presence of small quantities of **heavy elements,** such as carbon and oxygen, is crucial. These elements were formed in the cores of earlier generations of stars and have recycled through the ISM to become the raw material from which new stars and their retinues of worlds are formed.

interstellar molecules
More than one hundred different types of **molecule** have been found by **spectroscopy** in interstellar space, mainly in **molecular cloud**s:

Diatomic			
H_2	Molecular hydrogen	PN	Phosphorus nitride
OH	Hydroxyl radical	CS	Carbon monosulfide
CH	Methylidyne radical	SiS	Silicon sulfide
CH^+	Methylidyne cation	NS	Nitrogen sulfide
C_2	Carbon dimer	CSi	
CO	Carbon monoxide	CP	
CO^+	Carbon monoxide cation	HF	Hydrogen fluoride
SiO	Silicon monoxide	HCl	Hydrogen chloride
SO	Sulfur monoxide	NH	
SO^+	Sulfur monoxide cation	NaCl	Sodium chloride
NO	Nitric oxide	KCl	Potassium chloride
PO	Phosphorus monoxide	AlF	
CN	Cyanogen radical	AlCl	
SiN	Silicon nitride		

Triatomic			
C_3	Carbon trimer	HDO	Deuterated water
C_2H	Ethynyl radical	H_2S	Hydrogen sulfide
C_2O	Carbene	N_2O	Nitrous oxide
C_2S		CO_2	Carbon dioxide
CH_2		SO_2	Sulfur dioxide
HCN	Hydrogen cyanide	NH_2	
HNC	Hydrogen isocyanide	N_2H^+	Protonated nitrogen ion
HNO		H_3^+	
HCO	Formyl radical	c-SiC_2	
HCO^+	Formyl cation	OCS	Carbonyl sulfide
HCS^+		NaCN	Sodium cyanide
HOC^+		MgCN	Magnesium cyanide
H_2O	Water	MgNC	Magnesium isocyanide

4-Atomic			
c-C_3H	c-Propynlidyne	$HCNH^+$	Protonated hydrogen cyanide
l-C_3H	l-Propynlidyne	HNCO	Isocyanic acid
C_3N	Cyanoethynyl	HNCS	
C_3O	Tricarbon monoxide	$HOCO^+$	
C_3S	Tricarbon sulfide	H_2CN	
C_2H_2	Acetylene	H_2CS	Thioformaldehyde
H_2CO	Formaldehyde	H_3O^+	Hydronium ion
CH_2O^+		NH_3	Ammonia
HCCN			

5-Atomic			
C_5		CH	Methane
C_4H		HC_2NC	
C_4Si		HCOOH	Formic acid
C_4N	Butadiynyl	H_2C_2O	Ketene
c-C_3H_2	c-Cyclopropenyliden	HC_3N	Cyanoacetylene
l-C_3H_2	l-Cyclopropenyliden	H_2NCN	Cyanamide
CH_2CN		SiH_4	Silane
CH_2NH	Methylenimine	H_2COH^+	

6-Atomic			
C_5H		CH_3SH	
C_5O		HC_3NH^+	
l-C_2H_4	Ethene	HCH_2CHO	
CH_3CN	Methyl cyanide	$HCONH_2$	Formamide
CH_3OH	Methanol		
7-Atomic			
C_6H		CH_3CHO	Acetaldehyde
CH_2CHCN	Acrylonitrile	CH_3NH_2	Methylamine
CH_3C_2H	Methylacetylene	c-C_2H_4	
HC_5N	Cyanodiacetylene		
8-Atomic			
C_7H		$HCOOCH_3$	Methyl formate
C_6H_2		CH_3COOH	
CH_3C_3N			
9-Atomic			
C_8H		$(CH_3)_2O$	Dimethyl ether
CH_3C_4H		C_2H_5OH	Ethanol
CH_3CH_2CN	Propionitrile	HC_7N	Cyanotriacetylene
10-Atomic			
$CH_3C_5N(?)$		NH_2CH_2COOH	Glycine II
$(CH_3)_2CO$			
11-Atomic			
HC_9N	Cyanotetra-acetylene		
13-Atomic			
$HC_{11}N$			

interstellar probes

Four spacecraft launched from Earth—***Pioneer 10, Pioneer 11, Voyager 1,*** and ***Voyager 2***— have achieved solar **escape velocity** so that they are now on departure trajectories from the solar system. For as long as they remain functional, they afford the opportunity to explore the environment of space out to the limit of the Sun's magnetic influence, the **heliopause,** and beyond. Thereafter, although contact with them will be lost, they will continue to drift slowly toward the stars bearing messages (➜ ***Pioneer* plaque, *Voyager* interstellar record**) in the remote event that they are intercepted and recovered by an alien intelligence.

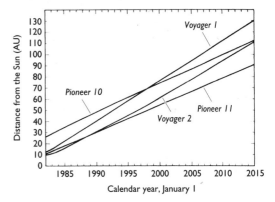

Heliocentric ranges of current solar system escapees. Originally presented at the 1983 AAS/AIA Astrodynamics Conference held August 22–25, 1983, Lake Placid, New York, and originally published in the AAS publication *Astrodynamics 1983,* American Astronautical Society (AAS), AAS Microfiche Series, vol. 45, paper no. AAS 83-308, "Prospects for *Voyager* Extra-Planetary and Interstellar Mission" by Robert J. Cesarone, Andrey B. Sergeyevsky, and Stuart J. Kerridge (JPL). Reprinted with permission of the AAS: American Astronautical Society Publications Office, P. O. Box 28130, San Diego, CA 92198.

interstellar travel

Journeying between the stars is made problematic at present by the immense distances involved (➔ **interstellar distances**) and the limited propulsion technologies that are available. Although it is increasingly hard to imagine a future in which human beings do not eventually journey to the stars, unless our species destroys itself first, it is also difficult to see how such a mission could be undertaken within the next century or so. For the foreseeable future, manned exploration will be concentrated on the Moon, Mars, and, beyond that, possibly the large moons of the outer planets. Robotic interstellar missions, on the other hand, may well become practicable over the next few decades. Already several spacecraft from Earth are heading slowly toward the stars (➔ **interstellar probes**), although they will be defunct long before they arrive anywhere near the vicinity of any extrasolar planetary systems. These early pioneers will rapidly be overtaken by a new generation of star probes based on advanced technology, including **artificial intelligence** and high-speed propulsion systems.[12, 13]

intracellular

Existing or taking place within a **cell.**

intrinsic variable

A **variable star** whose changes in brightness are due to actual fluctuations in the luminosity of the star itself, not to external processes as in the case of an **extrinsic variable.**

intron

A portion of **messenger RNA** (mRNA), as transcribed (➔ **transcription**) from the **DNA** of a **eukaryote,** that is removed by **enzymes** before the mRNA matures and is transplanted into **protein.** The portions of mRNA that remain after the excision of the introns are known as **exons.**

Invaders from Mars

Low-budget, high-impact 1953 science fiction film that both reflected and encouraged the xenophobia prevalent in postwar America. In it, a **flying saucer** lands and buries itself in the ground outside an unsuspecting town. Only a young boy sees its arrival, and of course at first no one believes his fantastic story. Then people start to disappear—a soldier, the commissioner of police, the boy's parents—only to reappear later, having been "taken over." Eventually, the Army is called in and the aliens are defeated. The people who had been abducted are returned to normal. If Hollywood had gone out of its way to produce an anti-Communist propaganda film, it could hardly have done a more effective job. The aliens are the Communists trying to compel everyone, against their will, to become part of a system in which individuality is crushed and merged with an authoritarian whole. Only American resolve and ingenuity stand in their way. And, naturally, the home side wins; freedom is preserved—for the moment. Although the metaphors seem transparent enough now, when the film was first shown people no doubt enjoyed it simply as pure sci-fi escapism. Nevertheless, the subliminal message (whether it was put there intentionally or not) would have got through and reinforced what everyone already feared: the United States, the last great guardian of liberty, was under imminent threat from sinister outside forces. ➔ **science fiction involving extraterrestrials, in films and on television; Cold War, linked to UFO reports**

Invasion of the Body Snatchers

1956 film, based on *The Body Snatchers* (1955) by Jack Finney, in which seedpods arrive on Earth from space (➔ **panspermia**) and begin forming emotionless duplicates of people. The human victims are then replaced as they sleep by their alien doppelgangers. In his analysis of the film, Ernesto Laura writes:

> It is natural to see the pods as standing for the idea of communism which gradually takes possession of a normal person, leaving him outwardly unchanged but transformed within.

Others have argued that the film reflects left-wing paranoia about McCarthyism. In any event, the theme is a popular one of this time—the threat to individuality and personal freedom. A good remake was released in 1978. ➔ **science fiction involving extraterrestrials,** in films and on television; Cold War, linked to UFO reports

inward orbital migration

A major reduction in the size of the orbits of some planets that may be a common collateral of the early development of planetary systems. Theories of inward orbital migration[350, 472] were hastily put forward following the unexpected discovery, from 1995 onward, of massive planets in extremely small orbits about their host stars (→ **epistellar Jovians**). Since it is hard to see how such large worlds, which are presumably **gas giant**s, could have formed in their present orbits of radii less than 2 AU, and in some cases less than 0.2 AU, the favored conclusion is that they formed further out and were then caused to move inward. Several processes have been suggested to account for this drastic orbital shift, including near encounters with other large worlds, resulting in an effect like the scattering of billiard balls,[617] and viscous drag as the new planet plowed its way through the remnants of the dusty nebula from which it formed, losing energy as it goes. Both theory and observation suggest that the migration time to a small orbit for a giant planet that formed at a radius of 5 AU is less than 1 million years. Researchers have also sought to explain how such a world manages to avoid terminal orbital decay and a disastrous collision with its central star. One possibility is that the giant planet raises a bulge on the surface of its primary. If the star rotates faster than the planet orbits, the tidal bulge would remain ahead and tend to speed the planet along, thus counteracting any tendency to spiral inward further. Alternatively, it may be that the magnetic field of the star sweeps the inner region of the nebula clear of gas and dust so that the drag on the planet stops abruptly when it reaches this open zone. While some large planets, similar to or greater than Jupiter in mass, may be affected in this way, others will form in the outskirts of their planetary systems and remain in distant orbits, as Jupiter itself has done. A number of astronomers, however, have cast doubt on whether the newly found **extrasolar planets** in tiny orbits are gas giants after all. In the ab-

sence of evidence to the contrary, it may that these worlds are, in the words of Paul **Butler,** "giant nickel-iron bowling balls" that actually formed in their present locations.

An intriguing question is whether, if inward orbital migration *has* taken place, this compromises the prospects for finding other potentially life-bearing worlds like the Earth. It may be that an inward-bound giant planet would eject or destroy any terrestrial-type neighbors that it encountered. On the other hand, it is also conceivable that other Earth-like worlds would form in its gravitational wake. → **planetary systems, formation of**

Io

The innermost and densest of **Jupiter**'s **Galilean satellites,** Io is similar in size and density to our own Moon. It has an iron core and a high-altitude ionosphere. The internal heat generated by the continual gravitational tug-of-war with Jupiter, **Europa,** and **Ganymede** makes Io the most volcanically active body in the solar system. When the *Voyager* spacecraft flew past, they recorded a total of eleven active volcanoes, the largest of which, Pele, ejected a plume of material 300 km (190

Discovery	January 7, 1610, by Galileo Galilei
Mean distance from Jupiter	421,600 km (262,026 mi.)
Diameter	3,630 km (2,256 mi.)
Equatorial diameter (Earth = 1)	0.285
Mass (Earth = 1)	0.0148
Mean density	3.55 g/cm³
Surface gravity (Earth = 1)	0.183
Escape velocity	2.56 km/s (9,216 km/h, 5,728 mi./h)
Orbital period	1.769 days (1 day 18 hours 27 minutes)
Orbital eccentricity	0.004
Orbital inclination	0.04°
Axial period	1.769 days
Albedo	0.61
Surface temperature	−135°C (−216°F) with "hot spots" of 27°C (81°F)
Surface composition	Sulfur/frozen sulfur dioxide

miles) high. Hundreds of volcanic calderas have been observed on the surface. Because the surface is continually being relaid, there are no visible impact craters. The surface colors of mottled red, orange, yellow, brown, and white are due to **sulfur** and frozen **sulfur dioxide.** The terrain consists mostly of flat plains rising to less than 1 km with some mountain ranges up to 9 km high. A torus of sodium gas and sulfur ions is spread out along Io's orbit. ➔ **Jupiter, moons of**

ion

Any **atom** or **molecule** containing an unequal number of **electron**s and **proton**s and therefore carrying a net positive or negative charge.

ionic bond

An attraction between **ion**s of opposite charge in an ionic compound. Such bonds, which result from the transfer of **electron**s, are not formed between particular ions but exist between an ion and all of the oppositely charged ions in its immediate vicinity. ➔ **covalent bond**

ionization

The formation of **ion**s by the removal or addition of one or more **electron**s from the outer parts of **atom**s. The stripping away of electrons can happen when atoms are exposed to short wavelength **electromagnetic radiation** as in the outer atmosphere of stars hotter than the Sun or in bright nebulas. Matter that has been completely ionized so that it is a mixture of bare nuclei and free electrons, as in the intensely hot interior of stars, is known as **plasma.**

ionized

Consisting of **ion**s.

ionized hydrogen
➔ **hydrogen ion**

ionizing radiation

High-energy radiation, including far **ultraviolet** and **X rays,** that is capable of causing **ionization.**

ionosphere

A region of charged particles in a planet's upper atmosphere. ➔ **Earth, atmosphere of**

IRAS
➔ **Infrared Astronomy Satellite**

iron

Metallic element; the fourth most abundant in the Earth's crust. Iron is required as a trace element by living organisms.

Atomic number 26; density relative to water 7.87; melting point 1,535°C; boiling point 2,750 °C

IRSI
➔ *Infrared Space Interferometer*

ISM
➔ **interstellar medium**

ISO
➔ *Infrared Space Observatory*

isotopes

Atoms of the same **element** that differ in the number of **neutron**s they contain. Nearly all elements found in nature are mixtures of several different isotopes. Of astrobiological interest is the fact that isotopic ratios of particular elements are affected by the presence of life. For example, **nitrogen** gas is enriched in ^{14}N when produced by denitrification, and **hydrogen sulfide** is enriched in ^{32}S when it results from **sulfate** reduction. Such patterns of fractionation provide clues for the remote sensing of life on other worlds. ➔ **extraterrestrial life, detection of**

isotropic

Having properties that are the same in all directions.

isotropic signal

A signal transmitted with equal strength in every direction in space. The energy required to broadcast an isotropic signal detectable over interstellar, or intergalactic, distances would be vastly greater than that needed to send a signal of equivalent strength from a **directional antenna.** Only a Type II or Type III **Kardashev civilization** would be capable of transmitting an easily detectable message in this way.

It Came from Outer Space

1953 film based on "The Meteor" by Ray

Bradbury that exploits the themes of alien subterfuge and human duplication, popular during this era of paranoia (➔ **Cold War, related to UFO reports**). By shape-shifting, the inhabitants of a crashed extraterrestrial spacecraft make copies of local inhabitants to assist in repairs. ➔ **science fiction involving extraterrestrials, in films and on television**

Ivuna meteorite

A 0.7-kg **carbonaceous chondrite** that landed near Ivuna, Tanzania, on December 16, 1938. It was one of four meteorites, including the **Orgueil meteorite,** in which Bartholomew Nagy and George Claus[119] claimed to have found evidence of primitive extraterrestrial fossils. Subsequent analysis led to this claim being discredited. ➔ **organic matter, in meteorites**

jansky (Jy)

The unit used by astronomers for measuring the radio flux density from radio sources. It equals 10^{-26} watts per square meter per **hertz** and is named after Karl **Jansky**.

Jansky, Karl Guthe (1905–50)

American radio engineer of Czech descent whose 1931 discovery of extraterrestrial radio emission while working for Bell Telephone Laboratories led to the eventual birth of radio astronomy and **SETI**. Jansky's announcement in 1933 that the source of the radio waves was the Milky Way galaxy itself received front-page coverage in the May 5 issue of *The New York Times*, which noted, "There is no indication of any kind, Mr. Jansky replied to a question, that these galactic radio waves constitute some kind of interstellar signaling, or that they are the result of some form of intelligence striving for intergalactic communication." Initially, astronomers showed little interest in Jansky's results and treated his galactic theory with skepticism. However, a young radio ham, Grote Reber, was encouraged by the findings to build in 1938 what was the world's first dedicated **radio telescope**—a 10-m (30-ft.) parabolic dish with which he discovered several new cosmic radio sources. Two decades later, the construction of giant versions of such in-struments would enable the search for artificial interstellar signals (→ **SETI**) to begin in earnest.

Janus

The fifth (equal) moon of **Saturn**, coorbital with **Epimetheus**. Janus displays few linear surface features but is extensively cratered, with several craters measuring up to 30 km (19 miles) across.

Discovery	1966, by Audouin Dollfus
Mean distance from Saturn	151,470 km (94,140 mi.)
Diameter	199 × 192 × 150 km (124 × 119 × 93 mi.)
Mean density	0.67 g/cm³
Escape velocity	0.052 km/s (187 km/h, 116 mi./h)
Orbital period	0.695 day (16 hours 41 minutes)
Orbital eccentricity	0.007
Orbital inclination	0.14°
Axial period	0.695 day
Visual albedo	0.8

Jeans, James Hopwood (1877–1946)

British astrophysicist, mathematician, and popularizer of science, whose theory of the origin of planets led, in the 1920s and 1930s, to a sharp decline in optimism among professional astronomers about the prospects for life beyond the solar system. In *The Universe Around Us* (1927) he wrote:

> [P]lanets…come into being as the result of the close approach of two stars, and stars are so sparsely scattered in space that it is an inconceivably rare event for one to pass near to a neighbour.

→ **Jeans-Jeffreys tidal hypothesis; prime number**

Jeans-Jeffreys tidal hypothesis
Championed by James **Jeans** and Harold **Jeffreys,** this explained the origin of the solar system as a result of a close encounter between the Sun and a second star. However, it differed significantly from the other major **catastrophic hypothesis** of the twentieth century, the **Chamberlin-Moulton planetesimal hypothesis.** As a result of a detailed mathematical analysis, Jeans concluded in 1916 that the tidal interaction between the Sun and a passing star would raise tides on the Sun resulting in the loss of a single cigar-shaped filament of hot gas, rather than separate streams of gas as in the Chamberlin and Moulton scenario. This hot gas would then condense directly into the planets instead of going through a **planetesimal** stage. The central section of the "cigar" would give rise to the largest planets—Jupiter and Saturn—while the tapering ends would provide the substance for the smaller worlds. This model had important repercussions for the possibility of life elsewhere in the Universe because if planetary systems came about only as a result of freak stellar encounters, there would be relatively few extrasolar worlds to provide biological platforms. In his 1923 lecture "The Nebular Hypothesis and Modern Cosmogony," Jeans said:

> Astronomy does not know whether or not life is important in the scheme of things, but she begins to whisper that life must necessarily be somewhat rare.

By the late 1920s, this opinion was shared by many astronomers. However, in 1935, Henry Norris **Russell** raised what would become fatal objections to the Jeans-Jeffreys hy-

pothesis. He pointed out that it was hard to see how a close stellar encounter could leave the Sun, which is a thousand times more massive than the planets, with such a tiny share of the solar system's **angular momentum.** Furthermore, he could not understand how the planets could condense out of hot material ejected from the Sun. The former objection was put into stronger form by Russell himself in 1943, while the latter was strengthened by Russell's student Lyman Spitzer in 1939.

Jefferson, Thomas (1743–1826)
U.S. president who accepted **pluralism** and whose library contained books on the subject by Bernard de **Fontenelle,** Christiaan **Huygens,** and William **Derham.** → **Adams, John**

Jeffreys, Harold (1891–1989)
British scientist who, from 1917 on, made original contributions to the tidal hypothesis of the origin of the solar system (→ **Jeans-Jeffreys tidal hypothesis**). He also developed early models of the structures of the outer planets and was the first to propose that the Earth's core is liquid.

Jet Propulsion Laboratory (JPL)
An establishment in Pasadena, California, operated by the California Institute of Technology for **NASA,** that plays a major role in the development, operation, and tracking of U.S. interplanetary space probes. JPL has responsibility for the Deep Space Network and has managed the *Viking, Voyager, Galileo,* and *Mars Pathfinder* missions. Among the current crop of projects it is involved with that have a direct bearing on the possibility of life in space are the *Mars Climate Observer,* the *Mars Polar Lander,* and the **Exploration of Neighboring Planetary Systems.** JPL was founded in 1944 for the purpose of missile development but became part of NASA in 1958.

Jodrell Bank
The site of the Nuffield Radio Astronomy Laboratory of the University of Manchester, near Macclesfield, Cheshire, England. The main instrument is the 76-m (250-ft.) **Lovell Telescope,** the second largest fully steerable **radio telescope** in the world.

Johnson Space Center (JSC)
→ **NASA Johnson Space Center**

Jones, Harold Spencer (1890–1960)
English astrophysicist and astronomer royal (1933–55) who become a strong advocate of the view that extraterrestrial life is probably common in the Universe. In the first edition of his influential *Life on Other Worlds*,[558] published in 1940, he echoed the conclusions of James **Jeans** and others, based on the then-popular **catastrophic hypothesis** that

> life is not widespread in the universe...not more than a small proportion of the stars are likely to have planets at all. With the usual prodigality of Nature, the stars are scattered far and wide, but only the favored few have planets that are capable of supporting life.

However, by the second edition in 1952, with the rise of Carl von **Weizsäcker**'s updated version of the **nebular hypothesis,** he was able to write:

> On this important problem of the origin of the solar system and of planetary systems in general, there has been a marked change in outlook in the past few years from that of twenty years ago. Astronomers then felt pretty confident that the solar system was something very exceptional; now it appears much more probable that the formation of a planetary system may occur as one of the normal courses of stellar evolution.

As to the likelihood of life evolving on the surface of a suitable planet, in 1940 Jones was already optimistic:

> [I]t seems reasonable to suppose that whenever in the Universe the proper conditions arise, life must inevitably come into existence. This is the view that is generally accepted by biologists.

Jong, H. G. Bungenburg de
Dutch chemist who, in 1932, first described the microscopic **cell**-like structures known as **coacervate**s that formed during his experiments on **colloidal dispersion**s.

Jovian
A planet similar to or greater than Jupiter in mass. The fact that the majority of **extrasolar planets** found to date are Jovians in small orbits is a selection effect, resulting from the fact that these objects exert a relatively large gravitational pull on their **host star**s and are therefore the easiest to detect. Numerous **Earth-class planet**s are expected to be found in the future through the use of more sensitive equipment, both on the ground and in space. Theory suggests that large Jovians, with masses several times that of Jupiter, should tend to occur around stars having a high abundance of elements heavier than hydrogen and helium. Such elements, in the **protoplanetary disk,** form dust particles and then, by agglomeration, **planetisimal**s and the rock-metal cores of **gas giant**s.

JPL
→ **Jet Propulsion Laboratory**

JSC
→ **NASA Johnson Space Center**

Juliet
The sixth known moon of **Uranus**. → **Uranus, moons of**

Discovery	1986, by *Voyager 2*
Mean distance from Uranus	64,400 km (40,000 mi.)
Diameter	84 km (52 mi.)
Orbital period	0.493 day (11 hours 50 minutes)
Orbital eccentricity	0.001
Orbital inclination	0.46°
Visual albedo	0.07

Jung, Carl Gustav (1875–1961)
Swiss psychologist and psychiatrist who founded analytic psychology. He believed that a direct encounter with intellectually superior beings would be disastrous for our race:

> [T]he reins would be torn from our hands and we would, as a tearful old medicine man once said to me, find ourselves "without dreams," that is, we would find our intellectual and spiritual aspirations so outmoded as to leave us completely paralyzed.

→ **extraterrestrial intelligence, implications following first contact**

Jupiter

A **gas giant** and the largest of the solar worlds, Jupiter accounts for two thirds of the planetary mass of the solar system. It has an extensive family of satellites (→ **Jupiter, moons of**) and a faint ring. Huge storms occur in its atmosphere, one of which, the **Great Red Spot,** is known to be at least 100 years old and may have been seen three centuries ago. Features such as the Great Red Spot are thought to be caused by plumes of warmer gas rising from deep in the planet's interior. The orange and brown colors may be due to **organic** compounds, or to **sulfur** or **phosphorus.** The topmost clouds of Jupiter are made of **ammonia** ice. Below this are believed to be ammonium–**hydrogen sulfide** crystals, and, deeper still, water ice and possibly liquid water. At great depths, **hydrogen,** which makes up the bulk of Jupiter's atmosphere, is believed to behave like a metal and may be the primary source of the immensely powerful Jovian magnetic field. One theory suggests that, rather than being solid, Jupiter's core is a high density liquid or slush.

Measurements by the *Galileo* descent probe in December 1995 have confirmed that Jupiter and the Sun have almost the same elemental composition and therefore formed from the same primordial mixture. However, not all of the probe's measurements tied in with theoretical predictions, the biggest surprise being the lack of water in the upper atmosphere. Several ideas have been put forward to explain this finding. Perhaps water concentrations vary with latitude, a suggestion that ties in with the observation that most of Jupiter's lightning (an activity associated with water clouds) occurs at middle latitude, whereas the probe descended near the planet's equator. Another possibility is that, during Jupiter's formation, water tended to be confined to the planet's core by the massive overlying blanket of hydrogen and helium.

Jupiter orbits the Sun five times further out than does the Earth, so that each unit area of its surface receives only about one twenty-fifth, or 4 percent, of the solar energy falling on a similar-sized patch of our own world. Although Jupiter has virtually the same elemental composition as the Sun, it would have needed at least ten times more mass in order to have become a **brown dwarf,** and about

Distance from Sun:	
Mean	778.3 million km (483.7 million mi., 5.20 AU)
Minimum	740.9 million km (460.4 million mi., 4.95 AU)
Maximum	815.7 million km (506.9 million mi., 5.46 AU)
Equatorial diameter	142,984 km (88,864 mi.)
Equatorial diameter (Earth = 1)	11.209
Mass (Earth = 1)	317.9
Mean density	1.3 g/cm^3
Escape velocity	60.2 km/s (216,720 km/h, 134,692 mi./h)
Orbital period	11.86 years
Orbital eccentricity	0.048
Orbital inclination	1.3°
Axial period	9.8 hours
Axial inclination	3.1°
Number of moons	16
Gravity at cloud tops (Earth = 1)	2.64
Atmospheric composition	~90% hydrogen, ~10% helium, traces of methane, other gases
Mean temperature (cloud tops)	−150°C (−238°F)
Albedo	0.43

eighty times more mass in order to have initiated nuclear reactions and shone as a star. Nevertheless, heat generated when Jupiter formed by gravitational collapse causes the planet to radiate 1.5 to two times as much energy as it receives through solar radiation. This internal source of heat is one of the reasons that scientists have not ruled out the possibility of life existing at some level within Jupiter's atmosphere (➔ **Jupiter, life on**).

Jupiter, life on

The possibility of "abundant biota" in the upper regions of **Jupiter**'s atmosphere was considered in a 1977 paper by Carl **Sagan** and Edwin E. Salpeter[504] prior to the arrival of the first Jupiter probe, *Pioneer 10.* Sagan and Salpeter compared the ecology of the Jovian atmosphere with that of terrestrial seas, which have simple **photosynthetic** plankton at the top level, fish at lower levels feeding on these creatures, and marine predators that hunt the fish. The three hypothetical Jovian equivalents of these organisms Sagan and Salpeter termed "sinkers," "floaters," and "hunters." They envisaged creatures like giant gas bags that move by pumping out **helium** and calculated that the "hunter" variety might grow to be many kilometers across (and therefore visible from space). Jovian aerial life-forms like these are portrayed in Arthur C. **Clarke**'s short story "A Meeting with Medusa" (in *The Wind from the Sun*). However in recent years, astrobiological interest in the Jovian system has shifted dramatically from Jupiter itself to its larger moons, especially **Europa** and **Callisto.**

Jupiter, moons of

See separate entries for each of the moons listed below.

Moon	Distance from Jupiter (km)	Orbital Period (days)	Orbital Eccentricity	Orbital Inclination (degrees)	Diameter (km)
Metis	127,600	0.295	0.000	0.00	40
Adrastea	128,400	0.298	0.000	0.00	25 × 20 × 15
Amalthea	181,300	0.498	0.003	0.40	270 × 168 × 150
Thebe	225,000	0.675	0.018	1.07	110 × 90
Io	421,600	1.769	0.004	0.04	3,630
Europa	670,900	3.551	0.009	0.47	3,138
Ganymede	1,070,000	7.155	0.002	0.20	5,262
Callisto	1,883,000	16.689	0.007	0.51	4,820
Leda	11,100,000	238.72	0.148	26.1	16
Himalia	11,470,000	250.57	0.158	27.6	186
Lysithea	11,710,000	259.22	0.107	29.0	36
Elara	11,743,000	259.65	0.207	24.8	76
Ananke	20,700,000	−631 (r)*	0.169	147	30
Carme	22,350,000	−692 (r)	0.207	163	40
Pasiphaë	23,300,000	−735 (r)	0.378	147	50

* r = retrograde.

Jupiter-type comet

A comet with a period of less than 20 years. Such comets differ from both **long-period comets** and **Halley-type comets** in that their orbits are inclined to the plane of Earth's orbit at no more than 40°, whereas the longer-period comets enter the planetary region randomly from all directions. Jupiter-type comets are believed to have come from the **Kuiper Belt.**

K

K star

An orange-red star of **spectral type** K. The spectrum contains strong **absorption line**s of neutral and ionized calcium and, particularly at the lower end of the temperature range, numerous lines of neutral metals and molecular bands. K-type **main sequence** stars are intermediate in size and temperature between M-type **red dwarf**s and type G Sun-like stars, with a mass of 0.5 to 0.8 M_S, a temperature of 3,600 to 4,900°C, and a luminosity of 0.1 to 0.4 L_S. Nearby examples include Epsilon Indi, **Epsilon Eridani,** and **Tau Ceti,** the latter two having been the **target stars** of Project **Ozma.** **Early-type** main sequence K stars within a few tens of light-years of the Sun are generally included in the list of target stars (→ **FGK stars**) of searches for **extrasolar planets** and targeted **SETI** programs, since if they have planets orbiting within their **habitable zone**s there is the possibility that these worlds support life of some kind. Familiar examples of K-type **giant stars** include **Arcturus, Aldebaran,** and **Pollux.**

Kaba meteorite

A **carbonaceous chondrite** that fell at Kaba, near Debrecen, Hungary, on April 15, 1857. Samples of it and the **Cold Bokkeveld meteorite** were examined and found to contain **or-ganic** substances by Friedrich **Wöhler,** who inferred a biological origin. Ironically, it was Wöhler who had shown that it was possible to make organic chemicals by inorganic means. However, it was only later appreciated that complex carbon molecules can be manufactured in space by purely chemical processes. → **organic matter, in meteorites**

Kamp, Peter van der

→ **van der Kamp, Peter**

Kant, Immanuel (1724–1804)

Great German philosopher, best known for his *Critique of Pure Reason,* who played an important part in the extraterrestrial life debate of the eighteenth century and in enlarging man's conception of the physical universe. The young Kant was strongly influenced by Thomas **Wright**'s speculations about life on other worlds and on the nature of the Milky Way. By 1755, in his *Universal Natural History and Theory of the Heavens,* he set out his revolutionary claims that the Milky Way was an optical effect due to our location within a large disk of stars and that the fuzzy patches known as nebulas were, in reality, other Milky Ways (external galaxies). He also put forward an early version of the **nebular hypothesis** (later developed by Pierre **Laplace**), though he applied this generally to the Milky Way and to the Universe as a whole, not just to planetary systems. On more metaphysical matters, Kant took the proponents of **natural theology** to task for seeking evidence of God's design in every detail of the cosmos. For him, the best evidence for God was the underlying lawfulness of the Universe: "There is a God precisely because nature can proceed even in chaos in no other way than regularly and orderly." His speculations in *Universal Natural History* regarding extraterrestrials are extraordinary. In the cosmology he develops, not only the solar system and the Milky Way have their centers, but so too does the entire Universe. Moreover, the creatures of worlds near to the centers of any system, having developed (he supposed) from less refined matter, are intellectually feeble, whereas those farther out are "the more perfect classes of rational beings." Thus Kant envisaged a hierarchy of intelligent life-forms developing throughout time and space. In our own solar system, he considered the inhabitants of Mercury and Venus to be dull and humans to be on "exactly the middle rung," while the Jovians and Saturnians are beings far in advance of ourselves. As to the problem of reconciling his views on **pluralism** with Christianity (especially the issues of **incarnation and redemption**), he speculates that the inhabitants of the outer planets might be "too noble and wise" to sin, whereas the miserable creatures living on Mercury and Venus were perhaps "grafted too fast to matter . . . to carry the responsibility of their actions before the judgment seat of justice?" Later in life, he moderated his views on extraterrestrial life without giving up his pluralist stance altogether. In his monumental *Critique of Pure Reason* (1781), he remarks, "I should not hesitate to stake all on the truth of the proposition . . . that, at least, some one of the planets, which we see, is inhabited." However, elsewhere in the same book, he acknowledges that all comments on extraterrestrial life are "a matter of opinion."

Kapteyn's Star

A nearby **red dwarf**, in the southern constellation of Pictor, that has an unusually high **radial velocity** of 246 km per second (153 miles per second) and the second largest known **proper motion** of any star (8.7 arc-seconds per year) after **Barnard's Star.** It was first studied in detail by the Dutch astronomer J. C. Kapteyn in 1897.

Kardashev civilizations

A scheme for classifying advanced technological civilizations proposed by Nikolai **Kardashev**[310] in 1964. He identified three possible types and distinguished among them in terms of the power they could muster for the purposes of interstellar communications. A Type I civilization would be able to marshal energy resources for communications on a planetwide scale, equivalent to the *entire* present power consumption of the human race, or about 10^{16} watts. A Type II civilization would surpass this by a factor of approximately 10 billion, making available 10^{26} watts, by exploiting the total energy output of its central star. Freeman **Dyson,** for example, has shown in general terms how this might be done with a **Dyson sphere.** Finally, a Type III civilization would have evolved far enough to tap the energy resources of an entire **galaxy.** This would give a further increase by at least a factor of 10 billion to about 10^{36} watts. Carl **Sagan** pointed out[493, ch. 34] that the energy gaps between Kardashev's three types were so enormous that a finer gradation was needed to make the scheme more useful. A Type 1.1 civilization, for example, would be able to expend a maximum of 10^{17} watts on communications, a Type 2.3 could utilize 10^{29} watts, and so on. He estimated that, on this more discriminating scale, the human race would presently qualify as roughly a Type 0.7.

Kardashev explored the consequences of a Type II or III civilization diverting all of its nonessential power resources into an effort to communicate with other races. A Type II civilization, he estimated, could send the information equivalent of a medium-sized library across the Galaxy in a transmission burst lasting just 100 seconds (though to travel from one side of the Galaxy to the other would take it tens of thousands of years). The same amount of information could be sent across an intergalactic distance of 10 million light-years with a transmission time of a few weeks. A Type

III civilization could broadcast a library of information across the entire observable Universe with a transmission time of 3 seconds (although the journey to the most distant receiver, in this case, would take about 10 billion years). Kardashev argued that an **Ozma**-like search would be unlikely to detect a Type I civilization and that **SETI** programs should concentrate instead on looking for the kind of intense radio signals that might emanate from Type II or III activity. He called attention to two unusual radio sources with the California Institute of Technology designation numbers CTA-21 and **CTA-102.** Subsequently, Gennady Sholomitskii used the Crimea Deep Space Station to examine CTA-102 at a frequency of 920 MHz and reported variability in its output. Kardashev's claim that this was indicative of a possible artificial origin caused a short-lived sensation.

Kardashev, Nikolai S. (1932–   )

Russian astrophysicist and deputy director of the Space Research Institute of the Academy of Sciences, Moscow, who conducted the first Soviet search for intelligent extraterrestrial signals in 1963. A graduate of Moscow University (1955), Kardaschev studied under Iosif **Shklovskii** at the **Sternberg State Astronomical Institute,** from where he obtained a Ph.D. in 1962. The following year he carried out the pioneering Soviet effort in **SETI,** examining quasar **CTA-102.** An early advocate of the idea that some alien races may be billions of years ahead of us, he proposed a classification for such supercivilizations (➔ **Kardashev civilizations**) and recommended that searches for them concentrate on the **infrared** and millimeter-wave ranges of the spectrum, rather than the centimeter-wave range. In 1963, Kardashev organized a SETI research group at the Sternberg Institute and initiated arrangements for the first All-Union Meeting on extraterrestrial civilizations (➔ **Byurakan SETI conferences**).

Kauffman, Stuart A.

Controversial biophysicist, external professor at the Santa Fe Institute, and founder of the Bios Group. He is a leading proponent of the idea, first advocated by Manfred **Eigen,** that life emerges spontaneously from **prebiotic** material as a consequence of **self-organization. Natural selection** and the continuing influence of self-organization, he maintains, then interact in a coevolving population.

Keck Interferometer

Over the next decade, the light entering the twin **Keck Telescopes** will be passed through a system of **adaptive optics** to correct for turbulence in the Earth's atmosphere, and combined by an **optical interferometer.** The result of this new technology will be to create an instrument with the **resolving power** of a single mirror 85 m (278.9 ft.) in diameter. This immensely powerful tool will play a significant part in **NASA**'s **Origins Program.**

Keck Observatory

A major new optical and **infrared** observatory, located at an altitude of 4,200 m (13,800 ft.) atop Mauna Kea in Hawaii. It is operated by the California Association for Research in Astronomy (CARA), a partnership involving the California Institute of Technology, the University of California, and **NASA,** and was funded by the W. M. Keck Foundation. The observatory is home to the twin **Keck Telescopes.**

Keck Telescopes

The two largest optical and **infrared** telescopes currently in use. Located at the **Keck Observatory** in Hawaii, both have primary mirrors 10 m (33 ft.) in diameter, made from thirty-six 1.8-m-wide hexagonal segments. A computer-controlled system of sensors and actuators adjusts the position of each segment relative to its neighbors, twice a second, to an accuracy of 4 nm. Each telescope has four times the light-gathering power of the famous 5-m (16.4-ft.) Hale Telescope and seventeen times that of the *Hubble Space Telescope.* Keck I began scientific observations in May 1993 and Keck II in October 1996. Attached to Keck I is HIRES, the **High Resolution Échelle Spectrometer,** used in the search for **extrasolar planets** (➔ **San Francisco State University Planet Search**). Among the instruments fitted to Keck II is MIRLIN, the **Mid-Infrared Large-well Imager,** capable of showing detail in **circumstellar disk**s and thereby shedding light on the process of planetary formation.

kelvin (K)

A unit of temperature that has the value 0 at **absolute zero** (−273.16°C). One kelvin corresponds to an interval of one degree on the Celsius scale, so that the freezing and boiling points of water, at standard pressure, are 273 K and 373 K, respectively.

Kelvin, Lord

→ **Thomson, William**

Kepler, Johannes (1571–1630)

German astronomer, famed for his discovery of the laws of planetary motion. Kepler exemplifies the resistance shown by some of the leading Renaissance scientists (including Nicolaus **Copernicus** and Galileo **Galilei**) to the idea that there might be innumerable inhabited worlds. Having accepted that the Earth and other known planets revolve around the Sun, he was enthusiastic about the possibility of life in other parts of the solar system. However, he was resistant to the notion that the stars might have planetary systems of their own and questioned **pluralism** on theological grounds: "If there are globes similar to our Earth . . . [t]hen how can we be masters of God's handiwork?" His relief upon hearing the details of Galileo's discovery of four satellites of Jupiter are evident in his published response: "If you had discovered any planets revolving around one of the fixed stars, there would now be waiting for me chains and a prison among [Giordano] **Bruno**'s innumerabilities. I should say, exile to his infinite space." In Kepler's opinion the newly found moons had been made by God for the benefit of the Jovian inhabitants: "Our Moon exists for us on Earth, not for the other globes. Those four little moons exist for Jupiter, not for us. Each planet in turn, together with its occupants, is served by its own satellites. From this line of reasoning we deduce with the highest degree of probability that Jupiter is inhabited."

His *Somnium seu astronomia lunari* (*The Dream, or Postumous Work on Lunar Astronomy*),[316] published posthumously in 1634, was a typical blend of reasoned seventeenth-century astronomy and lingering medieval supernaturalism. The hero of the piece, a young Icelander named Duracotus, travels to the Moon with the aid of his mother, who is an accomplished witch—an arrangement not unfamiliar to Kepler since his own mother was tried, though not convicted, of witchcraft. → **Moon, life on**

Kepler Mission

A proposed mission in NASA's **Discovery Program** designed to detect and characterize **Earth-class planet**s by **photometry**. *Kepler*'s specific objectives over its 4-year lifetime are to determine: (1) the frequency of Earth-class and larger planets in and near the **habitable zone** of a wide variety of **spectral type**s of stars; (2) the distribution of diameter and orbital size of Earth-class planets; (3) the distribution of diameter, mass, density, **albedo,** and orbital size of giant inner planets; (4) the frequency of planets orbiting **multiple star** systems; and (5) the properties of those stars that have planetary systems.

Kepler's proposed main instrument is a 1-m-aperture **photometer** with a 12° field of view that will continuously and simultaneously monitor the light from 90,000 **main sequence** stars brighter than fourteenth magnitude in a star field in Cygnus. Planets will be discovered and characterized by the tiny periodic variations their **transit**s cause in a star's measured light output. Detection of two transits will be taken as evidence of a candidate planet with a third and subsequent transits providing confirmation.[66]

Keyhoe, Donald E. (1897–1988)

Retired Marine Corps major and pilot turned freelance writer who became interested in the phenomenon of **unidentified flying objects** in 1949 following a meeting with Ken Purdy, the editor of *True* magazine, and a proponent of the **extraterrestrial hypothesis.** Keyhoe became convinced that UFOs were alien spacecraft and that the government was hiding this fact from the public to avoid mass panic. He set forth his conspiracy theory in an article, "The Flying Saucers Are Real," in *True*'s January 1950 issue, then in a book of the same name published later that year.[319] His claims, although unsupported by scientific evidence or named sources, attracted much popular interest and were given a boost by the wave of UFO sightings in the early 1950s (→ "**Washington Invasion**") and the instigation of Project **Blue Book**. In 1957, Keyhoe became the director of a UFO club known as the **National Investigations Committee on Aerial Phenomena.**

kHz
→ **kilohertz**

kilogram (kg)
A unit of mass. 1 kg = 1,000 g = 2.2 lb. 1 kg is the mass of 1 liter of water.

kilohertz (kHz)
A unit of **frequency.** 1 kHz = 1,000 **hertz** (cycles per second).

kilometer (km)
A unit of distance. 1 km = 1,000 m = 0.62 miles. Alternatively, 1 mile = 1.609 km.

kiloparsec (kpc)
A unit used for measuring large astronomical distances. 1 kpc = 1,000 **parsec**s = 3,259 light-years.

kingdom
One of the chief taxonomic categories, the other being **domain.** The older, five-kingdom classification scheme has now been largely superseded by one of six kingdoms. → **life, classification of**

Kitt Peak National Observatory (KPNO)
A facility located 90 km (56 miles) southwest of Tucson, Arizona, at an altitude of 2,120 m. Founded in 1958 as part of the National Optical Astronomy Observatories, it includes among its instruments the 4-m (13.1-ft.) Mayall Telescope.

Klass, Philip J.
American aviation journalist who, in the 1970s, became the foremost critic of ufology, taking over that mantle from Donald **Menzel.**[321]

Klein, Harold P. "Chuck"
First head of NASA's astrobiology program at the **NASA Ames Research Center,** head of the *Viking* biology science team, and later head of life sciences at Ames.

KPNO
→ **Kitt Peak National Observatory**

Kraus, John D. (1910–)
Professor of electrical engineering and astronomy at Ohio State University and director-founder of the **Ohio State University Radio Observatory,** which for many years has been at the forefront of **SETI** research. Kraus, a pioneer of radio telescope design since the 1940s, obtained a B.S. in physics in 1931 and a Ph.D. in 1933 from the University of Michigan and went to Ohio State in 1946. His involvement with SETI dates back to the time when Robert **Dixon** proposed the use of the **Big Ear** telescope, which Kraus designed, to search for **narrowband** extraterrestrial signals. He edited and published *Cosmic Search*, the first journal dedicated to SETI.

Krebs, Nikolaus
→ **Nicholas of Cusa**

Krüger 60
A nearby **binary star** system, in the constellation of Cepheus, consisting of two **red dwarf**s, one of which (Krüger 60B) is a **flare star.** The pair lie 13.1 light-years away and orbit around each other with a period of 44 years.

K-T Boundary
→ **Cretaceous-Tertiary Boundary**

Kuiper Belt
A large reservoir of **ice dwarf**s that is believed to form a ring between about 30 AU—the mean distance of Neptune—and 50 AU (7.5 billion km, or 4.7 billion miles) from the Sun. Astronomers began to suspect its existence following the discovery by David Jewitt of the University of Hawaii and Jane Luu of the **University of California, Berkeley,** in 1992, of a 200-km-wide object circling the Sun beyond the orbit of Pluto. Since then, more such objects have been found. Estimates suggest that as

many as 70,000 Kuiper objects with a diameter of more than 100 km may exist in this region (and possibly more beyond 50 AU). Probably they formed where they are today, unlike the ice dwarfs in the **Oort Cloud,** which are thought to have formed closer to the Sun, at higher temperatures, and then been hurled into remote orbits by close encounters with the gas giants.

Kuiper objects, too, are occasionally disturbed, by the gravitational influence of Neptune and Uranus. When this happens, they may take up much more elliptical paths and become **Jupiter-type comets,** such as Comet Encke. A newly discovered class of object, known as **Centaurs,** are believed to be onetime Kuiper objects that have been displaced less severely so that they do not come close enough to the Sun to develop cometary tails. They include **Chiron** and **Pholus.** It is also suspected that **Pluto** and its moon, **Charon,** may have come from the Kuiper Belt. Further studies of the Kuiper Belt, possibly involving a probe (➔ *Pluto-Kuiper Express*) will help shed light on what are extremely primitive remnants from the early accretional phase of the solar system (➔ **planetary systems, formation of**). In addition, future investigations of **comets** will provide chemical evidence to test the hypothesis that Jupiter-type comets formed at lower temperatures than their longer-period cousins.

Kuiper Disk
➔ **Kuiper Belt**

Kuiper, Gerard Peter (1905–73)

Dutch-born American astronomer and graduate of the University of Leiden, who worked at the **Yerkes Observatory** and later at the **McDonald Observatory.** His name rhymes with "viper." Early in his career, Kuiper studied **binary star** and **multiple star** systems. His observations led him to conclude in 1935 that the average separation between the components of binary stars was about 20 AU, which is similar to the distance of the **gas giants** from the Sun. Following renewed difficulties with the **catastrophic hypothesis** of planetary formation, Kuiper speculated in 1951 that "it almost looks as though the solar system is a degenerate double star, in which the second mass did not condense into a single star but was spread out—and formed the planets and comets." Extrapolating from the fact that about 10 percent of binaries contained companion stars that were one tenth as massive as the primaries or less, Kuiper suggested that there might be 100 billion planetary systems in our galaxy alone. Kuiper also discovered **methane** in **Titan**'s atmosphere (1944), **carbon dioxide** in the Martian atmosphere (1947), the Uranian moon **Miranda** (1948), and the Neptunian moon **Nereid** (1949). His **spectroscopic** studies of Mars led him to propose that lichenlike plants might exist on the Martian surface (➔ **Mars, vegetation on**).[327]

L1551 (IRS5)

An object previously believed to be a young star in a giant cloud of gas and dust lying at a distance of 450 light-years (140 parsecs) in the constellation of Taurus. In 1998, observations with the **Very Large Array** (VLA), by Luis Rodriguez of the Autonomous National University of Mexico and his colleagues,[485] showed that it was in fact a close binary pair of young stars separated by only 45 AU (6.75 billion km), or slightly more than the Sun-to-Pluto distance. Around each component, VLA images revealed an orbiting dust disk extending out to 10 AU, or about as far as the orbit of Saturn. Similar **protoplanetary disk**s have been observed around single stars, but the L1551 disks are about one tenth as large, their size being limited by the gravitational effect of the neighboring star. The discovery is important because it shows that protoplanetary disks, albeit of more restricted size, can exist in close binary star systems. Each disk contains about 0.05 M_S of material, which is similar to the mass content of the solar system. Had the stars been much closer together, the gravitational effects of both would have disrupted the disks. As a result, if planetary systems do form in the L1551 pair, they will be among the nearest neighboring sets of planets in the Galaxy. In commenting on the discovery, astrophysicist Alan Boss suggested that if a giant planet were to form close to the edge of one of the disks, it might be ejected from the system by the gravitational effect of the companion. Such an effect, he pointed out, might explain the possible **rogue planet TMR-1C.**

La Silla Observatory

The facility of the **European Southern Observatory** at La Silla, near La Serena, in Chile. Located at an altitude of 2,400 m in a region of dry climate and clear skies, its main instruments are a 3.5-m (11.5-ft.) and a 3.6-m (11.8-ft.) reflector. The **Leonard Euler Telescope,** involved with **extrasolar planet** detection, is also sited here.

Lacaille 9352

→ **stars, nearest**

La Tour, Cagniard de (1777–1859)

French baron and naturalist who helped undermine the theory of **spontaneous generation** by demonstrating that the fermentation of beer results from the activities of tiny organisms.

Lagrangian orbit

The orbit of an object located at one of the **Lagrangian points.**

Lagrangian points

Locations in space around a two-body system (such as that of the Earth and the Moon) where a small object can maintain a fixed position with respect to the two main gravitating masses. They are named after the Italian-French mathematician and astronomer Joseph-Louis Lagrange, who first indicated their existence in 1772. Although there are five Lagrangian points in total, three of these are of

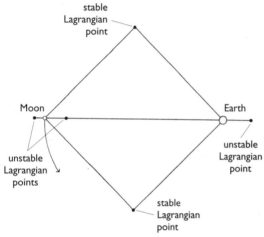

The location of the five Lagrangian points in the Earth-Moon system.

no practical significance since they are unstable. The slightest disturbance to any object located at one of these unstable points would cause the object to drift away permanently. The other two Lagrangian points, known as L4 and L5, lie at the vertices of equilateral triangles formed with the two main gravitating masses and in their orbital plane. These are stable Lagrangian points, also referred to as "libration points" since if any objects located at them were disturbed, the objects would simply wobble back and forth, or "librate." It has been argued that the L4 and L5 points in the Earth-Moon system would be good places to locate **space colonies** or to look for **Bracewell probe**s.

Lake Vostok
➔ Vostok, Lake

Lalande 21185

The fourth nearest star system to the Sun. Although Lalande 21185 is almost one two hundredth as bright as the Sun, it is among the brightest **red dwarf**s in the solar neighborhood. It has both a high **radial velocity,** of 86

Host Star		
Distance	8.25 light-years (2.53 parsecs)	
Spectral type	M2	
Mass (Sun = 1)	0.35	
Luminosity (Sun = 1)	0.0052	
Apparent magnitude	7.5	
Absolute magnitude	10.5	
Planets (To Be Confirmed)		
	a	*b*
Mass (Jupiter = 1)	0.9	1.6(?)
Semimajor axis	2.5 AU	10 AU(?)
Orbital period	5.8 years	30 years(?)
Discovery	1996, George Gatewood et al. at Allegheny Observatory	
Method of discovery	Astrometry	

km per second toward the Sun, and a high tangential velocity (**proper motion**) of 57 km per second. The former is bringing the star 0.028 light-years closer to us each century and to a closest approach of about 4.6 light-years in A.D. 22,000. After analyzing 50 years of **astrometric observation**s of the star, George **Gatewood** and colleagues of the **Allegheny Observatory** suggested (1996) that Lalande 21185 is orbited by two Jupiter-like planets, *a* and *b*, though the evidence for *b* is weaker than that for *a*.[213] There is also the possibility of a third, more remote object. If confirmed, these planets would be the nearest known extrasolar worlds to the Sun and the first to be discovered by astrometry. However, their existence has been questioned by researchers who have monitored Lalande 21185 by the **radial velocity method** and found no evidence of unseen companions. ➔ **stars, nearest**

Lalande, Joseph-Jérôme Le Français de (1732–1807)

Jesuit-trained French astronomer whose widely read *Traité d'astronomie* (published in three volumes under the title *Astronomie* in 1792) includes passages that argue in favor of intelligent life throughout the universe. He reconciles his support for **pluralism** with Christian doctrine by arguing that the glory of God is magnified by the presence of life on other worlds:

> If the extent of his works announces his power, can one supply any idea more magnificent and more sublime? We see with the naked eye many thousands of stars; an ordinary telescope reveals many more in every region of the sky.... [I]magination pierces beyond the telescope; it sees a new multitude of worlds infinitely larger.

Later, however, although continuing to support pluralism, he declared himself an atheist: "I have searched through the heavens, and nowhere have I found a trace of God." As director of the **Paris Observatory,** he published a list of observations of 50,000 stars, one of which, **Lalande 21185,** is among those now suspected of having **extrasolar planets.**

Lamarck, Jean-Baptiste-Pierre-Antoine de Monet de (1744–1829)

French naturalist and pre-Darwinian evolutionist. He served in the French Army, developed an interest in botany, and became keeper of the royal garden in 1774 and, in 1793, professor of invertebrate zoology at the Museum of Natural History, Paris. In his *Philosophie zoologique* (1809), he proposed that the environment causes organisms to acquire small changes, which are then passed on to their descendants. ➜ **evolutionary theory and extraterrestrial life**

Lambert, Johann Heinrich (1728–77)

German philosopher, described by Immanuel **Kant** as "the greatest genius of Germany." Lambert also ranked among the leading astronomers, mathematicians, and physicists of his day. In his *Cosmological Letters* (1761) he arrived, independently, at much the same conclusion as Kant and Thomas **Wright** concerning the disk-shaped form of the Milky Way and the existence of external systems of stars (galaxies) throughout space. Lambert's *Letters,* which reached a wider audience in eighteenth-century Europe than did the works of either Wright or Kant, is also replete with the most extreme kind of speculation about extraterrestrial life. No object in the universe, as far as Lambert was concerned, is devoid of life—and life, moreover, of every conceivable kind. "The Creator," he asserts in his *Letters,* "... is much too efficient not to imprint life, forces and activity on each speck of dust. ... [I]f one is to form a correct notion of the world, one should set as a basis God's intention in its true extent to make the whole world inhabited." The principle of **plenitude** he adopts without restraint: "[A]ll possible varieties which are permitted by general laws ought to be realized." Yet he is reasonable enough to acknowledge that he is being purely speculative: "And truly, have I not already rambled somewhat beyond the limits of what is credible? I drew conclusions and surely enough without having in each case appropriate observational evidence on hand." Like Wright and Kant, Lambert was driven to his extraterrestrial conclusions by the conviction that God in his omnipotence could not fail to populate every corner of the cosmos with all manner of beings. Indeed, these three pioneers of galactic and extragalactic astronomy seem to have been motivated as much by their desire to expand the number of planetary systems available for habitation as they were to populate the heavens with more stars.

Laplace, Pierre-Simon de (1749–1827)

French mathematician, astronomer, and physicist who, in 1796, announced an early version of the **nebular hypothesis,** the now generally accepted theory of how our planetary system formed. The solar system, Laplace said, originated out of a gradually cooling cloud of gas, with the planets most remote from the center condensing first. This theory had a strong influence on subsequent speculation about the nature of our neighboring worlds. It implied that the inner worlds were younger and that, in particular, cloud-covered Venus might be an immature version of the Earth—a virgin world. By contrast, planets further from the Sun, such as Mars, would have formed later and therefore could be expected to be more highly evolved. Laplace's theory also suggested that planets are a natural consequence of the evolution of stars, so that many stars ought to have planetary retinues. It therefore provided powerful support for the doctrine of **pluralism.**

Large Binocular Telescope (LBT)

An optical telescope employing two 8.4-m (27.6-ft.) mirrors on a common mount that is under construction on Mount Graham, Arizona. Scheduled to begin operation in 2003, the LBT is the result of a collaboration among the University of Arizona, Arcetri Astrophysical Observatory in Florence, Italy, and the Research Corporation of Tucson. Its twin mirrors, equipped with **adaptive optics** technology, will provide a light-gathering capacity equivalent to that of a single 11.8-m (39-ft.) mirror and a **resolving power** equivalent to that of a single 23-m (75.5-ft.) telescope. The LBT will be used with the technique of **nulling interferometry** in an effort to image **extrasolar planets** of Jupiter size or larger in orbit around nearby stars.

Large Magellanic Cloud (LMC)

The biggest of the satellite galaxies in orbit around the **Milky Way Galaxy.** The Large Magellanic Cloud lies about 150,000 light-years away and measures roughly 30,000 light-years in diameter. Its mass is estimated at about 1.5 billion M_S. → **Magellanic Clouds**

Large Southern Array (LSA)

→ **Atacama Large Millimeter Array**

Larissa

The fifth known moon of **Neptune.** Like the five other inner moons discovered during the 1989 flyby of *Voyager 2,* Larissa is among the darkest objects in the solar system. → **Neptune, moons of**

Discovery	1989, by Stephen Synnctt
Mean distance from Neptune	73,500 km (45,700 mi.)
Diameter	208 × 178 km (129 × 111 mi.)
Orbital period	0.555 day (13 hours 19 minutes)
Orbital eccentricity	0.0014
Orbital inclination	0.20°
Visual albedo	0.06

Las Campanas Observatory

An observatory at an altitude of 2,280 m on Cerro Las Campanas, 110 km northeast of La Serena, Chile, that is owned and operated by the Carnegie Institution of Washington, D.C. In addition to several smaller instruments already in place, it will be home to the **Magellan Telescopes.**

laser

A device that produces light or some other form of **electromagnetic radiation** that is monochromatic (of a single **wavelength**), coherent (in step), and contained in a narrow beam. It has been suggested that laser light, either continuous or pulsed, affords an effective means of communicating over interstellar distances, a concept that forms the basis of **optical SETI.** Paul **Horowitz,** for example, has proposed that a device such as the Helios laser being planned at the Lawrence Livermore National Laboratory would enable the generation of nanosecond-long pulses with 3,000 times the brightness of the Sun that would be detectable out to a distance of 1,000 light-years.

Lasswitz, Kurd (1848–1910)

German philosopher and historian who has been called the "father of German science fiction" for his 1897 novel *Auf zwei Planeten* (On Two Planets),[329] describing an encounter between humankind and an older, more advanced race of Martians. Lasswitz, like his English contemporary H. G. **Wells,** who published *The War of the Worlds* in the same year, adopts a **Kant**ian evolutionary view of the solar system in which Mars is a more ancient world than the Earth and its inhabitants technologically superior. But whereas Wells portrays his Martians as anatomically alien and morally degenerate, Lasswitz presents a much less threatening picture of humanoid creatures who have progressed as far in their societal and ethical development as they have in their science and engineering. Here there is no blitzkrieg by stalking tripods and deadly heat rays, no suggestion that biological evolution must inevitably create intellects that are as cold as they are huge. Yet when Lasswitz's

Martians place the Earth under a benign protectorate, humanity rebels and the extraterrestrials withdraw. Thereafter, communication is restricted to interplanetary signals until the two civilizations achieve equality and the prospect of a utopian future order. In an article on extraterrestrial life written years later, Lasswitz wrote of his view that not only was it inconceivable that there were no other intelligence-bearing worlds in the Universe but that "there should necessarily even be infinite gradations of intelligent beings inhabiting such worlds." Moreover, he was optimistic that the evolution of intelligence and of society went hand in hand and that we would have much to gain from contact with a superior race: "We do dream of a higher civilization, but we would also like to come to know it as something more than the hope for a distant future."

Last and First Men

Olaf **Stapledon**'s first novel (1930), which tells the story of eighteen species of mankind, some naturally evolved, others the product of eugenics, across a time span of 2 billion years.[561] Only with the Second Men, some 10 million years in the future, does humanity first meet extraterrestrial intelligence in the form, adopted by H. G. **Wells** 33 years earlier, of invaders from a drought-stricken **Lowell**ian Mars. Stapledon's Martians, however, are of an entirely different ilk from the repulsive creatures in *The War of the Worlds*. "Maintaining vital organization as a single conscious individual without continuity of living matter," they are evidently **noncorporeal life**-forms of the type often encountered in the science fiction of later decades. So different indeed are the Martian incursors from any terrestrial-type organisms that at first they are not even recognized *as* intelligence—another possibility that would exercise the imaginations of those to come (➔ **extraterrestrial intelligence, more advanced than we**). Later in Stapledon's saga, the descendants of the human race relocate to Venus, where they find a watery world straight out of the writings of Svante **Arrhenius** (➔ **Venus, life on**), inhabited by marine intelligence and other crea-

tures, "some sessile, others free-swimming, some microscopic, others as large as whales." All of these indigenous creatures are wiped out in the **terraforming** process employed to make the second planet fit for human habitation. Finally, mankind abandons Venus for Neptune before a supernova threatens its very existence. Here Stapledon again borrows from Arrhenius, suggesting that humanity's last hope of survival is **panspermia:** sending copies of its cells to the stars in the hope that there they will regenerate. Arthur C. **Clarke** recalled in later years, "With its multimillion-year vistas, and its role call of great but doomed civilizations, the book produced an overwhelming impact upon me."

Although aliens feature only sparingly in *Last and First Men*, some of the forms they are said to assume in other parts of the Universe are spectacularly nongeomorphic:

> In our own galaxy there have occurred hitherto some twenty thousand worlds that have conceived life. And of these a few score have attained or surpassed the mentality of the First Men.... [Beyond planets] we have evidence that in a few of the younger stars there is life, and even intelligence. How it persists in an incandescent environment we know not, nor whether it is perhaps the life of the star as a whole, as a single organism, or the life of many flame-like inhabitants of the star.

Such strange possibilities were to be explored much further in Stapledon's next and greatest work, *Star Maker.*

late-type

Descriptive of a star, of **spectral type** K or M, with a surface temperature cooler than that of the Sun.

LBT

➔ **Large Binocular Telescope**

Leda

The ninth known and smallest moon of **Jupiter**. ➔ **Jupiter, moons of**

Discovery	1974, by Charles Kowal
Mean distance from Jupiter	11,100,000 km (6,900,000 mi.)
Diameter	16 km (10 mi.)
Mean density	2.7 g/cm³
Escape velocity	0.0097 km/s (35 km/h, 22 mi./h)
Orbital period	238.72 days (238 days 17 hours 28 minutes)
Orbital eccentricity	0.148
Orbital inclination	26.07°

Lederberg, Joshua (1925–)

American geneticist at Stanford University who received the 1958 Nobel Prize for Physiology or Medicine. In 1958, while at the University of Wisconsin (where he was chairman of the medical genetics department), he was the first to raise the issue of biological **contamination** by space missions.[334] He was subsequently appointed chairman of **WESTEX** and then of the **Space Science Board**'s **Committee 14 on Exobiology.** In 1960, Lederberg introduced the term "**exobiology,**"[333] and in 1961 he was among the group of researchers who attended the first **SETI** conference at **Green Bank.**[584]

Leibniz, Gottfried Wilhelm (1646–1716)

German philosopher and mathematician who wrote extensively in favor of **pluralism.** He believed in a continuous gradation of life-forms from the simplest to creatures more advanced, physically, intellectually, and spiritually, than ourselves. In his *Essais de théodicée* (1710), he spoke of God having created the "best of all possible worlds"—by "world" meaning not simply the Earth but the Universe as a whole.

Lem, Stanisław (1921–)

Polish physician who turned to science fiction writing in about 1950 and explored in depth the possible nature of extraterrestrial intelligence. He suggested that we may have no common ground with alien races and that any signals we receive from them may prove meaningless. This was the central theme of his novel *Solaris.*

Leonard Euler Telescope

A 1.2-m (3.9-ft.) reflector built at the **Geneva Observatory,** located at **La Silla Observatory,** and named in honor of the famous Swiss mathematician. It is used specifically in conjunction with the **Coralie** spectrograph to conduct high-precision **radial velocity** measurements, principally to search for large **extrasolar planets** in the southern celestial hemisphere. Its first success was the discovery of a planet in orbit around **Gliese 86.**

Leucippus (fifth century B.C.)

Greek philosopher and originator, together with **Democritus of Abdera,** of the theory of **atomism,** which **Epicurus** later developed. Although no original writings of Leucippus or Democritus survive, fragments of their teachings have been transmitted by later scholars such as Diogenes Laertius of the third century A.D. who, in his *Lives of Famous Philosophers,* notes:

> Leucippus holds that the whole is infinite... part of it is full and part void.... Hence arise innumerable worlds, and are resolved again into these elements.

→ **ancient philosophy, related to the possibility of extraterrestrial life**

Leuschner Observatory

The student observatory run by the Astronomy Department of the **University of California, Berkeley.** Its main instruments are a 0.76-m (2.5-ft.) and a 0.5-m (1.6-ft.) reflecting telescope. Leuschner is one of the observatories from which a search has been conducted for **Dyson sphere**s.

Levin, Gilbert (1925–)

Onetime sanitation engineer in California who developed a technique to detect bacterial contaminants in water and went on to play a significant role in the *Viking* project as designer and team leader of the *Viking* **labeled release (LR) experiment.** In his detection method, the sample to be tested was mixed with a nutrient containing traces of radioactive carbon 14. Any bacteria present in the sample would feed on the nutrient and, as a waste product of their **metabolism,** give off radioactive **carbon dioxide** that could be detected with a radiation counter. Commercial interest in the technique proved disappointing, but then, at a cocktail party in 1959, Levin met T. Keith **Glennan,** NASA's first administrator. A discussion ensued about approaches to life detection by space probes that led, in 1961, to Levin being awarded a contract to develop an instrument to search for life on Mars. Known as "Gulliver" and eventually more formally as the "labeled release experiment," this was to provide the most intriguing data of the three experiments making up *Viking's* integrated biology package. Yet while the scientific consensus in the wake of *Viking* was that the remarkable activity found in the Martian soil was of a purely chemical nature, Levin stood firm in his conviction that the data suggested a biological interpretation (➔ **Levin's hypothesis, about the active nature of the Martian soil**). So strong were the disagreements between the different camps involved in the biology experiments on *Viking* that the dispute became acrimonious and was the subject of two consecutive issues of *The New Yorker* in 1979. To this day, Levin vociferously maintains that *Viking* found life on Mars.

Levin's hypothesis, about the active nature of the Martian soil

According to Gilbert **Levin,** the activity detected in the *Viking* soil samples by all three biology experiments is best understood in terms of the metabolism of living organisms. This puts him squarely at odds with the majority view that oxidizing chemicals on the surface can provide an adequate explanation (➔ **Oyama's hypothesis, about the active nature of the Martian soil**). Levin favored a biological interpretation of the *Viking* results from the outset. But over the years since the mission ended, he has become increasingly outspoken on the issue and, together with his *Viking* team member Patricia Straat, has made some remarkable and controversial claims. One is that the *Viking* **gas chromatograph–mass spectrometer** (GCMS), which failed to find any sign of organic matter in the Martian soil, was much less sensitive than officially stated and would have been incapable of detecting biological matter in samples containing a low density of microorganisms. Another of Levin's claims is that greenish patches seen on some of

the *Viking* photographs changed over time, suggesting that they were some kind of plant life, and furthermore, that spectral analysis of the patches compared favorably with the spectra of lichen-bearing rocks on Earth. Opponents of Levin point out that as an engineer who set out to design an instrument to prove that there was life on Mars, he has an intrinsically biased viewpoint. Further analysis of the Martian soil over the next few years should reveal who is right.

levorotatory
Rotating the plane of vibration of **polarized light** to the left (as seen by an observer looking toward the oncoming light).

Lewis, C(live) S(taples) (1898–1963)
Literature professor at Oxford from 1925 and professor of Medieval and Renaissance literature at Cambridge University after 1954 who wrote extensively as a Christian apologist. His cosmic trilogy, *Out of the Silent Planet*[344] (1938), *Perelandra*[345] (1943), and *That Hideous Strength*[346] (1945), explores the idea, popular among Catholic authorities during the early decades of the twentieth century, that the assumption of multiple inhabited worlds is compatible with Christian doctrine and that beings on other planets might be in a variety of different spiritual states. Some worlds, accordingly, might be in an Eden-like state of grace, others "fallen," redeemed, or in a condition of "integral nature" midway between man and angel. Some might even be so evil that they were beyond redemption. This was essentially an updated and expanded version of the idea proposed by some medieval Christian Aristotelians that the heavenly regions between the Moon and the *primum mobile* might be occupied by angelic intelligences. In Lewis's vision, Mars ("Malacandra") has yet to experience the fall of humankind, Venus ("Perelandra") has seen it averted, while Earth ("Thulcandra") is isolated by divine decree. Olaf **Stapledon**'s descriptions of Mars and Venus in *Last and First Men* are recognizable, but it was David **Lindsay**'s *A Voyage to Arcturus* that influenced Lewis most significantly. "From Lindsay," he wrote, "I first learned what other planets in fiction are really good for; for spiritual adventures." Although his primary

purpose was to defend Christian beliefs in the context of **pluralism,** Lewis also managed to populate his trilogy with a biologically interesting array of aliens, ranging from the froglike pfifltriggi to the ethereal eldil, with bodies made of light. Doubtless this contributed to the mounting public interest in extraterrestrial life at a time when astronomers, following the exposure of weaknesses in the **catastrophic hypothesis,** were beginning to believe again that planetary systems might be common.

Liais, Emmanuel (1826–1900)

French astronomer who spent much of his life in Brazil as director of the observatory of Rio de Janeiro. In 1860, he suggested that the dark regions on Mars, instead of being oceans and seas, as was widely believed at the time, might be tracts of vegetation (**→ Mars, vegetation on**). The summer meltwater from the poles, he believed, was irrigating the soil at lower latitudes and causing the dormant plant life there to rejuvenate and spread.

Lick Observatory

The first permanent mountaintop observatory, established in 1888 at an altitude of 1,283 m (4,169 ft.) above sea level on Mount Hamilton in California, with financial backing from James Lick of San Francisco. It houses a 91-cm (36-in.) refractor, the second largest in the world after that at **Yerkes Observatory.** This instrument was used extensively at the turn of the century in the investigation of Mars. Other instruments include a 3-m (120-in.) reflector, which is currently being used as part of the **San Francisco State University Planet Search** program, and the 0.9-m (36-in.) Crossley reflector. The observatory is run by the University of California, Santa Cruz.

Life, article on UFOs (1952)

One of the most influential pieces of journalism in the early history of **unidentified flying objects.** It appeared in the April 7, 1952, issue of *Life* magazine, just four days after the U.S. Air Force had issued a press release to announce that it would continue studying UFOs through the successor to Project **Grudge,** known as Project **Blue Book.** Under the title "Have We Visitors from Outer Space?" the ar-

ticle cited an unnamed general in the Pentagon who "strongly believed flying saucers were interplanetary spaceships." In his memoirs, Captain Edward **Ruppelt,** head of **Blue Book** at the time, asserted that a number of USAF generals who privately endorsed the **extraterrestrial hypothesis** had unofficially encouraged *Life* reporters to promote the "interplanetary aspect" and that these officers ranked "so high that their personal opinion was almost policy."[487] The article in *Life*, together with scores of others it spawned in newspapers around the country, may have been an important factor behind the increased rate of reports at this time. In his book *Watch the Skies!*[446] (1995) Curtiss Peebles describes the kind of feedback effect that may have been at work:

> *Life* said the Air Force was interested in flying saucers. People would then be more likely to report a sighting. The new regulations meant that reports that might have been ignored or thrown away before were now sent to *Blue Book*. The open press policy meant that questions were not brushed off as before. This, along with the increased number of reports, resulted in more newspaper articles which caused people to watch the skies.

Public interest in UFOs peaked later that year, following the **"Washington Invasion."**

life, classification of

Living things are placed in groups on the basis of similarities and differences at the organismic, cellular, and molecular levels. Taxonomic studies have led to the development of a system of classification in which all terrestrial life-forms (with the exception of **virus**es) are divided into several **kingdom**s. These are further divided into phyla, classes, orders, families, genera, and species. One of the most contentious issues is the classification of the kingdoms. Originally, there were just two of these: animals (Animalia) and vegetable (Plantae). Gradually, as new discoveries revealed the diversity of life, more were added until the five-kingdom system (including Monera, Protista, Fungi, Plantae, and Animalia) proposed in 1959 by the American biologist Robert H.

Whittaker won the support of most authorities. Even this, however, has now been superseded. Research concerning the organisms previously known as archaebacteria has led to the recognition that these creatures form an entirely distinct group. In the six-kingdom system, **archaen**s comprise their own kingdom on a par with those of **baceria, protists, fungi, plants,** and **animals.** Coexisting with this is a scheme put forward by Carl **Woese** in which all terrestrial life is divided into three **domains**— Archaea, Bacteria, and Eukaryota—each containing two or more kingdoms.[628]

life, detection of
➔ **exterrestrial life, detection of**

life, in space
According to a hotly disputed theory by Fred **Hoyle** and Chandra Wickramasinghe first put forward in 1974, life may have originated not on the surface of planets, such as Earth, but in the large **interstellar cloud**s of gas and dust from which stars and their planetary systems form.[290, 291, 292] Hoyle and Wickramasinghe believe that **molecular cloud**s, such as those present in the **Orion Nebula,** are the most natural cradles of life. In their view, inorganic **cosmic dust** grains composed of **silicate, graphite,** and iron particles, mixed with inorganic gases, act as assembly sites for **organic** molecules of increasing complexity. The organic molecules become **polymer**ized on the surface of the dust grains, they argue; then, as the density of the cloud rises during gravitational collapse, these polymer-coated grains collide with increasing frequency, leading to the growth of grain clumps with embedded **prebiotic** chemicals. Hoyle and Wickramasinghe point out that such clumps would have dimensions of a few microns, similar to the sizes of **cell**s in simple microorganisms. In their opinion, Darwinian-style selection and evolution would take place, involving competition between the growth of grain clumps and their division and destruction in the interstellar environment. The simplest self-replicable system, consisting of inorganic grains held together with organic polymer coatings, would dominate. Finally, they imagine that, given the right conditions, the organic polymer films,

which separate individual grains as well as surround entire clumps, could evolve into biological **cell membrane**s. Within each "protocell" all the essential ingredients of life would be present. These protocells would then become incorporated into meteorites and comets, which would act as delivery systems to bring the interstellar prebiota to the surface of newly formed worlds, such as the infant Earth. In support of their theory, they have pointed to the similarity between the **infrared** spectrum of interstellar grains and that of dried bacteria.
➔ **life, origin of; panspermia; epidemics, from space**

life, nature of
Inquiries into the origin of life and the possible existence of extraterrestrial life build upon assumptions made about life's very nature. It was once commonly believed that life was fundamentally different from nonlife: that living things possessed a "vital principle" that was absent from nonliving matter. This notion of "vitalism" began to seem less sustainable following the laboratory synthesis, in 1828, by Friedrich **Wöhler,** of an **organic** substance (urea). Although Henri **Bergson** and others continued to champion vitalism into the twentieth century, the overwhelming consensus emerged that life could ultimately be reduced to a complex series of physical and chemical processes. The debate focused onto what the fundamental unit of life might be. In the mid–nineteenth century, Thomas **Huxley** had maintained that it was "protoplasm." In the early decades of the twentieth century, smaller living entities were proposed, including **enzymes, virus**es, and **gene**s, though some researchers, including the American biochemist Edmund B. Wilson, argued that only a complete, functioning **cell** could properly be considered alive.

Today, there is still no agreement among biologists as to a clear definition of life. Several factors are generally reckoned to be involved, including the ability to self-replicate, to actively maintain a boundary between the inner environment of the organism and the outside world (➔ **cell membrane**), and to carry out **metabolism.** To these some might add the ability to mutate and evolve, or to be part of a community capable of Darwinian evolution. If all of these factors are required to be satisfied for something to be considered alive, then it is questionable, for example, whether viruses are alive. Viruses replicate not by themselves but by hijacking the cellular machinery of some host. Moreover, when dormant, they enter an inert, crystalline, nonmetabolizing state.

In addition to the general features we might expect of all life in the cosmos (the ability to metabolize, reproduce, differentiate "self" from the surroundings, and evolve), it may be that life, wherever it occurs, displays more specific features. For instance, it may be that life always utilizes cells; liquid **water;** the principal elements **carbon, hydrogen, oxygen, nitrogen, phosphorus,** and **sulfur;** a common set of **organic** molecules; a common set of metabolic reactants; and a common cell membrane structure. Some researchers posit that extraterrestrial life, in its biochemical, metabolic, and cellular makeup, will closely resemble the terrestrial variety, even though the gross appearance of life elsewhere might be different from anything we know. On the other hand, there are those who argue that extraterrestrial life might have a fundamentally different basis and therefore be alien not only in its external aspects but also in its basic constitution.

A further problem in establishing the limits of what may be considered alive is that "life" is a label of our own invention. Try as we might to impose a definition of life on nature, there are bound to be instances where the distinction between living and nonliving is blurred or indeterminate. Given that this is true even of terrestrial organisms, we can only guess what difficulties will arise in assessing the credentials of possible life elsewhere. In exploring other worlds, we may encounter life-forms far more different from any terrestrial species than, say, a sponge is from a condor. Some of these alien forms may, in spite of their unfamiliarity, obviously be alive. Yet others, like viruses, will challenge our definitions. Our real problem, however, may be not with simple biological systems on the lower margins of life but with entities that are vastly more evolved than ourselves (➜ **extraterrestrial intelligence, more advanced than we**), entirely different in appearance or composition (➜ **extraterres-**

trial life, variety of**), or perhaps even of a partially or wholly artificial nature. Regarding this last possibility, there have already been claims that some computer programs are, in a sense, alive (➜ **artificial life**). Other researchers have challenged this view, arguing that life must have a corporeal or material basis. In any event, we can envisage a time when genetic engineering, artificial body parts, and direct brain-computer links may lead to an exponential growth of human physical and intellectual capabilities. It is impossible to predict where such developments might lead if they were to continue for thousands or millions of years. Yet such technology-driven evolution may already have happened with other races in the Galaxy. The question, then, is whether the state to which such races may have evolved can be contained within any conventional notion of life or whether we will be forced to admit that there is another category of existence—one that is as far elevated above human life as we are, for example, above algae.[379, 401, 493, 518]

life, origin of

For much of human history it was common to believe that the creation of life was a divine event, and even today there are many who hold to the view that God fashioned humans and other terrestrial life-forms essentially in their present condition. Scientific opinion, however, has undergone a series of radical revisions from the seventeenth century to the present day. Moreover, it is only in this century that the questions of the origin of life and the existence of extraterrestrial life have been seen as closely intertwined.

At the beginning of the seventeenth century, the ultimate origin of life was considered primarily a theological issue. However, it was thought possible that small creatures, such as maggots and even mice, could arise from nonliving material by **spontaneous generation,** a theory first propounded by **Aristotle.** When the experiments of Francesco **Redi,** Louis **Pasteur,** and others undermined this theory, the notion that living things were somehow fundamentally different from inanimate matter became, for a while, difficult to avoid, and **vitalism** enjoyed a period of renaissance. Lack of data rendered scientific speculation about the origin of life problematic, though the possibility of a gradual, chemical origin of life was aired in the latter part of the nineteenth century by Thomas **Huxley,** John **Tyndall,** and Belgium's Leo Errera. An intriguing alternative, set out in detail by Svante **Arrhenius** (though the idea was not new to him), is that life is eternal and has been spread from world to world by the process of **panspermia.** However, this idea failed to attract widespread support at the time and seemed beset by technical difficulties. In the early decades of the twentieth century, it gave way to a more concerted exploration of the concept of a chemical origin of life on Earth, a theory whose rise coincided with a debate about the nature of life itself (➔ **life, nature of**) between vitalists and mechanists. This was eventually resolved in favor of the view that life was essentially a complex chemical and physical phenomenon, so that its origins might lie in relatively simple chemical and physical processes that took place on the young Earth. As early as 1868, Huxley had proposed that the basis of all terrestrial animal and plant life was "protoplasm." With the emergence of the new discipline of biochemistry between 1901 and 1905 came the idea that **enzymes** might better define the fundamental unit of living things, and in 1914, Leonard **Troland** put forward an explicit chemical theory for the origin of life in terms of **autocatalytic** enzymes. Others thought that the newly discovered **virus**es and, in particular, bacterial viruses known as "**bacteriophages,**" might represent the smallest living particles. In 1929, H. J. Muller suggested that the first living things on Earth might have been "little else than the gene." The parsing of life into simpler components—viruses, enzymes, or **gene**s—made it easier to accept the possibility that the first organisms might have come about as a result of a chance series of chemical reactions.

In the 1920s and early 1930s, Aleksandr **Oparin** in the Soviet Union and J. B. S. **Haldane** in Britain independently developed similar theories suggesting how conditions on the early Earth may have been conducive to the chemical evolution of life. Both postulated a primitive **reducing atmosphere** in which simple **organic** chemicals were synthesized. These organics, they argued, accumulated in the surface waters of the ocean, forming a "primordial soup" out of which, in time, life in its most elementary form emerged. In the 1950s, through the endorsement of Norman **Horowitz** in the United States, J. D. **Bernal** in Britain, and others, the **Oparin-Haldane Theory** achieved widespread recognition and was given powerful empirical support by the positive results of the **Miller-Urey Experiment** (1953). At the same time, James Watson and Francis **Crick** broke the **genetic code,** revealing the structure of **DNA,** and thus completed the knowledge of the structure of the basic chemical building blocks of terrestrial life.

The mid-1950s also saw the first integration of origin of life studies with those concerned with life on other worlds. George **Wald,** Haldane, and Oparin were prominent in making this connection, which was stimulated by the dawn of the Space Age and the prospect of searching for extraterrestrial life *in situ.* In 1964, Oparin wrote of the "inseparable connection" between **astrobiology** and the origin of life. Establishing how life arose on Earth was now seen as central to understanding where and how commonly life may have arisen elsewhere in the Universe.

A major obstacle was the inability of laboratory experiments in **prebiotic** synthesis to progress much beyond the production of **amino acids** and other relatively simple organic building blocks. As Lynn **Margulis** has commented, "To go from a bacterium to people is less of a step than to go from a mixture of amino acids to a bacterium." The gap between an amino acid molecule, containing fewer than 100 atoms, and the most primitive bacterium, containing around 100 billion atoms, posed a major obstacle to the Oparin-Haldane paradigm. Moreover, the need to seek new possible environments for and mechanisms of prebiotic evolution was spurred on by the gradual realization, based on geochemical evidence, that the Earth's primitive atmosphere was almost certainly not, after all, strongly reducing (➔ **Earth, early history of**).

There were two fundamental problems: first, to explain how the giant **polymers** that are essential to life, especially **proteins** and **nucleic acid**s, were synthesized under natural conditions from their subunits and, second, to understand the origin of cells. In 1947, Bernal argued that some way of concentrating the basic ingredients was needed and that lagoons and tidal pools around the early oceans would have served this purpose well. Polymerization, he suggested, may have taken place with the aid of clay minerals, which would have provided a surface for the adsorption of organic molecules, a means of holding them while they joined together, and protection from the disruptive effects of solar ultraviolet. The possible role played by clay (➔ **clay, role in prebiotic evolution**) and a semidry, lagoonlike environment has since been stressed by others, notably A. Graham **Cairns-Smith**[92] and Stanley **Miller.** Gradually, biologists also came to realize that there may have been earlier phases in the development of life that did not involve DNA. In particular, Thomas Cech's discovery of self-catalyzing **ribozymes** led to a sudden growth of interest in the possibility of a primordial "**RNA world**," a concept raised to prominence by Harvard biologist Walter Gilbert in 1986[216] but first suggested in 1968, long before Cech's breakthrough, by Francis Crick. However, although **RNA** has the combined properties of a self-catalyst and a self-replicator, its fragility has led researchers to consider alternative scenarios. Some have proposed that protein catalysts preceded any replicator molecules such as DNA or RNA, while others, such as Freeman **Dyson,**[174] have suggested that they appeared together. In vogue at present is the idea that before the RNA world, there was an even earlier era dominated by a substance such as **PNA.**

The second major problem surrounding the origin of life is how cells came about—in particular, the "containers" of cells, or **cell membrane**s. As early as 1932, primitive organic enclosures known as **coacervate**s were produced in the laboratory and touted as cell membrane precursors. An alternative candidate emerged in the 1950s in the form of **microspheres,** the properties and synthesis of which continue to be investigated, notably by Sidney **Fox** and his colleagues, with a view to establishing their biological credentials. Indeed, there is a school of thought that some

form of primitive cell container must have appeared first on the scene in order for the molecules that formed the basis of the earliest self-replicating life-forms to be sufficiently concentrated and protected from the external environment.

The discovery of **extremophiles** has prompted renewed speculation about the conditions under which the first terrestrial organisms appeared. Some researchers favor the hot environs of undersea **hydrothermal vent**s as a likely birthplace of life,[39] a hypothesis given further credence in 1999 with the announcement by Japanese researchers that they had managed to synthesize **peptide**s around an artificial deep-sea vent. Others, most vociferously Thomas **Gold,** have promulgated the notion of a deep (and also hot) subterranean place of origin. In contrast, there are those who have argued for a prebiotic genesis in "cold soup" conditions.

Parallel developments have led to a revival of interest in the possibility that some of the raw materials of life, and possibly even primitive life itself, may have come to the Earth from space. The discovery of increasingly complicated molecules between the stars (➔ **interstellar molecules**), meteorites (➔ **organic matter, in meteorites**), **comet**s, and the atmospheres of the giant planets has contributed to speculation that the seeds from which terrestrial life grew may have been planted during the early bombardment phase of our planet. In particular, recent experimental work at the **NASA Ames Research Center,** intended to replicate conditions in **interstellar cloud**s of gas and dust, has yielded possible early precursors of life, including cell-like bubbles, that are similar in structure to those found within the **Murchison meteorite.** Additional valuable data bearing on the possible extraterrestrial connection with life's origin will come from a number of current and planned space missions designed to collect samples of **primitive material** from comets or asteroids and return them for laboratory analysis. Other unmanned probes are scheduled to explore the environs of the biologically interesting worlds **Mars, Europa, Callisto,** and **Titan.** In addition, the identification of meteorites that have almost certainly come from the Moon and Mars (➔ **SNC meteorites**) has demonstrated that material may be routinely exchanged between worlds as a result of major impacts, giving rise to the possibility of **ballistic panspermia.** At the furthest extreme of speculation are the ideas of Fred **Hoyle** and Chandra Wickramasinghe, according to which primitive organisms may actually have evolved in space (➔ **life, in space**).[141, 206]

life, variety of
➔ **extraterrestrial life, variety of**

life zone
➔ **habitable zone**

lifetime, of civilizations
➔ **extraterrestrial civilizations, lifetime of**

light curve
A graph showing the way in which the brightness of an object, such as a **variable star,** changes with time. The light variations may be due to intrinsic changes in the source, as in the case of **Cepheid variable**s, or eclipses, when one member of a **binary star** system passes in front of the other. Modern techniques in **photometry** enable even the tiny fluctuations in the light received from a star by the **transit** of an orbiting planet to be detected.

light pressure
➔ **radiation pressure**

light-year (ly)
The distance traveled by light, moving at 300,000 km per second (186,282 miles per second), in one year—about 9.40 trillion km (5.88 trillion miles). The nearest star, **Proxima Centauri,** lies at a distance of 4.28 light-years, or just over 40 trillion km (25 trillion miles). A unit generally preferred by astronomers is the **parsec.**

Lilly, John C. (1915–)
American neurophysiologist and maverick researcher, previously of the Communication Research Institute, Coral Gables, Florida, who is best known for his efforts to understand the "language" of dolphins.[349] Lilly was an attendee at the **Green Bank conference (1961),** where he urged that dolphins represent another form of advanced intelligence on Earth (➔ **dolphins, as a form of alien intelligence**). Although this idea remains valid, as does the possibility that **cetaceans** engage in sophisticated forms of communication (➔ **humpback whales, songs of**), the scientific rigor of Lilly's research has been called into question and his conclusions are no longer considered reliable.

limb
The outer edge of the apparent disk of a celestial body.

Lincos
"Lingua Cosmica," a language for extraterrestrial communication developed by Hans Freudenthal, professor of mathematics at the University of Utrecht. Details of it are presented in Freudenthal's book[210] published in the Netherlands in 1960. Lincos represents an extension of the logistic language of mathematics developed by Alfred North Whitehead and Bertrand Russell. It is intended to be conveyed by unmodulated radio signals of varying duration and wavelength that represent phonemes. The signals would be combined to make up concepts or words.[273] ➔ **mathematics, as a universal language**

Lindsay, David (1878–1945)
Scottish-born writer of fantasy whose first novel, *A Voyage to Arcturus* (1920), is a deep metaphysical quest in an extraterrestrial setting. His description and characterization of the aliens of Tormance (a fictitious world circling Arcturus) are peripheral to the main journey of inner discovery. Nevertheless, Lindsay conjures up powerful images of novel senses and anatomies. C. S. **Lewis** is among those who have acknowledged his influence. ➔ **science fiction involving extraterrestrials, 1900–1940**

lipid bilayer
The structure of a **cell membrane,** in which two layers of **phospholipids** spontaneously align so that the **hydrophilic** head groups are exposed

to water, while the **hydrophobic** tails (consisting of **fatty acids**) are pointed toward the center of the membrane. This establishes a boundary separating the contents of the cell from its surroundings or an **organelle** within a cell from the general intracellular environment.

lipids

An important class of **organic** compounds, including oils, fats, waxes, and related substances, found in terrestrial organisms. Lipids are formed when molecules attach to **glycerol** by **condensation** reactions. Complex lipids, which contain long chains of **fatty acids,** are used in plants and animals for storing food and energy, and also, as **phospholipid**s, in the structure of **cell membrane**s. Simple lipids, such as steroids, are characterized by an absence of fatty acids.

Lippincott, Sarah Lee

Colleague of Peter **van der Kamp** at **Sproul Observatory** who conducted **astrometric** studies of nearby stars in the search for **extrasolar planets.** She was involved in observations leading to the reported discovery of several objects of substellar mass, including a 0.08-M_S companion to the **red dwarf** Ross 614 in 1955 and a 0.01-M_S companion of **Lalande 21185** in 1960.[352] These were not subsequently confirmed.

Listeners, The

Science fiction novel by James E. Gunn[246] (1972) that depicts the century-long effort by a **SETI** project on Earth to detect intelligent signals from space.

lithopanspermia

A version of the **panspermia** hypothesis in which it is argued that microscopic life can be conveyed from one world to another inside **meteorite**s. It attracted the support of several eminent scientists in the nineteenth century, including William **Thomson** (Lord Kelvin) and Hermann von **Helmholtz,** and has recently been revived in the guise of **ballistic panspermia.**

lithosphere

The **crust** and uppermost **mantle** of a planet or moon.

lithotrophs
→ endoliths

"little green men"

The meaning of the acronym LGM, used by Anthony Hewish of Cambridge University to designate a regularly pulsing radio source discovered in 1967 by his Ph.D. student Jocelyn Bell. The source was eventually identified as a **pulsar. → SETI, false alarms in**

Littrow, Joseph Johann von (1781–1840)

Austrian astronomer and director of the Vienna Observatory, who is supposed to have devised a method for signaling our presence to the inhabitants of either the Moon or Mars (→ **communication, with the Moon and planets**). The scheme often attributed to him called for canals to be dug in geometric shapes in the Sahara, filled with water, topped with kerosene, and set alight. This story, however, may be apocryphal, despite the fact that Littrow supported **pluralism** and possibly even the idea that the Moon was inhabited (→ **Moon, life on**). → **Gauss, Karl Friedrich**

LMC
→ **Large Magellanic Cloud**

Local Group

The small, gravitationally bound group of galaxies to which our **galaxy** belongs. It spans approximately 6 million light-years and contains about thirty members, the two largest of which are the **Andromeda Galaxy** and our own.

Locke, John (1632–1704)

English philosopher who supported the nonanthropocentric teleological argument of **pluralism,** popular in the Age of Enlightenment, that God created other worlds for the benefit of their own inhabitants rather than that of man:[357]

> It is more suitable to the wisdom, power, and greatness of God to think that the fixed stars are all of them suns, with systems of inhabitable planets moving about them, to whose inhabitants he displays the marks of his goodness as well as to us; rather than to

imagine that these very remote bodies, so little useful to us, were made only for our own sake.

Locke, Richard Adams (1800–71)

American-born writer and descendant of the philosopher John **Locke** who studied at the University of Cambridge before returning to the United States and pursuing a career in journalism. In 1835 he joined the *New York Sun* and subsequently perpetrated the infamous "**Moon Hoax.**"

locus

The position on a **chromosome** where a **gene** is located.

Lo'ihi Underwater Volcanic Vent Mission Probe

An instrumented underwater probe built at the **Jet Propulsion Laboratory** to examine deep **hydrothermal vent**s at the Lo'ihi Seamount, 27 km (20 miles) east of the Big Island of Hawaii, at a depth of about 1,300 m (4,250 ft.). A long-term objective of JPL engineers is to develop instruments for a probe that could be used to search for life in the underground oceans that may exist on Jupiter's moons **Europa** and **Callisto.**

The sensor end of the Lo'ihi probe, designed to withstand temperatures up to 400°C (750°F), contains a sophisticated thermometer and windows made of tough, heat-tolerant sapphire through which lights can be shone to illuminate the ocean floor. Images travel from the windows, up through fiber-optic rods to cameras mounted, together with other heat-sensitive electronic components, at the other end of the probe. Preliminary tests were carried out in August 1998 in the giant kelp forest exhibit at the Monterey Bay Aquarium in California. On October 17, 1998, a submersible from the University of Hawaii took the 52-kg (115-lb.) probe down to the Lo'ihi Seamount. The probe was controlled from the sub using a laptop computer. Following the success of this mission, it is planned to add an **ultraviolet** camera (for imaging **organic** matter) and a sensor to detect chemicals used by microbes in the vicinity of undersea vents to generate energy. The information gathered from experiments off Hawaii will be used to prepare for more challenging terrestrial investigations, including studies of a giant subice lake in Antarctica (→ **Vostok, Lake**), that will precede any explorations of oceans on other worlds (→ **Europa Vostok Initiative; Europa, future probes of**).

Lomonosov, Mikhail Vasilyevich (1711–65)

So-called father of Russian science who was deeply impressed by Bernard de **Fontenelle**'s writings on **pluralism** and, in the face of opposition from the Eastern Orthodox Church, expressed his belief in many inhabited worlds in his native country. He wrote pluralist poems, both scientific and satirical, and, more important, saw to it that the second edition of Fontenelle's *Conversations on the Plurality of Worlds* was translated into Russian. In this way, he may have had an important influence on future Russian scientists, including Otto **Struve,** who played a part in the modern search for extraterrestrial planets and life.

long-period comet

A **comet** with a period of more than 200 years and as much as several million years. Long-period comets, together with **Halley-type comet**s, are now believed to come from the **Oort Cloud,** an enormous reservoir of frozen cometary nuclei orbiting the Sun at a distance of tens of thousands of astronomical units. The gravitational influences of passing stars, giant **molecular cloud**s, and the central regions of the Galaxy are thought to be instrumental in occasionally perturbing the orbits of some of the Oort objects and causing them to plunge toward the inner solar system on highly elliptical paths characteristic of long-period comets. → **short-period comet**

"Los Angeles Air Raid"

The first incident involving unidentified aerial phenomena to spark a government investigation. Various radio reports and visual sightings of luminous objects in the sky over the Los Angeles area on the night of February 24–25, 1942, culminated in the firing of 1,430 antiaircraft shells. Although the incident has never been conclusively explained, it seems reasonable to assume that "war jitters" may have been at least partly to blame. Only two days earlier, a Japanese submarine had surfaced north of Santa Barbara and shelled fuel storage tanks for 20 minutes, and on that same evening President Franklin D. Roosevelt had made a nationwide broadcast warning that nowhere in the United States was safe from enemy action.

lost languages

The problem of understanding an extraterrestrial message is emphasized by the difficulty we have in deciphering lost languages on our own planet. This was discussed, for example, by Russell F. W. Smith, linguist and associate dean of general education at New York University at the 1963 convention of the Audio Engineering Society in New York. As Smith pointed out, the "code" of ancient Egyptian hieroglyphics was cracked only following the discovery of a basalt slab at Rosetta, near the mouth of the Nile, by Champollion. On the stone was an inscription written by the priests of Ptolemy V in three alphabets, including ancient hieroglyphic and Greek. Pictures sent via television could be used as a kind of cosmic Rosetta Stone, as might the universal language of mathematics (providing it is written in some form that can be decoded). → **mathematics, as a universal language**

Lovejoy, Arthur Oncken (1873–1962)

American historian who in *The Great Chain of Being*[359] (1936) argued that post-Copernican ideas about extraterrestrial life "were chiefly derivative from philosophical and theological premises" rather than due to observational evidence or scientific reasoning. → **SETI, religious dimensions of**

Lovell, (Alfred Charles) Bernard (1913–)

British radio astronomer, instrumental in the building of the world's first giant **radio telescope** at **Jodrell Bank.** An early skeptic of **SETI,** he responded coolly to a letter from Giuseppe **Cocconi,** dated June 29, 1959, proposing the use of the Jodrell Bank dish to search for interstellar signals.[360] However, he changed his views to the extent that on March 22, 1962, he was able to tell U.S. Congressman Emilio Daddario that "now one has to be sympathetic about an idea which only a few years ago would have seemed rather farfetched."[361]

Lovell Telescope

Previously known as the Mark I, the main instrument at **Jodrell Bank** in England. It is the world's second largest fully steerable **radio telescope** and has been in operation since 1957. Named after Bernard **Lovell,** through whose efforts it was built, it is employed principally for astrophysical research, especially **pulsar** observations. However, since mid-1998 it has also been used in conjunction with the **Arecibo radio telescope** as part of Project **Phoenix** (→ SETI).

Lovelock, James E. (1919–)

English independent scientist and inventor best known for his pioneering work on the **Gaia Hypothesis.**[362]

Lowell Observatory

Founded in 1894 by Percival **Lowell,** the observatory sits atop a mesa (now called "Mars Hill"), 2,210 m (7,180 ft.) above sea level, west of downtown Flagstaff, Arizona. From here, between 1912 and 1920, Vesto Slipher made observations of the **red shift**s of galaxies that helped lay the foundations for the theory of the expanding universe, while in 1930 Pluto was discovered by Clyde Tombaugh. But the observatory was set up with the prime objective of proving that Mars was inhabited by an intelligent, technological race and it is that burning quest of Lowell's for which the facility will always be best remembered. Its initial instruments were a 12-in. refractor leased from Harvard and an 18-in. refractor borrowed from John Brashear. These were replaced, in 1896, by a 24-in. Alvan Clarke refractor, which was temporarily erected at a site in Mexico for better viewing of the December 1896 **opposition** of Mars before being moved to its permanent home at Flagstaff.

Lowell, Percival (1855–1916)

Born into a wealthy and well-known Bostonian family, Lowell gave no early indication of the obsession that would come to dominate his life and create an enduring romance involving extraterrestrial canals (→ **Mars, canals of**) and an advanced Martian civilization (→ **Mars, life on**). At Harvard, where for twenty-four years his brother was president, he showed a talent for mathematics and even presented an astronomical address entitled "The Nebular Hypothesis." But following his graduation, he devoted the next seventeen years to family business concerns and three extended stays in the Orient. He served as foreign secretary and counselor to the first Korean diplomatic mission and, during his time in Korea and Japan, wrote four books on Eastern thought and culture. Then, for some reason that is not entirely clear, he caught the Mars bug. Perhaps he had been inspired by reading Camille **Flammarion**'s popular treatise on the planet. Or it may have been Giovanni **Schiaparelli**'s work that influenced him directly. Certainly, as early as 1890, he had begun to correspond with William **Pickering** on the subject. By the beginning of 1894, he determined to become actively involved in the study of Mars and made urgent preparations in order not to miss the favorable **opposition** that was due later that year. He stated his goal in an address to the Boston Scientific Society on May 22, 1894:

This may be put popularly as an investigation into the condition of life on other worlds, including last but not least their habitability by beings like [or] unlike man.... there is strong reason to believe that we are on the eve of pretty definite discovery in the matter.

As to the nature of Schiaparelli's *canali*, he had no doubt: "[I]n them we are looking upon the result of the work of some sort of intelligent beings."

Together with Pickering and Andrew **Douglass,** he set up two sizable telescopes (a 12-in. and an 18-in. refractor), both on loan, at a hastily erected observatory in Flagstaff, Arizona (➔ **Lowell Observatory**). By August, he was sketching canals and other intricate features on the Martian surface, including dark spots where the canals intersected. Pickering had first reported seeing these spots, which he referred to as "lakes," in 1892. Now Lowell saw them, too, and renamed them "**oases.**" In his mind, they were tracts of vegetation irrigated by meltwater brought by the canals from the poles. After seeing Mars at just one opposition, Lowell launched a publicity blitzkrieg to announce his theory about the grand hydro-

logical schemes of an alien race. Numerous articles, lectures, and a book, *Mars,*[365] by him in 1895 were greeted with fascination by the public and extreme skepticism, if not outright derision, by most astronomers. When asked which books he had enjoyed reading recently, British astronomer Norman Lockyer replied, "*Mars* by Percival Lowell, *Sentimental Tommy* by J. M. Barrie. (No Time for Reading Seriously)." And here is James Keeler, who became director of the **Lick Observatory** in California, speaking at the dedication ceremony of the **Yerkes Observatory** at Williams Bay, Wisconsin, in 1897:

It is to be regretted that the habitability of the planets, a subject of which astronomers profess to know little, has been chosen as a theme for exploitation by the romancer, to whom the step from habitability to inhabitants is a very short one. The result of his ingenuity is that fact and fantasy become inextricably tangled in the mind of the layman, who learns to regard communication with inhabitants of Mars as a project deserving serious consideration... and who does not know that it is condemned as a vagary by the very men whose labors have excited the imagination of the novelist.

Even as Lowell's theory began to take shape in the public consciousness, however, it was being undermined by the results of others during the 1894 opposition. At the Lick Observatory, William **Campbell** used a new **spectroscope** to search for water vapor in the Martian atmosphere—and found none, contradicting earlier results. Meanwhile, his colleague at Lick, Edward **Barnard,** one of the most respected observers of his day, scrutinized the Martian surface with the giant 36-in. refractor but failed to see any sign of straight narrow lines. Lowell countered by arguing that large telescopes were ill suited to planetary observation and that, in any case, much depended on the viewing conditions, which at Flagstaff, he asserted, were among the best available. Lowell claimed that the canals appeared to him only from time to time—rare and precious visions—when the viewing was excellent. Then the mystery markings would suddenly stand out, he said, "like the lines in a fine steel etching." Also in 1894, Edward **Maunder,** in England, suggested that the canals might be optical illusions and did some experiments with model disks to prove his point. But Lowell would have none of it and pressed on single-mindedly in his pursuit of proof that the network of waterways was both real and intelligently constructed. As many as five hundred canals eventually filled his Martian maps. He wrote:

Irrigation, unscientifically conducted, would not give us such truly wonderful mathematical fitness....A mind of no mean order would seem to have presided over the system we see—a mind certainly of considerably more comprehensiveness than that which presides over the various departments of our own public works. Party politics, at all events, have no part in them; for the system is planet-wide.

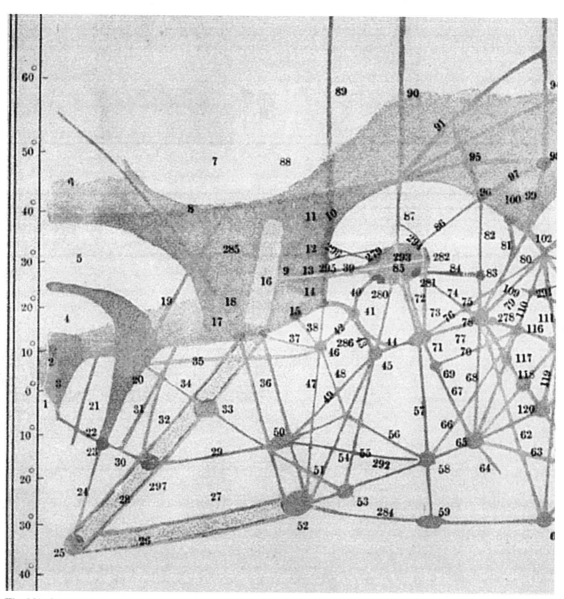

The Martian canals as mapped and numbered by Lowell in his book *Mars.*

From lines to canals to canal builders to world government! Lowell published two further books, *Mars and Its Canals*[366] (1906) and *Mars as the Abode of Life*[367] (1908), and continued to argue vociferously for the existence of a canal network until his death in 1916.

LSA
→ **Large Southern Array**

Lubbock Lights
One of the classic early cases of UFO sightings that received nationwide publicity despite the fact that the mystery was quickly solved—by the very people who had first reported it. One night in August 1951, three faculty members of Texas Technological University were watching the sky together and trying to count meteors. Suddenly, they saw fifteen to twenty faint, yellowish white lights moving from north to south. An hour later the spectacle was repeated, and again after another hour. The three scientists estimated the lights to be moving at a height of about 50,000 ft. and a speed of about 5 miles per second. Following a call to the *Lubbock Evening Avalanche,* the story snowballed. However, the three witnesses delved further into the incident and uncovered its true cause: birds. The lights turned out to be nothing more than flocks of migrating plovers reflecting the glow from newly installed mercury-vapor streetlamps. The fact that three professional scientists had so badly misjudged the scale of the phenomenon underscores the difficulties people face in gauging the height and speed of unidentified objects in the sky.

Lucian of Samosata (c. 120–c. 180 A.D.)
Syrian-Greek writer responsible for the first fictional accounts of extraterrestrial life. Lucian, whose parents had hoped he might become a sculptor, made a fortune by traveling around Asia Minor, Greece, Italy, and other lands giving entertaining speeches before settling down in Athens to study philosophy. This was a time—the second century A.D.—when faith in the old gods had all but evaporated, Greek culture and thought were in decay, and the great literature of Greece at its height had given way to shallow novels of adventure or romance. All this was grist to Lucian's satirical mill, and in

his two extraterrestrial stories—precursors of science fiction—he parodies the kind of feeble fantasy that had become popular. The concluding sentence of the preface to his *True History* reads, "I give my readers warning, therefore, not to believe me." With that he launches into a tale of a group of adventurers who, while sailing through the Pillars of Hercules (the Strait of Gibraltar), are lifted up by a giant waterspout and deposited on the Moon. There they find themselves embroiled in a full-scale interplanetary war between the king of the Moon and the king of the Sun over colonization rights to Jupiter, involving armies that boast such exotica as stalk-and-mushroom men, acorn dogs, and cloud centaurs. The human inhabitants of the Moon are also remarkable:

> Amongst them, when a man grows old he does not die, but dissolves into smoke and turns to air [a convenient ploy for disposing of dead aliens also used in more recent science fiction, such as "The Man Trap" and "Catspaw" episodes of the original **Star Trek** series]. They all eat the same food, which is frogs roasted on the ashes from a large fire; of these they have plenty which fly about in the air, they get together over the coals, snuff up the scent of them, and this serves for their victuals. Their drink is air squeezed into a cup, which produces a kind of dew.

Lucian may be off here in cloud-cuckoo-land (or almost—the trip to the city of Nephelo-coccygia [the cloud cuckoo] actually comes later in the book), but it is interesting that in his space odyssey he portrays the Moon and planets as being genuine worlds with unique life-forms of their own. In fact, for many centuries, Lucian's adventure was highly regarded not as pure fantasy but as speculative fiction, much as we might treat a science fiction novel by a respected scientist-author today. An example of this is buried in the footnotes of an 1887 edition of Lucian's work (Cassell's National Library series, p. 83). The original translator, one Thomas Franckling, Greek professor at the University of Cambridge, writing in 1780, had this to say at the point where the Earth is seen suspended in the lunar sky as if it were itself a mere satellite: "Modern astronomers are, I think, agreed, that we are to the moon just the same as the moon is to us. Though Lucian's history may be false, therefore, his philosophy, we see, was true." In parentheses after this, the editor of the Cassell edition has inserted the terse comment "The moon is not habitable, 1887."

In his second space story, *Icaro-Menippus*, Lucian is again bound for the Moon, this time in the footsteps, or rather the wing flaps, of his hero who has improved on the ill-fated scheme of Icarus. To his incredulous friend Menippus the hero explains, "I took, you know, a very large eagle, and a vulture also, one of the strongest I could get, and cut off their wings." Lucian, like many who followed him, made no distinction between *aeronautics* and *astronautics*, assuming that normal air-assisted flight and breathing are possible on voyages between worlds. Then, through his hero, he lets rip on the presumptuousness of earlier philosophers to know about the nature of the Universe and life beyond the Earth:

> [T]o think that men, who creep upon this Earth, and are not a whit wiser, or can see farther than ourselves ... should tell us the size and form of the stars ... that the sun is a mass of liquid fire, that the moon is inhabited.

➔ Moon, life on; Moon, voyages to; Plutarch

Lucky 13
Nickname given, by the British scientists who identified it, to the thirteenth known **SNC meteorite.** News of its identification was announced on August 12, 1998. The object, about the size of a softball and weighing 2.2 kg (4.8 lb.) was found in the Sahara Desert. It is important because it appears to have come from a different part of Mars and to be of a different age from the other known SNC meteorites. It is also the only Martian meteorite to have a private owner. Six of the others are owned by the U.S. government and six by museums.

Lucretius (c. 99–c. 55 B.C.)
Roman poet (Titus Lucretius Carus) who, in his *De rerum natura* (On the Nature of Things),[369] combined elegant Latin verse with the philosophy of **Epicurus** and that of the

early atomists **Leucippus** and **Democritus of Abdera** to explain his ideas, including the probability that other worlds and other lifeforms exist. On this subject, he wrote:

> Granted, then, that empty space extends without limit in every direction and that seeds innumerable are rushing on countless courses through an unfathomable universe ..., it is in the highest degree unlikely that this earth and sky is the only one to have been created.... So we must realize that there are other worlds in other parts of the universe, with races of different men and different animals.

Furthermore, he asserted that "when abundant matter is ready, when space is to hand, and no thing and no cause hinders, things must assuredly be done and completed." The latter is an early expression of what Arthur **Lovejoy** has termed the "principle of plenitude" (**➔ plentitude, principle of**). The publication in the West of *De rerum natura*, following its rediscovery in 1473, forced the Church to confront a powerful philosophy that seemed hard to reconcile with orthodox Christianity. **➔ ancient philosophy, related to the possibility of extraterrestrial life**

luminosity
The total amount of energy that an object, such as a star, radiates into space every second. Luminosity depends on both the surface area and the surface temperature of an object, so that, for example, two stars with the same surface temperature but different luminosity must differ in size.

luminosity class
➔ spectral type

luminosity function
The way in which **absolute magnitude** varies against the number of stars for a given volume of space.

Lunan, Duncan (Alasdair) (1945–)
Scottish writer of popular science and science fiction who, in his 1974 book *Man and the Stars*,[370] argued cogently that certain historical radio anomalies[86, 568, 603] could best be ac-

counted for in terms of long-delay echoes from a **Bracewell probe** located at one of the Earth-Moon **Lagrangian points.** The anomalies he referred to were subsequently explained in more mundane terms.[567]

Lunar Prospector

The third mission in NASA's **Discovery Program** and the first to be competitively selected. *Lunar Prospector* was launched on January 6, 1998, and 5 days later, entered a polar orbit around the Moon 101 km (63 miles) high at the start of its yearlong primary mission. The 1.4-m-by-1.2-m drum-shaped spacecraft is equipped with five instruments mounted on three 2.5-m-long booms. One of the instruments is a neutron spectrometer (the first device of this type to be carried aboard an interplanetary probe) designed to verify the existence of water ice at the lunar poles as first suggested by measurements made by *Clementine* in 1994. The neutron spectrometer detects water indirectly. When **cosmic rays** strike atoms in the lunar crust, they throw out **neutron**s and other particles at high energies. Such neutrons are said to be "hot" or "fast." Some of them escape directly into space, while others bounce around among atoms in the crust. If they collide with heavy atoms, they lose little energy and escape still "hot." However, if a dislodged neutron bumps into a **hydrogen** atom in the surface rocks, it loses much of its energy and then escapes into space as a "cool" or "epithermal" neutron. The neutron spectrometer aboard *Lunar Prospector* looks for these epithermal neutrons as a signature for hydrogen on the surface. Traces of hydrogen could be implanted in the Moon's rocks by the **solar wind,** but significant amounts of hydrogen could reasonably be accounted for only by

the presence of water ice. On March 5, 1998, came the announcement that *Lunar Prospector* had confirmed *Clementine*'s earlier discovery[190] (➔ **Moon, water on**). However, the controlled crash of *Lunar Prospector* onto the Moon's surface, on July 31, 1999, failed to splash up any detectable signs of water, leaving astronomers with an unresolved puzzle.

Lunar Sample Receiving Laboratory

An elaborate facility built to quarantine *Apollo* astronauts, spacecraft, and lunar samples following their return to Earth. Concern about the possibility of **back contamination** mandated that astronauts be kept in isolation for at least 3 weeks and that preliminary examination of samples be carried out behind absolute biological barriers. Only after the *Apollo 14* mission was the quarantine procedure abandoned.

lunarian

A hypothetical inhabitant of the Moon. ➔ **selenite; Moon, life on**

Lysithea

The eleventh known moon of **Jupiter.** ➔ **Jupiter, moons of**

Discovery	1938, by Seth Nicholson
Mean distance from Jupiter	11,710,000 km (7,280,000 mi.)
Diameter	36 km (22 mi.)
Mean density	3.1 g/cm^3
Escape velocity	0.0240 km/s (86 km/h, 54 mi./h)
Orbital period	259.22 days (259 days 5 hours)
Orbital eccentricity	0.107
Orbital inclination	29.02°

M

M 13 (NGC 6205)

A large **globular cluster** in the constellation of Hercules, located at a distance of about 25,000 light-years. Although it spans in total about 200 light-years, the bulk of its more than 1 million stars are concentrated into a core region whose diameter is less than 100 light-years. In this inner domain the average distance between stars is only about 1 light-year compared with a typical gap between stars in the solar neighborhood of just over 3 light-years. In 1974, a message was beamed toward M 13 using the giant **Arecibo radio telescope** (→ **Arecibo Message**).

M 33

A small **spiral galaxy** in the **Local Group** that was the initial target of a 1975 **SETI** investigation by Frank **Drake** and Carl **Sagan** using the **Arecibo radio telescope.** The study was extended, with negative results, to other nearby galaxies at **wavelength**s of 21, 18, and 12.6 cm.

M star

A cool red star of **spectral type** M, with a surface temperature of less than 3,600°C. Molecular absorption bands are prominent in the spectrum, with bands of titanium oxide becoming dominant at the lower end of the temperature range. **Main sequence** M stars, known as **red dwarf**s, have a mass of less than 0.5 M_S and a luminosity less than 0.08 L_S. M-type **giant star**s, known as **red giant**s, occur in the mass range 1.2 to 1.3 M_S and may exceed 300 L_S. The largest stars of all are M-type **supergiant**s, such as **Betelgeuse** and Antares, of mass 13 to 25 M_S and luminosity 40,000 to 500,000 L_S.

MACHO Project

A collaboration among American, Australian, and British astronomers to search for **MACHOs** using a special-purpose **charge-coupled device** camera on the 1.3-m (50-in.) telescope of the **Mount Stromlo and Siding Spring Observatories.** It is led by Charles Alcock at the Lawrence Livermore National Laboratory, California. The MACHO team has identified several dozen **microlensing** events in the **Galactic Bulge** and **Large Magellanic Cloud,** including a few that suggest the presence of planets in orbit around distant stars. Immediate notification of possible in-progress lensing events detected by the MACHO Project is made available to other interested groups through the **Global Microlensing Alert Network** (GMAN).

MACHOs

Massive Astronomical Compact Halo Objects; one possible form of **dark matter** in the Universe. MACHOs are believed by some astronomers to exist in large numbers in the halos of galaxies such as our own. They may occasionally give rise to **microlensing** events that can be used in the search for **extrasolar planets.** Several searches for lensing phenomena associated with MACHOs are in progress, including **EROS,** the **MACHO Project,** and **OGLE.**

Mack, John E. (1944–)

Professor of psychiatry at Harvard Medical School and author of the controversial *Abduction: Human Encounters with Aliens,*[371] (1992) in which he argued that alleged **alien abduction** reports refer to authentic encounters with extraterrestrials.

macroevolution

The development of new species, and the extinction of old ones. It contrasts with **microevolution.**

macromolecule

A very large **molecule** such as a **protein, polysaccharide, nucleic acid,** or **lipid.** Macromolecules are generally **carbon**-based and of biological importance.

Mädler, Johann Heinrich von (1794–1874)

German astronomer who was the main observer involved in the great lunar map (*Mappa Selenographica*) and accompanying descriptive volume (*Der Mond*) published by himself and Wilhelm **Beer** in 1930. Beer and Mädler also produced the first systematic map of Mars.

Magellan Telescopes

A pair of 6.5-m (21.3-ft.) reflectors jointly owned and operated by the Carnegie Institution, the Massachusetts Institute of Technology, and the Universities of Arizona, Harvard, and Michigan and located at the **Las Campanas Observatory.** The first was completed in 1998, while the second is scheduled for completion in 2002.

Magellanic Clouds

Two satellite galaxies of our own **galaxy** that are visible from the Southern Hemisphere as misty patches in the night sky. Riding at close quarters to each other, barely 100,000 light-years apart, it is possible that the Magellanic Clouds are destined at some time to merge into a single galaxy. Together with at least two other satellite galaxies, the Draco and Ursa Major systems, they move within an enormous river of hydrogen gas known as the Magellanic Stream. ➜ **Large Magellanic Cloud; Small Magellanic Cloud**

maghemite

A form of iron **oxide** also known as gamma Fe_2O_3, with the crystalline structure of magnetite but the composition of hematite, that can act as a powerful **catalyst.** On Earth, it is usually found only around the edges of regions of hydrothermal or magnetic activity, where the temperature ranges from 300 to 400°C. The abundance of water on Earth has converted much of the maghemite into a noncatalytic form, but on Mars it has survived virtually unaltered. It was cited by Vance **Oyama** in his explanation of the results of the *Viking* labeled release (LR) experiment (➜ **Oyama's hypothesis, about the active nature of the Martian soil**).

magnetosphere

The region of space in which the magnetic field of a planet dominates the **solar wind** or the magnetic field of a star dominates the interstellar magnetic field.

magnetotactic bacteria

Bacteria that effectively have internal compasses and are able to orient themselves with respect to a magnetic field.

magnetotaxis

The ability of some organisms to sense and respond to a magnetic field.

magnitude scale

A calibration of the brightness of objects in the sky. The first such scale was created by **Hipparchus of Nicaea** in about 120 B.C. He referred to the brightest stars visible to the eye as "first magnitude" and those at the limit of naked-eye visibility as "sixth magnitude." With the advent of **photometric** equipment (➜ **photometer**) that could accurately record the amount of light received from an object in the sky, it became possible to put this scheme on a scientific footing. In 1856, the magnitude scale was fixed so that a difference of five magnitudes corresponds to a ratio of apparent brightness of 100. This means that a difference of one magnitude corresponds to a brightness ratio of 2.512. → **absolute magnitude; apparent magnitude**

Main Asteroid Belt

A region between the orbits of Mars and Jupiter where the majority of **asteroid**s in the solar system are to be found. The Main Asteroid Belt extends from 1.7 to 4 AU (255 million to 600 million km) from the Sun and may contain more than a million objects bigger than 1 km across, the largest being Ceres (1,003 km), Pallas (608 km), and Vesta (538 km). The belt appears to have originated as a system of perhaps fifty large bodies in the 100-to-1,000-km size range. These accreted during the formation of the solar system and thereafter suffered collisions leading to fragmentation. This hypothesis suggests that only a few of the larger asteroids are still intact.

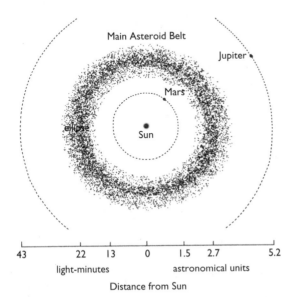

The Main Asteroid Belt shown to scale with the orbits of Mars and Jupiter.
NASA/JPL/Caltech

main sequence

A star on the main sequence is one that is generating light and heat by the conversion of **hydrogen** to **helium** by nuclear **fusion** in its core. The Sun and the bulk of the stars visible to the naked eye are main sequence stars.

major axis

The greatest diameter of an **ellipse**.

Malthus, Thomas Robert (1766–1834)

English economist who, in 1798, published anonymously his *Essay on the Principle of Population*, which argued that population has a natural tendency to rise faster than the means of its subsistence.

MANIA

Multichannel analyzer of nanosecond variation in brightness. A device used in a Russian search begun in 1989 for optical signals from intelligent extraterrestrials. → **optical SETI**

Mantell, Thomas F.

Pilot of an P-51 Mustang fighter killed on January 7, 1948, while pursuing an **unidentified flying object** near Godman Air Force Base, Kentucky. The object had previously been seen by numerous witnesses on the ground. At 15,000 ft., Mantell radioed the control tower that the UFO was "metallic and tremendous in size" and "appears to be moving about half my speed." Just after 5:00 P.M., the wreckage of Mantell's plane was found, with the port wing, rear fuselage, and tail ripped off. His body was in the cockpit, and his watch had stopped at 3:18, which was taken as the time of impact. Crash investigators thought it most likely that Mantell had blacked out at about 25,000 ft., while his P-51 continued to 30,000 ft., lost power, leveled off, and then circled before going into a power dive.

The newly established Project **Sign** concluded that the UFO had been the planet Venus, which was in the right place to concur with the witnesses' reports from Godman. However, this theory failed to account for many other aspects of the case, including Mantell's reference to a very large metallic object. A reexamination of the incident in the 1950s by Captain Edward **Ruppelt**[487] came to the conclusion that what Mantell had really been chasing was a U.S. Navy **Skyhook** balloon, probably launched from Camp Ripley, Minnesota. → **Cold War, linked to UFO reports**

mantle

That part of a planet or moon that lies between the core and the crust.

many-worlds interpretation

A way of explaining the results of **quantum mechanics** in terms of the creation of large numbers of **parallel universe**s. According to the many-worlds interpretation, first put forward by the physicist Eugene Wigner, every time a measurement or observation is made at the subatomic level, the entire Universe splits into two slightly different and independent realities in which the alternative outcomes of the measurement are played out. As in the case of the multiple universes predicted by **chaotic inflationary theory,** this vastly increases the number of places and forms in which life could occur.

MAP

→ **Multichannel Astrometric Photometer**

MAPS

→ **Multichannel Astrometric Photometer and Spectrometer**

Marconi, Guglielmo (1874–1937)

Italian physicist and Nobel Prize winner who, for several years, became involved with the possibility of radio communication with extraterrestrial intelligence. His first public comments on the subject appeared on the front page of *The New York Times* on January 20, 1919, under the headline "Radio to Stars, Marconi's Hope." Marconi expressed his belief that there might be many inhabited worlds, that mathematics might serve as a common language of communication (→ **mathematics, as a universal language**), and that unexplained signals he had detected might have been sent by intelligent beings in space. A year later the *Daily Mail* in London reported that Marconi had found "very queer sounds and indications, which might come from somewhere outside the Earth," including Morse code.

Subsequently, *The New York Times* followed up the story, stimulating comments from a number of scientists and engineers around the world. Although Marconi said nothing more on the subject, the possibility of radio communication with extraterrestrials created much public excitement at the coming close **opposition** of Mars in 1924. By this time, most professional astronomers agreed that there was little chance of finding advanced Martians. But one who had not yet given up hope of making contact with the inhabitants of the Red Planet was David P. **Todd.** → **communication, with the Moon and planets**

Marcy, Geoffrey W. (1954–)

Distinguished university professor at San Francisco State University, adjunct professor at the **University of California, Berkeley,** and primary researcher with the **San Francisco State University Planet Search** group. Together with Paul **Butler** and other colleagues, he has been responsible for the discovery of well over half the presently known **extrasolar planets** and for obtaining evidence that (1) the solar system may be unusual in its makeup, and (2) that **brown dwarf**s in orbit around stars are surprisingly rare. Since 1998, Marcy has served on the NASA working groups concerned with the *Terrestrial Planet Finder* and the origin of the solar system. He obtained a B.A. from the University of California, Los Angeles (1976), and a Ph.D. from the University of California, Santa Cruz (1982).

Marfa Lights

Unusual multicolored displays of aerial luminosity often seen near the town of Marfa, Texas. They appear to be examples of so-called **earthlights** and appear on such a frequent basis that the residents of Marfa hold an annual jamboree called the "Festival of Lights" to celebrate the phenomenon.

Margulis, Lynn

Microbiologist who is currently distinguished professor in the Department of Geosciences at the University of Massachusetts, Amherst. She originated the **endosymbiotic theory** and was one of the pioneers, along with James **Lovelock,** of the **Gaia Hypothesis.** From 1977 to

1980, she chaired the **Space Science Board** Committee on Planetary Biology and Chemical Evolution. Margulis obtained a B.A. from the University of Chicago in 1957, an M.S. from the University of Wisconsin in 1960, and a Ph.D. from the **University of California, Berkeley.** Her former husband was Carl **Sagan.**

maria

Large dark regions on the Moon's surface, once thought to be seas and now known to be lava-covered basins.

Mariner 9

Martian orbiter probe, launched May 30, 1971, that went into orbit around **Mars** on November 13, 1971, and subsequently returned 7,329 pictures of the planet's surface before contact was lost on October 27, 1972. These images showed a world very different from that seen in the lower-resolution images of the earlier *Mariner*s. In particular, they revealed a diversity of terrain, including channels and other features that indicated that there had once been liquid water on Mars (➔ **Mars, water on**). This discovery revitalized interest in the possibility of extant or past Martian life (➔ **Mars, life on**) at a time when preparations were being made to send *Viking* in search of it.[187]

Mars

The fourth and most remote of the terrestrial planets from the Sun, long considered to be the likeliest of our neighboring worlds to harbor life (➔ **Mars, life on**). Because Mars's orbit is significantly elliptical, the amount of solar heat received during the day at any given point on the planet's surface varies widely between **perihelion** and **aphelion.** Consequently, although the yearly average temperature over the whole surface is about $-55°C$ ($-67°F$), the temperature ranges from as low as $-133°C$ ($-207°F$) at the winter pole to about $27°C$ ($80°F$) at the equator on a summer day. These values are much lower than would occur on Earth if our planet orbited the Sun at the distance of Mars, due to the relatively feeble **greenhouse effect** of the thin Martian atmosphere (➔ **Mars, atmosphere of**). However, in the remote past, conditions on the fourth planet are known to have been more clement (➔ **Mars, past conditions on**) so that even if Mars proves to be sterile today, it may be that life evolved there, under a warmer and wetter regime, several billion years ago.

The seasonal waxing and waning of the Martian polar caps (➔ **Mars, polar caps on**) was seen by early observers to be accompanied by surface changes at lower latitudes (➔ **Mars, changes on**). The darkening of certain regions, following each spring thaw, prompted theories of inundation by floodwater and the growth of vast tracts of plant life (➔ **Mars, vegetation on**), while Giovanni **Schiaparelli**'s claims about the features he referred to as *canali* led, in time, to more florid speculation by Percival **Lowell** and others about the possible existence of artificial waterways (➔ **Mars, canals of**) and high intelligence. Although no trace of Lowell's canals appeared before the cameras of the first successful Martian probes, later robot missions, including *Mariner 9, Viking, Mars Pathfinder,* and *Mars Global Surveyor* have revealed the Red Planet to be the scene of remarkable geological, topographical, and chronological diversity. It boasts the largest volcano ever seen, Olympus Mons, 24 km (15 miles; 79,000 ft.) high; a collection of volcanoes in the northern Tharsis region so huge that they have deformed the planet's sphericity; an impact crater in the southern hemisphere, Hellas Planitia, which is more than 6 km deep and 2,000 km wide; and a rift valley, Valles Marineris (Valley of the Mariners) long enough to stretch from Los Angeles to New York—all this on a surface that is no bigger than the *land* area of Earth.

Mars is a planet of marked regional contrasts. Whereas the southern hemisphere consists mostly of ancient cratered highlands similar to those of the Moon, the northern hemisphere reveals a terrain of more complex history and generally lower elevation. In many places, there is incontrovertible evidence of erosion and a watery past, including floodplains and river channels, that tantalizes the astrobiologist. Valles Marineris, however, was created not by running water but by the stretching and cracking of the crust associated with the formation of the Tharsis bulge.

Distance from Sun:	
Mean	227.9 million km (141.6 million mi., 1.52 AU)
Minimum	206.7 million km (128.5 million mi., 1.38 AU)
Maximum	249.1 million km (154.8 million mi., 1.66 AU)
Equatorial diameter	6,786 km (4,217 mi.)
Equatorial diameter (Earth = 1)	0.532
Mass (Earth = 1)	0.107
Mean density	3.9 g/cm^3
Escape velocity	5.0 km/s (18,108 km/h, 11,254 mi./h)
Orbital period	686.98 days
Orbital inclination	1.85°
Orbital eccentricity	0.093
Axial period	24.6 hours
Axial inclination	23.9°
Number of moons	2
Atmospheric composition	95.3% carbon dioxide, 2.7% nitrogen, 1.6% argon, 0.15% oxygen, 0.03% water vapor
Surface temperature:	
Maximum (equatorial summer day)	27°C (80°F)
Minimum (polar winter night)	−133°C (−207°F)
Mean	−55°C (−67°F)
Surface gravity (Earth = 1)	0.38
Albedo	0.16

Inside, Mars may have a core roughly 1,700 km in radius, which the planet's relatively low density suggests contains a higher ratio of sulfur to iron than that in the cores of the other terrestrial worlds. Overlaying this is probably a molten, rocky mantle, somewhat denser than the Earth's, topped with a thin crust. Although tectonism has clearly played a major role in the planet's development, it has not involved the lateral movement of sliding plates as on our own world, but instead only vertical movement of hot lava pushing up to the surface. The lack of **plate tectonics,** as on Mercury and the Moon, has resulted in hot spots remaining fixed in certain locations beneath the crust. Large, but not planetwide, weak areas of magnetic activity have been one of the unexpected discoveries of *Mars Global Surveyor* and may represent isolated remnants of what was once a global magnetic field.

Mars, atmosphere of

It was William **Herschel** who offered the first scientific evidence that Mars might have an atmosphere. His observations of the planet in

1783 led him to suppose that some changes he had noted were due to "clouds and vapors."[269] Four years later, Johann **Schröter** arrived at the same conclusion:[519]

> The spots and streaks on the surface of Mars are always changing, even from hour to hour. But that they are the same regions is shown by the fact that the same shapes and positions develop and pass away again, as one would expect of the variable atmospheric appearances occurring above a solid surface.

These early results were disputed at the start of the next great phase of Martian observations, which was ushered in by the great mapmakers Wilhelm **Beer** and Johann **Mädler** and made possible by the construction of larger, better refracting telescopes. By 1830, Beer and Mädler had concluded, "The hypothesis, that the spots are similar to our clouds, appears to be entirely disproved." Yet the notion of an atmosphere rich in water vapor did not go away. In 1870, Richard **Procter** was still advocating the Herschelian view and from it extrapolating to Martian seas and life:

> [I]f we admit that the vaporous envelope which occasionally hides parts of Mars is aqueous, we must believe in the existence of aqueous oceans on Mars...the Martial lands are nourished by refreshing rainfalls; and who can doubt that they are thus nourished for the same purpose as our own fields and forests—namely, that vegetation of all sorts grow abundantly?

The final decade of the nineteenth century saw the rise of the canal controversy (➔ **Mars, canals of**) but, at the same time, serious doubts were cast by William **Campbell** that the Martian atmosphere was either substantial or contained water vapor. At the **opposition** of 1909, contradictory results came from Campbell, who reconfirmed his failure to find water vapor on Mars, and Vesto Slipher and Frank Very, who claimed a positive result. In any event, concluded Campbell,[95]

> these measurements do not prove that life does not or cannot exist on Mars. The question of life under these conditions is the biologist's problem rather than the astronomer's.

Percival **Lowell**'s 1908 estimate, based on **albedo** measurements, of a surface pressure on Mars of 87 millibars (0.087 of the Earth's barometric pressure) roughly agreed with those of later, pre–Space Age investigators, such as Gérard de **Vaucouleurs.** However, the composition of the atmosphere remained controversial. Spectroscopic studies by Walter **Adams** and Theodore **Dunham** in the 1930s found no trace of either water vapor or **oxygen.** In fact, the first substance to be positively identified in the Martian atmosphere was **carbon dioxide.** Observing from the **McDonald Observatory,** Gerard **Kuiper** found that there was about twice the concentration of this gas on Mars as there is on Earth. By analogy with Earth, it was assumed that the bulk of the Martian atmosphere was made up of **nitrogen,** a gas notoriously difficult to detect with a spectroscope. In 1950, the best guess as to the composition of the Martian atmosphere was made by Vau-couleurs: 98.5 percent nitrogen, 1.2 percent argon, 0.25 percent carbon dioxide, and less than 0.1 percent oxygen. But in fact there is very little nitrogen on Mars and the atmospheric pressure is therefore much lower than astronomers had estimated before the exploration of the planet by space probes. Measurements made by the *Viking* landers established the exact composition of the Martian atmosphere as 95.3 percent carbon dioxide, 2.7 percent nitrogen, and 1.6 percent argon, with traces of oxygen (0.15 percent) and water vapor (0.03 percent). The average surface pressure is only about 7 millibars (less than 1 percent of the Earth's), though it varies greatly with altitude from about 9 millibars in the deepest basins to about 1 millibar at the top of Olympus Mons. This is still thick enough to support strong winds and enable occasional planetwide dust storms to obscure the surface for months at a time. On the other hand, the Martian atmosphere results in only a weak **greenhouse effect** that raises the surface temperature by about 5°C. Consequently, most of Mars is well below the freezing point of water for most of the year. Moreover, even when the daytime temperature at low latitudes does climb significantly above freezing, the atmospheric pressure is so low that water ice turns directly into water vapor without first becoming liquid.

Mars, canals of

The saga of these elusive waterways began with Giovanni **Schiaparelli**'s claims following the **opposition** of Mars in 1877. Schiaparelli used the Italian word *canali* to describe linear markings that he observed in that year and at subsequent oppositions. He drew increasingly elaborate maps in which the canals became a more and more prominent feature, even seeming to double on a seasonal basis (➔ **"germination," of Martian canals**). On balance, he favored the view that they were natural waterways, although he never opposed the suggestion that they might have been intelligently constructed. To begin with, he received little encouragement from the astronomical community. Observers of the caliber of Asaph **Hall,** who first glimpsed the two tiny Martian moons, and Edward **Barnard,** discoverer of

Amalthea, a faint inner satellite of Jupiter, never saw linear markings on the Red Planet. In 1894, Barnard wrote:

> I have been watching and drawing the surface of Mars. It is wonderfully full of detail. There is certainly no question about there being mountains and plateaus. To save my soul I can't believe in the canals as Schiaparelli draws them. I see details where he has drawn none. I see details where some of his canals are, but they are not straight lines *at all*. When best seen these details are very irregular and broken up...I verily believe...that the canals...are a fallacy and that they will so be proved before many favorable oppositions are past.

Barnard's skeptical stance represented the majority position of professionals throughout the period of the canal debate. Yet enough reputable astronomers did verify Schiaparelli's *canali* to keep the controversy alive. Moreover, such was Schiaparelli's reputation as a skilled observer that, even among opponents, his claims concerning the mysterious lines were treated with respect and Mars became the subject of intense scrutiny at the world's leading observatories.

Several matters needed resolving, both intellectually and optically. First was the question of whether there really were lines on Mars at all. Many astronomers doubted it, suspecting that they were an illusion, but verification of Schiaparelli's markings came, in 1886, from Henri **Perrotin** and Louis **Thollon** in Nice and Herbert **Wilson** in Cincinnati. Next was the question of whether, if the lines were real, they were watercourses or some other phenomenon such as glacial crevasses or "stripes . . . due to differences in vegetation." The last suggestion was made by William **Pickering** in 1888 and won considerable support. Finally, came the question of whether, if the canals were waterways, they were natural or artificial. Although the latter view won very little support among professional astronomers, it proved irresistible to the general public, whose imagination was fired by the procanal writings of Camille **Flammarion** in France and especially of Percival **Lowell** in the United States. In his widely read and translated *La Planète Mars* (1892), Flammarion wrote:

> [I]t would be wrong to deny that [Mars] could be inhabited by human species whose intelligence and methods of action could be far superior to our own. Neither can we deny that they could have straightened the original rivers and built a system of canals with the idea of producing a planet-wide circulation system.

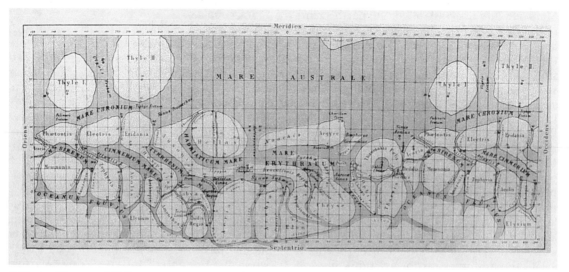

Schiaparelli's map of 1877.

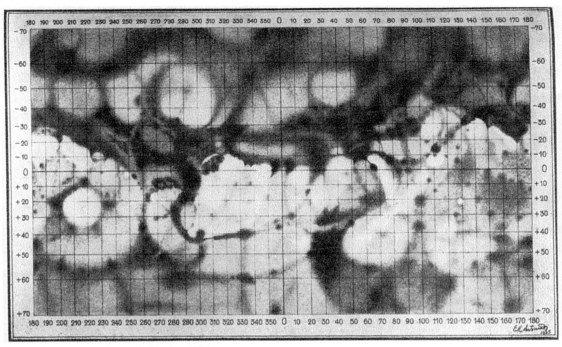

Antoniadi's master map published in 1930.

Even Flammarion's enthusiasm, however, paled beside that of Lowell, who from 1894 to his death in 1916 painted a picture of an extant Martian civilization infinitely more alluring than the prosaic (yet more accurate) portrayals by mainstream science (➔ **Mars, life on**).

Lowell managed to capture the mood of the age. By the closing decades of the nineteenth century, through a bombardment of extraordinary fact and fiction (➔ **Verne, Jules**), people had become habituated to high-speed technological progress and increasingly ambitious civil engineering schemes. So the suggestion that beings on another world who were more evolved than mankind might be able to carry out projects on a planetwide scale seemed perfectly credible. What humans could do, perhaps the Martians, older and wiser, could do bigger and better. Regarding transport systems, for instance, the year 1869 saw not only the term *canali* first applied (by Pietro **Secchi**) to a feature on Mars, but also the opening of the Suez Canal and the completion of the first

rail track linking the East and West Coasts of the United States. Ordinary folk were already primed to believe in advanced Martians, so that when Lowell speculated about a canal-building superrace, he found an eager and sympathetic audience.

Many people felt the haunting, other-worldly allure of the Martian canals and novelists were not slow to weave romantic tales around the theme, further stimulating public interest. Percy **Greg**, George **Griffith**, Garrett **Serviss**, H. G. **Wells** (most influentially), and others at the end of the nineteenth century, Edgar Rice **Burroughs** in the early decades of the twentieth, and, more recently, Ray **Bradbury** in *The Martian Chronicles*[76] and Robert Heinlein in *Stranger in a Strange Land*[266] drew inspiration from the Lowellian myth. For myth is what it proved to be. By the dawn of the twentieth century, it was becoming clear that the Martian atmosphere was too thin (➔ **Mars, atmosphere of**), the temperature too low, and water too sparse (➔ **Mars, water on**) to support any kind of life except possibly primitive vegetation (➔ **Mars, vegetation on**) and microbes. Hopes of finding canals or their builders had all but disappeared.[499]

Mars, changes on

William **Herschel**'s drawings of the Red Planet in the 1780s provided early evidence of changes on the planet in both the shape and coloration of surface features. These changes were studied in greater detail by the mapmakers Wilhelm **Beer** and Johann von **Mädler,** who noted that, between 1837 and 1839, the dark region surrounding the north polar cap appeared to shrink and fade. This could be explained, they suggested, if the dark region was marshy soil moistened by meltwater from the retreating snow. By the 1860s, the idea that Mars had both oceans and continents was commonplace. Emmanuel **Liais,** however, attributed the shifting appearance of the dark areas to the seasonal growth and decline of vegetation, a suggestion later elaborated in spectacular style by Percival **Lowell.** The vegetation hypothesis remained viable throughout the first half of the twentieth century. Yet sadly, Mars's coloration variations are now known to be due not to the presence of life but to great clouds of windborne dust that occasionally engulf the planet and leave behind dramatic evidence of their power, including vast dune fields, wind streaks, and wind-carved features.

Mars Climate Observer

One of the **Mars Surveyor 98** missions, launched on December 11, 1998, and lost on September 23, 1999, due to a navigational error. *Mars Climate Observer* was to have used a series of aerobraking maneuvers to achieve a stable Martian orbit but approached the planet too closely and is presumed to have disintegrated in the atmosphere.

Mars, communication with

➔ **communication, with the Moon and planets**

Mars Express

A **European Space Agency** mission scheduled for launch in May–June 2003 and arrival at Mars in late December of the same year. It will be the first spacecraft to use radar to penetrate the surface of Mars and map the distribution of possible underground water deposits and is expected to carry the **Beagle 2** lander.

Mars Global Surveyor (MGS)

An orbiter launched in November 1996 and designed, over the course of a full Martian year, to investigate the surface, atmosphere, and magnetic properties of Mars in unprecedented detail. It was the inaugural mission in a decade of planned intensive *in situ* research of the Red Planet. MGS carries four main science instruments. The Mars Orbiter Camera provides daily wide-angle images of Mars similar to weather photos of Earth and narrow-angle images of objects as small as 1.5 m (4.9 ft.) across. The Mars Orbiter Laser Altimeter bounces a **laser** beam off the surface to measure accurately the height of mountains and the depth of valleys. The Thermal Emission Spectrometer scans emitted heat to study both the atmosphere and the mineral composition of the surface. Finally, the Magnetometer and Electron Reflection experiment provides data on the magnetic state of the crustal rocks, which in turn sheds light on the early magnetic history of the planet. One of the conclusions suggested by high-resolution images from MGS is that, although Mars had a watery past, it may never have rained. The water that carved the channels first photographed by *Mariner 9* in 1972 may have welled up from inside the planet in one-off floods (➔ **Mars, water on**). Another surprise came in May 1999 with the announcement that Mars may once have had shifting tectonic plates,[127] making it appear even more Earth-like in its youth and raising hopes still further that life may have emerged. MGS data revealed parallel stripes of crust in the ancient southern highlands, about 200 km across and up to 2,000 km long, that are magnetized in alternating directions—the product of magma "freezing" the ancient Martian magnetic polarization as it periodically switched back and forth. No magnetic field exists on Mars now, but the MGS observations suggest that a strong active dynamo operated there for at least 0.5 billion years.

Mars, life on

Although advocates of **pluralism** from the seventeenth century on had built a case for Martian life on purely philosophical and theological grounds, it was William **Herschel** who first made astronomical observations of the planet that were detailed enough to be relevant to the debate. From his telescopic studies in 1783, he concluded:[269]

> The analogy between Mars and the earth is, perhaps, by far the greatest in the whole solar system. The diurnal motion is nearly the same; the obliquity of their respective ecliptics, on which the seasons depend, not very different; of all the superior planets the distance of Mars from the sun is by far the nearest alike to that of the earth.... If, then, we find that the globe we inhabit has its polar regions frozen and covered with mountains of ice and snow, that only partly melt when alternately exposed to the sun, I may well be permitted to surmise that the same causes may probably have the same effect on the globe of Mars.... I have often noticed occasional changes of partial bright belts... and also once a darkish one, in a pretty high latitude.... And these alterations we can hardly ascribe to any other cause than the variable disposition of clouds and vapors floating in the atmosphere of that planet.

Writing in 1870, Richard **Procter**[468] took Herschel's Mars-Earth parallels further and argued vehemently for advanced Martian life based on the assumption that Mars was well supplied with both water and atmosphere:

> Shall we recognize in Mars all that makes our own world so well fitted for our wants—land and water, mountain and valley, cloud and sunshine, rain and ice, and snow, rivers and lakes, ocean currents and wind currents—without believing further in the existence of those forms of life without which all of these things would be wasted?... [I]t is yet to speculate ten thousand times more rashly to assert... that Mars is a barren waste, either wholly untenanted by living creatures, or inhabited by beings belonging to the lowest orders of animated existence.

The astronomical evidence seemed to continue to favor life following Giovanni **Schiaparelli**'s announcement that he had seen regular linear markings on the surface, though no one could have imagined how far speculation over his *canali* would lead. By 1892, Camille **Flammarion**[196] had leaped to the conclusion that

> the present inhabitation of Mars by a race superior to ours is very probable.... The considerable variations observed in the network of waterways testify that this planet is the seat of an energetic vitality... we may hope that, because the world of Mars is older than ours, mankind there will be more advanced and wiser.

In the fertile imagination of Percival **Lowell,** this portrait of an intelligently populated planet attained its most elaborate form (➔ **Mars, canals of**). Though Lowell's Mars was far less hospitable than Procter's, this was seen by him as no barrier to its habitation. On the contrary, the difficulties imposed by the environment had led the Martians to engage in such heroic hydrological schemes that evidence of them was visible from Earth. By the early years of the twentieth century, professional opinion was shifting inexorably away from the notion of advanced life on Mars. Increasingly, Mars seemed too dry, airless, and cold to support anything more than primitive vegetation (➔ **Mars, vegetation on**). Yet as late as 1936, one of the founders of the **British Interplanetary Society** felt able to write:[120]

> On Mars, the crumbling remains of ancient civilizations may be found, mutely testifying to the one-time glory of a dying world.

Indeed, in the very decade the Space Age began, Willy Ley and Wernher von Braun's *The Exploration of Mars*[348] contained a haunting illustration by Chesley Bonestell of the ruins of a Martian temple. That dream, of finding the remnants of a long-dead race, quickly vanished as close-up pictures arrived in 1964 from the first successful Mars probe, *Mariner 4,* of a crater-strewn wilderness seemingly not unlike that of our own Moon. However, in 1971, *Mariner 9* brought renewed hope of finding past and even extant biological activity, with its images of what appeared to be dried-up river channels. Such was the revival of optimism that only a few weeks before the first *Viking* landing, Carl **Sagan** and Joshua **Lederberg** went so far as to suggest[501] that "Large organisms, possibly detectable by the Viking lander cameras, are not only possible on Mars; they may be favored." In the event, nothing so spectacular was found, although the *Viking* results are still open to a variety of interpretations, both chemical and biological.

More recently, attention has focused on the extraordinary possibility that life may have evolved first on Mars and then become seeded on the young Earth by the process of **ballistic panspermia.**[552] According to this idea, Mars afforded a safer haven for primitive life during the early, violent bombardment phase of the solar system, between about 4.6 and 3.8 billion years ago. Whereas the Earth was probably hit repeatedly by objects up to 500 km across that would have vaporized the oceans and created a deadly steam atmosphere (**→ Earth, early history of**), fewer giant impacts would have taken place on Mars (because it is a smaller target) and the absence of large amounts of surface water would have saved the planet from being as severely steam-sterilized. Any Martian **thermophile**s living just a few hundred meters below the surface, it has been suggested, would have been able to survive the trauma of collision with a 500-km-wide object. Furthermore, because of Mars's relatively cool interior and low gravity (allowing cracks in which microbes could reside to extend further down into the planet's interior), thermophilic subterranean organisms may have existed in a wide habitable zone extending to depths of several thousand meters. On Earth, by comparison, although thermophiles 1 km below the surface might have survived an ocean-boiling impact, this would have left an uncomfortably narrow habitable zone—much below 1 km—and microbes would probably have been cooked by the planet's hot interior.[225,254]

Mars, meteorites from
→ SNC meteorites

Mars Microprobe Mission
Also known as *Deep Space 2*, the second mission in NASA's **New Millennium Program.** It consisted of two basketball-sized aeroshells that piggybacked aboard the *Mars Polar Lander*. The aeroshells were supposed to crash at about 200 miles per second into the Martian surface at the northernmost boundary of the area near the south polar ice cap known as the Polar Layered Terrain, about 200 km from the landing site of the main spacecraft, and then send back information on subsurface conditions. In the event, no transmission was ever received.

Mars, moons of
There had been early (groundless) speculation about the existence of two Martian satellites (**→ Swift, Jonathan, and the moons of Mars**) but it was not until 1877 that diminutive **Phobos** and **Deimos** were discovered by Asaph **Hall** at the **U.S. Naval Observatory.**[217] Working at the same site, Bevan Sharpless concluded in 1944, after analyzing measurements made since Hall's discovery, that the orbit of Phobos was decaying.[535] Rapidly, his data suggested, the little moon was spiraling on a collision course with Mars. For a number of years, this result remained a minor curiosity. Then, in 1959, Soviet astrophysicist Iosef **Shklovskii** took up the challenge to explain *why* the orbit of Phobos was shrinking. He looked at the possibility that the thin upper regions of the Martian atmosphere might be gradually slowing Phobos down but decided that this effect would be too small to account for the results Sharpless had obtained. Among the alternatives he considered were the influence of the Sun, a tidal interaction with the gravity of Mars, and the effect of a hypothetical Martian magnetic field. However, none of these seemed able to provide a satisfactory mechanism. So Shklovskii went back to the idea that atmospheric drag might somehow be involved and came up with an audacious suggestion: What, he asked, if Phobos were not an ordinary moon? What if its average density were only a thousandth that of water, so that the thin outer atmosphere of Mars *could* act as an effective brake and destabilize the little moon's orbit? What, in fact, if Phobos were *hollow*? A hollow object 24 km (15 miles) across could not possibly be natural. It would have to

be the product of a technology well in advance of our own, surpassing even that required to build the great network of waterways and pumping stations envisaged by Percival **Lowell.** In *Intelligent Life in the Universe,* coauthored with Carl **Sagan,** Shklovskii writes:[540]

> Since Mars does not have a large natural satellite such as our moon, the construction of large, artificial satellites would be of relatively greater importance to an advanced Martian civilization in its expansion into space.... The launching of massive satellites from Mars would be a somewhat easier task than from Earth, because of the lower Martian gravity.

Shklovskii thought it unlikely that the creators of Phobos were still alive:

> Perhaps Phobos was launched into orbit in the heyday of a technical civilization on Mars, some hundreds of millions of years ago.

But the idea of advanced *extant* Martian life did not seem beyond belief to some others, including Frank Salisbury, professor of plant physiology at Colorado State University. He pointed out that neither of the Martian moons had been spotted in 1862, when Mars had been closer than in Hall's discovery year of 1877 and when large instruments had been trained upon it:

> Should we attribute the failure of 1862 to imperfections in the existing telescopes, or may we imagine that the satellites were launched into orbit between 1862 and 1877?

Sadly, close-up photographs of Phobos taken by the *Viking* orbiters and other probes have revealed a more prosaic truth. There is nothing suggestive of artifice about this rocky, pockmarked, potato-shaped moon. In all likelihood it was once, like Deimos, an asteroid that, during its solar peregrinations, strayed too far into the gravitational domain of Mars and became ensnared. Measurements made during the favorable opposition of Mars in 1988 confirmed that the orbit of Phobos is unstable. However, its rate of decay is only about half that claimed by Sharpless, so that it can be accounted for in terms of frictional forces acting on a natural solid body. Each year the little moon draws 2.5 cm closer to its parent planet. Phobos never came from the surface of Mars. But it will eventually end up there, blasting a crater roughly 500 km (300 miles) across sometime within the next 40 million years.

Mars, oppositions of

The Earth-Mars distance fluctuates between about 56 million and 400 million km (35 million and 250 million miles) as the two planets swing around their respective orbits. The best times for telescopic viewing are when Mars is in "opposition"—that is, close to the Earth and in the opposite part of the sky from the Sun. These happen every 780 days. But the most favorable oppositions of all, when the two planets approach as closely as possible, occur only at intervals of 15 to 17 years, and always in July, August, or September.

Mars, past conditions on

Early in the 4.6-billion-year history of the solar system, the conditions on the Earth and Mars were almost certainly much more similar than they are now. On both planets the primitive atmosphere is thought to have originated in large part from gases, mainly water vapor, **carbon dioxide,** and **nitrogen,** vented from volcanoes (**→ Mars, atmosphere of**). In the Earth's case, far more water was released than the atmosphere could hold, and the bulk of it condensed to form oceans, which remain to this day. Evidence suggests that an ocean also formed on Mars (**→ Mars, water on**), covering, according to some estimates, one third of the planet's surface to an average depth of 1,700 m (5,500 ft.). Early on, large amounts of carbon dioxide in the Martian atmosphere probably led to a vigorous **greenhouse effect** that kept the average temperature above 0°C. This fact, together with the substantial atmospheric pressure (perhaps similar to that presently found on Earth), would have enabled surface water to remain as a liquid. But whereas on Earth ongoing **plate tectonic**s have ensured that volcanoes and their release of fresh carbon dioxide play a crucial role in maintaining our planet's equable climate, on Mars the crust appears to consist of a single plate. Owing to its small size, Mars does not have enough internal heat to drive a significant level of tectonic and volcanic activity. Perhaps it did for a while, when it was young. But after the Martian volcanoes fell silent, no new carbon dioxide would have been pumped into the atmosphere, and that which was already there would have been gradually depleted. As happens all the time on Earth, large quantities of atmospheric carbon dioxide were probably taken up by liquid water on the surface and converted into **carbonate**s. Ironically, therefore, the Martian ocean and rivers may well have been instrumental in their own demise, for as they removed more and more carbon dioxide, they would have brought about a lowering of the atmospheric pressure and a reduction in the greenhouse effect, which had previously maintained the surface temperature above the freezing point of water.

Putting an accurate timescale on these dramatic changes in climate is not easy, and researchers continue to argue over when and for how long Mars was warm and wet. The original, volcanically vented Martian atmosphere was probably in place around 4 billion years ago, toward the end of the period of heavy primeval bombardment. Judging by the structure of the valley systems and the extent to which some craters from the early bombardment phase have apparently been eroded by running water, a strong greenhouse effect must have persisted for about 500 million years. Even after this, however, some surface water presumably remained for a long time, continuing to remove carbon dioxide, for the atmosphere to have thinned out to its present extent. According to one estimate, the last dregs of the once great ocean on Mars disappeared some 3 billion years ago.

Whether Mars has had an occasional wet spell since is a matter of controversy. It may be that Mars experiences periodic ice ages as does the Earth and that, at present, it is in the midst of a prolonged cold snap. There could be a number of reasons for this. Variations in the tilt of the Martian rotation axis, for example, are much more pronounced than in the case of the Earth due to the gravitational influence of Jupiter. Another possible source of climate change could be fluctuations in the amount of solar energy reflected back into space by the Martian polar caps. Wind-borne dust, which becomes trapped in the ice, causes the caps to darken and brighten on a seasonal basis. A gradual long-term reduction in the reflectivity of the poles could cause them to warm up and melt, releasing sufficient carbon dioxide to allow liquid water to exist on the surface again. (Some means of bringing this about artificially might one day be at the heart of a scheme to terraform the Red Planet.) Finally, it is conceivable that variations in the luminosity of the Sun have had their effect on Mars. Some of the channels presumed once to have contained water are pockmarked by occasional impact craters, the frequency of which provides a rough measure of the age of these particular channels—about 1 billion years, according to some estimates. This coincides more or less with the most recent era of high global temperatures on Earth, suggesting a common underlying process at work—a possible solar link.

In December 1999, researchers announced that, based on high-resolution images from *Mars Global Surveyor*, there was now powerful evidence that an ocean once filled the northern lowlands of Mars.

Mars Pathfinder

The second mission in NASA's **Discovery Program.** *Pathfinder* was launched on December 4, 1996, and landed on Mars on July 4, 1997. Shortly after its arrival, the miniature **Sojourner** rover was deployed. The primary goal of the mission was to study the Martian atmosphere, surface meteorology, elemental composition of the rocks and soil, and geology (or "areology") of the landing site. During almost 3 months of operation (nearly three times longer than its design lifetime of 30 days), *Pathfinder* returned more than 16,000 images from the lander and 550 from the rover, carried out fifteen chemical analyses of rocks, and gathered extensive data on winds and other aspects of the weather. Among the science highlights of the mission were the discoveries that the rock size distribution at the site was consistent with a flood-related deposit, that the rock chemistry might be different from that of the **SNC meteorites,** and that dust is the main absorber of solar radiation in the Martian atmosphere. *Pathfinder* was operated by the **Jet Propulsion Laboratory** and renamed the Sagan Memorial Station in honor of the late Carl **Sagan.**

Mars, polar caps on

Observations by space probes have confirmed that both permanent Martian ice caps are composed primarily of frozen carbon dioxide and consist of alternating layers of ice with varying concentrations of dark dust. In the northern summer, the carbon dioxide completely **sublimes**, leaving a residual layer of water ice. Whether a similar layer of water ice exists under the southern cap is unknown since the overlying carbon dioxide never completely disappears. The mechanism responsible for the polar layering is also still a mystery, though it may involve climatic changes linked to long-term variations in the **inclination** of Mars. Seasonal changes in the extent of the polar caps causes the global atmospheric pressure to fluctuate by as much as 25 percent.

Mars Polar Lander

A spacecraft launched on January 3, 1999, which was supposed to land on Mars on December 3, 1999, near the south polar cap. *Mars Polar Lander* was equipped with cameras, instruments, and a robotic arm to sample and analyze the composition of the Martian soil. The mission failed when no transmissions were received from the surface. Piggybacking aboard the spacecraft was the *Mars Microprobe Mission.*

Mars Surveyor 98

A two-part mission consisting of the *Mars Climate Observer* and the *Mars Polar Lander.*

Mars Surveyor 2001

A two-part mission, scheduled for launch in 2001, consisting of the *Mars Surveyor 2001 Orbiter* and the *Mars Surveyor 2001 Lander.*

Mars Surveyor 2001 Lander

Scheduled to arrive on Mars on January 22, 2002, if launch takes place as planned on April 10, 2001, the lander will carry out various experiments and observations directly relevant to an eventual human mission. As the vehicle descends, its Mars Descent Imager (MARDI) will take pictures of the surrounding terrain for geological analysis and to help in planning the initial operations and excursions by the rover. Once on the surface, the lander's main instru-

ments will be deployed. The Mars Environment Compatibility Assessment (MECA) will look closely at soil and dust samples with a view to characterizing their properties, such as adhesion and abrasion, that might pose problems to human explorers. The Martian Radiation Environment Experiment (MARIE) will quantify the risk to humans of the **ionizing radiation** that reaches the surface of Mars. Finally, the Mars In-Situ Propellant Production (MIP) will attempt to demonstrate that rocket propellant can be made on the spot using gases in the Martian atmosphere. The lander will also deploy the *Mars Surveyor 2001* **Rover.**

Mars Surveyor 2001 Orbiter

Scheduled to arrive at Mars on October 27, 2001, if launch takes place as planned on April 15, 2001. The orbiter will be the first space probe to take advantage of a new deceleration and orbital parking technique known as "aerocapture." Having attained a circular orbit 1 week after arrival, the orbiter will deploy its two main science instruments. The Thermal Emission Imaging System (THEMIS) will map the elemental composition and abundance of hydrogen (an indicator of the presence of water ice) in the shallow subsurface over the entire Martian surface. The orbiter's Gamma Ray Spectrometer (GRS) will map the mineralogy and morphology of the Martian surface using a high-resolution camera and a thermal infrared imaging spectrometer.

Mars Surveyor 2001 Rover

A **Sojourner**-class rover to be carried aboard the *Mars Surveyor 2001 Lander.* It will carry one of the instruments of the **Athena Precursor Experiment** (APEX).

Mars Surveyor 2003

A two-part NASA mission, consisting of the *Mars Surveyor 2003 Orbiter* and the *Mars Surveyor 2003 Lander.* The latter will deploy a sophisticated rover to collect Martian rock and soil samples which will then be returned to Earth. The 2003 rover will be similar in general design to the **Sojourner** and the *Mars Surveyor 2001* **Rover** but will be larger, better equipped, and capable of traveling further. During its planned 1-year lifetime, it is expected to cover 10 to 20 km. The package of instruments and tools that it will use to examine and collect the first Martian samples to be returned to Earth is known as **Athena.** Cameras mounted as high off the ground as adult human eyes will afford good visibility, while onboard computers will supply a limited amount of autonomous intelligence. The lander's robotic arm has the equivalent of wrist, elbow, and shoulder joints and a "hand" with four fingers that will be able to brush dust aside and touch rocks so that mission controllers can decide whether to take particular samples, including cores extracted with a miniature drill. Collected samples will be returned to Earth for laboratory analysis.

Mars, vegetation on

The possibility of Martian life was discussed as early as the mid–eighteenth century by Johann **Lambert,** who proposed that the vegetation was red—an idea later endorsed by Camille **Flammarion.** By the second half of the nineteenth century, some observers such as Emmanuel **Liais** began to suspect that the seasonal variations in Martian surface features might be due to the alternate growth and recession of vast tracts of vegetation. This thesis was embraced by Percival **Lowell** as part of his grand scheme of intelligently constructed canals. However, as it gradually became clear that the environment of Mars was probably too hostile for advanced forms of animal or plant life, astronomers in the pre–Space Age decades of the twentieth century came to suspect that, at most, lowly, lichenlike vegetation would be found. As late as the spring of 1956, Gerard **Kuiper,** using the 82-in. reflector at the **McDonald Observatory,** noted a "touch of moss green" in some of the equatorial regions. Such reports prompted a search for the **spectroscopic** signature of **chlorophyll,** which, for a brief period in the late 1950s, through the work of William **Sinton,** appeared to have been successful.

Mars, water on

Although, in previous centuries, astronomers believed that the dark markings on Mars might be seas, it was clear by the early decades of this century that little or no surface water exists on the Red Planet today. However, in

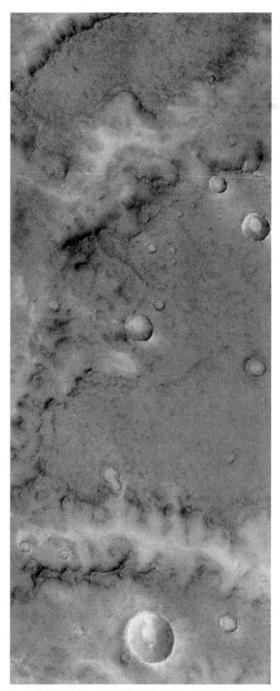

A typical valley network on Mars in central Terra Meridiani near the Martian equator. The image shows an area 11.5 km by 27.4 km (7.1 mi. by 17.0 mi.) in size and was taken by the *Mars Global Surveyor* in 1998. NASA/JPL/Caltech

1969, *Mariner 9* provided the first clear evidence that liquid water has existed on the Martian surface in the remote past. Among the thousands of images it sent back from orbit were those of flat-floored channels with eroded banks, sand bars and teardrop-shaped islands, channels with second- and third-order tributary systems, and braided channels that, had they been encountered on Earth, would unhesitatingly have been attributed to episodic flooding. Today, Mars is manifestly a desert planet, its atmospheric pressure so low that water cannot exist on its surface in liquid form. Even at the equator in midsummer, when the temperature can climb to a balmy 20°C or so, the slightest trace of water would evaporate almost instantly in the desperately low pressure. The fact that Mars once had rivers implies that conditions on the planet were once very different than they are at present (➜ **Mars, past conditions on**). Yet, curiously, there is no evidence that it ever rained on the fourth planet. The water-carved systems on Mars are short and stubby, dividing little upstream and ending abruptly, as if the water had suddenly appeared at that spot rather than having fallen over a large area and become collected. The assumption is that the Martian water came from beneath the surface, welling up as a result of volcanic eruptions or asteroid impacts and flooding to form channels and lakes.[100]

Martian Chronicles, The

Science fiction novel[76] by Ray **Bradbury** (1950) that has something of the dark psychological character of Stanisław **Lem**'s *Solaris*. Even at this late stage, Bradbury was still able to tap into the Lowellian, golden-age myth of canals and intelligent Martians, even though he and presumably most of his readers knew that the real planet Mars appeared incapable of supporting anything but the most primitive forms of life. Bradbury's main goal, however, is not to achieve astronomical accuracy but to contrast the "graceful, beautiful and philosophical" Martians and their love of the aesthetic with technology-obsessed humankind. Thus he explores how civilizations and intelligence elsewhere might have developed along completely different lines (➜ **extraterrestrial intelligence, more advanced than we**). ➜ **science fiction involving extraterrestrials, after 1940**

Martian "face"
➜ **"face," on Mars**

Martian "fossils" controversy

On August 7, 1996, a team of NASA scientists working at the **NASA Johnson Space Center** stunned the world by announcing that they had found evidence of past life on Mars.[392] Spokesman David S. **McKay** reported at a press conference that the group had detected four distinct signatures of Martian biology in the **SNC meteorite** designated **ALH 84001,** including

1. Dark specks known as "carbonate rosettes" on the sides of the cracks and crevices that perforate the meteorite's crust. Such formations, consisting of magnesium-rich cores surrounded by a layer of iron **carbonate** and a rind of iron **sulfide,** are similar to ones produced on Earth by **bacteria** in ponds as they metabolize minerals.
2. **Polycyclic aromatic hydrocarbons** (PAHs) in and around the rosettes.
3. Microscopic, teardrop-shaped crystals of magnetite and iron sulfide embedded in places where the iron carbonate had been dissolved, presumably by some kind of acid. Certain terrestrial bacteria manufacture crystals like these and use them as internal compasses (➜ **magnetotactic bacteria**).
4. Segmented, rod-shaped structures a few tens of nm long, interpreted by the team as the actual fossil remains of Martian microbial life.

On the day of the announcement, President Bill Clinton declared, "If this discovery is confirmed, it will surely be one of the most stunning insights into our universe that science has ever uncovered. Its implications are as far-reaching and awe-inspiring as we can imagine." However, the discovery was not confirmed. Although some researchers, including David **Black,** director of Houston's Lunar and Planetary Institute, initially supported the claims, others criticized them, pointing out that plausible explanations of the four main findings in terms of various **inorganic** chemical processes were to hand.

The most dramatic claim centered on the purported fossils. Under a scanning electron microscope, these appear as elliptical, rope-like, tubular structures in the carbonate rosettes and are extraordinarily small. Each measures a mere 20 to 100 nm across and has only one thousandth the volume of the smallest known terrestrial bacterium. Despite the recent claim that "**nanobes**" have been found, it is far from clear if anything this tiny has *ever* lived on Earth or even that something so small could encapsulate the minimum biochemical machinery needed to sustain and replicate a living organism. Moreover, no independent analysis carried out since the original announcement has produced evidence that the structures in question are anything other than fragments of inorganic minerals or clay.

Concerning the carbonate rosettes, it was the contention of the NASA group that these were (1) formed on Mars (rather than on Earth after the meteorite's arrival) and (2) were deposited by liquid water that infiltrated the rock billions of years ago. A Martian origin of the rosettes now seems beyond doubt, but controversy still surrounds the conditions under which the rosettes were laid down. In particular, there is strong evidence[260] to suggest that the carbonate formations grew at temperatures of more than 650°C (1,200°F), which would rule out a biological explanation. On the other hand, a low-temperature, possibly bacterial origin for the structures has not yet been discounted.

In addition to the purported fossils, McKay and his coworkers described two other features

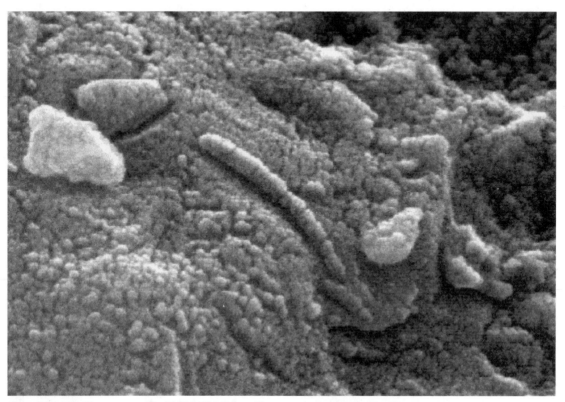

One of the tubelike structures in ALH 84001 claimed by some to be Martian fossils.
NASA/JSC

in and near the rosettes that they believe formed biogenically in a watery environment: microscopic mineral grains and PAHs. Noting that some terrestrial bacteria manufacture iron sulfide and magnetite, they interpreted the crystals of these substances in ALH 84001 as products of Martian microbial action. They conceded, however, that similar grains can result from purely inorganic processes. An analysis conducted in 1997[239] showed that the sulfides in the meteorite are too rich in sulfur 34, a heavy **isotope** of the element, to have come from microbes like any seen on Earth. Moreover, the long chains of magnetite that are characteristic of known bacterial activity have not been reported, although magnetite crystals *have* been observed growing directly out of other minerals in the meteorite—proof that at least some of them arose through simple chemical means. There is also the difficulty of understanding what use magnetite would be to a Martian organism, since Mars has virtually no magnetic field. Adrian J. Brearley of the University of New Mexico has suggested that a sharp blow to ALH 84001 (it is known to have suffered at least two) could have produced the effects seen by heating the rock to more than 550°C (1,020°F). This would have been sufficiently hot to break down the iron-rich carbonate into magnetite but would have left the more thermally stable magnesium-rich cores intact. When the iron subsequently crystallized, it would have released carbon dioxide and created tiny voids around the magnetite grains, as observed.[78]

As for the PAHs, it is true that they could have come from decomposed Martian microbes, particularly since the variety in the meteorite is unusual and very limited—just what would be expected, according to McKay and his group, of a biogenic origin. However, Edward Anders of the University of Chicago has shown how, given magnetite as a catalyst, such a blend could have come about inorganically.[11] If it did, this would explain the discovery by Thomas Stephan and his colleagues at the University of Münster of PAHs all through the meteorite.[564] The fact is that PAHs are not good **biomarkers** since they are so ubiquitous. For this reason, Jeffrey L. Bada and his colleagues of the Scripps Institution in La Jolla, California, looked instead for **amino acids** in ALH 84001.[31] Although he found some, they were present in virtually the same proportions as those in the Antarctic ice in which the meteorite had lain for 13,000 years, indicating extensive terrestrial contamination. If evidence of Martian life is eventually found, it will almost certainly have to come from elsewhere—probably in samples obtained fresh from the surface or subsurface of Mars and analyzed *in situ* or following their return to Earth.

Martian meteorites
→ SNC meteorites

Mascall, Eric Lionel (1905–1993)
Oxford lecturer in the philosophy of religion who rejected the notion that a unique earthly incarnation of Christ would be sufficient to redeem beings on other worlds (→ **incarnation and redemption**), as proposed, for example, by Edward A. **Milne.** For him, the significance of the incarnation of the Son of God on Earth was restricted to *Homo sapiens* alone and not exportable. As for intelligent creatures elsewhere, he cited the argument of Saint Thomas **Aquinas** that the incarnation could have involved any one of the Trinity (God the Father, the Son, or the Holy Ghost). Therefore, if such alternatives were not theologically excluded on Earth, he reasoned, there should be no bar to multiple incarnations throughout the Universe:[383]

It would be difficult to hold that the assumption by the Son of the nature of one rational corporeal species involved the restoration of other rational corporeal species.... The suggestion I wish to make... is that there are no conclusive *theological* reasons for rejecting the notion that, if there are, in some other part or parts of the universe, rational corporeal beings who have sinned and are in need of redemption, for those beings and for their salvation the Son of God has united (or one day will unite) to his divine Person their nature, as he has united it to ours.

→ **Coyne, George**

maser

A source of very intense, coherent **narrow-band,** microwave radiation.

mass extinction

An event in which large numbers of species, including entire genera, more or less suddenly vanish from the fossil record. Controversy surrounds the exact number and timing of mass extinctions in the Earth's history, though it is generally recognized that there have been at least six major ones. These occurred in the late Cambrian (500 million years ago), in the late Ordovician (440 million years ago), in the late Devonian (365 million years ago), at the end of the Permian (245 million years ago), in the late Triassic (208 million years ago), and the end of the Cretaceous (65 million years ago). A variety of causes have been proposed including sea-level changes, volcanic eruptions, ice ages, and asteroid or comet impacts (→ **cosmic collisions, biological effects of**). → Cretaceous-Tertiary Boundary

mathematics, as a universal language

It has often been pointed out that despite the great differences between cultures and natural languages on Earth, mathematics is the same the world over. In fact, scientists are inclined to believe that mathematics and the mathematical rules that underpin nature are universal, so that all intelligent races in space would have at least this much in common. Since the fundamental properties of numbers are the same everywhere, these can be used as the basis of interstellar messages. **Binary** numbers and **prime number**s, in particular, being so fundamental, are considered to be of great importance in **SETI.** They underpinned the **Arecibo Message** and provided the initial clues to the decipherment of the alien signals in Carl **Sagan**'s *Contact* and Fred **Hoyle** and John Elliot's *A for Andromeda.*

Matthew, William Diller (1871–1930)

Paleontologist at the American Museum of Natural History in New York (1895–1926) who later became professor of paleontology and head of the Paleontology Department at the **University of California, Berkeley.** Matthew cast doubt on the view expressed by some astronomers that life might be common in the Universe. He found it "noticeable that, as usual, the astronomers take the affirmative and the biologists the negative side of the argument"[387] and was certainly not alone among biologists in believing that the origin of life had come about as a result of "some immensely complex concatenation of circumstances so rare that even on earth it has occurred probably but once during the eons of geological time," a view first expressed by Alfred Russel **Wallace.** This cautious attitude, which emphasizes the difficulty in understanding how life came about even on our own planet, partly explains why biologists failed to join astronomers in debating the subject of extraterrestrial life until the 1950s with the dawn of the Space Age and the search for more universally applicable principles in the life sciences (→ **evolutionary theory and extraterrestrial life**). On the subject of extraterrestrial intelligence, Matthew thought that, if it existed at all,

> it probably—almost surely—would be so remote in its fundamental character and its external manifestations from our own, that we could not interpret or comprehend the external indications of its existence, nor even probably observe or recognize them.

→ **Beta Life**

Maunder, Edward Walter (1851–1928)

English astronomer best remembered for his studies of the cyclic variation of sunspot activity. He played a significant part in the Martian canal debate (→ **Mars, canals of**) by carrying out experiments with marked circular disks and concluding, as did Simon **Newcomb,** that the canals "are simply the integration by the eye of minute details too small to be separately and distinctly defined."

Mayor, Michel (1959–)

Swiss astronomer at the Geneva Observatory who was the codiscoverer, with Didier **Queloz,** of the first known planet around a Sun-like star (→ **51 Pegasi**). Mayor and his colleagues have since found several other **extrasolar planets** using the **Elodie** and **Coralie spectrographs** and their associated telescopes.

McDonald, James

Atmospheric physicist at the University of Arizona, Tucson, who was one of the few prominent scientists openly to support the **extraterrestrial hypothesis** of **unidentified flying objects** in the 1960s. He became closely involved with the subject in 1966 following a number of sightings in that year, including one over Tucson, and a visit to J. Allen **Hynek** and others involved with Project **Blue Book.** A lecture he delivered in Washington, D.C., in which he argued that UFOs were "the greatest scientific problem of our times," received widespread media coverage. He was particularly scathing of the **Condon Report,** considering it "seriously deficient" and its conclusions "almost incredible." In 1971, together with Gordon Thayer of the National Oceanic and Atmospheric Administration, he presented details of two case studies that he considered completely unresolved. On June 13, 1971, he was found to have committed suicide in the desert near Tucson.

McDonald Observatory

The observatory of the University of Texas located on the adjacent peaks of Mount Locke (altitude 2,070 m) and Mount Fowlkes (altitude 1,980 m) in the Davis Mountains near Fort David. It was established in 1932 and will be home to the **Hobby-Eberly Telescope.** Among its existing instruments are the 2.08-m (82-in.) Otto Struve Telescope, opened in 1939 and still in use, and a 2.72-m (107-in.) reflector opened in 1969.

McKay, Christopher P.

Research scientist in the Space Science Division at **NASA Ames Research Center** who has played a significant role in recent years in planetary investigations with a direct bearing on the possibility of extraterrestrial life. He has done extensive work on microorganisms in Antarctica, including cryptoendoliths, the atmosphere of **Titan,** and past conditions on Mars.

McKay, David S.

Geologist at the **NASA Johnson Space Center** who, on August 7, 1996, along with eight colleagues, created a worldwide sensation with the announcement of the results of their investigation into an **SNC meteorite** known as **ALH 84001.** "We have concluded," said McKay, "that there is evidence of early life on Mars." → **Martian "fossils" controversy**

M-class asteroid

So named because this type of **asteroid** is believed to be rich in the metals iron and nickel. M-class objects are common in the **Main Asteroid Belt** and are distinguished from the spectrally similar **E-class asteroid**s and **P-class asteroid**s by their moderate **albedo** of 0.10 to 0.18.

MCSA

→ **Multi-Channel Spectrum Analyzer**

medieval philosophy, related to the possibility of extraterrestrial life

Following the transmission of **Aristotle**'s cosmology to the West, it was customary to accept that there was only one world and that man was the prime focus of God's attention. By the late 1200s, however, some scholars in the new European universities were beginning to point out that an omnipotent deity must have had complete freedom of creative action and so, in principle, could have made more than one world—though, in fact, he had chosen not to do so. A more radical challenge to Aristotle's dictum came in the late fourteenth century, when it was suggested that multiple worlds might indeed be possible within the geocentric paradigm.[150] → **Buridan, Jean; Nicholas of Cusa; Ockham, William of; Oresme, Nicole d'; Vorilong, William**

mediocrity, principle of

The notion that our evolution (biological, cultural, and technological) and our surroundings, including the Earth and the Sun, are typical rather than exceptional. It is often invoked, together with two other principles (→ **plenitude, principle of; uniformity, principle of**), to support the claim that life and intelligence occur commonly throughout the Universe. It is also an implicit assumption of **SETI** that other beings exist who wish to communicate and are sufficiently technologically compatible with us to make communication possible. The principle of mediocrity remains largely a matter of opinion but has been bolstered by the discovery of **extrasolar planets** and that certain **organic** chemicals, such as **amino acids,** occur commonly throughout space.

megahertz (MHz)
One million **hertz** (cycles per second).

meiosis
Cell division in which the **chromosome**s are reduced from the **diploid** to the **haploid** number; the process of gamete formation.

Menzel, Donald Howard (1901–76)
American astrophysicist and director of Harvard Observatory (1954–66) who early in his career studied the surface properties of Mars and, in 1955, together with Fred Whipple, presented a maritime model of Venus (➔ **Venus, life on**). Menzel openly argued the case against the **extraterrestrial hypothesis** almost single-handedly, in the 1950s and '60s, first presenting his opinions on **unidentified flying objects** to Air Force officials in April 1952. Although he believed that the many reported sightings could be explained by mundane objects, he "saw no strong reason against the idea that planets inhabited by super-beings should not exist in great abundance" in the Universe.[397–9]

Mercury
The innermost planet of the solar system and second smallest after Pluto, Mercury follows a relatively elongated orbit around the Sun. What tiny trace of atmosphere it has consists of atoms ejected from the surface by the **solar wind.** Like the Moon, Mercury is heavily cratered except for some areas of smooth terrain where lava has flooded the surface. One of the largest features is the Caloris Basin, about 1,300 km (800 miles) in diameter, which resulted from an ancient asteroid impact. After the Earth, Mercury is the densest planet with an iron core, 1,800 to 1,900 km (1,120 to 1,180 miles) in radius. In 1991, radar measurements revealed that (like the Moon) Mercury might have ice in some deep craters at its north and south poles.

Distance from Sun:	
Mean	57.9 million km (35.9 million mi., 0.387 AU)
Minimum	45.9 million km (28.5 million mi., 0.306 AU)
Maximum	69.7 million km (43.3 million mi., 0.467 AU)
Equatorial diameter	4,880 km (3,033 mi.)
Equatorial diameter (Earth = 1)	0.382
Mass (Earth = 1)	0.0553
Mean density	5.44 g/cm^3
Escape velocity	4.3 km/s (15,480 km/h, 9,621 mi./h)
Orbital period	87.969 days
Orbital eccentricity	0.206
Orbital inclination	7.00°
Axial period	58.65 days
Axial inclination	2°
Number of moons	0
Atmospheric composition	Negligible—traces of sodium, helium, hydrogen, oxygen
Maximum temp. (day)	427°C (801°F)
Minimum temp. (night)	−183°C (−297°F)
Surface gravity (Earth = 1)	0.38
Albedo	0.11

Mercury, life on
The proximity of **Mercury** to the Sun did not deter some pluralists, before the twentieth century, from advocating the existence of life on the innermost planet. However, speculations of a more scientific nature followed Giovanni **Schiaparelli**'s attempts, in the 1880s, to map the Mercurian surface and his conclusion that Mercury always kept the same face toward the Sun (➔ **Mercury, rotation of**). This implied extreme permanent differences in temperature between the perpetually sunlit side of the planet, which would be unbearably hot, and the endlessly dark side, which would be almost unimaginably frigid. It also, crucially, implied the existence of a "twilight zone" where the temperature would be permanently moderate. Here, in this narrow margin between everlasting day and everlasting night, some astronomers speculated, there might exist prim-

itive forms of Mercurian life. Such hopes disappeared, however, as it became clear that Mercury lacks any substantial atmosphere.

Mercury, rotation of

Mercury is notoriously difficult to observe, being both small and always in the glare of the Sun as seen from Earth. At best it can be studied telescopically for only a few weeks each year, near sunrise or sunset. However, undeterred by these problems, astronomers from the late eighteenth century on did their best to glimpse features on Mercury's surface and, using these as fixed reference points, obtain the length of the Mercurian day. From his observations of the innermost planet between 1779 and 1813, Johann **Schröter** deduced the existence of a mountain 20 km high and a Mercurian rotation period of just over 24 hours. Later, William **Denning** reported surface markings "so pronounced that they suggest an analogy with those of Mars" and adjusted the period to 25 hours. But it was Giovanni **Schiaparelli**'s suggestion that Mercury's day might be 88 Earth days long, the same as its year, that was generally accepted from the 1880s until as recently as the early 1960s. Concomitant with this hypothesis of **gravitational lock** was the intriguing idea of a (possibly habitable) "twilight zone" (➔ **Mercury, life on**). Based on the assumption that Schiaparelli's period was correct, Eugène **Antoniadi** produced a map of dark and light areas of the planet, complete with wonderfully evocative names such as Aurora, Apollonia, Pieria, Liguria, and Cyllene. The first sign of trouble for the Schiaparellian model came in 1962, when measurements by W. E. Howard and his colleagues at the University of Michigan revealed that the night side of Mercury was warmer than it should have been if it never faced the Sun. Three years later, radar measurements, by Gordon Pettengill and Rolf Dyce of **Cornell University** using the **Arecibo radio telescope,** showed conclusively that Mercury is not locked in position relative to the Sun. It *is* in a gravitational resonance, but one in which its axial rotation period is about 58.6 Earth days, or two thirds of its orbital rotation period.

mesophiles

Microbes that reproduce and grow best in the temperature range 10 to 50°C (50 to 122°F). They represent the majority of microbial species on Earth, including all the **pathogen**s of mammals. Some mesophiles, said to be psychrotolerant, exhibit slow growth at lower temperatures; they include soil microbes that must be able to survive temperature extremes. ➔ **microbes, temperature ranges of**

messenger probe
➔ **Bracewell probe**

messenger RNA (mRNA)

A molecule of **RNA** that is transcribed (➔ **transcription**) from a **gene** and then translated (➔ **translation**) by **ribosomes** in order to manufacture **protein.**

META, Project

Megachannel Extraterrestrial Assay. A **SETI** program, conducted from 1985 to 1994 by the **Harvard SETI group,** using the **Harvard-Smithsonian radio telescope.** META was an **all-sky search** that covered much of the northern sky, between −30° and +60° **declination,** in **drift scan** mode, looking for **narrowband** signals near the **21-centimeter line** of neutral **hydrogen.** It overcame the deficiencies of its predecessor, Project **Sentinel,** by employing an 8.4-million-channel Fourier **spectrometer** of 0.05-Hz **resolution bandwidth** and 400-kHz **instantaneous bandwidth.** META was funded by the **Planetary Society** through a $100,000 donation from Steven **Spielberg** and by grants from NASA and the Bosack-Kruger Foundation. During its nine years of operation, META identified several dozen candidate events, but none of these was repeated at subsequent observations.[500] In 1995, META was superseded by Project **BETA,** although **META II** continues in the Southern Hemisphere.

META II, Project

META's sister program, which scans the southern sky. It uses a **radio telescope** at the Argentine Institute of Radio Astronomy near Buenos Aires.

metabolism

The combination of biochemical processes by which energy, obtained from an external source, is harnessed to maintain internal order and a state of chemical disequilibrium. It includes all of the chemosynthetic (*anabolic*) and degradative (*catabolic*) reactions that take place in living organisms. The ability to metabolize is generally considered to be one of the fundamental characteristics of life (→ **life, nature of**).

metempsychosis
→ **transmigration of souls**

meteor

A **meteoroid** or small icy particle that burns up in the Earth's atmosphere. It gives rise to a streak of light and is commonly referred to as a "shooting star" or "falling star." Very large, bright meteors are known as **fireball**s and **bolide**s.

meteorite

A natural object that survives its fall to Earth (or some other planet or moon) from space. Meteorites are fragments that were broken off during collisions between **asteroid**s, between asteroids and the surface of the Moon or Mars (→ **SNC meteorites**), or, in the case of **micrometeorite**s, from **comet**s. Some are similar to volcanic rocks on Earth, while others are alloys of iron and nickel similar to the material of the Earth's core. The most interesting variety in an astrobiological context, however, are **carbonaceous chondrites,** composed of **primitive material** from the time when the solar system was formed. Meteorites are usually named after the place near where they were seen to fall. They may come down individually and weigh anything from a few grams to many tons or be part of a meteorite shower.

meteorites, from Mars
→ **SNC meteorites**

meteorites, organic matter in
→ **organic matter, in meteorites**

meteorites, water in
→ **water, in meteorites**

meteoroid

A small rocky or metallic object in orbit around the Sun (or another star). A meteoroid that strikes the Earth (or other large body) is called a **meteorite.** As a meteoroid encounters the Earth's atmosphere frictional heating begins at an altitude of 100 to 120 km. What happens next depends on the speed, mass, and friability (tendency to break up) of the meteoroid. Micrometeoroids radiate heat so effectively that they survive unchanged to reach the surface as **micrometeorites.** Objects about the size of sugar grains burn up as **meteor**s, or "shooting stars." Friable meteoroids break up and are destroyed at altitudes of 80 to 90 km. Those that are tougher survive longer and produce **fireball**s as their surface is melted and eaten away at temperatures of several thousand degrees. If they avoid destruction high up, they enter the lower, denser part of the atmosphere, where they are rapidly decelerated. Finally, at subsonic speeds the fireball is extinguished and the residue falls to the ground as a meteorite. The last melted material on the surface of the object solidifies to form a thin, usually black rind known as a fusion crust.

methanal (HCHO)

A colorless gas, also known as formaldehyde.

Density relative to water (at −20°C) 0.82; melting point −92°C; boiling point −19°C

methane (CH$_4$)

A colorless, odorless gas; the simplest **hydrocarbon** and the first member of the alkane se-

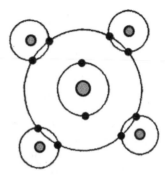

A molecule of methane comprising a central carbon atom and four hydrogen atoms.

ries. It occurs in the atmospheres of the **gas giant**s.

Melting point −182.5°C; boiling point −161°C

methanogens
Anaerobic archaeans that produce **methane.**

methanol (CH₃OH)
Also known as methyl alcohol. In considering whether some forms of extraterrestrial life might use **solvent**s other than **water,** methanol is one possible candidate.

Density relative to water 0.79; melting point −98°C; boiling point 64°C

Metis
The innermost moon of **Jupiter;** a small object of uneven shape. Together with **Adrastea,** it orbits inside the *synchronous orbit radius* of Jupiter, which means it orbits faster than Jupiter rotates on its axis. As a result, its orbit will eventually decay and Metis will fall into the planet. Metis and Adrastea also circle around

Discovery	1979, by Stephen Synnott
Mean distance from Jupiter	127,960 km (79,530 mi.)
Diameter	40 km (25 mi.)
Mean density	2.8 g/cm³
Escape velocity	0.025 km/s (90 km/h, 56 mi./h)
Orbital period	0.295 day (7 hours 5 minutes)
Orbital eccentricity	0.000
Orbital inclination	0.00°
Visual albedo	0.05

inside Jupiter's main ring and are undoubtedly the source of the material in this ring. → **Jupiter, moons of**

Metrodorus of Chios (fourth century B.C.)
Greek **atomist** philosopher who neatly summed up the attitude of his mentor, **Epicurus,** toward extraterrestrial life:

> To consider the Earth as the only populated world in infinite space is as absurd as to assert that in an entire field of millet, only one grain will grow.

→ **ancient philosophy,** related to the possibility of extraterrestrial life

Meudon Observatory
The French Observatory of Physical Astronomy, located near Paris. Its principal instrument is a 32.7-in. refractor that has a 24.4-in. photographic refractor coupled to it on the same mounting.

MHz
→ **megahertz**

microbe
A **unicellular** organism so small that it can be seen only with the aid of a microscope. Terrestrial microbes fall into the major categories of **bacteria, archaea,** and **virus**es. To a far greater extent than complex organisms, they are capable of coping with and even prospering from environmental change and extremes. Their high surface-to-volume ratio allows rapid rates of chemical exchange with the surroundings, so that they can exploit favorable conditions. Moreover, their diverse biochemistry enables them to survive and flourish, as **extremophiles,** under what to us appear hostile regimes, including environments that would have been common on the Earth at the time life first evolved (→ **Earth, early history of**). The adaptability of microbes, their ability to take advantage of a wide range of conditions, and their ability to survive in unexpected places, such as tiny interstices in deep underground rocks, suggests not only that microbes are the commonest form of life in the universe but that they evolve on worlds wherever conditions remotely allow.

microbes, temperature ranges of
Four categories of microbes are recognized according to the temperature range in which they can reproduce and grow:

	TEMPERATURE RANGE	
Type of Microbe	**Minimum °C (°F)**	**Maximum °C (°F)**
Psychrophile	−10 (14)	20 (68)
Mesophile	10 (50)	50 (122)
Thermophile	40 (104)	70 (158)
Hyperthermophile	60 (140)	115 (239)

microevolution

Also known as **adaptation;** evolution *within* a species. It is distinguished from **macroevolution.**

microlensing

An effect caused by a compact **gravitational lens** that can be exploited in the search for and characterization of **extrasolar planets.** The term "microlens" may refer to (1) massive compact objects located in external galaxies that bend and refocus the light of very distant light sources into multiple images separated by about a *microarc-second* or (2) compact lensing objects located within our own galaxy that (due to their relative proximity) create images with a separation of *milli*arc-seconds. The latter type are further subdivided into **galactic halo**-resident **MACHOs** and **galactic disk**-resident objects, which may include normal stars, **brown dwarf**s, and **black hole**s. It is disk-resident lenses that happen to be normal stars that are of specific interest in the detection of planetary systems.

Their role in the search for extrasolar planets has been widely discussed.[6, 30, 233, 442, 443, 595]

When aligned with a more distant star, a microlens deflects, distorts, and brightens the image of the background source in a way that is sensitive to the strength and geometry of the lensing star's gravitational field. If the lensing star is orbited by a planet, the result may be a microlensing anomaly known as a "binary lens," one of the characteristics of which is the appearance of so-called caustic curves in the plane of the source. As the source sweeps across the caustic curves, due to the relative motion of source and lens, sharp peaks appear in the **light curve.** Planets located at a distance between about 0.5 and 1.5 times the Einstein radius of their host star are said to be in the "lensing zone," since they are most likely to produce, with the help of the host, a sizable caustic structure. This distance is typically a few astronomical units, or approximately the distance of Jupiter from the Sun. Calculations (for example, by Bohdan Paczynski[442]) suggest

Advantages and Disadvantages of Microlensing for Planet Searching	
Advantages	*Disadvantages*
• There is no need to wait for planets at large separations to complete one orbit around their host stars.	• Since the alignment between lensing star/planetary system must be precise to produce significant lensing, a detectable microlensing signal will occur only once per planetary system. There is not usually a chance to repeat the observation if an opportunity is missed.
• Characterization can be achieved during an anomaly lasting only a few hours or days.	
• Planets around remote stars can be detected even when the stars themselves are too faint to be seen directly. Microlensing is the only technique that does not rely on detection of light from the star or its host star. Both components reveal themselves only through their lensing effect on a background source. Therefore, this technique is not biased against low-luminosity stars.	• Planets detected by microlensing will normally be too far away to allow other studies to be carried out that rely on detecting the light from the planets or their host stars.
• The mass ratio between a planet and host star, and the ratio of planetary separation to Einstein ring radius, can be determined directly from the shape of the light curve.	
• Microlensing is more sensitive to smaller-mass planets than most other techniques and is the only method (with the exception of pulsar timing) sensitive to Earth-mass planets with orbital radii of a few astronomical units.	

that microlensing anomalies due to Jupiter-mass planets in Jupiter-like orbits will last about 1 to 3 days and be detectable in 10 to 30 percent of cases where such planets are in orbit around a lensing star that is located roughly halfway between us and the center of the Galaxy. Smaller-mass planets will create smaller caustic structures, which (1) reduces the chance of the background source passing directly behind the anomaly and (2), in cases where the source *does* pass behind the anomaly, results in a shorter and less sharp increase in brightness. The probability of detection and the duration of the lensing peak decrease as the square root of the planet's mass. So an Earth-mass planet (1/320 times the size of Jupiter) orbiting at about the radius of its host's Einstein ring will give rise to a caustic structure one eighteenth the size of a Jupiter-mass planet in a similar orbit, and any light-curve variations caused by it will last for only a few hours rather than a few days.

Owing to the nature of this technique, the planetary systems it detects will typically be too remote for detailed studies to be carried out by other methods, such as **spectroscopy,** that might reveal signatures of life. On the other hand, microlensing is ideal for statistical studies aimed at determining the number and type of planets that exist in orbit around typical stars in the disk of the Galaxy, including planets that are similar to those within our own solar system.

Current searches, such as **PLANET** and **MOA,** are collecting data that, following extensive computer analysis, should result in the detection of a number of planets more massive than Neptune with orbital radii between about 2 and 10 AU. Indeed, several microlensing events have already been identified that may have been caused by massive extrasolar planets and one that may have been due to an Earth-sized world. Because microlensing events are impossible to predict, last for only a brief period, and do not repeat, their discovery is announced immediately (➔ **Global Microlensing Alert Network**) so that other interested groups can obtain data while an event is in progress. Future programs, probably involving special-purpose telescopes and dedicated computers,

are expected to be capable of finding many Earth-like planets.[50, 241]

Microlensing Observations in Astrophysics (MOA)

A collaborative project, involving researchers from New Zealand and Japan, to detect **microlensing** events from the Southern Hemisphere. One of its objectives is to search for **extrasolar planets** by this means, working closely with other groups in Australia and the United States. In January 1999, MOA, in collaboration with **Microlensing Planet Search,** announced that the microlensing event known as MACHO-98-BLG-35 was best interpreted as due to a planet with a mass somewhere between that of Neptune and the Earth, orbiting its host star at about twice the Earth-to-Sun distance.

Microlensing Planet Search (MPS) Project

A project affiliated with the **Global Microlensing Alert Network** (GMAN) to observe **microlensing** events that are in progress for light variations that might be caused by **extrasolar planets.** MPS uses the 1.9-m (6.2-ft.) telescope at **Mount Stromlo Observatory,** Australia, and the 1.5-m (4.9-ft.) telescope at Boyden Observatory, South Africa. Presently, MPS involves collaborators from the University of Notre Dame, the University of Washington, and Mount Stromlo Observatory.

Micromégas

Voltaire's satirical interplanetary romance in which a 20-mile-tall native of Sirius joins forces with a Saturnian "dwarf," a mere one mile in height, to explore the solar system. They discover that Mars has two moons—evidently a borrowing from Jonathan Swift (➔ **Swift, Jonathan, and the moons of Mars**).

micrometeorite

The smallest type of object that reaches the surface of the Earth (or some other planet or moon) from space. Two varieties occur: cosmic spherules and interplanetary dust particles. The former are round and about 1 mm or less in diameter. Interplanetary dust particles are irregular in shape and less than 0.05 mm in size. Micrometeorites are mineralogically different from larger **meteorite**s and probably originate in **comet**s. Their small size allows them to radiate heat away so that they are not melted during their passage through the atmosphere. Most are recovered from the clay beneath the oceans far from land and ice from Antarctica and Greenland. Others have been collected in the stratosphere.

microorganism
→ **microbe**

microscope argument
Used originally by Thomas **Chalmers** in his efforts to reconcile **pluralism** with Christian doctrine. The argument is that just as God has created and supervises a microcosm of life in a drop of water, so he is able to care for life not just on this Earth but on every world in space. → **Christian doctrine and pluralism**

microspheres
Microscopic, firm spherules that form on the cooling of hot saturated solutions of **proteinoids.** They were first reported in 1959 by Sidney **Fox,** K. Harada, and J. Kendrick, who proposed that microspheres might represent a significant early stage in precellular evolution[207] (→ **cell membranes, origin of**). It has been suggested that their greater stability makes them a better proposition in this regard than **coacervate**s. One mg of proteinoid can yield 100 million microspheres ranging from 1.4 to about 2.5 microns in diameter. Microspheres have been observed to retain their form for several weeks and, when sectioned, may display a double-walled structure. Recently, Fox has argued that microspheres also display characteristics of primitive nerve cells.

Microwave Observing Program (MOP)
The original name for the **SETI** program embarked upon jointly by **NASA Ames Research Center** and the **Jet Propulsion Laboratory** in the 1980s. In 1992, it became known as the **High Resolution Microwave Survey (HRMS).**

microwave radiation
Electromagnetic radiation with wavelengths between 30 cm and 1 mm, corresponding to frequencies between 1,000 MHz and 300,000 MHz (1 GHz to 300 GHz). Microwaves occupy the portion of the **electromagnetic spectrum** that lies between longer **radio waves** and **infrared** radiation. → **microwave window**

microwave window
The frequency band between 1,000 and 10,000 MHz. This is the favored portion of the **electromagnetic spectrum** to search for signals that might originate from extraterrestrial civilizations because the background noise (static) due to natural celestial sources is minimal at such frequencies. → **SETI**

Mid-Infrared Large-well Imager (MIRLIN)
A sensitive **infrared** camera built at the **Jet Propulsion Laboratory** that has been used in conjunction with the Palomar 5-m (16.4-ft.) telescope, the NASA Infrared Telescope Facility (IRTF), and the Keck II Telescope at the **Keck Observatory.** Among the applications to which it is well suited is the detection and investigation of **circumstellar disk**s of dust around Sun-like stars. The discovery of such a disk orbiting **HR 4796A** was made by MIRLIN attached to Keck II.

Milky Way Galaxy
→ **Galaxy**

Miller, Stanley Lloyd (1930–)
Professor of chemistry at the University of California, San Diego, who as a graduate student of Harold **Urey** at the University of Chicago, carried out the first practical investigation in **prebiotic** synthesis using a simulated **reducing atmosphere** (→ **Miller-Urey Experiment**). He continues to carry out research into the origin of life on Earth and has recently drawn attention to the possibility that certain key biochemicals, including **cytosine** and **uracil,** may have been manufactured under "dry beach" conditions. → **life, origin of**

Miller-Urey Experiment
Conducted in 1953 by Stanley **Miller** under the supervision of Harold **Urey,** this was the first experiment to test the **Oparin-Haldane Theory** about the evolution of **prebiotic** chemicals and the origin of life on Earth. A

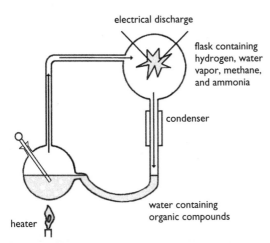

electrical discharge

flask containing hydrogen, water vapor, methane, and ammonia

condenser

water containing organic compounds

heater

The arrangement used in Miller and Urey's famous experiment.

mixture of **methane, ammonia, hydrogen,** and water vapor, to simulate the version of Earth's primitive **reducing atmosphere** proposed by Aleksandr **Oparin,** was introduced into a 5-liter flask and energized by an electrical discharge apparatus to represent **ultraviolet radiation** from the Sun. The products were allowed to condense and collect in a lower flask that modeled a body of water on the Earth's surface. Heat supplied to this flask recycled the water vapor just as water evaporates from lakes and seas before moving into the atmosphere and condensing again as rain. After a day of continuous operation, Miller and Urey found a thin layer of **hydrocarbon**s on the surface of the water. After about a week of operation, a dark brown scum had collected in the lower flask and was found to contain several types of **amino acids,** including **glycine** and alanine, together with **sugars,** tars, and various other unidentified **organic** chemicals.[403, 406]

millibar (mb)

A unit of pressure. 1 millibar is one thousandth of a **bar.** Standard sea-level pressure on Earth is 1,013 millibars.

millisecond pulsar

A **pulsar** with a pulse period of less than 25 milliseconds, equivalent to an axial rotation rate of 40 revolutions per second. Such a high spin rate may suggest that these pulsars are young, but in fact the opposite is true. Millisecond pulsars are typically a billion years or more old. They have been rejuvenated by a "spin-up process" involving the accumulation of matter from a companion star. Not only are the periods of millisecond pulsars much shorter than those of normal, young pulsars (the Crab Nebula pulsar, which is the youngest known, has a period of only 0.03 seconds), but their slowdown rate is very low because of their comparatively weak magnetic fields. Indeed, millisecond pulsars are so regular that their pulses can be averaged to create the most accurate clock known to man. Of more than seven hundred pulsars so far identified, fewer than twenty are of the millisecond variety. The first to be discovered, in 1982, PSR 1937+211, is also the fastest known, completing 642 revolutions per second. In recent years, several confirmed or suspected planets have been found by pulsar timing in orbit around millisecond pulsars (➜ **pulsar planets**).

Milne, Edward Arthur (1896–1950)

British mathematician and physicist who in his *Modern Cosmology and the Christian Idea of God* (1952) confronts the problem of the doctrine of incarnation in the light of the possible discovery of extraterrestrial intelligence (➜ **incarnation and redemption**):

> God's most notable intervention in the actual historical process, according to the Christian outlook, was the Incarnation. Was this a unique event, or has it been re-enacted on each of the countless number of planets? The Christian would recoil in horror from such a conclusion. We cannot imagine the Son of God suffering vicariously on each of a myriad of planets. The Christian would avoid this conclusion by the definite supposition that our planet is in fact unique. What then of the possible denizens of other planets, if the Incarnation occurred only on our own? We are in deep waters here, in a sea of great mysteries.

Milne offers a possible solution in the form of radio messages sent out from Earth into interstellar space. By this means, he suggests, we might convey the news of a unique terrestrial incarnation to other races. The idea was denounced by Eric L. **Mascall.** ➔ **Christian doctrine and pluralism**

Mimas

The seventh moon of **Saturn;** its low density suggests a composition that is primarily water ice. Mimas is heavily cratered, although the cratering is not uniform. While most of the

Discovery	1789, by William Herschel
Mean distance from Saturn	185,600 km (115,400 mi.)
Diameter	382 km (237 mi.)
Mean density	1.17 g/cm³
Escape velocity	0.161 km/s (580 km/h, 360 mi./h)
Orbital period	0.942 day (22 hours 36 minutes)
Orbital eccentricity	0.020
Orbital inclination	1.53°
Axial period	0.942 day
Visual albedo	0.5

surface is covered with craters up to and exceeding 40 km (25 miles) in diameter, in the southern polar region craters larger than 20 km (12 miles) are generally absent. Preeminent is the crater Herschel, which, at 130 km (80 miles) across, spans more than one third the diameter of the whole moon and has a central peak that rises 6 km (4 miles) above the crater floor. Had the impact that caused it been much bigger, it might have split Mimas apart. As it is, traces of fracture marks are evident on the opposite hemisphere. ➔ **Saturn, moons of**

Mira variable

A type of **red giant** or **red supergiant,** the surface of which pulsates and varies in brightness. Mira variables lose mass extensively in the form of powerful **stellar wind**s.

Miranda

The eleventh moon of **Uranus** and one of the most remarkable objects in the solar system. Its surface reveals huge fault canyons up to 20 km (12 miles) deep, terraced layers, and an extraordinary mixture of young and old terrain

Discovery	1948, by Gerard Kuiper
Mean distance from Uranus	130,500 km (81,100 mi.)
Diameter	472 km (293 mi.)
Mean density	1.15 g/cm³
Escape velocity	0.189 km/s (680 km/h, 423 mi./h)
Orbital period	1.413 days (1 day 9 hours 55 minutes)
Orbital eccentricity	0.0027
Orbital inclination	4.22°
Axial period	1.413 days
Visual albedo	0.27

seemingly jumbled together. The younger regions may have been produced by incomplete differentiation of the moon, a process in which upwelling of lighter material surfaced in certain areas. However, some scientists favor the view that Miranda has been shattered, perhaps as many as five times in its history. After each such catastrophe, the theory goes, the moon would have reassembled from the remains of its former self with portions of the core exposed and portions of the surface buried. ➔ **Uranus, moons of**

MIRLIN
➔ **Mid-Infrared Large-well Imager**

mirror life
➔ **mirror matter**

mirror matter

According to an idea first put forward in the 1980s, every particle in nature has an elusive, unseen partner. The discovery of mirror matter (not to be confused with antimatter, the existence of which is proven) would strengthen theories of how the four forces of nature—gravity, electromagnetism, and the strong and weak forces—were unified in the early Universe. In 1999 came the suggestion[412] that a small number of **MACHOs,** which had been detected on the outskirts of our galaxy, might be stars composed of this exotic stuff. Mirror matter would be subject to its own distinct set of physical laws. Although it would feel gravity in the ordinary way and therefore be able to condense into mirror stars and planets, its versions of the three other forces would be different. One consequence is that mirror stars would be invisible because they would not emit **electromagnetic radiation.** The only way their presence could become known to us is through their gravitational **microlensing** effects and their subsequent identification as MACHOs. Theoretical considerations suggest that the maximum mass of a stable mirror star would be about 0.5 M_S—just right to explain the dozen or so MACHOs that have been singled out as candidates. The possibility of mirror stars and planets opens up the bizarre possibility of mirror organisms that would be completely invisible to us (and we to them).

Mission of Gravity

Science fiction novel by Hal **Clement**[121] (1954) set on the giant, rapidly rotating planet of Mesklin, where the effective gravity varies between 700 G at the flattened poles and 3 G at the equator. Under these seemingly less than ideal conditions, life and intelligence have evolved. The Mesklinites are giant centipede-like creatures, derived from aquatic jet-propelled ancestors, that have diverged in biology and culture according to where they live on the planet. A spacecraft from Earth crashes at the planet's north pole, and a rescue mission ensues in which the Mesklinite known as Barlennan takes on the role of hero. Although Clement provides no great insight into novel extraterrestrial psychologies, his book is one of the earliest systematic attempts to invent a world with an ecology to match. ➔ **gravitational life**

mitochondria

Mobile **organelle**s in the **cytoplasm** of **eukaryotic cell**s, the main function of which is the production of **adenosine triphosphate** (ATP) by **aerobic respiration.**

mitosis

The normal process of somatic (**diploid**) cell division that results in two daughter cells, genetically identical to each other and to the parent cell.

MMT

➔ **Multiple Mirror Telescope**

MOA

➔ **Microlensing Observations in Astrophysics**

Mogul, Project

A secret program conducted by the U.S. Air Force and directed by Charles B. Moore, in the late 1940s, to develop balloon-borne equipment capable of giving early warning of distant Soviet nuclear explosions. Large helium-filled balloons were attached to instrument arrays and lofted into the stratosphere, where the acoustic signals from a remote nuclear detonation would have been detectable. They may have been responsible for a number of UFO reports around the time of the flying **saucer flap of 1947.** In particular, the 1996 Air Force investigation of the **Roswell Incident** concluded that the crash of a Mogul balloon array was probably to blame (➔ **Roswell Incident, USAF report on**). Somewhat bizarrely, the purplish flowers noted by the rancher who discovered the Roswell wreckage, and later referred to by others more luridly as "alien hieroglyphics," turned out to be decorations by the New York toy manufacturer who had supplied the tape used in assembling the arrays.[582] ➔ **Cold War, linked to UFO reports**

molecular cloud

An **interstellar cloud** in which most of the material present is in the form of **molecule**s. Both small and giant molecular clouds exist in the Galaxy, but it is only the latter that are associated with regions of active star formation, such as the **Orion Nebula.** Giant molecular clouds span between 150 and 250 light-years and may contain up to 10 million M_S of material. Although they consist mostly of **hydrogen,** they also contain large amounts of **carbon monoxide** and other substances. More than one hundred types of molecules have been found in some of the largest clouds (➔ **interstellar molecules**).

molecule

An aggregate of **atom**s held together by **covalent bond**s.

molecules, in space

➔ **interstellar molecules**

monochromatic

Of one wavelength or color.

Monod, Jacques-Lucien (1910–76)

French biologist who became director of the Pasteur Institute in Paris and, together with François Jacob and André Lwolff, won the 1965 Nobel Prize for Physiology or Medicine. In his influential book *Chance and Necessity*[407] (1971) he argued that the emergence of life on Earth was the result of a fantastically unlikely sequence of events: "the product of an enormous lottery presided over by natural selection, blindly picking the rare winners from among numbers drawn at utter random." This being the case,

> The universe was not pregnant with life, nor the biosphere with man. Our number came up in the Monte Carlo game.

A similar view, in which the human race is regarded as the outcome of a chain of accidents and its existence as pointless, has been expressed by, among others, Bertrand Russell and the Nobel physicist Steven Weinberg. → **evolutionary theory and extraterrestrial life**

monosaccharides

Simple sugars. They are classified by the number of **carbon** atoms in each of their **molecule**s: trioses (3), tetroses (4), **pentose**s (5), **hexose**s (6), and so on.

Montlivault, Sales-Guyon de

Early proponent of the idea of **panspermia** who suggested that life originated on Earth from seeds that came from the Moon. → **Moon, life on**

Moon

The Earth's only natural satellite and one that is unusually large relative to the size of its primary (being exceeded by **Charon** alone in this respect). Its origin remains a matter of debate, though the present consensus view is that it formed more than 4.5 billion years ago from debris resulting from the collision between the Earth and a Mars-sized body. The outer layers of the Moon, initially molten and comprising a global "magma ocean," cooled to form the 4.5-billion-year-old rocks now found in the lunar highlands. These ancient igneous rocks, known as anorthosites, are rich in the **silicate** mineral plagioclase and impart to the lunar highlands their characteristic light color. A period of intense bombardment followed that caused extensive cratering and fragmentation of the crust. About 4 billion years ago, the Moon suffered a number of major impacts that excavated the basins referred to as **maria.** Subsequent volcanic activity between about 4 and 2.5 billion years ago flooded these basins with molten lava, which then cooled and solidified to form dark basalt. Since that time, the Moon has changed little except for the occasional impact of a meteorite or comet.

However, the Moon is not completely inactive. Seismometers left on the lunar surface by the *Apollo* astronauts have recorded small seismic events, known as "moonquakes," occurring at depths of several hundred kilometers, that probably result from tidal stresses induced by the Earth's gravitational pull. In addition, there have been many reports over the years of unusual color changes and cloudlike obscurations associated with certain craters, including **Aristarchus** and **Alphonsus,** and referred to as **transient lunar phenomena.** Most unusually, Ken Mattingley, the command module pilot on *Apollo 16*, reported seeing flashes of light on the dark side of the Moon on two consecutive orbits of his craft.

Mean distance from center of Earth	384,400 km (238,906 mi.)
Diameter	3,476 km (2,160 mi.)
Mass (Earth = 1)	0.0122
Mean density	3.34 g/cm^3
Surface gravity (Earth = 1)	0.165
Escape velocity	2.38 km/s (8,568 km/h, 5,325 mi./h)
Orbital period	27.3 days
Orbital eccentricity	0.055
Orbital inclination	5.10°
Axial period	27.3 days (gravitational lock)
Max. surface temp.	117°C (243°F)
Min. surface temp.	−163 °C (−261°F)
Albedo	0.07

Mass concentrations, or "mascons," associated with the circular maria and thought to have been caused by layers of denser, basaltic lava, were discovered as a result of their gravitational effect on the orbital motions of *Lunar Orbiter* probes in the 1960s. Local magnetic areas have also been detected around some craters, although the Moon has no global magnetic field.

It was natural that philosophers and romantics alike should have long dreamed of traveling to the Moon (➔ **Moon, voyages to**) and there finding intelligent life (➔ **Moon, life on**). But the possibility of lunar life (except possibly for certain types of hardy microbes) died with the realization that the Moon has neither an atmosphere (➔ **Moon, atmosphere of**) nor any liquid water (➔ **Moon, water on**). Recent observations by *Lunar Prospector,* however, have confirmed the existence of substantial quantities of ice in deep craters at the lunar poles.

Moon, communication with
➔ **communication, with the Moon and planets**

"Moon Hoax"
Perpetrated in 1835 by Richard Adams **Locke,** a writer hired by the newly established *New York Sun*. As he had already dabbled in science fiction, it occurred to him to expand his activity in this direction without telling anyone. For his subject, he chose the astronomical expedition of John **Herschel** to the Cape of Good

An illustration from the *New York Sun* at the height of the "Moon Hoax" depicting winged hominids among other species.

Hope. Beginning with the August 25, 1835, issue of the *Sun,* Locke describes in detail all kinds of fantastic discoveries having been made by Herschel with a telescope of such power, he said, that it could see objects on the lunar surface as small as 18 in. across. In the second installment, the exotic variety of life supposedly found by Herschel is revealed, including a goatlike animal with a single horn and "an amphibious creature of spherical form, which rolled with great velocity across the pebbly beach." On August 29, Locke broke the news that lunar intelligence had been found in the guise of "Vespertilio-homo," or bat-men. Finally, on August 31, he spoke of the discovery of yet higher beings and of "the universal state of amity among all classes of lunar creatures." Huge interest was created by the articles, and the *Sun* briefly became the best-selling newspaper in the world. *The New York Times* believed the reports both "probable and possible," Yale was said to be "alive with staunch supporters," while, according to yet another report, an American clergyman was considering starting a collection for Bibles for the lunar inhabitants.[186]

The fact that the "Moon Hoax" was almost certainly nothing of the kind has been argued compellingly by Michael Crowe,[137] who cites an account of the affair written by William Griggs in 1852. According to Griggs, "we have the assurance of the author, in a letter published some years since, in the *New World,* that it was written expressly to satirize the unwarranted and extravagant anticipations upon this subject." The irony is that the hoax failed because the public had been primed for so long by the strident advocates of **pluralism** to *expect* intelligent life on other worlds. ➔ **Moon, life on**

Moon, life on

Among ancient philosophers to speculate about possible lunar inhabitants were **Anaxagoras of Clazomenae, Xenophanes,** Pythagoras and his followers, **Plutarch,** and (in fiction) **Lucian of Samosata.** In the late middle ages, **Nicholas of Cusa** favored life on the Moon. However, speculation became more intense following the **Copernican Revolution** and Galileo **Galilei**'s first lunar studies with the aid of a telescope (1608). In his *Discovery of a New World in the Moone* (1638), John **Wilkins** summarized what were then widely held beliefs:

> That those spots and brighter parts which by our sight might be distinguished in the Moon, do show the difference between the Sea and Land of that other World....
>
> The spots represent the Sea, and the brighter parts Land....
>
> That there are high mountains, deep valleys, and spacious plains in the body of the Moon....
>
> That there is an atmosphere, or an orb of gross vaporous air, immediately encompassing the body of the Moon....
>
> That it is probable there may be inhabitants in this other World, but of what kind they are is uncertain....

Even at this early stage, however, there was sharp disagreement over how to interpret what the telescope showed. The two great lunar mapmakers of the seventeenth century, Johannes **Hevelius** and Giovanni **Riccioli,** stood at opposite poles of the debate. Whereas Hevelius populated his chart with seas and "selenites" (as he called his lunar inhabitants), Riccioli's Moon was dry and dead. The battle over lunar life continued throughout the eighteenth century, Johann **Bode** and William **Herschel** being notable among the proselenites. By the turn of the nineteenth century, persuasive evidence was accumulating that the Moon lacked both sufficient air and water (➔ **Moon, water on**) to support substantial life. Yet the selenites had their champions, including the extremists Johann **Schröter** and Franz **Gruithuisen,** and the moderates Karl **Gauss,** Joseph von **Littrow,** and Wilhelm **Olbers.** Improved lunar maps in the 1830s, by Wilhelm Lohrmann and by Wilhelm **Beer** and Johann **Mädler,** helped persuade most astronomers that the Moon was unlikely to be inhabited. Even so, this did not prevent Richard **Locke** from creating a worldwide sensation in 1835 with his great **"Moon Hoax."** By the end of the nineteenth century, lunar life had passed more or less from the realm of science into that of science fiction. Jules **Verne** posed the question in *Around the Moon* (1870) and teased with his reply, George **Griffith**'s adventurers in *Stories of Other Worlds* (1900) find the ruins of a civilization and its bestial offspring, while, as late as 1901, in *First Men in the Moon,* H. G. **Wells** was able to exploit lingering public credulity with his tale of a hollow Moon, richly varied selenites, and massively cerebral Grand Lunar (➔ **Moon, voyages to**). Yet the romance did not quite end with these gaslight fantasies. In the 1920s, William H. **Pickering,** a staunch advocate of Martian vegetation (➔ **Mars, life on**), argued that certain dark areas on the Moon which changed shape were due to spreading plants,[454] while almost half a century later the remote possibility of microbial lunar life was still on the minds of NASA scientists when they quarantined the first *Apollo* astronauts and their rock samples (➔ **back contamination**)—a well-advised (but ill-performed) precaution in view of the bacterial survivors found on the returned camera of *Surveyor 3.* Arthur C. **Clarke** suggested remains of another kind on the Moon in his short story "The Sentinel,"[112] which blossomed into *2001: A Space Odyssey.*[111] In reality, it seems, the Moon has always been dead. However, the prospects of future intelligent (human) life on our nearest neighbor have been greatly improved by the discovery of billions of tons of ice in some deep lunar craters (➔ *Lunar Prospector*).

Moon, voyages to

Almost 1,500 years separated **Lucian**'s first imaginary lunar excursions from those of Ludovico **Ariosto** (1532), Johannes **Kepler** (1634), bishops Francis **Godwin** (1638) and John **Wilkins** (1640), and Savinien **Cyrano de Bergerac** (1656). All these tales involved the discovery of intelligent lunar beings (➔ **Moon, life on**) and assumed that air extends from the Earth to the Moon. Following the invention of the balloon in 1783, it became clear that humans could not survive unprotected at high altitude, and speculation focused for a while on terrestrial, atmospheric travel. By the second half of the nineteenth century, however, space sojourns were once again on the fictional agenda, with Jules **Verne,** George **Griffith,** H. G. **Wells,** and others offering varied glimpses of a world that would not be reached in reality until the 1960s.[402, 421]

Moon, water on

The belief that the dark lunar areas, or **maria,** might be seas was held by **Plutarch** and others in the ancient world. In his *Siderius Nunctius,* Galileo **Galilei** wrote that "[the] brighter part most fitly represents its land surface, but its darker part the watery surface." Later, he came to doubt this interpretation, but others, including John **Wilkins,** Johannes **Hevelius,** Johann **Schröter,** and William **Herschel** kept the idea of a maritime Moon alive for the next two centuries. The demise of lunar water accompanied that of a lunar atmosphere, since liquid water cannot exist where the atmospheric pressure is extremely low or zero. Ice, however, does exist in regions at the Moon's poles. This surprising fact, first suggested by data from the *Clementine* probe, in 1994, was confirmed, in March 1998, by observations made by *Lunar Prospector.* After further analysis,[190] the initial conservative estimate of 300 million t was increased by a factor of ten, to 3 billion t at each pole, enough to fill a lake about 100 m deep and 6 km across. The possibility also exists that there may be more. The instrument aboard *Lunar Prospector* used for this determination can detect the presence of water (or, more precisely, hydrogen) to a depth of 0.5 m. Since lunar soil has been turned over by meteorite impacts during the past couple of billion years to a depth of about 2 m, water could theoretically be present to this depth. However, if (as suspected) this water exists as crystals mixed in with the lunar regolith, larger amounts of pure water ice deposits could potentially exist at much greater depths.

The lunar ice is thought to have come from **comet**s that collided with the Moon in the remote past. Although most of the water deposited on the lunar surface in this way would long ago have been vaporized by the daytime heat of the Sun, in small, permanently shaded regions at the poles it has evidently survived. Its presence is further evidence that water, frozen or otherwise, is a common commodity on many worlds, and this, in turn, raises the prospects of extraterrestrial life. The availability of water on the Moon is also a major boost to any plans for establishing a self-sustaining lunar colony.

moons, atmospheres of
Of the sixty-four known moons in the solar system, four have been found to have atmospheres: Jupiter's volcanically active moon **Io** (tenuous **sulfur dioxide**); Jupiter's ice-coated moon **Europa** (tenuous **oxygen**); Saturn's largest moon, **Titan** (dense **nitrogen** and **methane**); and Neptune's largest moon, **Triton** (tenuous nitrogen and methane). The ability of a moon to retain an atmosphere is related to its mass and its distance from the Sun, although tenuous atmospheres may be regenerated by a variety of processes.

moons, life on
With biological or **prebiotic** chemical interest surrounding **Europa, Callisto, Titan,** and **Triton,** scientists are increasingly becoming interested in the possibility that large satellites, in addition to planets, might support conditions suitable for life.[107, 627] A number of giant worlds have been discovered circling relatively nearby Sun-like stars (→ **extrasolar planets**); although these seem to offer poor prospects for terrestrial-type biologies, it has been suggested that large moons in orbit around some of these newly found planets might fall into the **habitable zone,** where life can arise.

moons, tidal influences of
Large satellites such as the Earth's moon, it has been suggested, may play an important and even decisive role in the evolution of life on the planets they orbit around by giving rise to biologically fertile tidal zones.

MOP
→ **Microwave Observing Program**

Mormonism
Unusual among contemporary forms of Christianity in that it expounds a pluralist viewpoint. According to its founder, Joseph Smith, a multiplicity of inhabited worlds is part of God's plan of salvation. This truth supposedly came to Smith in a series of revelations and is said to be evinced by various Old Testament passages (for example, Moses 1:33, 35). The Mormon acceptance of the existence of other worlds created by God for a divine purpose has less in common with contemporary scientific extraterrestrial speculation than it does with theological arguments for **pluralism** put forward before the twentieth century. → **Christian doctrine and pluralism**

Morrison, Philip (1915–)
Theoretical astrophysicist and institute professor at the Massachusetts Institute of Technology who has played a significant role in advocating **SETI** for the past four decades. In 1959, while at **Cornell University,** he and Giuseppe **Cocconi** were the first scientists to call upon the professional community to carry out a coordinated search for intelligent extraterrestrial signals (→ **Morrison-Cocconi Conjecture**). Morrison recalled the genesis of this movement:[575]

> During a chamber music performance in the Cornell Student Center I began to think of the possibilities of gamma-ray astronomy. By the end of 1958, I had published a summary of what might be learned from gamma-ray astronomy.... [T]he paper was challenging, and a few months later, in the spring of 1959, Guiseppe Cocconi came into my office. We were thinking about gamma-rays of natural origin when we realized that we knew how to make them, too. We were making lots of them downstairs at the Cornell synchrotron. So Cocconi asked whether they could be used for communicating between the stars. It was plain that they would work, but they weren't very easy to use. My reply was enthusiastic but cautious. Shouldn't we look through the whole electromagnetic spectrum to find the best wavelength for any such communication? That was the germ of the idea.

Morrison received a B.S. from the Carnegie Institute of Technology in 1936 and a Ph.D. in theoretical physics from the **University of California, Berkeley,** in 1940, under the supervision of J. Robert Oppenheimer. From 1942 to 1946 he worked on the Manhattan Project, then joined the physics faculty of Cornell. Since 1965 he has been on the faculty of MIT. Aside from his role in instigating the modern SETI movement, Morrison has been a leader in organizing and chairing conferences on the subject, including those at Byurakan (1971) (➜ **Byurakan SETI conferences**) and Boston University (1973), various NASA symposia on SETI, and the IAU meetings on SETI (1980 and 1984).

Morrison-Cocconi Conjecture

A pivotal suggestion, put forward by Philip **Morrison** and Giuseppe **Cocconi,** in a September 1959 paper,[123] that the best frequency at which to search for signals from intelligent extraterrestrials is 1,420 MHz, corresponding to the **21-centimeter line** of neutral hydrogen:

> It is reasonable to expect that sensitive receivers for this frequency will be made at an early stage of the development of radio astronomy. That would be the expectation of operators of the assumed source, and the present state of terrestrial instruments indeed justifies the expectation.

They proposed that the search begin with seven reasonably Sun-like stars within a radius of 15 light-years and closed with this challenge:

> The reader may wish to consign these speculations wholly to the domain of science fiction. We submit, rather, that the foregoing line of argument demonstrates that the presence of interstellar signals is entirely consistent with all we now know, and that if signals are present the means of detecting them is now to hand.

Cocconi and Morrison's paper served to spark a debate among scientists that continues to this day. The year of its appearance coincided with the start of preparations for the first search for extraterrestrial signals, Project **Ozma,** by Frank **Drake.**

Morrison's radioglyph scheme

An elaboration, by Philip **Morrison,** of Lancelot Hogben's early **radioglyph** scheme,

Astraglossa, for communicating with extraterrestrials.[410] In Morrison's version, numbers are represented by square-shaped pulses (e.g., five square pulses for the numeral 5), and mathematical operations such as "plus," "minus," "the reciprocal" of, and so on, by other pulse shapes. Distant beings would be instructed in the meaning of these symbols through simple arithmetic. Next, pi (the ratio of the circumference to the diameter of a circle) would be introduced as the sum of an indefinite series of fractions. Morrison would then send a series of extended radio signals, each marked at its start and finish by a pulse, with occasional pulses in between. These he would intersperse with the symbol for pi in the hope that the recipients would catch his intent; namely, that the lines of radio emission should be aligned one below the other, so that the seemingly random pulses would form a circle. This would establish the "raster," or pattern of horizontal scanning lines, of a television screen, which could subsequently be used for more elaborate communications. ➜ **CETI**

Moulton, Forest Ray (1872–1952)

American astronomer at the University of Chicago who, with Thomas **Chamberlin,** developed the **Chamberlin-Moulton planetesimal hypothesis** about the origin of the planets.

Mount Hopkins Observatory

Renamed the Fred Lawrence **Whipple Observatory** in 1982.

Mount Palomar Observatory
➜ **Palomar Observatory**

Mount Stromlo and Siding Spring Observatories

Operated by the Australian National Observatories and located on Mount Stromlo, near Canberra, at an altitude of 770 m and on Siding Spring Mountain, New South Wales, at an altitude of 1,150 m. The main instruments are a 1.9-m (6.3-ft.) reflecting telescope (Mount Stromlo) and a 2.3-m (7.5-ft.) reflecting telescope (Siding Spring). The Siding Spring site is shared by the **Anglo-Australian Observatory.**

Mount Wilson Observatory

Located near Pasadena, California, at an altitude of 1,750 m (5,700 ft.). Mount Wilson is home to the famous 100-in. (2.54-m) Hooker telescope (refurbished in the early 1990s), a smaller, 60-in. (1.5-m) reflector, and two solar telescopes. Established by George **Hale** in 1905 with funds provided by Andrew Carnegie, it is now operated jointly by the University of Southern California, the University College of Los Angeles, and Harvard University.

MPS Project

→ **Microlensing Planet Search Project**

mRNA

→ **messenger RNA**

MSETI

Microwave **SETI**; the "traditional" way of conducting searches for extraterrestrial intelligence by tuning into the short radio wave region of the **electromagnetic spectrum.** Rising to more prominence recently has been **optical SETI.**

Muller, Hermann Joseph (1890–1967)

American geneticist at Indiana University and Nobel Prize winner who, influenced by Leonard **Troland**'s work, suggested in 1929 that the first life-form on Earth may have "consisted of little else than a gene or genes."[413] He later speculated on the differences and commonalities that might exist between higher life-forms on other worlds:[414]

> [They] may be expected to have followed radically different courses in regard to many of their features.... How much greater, then, might such differences be between the forms of Earth and those of another planet. These differences, affecting their whole internal economy, including the biochemistry within their cells, would also be expressed in their gross anatomy and in their outer form.... [Even so] it would certainly be capable of achieving much mutual understanding with our own, since both had been evolved to deal usefully with a world in which the same physico-chemical and general biological principles operate.

multicellular

Composed of many **cell**s.

Multichannel Astrometric Photometer (MAP)

A device developed and used at the **Allegheny Observatory** in the search for **extrasolar planets.**

Multichannel Astrometric Photometer and Spectrometer (MAPS)

An instrument developed at the **Allegheny Observatory** for detecting **extrasolar planets** that is unique in its simultaneous use of two techniques: the **radial velocity method** and **astrometry.** Capable of detecting planets of Uranian mass, it has been used on the Keck II Telescope (→ **Keck Telescopes**).

Multi-Channel Spectrum Analyzer (MCSA)

The detector, together with its software algorithms, that was at the heart of the instrumentation used in the targeted portion of NASA's **High Resolution Microwave Survey.** Developed at **NASA Ames Research Center** and built under contract to Ames by the Silicon Engines Company, the first operational version, known as MCSA 2.0, was capable of simultaneously analyzing 14 million 1-Hz channels. This represented a 10 million–fold increase in capability over the total of all previous searches.

Multiple Mirror Telescope (MMT)

An instrument located at the Fred Lawrence **Whipple Observatory** on Mount Hopkins, Arizona, at an altitude of 2,606 m (8,550 ft.). It employed six mirrors, each 1.82 m (6 ft.) across, working together to give the equivalent of a single mirror 4.45 m (14.6 ft.) in aperture. In 1998, the MMT was used in a pioneering demonstration of **nulling interferometry** to image the dust cloud around **Betelgeuse.** Following this, the telescope was closed and work began to upgrade it by replacing the six small mirrors with a single mirror 6.5 m (21.3 ft.) in diameter.

multiple star

A group of three (trinary) or more stars orbiting around one another because of their mutual gravitational attraction. Examples include the **Alpha Centauri** system and **Castor.**[255]

Murchison meteorite

A **carbonaceous chondrite** that exploded into fragments over the town of Murchison, 400 km north of Perth, Australia, on September 28, 1969. About 82 kg of the meteorite was recovered. Eyewitnesses arriving at the scene reported smelling something like **methanol** or pyridine, an early indication that the object might contain **organic** material. Subsequent analysis by NASA scientists and a group led by Cyril **Ponnamperuma** revealed the presence of six **amino acids** commonly found in **proteins** and twelve that did not occur in terrestrial life. All of these amino acids appeared in both **dextrorotatory** (right-handed) and **levorotatory** (left-handed) forms, suggesting that they were not the result of earthly contamination. The meteorite also contained **hydrocarbons** that appeared **abiotic** in character and was enriched with a heavy **isotope** of carbon, confirming the extraterrestrial origin of its organics. Initial studies suggested that the amino acids in the Murchison meteorite showed no bias between left- and right-handed forms. However, in 1997, John R. Cronin and Sandra Pizzarello of Arizona State University reported finding excesses of left-handed versions of four amino acids ranging from 7 to 9 percent,[135] a result confirmed independently by another group.[183] → **organic matter, in meteorites**

Murray, Bruce C. (1932–)

Professor of Planetary Science and Geology at the California Institute of Technology and faculty member since 1960, director of the **Jet Propulsion Laboratory** (1976–82), and current president of the **Planetary Society,** an organization he and Carl **Sagan** founded in 1979. Murray has been involved with planetary exploration since its inception in the 1960s and headed JPL during the *Viking* landings on Mars and the *Voyager* encounters with Jupiter and Saturn. He was among those scientists who openly supported the idea of further research into the problem of **unidentified flying objects** in the wake of the **Condon Report.** In a 1972

review of J. Allen **Hynek**'s book *The UFO Experience: A Scientific Inquiry,* he wrote:

> On balance, Hynek's defense of UFOs as a valid, if speculative, scientific topic is more credible than Condon's attempt to mock them out of existence.... From this juror's point of view, Hynek has won a reprieve for UFOs with his many pages of provocative unexplained reports and his articulate challenge to his colleagues to tolerate the study of something they cannot understand.

He attended the April 1975 Philip **Morrison** Workshop on Interstellar Communication dealing with planet detection and thereafter championed the idea of an **all-sky survey** component to NASA's **SETI** plans. Upon Murray's appointment as director of JPL, his personal interest in the field led to the establishment of a SETI office at the laboratory under Robert **Edelson.** A partnership subsequently developed between JPL and the **NASA Ames Research Center,** with JPL taking responsibility for the all-sky survey portion and Ames the **targeted search** portion of NASA's **High Resolution Microwave Survey.** Murray is currently involved with the development of a proposal for a **penetrator probe,** based on the **New Millennium Mars Microprobe,** to explore a site on the Valles Marineris system. Among his other interests is the societal impact of new information technology, including the Internet.

Murray meteorite

A **carbonaceous chondrite** that fell near Murray, Kentucky, in 1950. Its analysis by Melvin **Calvin** supported the conclusion that prebiotic molecules are able to form in space. → **organic matter, in meteorites**

MUSES-C

An innovative mission led by Japan that will use new flight technology, including solar electric propulsion, to rendezvous with the **asteroid** 4660 Nereus. Upon arrival, the smallest robotic space rover ever developed will be deployed on the asteroid's surface. So tiny it could be held in the palm of one's hand, the rover is being built by engineers at the **Jet Propulsion Laboratory.** The spacecraft will also fire projectiles onto the surface, collect the samples that are ejected, and return them to Earth for laboratory analysis. The mission is scheduled for launch in 2002.

mutation

A sudden, random change in the genetic material of a **cell.** It may include a change in the nucleotide sequence, alteration of **gene** position, gene loss or duplication, or insertion of a foreign sequence. Mutations in germline tissue are of enormous biological importance since they provide the initial material from which **natural selection** produces evolutionary change. → **evolutionary theory and extraterrestrial life**

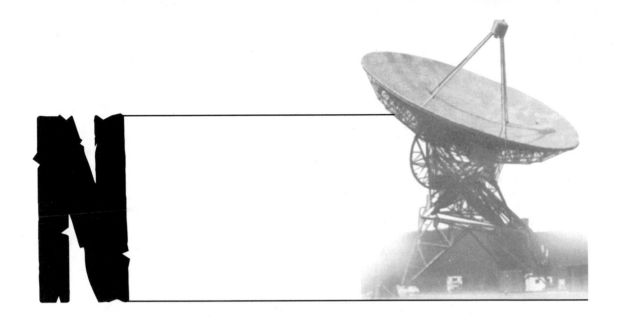

N

NABI
→ NASA Astrobiology Institute

Naiad
The innermost moon of **Neptune.** A small object of irregular shape, it orbits just 23,200 km (14,400 miles) above the Neptunian cloud tops. → **Neptune, moons of**

Discovery	1989, by *Voyager 2*
Mean distance from Neptune	47,900 km (29,800 mi.)
Diameter	58 km (36 mi.)
Orbital period	0.294 day (7 hours 3 minutes)
Orbital eccentricity	0.0003
Orbital inclination	4.74°
Visual albedo	0.06

NAIC Arecibo
→ Arecibo Observatory

Nakhla meteorite
An **achondrite** that exploded over the town of Nakhla, Egypt, on June 28, 1911, breaking into about forty fragments, one of which allegedly (though this has never been proved) killed a dog. The Nakhla meteorite was later identified as belonging to an exclusive group of objects, known as **SNC meteorites,** that are believed to have come from the surface of Mars. One of the fragments, a well-preserved 12-cm-wide specimen, in 1999 joined **ALH 84001** at the center of an intense debate concerning the nature of structures said by a team of NASA researchers to be the remains of microscopic Martian life (→ **Martian "fossils" controversy**).

nanobacteria
Hypothetical, microscopic life-forms smaller than the smallest confirmed viruses or bacteria. Their possible existence was first suggested in 1989 when Robert H. Folk, a geologist at the University of Texas, Austin, discovered tiny spheres, only about 50 nm across, in mineral deposits from a hot-water spring in Viterbo, Italy. More recent investigations, by Folk and his colleague F. Leo Lynch, have turned up similar minuscule spheres in the sub-200-nm range, which microbiologists have argued is below the smallest possible size for a self-sustaining organism. Further evidence that biological entities may exist at this tiny scale have come from an Australian team and their claims concerning **nanobes** and the discovery of carbon balls, 30 to 150 nm across, in freshly opened pieces of the **Allende meteorite.**

nanobes

Tiny filaments found in sandstone 3 km below the seabed off Western Australia and claimed by a team of geologists at the University of Queensland, Brisbane, to be the smallest known living organisms.[596] With diameters of 20 to 150 nm, the nanobes fall below the size range of the smallest known bacteria, *Mycoplasma*, which lack **cell wall**s and have a diameter of 150 to 200 nm. If the claim is verified, it would lend credence to the controversial 1996 announcement by NASA scientists of "**nanofossils**" in a Martian meteorite, some of which were just 20 nm across. The Queensland researchers said that the nanobes grew in the laboratory when exposed to air, moved away from the electron beam during scanning electron microscopy, and possess structures like cell walls. In addition, three different DNA analyses of them gave positive results. However, the claim remains controversial, with other experts warning that the DNA could be from contamination on the rock surface and pointing to the unusual fact that the filaments grow in air when their normal environment is **anaerobic.** If the nanobes are confirmed as being alive, they will break not just the record for small size but also the record for **hyperthermophiles** since at the depth they were found the temperature is more than 150°C.

nanofossils

A description applied to the extremely small structures found inside the **SNC meteorite** known as **ALH 84001** and claimed by some researchers to be the remains of tiny organisms that once lived on Mars. → **Martian "fossils" controversy**

nanometer (nm)

One billionth (10^{-9}) of a meter.

narrowband

Encompassing a small **frequency** range, typically less than 300 Hz—the narrowest natural maser lines. Narrowband radio signals tend to be characteristic of those produced by artificial sources and are therefore the type for which **SETI** equipment is designed to discriminate.

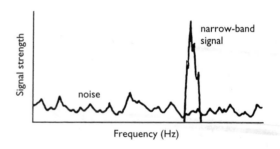

NASA

→ **National Aeronautics and Space Administration**

NASA Ames Research Center

A facility that for four decades has pioneered work in astrobiology, and also researched other new techniques and technologies of potential use to NASA. Located at Moffett Field in the heart of California's Silicon Valley, Ames was founded on December 20, 1939, as an aircraft research laboratory by the National Advisory Committee on Aeronautics (NACA). In 1958, it became part of the National Aeronautics and Space Administration and in 1960 the site of NASA's first life sciences laboratory, set up to study chemical evolution, the conditions under which life might survive, and a variety of related issues. Thus Ames was established as the center for NASA's astrobiology program, first under Harold P. **Klein** and then under Richard S. Young. Cyril **Ponnamperuma,** a student of Melvin **Calvin,** joined as a research associate and eventually headed a branch in chemical evolution. It was Ponnamperuma's group that confirmed the existence of extraterrestrial **amino acids** in the **Murchison meteorite.**

Following an earlier request by NASA to scientists around the country for proposals for ideas for remote life-detection equipment to be used in the search for possible Martian life, Ames set up a team in 1963 to evaluate the various concepts.[470] Subsequently, it played a major role in the *Viking* program, with Klein in charge of the mission's biology science team.

The involvement of Ames in **SETI** stemmed from John **Billingham,** head of the center's Biotechnology Division, who in 1970 convinced Ames Director Hans Mark that a small-scale study of the problem of interstellar communication was justified. This led, the following year, to the proposal for Project **Cyclops.** Eventually, a less ambitious scheme was developed jointly by Ames and the **Jet Propulsion Laboratory** known as the **High Resolution Microwave Survey,** the targeted portion of which was the responsibility of Ames.

Several interplanetary missions have been operated by Ames, including *Pioneer 10* and *Pioneer 11,* and the center now manages the newly established **NASA Astrobiology Institute.** Recently, researchers at Ames created cell-like bubbles in a laboratory simulation of an interstellar **molecular cloud (➔ life, origin of**) and reported finding **polycyclic aromatic hydrocarbons** in space.

NASA Astrobiology Institute (NAI)

A collaboration between NASA and academic and research organizations to carry out interdisciplinary research in **astrobiology.** The Astrobiology Institute, which began operations in July 1998, is managed by the **NASA Ames Research Center** and includes among its initial membership Arizona State University, the University of Colorado, the Scripps Research Institute, the University of California at Irvine and at Los Angeles, Pennsylvania State University, Harvard University, Woods Hole Marine Biology Laboratory, the Carnegie Institute, the **NASA Johnson Space Center,** and the **Jet Propulsion Laboratory.** It is designed to operate as a "virtual" institute, linking geographically dispersed scientific teams and laboratories by the Next Generation Internet and other modern communications tools. Institute members will pursue research in areas such as the origin of life in the universe, the formation and evolution of habitable worlds, the early evolution of Earth's oceans and atmosphere, and the potential for biological evolution beyond an organism's planet of origin. A major goal of the institute will be to develop concepts for new missions to search for life within the solar system, and for habitable planets and evidence of life outside the solar system. In May 1999, Baruch Blumberg, winner of the 1976 Nobel Prize for Medicine (for his discovery of the hepatitis B vaccine), was appointed the institute's director.

NASA Bioscience Advisory Committee

A committee appointed in July 1959 to provide recommendations on NASA's future direction in the life sciences. It reported in January 1960 that NASA's involvement should include not only **space medicine** in support of manned spaceflight but also "investigations of the effects of extraterrestrial environments on living organisms including the search for extraterrestrial life." In the spring of 1960, the **NASA Office of Life Sciences** came into existence, and by August NASA had authorized the **Jet Propulsion Laboratory** to investigate the type of spacecraft needed to land on Mars and search for life. To study the chemical evolution of life and related issues, a life sciences laboratory was set up at the **NASA Ames Research Center.**

NASA Johnson Space Center (JSC)

A complex of facilities in Houston, Texas, for the development, management, and control of U.S. space flights. It opened in March 1964 and for the first decade of operation was known as the Manned Spacecraft Center. On February 17, 1973, it was renamed the (Lyndon B.) Johnson Space Center after the president who, while a U.S. Senator, recommended a manned lunar landing in response to early Soviet space successes.

NASA Office of Life Sciences

Branch of NASA established in 1960 to deal with biological issues related to the exploration of neighboring worlds, including the search for extraterrestrial life and the problem of **contamination.** In the same year, NASA set up its first life-science laboratory at the **NASA Ames Research Center** and instructed the **Jet Propulsion Laboratory** to begin a study of an unmanned mission to look for life on Mars.

NASA-Brookings Study

A NASA-sponsored study carried out in the late 1950s by the Brookings Institution to identify long-range goals of the U.S. space program and their impact on American society. The resulting report, submitted to NASA in 1960 only a few months after the end of Project **Ozma,** included a discussion of the implications of the discovery of extraterrestrial life and intelligence.[400] The authors pointed out that the reactions of both individuals and governments would probably depend on their social, cultural, and religious backgrounds, as well as on the nature of the discovery. The finding of low forms of life, or "subhuman intelligence," it was thought, might be assimilated quickly. However, more profound effects might follow from the discovery of intelligence that was superior to our own (➜ **extraterrestrial intelligence, more advanced than we**). In particular, it was pointed out that

> Anthropological files contain many examples of societies, sure of their place in the universe, which have disintegrated when they had to associate with previously unfamiliar societies espousing different ideas and different life ways; others that survived such an experience usually did so by paying the price of changes in values and attitudes and behavior.
>
> Since intelligent life might be discovered at any time via the radio telescope research presently under way, and since the consequences of such a discovery are presently unpredictable because of our limited knowledge of behavior under even an approximation of such dramatic circumstances, two research areas can be recommended:
>
> 1. Continuing studies to determine emotional and intellectual understanding and attitudes—and successive alterations of them if any—regarding the possibility and consequences of discovering intelligent extraterrestrial life.
> 2. Historical and empirical studies of the behavior of peoples and their leaders when confronted with dramatic and unfamiliar events or social pressures. . . .

Such studies, the report recommended, should take account of public reactions to past hoaxes (➜ **"Moon Hoax"**), waves of **unidentified flying objects** (➜ **saucer flap of 1947; "Washington Invasion"**), and events such as *The War of the Worlds* radio play (1938). They should also consider how best to inform the public of contact with an extraterrestrial intelligence, or whether such knowledge should be withheld. International relations, the report concluded, might be permanently altered because of "a greater unity of men on earth, based on the 'oneness' of man or on the age-old assumption that any stranger is threatening." ➜ **extraterrestrial intelligence, implications following first contact**

NASA/Caltech Jet Propulsion Laboratory
➜ **Jet Propulsion Laboratory**

National Academy of Sciences
➜ **Space Science Board**

National Aeronautics and Space Administration (NASA)
Refer to individual NASA entries.

National Astronomy and Ionosphere Center
A national research center operated by **Cornell University.** Its main facility is the **Arecibo Observatory.**

National Investigations Committee on Aerial Phenomena (NICAP)
An amateur UFO club, formed in 1956 in Washington, D.C. In January 1957, it came under the directorship of retired major and flying saucer enthusiast Donald **Keyhoe.** NICAP achieved an unwarranted measure of prestige and credibility through its governing board of retired admirals, generals, and academics, enticed by Keyhoe to posts that were little more than sinecures. In reality, NICAP acted primarily as a vehicle for Keyhoe to promote the **extraterrestrial hypothesis** and press his claim that the U.S. Air Force and CIA were concealing information on alien spacecraft and their occupants.

National Radio Astronomy Observatory (NRAO)
The collective name for the government-owned radio astronomy facilities in the United States, which include **Green Bank,** the **Very Large Array,** and the Very Long Baseline Array. NRAO is operated by Associated Universities, Inc., a consortium of nine universities, on behalf of the National Science Foundation and has its headquarters in Charlottesville, Virginia.

natural selection

The differential reproduction of **genotypes** due to factors in the environment; the principle of "the survival of the fittest," as first expounded by Charles **Darwin.** Natural selection, in combination with random **mutation,** leads to evolutionary change.

natural theology

That branch of theology, also known as physicotheology, based on seeking evidence for God in the natural world. It played an important role, especially in the eighteenth and first half of the nineteenth centuries (prior to the publication of Charles **Darwin**'s *Origin of Species*), in the debate over **pluralism.** Supporters of natural theology maintained that the existence of life and, in particular, intelligent life on other worlds should be taken as evidence of God's omnipotence and generosity (➔ **teleology**). They sought to allay fears from religious traditionalists that pluralism undermined the view that God and man had a special relationship. But although natural theology was successful in persuading many of its case for a God of the Universe, it ran into problems in explaining how an incarnated redeemer—Jesus—could act to save souls throughout the cosmos (➔ **incarnation and redemption**). Among the principal advocates of natural theology were Johann **Bode,** David **Brewster,** Thomas **Chalmers,** William **Derham,** William **Herschel,** Johann **Lambert,** Johann **Schröter,** Emanuel **Swedenborg,** and Thomas **Wright.** Among those who combined natural theology with an antipluralist viewpoint was William **Whewell.** ➔ **Christian doctrine and pluralism**

Naval Observatory
➔ **U.S. Naval Observatory**

NEAR
➔ *Near-Earth Asteroid Rendezvous*

Near-Earth Asteroid Rendezvous (NEAR)

The first mission in NASA's **Discovery Program** and the first probe powered by solar cells to operate beyond the orbit of Mars. *NEAR* was launched in February 1996 and is operated by the Applied Physics Laboratory at Johns Hopkins University. On June 27, 1997, *NEAR* flew by the **asteroid** 253 Mathilde and found it to be composed of extremely dark material, with numerous large impact craters, including one about 9 km (nearly 6 miles) deep. A subsequent deep-space maneuver in July 1997 brought *NEAR* back around Earth for a **gravity assist** that put the spacecraft on course for its main mission: a rendezvous with the Manhattan-sized asteroid 433 Eros. On February 14, 2000 *NEAR* became the first probe ever to enter orbit around an asteroid and will study Eros from as close as just a few kilometers until early 2001.

Near-Earth Object (NEO)

An **asteroid** or extinct **short-period comet** in an orbit that may bring it close to the Earth. NEOs have **perihelion** distances of less than 1.3 AU and include asteroids belonging to the Apollo, Amor, and Aten groups. Three NEOs—Ganymed, Eros, and Eric—have diameters greater than 10 km, while estimates are that there may be at least 100,000 NEOs measuring 100 m or more across. Many of these will collide with the inner planets over the next 10 million years or so.

nearest stars
➔ **stars, nearest**

nebula

An extended interstellar object comprised of gas and dust. Among the specific types recognized are bright nebulas, including **emission nebula**s and **reflection nebula**s, and dark nebulas or **absorption nebula**s. Emission nebulas

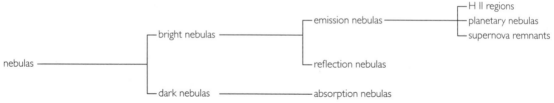

Classification of nebulas.

are further categorized as **H II region**s, **planetary nebula**s, and **supernova remnant**s.

nebular hypothesis

The idea put forward first in general terms by Immanuel **Kant** in 1775 and then more specifically by Pierre **Laplace** in 1796 that the solar system formed through the progressive condensation of a gassy nebula that once encircled the Sun. It was suggested that as this nebula rotated and contracted, rings of gas were cast off at various stages from which the planets subsequently condensed. Accordingly, the outer planets would have formed first, followed by Mars, the Earth, Venus, and Mercury. This notion of a sequential origin, from outermost planet to innermost, influenced subsequent debate about the nature of life on our neighboring worlds. In particular, it implied that Mars was more evolved than the Earth, so that if intelligent Martians existed they were likely to be more advanced than ourselves (➔ **Mars, life on**), whereas Venus, being a younger world, might support only primordial forms of life. The nebular hypothesis also implied, in sharp contrast with its great rival, the **catastrophic hypothesis,** that planets, and possibly life, around other stars might be common. In updated form, the nebular hypothesis has become the consensus model of planetary origin (➔ **planetary systems, formation of**).

neo-Darwinism

The modern version of Charles **Darwin**'s theory of evolution by **natural selection,** which incorporates genetic theory. It makes use of our current understanding of **gene**s and **chromosome**s to explain the source of the genetic variation upon which selection works. ➔ **evolution, theory of**

Neptune

Normally the eighth planet from the Sun, although **Pluto,** because of its elongated orbit, occasionally comes closer for periods of 20 years. Neptune is marginally the smallest of the **gas giant**s in the solar system, after **Uranus,** although its volume is still sixty times greater than that of the Earth. Its deep atmosphere, composed primarily of **hydrogen, helium,** and **methane,** overlies a layer of water and other melted ices, which in turn surrounds an approximately Earth-sized liquid core. Seasons on Neptune are extraordinarily long, the planet's north pole being bathed in continuous sunlight for 40 years during the northern summer, and the south pole enjoying a similar

Distance from Sun:	
Mean	4,488 million km (2,790 million mi., 30.1 AU)
Minimum	4,456 million km (2,769 million mi., 29.8 AU)
Maximum	4,537 million km (2,820 million mi., 30.3 AU)
Equatorial diameter	49,538 km (30,788 mi.)
Equatorial diameter (Earth = 1)	3.884
Mass (Earth = 1)	17.2
Mean density	1.7 g/cm^3
Escape velocity	23.9 km/s (86,040 km/h, 53,474 mi./h)
Orbital period	164.8 years
Orbital eccentricity	0.009
Orbital inclination	1.8°
Axial inclination	28.8°
Axial period	19.1 hours
Number of moons	8
Atmospheric composition	74% hydrogen, 24% helium, 2% methane
Mean temperature (cloud tops)	−220°C (−364°F)
Gravity at cloud tops (Earth = 1)	1.2
Albedo	0.35

exposure during the southern summer. Similar to the case of Uranus, the axis of Neptune's magnetic field is tilted 47 degrees away from the spin axis and offset from the planet's center by half a radius. Winds on the eighth planet, at up to 2,400 km per hour (1,500 miles per hour), are faster than anywhere else in the solar system. Neptune has four rings and eight known moons (→ **Neptune, moons of**), including **Triton.**

Neptune, moons of
See separate entries for each of the moons listed below.

Moon	Distance from Uranus (km)	Orbital Period (days)	Orbital Eccentricity	Orbital Inclination (°)	Diameter (km)
Naiad	47,900	0.294	0.0003	4.74	58
Thalassa	50,000	0.311	0.0002	0.21	80
Despina	52,400	0.335	0.0001	0.07	148
Galatea	61,900	0.429	0.0001	0.05	158
Larissa	73,500	0.555	0.0014	0.20	208 × 178
Proteus	118,000	1.122	0.0004	0.04	400
Triton	353,000	−5.877 (r)*	0.0000	157.35	2,700
Nereid	5,560,000	360.140	0.7512	27.60	340

* r = retrograde.

Nereid
The outermost moon of **Neptune** and the satellite with the most eccentric orbit of any in the solar system. Its surface is somewhat more reflective than that of our own moon and about twice as reflective as those of the six inner moons of Neptune. → **Neptune, moons of**

Discovery	1949, by Gerard Kuiper
Mean distance from Neptune	5,560,000 km (3,460,000 mi.)
Diameter	340 km (211 mi.)
Orbital period	360.14 days
Orbital eccentricity	0.7512
Orbital inclination	27.6°
Visual albedo	0.14

neural network
A network of densely interconnected processing elements that, like the brain, learns from experience rather than being rigidly programmed.

neutrino
A member of the lepton (lightweight) family of subatomic particles to which the **electron** also belongs. Neutrinos travel at the **speed of light** and have zero electric charge. Ghostlike in their ability to avoid interacting with matter, it has been estimated that neutrinos could pass through 100 light-years of solid lead with only a 50 percent chance of being absorbed. A vast number of them are produced every second in the cores of stars as a result of **proton**-to-**neutron** conversions—the hotter the core, the greater the proportion of total energy that neutrinos carry away. Neutrinos play an important role in the physics of **supernova**s.

neutrino communication
According to an idea proposed in 1994 by a group of physicists at the University of Hawaii at Manoa, advanced civilizations could be transmitting bursts of **neutrino**s across the Galaxy as timing pulses.[332] As a spokesman for the group pointed out:

> Accurate synchronized clocks are needed for a wide range of scientific measurements, particularly in astronomy. But any advanced civilization is bound to require standards that are more exacting.

Without some system of synchronization, clocks at different locations in the Galaxy would gradually drift out of step because of a **relativistic** effect that causes time to flow more slowly where the local gravitational field is more intense. To bring widely dispersed clocks regularly back into line with an extremely accurate galactic standard would mean exchanging timing signals at the limits allowed by physics, which is where neutrinos might come in. The fastest known process in (terrestrial) physics is the decay of a subatomic particle known as the Z^0 boson into a neutrino and an antineutrino. It takes just 10^{-21} seconds. Neutrinos also have the advantage that they are not blocked by material in space, such as **cosmic dust,** nor are they smeared out, or dispersed, by **ionized** gas. In addition, they can be produced with a higher luminosity than **electromagnetic radiation** can. The Hawaiian team suggested that neutrino pulses as narrow as 10^{-21} seconds could be sent across many thousands of light-years and be generated by a giant particle accelerator, about the size of the Earth, in which **electron**s and **positron**s were collided head-on. The Z^0 bosons produced by this device could be made in bursts synchronized by a master clock. If such interstellar neutrino signals are being transmitted, concluded the team, it might be possible to detect them using equipment such as DUMAND, the Deep Underwater Muon and Neutrino Detector, in the sea off Hawaii. Calculations showed that the detection of extraterrestrial neutrinos could be achieved with as little as 1 cubic km of seawater if there is a transmitter within about 3,000 light-years. Any artificial signals should be quite distinctive since the neutrinos would come from a single direction in the sky and have a very well defined energy.

neutron

An electrically neutral subatomic particle that, together with the **proton,** is found in the **nucleus** of **atom**s. It has a mass 1,838.65 times that of the **electron,** making it marginally more massive than the proton. In a free state the neutron is unstable with a half-life of about 12 minutes, decaying into a proton, an electron, and an anti-**neutrino.**

neutron spectrometer
→ *Lunar Prospector*

neutron star

One of the possible endpoints of stellar evolution (→ **stars, evolution of**). A neutron star, with a mass of 1.4 to 3 M_S, forms from the collapsing core of a massive star immediately following the star's exhaustion of its **fusion** energy reserves. With the outflow of radiation from the stellar core suddenly switched off, the core can no longer support the overlying layers against the inward force of gravity. The rapidly mounting pressure of the infalling layers squeezes the **electron**s and **proton**s of the core together to create **neutron**s and **neutrino**s. The neutrinos immediately escape into space but the neutrons crowd closer and closer together until they reach the density of an atomic **nucleus.** At this stage, if the compressed stellar core is less massive than about 3 M_S, the neutrons are able to resist further collapse. Otherwise, a **black hole** forms.

The star's collapsing middle layers rebound against the newly formed solid neutron core. This generates a shock wave that heats and blows off the surface layers as a **supernova** explosion. Left behind is a rapidly spinning neutron star that has a strong magnetic field with poles that are usually aligned with the poles of the star's rotation. Two oppositely directed beams of **radio waves** escape from the poles and sweep around like a lighthouse beam, producing a series of regular radio blips that can be detected from Earth. The result is a **pulsar.**

A neutron star is typically only about 20 km (12.5 miles) across, yet within this small region there may be more than 2 M_S of material. The result is a gravitational field at the surface of a neutron star about 70 billion times stronger than that on Earth. In structure, a neutron star more closely resembles a solid miniature planet than it does an ordinary star. Its core consists mainly of densely packed neutrons with a sprinkling of protons and an equal number of electrons, in a liquidlike state known as neutronium. Surrounding this is a mantle topped by a crust, perhaps 1 km thick, consisting of a stiff lattice of nuclei of the same elements as found on Earth through which flows a sea of electrons. The highest possible "mountains" (surface irregularities) rise to a height of about 5 mm (0.2 in.), while electrons and heavy nuclei evaporate in the surface temperature of 8,000°C to produce an "atmosphere" maybe a few micrometers thick. As a neutron star cools and shrinks, strains develop in the crust so that it buckles, causing **star-quake**s. Such events are marked by "glitches" in the otherwise remarkably steady periods of pulsars.

Life either on or in the vicinity of neutron stars may seem extremely unlikely. However, planets have been found around pulsars (➔ **pulsar planets**) and the possibility of life on a neutron star has been considered by Frank **Drake** and explored in fictional form by Robert L. **Forward** (➔ **neutron star, life on**).

neutron star, life on
An imaginative and tongue-in-cheek suggestion by the radio astronomer Frank **Drake**,[164] later developed and elaborated into two science fiction novels, ***Dragon's Egg*** and *Starquake!* by Robert **Forward.** In order to convey the idea that a **neutron star** was more like a planet than a normal star, Drake speculated that life might exist on its solid surface. The creatures he imagined were submicroscopic and made of tightly packed nuclei, rather than ordinary atoms, bound together as "nuclear molecules." Whether such bizarre molecules could exist and combine in ways complex enough to give rise to life is not known. However, if neutron star creatures did exist, they would live very rapidly. Nuclear reactions happen much faster than the chemical variety, so that any life-forms on a neutron star would evolve and live their lives a million times more quickly than human beings. ➔ **gravitational life**

neutronium
The densest possible kind of matter outside of a **black hole.** Neutronium, of which **neutron star**s are composed, consists entirely of **neutron**s packed closely together. In this state, the neutrons repel each by **degenerate neutron pressure.**

New Millennium Interferometer
Also known as *Deep Space 3*, this is the third mission in NASA's **New Millennium Program.** Its goal is to test the technologies and flight concepts needed to carry out space-based optical interferometry (➔ **interferometer**)—a technique of vital importance in future searches for Earth-sized **extrasolar planets** as part of the NASA's **Origins Program.** The *New Millennium Interferometer* will consist of two spacecraft capable of flying in formation to an accuracy of about 1 cm when separated by distances ranging from about 2 m to 1 km. Observations made by the spacecraft will be combined, so that the system will function as if it were a single giant telescope of extremely high resolving power. The *New Millennium Interferometer* will pave the way for more ambitious missions, including the **Space Interferometry Mission (SIM)**, the **Terrestrial Planet Finder (TPF)**, and the **Terrestrial Planet Imager (TPI)**.

New Millennium Program
A NASA program focused on the development and validation in space of advanced technologies that will be routinely used aboard unmanned spacecraft in the early part of the twenty-first century. Prototype scientific instruments, communications equipment, computer systems, and propulsion units will be tested during a series of actual space missions that will return data of relevance to understanding how the planets formed and life evolved. The first four missions in the program are **Deep Space 1,** the **Mars Microprobe Mission** (*Deep Space 2*), the **New Millennium Interferometer** (*Deep Space 3*), and **Champollion** (*Deep Space 4*).

New York Sun
➔ **"Moon Hoax"**

Newcomb, Simon (1835–1909)
Canadian-born American mathematical astronomer and one of the foremost exponents of celestial mechanics of his time who became superintendent of the Nautical Almanac Office in 1877. On the subject of other life and intelligence in the Universe, Newcomb was noncommittal, but he argued against the anthropocentric ideas of Alfred Russel **Wallace**

and was prepared to accept the possibility that Earth-like conditions may not be essential for the development of life. In the debate over the existence of the Martian canals (→ **Mars, canals of**), Newcomb made a significant contribution with his experiments involving artificial disks and his conclusion that any linear markings were probably optical illusions.

Newton, Isaac (1642–1727)

One of the most brilliant scientists of all time. Newton personally expressed almost no opinion on the question of whether life existed elsewhere in the Universe, preferring to consider it a theological rather than a physical issue. In the second edition of his *Philosophiae Naturalis Principia Mathematica* he writes:

> [I]f the fixed stars are the centres of other like systems, these, being formed by the like wise counsel, must be all subject to the dominion of the One.

Next Generation Sky Survey (NGSS)

A supercooled **infrared** space telescope designed to survey the entire sky with 1,000 times more sensitivity than previous missions. *NGSS* would result in the discovery of millions of new cosmic sources of infrared radiation including many **circumstellar disk**s, some of which are in the process of forming planetary systems. *NGSS,* which would be developed by a group at the University of California, Los Angeles, is among five mission proposals chosen by NASA as candidates for two medium-class *Explorer* (MIDEX) flights to be launched in 2003 and 2004.

Next Generation Space Telescope (NGST)

A large space-borne telescope of unprecedented sensitivity and **resolving power** that will carry out observations at wavelengths between those at the red end of the visible spectrum and the middle of the **infrared** range. Compared with the *Hubble Space Telescope,* its primary mirror will be about twice as large, it will be stationed much further from the Earth so that its equipment can remain cold and free from terrestrial infrared "noise," and it will operate at longer wavelengths. The *NGST* will

provide a vast amount of new information on the structure of **circumstellar disk**s around young stars, including high-resolution images showing details, such as gaps, which may indicate the presence of newly formed planets. It will also be capable of detecting the presence of **extrasolar planets** directly due to their infrared emission.[16] This is because planets are brighter relative to their central stars in the infrared part of the spectrum than they are at visible wavelengths. For example, Jupiter is one hundred millionth the brightness of the Sun in the optical region but only one ten-thousandth in the infrared. The *NGST* is expected to be launched in about 2007.

NGSS

→ *Next Generation Sky Survey*

NGST

→ *Next Generation Space Telescope*

NICAP

→ **National Investigations Committee on Aerial Phenomena**

niche

The role played by a particular species in its environment. An organism's niche is defined by factors such as its nutritional requirements, predators, and environmental tolerances. Two species cannot coexist stably if they have the same niche.

Nicholas of Cusa (1401–64) (Nikolaus Krebs)

Theologian who in his *De docta ignorantia* endorsed the idea of other inhabited worlds:

> Life, as it exists on Earth, in the form of men, animals and plants, is to be found, let us suppose, in a higher form in the solar and stellar regions.... Of the inhabitants then of worlds other than our own we can know less, having no standards by which to appraise them. It may be conjectured that in the Sun there exist solar beings, bright and enlightened denizens, and by nature, more spiritual than such as may inhabit the Moon—who are possibly lunatics.

He therefore went much further than those scholastics of the thirteenth and fourteenth centuries, including William of **Ockham,** Jean **Buridan,** and William **Vorilong,** who merely asserted that it would have been *possible* for God to have created other worlds should he have chosen to do so. Considering the fate of another medieval cleric, Giordano **Bruno,** who expounded **pluralism,** it might be assumed that Nicholas would have seriously upset the Church with his views. In fact, however, he went on to become a Catholic cardinal. → **medieval philosophy, related to the possibility of extraterrestrial life**

nitriles

Also known as cyanides; **organic** compounds containing the cyanogen group (CN). Nitriles are important precursors of **amino acids.**

nitrogen

A colorless, gaseous element; the most abundant gas in the Earth's atmosphere (78 percent by volume). Nitrogen is of central importance in the formation of **amino acids,** which are themselves essential components of **proteins** and **nucleic acid**s. As an element, nitrogen is not particularly reactive because of its great affinity for itself. Nitrogen molecules are composed of two nitrogen atoms, linked by a triple bond that is difficult to break. However, the nitrogen in the atmosphere can be converted without the expenditure of too much energy into **ammonia,** which is the source of nitrogen in biological compounds.

Atomic number 7; density 1.25 g/dm^3; melting point $-209.9°C$; boiling point $-195.8°C$

Niven, Larry (1938–)

American science fiction writer (Laurence van Cott Niven) whose novels are populated by a well-integrated variety of anatomically and neurologically diverse aliens from his *Known Space* stable, including tripedal Pierson's puppeteers; Outsiders, exposed to space in skeletal "spaceships"; and the racially paranoid Trinocs. Among his best-known works is *Ringworld*[422] (1970).

nocturnal light

One of the six categories of **unidentified flying object** in the classification scheme devised by J. Allen **Hynek** in the 1950s. Defined as any light or lights in the night sky that cannot be explained in terms of aircraft, astronomical objects, or any other familiar luminous source.

noncorporeal life

Hypothetical life that exists without material bodies. The idea has been extensively explored in science fiction (*Childhood's End*) but, from the viewpoint of science itself, the concept of life based on "pure energy," such as **electromagnetic radiation,** poses significant difficulties. A being made only of **photon**s, for example, could not move slower than the **speed of light** and would essentially exist outside of the normal time stream of the rest of the universe. **Artificial life** represents a possible alternative form of noncorporeal life with a basis in information.

nova

A star that suddenly and dramatically brightens before returning to its prenova state. Novas have been broadly classified into "slow" and "fast" types. An example of the former was Nova Herculis, first observed in 1934, which took 40 years to return to its original brightness. By contrast, Nova Persei 1901 was a classic case of the fast type, fading rapidly for 20 days, then declining more gradually over a period of 10 years to its prenova condition. All novas appear to be components of **binary star** systems and any theory to account for them must be built around this fact.

NRAO
→ **National Radio Astronomy Observatory**

NRAO Green Bank
→ **Green Bank**

NSCORT/Exobiology

NASA Specialized Center of Research and Training in Exobiology. A consortium of the University of California, San Diego, the Scripps Research Institute, and the Salk Institute to conduct research and train future researchers in this field.

nuclear fission
→ **fission (nuclear)**

nuclear fusion
→ **fusion (nuclear)**

nucleic acid
A long chain, or **polymer,** of **nucleotide**s. The two found in **cell**s are **DNA** (deoxyribonucleic acid), which is double-stranded, and **RNA** (ribonucleic acid), which is single-stranded.

nucleolus
The site of **ribosomal RNA** (rRNA) synthesis in **eukaryote**s. The nucleolus is spherical in shape and made up principally of rRNA that is in the process of being transcribed (→ **transcription**) from rRNA **gene**s. It is surrounded by the nuclear membrane.

nucleon
The generic name for a **neutron** or **proton.** Both particles are found in the **nucleus** of **atom**s and are bound together by the strong force. Protons and neutrons, along with many other subatomic particles that were once thought to be elementary (that is, not built up from smaller constituents), are now known to be composed of quarks—three quarks to each nucleon.

nucleoside
A **deoxyribose** or **ribose** sugar molecule to which a **purine** or **pyrimidine** is covalently bound.

nucleosynthesis
The formation of **element**s heavier than **hydrogen** and **helium** by means of nuclear **fusion** reactions in the interior of stars or in **supernova** explosions. As a star evolves, a contracting superdense core of helium is produced from the conversion of hydrogen nuclei into helium nuclei. Eventually, the temperature and pressure inside the core become high enough for helium to begin fusing into **carbon.** If the star has more than about twice the Sun's mass, a sequence of nuclear reactions then produces heavier elements such as oxygen, silicon, magnesium, potassium, and iron.

nucleotide
A **nucleoside** to which a **phosphate** group is attached at the 5′ position on the sugar. Nucleotides are the chemical building blocks of **nucleic acid**s.

nucleus (atomic)
The center of an **atom,** around which orbits a cloud of **electron**s. It consists of **proton**s and **neutron**s bound together by the strong force. Under the right conditions, nuclei may undergo nuclear **fission** or **fusion,** with the release of large amounts of energy.

nucleus (cell)
The membrane-bounded **organelle** that, in **eukaryotic cell**s, houses the chromosomal **DNA.**

nucleus (cometary)
The central and relatively small part of a comet. It is often described as a "dirty snowball" since it is made up of about 75 percent ice (including frozen water, ammonia, and carbon dioxide) and about 25 percent dust and rock.

nucleus, galactic
→ **galactic nucleus**

Nuffield Radio Astronomy Laboratory
→ **Jodrell Bank**

nulling interferometry
A starlight-shading technique first proposed by Ronald **Bracewell** and R. H. MacPhie in 1978. It can be used to search the region immediately around a star for **extrasolar planets** and circumstellar dust clouds by suppressing the star's glare. In a two-mirror interferometer, light is collected from the star and then combined using a system of secondary optics so that the light from one mirror is exactly half a wavelength out of step with the light from the other at the pointing center of the instrument. This causes the starlight to cancel out. However, light coming from objects near the star experiences a delay that is not half a wavelength and so is not suppressed. Nulling interferometry was pioneered at the **Center for**

Astronomical Adaptive Optics by Roger Angel and Neville Woolf and was applied by Philip Hinz and colleagues, using the **Astronomical Nulling Interferometer,** to provide the first direct view of the dust cloud around **Betelgeuse.** The same technique will be used with the **Large Binocular Telescope** to image Jupiter-size planets close to nearby stars and, in space, with NASA's *Terrestrial Planet Finder* and the **European Space Agency**'s *Infrared Space Interferometer* in an attempt to image extrasolar planets as small as the Earth.

O

O star

An extremely luminous blue star of **spectral type** O with a surface temperature of 30,000 to more than 50,000°C and a mass of 20 to about 100 M$_S$. The spectrum features **emission lines** of **ionized helium, oxygen,** and **nitrogen.** O stars have such short **main sequence** lifetimes, of typically a few million years, that there appears no chance that even the simplest form of life would be able to evolve on any associated planets. Examples include two of the stars in **Orion's Belt,** Alnitak and Mintaka.

Oak Ridge Observatory

A facility in Harvard, Massachusetts, operated by the Smithsonian Astrophysical Observatory, part of the **Harvard-Smithsonian Center for Astrophysics.** Among its principal instruments is a 26-m (84-ft.) steerable **radio telescope,** currently being used in Project **BETA.**

oases

A term introduced by Percival **Lowell** in 1895 to describe dark, round features on the surface of Mars that he claimed lay at the major intersections of a Martian canal network. These features had been referred to as "lakes" by William Henry **Pickering** in 1892. Lowell, however, believed they were extensive regions of vegetation irrigated by canal-borne polar meltwater. They were an important feature of his theory concerning an extant Martian civilization. ➔ **Mars, canals on**

OB association

A loose grouping of 10 to 100 **O star**s and **B star**s scattered across a region up to several hundred light-years across. The members of an OB association formed from the same **interstellar cloud** within the past few million years. ➔ **T association**s

OB stars

The collective name for **O star**s and **B stars.** These have similar properties and frequently occur together in space. ➔ **OB association**s

Oberon

The second largest and most remote moon of **Uranus.** Oberon shows less evidence of tectonic activity than does its neighbor **Titania** and differs also in that some of its major craters contain dark material. This may be a mixture of carbonaceous substances and ice

Discovery	1787, by William Herschel
Mean distance from Uranus	586,300 km (364,400 mi.)
Diameter	1,523 km (947 mi.)
Mean density	1.64 g/cm³
Escape velocity	0.729 km/s (2,624 km/h, 1,631 mi./h)
Orbital period	13.463 days (13 days 11 hours)
Orbital eccentricity	0.0008
Orbital inclination	0.10°
Axial period	13.463 days
Visual albedo	0.24

erupted from the interior. **→ Uranus, moons of**

Oberth, Hermann (1894–1989)

The father of German rocketry who began to consider the physics behind a possible lunar spacecraft after reading Jules **Verne**'s classic Moon adventure. Oberth later formed the opinion that **unidentified flying objects** were "definitely interplanetary vehicles."

Observatoire de Haute-Provence

→ Haute-Provence Observatory

occultation

An event in which one astronomical object passes in front of another.

occultation/transit photometry

→ photometry

oceans, origin of

Some of the water in the Earth's oceans came from condensation following the **outgassing** of water vapor from the surface of the planet, while some was delivered by impacting **comet**s. An important question in recent years has been the relative importance of these two sources. According to one school of thought, comets may have supplied the bulk of oceanic water during the heavy bombardment phase of the solar system, between about 4.5 and 3.8 billion years ago. If this is true, it increases the chances that **organic** matter, which is also found in comets, plays an important part in the origin of life generally. However, a study carried out by

scientists at the California Institute of Technology, the results of which were published in March 1999,[62] suggests that most of Earth's water probably did not have a cometary origin. Using Caltech's Owens Valley Radio Observatory (OVRO) Millimeter Array, cosmochemist Geoff Blake and his team found that Comet Hale-Bopp contains substantial amounts of **heavy water,** which is rich in the hydrogen isotope **deuterium.** If Hale-Bopp is typical in this respect and if cometary collisions were a major source of terrestrial oceans, it suggests that Earth's ocean water should be similarly rich in deuterium, whereas in fact it is not.

Ockham (Occam), William of (c. 1280–c. 1347)

Famous fourteenth-century intellectual, of Ockham's Razor fame, who joined the Franciscan order and studied at Oxford, where he was a contemporary of Jean **Buridan,** and Paris. He went further than Buridan in modifying **Aristotle**'s doctrine of natural place by arguing that the elements in each world would return to their natural place within their own world, without any intervention by God. Although he began by supporting **pluralism,** he later became a strong opponent of the idea, citing the view that neither other worlds nor the creation of man elsewhere were mentioned in the Scriptures. **→ medieval philosophy, related to the possibility of extraterrestrial life**

OGLE

→ Optical Gravitational Lensing Experiment

OH radical

→ hydroxyl radical

Ohio SETI Program

The longest-running **SETI** program conducted so far. It began on December 7, 1973, using the **Big Ear** of **Ohio State University Radio Observatory,** and ended in 1998 with the demolition of that instrument. It was initiated following a suggestion made by Robert **Dixon** to the observatory director, John **Kraus.** A number of candidate signals were detected but never confirmed during the course of the program, including the now-famous **Wow! signal.**

Ohio State University Radio Observatory

A facility until recently sited near Delaware, Ohio, and centered around the **Big Ear** telescope used in the **Ohio SETI Program.** The OSU Radio Observatory has now been relocated to the west campus of the university, where it shares a site with the Electroscience Laboratory. It is currently engaged in construction of the **Argus radio telescope.** The observatory's long-standing director is John **Kraus.**

Olbers, Heinrich Wilhelm Matthäus (1758–1840)

German doctor and skilled amateur astronomer who supported **pluralism** and the increasingly contentious idea that the Moon was inhabited by intelligent beings (→ **Moon, life on**). In the same 1823 paper in which he presents his famous paradox (Why is the night sky dark if the Universe is endless and full of stars?), he wrote that it is "most highly probable" that "all of infinite space is filled with suns and their retinues of planets and comets."

Oliver, Bernard "Barney" M. (1916–95)

For many years, vice president for research and development at the Hewlett-Packard Corporation and a leading advocate of **SETI.** Oliver was among the early pioneers to consider in detail the problems of interstellar communication and attended the seminal **Green Bank conference (1961).** Together with John **Billingham,** he developed the proposal for Project **Cyclops,** and subsequently he became chief of NASA's SETI program in the 1980s, managing the joint teams involved in the **High Resolution Microwave Survey** at the **NASA Ames Research Center** and the **Jet Propulsion Laboratory.** Oliver received a B.A. in electrical engineering from Stanford University (1935) and a Ph.D. from the California Institute of Technology (1940). He joined Hewlett-Packard in 1952 and served as head of R and D there for 25 years. He was also adjunct professor in the Astronomy Department at the **University of California, Berkeley.**

olivine

A magnesium iron silicate found in **carbonaceous chondrite**s.

Omega Centauri

At a distance of 20,000 light-years, the **globular cluster** nearest to the Sun.

omnidirectional antenna

A radio **antenna** capable of transmitting and/or receiving radio signals from all directions of the sky that are visible from its location, simultaneously. Omnidirectional *receiving* antennas will be used in the next generation of instruments used for **SETI** and the study of short-duration or fast-changing natural sources. These revolutionary new instruments will include the **Argus radio telescope,** the **One Hectare Telescope,** and the **Square Kilometer Array.** Omnidirectional *transmitting* antennas, if intended for communications with other technological civilizations in space, would require immense power to produce detectable signals at interstellar distances (→ **beacon, interstellar**).

omnidirectional signal
→ **isotropic signal**

One Hectare Telescope (1HT)

A planned array of 500 to 1,000 **radio telescope**s with a total collecting area of 10,000 square m, or 1 hectare (2.47 acres), that will be used extensively for **SETI** in parallel with other astronomy. The telescopes will consist of commercial satellite dishes fitted with sensitive but inexpensive, purpose-built receivers, enabling a high-performance instrument to be constructed at a fraction of the cost of a single large dish and receiver. The useful frequency range will be from less than 1 GHz to between 10 and 25 GHz. When completed, the $25 million 1HT will be the world's largest observatory facility devoted substantially to the search for intelligent signals from space. Its probable location will be the **Hat Creek Observatory** of the **University of California, Berkeley,** near Mount Lassen in northern California.

O'Neill, Gerard Kitchen (1927–1992)

American physicist at the Institute for Advanced Studies in Princeton, New Jersey, who in 1969 began to work out a strategy for the future expansion of the human race into space. He championed the idea of orbital settlements in several papers[427] and his book *The High Frontier*.[428]

ontogeny

The developmental course of an organism from fertilized egg through to maturity.

Oort Cloud

A vast reservoir of **ice dwarf**s that marks the material outer limit of the solar system and the maximum extent of the Sun's gravitational influence. Studies of the orbits of **long-period comet**s, which are believed to originate in the Oort Cloud, suggest that the cloud extends out from a heliocentric distance of about 20,000 to 100,000 AU, with a peak density of objects at 44,000 AU from the Sun. A variety of gravitational influences are thought to play a part in perturbing Oort Cloud objects so that their new orbits carry them into the inner solar system. These include passing stars, giant **molecular cloud**s,[85] and tidal forces due to the **galactic bulge** of the Milky Way.[79, 384] A star that approaches the Sun to within roughly the distance of the Oort Cloud might increase the rate of comet passages near the Earth by a factor of 300 for 2 to 3 million years, thus greatly increasing the risk of a catastrophic impact. Measurements of the accumulation in ocean sediments of interplanetary dust, most of which is thought to come from comets, suggest a sharp rise in the incidence of comets at the end of the Eocene epoch, about 36 million years ago. The discovery of several impact craters dating from this time and the occurrence of a moderate biological extinction in the late Eocene may be no coincidence. Several comet strikes may have been to blame. It is interesting to speculate how much the direction of evolution on Earth, as well as that on other life-bearing worlds in space, has been influenced indirectly by the random motion of stars.

The origin of the Oort Cloud is another unresolved problem. It seems clear that the Oort objects could not have formed in their present locations because the material at those distances would have been too sparse to condense. The only solution that makes sense is that these icy bodies coalesced in the vicinity of Jupiter, Saturn, Uranus, and Neptune and were subsequently hurled into the Oort Cloud by **gravity assist**s from the giant planets. If it were the case that the Oort Cloud comets originated at a wide range of distances, from the orbit of Jupiter to that of Neptune, and therefore at a wide range of ambient temperatures, this would explain the differences in composition observed in long-period comets. Recent work suggests that the Oort Cloud may even contain a small percentage of **asteroid**s, made of rock rather than predominantly of ice.[619] **→ Kuiper Belt; planetary systems, formation of**

Oort Limit

The outer boundary of the **Oort Cloud** and the furthest frontier of the Sun's domain. It is thought to lie at a heliocentric distance of about 100,000 AU (15 trillion km; 9 trillion miles), or more than one third of the distance to the nearest star.

Oparin, Aleksandr Ivanovich (1894–1980)

Russian biochemist who, in 1924, wrote a pamphlet on the origin of life (based on ideas presented at the Russian Botanical Society in 1922) and provided what J. D. **Bernal** called "the first and principal modern appreciation of the problem" (**→ life, origin of**). His writings reached the West, however, only in the late 1930s.[429]

Although Oparin began by reviewing the various **panspermia** theories, he was primarily interested in how life initially began. He asserted:

> There is no fundamental difference between a living organism and lifeless matter. The complex combination of manifestations and properties so characteristic of life must have arisen in the process of the evolution of matter.

But what was that process? Taking into account the recent discovery of **methane** in the atmospheres of Jupiter and the other giant planets, Oparin postulated that the infant Earth had possessed a strongly **reducing atmosphere,** containing methane, **ammonia, hydrogen,** and water vapor. In his opinion, these were the raw materials for the evolution of life:

At first there were the simple solutions of organic substances, the behavior of which was governed by the properties of their component atoms and the arrangement of those atoms in the molecular structure. But gradually, as the result of growth and increased complexity of the molecules, new properties have come into being and a new colloidal-chemical order was imposed on the more simple organic chemical relations. These newer properties were determined by the spatial arrangement and mutual relationship of the molecules.... In this process biological orderliness already comes into prominence. Competition, speed of growth, struggle for existence and, finally, natural selection determined such a form of material organization which is characteristic of living things of the present time.

Oparin outlined a way in which basic **organic** chemicals might form into microscopic localized systems—possible precursors of **cell**s—from which primitive living things could develop. He cited the work done by H. E. de **Jong** on **coacervates** and other experimental studies, including his own, into organic chemicals that, in solution, may spontaneously form droplets and layers. Oparin suggested that different types of coacervates might have formed in the Earth's primordial ocean and subsequently been subject to a selection process eventually leading to life. ➔ **Haldane, J. B. S.; Oparin-Haldane Theory**

Oparin-Haldane Theory

Working independently, in the 1920s, Aleksandr **Oparin** and J. B. S. **Haldane** proposed similar theoretical schemes for how life may have originated on Earth (➔ **life, origin of**). Hence, the term "Oparin-Haldane Theory" is sometimes used when referring to their views. The main similarities and differences between Oparin's and Haldane's suggestions are summarized below.

open cluster

A loose association of some 100 to 2,000 stars that have formed together in the fairly recent past and are destined to drift apart as the cluster slowly disintegrates. Open clusters are found in the disks of **spiral galaxies,** where star formation takes place, and so are sometimes referred to as "galactic" clusters.

Ophelia

The second known moon of **Uranus.** Ophelia acts as the outer **shepherd moon** for Uranus's epsilon ring. ➔ **Uranus, moons of**

Discovery	1986, by *Voyager 2*
Mean distance from Uranus	53,300 km (33,100 mi.)
Diameter	32 km (20 mi.)
Orbital period	0.376 days (9 hours 1 minute)
Orbital eccentricity	0.001
Orbital inclination	0.00°
Axial period	Unknown
Visual albedo	0.07

Öpik, Ernst Julius (1893–1985)

Estonian-born astronomer who, in 1950, put forward arguments for the existence of heavy cratering (later substantiated by the *Mariner* probes) and vegetation on Mars. Referring to the yellowish clouds that occasionally appeared to move across the surface and settle on

	Oparin	*Haldane*
Primitive atmosphere	Reducing, composed of methane, ammonia, hydrogen, and water vapor	Reducing, composed of carbon dioxide, ammonia, and water vapor
Source of carbon for life	Methane	Carbon dioxide
Site of prebiotic evolution	Atmosphere, then oceans	Atmosphere, then oceans
Mechanism	Spontaneous appearance of coacervates followed by evolution to cell-like state	Synthesis of increasingly complex organic molecules in presence of ultraviolet light

the dark regions, he suggested that the dark shading tended to reassert itself after a couple of weeks because the lighter dust had been shaken off or overgrown by plants. William **Sinton**'s citing of this idea at a symposium of the National Academy of Sciences drew the dry response from Harold **Urey** that he saw no reason why extraterrestrial plants should not have muscles and be able to dust themselves off. Öpik's lifelong interest in minor planets was rewarded by the naming of an asteroid after him. He wrote numerous articles, many of which were published in the *Irish Astronomical Journal*, on subjects ranging from life and intelligence in the Universe[430, 431, 433] to the possibility of interstellar travel.[432, 434] He was the first, in 1915, to compute the density of a **degenerate star** (the **white dwarf** 40 Eridani B) and the first, in 1922, to determine accurately the distance of an extragalactic object (the **Andromeda Galaxy**). Öpik was educated at Moscow Imperial University and after four years at Moscow Observatory became director of the Astronomy Department at Tashkent. From 1921 to 1944 he was associate professor at Tartu University, and from 1930 to 1934 a visiting scientist at Harvard. A former volunteer in the White Russian Army, he vehemently opposed the Bolshevik Revolution and, when the Soviet occupation of Estonia was imminent, moved first to Hamburg and then, in 1948, to Armagh Observatory in Northern Ireland, where he remained until 1981.

opinion polls, about extraterrestrials

A 1997 *Time*/Yankelovich poll revealed that one third of Americans are convinced that intelligent beings from other worlds have visited the Earth. Of these, nearly two thirds believe an alien spacecraft came down near Roswell (➔ **Roswell Incident**) and four fifths believe the U.S. government is not telling all that it knows about UFOs. In a 1998 poll conducted by the Marist Institute for the **Planetary Society,** 60 percent of those interviewed thought that there was intelligent life on other planets and of these, 47 percent thought that intelligence elsewhere would be more advanced than us (➔ **extraterrestrial intelligence, more advanced than we**), 40 percent thought it would be at about the same level, and only 13 percent

thought it would be less advanced. To the question "Do you think life on other planets is friendly or hostile?," 86 percent thought it would be friendly and 14 percent hostile (➔ **intelligence, nature of**).

opposition

The time when an outer planet or the Moon is located 180 degrees away from the Sun as seen from the Earth. It is then at its closest to us and in the best position for observing. The Moon is in opposition when it is full. ➔ **Mars, oppositions of**

Optical Gravitational Lensing Experiment (OGLE)

A search for **MACHOs** being conducted by a joint Polish and American team of astronomers, using a **charge-coupled device** on the 1-m (3.3-ft.) telescope at the **Las Campanas Observatory.** The team is headed by Bohdan Paczynski of Princeton University.

optical interferometer

An instrument that combines two separate light beams from the same object to form an interference pattern.

optical SETI

The search for pulsed and continuous wave **laser** beacon signals from intelligent extraterrestrials in the visible and **infrared** part of the spectrum. The idea was first suggested in 1961,[523] only a year after the Nobel Prize–winning invention of the **maser** by Charles H. **Townes** and Arthur L. Schalow but received little attention at the time because radio technology was in a much more mature state.[425] Indeed, over the past few decades there have been many large-scale **SETI** programs aimed at detecting artificial microwave signals (➔ **microwave radiation**) but only a handful designed to operate in the visible/infrared region. That situation is now changing as a result both of the rapid development of laser technology and the realization by astronomers that optical communication over interstellar distances makes good, practical sense.

As an alternative to radio waves for sending messages to the stars, lasers offer a number of advantages. They are not produced as "noise" by natural processes and are highly distinctive. Quasars, pulsars, and black holes were all found or confirmed because of their unique radiation characteristics, not because of their resemblance to ordinary stars. So it may be that a civilization wanting to send a message would choose an "unnatural" wavelength or technology to achieve maximum contrast to the natural environment (an argument directly counter to that used in support of **21-centimeter line** SETI). Lasers also have the advantage that they can be aimed accurately at a target, thereby enabling the best use of the transmitted energy. A well-designed laser would be very bright, with a high **signal-to-noise ratio.** Optical communication, enabling five times as much information to be carried, would be the logical choice for an advanced civilization, argued Russian astronomer Viktory Shvartsman. A search for such signals, begun in 1989, was carried out using the BTA-6 optical telescope (then the world's largest) of the Soviet Union's Special Astrophysical Observatory in the Caucasus, linked to a computer and another instrument, known as **MANIA.** The wide **bandwidth** available at optical frequencies could be exploited for sending complex, information-rich signals. This could even include, suggested John Rather of the Kaman Aerospace Corporation, the genetic code for a human being (➔ **genome, interstellar transmission of**).

Many of the most recent developments in optical SETI stemmed from the discussions of the 1998 SETI Science and Technology Working Group, sponsored by the SETI Institute. In the wake of this, the **Planetary Society** and the **SETI Institute** funded projects at the **University of California, Berkeley** (➔ **optical SETI at Berkeley**) and Harvard University (➔ **optical SETI at Harvard/Smithsonian**) to search for laser signals coming from nearby Sun-like stars, as well as from **globular clusters** and external galaxies. A separate search is under way at the **Columbus Optical SETI Observatory.**

optical SETI at Berkeley

Two **optical SETI** programs are currently in progress at the **University of California, Berkeley,** both supported by funds from the **SETI Institute** and the **Planetary Society.** The first is a search, directed by Geoffrey **Marcy,** for **laser** signals that are on continuously or at least a significant fraction of the time. It involves looking for ultra-**narrowband** visible signals in the radiation from 1,000 nearby Sun-like stars. Much of the data has already been obtained by Marcy and Paul **Butler** and their colleagues as a result of the **San Francisco State University Planet Search** and its Southern Hemisphere counterpart, the **Anglo-Australian Telescope Planet Search.** Further data will come from observations at the **Lick Observatory, Keck Observatory,** and **Anglo-Australian Observatory.**

The second search involves observing 2,500 objects for pulsed laser signals that might last only a billionth of a second or so. On the target list are nearby **FGK stars,** some **M star**s, and a few **globular cluster**s and external galaxies. Directed by Daniel Wertheimer, this project uses a 76-cm (30-in.) automated telescope at the **Leuschner Observatory** equipped with an instrument built for optical SETI in 1997.

optical SETI at Harvard/Smithsonian

An **optical SETI** program, funded by the **SETI Institute** and the **Planetary Society** and based at Harvard University and the **Oak Ridge Observatory,** that is currently searching for artificial pulsed **laser** signals that might be coming from nearby Sun-like stars. The project uses a relatively simple, high-speed optical detector attached to Harvard's 15-cm (6-in.) optical telescope, which is engaged in a continuing **radial velocity** survey of 2,500 solar-type stars conducted by David Latham and Robert Stefanik. The optical SETI "piggybacks" on this experiment, using about 25 percent of the light that is not used in the survey work.

orbit

A curved path followed by an object under the gravitational influence of another body. It is one of the **conic section** family of curves, including the circle, the **ellipse,** the **parabola,** and the **hyperbola.**

orbital period

The time taken for a body to go once around a closed orbit. The orbital period of a planet is its "year."

Note

For a body that is in an elliptical orbit of semimajor axis a, about a much more massive body of radius R, the orbital period P, is given by

$$P = 2\pi a^{3/2}\sqrt{(gR^2)}$$

orbital rotation

The movement of an object around its **primary.**

Order of the Dolphin

→ **Green Bank conference (1961)**

Oresme, Nicole d' (c. 1325–1382)

Paris prelate and bishop of Lisieux who reformulated **Aristotle**'s doctrine of natural place in a way that allowed for the possibility of other worlds. He taught that the doctrine was valid providing only that heavy bodies were located more centrally than light ones. Since there could be many centers, there could, in principle, be many different systems of worlds. However, almost all medieval scholastics stressed that God had in fact created only one world. → **medieval philosophy, related to the possibility of extraterrestrial life**

organelle

A specialized part of a **cell,** such as the **nucleus** or **mitochondria.** It is, literally, a small **cytoplasmic** organ analogous to the organs of **multicellular** animals.

organic

A term first applied by Jöns **Berzelius** to compounds, such as **sugars** and alcohols, that occur naturally in plant and animal "organisms." At the time, there was considered to be a fundamental difference between organic and **inorganic** materials. In modern parlance, organic refers to the chemistry of **carbon,** with the exception of a few simple carbon compounds.

organic matter, in meteorites

A series of eminent chemists, including Jöns **Berzelius,** Friedrich **Wöhler,** and Marcelin **Berthelot,** first identified the presence of organic materials in **carbonaceous chondrites** in the mid–nineteenth century. Wöhler's premature declaration that the substances he had identified were the products of extraterrestrial life seemed to be confirmed by the analysis by S. Cloëz of samples from the **Orgueil meteorite** that revealed the presence of substances analogous to lignite. However, hopes of discovering actual living matter in meteorites were dashed by the experiments of Louis **Pasteur** and later scientists that found no evidence of extant microorganisms. More recently, the possibility has been raised of there being microfossils inside several meteorites, including the **Orgueil** meteorite, the **Ivuna** meteorite, and **ALH 84001,** though these claims are strongly disputed.

Orgel, Leslie E. (1927–)

London-born senior fellow and research professor at the Salk Institute for Biological Studies, San Diego, whose research has focused on the chemical evolution of life. Orgel, together with Carl **Woese** and Francis **Crick,** was among the original group of scientists in the 1960s to suggest that **RNA** rather than **DNA** acted as the first replicative molecule, and continues to explore possible modes of protobiological evolution within the **"RNA world"** scenario today. In 1973, he and Crick put forward the remarkable idea of **directed panspermia.**[132] Orgel was a member of the *Viking* molecular analysis team and in 1998 chaired the Task Group on Sample Return from Small Solar System Bodies, a committee convened to make recommendations for protocols to avoid **back contamination.** After earning a B.A. (1949) and Ph.D. (1951) in chemistry from Oxford, Orgel became a reader in chemistry at Cambridge and subsequently the assistant director of research at Cambridge's Theoretical Chemistry Department (1955–63). Since 1964, he has been at the Salk Institute and has also served as adjunct professor at the University of California, San Diego.

Orgueil meteorite

A large **carbonaceous chondrite** that disintegrated and fell in fragments near the French town of Orgueil on May 14, 1864. About twenty pieces, totaling about 12 kg in mass, were subsequently recovered from an area of several square kilometers, some head-sized but most smaller than a fist. Specimens could be cut with a knife and, when sharpened, could be used like a pencil. One specimen was immediately examined by the French scientist S. Cloëz, who commented that its content "would seem to indicate the existence of organized substances in celestial bodies." Subsequently, several eminent chemists of the time, including Gabriel-Auguste Dubrée, Marcelin **Berthelot,** and Jöns **Berzelius,** analyzed samples and confirmed the existence of **organic** materials in the rock. Coming at the same time as Louis **Pasteur**'s famous announcement that he had experimentally disproven the theory of **spontaneous generation** on Earth, these findings prompted a scientific debate about whether such generation might be possible in space. Pasteur himself examined the Orgeuil meteorite, as recounted by Carl **Sagan:**

> [He] caused a special drill to be constructed, which, he hoped, would remove samples from the interior of the meteorite without contaminating them with microorganisms from outside. Using sterile techniques, Pasteur inoculated an organic medium to search for growth of any indigenous microorganisms which the meteorite interior might contain. The results were negative, and have relevance today: Pasteur extracted his sample shortly after the fall of the meteorite, and was, of course, a very careful experimentalist.

The possibility of biological remains in the Orgeuil stone resurfaced, however, a century later. At a meeting of the New York Academy of Sciences in March 1961, Bartholomew Nagy and Douglas J. Hennessy of the Department of Chemistry at Fordham University's Graduate School of Arts and Sciences in the Bronx, and Warren G. Meinschein, a petroleum chemist at the Esso Research and Engineering Company in Linden, New Jersey, announced that they had found in a sample of the meteorite "paraffinoid hydrocarbons" similar in type and distribution to those occurring in animal products such as butter.[417] From this, they concluded that "biogenic processes occur and that living forms exist in regions of the universe beyond the earth." More remarkably, Nagy and

George Claus, a microbiologist at New York University Medical Center, claimed shortly afterward that samples from the Orgeuil and **Ivuna meteorite**s contained "organized elements," including structures "resembling fossil algae."[119] A controversy ensued in which a minority of scientists, including J. D. **Bernal,** supported the microfossil theory, while most, including Philip **Morrison** and Harold **Urey,** were skeptical. Urey did, however, concede that it was possible the Orgeuil and Ivuna microstructures were evidence for biogenic activity and that, if so, these meteorites may have come from the Moon, which had become "contaminated temporarily with water and life-forms from Earth early in its history."[598] By 1975, Nagy himself had come to regard the biological interpretation as a "remote possibility." ➔ **organic matter, in meteorites**

Origins Program

A NASA initiative designed to explore, through a series of space projects over the first two decades of the twenty-first century, the origin and evolution of life, from the Big Bang to the present day. Included in this investigation are the formation of chemical elements, galaxies, stars, and planets, the formation and development of life on Earth, and the quest for **extrasolar planets** and extraterrestrial life. Missions associated with the Origins Program fall chronologically into four groups. Precursor missions, all scheduled to be operational by 2001, include the **Hubble Space Telescope,** the *Far Ultraviolet Spectroscopic Explorer* (*FUSE*), the *Wide Field Infrared Explorer* (*WIRE*), the *Stratospheric Observatory for Far Infrared Astronomy* (*SOFIA*), and the *Space Infrared Telescope Facility* (*SIRTF*). Following these will be the first-generation missions employing either large, lightweight optics or collections of small telescopes working in harness to provide images equivalent to those obtainable with a single, much larger instrument. They include the **Space Interferometry Mission** (*SIM*) and the **Next Generation Space Telescope** (*NGST*). Prior to *SIM*, a preliminary mission known as the **New Millennium Interferometer,** or *Deep Space 3* (*DS3*), will be launched to prove the technology of space-based interferometry (➔ **interferometer**). The first-generation missions will serve as technological stepping-stones to the second-generation missions, including the **Terrestrial Planet Finder** (*TPF*), and the third-generation missions, including the **Terrestrial Planet Imager** (*PI*).

Orion Arm

The **spiral arm** of the **Milky Way Galaxy** close to the inner edge of which the Sun is located. Its name derives from the fact that the stars closest to the Sun that actually lie within the arm are in the constellation of Orion, about 2,000 light-years away. These include the three bright stars of Orion's Belt, Alnilam, Alnitak, and Mintaka. It is important to recognize that the Orion Arm is not a physical structure but a zone where new stars have been created by the passage of a **density wave** and have subsequently illuminated the **interstellar medium** around them. The picturesque analogy has been drawn between spiral arms and bands of luminescent plankton churned up in the wake of a ship.

Orion Nebula (NGC 1976, M 42)

One of the nearest regions to the Sun in which stars are presently being formed. Lying at a distance of about 1,500 light-years, the Orion Nebula is **ionized** and made visible by a small group of **O stars** and **B stars** known as the Trapezium Cluster. A study of the **polarization** of light in a region of the Orion Nebula has provided a clue to the origin of "handedness" in some of the chemical building blocks of terrestrial life (➔ **chirality**). Other studies of the nebula have provided strong evidence that **protoplanetary disk**s are common around infant stars.

Orion, Project

A design for a nuclear-propelled rocket capable of **interstellar travel** conceived in 1955 by physicists Stanislaw Ulam and Frederick de Hoffman (both of whom had worked on the Manhattan Project) and developed by physicist Theodore Taylor over a 7-year period, beginning in 1958, with U.S. Air Force support. Other contributors to the project included Freeman **Dyson.** The Orion spacecraft was to be powered by the shocks from a series of nu-

clear **fission** explosions, each detonated roughly 60 m (200 ft.) behind the vehicle, which would be absorbed by a pusher plate. In one design, intended for a mission to a nearby star, a 40-million-t spacecraft was to be powered by the release of 10 million bombs. Project Orion fell from favor following the nuclear test-ban treaty of 1963 amid fears that its propulsion system could lead to serious contamination if operated in the vicinity of the Earth. However, the idea of the nuclear-pulse rocket was taken up again in the design for Project **Daedalus.**

Orion's Belt

The tight linear grouping of the prominent white stars Alnitak, Alnilam, and Mintaka in the constellation of Orion.

Orlando Furioso
➔ **Ariosto, Ludovico**

OSETI
➔ **optical SETI**

osmosis

The diffusion of a **solvent,** such as water, through a semipermeable membrane. The solvent usually travels from the side with the greater concentration of the solution to the side with the lesser concentration.

Outer Space Treaty of 1967

Treaty on Principles Governing the Activities of States in the Exploration and Use of Outer Space, Including the Moon and Other Celestial Bodies. An international treaty, enacted on October 10, 1967, Article IX of which asserts that:

> States Parties to the Treaty shall pursue studies of outer space, including the moon and other celestial bodies, and conduct exploration of them so as to avoid their harmful contamination and also adverse changes in the environment of the Earth resulting from the introduction of extraterrestrial matter....

➔ **contamination**

outgassing

The venting of gases from the crust of a planet or moon. Outgassing is believed to be a principal source of **secondary atmosphere**s.

Overwhelmingly Large Telescope (OWL)

A huge optical telescope with a mirror about 100 m (328 ft.) in diameter supported by a structure about 200 m (656 ft.) tall and weighing 40,000 t. It would have ten times more light-gathering power than all the other telescopes that have ever been built put together, could be completed by 2015 for a cost of less than $1 billion, and has been proposed by a team from the **European Southern Observatory.** Among its uses would be obtaining spectra of the atmospheres of **extrasolar planets** to allow astronomers to look for signatures of life, such as the presence of oxygen.

OWL

→ **Overwhelmingly Large Telescope**

oxidation

The loss of one or more **electron**s by an **atom** during a chemical reaction. In living organisms, chemical energy is stored in high-energy electrons that are transferred from one atom to another in reactions involving oxidation and **reduction.**

oxides

Compounds that form when **oxygen** reacts with other **element**s.

oxidizing

Descriptive of a substance or environment that causes **oxidation.**

oxygen (O)

A colorless, odorless, gaseous **element,** the most abundant in the Earth's crust (49.2 percent by mass) and the second most abundant in the atmosphere (28 percent by volume). **Free oxygen** is essential to the survival of all **aerobic** organisms.

Atomic number 8; density 1.14 g/dm^3; melting point −214.4°C; boiling point −183.0°C

Oyama, Vance I.

Astrobiologist at **NASA Ames Research Center,** a veteran of life detection experiments on *Apollo* lunar samples, and father of the *Viking* **gas exchange (GEX) experiment** (GEX). Along with Wolf **Vishniac** and Harold **Klein,** Oyama was among the most optimistic of the scientists working on the *Viking* biology experiments about the prospects of detecting Martian life. Ironically, his experiment gave the least biologically favorable result of the three on board the spacecraft, and Oyama subsequently became convinced that the activity registered in the soil samples could best be explained chemically (→ **Oyama's hypothesis, about the active nature of the Martian soil**).

Oyama's hypothesis, about the active nature of the Martian soil

In an effort to explain the puzzling results obtained by the *Viking* biology experiments, Vance **Oyama** began by assuming that intense solar **ultraviolet** radiation breaks down, by **photodissociation, carbon dioxide** (CO_2) in the Martian atmosphere into activated **carbon monoxide** (CO) and single atoms of **oxygen** (O). The carbon monoxide is further broken down into its constituents, carbon and oxygen. Some of the single-atom carbon then combines with carbon monoxide to produce carbene (C_2O). This in turn combines with carbon monoxide to form carbon suboxide (C_3O_2), which links together to make a carbon suboxide **polymer**—a substance that, interestingly, has a reddish cast. The presence of this polymer in the Martian soil, together with the use of radioactive carbon 14 as a labeler, are the keys to understanding the curious results of the *Viking* **pyrolytic release (PR) experiment,** claimed Oyama. The decay of carbon 14 into nitrogen 14 releases beta particles, which have enough energy to break carbon-carbon, carbon-hydrogen, and carbon-oxygen bonds, and thus activate the carbon suboxide polymer. In this energized state, the polymer is able to incorporate the labeled carbon monoxide gas made available to the sample. Upon pyrolysis, the polymer produces about 4 percent of the original carbon suboxide (monomer) with a carbon 14 label. This molecule adheres to the experiment's organic vapor trap and with subsequent heating is released, giving rise to a "second peak" seen in the *Viking* PR data.

To account for the results of his own *Viking gas exchange (GEX) experiment,* Oyama assumed that the same photochemical breakdown that produces carbon suboxide also leads to the formation of activated oxygen atoms. When these atoms strike alkaline earths, such as the oxides of magnesium or calcium in the surface soil, they combine to form superoxides that release oxygen upon exposure to water vapor. Less oxygen was released by the GEX experiment at the *Viking 2* site (**Utopia Planitia**) than at the *Viking 1* site (**Chryse Planitia**), suggested Oyama, because the larger amount of water vapor at the more northerly site had already freed some of the oxygen in the superoxides near the surface.

In his explanation of the most intriguing of the biology tests, the *Viking* **labeled release (LR) experiment,** Oyama built upon an idea first suggested by John Oro, of the molecular analysis team (responsible for the *Viking* **gas chromatograph–mass spectrometer**). Oro had suggested early on that the results from both the GEX and LR experiments were due to the presence of peroxidelike materials in the Martian soil. In Oyama's view, **hydrogen peroxide** formed photochemically in the atmosphere and reacted with a catalyst on the surface of the soil grains to form oxygen, which then diffused into the grains, reacting with the alkaline earths and metals to form superoxides. Atmospheric water vapor converted the superoxides to peroxides, which combined with water in the LR nutrient to form hydrogen peroxide. This in turn oxidized the labeled components of the nutrients to release the observed labeled carbon dioxide. As for the observed release of oxygen, Oyama pointed to what happens when hydrogen peroxide, a commonly used disinfectant, is applied to a wound. Bubbles of oxygen form as a result of the catalytic action of iron (present in blood hemoglobin) on hydrogen peroxide. A similar process operates on Mars, but in this case, suggested Oyama, the catalyst is probably a form of iron oxide known as **maghemite.**

Ozma, Project

The first systematic attempt to detect artificial radio signals from nearby stars. Named after the princess in L. Frank Baum's *The Land of Oz,* it was the brainchild of American radio astronomer Frank **Drake,** working at the **Green Bank** observatory in West Virginia. Drake began preparations for Ozma in 1959, the same year in which the seminal theoretical paper on **SETI** by Philip **Morrison** and Giuseppe **Cocconi** was published in the British journal *Nature* (➔ **Morrison-Cocconi Conjecture**). These developments, although occurring more or less simultaneously (the paper appeared about 6 months after Drake began his work), were quite independent of one another. Both, however, concluded that the best chance of success would come from searching at a radio wavelength of 21.1 cm (corresponding to a frequency of 1,420 MHz) since the **21-centimeter line** of neutral **hydrogen** in the Galaxy might represent a natural hailing wavelength at which intelligent species

The 85-foot Howard Tatel radio telescope used in Project Ozma.
NRAO/AUI

would try to communicate. As his target, Drake chose two nearby, reasonably Sun-like stars, **Epsilon Eridani** and **Tau Ceti.** From April to July 1960, he tuned in to both for 6 hours a day, using the 85-foot Howard Tatel **radio telescope** at Green Bank equipped with a receiver that had just a single channel and a **bandwidth** of only 100 Hz. Although, after 150 hours of listening, Ozma drew a blank, it would be the starting point for many other, increasingly more sophisticated searches that continue to this day.[162] ➔ **Berkner, Lloyd; Struve, Otto**

ozone (O$_3$)

The triatomic form of **oxygen.** It forms a stratospheric layer in the Earth's atmosphere and is responsible for filtering out **ultraviolet** radiation from the Sun that would otherwise make advanced life on the planet impossible. Among the strategies that will be used in the future to search for signs of life on extraterrestrial **Earth-class planet**s will be to look for the spectral **absorption line**s that are characteristic of ozone (➔ *Darwin*).

Melting point −192.7°C; boiling point −111.9°C

PAHs
→ polycyclic aromatic hydrocarbons

Paine, Thomas (1737–1809)
English-born radical political writer who moved to Philadelphia in 1774 and subsequently argued for American independence. After serving with the American Army, he returned to England in 1787 and wrote in support of the French Revolution. Arraigned for treason, he fled to Paris but was imprisoned for offering the French king asylum in the United States. While incarcerated, he wrote *The Age of Reason* (1794), in which he argued aggressively that Christianity and **pluralism** were incompatible:

> [T]o believe that God created a plurality of worlds at least as numerous as what we call stars, renders the Christian system of faith at once little and ridiculous and scatters it in the mind like feathers in the air. The two beliefs cannot be held together in the same mind; and he who thinks that he believes in both has thought but little of either.

→ **Christian doctrine and pluralism**

paleocontact hypothesis
The notion originally proposed by Matest M. **Agrest** and others on a serious academic level, and frequently put forward in pseudoscientific and pseudohistoric literature since the 1960s, that advanced extraterrestrials have played an influential role in past human affairs. Its most outspoken and commercially successful advocate has been the writer Erich von **Däniken.** Although not an unreasonable idea in principle (→ **sentinel hypothesis; artifacts, alien**), there is a lack of convincing, substantive evidence to support it. Moreover, when specific claims are examined in detail, other, less exotic explanations can usually be found.[560, 569] A case in point concerns the Dogon tribe and their remarkable knowledge of the star Sirius (→ **Sirius, mystery of red color of**).

palingenesis
→ **transmigration of souls**

Palmer, Raymond (Arthur) (1910–1977)
Eccentric editor in the 1940s of *Amazing Stories,* then the world's oldest and worst science fiction pulp. The magazine was facing extinction when, in an effort to boost sales, Palmer began running crazy stories, by Richard **Shaver,** of beings who lived underground and controlled people on the surface by means of invisible rays. These outlandish accounts he presented not as fiction but as unadulterated fact, and many readers, it seems, were pre-

pared to take them seriously. *Amazing*'s circulation soared to more than a quarter of a million, testimony to the widespread paranoia and culture of mistrust that had infected the nation at this time (→ **Cold War, linked to UFO reports**). From aliens under the ground, Palmer progressed to aliens in the sky. His stories hammered away at three main themes: aliens who abduct unsuspecting citizens (→ **alien abduction**), inexplicable memory losses, and mysterious men from the government who were really alien agents. These same ideas also pervaded *Amazing*'s "readers' letters"—not surprisingly, since many of them were written by Palmer himself. By taking advantage of the national postwar mood of insecurity and repeating his bizarre claims often enough, Palmer contributed to an undercurrent of suspicion that, by the start of the **saucer flap of 1947,** made it easier for people to accept the possibility of clandestine alien activity. → **science fiction involving extraterrestrials, 1900–1940; science fiction involving extraterrestrials, after 1940**

Palomar Observatory

A facility built with funds from the Carnegie Institution of Washington and the California Institute of Technology to house the 5-m (16.4-ft.) Hale telescope, which was inaugurated in 1948. It is located on Palomar Mountain at an altitude of 1,706 m, 80 km (50 miles) northeast of San Diego, California, and operated by the California Institute of Technology. Other instruments at the site include a 1.5-m (4.9-ft.) reflector, opened in 1970, and the 1.2-m (3.9-ft.) Oschin Schmidt Telescope, opened in 1948.

Palomar Testbed Interferometer (PTI)

An experimental arrangement at **Palomar Observatory,** funded by NASA, to demonstrate key technologies that will be used in the **Keck Interferometer** and eventually in future space-based interferometers, such as the *Space Interferometry Mission.* Light from a cosmic source is collected by three small telescopes located in separate buildings about 110 m (360 ft.) apart and directed through pipes to a central building where the beams are combined.[126]

Pan

The innermost of **Saturn**'s moons; it lies within the Encke gap of Saturn's A-ring (→ **Saturn, rings of**). Pan is a shepherd moon responsible for keeping the Encke gap open. → **Saturn, moons of**

Discovery	1990, by Mark R. Showalter from 1981 *Voyager 2* images
Mean distance from Saturn	131,940 km (82,000 mi.)
Diameter	20 km (12 mi.)
Orbital period	0.575 day (13 hours 48 minutes)
Orbital eccentricity	0.000
Orbital inclination	0.00°
Visual albedo	0.5

Pandora

The fourth of **Saturn**'s moons and the outer shepherd moon for the F-ring (→ **Saturn, rings of**). Although no linear ridges or valleys have been identified on Pandora, its surface appears to be heavily cratered, with the two largest craters measuring about 30 km (19 miles) across. → **Saturn, moons of**

Discovery	1980, by S. Collins et al. from *Voyager 1* data
Mean distance from Saturn	141,700 km (88,070 mi.)
Diameter	114 × 84 × 62 km (71 × 52 × 39 mi.)
Mean density	0.7 g/cm^3
Escape velocity	0.023 km/s (83 km/h, 51 mi./h)
Orbital period	0.629 day (15 hours 6 minutes)
Orbital eccentricity	0.004
Orbital inclination	0.00°
Visual albedo	0.9

Panel on Extraterrestrial Life

A committee established in 1958 by the **Space Science Board** to recommend approaches to the study of extraterrestrial life and, in particular, issues related to the problem of **contamination.** It consisted of two geographically distinct panels, **EASTEX** and **WESTEX.** For about two years, it ran in parallel with **Panel 2** on **Extraterrestrial Life** but then took over the activities of the latter.

Panel 2 on Extraterrestrial Life

One of the first two groups set up in the late 1950s to study problems related to life beyond the Earth, the other being the **Space Science Board**'s **Panel on Extraterrestrial Life.** Panel 2 operated under the auspices of the Joint Armed Forces–National Research Council Committee on Bio-Astronautics and was chaired by Melvin **Calvin.** Its eight member scientists, including Carl **Sagan,** Henry Linschitz, Richard E. Lord, Matthew Messelson, Malcolm Ross, Wolf **Vishniac,** and Harold F. Weaver, who were interested primarily in extraterrestrial life, the origin of life, and **SETI,** had to contend with other colleagues and military officers who were more concerned with the effects of space travel on human beings (➜ **space medicine**). Panel 2 was dissolved in August 1960 so that the National Academy of Sciences would have a single representative in this field, the Space Science Board. The activities of Panel 2 were taken over by **Committee 14 on Exobiology** on August 12, 1960.

panspermia

An idea, with ancient roots, according to which life arrives, ready-made, on the surface of planets from space.[308] **Anaxagoras of Clazomenae** is said to have spoken of the "seeds of life" from which all organisms derive. Panspermia began to assume a more scientific form through the proposals of Jöns **Berzelius** (1834), H. E. **Richter** (1865), William **Thomson** (1871), and Hermann **Helmholtz** (1871), finally reaching the level of a detailed, widely discussed hypothesis through the efforts of the Swedish chemist Svante **Arrhenius.** Originally in 1903,[22] but then for a wider audience through a popular book in 1908,[24] Arrhenius urged that life in the form of spores could survive in space and be spread from one planetary system to another by means of **radiation pressure.** He generally avoided the problem of how life had come about in the first place by suggesting that it might be eternal, though he did not exclude the possibility of living things generating from simpler substances some-

where in the Universe. In Arrhenius's view, **spores** escape by random movement from the atmosphere of a planet that has already been colonized and are then launched into interstellar space by the pressure of starlight ("radiopanspermia"). Eventually, some of the spores fall upon another planet, such as the Earth, where they inoculate the virgin world with new life or, perhaps, compete with any life-forms that are already present.

Arrhenius's ideas prompted a variety of experimental work, such as that of Paul **Becquerel,** to test whether spores and bacteria could survive in conditions approximating those in space. A majority of scientists reached the conclusion that stellar **ultraviolet** would probably prove deadly to any organisms in the inner reaches of a planetary system and, principally for this reason, panspermia quietly faded from view—only to be revived some four decades later. In the early 1960s, Carl **Sagan** analyzed in detail both the physical and biological aspects of the Arrhenius scenario. The dynamics of a microorganism in space depend on the ratio p/g, where p is the repulsive force due to the radiation pressure of a star and g is the attractive force due to the star's gravitation. If $p > g$, a microbe that has drifted into space will move away from the star; if $p < g$, the microbe will fall toward the star. For a microbe to escape into interstellar space from the vicinity of a star like the Sun, the organism would have to be between 0.2 and 0.6 microns across. Though small, this is within the range of some terrestrial **bacterial spores** and **virus**es. The ratio p/g increases for more luminous stars, enabling the ejection of larger microbes. However, **main sequence** stars brighter than the Sun are also hotter, so that they emit more **ultraviolet** radiation, which would pose an increased threat to spaceborne organisms. Additionally, such stars have a shorter main sequence lifespan, so that they provide less opportunity for life to take hold on any worlds that might orbit around them. These considerations, argued Sagan, constrain "donor" stars for Arrhenius-style panspermia to **spectral type**s G5 (Sun-like) to A0. Stars less luminous than the Sun would be unable to eject even the smallest of known living particles. "Acceptor" stars, on the other hand, must have lower *p/g* ratios in order to allow microbes, approaching from interstellar space, to enter their planetary systems. The most likely acceptor worlds, Sagan concluded, are those circling around **red dwarf**s (dwarf **M star**s), or in more distant orbits around **G star**s and **K star**s. In the case of the solar system, he surmised, the best place to look for life of extrasolar origin would be the moons of the outer planets, in particular **Triton.**

Many variations on the panspermia theme have been put forward. William Thomson (Lord Kelvin) proposed that spores might travel aboard **meteorite**s ("lithopanspermia"), thus affording them better protection from high-energy radiation in space. Whether events violent enough to hurl rocks from the surface of a biologically active planet into *interstellar* space ever occur is not clear. But there is now overwhelming evidence that **ballistic panspermia** occasionally operates between worlds of the same planetary system. This follows the discovery of meteorites on Earth that have almost certainly come from the surface of Mars (➔ **SNC meteorites**) and the Moon.

In the 1960s, Thomas **Gold** pointed out another way in which life might travel from world to world (➔ **"garbage theory," of the origin of life**). A team of explorers from an advanced, interstellar-faring race might land on the planet of a foreign star and, unwittingly, leave behind "bugs," which would then adapt to the local conditions. He imagined, for example, the visitors having a picnic and not clearing up afterward. What effect microscopic alien fauna and flora might have on the indigenous species is impossible to predict, but such considerations were foremost in the minds of scientists receiving the first samples of rock and soil from the Moon. Precautions against alien contamination will be even more important when the first spacecraft return from Mars or **Europa,** where the possibility of extant life is far greater (➔ **back contamination**). And there is the reverse problem (➔ **forward contamination**). The remarkable case of *Surveyor 3* makes it clear that some terrestrial microbes can survive for significant periods in hostile conditions on other worlds. What if such a world (such as Mars) had life-forms of its own? What chaos might the "alien" microbes from Earth wreak? It would be tragic indeed if the very means of discovering the first examples of extraterrestrial life were also to be the vehicle of its extinction. On the other hand, as Sagan pointed out, if Gold's "picnic scenario" had actually happened in the Earth's past "some microbial resident of a primordial cookie crumb may be the ancestor of us all." Just as the chance of accidental contamination arising from intelligent activity cannot be ruled out, there is the complimentary possibility of intentional or **directed panspermia.**

Today, the panspermia hypothesis has finally achieved some measure of scientific respectability. Although it remains the orthodox view that life evolved *in situ* on this world and, possibly, many others, there is mounting evidence of at least some extraterrestrial input into the formative stages of planet-based biology. **Prebiotic** chemicals have been detected in **interstellar cloud**s (similar to that from which the solar system formed), **comet**s, and meteorites. At the very least, it seems that some of the raw ingredients for life, such as **amino acids,** may have fallen from the sky in addition to being manufactured here on Earth. But some researchers have gone much further in their speculations. Most notably, Fred **Hoyle** and Chandra Wickramasinghe have argued persistently since the 1970s that complex **organic** substances, and perhaps even primitive organisms, might have evolved on the surface of **cosmic dust** grains in space and then been transported to the Earth's surface by comets and meteorites (➔ **life, in space**). The extraordinary durability of some **extremophiles, bacterial spores,** and even exposed **DNA** lends credence to the view that simple life-forms may have originated between the stars or been capable of surviving long interstellar journeys.

parabola

A curve with an **eccentricity** equal to 1 that is obtained by slicing a cone with a plane parallel to one side of the cone. A parabola can be considered an **ellipse** with an infinite **major axis.** ➔ **conic sections**

parabolic orbit

An orbit around a central mass which is followed by an object that, at any point on its path, has the minimum velocity needed to escape from the gravitating mass. → **conic sections**

parabolic velocity

The velocity which an object at a given point would require in order to describe a **parabola** about the center of attraction. This is also the **escape velocity** since it is the upper limit of velocity on a closed curve. It is obtained by multiplying the velocity of an object moving in a circular orbit by the square root of 2 (approximately 1.414). For example, if the Earth's mean velocity around the Sun of 29.8 km per second (18.5 miles per second), in a near-circular orbit, were increased to 42 km per second (26 miles per second), the Earth would move to a parabolic path and escape from the solar system.

parallax

The apparent shift in position of an object due to the actual movement of the observer. Stellar parallax results from the movement of Earth around the Sun and, in the case of the nearest stars, can be used to give a reasonably accurate measure of distance. → **61 Cygni**

parallel universe

A hypothetical universe, entirely separate in space and time from our own. Such universes, the existence of which is predicted by the **many-worlds interpretation** of **quantum mechanics** and also by **chaotic inflationary theory,** could contain life-forms that conform to a totally different set of physical laws.

parametric amplifier

A sensitive amplifying device that employs the properties of nonlinear elements.

parent star

→ **host star**

Paris Observatory (Observatoire de Paris)

Founded in 1667, the oldest astronomical observatory still in use. Observations are also carried out at **Meudon,** 9 km (5.6 mi.) south of Paris.

Parkes Observatory

The principal radio astronomy observatory of the Southern Hemisphere. Operated by the Australia Telescope National Facility and located near Sydney, New South Wales, its main instrument is the **Parkes Radio Telescope.**

Parkes Radio Telescope

A fully steerable 64-m (208-ft.) **radio telescope** at the **Parkes Observatory** in Australia. The largest of its kind in the Southern Hemisphere, it was completed in 1961. In addition to its use for astrophysical research, it is actively involved in **SETI** work (→ **Southern SERENDIP**).

parsec (pc)

An astronomical unit of length, equal to the distance at which the radius of the Earth's orbit subtends an angle of one **arc-second.** The name is a contraction of "parallax-second." One parsec = 3.259 **light-year**s, or 30.83 trillion km (19.16 trillion miles). It is generally used by astronomers in preference to the light-year. 1,000 parsecs = 1 kiloparsec (kpc).

Pasiphaë

The fifteenth known moon of **Jupiter.** It is one of the group of four outer Jovian moons that exhibit **retrograde** motion and are therefore suspected of being captured asteroids. → **Jupiter, moons of**

Discovery	1908, by Philibert Jacques Melotte
Mean distance from Jupiter	23,300,000 km (14,480,000 mi.)
Diameter	50 km (31 mi.)
Mean density	2.9 g/cm^3
Escape velocity	0.0319
Orbital period	−735 days (retrograde)
Orbital eccentricity	0.378
Orbital inclination	147°

Pasteur, Louis (1822–95)

Great French chemist and microbiologist who carried out an experiment in 1862 that finally disproved the ancient theory of **spontaneous generation.** To address the criticism leveled at Lazzaro **Spallanzani**'s early experiments, namely that boiling might destroy some "vital principle" in air, Pasteur devised a long swan-necked flask. Air could reach the flask through the opening, but dust particles and microorganisms could not because the curved neck served as a trap. Pasteur placed some broth in the flask, attached the swan neck, boiled the broth until it steamed (to kill any microorganisms in the neck as well as in the broth), and waited to see what happened. The broth remained sterile, demonstrating that there was no vital principle in air. Scientists now faced the problem of explaining how, if spontaneous generation was wrong, life could originate (➔ **life, origin of**).

Pathfinder
➔ *Mars Pathfinder*

pathogen

A **microbe** capable of causing disease. Pathogens include many **virus**es, **bacteria, fungi,** and protozoans.

Pauli exclusion principle

A fundamental law of physics that states that no two basic particles, such as **electron**s or **neutron**s, with the same spin and speed, can occupy the same place at the same time.

P-class asteroid

A type of **asteroid,** commonest in the outer part of the **Main Asteroid Belt** at a solar distance of about 4 AU, with a spectrum intermediate between that of **C-class asteroid**s and **D-class asteroid**s. P-class objects are distinguished from the spectrally similar **E-class asteroid**s and **M-class asteroid**s by their lower **albedo** (in the range 0.02 to 0.06).

51 Pegasi

A Sun-like star around which has been discovered a planet, 51 Pegasi b, with about half the mass of Jupiter. With the exception of some **pulsar planets,** 51 Pegasi b was the first **extra-solar planet** to be found. It is the prototype of a new and previously unsuspected class of planet known as **epistellar Jovians** with remarkably small orbits. The existence of giant planets very close to their host stars has led to the suggestion that **inward orbital migration** is a common feature of young planetary systems. 51 Pegasi b orbits its host star at less than one eighth the distance of Mercury from the Sun so that, assuming it has a radius 1.2 to 1.4 times that of Jupiter, it must have a surface temperature of around 1,000°C. Even so, calculations show that it should still be able to retain a massive atmosphere of predominantly light gases.[67, 261, 389]

Host Star	
Distance	50.2 light-years (15.4 parsecs)
Spectral type	G2.5 IVa
Apparent magnitude	5.49
Temperature	5,480 °C (5,750 K)
Luminosity	1.32 L_s
Mass	1.05 M_s
Planet	
Mass	0.47 M_j
Semimajor axis	0.052 AU (7.8 million km, 4.8 million mi.)
Orbital period	4.23 days
Eccentricity	0.015
Discovery	1995, by Michel Mayor and Didier Queloz, Geneva Observatory
Method of discovery	Radial velocity

51 Pegasi–type planets
➔ **epistellar Jovians**

penetrator probe

A device that, by impact, tunneling, or melting, penetrates beneath the surface of a planet, moon, asteroid, or comet to investigate the subsurface environment. Among missions currently in progress or under development that will deploy penetrator probes are the *Mars Polar Lander* and the *Europa Ocean Explorer* (➔ **Europa, future probes of**).

Pennsylvania State Pulsar Group

The team, led by Alexander **Wolszczan** at Pennsylvania State University, responsible for the discovery of the **pulsar planets** around **PSR 1257+12** by the pulsar-timing method.

pentose
A **monosaccharide** (simple **sugar**) containing five **carbon** atoms in the molecule.

peptide
A sequence of **amino acids** held together by **peptide bond**s. Peptides can vary in length from dipeptides, with two amino acids, to **polypeptide**s, with several hundred.

peptide bond
A chemical bond formed by the **condensation** of the **amino group** and **carboxyl group** of a pair of **amino acids.** It is a special case of the **amide bond. → peptide**

The formation of a peptide bond.

peptide nucleic acid
→ **PNA**

peptidoglycan
A cross-linked complex of **polysaccharides** and **peptide**s found in the **cell wall**s of **bacteria.** It occurs in particularly high concentration in gram-negative bacteria.

periapsis
The point of closest approach between an orbiting body and its **primary.**

periastron
The point in the orbital motion of a **binary star** system when the two stars are closest together.

perihelion
The point in the solar orbit of a planet, comet, or other object when it is nearest to the Sun.

period
The time required for one complete cycle of a regularly occurring event. For example, the period of a planet's axial rotation is its "day," while the period for its orbital rotation is its "year."

permafrost
Permanently frozen soil, such as exists in Arctic, subarctic, and Antarctic regions on Earth and in the upper part of the crust on Mars.

peroxides
A group of **inorganic** compounds that contain the O_2^{2-} **ion.**

Perrotin, Henri (1845–1904)
French astronomer who, in 1886, while working with Louis **Thollon** at the Nice Observatory, reported having seen many canals and some "germinations" on Mars in positions agreeing with the map produced by Giovanni **Schiaparelli** in 1882 (→ **Mars, canals of**). On receiving the news, Schiaparelli was delighted:

> I attach very great importance to this confirmation for people will hereafter cease to scoff at me in certain places. The germinations are very difficult to explain, but it is indeed necessary to admit their existence.

In 1888, using what was then the largest refracting telescope in Europe, Perrotin described having observed dramatic changes in a feature, named "Libya" by Schiaparelli and assumed to be a continental land mass. "Clearly visible two years ago, it no longer exists today," claimed Perrotin. "The nearby sea (if sea it is) has totally inundated it." By 1892, Perrotin had switched his attention to watching for "bright projections" on Mars, reporting three in the summer of that year. These observations attracted widespread press coverage, especially in the light of similar announcements from the **Lick Observatory** and the recent announcement of the **Guzman Prize.**

Perseus Arm

One of the **spiral arm**s of our galaxy, the nearest part of which lies in the direction of the constellation Perseus at a distance of about 7,000 light-years. The Perseus Arm winds around to the other side of the Galaxy.

Persinger, Michael

Canadian neurophysiologist at Laurentian University in Sudbury, Ontario, whose research has shed light on phenomena that may have some bearing on reports of **alien abduction** and **unidentified flying objects.** Persinger believes that some individuals may have an abduction experience because of high **temporal lobe lability** and claims to be able to replicate the abduction experience and related phenomena by arranging pulsed magnets around a subject's skull. He has also investigated the relationship between UFO sightings and tectonic activity (➔ **earthlights**).

perturbation

Any small disturbance of the regular motion of an object in space.

pH

A measure of the positive **hydrogen ion** (H+) concentration in water. More precisely, pH equals the negative logarithm of the H+ concentration. Solutions with a high H+ concentration have a low pH (less than 7) and are said to be acidic (➔ **acid**), while those with a low H+ concentration have a high pH and are said to be basic (➔ **base**) or alkaline (➔ **alkali**). pH values range from 1 for the strongest acids to 14 for the strongest alkalis. Pure water has a pH of 7.

phage

➔ **bacteriophage**

phenotype

The realized expression of the **genotype.**

Phobos

The larger of the two small moons of **Mars.** Its most impressive feature is the crater Stickney, some 9 km (6 miles) in diameter, the formation of which would have involved an impact that almost shattered the little satellite. High-resolution images of Stickney, obtained by the *Mars Global Surveyor,* have shown the crater to be filled with fine dust and provided evidence of boulders sliding down its steep sides. The temperature varies between about −4°C (25°F) on the sunlit side of the moon and −112°C (−70°F). Like **Deimos,** Phobos has the dark appearance of a **C-class asteroid** and may well be such an object that was captured by the gravitational field of its primary in the remote past. Every century, Phobos draws 2.5 meters closer to Mars, so that it will probably impact into the surface within the next 40 million years. ➔ **Mars, moons of**

Discovery	August 16, 1877, by Asaph Hall
Mean distance from center of Mars	9,270 km (5,761 mi.)
Diameter	20 × 23 × 28 km (12 × 14 × 17 mi.)
Escape velocity	0.016 km/s (58 km/h, 36 mi./h)
Orbital period	7.65 hours (7 hours 39 minutes)
Orbital eccentricity	0.021
Orbital inclination	1.1°

Phoebe

The outermost moon of **Saturn** and the only one that orbits in a **retrograde** direction. It rotates once every 9 hours or so during each orbit of 550 days so that, unlike Saturn's other moons (with the exception of **Hyperion**), it does not always show the same face to the planet. It is dark, quite red, resembles in appearance the common class of carbonaceous asteroids, and may be a captured asteroid. According to one idea, the dark material on the leading hemisphere of **Iapetus** may have originated on Hyperion and been dislodged by micrometeorite impacts. ➔ **Saturn, moons of**

Discovery	1898, by William Henry Pickering
Mean distance from Saturn	12,950,000 km (8,048,000 mi.)
Diameter	220 km (137 mi.)
Mean density	0.7 g/cm^3
Escape velocity	0.070 km/s (252 km/h, 157 mi./h)
Orbital period	−550.48 days (retrograde)
Orbital eccentricity	0.163
Orbital inclination	175.3° (retrograde)
Axial period	~9 hrs
Visual albedo	0.06

Phoenix, Project

The **SETI Institute**'s privately funded research project to search for extraterrestrial intelligence. The name derives from the mythological Egyptian bird that rose from its own ashes—in this case, the ashes of NASA's **High Resolution Microwave Survey** (HRMS), which was canceled in 1993. After the demise of HRMS, the SETI Institute acted to retain the core science and engineering team of NASA's project and, with the aid of its subcontractors, upgraded and expanded the targeted search electronics and software. Project Phoenix is currently the only **targeted search** for extraterrestrial intelligence in operation. Its core program involves examining nearly 1,000 nearby Sun-like stars (➔ **target stars**), in the "Microwave Window" from 1.2 to 3.0 GHz, for **narrowband** signals that would indicate an artificial origin.

The initial phase of the project, which ran from November 1993 to June 1995, involved making ready for use the instrumentation from the terminated NASA program and spending 5 months conducting observations of two hundred Sun-like stars in the southern sky using the **Parkes Radio Telescope** in Australia. These observations were the first to utilize real-time confirmation with an independent processing system and antenna. The Mopra 22-m (72-ft.) antenna, about 200 km north of Parkes, checked any candidate signals detected at Parkes with a **Follow-Up Detection Device** (FUDD).

At the conclusion of the Australian observations, the Phoenix receiving equipment, known as the Mobile Research Facility (MRF),

was shipped back to California. There it was upgraded to improve performance, increase system reliability, and eventually allow automatic observing with little or no operator assistance. In early September 1996, the observing system was moved to the 43-m (141.1-ft.) telescope at **Green Bank.** In mid-1998, it was moved again to the 305-m (1,000-ft.) **Arecibo radio telescope,** from which the search continues. Each star on the target list is observed for about 1.5 hours, during which time a multimillion-channel receiver steps across the 1.2-to-3-GHz band in 10-MHz steps, each observation taking about 5 minutes. Many signals are detected in each 5-minute period, and their characteristics are compared with a database of known signals from the Earth and orbiting satellites. Having eliminated known sources, a few are usually left that are then analyzed by FUDD. Parallel observations are made using the 72-m (236.2-ft.) **Lovell Telescope** in England, which is equipped with an identical FUDD system. The use of such powerful and widely spaced instruments enables the quick and efficient discrimination between extraterrestrial signals and those that are local or due to satellites in Earth orbit. During a 3-week observation period each year, the two giant telescopes are trained simultaneously on the same target stars. If the instrument at Arecibo detects a potentially interesting signal, this information is passed immediately to the FUDD at Jodrell Bank. The large spatial separation of the telescopes is sufficient to allow nearby signals to be distinguished from any that are coming from outside the solar system. The observational phase of Project Phoenix is expected to run until at least the year 2001.

Pholus

A **Centaur** about 200 km in diameter that was discovered in 1992 in orbit between Saturn and Neptune. Its dark red coloration suggests that its surface has been subjected to bombardment by **cosmic rays** from the earliest days of the solar system, when Pholus was formed in the **Kuiper Belt** beyond the orbit of Neptune. The continuous irradiation has led to the selective loss of hydrogen from the surface layers and the synthesis of complex organic **polymers.**

phosphate
A salt of **phosphoric acid.**

phospholipid
One of a group of **lipids** having both a **phosphate** group and one or more **fatty acids.** With their hydrophilic polar phosphate groups and long hydrophobic hydrocarbon chains, phospholipids readily form membranelike structures in water. They are crucial in the formation and functioning of **cell membranes.**

phosphoric acid (H₃PO₄)
A white solid that is highly soluble in water.

Density relative to water 1.83; melting point 42.3°C

phosphorus (P)
A highly reactive nonmetallic element.

Atomic number 15; density relative to water 1.82 (yellow), 2.20 (red); melting point 44.2°C (white); boiling point 280°C (white)

photoautotrophs
Autotrophic organisms that are capable of obtaining their energy directly from sunlight. Green **plants** are photoautotrophs.

photochemical
Refers to the effect of light in causing or modifying chemical reactions.

photodissociation
The breaking up of molecules by exposure to light.

photometer
An instrument used to measure the intensity of light from a source.

photometry
The accurate quantitative measurement of the amount of light received from an object. It can be applied to the detection and characterization of **extrasolar planets,** since planets in **transit** cause tiny periodic variations in the apparent light output of their host stars. From the period and depth of the transits, the orbit and size of the planetary companions can be calculated: the smaller the planet, the smaller the photometric effect. Transits by **Earth-class planets,** for example, are expected to produce only a tiny drop in stellar brightness of 0.005 percent to 0.04 percent and lasting for 4 to 16 hours. Among current or proposed planetary searches that employ photometry are the **Transits of Extrasolar Planets** (TEP) **Network,** the **Wyoming Arizona Search for Planets** (WASP), and the **Kepler Mission.** This technique achieved its first major success with the confirmation of a planet in orbit around **HD 209458.**

photon
A particle of light or, more precisely, a quantum of the electromagnetic field. It has zero rest mass and a spin of 1. Apart from its obvious role as the carrier of virtually all the information that we have so far been able to ascertain about phenomena beyond the solar system (with the exception of **cosmic dust, cosmic rays, neutrinos,** and, possibly, **gravitational waves**), the photon is also the exchange particle of the electromagnetic force acting between any two charged particles. ➔ **electromagnetic radiation**

photopolarimeter
A **photometer** combined with a **polarimeter.**

photosphere
The visible surface of a star.

photosynthesis
The natural process by means of which **carbon dioxide** and water are converted into **carbohydrates** by plants with the aid of sunlight.

photosynthetic
Descriptive of organisms that carry out, or processes that are connected with, **photosynthesis.**

photosynthetic pigments
The plant pigments responsible for the capture of light during the light reactions of **pho-**

tosynthesis. They include **chlorophyll** and the **carotenoid**s.

phylogeny
The evolutionary development of groups of organisms.

physicotheology
→ **natural theology**

Pic-du-Midi Observatory
A facility located in the Pyrénées at an altitude of 2,860 m (9,300 ft.) and operated by the University of Toulouse. It is historically famous for its planetary, lunar, and solar studies.

Pickering, William Henry (1858–1938)
American astronomer, brother of Harvard College Observatory director E. C. Pickering and the first to discover a satellite (Saturn's moon **Phoebe**) by photographic means. He played a prominent part in the Martian canal controversy (→ **Mars, canals on**), asserting in 1888, on the basis of observations made by others, that the canals were made visible by adjacent strips of vegetation (→ **Mars, vegetation on**). At the favorable **opposition** of 1892, he claimed to have seen forty "lakes" and clouds high in the Martian atmosphere. Percival **Lowell** later used these observations in formulating his theory of an advanced Martian civilization, with which Pickering fully concurred. Up to his death, Pickering also maintained that there was plant life in specific areas on the Moon, including the crater Eratosthenes[454] (→ **Moon, life on**).

Pierce, John R. (1910–)
Leading applied physicist and executive director of the Research-Communications Principles Division at the Bell Telephone Laboratories who, in the early years of the Space Age, cast doubt on the feasibility of interstellar travel.[456] A similar position was adopted by Edward **Purcell** and Sebastian von **Hoerner.**

"piggyback" search
A **SETI** technique that does not require the dedicated use of a **radio telescope.** Instead, during routine astronomical observations, a computer program automatically checks for **narrowband** signals of the type that are unlikely to arise from natural objects in space. This approach means that the search is restricted to whatever wavelengths and parts of the sky are of interest to the astronomers, but as there is no way of ensuring where it is best to look in the first place, this is no great disadvantage. On the contrary, it avoids what might otherwise be a human bias in the choice of target. → **SERENDIP**

Pioneer 10
Launched on March 2, 1972, the first spacecraft to cross the **Main Asteroid Belt** and to fly close by Jupiter (December 3, 1973). It is now on an exit trajectory from the solar system, together with three other probes, *Pioneer 11, Voyager 1,* and *Voyager 2.* Of this interstellar quartet, only *Pioneer 10* is heading in the opposite direction to the Sun's motion through the Galaxy. It continues to be tracked in an effort to learn more about the interaction between the **heliosphere** and the local **interstellar medium.**

Pioneer 10 is heading for interstellar space at a speed of 12.24 km per second (7.61 miles per second). At this rate it would take about 105,000 years to reach what is currently the nearest star to the Sun, **Proxima Centauri.** However, *Pioneer 10*'s course is taking it generally toward **Aldebaran** (65 light-years away) in the constellation of Taurus, and a remote encounter about 2 million years from now. The closest that it will come to another star system within the next 100,000 years is 3.27 light-years (1.00 parsec) from the **red dwarf** Ross 248 in approximately the year A.D. 32,608. Even then, this distant passage will owe more to the relative motions of the stars themselves than the probe's own efforts. It so happens that Ross 248 is approaching the Sun at about 80 km per second (50 miles per second), so that by A.D. 34,923 the gap between the Sun and the red dwarf will have narrowed from its present value of 10.3 light-years (3.2 parsecs) to just 2.9 light-years (0.9 parsec). Uncertainties in the movements of stars over long periods are one of the main reasons that mission specialists cannot be absolutely sure when and at what range future stellar flybys of escaping probes will take place. In January 2000, *Pioneer 10* was 74 AU (11.1 billion km; 6.9 billion miles) from the Sun, equivalent to a round-trip light-travel time of 20 hours, 20 minutes. It was superseded as the most distant human-made object by *Voyager 1* in mid-1998.[104] ➔ *Pioneer* **plaque; interstellar probes**

Pioneer 11

Launched on April 5, 1973, flew past Jupiter (December 2, 1974), and became the first spacecraft to rendezvous with Saturn (September 1, 1979). The last communication was received from the probe on November 30, 1995; its electric power source exhausted, it could no longer operate any of its experiments or point its antenna toward Earth. *Pioneer 11* is headed in the direction of Aquila and may pass relatively near one of the stars in that constellation in about 4 million years. On a shorter timescale, *Pioneer 11* will achieve its first stellar encounter of sorts when it passes about 1.65 light-years (0.51 parsec) from the **red dwarf** AC +79° 3888 in the year A.D. 42,405. At present, AC +79° 3888 is 16.6 light-years (5.1 parsecs) from the Sun but is approaching so rapidly that by A.D. 40,598 it will be just under 3 light-years (0.9 parsecs) away—roughly the same distance *Pioneer 11* will be from the Sun at that time. At the start of 2000, *Pioneer 11* was approximately 52 AU (7.8 billion km; 4.9 billion miles) from the Sun.[104] ➔ *Pioneer* **plaque; interstellar probes**

Pioneer plaque

A 15-cm-by-23-cm (6-in.-by-9-in.) gold-anodized aluminum plate fixed to the antenna support struts of ***Pioneer 10*** and ***Pioneer 11.*** It carries an information-rich message, devised by Carl **Sagan** and Frank **Drake,** in the event that either of the spacecraft is detected and recovered in the remote future by advanced extraterrestrials. The message is intended to communicate the location of the human race, the appearance of an adult male and female of our species, and the approximate era when the probe was launched. A line drawing of a naked couple standing in front of the *Pioneer* probe is accompanied by an ingenious scheme for con-

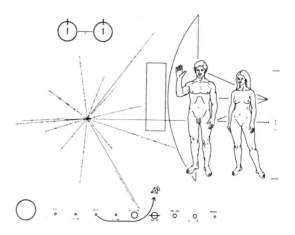

veying distance, direction, and time information about the spacecraft's origins.

At the top left of the plaque is a schematic representation of the energy transition between the parallel and antiparallel **proton** and **electron** spins in the neutral **hydrogen** atom. It is this transition that is responsible for the **21-centimeter line** (giving a standard distance) at 1,420 MHz (giving a standard time) by clouds of atomic hydrogen in space. Any spacefaring race, it is assumed, would be aware of the significance of this most fundamental transition. As a check, the plaque also shows the number 8 in **binary** (1---) between two tote marks indicating the height of the *Pioneer* probe. The fact that this height is close to eight times 21 cm will serve to verify that the symbol at the top left does indeed represent the 21-cm hydrogen transition. Further binary numbers accompany the lines in the spokelike pattern to the left of center of the message. Evidently, they must be either distances or times in terms of the characteristic wavelength or frequency of the hydrogen transition. If interpreted as distances, they correspond roughly to interplanetary ones. This would not be reasonable information to communicate since the separations between objects in a planetary system are continually changing. If (correctly) interpreted as times, however, they yield values in the range 0.1 to 1 second. These are characteristic of the periods of **pulsar**s, which are very precise and slow down, over long periods of times, at a predictable rate. An intelligent recipient civilization, it is hoped, would be able to compare its current maps and timings of pulsars with the relative positions and timings given on the *Pioneer* plaque and, as a result, pinpoint the probe's home star and its year of launch. ➔ **mathematics, as a universal language;** *Voyager* **interstellar record**

planet

A large body orbiting a star and shining by its reflected light. At the low end of the planetary size range are objects such as Pluto, which may be smaller than large moons. Their status as true planets may be called into question, especially if it can be shown that they are actually escaped moons or objects displaced from the **Kuiper Belt.** At the high end of the planetary size range are objects with masses up to about thirteen times that of Jupiter. Beyond this, objects would be classified as **brown dwarf**s. ➔ **Earth-class planet; gas giant; extrasolar planets**

PLANET
➔ **Probing Lensing Anomalies Network**

planet migration

A major shift in the orbit of a planet. This could be caused by the collision or near miss of another sizable object or by interaction with the dust of a **protoplanetary disk.** Most planet migration is likely to take place in very young planetary systems (➔ **planetary systems, formation of**) and is the favored explanation for the small orbits of most **extrasolar planets** found to date (➔ **inward orbital migration**).[591]

planet swallowing

The destruction of a planet through collision with its central star. Such an event may not be uncommon in the early stages of a planetary system, when the orbits of newly formed planets may be altered dramatically by near encounters with other worlds or as a result of interaction with the remains of the **protoplanetary disk** (➔ **inward orbital migration**).[544] Possible evidence for planet swallowing came in 1999 from Luca Pasquini and colleagues working at the **European Southern Observatory.** Spectroscopic studies of a 2-billion-year-old star named S50 revealed that its atmosphere contains 100 to 1,000 times more lithium than normal. Since S50 shows no other unusual features, the researchers believe that its extra lithium may have come from a large planet or **brown dwarf** that fell into the star.

Planet X

A hypothetical tenth planet of the solar system. What were thought to have been unexplained perturbations in the orbits of Neptune and Uranus at the turn of the twentieth century led to the search for a trans-Neptunian planet. But upon the discovery of this planet—Pluto—the mystery only seemed to deepen. Pluto proved to be much too small to account for the wobbles thought to exist in the movements of Neptune and Uranus. Over the next few decades, speculation continued about the possible existence of "Planet X." However, today, it seems clear that the supposed perturbations were fictitious, and therefore there are no grounds to suspect that a tenth planet exists. ➔ **Kuiper Belt**

planetary nebula

A shell or bubble of glowing gas expanding outward from a dying star from which it was ejected (➔ **stars, evolution of**). The planetary nebula stage is typical of highly evolved stars of intermediate mass, between about 0.8 and 8 M_S. It follows the growth of the star into a **red giant** and the subsequent sloughing off of its distended outer atmosphere. The exposed hot core of the star pours out large amounts of **ultraviolet** radiation that serves to photoionize the expanding gaseous shell. As the **ions** in the nebular gas recombine with free **electron**s, they emit radiation at a variety of characteristic wavelengths imparting to the expanding cloud a multicolored glow. The rate of expansion is usually around 30 km per second (20 miles per second), though expansion speeds ranging from 5 to 100 km per second (3 to 60 miles per second) have been measured. The lightest planetary nebulas have a mass of about 0.01 M_S and a radius of about 0.05 light-years; the most massive ones contain about 1 M_S of material and span several light-years. After 10,000 to 30,000 years, the expanding matter dissipates to the extent that the central star can no longer photoionize it, at which point the nebula fades from view and all that remains to be seen is a slowly cooling **white dwarf.**

Planetary nebulas have nothing whatever to do with planets. Their name was coined by William **Herschel** in the 1780s because their appearance suggested to him the disks of remote worlds. More than 1,600 examples have been identified in our galaxy out of an estimated total galactic population of some 30,000. Among the best known are the **Dumbbell Nebula,** the Helix Nebula, and the **Ring Nebula.** In all they return to the **interstellar medium** about 5 M_S of material each year (about 15 percent of all the matter expelled by all sorts of stars)—flotsam from which a new generation of stars will eventually form. The Sun itself will probably eject a planetary nebula in about 5 billion years' time.[556]

planetary protection

Measures designed to protect the Earth (➔ **back contamination**) and other bodies in the solar system (➔ **forward contamination**) from cross-contamination. The need for planetary protection was first considered in 1959 (➔ **Committee on Contamination by Extraterrestrial Exploration**), was expressed in the **Outer Space Treaty of 1967,** and has been reconsidered and refined in the light of more recent developments. For many years, the **Space Science Board** has served as NASA's primary adviser on planetary protection and quarantine.

Planetary Society

A nonprofit, public organization established in 1979 to encourage and support, through education, public information events, and special events, the exploration of the solar system and the search for extraterrestrial life. With a membership of nearly 100,000 from more than one hundred countries, the Planetary Society is the largest space interest group in the world.

planetary system

A collection of planets and smaller objects, such as moons, **asteroid**s, and **comet**s, orbiting around a star. Planetary systems are believed to originate from rotating clouds of dust and gas that encircle stars shortly after their birth (➔ **planetary systems, formation of**). Evidence is

gathering that they are relatively common. ➔ **extrasolar planets**

planetary systems, formation of

The frequency with which stars are attended by planets is a key factor in the extraterrestrial life debate. This frequency, in turn, is dependent on the mechanism by which planets are generally formed. For about 300 years, from the middle of the seventeenth century to the middle of the twentieth, there were two fundamentally different, competing scenarios. The **nebular hypothesis** argued for the formation of planets from residual (or, in earlier versions, spin-ejected) circumstellar material and suggested that planetary systems may be common. The **catastrophic hypothesis,** by contrast, regarded planets as condensates from material torn out of a star by a close encounter or collision with another star and implied that the solar system may be exceptional.[578]

A consensus theory of planetary formation is now to hand based on the nebular hypothesis. It envisages the gradual **accretion** of planets, moons, and smaller objects from **cosmic dust** grains and gas particles within a primarily gaseous **protoplanetary disk** that is itself a by-product of the formation of the parent star from a dense, rotating **interstellar cloud.** Calculations suggest that dust grains grow by "sticky" collisions into **planetesimals** of the order of 10 km across (although there are still theoretical difficulties with the later stages of this process). These planetesimals then begin to interact with each other through gravity, leading to a phase of runaway accretion and rapid growth.[351] Confidence in this theory has been boosted by the discovery and study of numerous **circumstellar disk**s, with masses in the range 0.01 to 0.1 M_S, needed to produce a planetary system like that of the Sun, around young stars of widely differing **spectral type.** However, the theory has been investigated in only a narrow range of initial conditions and still has little predictive capability—a fact illustrated by the unexpected discovery of massive planets in very small circular orbits (➔ **epistellar Jovians**) around Sun-like stars.

The solar system, it is thought, began as a subcondensation (➔ **globule**) in an interstellar cloud of gas and dust, from which probably hundreds of other stars also formed. To begin with, this presolar cloud was spheroidal, slowly rotating, and quite large, with a diameter of perhaps 1 or 2 light-years. As it condensed, its rotation rate increased as a result of the law of conservation of angular momentum, causing it to become increasingly flattened. In the middle of the disk, where the density was greatest, the protosun began its final condensation. By the time the Sun had initiated nuclear **fusion** reactions in its core (➔ **T Tauri star**), the pancake-shaped protoplanetary disk had started to form agglomerations at various distances from the center.

Two key factors determine what kind of planet a protoplanet will become: its mass and its distance from the central star. Planets of low mass cannot retain **hydrogen** and **helium,** the lightest and most abundant gases, especially if their temperature rises to the point at which the lightest molecules escape. When the planets were in their early accretional phase, the mass that agglomerated before the Sun began to shine helped determine how well the planet would retain its hydrogen and helium. The other crucial factor, the distance of the planet from the Sun, also influenced the escape of hydrogen and helium from the planet's gravity, because inner planets become hotter and so have more difficulty in retaining the lightest gases with a given amount of gravitational force. These considerations explain well the overall structure of the solar system. The four small, inner planets were unable to hold on to any free hydrogen and helium with which they may have started out. However, the four **gas giant**s, lying much further out from the Sun and therefore having much lower temperatures, not only retained their light gases but, through their powerful gravitational pulls, continued to draw in more material after the Sun had turned on.

Based on these ideas, we might expect *any* planetary system to follow the general plan of our own, with small, dense, rocky worlds occupying orbits close to the central star and large, low-density, gassy worlds orbiting at much greater distances. However, the majority of the first **extrasolar planets** to be confirmed do not conform at all to this scheme. Planets with masses even greater than that of Jupiter have

been found in near-circular orbits within 2 AU (and, in some cases, within 0.1 AU) of their host stars. Since it is hard to conceive how these giant worlds could have formed *in situ,* the consensus is emerging that they formed further out, beyond several astronomical units, but then underwent **inward orbital migration.** Indeed, evidence is rapidly mounting that catastrophic events, involving planets being hurled into radically different orbits or even expelled altogether into interstellar space (➔ **rogue planet**), is a common, and perhaps universal, aspect of planet formation.[353]

planetesimals
Intermediate-size objects that form from the accretion of dust in a **circumstellar disk** and are the precursors of larger bodies, including planets, moons, and asteroids.

planets, as living beings
The extraordinary notion that an entire planet might be alive or even conscious has been explored in fiction, philosophy, and science. One of the first stories based on this theme was Arthur Conan **Doyle**'s "When the Earth Screamed" (1929), in which a deep shaft is drilled through the crust to expose the planet's supposed living flesh. According to the controversial **Gaia Hypothesis,** the biosphere of the Earth can be considered to act as a single integrated life-form. Among those to develop fictionally the idea of intelligent and conscious worlds are Olaf **Stapledon** in *Star Maker,* Stanisław **Lem** in *Solaris,* and David Brin in *Earth* (1990).

plants
Organisms belonging to the kingdom Plantae, characterized by their ability to manufacture **carbohydrates** by **photosynthesis.**

plasma (physics)
Sometimes referred to as the "fourth state" of matter, plasmas consist of a fluid of **ions** and free **electron**s. They occur in the interior of stars and in other places, such as **H II region**s, where the temperature is very high or there is an intense bombardment by **ionizing radiation.**

plasma membrane
→ cell membrane

plasmid
A small fragment of extrachromosomal **DNA,** usually circular, that replicates independently of the main **chromosome,** although it may have been derived from it. Plasmids make up about 5 percent of the DNA of many **bacteria** but are relatively rare in **eukaryotic cell**s.

plate tectonics
A geological model in which a planet's **lithosphere** is divided into a number of more or less rigid segments that move in relation to one another.

Plato (c. 428–348 B.C.)
Greek philosopher who opposed the claims of **atomism,** put forward by **Leucippus, Democritus of Abdera,** and others, that there are other inhabited worlds. In the *Timaeus,* he writes, "There is and ever will be one only-begotten and created heaven." This statement derived partly from Plato's belief that a unique Creator implies a unique creation. His student **Aristotle** also argued vigorously in favor of a single *kosmos* and a single seat of life throughout all of space and time. → **ancient philosophy, related to the possibility of extraterrestrial life**

Pleiades (M 45)
An **open cluster,** containing three hundred to five hundred young stars located about 380 light-years (120 parsecs) from the Sun in the constellation of Taurus. It is sometimes referred to as the Seven Sisters, although most observers can distinguish only six stars in the group with the naked eye. The stars of the Pleiades were formed only about 50 million years ago from the same **interstellar cloud** of gas and dust, the remaining fragments of which can still be seen as a **reflection nebula** illuminated by the brighter members of the cluster.

plenitude, principle of
The name given by historian Arthur O. **Lovejoy**[359] to the philosophical doctrine according to which the nature of God, or the fecundity of nature, is such that every situation that can be

realized *will* be realized. Throughout history, it has been a central tenet of those arguing in favor of **pluralism.** First employed by supporters of **atomism,** including **Epicurus** and **Lucretius,** it was used in a theological sense to support the case for numerous inhabited worlds by **Nicholas of Cusa** and by others following the **Copernican Revolution.** In a more restrained way, it is now espoused by many researchers involved in **astrobiology** and **SETI** who contend that wherever conditions are not opposed to the development of life, life will be likely to appear. According to Carl **Sagan:**

> The available evidence strongly suggests that the origins of life should occur given the initial conditions and a billion years of evolutionary time. The origin of life on suitable planets seems built into the chemistry of the universe.

Proponents of the ubiquity of extraterrestrial life and intelligence also commonly appeal to two other principles (→ **mediocrity, principle of; uniformity, principle of**).

pluralism
In an astronomical context, the belief that there exist numerous other worlds harboring life and, in particular, intelligent life. The debate over pluralism, or "the plurality of worlds," extends back at least two and a half thousand years, to the time of ancient Greece, and continues vigorously today. For most of this period, a lack of hard scientific data forced the discussion entirely onto a philosophical and theological footing. Only in relatively recent times have astronomical and biological considerations come to the fore.

The first strong pluralist stance was taken by the early proponents of **atomism** and its associated doctrines, notably **Leucippus, Democritus of Abdera,** and **Epicurus.** The opposing view—that the Earth is unique and that there can be no other systems of worlds— was championed by a number of other prominent Greek philosophers, including **Plato** and **Aristotle.** The possibility of lunar inhabitants was raised by **Anaxagoras of Clazomenae, Plutarch,** and **Lucian of Samosata.** It is important to recognize that "other systems of worlds" in the classical sense did not imply

SOME SIGNIFICANT ADVOCATES OF PLURALISM*

Pre–17th Century	17th Century	18th Century	19th Century
Anaxagoras	Joseph Addison	John Adams	François Arago
Giordano Bruno	Richard Bentley	Jean Le Rond d'Alembert	Robert Stawell Ball
Tommaso Campanella	Pierre Borel	Henry Baker	Honoré de Balzac
Democritus of Abdera	Savinien Cyrano de Bergerac	Jean-Jacques Barthélemy	Jacques-Henri Bernadin de Saint-Pierre
Epicurus	Bernard Fontenelle	James Beattie	David Brewster
Johannes Kepler	Francis Godwin	George Berkeley	Thomas Chalmers
Leucippus	Christiaan Huygens	Johann Elert Bode	Humphry Davy
Lucretius	John Locke	Henry St. John Bolingbroke	Januarius De Concilio
Nicholas of Cusa	John Wilkins	Charles Bonnet	Thomas Dick
Teng Mu		Ruggiero Giuseppe Boscovich	Camille Flammarion
Xenophanes		Georges-Louis Leclerc de Buffon	Karl Friedrich Gauss
		William Derham	Franz von Paula Gruithuisen
		William Herschel	Hermann von Helmholtz
		Immanuel Kant	John Herschel
		Joseph-Jérôme Le Français de Lalande	Joseph Johann von Littrow
		Johann Heinrich Lambert	Heinrich Wilhelm Matthäus Olbers
		Mikhail Vasilyevich Lomonosov	Richard A. Procter
		Johann H. Schröter	Jean Reynaud
		Emanuel Swedenborg	Pietro Angelo Secchi

* Refer to individual entries for details.

planets going around remote stars. As far as most Greeks were concerned, the stars of the night sky were small lights located in a vault that immediately surrounded the "sphere" of Saturn. The multitude of life-bearing worlds envisaged by the atomists was invisible and inaccessible from Earth, rather like the parallel universes of modern scientific speculation. These supposed other worlds might exist contemporaneously with the Earth (as the Stoics believed) or form a linear succession in time (as, for example, the Roman orator Cicero maintained). → **ancient philosophy, related to the possibility of extraterrestrial life**

Throughout the early Christian era and into the late Middle Ages, there was little discussion of the possibility of extraterrestrial life beyond that of angels and demons. The conventional **geocentric** model of the cosmos, based on the teachings of Aristotle and **Ptolemy,** suited the Church well. Allowing, as it did, for only one Earth and therefore a privileged position for mankind, it avoided serious theological concerns having to do with the **incarnation and redemption** that surrounded the notion that there might be intelligent corporeal life-forms elsewhere (→ **Christian doctrine and pluralism**). Despite these concerns, however, a number of prominent scholastics eventually came to question the Ptolemaic-Aristotelian cosmos in its original form. William of **Ockham,** Jean **Buridan,** Nicole d'**Oresme,** and William **Vorilong** were among those who pointed out that Aristotle's insistence on the impossibility of there being more than one *kosmos* placed unacceptable restrictions on God's power. An omnipotent Creator, they said, must at least be credited with having had the *option* to make multiple worlds—a point of view officially sanctioned in 1277 by Étienne Tempier, the bishop of Paris, acting on papal authority. With this change to the Aristotelian scheme in place, the consensus became that while God *could* have created other inhabited worlds, *in reality* he chose not to do so. But then, in 1440, **Nicholas of Cusa** took a bolder step by arguing that whatever lay in God's power must have been realized—a principle that has come to be known as **plenitude.**

Following the demise of the geocentric theory at the hands of Nicolaus **Copernicus** and

the realization that the Earth is just another planet, speculation about life on other worlds, both within the solar system and beyond, flourished. Giordano **Bruno,** Johannes **Kepler,** Tommaso **Campanella,** John **Wilkins,** Pierre **Borel,** Savinien **Cyrano de Bergerac,** Christiaan **Huygens,** Bernard **Fontenelle,** and others used the heliocentric worldview as a logical basis for extraterrestrial speculation. For the first time, astronomical observations, made with the help of early telescopes, began to play a part in the pluralism debate. However, theological and philosophical arguments continued to hold sway. Those opposed to pluralism insisted that although the Earth may have been displaced from the center of the cosmos, humanity and its planet were still the unique focus of God's attention and love. Conversely, post-Copernican pluralists saw multiple life-bearing worlds as an expression of God's creative power and generosity. Other propluralism arguments included **analogy,** belief in a cosmic **chain of being,** and **teleology.** By the second half of the nineteenth century, science began to play a far more decisive role in the pluralism debate, leading to a new climate of skeptical and rigorous inquiry.

plurality of worlds
→ **pluralism**

Plutarch (c. 46–c. 120 A.D.)
Greek historian and biographer who wrote about the possibilities of lunar life (→ **Moon, life on**) in his *De facie in orbe lunae* (On the Face That Appears in the Moon) in A.D. 70. He wondered whether the Moon's apparent lack of clouds might mean it was intolerably dry, but decided on balance that the dark areas were probably seas (→ **Moon, water on**). Today, that description still survives in the naming of these regions as *maria*. → **Lucian of Samosata; ancient philosophy, related to the possibility of extraterrestrial life**

Pluto
The smallest and usually the most remote known planet in the solar system, although between February 1979 and February 1999 its elongated orbit brought it closer to the Sun than Neptune. It was discovered in 1930 by

Distance from Sun:	
Mean	5,910 million km (3,673 million mi., 39.4 AU)
Minimum	4,425 million km (2,750 million mi., 29.6 AU)
Maximum	7,375 million km (4,584 million mi., 49.2 AU)
Equatorial diameter	2,320 km (1,442 mi.)
Equatorial diameter (Earth = 1)	0.182
Mass (Earth = 1)	0.002
Mean density	2.02 g/cm³
Escape velocity	1.1 km/s (4,055 km/h, 2,520 mi./h)
Orbital period	247.7 years
Orbital eccentricity	0.248
Orbital inclination	17.2°
Axial period	6.39 days
Axial inclination	122°
Number of moons	1
Atmospheric composition	Mostly nitrogen, with some carbon monoxide, methane
Mean temperature	−230°C (−382°F)
Albedo	0.4

Clyde Tombaugh at the **Lowell Observatory.** Given its extremely small size—smaller even than our moon—and the unusually high **eccentricity** and **inclination** of its orbit, there has been much speculation about its nature and origin, and indeed whether it should even be properly classified as a planet. A popular theory in the past was that it had been a moon of Neptune that escaped when another large object passed close by. However, it now seems that both Pluto and its solitary moon, **Charon,** were among the largest **ice dwarfs**, or trans-Neptunian objects, that formed in the **Kuiper Belt.** Subsequently, their orbits were altered, perhaps through the gravitational influence of Neptune, into those seen today. The fact that Pluto is much brighter than other known Kuiper objects is thought to be due to a layer of frost. However, its surface displays such extreme variations in reflectivity that it has the second highest contrast level in the solar system, after **Iapetus.** Pluto's atmosphere, which turns completely to frost as the planet recedes from the Sun, consists mostly of **nitrogen,** a distinction it shares with the Earth, Saturn's largest moon, **Titan,** and Neptune's largest moon, **Triton.** On both Pluto and Triton, the composition of the atmosphere is very similar to that of the surface. The main atmospheric constituents, nitrogen, **carbon monoxide,** and **methane,** are also relatively common substances in the **molecular cloud**s from which new star systems are made. This suggests that Pluto and Triton, being so cold and far from the Sun, managed to retain more or less the original molecular mix from which the solar system was made. Pluto's distinction of being the only planet not to have been visited by a spacecraft will be lost in 2014, when the ***Pluto-Kuiper Express*** is scheduled to fly by.

Pluto, moon of
→ **Charon**

Pluto-Kuiper Express
A proposed NASA mission to explore the Pluto-Charon system and the **Kuiper Belt**, scheduled for launch in 2004 and arrival at Pluto in about 2014. Mission planners were anxious to intercept the outermost planet while it is still in the near-**perihelion** part of its orbit; at greater distances from the Sun, its atmosphere will freeze and any surface activity, such as ice geysers, will become less frequent.

PNA
A substance that contains the same **base**s as those found in biological **nucleic acid**s but whose backbone is held together by **amide bond**s. PNAs are currently of interest in discus-

sions about the chemical precursors of **DNA** and **RNA**.[65, 420] PNAs form double-stranded complexes that closely resemble those of DNA. Moreover, the laboratory demonstration that DNA serves as a template for PNA synthesis, and vice versa, lends support to the view that one genetic polymer could have replaced another on the **prebiotic** Earth. ➔ **life, origin of**

poikilotherm

An animal whose body temperature fluctuates with that of the environment. ➔ **ectotherms**

polar molecule

A **molecule** in which there is some separation of charge in the chemical bonds, so that one part of the molecule has a slight positive charge and the other a slight negative charge. ➔ **polar solvent**

polar solvent

A compound, such as **water** or liquid **ammonia,** that is composed of **polar molecule**s. Polar solvents can dissolve ionic compounds or covalent compounds that ionize. *Nonpolar solvents,* such as benzene, will dissolve only nonpolar covalent compounds.

polarimeter

An instrument for measuring the state of **polarization** of a beam of light or other form of **electromagnetic radiation.**

polarimetry

The measurement of the state of **polarization** of a beam of **electromagnetic radiation.**

polarization

(1) The phenomenon in which waves of **electromagnetic radiation** vibrate in a preferred plane or planes; (2) the process of confining the vibrations to certain planes.

polarized light

Light in which the (electric and magnetic field) vibrations are confined to certain directions. In plane polarized light, the vibrations are confined to a single plane. In circular polarized light, this plane rotates continuously. Plane polarized light can be used to distin-

guish between the two forms of chiral molecules (➔ **chirality**). Polarized **ultraviolet** radiation can influence chemical reactions that normally produce both left- and right-handed forms of a molecule, so that a preponderance of molecules of a particular handedness results.

Pollux

Beta Geminorum; a **K star** that is one of the **giant star**s nearest to the Sun. ➔ **stars, brightest**

polycyclic aromatic hydrocarbons (PAHs)

A group of **hydrocarbon**s made up from multiple interconnected 6-carbon (benzene) rings, like pieces of chicken wire, the simplest of which is napthalene (the chemical in mothballs). More complex PAHs may contain elements other than **carbon** and **hydrogen,** including **nitrogen** and **sulfur.** PAHs can form in a variety of ways, as a result of both biological and nonbiological processes. On Earth they can cause pollution and cancer and are found, for example, in diesel exhaust, burned pots and pans, charred hamburgers, and cigarette smoke. Among cosmic sources of PAHs are **carbonaceous chondrite**s, which originated in the **Main Asteroid Belt** and are not associated with life as far as we know. On the other hand, David **McKay** and his colleagues have tried to show that the PAHs in the meteorite **ALH 84001** are derived from ancient Martian **bacteria,** though this has been strongly disputed (➔ **Martian "fossils" controversy**).

In December 1998, scientists from the **NASA Ames Research Center** and the Astrophysikalisches Institut in Germany reported finding the **spectroscopic** signatures of PAHs in interstellar space.[267] Ames researchers simulated conditions in space using extreme cold, a near vacuum, and artificial starlight. Then they measured the spectra of large, carbon-bearing molecules in the **ultraviolet** and visible bands of the spectrum and compared their results to astronomical data from **Kitt Peak National Observatory** and other observatories. The German scientists carried out a similar study using other forms of carbon molecules. The result of the collaboration was the conclusion that previously unidentified absorption features in the spectra of the interstellar medium, known as **diffuse interstellar bands,** are due to PAHs in space that originated in the atmospheres of **red giant**s. This adds to the growing impression that complex carbon chemistry is a universal phenomenon and that carbon-based life may also be common throughout space.

polymerization

The process by which many similar or identical small **molecule**s link together to form much larger **polymers.**

polymers

Long-chain **molecule**s composed of many similar or identical molecular subunits. **Starch,** for example, is a polymer of **glucose.**

polypeptide

A molecule consisting of many joined **amino acids.** One or more polypeptide chains link together to form a **protein.** → **proteinoids**

polysaccharides

Polymers made from simple sugar molecules (→ **monosaccharides**) linked by **glycosidic bond**s. Polysaccharides are insoluble and may serve as a store of energy, as in the case of **starch** and **glycogen,** or as a structural component, as in the case of **cellulose,** which is found in the **cell wall**s of plants. A single cellulose chain may contain as many as 10,000 units of **glucose.** Polysaccharides are part of the larger family of **carbohydrate**s.

Ponnamperuma, Cyril (1923–95)

Sri Lankan–born professor of chemistry and director of the Laboratory of Chemical Evolution at the University of Maryland, College Park, and former director of the program in Chemical Evolution in the Exobiology Division at **NASA Ames Research Center.** Ponnamperuma's interest in **prebiotic** synthesis went back to his undergraduate days at Birckbeck College, University of London, where he studied under J. D. **Bernal,** receiving a B.Sc. in 1959. He then joined Melvin **Calvin**'s group at the **University of California, Berkeley,** receiving a Ph.D. in 1962, before moving to Ames as a postdoctoral associate and carrying out pioneering experiments on the origin of life. In the preface to *Exobiology*[462] (1972), he points out that

> our primary objective becomes the understanding of the origin of life in the universe. This is the scientifically broader question before us. If we can understand how life began on the Earth, we can argue that the sequence of events which lead to the appearance of terrestrial life may be repeated in the staggering number of planetary systems in our universe.

Ponnamperuma thus aligned himself with others, including Leonard **Troland,** Harold Spencer **Jones,** and Calvin, who regarded the evolution of life as almost inevitable, given the right starting conditions. In 1971 he joined the faculty at Maryland.[461]

Pope, Gustavus W.

American physician and author of many books in the Victorian era, including two interplanetary tales that adopt the conventional evolutionist line of that time. In *A Journey to Mars,*[464] an American officer falls in love with an advanced Martian on a world strongly reminiscent of that portrayed two decades later by Edgar Rice **Burroughs,** while in *A Journey to Venus* (1895) his explorers find themselves on a primeval planet inhabited by all manner of creatures taken from prehistory and myth.

Population I

A term used to describe objects found in, or near to, the plane of a **spiral galaxy.** *Extreme* Population I objects include **OB stars,** the brilliant light of which illuminates the **spiral arm**s. *Older* Population I objects include stars like the Sun. All Population I stars are relatively rich in **heavy element**s, since they formed from clouds of gas and dust that contained the products of **nucleosynthesis** from previous generations of stars. The presence of heavy elements in **protoplanetary disk**s is believed to be a key factor in the formation of planets (→ **planetary systems, formation of**), so that only Population I objects are expected to harbor planetary systems, and possibly life, similar to our own.

Population II

A term used to describe old, red stars found in the **galactic halo** of a **spiral galaxy,** such as our own, near the galactic center, and in parts of the disk of the Galaxy that are well away from the galactic plane. The halo contains individual old stars and large groupings known as **globular clusters**. Population II stars are relatively deficient in elements heavier than hydrogen or helium because they formed when the Galaxy was young, before much stellar **nucleosynthesis** had taken place. The importance of **heavy elements** in planet formation (→ **planetary systems, formation of**) suggests that few, if any, Population II stars have worlds in orbit around them.

population types

It was Walter Baade, in 1944, who first distinguished between the two main types of stars found in a **spiral galaxy,** referring to them as **Population I** and **Population II**. In reality, there is a continuous gradation of stars from one type to the other.

porphin

A chemical made up of four **pyrrole** molecules linked by **carbon-hydrogen** bridges. The bonding arrangement within porphin is responsible for the reddish color of its derivatives.

An outline of the porphin molecule. A carbon atom lies at each corner, except where nitrogen atoms are shown.

porphyrins

Organic compounds of great biological importance that are found in a variety of pigments,

The general structure of a porphyrin molecule formed by four pyrrole rings linked by carbon-hydrogen bridges.

including hemoglobin, **chlorophyll,** and the **cytochromes** (these last concerned with **respiration** in **cell**s). Porphyrins are variations on the basic structure of **porphin**. A variety of side groups can be attached at eight different locations around the molecule and a complex can be formed with a centrally located, heavy metal atom. In hemoglobin this metal is iron, while in chlorophyll it is magnesium.

Portia

The seventh known moon of **Uranus**. → **Uranus, moons of**

Discovery	1986, by *Voyager 2*
Mean distance from Uranus	66,100 km (41,100 mi.)
Diameter	110 km (68 mi.)
Equatorial diameter (Earth = 1)	0.00862
Orbital period	0.513 day (12 hours 19 minutes)
Orbital eccentricity	0.000
Orbital inclination	0.09°
Visual albedo	0.07

positron

The positively charged **antiparticle** of the **electron**. When a positron and electron meet they destroy one another instantly and produce a pair of high-energy **gamma rays**. The existence of the positron was first predicted by Paul Dirac in 1930 as a result of his work on the application of the **special theory of relativity** to **quantum mechanics**. It was discovered in 1933 by Carl Anderson.

potential energy
Stored energy or energy possessed by an object due to its position, for example, in a gravitational field.

prebiotic
Not yet alive; a chemical system or environment that is a precursor of life.

prebiotic evolution
The development of increasingly complex molecules and aggregates of molecules that, if continued, might lead to living systems.

presolar grains
Microscopic grains of matter that existed in the interstellar cloud from which the Sun formed.

Prigogine, Ilya (1917–)
Moscow-born professor of physics and chemical engineering at the University of Texas, Austin, and winner of the 1977 Nobel Prize for Chemistry for his research in the field of non-equilibrium thermodynamics. Prigogine's work on dissipative structures has stimulated other scientists to examine the role of systems far from equilibrium in the origin of life. Among his books are *Order Out of Chaos*[466] (1983) and *The End of Certainty: Time, Chaos, and the New Laws of Nature* (1997), both with Irene Stenger.

primary
The largest gravitating mass within a given system. In a **binary star** system, it is the more massive of the two components. The planet around which a moon revolves is also known as the primary.

prime number
A number with no factors other than itself and 1. In 1941, James **Jeans** pointed out that the attention of intelligent Martians "if any such there be" could be attracted by using powerful searchlights to flash, in sequence, the first prime numbers: 2, 3, 5, 7, 11, 13, 17, 19, 23. . . . Likewise, it has been suggested that the occurrence of sequences of prime numbers in an extraterrestrial radio signal would immediately imply an artificial and intelligent origin.

The reception of such a signal occurs in the novel (and film) **Contact.**[495] Prime numbers were also used in the construction of **Drake's cryptogram** and the **Arecibo Message.**

primitive material
Material that has survived from the time of the earliest **accretion** of the planets of the solar system (or some other planetary system). It may include **presolar grains, organic** matter that might preserve the signature of interstellar chemistry, and once molten **chondrule**s with composition, size, and mineralogy diagnostic of the preaccretionary environment.

primordial atmosphere
An atmosphere made from the original material in a **protoplanetary disk** and retained since the formation of a planet. **Gas giant**s, such as Jupiter and Saturn, have primordial atmospheres. → **secondary atmosphere**

Probing Lensing Anomalies Network (PLANET)
An international collaboration of astronomers with access to Dutch, South African, and Australian telescopes for monitoring the sky from the Southern Hemisphere for **microlensing** events, some of which are believed to provide evidence for **extrasolar planets.** After analysis of its first 3 years of data is complete, PLANET should enable limits to be placed on the numbers of lensing stars in the Galaxy that have Jupiter-type planets in their lensing zones.[5]

Procter, Richard Anthony (1837–88)
Cambridge-educated author of numerous books and articles on astronomy and one of the most influential commentators of his day on the subject of life on other worlds. Only Camille **Flammarion** was more prolific in popular output at this time. Procter was frank about his reasons for entering the debate on **pluralism.** It was, he said "a convenient subject with which to associate scientific researches which I could in no other way bring before the notice of the general reading public." His personal financial crisis (precipitated by the collapse of the bank in which he was a major shareholder) meant that he had to write for a commercial end, and, like authors today, he

found that speculation about life beyond the Earth sold well. In his first successful book, *Other Worlds than Ours* (1870),[468] he stated his basic position that a planet should be assumed inhabited until proven lifeless. Mercury he thought possibly sterile because of its intense bombardment by solar rays. Regarding the likelihood of Venusians, he was more hopeful, while Mars "exhibits in the clearest manner the traces of adaptation to the wants of living beings such as we are acquainted with" (➔ **Mars, life on**). Moving to the giant outer planets, he dismissed the theories of both David **Brewster** and William **Whewell** on these bodies, arguing that their surfaces were hot as a result of immense internal sources of heat. This view was subsequently taken up by others, including Robert **Ball**. Procter likened both Jupiter and Saturn to miniature suns, bestowing both warmth and life on their systems of moons. By 1875, he had incorporated these ideas into a theory of planetary evolution, powerfully influenced by the new Darwinian paradigm:

> Each planet, according to its dimensions, has a certain length of planetary life, the youth and age of which include the following eras:—a Sun-like state; a state like that of Jupiter or Saturn, when much heat but little light is evolved; a condition like that of our earth; and lastly, the stage through which our moon is passing, which may be regarded as planetary decrepitude.

Although this theory suggested that the Earth might presently be the only inhabited world in the solar system (smaller planets being dead and larger ones not yet alive), it did not mean that Procter had moved away from pluralism. In *Our Place Among Infinities* (1875), he writes:

> Have we then been led to the Whewellite theory that our earth is the sole abode of life? Far from it. For not only have we adopted a method of reasoning which teaches us to regard every planet in existence, every moon, every sun, every orb in fact in space, as having *its period* as the abode of life, but the very argument from probability which leads us to

regard any given sun as not the centre of a scheme in which at this moment there is life, forces upon us the conclusion that among the millions on millions … of suns which people space, millions have orbs circling round them which are at this present time the abode of living creatures.

Despite his tendency toward metaphysical speculation, Procter played an important role, as Whewell had done and as Flammarion was doing in France, in shifting the extraterrestrial life debate onto a more scientific footing.

Procyon
Alpha Canis Minoris; a yellow-white **F star** that is one of the Sun's nearest stellar neighbors. It has a **white dwarf** companion (Procyon B) with a period of 40.23 years. ➔ **stars, nearest**

	A	**B**
Distance	11.4 light-years (3.5 parsecs)	
Spectral type	F5 IV–V	wdF8
Apparent magnitude	0.34	
Absolute magnitude	2.7	
Luminosity (Sun = 1)	7.6	0.0005
Mass (Sun = 1)	1.77	0.63
Radius (Sun = 1)	1.7	0.01

Project Argus
➔ **Argus, Project**

Project BETA
➔ **BETA, Project**

Project Blue Book
➔ **Blue Book, Project**

Project Cyclops
➔ **Cyclops, Project**

Project Daedalus
➔ **Daedalus, Project**

Project Grudge
➔ **Grudge, Project**

Project META
➔ **META, Project; META II, Project**

Project Mogul
→ **Mogul, Project**

Project Orion
→ **Orion, Project**

Project Ozma
→ **Ozma, Project**

Project Phoenix
→ **Phoenix, Project**

Project Sentinel
→ **Sentinel, Project**

Project Sign
→ **Sign, Project**

Project Skyhook
→ **Skyhook, Project**

Project Twinkle
→ **Twinkle, Project**

prokaryote
An organism consisting of one or more **prokaryotic cell**s. Prokaryotes include **archaea** and **bacteria.**

prokaryotic
Pertaining to a **prokaryote** or a **prokaryotic cell.**

prokaryotic cell
A **cell** lacking a membrane-bounded **nucleus** or membrane-bounded **organelle**s. Prokaryotic cells are more primitive than **eukaryotic cell**s, which evolved from them.

Prometheus
The third of **Saturn**'s moons; it acts as a **shepherd moon** for the inner edge of Saturn's F-ring. Prometheus is extremely elongated and has a number of ridges and valleys on its northern side. Although craters up to 20 km (12 miles) across mark its surface, it appears to be less heavily cratered than its neighboring moons **Pandora, Janus,** and **Epimetheus.** Its low estimated density suggests that it may be a porous, icy body. → **Saturn, moons of**

Discovery	1980, by S. Collins et al.
Mean distance from Saturn	139,350 km (86,610 mi.)
Diameter	145 × 85 × 65 km (90 × 53 × 40 mi.)
Mean density	0.7 g/cm^3
Escape velocity	0.022 km/s (79 km/h, 49 mi./h)
Orbital period	0.613 day (14 hours 43 minutes)
Orbital eccentricity	0.003
Orbital inclination	0.00°
Visual albedo	0.6

proper motion
The apparent motion of a star across the sky. Only two hundred stars have proper motions exceeding one arc-second per year. **Barnard's Star** has the largest proper motion (10.3 arc-seconds per year), followed by **Kapteyn's Star.** Periodic perturbations, or wobbles, in a star's proper motion are indicative of an unseen companion, which may be a dim star, a **brown dwarf,** or a planet. In 1844, Friedrich **Bessel** reported variations in the proper motions of **Sirius** and **Procyon,** now known to be due to **white dwarf** companions. The use of **astrometry** to detect **extrasolar planets,** however, is much more problematic, because of the extremely small deviations involved.

proplyd
Abbreviation of "**protoplanetary disk.**"

prosthetic group
A tightly bound non-**peptide** component of a **protein.** Prosthetic groups may be **lipid**s, **carbohydrate**s, metal ions (e.g., iron in hemoglobin), or **inorganic** groups such as phosphates.

proteinoids
The term originally used to describe substances now known as **thermal proteins.**

proteins
Macromolecules that play a central role in the structure and functioning of all living **cells** on Earth. Together with **nucleic acid**s, **carbohydrate**s, and **lipids,** they form the biochemical basis of terrestrial life. Proteins are **polymers** made of **amino acid** subunits linked by **pep-**

Part of a protein molecule. Any of a variety of different side groups may be attached at R. Dashed lines between O and H represent hydrogen bonds.

tide bonds to give polypeptide chains. Their synthesis takes place on ribosomes within the cell cytoplasm, each polypeptide chain being generated by the joining of amino acids in an order specified by the nucleic acids of the cell. The specific amino acid sequence of a protein is referred to as its *primary structure.* Since, in principle, a protein can be formed from *any* long sequence of any or all of the twenty different amino acids found in terrestrial organisms, the potential diversity of proteins is enormous. For example, a protein containing 100 amino acids could have 20^{100} (about 1 followed by 130 zeros) different sequences. This almost unlimited diversity is perhaps the most important property of proteins since it enables them to perform such a wide range of functions in living organisms.

The amino acid sequence of a protein encourages the formation of hydrogen bonds between nearby amino acids. This results in two distinct types of structures. In the first, hydrogen bonds are established between different parts of the same polypeptide chain, which pulls the chain into a spiral shape, known as an "α-helix." In the second, hydrogen bonds form between two adjacent chains, resulting in a pleated configuration called a "β-sheet." These types of folding are referred to as the protein's *secondary structure.* A more complex pattern of folding organizes the protein into its final, unique, three-dimensional configuration, or *tertiary structure.* The details of this final configuration are determined by the chemical nature of the side groups of the amino acids making up the primary structure. Many proteins associate with other polypeptide chains in clusters. Each contributing chain is referred to as a subunit and the overall struc-

ture of the cluster as the *quarternary structure.*

Since many of the bonds holding a protein in its normal shape are weak, they are easily broken by changes in the protein's environment, including the pH, the temperature, or the concentration of ions in the surrounding solution. When this happens, the protein undergoes a process called "denaturation"; that is, it changes shape or may even unfold and, as a result, usually becomes biologically inactive. This has particularly serious consequences if the protein is an enzyme, since such substances regulate the metabolism of living cells.

Proteus

The sixth known moon of Neptune. Like the five other inner moons discovered during the 1989 flyby of *Voyager 2,* Proteus is among the darkest objects in the solar system. It is thought to be about as large as a satellite can be without being drawn into a spherical shape by its own gravity. → Neptune, moons of

Discovery	1989, by Stephen Synnott from *Voyager 2* data
Mean distance from Neptune	118,000 km (73,300 mi.)
Diameter	400 km (249 mi.)
Orbital period	1.122 days (1 day 2 hours 56 minutes)
Orbital eccentricity	0.0004
Orbital inclination	0.04°
Visual albedo	0.06

protists

Relatively simple, eukaryotic organisms that are distinct from animals, plants, or fungi. They form their own kingdom, Protista.

protobiological

Pertaining to a time or environment when life has just begun to emerge.

protobionts

A term first used by Aleksandr Oparin to describe the early environmentally isolated, chemical-concentrating structures from which cells are presumed to have evolved. → protocells

protocells

Encapsulating structures, or **vesicle**s, made of simple membrane-forming material that could have self-assembled in the **protobiological** environment. The presence of such membrane-forming material in **carbonaceous chondrite**s is consistent with this idea. Moreover, recent experiments have shown that vesicular **lipid** bilayer structures can grow by spontaneous addition of membrane-forming material from the surrounding medium, and can encapsulate both **ion**s and **macromolecule**s. ➔ **cell membranes, origin of**

proton

A positively charged subatomic particle found, together with **neutron**s, in the nuclei of atoms. Its mass is 1,836.12 times that of the **electron.** ➔ **nucleon**

protoplanet

A planet in the process of **accretion** from material in a **protoplanetary disk.**

protoplanetary disk

A circumstellar disk of matter, including gas and dust, from which planets may eventually form or be in the process of forming. The existence of such disks was long suspected (➔ **planetary systems, formation of**) but was confirmed by direct imaging in 1994, when C. Robert O'Dell and his colleagues at Rice University used the *Hubble Space Telescope* (HST) to examine newborn stars in the **Orion Nebula.** About half of those observed were found to be surrounded by disks of gas and dust. Before this, in the 1980s, dust disks, believed to be **regenerated disk**s, had been discovered around a number of more mature stars using the *Infrared Astronomy Satellite.* Additionally, **infrared** studies of nearby star-forming regions by Stephen and Karen Strom's group at the University of Massachusetts, Amherst, had revealed that at least 50 percent of all 1-million-year-old stars have excess infrared emission, suggesting that they are surrounded by warm dust. In 1994, John Stauffer and associates of the **Harvard-Smithsonian Center for Astrophysics** reported that 70 to 80 percent of infant stars at the center of the Orion Nebula showed signs of having disks. This high fraction has since been confirmed by more sensitive observations by the *Infrared Space Observatory.*

In 1999, some of the clearest views yet seen of protoplanetary disks came from observations by the HST. A group at the California Institute of Technology's Image Processing and Analysis Center in Pasadena used NICMOS (Near Infrared Camera and Multi-Object Spectrometer) to peer through obscuring dust clouds surrounding six extremely young stars in a stellar nursery in Taurus, 450 light-years away.[444] Evidence of dusty disks eight to sixteen times the diameter of Neptune's orbit was found in all six in the form of dark bands, believed to be dust lanes, crossing the bright areas around each star. Dark clumps and bright streamers above and below the dust lanes, apparent in the NICMOS images, suggest that raw material is still falling into the disks and driving outflowing jets of gas from the young stars. At about the same time, another group using *Hubble* took very sharp visible-light pictures of disks in the same region. John Krist of the Space Telescope Science Institute in Baltimore found that the young star Haro 6-5B is actually a small nebula crossed by a dust lane about ten times the size of Neptune's orbit. Also in 1999, Karl Stapelfeldt of the **Jet Propulsion Laboratory** used *Hubble*'s Wide Field and Planetary Camera 2 to spot the first example of an edge-on disk in a young **binary star** system. The disk is centered on the fainter component and has a diameter of only thirty-one times the diameter of Neptune's orbit. This offers further evidence that, in spite of theoretical predictions that the gravitational forces in binaries ought to tear apart fragile protoplanetary disks, planetary formation may well be able to occur in two-star systems.

Conventional theory suggests that about 10 million years are required for a planetary system to form completely from a protoplanetary disk, so that, on this basis, the disks mentioned above might not yet be old enough to contain planets. They should, however, be at the stage where dust grains are accreting to give larger particles. This was confirmed in 1998 by observations carried out with the HST by Larry Esposito and colleagues at the University of Colorado that showed that the disks around three stars in the Orion Nebula contain dust at least 10 microns across, or nearly one hundred times larger than dust grains in interstellar space.

Some young protoplanetary disks are thought to have a mass of 0.01 to 0.1 M_S, or more than ten times that needed to make a planetary system like our own. Much of this material will eventually be blown away by the strong **stellar wind** from the central star. Dust accounts for about 1 percent of the disk's initial mass, the rest being made up of gas, mainly hydrogen and helium. Young disks imaged by the HST, in Orion and Taurus, are seen at many different angles, from edge-on to nearly face-on, and are typically a few hundred AU in diameter. Two of the most spectacular edge-on disks surround HH 30 and the "Butterfly Star," both of which are narrow in their central parts but flare gently at distances of about 100 AU. Such flaring was predicted as a result of heating by the host star by Harvard-Smithsonian astronomers Lee Hartman and Scott Kenyon in the late 1980s.

As accretion within a protoplanetary disk continues, sizable objects known as **planetesimals** form; after several million years, these give rise to small, rocky planets close to the host star. Further out, where it is cold enough for ice to form in the disk, more solid material is available for world building. **Gas giant**s, such as Jupiter and Saturn, may start with cores of rock and ice of about ten Earth masses and then sweep up large quantities of light gases to form thick atmospheres. This should result in the creation of a central cavity within the circumstellar disk, similar in size to the solar system, and a drastic depletion of the disk's gas content. Recent observations, for example of the 10-million-year-old star **HR 4796A,** provide evidence for this view.

Studies of more mature stars around which dust rings have been detected, including **Beta Pictoris, Vega,** and **Epsilon Eridani,** suggest that the circumstellar material is in the form of **regenerated disk**s. There is also indirect evidence of planets in these systems.

protoplanetary nebula
→ **protoplanetary disk**

protoplasm
An obsolete term for the principal living substance of a **cell.** → **Huxley, Thomas**

protostar
A stage in the evolution of a young star after it has fragmented from a gas cloud but before it has collapsed sufficiently for nuclear **fusion** reactions to begin. It may last from 100,000 years to 10 million years, depending on the mass of the star. → **globule; T Tauri star**

Proxima Centauri
A **red dwarf** that, at 270,000 AU, is the star nearest to the Sun. It is also a **flare star** and an intense source of low-energy **X rays** and high-energy **ultraviolet.** Proxima is a remote member of the **Alpha Centauri** system, orbiting Alpha Centauri A and B at a distance of 0.11 light-year (about 10,000 AU), with a period of about 1 million years. In 1998, Al Schulz and coworkers at the Space Science Institute in Baltimore, using the Hubble Space Telescope, reported having seen a point of light near Proxima on two occasions three months apart that they suggested might be a planetary companion.[520] Searches by other groups, however, have failed to verify this.[227] → **stars, nearest**

Distance	4.28 light-years (1.31 parsecs, or 40 trillion km)
Spectral type	M5e V
Apparent magnitude	10.7
Absolute magnitude	15.1
Luminosity (Sun = 1)	0.00006
Mass (Sun = 1)	0.1
Radius (Sun = 1)	0.093

PSR 1257+12
A **millisecond pulsar** in the constellation of Virgo discovered in 1990 by Alexander **Wolszczan** of the **Arecibo Observatory.** Around it, in 1991, Wolszczan and Dale Frail of the National Radio Astronomy Observatory in New Mexico found the first planets to be subsequently confirmed outside the solar system. The initial announcement was of two objects (b and c) similar in mass to the Earth.[631] This was followed by claims for a third, Moon-sized

Pulsar				
Distance	1,000 light-years (300 parsecs)			
Period	6.2 ms (= 160 rev/s)			
Planets	*a*	*b*	*c*	*d*
Mass (Earth = 1)	0.015(?)	3.4	2.8	95
Semimajor axis (AU)	0.19(?)	0.36	0.47	35
Orbital period	25.34 d	66.54 d	98.22 d	~170 y
Eccentricity	0.00(?)	0.02	0.03	—

body (a) in 1994[629] and a possible fourth, Saturn-sized planet (d) in 1996. The planets were discovered by the pulsar timing method. The existence of the innermost, lunar-mass member of the system has been called into question by Klaus Scherer of the Max Planck Institute in Katlenburg-Linda, Germany. The period of this supposed planet, 25.3 days, is the same as the rotational period of the Sun, leading Scherer to suggest that the 25.3-day periodicity in PSR 1257+12's timing is an artifact caused by the solar wind. A similar effect has been found in the measured velocity of the deep space probe *Pioneer 10.* No doubt remains about the reality of the Earth-mass planets, however, following the matching of a gravitational perturbation model with the pulsar timings. → **pulsar planets**

PSR B1620-26
A remote **millisecond pulsar** with a **white dwarf** companion, located in the **globular cluster** M4. Measurements using the pulsar-timing method indicate that the pulsar is orbited by three massive planets.[471, 586]

Pulsar			
Distance	12,400 light-years (3.8 kiloparsecs)		
Period	11 ms (= 90 rev/s)		
Planets	*a*	*b*	*c*
Mass (Jupiter = 1)	1.2	3.4	6.7
Semimajor axis (AU)	~10	30	64
Orbital period (years)	61.8	129	389
Eccentricity	0.0	0.2	0.5

psychrophiles
Microbes that reproduce and grow best at low temperatures, in the range of −10 to 20°C (14 to 68°F). Psychrophiles thrive in the Arctic and Antarctic Oceans, which remain frozen for much of the year. Typically, they have **enzymes** that are adapted to function at lower temperatures and are denatured at moderate temperatures. They also exhibit polyunsaturated **fatty acids** in their **lipids.** *Psychrotolerant* organisms, by contrast, are **mesophiles** that can survive at low temperatures but grow more slowly. → **extremophiles**

PTI
→ **Palomar Testbed Interferometer**

Ptolemy (c. 100–c. 168)
Egyptian astronomer and geographer, who worked at the great library in Alexandria. His thirteen-volume *Almagest,* a compendium of the astronomical works of **Hipparchus of Nicaea, Aristotle,** and others, represents the most complete description of the Universe as it was then understood. It also promulgated a sophisticated version of the Aristotelian, geocentric theory that held sway in the West until the **Copernican Revolution.**

Puck
The tenth known moon of **Uranus.** → **Uranus, moons of**

Discovery	1986, by *Voyager 2*
Mean distance from Uranus	85,900 km (53,400 mi.)
Diameter	154 km (96 mi.)
Orbital period	0.762 day (18 hours 17 minutes)
Orbital eccentricity	0.000
Orbital inclination	0.31°
Visual albedo	0.07

pulsar

A rapidly rotating **neutron star** emitting radio beams from its poles, which periodically sweep past the Earth like the beam from a lighthouse. Pulsar periods have been found in the range of 30 milliseconds to 4 seconds. To the surprise of everyone, the first confirmed **extrasolar planets** were found in orbit around pulsars. → **pulsar planets**

pulsar planets

Against all expectations, the first confirmed planetary system beyond our own was found, in 1991, in orbit around a **pulsar.** The object in question is a **millisecond pulsar** known as **PSR 1257+12.** The discoveries of several other planets around millisecond pulsars, made using the pulsar timing method, have since been announced, though in most cases these are awaiting confirmation. The nature and origin of these strange worlds are a matter of debate.[40, 452, 453] One possibility is that the pulsar planets formed in the normal way (→ **planetary systems, formation of**) before their host star exploded as a **supernova.** However, it is hard to see how this could be so. The problem is not that the supernova would destroy any nearby planets (though it would certainly incinerate any surface life) but that it would effectively loosen the gravitational glue holding the planetary system together. A planet orbiting a star that suddenly lost a large fraction of its mass would fly off into space. The alternative, and more likely, scenario is that pulsar planets formed *after* the pulsar came into existence. Millisecond pulsars are believed to spin so fast because they have acquired material from a companion star. Planets could condense from some of this material as it entered an **accretion disk** in orbit around the pulsar. However they were made, these strange and unexpected worlds are of little direct biological interest. The **main sequence** life spans of massive stars that are the precursors of pulsars are probably too short to allow any kind of life to develop, even given the availability of suitable planets nearby. On the other hand, planets that formed around a pulsar would be permanently strafed by high-energy radiation, including **X rays** and **gamma rays,** leaving them barren and inhospitable.

The table below shows the pulsar planets confirmed or suspected as of January 1999.[630]

pulsar-timing noise

Slight irregularities in the arrival times of radiation from a **pulsar** due to irregularities in the pulsar's rotation that are believed to be caused by changes in the extent to which the pulsar's superfluid core is connected to its surface. In searching for **pulsar planets,** it is important to discriminate between possible effects due to timing noise and the more regular changes in a pulsar's period that may indicate the presence of a planetary companion.

Host Star	Distance (light-years)	Mass (Earth = 1)	Semimajor Axis (AU)	Period	Eccentricity
Confirmed:					
PSR 1257+12	1,000	0.015	0.19	25.3 days	0
		3.4	0.36	66.5 days	0.02
		2.8	0.47	98.2 days	0.03
		~100	~40	~170 years	—
PSR B1620-26	12,400	?	~38	~100 years	—
Suspected:					
Geminga	512	1.7	3.3	5.1 years	0.04
PSR 0329+54	2,540	0.2	2.3	3.3 years	—
		2.2	7.3	16 years	—
PSR 1828-11	11,700	3	0.93	0.68 years	—
		12	1.32	1.35 years	—
		8	2.1	2.71 years	—

punctuated equilibrium

A hypothesis of the mechanism of evolutionary change put forward in 1971 by Niles Eldridge and Stephen Jay Gould, then of Columbia University, New York, that disputes the standard Darwinian idea (➔ **evolution, theory of**) that major adaptations and the appearance of new species come about through the slow accumulation of small, random changes.[182] Punctuated equilibrium posits that species are relatively stable over long periods of time but undergo rapid bursts of change, leading to the sudden appearance of new species, when genetically distinct subgroups become geographically isolated. In 1999, U.S. paleontologist Jeffrey Schwartz, of the University of Pittsburgh, strengthened the case for punctuation with his suggestion[522] that new species arise abruptly because of **mutation**s in the **gene**s that control the development of embryos. If such mutations occur in several individuals that then interbreed, they may lead to a new, taxonomically distinct organism. Schwartz cites the case of the origin of the backbone as a notochord in the free-swimming larva of sea squirts. The growth of a notochord is triggered by a specific gene, called *Manx,* that regulates embryonic development. If this gene is deactivated, the larva remains as a sessile-notochordless animal. According to Schwartz, a minor random variation in the gene that regulates *Manx* could have led to a subgroup of sea squirts with primitive backbones and so to the evolution of all vertebrates (including ourselves).

Purcell, Edward M. (1912–)

Codiscoverer with Harold I. Ewen at Harvard in 1951 of the **21-centimeter line** of hydrogen, for which he shared the 1952 Nobel Prize in Physics (with Felix Bloch, who had done similar work at Stanford). In a lecture delivered at Brookhaven National Laboratory in 1960, Purcell attacked the notion that **interstellar travel** would ever be possible, arguing that radio signals were probably the best way of establishing contact with other intelligent races.[469] A similar discouraging outlook for flight between the stars was expressed by John **Pierce** and Sebastian von **Hoerner.**

purines

Nitrogen-containing organic **bases**, the molecules of which have a double-ring structure. They are the larger of the two types of nitrogenous bases found in **DNA** and **RNA** (the other being **pyrimidines**). **Adenine** and **guanine** are purines.

Adenine   Guanine

pyrimidines

The smaller of the two kinds of nitrogenous **bases** found in **DNA** and **RNA** (the other being **purines**). Their molecules have a single-ring structure. **Cytosine, thymine,** and **uracil** are pyrimidines.

Thymine   Cytosine

pyrrole

A colorless liquid that smells like chloroform, the molecules of which contain a ring of four **carbon** atoms and one **nitrogen.** Many natural coloring materials are derived from pyrrole, including **chlorophyll** and hemoglobin.

Q0957+561 A,B

A **quasar,** one component of which (A) was seen to undergo a change in brightness possibly as a result of **microlensing** by a planet-sized body located in a foreground galaxy.[513] If the lensing object, estimated to have a mass about 0.01 times that of Jupiter, exists, it may be a **rogue planet** since no lensing effect was observed that could be attributed to a **host star.** However, this interpretation would imply that there are about 1 million rogue planets per star, a number far greater than that predicted by our present understanding of planet formation. On the other hand, it has been suggested that the **light curve** variations could have been caused by a drop in the quasar's energy flux.[328]

"Q" waves

A whimsical term coined in the early 1960s by Philip **Morrison** during the scientific debate on the best method for communicating with extraterrestrial races. Morrison pointed out that the most effective way might be "Q" waves "that we're going to discover ten years from now!" His point was that, although we are presently constrained to using electromagnetic communication—and, in particular, **radio waves**—this limitation may be lifted by future technological developments. Conceivably, the reason we have not so far detected artificial electromagnetic signals from space is that the vast majority of advanced races out there are using a form of communication of which we are unaware and that we are presently unequipped to detect. One form, for example, that such communication might take is the "subspace" messages—signals that travel outside of normal **space-time**—familiar from the fictional universe of *Star Trek.* ➜ **extraterrestrial intelligence, more advanced than we**

quantum mechanics

A major branch of modern physics concerned with phenomena at the atomic and subatomic scale.

quasar

An object that typically resembles a blue star (hence the name, which is a contraction of "quasistellar") but whose **spectral lines** display a very large **red shift.** Interpreted as due to the overall expansion of the universe, this red shift indicates that quasars are extremely remote and luminous. They are now widely recognized as being the nuclei of young galaxies going through a violent stage during or immediately following their formation. Support for this idea has been lent by the discovery of distant galaxies that closely resemble quasars in their energy output and appearance. The source of a quasar's great luminosity is believed to be a supermassive **black hole** surrounded by a brightly glowing **accretion disk** of captured material. This suggests that many normal galaxies, including our own, may still harbor black holes in their cores.

Queloz, Didier

Swiss astronomer at the Geneva Observatory who, as a postgraduate student from 1991 to 1995, worked with Michel **Mayor** and codiscovered the first **extrasolar planet** around a star similar to the Sun (➜ **51 Pegasi**). From 1998 to 1999, Queloz was a distinguished visiting scientist at the **Jet Propulsion Laboratory.**

R

radar-visual UFO

One of the six categories of **unidentified flying object** in the classification scheme devised by J. Allen **Hynek** in the 1950s. Defined as a UFO tracked on radar and simultaneously seen visually at the same location.

radial velocity

The component of the velocity of a celestial object, such as a star, that is directly toward or away from the observer. By convention, it is positive if receding, negative if approaching. ➔ **transverse velocity**

radial velocity method

One of the principal techniques being applied in the search for **extrasolar planets** and the most successful to date in terms of the number of confirmed detections. It is also known as Doppler spectroscopy. Just as a star causes a planet to move in an orbit around it, so a planet causes its host star to move in a small counterorbit resulting in a tiny additional, regularly varying component to the star's motion. Jupiter, for example, causes an additional movement of the Sun with an amplitude of 13 m per second and a period of 12 years. The Earth's effect is much smaller, amounting to fluctuations with a 10-cm-per-second amplitude over a period of 1 year. If a star is accompanied by a planet, the **radial velocity** of the star will periodically change as the star moves toward and then away from a distant observer. If the effect of the planet is sufficiently large as a result of the combination of its mass and orbital radius, the back-and-forth movement of the star is detectable as a small periodic **blue shift** and **red shift** in the star's **spectral lines.** Historically, radial velocity measurements had errors of 1,000 m per second or more, making them useless for the detection of orbiting planets. However, beginning in 1980, Bruce Campbell and Gordon Walker developed a method capable of measuring radial velocities to a precision of 15 m per second. A number of groups around the world are now using the radial velocity method with a precision in the range of 3 to 10 m per second in the search for extrasolar planets (➔ **extrasolar planets, searches for**).

A drawback of the technique is that because it measures movement exclusively along the line of sight, it allows only a *lower* mass limit to be assigned to any invisible companions that it detects. If the orbital plane of the orbiting object happens to lie along our line of sight, the measured speed is the true speed of the wobble. However, if the orbital plane is tilted with respect to the Sun, the true speed is higher and the companion is more massive by a factor of $1/\sin i$, where i is the angle of inclination. To

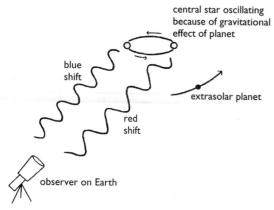

blue shift

red shift

central star oscillating because of gravitational effect of planet

extrasolar planet

observer on Earth

The shift in the wavelength of light from a star caused by an orbiting planet can be detected on Earth.

determine the value of i, and therefore the true mass, radial velocity measurements must be combined with **astrometric observations** that track the movement of the host star across the sky. Only in this way can researchers check that what might appear to be high-mass planets are not actually in the mass range that would suggest that they are more likely to be **brown dwarf**s.

radiation
A stream of particles or waves. Included in this general description are **electromagnetic radiation** and the various types of radioactivity.

radiation pressure
The minute pressure exerted on a surface at right angles to the direction of travel of the incident **electromagnetic radiation**. Its existence was first predicted by James Maxwell and demonstrated experimentally by Pyotr Lebedev. In **quantum mechanics,** radiation pressure can be interpreted as the transfer of momentum from **photons** as they strike a surface.

radio interferometer
An array of **antenna**s that operate together as if they were a single instrument of very large **aperture.**

radio telescope
An instrument designed to collect and focus **radio waves** arriving at Earth from space. Its

principle of operation is broadly similar to that of an optical telescope, the major practical differences being forced by the fact that radio waves are much longer than waves of visible light. Since **resolving power** decreases as **wavelength** increases, very large instruments are needed to provide useful information about the structure of radio sources. Indeed, to distinguish the same level of detail in a source emitting 21-centimeter radio waves as can be achieved by a large optical telescope, a radio dish would need a diameter of about 100 km (60 miles). In practice, fully steerable dishes are limited by weight considerations to about 100 m (328 feet) across. Fixed dishes, such as that of the **Arecibo Observatory,** may be considerably larger. However, to achieve much higher levels of resolution, arrays of separate instruments are linked to form **radio interferometer**s.

radio waves
Electromagnetic radiation spanning a vast frequency range from about 3 kHz to about 300 GHz, corresponding to a wavelength range of 100 km to 0.1 cm.

radioactivity
The emission of nuclear particles and rays by unstable atoms as they decay into more stable forms.

radioglyph
A picture sent across interstellar space by means of a code carried by **radio waves.** One of the earliest schemes was devised by the British mathematician Lancelot Hogben (➔ **Astraglossa**). Later developments included **Drake's cryptogram** and the **Arecibo Message.**

radiopanspermia
A version of the **panspermia** hypothesis in which it is argued that microorganisms or **spores** can be spread from one star system to another by **radiation pressure.** It was developed in detail by Svante **Arrhenius.**

radioresistant
Able to withstand high doses of **ionizing radiation** without serious injury, as demonstrated

by certain bacteria such as *Micrococcus radiodurans.*

radiosensitive
Quickly injured by exposure to **ionizing radiation.**

radius vector
An imaginary straight line connecting an orbiting body with its **primary.**

R-class asteroid
A rare class of **asteroid** of moderately high **albedo.**

red Centaurs
A rare class of **Centaurs** that appear to be covered in **organic** substances and pristine materials that have hardly changed since the birth of the solar system. Among them are **Pholus** and 1995 G0, observations of which by David Weintraub and his colleagues at Vanderbilt University in Nashville, Tennessee, using the 3-m (9.8-ft.) infrared telescope on Mauna Kea, Hawaii, and an optical telescope at **Steward Observatory,** revealed that they are redder than any other **asteroid**s in the solar system. Red Centaurs colliding with the Earth in the remote past may have contributed to the **prebiotic** mixture out of which terrestrial life eventually arose.

red dwarf
A small, dim, **main sequence** star of **spectral type M** (➔ **M star**) or late K (➔ **K star**). The characteristic properties of red dwarfs stem ultimately from their low mass, which is approximately in the range 0.1 to 0.5 M_S. Their low surface temperature, in the range of 2,500 to 3,500°C, imparts to them a ruddy hue, while their combination of low temperature *and* small surface area results in their being very faint. Red dwarfs survive longer (➔ **stars, lifetimes of**) and are more numerous (➔ **stars, numbers of**) than any other kind of star. Of the thirty nearest stars to the Sun, for example, twenty-one fall into this category (➔ **stars, nearest**). Like other types of stars, red dwarfs may be accompanied by planets. Indeed, a red dwarf planetary system may already have been found, in the case of **Lalande 21185.** However,

there are doubts whether any worlds in orbit around such faint stars could harbor life.[325] These doubts arise because of the extremely small **habitable zone** that would surround a red dwarf. It is not known whether a planet can form so close to its parent star. If it can, it will almost certainly end up in a **gravitational lock,** with one side permanently turned toward the star. Under such circumstances, it is not clear whether life would be able to evolve.

red giant
A **giant star** with a surface temperature of 2,500 to 3,500°C and a diameter between ten and one hundred times that of the Sun. Red giants represent a late stage in the evolution of normal stars with a range of masses, from just under the mass of the Sun to tens of M_S (➔ **stars, evolution of**). The largest red giants, which form from the most massive of stars, are known as **red supergiant**s.

Red Rectangle
A **reflection nebula** in the center of which observations made by the *Infrared Space Observatory* have revealed a region of oxygen-rich dust.[614] It has been suggested that the dust's properties are similar to those of **dust disk**s around young stars and that grain processing and even planet formation may be taking place.

red shift
The displacement of **spectral lines** in the **spectrum** of an object toward longer **wavelength**s. If caused by the line-of-sight recession of the object (➔ **Doppler effect**), as is usually the case, this displacement, when measured, allows the recessional velocity to be calculated. ➔ **blue shift**

red supergiant
Similar in nature to but bigger and more massive than a **red giant.** Red supergiants may be more than one hundred times larger than the Sun. They end by exploding as **supernova**s (➔ **stars, evolution of**). Well-known examples include **Betelgeuse** and Antares.

Redi, Francesco (1626–97)
Italian physician whose experiments in 1668 on the putrefaction of meat showed that mag-

gots were not produced by the meat but came from small eggs laid by flies. His work was followed by that of Lazzaro **Spallanzani** (1765), Louis **Pasteur** (1862), and John **Tyndall** (1869), which finally dispelled the old notion of **spontaneous generation.** → **abiogenesis**

redox sensor

An instrument capable of detecting the kind of nonequilibrium concentrations of reduced iron and manganese, along with the **oxides** of **nitrogen** and **sulfur,** that are strongly indicative of life processes on Earth. Miniature redox sensors have recently been developed that are capable of withstanding high-pressure liquid environments. It is thought that arrays of such sensors could form part of the instrumentation on a probe to search for life in Lake **Vostok** and eventually in oceans that might exist on Jupiter's moons **Europa** and **Callisto.**

reducing atmosphere

An atmosphere of a planet or moon that has a high hydrogen content in the form of either free hydrogen or hydrogen-containing compounds such as **methane** or **ammonia.**

reduction

The gain of one or more electrons by an **atom** during a chemical reaction. In living organisms, chemical energy is stored in high-energy electrons that are transferred from one atom to another in reactions involving **oxidation** and reduction.

reflecting telescope

An instrument that uses a curved mirror to collect light from a distant object and bring it to a focus. The image may be looked at through an eyepiece, photographed, detected by **charge-coupled devices,** or otherwise analyzed.

reflection nebula

An **interstellar cloud** of gas and dust that shines solely because light from nearby bright stars is reflected toward the observer by **cosmic dust** particles contained in the cloud. A familiar example is the nebulosity seen around some of the stars in the **Pleiades.**

reflector

→ **reflecting telescope**

refracting telescope

An instrument that uses a lens or system of lenses to gather light from a distant object and bring it to a focus. The earliest refractors, based on a single lens, suffered from false coloring known as *chromatic aberration.* In 1756, John Dolland introduced the first achromatic lenses consisting of a combination of two lenses made from crown and flint glass. By the early 1800s, Joseph von Fraunhofer succeeded in applying Dolland's technique to lenses of substantial size. This ushered in the era of giant refracting telescopes, which reached its height at the end of the nineteenth century with the instruments of Alvan **Clark,** including those at the **Lick Observatory** and **Yerkes Observatory.** Before large reflecting telescopes took over in the twentieth century, refractors were generally preferred for detailed observations of the planets since, having an enclosed tube, they produced a steadier image.

refractor

→ **refracting telescope**

regenerated disk

A circumstellar disk of dust orbiting a relatively mature star. Also known as a debris disk. Regenerated disks have been found around a number of young **main sequence** stars, including **Beta Pictoris, Fomalhaut, Vega,** and BD +31°643. The dust in these disks may have come from a variety of sources, including the collisional grinding of **asteroid**s and of ice objects in an unseen **Kuiper Belt,** and the ejection of dust from star-grazing **comet**s. Such material forms a tenuous disk around our own Sun known as the **Zodiacal Cloud.**

regolith

The layer of rocky or icy debris made by meteoric impact that forms the uppermost surface of planets, moons, and asteroids.

Regulus

Alpha Leonis; a bluish-white **B star** with an orange companion that itself has a faint companion. It ranks twenty-first in brightness of the stars visible from Earth. **→ stars, brightest**

relativistic
A term used to describe any situation in which Einstein's theory of relativity makes predictions that are significantly different from those of classical (Newtonian) physics.

Rendezvous with Rama
Science fiction novel by Arthur C. **Clarke**[113] (1973) in which a vast and apparently derelict alien spacecraft arrives in the solar system.

resolution
The ability to distinguish visual detail, usually expressed in terms of the size of the smallest features that can be seen.

resolution bandwidth
The narrowest **frequency** band within the **instantaneous bandwidth** of a **radio telescope** that can be discriminated and analyzed by the detection system.

resolving power
The ability of a telescope to distinguish between two closely separated objects. It is ultimately limited by **diffraction** but, in the case of ground-based instruments, is also compromised by the smearing effect of the Earth's atmosphere. The use of **interferometer**s and new techniques such as **adaptive optics** allows dramatic improvements in resolving power.

respiration
The metabolic process in which complex **organic** substances are broken down into simpler products with the release of energy. This energy is incorporated into the energy-carrying substance **ATP** and subsequently used for other metabolic processes.

resurfacing
The creation of a new surface on a planet or moon by volcanic or tectonic processes.

retrograde (motion)
That which is contrary to the usual sense. In the case of the **orbital rotation** of moons or the **axial rotation** of planets or moons in the solar system, this means clockwise motion as seen from the north side of the solar system. For example, Venus displays retrograde axial rotation and the outer four moons of Jupiter display retrograde orbital rotation.

revolution
The motion of one body around another.

Reynaud, Jean (1806–63)
French statesman and writer who, in his *Terre et ciel* (1854), set out a religious system based on the **transmigration of souls** that he believed was reconcilable with both Christianity and **pluralism.** He believed that at death souls pass from planet to planet, progressively improving at each new incarnation. Among those on whom the book had a strong influence was Camille **Flammarion.**

Reynolds, James Emerson (1844–1920)
English chemist who spent the latter part of his life studying **silicon** compounds and speculated on the possibility of **silicon-based life.**

Rhea
The second largest moon of **Saturn;** it appears to resembles **Dione** in composition, **albedo** features, and variety of terrain. Rhea probably has a rocky core extending out to about one third of the way from the center, the rest of the moon being composed primarily of water ice. Its surface is heavily cratered with bright, wispy markings. Of the two main types of terrain,

Discovery	1672, by Giovanni Cassini
Mean distance from Saturn	527,200 km (327,700 mi.)
Diameter	1,530 km (951 mi.)
Mean density	1.33 g/cm³
Escape velocity	0.659 km/s (2,372 km/h, 1,474 mi./h)
Orbital period	4.518 days (4 days 12 hours 26 minutes)
Orbital eccentricity	0.001
Orbital inclination	0.35°
Axial period	4.518 days
Visual albedo	0.7

one contains craters up to and exceeding 40 km (25 miles) in diameter; the other, in parts of the polar and equatorial regions, has no craters larger than 40 km. This suggests that a major **resurfacing** event took place early in the moon's geological history. → **Saturn, moons of**

rho¹ Cancri

A **binary star** system consisting of a middle-aged, Sun-like **primary,** rho¹ Cancri A, and a **red dwarf** companion, rho¹ Cancri B.[230] The component stars are separated by a mean distance of about 1,150 AU (172 billion km, 108 billion miles). In orbit around the primary is at least one, and possibly two, planets (Ab and Ac).[90] Ab is an **epistellar Jovian** circling around its host star at less than one third the distance of Mercury from the Sun. The second planet, Ac, still to be confirmed, is a high-mass **classical Jovian.** Also surrounding the primary star is a dust disk, presumably a **regenerated disk,** extending out to about 40 AU from the star[36, 160, 592] with an inclination of about 25 degrees. If the planets orbit in the same plane as the dust disk, this gives a mass for the first planet of approximately twice that of Jupiter. → **extrasolar planets**

rho Coronae Borealis

A star similar to the Sun but of greater age, around which has been found a planet marginally more massive than Jupiter.[423] This **epistel-**

Host Star	
Distance	55 light-years (16.7 parsecs)
Spectral type	G0V or G2V
Apparent magnitude	5.4
Temperature	5,480°C (5,750 K)
Luminosity	1.80 L_s
Mass	0.89 M_s
Planet	
Mass	1.13 M_J
Semimajor axis	0.25 AU (37.5 million km, 23.3 million mi.)
Orbital period	39.65 days
Eccentricity	0.028
Discovery	1997, by Robert Noyes et al., Smithsonian Astrophysical Observatory. Independently by teams at the National Center for Atmospheric Research and Penn. State University
Method of discovery	Radial velocity

Host Star (rho¹ Cancri A)	
Distance	43.7 light-years (13.4 parsecs)
Spectral type	G8V
Apparent magnitude	5.95
Temperature	4,980°C (5,250 K)
Luminosity	0.61 L_s
Mass	0.95 M_s

Planets	rho¹ Cancri Ab (confirmed)	rho¹ Cancri Ac (unconfirmed)
Mass	0.84 M_J	~5 M_J
Semimajor axis	0.11 AU (16 million km; 10 million mi.)	>4 AU (600 million km; 375 million mi.)
Orbital period	14.64 days	15–20 years
Eccentricity	0.05	—
Discovery	1996, by Geoffrey Marcy and Paul Butler, San Francisco State University Planet Search	1996, by Geoffrey Marcy and Paul Butler, San Francisco State University Planet Search
Method of discovery	Radial velocity	Radial velocity

lar Jovian, the fourth of its type to be discovered, occupies a nearly circular, sub-Mercurian orbit around its host. → **extrasolar planets**

ribonucleic acid
→ **RNA**

ribose ($C_5H_{10}O_5$)
A **pentose** sugar, the **dextrorotatory** form of which is of great biological importance as it occurs in the **nucleotide**s of **RNA** (ribonucleic acid).

ribosomal DNA
Genes that code for the various forms of **ribosomal RNA.**

ribosomal RNA
RNA that is transcribed from the **DNA** of the **nucleolus** and is found, together with characteristic **proteins,** in the **ribosomes** (→ **transcription**).

ribosome
The site of **protein** synthesis in the living **cell.** Ribosomes are complex, beadlike structures composed of proteins and three different kinds of **ribosomal RNA** molecule. In **eukaryotes,** they are often attached to the membranes of the endoplasmic reticulum to form rough ER, while in prokaryotes, they are free in the **cytoplasm.**

ribozymes
Certain types of naturally occurring **RNA** molecules that can behave as **enzymes,** catalyzing their own assembly. The discovery of ribozymes, by Thomas Cech at the University of Colorado and Sidney Altman at Yale University, provided an empirical basis for the concept of the **"RNA world."**[103] At first it seemed that ribozymes were limited in their enzymatic behavior to the catalysis of only the RNA sugar-phosphate backbone. However, in April 1995, Jack W. Szostak and Charles Wilson of the University of California announced[576] that they had manufactured ribozymes capable of a broad class of catalytic reactions, including ones that promoted the formation of **peptide bond**s (needed to form **proteins**). Szostak's work was criticized on the basis that it would be

unlikely for nature to select, from a primordial pool of trillions of different sequences of RNA, just those ones that would give rise to catalytically versatile ribozymes. However, the Colorado team countered by arguing that the ease with which these ribozymes "evolved" in the laboratory suggested that they were almost certainly part of a larger class of similar molecules that nature was capable of creating spontaneously, given the right conditions.[181]

Riccioli, Giovanni Battista (1598–1671)
Italian astronomer best known for his lunar atlas, the *Almagestum novum* (1651). The only map of comparable quality was created by Johannes **Hevelius,** with whom Riccioli profoundly disagreed over the question of lunar water and life. Above his map, Riccioli declared, "No Man Dwell on the Moon." → **Moon, life on; Moon, water on**

Richter, H. E.
German physician who was among the first to argue the case for **panspermia** from a scientific standpoint. He was influenced by Camille **Flammarion**'s popularization of the idea in the 1864 edition of his book *The Plurality of Inhabited Worlds,* which, in turn, derived from a suggestion by Jöns **Berzelius.** In 1865, Richter pointed out that not all **meteor**s that enter the Earth's atmosphere necessarily fall to the ground as **meteorite**s. Some might approach at such a glancing angle that they penetrated only partway through the atmosphere before bouncing off again into space. During their encounter, Richter surmised, such meteors might pick up living cells from the air and then carry them away, possibly to deliver them, in time, to the surface of another world. The possibility of **lithopanspermia** on a grander scale was later envisaged both by William **Thomson** (Lord Kelvin) and Hermann von **Helmholtz.**

rift valley
An elongated valley formed by the depression of a block of a planet's crust between two faults or groups of approximately parallel faults. Examples include the Great Rift Valley on Earth and Valles Marineris on Mars.

Rigel

Beta Orionis; a massive, luminous, and remote **blue supergiant.** This **B star** is one of the most intrinsically bright stars visible to the naked eye. Within a few million years, it will probably evolve to become a **red supergiant** like its neighbor in Orion (though not in physical space), **Betelgeuse. → stars, brightest**

Rigel Kentaurus

Often abbreviated to "Rigel Kent." An alternative name, used by navigators, for the star **Alpha Centauri.**

right ascension

One of two coordinates commonly used to define the position of an object in the sky, the other being **declination.** Right ascension is the equivalent of longitude on Earth but is measured in hours, minutes, and seconds from an arbitrary point that is taken as the intersection of the **celestial equator** with the **ecliptic.**

ringworld

A compromise between a normal planet and a **Dyson sphere.** A ringworld would be an artificial band-shaped structure placed around a star within the star's **habitable zone.** Although, unlike a Dyson sphere, it would intercept only a small fraction of the total radiation output of the star, the incident energy would still be many millions of times greater than that falling onto a planet. The ringworld would be easier to build than a Dyson sphere, allow freer access to open space, and be completely habitable (in contrast with most of the interior surface of a Dyson sphere, which would be subject to reduced gravity conditions). As a bonus, those living on a ringworld would be able to see the stars. Larry **Niven** speculated about

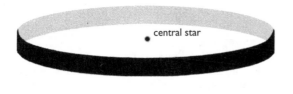

2 AU

A ringworld surrounding a Sun-like star.

such a structure in his novels *Ringworld*, *The Ringworld Engineers*, and *The Ringworld Throne*.

Ringworld

Novel by Larry **Niven**[422] (1970), the centerpiece of which is a **ringworld** 1 million miles wide and 600 million miles in circumference circling around a remote star.

RNA (ribonucleic acid)

A class of **nucleic acid**s characterized by the presence of the sugar **ribose** and the organic **base uracil.** By contrast, **DNA** contains **deoxyribose** and **thymine,** respectively. Most RNA molecules, including **messenger RNA** and **transfer RNA,** act as cellular intermediaries; that is, they convert the genetic information stored in DNA into the **proteins** that provide cells with structure and enable them to carry out **metabolism.** In some **virus**es, RNA also serves as the hereditary material. Biologists believe that RNA evolved on Earth before DNA. However, a major debate is in progress about the sequence of events leading to the first cellular life-forms, and, in particular, about which came first, RNA or proteins. **→ "RNA world"**

"RNA world"

One of the scenarios suggested for the protobiological regime that existed on Earth nearly 4 billion years ago, before the appearance of **DNA.** The term "RNA world" was coined in 1986 by Walter Gilbert,[216] who had earlier shared a Nobel Prize in Chemistry with Frederick Sanger. Advocates of this hypothesis argue that **RNA** must have come before the first **proteins,** since without it there would have been no molecule of heredity—no "blueprint" molecule—and therefore no way for other molecules to have been manufactured consistently. According to this idea, there was a time when RNA alone handled all of the tasks required for a cell to survive, acting as both a genetic material and a **catalyst** for the various reactions involved in **metabolism** and for its own assembly. This last possibility was given credence by the discovery of some varieties of RNA, known as **ribozymes,** that can act as their own **enzymes,** snipping themselves in two and splicing themselves back together. Only with the evolution of DNA, the theory goes, was there a reallocation of labor, with the more stable DNA molecule assuming the role of **genome** carrier and the more versatile protein-based enzymes taking on the job of biochemical catalysts.

A significant sticking point is how RNA, self-catalyzing or not, arose in the first place. Until recently, two of RNA's building blocks, **cytosine** and **uracil,** had proven difficult to synthesize under the sort of conditions that might have prevailed on Earth about 4 billion years ago. However, in June 1995, Stanley **Miller** and Michael P. Robertson, at the University of California, San Diego, reported[405] that they had been able to synthesize cytosine and uracil under plausible **prebiotic** conditions. The technique involved placing urea and cyanoacetaldehyde in an environment equivalent to that of a warm tidal pool. As evaporation concentrated the mixture, the chemicals reacted to yield cytosine and uracil in large amounts.

Further support for the "RNA world" view came in 1998 from researchers at Massey University in New Zealand.[463] They developed a picture of a hypothetical RNA-based organism, which they named *Riborgis eigensis* after the German biologist Manfred Eigen. In their view, *R. eigensis* would have had its **gene**s strung out along a set of *linear* **chromosome**s, so that it had more in common with the genetic organization of **eukaryote**s than it did with the single, circular chromosome found in the cells of **prokaryote**s. Their reasoning stems from the fact that RNA, being less stable than DNA, is less reliable as a basis for molecular replication. Moreover, there is a limit to the size of a genome, known as the Eigen limit, determined by the propensity for error of the replicating mechanism. Since the Eigen limit for RNA is relatively low, an RNA-based organism might best get around this problem by holding its genome on several short chromosomes and also by keeping several copies of these in case one or two become corrupted. A drawback of linear chromosomes is that they suffer from a tendency toward frayed ends. Eukaryotes counter this tendency with **telomerase,** an enzyme that maintains the **telomere**s with which the ends of chromosomes are capped. Telomerase, as it happens, is guided in its task by an RNA molecule, suggesting that a similar substance might have been used for

chromosome maintenance by *R. eigensis*. This would tie in with the Massey team's unconventional idea of linear chromosomes in RNA-based organisms *predating* the simple chromosome rings of bacteria. Once proteins evolved, so the argument goes, they took on all the new catalytic functions of evolving organisms, leaving RNA with only the jobs it performed in the preprotein era. So if terminating chromosomes requires RNA, chromosome ends must have been in existence before there were proteins. Since prokaryotes lack telomerase, the implication is that they lost their catalytic RNA *after* they had evolved from more complex cells.

Similar reasoning can be applied to the evolutionary history of **ribosome**s. If the "RNA world" view is correct, these most elaborate of RNA-containing structures, which are now involved with protein synthesis, must have had a different role before proteins existed. One possibility is that they were used to replicate RNA. Protoribosomes may have taken small strands of RNA from their surroundings and cut and pasted those that matched their template into a new, duplicate strand.

Opponents of the "RNA world" picture point to the chemical fragility of RNA and the fact that it is difficult to synthesize **abiotic**ally. According to some biologists, proteins must have evolved first because only they can furnish the full range of enzymatic capabilities needed to support even the most primitive form of life. Other researchers believe that instead of evolving independently, RNA and proteins may have evolved together in the earliest of protocells. Yet if such was the case, it is not clear how the division of cellular functions between these molecules took place.

Even supporters of the "RNA world" suspect that a molecule as complex as RNA was not manufactured at a stroke but evolved from some simpler self-replicating molecule. Stanley Miller and Leslie **Orgel** are among those who have suggested that RNA probably took over from some more primitive precursor. Orgel and his group at the Salk Institute for Biological Studies in San Diego have studied a compound known as peptide nucleic acid (PNA) that has the ability to replicate itself and catalyze reactions but is much simpler than

RNA. They showed that PNA can act as a template both for its own replication and for the formation of RNA from its subcomponents. Although Orgel's team has not claimed that PNA itself may have been the primordial replicator (since it is not clear how this substance could have arisen under plausible prebiotic conditions) their work demonstrates that the evolution of a more complex self-replicating molecule from a simpler precursor is at least possible. → **life, origin of**

Robertson Panel
→ **Scientific Advisory Panel on Unidentified Flying Objects**

Roche limit
The smallest distance that a fluid satellite can orbit from the center of a planet without being torn apart by **tidal force**s. For a planet and moon with equal densities, the Roche limit is about twenty-one times the radius of the planet. In practice, since moons tend to be solid, the tensile force of the rock and ice of which they are composed helps prevent their breakup. Even so, the shattering of satellites in orbits well inside the Roche limit may explain the origin of some planetary ring systems.

rogue planet
A planet that has escaped the gravitational pull of its **host star** and is moving freely through interstellar space. Evidence is mounting that such freelance worlds may be common. New theoretical models devised to account for the unusual orbits of **epistellar Jovians** and **eccentric Jovians** suggest that planetary formation (→ **planetary systems, formation of**) may be a much more dynamic process than had previously been supposed. The interplanetary billiards that, it seems, routinely take place in embryonic systems of worlds (especially those that initially have several Jupiter-class objects) may often lead to planets being hurled away from their home stars on exit trajectories. An actual example of a rogue planet may have been found in the case of **TMR-1C,** which appears to have been thrown out from the vicinity of a pair of **protostar**s. If this is a normal phenomenon associated with newly formed binary or multiple star

systems, then, considering that the majority of stars in the Galaxy belong to such systems, rogue planets must be numerous.[142, 224]

At first sight, it seems that escaped worlds, without Sun-like stars to warm them, would surely be lifeless. Yet according to one recent suggestion, the possibility of inhabited Earth-like worlds roaming the interstellar void cannot be ruled out. If a terrestrial-sized planet was thrown free of its planetary system within a few million years of its formation it might still be swathed in hydrogen. This hydrogen envelope would prevent much of the heat generated internally by radioactivity from escaping, keeping the rogue planet warm and possibly replete with liquid water. Volcanic activity and lightning might supply the local temperature variations conducive to the emergence of at least primitive forms of life. → **L1551 (IRS5)**

Rosalind
The eighth known moon of **Uranus.** → **Uranus, moons of**

Discovery	1986, by *Voyager 2*
Mean distance from Uranus	70,000 km (43,500 mi.)
Diameter	54 km (34 mi.)
Orbital period	0.558 day (14 hours 8 minutes)
Orbital eccentricity	0.000
Orbital inclination	0.28°
Visual albedo	0.07

Rosetta
A European Space Agency and French mission to land a probe on the nucleus of Comet Wirtanen, scheduled for launch in 2003.

Rosny, J. H. (the Elder) (1856–1940)
Pseudonym of the Belgian writer Joseph-Henri Boëx, who, like Camille **Flammarion,** was encouraged by the evolutionary philosophy of Jean **Lamarck** to pioneer the theme of genuinely alien life. In his first work, *Les Xipéhuz* (The Shapes, 1887), he describes the arrival on Earth in prehistoric times of strange translucent beings which threaten the survival of the human race. Further bizarre life-forms appear in his *Un Autre monde* (Another World, 1910) and *La Mort de la terre* (The Death of the

Earth, 1910). The influence of Rosny's work in France in the 1880s and 1890s has been cited as a factor in the decline of the popularity of Jules **Verne**'s fiction in this same period. → **science fiction involving extraterrestrials, up to 1900; science fiction involving extraterrestrials, 1900–1940**

Ross 128
→ **stars, nearest**

Ross 154
→ **stars, nearest**

Roswell Incident
The most widely discussed series of events and purported events in the annals of ufology, the Roswell Incident has now achieved the status of a major modern myth. On June 14, 1947, 10 days before Kenneth **Arnold**'s seminal sighting of "**flying saucer**s," William "Mac" Brazel came across some debris scattered across a 200-m swathe of field while doing rounds on the Foster Ranch, 120 km (75 miles) northwest of Roswell, New Mexico. Later, accompanied by his wife and two children, he returned to the scene, collected some of the fragments, and took them home. As Brazel did not have access to a radio or phone, it was only on July 5, when he drove into the nearby town of Corona, that he heard news of Arnold's saucers and the many subsequent reports of mysterious disks in the skies over America. Two days later, while in Roswell to sell wool,

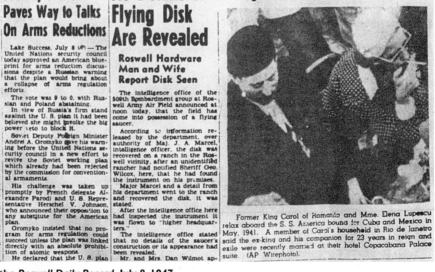

The front-page story of the *Roswell Daily Record*, July 8, 1947.
Roswell Daily Record

Brazel dropped in at the office of Sheriff Wilcox and confided that he might have come across the wreckage of a disk. Wilcox contacted Major Jesse Marcel, the group intelligence officer for Roswell Army Air Field (RAAF), home to what was then the world's only atomic bomb squadron, who subsequently drove out to the Foster Ranch with Counter-Intelligence Corps officer Sheridan Cavitt to inspect the crash site and collect the debris that Brazel had found. The following day an extraordinary press release was put out on the orders of Colonel Blanchard, RAAF's base commander:

> The many rumors regarding the flying disks became a reality yesterday when the intelligence office of the 509th bomb group of the eighth air force, Roswell Army Air Field, was fortunate enough to gain possession of a disk through the cooperation of one of the local ranchers and the Sheriff's office of Chaves county. The flying object landed on a ranch near Roswell sometime last week.... It was inspected at the Roswell Army Air Field and subsequently loaned by Major Marcel to higher headquarters.

The headline of the *Roswell Daily Record* for July 8, 1947, announced, "RAAF Captures Flying Saucer on Ranch in Roswell Region." America was stunned. Radio stations around the United States carried hourly bulletins. Reported one:

> The Army Air Force has announced that a flying saucer has been found and is now in possession of the army. Army officers say that the missile...has been...sent to Wright Field, Ohio, for further inspection. Russia has demanded UN action.

The news spread swiftly around the globe. Editors of major newspapers in London, Paris, Rome, and Tokyo bombarded the normally quiet editorial offices of Roswell's two local papers with calls for more details.

While this was happening, Marcel had flown with his crash samples to the headquarters of the Eighth Air Force at Fort Worth, Texas. There the incident would take another abrupt and unexpected turn. Brigadier General Roger Ramey, the commanding officer, hur-

riedly convened a press conference at which Marcel displayed what was said to be the material brought from Roswell while the base duty weather officer explained that the fragments were from a radar targeting balloon used for meteorological purposes. As two official investigations into the incident would conclude four decades later, this story had been invented to conceal a military secret (➔ **Roswell Incident, USAF report on; Roswell Incident, GAO report on**). ➔ **Cold War, linked to UFO reports**

Roswell Incident, GAO report on

The outcome of an independent inquiry by the General Accounting Office (GAO), the investigative arm of the U.S. Congress, into the **Roswell Incident** almost half a century earlier. Published in July 1995, the report effectively closed the casebook on the matter—at least, at an official level. Its conclusion: the Air Force was now telling the truth (➔ **Roswell Incident, USAF report on**). The crash had involved not a weather balloon, as originally claimed, but a covert military balloon intended to supply early warning of a nuclear attack. Bizarrely, some of the minor components of the balloon's payload had been supplied by a New York novelty company, whose fancy labels had been misinterpreted by eyewitnesses at the crash site as alien inscriptions. The GAO also concluded that a document known as "Majestic 12," which some UFO buffs claim is a secret government document outlining procedures to be followed when handling the putative Roswell craft and its occupants, is a forgery. ➔ **Schiff, Steven**

Roswell Incident, USAF report on

In July 1994, the U.S. Air Force released the results of its own investigation into the **Roswell Incident** of 1947 and concluded that while the original official account of a crashed weather balloon was indeed a cover story, there was no reason to suspect extraterrestrial involvement. In *The Roswell Report: Case Closed*, the Air Force investigators state that "Project Mogul offers the most likely explanation for the Roswell Incident" (➔ **Mogul, Project**). In particular, the finger of suspicion is pointed at Flight 4 of this secret Pentagon program as being the source of the debris that spawned the myth of a crashed flying saucer. According to the project's director, Flight 4 was launched on June 4, 1947, and never recovered. Its last airborne position, as recorded by a B-17 that had been tracking it, was about 27 km from the site where wreckage was found 10 days later. "This research indicated absolutely no evidence of any kind that a spaceship crashed near Roswell or that any alien occupants were recovered therefrom," concluded Richard Weaver, director of security at the Air Force. ➔ **Schiff, Steven; Roswell Incident, GAO Report on**

rotation
The turning or spinning of a body about an axis running through it.

rotation period
The time taken for one complete turn through 360 degrees. It may refer to either an object's **axial period** or its **orbital period.**

rRNA
➔ **ribosomal RNA**

runaway greenhouse effect
Massive overheating of a planet caused by a high atmospheric concentration of **greenhouse gases.** Such an effect operates on **Venus** and is responsible for the surface temperature on this planet being several times higher than would otherwise be expected given its distance from the Sun.

runaway planet
➔ **rogue planet**

runaway star
A young, hot star moving through space at an unusually high speed. One possibility is that such stars were members of **binary star** or **multiple star** systems before a **companion** exploded as a **supernova.** Examples include Mu Columbae, AE Aurigae, and 53 Arietis, which, from their speeds and trajectories, appear to have been ejected from a common point in the constellation of Orion about 3 million years ago.

Ruppelt, Edward J.
Head of the U.S. Air Force's investigation into **unidentified flying saucers** from 1951 to 1953. Upon taking charge of Project **Blue Book** in 1952, he insisted upon the use of the term "unidentified flying object" instead of "flying saucer" and introduced more rigorous procedures for reporting and analyzing information on sightings. His experiences are related in his 1956 book, *Report on Unidentified Flying Objects.*[487]

Russell, Henry Norris (1877–1957)
Eminent American astronomer, director of Princeton Observatory (1912–47), who made many significant contributions to astrophysics. In the 1920s, he was persuaded by the **Jeans-Jeffreys tidal hypothesis** to affirm that planetary systems are "infrequent" and inhabited planets "matters of pure speculation." Two decades later, however, on the back of independent claims by Frank Schlesinger at Yale and Kaj **Strand** at the **Sproul Observatory** of the discovery of planetary systems around two nearby stars (later demonstrated to be unfounded), he declared that it was time to reverse this view and consider that there may be a very large number of extrasolar worlds.[488] Regarding our planetary neighbors, Russell, in the 1920s and '30s, considered Venus almost certainly nonbiological but Mars the possible abode of vegetation and other low forms of life.

Ryle, Martin (1918–84)
English radio astronomer, Nobel laureate (1974), and outspoken critic of attempts to communicate with intelligent extraterrestrials (➔ **CETI, opposition to**).

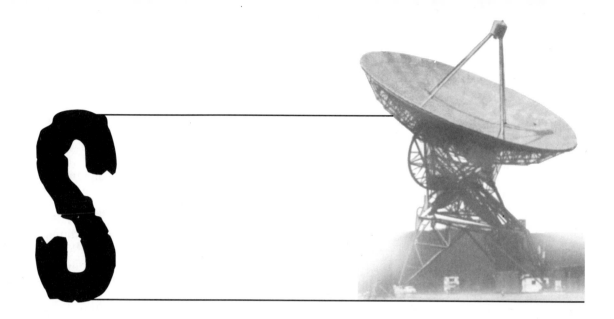

Sagan, Carl Edward (1934–96)

American astronomer and planetary scientist who was professor of Astronomy and Space Sciences and director of the Laboratory for Planetary Studies at **Cornell University.** Widely known for his popularization of science in books and on television, he made many important contributions to planetary exploration, astrobiology, and **SETI.** He coauthored with Iosif **Shklovskii** the influential *Intelligent Life in the Universe* (1966), participated in sending the **Arecibo Message,** and helped design the *Pioneer* **plaque** and the *Voyager* **interstellar record.** In the field of planetary science, he established the greenhouse model of the Venusian atmosphere (➔ **Venus, atmosphere of**) and helped show that seasonal changes on Mars are due to windblown dust (➔ **Mars, changes on**) and that the orange color of Titan's atmosphere is caused by complex **organic** chemicals. Sagan worked as a consultant and adviser to NASA for almost four decades, beginning in the 1950s, and played a prominent role in the *Mariner 9, Viking, Voyager,* and *Galileo* missions to the planets. He was cofounder and first president of the **Planetary Society.** His novel *Contact* (1985) was made into a successful film.

Sagan Memorial Station
➔ *Mars Pathfinder*

Sagan's Response

A rebuttal of **Tipler's Argument** put forward by Carl **Sagan** and William Newman of **Cornell University.**[502] They first pointed out that Frank Tipler had *underestimated* the number of **von Neumann probes** there ought to be. With exponential growth, a single self-replicating probe could be expected to convert *the entire mass of the Galaxy* into copies of itself within 2 million years. Any species intelligent enough to build such a probe, Sagan and Newman argued, would also be intelligent enough to realize the danger of it and so would not embark upon the project in the first place. In the event of a von Neumann probe being released either accidentally or maliciously, it would be a prime duty of other, responsible civilizations, said Sagan and Newman, to stamp out the "infection" before it could spread.

Sagittarius Arm

One of the **spiral arm**s of the Galaxy. It lies between the Sun and the center of the Galaxy in the direction of the constellation of Sagittarius.

Sagittarius B2

A giant **molecular cloud** located near the center of our galaxy. It may be part of a shell of material ejected by a large explosion. Many different types of **interstellar molecules** have been identified within Sagittarius B, including **glycine,** the simplest **amino acid** (➔ **amino acids, in space**).

Sakurai, Kunitomo (1933–   )

Physics professor at Kanagawa University, Yokohama, Japan, and one of the first scientists in Japan to consider seriously the possibility of extraterrestrial intelligence. He obtained a Ph.D. at Kyoto University (1961), where he remained until 1968, becoming an associate professor. From 1968 to 1974, he was a senior research associate and then visiting scientist at the NASA Goddard Space Flight Center, before moving to the University of Maryland's Institute of Fluid Dynamics and Applied Physics (1975–77). Subsequently, he joined the Institute of Physics at Kanagawa. His interest in **SETI** was stimulated in the 1960s by reading several seminal texts, including Walter Sullivan's *We Are Not Alone,* Alastair **Cameron**'s *Interstellar Communication,* and Carl **Sagan** and Iosif **Shklovskii**'s *Intelligent Life in the Universe.* Sakurai's own book on the subject, *Search for Life in the Universe,* was published in 1975.

sample-return mission

An unmanned mission designed to collect material from another celestial body and bring it back to Earth. The first successful project of this kind was *Lunokhod.* Over the next decade or so, a number of sample-return missions are scheduled to harvest dust and/or rock from comets (➔ **comet sample-return probe**), Mars (➔ *Mars Surveyor 2003*), and other bodies in the solar system, leading to increased concern over the possibility of **back contamination.**

San Francisco State University Planet Search

An ongoing observational program to detect **extrasolar planets** by means of a high-precision **radial velocity method.** It was initiated in 1987 by Geoffrey **Marcy** and R. Paul **Butler** using detection equipment they had constructed in the chemistry laboratories of San Francisco State University (SFSU) and attached to the 3-m (9.8-ft.) telescope at **Lick Observatory.** Over an 8-year period, Marcy and Butler collected data on 100 nearby Sun-like stars. Following computer analyses of these data, they were able to announce that six of the observed stars were accompanied by planets. The 3-m Lick telescope continues to be used by the SFSU group to monitor the 300 brightest Sun-like stars in the Northern Hemisphere, while since July 1996 an additional 430 stars have been monitored using the Keck I telescope at the **Keck Observatory,** equipped with Steven **Vogt**'s **High Resolution Échelle Spectrometer.** In October 1997, the group extended its work, in the form of the **Anglo-Australian Planet Search,** to include the 150 brightest Sun-like stars in the Southern Hemisphere. Surveying with a current precision of 3 m per second will enable the detection of systems similar to the solar system with Jupiter-mass and Saturn-mass worlds.

satellite

Any object, natural or artificial, that orbits another body.

satellite galaxy

A small galaxy in orbit around a much larger one. Our own galaxy, for example, has several satellite galaxies, including the Large and Small **Magellanic Clouds.**

Saturn

The sixth planet from the Sun and a **gas giant,** second only in size to **Jupiter.** It has a prominent system of rings and the largest collection of satellites in the solar system (➔ **Saturn, moons of**). Its atmosphere consists primarily of **hydrogen** and **helium,** with traces of other elements. Alternate jet streams of east–west and west–east circulation, with speeds of up to about 1,800 km per hour (1,100 miles per hour), have been traced in the motion of the cloud tops and are responsible for the banded appearance of the planet. Electrical processes and heat from within Saturn enrich the layered chemical mixture of the atmosphere, which probably transitions from superheated water near the core to ammonia ice at the observed cloud tops.

Distance from Sun:	
Mean	1,427 million km (886.9 million mi., 9.54 AU)
Minimum	1,347 million km (837.1 million mi., 9.01 AU)
Maximum	1,507 million km (936.6 million mi., 10.01 AU)
Equatorial diameter	120,536 km (74,913 mi.)
Equatorial diameter (Earth = 1)	9.449
Mass (Earth = 1)	95.2
Mean density	0.69 g/cm³
Escape velocity	35.47 km/s (127,690 km/h, 79,360 mi./h)
Orbital period	29.46 years
Orbital eccentricity	0.056
Orbital inclination	2.5°
Axial period	10.2 hours
Axial inclination	26.7°
Number of moons	18
Gravity at cloud tops (Earth = 1)	0.92
Atmospheric composition	97% hydrogen, 3% helium, traces of methane
Mean temperature (cloud tops)	−180°C (−292°F)
Albedo	0.61

Saturn, moons of

See separate entries for each of the moons listed below.

saucer flap of 1947

Extensive media coverage of the first so-called **flying saucer**s observed, on June 24, 1947,

Moon	Distance from Saturn (km)	Orbital Period (days)	Orbital Eccentricity	Orbital Inclination (degrees)	Diameter (km)
Pan	131,940	0.575	0.000	0.00	20
Atlas	137,670	0.602	0.000	0.00	40 × 30
Prometheus	139,353	0.613	0.003	0.00	145 × 85 × 65
Pandora	141,700	0.629	0.004	0.00	114 × 84 × 62
Epimetheus	151,422	0.694	0.009	0.34	144 × 108 × 98
Janus	151,472	0.695	0.007	0.14	196 × 192 × 150
Mimas	185,600	0.942	0.020	1.53	382
Enceladus	238,100	1.376	0.065	0.02	500
Tethys	294,700	1.888	0.000	1.09	1,060
Telesto	294,700	1.888	0.000	0.00	34 × 28 × 26
Calypso	294,700	1.888	0.000	0.00	34 × 22 × 22
Dione	377,500	2.737	0.002	0.00	1,120
Helene	378,000	2.737	0.005	0.20	36 × 32 × 30
Rhea	527,200	4.518	0.001	0.35	1,530
Titan	1,221,600	15.950	0.029	0.33	5,140
Hyperion	1,483,000	21.280	0.104	0.43	400 × 250 × 240
Iapetus	3,560,000	79.330	0.028	14.72	1,460
Phoebe	12,950,000	550.480	0.163	175.30	220

near Mount Rainier by businessman Kenneth **Arnold** opened the floodgates to a deluge of similar sightings. Within three weeks of the Arnold incident, the U.S. military had logged 850 reports from around the nation. Most of these were readily accounted for in terms of astronomical objects, aircraft, hoaxes, and the like. However, inevitably, a few cases proved more difficult to resolve and these provided fertile ground for speculation.

Several factors conspired to see the United States, in the summer of 1947, firmly in the grip of saucer fever. It was only a decade since the mass panic instigated by *The War of the Worlds* **radio play.** That broadcast had gone out on the eve of war in Europe, at a time when the sight and sound of Hitler's fanatical stormtroopers in Berlin was bringing home to people everywhere the very real possibility of invasion by a powerful, single-minded enemy. Now that the war was over, Germany and Japan had been defeated but a general nervousness pervaded America about the new threat of communism. The public and military alike were alive to the possibility of a preemptive aerial attack by the Soviets, perhaps using weapons of advanced design smuggled out of Nazi Germany. It is not difficult to understand, following the media hype surrounding Arnold's sighting, people's preoccupation with what might be going on in the skies overhead, or the ease with which, in all the excitement, it was possible for even commonplace phenomena to be misinterpreted. Those who believed that the saucers (or "flying disks," as they were also known) were both real and artificial could choose between the theory that they were man-made and the **extraterrestrial hypothesis.** → **Cold War, related to UFO reports**

Schiaparelli, Giovanni Virginio (1835–1910)

Prolific Italian astronomer whose research ranged widely but whose name is forever associated with Mars, and the controversy over the Martian "canals," which, unwittingly, he helped unleash. Born in Savigliano, Piedmont, Schiaparelli graduated from the University of Turin and studied at the Royal Observatory in Berlin under Johann Encke, discoverer of a short-period comet that now bears his name.

After a brief spell at Pulkova Observatory in Russia under Otto **Struve,** he joined the staff of Milan's Brera Observatory in 1860 and two years later became its director. The small instruments at Brera led Schiaparelli to focus his research initially on meteors and comets. Indeed, probably his most important contribution to astronomy was his discovery that swarms of meteors, which give rise to annual showers on Earth, and comets follow similar paths through space. His reward for this breakthrough was the installation of a more powerful (8.6-in.) refractor at Brera, which allowed him to engage in serious planetary work. He first wanted to test the powers of the new instrument, to see if it "possessed the necessary optical qualities to allow for the study of the surfaces of the planets." The year 1877 brought the ideal opportunity in the form of a particularly favorable **opposition** of Mars. Schiaparelli prepared for it almost like a prizefighter, avoiding "everything which could affect the nervous system, from narcotics to alcohol, and especially . . . coffee, which I found to be exceedingly prejudicial to the accuracy of observation."

What emerged from Schiaparelli's long hours at the eyepiece in September 1877 was the most (optimistically) detailed map of Mars ever published. With the additional features he filled in over the next decade, it became a standard reference in planetary cartography, still in use until the dawn of the space probe era, and the scheme he devised for naming major Martian features survives to this day. He used Latin and Mediterranean place-names taken from ancient history, mythology, and the Bible. A light spot in the southern hemisphere, for example, he called Nix Olympia—the Snows of Olympus (now known to be the largest volcano in the solar system and rechristened Mons Olympus). The great triangular feature first observed by Christiaan **Huygens** in 1669 became **Syrtis Major,** while large, bright patches earned the picturesque labels of Elysium, Cydonia, Tharsis, and Thyle. What was most striking about Schiaparelli's original map, however, was a curious network of linear markings that crisscrossed the Martian surface and joined one dark area to another. These lines he referred to as *canali,* and he named them after famous rivers, both fictional and real: Gehon, Hiddekel, and Phison from the rivers in the Garden of Eden, Lethes and Nepenthes from the underground realm of Hades, and Ganges, Euphrates, and Nilus from actual geography.

Schiaparelli insisted that his nomenclature was not intended to prejudge the nature of the features he saw on the Martian surface:

> [T]hese names may be regarded as a mere artifice.... After all, we speak in a similar way of the seas of the Moon, knowing very well that they do not consist of liquid masses.

However, the romantic and evocative names he chose would prove to have a powerful influence over some of his contemporaries. Moreover, Schiaparelli himself clearly favored a maritime view of Mars in which the dark areas were seas and the brighter regions land.

During the opposition of 1879, Schiaparelli refined his original map, noting some changes such as the apparent invasion of a bright area known as Libya by Syrtis Major. This encouraged him in his belief that Syrtis Major was a shallow sea that at times flooded the lands around. He drew in more canals and for the first time reported what he called a "germination," or doubling, of one of these features. Of the reality of the *canali,* if not their exact nature, he was utterly convinced: "It is [as] impossible to doubt their existence as that of the Rhine on the surface of the Earth."

So began the great canal controversy. Were the *canali* real? And if so, what were they? (➔ **Mars, canals of**) In an influential 1893 article, Schiaparelli maintained that Mars is a planet of seasonal changes, with a temporary sea forming around the northern polar cap as it melted each spring. In support of his belief in a Martian atmosphere rich in water vapor, he pointed to the **spectroscopic** observations of Hermann Vogel. The canals, he asserted, made up "a true hydrographic system" and perhaps "the principal mechanism . . . by which water (and with it organic life) may be diffused over the arid surface of the planet." As to their origin, he leaned toward a natural explanation:

> [W]e are inclined to believe them to be produced by an evolution of the planet, just as on the Earth we have the English Channel and the Channel of Mozambique.

However, he did not rule out the possibility that they might be artificial:

> Their singular aspect, and their being drawn with absolute geometrical precision, as if they were the work of rule or compass, has led some to see in them the work of intelligent beings.... I am very careful not to combat this supposition, which includes nothing impossible.

Cautious and unflamboyant though he was—in sharp contrast to Percival **Lowell**—Schiaparelli nevertheless seems to have been biased in his Martian studies by an underlying desire to prove the habitability (if not the actual habitation) of other worlds in the solar system. This willingness to see what was often not there is also suggested by his observations of **Mercury.** From these, Schiaparelli deduced that Mercury spins on its axis once every 88 days, the same time it takes to go around its orbit (➔ **gravitational lock**), so that it must always keep one face toward the Sun (➔ **Mercury, rotation of**). Furthermore, he claimed that Mercury shows librations of 47 degrees; that is, it rocks back and forth considerably, so that there is a broad, temperate "twilight" zone between perpetual day and perpetual night. Only such an arrangement, Schiaparelli presumably realized, together with a Mercurian atmosphere (in which he also believed), would provide a tolerable environment for life (➔ **Mercury, life on**).

Scheiner, Julius (1858–1913)

Astrophysicist at the University of Potsdam who, in an 1891 essay, wrote on the likelihood of extraterrestrial life adapting itself to a wide variety of environments. He considered the possibility of life based on **silicon** rather than **carbon** (➔ **silicon-based life**). Of the other planets within the solar system, he thought it beyond doubt that Mercury, Venus, and Mars were inhabited, while Jupiter, Saturn, and Uranus, he decided, might be capable of supporting life. Since, in his estimation, the Sun was orbited by at least three inhabited worlds, he thought it reasonable to suppose that every other star in space should be orbited by at least one.

Schiff, Steven H. (1947–98)

U.S. Congressman for New Mexico who represented the Roswell area. Schiff complained that the government had fueled speculation about the **Roswell Incident** by keeping files of the affair secret. At his request, the U.S. Air Force carried out an investigation and publicly reported its findings in 1994 (➔ **Roswell Incident, USAF report on**). Still concerned that the Air Force might be withholding confidential files, Schiff asked for an independent investigation into the matter by the General Accounting Office. The results of this appeared the following year (➔ **Roswell Incident, GAO report on**).

Schröter, Johann Hieronymous (1745–1816)

German astronomer with a passion for lunar and planetary observation who set up a private observatory at Lilienthal, near Bremen, and produced the most detailed study of the Moon up to that time. Schröter was an enthusiastic pluralist who wrote that he was "fully convinced that every celestial body may be so arranged physically by the Almighty as to be filled with living creatures." He claimed to have detected an atmosphere, mountains, and an Earth-like period of rotation on Venus and Mercury, both of which he considered to be inhabited (➔ **Venus, life on; Mercury, life on**). Color changes he reported seeing on the Moon were attributed to areas under cultivation (➔ **Moon, life on**), and although in 1792 he estimated that the lunar atmosphere was one twenty-ninth as dense as that of Earth, he felt confident enough to write that

> I at least imagine... [the] gray surface of Maris Imbrium to be just as fruitful as the Campanian plain [of Italy]. Here nature has ceased to rage, there is a mild and beneficial tract given over to the calm culture of rational creatures.

Like his compatriot Franz **Gruithuisen,** who followed him on the proselenite trail, and

Percival **Lowell,** a century later, he too often allowed his preconceived ideas about the presence of extraterrestrial life to color his observations and the inferences he drew from them.

Schwann, Theodor Ambrose Hubert (1810–1892)

German naturalist who established that cells were the fundamental units of life and played a part in disproving the idea of **spontaneous generation.** Schwann showed that the putrefaction of meat required the presence of microscopic organisms and that if these were rigorously excluded the meat would remain fresh for long periods of time.

science fiction involving extraterrestrials, up to 1900

Before the nineteenth century, the concept of authentically alien creatures—beings unlike anything on Earth—never arose. **Lucian,** Ludovico **Ariosto,** Johannes **Kepler,** John **Wilkins,** Francis **Godwin,** and others all told of voyages through space and meetings with the inhabitants of other worlds in stories that are precursors of modern science fiction, but none of their extraterrestrials were anything more than strangely attired humans or animals obviously modeled on terrestrial forms. In the latter part of the nineteenth century, however, science fiction began to reflect the influence of three key scientific paradigms and breakthroughs: the notion of biological evolution (➔ **evolutionary theory and extraterrestrial life**), the **nebular hypothesis** (which, in the form it then took, suggested that the planets of the solar system might be at different stages of development), and the confirmation by **spectroscopy** that the same chemical elements occur throughout the Universe. To these underlying themes must be added the specific and powerful effect that Percival **Lowell**'s vision of Mars exerted on the public (and scientific) imagination.

The Frenchmen Camille **Flammarion** and J. H. **Rosny** were among the first to portray in fiction alien life that was radically different from any terrestrial variety. Yet both, in keeping with the views of their compatriots Jean **Lamarck** and Henri **Bergson,** offered a positive perspective in which humans and extraterrestrials were part of a broader, cosmic scheme of evolution. A darker possibility was suggested by H. G. **Wells,** who was deeply influenced by the Darwinian principle of the "survival of the fittest" as taught to him directly by Thomas **Huxley.** His *The War of the Worlds* of 1897 makes a striking contrast with another great Martian story, *Auf zwei Planeten* (On Two Planets), published in the same year by Kurd **Lasswitz.** Both novels were (and still are) widely read, but they stand at opposite poles in imagining the consequences that might ensue from first contact between humankind and a superior alien intelligence. For the most part, the many science fiction tales written in the last two decades of the nineteenth century, by authors such as Percy **Greg,** George **Griffith,** and Gustavus **Pope,** were lightweight extraterrestrial romances and fantasies written for the amusement of an urban middle class enamored with the wonders of technology and travel.[7, 42, 122, 248]

science fiction involving extraterrestrials, 1900–1940

The first three decades of the twentieth century saw the decline in interest in extraterrestrial life among scientists reflected in a stagnation of innovative fictional output. H. G. **Wells**'s *First Men in the Moon* (1901), though interesting because of its detailed depiction of a **hive intelligence,** is regressive in being built around the outmoded notion of a lunar civilization. Similarly, the early American pulp magazines featured tales, such as those by Edgar Rice **Burroughs,** often set in a Martian environment extrapolated from Percival **Lowell**'s theories that was no longer scientifically credible. However, there were exceptions, including Abraham Merritt's description of a collective alien being made from millions of metal components in *The Metal Monster* (1920) and his account of an ancient, semireptilian race in *The Face of the Abyss* (1923), both first published in *Argosy*. Yet it was not until the 1930s that writers began to give full rein to their extraterrestrial speculations. Stanley **Weinbaum,** for example, was notable for his detailed accounts of alien ecologies and unfamiliar forms of intelligence, beginning with "A

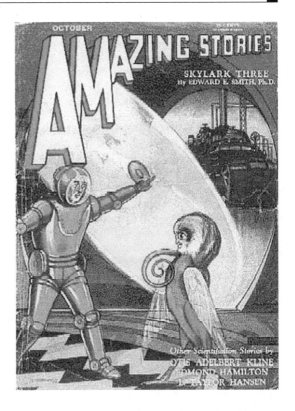

Martian Odyssey" (1934), while Olaf **Stapledon,** in *Star Maker* (1937), projected a future of the Universe in which humans and aliens evolve together toward a single cosmic mind. Clifford Simak's first venture into pseudotheological waters, "The Creator" (1935), in which the Earth and other worlds are revealed to be the product of a godlike alien, was considered by some editors too blasphemous to print. On the other hand, David **Lindsay,** in *A Voyage to Arcturus,* and C. S. **Lewis,** in his cosmic trilogy, used allegory and symbolism in their extraterrestrial settings to convey more conventional religious viewpoints.[7, 42, 122, 248]

science fiction involving extraterrestrials, after 1940

Alien invasion and subversion became popular themes in American and British (though not Russian) science fiction during the Second World War and the Cold War years that followed (➔ **Cold War, linked to UFO reports**). John W. **Campbell**'s "Who Goes There?" served as an inspiration for many subsequent tales of aggressive extraterrestrial monsters and shape shifters, both in print and film. Paranoia and the fear of loss of self-identity, engendered both by the perceived Communist threat and the reactionary right-wing excesses of McCarthyism, found ample expression in the alien motif. Robert Heinlein's *The Puppet Masters,* for example, envisages sluglike parasites that fasten themselves to their victim's back and thereafter assume control over the person's body and brain. The idea of individuals being "taken over," or invasion by insinuation, also underlies Jack Finney's *The Body Snatchers,* better known for its two cinematic interpretations as *Invasion of the Body Snatchers.* The postwar years, however, saw further exploration of the more optimistic concept of advanced extraterrestrials as facilitators of future human evolution. This became a favorite theme of Arthur C. **Clarke,** as exemplified in his short story "The Sentinel"—the inspiration for *2001: A Space Odyssey*—and *Childhood's End.* As for the aliens themselves, portrayals of their possible forms, habitats, behaviors, and minds became ever more adventurous and diverse. James White's Sector General stories, set in a huge space station–hospital on the galactic rim, ingeniously and humorously depicts the medical dramas that accompany the treatment of all manner of exotic species, while Hal **Clement,** Larry **Niven,** and Robert **Forward** were among those to speculate on life in the most unexpected and bizarre locations. Other writers, such as Stanisław **Lem** and Ray **Bradbury,** used aliens as a means of throwing into sharp relief humanity's own strengths and weaknesses. The consequences of **first contact** were also investigated by Fred **Hoyle,** James Gunn, Carl **Sagan,** and others, often leading to disquieting conclusions.[7, 42, 122, 248]

science fiction involving extraterrestrials, in films and on television

The dawn of the Space Age was preceded by a spate of films in the early 1950s, beginning with *Destination Moon* (1950), centered on the theme of space exploration. Extraterrestrials also came onto the cinematic agenda at this time, but not simply or even mainly as an accompaniment to the idea of interplanetary travel. To a large extent, the alien films produced during the late Truman and early Eisenhower years captured in metaphor the American fear of Communist invasion and infiltration[368]—a fear that was itself a stimulus to and corollary of the first modern wave of UFO sightings in the late 1940s (➔ **saucer flap of 1947**). The threat of takeover by outwardly benign but inwardly hostile agents supplied the emotional cutting edge to such classic monster-alien movies as *The Thing* (1951), *It Came from Outer Space* (1953), *Invaders from Mars* (1953), and *Invasion of the Body Snatchers* (1956). As Frederic Jameson has noted:[301]

Arguably, the golden age of the fifties science fiction film with its pod people and brain-eating monsters, testified to a genuine collective paranoia, that of the fantasies of the Cold War period.... The enemy within is then paradoxically marked by non-difference. "Communists" are people just like us save for the emptiness of the eyes and a certain automation which betray the appropriation of their bodies by alien forms.

Yet not all the Hollywood aliens of the fifties were menacing in appearance or intent. In *The Day the Earth Stood Still* (1951), humanity emerges as the source of aggression. The powerful image in this film of a spacecraft landing near the White House may have played a part in inciting the **"Washington Invasion"** flap of 1952, which in turn, formed the basis of the plot of *Earth versus the Flying Saucers* (1956). Aliens were also occasionally depicted as the victims of their own technological ingenuity, thus serving as a moral to our own kind. In *This Island Earth* (1955), two extraterrestrial races are terminally locked in a devastating interplanetary war, while in *Forbidden Planet* (1956) an advanced civilization is found to have destroyed itself through misuse of an intellect-enhancing device.[508]

The late 1950s and early 1960s saw a lull in serious alien representations on the big screen but the beginnings of imaginative exploration of the theme on television. The first episode of *The Outer Limits* (1963–65) concerned a **non-corporeal life**-form that is accidentally "received" by a radio telescope on Earth. Other aliens from the *Outer Limits* stable followed, generally of the unpleasant-looking, anthropophobic variety. On British TV, the *Quatermass* series left a similarly dark and memorable impression of otherworldly beings. In 1966 the *Star Trek* phenomenon began, though none at the time could have imagined how popular or influential it would eventually become. The late 1960s also saw a revival of film interest in extraterrestrials, 1968 being a particularly vintage year with the release of *Planet of the Apes* and, most notably, *2001: A Space Odyssey,* with its remarkably scientifically authentic special effects and unusually subtle treatment of alien intervention in human affairs. Another notable year for cinematic extraterrestrials was 1977, though the approach adopted in *Star Wars* (in which the aliens play a tangential and generally humorous role) and *Close Encounters of the Third Kind* (in which they are central and profound) could hardly be more different. Extraterrestrial benignity continued in *E.T. The Extra-Terrestrial* (1982) but had already been devastatingly contrasted to its polar opposite in *Alien* (1979). For the most part, the demands of commercialism have precluded complex cinematic inquiries into the possible nature of alien life and intelligence of the type successfully accomplished by Andrei Tarkovsky in *Solaris* (1972), the film of Stanisław **Lem**'s novel.[27]

science fiction involving extraterrestrials, on radio
➔ *War of the Worlds, The,* **radio play**

Scientific Advisory Panel on Unidentified Flying Objects
A panel of scientific experts set up, following a CIA proposal to the Intelligence Advisory Committee on December 4, 1952, to review the issue of **unidentified flying objects** and assess any possible threat to national security. The CIA's proposal was in response to a September 24 memo from the assistant director for scientific intelligence, H. Marshall Chadwell, to the CIA's director, General Walter Bedell Smith. Chadell expressed concern that the Soviets might be able to orchestrate a flying saucer flap in order to confuse the U.S. Air Warning System and thus camouflage a surprise attack given that "a fair share of our population is mentally conditioned to the acceptance of the incredible." In the wake of the CIA's response, Chadwell asked H. P. Robertson, a specialist in cosmology and relativity theory at the California Institute of Technology, to assemble a suitable group of consultants. To this end, Robertson brought together physicists Luis **Alvarez** and Samuel A. **Goudsmit,** geophysicist Lloyd **Berkner,** and astronomer Thornton Page, together with associate panel members J. Allen **Hynek** and rocketry expert Frederick C. Durant. From January 14 to 17, 1953, in Washington, D.C., the scientists met in secret to consider the evidence. They concluded that "reasonable explanations could be suggested for most sightings" but that "the continued emphasis of the reporting of these phenomena does, in these parlous times, result in a threat to the orderly functioning of the protective organs of the body politic." The panel recommended that the national security agencies adopt a program

to reassure the public of the total lack of evidence of inimical forces behind the phenomena, to train personnel to recognize and reject false indications quickly and effectively, and to strengthen regular channels for the evaluation of and prompt rejection to true indications of hostile measures.

The fact that the CIA did not declassify the whole of the panel's report until 1979 and that the panel advocated a debunking education program was later seized upon by some ufologists as more evidence of a cover-up. But there were good reasons for these actions. The CIA would not have wanted, by revealing its involvement with the panel at the time, to give further ammunition to those, such as Donald **Keyhoe,** who in the early 1950s were energetically promulgating the theory of an extraterrestrial conspiracy. More importantly, the CIA would have been keen not to hand the idea of spreading UFO hysteria among the American populace to the Soviets, given that the enemy might not in fact have thought of it. As for the panel's recommendations for greater openness and a more analytical approach to handling UFO reports, these were nothing more than one would expect from a team of professional scientists.[167]

S-class asteroid

A type of **asteroid,** reddish in color, with an **albedo** in the range 0.10 to 0.28, that is common in the inner part of the **Main Asteroid Belt.** The "S" stands for "silicaceous," as these objects are believed to be rich in **silicates** such as olivine and pyroxene. S-class asteroids may be the parent objects of stony-iron meteorites.

18 Scorpii

The nearest star that is virtually identical to the Sun.[465] It lies 46 light-years away and closely matches the Sun in mass, luminosity (just 5 percent brighter), temperature, color, surface gravity, speed of rotation, surface activity, abundance of iron, and the fact that it is solitary.

Scully, Frank

Columnist on the show-business magazine *Variety* who in 1950 published his best-selling *Behind the Flying Saucers.* A centerpiece of the book was Scully's claim that a spacecraft containing sixteen dead aliens had been found on a plateau close to the small town of Aztec, New Mexico. According to his informants, "Texas oilman" Silas M. Newton and his colleague "Dr. Gee" (the latter a pseudonym for a "specialist in magnetism"), the bodies were in the custody of the U.S. military along with two other crashed disks. Newton and Dr. Gee (real name: Leo GeBauer) turned out to be convicted confidence tricksters who had embellished a story that had originated with a Hollywood actor named Mike Conrad. Around 1948, Conrad had hit upon the idea of making a movie about UFOs with a base in Alaska (➜ **Keyhoe, Donald**). To generate interest in the project, Conrad claimed that the film would include footage of genuine UFOs. He also hired a promoter to pose as an FBI agent to spread the story that the FBI had custody of this footage. Newton and GeBauer were unaware that Conrad's story was a hoax, while Scully knew nothing about Conrad's publicity ploy. Newton and GeBauer's motive for elabo-

rating the tale was purely commercial. GeBauer had built a gadget that, he said, was based on technology found in the downed saucer and could detect oil and gold deposits. Ironically, the FBI took an interest in the affair and, in due course, its chief, J. Edgar Hoover, received a memo on the subject. This document—a commentary on a piece of hearsay—was later often cited as proof that the U.S. government was holding saucer wreckage and alien corpses.

Search for Life in the Universe, The

A standard, highly accessible work on **SETI** and **astrobiology** by Donald Goldsmith and Tobias Owen.[226] It presents, in updated form, many of the topics dealt with in Carl **Sagan** and Iosif **Shklovskii**'s somewhat more technical *Intelligent Life in the Universe.*

Secchi, Pietro Angelo (1818–78)

Prolific Italian astronomer, pioneer of stellar **spectroscopy,** Jesuit priest, and director of the Roman College Observatory, who saw his religion as being fully compatible with **pluralism.** In 1856, he wrote:

> It is with sweet sentiment that man thinks of these worlds without number, where each star is a sun which, as minister of the divine bounty, distributes life and goodness to the other innumerable beings, blessed by the hand of the Omnipotent.

In fact, Secchi was such a committed pluralist that he often seemed to ignore the evidence of his own research. He was the first to classify stars according to their spectra and therefore knew as well as anyone how different they could be. Still he concluded:

> The atmospheric constitution of the other planets which, in certain points, is so similar to ours as that of the stars is similar to that of the sun, persuades us that these bodies are in a state similar to that of our system.

In 1859, Secchi became the first to use the term *canali* to describe two fine lines he had seen on the surface of Mars (➜ **Mars, canals of**).

secondary atmosphere

An atmosphere produced by the **outgassing** of volatile compounds from the rocky material of a terrestrial-type planet. Venus, Earth, and Mars, for example, all possess secondary atmospheres. ➔ **primordial atmosphere**

sediment exploration station

➔ **cryobot**

Seeger, Charles L. (1912–)

Radio astronomer who played a leading role in the **SETI** Program Office at NASA. He was a codeveloper of the first ultrastable, high-gain, low-noise **parametric amplifier**s needed for radio astronomy and for SETI and took part in the 1971 Stanford-Ames ASEE summer study that produced Project **Cyclops.** Seeger obtained a B.S. in electrical engineering from **Cornell University** (1946) and carried out graduate studies at Leiden University in the Netherlands under Jan Oort.

selenite

A hypothetical lunar inhabitant. The name was coined by Johannes **Hevelius** and later used by many others, both in philosophical discourse and fiction (including, as recently as 1901, H. G. **Wells** in *First Men in the Moon*).

self-organization

The phenomenon by which many physical and chemical systems can, under certain circumstances, jump spontaneously to states of greater organizational complexity. Self-organization tends to occur in nonlinear, open systems that have been driven far out of thermodynamic equilibrium by their surroundings. One possible conclusion is that the laws of nature are, in a sense, biased, so that they tend locally to direct matter toward states of increasing complexity and order. Some researchers have concluded from this that the probability of **abiogenesis** is very much greater than that expected from the random shuffling of molecules in a **prebiotic** environment (➔ **life, origin of**). Manfred **Eigen** is among those who have investigated the effect of connected, self-organizing chemical processes in generating complex molecular arrangements.[178, 179]

His ideas have been taken further by Stuart **Kauffman**[315] and Per Bak[34] and are supported by Robert **Shapiro** and others.

semimajor axis

Half of the longest distance across an ellipse.

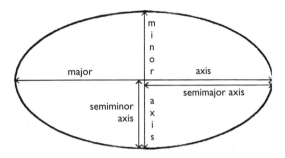

sentinel hypothesis

The suggestion that if advanced alien civilizations exist they might place intelligent monitoring devices on or near the worlds of other evolving species to track their progress. A robot sentinel might establish contact with a developing race once that race had reached a certain technological threshold, such as large-scale radio communication or interplanetary flight.

Already, scientists are beginning to understand the basic conditions necessary for **carbon**-based life to develop. They can identify those stars in the solar neighborhood most like the Sun and can delineate approximately the **habitable zone** around any given star in which complex biochemistry might be expected to flourish. Scientists are also starting to acquire the ability to detect **extrasolar planets.** More advanced species would presumably be able to stake out with reasonable accuracy those stars and their associated worlds upon which intelligent life had a good chance of eventually developing, particularly if scout ships had revealed the presence of protointelligence. Such promising locations might then be expected to come under increasingly intense scrutiny by automatic sentinels. This idea was used by Arthur C. **Clarke** in his short story "The Sentinel,"[112] which subsequently formed the basis of the motion picture *2001: A Space Odyssey* and its novelization.[105]

Ronald **Bracewell** has discussed a specific strategy by which devices could be used to monitor star systems for evolving technological races and also how we might go about trying to find sentinels that had been placed in the solar system. → **Bracewell probes**

Sentinel, Project

A dedicated **all-sky search** conducted from 1983 to 1985 using the **Harvard-Smithsonian radio telescope** and a reconfigured version of **"Suitcase SETI."**[284] Covering the northern sky in **drift scan** mode around the frequency of the **21-centimeter line,** this was the first dedicated high-resolution **SETI** program. An all-sky search was chosen, unlike the earlier **Harvard-Arecibo off-line SETI,** which was a **targeted search,** because the larger beam size (30 arc-minutes at Harvard, compared with 3 arc-minutes at Arecibo) enabled a full-sky search in about 200 days. Like its predecessors, Sentinel achieved high resolution at the expense of total frequency coverage (2 kHz **instantaneous bandwidth** for Sentinel and "Suitcase SETI," 1 kHz for the off-line search), requiring a transmitting civilization to target the Sun specifically in order to adjust the frequency of its signals to take account of the relative motion of the local and **heliocentric** frames. Moreover, the long **integration time** of about 30 seconds prevented immediate reobservations of interesting candidate signals. These problems were addressed in a subsequent Harvard search known as Project **META.**

SERENDIP

Search for Extraterrestrial Radio Emission from Nearby Developed Intelligent Populations; an ongoing **SETI** program conducted by the **University of California, Berkeley.** It is unusual in being a "piggyback" search operating alongside conventional radio astronomy observations. Since it began in 1979, with **SERENDIP I,** it has undergone three major improvements and upgrades, **SERENDIP II** (1986–88), **SERENDIP III** (1992–96), and the current **SERENDIP IV.**[71]

SERENDIP I

The first phase of the **SERENDIP** program, which began in 1979 using a 100-channel **spectrum** analyzer installed at the **Hat Creek Observatory.** It was succeeded by **SERENDIP II.**

SERENDIP II

Thousands of times more powerful than its predecessor, **SERENDIP I,** this second phase of Berkeley's **SERENDIP** program ran from 1986 to 1988 and was primarily located at the 92-m (300-ft.) radio telescope at **Green Bank.** It was capable of searching 65,000 channels simultaneously.

SERENDIP III

The third incarnation of **SERENDIP,** led by Stuart Bowyer, which began piggyback operation at the **Arecibo radio telescope** on April 15, 1992. The SERENDIP III equipment examined 4.2 million channels every 1.7 seconds in a 12-MHz-wide band centered at 429 MHz (equivalent to a wavelength of 70 cm). During 10,000 hours of observation time between 1992 and 1996, the project looked at 93 percent of the sky visible from Arecibo at least once and 43 percent of the visible sky at least five times. Around 100 trillion channels were examined at very high sensitivity. Data analysis, which is still in progress, has turned up a few interesting candidate signals but nothing that strongly suggests an artificial extraterrestrial origin.

SERENDIP IV

The latest phase of Berkeley's **SERENDIP** endeavor, installed at the **Arecibo radio telescope** in June 1997. It is forty times more sensitive than its predecessor, **SERENDIP III,** and examines 168 million frequency channels every 1.7 seconds in a 100-MHz band centered at 1.42 GHz. Signals that peak significantly above the background noise are stored and the data transferred across the Internet to the SERENDIP laboratory at Berkeley. There the data are passed through a series of algorithms designed to reject radio frequency interference and sift out signals that have some possibility of being both artificial and extraterrestrial. SERENDIP IV instrumentation is also being used by the Australian SETI group at the **Parkes Radio Telescope** and by the Italian SETI group at Medicina. A 4-million-channel version of SERENDIP IV is in operation at the **Ohio State University Radio Observatory.**

Serviss, Garrett Putnam (1851–1929)

American journalist and writer of popular astronomy fiction and nonfiction, with a science degree from **Cornell University,** who, in his *Other Worlds*[526] (1901), draws upon Pierre **Laplace**'s **nebular hypothesis** and Darwinian biology in arguing the case for varying degrees of habitability and evolutionary progress on the planets of the solar system. Mercury is uninhabitable by life as we know it, whereas Venus, he suggests, may be

> passing through some such period in its history as that at which the earth had arrived in the age of the carboniferous forests, or the age of the gigantic reptiles.

Since Mars, according to the Laplacian scheme of planetary evolution, formed and cooled earlier than the Earth, its inhabitants were biologically older and possessed of "superhuman powers," as evidenced by the canals in which Serviss believed. The outer planets, he concluded, were Sun-like bodies that are burned out and are still in the process of becoming worlds. His fictional tales include a sequel to **Wells**'s *The War of the Worlds,* called *Edison's Conquest of Mars*[528] (1898), and *A Columbus in Space*[527] (1909), published in *All-Story Magazine,* which portrays Venus as having progressed well beyond the Carboniferous stage and become populated by two tribes, one subhuman and the other human.

SETI

Search for Extraterrestrial Intelligence. The first practical proposals in SETI were made in the nineteenth and early twentieth centuries but were aimed only at *interplanetary* communication (➔ **communication, with the Moon and planets**). The roots of SETI in its modern form, as a search for artificial signals over interstellar and even intergalactic distances, can be traced back to the 1930s with the discovery by Karl **Jansky** of **radio waves** coming from a source outside the solar system. This led, in time, to the birth of radio astronomy and to the construction, in the late 1950s, of the first

large **radio telescopes** such as those at **Jodrell Bank** and **Green Bank.** Only with such powerful instruments was it feasible to start looking for Earth-type signals from nearby stars. As a serious scientific enterprise, SETI began in 1959 with two independent events. The first was the publication of a paper in which Cornell researchers Philip **Morrison** and Giuseppe **Cocconi** discussed the suitability of radio waves as a communication medium, man's newly acquired ability to eavesdrop on interstellar radio conversations, and the optimum frequency at which to conduct a search (➔ **Morrison-Cocconi Conjecture**). They argued:

> If signals are present, the means of detecting them is now at hand. Few will deny the profound importance, practical and philosophical, which the detection of interstellar communications will have. We therefore feel that a discriminating search for signals deserves a considerable effort. The probability of success is difficult to estimate; but if we never search, the chance of success is zero.

Meanwhile, at the National Radio Astronomy Observatory, Green Bank, Frank **Drake** had independently arrived at the same conclusion. Indeed, Drake had already begun to assemble the equipment he would use in Project **Ozma,** the first observational SETI program, carried out in 1960. Despite Ozma's failure to detect any extraterrestrial transmissions from its two target stars, it served to stimulate widespread public interest and lively (often critical) scientific debate. In 1961, an informal conference sponsored by the **Space Science Board** was held at Green Bank [➔ **Green Bank conference (1961)**]. A dozen scientists and engineers deeply interested in the possibility of extraterrestrial life were invited to attend, including Drake himself, Morrison, Cocconi, Carl **Sagan,** Su-Shu **Huang,** Melvin **Calvin,** John **Lilly,** Bernard **Oliver,** Dana **Atchley,** and J. P. Pearman. At the conference, the now-famous **Drake Equation** was discussed for the first time.

The dawn of the SETI era stimulated scientists to consider the pros and cons of searching at all, the best strategy involving radio wave

SETI OBSERVING PROGRAMS: 1960 TO THE PRESENT*

Date	Investigator(s)	Location	Antenna Diameter (m)	Search Frequency	Frequency Resolution	Targets	Comments
1960	Drake	Green Bank	26	1420 MHz	100 Hz	ε Eridani τ Ceti	Project Ozma
1963–64	Kardashev, Sholomitskii	Crimea Deep Space Station	16 × 8 antennas	923 MHz	10 MHz	2 quasars	CTA 102—initial report of type III civilization
1966	Kellerman	Parkes	64	350–5000 MHz	full bandwidth	1 galaxy (1934–63)	
1968–69	Troitskii, Rakhlin, Gershtejin, Starodubstev	Zimenkie	5	926–8 Hz, 1421–23 MHz	13	11 stars and M31	
1968–82	Troitskii	Gorky	dipole	1, 1.875, 3.75, 10 GHz		all-sky	
1969–83	Troitskii, Bondar, Starodubstev	Gorky, Crimea, Mumansk, Primorskij	dipoles	600, 927, 1863 MHz		all-sky	search for pulsed signals
1970–72	Slysh, Pashchenko, Rudnitskii, Lekht	Nancay	40 × 240 antennas	1665, 1667 MHz	4 kHz	5 OH masers	search for unnatural emission characteristics
1970–72	Slysh	Nancay	40 × 240 antennas	1665, 1667 MHz	4 kHz	10 nearest stars	
1971, 1972	Verschuur	Green Bank	91 43	1420–21 MHz 1410–30 MHz	490 Hz 6.9 kHz	9 stars	Project Ozpa
1972	Kardashev, Popov, Soglasnov, et al.	Crimea, RT-22	22	8570 MHz		galactic center	search for statistical anomalies
1972–74	Kardashev, Gindilis, Popov, Soglasnov, Spangenberg, et al	Caucasus, Pamir, Kamchatka, Mars 7	38, 60	371, 408 458, 535 MHz	5 MHz	omnidirectional	eavesdropping search for pulses
1972–76	Zuckerman, Palmer	Green Bank	91	1413–25, 1420–21 MHz	6.4×10^4 4 kHz	674 stars	Project Ozma II
1972–76	Bridle, Feldman	Algonquin	46	22,235 MHz	30 kHz	70 stars	first search at the water wavelength
1973–74	Shvartsman, et al.	Special Astrophysical Observatory, MANIA	0.6	optical		21 peculiar objects	optical search for short pulses and laser lines

Year	Observers	Telescope	Diameter	Frequency	Resolution	Target	Description
1973–98	Dixon, Ehman, Raub, Kraus	Ohio State	53	1420 MHz	10 kHz, 1 kHz	all sky	Wow! signal in 1976
1974	Wishnia	Copernicus	1	UV		nearby stars	search for UV laser lines
1975	Drake, Sagan	Arecibo	305	1420, 1667, 2380 MHz	1 kHz	4 galaxies	search for type II civilizations
1975–79	Israel, de Ruiter	WRST	1500	1415 MHz	4×10^6	50 star fields	
1976	Wielebinski, Seiradakis	Max Planck Institute	100	1420 MHz	20 MHz	three Sun-like stars	search for pulsed signals with periods of 0.3–1.5 seconds
1976	Black, Cuzzi, Clark, Tarter	Green Bank	43	8522–23 MHz	5 Hz	4 stars	
1977	Black, Cuzzi, Clark, Tarter	Green Bank	91	1665–67 MHz	5 Hz	200 stars	
1977	Drake, Stull	Arecibo	305	1664–68 MHz	0.5 Hz	6 stars	
1978	Shvartsman, et al.	Special Astrophysical Observatory, MANIA	6	optical			optical search of 30 radio objects for pulses from Kardashev II or III civilization
1978	Horowitz	Arecibo	305	1420 MHz	0.015 Hz	185 stars	
1978	Cohen, Malkan, Dickey	Arecibo, HRO, Parkes	305, 36, 64	1665–67 MHz, 22235 MHz, 1612 MHz	9.5 kHz, 65 kHz, 4.5 kHz	25 globular clusters	passive search for type II and III civilizations
1978	Knowles, Sullivan	Arecibo	305	130–500 MHz	1 Hz	2 stars	
1978	Makovetskij, Gindilis, et al.	Zelenchukskaya, RATAN-600	7.4 × 450			Barnard's Star	
1978–80	Harris	Pioneer Venus, Venera 11 and 12		20 keV–1 MeV		54 γ-ray bursters	search for 3 linear events as sign of i/s spacecraft
1979	Cole, Ekers	Parkes	64	5000 MHz	10 MHz, 1 MHz	nearby FGK stars	
1979	Freitas, Valdes	Leuschner Observatory	0.76	optical		Lagrangian points	Bracewell probes

Date	Investigator(s)	Location	Antenna Diameter (m)	Search Frequency	Frequency Resolution	Targets	Comments
1979–81	Tarter, Clark, Duquet, Lesyna	Arecibo	305	1420 MHz, 1666 MHz	5 Hz, 600 Hz	200 stars	
1979–85	Bowyer et al.	Hat Creek	26	917–37, 1410–30, 1602–5 MHz, etc.	2 × 500	all-sky	SERENDIP piggyback
1980	Witteborn	NASA—Univ. of Arizona, Mt. Lemon	1.5	infrared		20 stars	infrared excess from Dyson spheres
1980–81	Suchkin, Tokarev, et al.	Nirfi, Gorkii, Gaish, Moscow		9.3 MHz	1.5 kHz	Lagrangian points	Bracewell probes
1981	Lord, O'Dea	Univ. of Mass.	14	115 GHz	20 kHz, 125 kHz	north galactic rotational axis	
1981	Israel, Tarter	WRST	3,000 max. baseline	1420 MHz	4 MHz, 10 MHz	85 star fields	piggyback search
1981–82	Biraud, Tarter	Nancay	40 × 240	1420 MHz	49 Hz	343 stars	
1981	Shostak, Tarter	WRST	3,000 max. baseline	1420 MHz, 1665–67 MHz	1.2 kHz	galactic center	interferometer search for pulsed signals
1981	Talent	Kitt Peak National Obser.	2.1	optical		3 stars	search for enhanced stellar lines of rare earth elements as evidence of ET nuclear waste disposal
1981–82	Valdes, Freitas	Kitt Peak	0.61	optical		Langrangian points	Project SETA; search for Bracewell probes
1982	Horowitz, Teague, Linscott, Chen, Backus	Arecibo	305	2841 MHz, 1420 MHz	0.03 Hz, 0.03 Hz	250 stars, 150 stars	Suitcase SETI
1982	Vallee, Simard-Normandin	Algonquin	46	10522 MHz	185 MHz	galactic center meridian	search for strongly polarized signals
1983–85	Horowitz	Oak Ridge	26	1420 MHz, 1667 MHz	0.03 Hz	sky survey	Project Sentinel
1983	Damashek	Green Bank	92	390 MHz	2×10^6 Hz	sky survey	search for single pulses and telemetry
1983	Valdes, Freitas	Hat Creek	26	1516 MHz	4.9 kHz, 76 k	80 stars, 12 stars	search for radioactive tritium from ET fusion technology

Year	Name	Telescope	Size	Frequency	Resolution	Target	Notes
1983	Gulkis	DSS 43	64	8 GHz 2380 MHz	40 kHz	southern sky survey	
1983–88	Gray	Small SETI Obser.	4	1419–21 MHz	1–40 Hz	sky survey	amateur meridian transit search
1983–84	Cullers	AMSETI	2	1420 Hz, <1000 MHz			amateur SETI based on satellite TV dishes
1983–88	Stephens	Hay River, NWT	Two 18 × 18	1415–25 MHz	30 kHz	northern sky survey	amateur SETI observatory using two 64-ft. square dishes
1984	Slysh	Satellite radiometer		37 GHz	400 MHz	all sky	Dyson spheres radiating > 1 sol. lum. within 100 pc
1985–95	Horowitz	Oak Ridge	26	1420, 1665 1667, 2841 MHz	0.05	sky survey	META
1986–88	Bowyer, Wertheimer, Lampton	Green Bank	92	400–3,500 MHz	1 Hz	various sky areas	SERENDIP II
1986	Mirabel	Green Bank	43	4830 MHz	76 Hz	galactic center 33 stars	
1986	Betz	Mount Wilson	1.65	infrared	3.5 MHz	100 Sun-like stars	search for IR beacons at carbon dioxide laser frequency
1986–	Colomb, Martin, Lemarchand	Argentina	30	1415 MHz 1425 MHz 1667 MHz	2.5 kHz	78 Sun-like stars	
1987	Tarter, Kardashev, Slysh	VLA	26 ×9	1612 MHz	6.1 kHz	G357.3-1.3	obs. of IR source near galactic center to check if Dyson sphere
1987	Gray	Oak Ridge	26	1420 MHz	0.05 Hz	sky positions of Wow! signal	used META system
1988	Bania, Rood	Green Bank	43	8665 MHz	305 Hz	24 Vega-like stars with IR excess	search for narrow-band signal at freq. of spin-flip of 3He+
1990	Colomb et al.	Argentina	30	1420 MHz	0.05 Hz	all sky	META II (Southern Hemis.)

Date	Investigator(s)	Location	Antenna Diameter (m)	Search Frequency	Frequency Resolution	Targets	Comments
1990	Blair et al.	Parkes	64	4462 MHz	100 Hz	100 Sun-like stars	search at $\pi \times 21$-cm hydrogen line frequency
1990	Gray	Oak Ridge	26	1420 MHz	0.05 Hz	M31, M33	
1990–	Kingsley	Bexley, Ohio	0.25	optical		nearby stars	COSETI
1992	NASA Ames	Arecibo	305	1.3–2.4 GHz	1.7, 28 Hz	78 Sun-like stars	HRMS targeted search
1992	JPL	Goldstone	26, 34	1.7 GHz 8.3–8.7 GHz	30 Hz	all sky	HRMS sky survey
1992–96	Bowyer, Wertheimer, Donnelly	Arecibo	305	423–35 MHz	0.6 Hz	all sky	SERENDIP III
1993	Steffes, Deboer	NRAO/Tucson	12	203 GHz	32 Hz	40 stars and 3 locations near galactic center	search near positronium line
1995–	SETI Institute	Parkes-Mopra Green Bank-Woodbury Arecibo-Jodrell Bank	64,22 43,30 305,76	1.2–3 GHz 1.2–3 GHz 1.2–3 GHz	1 Hz	206 stars 192 stars 600 stars	Project Phoenix
1995	Gray	VLA	26	1420 MHz	381 Hz	Wow! signal region	
1995	Beskin	Special Astrophysical Observatory	6	optical	6.1 kHz	several objects	
1995	Mauersberger; Wilson, Rood, Bania, Hein, Linhart	IRAM	30	203 GHz	9.7 kHz	17 stars and positions	search at spin-flip frequency of positronium
1995–99	Horowitz et al.	Oak Ridge	26	1.4–1.7 GHz	0.5 Hz	northern all-sky	BETA; covered full waterhole (damaged by wind storm)
1996	Blair, Zadnik	Perth, Australia	0.64	optical		nearby stars	
1997–ongoing	Wertheimer, et al	Arecibo	305	1.37–1.47 GHz	0.6	all-sky equatorial	SERENDIP IV, random sky survey
1998–	SETI League	amateur dishes (up to 5,000)	3–5	1.42 GHz	10 Hz	all directions in real time	Project Argus

1998–	Stootman et al.	Parkes	64	1.418–1.420 MHz	0.6 Hz	southern all-sky	Southern SERENDIP; uses 13 beams on sky from focal plane array in random sky survey
1999–	Wertheimer	Leuschner	0.76	optical		nearby stars	search for pulsed signals
1999–	Marcy	Lick and Keck	4 and 10	optical		nearby stars	search for narrowband continuous wave signals in data archive of radial velocity extrasolar planet search
1999–	Horowitz	Harvard Smithsonian	1.55	optical		nearby stars	search for nanosecond pulsed signals
1999–	Montebugnoli	Medicina	32	1415–25 MHz 4255–65 MHz	0.6 Hz	northern sky survey	SETI Italia; SERENDIP-type random sky survey at 21 cm and 7 cm
1999–	Wertheimer and Anderson	Arecibo	305	1.419–1.421 GHz	0.1 Hz	all sky	SETI@home (2.5 MHz of SERENDIP IV data analyzed by screen-saver analysis on up to 1 million home PCs)

* Based on data compiled by Jill Tarter of the SETI Institute.

searches, and alternative approaches to finding evidence of extraterrestrial intelligence.[73] Into the last category came the suggestions of **Dyson spheres** and **Bracewell probes.** The feasibility of interstellar travel was also considered around this time by Robert **Bussard,** Freeman **Dyson,** Sebastian von **Hoerner,** John **Pierce,** Edward **Purcell,** and Carl Sagan.

In the Soviet Union, SETI was seen as a natural outcome of Communist philosophy and, partly for this reason, became quickly established as a respectable field of research. Interest there was initially sparked by the writings of Iosef **Shklovskii** and tended to focus on the possibility of civilizations far in advance of our own. In 1963, a radio wave search was carried out for **Kardashev civilizations,** though at a different frequency to that employed by Project Ozma.

Within the radio search paradigm, which by the mid-1960s was well established as the standard approach to SETI, much debate focused on methodology. An artificial signal, unlike one of natural origin, would be expected to have a narrow **bandwidth** so that it could be detected only by an antenna tuned to one particular frequency. The question was *which* frequency offered the best chance of success. Morrison and Cocconi had argued for 1,420 MHz, corresponding to the ubiquitous **21-centimeter line** of neutral hydrogen, but the subsequent discovery of other common natural radio frequencies (➔ **waterhole**) complicated the decision. Moreover, the merits of **targeted search**es had to be weighed against those of **all-sky survey**s. In the decades following Project Ozma, many different approaches were tried.

In 1970, NASA's involvement with SETI began through some preliminary work carried out by John **Billingham.** This led, in 1973, to an ambitious proposal by Billingham and Oliver, known as Project **Cyclops,** to detect extraterrestrial civilizations by eavesdropping on their stray electromagnetic signals. Although the proposal failed, it served to stimulate interest in a NASA SETI program of more modest scale. This eventually led to the **High Resolution Microwave Survey** and, when this had to be abandoned because of budget cuts,

its privately funded successor, Project **Phoenix.**

In 1973, what was to become the longest-running SETI program to date began at the **Ohio State University Radio Observatory.** Its most dramatic moment came in 1977 with the detection of the mysterious **Wow! signal.** Meanwhile, Drake and Sagan employed the giant **Arecibo radio telescope** to search for emissions from advanced civilizations in other galaxies. The mid-1970s also saw the very foundations of SETI challenged by a revival of interest in the **Fermi Paradox.**

Interest in SETI has never been greater than today. A number of programs are active, including the **SETI Institute**'s Project Phoenix, Harvard's Project **BETA,** Berkeley's **SERENDIP,** and the **SETI League**'s Project **Argus,** the last unique in that it relies upon data gathered worldwide by a growing army of amateur observers. The public's interest in SETI has been heightened by the suggestion of possible life on Mars and the giant moons of Jupiter, as well as by fictional portrayals, such as Sagan's *Contact.*[495] Finally, there is a sense in which SETI, in addition to being a scientific quest, answers a modern spiritual need (➔ **SETI, religious dimensions of**).[70, 96, 492]

SETI@home

A screen-saver program for personal computers that analyzes data collected by the **SERENDIP IV** project and looks for potential signals from an extraterrestrial civilization. It was developed by David Anderson and Daniel Wertheimer at the **University of California, Berkeley,** and is sponsored by Paramount Pictures, as part of the promotion for *Star Trek: Insurrection,* with support from the **Planetary Society.** The director and costar of the film, Jonathon Frakes ("Commander Riker") pulled the switch to start operations on October 19, 1998. Following testing and debugging of the software, SETI@home will be available free from the Planetary Society to anyone wishing to participate.

SETI Australia Centre

A facility established in 1995 and located in the Faculty of Informatics, Science, and Technology at the Campbelltown campus of the University of Western Sydney Macarthur. It is the first center of its kind in Australia and has links with the **SETI Institute** and the **SERENDIP** group at the **University of California, Berkeley.** It operates the **Southern SERENDIP** project.

SETI, false alarms in

Two incidents stand out in the chronicles of **SETI** that, at the time, suggested that signals might have been detected from an extraterrestrial intelligence. The first was in 1963, when the radio source designated **CTA-102** was claimed by Soviet astronomers to be evidence of a highly advanced alien civilization. In 1967, S. Jocelyn Bell (now Bell Burnell) recorded a regular pulsating signal using a **radio telescope** in Cambridge, England, designed by Anthony Hewish to look for rapid variations in the radio wave emission of **quasar**s. An early theory was that the pulses might be coming from an **interstellar beacon,** and the source was tentatively cataloged as LGM, for "little green men." However, it quickly became clear that this and other similar sources that were detected soon after could be explained naturally in terms of rotating neutron stars, or **pulsar**s. → **SETI, unexplained signals**

SETI Institute

A nonprofit corporation based in Mountain View, California, that conducts research in various fields related to the study of life in the universe, including astronomy and planetary sciences, chemical evolution, the origin of life, biological evolution, and cultural evolution. The institute's projects have been sponsored by NASA, JPL, the National Science Foundation, the Department of Energy, and others. The SETI Institute's search for extraterrestrial intelligence, Project **Phoenix,** is effectively a resurrection of NASA's **High Resolution Microwave Survey** that was dropped in 1993 following the removal of government funding for the program. In collaboration with the **University of California, Berkeley,** the SETI Institute is about to embark on the construction of the **One Hectare Telescope,** the first large instrument to be primarily devoted to the search for intelligent signals. → **Chyba, Christopher; Drake, Frank; Tarter, Jill; Welch, William**

SETI League

A nonprofit, membership-supported organization dedicated to the search for radio signals from extraterrestrial intelligence. The SETI League launched its first search program, Project **Argus,** in April 1996.

SETI, religious dimensions of

It has been suggested that **SETI,** and **pluralism** in general, has some of the hallmarks of an alternative or quasi religion. As pointed out by Frank **Tipler,**[588] this tends to be supported by some of the statements made by leading researchers in the field, including Frank **Drake** and Carl **Sagan.** Drake, for example, writes:

> I fear we have been making a dreadful mistake by not focusing all searches…on the detection of the signals of the immortals. For it is the immortals we will most likely discover.…An immortal civilization's best assurance of safety would be to make other species immortal like themselves, rather than risk hazardous military adventures. Thus we could expect them to spread actively the secrets of their immortality among the young, technically developing civilizations.

Sagan, too, although scathing of the messianic motives of some saucer enthusiasts, has suggested that the mere detection of an extraterrestrial radio signal would provide "an invaluable piece of knowledge: that it is possible to avoid the dangers of the period through which we are now passing." Furthermore, according to Sagan, "it is possible that among the first contents of such a message may be detailed prescriptions for the avoidance of technological disaster, for a passage through adolescence to maturity."

If the *search* for other intelligent life has some of the elements of a religious or spiritual quest, then **first contact** is the closest equivalent of the sought-for epiphany. This idea is apparent, for example, in Sagan's novel *Contact*[495] and, even more so, in the motion picture based upon it.[426, 542] → **extraterrestrial intelligence, implications following first contact**

SETI, unexplained signals

Over the past few decades, many intriguing signals have been picked up by the various **SETI** programs that are compatible with an artificial origin but remain unidentified. Of these, the most famous is the **Wow! signal.** Although in the majority of cases the possibility of interference cannot be ruled out, these anomalous sources tend to be concentrated toward the plane of the Milky Way, as would be expected if they were galactic in origin. → **SETI, false alarms in**

Shapiro, Robert (1935–)

Professor of chemistry at New York University who has argued strongly against conventional origin-of-life theories that are based on the spontaneous—and to him, highly unlikely—generation of complex entities such as **RNA, DNA,** or **gene**s. In his *Origins: A Skeptic's Guide to the Creation of Life on Earth*[530] (1987), he presented a pessimistic view of the possibility of life on Earth having emerged by chance. By 1999, in *Planetary Dreams*,[531] he had elaborated his thesis to argue that universal self-organizing principles operating on basic **organic** materials would serve to generate life under a wide variety of circumstances. Given a liquid or dense gaseous medium, a suitable energy source, and a system of matter capable of using the energy to structure itself, primitive organisms *will* inevitably emerge—an idea he terms the "Life Principle." He further maintains that, following its elementary genesis, life will evolve in ways and directions that are wholly unpredictable.

Shapley, Harlow (1885–1972)

American astronomer who, while working at **Mount Wilson Observatory,** made observations of **variable star**s in **globular cluster**s to obtain, in 1918, a new estimate of the size and shape of the **Galaxy.** His demonstration that the Sun lay closer to the periphery of the Galaxy than its center marked another step in the movement away from anthropocentrism in a cosmological context. In 1921, he became di-

rector of **Harvard College Observatory,** a post he held for 31 years. In that period, he switched from a pessimistic view about the likelihood of **extrasolar planets** and life, influenced by the **Jeans-Jeffreys tidal hypothesis,** to one of great optimism. His widely read *Of Stars and Men*[533] (1958) urges that "millions of planetary systems exist, and billions is the better word" and that "whenever the physics, chemistry and climates are right on a planet's surface, life will emerge, persist and evolve." Shapley also speculated on the possibility that life might exist on the surface of objects, now known as **brown dwarf**s, that are intermediate between planets and stars.

Shaver, Richard S(harpe) (1907–75)

American science fiction writer now remembered infamously for the conspiracy-oriented "Shaver Mystery" tales, presented as fact, which Raymond **Palmer** published in *Amazing Stories* (1945–47). In these, Shaver describes a hidden underground world of warring Deros and Teros—"deranged" and "integrated" robots—whose extraterrestrial ancestors had lived on the lost continents of Atlantis and Lemuria.

shepherd moon

A small satellite, the gravitational influence of which acts to constrain a planetary ring and prevent it from dispersing.

Shklovskii, Iosef Samuilovich (1916–85)

Eminent Ukrainian astrophysicist who was largely responsible for making **SETI** a subject of serious scientific concern in the old Soviet Union. After graduating from Moscow State University in 1938, he began work at the **Sternberg State Astronomical Institute,** but following the Nazi invasion he moved to Central Asia with a number of other students, including Andrei Sakharov. After the war, he returned to Sternberg, obtained a Ph.D. in mathematical physics (1950), and became head of the Department of Radio Astronomy. He carried out early studies of planetary atmospheres, proposed that nearby **supernova** explosions may have played an important role in the evolution of terrestrial life, predicted the existence of astronomical **maser**s, and, in 1965, put forward the modern idea that **planetary nebula**s represent a transitional stage from **red giant**s to **white dwarf**s. In a country of tight censorship, Shklovskii was never afraid to give voice to his fertile imagination. Among his many less orthodox suggestions were that the moons of Mars might be artificial (➔ **Mars, moons of**) and that advanced civilizations might obtain new resources by intentionally triggering supernovas using gamma-ray lasers. He pioneered SETI in the Soviet Union following early developments in the United States.[539] One of his students was Nikolai **Kardashev**.[575]

short-period comet

A **comet** with a period of less than 200 years. Short-period comets are now subdivided into **Jupiter-type comet**s, such as comets Encke and Tempel 2, which have periods of less than 20 years, and intermediate-period or **Halley-type comet**s, with periods between 20 and 200 years. Jupiter-type comets are believed to originate in the **Kuiper Belt,** which surrounds the Sun at distances between about 30 AU (the distance of Neptune) and 50 AU (7.5 billion km, 4.7 billion miles). The gravitational influence of the outer planets Neptune and Uranus is thought occasionally to perturb some of the Kuiper objects, causing them to take up the orbits characteristic of comets in the Jupiter family. Halley-type comets, together with **long-period comet**s, however, appear to come from the **Oort Cloud.**

Siding Spring Observatory

Located on Siding Spring Mountain in New South Wales, Australia, at an altitude of 1,165 m (3,785 ft.). Its main instruments are the 3.9-m (12.8-ft.) **Anglo-Australian Telescope** and the 1.2-m (3.9-ft.) U.K. Schmidt telescope.

Sigma 2398

➔ **stars, nearest**

Sign, Project

The first official investigation carried out by the U.S. Air Force into reports of "**flying disk**s." Project Sign was established on December 30, 1947, in response to the massive wave of sightings that year (➔ **saucer flap of 1947**) and following recommendations by Lieutenant General Nathan F. **Twining,** the head of **Air Materiel Command** (AMC). It was staffed by members of AMC's **Technical Intelligence Division,** based at Wright Field (now Wright-Patterson Air Force Base) in Dayton, Ohio, and began work on January 22, 1948. At the outset, the consensus among Sign researchers seems to have been that the flying disks (UFOs) were real and were most likely advanced Soviet aircraft, possibly developed from German prototypes captured at the end of World War II. During the 368 days of Sign's existence, however, opinion shifted to the extent that in a secret document entitled *Estimate of the Situation,* which reached U.S. Air Force Chief of Staff General Hoyt S. Vandenberg in early October 1948, it was suggested that the **extraterrestrial hypothesis** offered the best solution to the mystery of the flying disks. Vandenberg rejected this conclusion, the document was declassified a few months later, and all copies of it were ordered burned. When the destruction order became public knowledge, in the mid-1950s, it served to inflame a growing belief that the government was orchestrating a cover-up as to the true nature of UFOs. Subsequent denials by the Air Force that the *Estimate* document had ever existed only exacerbated the situation further. Following Vandenberg's rejection of the extraterrestrial hypothesis, supporters of this view at Sign were gradually reassigned to other duties until skeptics became the majority. In its final report, Project Sign expressed itself guardedly on the extraterrestrial issue:

It is hard to believe that any technically accomplished race would come here, flaunt its ability in mysterious ways and then simply go away.... Only one motive can be assigned; that the spacemen are "feeling out" our defenses without wanting to be belligerent. If so, they must have been satisfied long ago that we can't catch them.... Although visits from outer space are believed to be possible, they are believed to be very improbable. In particular, the actions attributed to the "flying objects" reported during 1947 and 1948 seem inconsistent with the requirements for space travel.

On February 11, 1949, Project Sign gave way to its successor, Project **Grudge.**

signal verification

The process of checking candidate signals, detected by **SETI** receiving equipment, to eliminate the possibility that they may be of natural or local, man-made origin.

signal-to-noise ratio (SNR)

The ratio of the strength of a signal to the strength of any **background noise** that might also be present. The higher the SNR, the more easily the signal can be distinguished.

silane (SH₄)

A colorless gas, insoluble in water, that is stable in the absence of air but spontaneously flammable even at low temperatures.

Density relative to water 0.68 (liquid); melting point −185°C; boiling point −112°C

silicates

The largest group of minerals, wide-ranging and often complex in composition. All contain **silicon, oxygen,** and one or more metals, and may contain **hydrogen.**

silicon (Si)

A metalloid element, the second most abundant element in the Earth's crust (25.7 percent by mass). Silicon occurs in various forms, including **silicate** minerals and quartz. It has a diamondlike crystal structure, although it can also exist in an amorphous state. Many organosilicon compounds are known, and there has been much speculation over the years on the possibility of **silicon-based life.**

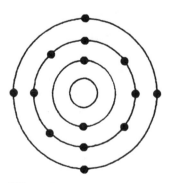

Silicon atom.

Atomic number 14; density relative to water 2.33; melting point 1,410°C; boiling point 2,355°C

silicon-based life

All life on Earth is built upon **carbon** and carbon-based compounds. Yet the possibility has been discussed that life elsewhere may have a different chemical foundation. In 1891, Julius **Scheiner** became perhaps the first to speculate on the suitability of **silicon** as a basis for life. This idea was taken up by James Emerson **Reynolds,** who, in 1893, in his opening address to the British Association for the Advancement of Science,[479] pointed out that the heat stability of silicon compounds might allow life to exist at very high temperatures (➜ **thermophiles**). In an 1894 article[620] drawing on Reynolds's ideas and also those of Robert **Ball,**[38] H. G. **Wells** wrote:

> One is startled towards fantastic imaginings by such a suggestion: visions of silicon-aluminium organisms—why not silicon-aluminium men at once?—wandering through an atmosphere of gaseous sulphur, let us say, by the shores of a sea of liquid iron some thousand degrees or so above the temperature of a blast furnace.

Thirty years later, J. B. S. **Haldane** suggested that life might be found deep inside a planet based on partly molten **silicates,** the **oxidation** of iron perhaps providing it with energy.

At first sight, silicon does seem a promising organic alternative to carbon. It is common in the universe and lies directly below carbon in the periodic table of elements, so that much of its basic chemistry is similar. For instance, just as carbon combines with four hydrogen atoms to form **methane,** CH₄, silicon yields **silane,** SiH₄. Silicates are analogues of **carbonate**s, silicon chloroform of chloroform, and so on. Both elements form long chains, or **polymers,** in which they alternate with oxygen. In the simplest case, carbon-oxygen chains yield polyacetal, a plastic used in synthetic fibers, while from a backbone of alternating atoms of silicon and oxygen come polymeric silicones.

Conceivably, some strange life-forms could be built from siliconlike substances were it not for an apparently fatal flaw in silicon's biological credentials. This is its powerful affinity for **oxygen.** When carbon is oxidized during the respiratory process of a terrestrial organism (➔ **respiration**), it becomes the gas **carbon dioxide**—a waste material that is easy for a creature to remove from its body. The oxidation of silicon, however, yields a solid because, immediately upon formation, silicon dioxide organizes itself into a lattice in which each silicon atom is surrounded by four oxygens. Disposing of such a substance would pose a major respiratory challenge.

Life-forms must also be able to collect, store, and utilize energy from their environment. In carbon-based biota, the basic energy storage compounds are **carbohydrate**s in which the carbon atoms are linked by single bonds into a chain. A carbohydrate is oxidized to release energy (and the waste products water and carbon dioxide) in a series of controlled steps using **enzymes.** These enzymes are large, complex molecules **(proteins)** that catalyze specific reactions because of their shape and "handedness." A feature of carbon chemistry is that many of its compounds can take right-hand or left-hand forms; it is this handedness, or **chirality,** that gives enzymes their ability to recognize and regulate a huge variety of processes in the body. Silicon's failure to give rise to many compounds that display handedness makes it hard to see how it could serve as the basis for the many interconnected chains of reactions needed to support life.

The absence of silicon-based biology, or even silicon-based **prebiotic** chemicals, is also suggested by astronomical evidence. Wherever astronomers have looked—in **meteorite**s, in **comet**s, in the atmospheres of the giant planets, in the **interstellar medium,** and in the outer layers of cool stars—they have found molecules of oxidized silicon (silicon dioxide and silicates) but no substances such as silanes or silicones, which might be the precursors of a silicon biochemistry.

Even so, it has been pointed out, silicon may have had a part to play in the origin of life on Earth. A curious fact is that terrestrial life-forms utilize exclusively right-handed carbohydrates and left-handed **amino acids.** One theory to account for this is that the first prebiotic carbon compounds formed in a pool of

"primordial soup" on a silica surface having a certain handedness. This handedness of the silicon compound determined the preferred handedness of the carbon compounds now found in terrestrial life. An entirely different possibility is that of **artificial life** or intelligence with a significant silicon content.

Notwithstanding the gloomy prognosis of chemists, silicon-based life has flourished in the imaginary worlds of science fiction. In one of its earliest outings, Stanley **Weinbaum**'s "A Martian Odyssey," the creature in question is half a million years old and moves once every ten minutes to deposit a brick—Weinbaum's answer to one of the major problems facing siliceous life. As one of the watching scientists observes:

> Those bricks were its waste matter.... We're carbon, and our waste is carbon dioxide, and this thing is silicon, and its waste is silicon dioxide—silica. But silica is a solid, hence the bricks. And it builds itself in, and when it is covered, it moves over to a fresh place to start over.

More recently, a silicon-based life-form, the Horta, was discovered by miners on Janus IV in "Devil in the Dark" (original *Star Trek* series, episode 26). Every 50,000 years, all the Horta die except for one individual, who survives to look after the eggs of the next generation.[9]

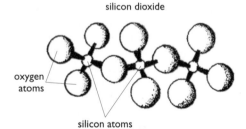

Part of a macromolecule of silicon dioxide.

SIM
➔ *Space Interferometry Mission*

Simpson, George Gaylord (1902–84)
Professor of vertebrate paleontology at Harvard who, in the 1960s, expressed pessimism at the suggestion that life would readily arise on any suitably Earth-like planet. Although allowing that the early stages of **prebiotic** synthesis

(simple molecules to polymeric chains) might occur commonly, he agreed with Harold **Blum** that the step from **macromolecule**s to simple living cells was so great as to be a rarity. This led him to criticize NASA's proposed attempts to search for extraterrestrial life by spacecraft as a waste of money. Concerning, in particular, the search for life on Mars, he wrote in 1964:[546]

> I cannot share the euphoria current among so many, even among certain biologists.... Let us face the fact that this is a gamble at the most adverse odds with history. Then if we want to go on gambling, we will at least recognize that what we are doing resembles a wild spree more than a sober scientific program.

Of astrobiology in general, he remarked that it was "a science looking for a subject." Simpson also pointed out that even if life had arisen elsewhere, the odds were stacked against it developing along anything like terrestrial lines. Echoing an argument put forward by Alfred Russel **Wallace** at the beginning of the century, Simpson concluded, "If the causal chain had been different, *Homo sapiens* would not exist."

Single Telescope Extrasolar Planet Survey (STEPS)

A project, under development, to detect **extrasolar planets** with high-precision **astrometry**. A successful feasibility study was carried out in 1996 with the Palomar 5-m telescope.

Sinope

The sixteenth and outermost moon of **Jupiter.** Sinope orbits Jupiter at more than a third of the distance of Mercury from the Sun. Like its three inner neighbors, **Ananke, Carme,** and **Pasiphaë,** Sinope has a **retrograde** motion, so it is unquestionably a captured asteroid. → **Jupiter, moons of**

Sinton, William M.

Harvard astronomer whose **spectroscopic** studies of Mars in 1956 and 1958 appeared to support the hypothesis of Martian plant life[548, 549] (→ **Mars, vegetation on**). From **infrared** measurements made using a photoconductive cell, cooled by liquid nitrogen to make it more sensitive, he reported strong **absorption band**s in the spectrum of the dark areas of Mars that he interpreted as being due to organic compounds, and in particular the presence of plants. Although his results led to much excitement, they were also controversial and open to interpretation. In 1963, an alternative explanation was put forward in terms of compounds in the Earth's atmosphere,[475] and by 1965 Sinton himself agreed that two of his observed bands had been caused by terrestrial atmospheric "deuterated" water (HDO).[476]

Sirius

Alpha Canis Majoris; commonly known as the Dog Star. It is the brightest star in the sky and one of the nearest to the Sun. Sirius is a **binary star** system. The primary (Sirius A) is a white **A star.** The companion (Sirius B, or "the Pup") orbits with a period of 49.97 years and was the first **white dwarf** to be discovered. Following Friedrich **Bessel**'s suggestion (1844) that Sirius had a dark companion to account for the star's wobbling movement, this object was optically identified by Alvan G. **Clark** in 1862. **Spectroscopic** measurements of Sirius B, by Walter S. **Adams,** Jr., in 1925, revealed its true nature.[48] → **Sirius, mystery of red color of; stars, nearest; stars, brightest**

Discovery	1914, by Seth Nicholson
Mean distance from Jupiter	23,700,000 km (14,730,000 mi.)
Diameter	36 km (22 mi.)
Mean density	3.1 g/cm³
Escape velocity	0.0240 km/s (87 km/h, 54 mi./h)
Orbital period	−758 days (retrograde)
Orbital eccentricity	0.275
Orbital inclination	153°

Distance	8.70 light-years (2.67 parsecs)	
	A	**B**
Spectral type	A1 V	wdA5
Apparent magnitude	−1.46	8.67
Absolute magnitude	1.41	11.54
Luminosity (Sun = 1)	26	0.002
Mass (Sun = 1)	2.31	0.98
Radius (Sun = 1)	1.7	0.022

Sirius, mystery of red color of

A puzzle regarding the brightest star in the sky, **Sirius,** that has been put forward by some as evidence in support of the **paleocontact hypothesis.** As Carl **Sagan** and others have pointed out, however, explanations more mundane than those involving extraterrestrial encounters may be to hand.

In the 1930s, the French anthropologist Marcel Griaule began a study of the Dogon tribe in what is now the Republic of Mali. Like most native peoples, the Dogon had an extensive body of folklore concerning the heavens. The problem was, much of their knowledge was not only correct but far beyond what they could possibly have acquired for themselves. They knew that the Earth rotates on its axis, the planets revolve around the Sun, Jupiter has four major satellites, and Saturn has a system of rings. They also spoke about an invisible companion of Sirius, which was very small and heavy and circled around the bright star every 50 years. Such a claim would have been treated as sheer fantasy by any Western scientist of the early nineteenth century. But in 1844, Friedrich **Bessel** detected wobbles in the movement of Sirius that could be explained only by the presence of an unseen companion with a period of about half a century. Eighteen years later, Sirius B was glimpsed for the first time during the testing of a new powerful telescope. Orbital calculations revealed that it has a mass similar to that of its illustrious neighbor but is one ten-thousandth as bright. In fact, it is now known to be a highly evolved type of star called a **white dwarf.**

How could the Dogon, without any technological aids, have uncovered the secrets of Sirius B? In his book *The Sirius Mystery,* author Richard Temple argued the case for alien involvement.[579] On a past visit to Earth, claimed Temple, extraterrestrials gave the ancient Egyptians a crash course in astronomy. This information (though surprisingly not referred to in any Egyptian records) filtered through to the Dogon, who are believed to have migrated to their present location from somewhere in North Africa, possibly Libya, several hundred years ago. Although this is an intriguing possibility, Sagan has pointed out that many travelers came to what was previously known as

French West Africa in the late nineteenth and early twentieth centuries. Explorers, missionaries, and diplomats, many of them well educated, would undoubtedly have come into contact with the Dogon, and during such encounters it is not unreasonable to suppose that the parties would have exchanged stories and beliefs. The Dogon would doubtless have been keen to learn more about the objects in the heavens that figured prominently in their own beliefs, including Venus, Jupiter, Saturn—and Sirius. In this way, they may have come to hear about the true movements of the Earth, the Galilean moons of Jupiter, and the rings encircling the sixth planet. Furthermore, even if their mentors had no more than a casual interest in astronomy, they may well have been carrying reference books or have recently read about the discovery that the Dog Star had a tiny, superdense companion. It is not hard to imagine, argued Sagan, that the Dogon incorporated such details into their mythological framework and then, a generation or two later, repeated them to an anthropologist who was unaware that there had been any cultural contamination.

This, however, is not the end of the Sirius mystery because the Dogon include in their traditions the belief that Sirius once appeared red, as indeed it would have done when it passed through its **red giant** phase in the remote past (→ **stars, evolution of**). Long ago, as a red giant, Sirius B would have greatly outshone its conventionally sized white companion so that the combined system, as seen from Earth, would have looked like a single brilliant red star. The trouble is that according to current theories of stellar evolution, there is no way that Sirius B could have evolved from a red giant to its present white dwarf stage in a matter of a few thousand years. Therefore, the Dogon ought not to have any knowledge of its previous color. One way out of the dilemma, it might be assumed, is to extend Sagan's hypothesis to include the possibility that the Dogon learned about Sirius B having once been a red giant from early European travelers. But that explanation fails on two counts. First, more than half a century ago, when Griaule first noted the Dogon reference to the red color of Sirius, astronomers had not established the red giant/white dwarf evolutionary link (in fact, the consensus at the time was that red giants were very young stars). Second, historical references to a red Sirius are not confined to the Dogon. In ancient Babylonian, Greek, and Roman literature, the appearance of Sirius is likened to that of Mars and the orange-red star Arcturus. Both Seneca, in the first century A.D., and **Ptolemy,** in the second, mention Sirius as being red, while in the sixth century A.D., Gregory of Tours, in a text intended to guide monks in their vespers duties, gives Sirius the nickname Rubela, meaning "ruddy."

Unfortunately, even this additional mystery does not require the theory of alien intervention. A credible astrophysical explanation has been put forward according to which although Sirius B could not have been a red giant in historical times, it may nevertheless have taken on the appearance of one. A white dwarf is made up of a highly compressed carbon-oxygen core surrounded by a thin layer of helium topped with a very thin "atmosphere" of hydrogen. The suggestion is that it might be possible for a small amount of hydrogen to percolate down into the interior and then, with carbon and oxygen acting as nuclear catalysts, to begin fusing into helium. This sudden, brief resumption of energy making would release a pulse of heat that, upon reaching the surface, would cause the hydrogen atmosphere to billow out to thousands of times its normal size. As the atmosphere expanded, it would cool and glow bright red. Calculations indicate that after about 250 years the atmosphere would again collapse, losing its ruddy brilliance and returning the white dwarf to its previous state of dim anonymity.

SKA
→ **Square Kilometer Array**

Skyhook, Project
A secret U.S. Navy program of the late 1940s to develop giant balloons for carrying out photoreconnaissance over the Soviet Union. Launched partially inflated, Skyhooks expanded as they rose until they reached their maximum size of up to 600 ft. tall and 100 ft. in diameter at an altitude of 60,000 ft. Almost certainly, they were behind many UFO sightings in the postwar years, including the UFO chased, with fatal consequences, by Air National Guard captain Thomas **Mantell.** → **Cold War, linked to UFO reports; Mogul, Project**

slingshot effect
→ **gravity assist**

Slipher, Earl C. (1883–1964)
American astronomer who was the leading Mars observer at **Lowell Observatory** in the twentieth century. Between 1905 and his death in 1964, he took more than 100,000 photographs of the planet and remained convinced of the existence of Percival **Lowell**'s canals. In *Mars: The Photographic Story,* he wrote optimistically:

> Each opposition adds something to what we knew before. Since the theory of life on the planet was first enunciated some fifty years ago, every new fact discovered has been found to be accordant with it. Not a single thing has been detected which it does not explain.

His map from the late 1950s, which formed the basis of the official chart for use with the early Mars spacecraft, shows an extensive canal network. → **Mars, canals of**

Small Magellanic Cloud (SMC)
One of the two **Magellanic Clouds** and a satellite galaxy of our own. The SMC lies about 250,000 light-years from the Sun, measures about 25,000 light-years across, and has a mass roughly 1 billion times that of the Sun.

Smithsonian Astrophysical Observatory
Founded by the Smithsonian Institution in 1890 and originally located in Washington, D.C. In 1955, it moved to Cambridge, Massachusetts, and in 1973 it combined with the **Harvard College Observatory** to form the **Harvard-Smithsonian Center for Astrophysics.**

SNC meteorites
Achondrites thought to have come from the surface of **Mars** and named after the initials of the places where the first three were found:

Shergotty, India, in 1865; Chassigny, France, in 1815; and **Nakhla,** Egypt, in 1911. Only fourteen SNC meteorites have been found to date, including several from Antarctica.

Their ages give the first hint of an unusual origin. The vast majority of meteorites found on Earth are thought to be bits that broke off when **asteroid**s, chiefly in the **Main Asteroid Belt** between Mars and Jupiter, collided with each other at various times in the past. Like the planets, asteroids formed about 4.5 billion years ago, not long after the Sun itself began to shine. However, being much smaller than planets, they quickly lost their original supply of internal heat. Except for the few largest ones, asteroids have been cold and completely solid, inside and out, virtually since the birth of the solar system. This is reflected in the fact that most meteoric rock seems to have been crystallized for all of the last 4.5 billion years.

But the SNC meteorites are different. With one exception, they appear to have solidified from molten rock between about 1.3 billion years and 200 million years ago. The only place where molten rock has existed in the solar system in such relatively recent times is inside planets—so presumably, this is where the SNC meteorites have come from. Because of their proximity to Earth, Mars and Venus are the obvious candidates. And of these two Mars is much the more likely prospect, as its lower gravity and much thinner atmosphere would make it a far easier place from which to eject rocks from the surface into space. But the most compelling evidence came when scientists examined tiny samples of gas that had been trapped within EETA 79001, a 7.9 kg (17-lb.) SNC meteorite found in Antarctica's Elephant Moraine in 1980. The composition of this gas exactly matched measurements of the Martian atmosphere made by the *Viking* landers.

In *The War of the Worlds,* H. G. **Wells** imagines the Martians firing their invading ships Earthward out of a great cannon (much like the *Columbiad* of Jules **Verne**'s lunar classic). But could a natural collision similarly have blasted pieces of Mars into space? Photos of the Martian surface taken by the *Viking* orbiters revealed scores of craters that are obviously the result of oblique impacts. One of these is a crater measuring 14 by 31 km, located at the southern approaches to a volcano known as Ceraunius Tholus, about 950 km west of the *Viking 1* landing site. Conceivably, some of the lava that flowed out of this volcano, 1.3 billion years ago, cooled to form the **basalt** contained within EETA 79001, although a number of other craters have also been identified as possible sources of the rock.

KNOWN SNC METEORITES			
Meteorite	*Location Found*	*Date Found*	*Mass (kg)*
Chassigny	Chassigny, France	October 3, 1815	~4
Shergotty	Shergotty, India	August 25, 1865	~5
Nakhla	Nakhla, Egypt	June 28, 1911	~10
Lafayette	Lafayette, Indiana	1931	~0.8
Governador Valadares	Governador Valadares, Brazil	1958	0.158
Zagami	Zagami, Nigeria	October 3, 1962	~18
ALH 77005	Allan Hills, Antarctica	December 29, 1977	0.482
Yamato 793605	Yamato Mountains, Antarctica	1979	0.016
EETA 79001	Elephant Moraine, Antarctica	January 13, 1980	7.9
ALH 84001	Allan Hills, Antarctica	December 27, 1984	1.940
LEW 88516	Lewis Cliff, Antarctica	December 22, 1988	0.013
QUE 94201	Queen Alexandra Range, Antarctica	December 16, 1994	0.012
Dar al Gani 476	Sahara Desert, Libya	May 1, 1998	2.015
Dar al Gani 489	Sahara Desert, Libya	1998	2.146

The mechanics of how SNC meteorites might have been ejected were first investigated in detail in the early 1980s by Laurence Nyquist at the **NASA Johnson Space Center** in Houston. A large object striking Mars at 35,000 km per hour could, he showed, hurl material from the surface at a speed in excess of the 18,000-km-per-hour Martian **escape velocity.** In fact, his calculations revealed, the escape velocity would be easily surpassed if heat from the impact vaporized permafrost below the Martian surface and so gave rise to a massive gas explosion. These conclusions were confirmed by the work of John O'Keefe and Thomas Ahrens at the California Institute of Technology in 1986[424] (➔ **ballistic panspermia**). Intense interest was focused on SNC meteorites by claims, first made in 1996, of evidence of past Martian activity in ALH 84001.

Socorro Incident

One of the most frequently recounted UFO events, since it involved a police witness and heralded the start of the great wave of **flying saucer** reports of the mid-1960s. At about 5:45 P.M. on April 24, 1964, patrolman Lonnie Zamora was in pursuit of a speeding motorist south of Socorro, New Mexico, when he heard a brief roar and saw a "flame in the sky" over a mesa less than a mile away. A shack containing dynamite was nearby, and at first Zamora thought that this had blown up. Abandoning his chase, he drove up a steep road to the mesa top, from which he observed "a shiny object to [the] south" 90 to 180 m (300 to 600 ft.) away, below him in a gully. "It looked," Zamora told an FBI agent later that day, "like a car turned upside down." Next to the object were "two people in white coveralls." They seemed "normal in shape—but possibly they were small adults or large kids." Zamora approached to within 30 m of the object and saw that it was smooth and oval, with red insignia on its side, and standing on girderlike legs. Then the roar began again, rising in pitch and growing "very loud." Finally, the UFO moved away in a southwesterly direction "possibly ten to fifteen feet above the ground, and it cleared the dynamite shack by about three feet." Two other police officers and the FBI agent ar-

rived on the scene shortly after and found four burn marks, and four V-shaped depressions, 25 to 50 mm (1 to 2 in.) deep and roughly 50 cm (18 in.) long. In his interview with Zamora, chief Air Force consultant J. Allen **Hynek** found him "basically sincere, honest, and reliable." Project **Blue Book** finally classified the sighting as an "unknown" and the incident remains unexplained, although its authenticity can be challenged on the grounds that there was only one witness and that a couple in their home only 300 m (984 ft.) away from the supposed landing site saw and heard nothing. Attention has also been drawn to the fact that the landing site happened to be owned by the town's mayor, who therefore had a vested interest in attracting tourism to the spot.

Sojourner

The first roving vehicle to explore the Martian surface. It was carried by *Mars Pathfinder,* weighed 10 kg (22 lb.), and sent back its last transmission on September 27, 1997.

sol

The length of a Martian day. One sol = 24 hours, 37 minutes, 22.6 seconds, which is 39.6 minutes longer than an Earth day.

Sol

An alternative name for the Sun.

solar flare
➔ **flare**

solar mass

The mass of the Sun: approximately 2,000 trillion trillion metric tons.

solar nebula

The rotating cloud of gas and dust that began to collapse about 5 billion years ago to form the solar system.

solar system, formation of
➔ **planetary systems, formation of**

solar wind

A continuous stream of charged particles, mostly **proton**s and **electron**s, that is ejected by the Sun and flows radially out at speeds of 200 to 850 km per second. The Sun's magnetic field is transported by the solar wind and becomes the interplanetary magnetic field, the lines of which are wound into spirals by the Sun's rotation. → **heliosphere**

solarion

A hypothetical inhabitant of the Sun. → **Sun, life on**

Solaris

Science fiction novel (1961) by Stanisław **Lem**[337] in which human explorers encounter

a monstrous entity endowed with reason, a protoplasmic ocean-brain enveloping the entire planet and idling its time away in extravagant theoretical cognitation [*sic*] about the nature of the universe.

Lem develops the notion of an intelligence so huge and alien that any form of communication with it proves virtually impossible, "like wandering about in a library where all the books are in an indecipherable language." But beyond the issue of *how* a dialogue with extraterrestrial intelligence might be established, Lem explores the motives behind *why* humans should seek such contact. In the words of one of his characters:

We are seeking only man. We have no need of other worlds.... We are seeking for an ideal image of our own world: we go in quest of a planet, of a civilization superior to our own but developed on the basis of a prototype of our primeval past.

Lem's warnings that aliens might be incomprehensible and that we should endeavor to understand ourselves before we look to the stars contrasts with a more positive approach to the cosmic quest found in the twentieth-century writings of such authors as David **Lindsay,** Olaf **Stapledon,** C. S. **Lewis,** and Arthur C. **Clarke.**

solute

A substance that is dissolved in a **solvent** to form a solution.

solvent

The medium in which **solute**s are dissolved. In terrestrial living systems, the solvent of overwhelming biological importance is **water.** It provides a fluid in which molecules of nutrients and waste products can be dissolved and transported, helps regulate the temperature and preserve chemical equilibrium within living cells, and makes up a major fraction of the body weight of every organism on Earth. For more than a century, there has been speculation about whether life on other worlds might use substances other than water to fulfill the same role. Many different solvents are known, including **hydrogen sulfide** (H_2S), the closest chemical analogue of water, and hydrogen chloride (HCl). But two major problems affect the majority of these potential rivals. First, they contain elements such as **sulfur** and **chlorine** that are much rarer than the main biological elements of **carbon, hydrogen, oxygen,** and **nitrogen.** Second, they break up into their constituent atoms more easily. Having said this, at least two possible candidates for alternative biological solvents can be identified: **ammonia** (NH_3) and **methanol** (CH_3OH).

To be effective in sustaining life, a solvent must remain liquid over a wide temperature range, so that inevitable variations in the conditions on a planet or moon do not cause the solvent to freeze or boil. This range should include those temperatures that allow the chemical processes of metabolism to take place at an optimum rate without disrupting ("denaturing") essential **organic** molecules. The solvent should also be able to cushion the organism against changes in external temperature by having a high **heat capacity** and high **heat of vaporization.** Finally, it must be able to dissolve a great variety of chemical compounds, including nutrients and waste materials, so that these can be transported internally within an organism.

Both ammonia and methanol remain liquid at temperatures well below the freezing point of water. This might appear to be an advantage on a world that was generally much colder than the Earth. However, it is not clear how metabolic processes could take place quickly enough to sustain life at very low temperatures. Ammonia has much the narrower range

PROPERTIES OF SOME SOLVENTS					
Solvent	Temperature at Which Liquid (°C)	Temperature Range (°C)	Heat Capacity (cal/g-°C)	Heat of Vaporization (cal/g)	Surface Tension (water = 1)
Water	0 to 100	100	1.00	586	1
Ammonia	−78 to −33	45	1.23	300	0.3
Methanol	−94 to +65	159	0.60	290	0.3

of the two and will remain liquid only at temperatures below *minus* 33°C. Methanol, by contrast, is liquid over all of the normal temperature range experienced by terrestrial life, with the exception of some **hyperthermophiles.** Regarding heat capacity, ammonia has the advantage over both water and methanol. Yet a solvent's ability to act as a thermal buffer, and thereby regulate the internal temperature of an organism, depends also upon the heat of vaporization. In this respect, water is far superior to its two rivals. Water's high heat of vaporization means that only a small amount of evaporation from an organism is needed to carry away the heat released by cells as a result of their metabolic processes. Temperature regulation is especially important to the highest forms of terrestrial life, notably mammals and birds, which are **homeotherm**s, and has been crucial to the rise of intelligent, large-brained animals such as ourselves.

Another property of biological significance is **surface tension,** a measure of the ability of a liquid to form droplets. Water has a very high surface tension, a fact that was probably crucial in the formation of aggregates of **organic** compounds before cells evolved. It would have forced some chemicals together while, at the same time, preserving boundaries between mixtures of different molecules. In living organisms today it continues to play an important role in concentrating solutions of substances at the boundaries of different media in an organism; for example, at a **cell membrane.**

Of all the features of a solvent, however, the most biologically important is that which defines it: its ability to dissolve other chemicals. In this respect, water is superior to both ammonia and methanol by about a factor of two.

Somnium
→ **Kepler, Johannes**

Southern SERENDIP

A **SETI** project operated by the **SETI Australia Centre** in collaboration with **SERENDIP** at the **University of California, Berkeley.** It is a **"piggyback" search** that scans across 8.4 million channels using the **Parkes Radio Telescope.**

space biology

A term originally applied to the study of the medical problems posed to human beings by space travel. In the 1960s, a separate term, **exobiology,** was introduced to refer to the study of life beyond the Earth.

space colony

A large, self-contained, artificial environment in space that is the permanent home of an entire community.

Space Interferometry Mission (SIM)

A major space-based observatory in NASA's **Origins Program,** *SIM* will be the first space mission to carry an **optical interferometer** as its main instrument. Designed specifically for the precise measurement of star positions, one of its prime goals will be to search for **extrasolar planets** as small as the Earth in orbit around nearby stars. *SIM* will combine the light from two sets of four 30-cm- (1-ft.-) diameter telescopes arrayed across a 10-m (33-ft.) boom to achieve a resolution approaching that of a 10-m-diameter mirror. This will allow it to perform extremely sensitive **astrometry** so that it will be able to detect very small wobbles in the movement of a star due to unseen companions. Objects of Earth mass could be inferred around a star up to 30 light-years (9 parsecs) away. Through a process known as "synthesis imaging," *SIM* will also be able to generate images of objects such as **dust disk**s around stars and look for gaps or clearings in the debris that might indicate the presence of unseen worlds. Scheduled for launch in 2005, *SIM* will conduct its 7-year mission from a heliocentric, Earth-trailing orbit.

space medicine

A field with roots in aviation medicine that came of age in the 1940s and 1950s with the advent of high-altitude, high-performance atmospheric flight. The need to evaluate the physiological and psychological effects of such factors as weightlessness, sustained high acceleration and deceleration, and radiation exposure became crucial as the dawn of manned spaceflight approached. But in those early days, space medicine also embraced other areas of extraterrestrial biology. Hubertus Stughold, a pioneer of aviation medicine, used his background in medicine and physiology to inquire into the possibility of life on Mars—previously a subject discussed mainly in astronomical circles—and suggested in 1953 that a laboratory based on the test chambers used in aviation medicine be set up to simulate the Martian environment.[571] In the late 1950s, as the prospect of planetary exploration by probes moved closer, attention also focused on the issue of **back contamination** by alien microorganisms. It was becoming clear that this new, heightened interest in the possible biology of other worlds fell outside the domain of space medicine, with its focus on human problems in space. In 1960, Joshua **Lederberg** proposed a formal distinction between space medicine and "exobiology" (➜ **astrobiology**).[94]

space missions, linked to UFO reports

On October 4, 1957, the Soviet Union rocked the world—and rocketed out of the world—with the launch of the first Earth-orbiting satellite, *Sputnik 1*. From then on there would be two races, in arms and in space, that would be intimately linked. American pride and morale demanded a swift reply. It came on January 31, 1958, with the launch by a Jupiter-C booster of the *Explorer 1* satellite. Suddenly,

the possibility of traveling to the planets and eventually even to the stars seemed more real—as, too, did the possibility that other beings might have visited the Earth.

Space Science Board

A committee formed by the National Academy of Sciences in 1958, shortly after the launch of the first Earth satellites, to help establish national goals in space science. For more than four decades, it has served as NASA's primary adviser on planetary protection. Initially, chaired by Lloyd **Berkner,** its membership also included Harold **Urey,** Joshua **Lederberg,** and J. P. T. Pearman. The Space Science Board's **Panel on Extraterrestrial Life** was set up principally to address the problem of **back contamination** by spacecraft and consisted of two groups, **EASTEX** on the East Coast, chaired by Lederberg, and **WESTEX** on the West Coast, chaired by Melvin **Calvin,** which met from 1958 to 1960. In August 1960, these groups were merged into **Committee 14 on Exobiology,** following the dissolution of **Panel 2 on Extraterrestrial Life.** The following year, the Space Science Board sponsored the **Green Bank conference (1961)** to assess the prospects for extraterrestrial communication in the wake of the publication of Giuseppe **Cocconi** and Philip **Morrison**'s seminal paper (➜ **Morrison-Cocconi Conjecture**) and Project **Ozma.** In 1962, the prestigious National Academy Space Science Summer Study at Iowa State University produced a set of detailed recommendations for research in space biology, including the quest to find life elsewhere in the solar system, which would entrench the subject within NASA's space program.[418] At NASA's request, a study was initiated in June 1964 by a steering committee of the Space Science Board, which included Lederberg and Calvin, "to recommend to the government . . . whether or not a biological exploration of Mars should be included in the nation's space program over the next few decades; and further, to outline what that program, if any, should be." The committee's conclusion that such an exploration merited "the highest scientific priority" increased the urgency to develop an unmanned spacecraft capable of Martian life detection.[459] In 1968, the Space Science Board recommended the three key experiments that would be used aboard the *Viking* spacecraft to search for microorganisms on Mars. Two decades later, the Space Science Board's **Committee on Planetary and Lunar Exploration** (COMPLEX) urged that preparations be made to search in earnest for planetary systems around other stars.

Space Travel Argument
→ **Fermi Paradox**

space-time
The union of space and time into a four-dimensional whole.

Spallanzani, Lazzaro (1729–99)
Italian naturalist whose experiments were the first to cast doubt on the long-held belief that microorganisms can arise by **spontaneous generation.** In 1765, he set out two sets of vessels containing a broth. One was left open to the air, while the other was sealed after the broth in it had first been boiled to kill any bacteria that might already be present. Spallanzani observed that only the broth that had been sealed remained sterile. Proponents of spontaneous generation, however, remained unconvinced, arguing that the boiling had destroyed some "vital principle" in the air, which explained why no microbes appeared in the closed container. It remained for Louis **Pasteur,** almost a century later, to finally settle the issue.

special theory of relativity
A theory put forward by Albert Einstein in 1905 centered on the proposition that the speed of light in a vacuum is the same for all observers, no matter how they are moving. Among its predictions is that no material object can be accelerated to reach light speed—a result that appears to rule out practical interstellar travel for all but the nearest stars. However, the special theory provides an escape clause in that for objects (such as a very fast spacecraft and its crew) moving at significant fractions of the speed of light, time slows down. In principle, this would allow astronauts to travel as far as they liked within as short a

period as they liked, simply by moving at a sufficiently high speed. The problem is that the time "dilation" effect does not operate for those who stay at home, so that the star-hopping astronauts would suffer the disturbing phenomenon of **time dislocation.**

specific heat
The amount of heat needed to raise the temperature of one gram of a substance by one degree Celsius. The specific heat of water is 1 cal/°C.

spectral lines
Dark **absorption line**s or bright **emission line**s in the **spectrum** of a star or other luminous object. They are uniquely characteristic of the types of **atom**s, **molecule**s, or **ion**s that give rise to them.

spectral type
The category to which a star is assigned depending on the characteristics of its **spectrum.** The classification scheme in use today has evolved from that devised at Harvard Observatory at the end of the nineteenth century in which stars were grouped into sixteen classes from A to Q. Advances in stellar astronomy led to many of these original spectral classes being dropped and others rearranged, so that the modern classification scheme (see Table 1) of stellar spectra consists of seven main groups that form a temperature sequence (→ **stars, temperatures of**). From hottest to coolest they are: O, B, A, F, G, K, and M. Each class is characterized by the appearance of certain types of **spectral lines** and is further subdivided into ten subclasses numbered from 0 to 9. The Sun, for example, is assigned the spectral class G2 in the modern Harvard classification, corresponding to a surface temperature of about 5,700°C. Other spectral characteristics, such as the presence of emission lines, are indicated by an additional lowercase letter placed after the spectral type (see Table 2).

In the 1890s, it was realized that stars of a particular spectral type could differ widely in luminosity. As a result, systems of **luminosity** classification were developed. That used today was introduced in the 1930s (see Table 3).

TABLE 1: MAIN SPECTRAL TYPES

Type	Features of Spectrum	Surface Temperature (°C)	Color
O	Both emission and absorption lines of ionized helium and other highly ionized ions of light elements	30,000–>50,000	Bluish white
B	No emission lines; absorption line of ionized helium disappears after B5; neutral helium reaches a maximum at B2; hydrogen becomes more prominent	9,400–30,000	Bluish white or white
A	Neutral hydrogen lines dominant	6,900–9,400	White
F	Many lines of neutral and singly ionized metals such as calcium, iron, chromium, and titanium	5,800–6,900	White or yellowish white
G	Lines of neutral metals dominate	4,200–5,200 5,000–5,800	Yellow giants Yellow main sequence
K	Increasing numbers of lines of neutral metals and bands due to molecules such as titanium oxide	3,200–4,600 3,600–5,000	Orange giants Orange main sequence
M	Numerous neutral metal lines and prominent molecular bands	<3,000 <3,600	Red giants Red main sequence

TABLE 2: NONSTANDARD SPECTRAL FEATURES

c	Sharp lines	n	Diffuse lines
d	Dwarf (i.e., main sequence) star	p	Peculiar spectrum
e	Emission lines of hydrogen	s	Sharp lines
f	Emission lines of helium and neon	sd	Subdwarf
g	Giant	v	Variable
k	Interstellar lines	wd	White dwarf
m	Emission lines of metals	wk	Weak lines

TABLE 3: LUMINOSITY CLASSES

Ia	Bright supergiants	IV	Subgiants
Ib	Supergiants	V	Main sequence (dwarfs)
II	Bright giants	VI	Subdwarfs
III	Giants	VII	White dwarfs

spectrograph

A instrument that splits apart light into a **spectrum** so that the intensity at each **wavelength** can be recorded.

spectrometer

A **spectrograph** in which the resultant spectrum is scanned by a **photometer** to produce a graph of how the intensity of light varies with wavelength. Such devices are used, for example, in the **radial velocity method.**

spectroscope

An instrument used for breaking down light or other **electromagnetic radiation** into its component **wavelengths**. The basic parts of a spectroscope are a slit and collimator (a lens) for producing a parallel beam, a prism or **diffraction grating** for dispersing different wavelengths through different angles of deviation, and a telescope, camera, or counter tube for observing the dispersed radiation. → **spectroscopy**

spectroscopic

Connected with the use of a **spectroscope.**

spectroscopic binary

A **binary star** system in which the two components are so close together or so far from the Sun that they cannot be resolved simply by looking at them, even through a powerful telescope. Their binary nature can, however, be established because of the **Doppler shift** of their **spectral lines.** As the stars revolve around their common center of gravity, they alternately approach and recede in the line of sight. This motion shows up in their combined spectra as a regular oscillation or doubling of the spectral lines. In most cases, the components of a spectroscopic binary are so close together that each is distorted into a nonspherical shape.

spectroscopic companion

A companion star, **brown dwarf,** or planet, the presence of which is inferred by the effect it produces on the **spectral lines** of the **primary.** As the companion revolves around the primary, it causes the latter alternately to approach and recede along the line of sight. This in turn results in a small periodic **Doppler shift** in the primary's spectrum. → **radial velocity method**

spectroscopy

The study of the nature of objects by analyzing the light and other radiation they produce. It involves the use of a **spectroscope** to reveal the **spectral lines** present in the radiation from a particular source. The advent of spectroscopy in the 1860s brought a powerful new scientific tool to bear on the question of whether there might be life elsewhere in the Universe by enabling the chemical composition and physical state of stars, nebulas, and planetary atmospheres to be probed for the first time.

spectrum

A representation of how the strength of **electromagnetic radiation** from a source, such as a star, varies with **wavelength.** In addition to a continuous spectrum of color, the light from a star is crossed by numerous **spectral lines** corresponding to specific wavelengths at which particular **atom**s or **ion**s in the star's atmosphere absorb or emit radiation. By a detailed analysis of these lines, the **spectral type** and, therefore, the surface temperature of a star can be worked out. → **stars, temperatures of**

speed of light

Designated by the letter c. In empty space it equals 299,790 km per second (186,282 miles per second).

Spencer, Herbert (1820–1903)

English philosopher who coined the phrase "survival of the fittest" and robustly defended the notion of evolution both in terrestrial biology and the universe at large. He maintained that some unknown (and unknowable) force generated order from chaos and drove the development of higher forms from lower ones. His beliefs overlapped with those of Friedrich Engels and Pierre **Teilhard de Chardin** and are not dissimilar to those held today by proponents of **complexity theory.**

Spica

Alpha Virginis; an **eclipsing binary** with a period of 4.014 days. The primary is a bright, bluish white **B star.** → **stars, brightest**

Spielberg, Steven (1947–)

American director (born in Cincinnati and raised in Arizona) of several populist and influential motion pictures with an extraterrestrial theme, including *Close Encounters of the Third Kind* and *E.T. The Extra-Terrestrial.* After being approached by Carl **Sagan** and Ann Druyan, Spielberg donated $100,000 to support Project **META**, a **SETI** program at Harvard University.

spiral arm

A luminous spiral pattern in the disks of **spiral galaxies** that lends them their name. Spiral galaxies typically have two major arms, though these may be fragmented into highly complex forms.

spiral galaxy

A galaxy possessing a flattened disk, marked by a pattern of **spiral arm**s. As well as stars, the disk harbors extensive **interstellar cloud**s of gas and dust. Surrounding the disk is an extensive **galactic halo.**

spontaneous generation

The belief that lower forms of life might spontaneously arise from nonliving material. It stemmed from everyday (but incomplete) observations such as that insects and worms appeared in rotting meat, frogs in mud, and mice in rotting wheat. Spontaneous generation was proposed by **Aristotle,** espoused by theologians in the Middle Ages, including Thomas **Aquinas,** and upheld by the likes of William Harvey and Isaac **Newton.** Only when the hypothesis was properly put to the test by experiments, such as those of Francesco **Redi** (1668), Lazzaro **Spallanzani** (1765), Cagniard de **La Tour** (1837), Theodor **Schwann,** and, most decisively, Louis **Pasteur** (1862), was it seen to be in error. Any lingering doubts were removed by the work of John **Tyndall.** However, the notion that life can develop from nonlife, albeit over many millions of years, has been revived in the modern concept of the origin of life from **prebiotic** chemicals.[188]

spores

Single-celled bodies that result from **meiosis.** Spores, which may be produced by **bacteria, fungi,** or **plants,** are **haploid** reproductive **cell**s that grow into new individuals without fusion with another cell. **Bacterial spores,** in particular, can survive exposure to a variety of extreme conditions.

Sproul Observatory

The observatory at Swarthmore College, near Philadelphia, where Peter **van der Kamp**, Kaj **Strand,** and Sarah Lee **Lippincott** worked in the middle decades of this century to try to detect planets around nearby stars. Its main instrument during this period was a 24-in. refractor.

Square Kilometer Array (SKA)

A proposed giant **radio telescope** with a collecting area of 1 million square m (1 square km), preliminary designs for which are being explored at various sites around the world. A Memorandum of Agreement has been signed by the directors of eight institutions including the **National Astronomy and Ionosphere Center,** the **SETI Institute,** the **Ohio State University Radio Observatory,** the Australia Telescope National Facility, and observatories in Canada, China, and India, to cooperate in a technology study program for a future very large radio telescope. In addition to many conventional astronomy uses, including observations on the formation and evolution of galaxies and stars, the SKA would be ideally suited to **SETI.** Two basic approaches are being considered. The first, which also forms the basis of the **One Hectare Telescope,** involves a linked collection of many thousands of small dishes, similar to satellite dishes. The second, and more revolutionary, approach calls for the construction of a flat array of antenna elements known as a "phased array." This latter concept will be tested by the **Argus radio telescope,** under construction at the Ohio State University Radio Observatory.

Stapledon, (William) Olaf (1886–1950)

English philosopher and novelist whose groundbreaking ideas, not least concerning the anatomical, mental, and moral diversity that might exist among intelligent extraterrestrials, served as a fertile source of inspiration for many subsequent science fiction writers. After earning degrees in history from Oxford and philosophy from Liverpool College, Stapledon spent most of his life near Liverpool. His first novel, *Last and First Men*[561] (1930), spans 2 billion years of human history but is eclipsed in scope and style by *Star Maker*[563] (1937). Although in these works, alien creatures play a secondary role to the philosophical, political, and religious themes that Stapledon explores, the sheer imaginative power brought to bear in conjuring up, page after page, innovative otherworldly beings has never been surpassed. Almost as the Greek philosophers did, Stapledon seems to touch upon every conceivable possibility, up to and including a single, cosmoswide entity, so that future writers can only play with variations upon the same ideas. Among those to be most directly influenced by his breadth of vision were his compatriots, C. S. **Lewis** and Arthur C. **Clarke.**

star

A luminous body of gas sufficiently compressed by its own gravity for nuclear **fusion** to take place in its interior. Stars exist in a wide range of sizes (➔ **stars, sizes of**), luminosities, temperatures (➜ **stars, temperatures of**), and environments. However, the single most important property of a star, which largely determines its life course, appearance, and behavior, is its mass (➜ **stars, masses of**).

The energy source of stars, during that phase of their life cycle for which their radiative output remains more or less constant, is the fusion of **hydrogen** into **helium.** When the supply of hydrogen in the stellar core becomes depleted, the character and appearance of the star change dramatically. The star swells to become a **red giant** or, if massive enough, a **red supergiant.** Finally, the star reaches a stage at which it can no longer produce energy by any kind of fusion reaction. It then effectively dies. This death may be gradual, as in the case of a Sun-like star, which ejects a **planetary nebula** before gradually cooling to become a **white dwarf.** Or the death throe may be sudden and spectacular, as happens with very massive stars, which undergo **supernova** explosions at the same time as their cores collapse to form **neutron star**s or **black hole**s.

Roughly half of all stars occur in **binary star** or **multiple star** systems. The neighboring stars **Alpha Centauri** (trinary), **Sirius** (binary), **Procyon** (binary), and **61 Cygni** (binary) are all of this type. On a larger scale, stars may be aggregated into gravitationally bound **globular cluster**s or smaller, gravitationally unbound **open cluster**s, the latter consisting of stars that have formed relatively recently from the same **interstellar cloud.**

Many stars, known as **variable star**s, undergo changes in brightness. These changes result from a variety of physical processes, may be regular, semiregular, or irregular, and may occur gradually or suddenly.

Astronomers now believe that a significant fraction of stars possess planetary systems (➜ **extrasolar planets**), some of which may support life. The existence of **brown dwarf**s—"missing links" between stars and planets—has also recently been confirmed.

star cluster
➜ **cluster**

Star Maker
Science fiction novel of prodigious scope, or work of speculative philosophy, by Olaf **Sta-**

pledon[563] (1937). Unlike its predecessor, *Last and First Men,* it presents a panoply of intelligent alien life across the Galaxy with each race striving toward the common goal of achieving "a more awakened state." The physical repositories of intelligence prove to be astonishingly diverse and Stapledon's human protagonist encounters sentient arachnoids, nautiloids, echinoderms, fishlike creatures, plant men, and many others. All these species, however, are ultimately engaged in the same struggle: to evolve to new levels of mental capacity, a progression that Stapledon overtly equates with spiritual development. Only a tiny minority of civilizations survive the "familiar crisis" now facing modern man, achieve a well-organized, utopian world order, and evolve to become part of a growing community of linked minds. Over vast epochs of time, individual creatures and races, and even planets, stars, and galaxies, expand in consciousness and merge telepathically until, in the far future, the Universe as a whole becomes aware—and aware of its creator, the Star Maker. Thus Stapledon arrives at a scenario strangely reminiscent of that envisaged, decades later, by the more enthusiastic proponents of the **anthropic principle.** Moreover, his imagination is broad enough to encompass numerous universes, each with subtle variations, some sterile, others with life, again presaging late-twentieth-century thought on this issue (➜ **chaotic inflationary theory**).

Star Maker's influence, and that of its predecessor, are difficult to gauge or overestimate. Arthur C. **Clarke** and C. S. **Lewis** are just two of the many writers who continued, in different ways, its cosmic quest for truth using a variety of extraterrestrial life-forms as players. Less obviously, the entire **SETI** movement represents, in a sense, a Stapledonian attempt to make contact with a cosmoswide community of intelligence and so enable mankind to become an integral part of a larger adventure.

Star Trek
A three-season TV series (1966–69) about the adventures of the superluminal starship *Enterprise* and her crew that eventually spawned a number of motion pictures and three derivative series: *Star Trek: The Next Generation, Star*

Trek: Deep Space Nine, and *Star Trek: Voyager*—set in the same "universe" but about 80 years further in the future. The need for interesting plots demands that inhabited planets abound. But although a variety of unusual extraterrestrials have appeared on *Star Trek* over the years, including **cyborg**s, **silicon-based life**-forms, and **noncorporeal life**-forms, the stock alien is basically human with a modified forehead, ears, or nose (**→ anthropomorphism**).

Star Wars

Popular motion picture (1977) in the swashbuckling, "space opera" tradition of Edgar Rice **Burroughs**'s Martian yarns. Morphologically diverse aliens feature prominently, notably in the bar scene, but for decorative purposes only. *The Empire Strikes Back* (1980) and *Return of the Jedi* (1983) completed the original trilogy, which was followed by the first *Star Wars* "prequel," *The Phantom Menace,* in 1999.

starch

A **carbohydrate** built up of simple **sugars** that is the main energy storage compound in green plants.

Stardust

Launched on February 7, 1999, with the object of encountering Comet Wild-2 in December 2004 and returning samples of it to Earth. The spacecraft will make three loops around the Sun. On the second loop, it will pass within 160 km of Wild-2, send back pictures, take counts of the number of **comet** particles striking it, and analyze in real time the composition of substances in the comet's tail. It will also capture samples of cometary material using a spongelike cushioning substance called **aerogel** that is attached to panels on the spacecraft. Additionally, the *Stardust* probe will obtain samples of cosmic dust, including the recently discovered interstellar dust streaming into the

The *Stardust* probe close to its rendezvous with Comet Wild-2.
NASA/JPL/Caltech

solar system from the direction of Sagittarius. Having been "soft caught" and preserved by the aerogel, these samples will be brought back to Earth by a reentry capsule, which will land in Utah in January 2006. Analysis of the material from Wild-2 and interstellar space, which will include **presolar grains** and condensates left over from the formation of the solar system, is expected to yield important insights into the evolution of the Sun and planets and possibly the origin of life itself. *Stardust*, the fourth mission in NASA's **Discovery Program,** following *Mars Pathfinder,* the *Near Earth Asteroid Rendezvous* (*NEAR*) probe, and *Lunar Prospector,* represents an international collaboration between NASA and university and industry partners.

starquake

A phenomenon analogous to an earthquake— a powerful tremor in a solid—might not be ex-

pected to occur in stars. However, in the exceptional case of **neutron star**s, the stellar material is so tightly compressed that it behaves like a solid. As a neutron star cools and shrinks, strains develop in its crust so that it buckles, giving rise to starquakes. This is not merely a theoretical possibility; rotating neutron stars are observed as **pulsar**s, and their pulsation period is normally remarkably constant. However, some pulsars have been shown to experience glitches—sudden changes in the interval between their pulses. These have been attributed by astronomers to shifts in mass caused by starquakes.

stars, brightest

Stars that appear brightest in the night sky do so for one or both of two reasons. Either they are intrinsically very luminous or quite close to the Sun or both. Without exception, every one of the fifty brightest stars in the night sky is in-

THE BRIGHTEST STARS AS SEEN FROM EARTH						
Star	Scientific Name	Apparent Magnitude	Absolute Magnitude	Luminosity (Sun = 1)	Spectral Type	Distance (light-years)
Sirius*	α CMa	−1.46	1.4	26	A1 V	8.6
Canopus	α Car	−0.62	−3.1	200,000	F0 Ib	1,200
Alpha Centauri*	α Cen	−0.28	4.2	1.5 and 0.4	G2 V and K1 V	4.4
Arcturus*	α Boo	−0.05v	−0.3	115	K2 V	37
Vega*	α Lyr	0.03v	0.5	52	A0 V	25.3
Capella*	α Aur	0.08v	−0.6	70	G8 III	42
Rigel*	β Ori	0.18v	−7.1	60,000	B8 Ia	900
Procyon*	α CMi	0.40	2.7	11	F5 IV–V	11.4
Achernar	α Eri	0.45v	−2.2	780	B5 V	144
Betelgeuse*	α Ori	0.45v	−5.9	10,000	M2 Iab	520
Agena	β Cen	0.61v	−5.0	10,500	B1 III	460
Altair*	α Aql	0.76	2.3	10	A7 IV–V	16.8
Acrux	α Cru	0.77	−3.7	3,200 and 2,000	B1 IV and B3 IV	360
Aldebaran*	α Tau	0.87	−0.8	100	K5 III	65
Spica*	α Vir	0.98v	−3.1	2,100	B1 V	260
Antares	α Sco	1.06v	−4.7	7,500	M1 Ib	330
Pollux*	β Gem	1.16	1.0	60	K0 III	34
Fomalhaut*	α PsA	1.17	1.9	13	A3 V	25.1
Deneb*	α Cyg	1.25	−7.2	70,000	A2 Ia	1,800
Beta Crucis	β Cru	1.25v	−4.3	8,200	B0 IV	425
Regulus*	α Leo	1.36v	−0.8	130	B7 V	78
Adhara	ε CMa	1.50	−5.0	5,000	B2 II	490
Castor*	α Gem	1.58	0.8	45	A0 V	52

* Refer to individual entry.

trinsically brighter than the Sun (although in the case of **Alpha Centauri,** the nearest bright star of all, the difference is not great). However, their distances vary enormously. Those in the list below that lie furthest away compensate for their remoteness by their exreme brilliance.

stars, classification of
➔ **spectral type**

stars, evolution of

Like people, stars are born, frequently have a tempestuous youth, live most of their lives in relative stability, then grow old and die. The stellar equivalents of human fetuses are **protostar**s, which form out of dense clouds of gas in the **interstellar medium.**

At some point, the temperature in the core of a protostar becomes high enough for **hydrogen** to begin undergoing nuclear **fusion** into **helium,** with the release of large quantities of light and heat. The period of core "hydrogen burning" accounts for about 90 percent of a star's active life during which it is said to be on the **main sequence.** How long is spent on the main sequence depends critically on the star's initial mass. More massive stars have shorter lives because they consume their stocks of fusion fuel more rapidly than do smaller stars. For example, a star with the same mass as the Sun will remain on the main sequence for about 10 billion years, whereas a star of 5 M_S will race through its main sequence phase in only about 60 million years—less time than that separating man from the dinosaurs (➔ **stars, masses of**).

Once a star has exhausted its central hydrogen reserves, the core fusion reactor temporarily shuts down. The now helium-rich core begins to shrink under its own gravity and becomes hotter. Fusion continues in a shell surrounding the core, where hydrogen-rich material is still present. During this hydrogen-shell-burning phase, the star expands to several tens of times the diameter of the Sun. Its surface layers, now remote from the central energy source, cool to about 3,000°C and glow red. Each unit area of the star's surface radiates less energy than before but because the total surface area has grown more than 1,000-

fold, the star as a whole is about one hundred times brighter than it was on the main sequence. It has become a **red giant,** or, in the case of a very massive star, a **red supergiant.**

Helium "ashes" from the hydrogen-burning shell are dumped onto the core, which as a result becomes hotter and more massive. When its temperature finally reaches about 100 million degrees, helium nuclei suddenly begin fusing to form **carbon** and **oxygen** in an event known as the "helium flash." At the same time, the outer parts of the star fall back down and reheat, becoming even hotter than when the star was on the main sequence, so that they shine white or blue-white.

Eventually, the central helium reserves are depleted and the core again ceases to generate light and heat. Gravity squeezes the core harder, causing it to shrink and increase in density, while at its margin a helium-burning shell begins to work its way outward in pursuit of the still active hydrogen-burning shell. Again the outer layers swell, but even more than before. The star becomes what is known as an "asymptotic giant branch star." For reasons still unclear, an intense **stellar wind** begins to blow. At the same time, the surface layers start to oscillate in radius, temperature, and luminosity, and the star becomes a **Mira variable.**

What happens next depends on the star's mass. In the case of a star with about 0.8 to 8 M_S, the outer layers of the star are shed into space over a period of several thousand years. Eventually, this lost material is caused to glow as a **planetary nebula** by **ultraviolet** radiation pouring out from the exposed hot core. The spent core gradually cools to become a **white dwarf,** a star with perhaps two thirds the mass of the Sun but only about twice the diameter of the Earth. Since the white dwarf has no further source of energy, it simply cools over many billions of years and fades to a solid, inert lump—a **black dwarf.**

If the star has a mass of more than about 8 M_S, however, it suffers a more spectacular fate. In old age, the star swells to become a red supergiant and "burns" successively heavier nuclei in its interior until its core is choked full of iron. No further fusion is possible beyond this point because iron nuclei actually have to be supplied with energy in order to fuse together. In a fraction of a second, the core collapses to become a **neutron star** or possibly even a **black hole,** while the outer layers are violently expelled in a **supernova** explosion.

Material lost by stars, whether in the form of stellar winds, planetary nebulas, or supernovas, is returned to the interstellar medium to begin the process of star formation all over again. Moreover, as it is only within the interior of stars that **heavy element**s such as carbon and oxygen are formed, this dissemination and recycling of star matter is crucial to the development of life as we know it. → **nucleosynthesis**

stars, lifetimes of

Type	Typical Mass (Sun = 1)	Surface Temperature (°C)	Estimated Main Sequence Lifetime (years)
O	32	35,000	10,000,000
B	6	14,000	270,000,000
A	2	8,100	810,000,000
F	1.25	6,500	4,200,000,000
G	0.9	5,400	10,000,000,000
K	0.6	4,000	32,000,000,000
M	0.22	2,600	210,000,000,000

stars, masses of

The life span of a star depends crucially upon its mass: the greater the mass, the shorter the lifetime. This may seem strange, since a more massive star obviously starts out with more available fuel for nuclear **fusion.** However, such a star consumes its fuel at a faster rate. The more massive the star, the greater the pressure exerted on its core due to the weight of the overlying layers. Higher pressures result in higher temperatures (just as pumping a bicycle pump causes the compressed air inside to heat up). In turn, higher temperatures cause nuclear fusion reactions to take place at a more rapid rate, which increases the energy output of the core and hence the star's **luminosity.** The effect is dramatic. Observations have shown that, in the case of stars with a mass more than about 3 M_S, a star's luminosity varies as the cube of its mass. This means that a star of, say, 10 M_S must consume its fusion fuel about 1,000 times faster than does a Sunlike star. Its lifetime is, therefore, only about one hundredth as long, or roughly 100 million years, compared with the Sun's 10 billion years. For a star of 30 M_S, the observed mass-to-luminosity relationship indicates that fusion fuel is "burned" 30^3, or 27,000, times faster than in the Sun, resulting in a lifetime of little over 10 million years. Low-mass stars, on the other hand, are energy misers, destined to spin out their meager fuel reserves over colossal periods of time. For example, **Proxima Centauri,** a **red dwarf** that is the nearest star to the Sun, has a predicted life span of about 16 trillion years, roughly 1,000 times the present age of the universe.

The total range of star masses is believed to be from about 0.08 to 70 M_S. Below the lower limit, an object would not be able to attain a sufficiently high core temperature to trigger fusion reactions and so would exist as either a **brown dwarf** or simply a large planet such as Jupiter. The upper limit is less certain, and there may be a few stars, such as Eta Carinae, that have masses of more than 100 M_S. Such supermassive stars, however, must be highly unstable and extremely short-lived.

stars, nearest

Recent observations by the *Hipparcos* satellite have provided vastly more accurate data on the distances and other characteristics of nearby stars. Refer to entries on individual stars for more information.

THE STARS NEAREST TO THE SUN

Star	Distance (light-years)	Spectral Type	Apparent Magnitude	Absolute Magnitude	Luminosity (Sun = 1)	Mass (Sun = 1)	Radius (Sun = 1)	Radial Velocity (km/s)
Proxima Centauri	4.22	M5e V	11.01	15.45	0.00006	0.1		−16
Alpha Centauri B	4.40	K2 V	1.35	5.70	0.44	0.89	0.87	−22
Alpha Centauri A	4.40	G2 V	−0.01	4.34	1.53	1.1	1.23	−22
Barnard's Star	5.94	M5 V	9.54	13.24	0.00044			−109
Lalande 21185	8.31	M2 V	7.49	10.46	0.0052	0.35		−87
Sirius A	8.60	A1 V	−1.44	1.45	23.0	2.31	1.8	−8
Sirius B	8.60	wdA	7.20	11.50	0.002	0.98	0.022	−8
Ross 154	9.69	M4e V	10.37	13.00	0.0004			−5
epsilon Eridani	10.50	K2 V	3.72	6.18	0.3	0.98		+16
Lacaille 9352	10.70	M2 V	7.35	9.76	0.012			+10
Ross 128	10.90	M5e V	11.12	13.50	0.00033			−13
61 Cygni A	11.40	K5 V	5.20	7.49	0.082	0.63		−64
Procyon A	11.41	F5 IV-V	0.40	2.68	7.6	1.77	1.7	−3
Procyon B	11.41	wdA	10.80	13.10	0.0005	0.63	0.01	−3
61 Cygni B	11.43	K7 V	6.05	8.33	0.038	0.60		−64
Sigma 2398B	11.64	M5 V	9.70	11.97	0.002			+2
Sigma 2398A	11.47	M4 V	8.94	11.18	0.003			+2
Groombridge 34A	11.64	M1 V	8.09	10.33	0.006			+14
Groombridge 34B	11.64	M6 V	11.00	13.30	0.0004			+21
epsilon Indi	11.83	K5 V	4.69	6.89	0.14			−40
tau Ceti	11.90	K0 V	3.49	5.68	0.47			−16

stars, numbers of

The exact number of stars in the **Galaxy** is not known but probably lies in the range of 200 to 400 billion. Just as smaller creatures tend to be more numerous than larger ones, so there is a direct relationship between the mass (and **luminosity**) of **main sequence** stars and their abundance. The figures in the table below assume a total stellar population in our galaxy of 400 billion stars.

stars, populations of
→ **population types**

stars, sizes of

Considering that the range of stellar masses is quite narrow (→ **stars, masses of**), stars vary in size to a surprising extent. Near the small end of the scale are **white dwarf**s with only about one hundredth the radius of the Sun (R_S). More compact still, **neutron stars** may measure only about

APPROXIMATE ABUNDANCE OF THE TYPES OF MAIN SEQUENCE STARS

Spectral Type	Mass (Sun = 1)	Brightness (Sun = 1)	Percentage of Total	Number of Stars
O	32	50,000	0.00002	56,000
B	6	300	0.09	360,000,000
A	2	10	0.6	2,400,000,000
F	1.25	2	2.9	12,000,000,000
G	0.9	0.9	7.3	28,000,000,000
K	0.6	0.2	15.1	60,000,000,000
M	0.2	0.005	73.2	293,000,000,000

24 km (15 miles) across. In contrast, the largest **red supergiant**s may have a radius of about 1,000 R$_S$, so that if they were put in place of the Sun they would engulf the orbit of Mars and possibly even that of Jupiter. The sizes of stars may be deduced theoretically or, in the case of a few relatively nearby supergiants, such as **Betelgeuse** and Antares, measured by the technique of speckle **interferometry**. Stellar radii can also be obtained, and with greater precision, by analyzing the light curves of eclipsing binaries, provided that the lengths of their orbits are known.

stars, temperatures of

The overwhelming majority of stars have surface temperatures between about 2,500 and 40,000°C. At the low end of the temperature range are two types of stars, **red dwarf**s and **red giant**s, that could hardly differ more in size and luminosity. A similar disparity exists between **blue supergiant**s and the central stars of **planetary nebula**s, which together account for some of the hottest stars known.

Rising temperature implies changing color from red through orange, yellow, and white to bluish white. Some stars, however, emit a large portion of their total energy output beyond the visible range of the spectrum. **Protostar**s and **brown dwarf**s, for example, give off mostly **infrared** radiation, whereas **Wolf-Rayet stars**, **O stars**, and the central stars of **planetary nebula**s are powerful emitters of **ultraviolet** radiation.

stellar evolution
→ **stars, evolution of**

stellar wind

All stars shed matter into space in the form of a high-speed "wind" of particles from their surface. This represents an important way in which material is returned to the **interstellar medium** to be recycled as a new generation of stars and planets. The **solar wind** from the Sun moves outward at a rate of several hundred km per second and carries away a modest one ten trillionth of a solar mass each year.

Sternberg State Astronomical Institute

A Russian research institute in Moscow with observing facilities in the Crimea and Kazakhstan.

Steward Observatory

The observatory of the University of Arizona, founded in Tucson in 1922. It currently operates telescopes at five main sites in Arizona, including Kitt Peak, Mount Hopkins, and Mount Graham. The Steward Observatory Mirror Laboratory has produced a new 6.5-m single mirror for the **Multiple Mirror Telescope** and is engaged in manufacturing mirrors for the **Large Binocular Telescope** and the **Magellan Telescopes**.

Stoney, George Johnstone (1826–1911)

Irish physicist who applied the kinetic theory of gases to the analysis of planetary atmospheres. His work had important implications for the habitability of other worlds. Using the kinetic theory, which treats gases as collections of randomly moving particles, Stoney was able to draw conclusions about which gases would tend to escape from the atmosphere of a given planet or satellite. Beginning in 1870, he presented a series of papers to the Royal Dublin Society in which he (1) accounted for the Moon's lack of atmosphere in terms of the low lunar gravity, (2) explained the absence of hydrogen from the Earth's atmosphere in terms of the high average velocity of hydrogen molecules (→ **Earth, atmosphere of**), and (3) concluded that probably no water exists on Mars (→ **Mars, water on**). It was not until 1898 that these results were published, together with other conclusions about the remaining objects in the solar system, including that Jupiter can retain all known gases (→ **gas giant**), whereas most moons and all asteroids are devoid of an atmosphere.

stony meteorite

A **meteorite** that is composed mainly of **silicate** minerals but may contain up to 25 percent metal (iron and nickel) by weight. Stony meteorites account for 95 percent of all known falls. The majority (86 percent of all falls) are **chondrite**s, the rest **achondrite**s.

stony-iron meteorite

A **meteorite** composed of **silicate** minerals and metal (iron and nickel) in roughly equal proportions. They are rare, comprising only about 1 percent of all known falls.

Strand, Kaj Aage Gunnar

Danish astronomer who began his research career working with Ejnar Hertzsprung (➔ **Hertzsprung-Russell diagram**) using photography to measure precisely the relative motions of nearby stars. In 1938, Strand brought knowledge of the technique to **Sproul Observatory,** where it was used in the search for **extrasolar planets.** Strand himself concentrated on **61 Cygni** and, in 1943, announced that he had detected wobbles in the movement of this **binary star** which indicated the presence of a planetary companion.[570]

Strieber, Whitley (1945–)

American novelist whose book *Communion: A True Story* (1987), which attracted a $1 million advance, purportedly recounted the author's experience of **alien abduction** discovered under hypnosis a year later. More revelations of sinister extraterrestrial goings-on followed in *Transformation: The Breakthrough* (1988). In 1993, however, Strieber confessed that his writings had been entirely fictional.

stromatolites

Rounded, multilayered, sedimentary structures, up to about 1 m (39 in.) across, found in rocks dating back at least 2,800 million years. Present-day equivalents are formed by the life activities of algal mats.

Struve, Otto (1897–1963)

The last of four famous Struve astronomers[572] and effectively the father of modern **SETI.** He was one of the few eminent astronomers in the pre–Space Age era to publicly express his belief that extraterrestrial intelligence was abundant. Struve emigrated from the USSR to the United States in 1921, obtained a Ph.D. from the University of Chicago, and eventually became head of the Astronomy Department there. In 1932, he was made joint director of the university's **Yerkes Observatory** and **McDonald Observatory.** In 1950, he moved to the **University of California, Berkeley,** and in 1959 he became the first regular director of the **National Radio Astronomy Observatory** at **Green Bank.** Struve's belief in the widespread existence of life and intelligence in the Universe stemmed from his studies of slowly

rotating stars. Many stars, including the Sun, spin at a much lower rate than was predicted by contemporary theories of early stellar evolution. The reason for this, claimed Struve, was that they were surrounded by planetary systems that had carried away much of the stars' original angular momentum (➔ **extrasolar planets**). So numerous were the slow-spinning stars that Struve estimated, in 1960, that there might be as many as 50 billion planets in our **galaxy** alone. As to how many might harbor intelligent life, he wrote:[573]

> An intrinsically improbable event may become highly probable if the number of events is very great.... It is probable that a good many of the billions of planets in the Milky Way support intelligent forms of life. To me this conclusion is of great philosophical interest. I believe that science has reached the point where it is necessary to take into account the action of intelligent beings, in addition to the classical laws of physics.

Having become director of the Green Bank observatory during the time that preparations were being made for Project **Ozma,** Struve enthusiastically endorsed and publicized Frank **Drake**'s pioneering work. He thus helped, from the outset, to give legitimacy and respectability to the SETI enterprise. Before this, through his lectures and discussions at Berkeley and **Cornell University,** he helped inspire a number of key researchers, including Drake himself and Ronald **Bracewell,** whom he invited to Berkeley in 1954.

subdwarf

A star that is smaller and about one fifth as bright as a normal dwarf (main-sequence) star of the same **spectral type.** Subdwarfs are mainly old (**galactic halo Population II**) objects and are denoted by the prefix "sd," as in sdK7.

subgiant

A giant star of smaller size and lower luminosity than normal giants of the same **spectral type.** Subgiants form luminosity class IV.

sublime (or sublimate)

To change directly from a solid to a gas without passing through a liquid phase.

subluminous star

A star, such as a **white dwarf, subdwarf,** or central star of a **planetary nebula,** that is fainter than a **main sequence** star of the same spectral type. Most subluminous stars are old **(Population II)** objects.

substrate

The substance upon which an **enzyme** acts in biochemical reactions.

sugars

Simple, water-soluble **carbohydrate**s.

"Suitcase SETI"

A portable, high-resolution **spectrometer** developed in 1981–82 by Harvard physicist Paul **Horowitz** and colleagues from Stanford University and NASA with support from NASA and the **Planetary Society** for use in **SETI.** It enabled the kind of signal processing used in the earlier **Harvard-Arecibo off-line SETI search** to be carried out in real time. "Suitcase SETI" was capable of 64,000-channel spectrum analysis (0.03-Hz **resolution bandwidth,** 2-kHz **instantaneous bandwidth**) in each of two **polarization**s, equivalent to searching 131,000 extremely **narrowband** channels. It was connected to the **Arecibo radio telescope** in March 1982 and used to search 250 candidate objects (stellar and other), mostly at the second harmonic (2.84 GHz) of the **21-centimeter line.** "Suitcase SETI" was later reconfigured and used in Project **Sentinel.**[283]

sulfides

Compounds formed when **sulfur** reacts directly with another element. Sulfides can be important indicators of the presence of life since there is no way that they can be formed at normal temperatures except biologically.

sulfur (S)

A nonmetallic element that chemically resembles oxygen and can replace the latter in many compounds, **organic** and **inorganic.** It is abundant and widely distributed in nature (➔ **elements, cosmic abundance of**), occurring in elemental form as hydrogen sulfide, and as sulfur oxides in volcanic regions, fumaroles, hot springs, and **hydrothermal vent**s.

Atomic number 16, density relative to water 2.07; melting point 113°C (rhombic), 119°C (prismatic); boiling point 445°C (rhombic)

sulfur dioxide (SO_2)

A colorless, pungent gas that dissolves in water to give a mixture of sulfuric and sulfurous acids.

Density relative to water 1.43; melting point −72.7°C; boiling point −10°C

Sun

The central star of the solar system; a solitary, yellow **dwarf star** of **spectral type** G2 that has been on the **main sequence** for about 5 billion years. Since the Sun is unique in having a known (to humans!) habitable planet, it is natural that scientists first turn to stars similar to the Sun (➔ **FGK stars**) in their search for extraterrestrial life. Superficially, there are many such stars, including a handful that are less than 20 light-years away (➔ **Sun-like stars**). Over the next decade, attention will be focused on trying to detect Earth-like planets orbiting within the **habitable zone**s of such solar look-alikes. However, it may be that in at least one respect the Sun is abnormal. A consensus is emerging that our star is exceptionally stable. Although like all stars it sends out **flares** from time to time, these tend to be on a very modest scale by stellar norms. What is still unknown is *why* the Sun is so well behaved and whether we just happen to be enjoying a tranquil phase in its career.

Distance	149,597,900 km (92,975,699 mi., 8.3 light-min.)
Spectral type	G2 V
Diameter	1,392,000 km (865,000 mi.)
Surface temperature	5,400°C (9,800°F)
Central temperature	14 million°C (25 million°F)
Mass (Earth = 1)	332,946
Density (water = 1)	1.409
Surface gravity (Earth = 1)	27.90
Escape velocity	617.5 km/s (383.8 mi./s)
Rotation period	25.38 days
Apparent magnitude	−26.8
Absolute magnitude	4.83

Sun, as a gravitational lens for focusing interstellar signals

A possibility suggested, in 1979, by Von R. Eschelman of Stanford University, California.[185] Since the Sun can act as a **gravitational lens,** why not use it, asked Eschelman, in the search for messages arriving in our direction from other stars? His calculations showed that the focusing produced by the Sun would yield signals easily detectable by existing interplanetary probes such as *Voyager* and *Pioneer.* Yet a formidable problem would remain: the nearest appropriate focal point is 550 times as far from the Sun as the Earth is, and the area in which the detectable signal would be focused would be at most a few kilometers across. Commenting on this, Eschelman said that although it might prove an insurmountable technological difficulty to us at present, radar and microwave communications signals leaking out from the Earth could be picked up by a race slightly more advanced than ours using its own stellar gravitational lens.

Sun, life on

Before the nature of the Sun was properly understood, there was no shortage of speculation that it might be inhabited. **Lucian** played with the idea in his *True History,* while Tommaso **Campanella** built an entire utopian narrative around it in his *City of the Sun.* More remarkably, as late as 1795, William **Herschel** maintained that the Sun was essentially a large planet with a solid surface, surrounded by two layers of clouds. An opaque lower layer shielded the solar inhabitants from the heat and light of the glowing upper layer, which, he thought, was similar in nature to the Earth's aurora though on a grander scale. Wrote Herschel:[270]

> The Sun... appears to be nothing else than a very eminent, large, and lucid planet.... Its similarity to the other globes of the solar system... leads us to suppose that it is most probably... inhabited... by beings whose organs are adapted to the peculiar circumstances of that vast globe.

Among others who shared this belief in the Sun as a life-bearing planet were François **Arago** and David **Brewster.** In fact, such weight did Herschel's views carry that serious proponents of an inhabited Sun were still to be found in the 1860s. More recently, with the realization that alien life might run along completely different lines than the terrestrial variety, scientifically informed writers have revisited the possibility of organisms living inside or on the surface of stars. Among these are David Brin, with *Sundiver,*[81] (1980) and Robert **Forward,** with his novels about a technological civilization on a **neutron star** (→ **neutron star, life on**).

Sun-like stars

SUN-LIKE STARS LESS THAN 24 LIGHT-YEARS AWAY		
Star	Distance (light-years)	Mass (Sun = 1)
Epsilon Eridani	10.8	0.80
Tau Ceti	12.2	0.82
Sigma Draconis	18.2	0.82
Delta Pavonis	19.2	0.98
82 Eridani	20.9	0.91
Beta Hydrae	21.3	1.23
Zeta Tucanae	23.3	0.90

supercivilizations
→ **Kardashev civilizations**

supergiant
The biggest and most luminous type of star. Supergiants are at least ten times more massive than the Sun and have became grossly distended following the exhaustion of hydrogen in their cores. So large are some members of this category that if they were put in place of the Sun, their outer layers would extend out as far as the orbit of Mars or even of Jupiter.

supernova
The explosion of a massive star at the end of its life (→ **stars, evolution of**). A supernova occurs when a star with many times the mass of the Sun runs out of usable nuclear fuel. → **supernova remnant**

supernova remnant
Material cast into space by the explosion of a star as a **supernova.** The best-known example is the **Crab Nebula.**

superorganism

A collection or community of highly interdependent life-forms that behaves as if it were a single organism of a higher order. Familiar examples include the colonies of social insects such as ants. These appear to display an organizational ability and collective will (➔ **hive intelligence**) that is not evident in the individuals of which they are composed. More controversial is the suggestion that the entire terrestrial biosphere (and presumably those of other planets that support life) acts as a superorganism (➔ **Gaia Hypothesis**).

surface gravity

The local gravitational field strength at the surface of an astronomical body. It determines, for example, how much a person would weigh if he or she were to stand on that object. In the case of a **gas giant** or a star, the surface gravity is calculated as if there were a solid surface at the top of the atmosphere.

Note

Local gravitational field strength is given by g, the force acting on a mass of 1 kg at the surface, according to the formula $g = GM/r^2$, where M is the mass of the body, r its radius, and G the gravitational constant (6.67×10^{-11} Nm^2). For the Earth, g has a value of about 9.8 newtons/kg. For Mars, by contrast, g is only about 3.7 N/kg, or 0.38 as much.

surface tension

The property of a liquid that makes it behave as if its surface were enclosed in an elastic skin. It is responsible for the formation of liquid drops and bubbles. Surface tension arises from the fact that a **molecule** in the interior of a liquid is pulled equally from all sides by its neighbors, whereas a molecule at the surface is only attracted by molecules below it in the liquid.

Surveyor 3

An unmanned lunar probe that soft-landed on the Moon near Oceanus Procellarum on April

NASA

20, 1967. Two and a half years later, on November 20, 1969, *Apollo 12* astronauts Pete Conrad and Alan L. Bean recovered the camera from *Surveyor 3* and brought it back to Earth. When NASA scientists examined the camera, they found that the polyurethane foam insulation covering its circuit boards contained fifty to a hundred viable specimens of *Streptococcus mitis*, a harmless **bacterium** commonly found in the human nose, mouth, and throat. Since the camera had been returned under strictly sterile conditions, it is evident that the microbes must have been on the probe since it had departed the Earth and had survived 31 months in the absence of air or water while being subjected to huge monthly temperature variations and bombardment by hard **ultraviolet** radiation from the Sun. Conrad later commented, "I always thought the most significant thing that we ever found on the whole . . . Moon was that little bacteria who came back and living and nobody ever said [anything] about it." This is one of a number of remarkable examples of the extreme survivability of bacteria and their spores (➔ **bacterial spores**).

suspended animation
A state in which the metabolic functions (➔ **metabolism**) of an organism slow to such an extent that they almost cease.

Swedenborg, Emanuel (1688–1772)
Swedish mystic and scientist who, early in his career, wrote books on mathematics, navigation, astronomy, chemistry, and mineralogy, and formulated a version of the **nebular hypothesis,** though this received little attention at the time. He then became convinced, through a series of strange dreams in 1743–45, that he had been contacted by spirits, who had described to him the existence of countless inhabited worlds. In *Heavenly Arcana* he describes a visionary trip to the planets and recounts being told that on Venus there were two races, one gentle and humane, the other savage and cruel, while on Mars lived the noblest creatures in the solar system, resembling in piety the early Christians. Thereafter, Swedenborg devoted his life to expounding his revelations in works such as *The New Jerusalem* (1758).

Swedenborgians
Followers of the doctrines of Emanuel **Swedenborg** who in 1787 formed the Church of the New Jerusalem.

Swift, Jonathan, and the moons of Mars
Irish clergyman and social and political commentator, best known for his satirical fantasy *Gulliver's Travels*, originally entitled *Travels into Several Remote Nations of the World in Four Parts . . . by Lemuel Gulliver* (1726), in which reference is made to two (then-undiscovered) moons of Mars. The astronomers on the flying island of Laputia, says Gulliver, have

> discovered two lesser stars, or satellites, which revolve around Mars, whereof the innermost is distant from the center of the primary exactly three of his diameters, and the outermost five: the former revolves in the space of ten hours, and the latter in twenty-one and a half.

When the two Martian moons, **Phobos** and **Deimos,** were eventually found, by Asaph **Hall** at the **U.S. Naval Observatory,** their orbits proved to be quite similar to those described in Swift's novel, as shown below.

Some cult literature has sprung up specifically to address how Swift could have "known" about the Martian moons and has arrived at some spectacular solutions, including the remarkable idea that Swift himself was a Martian! In fact, the idea that Mars might have two satellites goes back to Johannes **Kepler** and a memoir he published in 1610 in which he misconstrued an anagram devised by Galileo

	DISTANCE FROM SURFACE OF MARS (KM)		ROTATION PERIOD (HOURS)	
	Swift	Actual	Swift	Actual
Phobos	13,600	6,000	10	7.7
Deimos	27,200	20,100	21.5	30.3

Galilei in order to announce secretly a new discovery to his correspondents (who also included the Jesuit Fathers at the Collegio Romano). What Galileo had actually found were features connected with the planet Saturn that we now know to be its rings. His anagram was

s m a i s m r m i l m e p o e t a l e u m i b u n e n u g t t a u i r a s

the correct solution of which was

Altissimum planetam tergeminum observavi.
I have observed the most distant planet [Saturn] to have a triple form.

However, Kepler misconstrued the scrambled message to mean

Salue umbistineum geminatum Martia proles.
Hail, twin companionship, children of Mars.

and therefore assumed that Galileo had discovered two Martian moons. Although the true meaning of the anagram became known half a century later, Kepler's mistranslation endured and, it seems, came down to Swift, who may (although this is purely conjecture) have added some reasoning of his own. Since no Martian moons had been found by the early eighteenth century, it would have been reasonable to assume that they must be very small, very close to the planet, or both. Whatever the case, Swift's fictional moons turned out to be sur-

prisingly like their real counterparts. A more recent example of satellite prescience is Arthur C. **Clarke**'s description of a solitary moon of Pluto in ***Rendezvous with Rama***,[113] made in advance of the discovery of Charon. ➔ **Cyrano de Bergerac, Savinien; Voltaire**

Sycorax (97U2)

The outermost moon of **Uranus.** It moves in a highly elongated orbit and, together with **Caliban,** it is the most recently discovered by a ground-based telescope. ➔ **Uranus, moons of**

Discovery	1997 by B. J. Gladman, P. D. Nicolson, J. A. Burns and J. J. Kavelaars
Mean distance from Uranus	12,175,000 km (7,567,000 mi.)
Diameter	~80 km
Orbital period	1,284 days (3.5 years)
Orbital eccentricity	0.509
Orbital inclination	152.7°

Syrtis Major

Formerly known as the Kaiser Sea; one of the most conspicuous dark markings on the surface of **Mars.** Its existence was first noted by Christiaan **Huygens.** Later observers noticed that Syrtis Major, and features surrounding it, were subject to seasonal changes, the nature of which was the cause of much speculation (➔ **Mars, changes on**).

T association

A stellar association consisting of numerous low-mass **T Tauri star**s.

T Tauri star

Named after the prototype discovered in the constellation of Taurus. T Tauri stars represent an early stage in the evolution of stars that are similar to the Sun. The nearest occur in the Taurus **molecular cloud** and the Rho Ophiuchus Cloud, both about 460 light-years (140 parsecs) away.

Many T Tauri stars give off large amounts of **infrared** radiation, indicating that they are surrounded by dusty clouds that have become warm by absorbing starlight and reemitting it in the infrared part of the spectrum. T Tauri stars also vary erratically in brightness, as if they are being intermittently obscured. One way to interpret these and other observations is that the stars are circled by rotating disks of gas and dust—disks that may one day give rise to families of planets. According to one estimate, about 60 percent of T Tauri stars younger than 3 million years may possess dust disks, compared with only 10 percent of stars that are 10 million years old. The implication is that the disappearance of disks in older stars is linked to the appearance of (unseen) planets.

tachyon

A hypothetical particle that travels faster than the **speed of light** (and therefore also travels back in time). The existence of tachyons is allowed by the equations of Einstein's **special theory of relativity.** However, although searches have been carried out for tachyons, the results have so far proved negative.

target stars

In planning a **targeted search,** either for **extrasolar planets** of potential biological interest or signals from an extraterrestrial intelligence (➔ **SETI**), two major factors to be considered are (1) the likelihood that a given star could support life on a world of suitable size orbiting within the **habitable zone,** and (2) the star's proximity to the Sun. Since the only known examples of life have evolved on a world circling around a solitary, 5-billion-year-old **G star,** this type of star or ones similar to it appear to offer the best chances of success. Targeted searches for other planets and targeted SETI programs have therefore tended to focus on **Sun-like stars** (➔ **FGK stars**) within a few tens of light-years of the Earth (➔ **stars, nearest**).

Of the stars within a radius of 12 light-years (3.7 parsecs), only three are solitary and reasonably similar to the Sun in temperature and brightness: **Epsilon Eridani** (slightly cooler and dimmer, at 10.7 light-years), **Epsilon Indi** (slightly cooler and significantly dimmer, at 11.2 light-years), and **Tau Ceti** (slightly cooler and about half the solar brightness, at 11.9 light-years). The nearest star system of all is the triple-sunned **Alpha Centauri,** but it remains unclear how likely life is to evolve on a world subject to the complex gravitational perturbations of a binary or multiple star.

Of course, for all we know, it might be that a solitary star very different from the Sun, with a complement of orbiting worlds, could nurture the evolution of some form of life. Inhabited planets around **red dwarf**s, for example, the commonest type of star, cannot be ruled out.

targeted search

A search that involves aiming observation equipment at specific locations or objects in the sky and tracking these over extended periods of time. This contrasts to an **all-sky survey.** Targeted searches are used, for example, in the search for **extrasolar planets** and in some **SETI** programs, such as Project **Phoenix.** Targeted SETI is well suited to large, steerable **radio telescopes** with their narrow **bandwidth**s and high sensitivities. Providing the guess is right, a targeted search offers the greatest likelihood of success. On the other hand, it involves making assumptions that, if wrong, would result in more interesting objects or signals being missed.[168] **→ target stars**

Targeted Search System

A transportable **SETI** system that is used in conjunction with existing **radio telescope**s for high sensitivity observations in Project **Phoenix.** It is composed of several subsystems, each responsible for one aspect of the signal processing. Among these subsystems are the **Multi-Channel Spectrum Analyzer** (MCSA) and the **Follow-Up Detection Device** (FUDD).

Tarter, Jill Cornell (1944–)

Science team leader at the **SETI Institute,** holder of the institute's Bernard M. Oliver Chair for **SETI,** and director of Project **Phoenix.** Tarter received a B.S. in engineering physics from **Cornell University** (1965) and an M.S. (1971) and Ph.D. (1975) in theoretical astrophysics from the **University of Califor-**nia, **Berkeley,** where, as a graduate student, she carried out work on Project **SERENDIP.** From 1975 to 1977 she held a postdoctoral National Research Council Fellowship at **NASA Ames Research Center** and was subsequently contracted to work on NASA's **High Resolution Microwave Survey.** She has been on the staff at Berkeley since 1977 and has been principal investigator for the SETI Institute since 1985. Tarter is married to another leading SETI investigator, William "Jack" **Welch.**

Task Group on Sample Return from Small Solar System Bodies
→ back contamination

tau Bootis

A nearby **binary star** system, consisting of an **F star primary,** tau Bootis A, and a **red dwarf** companion, tau Bootis B. The red dwarf moves around the primary in an extraordinarily elongated path (**eccentricity** = 0.91), taking about 2,000 years to complete each circuit at an average distance of 245 AU (37 billion km, 23 billion miles). A massive planet has been found in orbit around the primary at less than one eighth the distance of Mercury from the Sun, making it one of the most extreme examples yet found of an **epistellar Jovian. → extrasolar planets**

Host Star	
Distance	51 light-years (15.6 parsecs)
Spectral type	F9 V
Apparent magnitude	4.5
Temperature	6,280°C (6,550 k)
Luminosity	3.01 L$_s$
Mass	1.37 M$_s$
Planet	
Mass	3.66 M$_J$
Semimajor axis	0.04 AU (6.1 million km, 3.8 million mi.)
Orbital period	3.31 days
Eccentricity	0.015
Discovery	1996, by Paul Buter et al., San Francisco State University Planet Search
Method of discovery	radial velocity

tau Ceti

At a distance of 11.9 light-years (3.7 parsecs), the most Sun-like of the thirty nearest stars to Earth. It is a **main sequence** star of **spectral type** K0, about half as bright as the Sun, that has been the target of many **SETI** attempts including the very first (➔ **Ozma, Project**). ➔ **stars, nearest**

Technical Intelligence Division (TID)

The group within Air Materiel Command, based at Wright Field (now Wright-Patterson Air Force Base), to which all reports of unidentified aerial activity were forwarded following a serious of sightings by personnel at Muroc Field (now Edwards AFB) on July 8, 1947. That same month, two TID officers visited Kenneth **Arnold** and concluded, "If Mr. Arnold could write a report of such a character and did not see the objects he was in the wrong business and should be engaged in writing Buck Rogers fiction." As the **saucer flap of 1947** gathered momentum, staff at TID began to speculate on the origin of what were then commonly called "**flying disks.**" One faction put forward the **extraterrestrial hypothesis,** although the consensus quickly emerged that advanced Soviet aircraft, possibly based on Nazi designs, were to blame.

technological developments, influence on extraterrestrial speculation

Whatever has been the leading-edge technology or scientific speculation of the day has colored how we imagine intelligent extraterrestrials to be. The Victorians began this trend in an age when no scheme, however crazy or ambitious, seemed impossible. A host of engineering marvels and scientific breakthroughs had convinced the public that the potential of technology was almost limitless. Between 1860 and 1900 came the invention of the internal combustion engine and automobile, telephone, electric motor, phonograph, radio, motion pictures, handheld camera, electric lamp, typewriter, microphone, rigid airship, and electric tram. During the same period, the first skyscrapers were built, the Statue of Liberty and the Eiffel Tower were erected, dynamite came into use, antiseptic surgery and anesthetics were introduced, and X rays, radioactivity, and the electron were discovered. Suddenly it seemed there might be nothing to which humans could not turn their hands and minds. The same capabilities, but to a higher degree, were projected onto other races in space. Thus Martians could not only build canals, they could construct a global network of them and irrigate their entire world by this means. As radio and telephony became a routine form of communication, so speculation began that beings on other worlds might be trying to send us radio messages. Nor is it coincidental that the first wave of **unidentified flying object**s, described as "mystery airships," appeared in the skies at the same time as airship technology reached a practical level on Earth. Fifty years later, as the first giant radio telescopes came into use, the talk of the times switched to interstellar communication by powerful, beamed radio waves, while UFOs had made a quantum jump in performance, just as humans had harnessed the jet engine and were learning how to escape the confines of their planet.

tectonic

Pertaining to the deformation of a planet's crust by internal forces.

tectonism

The processes of faulting, folding, or other deformation of the **lithosphere** of a planet or moon, often resulting from large-scale movements below the lithosphere.

Teilhard de Chardin, Pierre (1881–1955)

French Jesuit priest whose philosophical vision of the universe encompassed both Christian and evolutionary ideas. He believed that cosmic evolution proceeded slowly and gradually until it reached a critical point at which further developments would take place in the "noosphere," or the sphere of the mind. His book *The Phenomenon of Man* provoked such disapproval within the Catholic Church that it was published posthumously.

teleology

The doctrine that phenomena occur for a purpose. It was often used, from the seventeenth century on, as a theological argument in favor of **pluralism,** the argument being that God would not have gone to the trouble of creating uninhabited worlds. Among those to give prominence to teleological reasoning were Jacques-Henri **Bernardin de Saint-Pierre** and John **Locke.** Opponents of it included Ludwig **Büchner.**

telepathic species

A favorite theme of science fiction is the mega-cephalic alien telepath. At some stage, the supposition goes, intelligent beings reach the stage at which they can communicate with each other by thought alone. The question is whether this is a realistic possibility. There have been many claims, stemming from parapsychology experiments carried out in laboratories in the United States and Europe since the 1930s, of a weak telepathic ability in some human subjects. Among the best known are those conducted in the 1940s by J. B. Rhine at Duke University and more recently by Robert Jahn at Princeton. The wider scientific community has never been convinced by the reported positive results, suspecting instead that the experimental procedures or the statistical handling of data were flawed. The problem remains unresolved. However, it is interesting to consider the case for telepathy purely on evolutionary grounds. If humans *do* have telepathic abilities (or other paranormal powers, such as telekinesis or clairvoyance), it is reasonable to suppose that, like our other senses and skills, these developed at some point in the course of our evolution for sound survival-oriented reasons. Clearly, it would be useful to be able to read other people's thoughts, or even simply sense their emotions, when they were out of sight. An individual who is more telepathic than his adversary stands a better chance of outflanking him. A group of mildly telepathic hunters who are able to communicate without making a noise stand a better chance of catching their prey. The point is that if some primitive telepathic ability took root in our ancestors, it would have been so valuable that it is surprising not to find it fully developed in modern humans. A counterargument might be that telepathy is present to a greater extent in other animals and that, as in the case of the olfactory

sense, humans have lost the telepathic abilities once enjoyed by their predecessors. A reason for this could be that, following the emergence of a sophisticated spoken language, people had less need to rely on a purely mental (and possibly much less precise) method of conveying thoughts. It seems much more likely, however, in the absence of secure evidence to the contrary, that our species is nontelepathic.

Although it is true that certain other species on Earth, such as ants and flocking birds, can demonstrate such extraordinarily well choreographed behavior that it may *seem* as if they are linked by some form of extrasensory perception, alternative, more mundane explanations are to hand. The question remains whether extraterrestrials, having followed an entirely different evolutionary path, may have acquired a telepathic power. One difficulty is that it is not easy to see, in terms of our present scientific knowledge, how biological telepathy could work. That brains produce weak electromagnetic fields is beyond doubt. But even if another brain were sensitive enough to detect these fields, it strains credibility to imagine that any meaningful information could be extracted from them. Far more likely is that an intelligent species might develop a form of telepathy through the use of advanced computer technology. Such a prospect no longer seems fantastic given recent progress in establishing brain-computer links. **→ cyborg; extraterrestrial intelligence, forms of; artificial intelligence**

Telesto

A small moon of **Saturn.** Telesto and **Calypso** are known as the **Tethys** trojans due to the fact

Discovery	1981, by B. Smith and others
Mean distance from Saturn	294,700 km (183,200 mi.)
Diameter	34 × 28 × 26 km (21 × 17 × 16 mi.)
Orbital period	1.888 days (1 day 21 hours 19 minutes)
Orbital eccentricity	0.000
Orbital inclination	0.00°
Visual albedo	0.5

that they share the same orbit as Tethys; Telesto moves about 60 degrees ahead of the large moon and Calypso about 60 degrees behind. → **Saturn, moons of**

telomerase
The **enzyme** that catalyses for the synthesis of **telomere**s.

telomere
A specialized structure that caps each end of the **DNA** molecule, thus forming the end of a **chromosome** and helping to ensure that the DNA molecule is completely replicated.

temporal lobe lability
The amount of spontaneous electrical activity taking place in the temporal lobes of the brain (located behind the ears). According to some researchers, such as neuroscientist Michael **Persinger** at Laurentian University, it may play a significant role in the phenomenon of **alien abduction.** Temporal lobe lability is known to vary widely between individuals. In the most extreme cases, violent, synchronized electrical storms flare up in the temporal lobes and cause epileptic fits. Immediately before a seizure, epilepsy sufferers sometimes report strange feelings such as déjà vu or a mystical oneness with their surroundings.[550] Other people who are not epileptic but who nevertheless have a high lability as measured by an electroencephalograph tend on the whole to be unusually artistic and imaginative. They are also more prone than normal to having out-of-body experiences and other such dramatic psychotic episodes. Research by Persinger suggests that these effects can be induced in *anyone* by artificially stimulating the temporal lobes. At Laurentian, Persinger has set up an isolation chamber in an effort to simulate such experiences. Subjects relax in the darkened room while wearing a helmet in which three solenoids are used to produce a pulsating electromagnetic field. Although effects vary from one person to the next, frequently reported sensations include the feeling that others are present, of being pulled by someone or something, and of sudden, powerful bursts of emotion—fear or anger—over which the individual has no control. Persinger believes that in people who have a naturally high temporal lobe lability, such strong sensations if experienced at home, alone, and in the middle of the night could be enough to explain many abduction accounts.[448, 449, 483] This hypothesis becomes especially compelling when considered together with the possibility of **false memory syndrome.**

Teng Mu
Chinese scholar of the Sung Dynasty who adopted a position similar to that of **Lucretius** and other proponents of **atomism** with respect to extraterrestrial worlds. He wrote:[580]

> Empty space is like a kingdom, and earth and sky are no more than a single individual person in that kingdom. Upon one tree are many fruits, and in one kingdom there are many people. How unreasonable it would be to suppose that, besides the earth and the sky which we can see, there are no other skies and no other earths.

tenth planet
→ **Planet X**

terminal shock
The shock front that surrounds the Sun at an estimated distance of 80 to 100 AU. It marks the transition where the **solar wind** slows from supersonic to subsonic speed, and where there are large changes in the orientation of the Sun's magnetic field and the direction of flow of charged particles. *Voyager 1* is expected to reach the terminal shock in the year 2000 or shortly after. Beyond the terminal shock lies the magnetosheath.

terminator
The dividing line between the illuminated and dark part of a planet's or moon's disk.

terraforming
The process of altering the environment of a planet to make it more clement and suitable for human habitation. The possible future terraforming of Mars and Venus has been widely discussed. A major consideration before starting such a project would be its effects on any indigenous life.

terrestrial planet

A small planet of high density with a solid, rocky surface. The terrestrial planets in the solar system are Mercury, Venus, Earth, and Mars.

Terrestrial Planet Finder (TPF)

A mission, under study, that would form an important future part of NASA's **Origins Program.** It would employ an **optical interferometer** consisting of four 8-m telescopes (with a total surface area of 1,000 square m). The goal of *TPF* would be to identify **Earth-class planets** around nearby stars and analyze their spectra for the signatures of terrestrial-type life (➜ **biospheres, recognition of**). Its earliest launch date is 2009.

Terrestrial Planet Imager

A possible future NASA mission, part of the **Origins Program,** that would follow on from the *Terrestrial Planet Finder (TPF)* and produce images of Earth-like planets. To obtain a 25-by-25-pixel image of an **extrasolar planet** would call for an array of five TPF-class **optical interferometer**s flying in formation. Each interferometer would consist of four 8-m (26.2-ft.) telescopes to collect light and null it (➜ **nulling interferometry**) before passing it to a single 8-m telescope that would relay the light to a combining spacecraft. The five interferometers would be arranged in a parabola, creating a very long baseline of 6,000 km with the combining spacecraft at the focal point of the array.

tertiary structure

The unique, three-dimensional structure of a **protein** or other **polymer.** It is determined by

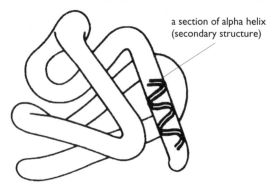

a section of alpha helix (secondary structure)

The folded three-dimensional form of a protein that is its tertiary structure.

the weak chemical bonds that act between the subunits along the polymer chain.

Tesla, Nikola (1856–1943)

Brilliant but enigmatic Serbian-born American electrical inventor who was the first to attempt to communicate with neighboring worlds using **radio waves.** In the February 9, 1901, issue of *Collier's Weekly,* he published "Talking with the Planets," in which he claimed he had detected an artificial signal from Mars, or possibly Venus, using high-voltage equipment he had set up at Colorado Springs, Colorado. He also predicted that interplanetary communication would "become the dominating idea of the century that has just begun." He went on, "With an expenditure not exceeding two thousand horsepower, signals can be transmitted to a planet such as Mars with as much exactness and certitude as we now send messages by wire from New York to Philadelphia." The local newspaper expressed its delight at Tesla's breakthrough: "If there be people on Mars, they certainly showed most excellent taste in choosing Colorado Springs as the particular point . . . with which to open communication." However, the scientific community responded more skeptically. The former director of the **Lick Observatory** Edward S. Holden commented, "It is a rule of sound philosophizing to examine all probable causes for an unexplained phenomenon before invoking improbable ones. Every experimenter will say that it is 'almost' certain that Mr. Tesla has made an error." Two decades later, the idea of interplanetary communication was revived by Guglielmo **Marconi.** ➜ **communication, with the Moon and planets; CETI**

Tethys

A medium-sized moon of **Saturn;** ninth in order of distance from the planet. It is composed primarily of water ice and is marked by a huge, globe-encircling canyon and numerous impact craters. The giant canyon, named Ithaca Chasma, is about 2,500 km (1,550 miles) long (three quarters of the circumference of the moon), and has an average width of about 65 km (40 miles) and a depth of 3 to 5 km (about 2 to 3 miles). If Tethys were once a ball of liquid water covered with a thin, solid

Discovery	1684, by Giovanni Cassini
Mean distance from Saturn	181,300 km (112,680 mi.)
Diameter	1,060 km (660 mi.)
Mean density	1.21 g/cm³
Escape velocity	0.436 km/s (1570 km/h, 976 mi./h)
Orbital period	1.888 days
Orbital eccentricity	0.000
Orbital inclination	1.09°
Axial period	1.888 days
Visual albedo	0.9

crust, freezing of a thick, watery mantle would have produced enough surface expansion to account for the area of the trough. But it is unclear why all the expansion would have taken place in a single band rather than in widely distributed faults. Also prominent is a large crater, Odysseus, about 400 km (250 miles) across, or more than one third the diameter of Tethys. A line drawn through the center of Odysseus would lie roughly at right angles to Ithaca Chasma, suggesting a possible link between the two features. The temperature on the surface is −187°C (−305°F). → **Saturn, moons of**

Thalassa

The second known moon of **Neptune.** Like the five other inner moons discovered during the 1989 flyby of *Voyager 2,* Thalassa is among the darkest objects in the solar system. → **Neptune, moons of**

Discovery	1989, by *Voyager 2*
Mean distance from Neptune	50,000 km (31,100 mi.)
Diameter	80 km (50 mi.)
Orbital period	0.311 days (7 hours 28 minutes)
Orbital eccentricity	0.0002
Orbital inclination	0.21°
Visual albedo	0.06

Thales of Miletus (c. 624–c. 545 B.C.)

Traditionally regarded as the founder of Greek philosophy and therefore of Western rational speculation about the nature of the universe. His home was Ionia, a region that included the coastal strip and islands to the east of the Aegean in what is present-day Turkey. Half a dozen major city-states, together with as many smaller ones, had banded together to make a loose federation known as the Ionian League. Of these, Miletus, a large commercial center near the mouth of the Meander, was chief, and it was here that Thales lived and taught. What we know of him and his works comes through the commentaries of others, since none of Thales's original writings has survived. He asked: What is the raw material from which all the Universe is made? He thought the answer was "water." But the crucial point is that he broke new ground by suggesting that the Earth and everything beyond it had a common physical basis and was subject to natural, rather than supernatural, laws. Thales is said to have proposed that the stars were other worlds—an important departure from the view that they were simply lights suspended from a celestial vault. Following his lead, other philosophers began to rally behind rationalism and put forward their own views as to the fundamental essence of matter and the nature of objects in the sky. This led quickly to speculation about extraterrestrial life. → **Anaximander of Miletus; Leucippus; ancient philosophy, related to the possibility of extraterrestrial life**

Thebe

The third moon of **Jupiter.** Together with **Amalthea,** Thebe appears to have supplied the material for Jupiter's Gossamer Ring. → **Jupiter, moons of**

Discovery	1979, by Stephen Synnott
Mean distance from Jupiter	225,000 km (139,800 mi.)
Diameter	110 × 90 km (68 × 56 mi.)
Mean density	1.5 g/cm³
Escape velocity	0.043 km/s (155 km/h, 96 mi./h)
Orbital period	0.675 days (16 hours 12 minutes)
Orbital eccentricity	0.0183
Orbital inclination	1.066°
Axial period	0.675 days
Visual albedo	0.05

theory of evolution

→ **evolutionary theory and extraterrestrials**

thermal probe
→ **cryobot**

thermal proteins

Synthetic **polypeptide**s, previously referred to as "proteinoids," made by heating certain mixtures of **amino acids.** In **proteins,** amino acids are linked by **peptide bond**s that form as a result of the loss of water. Following the much-publicized success of the **Milller-Urey experiment** (1953), it was hoped that by heating amino acids to a sufficiently high temperature, to drive off water, the next great step in retracing the chemical evolution of life—the synthesis of proteins—might be achieved in the laboratory. However, early work in this direction was discouraging and resulted only in the production of tarry materials. A breakthrough came in 1956 following the observation by Sidney **Fox** and his colleagues that of the twenty amino acids found in proteins, two, aspartic acid and glutamic acid, were especially prevalent, accounting for a quarter to a half of the amino acid content of protein molecules in general. It was also known that aspartic and glutamic acids play key roles in certain biological processes. Therefore, in their experiments in prebiological synthesis, Fox and his group tried heating a mixture of amino acids in which aspartic and glutamic acids were present in excess. After three hours of heating at about 180°C, they obtained an amber-colored liquid in which they discovered a complex **polymer** with a structure like that of a protein. Further experiments revealed that these "proteinoids," which later became known as thermal proteins, had molecular weights from 3,000 to 10,000, and always contained some of each of the amino acids present in the starting mixtures.[204] Moreover, against all expectations, the particular arrangements of amino acids making up thermal proteins turned out not to be random, but orderly and reproducible: the same mixture of amino acids would always combine in the same way.

Fox pointed out that the reactions in heated amino acid mixtures were not confined to the solid phase because, at the temperatures used, glutamic acid becomes a liquid. Also, the inclusion of **phosphoric acid,** which facilitated some of the reactions, served to provide a liq-

uid environment. Fox quoted features of the proteinoid thermal synthesis reactions that were discovered in the biochemical mechanisms of living organisms only afterward. Most interesting of all were the later studies by Fox, K. Harada, and J. W. Kendrick that resulted in the production of rudimentary cell-like structures known as **microspheres.**[207]

Until 1979, it was thought that the thermal proteins produced by heating amino acids were entirely synthetic and without counterparts in the biological world. Then the German biochemist Klaus Dose and his associates succeeded in showing that one of the products of Fox's experiments was flavin, a naturally occurring protein. Indeed, flavins play a significant role in the energy **metabolism** of cells, and **riboflavin,** in particular, is a standard component of the human diet.

thermophiles

Microbes that reproduce and grow in the temperature range of 40 to 70°C (104 to 158°F). A key thermophilic adaptation of an organism is the presence of heat stable **proteins.** These proteins are more densely packed to exclude internal water, are more hydrophobic, have more salt bridges, and have more saturated and longer-chained **fatty acids.** Thermophilic **archaea** have ether-linked, branched-chain fatty acids that are more hydrophobic still. Capable of thriving at even higher temperatures than thermophiles are **hyperthermophiles. → extremophiles; microbes, temperature ranges of**

thermophilic life
→ **thermophiles; hyperthermophiles**

Thing, The

The first and one of the best monster-alien movies (1951), based on John W. **Campbell's** "Who Goes There?," in which a humanoid vegetable arrives by spacecraft in the Arctic and terrorizes the inhabitants of a research station.

Thollon, Louis (1829–87)

French astronomer at the Nice Observatory who in 1886, together with his colleague Henri **Perrotin,** provided the first observational support for Giovanni **Schiaparelli's** claims about Martian canals and their "germination." → **Mars, canals of**

Thomson, William, Lord Kelvin (1824–1907)
Scottish theoretical and experimental physicist who, in his 1871 presidential address to the British Association for the Advancement of Science,[585] surprised the scientific community by declaring his support for a version of **panspermia:**

> Should the time come when this earth comes into collision with another body, comparable in dimensions to itself…many great and small fragments carrying seeds of living plants and animals would undoubtedly be scattered through space. Hence, and because we all confidently believe that there are at present, and have been from time immemorial, many worlds of life besides our own, we must regard it as probable in the highest degree that there are countless seed-bearing meteoric stones moving about through space. If at the present instance no life existed upon this earth, one such stone falling upon it might, by what we blindly call *natural* causes, lead to its becoming covered with vegetation.

Witty and derisive replies were not slow in coming. That archsupporter of Darwinism Thomas **Huxley** (who, ironically, had introduced Thomson to the BAAS meeting) wrote in a private letter, "What do you think of Thomson's 'creation by cockshy'—God almighty sitting like an idle boy at the seaside and shying aerolites (with germs), mostly missing, but sometimes hitting a planet!" Thomson, however, continued to argue his case, even urging that he considered it "not in any degree antagonistic to . . . Christian belief." Friedrich **Zöllner's** attack on Thomson's thesis prompted a rebuttal from Hermann von **Helmholtz,** who had independently put forward a similar theory of panspermia. In recent years, with the discovery of meteorites that have come from Mars (→ **SNC meteorites**), the concept of microbes hitching a ride from one world to another aboard impact fragments has become scientifically respectable (→ **ballistic panspermia**).

thymine
A **pyrimidine** that is one of five organic **bases** found in the **nucleic acid**s of **cells**. In **DNA,** it pairs with **adenine.**

TID
→ **Technical Intelligence Division**

tidal force
The ability of one massive object to cause tides on another object nearby. If the tidal force is large enough it can give rise to **tidal heating.**

tidal heating
The frictional heating of a moon's interior due to flexure caused by the gravitational pull of its parent planet and possibly neighboring satellites. The most dramatic example in the solar system is the tidal heating induced in each of the four **Galilean satellites** by their mutual pull and, more significantly, by the powerful attraction of Jupiter. In the case of **Io,** the result is global volcanism. In the case of **Europa,** and perhaps also **Ganymede** and **Callisto,** the effects of tidal heating are less dramatic but possibly much more profound in that they give rise to a suspected under-ice ocean that might conceivably support life.

tidal lock
→ **gravitational lock**

time dilation
A phenomenon predicted by the **special theory of relativity** in which the passage of time in the frame of reference of a moving object slows down as the object approaches the speed of light. Effectively, this makes it possible to spend energy to buy time. A potentially impor-

SHIPBOARD TRAVEL TIMES TO ARCTURUS AT VARIOUS SPEEDS	
Speed	*Travel time (years)*
0.1 c	35.8 years
0.5 c	31.2 years
0.9 c	15.7 years
0.99 c	5.1 years
0.999 c	1.6 years

tant consequence follows for future **interstellar travel.** Simply by traveling fast enough, an astronaut can reach *any* destination within a specified amount of (shipboard) time. The table below gives the travel times, as measured by onboard clocks, to Arcturus, located 36 light-years (11 parsecs) from the Sun, for a spacecraft traveling at various speeds (given as fractions of the speed of light, *c*).

Impressive though these results seem, they do not take into account the profound human problems that would surely follow from **time dislocation.**

time dislocation

A major drawback of exploiting the effect of **time dilation** to achieve manned **interstellar travel** is that those who make the journey age less than those, including friends and family members, who remain behind. For very long journeys at high fractions of the speed of light, the time dislocation may be so great that many generations, and even millennia, pass on the home planet before the interstellar travelers return. For example, an excursion from Earth to Rigel, 900 light-years away, and back, at (a constant) 99.99 percent of light speed, would take 1,800 years as measured on Earth but only about 28 years as experienced by those on the spacecraft. It has been argued, for example by Sebastien von **Hoerner,** that such acute time dislocations—effectively hurling the travelers into the future—will prevent interstellar travel beyond a few tens of light-years and, therefore, the colonization of the Galaxy. However, there may be other ways to circumvent the light barrier.

Tipler, Frank J.

American physicist at Tulane University, New Orleans. He is a strong advocate of the **anthropic principle** in its most extreme form and a critic of **SETI.** → **Tipler's Argument**

Tipler probe

→ **von Neumann probes**

Tipler's Argument

A thesis put forward by Frank **Tipler** in 1981[587] in opposition to the view that the Galaxy is populated by other intelligent races.

It is based on the supposition that the most effective and economical way to explore the Galaxy is with autonomous self-replicating spacecraft known as **von Neumann probes.** The fact that no evidence of such probes has yet been found is proof, said Tipler, that we are alone. His argument was cited by Senator William Proxmire in his efforts, in the early 1980s, to halt funding for NASA's **SETI** program. Tipler's argument was effectively countered, however, by Carl **Sagan** and William Newman (→ **Sagan's Response**).

Titan

The largest moon of **Saturn** and the second largest moon in the solar system, after **Ganymede.** It is the only moon in the solar system to have a dense atmosphere. The existence of this atmosphere, first suggested by José **Comas Solá** in 1903, following his observation that Titan appeared brighter at the center than at the limb, was confirmed spectroscopically by Gerard **Kuiper** in 1944. Vastly more information about the moon was returned by the *Voyager* probes following their flybys in 1980 and 1981. Titan is now known to be surrounded by a dense atmosphere of **nitrogen** (the major component), **methane,** and **hydrogen** that traps some of the Sun's heat and gives rise to a **greenhouse effect.** These gases take part in a cycle of **organic** chemistry to which the stability of Titan's climate is linked. In particular, methane is being steadily depleted. If it is not replenished, or replenished only irregularly, Titan's atmosphere may occasionally thin and cool as methane's greenhouse contribution is lost. An opaque, orange **photochemical** haze, thickest at an altitude of about 300 km (200 miles) hides the big moon's surface at visible wavelengths. However, **infrared** observations by the *Hubble Space Telescope* and, more recently by one of the **Keck Telescopes** have provided a map of bright and dark regions with a resolution of 240 km (150 miles). These images support the view that oceans or lakes of liquid **ethane** may cover a large fraction of the moon's surface and that liquid methane may fall as rain. According to another model, the bright areas glimpsed by *Hubble* and Keck are water ice plateaus thrust above lowlands darkened by solid and liquid

Discovery	1655, by Christiaan Huygens
Mean distance from Saturn	1,221,830 km (759,210 mi.)
Diameter	5,150 km (3,200 mi.)
Equatorial diameter (Earth = 1)	0.403
Mass (Earth = 1)	0.0227
Density	1.9 g/cm^3
Escape velocity	2.47 km/s (8,892 km/h, 5,526 mi./h)
Orbital period	15.95 days (15 days 23 hours)
Orbital eccentricity	0.029
Orbital inclination	0.33°
Axial period	15.95 days
Surface temperature	About −178°C (−288°F)
Atmospheric composition	Mainly nitrogen, plus methane, hydrogen, and other gases
Atmospheric pressure at surface	60% greater than Earth's at sea level
Depth of atmosphere	About ten times that of Earth's
Albedo	0.2

organic molecules. Sunlight and **cosmic rays** acting on molecules in the atmosphere, together with impacts and possibly volcanism at ground level, provide energy for the synthesis of more complex organic chemicals that may accumulate on the surface.[439] ➔ **Titan, prebiotic evolution on;** *Huygens* **probe; Saturn, moons of**

Titan, prebiotic evolution on

Together with **Mars, Europa,** and **Callisto, Titan** is considered one of the most promising locations in the solar system to look for signs of significant **prebiotic evolution.** It provides perhaps the closest analogue to the environment on Earth immediately before the appearance of the first organisms, and so offers a natural laboratory in which scientists can observe some of the crucial chemical steps leading to life. It is thought that Titan's **methane,** through ongoing photochemistry, is converted to **ethane,** acetylene, ethylene, and (when

combined with **nitrogen**) **hydrogen cyanide.** The last is an especially important molecule, since it is a building block of **amino acids.**

Some laboratory work has also been done to simulate what may be happening on Titan. In 1988, Carl **Sagan** and colleagues at **Cornell University** carried out experiments in which they simulated the chemistry of Titan's atmosphere.[506] Starting with a mixture of nitrogen, methane, hydrogen, and helium at the appropriate pressures and concentrations, they subjected this to a high voltage to mimic the effect of an **aurora.** Various **organic** materials were produced, including **hydrocarbon** chains up to seven **carbon** atoms long, **nitriles,** and a brownish-orange solid with optical properties similar to those of Titan's haze established by *Voyager* and ground-based observations. Titan's low temperature and consequent lack of liquid water may have inhibited more complex organic chemistry, though it is not clear to what extent volcanism and major impacts may have furnished locally more favorable conditions for prebiotic development. The *Cassini* mission and, in particular, the arrival on Titan of the *Huygens* **probe,** should provide some of the answers.[473, 609]

Titania

The fourteenth and largest moon of **Uranus.** Although Titania has a few large impact basins, it is generally covered with small craters and rough terrain. Numerous faults on the moon indicate that internal forces have helped mold its surface. ➔ **Uranus, moons of**

Discovery	1787, by William Herschel
Mean distance from Uranus	438,400 km (272,500 mi.)
Diameter	1,578 km (981 mi.)
Mean density	1.70 g/cm^3
Escape velocity	0.768 km/s (2,765 km/h, 1,718 mi./h)
Orbital period	8.706 days (8 days 16 hours 57 minutes)
Orbital eccentricity	0.0022
Orbital inclination	0.14°
Axial period	8.706 days
Visual albedo	0.27

TLPs
→ **transient lunar phenomena**

TMR-1A and B
A **binary star** system consisting of two **proto-stars** located in the so-called Taurus Molecular Ring at a distance of 450 light-years (136 parsecs). → **TMR-1C**

TMR-1C
An object which appears to be a large planet, or possibly a **brown dwarf,** that has been ejected from a binary pair of young **proto-stars, TMR-1A and B.** The discovery was made by Susan Tereby and her colleagues at the Extraterrestrial Research Corporation while examining an image of a star-forming region obtained using the *Hubble Space Telescope* NICMOS (Near Infrared Camera and Multi-Object Spectrometer).[581] A narrow filament of nebulosity about 1,400 AU (21 billion km, 13 billion miles) long connects TMR-1C to the region near the embryonic stars from which it is presumed to have come. TMR-1C is self-luminous. However, its effective temperature of about 1,300°C (determined from the radiation spectrum it emits) is much less than the 2,200°C expected of the lowest-mass stars and is within the limits prescribed by models of giant planets and **brown dwarf**s in the early stages of their evolution. Using conventional theory of how the temperature of a young planet depends on its age and mass, and assuming that, like the nearby protostellar binary system, TMR-1C is a few hundred thousand years old, Tereby and her colleagues obtained a mass for the ejected object of two to three times that of Jupiter. The uncertainties involved, however, could mean that this estimate is much too low and that TMR-1C is really a brown dwarf. Either way, it is a double first: the first extrasolar world or brown dwarf to be discovered by direct visual observation and the first known **rogue planet** or brown dwarf, implying that interstellar space may have a large population of substellar objects that have escaped their parent stars at an early stage in their development.
→ **L1551 (IRS5)**

Todd, David P. (1855–1939)
American astronomer, director of the observatory at Amherst College, who was interested in the possibility of radio communication with Mars. In 1907, Todd led the **Lowell** expedition to Chile to photograph the Martian canals. Two years later, he suggested that the Martians might use radio waves to communicate with Earth and that sensitive receivers carried to high altitude by balloon would have the best chance of picking up these signals. Although Todd revived his plan in 1920, around the time Guglielmo **Marconi** was discussing extraterrestrial signals, no balloon was ever launched. In August 1924, during an opposition of Mars, Todd persuaded the U.S. Army and Navy to use their receiving stations to listen in for any unusual signals. → **communication, with the Moon and planets**

Townes, Charles Hard (1915–)
American physicist at the **University of California, Berkeley,** who developed the **maser** in the 1950s and won a Nobel Prize for this work in 1964. He was a pioneer in microwave and infrared astronomy and led the team at Berkeley that, in 1968, discovered water and ammonia molecules in interstellar space. Townes has a long-standing interest in the possibly of **optical SETI** and while at the Massachusetts Institute of Technology in the early 1960s was the first, together with R. N. Schwarz, to suggest the possibility of using **lasers** for interstellar communication. He is presently involved in a project, funded by the **Planetary Society,** to search for artificial laser pulses coming from a variety of sources, including nearby stars, **globular clusters**, and external galaxies.

TPF
→ *Terrestrial Planet Finder*

trace element
Any of a number of **elements** required by living organisms, in small amounts, to ensure normal growth, development, and maintenance. They do not include the basic elements of organic compounds (carbon, hydrogen, oxygen, and nitrogen) or the other major elements present in quantities greater than about

0.005 percent (calcium, phosphorus, potassium, sodium, chlorine, sulfur, and magnesium). Among the most important trace elements in terrestrial organisms are **iron, manganese, zinc, copper, iodine, cobalt, molybdenum, selenium, chromium,** and **silicon** (➔ **elements, biological abundance of**). Because living things serve to locally concentrate trace elements, accumulations of these elements in rocks provide a **biomarker** that astrobiologists will be able to use in their search for extraterrestrial life.

transcription

The process in which the genetic information in **DNA** is transferred to a molecule of **messenger RNA** (mRNA) as the first stage in **protein** synthesis. Transcription takes place in the cell **nucleus** or nuclear region. An **enzyme** (transcriptase) moves along the DNA strand and assembles the **nucleotide**s needed to make a complementary strand of mRNA.

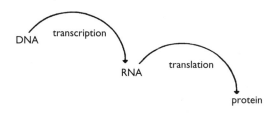

transduction

The uptake of **DNA** mediated by a **bacteriophage**; one of the three modes of **gene transfer.**

transfer RNA (tRNA)

A type of **RNA** that translates (➔ **transcription**) the language of **nucleotides** into the language of **amino acids** and places them in a **protein** that is being produced according to the instructions of **messenger RNA** (mRNA).

transformation

The uptake of "naked" **DNA** into a cell thereby altering the cell **genotype** of a **prokaryote** or **eukaryote**; one of the three modes of **gene transfer.**

transient lunar phenomena (TLPs)

Changes occasionally reported on the Moon's surface, most notably in the regions of the craters **Alphonsus, Aristarchus,** and Gassendi. TLPs are said to take the form of colored patches or obscurations, but it remains unclear whether they represent real physical phenomena.

transit

The movement of a smaller object, such as a planet, across the illuminated face of a larger object, such as a star.

Transits of Extrasolar Planets (TEP) Network

An international group of collaborators searching for **transit**s of **extrasolar planets.** A major effort of the group involves making observations of the **eclipsing binary** CM Draconis for signs of orbiting worlds.

translation

The assembly of a **protein** on the **ribosome**s, using **messenger RNA** to specify the sequence of **amino acid**s.

translocation

A **mutation** that moves a portion of a **chromosome** to a new location, generally on a different chromosome.

transmigration of souls

A theological doctrine (also known as "metempsychosis" or "palingenesis") that became popular during the Enlightenment as the scale of the Universe and the vast number of planets that might exist began to become clear. It taught that the soul, after death, would inhabit a succession of other worlds, becoming progressively more perfect. As Karl Guthe[248] writes:

> Such a concept of perfectibility linked to migration between planets offers a perspective in which the fears of inferiority, or isolation, or of being lost in a cosmos are transformed into ultimate triumph for the immortal part of man's being.

It was embraced in various forms by, among others, Thomas **Wright,** Charles **Bonnet,** Immanuel **Kant,** Humphry **Davy,** Jean **Reynaud,** and Camille **Flammarion.** The vast public readership of Flammarion's writings, in particular, ensured that belief in transmigration remained in circulation until the beginning of the twentieth century.

transmitter

Equipment used to generate and broadcast **radio wave** signals for use in communications. It consists of a **carrier wave** generator, a device for modulating the carrier wave according to the information to be transmitted, amplifiers, and an **antenna** system.

transverse velocity

The component of an object's velocity that is at right angles to the line of sight of the observer.

Trapezium

The popular name of the **multiple star** system Theta Orionis, which is located within, and illuminates, the **Orion Nebula.** Its name comes from the pattern of its four brightest stars. Two fainter stars also form part of the system.

Triton

The largest moon of **Neptune** and the only major satellite in the solar system to display **retrograde** motion about its primary. To add to this peculiarity, Triton's axis is tilted to that of Neptune by 157 degrees. These unusual facts suggest that Triton may once have been an independent body that was captured by Neptune's gravity. Triton's density of more than twice that of water indicates that it has a rocky interior surrounded by water ice. Its pink coloration may be due to evaporation of a surface layer of frozen **nitrogen.** Dark streaks across the south polar cap may be due to the eruptions of ice geysers, the ejecta of which probably consist of liquid nitrogen, dust, or **methane.** Icy plains have the appearance of lakes, suggesting that regions of the surface were once fluid. Triton's thin nitrogen atmosphere, with only about 1/70,000th the surface pressure of Earth's atmosphere, may give rise

to thin clouds of nitrogen ice particles a few kilometers above the surface. ➔ **Neptune, moons of**

Discovery	1846, by William Lassell
Mean distance from Neptune	353,000 km (219,000 mi.)
Diameter	2,700 km (1,678 mi.)
Equatorial diameter (Earth = 1)	0.212
Mass (Earth = 1)	0.0036
Mean density	2.07 g/cm³
Escape velocity	1.45 km/s (5,220 km/h, 3,244 mi./h)
Orbital period	−5.877 days (5 days 21 hours 3 minutes) (retrograde)
Orbital eccentricity	0.000
Orbital inclination	157.35°
Axial period	−5.877 days (gravitational lock)
Albedo	0.7
Atmosphere	Mostly nitrogen; small amount of methane
Atmospheric pressure at surface	14 microbars (about fourteen millionths that of Earth)
Surface temperature	−235°C (−391°F)

tRNA
➔ **transfer RNA**

Troitskii, Vsevolod Sergeyevich (1913–)

Vice director of the Radiophysical Institute at Gorky and, together with Iosif **Shklovskii** and Nikolai **Kardashev,** one of the pioneers of **SETI** in the Soviet Union. In contrast to Kardashev's belief in supercivilizations and Shklovskii's revised belief that the human race is alone, Troitskii argued that the majority of technological civilizations are probably at about our level of advancement or slightly higher. In their attempts to establish interstellar contact, such civilizations, he suggested, would send out highly directed **narrowband** signals toward the star systems they deemed most likely to be inhabited. After completing technical school in 1932, Troitskii worked in the Central Radio Laboratory at Nizhny Novgorod (later renamed Gorky) until 1936. He graduated from the University of Gorky in 1941 and joined the staff of the Gorky Radio-physical Institute in 1948. His thinking about the possibility of extraterrestrial signals began just prior to the 1964 All-Union Meeting on Extraterrestrial Civilizations at Byurakan (➔ **Byurakan SETI conferences**). Subsequently, he became the first chairman of the section of the Soviet Academy of Sciences responsible for **SETI.** In 1968, he began a **targeted search** of the twelve nearest star systems and in 1970 an **all-sky survey,** the most ambitious SETI project at that time, which eventually logged more than 700 hours of observations.

Trojan asteroids

Two groups of **asteroid**s that share the same orbit as Jupiter. They are clustered around the **Lagrangian points,** 60 degrees ahead of and 60 degrees behind the giant planet. More than two hundred are known, the majority being in the preceding group.

Troland, Leonard Thompson (1889–1932)

Harvard biochemist who put forward one of the earliest theories describing a chemical origin for life on Earth. Troland suggested that **autocatalytic enzymes** (enzymes capable of catalyzing their own manufacture), bathed in an oily liquid produced in the Earth's primordial seas, might be considered the earliest "primitive living bodies." ➔ **life, origin of**

Tsiolkovskii, Konstantin Eduardovich (1857–1935)

Russian rocket pioneer and research scientist in aeronautics and astronautics who produced some of the earliest scientific literature on spaceflight, including the classic work *Exploration of Space by Means of Reactive Apparatus* (1896). He also wrote extensively and far ahead of his time on the possibility of life on other worlds. Some extraterrestrial life-forms, he proposed, might consist entirely of **hydrogen** (like the intelligent nebula in Fred **Hoyle**'s *The Black Cloud*). Tsiolkovskii also wondered if there might be beings so advanced that they were essentially a disembodied consciousness. In his *Monism of the Universe* (1925), he suggests that superior entities might systemati-

cally eliminate lower creatures, such as animals and bacteria, rather than have them endure the painful process of biological evolution. Furthermore, he argued that somewhere a race had progressed technologically to the point at which it could "overcome the force of gravity and . . . colonize the Universe." Although he believed that **interstellar travel** was achievable, he argued in a letter to the Organization of Young Technicians in 1920 that "In the near future short radio waves will penetrate our atmosphere and . . . be the main means of stellar communication." ➔ **SETI**

Tunguska Phenomenon

A violent explosion that took place over the valley of the Stony Tunguska river, in central Siberia, at 7:17 A.M. on June 30, 1908, and is now generally attributed to the detonation of icy material from a **comet** in the Earth's atmosphere. The blast, which stripped or felled trees out to a radius of 40 km, burned reindeer to death, and sent the tents of nomads flying through the air, was preceded by the observed passage across the sky of a dazzling blue **bolide** trailing a column of dust. Soviet mineralogist Leonid Kulik, who first investigated the event, initially assumed that it had been caused by the fall of a giant iron meteorite but the absence of any crater quickly led to this idea being abandoned. The cometary theory was first put forward in the 1930s by Soviet astronomer I. S. Astapovich and English meteorologist Francis Whipple. However, other more exotic explanations later stemmed from the rumored existence of anomalous radiation at the site. In a science fiction story of 1946, Soviet author Alexander Kazantsev developed the idea that a nuclear-powered spacecraft from Mars, on a visit to collect fresh water from Lake Baikal, had exploded, showering the area in radioactivity. A similar scenario has been advocated as a genuine scientific hypothesis by Mikhail **Agrest** and others. Geochemist Kirill Florensky of the Soviet Academy of Sciences, who led expeditions to the site in 1958, 1961, and 1962, reported that the only radioactivity in the Tunguska trees could be explained as fallout from atomic bomb tests. More interesting was the discovery, by Clyde Cowan, C. R.

Atluri, and Willard Libby,[130] of a 1 percent jump in the radiocarbon content of the rings of two trees, one in Los Angeles and the other in Tucson, for 1909, the year following the explosion. A possible explanation of this was suggested in 1977 by John Brown and David Hughes of the University of Sheffield, who pointed out that sufficient neutrons to account for the American radiocarbon data could have come from the hot **plasma** generated by a comet's passage.

21-centimeter line

An **emission line** in the radio region of the spectrum that is due to the "spin-flip" transition in neutral **hydrogen** atoms. The **proton** and **electron** making up a hydrogen atom both spin. When their spins are parallel, the atom has slightly more energy than when their spins are antiparallel. As the atom flips from the parallel to the antiparallel state, it emits a **radio wave photon** with a wavelength of 21.1 cm, equivalent to a frequency of 1,420 MHz. Most of what is known about the distribution of cold gas in the **Galaxy,** including the mapping of the nearby **spiral arm**s, has come from detailed studies of the variation of 21-cm emission across the sky. In 1959, the famous **Morrison-Cocconi Conjecture,** concerning the possibility of detecting artificial signals at this wavelength, heralded the birth of **SETI** in its modern form.

Twining, Nathan F. (1897–1982)

Head of **Air Materiel Command** (AMC) at the time of the flying **saucer flap of 1947.** On September 23, 1947, Twining sent a memo to Brigadier General George Schulgen, commanding general of the U.S. Air Force, summarizing what were then AMC's opinions on the phenomenon of "**flying disks.**" These included:

a. The phenomena reported is [sic] something real and not visionary or fictitious.
b. There are objects probably approximately the shape of a disc, of such appreciable size as to appear to be as large as a man-made aircraft.
c. There is the possibility that some of the incidents may be caused by natural phenomena, such as meteors.
d. The reported operating characteristics such as extreme rates of climb, maneuverability (particularly in roll), and action which must be considered evasive when sighted or contacted by friendly aircraft and radar, lend belief to the possibility that some of the objects are controlled either manually, automatically or remotely.

Twining asked for the following points to be considered:

1. The possibility that these objects are of domestic origin—the product of some high

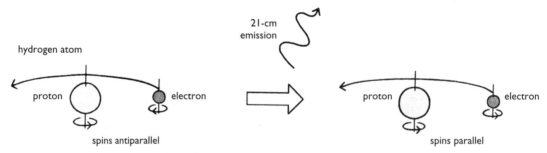

A 21-cm radio-wave photon is emitted as an electron "flips" from an antiparallel to a parallel state.

security project not known to . . . this command.

2. The lack of physical evidence in the shape of crash recovered exhibits which would undeniably prove the existence of these objects.

3. The possibility that some foreign nation has a form of propulsion, possibly nuclear, which is outside of our domestic knowledge.

Finally, Twining recommended that

Headquarters, Army Air Forces issue a directive assigning a priority, security classification and code name for a detailed study of this matter.

On December 30, 1947, Twining's recommendation was put into effect with the launch of Project **Sign.**

Twinkle, Project

An investigation, begun in 1950, into reports, from late 1948 to 1951, of the appearance of green "fireballs" in the general area of Holloman Air Force Base and Vaughn, New Mexico. It was conducted by the **Air Materiel Command** (AMC) and Air Research and Development Command (ARDC) and headed by Lincoln La Paz, a meteor specialist, who became convinced that the fireballs were not natural phenomena. However, as a memo to the commanding general of AMC, dated September 15, 1950, points out, "It may be considered significant that fire balls have ceased abruptly as soon as a systematic watch was set up." ➔ **"foo fighters"; earthlights**

2001: A Space Odyssey

Epic science fiction film (1968) directed by Stanley Kubrick[3, 115, 492 (ch. 25)] and based on Arthur C. **Clarke's** short story "The Sentinel"[112] (1948). In Clarke's tale, a crystal pyramid placed on the Moon long ago by an advanced extraterrestrial race serves to notify its creators when it is finally disturbed by explorers from Earth (➔ **sentinel hypothesis**):

They left a sentinel, one of millions they have scattered throughout the universe, watching over all the worlds with the promise of life. It

was a beacon that down the ages has been patiently signaling the fact that no one had discovered it. . . . We found the pyramid and forced it open. Now its signals have ceased, and those whose duty it is will be turning their minds upon Earth.

In the film, the sentinels take the form of enigmatic black monoliths that monitor human evolution, from cave-dwelling to space-faring stage, and also influence and accelerate mankind's development by supplying valuable information at crucial moments. The aliens themselves are never shown, and the film ends, in surreal style, with the transformation of astronaut Dave Bowman into a "star child." Clarke produced a novelization of the film[111] but located the "Star Gate" near Saturn's moon **Iapetus** rather than, as in the screen version, in orbit around Jupiter—a serendipitous choice, given that Iapetus was subsequently found to have the highest visual contrast of any moon in the solar system, leading to some half-serious suggestions that it might be artificial.[226] Although the sequel novels and film, *2010: Odyssey Two*[116] (1982; film, 1984), *2061: Odyssey Three*[117] (1988), and *3001: The Final Odyssey*[118] (1997), were less successful, the impact of *2001* itself continues to be felt today. ➔ **science fiction involving extraterrestrials, in films and on television**

Tyndall, John (1820–93)

Irish physicist who championed the now accepted notion that there is no fundamental difference between animate and inanimate matter, and that the origin of life was chemical:[594]

[T]he matter of the animal body is that of inorganic nature. There is no substance in the animal tissues which is not primarily derived from the rocks, the water and the air. . . . [A] perfect reversal of this process of reduction would carry us from the inorganic to the organic, and such a reversal is at least conceivable.

Carrying on from where Lazzaro **Spallanzani,** Cagniard de **La Tour,** and Louis **Pasteur** had left off, Tyndall also finally disposed of the old idea of **spontaneous generation** by answering the last objection raised by supporters of that view. It had been observed that microbes sometimes began growing in infusions, such as those of hay, even after the latter had been boiled. Tyndall showed that the reason for this was that the hay contained **spores,** which can survive even after long exposure to high temperature.

U

UFOs
→ unidentified flying objects

ultramicrobacteria
→ dwarf bacteria

ultraviolet (UV)
That part of the **electromagnetic spectrum** lying between the regions of visible light and **X rays,** with **wavelength**s between approximately 400 and 10 nm. It is divided into near ultraviolet (400 to 300 nm), middle ultraviolet (300 to 200 nm), and far ultraviolet (200 to 10 nm).

ultraviolet lasers, interstellar signaling via
An idea proposed by American electro-optical engineer Herbert F. Wischnia, a guest investigator on the *OAO-3* (*Orbiting Astronomical Observatory*) satellite (also known as *Copernicus*). According to Wischnia, **ultraviolet laser**s would provide an effective and logical method of sending interstellar messages. "Stars with a temperature near that of our own Sun radiate very little energy in the ultraviolet," he pointed out, "so that the telescope receivers are not blinded by natural stellar radiation." He made his first scans with *OAO-3* in November 1974, first turning the spacecraft's spectrometer toward **Epsilon Eridani** before moving on to look for UV signals from **Tau Ceti** and **Epsilon Indi,** though without success. → **optical SETI**

Umbriel
The thirteenth and darkest moon of **Uranus.** Its size and density are about the same as those of **Ariel,** while its surface is old with little variation in the type of terrain from one region to another. A puzzling bright ring in Umbriel's surface, nicknamed the "fluorescent Cheerio," may be the floor of a crater. → **Uranus, moons of**

Discovery	1851, by William Lassell
Mean distance from Uranus	267,200 km (166,100 mi.)
Diameter	1,190 km (740 mi.)
Mean density	1.52 g/cm³
Escape velocity	0.540 km/s (1,944 km/h, 1,208 mi./h)
Orbital period	4.144 days (4 days 3 hours 27 minutes)
Orbital eccentricity	0.005
Orbital inclination	0.36°
Axial period	4.144 days
Visual albedo	0.18

unicellular

Descriptive of tissues, organs, or organisms that consist of a single **cell.** Unicellular organisms include **bacteria, archaea, protists,** and certain **algae** and **fungi.** Certain algae and fungi that are **multicellular** have unicellular reproductive organs.

unidentified flying objects (UFOs)

Although the term "UFO" dates back only as far as 1952, mysterious aerial phenomena have been reported on and off for centuries. The notion that unidentified objects or lights in the sky might be craft from other worlds appears to have been first suggested following the earliest wave of such sightings—that of the "mystery airships"—in 1896–97. Perhaps it is no coincidence that this wave came at a time when Percival **Lowell** was advocating the existence of an advanced race on Mars and there was increasing discussion of the feasibility of heavier-than-air flight. The modern debate about the nature of UFOs began in 1947 with Kenneth **Arnold's** sighting of the first so-called **flying saucer**s (➔ **Cold War, linked to UFO reports**). Explanations for the saucers, or "**flying disk**s," as they were also known at the time, included natural phenomena, such as Venus or unusual clouds, illusions, hoaxes, balloons, prototype aircraft and secret weapons (friendly or hostile), and the **extraterrestrial hypothesis.** The last possibility was not initially given much credence but rapidly gained in favor as a result of intense media speculation.

From the outset, the systematic investigation of UFOs was made problematic by the fact that the alleged phenomenon was both transient and unpredictable. Although data were plentiful, these largely took the form of individual and uncorroborated eyewitness reports—a notoriously unreliable source of information. Yet enough sightings were made by what appeared to be reliable, experienced observers, including military personnel and police officers, for the phenomenon to be taken seriously (➔ **Roswell Incident; Mantell, Thomas F.**). The U.S. military, concerned about a possible threat to national security and following the recommendations of General Nathan F. **Twining,** launched the first of its investigations, Project **Sign.** This was followed by Project **Grudge** and, finally, beginning in 1952, by Project **Blue Book.** J. Allen **Hynek,** the astronomical consultant for Blue Book, devised a classification scheme for UFO reports:

Type of UFO Sighting	Description
Nocturnal lights	Bright lights seen at night
Daylight disks	Usually oval or disklike
Radar-visual	Those detected by radar
Close encounters of the first kind	Visual sightings of an unidentified object
Close encounters of the second kind	Visual sightings plus physical effects on animate and inanimate objects
Close encounters of the third kind	Sightings of occupants in or around the UFO

Although military and CIA interest in UFOs declined steeply after the **"Washington Invasion"** of 1952, public interest was maintained by the increasingly sensational claims of amateur investigators such as Donald **Keyhoe** and "contactees" such as George **Adamski.** A large body of saucer mythology began to accrete around claims of government cover-ups and certain improperly explained sightings. Meanwhile, professional scientists continued, with a few notable exceptions such as Donald **Menzel,** to distance themselves from the subject.[102, 503]

uniformity, principle of

The assertion that the laws of nature discovered on Earth apply throughout the rest of the Universe. From this it is a reasonable, though not inevitable, conclusion that the same physical, chemical, and biological processes that gave rise to terrestrial life could also produce life elsewhere. The principle of uniformity is a fundamental tenet of science. Together with two other basic beliefs (➔ **mediocrity, principle of; plenitude, principle of**) it is used by most **SETI** proponents to argue that life and intelligence are not uncommon throughout space.

universe

A term that is becoming increasingly difficult to define, given the possibility that there may be many different universes. *The* Universe could be said to be all of **space-time** that is contiguous with that portion of space-time in which we live. However, the presence of **wormholes,** capable of linking universes, would provide an extra complication.

University of California, Berkeley

An institution that has played a prominent role, over several decades, in the development of both **astrobiology** and **SETI.** It was here, in the 1960s, that Melvin **Calvin** carried out important work in **prebiotic** evolution. Earlier still, in the mid-1950s, important research and discussions on the likelihood and habitability of **extrasolar planets** took place at Berkeley involving Otto **Struve,** Su-Shu **Huang,** and Ronald **Bracewell.** Charles **Townes,** inventor of the **maser,** has long supported the idea that intelligent races might use **lasers** for interstellar communication and is presently engaged in a search for artificial laser signals. The university's **Leuschner Observatory** has been used in an effort to detect **Dyson sphere**s, while Berkeley's long-running **SERENDIP** program has employed some of the world's largest **radio telescope**s, including the **Arecibo radio telescope.** Leading SETI investigators, including Jill **Tarter** and William ("Jack") **Welch,** are on Berkeley's faculty, as are Geoffrey **Marcy** and R. Paul **Butler,** who have figured prominently in the search for extrasolar planets. In the near future, the university's Radio Astronomy Laboratory will embark on a joint effort with the **SETI Institute** to build the world's most powerful instrument dedicated primarily to the search for intelligent signals: the **One Hectare Telescope.**

University of St. Andrews Planet Search

A program to detect **extrasolar planets** using both **microlensing** and **transit** techniques. The microlensing data were gathered at various sites, including the **McDonald Observatory,** Texas, and the IAC Observatory, Tenerife, while the transit data were collected in the summer of 1999 at the ING Observatory, La Palma.

unseen companion

An object, such as an **extrasolar planet, brown dwarf,** low-luminosity star, or **black hole,** that is too dim or near to its **primary** to be imaged but the existence of which can be inferred by other means, such as **Doppler spectroscopy, astrometry,** or **photometry.**

upsilon Andromedae

The first **main sequence** star around which an extrasolar planetary system has been found. The discovery was announced in 1999 by a team from the **San Francisco State University Planet Search** group and independently by astronomers from the **Harvard-Smithsonian Center for Astrophysics** and the High Altitude Observatory in Boulder, Colorado, who had been studying the star for more than four years at the **Whipple Observatory.** Prior to this, only single **extrasolar planets** had been confirmed around Sun-like stars, together with two planetary systems around **pulsar**s. A planet of about two thirds the mass of Jupiter was found around upsilon Andromedae by the SFSU group in mid-1996. This became the fourth known **epistellar Jovian,** having an orbit that brings it seven times closer to its host star than Mercury is to the Sun. Three years later, two companions of larger mass were announced orbiting at about 0.8 and 2.5 AU.[376] As one of the SFSU researchers, Debra Fischer, pointed out, this important discovery "implies that planets can form more easily than we ever imagined, and that our Milky Way is teeming with planetary systems." The greatest surprise is the presence in one system of so many giant worlds. Theorists had only just begun to adjust to the idea of Jupiter-size planets in very small or highly elongated orbits. But this new triple-Jovian system promises to cause an even bigger shake-up of ideas of planet formation. As to whether there might be life around upsilon Andromedae, that is impossible to say. The star's age is about 3 billion years, old enough for life to have evolved; however, further study will be needed to establish whether any Earth-like worlds are present.

Host Star	
Distance	43.9 light-years (13.5 parsecs)
Spectral type	F7 V
Apparent magnitude	4.63
Temperature	5,980°C (6,250 K)
Luminosity	3.33 L_s
Mass	1.34 M_s

Planets			
	b	**c**	**d**
Mass	0.71 M_J	2.11 M_J	4.61 M_J
Semimajor axis (AU)	0.059	0.83	2.50
Orbital period	4.62 days	241 days	1,267 days
Eccentricity	0.034	0.18	0.41
Discovery:			
Year	1996	1999	1999
Group	San Francisco State University Planet Search	San Francisco State University, Smithsonian Center for Astrophysics High Altitude Observatory	
Method	Radial velocity	Radial velocity	Radial velocity

uracil

A **purine,** one of five organic bases found in the **nucleic acid**s of **cell**s. In **RNA,** it pairs with **adenine.** The difficulty of synthesizing uracil and **cytosine** in laboratory experiments intended to mimic conditions on the primor-dial Earth has left a question mark over current models of **prebiotic** evolution.

Uranus

The seventh planet from the Sun and one of the four **gas giant**s. It is unique in the solar

Discovery	1781, by William Herschel
Distance from Sun:	
Mean	2,869 million km (1,783 million mi., 19.2 AU)
Minimum	2,735 million km (1,700 million mi., 18.3 AU)
Maximum	3,004 million km (1,867 million mi., 20.1 AU)
Equatorial diameter	51,108 km (31,764 mi.)
Equatorial diameter (Earth = 1)	4.007
Mass	14.6 M_e
Mean density	1.3 g/cm^3
Escape velocity	22.5 km/s (81,000 km/h, 50,342 mi./h)
Orbital period	84 years
Orbital eccentricity	0.047
Orbital inclination	0.8°
Axial period	17.9 hours
Axial inclination	97.9°
Number of moons	18
Atmospheric composition	83% hydrogen, 15% helium, 2% methane
Mean temperature (cloud tops)	−197°C (−323 °F)
Gravity at cloud tops (Earth = 1)	1.17
Albedo	0.35

system in having its equator tilted at 98 degrees with respect to its orbit, suggesting that it suffered a major impact early in its career that knocked it onto its side. Since the plane containing its eleven rings and eighteen known moons (→ **Uranus, moons of**) is similarly tilted, this impact presumably took place during or shortly after the **accretion**ary phase of the planets. Although Uranus may have a small **silicate**-rich core, most of its mass is believed to consist of water, **ammonia,** and **methane.** Its atmosphere contains **hydrogen** and **helium** in the same ratio as that found on the Sun, while its blue-green color is due to a high haze of methane (which absorbs red light and reflects blue). The magnetic field of Uranus is unusual in that it is tilted 60 degrees from the planet's spin axis, and offset from the center of the planet by one third of the radius.

Uranus, moons of

See separate entries for each of the moons listed below.

urea [CO(NH₂)₂]

A white crystalline solid, soluble in water, that is the major end product of **nitrogen** excretion in mammals. It was the first **organic** substance to be synthesized in the laboratory (→ **Wöhler, Friedrich**).

Urey, Harold Clayton (1893–1981)

American physical chemist and Nobel laureate (1934) who, along with Stanley **Miller,** carried out research into the possible makeup of Earth's primeval atmosphere and **prebiotic evolution.** During the birth of the Space Age in the 1950s, he was a major proponent of solar system exploration and the search for extraterrestrial life, becoming involved with the Apollo and *Viking* missions. He also investigated organic matter in meteorites.[597]

47 Ursae Majoris

One of the first Sun-like stars to be confirmed as having a planet. This companion was the first planet found orbiting another star to fall into the category of a **classical Jovian**—that is, one

Moon	Distance from Uranus (km)	Orbital Period (days)	Orbital Eccentricity	Orbital Inclination (degrees)	Diameter (km)
Cordelia	49,200	0.335	0.140	0.00	26
Ophelia	53,300	0.376	0.001	0.09	32
Bianca	59,100	0.435	0.001	0.16	44
Cressida	61,800	0.464	0.000	0.04	66
Desdemona	62,800	0.474	0.000	0.16	58
Juliet	64,400	0.493	0.001	0.06	84
Portia	66,100	0.513	0.000	0.09	110
Rosalind	70,000	0.558	0.000	0.28	54
Belinda	75,100	0.624	0.000	0.03	68
S/1986U10	76,200	0.638	—	—	~40
Puck	85,900	0.762	0.000	0.31	154
Miranda	130,500	1.413	0.003	4.22	472
Ariel	191,800	2.520	0.003	0.31	1,158
Umbriel	267,200	4.144	0.005	0.36	1,170
Titania	438,400	8.706	0.002	0.14	1,578
Oberon	586,300	13.463	0.001	0.10	1,523
Caliban	7,165,000	579.4	0.082	139.2	~40
Sycorax	12,175,000	1284	0.509	152.7	~80

Host Star	
Distance	46.4 light-years (14.1 parsecs)
Spectral type	G I V
Apparent magnitude	5.1
Temperature	5,530°C (5,800 K)
Luminosity	1.82 L_s
Mass	1.03 M_s

Planet	
Mass	2.39 M_j
Semimajor axis	2.11 AU (316 million km, 196 million mi.)
Orbital period	1,088 days (2.98 years)
Eccentricity	0.03
Discovery	1996, by Geoffrey Marcy and R. Paul Butler, San Francisco State Planet Search
Method of discovery	Radial velocity

that roughly resembles Jupiter in both its mass and orbit. Its location around its host star is approximately the same as that of the asteroid belt in the solar system.[88] → **extrasolar planets**

U.S. Naval Observatory
First established at the aptly named Foggy Bottom on the banks of the Potomac River in Washington, D.C. It was from here, using the 26-in. Clarke refractor—the largest refracting telescope in the world at that time—that Asaph **Hall** discovered the two tiny moons of Mars, **Phobos** and **Deimos,** in 1877. The atrocious seeing conditions at the original site led to the observatory being relocated to the northwest of the capital in 1893.

Utopia Planitia
A smooth Martian plain situated northwest of the Elysium Planitia volcanoes and chosen as the landing site for *Viking* 2 in 1976.

UV Raman and fluorescence spectroscopy
Analytical methods that are exceptionally sensitive to the presence of large biological molecules and **bacteria.** Recent work has shown that under suitable conditions, it is possible by these means to detect as few as five to ten bacteria on a surface and acquire some classification information at the same time. As progress is made in these analytical approaches over the next few years, it seems likely that an instrument of small size (c. 1 to 2 liters volume, 2 kg mass, and 4 to 5 watts power consumption) may become available that could be fitted within a probe to detect life in unusual environments, both on Earth, such as Lake **Vostok,** and on other worlds, such as **Europa.** Miniature UV **laser**s and flash lamps already exist, and as their operational wavelengths reach 220 to 250 nm, the detection of fragments of **RNA** and **DNA** will become possible.

UX Orionis
The prototype of a class of pre–**main sequence** stars ("UXORs") that may eventually evolve into **Beta Pictoris**–like systems. Photometric, spectroscopic, and polarimetric studies indicate that UXORs have **circumstellar disk**s seen edge-on that may be in the protoplanetary stage.[243]

valence electron

An **electron** in one of the outer shells of an **atom** that takes part in forming chemical bonds.

Vallée, Jacques F. (1939–)

French astronautics engineer who has made a study of ancient folklore and religious belief systems in the context of twentieth-century UFO reports. He claims that contemporary accounts of UFOs and their occupants are merely a modern variant of a complex of experiences that infuse the folk memories of all cultures. A similar conclusion was reached by Carl **Jung.**[599]

van Biesbroeck 8

A nearby, low-luminosity star that appears in the catalogue of ultrafaint objects discovered by astronomer George van Biesbroeck. In 1984, independent announcements were made of the discovery of an unseen companion, van Biesbroeck 8b (VB 8b), which was suspected of being a **brown dwarf.** The claims were made by Robert Harrington of the **U.S. Naval Observatory,** based on **astrometric observations,** and by Donald McCarthy and colleagues at the University of Arizona, from a study using infrared speckle interferometry. Despite this persuasive double sighting, however, subsequent observations of greater sensitivity failed to uncover any further trace of the object. As a result, it is now generally accepted that VB 8b does not exist.

van der Kamp, Peter (1901–95)

Planetary astronomer, director of **Sproul Observatory,** and pioneer in the search for **extrasolar planets.** In 1937, using a technique brought to Sproul by Kaj **Strand,** he initiated a search for unseen companions of fifty-four stars known to lie within 16 light-years (5 parsecs) of the Sun (➔ **stars, nearest**). Over the next two decades, the Sproul group, which also included Sarah Lee **Lippincott,** reported evidence for planetary bodies around several of the target stars, including **61 Cygni,** Ross 614, and **Lalande 21185.** In 1963, van der Kamp claimed that a giant planet about eleven times the mass of Jupiter was in a 24-year orbit around **Barnard's Star,**[600] a stellar neighbor of the Sun in which he had a special interest. Over the next few years, he published further evidence for unseen companions around other nearby stars. However, doubts began to grow among fellow astronomers about the validity of his data. In particular, Robert Harrington pointed out that all of the "wobbles" supposedly caused by van der Kamp's planets were of an identical form, suggesting a systematic instrumentation effect. Undeterred, van der Kamp further analyzed his data on Barnard's Star and, in 1976, claimed he now had evidence for two companions—a 0.7-Jupiter-mass planet with a period of 12 years and a 1.2-Jupiter-mass planet with a period of 26 years, orbiting at distances of three and five times that of the Earth from the Sun, respectively. Three years earlier, he suggested that the nearby Sun-like star **Epsilon Eridani** had a planetary companion six times as massive as Jupiter. Though the planetary discoveries claimed by van der Kamp and his contemporaries at Sproul were all subsequently rejected, van der Kamp's optimism in general has been vindicated. In a 1963 article he argued that there was no reason to doubt the existence of "large numbers" of extrasolar bodies larger than Jupiter and smaller than stars. Recent confirmation of the existence of giant planets and **brown dwarf**s beyond the solar system have vindicated that view.[601, 602]

van Maanen's Star

A nearby solitary **white dwarf,** lying at a distance of 14.37 light-years (4.41 parsecs) discovered by the Dutch astronomer Adriaan van Maanen. ➔ **stars, nearest**

variable star

A star or star system the brightness of which alters measurably over time. Many different types are known. A principal distinction is between **intrinsic variable**s and **extrinsic variable**s.

Vaucouleurs, Gérard Henri de (1918–95)

French-born American astronomer whose survey of bright, relatively nearby galaxies led to the discovery of the Local Supercluster. In his influential *Physics of the Planet Mars* (1954) he adopted a cautious position on the question of Martian life, arguing that while low forms of vegetation remained a possibility (➔ **Mars, vegetation on**), the "overwhelming majority" of terrestrial organisms would not be able to survive there. However, he pointed out that a second school of thought in the 1950s was more optimistic and emphasized the adaptability of life.

Vega

Alpha Lyrae; a nearby, bluish white **A star** that is about fifty times as luminous as the Sun. It ranks as the fifth brightest star in the sky and has the distinction of being the first star ever to be captured on a photographic plate (in 1850). At one time, Vega was the pole star, and it will be so again in about 11,500 years.

Infrared observations by the *Infrared Astronomy Satellite* in 1983 revealed that Vega, as well as some other young **main sequence** stars such as **Fomalhaut** and **Beta Pictoris,** is encircled by a swarm of dust particles that may be either a **regenerated disk** (perhaps containing embedded worlds which have not yet been detected) or material which failed to form into a planetary system. Observations carried out by Helen Walker of the Rutherford Appleton Laboratory, England, and associates, using the *Infrared Space Observatory,* have shown that the Vegan disk contains particles 200 microns across, or two hundred times larger than a typical interstellar dust grain. If planets are present, they are unlikely to harbor life. With a mass of more than 3 M_S, Vega has a life-expectancy as a main sequence star of only about 200 million years, which is probably too short to allow even primitive creatures to evolve.

A beacon in orbit around Vega was the source of the radio message picked up by the SETI team in Carl **Sagan's** novel *Contact.*[495] ➔ **stars, brightest**

Velikovsky, Immanuel (1895–1979)

Russian author of a number of books, including *Worlds in Collision,* in which he claimed that impacts and near encounters between bodies in the solar system can explain various dramatic events in human history. His theories have been effectively demolished by Carl **Sagan** and others.[223]

Venus

The second planet from the Sun and the hottest due to its dense atmosphere, predominantly of **carbon dioxide,** which traps the heat radiating from the surface. The **runaway greenhouse effect** on Venus gives rise to temperatures high enough to melt lead, while the

Distance from Sun:	
Mean	108.2 million km (67.3 million mi., 0.723 AU)
Minimum	107.4 million km (66.7 million mi., 0.718 AU)
Maximum	109.0 million km (67.7 million mi., 0.728 AU)
Equatorial diameter	12,104 km (7,523 mi.)
Equatorial diameter (Earth = 1)	0.949
Mass (Earth = 1)	0.815
Mean density	5.25 g/cm³
Escape velocity	10.36 km/s (37,296 km/h, 23,180 mi./h)
Orbital period	224.70 days
Orbital eccentricity	0.007
Orbital inclination	3.4°
Axial period	243.0 days
Axial inclination	177.3°
Number of moons	0
Atmospheric composition	96% carbon dioxide, 3.5% nitrogen
Mean surface temperature	450°C (842°F)
Surface gravity (Earth = 1)	0.903
Albedo	0.76

weight of the atmosphere results in a surface pressure ninety times greater than that of Earth (equivalent to standing on the ocean floor at a depth of about 900 m, or 3,000 ft.). Droplets of sulfuric acid also occur in the atmosphere, but there is virtually no water vapor. Earth and Venus are similar in density and chemical composition, and both have relatively young surfaces. That on Venus is no more than 300 to 500 million years old and has been shaped by volcanism, impacts, and deformation of the crust. Approximately 70 percent of the surface is covered by rolling hills, 20 percent by lowland plains, and 10 percent by highlands. Although there is no direct evidence of active volcanoes, variations of **sulfur dioxide** concentrations in the atmosphere have been taken by some researchers as an indication of volcanic activity. Some weathering takes place due to the corrosive effects of the acid rain and to gentle winds of a few kilometers per hour, which are just strong enough to carry small dust grains. No craters exist on Venus with diameters less than about 1.5 to 2 km, since meteors that would create smaller impacts burn up in the dense atmosphere. Among the largest surface features are Ishtar

Terra, an elevated, lava-filled basin bigger than the continental United States, and Aphrodite Terra, a highland region near the equator that is half the size of Africa. Giant calderas, more than 100 km (60 miles) across, tens of thousands of small shield volcanoes, and hundreds of larger volcanoes, including Maxwell Montes, which is taller than Mount Everest, dot the surface, while sinuous channels, sculpted by lava flows, extend for hundreds of kilometers. Internally, Venus is probably much like the Earth, with an iron core about 3,000 km (1,900 miles) in radius and a molten rocky mantle comprising the planet's bulk. Although Venus lacks an intrinsic magnetic field, a pseudofield is set up around the planet by its interaction with the **solar wind.**

Venus, ashen light of

A faint glow occasionally observed on the dark side of Venus. First reported by Giovanni **Riccioli** in 1643, it has been explained over the years in terms of various effects from fires lit by the inhabitants (→ **Gruithuisen, Franz von Paula**) to electrical phenomena in the upper atmosphere. While some astronomers dismiss the ashen light as nothing more than an optical illusion, there remains the possibility that it is a genuine physical effect, perhaps similar to the airglow seen in the Earth's atmosphere.

Venus, atmosphere of

That Venus is permanently enveloped in what appeared to be thick, white clouds soon became clear following the development of the telescope. By analogy with the Earth, it was generally assumed that these clouds were made of water vapor, a conclusion supported by early **spectroscopic** studies by Pietro **Secchi.** The main composition of the atmosphere remained a matter for conjecture until spectroscopic observations by Walter **Adams** and Theodore **Dunham,** in 1932, established that it was **carbon dioxide.** Speculation about the makeup of the clouds continued. In 1937, R. Wildt suggested **formaldehyde,** while in 1954 Fred Whipple and Donald **Menzel** proposed ice crystals. Today, they are known to consist primarily of sulfuric acid.

Venus, life on

The similarity in size between Venus and Earth and the presence, evident even to early telescopic observers, of a substantial atmosphere on the second planet encouraged speculation about Venusian life. Temperatures on Venus were assumed to be generally higher than those on Earth but not so high as to pose a major obstacle to habitation, as Richard **Procter,** writing in 1870, affirmed:[468]

It is clear that, merely in the greater proximity of Venus to the sun, there is little to render at least the large portion of her surface uninhabitable by such beings as exist upon our earth. This undoubtedly would render [the Sun's] heat almost unbearable in the equatorial regions of Venus, but in her temperate and subarctic regions a climate which we should find well suited to our requirements might very well exist.... I can find no reason... for denying that she may be considered the abode of creatures as far advanced in the scale of creation as any which exist upon the earth.

In 1918, the Swedish chemist and Nobel laureate Svante **Arrhenius** concluded that[25]

everything on Venus is dripping wet.... A very great part of the surface... is no doubt covered with swamps corresponding to those on the Earth in which the coal deposits were formed.... The constantly uniform climatic conditions which exist everywhere result in an entire absence of adaptation to changing exterior conditions. Only low forms of life are therefore represented, mostly no doubt, belonging to the vegetable kingdom; and the organisms are nearly of the same kind all over the planet.

This evocative portrait of a world trapped in a kind of Carboniferous time warp was the first of a number of intriguing Venusian dioramas to emerge in the first half of the twentieth century.

During the 1920s, **spectroscopic** searches were carried out to try to detect water vapor in the Venusian clouds. But to everyone's surprise, none was found. What did show up were large quantities of **carbon dioxide.** This seemed to put paid to the swamp theory, and a radically new picture emerged in which the clouds of Venus were assumed to be dust and the surface a dry, windswept desert. According to another theory the clouds were made of **formaldehyde,** prompting the comment that Venus was not only dead but pickled.

More speculation followed. In 1955, the American astronomers Frank Whipple and Donald **Menzel**[624] argued that the Venusian atmosphere might be rich in ice crystals that would not show up spectroscopically. For them, Venus was a world *completely* covered by a carbonated ocean—a globe-encircling seltzer sea. Any protruding landmasses, they claimed, would have removed most of the carbon dioxide from the atmosphere and fixed it in the rocks in the form of **carbonate**s (as has happened on our own world). Encouraged by this vision of a planetwide Pacific, it became fashionable to speculate on a world inhabited by marine organisms, similar perhaps to those that existed on Earth in the Cambrian era, 500 million years ago. Isaac **Asimov** gave the aqueous theory center stage in his 1954 novel *Lucky Starr and the Oceans of Venus.*

Yet any hopes of finding even a puddle of surface water on Venus, let alone antediluvian life, quickly evaporated in the late 1950s and early 1960s. Measurements, first from radio telescopes on the ground and later from spacecraft on flyby missions, revealed that far from being balmy, the Venusian climate is hostile in the extreme. Astronomers had previously thought that much of the extra heat arriving at Venus because of its proximity to the Sun would be reflected back into space by the enveloping white clouds. But it soon became clear that this is not the case. The dense carbon dioxide atmosphere—ninety times thicker than Earth's—creates a **runaway greenhouse effect** that traps the Sun's radiation and drives the surface temperature up to around 600°C, easily hot enough to melt lead—or fry flesh. Far from being a haven for life, Venus is a planet from hell.

Verne, Jules (1828–1905)

Borne in Nantes, France, and trained in law, Verne may not have been the first science fiction writer (**Lucian of Samosata,** Mary Shelley, and Edgar Allan Poe all having prior claims to that accolade) but he was certainly the first to explore the genre systematically and to make a fortune from it. Although he must have been familiar with the enthusiasm of his Parisian contemporary Camille **Flammarion** for the possibility of life on other worlds, Verne barely touches upon the alien theme in his novels. The one minor exception is to be found in his only extraterrestrial venture, *From the Earth to the Moon* (1865) and its sequel *Around the Moon* (1870). In the latter, he exploits Hansen's hypothesis that the Moon's far side has an atmosphere, water, and, possibly, life. His astronauts glimpse "real seas, oceans, widely distributed, reflecting on their surface all the dazzling magic of the fires of space; and, lastly, on the surface of the continents, large dark masses, looking like immense forests." In other respects, his lunar novels remarkably presaged *Apollo,* even to the extent of describing a three-man crew, a Florida launch site, and a splashdown point in the Pacific just three miles from where *Apollo 11* landed. All of Verne's early novels captured the Victorian enthusiasm for science and technology, though the optimistic ideology in them may have stemmed more from the urging of Verne's publisher, the com-

mercially minded Pierre-Jules Hetzel, than from Verne himself, who seems by nature to have been a technoskeptic. ➔ **science fiction involving extraterrestrials, up to 1900**

Very Large Array (VLA)

A radio **interferometer** located near Socorro, New Mexico. It consists of twenty-seven dish **antenna**s, each 25 m (81 ft.) in diameter and weighing 230 t, spaced along a Y-shaped track with two arms 21 km (13.02 miles) long and the other 18.9 km (11.7 miles) long. It was well established that the VLA had the **resolving power** to produce radio images of circumstellar **dust disk**s, but until 1993 it had no receivers that could operate at the required wavelength. Such receivers were installed in 1993 and 1994 on thirteen of the antennae, enabling the VLA to show ten times more detail in this part of the spectrum than any previous observations.

Very Large Telescope (VLT)

A set of four connected optical telescopes, each 8 m (26.2 ft.) across, that will be equivalent to a single instrument with a mirror 16 m (52.5 ft.) in diameter. It is being built by the **European Southern Observatory** on Cerro Paranal, Chile, at an altitude of 2,600 m and is due to become operational in 2000.

vesicle

A small intracellular sac, bounded by a membrane, in which various substances are stored or transported. The term is sometimes used more generally to mean any structure surrounded by a membrane.

Viking

Twin spacecraft, *Viking 1* and *Viking 2,* launched toward Mars on August 20 and September 8, 1975. Each consisted of an orbiter and a lander (with a combined mass, less propellant, of 600 kg), the latter carrying a sophisticated package of instruments, including several experiments designed to search for traces of life in the Martian soil (➔ **Mars, life on**). After arrival in orbit around the planet on June 19 and August 7, 1976 (*Viking 1* having departed second but arrived first), a detailed reconnaissance was carried out to identify suitable and safe landing sites, during which the United States celebrated its bicentennial. On July 20, the *Viking 1*'s lander touched down in the western part of **Chryse Planitia,** at latitude 22.4° N and longitude 47.5° W, followed, on September 3, by its sister craft 7,420 km to the northeast, in **Utopia Planitia,** at latitude 48° N and longitude 226° W.

The *Viking* project, managed by the NASA Langley Research Center, was the first space mission to have as one of its primary goals the attempt to find extraterrestrial life. Although initiated in 1968, its origins actually extended back to the late 1950s, when the newly formed NASA set up a Bioscience Advisory Committee and then, in 1960, the **NASA Office of Life Sciences.** The latter authorized the **Jet Propulsion Laboratory** to study the type of spacecraft needed to land on Mars and conduct a search for life. To **NASA Ames Research Center** fell the task of evaluating early proposals for life detection equipment. In the end, diverse opinions about the possible nature of Martian life

led to the **Space Science Board** selecting and recommending a package of three experiments that would test for life using different philosophies and methodologies (→ *Viking* **gas exchange (GEX) experiment;** *Viking* **labeled release (LR) experiment;** *Viking* **pyrolytic release (PR) experiment**) and thereby cast an investigative net widely. A fourth experiment, the *Viking* **gas chromatograph–mass spectrometer** (GCMS), was included to look for the presence of organic (not necessarily biogenic) material.

Preliminary tests on the first soil sample, collected by *Viking 1* on July 28, 1976, immediately brought surprises. Gas was given off following the introduction of nutrient in the LR experiment, before the reaction tapered off—exactly the outcome expected if microorganisms had been present in the soil. The PR experiment also gave a positive result that was compatible with metabolic activity in the sample. In the case of the GEX experiment, both carbon dioxide *and* oxygen were evolved, the

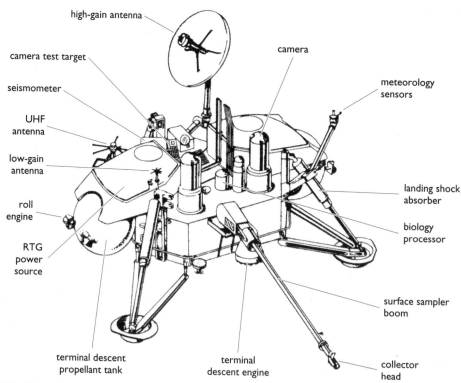

The *Viking* lander.

latter being a reaction never before seen in tests on either terrestrial or lunar soils. The speed and course of the reaction, however, suggested that it might be due to an **oxidizing** chemical rather than a biological process. On the face of it, then, two of the three biology experiments gave indications of life. But the results of the first GCMS tests were curiously negative. *No* organics were detected in the Martian soil to the level of a few parts in a billion, prompting Viking project scientist Gerald A. Soffen to comment, "All the signs suggest that life exists on Mars, but we can't find any bodies!"

Ten weeks later, following more tests at both landing sites, researchers were still undecided about what their results meant. Soffen summed up the general feeling:[554]

> The tests revealed a surprisingly chemically active surface—very like oxidizing. All experiments yielded results, but these are subject to wide interpretation. No conclusions were reached concerning the existence of life on Mars.

At the end of 8½ months of investigations on the Martian surface, including twenty-six biology experiments, the jury was still out—and remains so to this day. The most widely held opinion is that some highly oxidizing chemical, such as **hydrogen peroxide,** was responsible for the activity registered by the biological experiments. A cogent theory based on this idea has been put forward by Vance **Oyama** but has yet to be confirmed either by laboratory simulations or further *in situ* tests. On the other hand, a small minority of researchers, most notably Gilbert **Levin,** continue to argue that the Viking data are better explained in biological terms. Intense investigation of the Red Planet over the next decade seems likely to settle this issue once and for all.[56, 129, 187, 555] → **Mars, life on**

Viking gas chromatograph–mass spectrometer (GCMS)

A device capable of detecting even minute concentrations of **organic** compounds in the Martian soil. The GCMS baked a small soil sample in an oven to drive off any volatile gases present, separated those volatiles using a gas chromatograph, and analyzed their composition with a mass spectrometer. It provided a way of resolving any ambiguities that might arise from the three biology experiments. In particular, the failure of the GCMS to detect organics would strongly suggest an absence of life whatever were the indications from one or more of the biology tests. On the other hand, the detected presence of organics would not, by itself, constitute evidence for biological activity, since many organic compounds (such as those found in meteorites) are **abiotic.** Responsibility for GCMS was with a molecular analysis team, separate from the three biology teams, headed by Klaus Biemann of the Massachusetts Institute of Technology.

Viking gas exchange (GEX) experiment

Developed by Vance **Oyama** at **NASA Ames Research Center** and designed to test for life under two different conditions.[440] In the first mode, it was assumed that organisms that had been dormant for a very long time under dry conditions on Mars would be revived and stimulated back into metabolic activity by the addition of moisture alone. The effect of any subsequent Martian life processes would be to alter the composition of the gases (such as carbon dioxide, nitrogen, and methane) above the sample in a way that would be measurable by the onboard gas chromatograph. During a 10-day incubation period, the gas composition was determined five times. In the second, wet-nutrient (or "chicken soup") mode, a rich organic broth (containing nineteen amino acids,

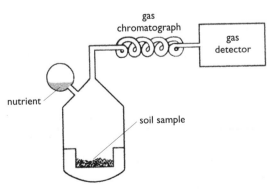

Tobias Owen

vitamins, a number of other organic compounds, and a few inorganic salts) was "fed" to the sample as a further encouragement to induce metabolism. Again, a change in the gas mixture might indicate that some kind of organism was stirring into life.[441]

Viking labeled release (LR) experiment

Also known as "Gulliver";[341] developed by Gilbert **Levin** and designed to detect **carbon dioxide** released by microorganisms as a result of their metabolic activity.[339] On Earth, this would be classed as a respiration experiment. A sample of soil was placed inside a culture chamber and a broth of seven organic nutrients (formate, glycolate, **glycine**, D-alanine, L-alanine, D-lactate, and L-lactate), labeled with radioactive carbon 14, was allowed to drip onto it. If microbes were present in the sample, it was assumed they would metabolize the organic compounds in the nutrient and release radioactive carbon dioxide which would be trapped on a chemically coated film at the window of a Geiger counter. The LR experiment had the virtue of being able to detect growth, as well as metabolism, since the rate of carbon dioxide production would increase exponentially with a growing culture. Like the *Viking* **gas exchange (GEX) experiment,** however, it assumed that Martian microbes would be (1) activated by liquid water (which might not be true since any organisms on Mars might have adapted to a completely waterless environment), and (2) able to metabolize the same organic nutrients as terrestrial organisms (whereas, in fact, such Earthly foodstuffs might

be toxic to life based on a different biochemistry). These drawbacks were avoided by the *Viking* **pyrolytic release (PR) experiment.**[342]

Viking pyrolytic release (PR) experiment

Headed by Norman **Horowitz** and also known as the "carbon assimilation" experiment.[282] Of the three *Viking* biology experiments, this was the only one to attempt to detect signs of life in the complete absence of water and organic nutrients. It was assumed that any organisms on Mars would have developed the ability to assimilate **carbon dioxide** and **carbon monoxide** from the atmosphere and convert these, in the absence of water, to organic matter. Therefore, the PR experiment exposed a small sample of Martian soil to quantities of these two gases, which had been labeled with radioactive carbon 14 for detection purposes. After 120 hours of incubation under an artificial sun (a xenon arc lamp), the soil chamber was heated to about 625°C to break down (pyrolize) any organic matter and release the volatile organic products for subsequent testing by a radiation counter. Since any organisms present would be expected to carry out metabolic processes during which they would take in carbon 14 from the gas in the chamber, detection of carbon 14 would be a positive result. It would not, however, be conclusively biological, since a first peak of radioactivity might equally be due to purely chemical processes. In order to rule out this possibility, other samples, serving as controls, were sterilized by heating before the carbon source was admitted.

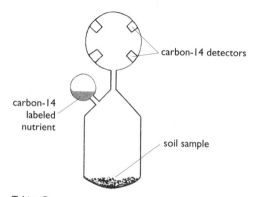

carbon-14 detectors

carbon-14 labeled nutrient

soil sample

Tobias Owen

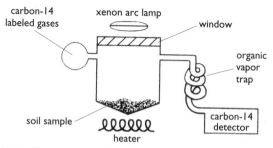

carbon-14 labeled gases

xenon arc lamp

window

organic vapor trap

soil sample

heater

carbon-14 detector

Tobias Owen

Viking sampler arm

A device used to acquire specimens of soil from the Martian surface for use in the chemical and biological investigations carried out by the *Viking* landers. The sampler could also dig trenches (which, as the lunar *Surveyor* spacecraft had shown, was a valuable way of learning about the surface) and provide other data about the physical properties of the surface materials using a temperature sensor, brush, and magnets. It consisted of a head attached to the end of a 3-m retractable boom.

VIM
→ *Voyager* **Interstellar Mission**

70 Virginis
A Sun-like star around which has been found a high-mass planet in a very eccentric orbit. The companion of 70 Virginis is the prototype for the **eccentric Jovian** class of **extrasolar planets.** Although this world may lie within the **habitable zone** of its host star—earning it the nickname "Goldilocks," since its orbital distance is "just right"—two other factors argue against the possibility of it harboring life. First, the planet moves in such a stretched-out orbit that it must experience severe seasonal variations in climate. Second, being so massive, it almost certainly has an immense, crushing atmosphere. It appears to be similar in nature to the companion of **HD 114762**.[374]

Host Star	
Distance	59.0 light-years (18.1 parsecs)
Spectral type	G4 V
Apparent	
magnitude	5.0
Temperature	5,230°C (5,500 K)
Luminosity	2.86 L_S
Mass	1.10 M_S
Planet	
Mass	6.6 M_J
Semimajor axis	0.43 AU (9.0 million km, 5.6 million mi.)
Orbital period	116.6 days
Eccentricity	0.40
Discovery	January 1996, by Geoffrey Marcy, and R. Paul Butler, San Francisco State Planet Search
Method of discovery	Radial velocity

virus
A disease-causing entity on the borderline between life and nonlife. Viruses are capable of reproducing only within a living host **cell.** They effectively reprogram the cells they invade, turning the cellular machinery into a biological factory for manufacturing fresh copies of themselves. The simplest viruses consist of a single helical strand of **RNA** coated with **protein** molecules. Other viruses are more complex and may have a diameter of up to 0.2 micron.

Conceivably, complex combinations of molecules could exist on other worlds which, although not living organisms in any familiar sense, could behave like viruses given a suitable host. This would present a threat to humans and other terrestrial life-forms, which would have no immunity to such alien infection. It was the reason that elaborate quarantine precautions were planned for the return of the first astronauts from the Moon. Even more care will be required when people first come into contact with Martian rocks and soil (→ **back contamination**).

The possibility that terrestrial viruses could mutate into dangerous, "alien" forms if subjected to highly **ionizing radiation,** such as that present above the protective blanket of the Earth's atmosphere, was exploited by Michael Crichton in *The Andromeda Strain.*

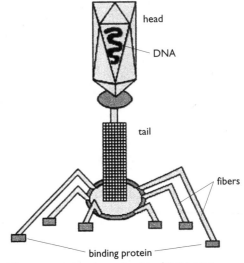

The general structure of a virus known as a bacteriophage.

viruses, from space
→ **epidemics, from space**

Vishniac, Wolf

Professor of biology at the University of Rochester and attendee at the **EASTEX** meetings in 1958, who received a NASA grant to develop a prototype system for detecting life on other planets. His "Wolf Trap" was designed to introduce a nutrient broth into a test chamber containing a sample of soil or dust. The presence of microscopic life could be detected by observing either an increased cloudiness of the broth or changes in its acidity.

visible light

Electromagnetic radiation that can be detected by the human eye. It extends from a wavelength of about 780 nm (red light) to one of 380 nm (violet light) and bridges the divide between **infrared** and **ultraviolet.**

vitalism

The now-discredited hypothesis that only living tissue, by virtue of possessing some "life force," can produce **organic** compounds. Among its greatest advocates was Jöns **Berzelius** and, more recently, Henri **Bergson.** Although Friedrich **Wöhler**'s synthesis of urea posed a serious empirical challenge to this point of view, it was only with the production of an organic substance, acetic acid, from its **element**s by the German chemist Adolph Wilhelm Hermann Kolbe in 1845 that belief in vitalism was finally undermined.

VLA
→ **Very Large Array**

VLT
→ **Very Large Telescope**

volatile

A substance that is gaseous at normal Earth temperatures.

Voltaire (1694–1778)

Great French poet, philosopher, and dramatist (originally François-Marie Arouet) who was an outspoken critic of political and religious intolerance. In his satirical novel *Micromégas,* he shrugged off the religious dogma of his time and speculated freely and humorously on the subject of extraterrestrial life.

von Neumann probes

Named after the Hungarian-born American mathematician John von Neumann, who, among many other achievements, developed a theory of machines that can make exact copies of themselves. Attention was first focused on the potential advantages of using self-replicating robot spacecraft for galactic exploration by Frank **Tipler** in 1975. He envisaged the following scenario: Initially, a von Neumann probe, consisting of an interstellar propulsion system and a universal von Neumann replicator with human-level intelligence, would be launched from the home star toward a neighboring stellar system. Upon arrival it would seek out raw materials from local sources such as **asteroid**s and use these to make several copies of itself (including its rocket engines). The copies would then be launched at the next set of neighboring stars. This process would be repeated over and over again, so that increasing numbers of identical probes would be involved in penetrating ever more remote regions of the Galaxy. Having dispatched copies of itself, a probe would begin to explore the star system in which it found itself. It would conduct scientific research and transmit the results back to the point of origin. It could also be used as a means of colonization by constructing an artificial life-sustaining environment and then implanting this with synthesized fertile egg cells bearing **genome**s transcribed from the probe's computer memory. Loren **Eiseley** has suggested that the embryonic individuals of such a colony could be tended by robots, also built by the probe, until they were old enough to function independently. They would then be free to develop their own civilization around the host star. As Tipler has pointed out, a great advantage of a von Neumann probe is that, being a universal machine, it can be used for *any* purpose at its target system depending on the instructions sent out to it from its ultimate creators. Consequently, as the creators made technological advances at home they could reprogram a remote von Neumann probe, for example, to build faster rocket engines for the next generation of probes or more sensitive sensing equipment with which to study its host stellar system. How rapidly the Galaxy could be completely explored and colonized in this way depends on several factors, including the interstellar transit times of the probes (➔ **interstellar travel**), the speed at which they reproduce and carry out other tasks within the host systems, and the specific strategy used for **interstellar colonization.** Tipler proposes a conservative value of 300 million years, or less than 5 percent of the present age of the Galaxy, for complete galactic colonization. He considers the von Neumann probe approach to be so logical and economical that it would be commonly adopted by advanced civilizations. According to this view, there should be a significant and obvious presence of such devices within the solar system. Yet, no such presence has been detected. Tipler therefore draws the conclusion that we are the *only* intelligent race among the Galaxy's several hundred billion stars (➔ **Tipler's Argument**). The validity of this conclusion has been questioned by, among others, Carl **Sagan** and William Newman (➔ **Sagan's Response**).

The idea of using automatically exponentiating systems has been investigated for extraterrestrial mining by Georg von Tiesenhausen and Wesley A. Darbro at NASA's Marshall Spaceflight Center.[608] ➔ **Bracewell probes**

Vorilong, William (d. 1463)

French theologian who examined the idea of extraterrestrial life in the light of Christian beliefs about a divine **incarnation and redemption.** He concluded that although God *could* create another inhabited world, he would not in fact do so:

> If it be inquired whether men exist on that [other] world, and whether they have sinned as Adam sinned, I answer no, for they would not exist in sin and did not spring from Adam.... As to the question whether Christ by dying on this Earth could redeem the inhabitants of another world, I answer that he is able to do this even if the worlds were infinite, but it would not be fitting for Him to go unto another world that he must die again.

➔ **Nicholas of Cusa; Christian doctrine and pluralism; medieval philosophy, related to the possibility of extraterrestrial life**

Vostok, Lake

An underground Antarctic lake near the Russian Vostok Station, discovered in 1977 during an airborne radio-echo survey of ice depths over central East Antarctica. In 1993, altimetry measurements from the ERS-1 satellite verified the lake's existence and extent, confirming it to be by far the largest deep subice body of water on the planet. In 1996, Russian and British scientists combined radio sounding, altimetric, and seismic data to provide the most comprehensive picture of the lake currently available.[309]

Lake Vostok extends over about 14,000 square km (roughly the size of Lake Ontario) and is overlaid by 3,710 m (12,170 ft.) of ice. It has a maximum depth of 510 m, an average depth of 125 m, a volume of 1,800 cubic km, and a bed that is 710 m below sea level. It may be 500,000 to 1 million years old and, based on density measurements, is composed of fresh water.

Researchers hope that, aside from its intrinsic interest, Lake Vostok will serve as a natural terrestrial laboratory to help understand the conditions that may exist in the putative subsurface oceans on Jupiter's moons **Europa** and **Callisto.** In particular, NASA has identified four objectives in its Europa Vostok Initiative. These are to investigate the nature and origin of the lake, obtain evidence of long-term climatic change associated with it, identify a site suitable for *in situ* microbiological exploration, and validate the design of planetary radar sounders for exploration of Europa. A first step toward developing instrumentation for exploring Lake Vostok was taken in 1998 with the deployment of the **Lo'ihi Underwater Volcanic Vent Mission Probe.**

Of primary concern is that any vehicle and instrumentation introduced into Lake Vostok be scrupulously clean of biological material to avoid contaminating any indigenous life (➔ **forward contamination**). Among the instruments and measurement methods that may be used on the first entry probe into the lake are **redox sensors** and **UV Raman and fluorescence spectroscopy.**

At the time of writing, the lake remains un-penetrated, although 400,000-year-old deep ice samples have been obtained from just 100 m above its liquid surface. Within these samples, Richard Hoover of NASA's Marshall Space Sciences Laboratory and S. S. Abyzov of the Russian Academy of Sciences found a variety of microbial life-forms, some of them read-ily recognizable (including cyanobacteria, bacteria, fungi, spores, pollen grains, and diatoms) but others unlike anything ever seen before.[566]

Voyager I

Launched on September 5, 1977, flew past Jupiter (March 5, 1979) and Saturn (Novem-

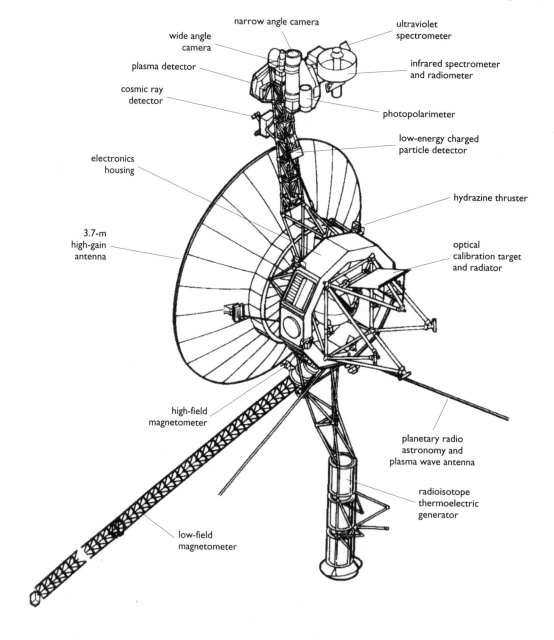

narrow angle camera

wide angle camera

plasma detector

cosmic ray detector

ultraviolet spectrometer

infrared spectrometer and radiometer

photopolarimeter

low-energy charged particle detector

electronics housing

hydrazine thruster

3.7-m high-gain antenna

optical calibration target and radiator

high-field magnetometer

planetary radio astronomy and plasma wave antenna

radioisotope thermoelectric generator

low-field magnetometer

ber 12, 1980). It is now one of four probes, including **Pioneer 10, Pioneer 11,** and **Voyager 2,** that are heading out of the solar system. *Voyager 1* became the most remote human-made object when, in mid-1998, it surpassed the heliocentric distance of *Pioneer 10*. In January 2000, *Voyager 1* was 74.7 AU (11.2 billion km, 7.0 billion miles) from the Sun, equivalent to a round-trip light-travel time of just over 20.8 hours. It is traveling at a speed of 17.3 km per second (38,711 miles per hour) away from the Sun in the general direction of the solar apex (the direction of the Sun's motion relative to nearby stars), so that it will probably be the first of the four present star-bound craft to reach the **heliopause** and enter true interstellar space. Thereafter, it will have a journey lasting almost 40,000 years before it passes the M4 dwarf AC +79° 3888 at the remote distance of 1.64 light-years (0.5 parsecs). Together with its sister craft, *Voyager 1* is currently engaged on the **Voyager** Interstellar **Mission.** → *Voyager interstellar record; interstellar probes*

Voyager 2

Launched on August 20, 1977, flew past Jupiter (July 9, 1979) and Saturn (August 25, 1981), and became the first spacecraft to encounter Uranus (January 24, 1986) and Neptune (August 24, 1989). In January 2000, *Voyager 2* was 8.8 million km (5.5 million miles) from the Sun, equivalent to a round-trip light-travel time of just over 16 hours. Its departure speed from the solar system is 15.9 km per second (35,453 miles per hour). The future trajectory of *Voyager 2* among the stars was determined by its final planetary encounter, with Neptune. An earlier planned route past Neptune would have resulted in the probe coming within 0.8 light-years of **Sirius** in just under 500,000 years from now—easily the closest and most interesting foreseeable stellar encounter of the four escaping probes. However, the Neptune flyby trajectory actually chosen (the "polar crown" trajectory) means that the nearest *Voyager 2* will come to any star in the next million years is 1.65 light-years, when it will pass Ross 248 in about 40,000 years. Like *Voyager 1*, it is now

involved in the **Voyager** Interstellar Mission. → *Voyager interstellar record; interstellar probes*

Voyager Interstellar Mission (VIM)

An extension of the *Voyager* primary mission following the flyby of Neptune by **Voyager 2** in 1989. The objective of the VIM is to extend NASA's exploration of the solar system beyond the neighborhood of the outer planets to the limits of the **heliosphere** and possibly beyond. Data received from the two *Voyagers* (and **Pioneer 10**) into the first decade or two of the twenty-first century will be used to characterize the outer solar system environment and search for the **heliopause** boundary, where the **solar wind** meets the **interstellar medium.** Penetration of the heliopause by either or both spacecraft, while still active, would allow the first-ever measurements to be made of the interstellar fields and particles. At the start of the VIM, the two *Voyagers* had been in flight for more than 12 years. *Voyager 1* was at a distance of approximately 40 AU (6 billion km, 3.7 billion miles), and *Voyager 2* at a distance of ap-

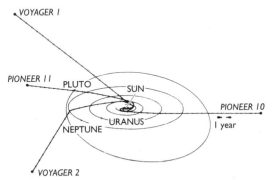

The trajectories and locations (in 2000) of the four probes currently leaving the solar system.
Originally presented at the 1983 AAS/AIA Astrodynamics Conference held from August 22 to 25, 1983, Lake Placid, New York, and originally published in the AAS publication *Astrodynamics 1983*, American Astronautical Society (AAS), AAS Microfiche Series, vol. 45, paper no. AAS 83-308, "Prospects for *Voyager* Extra-Planetary and Interstellar Mission" by Robert J. Cesarone, Andrey B. Sergeyevsky, and Stuart J. Kerridge (JPL). Reprinted with permission of the AAS: American Astronautical Society Publications Office, P. O. Box 28130, San Diego, CA 92198.

proximately 31 AU (4.7 billion km, 2.9 billion miles).[104] ➔ **interstellar probes**

Voyager interstellar record

A gold-coated phonograph record containing, in audio-encoded form, 117 pictures explaining our planet and ourselves; greetings in fifty-four different human languages and "songs" of the **humpback whales;** a representative selection of sounds, from an elephant's trumpet to a rocket launching; and almost ninety minutes of some of the world's greatest music. Copies of the record were attached to the side of *Voyager 1* and *Voyager 2* in the event of these craft being intercepted at some point in the remote future by an extraterrestrial intelligence. Among those involved in the preparation of the disk were Frank **Drake,** Carl **Sagan,** and Bernard **Oliver.**[498]

Vogt, Steven S. (1949–)

Professor of astronomy and astrophysics at the University of California, Santa Cruz, who has been involved with the discovery of many of the first **extrasolar planets** to be found. Essential to these breakthroughs have been the Hamilton Spectrometer at the **Lick Observatory** and the **High Resolution Échelle Spectrometer (HIRES)** at the **Keck Observatory,** both of which Vogt designed and built. His first Ph.D. student, in the early 1980s, was another extrasolar planet pioneer, Geoffrey **Marcy.**

Vulcan

A hypothetical intra-Mercurian planet,[44] the existence of which was proposed by the nineteenth-century French mathematician Urbain Le Ferrier to explain anomalies in Mercury's orbit (now accounted for by the general theory of relativity). Alleged sightings of Vulcan in 1859 inspired many astronomers to look for it during the total solar eclipse of 1860. Nothing was found. In recent years, however, a number of **extrasolar planets** have been discovered with orbits much smaller than that of Mercury. These so-called **epistellar Jovians,** also known as 51-Pegasi-type planets or "hot Jupiters," have forced scientists to reconsider their models of planetary system formation.

Vulcan Camera Project

An effort, supported by **NASA Ames Research Center,** to detect large **extrasolar planets** by **photometry.** The Vulcan photometer employs a 4-in.-aperture telescope and **charge-coupled device** imager for demonstrating the feasibility of this technique. Specific objectives are to determine the frequency of Jupiter- and Saturn-sized planets in inner orbits around a variety of stellar types and to characterize those planets in terms of size, density, and **semimajor axis,** in order to try to correlate the nature of the planets found with the **spectral type** of their host stars. If the project is successful it will provide impetus to the space-based *Kepler* **Mission.**

W

W. M. Keck Observatory
→ **Keck Observatory**

W star
→ **Wolf-Rayet star**

Wald, George (1906–)
Harvard biologist and Nobel laureate (1967) who, while allowing that life in the Universe was probably common, argued strongly against any attempt to establish contact with an extraterrestrial race. At a 1972 symposium, "Life Beyond Earth and the Mind of Man," sponsored jointly by NASA and Boston University, he said that he could "conceive of no nightmare as terrifying as establishing such communication with a so-called superior (or if you wish, advanced) technology in outer space." His fear was that human enterprise in arts, sciences, and other fields would come to an end once our race became "attached as by an umbilical cord to that 'thing out there.'" → **extraterrestrial intelligence, implications following first contact**

Wallace, Alfred Russel (1823–1913)
Cofounder with Charles **Darwin** of the theory of evolution by **natural selection** and the first great biologist to consider in depth the possibility of extraterrestrial life. Wallace differed from Darwin in that he regarded mankind as more than just the product of evolution and "that some higher intelligence may have directed the process by which the human race was developed." In his influential work *Man's Place in the Universe: A Study of the Results of Scientific Research in Relation to the Unity or Plurality of Worlds* (1903), Wallace presented a view of the Milky Way system that was coextensive with the Universe and at the center of which lay the Sun. By a series of arguments based on this anthropocentric scheme, he deduced that the Earth and its inhabitants were unique. Even at the time, his conclusions were greeted with skepticism. Fifteen years later, with the discoveries that the Sun lay in the outskirts of the Milky Way rather than at its heart and that our galaxy is but one of many, most of Wallace's central assumptions were shown to be false.

War of the Worlds, The, novel
Science fiction tale by H. G. **Wells** that is one of his darkest evolutionary visions and was to have a powerful effect on public conceptions of alien life.[621] It was originally serialized in *Pearson's Magazine*, from April to December 1897, before being published as a book in 1898. The title of the opening section, "The Coming of the Martians," the title of the opening chapter,

"The Eve of War," and the very first sentence foreshadow the horror that is about to descend:

> No one would have believed, in the last years of the nineteenth century, that human affairs were being watched keenly and closely by intelligences greater than man's.

Cleverly, Wells weaves scientific fact into his tale so that the reader is left wondering where the real world ends and glimpses of another possible truth begin. Some familiar names make their appearance:

> Men like Schiaparelli watched the red planet—it is odd, by the by, that for countless centuries Mars has been the star of war—but failed to interpret the fluctuating appearances of the markings they mapped so well. All the time the Martians must have been getting ready. During the opposition of 1894 a great light was seen on the illuminated part of the disc, first at the Lick Observatory, then by Perrotin of Nice....I am inclined to think that the appearance may have been the casting of the huge gun [a borrowing from Verne]...from which their shots were fired at us.

Swept aside here is the heroic, isolated, near-human race of Percival **Lowell.** In its place is a truly alien species with an intellect "vast and cool and unsympathetic." As for the anatomy of this otherworldly creature, Wells had already warned in an earlier article to expect a nasty shock. Now the thing was revealed:

> A big, greyish rounded bulk, the size, perhaps of a bear, was rising slowly and painfully out of the cylinder. As it bulged up and caught the light, it glistened like wet leather. Two large dark-coloured eyes were regarding me steadfastly. The mass that framed them, the head of the thing, it was rounded, and had, one might say, a face. There was a mouth under the eyes, the lipless brim of which quivered and panted, and dropped saliva. The whole creature heaved and pulsated convulsively. A lank tentacular appendage gripped the edge of the cylinder, another swayed in the air.

With his appreciation of how living things were shaped and selected by their circumstances, Wells realized that where life arose on other planets it would develop to suit the local conditions, such as gravitational pull and atmospheric makeup. Therefore it would not be easy for a creature that had evolved in one place to adjust to the environment elsewhere:

> Those who have never seen a living Martian can scarcely imagine the strange horror of their appearance. The peculiar V-shaped mouth with its pointed upper lip, the absence of brow ridges, the absence of a chin beneath the wedge-like lower lip, the incessant quivering of this mouth, the Gorgon groups of tentacles, the tumultuous breathing of the lungs in a strange atmosphere, the evident heaviness and painfulness of movement, due to the greater gravitational energy of the earth—above all, the extraordinary intensity of the immense eyes—culminated in an effect akin to nausea. There was something fungoid in the oily brown skin.... Even at this first encounter, this first glimpse, I was overcome with disgust and dread.

Thus was spawned the nightmare of the pulsating brain, of the malicious anatomy—the alien from hell—and the nightmare, too, that might follow were it to transpire that humankind was far from being near the pinnacle of cerebral development. Elsewhere in space, there could be, as Wells put it, species with "minds that are to our minds as ours are to the beasts that perish." And what if those minds meant us no good? How could we possibly stand against them? This is the fear that Wells so skillfully implanted: an alien race, alien in appearance and with an intelligence and technology frighteningly superior to our own. Wells had not had to look far for a precedent for his usurping aliens. In the final decades of the nineteenth century, "technologically advanced" European powers such as Britain and France had been busily carving up Africa, invading territories at will and trampling on the rights of the indigenous folk whom, in true imperialist style, they considered culturally and intellectually inferior to themselves. As Wells asks in the prelude to the Martian mayhem, "Are we such apostles of mercy as to complain if the Martians warred in the same spirit?"

Partly this urge to grab new resources and strategic land around the world was a response to instabilities within Europe itself. Thus Wells was able to touch another raw nerve. Throughout the latter part of the nineteenth century, the continent was in a perpetual state of tension, its major powers playing a dangerous game of shifting alliances and rivalries. War never seemed more than a careless gunshot away. It might even come from the air, given that gas balloons had been used by the Germans during the Siege of Paris in 1870. So just as Lowell's concept of a worldwide canal network and giant pumping stations had seemed all the more credible (and had been conceived) against a backdrop of rapid engineering and industrial progress, it was to a public all too familiar with news of international unrest and threats of invasion that Wells directed his menacing tale.

Until *The War of the Worlds,* stories of visitors to Earth had generally portrayed the outsiders as gentle peace-lovers, interested only in watching us, perhaps with mild amusement or concern (➔ *Micromégas*). But in Wells's novel, the extraterrestrials are suddenly painted in an altogether different light: as a terrifying threat, capable of bringing merciless death and destruction. No human weapon could stand against them, any more than a spear or shield could provide protection against a gun. Wells showed how pathetically helpless we would be if a malignant alien race, centuries ahead of us, *did* decide to attack the Earth. In doing so he caused something to stir that had been buried deep within our animal subconscious—the naked fear of the prey when confronted by the irresistible predator. To Technological Man the effect of this sudden exposure to a long-suppressed dread was devastating. Humankind had begun to imagine that it was secure in its role as master of the planet. But Wells revealed how feeble our tenure might be should superior beings from elsewhere choose to come and wrest control of the Earth away from us.

Speculation about the Martian canals and their creators had titillated public interest. But the idea of invasion from space had an altogether more serious and long-lasting effect. It

Martian tripods move toward Windsor Castle.

buried itself like a barbed sting beneath the surface of popular culture, so that it would be felt in future whenever there came a hint of the possibility of alien incursion. ➔ *War of the Worlds, The,* **radio play; saucer flap of 1947**

War of the Worlds, The, radio play

Broadcast across the United States on October 30, 1938, this production revealed the extent to which the fear of hostile aliens had become entrenched in the public mind. For several months, the CBS radio network had been staging plays by Orson Welles, John Houseman, and their *Mercury Theatre of the Air.* Now it was Halloween, time for something a little special and scary: an updated version of H. G. **Wells**'s classic, scripted by Howard Koch (who later cowrote the screenplay for *Casablanca*).

At 8:00 P.M. Eastern Standard Time, the production began, innocently enough, with a weather forecast that commented on slightly unusual happenings for the time of year. Then the smooth-talking announcer led into an outside broadcast from a New York hotel, where Raymond Raquello and his orchestra were playing ballroom dance music. The bandleader introduced the tune, but abruptly the sound faded. A studio announcer broke in, apologized for the interruption, and read a news flash about explosions on Mars seen from observatories at Mount Jennings and Princeton. More snatches of music followed, punctuated by increasingly alarming news reports. The Government Meteorological Bureau requested that all observatories across the nation train their instruments on Mars. A meteorite, subsequently described as a "huge, flaming object" had landed on a farm at Grovers Mill, New Jersey, not far away. The station's reporter, Carl Phillips, was on his way there with a mobile crew.

Relentlessly, the tension grew. Amid the hubbub of an excited crowd, Phillips spoke in turn to a semicoherent eyewitness and to an expert, interviewed earlier in his observatory but now clearly shaken by the turn of events, a Professor Richard Pearson (played by Welles). And then the meteorite, now revealed to be an alien spacecraft, opened. Phillips described the frenzied scene, the monster crawling out, the pointing by it of some kind of device at the radio crew and . . . silence. The similarity in tone with that of the commentary on the *Hindenburg* airship disaster, a year earlier, was striking—and entirely uncoincidental: Welles and his company had thoroughly studied the unforgettable recording of that event. "Due to circumstances beyond our control . . . ," a studio voice cut in, followed by piano music, interspersed with more confused and totally credible reporting. An official statement from

New York Times report on the aftermath of Welles's broadcast.

Washington referred to the "gravity of the situation." Seven thousand soldiers had surrounded the object. Most had been killed. Washington warned that New Jersey was seeing "the vanguard of an invasion from Mars."

Many listeners tuning in late hadn't heard Welles introduce the play for what it was and took the events to be real. Thousands of families in New York and New Jersey fled their homes, freeways were jammed, people called each other on the phone to wish fond farewells, one distraught individual tried to commit suicide, and groups gathered in New England, Harlem, and the Deep South to pray for divine intervention. There were miscarriages, heart attacks, lootings, and brawls. In New Jersey, the National Guard was called out. The CBS switchboard was jammed with callers, some frantic with fear, others bravely volunteering to help repel the alien onslaught. Even weeks later, Red Cross volunteers were trying to persuade families who had fled to the mountains that it was safe to return home. According to research based on interviews begun by Princeton University in the week following the broadcast, well over 1 million listeners, or more than one in ten of the audience, had been actively frightened by what they heard.[98]

In the aftermath, CBS publicly apologized, Welles (saved from a sacking and police prosecution only by the skin of his contract) vowed it would never happen again, and the Federal Communications Commission passed rules to ensure that it never could. But legislating against human nature is not so simple. The panic triggered by Welles's superb performance graphically exposed the ease with which large numbers of people can be misled and driven over the edge into mass hysteria. With hindsight, it seems obvious that events could not have unfolded in real life with the speed depicted in the play. One moment there are explosions on Mars, a few minutes later a spacecraft has arrived on earth, and a few minutes later still a large contingent of troops is at the scene. It is hard to imagine listeners being so utterly convinced that it was live action. But when people have been conditioned to believe that something is possible, and when, in addition, they *want* to believe in the extraordinary,

surprisingly little is needed to evoke a spectacular response. Nine years after the Halloween scare, the Martians would be back—with a vengeance (➔ **saucer flap of 1947**). ➔ *War of the Worlds, The,* **novel**

"Washington Invasion"

A series of incidents in the latter part of July 1952, centered on Washington, D.C., that came at the peak of a major flying saucer flap that year. Events began in the early hours of July 20, when two radar stations covering the capital picked up eight UFOs in restricted airspace, flying at a few hundred km per hour and suddenly accelerating to a tremendous speed. A number of military and civilian pilots reported seeing strange lights in the sky around the same time. On the night of July 26–27, more strange lights and radar contacts were logged. Interceptor planes from Wilmington, Delaware, were scrambled. One pilot, Lieutenant William Patterson, reported himself surrounded by a ring of great blue-white lights, which disappeared before he was given permission to fire on them. In its investigation of the incidents, the Civil Aviation Authority's Technical Development and Evaluation Center concluded that the radar images had been the result of temperature inversions that could cause radar signals to be reflected back to the ground. Excitement caused by the radar anomalies could have led to misidentification of ordinary bright sources of light as mysterious aerial objects.

WASP
➔ **Arizona Search for Planets**

water (H₂O)

A colorless liquid at room temperature, each molecule of which consists of an **oxygen** atom and two **hydrogen** atoms joined by **covalent bond**s. Terrestrial organisms are composed primarily of water (about 65 percent in the case of humans), and water is essential for life as we know it. Most biologically significant chemical reactions take place in an aqueous environment and have done so on Earth for the past 4 billion years. Indeed, according to the standard theory of the chemical evolution of life (➔ **life, origin of**), water provided the medium in which **prebiotic** molecules could move around and interact without being locked in place by strong covalent or **ionic bond**s.

So familiar is water that we tend to forget how unusual a substance it really is. Of all of water's properties, the most significant is its ability to form weak chemical associations, known as **hydrogen bond**s, with about 5 to 10 percent of the strength of covalent bonds. This ability stems from the fact that water consists of **polar molecule**s, in each of which the oxygen atom has a slight negative charge and the two hydrogen atoms slight positive charges. The polarity of water causes it to be attracted to other polar molecules. When these other molecules are also water, the attraction is referred to as *cohesion;* when they are different, it is known as *adhesion*. The cohesiveness of water is what allows it to remain a liquid at moderate temperatures (whereas **hydrogen sulfide,** for example, which is chemically similar, exists as a gas). Water molecules always tend to form the maximum possible number of hydrogen bonds. When nonpolar molecules such as oils, which do not form hydrogen bonds, are placed in water, the water molecules act to exclude them. This forces the nonpolar molecules into association with one another, a tendency to aggregate known as **hydrophobic** exclusion. Hydrophobic forces arising from the polar nature of water are thought to have been of central importance in the evolution of life. First, they seem to have encouraged the formation of **protocells** and, in particular, the boundaries that enclosed them (➔ **cell membranes, origin of**). Second, their influence is evident in the fact that some of the exterior portions of many of the molecules on which life came to be based are nonpolar. By forcing the hydrophobic portions of molecules into proximity with one another, water caused such molecules to assume particular shapes.

Whereas water organizes and orchestrates the geometry of nonpolar molecules, it acts as a **solvent** for substances that consist of ions or polar molecules. It does this by surrounding the charged parts of the substance with a cluster of water molecules known as a *hydration*

shell. Such shells prevent the ions or polar molecules of the solute from reassociating.

Another crucial property of water, which is again a result of its polar nature, is its ability to resist changes in temperature. That is to say, water has a high **specific heat.** A lot of thermal energy has to be supplied to break the hydrogen bonds between water molecules and cause them to move around faster (resulting in a temperature rise). Even so, only about 20 percent of the hydrogen bonds are broken in heating water from its freezing point to its boiling point. By the same token, water holds its temperature longer than do most other substances when heat is no longer supplied. Only **ammonia,** which is more polar than water, has a higher specific heat.

Extensive hydrogen bonding also means that water has a high **heat of vaporization.** From this it follows that the evaporation of only a small amount of water is sufficient to carry away a great deal of heat, enabling organisms to rid themselves of excess body heat through evaporative cooling.

Relative density 1.00; temperature at maximum density 3.98°C; melting point 0.0°C; boiling point 100.0°C; specific heat 1 cal/g/°C; heat of vaporization 586 cal/g

water, in meteorites
In 1999, scientists at the **NASA Johnson Space Center** uncovered the largest crystals of a water-containing substance ever found in an extraterrestrial specimen. The 3-mm-diameter crystals of halite, estimated to be 4.5 billion years old, turned up in a meteorite that had fallen in Texas on March 22, 1998, and demonstrate that a brine solution was present at the time the solar system formed. This solution may have flowed within the parent **asteroid** from which the meteorite came, or may have been deposited on the asteroid's surface by a passing **comet.**

waterhole
The radio frequency band between the neutral **hydrogen** line at 1,420 MHz (**21-centimeter line**) and the **hydroxyl radical** (OH) line at 1,662 MHz. It lies in a part of the radio spec-

trum in which there is relatively little noise from natural celestial sources, so that a directional transmitter of only modest power would be needed to produce a detectable signal over interstellar distances. The waterhole was first identified as a prime region of the radio spectrum in which to carry out searches for intelligent signals in the Project **Cyclops** report prepared in 1971 by Bernard **Oliver** and John **Billingham:**

> Nature has provided us with a rather narrow band in this best part of the spectrum that seems especially marked for interstellar contact.... Standing like the Om and the Um on either side of a gate, these two emissions of the disassociation products of water beckon all water-based life to search for its kind at the age-old meeting place of all species: the waterhole.

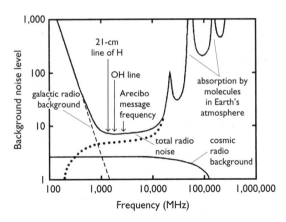

Watson and Marilyn Alberts Chair
The first academic position devoted to **SETI.** It was established in the Department of Astronomy at the **University of California, Berkeley,** as a result of a gift from two alumni with a long-standing interest in the field. The first holder of the chair is William "Jack" **Welch.**

wavelength
The distance between successive peaks (or troughs) of a wave. Wavelength is related to the **frequency** and speed of a wave by the equation

$$speed = wavelength \times frequency$$

For example, a radio wave of wavelength 300 m traveling at 300 million m per second (the speed of light) has a frequency of 1 MHz.

We Are Not Alone
Authoritative and best-selling account of the search for extraterrestrial life and intelligence by Walter Sullivan, science editor of *The New York Times*.[574] First published in 1964, it was destined to become an early SETI classic, alongside Carl **Sagan** and Iosif **Shklovskii**'s more technical *Intelligent Life in the Universe.*

weight
The force with which a body such as a planet attracts a given **mass.** Weight is experienced as a reaction to this force against a solid surface. Although the mass of an object is independent of location, its weight varies depending on the strength of the local gravitational field.

Weinbaum, Stanley G(rauman) (1902–35)
Student of chemical engineering at the University of Wisconsin (where he was in the same class as Charles Lindbergh) and science fiction author who was among the first to explore in depth the possible mentalities and motives of genuinely alien beings. His first published story, "A Martian Odyssey," published just fifteen months before his death from throat cancer at the age of thirty-three, is set on a Lowellian Mars and populated by a remarkable diversity of extraterrestrials, from Tweel, a birdlike creature who attempts to communicate with the explorers from Earth, to a **silicon-based life**-form whose respiratory waste consists of silica bricks. As the science fiction writer and critic Sam Moskowitz pointed out in his introduction to a 1966 edition of Weinbaum's classic:[618]

> Many devotees... believe that the true beginning of modern science fiction, with its emphasis on polished writing, otherworldly psychology, philosophy and stronger characterization began with Stanley G. Weinbaum. Certainly few authors in this branch have exercised a more obvious and pervasive influence on the attitudes of his contemporaries.

In 1935, Weinbaum's "The Lotus Eaters" offered a glimpse into the mind of an intelligent Venusian plant.

Weismann, August Friedrich Leopold (1834–1914)

German biologist who, in 1886, put forward the notion of the "continuity of the germ plasm." His experiments, which involved cutting off the tails of mice for generation after generation, disposed of Jean **Lamarck**'s hypothesis. (Although, as Isaac **Asimov** has pointed out, he could have saved himself the trouble by considering the fact that after many generations of circumcision, Jewish males display no reduction in their foreskin at birth.) Weismann proposed instead that the reproductive cells of an organism pass on their contents to the succeeding generation, unaltered by any changes that may have taken place to the rest of the body, a tenet that has become fundamental to **neo-Darwinism.**

Weizsäcker, Carl Friedrich von (1912–)

German physicist and philosopher at the University of Strasbourg who, in 1944, published an important new version of the **nebular hypothesis** that explained the puzzling discrepancy between the comparatively low **angular momentum** of the Sun and the high angular momentum of the outer planets.

Welch, William "Jack"

Vice president of the **SETI Institute** and professor of Astronomy and Electrical Engineering and holder of the Watson and Marilyn Alberts Chair for **SETI** at the **University of California, Berkeley.** Welch earned a Ph.D. in electrical engineering from Berkeley in 1960 and, as director of the Radio Astronomy Laboratory there from 1971 to 1996, was the key figure in setting up the BIMA (Berkeley-Illinois-Maryland Association) Array. Among his current activities is supervising the construction of the **One Hectare Telescope.** He is married to another leading SETI researcher, Jill **Tarter.**

Welles, (George) Orson (1915–85)

American film director and actor who made his acting debut in Ireland (1931) before returning to the United States to become a radio producer (1934). In 1938, his *Mercury Theatre of the Air* put on a radio production of H. G. **Wells**'s *The War of the Worlds* that was so convincing it plunged the nation into panic. ➔ *War of the Worlds, The,* **radio play**

Wells, Herbert George (1866–1946)

English writer whose science fiction stories played an important role in influencing popular conceptions of the nature of extraterrestrial life. The first novelist of his genre to receive a thorough scientific education, he held a bachelor's degree from the Normal School of Science (later renamed the Royal College of Science) in London and had been tutored by none other than the biologist Thomas **Huxley,** famed for his epic public encounter with the creationist Bishop Samuel "Soapy Sam" Wilberforce at Oxford in 1860. Huxley had been a close friend of Charles **Darwin.** Now, following Darwin's death in 1882—the year Wells first began attending Huxley's lectures—he was the new chief standard-bearer for Darwinism. Wells, therefore, could not have found a better teacher from whom to learn about the theory of evolution and all that it implied.

For Wells, as for his contemporaries, evolutionary theory was at the hub of biological thinking. It dominated much of what he wrote, both in the form of fiction and science journalism. In essay after essay, especially in his first decade of professional writing from 1887 to 1896, he attacked the traditional anthropocentric viewpoint that man was somehow special and that nature was teleologically oriented toward our species. What was *Homo sapiens,* he asked, but just another, accidental episode in the panoramic sweep of history? That was Wells's fundamental premise, and from it he went on to contemplate the precariousness of man's tenure on Earth. In an early piece, "Zoological Regression," he writes:

> There is … no guarantee in scientific knowledge of man's permanence or permanent ascendancy. … [I]t may be that … Nature is, in unsuspected obscurity, equipping some now humble creature … to rise in the fullness of time and sweep *homo* away. … The Coming Beast must certainly be reckoned in any anticipatory calculations regarding the Coming Man.

But the threat to humankind, Wells realized, might come not only from some lower species that subsequently evolved to take our place. In *The Time Machine*, the "Coming Beast" is man himself, or at least a bestial form of *Homo* that, in the far future, has diverged from a gentler, feebler strain of humanity that represents the other extreme end point of our development. Then again, perhaps the challenge to humanity would come from beyond the Earth and from a creature that was our intellectual superior.

On April 4, 1896, Wells's article "Intelligence on Mars" appeared in the *Saturday Review*. It begins by referring to a "luminous projection on the southern edge of the planet" seen by M. Javelle at Nice. The report of Javelle's sighting in *Nature*, some eighteen months earlier, had led to a flurry of speculation that the light was an attempt by Martians to signal to us (→ **Mars, changes on**). Wells went on in his article to ask what sentient life on Mars might be like. He was scornful of earlier suggestions that the inhabitants might resemble ourselves:

> No phase of anthropomorphism is more naïve than the supposition of men on Mars. The place of such a conception in the world of thought is with the anthropomorphic cosmogonies and religions invented by the childish conceit of primitive man.

The Martians, he concluded, "would be different from the creatures of earth, in form and function, in structure and in habit, different beyond the most bizarre imaginings of nightmare." A year later, he gave full rein to such speculation in *The War of the Worlds*.

Wells further explored the variety of forms that extraterrestrials might take in his writings on **silicon-based life** and his 1901 novel, ***First Men in the Moon.*** → **science fiction involving extraterrestrials, before 1900; science fiction involving extraterrestrials, 1900–1940**

WESTEX

The West Coast group of the **Panel on Extraterrestrial Life,** chaired by Joshua **Lederberg** and also including Melvin **Calvin,** Richard Davies, Norman **Horowitz,** A. G. Marr, Daniel Mazia, Aaron Novick, Carl **Sagan,** William **Sinton,** Roger Stanier, Gunther Stent, C. S. van Niel, and Harold F. Weaver. It held its first meeting on February 21, 1958, and produced the "WESTEX Summary Report." In August 1960, WESTEX was merged with **EASTEX** into **Committee 14 on Exobiology.**

Whewell, William (1794–1866)

English philosopher and Master of Trinity College, Cambridge, who, in his *On Plurality of Worlds: An Essay,* published anonymously in 1853, sparked off one of the most intense periods of debate on the issue of life on other worlds. Whewell, who until this time had argued in favor of **pluralism,** suddenly presented a range of scientific and theological arguments against it.

Whewell's early support for the pluralist position is reflected in a sermon he delivered in 1827:

> The earth . . . is one among a multitude of worlds . . . with resemblances and subordinations among them suggesting . . . that [they may be inhabited by] crowds of sentient . . . beings.

He employed the **microscope argument** of Thomas **Chalmers:**

> Does not even science herself compel us to expand our notion of God's vivifying and cherishing care, when she . . . shews us the myriads of animals that live in . . . the drop of water?

His acceptance of extraterrestrial life at this stage is also clear from passages in his *Astronomy and General Physics* (1833):

> [The stars] . . . may . . . have planets revolving around them; and these may, like our planet, be the seats of vegetable and animal and rational life:—we may thus have in the universe worlds, no one knows how many, no one can guess how varied.

By 1850, however, Whewell's difficulties in reconciling traditional Christian doctrines, especially the **incarnation and redemption,** with

pluralism and also with Pierre **Laplace**'s **nebular hypothesis** were beginning to emerge. In an unpublished manuscript, "Astronomy and Religion," he writes:

> God has interposed in the history of mankind in a special and personal manner;...that one, having a special relation to God, came from God to men in the form of a man.... [Consequently] what are we to suppose concerning the other worlds which science discloses to us? Is there a like scheme of salvation provided for all of them? Our view of the saviour of man will not allow us to suppose that there can be more than one saviour. And the saviour coming as a man to men is so essential a part of the scheme...that to endeavour to transfer it to other worlds and to imagine there something analogous as existing, is more repugnant to our feeling than to imagine those other worlds not to be provided with any divine scheme of salvation.

Later in the same manuscript, he introduces an argument that in subsequent years he applied against pluralism. He points to the vast eras of time which preceded the appearance of human beings on Earth. Such a hiatus without intelligent life might appear problematic if the world had been designed by God specifically for man. But Whewell stresses that wastage in nature is common: many seeds must fall, for example, in order that a few may germinate. If, Whewell argues, God has placed man on Earth for only a tiny fraction of our planet's history, is it not possible that intelligent life may exist on only a proportionately small number of other worlds?

Although Whewell's emergent antipluralist stance was firmly rooted in theological concerns, he was aware that religious arguments alone would not win the day against his critics. Consequently, he marshaled an array of often impressive scientific and philosophical objections against the view that intelligence (as distinct from lower life-forms) was common throughout the Universe. In addition to the geological argument mentioned above, Whewell called into question the hypothesis, gaining ground at the time, that some nebulas were "island universes," or external galaxies. He also doubted that "star clusters" were really made of separate stars rather than pieces of a single star in the process of formation. Regarding the nature of stars themselves, he pointed out that some were variable, while others, such as the **61 Cygni** pair, were known to be much less massive than the Sun. What assurance did we have, then, that most stars were similar to the Sun and therefore attended by planets, let alone by planets capable of supporting intelligent life? Some of his arguments are still relevant today. For example, he questioned whether the gravitational field around binary stars would be suited to providing stable conditions for planets. He also raised a valid objection concerning **Algol**, the light variations of which had been interpreted as due to eclipses of the star by a *planetary* companion. Turning to the solar system, he dismissed the outer planets as possible habitats of intelligent life on account of either their low temperature (Uranus and Neptune) or their low density (Jupiter and Saturn). Jupiter, he thought perhaps "a mere sphere of water," home at best to "boneless, watery, pulpy creatures." Mercury and Venus were too hot, though he allowed that Venus might harbor heat-resistant "microscopic creatures, with siliceous coverings." The Moon he considered uninhabitable because of evidence (for example, from Friedrich **Bessel**'s research) that it lacked both water and an atmosphere. Only Mars caused him some doubt: he suggested it might resemble the primordial Earth and be populated by dinosaurs.

Although Whewell's objections to pluralism were grounded in theology, it is just as true to say that those in favor of pluralism looked to support their cause with their own special interpretations of Christian doctrine. Science and religion were called upon to give evidence on both sides of the extraterrestrial life debate. But it was only with Whewell that the full strength of the scientific case *against* pluralism, as it stood in the mid–nineteenth century, was brought to bear. Whewell was successful in showing that the limited observational evidence to hand could be used just as effectively to dispute the view that (1) planets and (2) intelligent life were ubiquitous. In some cases, his scientific arguments (for example, regarding the nature of stars and external galaxies) came to be rejected, while in other cases (such as his caution about the habitability of other planets in the solar system and his suggestion of the nonsolidity of Jupiter and Saturn) he was eventually vindicated. Whewell was an important figure in the field, not because he was always right but because his *Essay* and subsequent *Dialogue on the Plurality of Worlds* (1854) led to a much-needed period of reevaluation on the question of extraterrestrial life and intelligence.[623] ➔ **Christian doctrine and pluralism; Brewster, David**

Whipple (Fred Lawrence) Observatory

Formerly known as Mount Hopkins Observatory and located on Mount Hopkins, Arizona, at an altitude of 2,600 m, it is operated by the Smithsonian Institution. Its main instrument is the **Multiple Mirror Telescope** (MMT).

white dwarf

A small, dim star in an advanced stage of evolution (➔ **stars, evolution of**). White dwarfs form from **main sequence** stars with masses similar to that of the Sun. The first such object to be discovered was the companion of **Sirius** in 1862. A white dwarf may contain up to 1.4 M_S (➔ **Chandrasekhar Limit**) of compressed material, mainly **carbon,** supported from further collapse by **degenerate electron pressure,** within a sphere approximately the size of the Earth.[304]

Wilkins, John (1614–72)

Brother-in-law of Oliver Cromwell and Oxford graduate who became master of Trinity College, Cambridge, and eventually bishop of Chester. Wilkins was among the new wave of thinkers who voiced freely their opinions on the implications of the **Copernican Revolution.** As a young author he was one of several men, including Johannes **Kepler,** who, following Galileo **Galilei**'s telescopic observations, were inspired to speculate about the possibility of lunar life (➔ **Moon, life on**) and of traveling to the Moon (➔ **Moon, voyages to**). He expounded upon the former in the first edition of his book *The Discovery of a World in the Moone,*

or, A Discourse Tending to Prove That 'Tis Probable There May Be Another Habitable World in That Planet,[626] published anonymously in 1638. Two years later, having read Francis **Godwin**'s contemporaneous fantasy about a lunar journey, he was encouraged to set down his own thoughts on such a possibility in the third edition of *The Discovery*. Wilkins saw no reason why men should not one day invent a means of transport—a "flying chariot," as he called it—that could reach the Moon. He even suggested that colonies might be established there, a proposal that, not surprisingly, drew derogatory comments from foreign writers about British imperialism. Among those who poured scorn on his ideas was the orator and sermonizer Robert South, who suggested that Wilkins had ambitions to obtain a bishopric on the Moon. About the same time, Samuel Butler penned his comic poem "The Elephant in the Moon," about a lunar beast discovered by astronomers that turns out to be a mouse inside their telescope. However, Wilkins's ideas proved highly influential. He discussed them at weekly meetings of the Philosophical Society of Oxford with other savants, including Robert Boyle, Christopher Wren, and Samuel Pepys—a group that was eventually chartered and became the Royal Society of London—and echoes of them are to be found throughout later-seventeenth-century writings on **pluralism.** ➔ **Campanella, Tommaso**

Wilson, Herbert C. (1858–1940)

American astronomer who, in 1886, reported seeing canals on Mars, thus giving support to Giovanni **Schiaparelli**'s claim. He was later among the few professional astronomers to argue in favor of the theories of Percival **Lowell.** (➔ **Mars, canals of**)

Woese, Carl

Professor of microbiology at the University of Illinois, Urbana-Champaign, whose research is focused on the molecular evolution of **prokaryote**s and the mechanism of **protein translation.** By sequencing the **ribosomal RNA** of various prokaryotes in his laboratory, he and his colleagues have demonstrated that **archaea** form a fundamentally distinct group of organisms that appear to lie at the root of the tree of life.

Wöhler, Friedrich (1800–82)

German chemist and student of Jöns **Berzelius** who, in 1828, synthesized **urea** by evaporating a solution of ammonium isocyanate and thereby demonstrated that there is no sharp distinction between **organic** and **inorganic** matter. Although this did not put an end to belief in **vitalism,** it showed that some organic substances, at least, could be produced independently of living organisms. In 1858, Wöhler became one of the first scientists to identify **organic matter in meteorites** (the first of all having been Berzelius in 1834). The fact that he (erroneously) concluded without hesitation that the organics were biological in origin reflects the strength of preconceived notions about extraterrestrial life at this time.

Wolf-Rayet star

An extremely hot star that is surrounded by an expanding envelope of gas.

Wolszczan, Alexander (1943–)

Professor of astronomy and astrophysics at Pennsylvania State University and codiscoverer, with Dale Frail, in 1991, of the first confirmed planets beyond the solar system. These are **pulsar planets** in orbit around **PSR 1257+12.**

wormhole

As early as 1916, Ludwig Flamm, an obscure Viennese physicist, looked at the simplest possible theoretical form of a **black hole**—the Schwarzschild black hole—and discovered a remarkable effect. By adjusting the solution, he could make the flexible surface of **space-time** drop down through hyperspace and connect to another universe. This kind of connecting tube is now known as a "wormhole." In 1957, the American physicist John Wheeler showed that a wormhole might also connect two different regions within our own universe, possibly separated by immense gulfs in both space and time. It is not known if wormholes actually exist. However, this has not deterred speculation, both theoretical and fic-

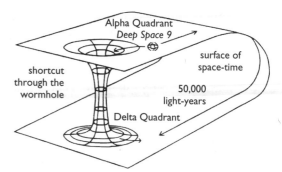

A wormhole connects the space station to the distant Delta Quadrant in *Star Trek: Deep Space Nine.*

tional (➔ *Contact*) about the possibility of using these esoteric structures as a form of rapid transit system around the cosmos.

Wow! signal

An anomalous, **narrowband** burst of radio noise picked up on August 15, 1977, during **SETI** observations by the **Big Ear** of the **Ohio State University Radio Observatory.** The signal, which lasted 37 seconds and came from the direction of Sagittarius, attracted the attention of Ohio State astronomer Jerry **Ehman,** who scrawled "Wow!" in the margin of the printout. It was, said Ehman,

> the strangest signal I had ever seen.... At first, I thought it was an earth signal reflected from space debris, but after I studied it further, I found that couldn't be the case.

The signal was near the **21-centimeter line** (1,420-MHz) of **hydrogen,** where all radio transmissions are prohibited both on and off the Earth by international agreement; unlike the broadband emission typical of most natural radio sources, it covered only a narrow spread of frequencies; and it came from beyond the distance of the Moon. The nearest star in the direction in which the telescope was pointing is 220 light-years (68 parsecs) away. A source at this distance using a transmitting dish as big as the **Arecibo radio telescope** (the largest in the world) would require a 2.2-gigawatt transmitter—extraordinarily powerful but not out of the question. Another possibility is that a much weaker signal from a more remote source may have experienced **gravitational microlensing** by an intervening star. More than one hundred subsequent searches of the same region of sky have failed to recover the signal. However, this is not surprising. A telescope such as the Big Ear listens to only about one millionth of the sky at a time and a similar dish on another planet would broadcast to only about one millionth of the sky. The chance of an alignment between receiver and transmitter, therefore, would be only about one in a trillion. On the other hand, it is possible that many such similarly strong, intermittent, and highly directional signals are arriving at the Earth every day. Although the Wow! signal remains unexplained, Paul Shuch of the **SETI League** has made the interesting observation:

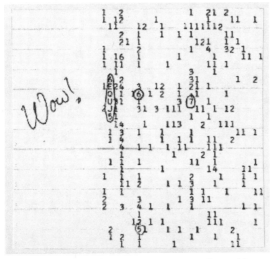

The Wow! computer printout with Ehman's markings.

Either the Wow! signal was the intercepted radiation from another civilization, or it's a previously undiscovered astrophysical phenomenon. Either possibility is mind-boggling.

The Wow! signal is used as a benchmark for calibrating the sensitivity of systems being used in Project **Argus**. → **SETI, false alarms in**

Wright, Thomas (1711–86)

English amateur astronomer, private tutor, and instrument maker who, in *An Original Theory or New Hypothesis of the Universe*[632] (1750), was the first to propose a reasonably modern view of the Milky Way in which the Sun is not centrally located. He suggested that the Milky Way is a slab of stars shaped like a mill wheel with the Sun lying between the two planes, though not necessarily at the hub. He further suggested that there might be other collections of stars (external galaxies) like the Milky Way, citing as evidence "the many cloudy spots [nebulae], just perceivable by us . . . in which . . . no one star or particular constituent can possibly be distinguished." His later description of the Universe in terms of systems of spheres and rings of stars was taken up by Immanuel **Kant**. Wright also speculated about the existence of life on other worlds, but from a theological rather than a scientific standpoint. Despite having relegated the Earth to a mundane site within a giant collection of similar stars, he returned to a form of anthropocentrism with his ideas on the **transmigration of souls**.

Wyoming Arizona Search for Planets
→ **Arizona Search for Planets**

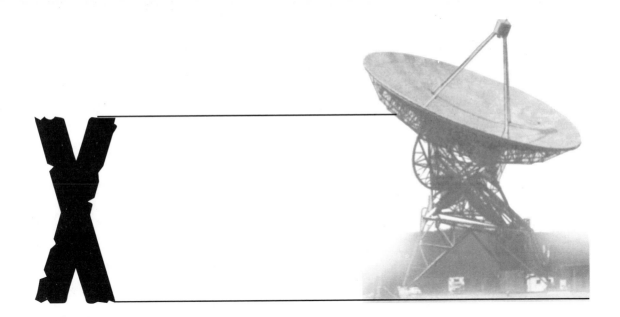

X

X rays
Electromagnetic radiation of wavelengths shorter than that of **ultraviolet** rays and longer than that of **gamma rays.** X-ray wavelengths range from .001 nm to 10 nm.

xenobiology
→ **astrobiology**

Xenophanes (c. 570–c. 475 B.C.)
Greek philosopher and native of the city of Colophon. Xenophanes had a particular gripe against the anthropomorphism of popular religion. Why, he asked, did people suppose their gods to be human in appearance? Wouldn't cows, if they were inclined to pray, worship bovine gods? Xenophanes urged that people should stop assuming they were the center of cosmic attention or that either they or the Earth were unique. To him, the idea of unlimited worlds was irresistibly attractive, and he added a new possibility: that the Moon might support life (→ **Moon, life on**).
→ **ancient philosophy, related to the possibility of extraterrestrial life**

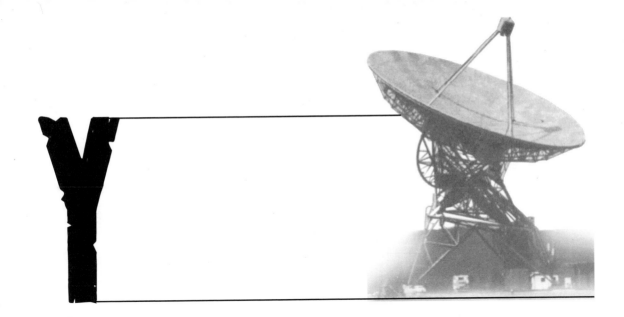

Yamato 791198

A **carbonaceous chondrite** weighing 180 g that was recovered in 1979 by the Japanese Antarctic Research Expedition. Analysis showed that it contained twenty different kinds of **amino acids** of extraterrestrial origin, in concentrations greater than those recorded in any other meteorites up to that time.[538] The highest concentrations were found for alpha-amino-isobutyric acid, **glycine,** and alanine.

The presence of both **enantiomers** of the first two proved conclusively that the substances were not earthly contaminants.

Yerkes Observatory

Founded by George Ellery **Hale** in 1897 with funds from Charles T. Yerkes and located near Chicago. Its 1.02-m (40-in.) refracting telescope is the largest of its kind ever built.

Zeeman effect
The broadening or splitting of radiation from a substance into several wavelengths due to the presence of a magnetic field.

Zodiacal Cloud
A tenuous disk that surrounds the Sun and is composed of dust released from active **comets** and colliding **asteroid**s.

Zöllner, Johann Karl Friedrich (1834–82)
German astronomer at the University of Leipzig who used **photometry** to measure the reflectivity of the planets. In a 1874 paper, he concluded from Mercury's low **albedo** that the innermost planet probably had no significant atmosphere. This dealt a severe blow to the prospects for Mercurian habitation (➔ **Mercury, life on**). In 1872, Zöllner outspokenly criticized the **lithopanspermia** hypothesis of William **Thomson,** Lord Kelvin, on two grounds: (1) that it offered no explanation as to how life arose in the first place (merely shifting that problem from the Earth to some other world) and (2) that it failed to explain how organisms could survive the high-temperature passage of a meteorite through the Earth's atmosphere. ➔ **Helmholtz, Hermann von**

zone of habitability
➔ **habitable zone**

zoo hypothesis
One of a number of suggestions that have been put forward to explain the fact that we have so far found no evidence for advanced extraterrestrials (➔ **Fermi Paradox**).[37] According to this idea, alien races are taking good care to avoid making their presence known to us or exerting an influence on our development (just as the Federation in *Star Trek* has a strict policy of nonintervention with the less technologically sophisticated cultures it encounters). Our planet and our species, it is hypothesized, may be under close scrutiny, like the animals in a zoo, without us being aware of it. One way this monitoring could be carried out would be through automatic equipment surreptitiously located on the Earth or elsewhere in the solar system that relays back to its masters news of our progress. Only when we are sufficiently advanced, it is suggested, may we be let into the secret and inducted into the galactic society of beings capable of interstellar travel.

Zuckerman, Benjamin M.

Professor of astronomy at the University of California, Los Angeles, whose work is centered on the search for evidence, in the form of circumstellar gas, dust, and **brown dwarf**s, of extrasolar planetary systems. Together with colleagues from UCLA and the United Kingdom, he has produced images of dust disks around the stars **Vega, Fomalhaut,** and **Beta Pictoris.**

References

1. Acuna, M. H., Connerney, J. E. P., Ness, N. F., Lin, R. P., Mitchell, D., Carlson, C. W., McFadden, J., Anderson, K. A., Rème, H., Mazelle, C., Vignes, D., Wasilewski, P., and Cloutier, P. "Global Distribution of Crustal Magnetization Discovered by the Mars Global Surveyor MAG/ER Experiment," *Science*, **284**, 284 (1999).

2. Aczel, Amir D. *Probability 1: Why There Must Be Intelligent Life in the Universe*. New York: Harcourt, Brace (1998).

3. Agel, Jerome, ed. *The Making of Kubrick's 2001*. New York: Signet (1970).

4. Aitken, R. G. "Life on Other Worlds," *Journal of the Royal Astronomical Society of Canada*, **5**, 291 (1911).

5. Albrow, M., et al. "Searching for Anomalies Through Precise, Rapid, Round-the-Clock Monitoring," *Astrophysical Journal*, **509**, 687 (1998).

6. Alcock, C., et al. "Possible Gravitational Microlensing of a Star in the Large Magellanic Cloud," *Nature*, **365**, 621 (1993).

7. Aldiss, Brian W., and Wingrove, David. *Trillion Year Spree: The History of Science Fiction*. London: Victor Gollancz (1986).

8. Allard, F., Hauschildt, P. H., Baraffe, I., and Chabrier, G. "Synthetic Spectra and Mass Determination of the Brown Dwarf GL229B," *Astrophysical Journal Letters*, **465**, L123 (1996).

9. Allison, A. "Possible Forms of Life," *Journal of the British Interplanetary Society*, **21**, 48 (1968).

10. Amy, Penny S., and Haldeman, Dana L., eds. *The Microbiology of the Terrestrial Deep Subsurface*. Boca Raton, Fla.: CRC Press (1997).

11. Anders, E. Letter in *Science*, **274**, 2119 (1966).

12. Anderson, Poul. *Tau Zero*. New York: Lancer Books (1970).

13. Andreadis, Athena. *To Seek Out New Life: The Biology of Star Trek*. New York: Crown (1998).

14. Angel, J. R. P. "Ground-Based Imaging of Extrasolar Planets Using Adaptive Optics," *Nature*, **368**, 203 (1994).

15. Angel, J. R. P. "Taking Adaptive Optics to the Limit to Image Extrasolar Planets," *Astrophysics & Space Science*, **223**, 136 (1995).

16. Angel, R., and Woolf, N. "Sensitivity of an Active Space Telescope to Faint Sources and Extrasolar Planets." In E. P. Smith and A. Koratkar, eds., *Science with the NGST (Next Generation Space Telescope)*, ASP Conference Series **133**. San Francisco: Astronomical Society of the Pacific Publications (1998).

17. Annis, James. "An Astrophysical Explanation for the Great Silence," *Journal of the British Interplanetary Society,* **52,** 19 (1999).

18. Antoniadi, E. M. "Sixth Interim Report for 1909, Dealing with Some Further Notes on the So-called 'Canals,' " *Journal of the British Astronomical Association,* **20,** 189 (1910).

19. Antoniadi, E. M. *La Planète Mars; étude basée sur les resultats obtenus avec la grande lunette de l'observatoire de Meudon et expose analytique de l'ensemble des travaux éxécutés sur cet astre depuis 1659.* Paris: Librairie scientifique Hermann et cie (1930). 1st English language ed., *The Planet Mars,* trans. by Patrick Moore. Keith Reid Ltd. (1975).

20. Antoniadi, E. M. *La Planète Mercure et la rotation des satellites; étude basée sur les resultats obtenus avec la grande lunette de l'observatoire de Meudon.* Paris: Gauthier-Villars (1934).

21. Archer, M. "Slime Monsters Will Be Human Too," *Nature Australia,* **22,** 546 (1989).

22. Arrhenius, S. "The Propagation of Life in Space," *Die Umschau,* **7,** 481 (1903). Reprinted in Donald Goldsmith, ed., *The Quest for Extraterrestrial Life,* q.v.

23. Arrhenius, S. "Panspermy: The Transmission of Life from Star to Star," *Scientific American,* **96,** 196 (1907).

24. Arrhenius, Svante. *Worlds in the Making: The Evolution of the Universe.* New York: Harper & Row (1908).

25. Arrhenius, Svante. *The Destinies of Stars,* trans. by J. E. Fries. New York: G. P. Putnam's Sons (1918).

26. Ascher, R., and Ascher, M. "Interstellar Communication and Human Evolution." In A. G. W. Cameron, ed., *Interstellar Communication,* q.v.

27. Ash, Brian, ed. *The Visual Encyclopedia of Science Fiction.* New York: Harmony (1977).

28. Asimov, Isaac. *The Gods Themselves.* New York: Fawcett Crest (1972).

29. Asimov, Isaac. *Extraterrestrial Civilizations.* New York: Crown (1979).

30. Auborg, E., et al. "Evidence for Gravitational Microlensing by Dark Objects in the Galactic Halo," *Nature,* **365,** 623 (1993).

31. Bada, J. L., Glavin, D. P., McDonald, G. D., and Becker, L. "A Search for Endogenous Amino Acids in Martian Meteorite ALH 84001," *Science,* **279,** 362 (1998).

32. Bailey, J., Chrystostomou, A., Hough, J. H., Gledhill, T. M., McCall, A., Clark, S., Menard, F., and Tamura, M. "Circular Polarization in Star-Formation Regions: Implications for Biomolecular Homochirality," *Science,* **281,** 672 (1998).

33. Baird, John. *The Inner Limits of Outer Space.* Hanover, N.H.: University Press of New England (1987).

34. Bak, Per. *How Nature Works: The Science of Self-Organized Criticality.* New York: Springer-Verlag (1996).

35. Balázs, Béla A. "SETI and the Galactic Belt of Intelligent Life," a paper presented at Bioastronomy 99: A New Era in Bioastronomy, Kohala Coast, Hawaii, August 2–7, 1999.

36. Baliunas, S., Henry, G. W., Donahue, R. A., Fekel, F. C., and Soon, W. H. "Properties of Sunlike Stars with Planets," *Astrophysical Journal Letters,* **474,** L119 (1997).

37. Ball, J. A. "The Zoo Hypothesis," *Icarus,* **19,** 347 (1973).

38. Ball, R. S. W. "The Possibility of Life in Other Worlds," *Fortnightly Review,* **78,** 676 (1894).

39. Balter, M. "Did Life Begin in Hot Water?," *Science,* **280,** 31 (1998).

40. Banit, M., Ruderman, M. A., Shaham, J., and Applegate, J. H. "Formation of Planets Around Pulsars," *Astrophysical Journal,* **415,** 779 (1993).

41. Barrat, J. A., Gillet, C., Lécuyer, C., Sheppard, S. M. F., and Lesourd, M. "Formation of Carbonates in the Tatahouine Meteorite," *Science,* **280,** 412 (1998).

42. Barron, Neil, ed. *Anatomy of Wonder: A Critical Guide to Science Fiction,* 4th ed. New York: Bowker (1995).

43. Barrow, John D., and Tipler, Frank. *The Anthropic Cosmological Principle.* New York: Oxford University Press (1986).

44. Baum, Richard, and Sheehan, William. *In Search of Planet Vulcan: The Ghost in Newton's Clockwork Universe.* New York: Plenum (1997).

45. Benest, D. "Planetary Orbits in the Alpha Centauri System," *Bulletin of the American Astronomical Society,* **18,** 810 (1986).

46. Benest, D. "Stable Planetary Orbits Around One Component in Nearby Binary Stars," *Celestial Mechanics*, **43,** 47 (1988).

47. Benest, D. "Planetary Orbits in the Elliptic Restricted Problem. I—The Alpha Centauri System," *Astronomy & Astrophysics*, **206,** 143 (1988).

48. Benest, D. "Planetary Orbits in the Elliptic Restricted Problem. II—The Sirius System," *Astronomy & Astrophysics*, **223,** 361 (1989).

49. Benest, D. "Planetary Orbits in Double Star Systems," *Bulletin of the American Astronomical Society*, **24,** 983 (1992).

50. Bennet, D. P., and Rhie, S. H. "Detecting Earth-mass Planets with Gravitational Microlensing," *Astrophysical Journal*, **472,** 660 (1996).

51. Bergson, Henri. *Creative Evolution*, trans. by A. Mitchell. New York: H. Holt (1913).

52. Bernal, J. D. "The Problem of Stages in Biopesis," *Proceedings of the First International Symposium on the Origin of Life on Earth*, Pergamon Press: London (1959).

53. Bernal, J. D. "Significance of Carbonaceous Meteorites in Theories on the Origin of Life," *Nature*, **190,** 129 (1961).

54. Bernal, J. D. *The World, the Flesh, and the Devil: An Enquiry into the Future of the Three Enemies of the Rational Soul*, 2nd ed. Bloomington: University of Indiana Press (1969) (first published 1929).

55. Beust, H., Vidal-Madjar, A., Ferlet, R., and Lagrange-Henri, A. M. "Cometary-like Bodies in the Protoplanetary Disk Around Beta Pictoris," *Astrophysics & Space Science*, **212,** 147 (1994).

56. Biemann, K., et al. "The Search for Organic Substances and Inorganic Volatile Compounds in the Surface of Mars," *Journal of Geophysical Research*, **82,** 4641 (1977).

57. Billingham, J., and Oliver, B. M. "Project Cyclops: A Design Study of a System for Detecting Extraterrestrial Intelligent Life," Moffett Field, Calif.: NASA/Ames Pub. CR-114445 (1972).

58. Billingham, John, ed. *Life in the Universe*. Cambridge, Mass.: MIT Press (1981).

59. Billingham, J. "The Demography of Extraterrestrial Civilizations." In L. G. Napolitano, ed., *Space: Mankind's Fourth Environment*. New York: Pergamon Press (1983).

60. Billingham, J., Heyns, R., Milne, D., et al. *Social Implications of Detecting an Extraterrestrial Civilization: A Report of the Workshop on the Cultural Aspects of SETI*. Mountain View, Calif.: SETI Institute (1994).

61. Black, D. "Completing the Copernican Revolution: The Search for Other Planetary Systems," *Annual Review of Astronomy and Astrophysics*, **33,** 359 (1995).

62. Blake, G. A., Qi, C., Hogerheijde, M. R., Gurwell, M. A., and Muhleman, D. O. "Sublimation from Icy Jets as a Probe of the Interstellar Volatile Content of Comets," *Nature*, **398,** 213 (1999).

63. Blum, Harold F. *Time's Arrow and Evolution*, 3rd ed. Princeton, N.J.: Princeton University Press (1968) (first published 1951).

64. Bock, G., Goode, J. A., and Walker, M., eds. *Evolution of Hydrothermal Ecosystems on Earth (and Mars?)*, Ciba Foundation Symposium, No. 202. New York: John Wiley & Sons (1996).

65. Böhler, C., Nielsen, P. E., and Orgel, L. E. "Template Switching Between PNA and RNA Oligonucleotides," *Nature*, **376,** 578 (1995).

66. Borucki, W. J., Koch, D. G., Dunham, E. W., and Jenkins, J. M. "The Kepler Mission: A Photometric Mission to Determine the Frequency of Inner Planets Near the Habitability Zone of Solar-like Stars." In David Soderblom, ed., *Proceedings of ASP Conference 119: Planets Beyond the Solar System and the Next Generation of Space Missions*. San Francisco: Astronomical Society of the Pacific Publications (1996).

67. Boss, A. "Forming a Jupiter-like Companion for 51 Peg," *Lunar and Planetary Science*, **27,** 139 (1996).

68. Boss, A. "Astrometric Signatures of Giant-Planet Formation," *Nature*, **393,** 141 (1998).

69. Boss, Alan. *Looking for Earths: The Race to Find New Solar Systems*. New York: John Wiley & Sons (1998).

70. Bova, Ben, and Preiss, Byron. *First Contact: The Search for Extraterrestrial Intelligence*. New York: NAL Books (1990).

71. Bowyer, S., Zeitlin, G., Tarter, J., Lampton, M., and Welch, W. "The Berkeley Parasitic SETI Program," *Icarus*, **53**, 147 (1983).

72. Bracewell, R. N. "Communications from Superior Galactic Communities," *Nature*, **186**, 670 (1960).

73. Bracewell, R. N. "Radio Signals from Other Planets," *Proceedings of the Institute of Radio Engineers*, **50**, 214 (1962), reprinted in A. G. W. Cameron, ed., *Interstellar Communication*, q.v.

74. Bracewell, Ronald N. *The Galactic Club*. San Francisco: W. H. Freeman (1975).

75. Bracewell, R. "Detecting Nonsolar Planets by Spinning Infrared Interferometer," *Nature*, **274**, 780 (1978).

76. Bradbury, Ray. *The Martian Chronicles*. New York: Doubleday (1950).

77. Bradbury, R. J. "Dyson Shell Supercomputers as the Dominant 'Life Form' in Galaxies," paper presented at Bioastronomy 99: A New Era in Bioastronomy, Kohala Coast, Hawaii, August 2–6, 1999.

78. Bradley, J. P., Harvey, R. P., and McSween, H. Y., Jr. "Magnetite Whiskers and Platelets in ALH 84001 Martian Meteorite: Evidence of Vapor Phase Growth," *Geochimica et Cosmochimica Acta*, **60**, 5149 (1996).

79. Breiter, S., Dybczynski, P. A., and Elipe, A. "The Action of the Galactic Disk on the Oort Cloud Comets," *Astronomy & Astrophysics*, **315**, 618 (1996).

80. Brewster, David. *More Worlds Than One, the Creed of the Philosopher and the Hope of the Christian*. New York: Robert Carter and Brothers (1854).

81. Brin, David. *Sundiver*. New York: Bantam (1980).

82. Brown, H.. "Planetary Systems Associated with Main-Sequence Stars," *Science*, **145**, 1177 (1964).

83. Brown, Harrison, and Zerwick, Clöe. *The Cassiopeia Affair*. New York: Doubleday (1968).

84. Brown, T. M., Noyes, R. W., Nisenson, P., Korzennik, S. G., and Horner, S. "The AFOE: A Spectrograph for Precise Doppler Studies," *Publications of the Astronomical Society of the Pacific*, **106**, 1285 (1994).

85. Brunini, A., and Fernandez, J. A. "Perturbations on an Extended Kuiper Disk Caused by Passing Stars and Giant Molecular Clouds," *Astronomy & Astrophysics*, **308**, 988 (1996).

86. Budden, K. G., and Yates, G. G. "A Search for Radio Echoes of Long Delay," *Journal of Atmospheric and Terrestrial Physics*, **2**, 272 (1952).

87. Bussard, R. W. "Galactic Matter and Interstellar Flight," *Astronautica Acta*, **6**, 179 (1960).

88. Butler, P., and Marcy, G. "A Planet Orbiting 47 UMa," *Astrophysical Journal Letters*, **464**, L153 (1996).

89. Butler, P., Marcy, G., Vogt, S., and Apps, K. "A Planet with a 3.1 Day Period Around a Solar Twin," *Publications of the Astronomical Society of the Pacific*, **110**, 1389 (1998).

90. Butler, P., Marcy, G., Williams, E., Hauser, H., and Shirts, P. "Three New 51 Peg-type Planets," *Astrophysical Journal Letters*, **474**, L115 (1997).

91. Cairns-Smith, A. G. *Genetic Takeover and the Mineral Origins of Life*. New York: Cambridge University Press (1982).

92. Cairns-Smith, A. G. *Seven Clues to the Origin of Life*. Cambridge, England: Cambridge University Press (1985).

93. Calvin, Melvin. *Chemical Evolution: Molecular Evolution Towards the Origin of Life on the Earth and Elsewhere*. New York: Oxford University Press (1969).

94. Calvin, Melvin, and Gazenko, O. G., eds. *Foundations of Space Biology and Medicine*. Washington, D.C.: National Aeronautics and Space Administration (1975).

95. Campbell, W. W. "Water Vapor in the Atmosphere of Mars," *Science*, **30**, 474 (1909).

96. Cameron, A. G. W. *Interstellar Communication*. New York: W. A. Benjamin (1963).

97. Cano, R. J., and Borucki, M. K. "Revival and Identification of Bacterial Spores in 25- to 40-Million-Year-Old Dominican Amber," *Science*, **268**, 1060 (1995).

98. Cantril, Howard. *The Invasion from Mars: A Study in the Psychology of Panic, with the Complete Script of the Famous Orson Welles Broadcast*. Princeton, N.J.: Princeton University Press (1940).

99. Carlotto, M. "Digital Imagery Analysis of Unusual Martian Surface Features," *Applied Optics*, **27**, 1926 (1988).

100. Carr, Michael H. *Water on Mars*. New York: Oxford University Press (1996).

101. Carter, B. "Large Number Coincidences and the Anthropic Principle in Cosmology." In M. S. Longair, ed., *Confrontation of Cosmological Theories with Observational Data*. Dordrecht: D. Reidel (1974).

102. Catoe, Lynn E. *UFOs and Related Subjects: An Annotated Bibliography*. Washington, D.C.: U.S. Government Printing Office (1969).

103. Cech, T. R. "A Model for the RNA-catalyzed Replication of RNA," *Proceedings of the National Academy of Sciences*, **83**, 4360 (1986).

104. Cesarone, R. J., Sergeyevsky, A. B., and Kerridge, S. *Prospects for the Voyager Interstellar Mission*, AAS/AIAA Astrodynamics Specialist Conference Paper 83-308, Lake Placid, N.Y., Aug. 22–25, 1983.

105. Christian, James, ed. *Extraterrestrial Intelligence: The First Encounter*. Buffalo, N.Y.: Prometheus Books (1976).

106. Chyba, C. "Impact Delivery and Erosion of Planetary Oceans in the Early Solar System," *Nature*, **343**, 129 (1990).

107. Chyba, C. "Exobiology: Life on Other Moons," *Nature*, **385**, 201 (1997).

108. Clark, Stuart. *Extrasolar Planets*. London: Wiley (1999).

109. Clarke, Arthur C. *Childhood's End*. New York: Harcourt, Brace and World (1963) (first published 1953).

110. Clarke, Arthur C. *The City and the Stars*. New York: Harcourt, Brace (1956).

111. Clarke, Arthur C. *2001: A Space Odyssey*. New York: New American Library (1968).

112. Clarke, Arthur C. "The Sentinel." In *Expedition to Earth*. New York: Harcourt, Brace and World (1970).

113. Clarke, Arthur C. *Rendezvous with Rama*. New York: Harcourt, Brace, Jovanovich (1973).

114. Clarke, Arthur C. *Imperial Earth*. New York: Harcourt, Brace, Jovanovich (1976).

115. Clarke, Arthur. C. *The Lost Worlds of 2001*. Boston: Gregg Press (1979).

116. Clarke, Arthur C. *2010: Odyssey Two*. New York: Ballantine (1982).

117. Clarke, Arthur C. *2061: Odyssey Three*. New York: Ballantine (1991).

118. Clarke, Arthur C. *3001: The Final Odyssey*. New York: Del Rey (1997).

119. Claus, G., and Nagy, B. "A Microbiological Examination of Some Carbonaceous Chondrites," *Nature*, **192**, 594 (1961).

120. Cleator, P. E. *Rockets Through Space*, p. 195. New York: Simon & Schuster (1936).

121. Clement, Hal. *Mission of Gravity*. New York: Doubleday (1954).

122. Clute, John, and Nicholls, Peter, eds. *The Encyclopedia of Science Fiction*. New York: St. Martin's Press (1993).

123. Cocconi, G., and Morrison, P. "Searching for Interstellar Communication," *Nature*, **184**, 844 (1959).

124. Cochran, W., Hatzes, A., and Hancock, J. "Constraints on the Companion Object to HD 114762," *Astrophysical Journal Letters*, **380**, L35. (1991).

125. Cohen, Philip. "An Alien Diet," *New Scientist*, 14 (Aug. 1, 1998).

126. Colavitta, M., et al. "The Palomar Testbed Interferometer," *Astrophysical Journal*, **510**, 505 (1999).

127. Connerney, J. E. P., Acuna, M. H., Wasilewski, P. J., Ness, N. F., Rème, H., Mozelle, C., Vignes, D., Lin, R. P., Mitchell, D. L., and Cloutier, P. A. "Magnetic Linearities in the Ancient Crust of Mars," *Science*, **284**, 790 (1999).

128. Connes, P. "Development of Absolute Accelerometry," *Astrophysics & Space Science*, **212**, 357 (1994).

129. Cooper, Henry S. F., Jr. *The Search for Life on Mars*. New York: Holt, Rinehart and Winston (1980).

130. Cowan, C., Atluri, C. R., and Libby, W. "Possible Antimatter Content of the Tunguska Meteor of 1908," *Nature*, **206**, 861 (1965).

131. Crawford, I. A. "Interstellar Travel: A Review for Astronomers," *Quarterly Journal of the Royal Astronomical Society*, **31**, 377 (1990).

132. Crick, F. H. C., and Orgel, L. E. "Directed Panspermia," *Icarus*, **19**, 341 (1973).

133. Crifo, F., Vidal-Madjar, A., Lallement, R., Ferlet, R., and Gerbaldi, M. "Beta Pictoris Revisited by Hipparcos. Star properties," *Astronomy & Astrophysics*, **320**, L29 (1997).

134. Cromie, Robert. *A Plunge into Space*. London: Frederick Warne (1890).

135. Cronin, J. R., and Pizzarello, S. "Enantiomeric Excesses in Meteoritic Amino Acids," *Science*, **275**, 951 (1997).

136. Croswell, Ken. *Planet Quest: The Epic Discovery of Alien Solar Systems.* New York: Free Press (1997).

137. Crowe, Michael. *The Extraterrestrial Life Debate, 1750–1900.* Cambridge, England: Cambridge University Press (1986).

138. Davies, Paul. *Are We Alone? Philosophical Implications of the Discovery of Life.* New York: Basic Books (1995).

139. Dawkins, Richard. *The Selfish Gene.* New York: Oxford University Press (1977).

140. Dawkins, Richard. *The Blind Watchmaker.* New York: W. W. Norton (1987).

141. Deamer, David W., and Fleischaker, Gail R., eds. *Origins of Life: The Central Concepts.* Boston: Jones and Bartlett (1994).

142. De La Fuente, M. C., and De La Fuente, M. R. "Runaway Planets," *New Astronomy*, **4**, 21 (1998).

143. del Rey, Lester. *The World of Science Fiction: The History of a Subculture.* New York: Ballantine (1979).

144. Delfosse, X., Forveille, T., Mayor, M., Perrier, C., Naef, D., and Queloz, D. "The Closest Extrasolar Planet: A Giant Planet Around the M4 Dwarf Gl 876," *Astronomy & Astrophysics*, **338**, L67 (1998).

145. Derbyshire, G. A. "Resumé of Some Earlier Extraterrestrial Contamination Activities." In *A Review of Space Research*, ch. 10, p. 11. Washington, D.C.: National Academy of Sciences (1962).

146. Derr, J. S. "Earthquake Lights: A Review of Observations and Present Theories," *Bulletin of the Seismological Society of America*, **63** (6), 2177 (1973).

147. Derr, J. S. "Geophysical Variables and Behavior: LXXVI. Seasonal Hydrological Load and Regional Luminous Phenomena (UFO Reports) with River Systems, The Mississippi River Test," *Perceptual and Motor Skills*, **77**, 1163 (1993).

148. "Development of International Efforts to Avoid Contamination of Extraterrestrial Bodies," *Science*, **128**, 887 (1958).

149. Devereux, Paul. *Earth Lights Revelation.* New York: Blandford Press (1990).

150. Dick, Steven J. *Plurality of Worlds: The Extraterrestrial Life Debate from Democritus to Kant.* Cambridge, England: Cambridge University Press (1982).

151. Dick, S. J. "The Search for Extraterrestrial Intelligence and the NASA High Resolution Microwave Survey (HRMS): Historical Perspectives," *Space Science Reviews*, **64**, 93 (1993).

152. Dick, Steven J. *The Biological Universe: The Twentieth-Century Extraterrestrial Life Debate and the Limits of Science.* Cambridge, England: Cambridge University Press (1996).

153. Dick, S. J. "Cultural Aspects of Astrobiology," paper presented at Bioastronomy 99: A New Era for Bioastronomy, Kohala Coast, Hawaii, August 2–6, 1999.

154. Dicke, R. H. "Dirac's Cosmology and Mach's Principle," *Nature*, **192**, 440 (1961).

155. Dickinson, Terence, and Schaler, Adolf. *Extraterrestrials: A Field Guide for Earthlings.* London: Camden House (1994).

156. Dixon, R. S. "A Search Strategy for Finding Extraterrestrial Radio Beacons," *Icarus*, **20**, 187 (1973).

157. Dixon, R. S., and Cole, D. M. "A Modest All-Sky Search for Narrowband Radio Radiation Near the 21-cm Hydrogen Line," *Icarus*, **30**, 267 (1977).

158. Dobzhansky, T. "Darwinian Evolution and the Problem of Extraterrestrial Life," *Perspectives in Biology and Medicine*, **15**, 157 (1972).

159. Dole, Stephen. *Habitable Planets for Man.* New York: American Elsevier (1964).

160. Dominik, C., Laureijs, R. J., Jourdain de Mouizon, M., and Habing, H. J. "A Vega-like Disk Associated with the Planetary System of Rho^1 Cancri," *Astronomy & Astrophysics*, **329**, L53 (1998).

161. Doyle, L. R., ed. *Circumstellar Habitable Zones*, Proceedings of the First International Conference on Habitable Zones, San Francisco. Menlo Park, Calif.: Travis House (1996).

162. Drake, F. D. "Project Ozma," *Physics Today*, **14**, 140 (1961).

163. Drake, Frank D. *Intelligent Life in Space.* New York: Macmillan (1962).

164. Drake, F. D. "Life on a Neutron Star," *Astronomy*, 5 (December 1973).

165. Drake, Frank, and Sobel, Dava. *Is Anyone Out There? The Scientific Search for Extraterrestrial Intelligence.* New York: Delacorte (1993).

166. du Prel, Carl. *Die Planetenbewohner und die Nebularhypothese.* Leipzig: Philipp Reclam (1880).

167. Durant, F. C. *Report on Meetings of Scientific Advisory Panel on Unidentified Flying Objects.* Washington, D.C.: CIA (1953).

168. Dutil, Y., and Dumas, S. "Active SETI: Targets Selection and Message Conception," paper presented at 193rd American Astronomical Society Meeting, Austin, Tex., January 9, 1999.

169. Dyson, F. J. "Search for Artificial Sources of Infrared Radiation," *Science,* **131,** 1667 (1959).

170. Dyson, F. J. Letter, *Scientific American* (1964).

171. Dyson, Freeman J. "The Search for Extraterrestrial Technology." In R. E. Marshak, ed., *Perspectives in Modern Physics: Essays in Honor of Hans Bethe.* New York: John Wiley & Sons (1966).

172. Dyson, F. J. "Interstellar Transport," *Physics Today,* **21,** 41 (1968).

173. Dyson, Freeman. *Disturbing the Universe.* New York: Harper & Row (1979).

174. Dyson, Freeman. *Origins of Life.* New York: Cambridge University Press (1985).

175. Dyson, Freeman. *Infinite in All Directions.* New York: Harper & Row (1988).

176. Edelson, R. E. "At the Technological Frontier: The JPL Search for Extraterrestrial Intelligence," *Mercury,* **6** (4), 8 (1977).

177. Edie, L. C. "Messages from Other Worlds," letter in *Science,* **136,** 184 (1962).

178. Eigen, M., and Schuster, P. "Stages of Emerging Life—Five Principles of Early Organization," *Journal of Molecular Evolution,* **19,** 47 (1982).

179. Eigen, Manfred, and Winkler, Ruthild. *Laws of the Game: How the Principles of Nature Govern Chance.* Princeton, N.J.: Princeton University Press (1993).

180. Eiseley, Loren. *The Immense Journey.* New York: Vintage Books (1946).

181. Ekland, E. H., Szostak, J. W., and Bartel, D. P. "Structurally Complex and Highly Active RNA Ligases Derived from Random RNA Sequences," *Science,* **269,** 364 (1995).

182. Eldridge, Niles. *Time Frames: The Evolution of Punctuated Equilibrium.* Princeton, N.J.: Princeton University Press (1985).

183. Engel, M. H., and Macko, S. A. "Isotopic Evidence for Extraterrestrial Non-Racemic Amino Acids in the Murchison Meteorite," *Nature,* **389,** 265 (1997).

184. Epstein, I. R., Kustin, K., De Kepper, P., and Orban, M. "Oscillating Chemical Reactions," *Scientific American,* 112 (March 1983).

185. Eschelman, V. R. "Gravitational Lens of the Sun: Its Potential for Observations and Communications over Interstellar Distances," *Science,* **205,** 1133 (1979).

186. Evans, David S. "The Great Moon Hoax," *Sky & Telescope,* 196 (September 1981) and 308 (October 1981).

187. Ezell, E. C., and Ezell, L. N. *On Mars: Exploration of the Red Planet, 1958–1978.* Washington, D.C.: National Aeronautics and Space Administration (1984).

188. Farley, J. *The Spontaneous Generation Controversy from Descartes to Oparin.* Baltimore: The Johns Hopkins University Press (1977).

189. Feinberg, Gerald, and Shapiro, Robert. *Life Beyond Earth: The Intelligent Earthling's Guide to Life in the Universe.* New York: William Morrow (1980).

190. Feldman, W. C., Maurice, S., Binder, A. B., Barraclough, B. L., Elphic, R. C., and Lawrence, D. J. "Fluxes of Fast and Epithermal Neutrons from Lunar Prospector: Evidence for Water Ice at the Lunar Poles," *Science,* **281,** 1496 (1998).

191. Ferris, J. P., Hill, A. R., Jr., Liu, R., and Orgel, L. "Synthesis of Long Prebiotic Oligomers on Mineral Surfaces," *Nature,* **381,** 59 (1996).

192. Firsoff, V. A. *Life Beyond the Earth.* New York: Basic Books (1963).

193. "First Soviet-American Conference on Communication with Extraterrestrial Intelligence," *Icarus,* **16,** 412 (1972).

194. Fischer, D., Marcy, G., Butler, P., Vogt, S., and Apps, K. "Planetary Companions Around Two Solar Type Stars: HD 195019 and HD 217107," *Publications of the Astronomical Society of the Pacific,* **111,** 50 (1999).

195. Fisk, M., and Giovannoni, S. "Microbial Weathering of Igneous Rocks: A Tool for Locating Past Life on Mars," paper presented at 30th Annual Lunar and Planetary Science Conference, Houston, Tex., March 15–29, 1999.

196. Flammarion, Camille. *La planète Mars et ses conditions d'habitabilité.* Paris: Gauthier Villars et Fils (1892).

197. Florkin, M., et al. "Contamination by Extraterrestrial Exploration," *Nature,* **183,** 925 (1959).

198. Fontenelle, Bernard Le Bovier de. *Conversations on the Plurality of Worlds,* trans. by H. A. Hargeaves. Berkeley: University of California Press (1990).

199. Ford, E., Rasio, F. and Sills, A. "Structure and Evolution of Nearby Stars with Planets," *Astrophysical Journal,* **514,** 411 (1998).

200. Forward, Robert L. *Dragon's Egg.* New York: Del Rey (1980).

201. Forward, Robert L. *Starquake!* New York: Del Rey (1985).

202. Forward, R. "When You Live Upon a Star," *New Scientist,* 36 (December 24/31, 1987).

203. Forward, Robert L., and Davis, Joel. *Mirror Matter: Pioneering Antiphysics.* New York: Wiley (1988).

204. Fox, S. W. "Evolution of Protein Molecules and Thermal Synthesis of Biochemical Substances," *American Scientist,* **44,** 347 (1956).

205. Fox, Sidney. *The Emergence of Life: Darwinian Evolution from the Inside.* New York: Basic Books (1988).

206. Fox, S. W., and Dose, K. *Molecular Evolution and the Origin of Life.* New York: Marcel Dekker (1977).

207. Fox, S. W., Harada, K., and Kendrick, J. "Production of Spherules from Synthetic Proteinoid and Hot Water," *Science,* **129,** 1221 (1959).

208. Frederickson, J. K., and Onstott, T. C. "Microbes Deep Inside the Earth," *Scientific American,* 68 (October 1996).

209. Freitas, Robert A., Jr., and Valdes, Francisco. "The Search for Extraterrestrial Artifacts (SETA)," *Acta Astronautica,* **12** (12), 1027 (1985).

210. Freudenthal, Hans. *Lincos, Design of a Language for Cosmic Intercourse.* Amsterdam: North-Holland (1960).

211. Fuller, John. *The Interrupted Journey.* New York: Berkley (1966).

212. Galtier, N., Tourasse, N., and Gouy, M. "A Nonhyperthermophilic Common Ancestor to Extant Life Forms," *Science,* **283,** 220 (1999).

213. Gatewood, G. D. "Lalande 21185," *Bulletin of the American Astronomical Society,* **28,** 885 (1996).

214. Geiger, P. J., Jaffe, L. D., and Mamikunian, G. "Biological Contamination of the Planets." In Mamikunian, G., and Briggs, M. H., eds., *Current Aspects of Biology.* Oxford: Oxford University Press (1965).

215. Gesteland, R. F., and Atkins, J. F., eds. *The RNA World.* Cold Spring Harbor, N.Y.: Cold Spring Harbor Laboratory Press (1993).

216. Gilbert, W. "The RNA World," *Nature,* **319,** 618 (1986).

217. Gingerich, O. "The Satellites of Mars: Prediction and Discovery," *Journal of the History of Astronomy,* **1,** 109 (1970).

218. Gladman, B. "Twenty-eight Ways to Build a Solar System," *Nature,* **396,** 513 (1998).

219. Glanz, J. "Six Strange New Worlds," *Science,* **280,** 2037 (1998).

220. Gold, T. "Cosmic Garbage," *Air Force and Space Digest,* 65 (May 1960).

221. Gold, Thomas. *The Deep Hot Biosphere.* New York: Springer-Verlag (1999).

222. Goldsmith, Donald, ed. *The Quest for Extraterrestrial Life: A Book of Readings.* Mill Valley, Calif.: University Science Books (1980).

223. Goldsmith, Donald, ed. *Scientists Confront Velikovsky.* Ithaca, N.Y.: Cornell University Press (1989).

224. Goldsmith, Donald. *Worlds Unnumbered: The Search for Extrasolar Planets.* Sausalito, Calif.: University Science Books (1997).

225. Goldsmith, Donald. *The Hunt for Life on Mars.* New York: Penguin Books (1997).

226. Goldsmith, Donald, and Owen, Tobias. *The Search for Life in the Universe.* Menlo Park, Calif.: Benjamin/Cummings (1980).

227. Golimowski, D., and Schroeder, D. "WFPC2 Observations of Proxima Centauri: No Evidence of the Possible Substellar Companion," *Astronomical Journal,* **116,** 440 (1998).

228. Gonzalez, G. "Extrasolar Planets and ETI," *Astronomy & Geophysics*, **39**, 68 (1998).

229. Gonzalez, G. "Spectroscopic Analyses of the Parent Stars of Extrasolar Planetary System Candidates," *Astronomy & Astrophysics*, **334**, 221 (1998).

230. Gonzalez, G., and Vanture, A. "Parent Stars of Extrasolar Planets III: Rho[1] Cancri Revisited," *Astronomy & Astrophysics*, **339**, L29 (1998).

231. Gonzalez, G., Wallerstein, G., and Saar, S. "Parent Stars of Extrasolar Planets IV: 14 Herculis, HD 187123, and HD 210277," *Astrophysical Journal Letters*, **511**, L111 (1999).

232. Gore, John Ellard. *The Worlds of Space.* London (1894).

233. Gould, A. "Microlensing and the Stellar Mass Function," *Publications of the Astronomical Society of the Pacific*, **108**, 465 (1996).

234. Gould, Stephen Jay. *The Flamingo's Smile: Reflections in Natural History,* chapter "SETI and the Wisdom of Casey Stengel." New York: W. W. Norton (1985).

235. Gould, Stephen Jay. *Wonderful Life: The Burgess Shale and the Nature of History.* New York: W. W. Norton (1989).

236. Greaves, J., Holland, W., Moriarty-Schiven, G., Dent, W., Zuckerman, B., McCarthy, C., Webb, R., Butner, H., Gear, W., and Walker, H. "A Dust Ring Around Epsilon Eridani: Analogue to the Young Solar System," *Astrophysical Journal Letters*, **506**, L133 (1998).

237. Green, H. W. II, Radcliffe, S. V., and Heuer, A. H. "Allende Meteorite: A High-Voltage Electron Petrographic Study," *Science*, **172**, 936 (1971).

238. Green, N. "On Some Changes in the Markings of Mars, Since the Opposition of 1877," *Monthly Notices of the Royal Astronomical Society*, **40**, 331 (1880).

239. Greenwood, J. P., Riciputi, L. R., and McSween, H. Y., Jr. "Sulfide Isotopic Compositions in Shergottites and ALH 84001, and Possible Implications for Life on Mars," *Geochimica et Cosmochimica Acta*, **61**, 4449 (1997).

240. Greg, Percy. *Across the Zodiac.* London: Trubner (1880). Reprinted with introduction in the series *Classics of Science*, Westport, Conn.: Hyperion Press (1974).

241. Griest, K., and Safizadeh, N. "The Use of High-Magnification Microlensing Events in Discovering Extrasolar Planets," *Astrophysical Journal*, **500**, 37 (1998).

242. Griffith, C., Yelle, R., and Marley, M. "The Dusty Atmosphere of the Brown Dwarf Gliese 229B," *Science*, **282**, 2063 (1998).

243. Grinin, V. P., et al. "The Beta Pictoris Phenomenon Among Young Stars. 1. The Case of the Herbig Ae Star UX Orionis," *Astronomy & Astrophysics*, **292**, 165 (1994).

244. Gross, Michael. *Life on the Edge: Amazing Creatures Thriving in Extreme Environments.* New York: Plenum (1998).

245. Guinan, E., McCook, G. P., Wright, S., and Schneider, J. "Possible Planetary Transit Eclipse for CM Draconis," *Bulletin of the American Astronomical Society*, **189**, 3201 (1996).

246. Gunn, James. *The Listeners.* New York: Scribner's (1972).

247. Gunn, James. *Isaac Asimov: The Foundations of Science Fiction.* Oxford: Oxford University Press (1982).

248. Guthke, Karl S. *The Last Frontier: Imagining Other Worlds from the Copernican Revolution to Modern Science Fiction.* Ithaca, N.Y.: Cornell University Press (1990).

249. Haldane, J. B. S. *Possible Worlds.* New York: Hugh & Bros. (1928).

250. Haldane, J. B. S. "The Origin of Life," *Rationalist Annual* (1929). Reprinted in J. B. S. Haldane, *The Inequality of Man.* London: Penguin Books (1937).

251. Haldane, J. B. S. "The Origins of Life," *New Biology*, **16**, 12 (1954).

252. Hale, A. "On the Nature of the Companion to HD 114762," *Publications of the Astronomical Society of the Pacific*, **107**, 22 (1995).

253. Halpern, Paul. *The Quest for Alien Planets.* New York: Plenum (1997).

254. Hansson, Anders. *Mars and the Development of Life*, 2nd ed. New York: John Wiley & Sons (1997).

255. Harrington, R. S., and Harrington, B. J. "Can We Find a Place to Live Near a Multiple Star?" *Mercury*, **7**, 34 (1978).

256. Harrington, R. "Planetary Motion in Alpha Centauri," *Journal of Astronautic Science*, **35**, 359 (1987).

257. Harrison, Albert. *After Contact: The Human Response to Extraterrestrial Life.* New York: Plenum (1997).

258. Hart, M. "An Explanation for the Absence of Extraterrestrial Life on Earth," *Quarterly Journal of the Royal Astronomical Society,* **16,** 128 (1975).

259. Hart, M. "Habitable Zones Around Main Sequence Stars," *Icarus,* **37,** 351 (1979).

260. Harvey, R. P., and McSween, H. Y., Jr. "A Possible High-Temperature Origin for the Carbonates in the Martian Meteorite ALH 84001," *Nature,* **382,** 49 (1996).

261. Hatzes, A., Cochran, W., and Bakker, E. "Further Evidence for the Planet Around 51 Pegasi," *Nature,* **391,** 154 (1998).

262. Hauser, H., and Marcy, G. "The Orbit of 16 Cygni AB," *Publications of the Astronomical Society of the Pacific,* **111,** 321 (1999).

263. Heidmann, Jean. *Life in the Universe.* New York: McGraw-Hill (1992).

264. Heidmann, J. *Extraterrestrial Intelligence.* New York: Cambridge University Press (1995).

265. Heidmann, J., and Klein, M. J., eds. *Bioastronomy.* New York: Springer Verlag (1991).

266. Heinlein, Robert. *Stranger in a Strange Land.* New York: Putnam (1961).

267. Henning, T., and Schnaiter, M. "Carbon—from Space to Laboratory." In P. Ehrenfreund, K. Krofft, H. Kochan, and V. Pironello, eds., *Laboratory Analysis and Space Research, Astrophysics and Space Science Library,* **236,** 249, Dortrecht: Kluwer Academic (1999).

268. Herbig, G. H. "The Diffuse Interstellar Bands," *Annual Review of Astronomy and Astrophysics,* **33,** 359 (1995).

269. Herschel, W. "On the Remarkable Appearances at the Polar Regions of the Planet Mars, the Inclination of its Axis, the Position of its Poles, and its spheroidical Figure; with a few Hints relating to its real Diameter and Atmosphere," *Philosophical Transactions of the Royal Society of London,* **74,** 233 (1784).

270. Herschel, W. *Philosophical Transactions of the Royal Society of London* (1795).

271. Hinz, P. M., Angel, J. R. P., Hoffmann, W. F., McCarthy, D. W., Jr, McGuire, P. C., Cheselka, M., Hora, J. L., and Woolf, N. J. "Imaging Circumstellar Environments with a Nulling Interferometer," *Nature,* **395,** 251 (1998).

272. Hipolito, J., and McNelly, W. E., eds. *The Book of Mars.* London: Futura (1976).

273. Hogben, L. Review of *Lincos* by Hans Friedenthal, *Nature,* **192,** 826 (1961).

274. Hogben, Lancelot. *Science in Authority.* New York: W. W. Norton (1963).

275. Holm, N. G. "Why Are Hydrothermal Systems Proposed as Plausible Environments for the Origin of Life?" *Origins of Life and Evolution of the Biosphere,* **22,** 5 (1992).

276. Holman, M., and Wiegert, P. "Long-term Stability of Planets in Binary Systems," *Bulletin of the American Astronomical Society,* **28,** 1113 (1996).

277. Horowitz, N. H. "On the Evolution of Biochemical Syntheses," *Proceedings of the National Academy of Science,* **31,** 153 (1945).

278. Horowitz, N. "The Search for Life on Mars," *Scientific American,* 52 (November 1977).

279. Horowitz, Norman. *To Utopia and Back: The Search for Life in the Solar System.* New York: Freeman (1986).

280. Horowitz, N. H., et al. "Planetary Contamination I: The Problem and the Agreements," *Science,* **155,** 1501 (1967).

281. Horowitz, N. H., et al. "Microbiology of the Dry Valleys of Antarctica," *Science,* **176,** 242 (1972).

282. Horowitz, N. H., Hubbard, J. S., and Hobby, G. L. "The Carbon-Assimilation Experiment: The Viking Mars Lander," *Icarus,* **16,** 147 (1972).

283. Horowitz, P. "A Search for Ultra-Narrowband Signals of Extraterrestrial Origin," *Science,* **201,** 733 (1978).

284. Horowitz, P., Matthews, B. S., Forster, J., Linscott, I., Teague, C., Chen, K., and Backus, P. "Ultranarrowband Searches for Extraterrestrial Intelligence with Dedicated Signal-Processing Hardware," *Icarus,* **67,** 525 (1986).

285. Hoyle, Fred. *Frontiers of Astronomy.* New York: Harper's (1955).

286. Hoyle, Fred. *The Black Cloud.* New York: Signet (1959).

287. Hoyle, Fred. *Of Men and Galaxies.* Seattle: University of Washington Press (1964).

288. Hoyle, Fred, and Elliott, John. *A for Andromeda*. New York: Harper & Row (1962).

289. Hoyle, Fred, Watkins, John, and Wickramasinghe, Chandra. *Viruses from Space*. Cardiff: University College Cardiff Press (1986).

290. Hoyle, F., and Wickramasinghe, C. "Prebiotic Molecules and Interstellar Grains," *Nature*, **266,** 241 (1977).

291. Hoyle, Fred, and Wickramasinghe, Chandra. *Lifecloud*. New York: Harper & Row (1979).

292. Hoyle, Fred, and Wickramasinghe, Chandra. *Evolution from Space*. London: J. M. Dent & Sons (1981).

293. Hoyle, Fred, and Wickramasinghe, Chandra. *Living Comets*. Cardiff: University College Cardiff Press (1985).

294. Huang, S. S. "Occurrence of Life Outside the Solar System," *American Scientist*, **47,** 397 (1959).

295. Huang, S. S. "Life-Supporting Regions in the Vicinity of Binary Systems," *Publications of the Astronomical Society of the Pacific*, **72,** 106 (1960).

296. Huang, S. S. "The Limiting Sizes of the Habitable Planets," *Publications of the Astronomical Society of the Pacific*, **72,** 489 (1960).

297. Hynek, J. Allen. *The UFO Experience*. Chicago: Henry Regnery (1973).

298. Ida, S., and Lin, D. "On the Origin of Massive Eccentric Planets," *Bulletin of the American Astronomical Society*, **28,** 1112 (1996).

299. Imai, E., Honda, H., Hatori, K., Brack, A., and Koichiro, M. "Elongation of Oligopeptides in a Simulated Submarine Hydrothermal System," *Science*, **283,** 831 (1999).

300. Jackson, C., and Hohmann, R. "An Historic Report on Life in Space: Tesla, Marconi, Todd," paper presented at 17th Annual Meeting of the American Rocket Society, Los Angeles, November 13–18, 1962.

301. Jameson, Frederic. *Signatures of the Visible*. New York: Routledge (1990).

302. Jastrow, Robert. *Until the Sun Dies*, pp. 154ff. New York: W. W. Norton (1977).

303. Jeans, J. "Is There Life on the Other Worlds?" *Science*, **95,** 589 (1942).

304. Jianke, L., Ferrario, L., and Wickramasinghe, D. "Planets Around White Dwarfs," *Astrophysical Journal Letters*, **503,** L151 (1998).

305. Jones, D. L., Lestrade J.-F., Preston, R. A., and Phillips, R. B. "Searching for Planets with VLBI," *Astrophysics and Space Science*, **223,** 166 (1995).

306. Jugaku, J. and Nishimura, S. "A Search for Dyson Spheres Around Late-Type Stars in the Solar Neighborhood. III," paper presented at Bioastronomy 99: A New Era in Bioastronomy, Kohala Coast, Hawaii, August 2–6, 1999.

307. Kalas, P. "Dusty Disks and Planet Mania," *Science*, **281,** 182 (1998).

308. Kamminga, H. "Life from Space—A History of Panspermia," *Vistas in Astronomy*, **26,** 67 (1982).

309. Kapitza, A. P., Ridley, J. K., Robin, G. de Q., Siegert, M. J., and Zotikov, I. A. "A Large, Deep Freshwater Lake Beneath the Ice of Central East Antarctica," *Nature*, **381,** 684 (1996).

310. Kardashev, N. S. "Transmission of Information by Extraterrestrial Civilizations," *Soviet Astronomy*, **8,** 217 (1964).

311. Kargel, J. S. "The Salt of Europa," *Science*, **280,** 1211 (1998).

312. Kasting, J. F. "The Early Mars Climate Question Heats Up," *Science*, **278,** 1245 (1997).

313. Kasting, J. F., Whitmire, D. P., and Reynolds, R. T. "Habitable Zones Around Main Sequence Stars," *Icarus*, **101,** 108 (1993).

314. Kauffman, Stuart. *The Origins of Order: Self-Organization and Selection in Evolution*. New York: Oxford University Press (1993).

315. Kaufmann, Stuart. *At Home in the Universe: The Search for the Laws of Self-Organization and Complexity*. New York: Oxford University Press (1995).

316. Kepler, Johann. *Kepler's Somnium*, trans. with commentary by Edward Rosen. Madison, Wis.: University of Wisconsin Press (1967).

317. Kerr, R. A. "Life Goes to Extremes in the Deep Earth—and Elsewhere?," *Science*, **276,** 703 (1997).

318. Kerr, R. A. "An Ocean for Old Callisto," *Science*, **280,** 1695 (1998).

319. Keyhoe, Donald. *The Flying Saucers Are Real*. New York: Fawcett (1950).

320. Kivelson, M. G., Khurana, K. K., Stevenson, D. J., Bennett, L., Joy, S., Russell, C. T.,

Walker, R. J., Zimmer, C., and Polanskey, C. "Europa and Callisto: Induced or Intrinsic Fields in a Periodically Varying Plasma Environment," *Journal of Geophysical Research,* **104,** No. A3, 4609 (1999).

321. Klass, Philip. *UFOs Explained.* New York: Vintage (1974).

322. Klass, Philip J. *UFO Abductions: A Dangerous Game.* Buffalo, N.Y.: Prometheus (1988).

323. Klemaszewski, J. E., et al. "Galileo at Callisto: Overview of Nominal Mission Results," *29th Annual Lunar and Planetary Society Conference,* Houston, Tex., abstract no. 1866 (1998).

324. Kreifeldt, J. G. "A Formulation for the Number of Communicative Civilizations in the Galaxy," *Icarus,* **14,** 4190 (1971).

325. Ksanfomality, L. "Problem of Habitation on Planetary Systems of Red Dwarf Stars," *Journal of the British Interplanetary Society,* **39,** 416 (1987).

326. Kubat, J., Holmgren, D., and Rentzsch-Holm, I. "On the Planetary Companions of Solar-type Stars," *Astronomy & Astrophysics,* **332,** 842 (1998).

327. Kuiper, Gerard. P. *The Atmospheres of the Earth and Planets,* rev. ed. Chicago: University of Chicago Press (1952).

328. Kundic, T., et al. "An Event in the Light Curve of 0957 +561A and Prediction of the 1996 Image B Light Curve," *Astrophysical Journal Letters,* **455,** L5 (1996).

329. Lasswitz, Kurd. *Auf zwei Planeten.* 1st ed. Leipzig: Verlag B. Elischer Nachfolger (1897). *Two Planets,* only English lang. ed., abridged by Erich Lasswitz, trans. by Hans Rudruick. Carbondale, Il.: Southern Illinois University Press (1971).

330. Latham, D. W., Stefanik, R. P., Mazeh, T., Mayor, M., and Burki, G. "The Unseen Companion of HD 114762," *Nature,* **339,** 38 (1989).

331. Lazzaro, D., Sicardy, B., Roques, F., and Greenberg, R. "Is There a Planet Around Beta Pictoris? Perturbations of a Planet Circumstellar Disk. 2: The Analytical Model," *Icarus,* **108,** 59 (1994).

332. Learned, J. G., Pakvasa, S., Simmons, W. A., and Tata, X. "Timing Data Communication with Neutrinos—A New Approach to SETI," *Quarterly Journal of the Royal Astronomical Society,* **35,** 321 (1994).

333. Lederberg, J. "Exobiology: Approaches to Life Beyond the Earth," *Science,* **132,** 398 (1960).

334. Lederberg, J., and Cowie, D. B. "Moondust," *Science,* **127,** 1473 (1958).

335. Leger, A., Mariott, J. M., Menesson, B., Ollivier, M., Puget, J. L., Rouan, D., and Schneider, J. "Could We Search for Primitive Life on Extrasolar Planets in the Near Future? The Darwin Project," *Icarus,* **123,** 249 (1996).

336. Leger, A., Ollivier, M., Altwegg, K., and Woolf, N. "Is the Presence of H_2O and O_3 in an Exoplanet a Reliable Signature of a Biological Activity?," *Astronomy & Astrophysics,* **341,** 304 (1998).

337. Lem, Stanisław. *Solaris,* trans. by Joanna Kilmartin and Steve Cox. New York: Walker (1970).

338. Lemonick, Michael D. *The Search for Life in the Universe.* New York: Simon & Schuster (1998).

339. Levin, G. V. "Detection of Metabolically Produced Labeled Gas: The Viking Mars Lander," *Icarus,* **16,** 153 (1972).

340. Levin, G. V. "The Viking Labeled Release Experiment and Life on Mars," *Proceedings SPIE,* **3111,** 146 (1997).

341. Levin, G. V., Heim, A. H., Clendenning, J. R., and Thompson, M.-F. " 'Gulliver'—A Quest for Life on Mars," *Science,* **138,** 114 (1962).

342. Levin, G. V., and Straat, P. A. "Recent Results from the Viking Labeled Release Experiment on Mars," *Journal of Geophysical Research,* **82,** 4663 (1977).

343. Levison, H., Lissauer, J., and Duncan, M. "Modeling the Diversity of Outer Planetary Systems," *Astronomical Journal,* **116,** 1998 (1998).

344. Lewis, C. S. *Out of the Silent Planet.* New York: Macmillan (1943) (first published 1938).

345. Lewis, C. S. *Perelandra.* New York: Macmillan (1944) (first published 1943).

346. Lewis, C. S. *That Hideous Strength.* New York: Macmillan (1946) (first published 1945).

347. Lewis, J. S. "Satellites of the Outer Planets: Their Physical and Chemical Nature," *Icarus*, **15** (1971).

348. Ley, Willy, and von Braun, Wernher. *The Exploration of Mars*. New York: Viking (1956).

349. Lilly, John C. *Man and Dolphin*. New York: Doubleday (1961).

350. Lin, D. N. C., Bodenheimer, P., and Richardson, D. C. "Orbital Migration of the Planetary Companion of 51 Pegasi to Its Present Location," *Nature*, **380,** 606 (1996).

351. Lin, D. N. C., Laughlin, G., Bodenheimer, P., and Rozyczka, M. "The Formation of Substellar Objects Induced by the Collision of Protostellar Disks," *Science*, **281,** 2085 (1998).

352. Lippincott, S. L. "Astrometric Analysis of Lalande 21185," *Astrophysical Journal,* **65,** 445 (1960).

353. Lissauer, J. J. "Planet Formation," *Annual Review of Astronomy and Astrophysics,* **31,** 129 (1993).

354. Lissauer, J. J. "Urey Prize Lecture: On the Diversity of Plausible Planetary Systems," *Icarus,* **114,** 217 (1995).

355. Lissauer, J. "Seeking Planetary Systems," *Science,* **282,** 1832 (1998).

356. Livio, M. "How Rare Are Extraterrestrial Civilizations and When Did They Emerge?," *Astrophysical Journal,* **511,** 429 (1999).

357. Locke, John. "Elements of Natural Philosophy." In *The Works of John Locke*, vol. 3, p. 309. London: T. Tegg (1823).

358. Locke, Richard Adams. *The Moon Hoax: A Discovery That the Moon Has a Vast Population of Human Beings*. Reproduced, with intro. by Ormond Seavey. Boston: Gregg Press (1975).

359. Lovejoy, Arthur O. *The Great Chain of Being*. Cambridge, Mass.: Harvard University Press (1971) (first published 1936).

360. Lovell, Bernard. *The Exploration of Outer Space* (appendix). Oxford: Oxford University Press (1962).

361. Lovell, Bernard. *Out of the Zenith*. New York: Harper & Row (1973).

362. Lovelock, J. "Thermodynamics and the Recognition of Alien Biospheres," *Proceedings of the Royal Society of London,* **B 189,** 167 (1975).

363. Lovelock, J. E. *Gaia: A New Look at Life on Earth*. Oxford: Oxford University Press (1979).

364. Lovelock, J. and Margulis, L. "Is Mars a Spaceship, Too?," *Natural History,* 86 (June–July 1976).

365. Lowell, Percival. *Mars*. New York: Houghton-Mifflin (1895).

366. Lowell, Percival. *Mars and Its Canals*. New York: Macmillan (1906).

367. Lowell, Percival. *Mars as the Abode of Life*. New York: Macmillan (1910).

368. Luciano, Patrick. *Them or Us: Archetypal Interpretations of Fifties Alien Invasion Films*. Bloomington, Ind.: Indiana University Press (1987).

369. Lucretius. *The Nature of the Universe*, trans. by Ronald Latham. Baltimore: Penguin Books (1951).

370. Lunan, Duncan. *Interstellar Contact*. Chicago: Regnery (1975).

371. Mack, John E. *Abduction: Human Encounters With Aliens*. New York: Scribner's (1992).

372. Mammana, Dennis L., and McCarthy, Donald W., Jr. *Other Suns, Other Worlds?* New York: St. Martin's Press (1996).

373. Marcy, G. W. "Extrasolar Planets," *Nature*, **391,** 127 (1998).

374. Marcy, G. W., and Butler R. P. "A Planetary Companion to 70 Virginis," *Astrophysical Journal Letters*, **464,** L147 (1996).

375. Marcy, G. W., and Butler, R. P. "The Diversity of Planetary Systems," *Sky & Telescope*, **95** (3), 30 (1998).

376. Marcy, G., Butler, P., and Fischer, D. "Three Jupiter-Mass Companions Orbiting Upsilon Andromedae," paper presented at the American Astronomical Society Meeting No. 194. Washington, D.C.: American Astronomical Society Publications (1999).

377. Marcy, G. W., Butler, R. P., Vogt, S. S., Fischer, D., and Lissauer, J. "A Planetary Companion to the M4 Red Dwarf, Gliese 876," *Astrophysical Journal Letters*, **505,** L147 (1998).

378. Marcy, G. W., Butler, R. P., Vogt, S. S., Fischer, D., and Liu, M. C. "Two New Planets in Eccentric Orbits," *Astrophysical Journal*, **520,** 239 (1999).

379. Margulis, Lynn. *What Is Life?* New York: Simon & Schuster (1995).

380. Margulis, Lynn. Interview in John Horgan, *The End of Science*, p. 140. New York: Addison-Wesley (1996).

381. Margulis, Lynn, and Sagan, Dorion. *Microcosmos: Four Billion Years of Microbial Evolution.* New York: Simon & Schuster (1986).

382. Marten, K., et al. "Ring Bubbles of Dolphins," *Scientific American,* **275** (2), 64 (1996).

383. Mascall, E. L. *Christian Theology and Natural Science—Some Questions on Their Relations.* London: Green (1956).

384. Matese, J., and Whitmire, D. "Tidal Imprint of Distant Galactic Matter on the Oort Comet Cloud," *Astrophysical Journal Letters,* **472,** L41 (1996).

385. Matthews, C., Nelson, J., Varma, P., and Minard, R. "Deuterolysis of Amino Acid Precursors: Evidence for Hydrogen Cyanide Polymers as Protein Ancestors," *Science,* **198,** 622 (1977).

386. Matthews, K., Nakajima, T., Kulkarni, S. R., and Oppenheimer, B. R. "Spectral Energy Distribution and Bolometric Luminosity of the Cool Brown Dwarf Gliese 229B," *Astrophysical Journal,* **112,** 1678 (1996).

387. Matthews, W. D. "Life in Other Worlds," *Science,* **44,** 239 (1921).

388. Mattox, J. R. "Possible Detection of a Planet Orbiting the Geminga Gamma-Ray Pulsar," *Detection and Study of Planets Outside the Solar System,* 23rd Meeting of the IAU, Joint Discussion 13, Kyoto, Japan, August 25–26, 1997.

389. Mayor, M., and Queloz, D. "A Jupiter-mass Companion to a Solar-type Star," *Nature,* **378,** 355 (1995).

390. McCollum, Michael. *LifeProbe.* New York: Ballantine Books (1983).

391. McKay, C. P. "The Search for Life on Mars," *Origins of Life and Evolution of the Biosphere,* **27,** 263 (1997).

392. McKay, D. S., Gibson, E. K., Jr., Thomas-Keprta, K. L., Vali, H., Romanek, C. S., Clemett, S. J., Chillier, X. D. F., Maechling, C. R., and Zare, R. N. "Search for Past Life on Mars: Possible Relic Biogenic Activity in Martian Meteorite ALH 84001," *Science,* **273,** 924 (1996).

393. McKay, D. S., Wentworth, S. W., Thomas-Keprta, K., Westall, F., and Gibson, E. K., Jr. "Possible Bacteria in Nakhla [#1816]," *Proceedings of the 30th Lunar and Planetary Conference,* Houston, Tex., March 14–19, 1999.

394. McKinnon, W. B. "Sighting the Seas of Europa," *Nature,* **386,** 765 (1997).

395. Medawar, Peter B. *The Future of Man,* p. 108. London: Methuen (1960).

396. Melosh, H. J. "Multi-Ringed Revelation," *Nature,* **390,** 439 (1997).

397. Menzel, Donald H. *Flying Saucers.* Cambridge, Mass.: Harvard University Press (1953).

398. Menzel, Donald H., and Boyd, Lyle B. *The World of Flying Saucers: A Scientific Examination of a Major Myth of the Space Age.* New York: Doubleday (1963).

399. Menzel, Donald H., and Taves, Ernest H. *The UFO Enigma.* New York: Doubleday (1977).

400. Michael, Donald N., ed. *Proposed Studies on the Implications of Peaceful Space Activities for Human Affairs* by the Brookings Institution to the 87th U.S. Congress, report No. 242. Washington, D.C.: National Aeronatics and Space Administration (1961).

401. Miller, J. G. *Living Systems.* New York: McGraw-Hill (1978).

402. Miller, Ron. "Astronauts by Gaslight," *Ad Astra,* 42 (September–October 1994).

403. Miller, S. L. "Production of Amino Acids Under Possible Primitive Earth Conditions," *Science,* **117,** 528 (1953).

404. Miller, Stanley, and Orgel, Leslie E. *The Origins of Life on the Earth.* Englewood Cliffs, N.J.: Prentice-Hall (1974).

405. Miller, S. L., and Robertson, M. P. "An Efficient Prebiotic Synthesis of Cytosine and Uracil," *Nature,* **375,** 772 (1995).

406. Miller, S. L., and Urey, H. C. "Organic Compound Synthesis on the Primitive Earth," *Science,* **130,** 245 (1959).

407. Monod, Jacques. *Chance and Necessity.* New York: Alfred A. Knopf (1971).

408. Moravec, Hans. *Robot: Mere Machine to Transcedent Mind.* New York: Oxford University Press (1998).

409. Morowitz, Harold J. *Cosmic Joy and Local Pain.* New York: Charles Scribner's (1987)

410. Morrison, P. "Interstellar Communication," *Bulletin of the Philosophical Society of Washington,* **16,** 78 (1962). Reprinted in A. G. W. Cameron, ed., *Interstellar Communication,* q.v.

411. Morrison, P., Billingham, J., and Wolfe, J., eds. *The Search for Extraterrestrial Intelligence.* New York: Dover (1979).

412. Muir, Hazel. "There Could be Whole Worlds of Invisible Matter Out There," *New Scientist,* 17 (February 13, 1999).

413. Muller, H. J. "The Gene as the Basis of Life," *Proceedings of the International Congress of Plant Science,* **1,** 897 (1929). Reprinted in *Studies in Genetics: The Selected Papers of H. J. Muller,* Bloominton, Ind.: University of Indiana Press (1962).

414. Muller, H. J. "Life Forms to Be Expected Elsewhere than on Earth," *The American Biology Teacher,* **23,** 74 (1961).

415. Murray, B. C., et al. "Planetary Contamination II: Soviet and U.S. Practices and Policies," *Science,* **155,** 1505 (1967).

416. Murray, N., Hansen, B., Holman, M., and Tremaine, S. "Migrating Planets," *Science,* **279,** 69 (1998).

417. Nagy, B., Hennessy, D. J., and Meinschein, W. G. "Mass Spectroscopic Analysis of the Orgueil Meteorite: Evidence for Biogenic Hydrocarbons," *Annals of the New York Academy of Sciences,* **93,** 25 (1961).

418. National Academy of Sciences. *A Review of Space Research: The Report of the Summer Study Conducted Under the Auspices of the Space Science Board of the National Academy of Sciences at the State University of Iowa, Iowa City, Iowa, June 17–August 10, 1962.* Washington, D.C.: U.S. Government Printing Office (1962).

419. Nelson, A., Benz, W., Adams, F., and Arnett, D. "Dynamics of Circumstellar Disks," *Astrophysical Journal,* **502,** 342 (1998).

420. Nielsen, P. E. "Peptide Nucleic Acid (PNA). From DNA Recognition to Antisense and DNA Structure," *Biophysical Chemistry,* **68,** 103 (1997).

421. Nicolson, Marjorie Hope. *Voyages to the Moon.* New York: Macmillan (1948).

422. Niven, Larry. *Ringworld.* New York: Ballantine Books (1970).

423. Noyes, R., et al. "A Planet Orbiting the Star Rho Coronae Borealis," *Astrophysical Journal,* **483,** 111 (1997).

424. O'Keefe, J., and Ahrens, T. "Oblique Impact: A Process for Obtaining Meteorite Samples from Other Planets," *Science,* **234,** 346 (1986).

425. Oliver, B. M. "Some Potentialities of Optical Masers," *Proceedings of the Institute of Radio Engineers,* **50,** 135 (1962). Reprinted in A. G. W. Cameron, ed., *Interstellar Communication,* q.v.

426. O'Malley, W. J. "Carl Sagan's Gospel of Scientism," *America,* **144,** 95 (February 7, 1981).

427. O'Neill, G. K. "The Colonization of Space," *Physics Today,* **27** (9), 32 (1974).

428. O'Neill, Gerard K. *The High Frontier.* New York: William Morrow (1977).

429. Oparin, A. I. *The Origin of Life.* New York: Dover (1952) (first published 1938).

430. Öpik, E. J. "Life and Its Evolution from an Astronomical Viewpoint," *Irish Astronomical Journal,* **2** (1), 9 (1952).

431. Öpik, E. J. "The Destiny of Life," *Irish Astronomical Journal,* **2** (3), 65 (1952).

432. Öpik, E. J. "Is Interstellar Travel Possible?," *Irish Astronomical Journal,* **6,** 299 (1964).

433. Öpik, E. J. "Life and Intelligence in the Universe," *Irish Astronomical Journal,* **8** (4), 128 (1967).

434. Öpik, E. J. "Space Travel and Life Beyond the Earth," *Irish Astronomical Journal,* **11** (7–8), 220 (1974).

435. Oppenheimer, B. R., Kulkarni, S. R., Matthews, K., and Nakajima, T. "Near IR Spectrum of the Cool Brown Dwarf GL 229B," *Science,* **270,** 1478 (1995).

436. Oppenheimer, B. R., Kulkarni, S. R., Matthews, K., and Van Kerrwijk, M. H. "The Spectrum of the Brown Dwarf Gliese 229B," *Astrophysical Journal,* **502,** 932 (1998).

437. Orgel, L. E. *The Origins of Life: Molecules and Natural Selection.* New York: John Wiley & Sons (1973).

438. Orgel, L., et al. *Evaluating the Biological Potential in Returned Samples from Planetary Satellites and Small Solar System Bodies: Framework for Decision Making.* Washington, D.C.: National Academy Press (1998).

439. Owen, T., Gautier, D., Raulin, F., and Scattergood, T. "Titan." In G. Carle, D. Schwartz, and J. Huntington, eds., *Exobiology in Solar System Exploration,* NASA Special Publication 512, p. 127. Moffett Field, Calif.: NASA, Ames Research Center (1988).

440. Oyama, V. I. "The Gas Exchange Experiment for Life Detection," *Icarus,* **16,** 167 (1972).

441. Oyama, V. I., and Berdahl, B. J. "The Viking Gas Exchange Experiment Results from Chryse and Utopia Surface Samples," *Journal of Geophysical Research,* **82,** 4669 (1977).

442. Paczynski, B. "Gravitational Microlensing by the Galactic Halo," *Astrophysical Journal,* **304,** 1 (1986).

443. Paczynski, B. "Gravitational Microlensing in the Local Group," *Annual Review of Astronomy & Astrophysics,* **34,** 415 (1996).

444. Padgett, D. L., Brandner, W., Stapelfeldt, K. R., Strom, S. E., Tereby, S., and Koerner, D. "Hubble Space Telescope/NICMOS Imaging of Disks and Envelopes Around Very Young Stars," *Astrophysical Journal,* **117,** 1490 (1999).

445. Papaloizou, J., and Terquem, C. *Protostellar Discs and Planetary System Formation.* Chichester, England: Praxis (1998).

446. Peebles, Curtis. *Watch the Skies! A Chronicle of the Flying Saucer Myth.* Washington, D.C.: Smithsonian Institution Press (1995).

447. Perryman, M. A. C., et al. "Searching for Planets Beyond Our Solar System: How Astrometry Helps," *ESA Bulletin,* **87,** 25 (1996).

448. Persinger, M. A. "Vectorial Cerebral Hemisphericity as Differential Sources for the Sensed Presence, Mystical Experiences and Religious Conversion," *Psychological Reports,* **76,** 915 (1993).

449. Persinger, M. A., Bureau, Y. R. J., Peredery, O. P., and Richards, P. M. "The Sensed Presence as Right Hemisphere Intrusions in the Left Hemisphere Awareness of Self: An Illustrative Case," *Perceptual and Motor Skills,* **78,** 999 (1994).

450. Persinger, M. A., and Derr, J. S. "Geophysical Variables and Behavior: LXXIV. Man-made Fluid Injection into the Crust and Reports of Luminous Phenomena (UFO Reports)—Is the Strainfield an Aseismically Propagating Pulse?," *Perceptual and Motor Skills,* **77,** 1059 (1993).

451. Phillips, C. R. *The Planetary Quarantine Program: Origins and Achievements, 1956–1973.* Washington, D.C.: National Aeronautics and Space Administration (1974).

452. Phillips, J. A., and Thorsett, S. E. "Planets Around Pulsars: A Review," *Astrophysics & Space Science,* **212,** 91 (1994).

453. Phinney, E. S., and Hansen, B. M. S. "The Pulsar Planet Production Process." In *Planets Around Pulsars,* proceedings of the conference, California Institute of Technology, Pasadena, ASP Conference Series, p. 321, April 30–May 1, 1992.

454. Pickering, W. H. "Eratosthenes," 1 to 6, *Popular Astronomy,* nos. 269, 287, 312, and 317 (1919–25).

455. Pickover, Clifford. *The Science of Aliens.* New York: Basic Books (1999).

456. Pierce, J. R. "Relativity and Space Travel," *Proceedings of the Institute of Radio Engineers,* **47,** 1053 (1959).

457. Pimentel, G. C., et al. In C. S. Pittendrigh, W. Vishniac, and J. P. T. Pearman, eds., *Biology and the Exploration of Mars,* Publication 1296. Washington, D.C.: National Research Council (1966).

458. Pirie, N. W. "Introductory Remarks in a Discussion on the Recognition of Alien Life," *Proceedings of the Royal Society of London, Series B,* **189,** 137 (1975). Other papers on this subject by C. Sagan, A. G. Cairns-Smith, J. E. Lovelock, and C. H. Waddington.

459. Pittendrigh, C. S., Vishniac, W., and Pearman, J. P. T., eds. *Biology and the Exploration of Mars: Report of a Study Held under the Auspices of the Space Science Board, National Academy of Sciences, National Research Council, 1964–1965.* Washington, D.C.: National Aeronautics and Space Administration (1966).

460. Pizor, Faith K., and Comp, T. Allan, eds. *The Man in the Moone and Other Lunar Fantasies: An Anthology of Antique Science Fiction.* New York: Praeger (1971).

461. Ponnamperuma, Cyril. *The Origins of Life.* New York: E. P. Dutton (1972).

462. Ponnamperuma, Cyril, ed. *Exobiology.* Amsterdam: North-Holland (1972).

463. Poole, A. M., Jeffares, D. C., and Penny, D. "The Path from the RNA World," *Journal of Molecular Evolution,* **46,** 1 (1998).

464. Pope, Gustavus W. *Romances of the Planets, No. 1: Journey to Mars, the Wonderful World: Its Beauty and Splendor: Its Mighty Races and Kingdoms: Its Final Doom.* Westport, Conn.: Hyperion (1974) (first published 1894).

465. Porto de Mello, G. F., and da Silva, L. "The Closest Ever Solar Twin?," *Astrophysical Journal Letters,* **482,** 89 (1997).

466. Prigione, Ilya, and Stengers, Isabelle. *Order Out of Chaos.* New York: Bantam (1984).

467. Pritchard, Andrea. *Alien Discussions* (proceedings of the MIT Abduction Study Conference). Cambridge, Mass.: North Cambridge Press (1993).

468. Procter, Richard. *Other Worlds Than Ours.* New York: P. F. Collier (1900) (first published 1894).

469. Purcell, Edward. "Radio Astronomy and Communication Through Space." In A. G. W. Cameron, ed., *Interstellar Communication,* q.v. (1963).

470. Quimby, F. H. *Concepts for Detection of Extraterrestrial Life,* NASA Document SP56. Washington, D.C.: U.S. Government Printing Office (1964).

471. Rasio, F. A. "New Evidence for a Planet or Brown Dwarf in Orbit Around PSR B1620-26." In A. Olinto et al., eds., *Proceedings of the Texas Symposium on Relativistic Astrophysics, Annals of the New York Academy of Science* (1998).

472. Rasio, F., Tout, C., Lubow, S., and Livio, M. "Tidal Decay of Close Planetary Orbits," *Astrophysical Journal,* **470,** 1187 (1996).

473. Raulin, F., Coll, P., Gazeau, M.-C., and Smith, N. "Bioastronomical Aspects of Titan and the Giant Planets," paper presented at Bioastronomy 99: A New Era in Bioastronomy, Kohala Coast, Hawaii, August 2–6, 1999.

474. Raulin, F., Maurel, M.-C., and Schneider, J. "From Panspermia to Bioastronomy: The Evolution of the Hypothesis of Universal Life," *Origins of Life,* **28,** 597 (1998).

475. Rea, D. G., Belsky, T., and Calvin, M. "Interpretation of the 3- to 4-Micron Infrared Spectrum of Mars," *Science,* **141,** 923 (1963).

476. Rea, D. G., O'Leary, B. T., and Sinton, W. M. "The Origin of the 3.58- and 3.69-Micron Minima in the Infrared Spectrum," *Science,* **147,** 1286 (1965).

477. Regis, Edward, Jr. *Extraterrestrials: Science and Alien Intelligence.* Cambridge, England: Cambridge University Press (1986).

478. "Report of the Committee on the Exploration of Extraterrestrial Space (CETEX) 1959," *ICSU Review,* **1,** 100 (1959).

479. Reynolds, J. E. *Nature,* **48,** 477 (1893).

480. Reynolds, R. T., McKay, C. P., and Kasting, J. F. "Europa, Tidally Heated Oceans, and Habitable Zones Around Giant Planets," *Advances in Space Research,* **7** (5), 125 (1987).

481. Reynolds, R. T., Squyres, S. W., Colburn, D. S., and McKay, C. P. "On the Habitability of Europa," *Icarus,* **56,** 246 (1983).

482. Rhie, S. H., et al. "A Report from Microlensing Planet Search Collaboration: A Possible Earth Mass Planetary System Found in MACHO-98-BLG-35?," paper presented at 193rd American Astronomical Society Meeting, Austin, Tex., January 6–9, 1999.

483. Richards, P., Persinger, M. A., and Koren, S. A. "Modification of Activation and Evaluation Properties of Narratives by Weak Complex Magnetic Field Patterns that Simulate Limbic Burst Firing," *International Journal of Neuroscience,* **71,** 71 (1993).

484. Robertson, Michael P., and Miller, Stanley L. "An Efficient Prebiotic Synthesis of Cytosine and Uracil," *Nature,* **375,** 772 (1996).

485. Rodrigez, L., et al. "Compact Protoplanetary Disks Around the Stars of a Young Binary System," *Nature,* **395,** 355 (1998).

486. Ross, M. N., and Schubert, G. "Tidal Heating in an Internal Ocean Model on Europa," *Nature,* **325,** 133 (1987).

487. Ruppelt, Edward. *The Report on Unidentified Flying Objects.* New York: Doubleday (1956).

488. Russell, Henry Norris. "Anthropocentrism's Demise," *Scientific American,* **19,** 18 (1943).

489. Sagan, C. "Biological Contamination of the Moon," *Proceedings of the National Academy of Science,* **46,** 396 (1960).

490. Sagan, C. "Direct Contact Among Galactic Civilizations by Relativistic Interstellar Spaceflight," *Planetary and Space Science,* **11,** 485 (1963).

491. Sagan, Carl, ed. *Communication with Extraterrestrial Intelligence.* Cambridge, Mass.: MIT Press (1973).

492. Sagan, Carl. *The Cosmic Connection: An Extraterrestrial Perspective.* New York: Dell (1975).

493. Sagan, Carl. "Life." In *Encyclopedia Britannica,* 15th ed., Macropedia, vol. 10 (1974), p. 908.

494. Sagan, Carl. *The Dragons of Eden.* New York: Random House (1977).

495. Sagan, Carl. *Contact.* New York: Simon & Schuster (1985).

496. Sagan, Carl, and Coleman, Sydney. "Decontamination Standards for Martian Exploration Programs." Washington, D.C.: National Aeronautics and Space Administration (1966).

497. Sagan, C., et al. "Contamination of Mars," *Science,* **159,** 1191 (1968).

498. Sagan, Carl, Drake, Frank, Druyan, Ann, Ferris, Timothy, Lomberg, Jon, and Sagan, Linda. *Murmurs of Earth: The Voyager Interstellar Record.* New York: Random House (1978).

499. Sagan, C., and Fox, P. "The Canals of Mars: An Assessment After *Mariner 9,*" *Icarus,* **25,** 601 (1971).

500. Sagan, C., and Horowitz, P. "Five Years of Project META: An All-Sky Narrowband Radio Search for Extraterrestrial Signals," *Astrophysical Journal,* **415,** 218 (1993).

501. Sagan, C., and Lederberg, J. "The Prospects for Life on Mars: A Pre-Viking Assessment," *Icarus,* **28,** 291 (1976).

502. Sagan, C., and Newman, W. "The Solipsist Approach to Extraterrestrial Intelligence," *Quarterly Journal of the Royal Astronomical Society,* **24,** 113 (1983).

503. Sagan, Carl, and Page, Thornton, eds. *UFOs: A Scientific Debate.* New York: Norton (1974).

504. Sagan, C., and Salpeter, E. E. "Particles, Environments and Possible Ecologies in the Jovian Atmosphere," *Astrophysical Journal Supplement,* **32,** 737 (1976).

505. Sagan, C., Thompson, W. R., Carlson, R., Gurnett, D., and Hord, C. "A Search for Life on Earth from the Galileo Spacecraft," *Nature,* **365,** 715 (1993).

506. Sagan, C., Thompson, W. R., and Khare, B. N. "Titan: A Laboratory for Prebiological Organic Chemistry," *Accounts of Chemical Research,* **25,** 286 (1992).

507. Sagan, C., and Walker, R. G. "The Infrared Detectability of Dyson Civilizations," *Astrophysical Journal,* **144,** 1216 (1966).

508. Salen, Dennis. *Science Fiction Gold: Film Classics of the '50's.* New York: McGraw Hill (1979).

509. Santos, F. "Giant Planets to Brown Dwarfs: What Is in Between?," *Science,* **281,** 359 (1998).

510. Sartoretti, P., and Schneider, J. "On the Detection of Satellites of Extrasolar Planets with the Method of Transits," *Astronomy & Astrophysics,* **134,** 553 (1998).

511. Saumon, D., Marley, M., Guillot, T., and Freedman, R. "The Remarkable Spectrum of the Brown Dwarf Gliese 229B," *Bulletin of the American Astronomical Society,* **28,** 1114 (1996).

512. Scheffer, L. K. "Machine Intelligence, the Cost of Interstellar Travel and Fermi's Paradox," *Quarterly Journal of the Royal Astronomical Society,* **35** (2), 157 (1994).

513. Schild, R. E. "Microlensing Variability of the Gravitationally Lensed Quasar Q0957+561 A, B," *Astrophysical Journal,* **464,** 125 (1996).

514. Schnier, P. D., Klassen, J. S., Strittmatter, E. F., and Williams, E. R. "Activation Energies for Dissociation of Double Strand Oligonucleotide Anions: Evidence for Watson-Crick Base Pairing in Vacuo," *Journal of the American Chemical Society,* **120** (37), 9605 (1998).

515. Schopf, J. W. "The Evolution of the Earliest Cells," *Scientific American,* **239,** 110 (1978).

516. Schopf, J. W., ed. *Earth's Earliest Biosphere: Its Origin and Evolution.* Princeton, N.J.: Princeton University Press (1983).

517. Schopf, J. W. "Microfossils of the Early Archaen Apex Chert: New Evidence of the Antiquity of Life," *Science,* **260,** 640 (1993).

518. Schrödinger, Erwin. *What is Life?* New York: Anchor Books (1956).

519. Schröter, J. H. *Areographische Beiträge zur genauern Kenntnis und Beurtheilung des Planeten Mars,* H. G. van de Sande Bakhuyzen, ed., Leiden (1881).

520. Schultz, A. B., Hart, H. M., Hershey, J. L., Hamilton, F. C., Kochte, M., Bruhweiler, F. C., Benedict, G. F., Caldwell, J., Cunningham, C., Nailong, W., Franz, O., Keyes, C., and Brandt, J. "A Possible Companion to Proxima Centauri," *Astronomical Journal,* **11,** 345 (1998).

521. Schwartz, A. W. "Speculation on the RNA Precursor Problem," *Journal of Theoretical Biology,* **187,** 523 (1997).

522. Schwartz, J. "Homeobox Genes, Fossils, and the Origin of Species," *The Anatomical Record,* **257,** 15 (1999).

523. Schwartz, R. N., and Townes, C. H. "Interstellar and Interplanetary Communication by Optical Maser," *Nature,* **190,** 205 (1961).

524. Seager, S., and Sasselaw, D. "On Spectrum Formation of Giant Extra-solar Planets under Strong Irradiation by Their Parent Star," *Astrophysical Journal Letters,* **502,** L157 (1998).

525. Seckbach, J. "Search for Life in the Universe with Terrestrial Microbes Which Thrive Under Extreme Conditions." In Cristiano Batalli Cosmovici, Stuart Bowyer, and Dan Wertheimer, eds., *Astronomical and Biochemical Origins and the Search for Life in the Universe,* p. 511. Milan: Editrice Compositori (1997).

526. Serviss, Garrett P. *Other Worlds, Their Nature, Possibilities and Habitability in the Light of the Latest Discoveries.* New York (1901).

527. Serviss, Garrett P. *A Columbus in Space.* Westport, Conn.: Hyperion Press (1974) (first published 1909).

528. Serviss, Garrett P. *Edison's Conquest of Mars.* Reprinted Carcosa House (1947).

529. Shabanova, T. "Evidence for a Planet Around the Pulsar PSR B0329+54," *Astrophysical Journal,* **453,** 779 (1995).

530. Shapiro, Robert. *Origins: A Skeptic's Guide to the Creation of Life on Earth.* New York: Bantam (1987).

531. Shapiro, Robert. *Planetary Dreams.* New York: John Wiley & Sons (1999).

532. Shapiro, R. "Prebiotic Cytosine Synthesis: A Critical Analysis and Implications for the Origin of Life," *Proceedings of the National Academy of Science,* **96** (8), 4396 (1999).

533. Shapley, Harlow. *Of Stars and Men.* Boston: Beacon Press (1958).

534. Shapley, H. "Crusted Stars and Self-Heating Planets," *Matemática y Física Teorética, Serie A* (Tucumán National University, Argentina), **14** (1962).

535. Sharpless, B. P. "Secular Accelerations in the Longitudes of the Satellites of Mars," *Astronomical Journal,* **51,** 185 (1945).

536. Sheehan, William. *The Planet Mars: A History of Observation and Discovery.* Tucson: University of Arizona Press (1996).

537. Shibata, T., Yamamoto, J., Matsumoto, N., Yonekubo, S., Osanai, S., and Soai, K. "Amplification of a Slight Enantiomeric Imbalance in Molecules Based on Asymmetric Autocatalysis: The First Correlation Between High Enantiomeric Imbalance in a Chiral Molecules Based and Circularly Polarized Light, *Journal of the American Chemical Society,* **120** (46), 12157 (1998).

538. Shimoyama, A., and Harada, K. "Amino Acids from the Yamato-791198 Carbonaceous Chondrite from Antarctica," *Chemistry Letters,* 1183 (1985).

539. Shklovskii, I. S. "Is Communication Possible with Intelligent Beings on Other Planets?," *Priroda,* **7,** 21 (1960). Translated and reprinted in A. G. W. Cameron, ed., *Interstellar Communication,* q.v.

540. Shklovskii, I. S., and Sagan, Carl. *Intelligent Life in the Universe.* New York: Dell (1966).

541. Sholomitskii, G. B. "Variability of the Radio Source CTA-102," *Information Bulletin on Variable Stars,* Commission 27 of the IAU, no. 83 (February 27, 1965).

542. Short, Robert. *The Gospel from Outer Space.* San Francisco: Harper & Row (1982).

543. Shostak, Seth. *Sharing the Universe: Perspectives in Extraterrestrial Life.* Berkeley, Calif.: Berkeley Hills Books (1998).

544. Siess, L., and Livio, M. "The Swallowing of Planets by Giant Stars." In M. Livio, ed.,

Unsolved Problems in Stellar Evolution. Cambridge, England: Cambridge University Press (1998).

545. Sigurdsson, S. "Planets in Globular Clusters?" *Astrophysical Journal Letters,* **399,** L95 (1992).

546. Simpson, G. G. "The Non-Prevalence of Humanoids," *Science,* **143,** 769 (1964).

547. Sinnott, R. W. "Mars Mania of Oppositions Past," *Sky & Telescope,* **76,** 244 (1988).

548. Sinton, W. M. "Spectroscopic Evidence for Vegetation on Mars," *Astrophysical Journal,* **126,** 231 (1957).

549. Sinton, W. M. "Further Evidence of Vegetation on Mars," *Science,* **130,** 1234 (1959).

550. Skirda, R. J., and Persinger, M. A. "Positive Associations Between Dichotic Listening Errors, Complex Partial Epileptic-like Signs and Paranormal Beliefs," *Journal of Nervous and Mental Disease,* **181,** 663 (1993).

551. Slater, A. E. "The Evolution of Life in the Universe," *Journal of the British Interplanetary Society,* **12,** 114 (1953).

552. Sleep, N. H., and Zahnle, K. "Refugia from Asteroid Impacts on Early Mars and the Early Earth," *Journal of Geophysical Research,* **103,** no. E12, 28529 (1998).

553. Smith, J. M., and Szathmáry, E. "On the Likelihood of Habitable Worlds," *Nature,* **384,** 107 (1996).

554. Soffen, G. A. "Scientific Results of the Viking Missions," *Science,* **194,** 1274 (1976).

555. Soffen, G. A. "The Viking Project," *Journal of Geophysical Research,* **82,** 3959 (1977).

556. Soker, N. "What Planetary Nebulae Can Tell Us About Planetary Systems," *Astrophysical Journal Letters,* **460,** L53 (1996).

557. Spanos, N. P., et al. "Close Encounters: An Examination of UFO Experiences," *Journal of Abnormal Psychology,* **102,** 624 (1993).

558. Spencer Jones, Harold. *Life on Other Worlds,* 3rd ed. London: Hodder & Stoughton (1956).

559. Spielberg, Steven. *Close Encounters of the Third Kind.* New York (1977).

560. Sprague de Camp, L. *The Ancient Engineers.* New York: Ballantine (1973).

561. Stapledon, Olaf. *Last and First Men.* New York: Dover (1931).

562. Stapledon, Olaf. "The Flames." Reprinted in *Worlds of Wonder.* Los Angeles: Fantasy Publishing (1949).

563. Stapledon, Olaf. *Star Maker.* Los Angeles: Jeremy P. Tarcher (1987).

564. Stephan, T., Rost, D., Jessberger, E. K., and Greshake, A. "Polycyclic Aromatic Hydrocarbons in ALH84001 Analyzed with Time-of-Flight Secondary Ion Mass Spectrometry," paper presented at 29th Annual Lunar and Planetary Science Conference, Houston, Tex., March 16–20, 1998.

565. Stevens, T. O. "Subsurface Lithoautotrophic Microbial Ecosystems (SLiMEs) in Igneous Rocks: Prospects for Detection," *Proceedings of SPIE,* **311,** 358 (1997).

566. Stone, R. "Russian Outpost Readies for Otherworldly Quest," *Science,* **279,** 650 (1998).

567. Stonely, Jack, and Lawton, Anthony T. *CETI: Communication with Extraterrestrial Intelligence.* New York: Warner Books (1976).

568. Stormer, C. "Short Wave Echoes and the Aurora Borealis," *Nature,* **122,** 681 (1928).

569. Story, Ronald. *The Space Gods Revealed: A Close Look at the Theories of Erich von Däniken.* New York: Harper & Row (1976).

570. Strand, K. "61 Cygni as a Triple System," *Publications of the Astronomical Society of the Pacific,* **55,** 29 (1943).

571. Strughold, Hubertus. *The Red and Green Planet: A Physiological Study of the Possibility of Life on Mars.* Albuquerque, N.M.: New Mexico Press (1953).

572. Struve, Otto. *Stellar Evolution.* Princeton, N.J.: Princeton University Press (1950).

573. Struve, O. "Astronomers in Turmoil," *Physics Today,* **13,** 22 (1960).

574. Sullivan, Walter. *We Are Not Alone,* 2nd ed. New York: McGraw-Hill (1993) (first published 1966).

575. Swift, David. *SETI Pioneers: Scientists Talk About Their Search for Exterrestrial Intelligence.* Tucson: University of Arizona Press (1990).

576. Szostak, J. W., and Wilson, C. "*In vitro* Evolution of a Self-Alkylating Ribozyme," *Nature,* **374,** 777 (1995).

577. Tarter, J. "The Search for Extraterrestrial Intelligence," paper presented to 193rd American Astronomical Society Meeting, Austin, Tex., January 6–9, 1998.

578. Tel Haar, D., and Cameron, A. G. W. "Historical Review of Theories of the Origin of the Solar System." In Robert Jastrow and A. G. W. Cameron, eds., *Origin of the Solar System, Proceedings of a Conference Held at the Goddard Institute for Space Studies, New York, January 23–24, 1962.* New York: Academic Press (1963).

579. Temple, Robert K. G. *The Sirius Mystery.* New York: St. Martin's Press (1976).

580. Teng Mu, quoted by P. Morrison in *Bulletin of the Philosophical Society of Washington,* **18,** 81 (1962).

581. Tereby, S., van Buren, D., Hancock, T., Padgett, D., and Brundage, M. "A Candidate Protoplanet in the Taurus Star Forming Region," *Astrophysical Journal Letters,* **507,** L71 (1998).

582. Thomas, D. "The Roswell Incident and Project Mogul," *Skeptical Inquirer,* 15 (July–August 1995).

583. Thomas, P. J., Chyba, C. F., and McKay, C. P., eds. *Comets and the Origin and Evolution of Life.* New York: Springer-Verlag (1997).

584. Thomas, Shirley. *Men of Space: Profiles of Scientists Who Search for Life in Space.* Philadelphia: Chilton (1960).

585. Thomson, W. "Presidential Address to the British Association for the Advancement of Science," *Nature,* **4,** 262 (1871).

586. Thorsett, S., Arzoumanian, Z., Camilo, F., and Lyne, A. "The Triple Pulsar System PSR B1620-26 in M4," *Astrophysical Journal* (submitted 1999).

587. Tipler, F. J. "Extraterrestrial Beings Do Not Exist," *Quarterly Journal of the Royal Astronomical Society,* **21,** 267 (1981).

588. Tipler, F. J. "Additional Remarks on Extraterrestrial Intelligence," *Quarterly Journal of the Royal Astronomical Society,* **22,** 288 (1981).

589. Tovmasyan, G. M., ed. *Extraterrestrial Civilizations: Proceedings of the First All-Union Conference on Extraterrestrial Civilizations and Interstellar Communication, May 20–23, 1964,* trans. from the Russian. Jerusalem: Israel Program for Scientific Translations (1967).

590. Trefil, James. *Are We Unique?* London: Wiley (1997).

591. Trilling, D., Benz, W., Guillot, T., Lunine, J., Hubbard, W., and Burrows, A. "Orbital Evolution and Migration of Giant Planets: Modeling Extrasolar Planets," *Astrophysical Journal,* **500,** 428 (1997).

592. Trilling, D., and Brown, R. "A Circumstellar Dust Disk Around a Star with a Known Planetary Companion," *Nature,* **395,** 775 (1998).

593. Troland, L. "The Chemical Origin and Regulation of Life," *The Monist,* **24,** 92 (1914).

594. Tyndall, J. *Fragments of Science,* p. 459. London: Longmans, Green (1876).

595. Udalski, A., et al. "The Optical Gravitational Lensing Experiment. Discussion of the First Candidate Microlensing Event in the Direction of the Galactic Bulge," *Acta Astronomica,* **43,** 289 (1993).

596. Unwins, P. J. R., Webb, R. I., and Taylor, A. P. "Novel Nano-organisms from Australian Sandstones," *American Mineralogist,* **83,** 1541 (1999).

597. Urey, H. C. *The Planets, Their Origin and Development.* New Haven, Conn.: Yale University Press (1952).

598. Urey, H. C. "Biological Material in Meteorites: A Review," *Science,* **151,** 157 (1966).

599. Vallée, Jacques. *Anatomy of a Phenomenon: Unidentified Objects in Space—A Scientific Appraisal.* Chicago: Henry Regnery (1965).

600. van der Kamp, P. "Astrometric Study of Barnard's Star from Plates Taken with the 24-inch Sproul Refractor," *Astronomical Journal,* **68,** 515 (1963).

601. van der Kamp, P. "The Nearby Stars," *Annual Reviews of Astronomy and Astrophysics,* **9,** 103 (1971).

602. van der Kamp, P. "Unseen Astrometric Companions of Stars," *Annual Reviews of Astronomy and Astrophysics,* **13,** 295 (1975).

603. van der Pol, B. "Short Wave Echoes and the Aurora Borealis," *Nature,* **122,** 878 (1928).

604. Vidal-Madjar, A., Lecavelier des Etangs, A. and Ferlet, R. "Beta Pictoris, A Young Planetary System: A Review," *Planetary and Space Science,* **46,** 629 (1998).

605. Viewing, D. "Directly Interacting Extraterrestrial Technological Communities," *Journal of the British Interplanetary Society,* **28,** 735 (1975).

606. von Hoerner, S. "The Search for Signals from Other Civilizations," *Science,* **134,** 1839 (1961).

607. von Hoerner, S. "The General Limits of Space Travel," *Science*, **137**, 18 (1962).

608. von Tiesenhausen, G. and Darbro, W. A. "Self-Replicating Systems," NASA Technical Memorandum 78304. Washington, D.C.: National Aeronautics and Space Administration (1980).

609. Vonnegut, Kurt, Jr. *The Sirens of Titan*. New York: Dell (1959).

610. Wald, G. "Life and Light," *Scientific American* (October 1959).

611. Wald, G. *Proceedings of the National Academy of Sciences*, **52**, 595 (1964).

612. Wallace, Alfred Russell. *Is Mars Habitable?* London: Macmillan (1907).

613. Wallis, M. K., and Wickramasinghe, C. R. "Role of Major Terrestrial Cratering Events in Dispersing Life in the Solar System," *Earth and Planetary Science Letters*, **130**, 69 (1995).

614. Waters, L., Waelkens, C., van Winckel, H., Molster, F., Tielens, A., van Loon, J., Morris, P., Cami, J., Bouwman, J., de Koter, A., de Jong, T., and de Graauw, Th. "An Oxygen-Rich Dust Disk Surrounding an Evolved Star in the Red Rectangle," *Nature*, **391**, 868 (1998).

615. Watson, A. "Seeking a Snapshot of an Alien World," *Science*, **281**, 1940 (1998).

616. Watson, James D. "Prologue: Early Speculations and Facts about RNA Templates," pp. xv–xxiii, *The RNA World*, R. F. Gesteland and J. F. Atkins, eds., q.v.

617. Weidenshelling, S., and Marzari, P. "Gravitational Scattering as a Possible Origin for Giant Planets at Small Stellar Distances," *Nature*, **384**, 619 (1996).

618. Weinbaum, Stanley G. *A Martian Odyssey*, 1st ed. New York: Fantasy Press (1949). S. G. Weinbaum and S. Moskowitz, eds., *A Martian Odyssey and Other Science Fiction Tales*. Westport, Conn.: Hyperion Press (1974).

619. Weissman, P. R. "The Oort Cloud," *Scientific American*, 62 (September 1998).

620. Wells, H. G. "Another Basis for Life," *Saturday Review*, p. 676 (December 22, 1894).

621. Wells, H. G. *The War of the Worlds*. New York: Berkeley Publishing Company (1964).

622. Wells, H. G., Huxley, Julian, and Wells, G. P. "Is There Extra-terrestrial Life?" In H. G. Wells, Julian Huxley, and G. P. Wells, eds., *The Science of Life*, p. 11. New York: Doubleday (1931).

623. Whewell, Willam. *The Plurality of Worlds*. Boston: Gould and Lincoln (1854).

624. Whipple, F. L., and Menzel, D. H. "The Case for H_2O Clouds on Venus." *Publications of the Astronomical Society of the Pacific*, **67**, 161 (1955).

625. Whitmire, D., Matese, J., Criswell, L., and Mikkola, S. "Habitable Planet Formation in Binary Star Systems," *Icarus*, **132**, 196 (1998).

626. Wilkins, John. *Discovery of a New World in the Moone*. Delmar, New York: Scholar's Facimiles & Reprints (1973) (first published 1638).

627. Williams, D. M., Kasting, T. F., and Wade, B. H. "Habitable Moons Around Extrasolar Giant Planets," *Nature*, **385**, 234 (1997).

628. Woese, C. R., Kandler, O., and Wheelis, M. L. "Towards a Natural System of Organisms: Proposal for the Domains Archaea, Bacteria, and Eucarya," *Proceedings of the National Academy of Science*, **87**, 4576 (1990).

629. Wolszczan, A. "Towards Planets Around Neutron Stars," *Astrophysics & Space Science*, **212**, 67 (1994).

630. Wolszczan, A. "Confirmation of Earth-Mass Planets Orbiting the Millisecond Pulsar PSR1257+12," *Science*, **264**, 538 (1994).

631. Wolszczan, A., and Frail, D. "A Planetary System Around the Millisecond Pulsar PSR1257+12," *Nature*, **255**, 145 (1992).

632. Wright, Thomas. *An Original Theory or New Hypothesis of the Universe*. Reprinted with an introduction by Michael A. Hoskin. New York: American Elsevier (1971) (first published 1750).

633. Zuckerman, Ben and Hart, Michael H., eds. *Extraterrestrials: Where Are They?* 2nd ed. Cambridge, England: Cambridge University Press (1995).

634. Zubrin, R. "Detection of Extraterrestrial Civilizations via the Spectral Signatures of Advanced Interstellar Spacecraft," *Astronomical Society of the Pacific*, **74**, paper presented at Progress in the Search for Extraterrestrial Life, 1993 Bioastronomy Symposium, Santa Cruz, Calif., Seth Shostak, ed., August 16–20, 1993.

Web Sites on Topics in the Encyclopedia

Web site addresses may change. Links to all of the sites listed below (all Web site addresses listed begin with http://), and others relevant to the search for life in space, are maintained and updated by the author at his Web site (www.angelfire.com/on2/daviddarling).

adaptive optics	www.eso.org/projects/aot/introduction.html
Adrastea	sse.jpl.nasa.gov/features/planets/jupiter/adrastea.html
Advanced Fiber-Optic Échelle Spectrometer (AFOE)	cfa-www.harvard.edu/afoe
aerogel	science.msfc.nasa.gov/aerogel
ALH 84001	cass.jsc.nasa.gov/lpi/meteorites/alhnpap.html
Allan Hills	cass.jsc.nasa.gov/pub/publications/amlamp/amlamp1.html
Allegheny Observatory	isi9.mtwilson.edu/~david/AO/ao.html#research
Alpha Centauri	monet.physik.unibas.ch/~schatzer/Alpha-Centauri.html
Amalthea	sse.jpl.nasa.gov/features/planets/jupiter/amalthea.html
Ananke	sse.jpl.nasa.gov/features/planets/jupiter/ananke.html
Andromeda Strain, The	www.scifi.com/sfw/issue80/classic.html
Anglo-Australian Observatory	www.aao.gov.au
Anglo-Australian Planet Search	www.aao.gov.au/local/www/cgt/planet/aat.html
Antarctic Search for Meteorites (ANSMET)	www.cwru.edu/affil/ansmet
Antarctic ice, microbes in	science.nasa.gov/newhome/headlines/ast12mar98_1.htm
archaea	www3.ncbi.nlm.nih.gov/htbin-post/Taxonomy/wgetorg?name=Archaea
Arecibo Observatory	www.naic.edu
Argus, Project	www.setileague.org/general/whargus.htm
Argus radio telescope	bigear.org/argus_menu.htm
Ariel	seds.lpl.arizona.edu/nineplanets/nineplanets/ariel.html
artifacts, alien	easyweb.easynet.co.uk/~portwin/Pages/ASTRA/seti.html
artificial life	alife.santafe.edu/alife/alife-def.html
asteroid and comet collisions	www.reston.com/astro/impacts.html
astrobiology (Astro. Web)	www2.astrobiology.com/astro
astrobiology (NASA Ames)	astrobiology.arc.nasa.gov
Astrobiology Institute	nai.arc.nasa.gov

Chronology

The Search for Life in Space	Science Fiction	World/Scientific Events
		476 Fall of Western Roman Empire.
		529 Plato's Academy closed down.
		1295 Marco Polo returns to Venice after exploring China for 17 years.
1450 (c.) Nicholas of Cusa revives the idea that planets may be inhabited.		
		1453 End of Byzantine Empire and Hundreds Years' War. End of Middles Ages.
		1454 Gutenberg Bible printed.
		1469 Renaissance at its height in Florence under Medici family.
		1478 Spanish Inquisition established.
		1492 Columbus in New World. Dawn of age of exploration.
	1516 *Utopia*, More	
		1522 Magellan's expedition completes circumnavigation of the globe.
	1532 *Orlando Furioso*, Ariosto	
1543 Copernicus espouses heliocentric theory in *On the Revolution of Heavenly Bodies*.		
		1589 Galileo experiments with falling objects.
1600 Bruno burnt at stake for his views.		
1609 Galileo views Moon through his telescope.		**1609** Kepler's laws of planetary motion.
1610 Galileo observes Jupiter and its four largest moons.		
		1620 Pilgrims land at Plymouth Rock.
1633 Inquisition forces Galileo to recant.		
	1634 *Somnium*, Kepler	
	1638 *The Man in the Moone*, Godwin	
1640 John Wilkins publishes *A Discussion Concerning a New World*.		
		1642 Newton born.
		1644 Descartes publishes his *Principles of Philosophy*.
1647 Hevelius publishes his *Selenographica*.	**1647** *Voyages to the Sun and the Moon*, Cyrano de Bergerac	
		1650 Archbishop Usher calculates biblical creation date as 4004 B.C.
		1651 Ricciolo begins modern naming of Moon's features.
1655 Titan discovered by Huygens.		

The Search for Life in Space

1659 Huygens observes Syrtis Major, first permanent feature on another world (Mars).
1661 Cassini sees Martian icecap.
1665 Cassini determines rotation period of Mars and Jupiter.

1668 Theory of spontaneous generation refuted by Redi.
1676 Cassini establishes fairly accurate distances of planets.

1686 De Fontenelle publishes *A Plurality of Worlds*.

1745 De Buffon suggests Earth formed by collision of comet with Sun.

1756 Swedenborg publishes *Heavenly Arcana*.

1767 Spallanzani's experiments refute idea of spontaneous generation.

1796 Laplace: nebular hypothesis of formation of solar system.

1802 Gauss: idea of signaling to Martians in Siberian tundra.

Science Fiction

1726 *Gulliver's Travels*, Swift

1752 *Micromégas*, Voltaire

World/Scientific Events

1660 Royal Society founded.

1665 Hooke describes cells.

1666 Hooke sees Jupiter's red spot.

1683 Bacteria discovered by Leeuwenhoek.

1687 Newton publishes *Principia*, establishing law of gravity.
1692 Salem witch trials.
1718 Halley discovers that stars move through space.

1727 Newton dies.

1755 Gauss suggests Sun is one of many stars in lens-shaped galaxy.
1765 Watt develops an improved steam engine.
Industrial Revolution gathers pace.

1776 American Declaration of Independence.
1781 Herschel discovers Uranus.
1783 Montgolfier brothers begin building flying balloons.
1785 First balloon crossing of English Channel.
1794 Chladni suggests meteorites fall from sky.
1796 Presidency of George Washington ends.
1801 Discovery of first asteroid, Ceres.

The Search for Life in Space	Science Fiction	World/Scientific Events
		1804 Lewis and Clark begin their exploration of American West.
	1818 *Frankenstein*, Shelley	
1819 Von Littrow: Martian signals using fires in Sahara.		
		1825 First passenger train (Britain).
	1827 *A Voyage to the Moon*, Joseph Atterley	**1828** United States begins construction of its first commercial railroad.
1830 Beer and Mädler produce first maps of Mars.		**1830** World population 1 billion.
		1831 First practical electric motor.
		1833 Invention of the telegraph.
1835 *New York Sun* runs hoax story about life on Moon.		
		1838 First accurate measurement of star distances.
		1846 Discovery of Neptune.
		1849 California gold rush.
1853 Whewell publishes *The Plurality of Worlds*.		
		1858 First transatlantic telegraph cable.
		1859 Darwin publishes *Origin of Species*.
1860 Liais suggests dark areas on Mars are vegetation.		**1860** Internal combustion engine invented.
1862 Flammarion publishes *The Plurality of Inhabited Worlds*.		
		1863 World's first subway opened in London.
	1865 *From the Earth to the Moon*, Verne	
1869 Secchi first uses term *canali*.		**1866** Transatlantic cable laid.
		1869 Suez Canal opened.
		1871 Human evolution discussed by Darwin in *The Descent of Man*.
	1872 *Around the World in Eighty Days*, Verne	
		1873 World's first streetcars in San Francisco.
		1876 Telephone first used to send speech.
1877 Schiaparelli reports seeing *canali* on Mars.		**1877** Hall discovers Phobos and Deimos.
		1879 Edison invents electric light.
	1880 *Across the Zodiac*, Greg	**1880** Population of China 400 million.

The Search for Life in Space

1886 Perrotin and Wilson see canals
on Mars.

1892 Flammarion talks about a race of
canal builders in *The Planet Mars*.
1894 Lowell Observatory founded.
Lowell's first book: *Mars*.

1900 Prize offered in France for first
communication with alien race.
Tesla suggests communicating
between worlds by radio waves.

1903 Comas Solá: first suggestion
of atmosphere on Titan.

1906 Lowell publishes
Mars and Its Canals.
1908 Arrhenius: panspermia theory.
Meteorite from Mars falls at
Nakhla, Egypt.
1909 Reynolds suggests life
could be based on silicon.

1916 Lowell dies.

1918 Arrhenius: ideas about life on
Venus.

1923 Menzel concludes Jupiter and
Saturn are cold.
1924 First search for radio signals from
Mars.

Science Fiction

1892 "On the Moon,"
Tsiolkovsky

1895 *The Time Machine*, Wells
1897 *The War of the Worlds*, Wells
On Two Planets, Lasswitz
Edison's Conquest of Mars,
Serviss
1900 *A Honeymoon in Space*,
Griffith

1901 *The First Men in the Moon*,
Wells
1903 Film: *A Trip to the Moon*

1912 *The Lost World*, Conan Doyle

1917 *A Princess of Mars*, Burroughs

1920 *A Voyage to Arcturus*, Lindsay

World/Scientific Events
1885 First working automobile.

1889 Eiffel Tower completed.
World's first skyscraper in New York.
1890 U.S. troops kill over 200
Sioux at Battle of Wounded Knee.
1894 Sino-Japanese War begins.

1895 X rays discovered.
1897 British Empire at its peak.
1898 Marie and Pierre Curie
discover radium.

1901 First transatlantic radio
message.
1903 First powered flight by Wright
brothers.
Ideas on rocketry, colonization of
solar system by Tsiolkovskii.
1905 Einstein's special theory of
relativity.
1908 Comet explodes above central
Siberia (Tunguska).

1911 Amundsen reaches South Pole.

1914 Completion of Panama Canal.
World War I begins.
1916 Einstein's general theory of
relativity.
1917 Population of United States
100 million.
1918 Worldwide flu epidemic
kills 20 million.
1921 Airmail begins in the United
States.
1922 Joyce publishes *Ulysses*.

1924 Lenin dies.

The Search for Life in Space

1929 Haldane speculates about chemical origin of life.

1932 Carbon dioxide found in atmosphere of Venus.

1937 van der Kamp begins search for extrasolar planets.

1943 Kuiper: atmosphere on Titan.
Strand: planet around 61 Cygni.
1944 Phobos's orbit found to be decaying.
Weizsäcker revives nebular hypothesis.

1947 Arnold sees first "flying saucers."
Roswell incident.
Kuiper: analysis of Martian atmosphere.
1948 U.S. Air Force launches Project Sign.
1949 Project Grudge begins.

1950 Prebiotic experiment begun by Calvin.
Murray meteorite falls in Kentucky.

1952 Start of Project Blue Book.
Washington UFO scare.
1953 Miller and Urey: simulation of primitive Earth atmosphere.

Science Fiction

1926 Film: *Metropolis*
Journal: *Amazing Stories*
1929 Film: *Girl in the Moon*

1930 *Last and First Men*, Stapledon
1932 *When Worlds Collide*, Wylie

1936 Film: *Things to Come*
Film: *Flash Gordon*
1937 *Star Maker*, Stapledon
1938 Radio: *The War of the Worlds*
Out of the Silent Planet, Lewis
1939 Film: *Buck Rogers*
1942 "Runaround," Asimov
1943 *Perelandra*, Lewis

1946 *The Skylark of Space*, Smith
Slan, Van Vogt

1949 *1984*, Orwell
A Martian Odyssey, Weinbaum

1950 *I, Robot*, Asimov
Film: *Destination Moon*
The Martian Chronicles, Bradbury

1951 Film: *The Day the Earth Stood Still*
Film: *When Worlds Collide*
Film: *The Thing*

1953 *Childhood's End*, Clarke
Fahrenheit 451, Bradbury
Film: *The War of the Worlds*
Film: *Invaders from Mars*

World/Scientific Events

1926 Goddard flies his first liquid-fueled rocket.

1930 Discovery of Pluto.
1932 Radio waves detected from Galaxy by Jansky.

1937 First radio telescope (Reber).

1939 World War II begins.

1944 V-2s used to bomb London.

1945 End of World War II.
Arthur C. Clarke proposes idea of communications satellites.
1946 Churchill speaks of "Iron Curtain" descending.
1947 Truman Doctrine announced.
Yeager breaks sound barrier in Bell X-1 rocket-plane.

1948 Hale Telescope operational.

1949 Soviet Union sets off atomic bomb.
NATO formed.
Rocket testing ground established at Cape Canaveral.
1950 Truman orders development of hydrogen bomb.
Start of Korean War.
McCarthy alleges 57 "card-carrying Communists."
1951 21-cm radiation discovered.
1952 Everest climbed for first time.

1953 Moscow announces explosion of H-bomb.
Korean War ends.

The Search for Life in Space

1954 Haldane suggests ammonia-based life.

1955 Menzel and Whipple: theory of Venus as an ocean world.
1956 High temperature of Venus established.

USSR launches *Sputnik 1*.
  issue of contamination.

1959 Shklovskii proposes that Phobos is artificial.
Cocconni and Morrison's SETI ideas in letter to *Nature*.
"Dyson spheres" proposed.
1960 Project Ozma begins.
Bracewell probes suggested.
1961 "Drake Equation" devised.

1962 *Mariner 2* flies past Venus.

1963 First interstellar molecule found.
NASA sets up team to evaluate ideas for detection of life on Mars.
1964 Kardashev proposes types of advanced interstellar civilizations.
1965 *Mariner 4* flyby of Mars.

1966 Sagan and Shklovskii publish *Intelligent Life in the Universe*.
1967 *Venera 4* enters Venus's atmosphere.

1968 Water molecules and ammonia found in space.

Science Fiction

1954 *Lucky Starr and the Oceans of Venus*, Asimov
Film: *Them!*

1955 Film: *Conquest of Space*
Film: *This Island Earth*
1956 *The City and the Stars*, Clarke
Film: *Forbidden Planet*

1957 Lederberg raises

The Seedling Stars, Blish
Foundation, Asimov
1958 *A Case of Conscience*, Blish
Film: *It! The Terror from Beyond Space*
1959 *The Sirens of Titan*, Vonnegut

1960 TV: *The Twilight Zone*
A Canticle for Leibowitz, Miller
1961 *Stranger in a Strange Land*, Heinlein
1962 *A for Andromeda*, Hoyle and Elliot
The Listeners, Gunn
1963 *Planet of the Apes*, Boulle
TV: *The Outer Limits*
TV: *My Favorite Martian*

1964 Film: *Dr. Strangelove*
Way Station, Simak
1965 *Dune*, Herbert
TV: *Lost in Space*

1966 TV: *Star Trek* (first season)

1967 TV: *The Invaders*
Film: *Five Million Years to Earth*

1968 Film: *2001: A Space Odyssey*

World/Scientific Events

1954 McCarthy discredited.
First atomic submarine, *Nautilus*, launched.

1955 Warsaw Pact signed.

1956 First aerial H-bomb tested over Bikini Atoll.
Anticommunist rebellion crushed in Hungary.
1957 *The Black Cloud*, Hoyle **1957**

Jodrell Bank becomes operational.
1958 First U.S. satellite, *Explorer 1*.

1959 *Lunik 1* flies past the Moon.
St. Lawrence Seaway opens.

1960 American U-2 spy plane shot down over Russia.
1961 Gagarin is first man in space.
U.S. suborbital flight by Shepard.
1962 Glenn in orbit.
Cuban missile crisis.
1963 Kennedy assassinated.
Discovery of quasars (Schmidt and Greenstein).

1964 Radar measurements of Mercury.
1965 First communications satellite.
Cosmic background radiation discovered.
Malcolm X killed.
1966 Cultural Revolution begins in China.
1967 Grissom, White, Chaffee killed during *Apollo* test.
Pulsars discovered.
1968 *Apollo 8* travels around Moon.
Martin Luther King assassinated.

The Search for Life in Space
1969 Condon Report on UFOs.
Mariner 6 and *7* flybys of Mars.
Formaldehyde found in space.

1970 Amino acids found in Murchison
  meteorite.
1971 *Mariner 9* in Martian orbit.
launched.
Mars 3 lands but fails.
First international SETI
  conference, Armenia.
Proposal for Project Cyclops.
1972 Attempt to detect radio signals
  from five nearby stars.
1973 Drake and Sagan suggest "water
  hole" frequency for SETI searches.

1974 Hoyle and Wickramasinghe
  revive panspermia hypothesis.
Radio message sent to Hercules
  star cluster from Arecibo.
Theory about organic molecules
  on Titan (Sagan).
1975 *Viking* probes launched.

1976 *Viking 1* and *2* on Mars.
1977 Wow! signal detected.

1978 Microbes discovered in Dry
  Valleys of Antarctica.

1981 Nyquist models how Martian
  meteorites traveled to Earth.
1982 First suggestion that there could
  be life on Europa.
1983 Dust rings found around several
  stars, possible protoplanetary systems.

1985 Experiments show bacteria could
  survive in space.

1987 Polymer found in dust from
  Halley's Comet.
1988 Carlotto suggests Martian
  "face" is artificial.

Science Fiction
1969 *Slaughterhouse-Five*, Vonnegut

1970 *Ringworld*, Niven
Solaris, Lem
1971 Film: *The Andromeda Strain*

1972 *The Gods Themselves*, Asimov
Film: *Silent Running*
1973 *Rendezvous with Rama*, Clarke
Gravity's Rainbow, Pynchon

1974 *The Dispossessed:
  An Ambiguous Utopia*,
  Le Guin

1975 *Imperial Earth*,
  Clarke

1977 Film: *Close Encounters of the
  Third Kind*
Film: *Star Wars*

1979 Film: *Alien*
1980 *Timescape*, Gregory
  Benford

1982 Film: *E.T. The
  Extra-Terrestrial*

1984 *Startide Rising*,
  David Brin

1986 *Contact*, Sagan
1987 *Communion*, Strieber
TV: *Star Trek: The Next Generation*

World/Scientific Events
1969 *Venera 5* and *6* land on Venus.
Apollo 11 lands on the Moon.
American involvement in
  Vietnam reaches its peak.
1970 Near disaster of *Apollo 13*.

1971 *Salyut 1* space station
First black hole detected.

1972 *Pioneers 10* and *11* launched.

1973 *Pioneers 10* and *11* reach
  Jupiter.
United States withdraws from
  Vietnam.
1974 Richard Nixon resigns.
Mariner 10 reaches Mercury.

1975 *Apollo-Soyuz* rendezvous.

1977 Rings of Uranus discovered.

1978 Pluto's moon Charon
  discovered.
1979 *Voyager* flybys of Jupiter.
1980 Very Large Array becomes
  operational.
1981 First launch of space shuttle.
Voyager flybys of Saturn.

1983 Theoretical predictions of a
  nuclear winter.

1985 *Giotto* photographs Halley's
  nucleus.
1986 *Voyager 2* flyby of Uranus.
1987 Supernova 1987A visible to
  unaided eye.
1988 Bomb explodes aboard Pan-
  Am 747

The Search for Life in Space

1989 Set of guidelines drawn up in case of discovery of extraterrestrial intelligence.

1991 First suggestion of water/life on Titan (Sagan and Reid-Thompson).
1993 SETI funding cut by NASA.

1994 Amino acid found in space.
ALH 84001 recognized to be a Martian meteorite.
Ice found on the Moon.
1995 GAO report on Roswell Incident.
Mayor and Queloz find first extrasolar planet around 51 Pegasi.
1996 Martian "fossils" claim.
Galileo probe arrives at Jupiter.
1997 *Pathfinder* probe lands on Mars.
Project Argus commences.
Red "Centaur" asteroids said to be coated with organic matter.
Cassini/Huygens probe launched.
1998 First planet observed around another star.
Lunar Prospector finds more ice on Moon.
Ocean on Callisto proposed.
1999 Extrasolar planetary system found around main sequence star.
Peptides synthesized around artificial hydrothermal vent.
Stardust probe launched.
2000 *Mars Global Surveyor* finds ancient subterranean channels on Mars.
Extrasolar planet count exceeds 30.

Science Fiction

1992 TV: *Star Trek: Deep Space Nine*
1993 Film: *Jurassic Park*
Star Trek: Voyager
1994 Film: *Star Trek: Generations*

1996 *Excession*, Banks
Film: *Independence Day*
1997 Film: *Men in Black*
Film: *Contact*

1999 Film: *Star Wars: The Phantom Menace*

2000 Film: *Mission to Mars*

World/Scientific Events

1989 *Voyager 2* flyby of Neptune.

1990 *Hubble Space Telescope* launched.
1991 Collapse of Soviet Union.

1993 Cloning of human embryo.

1994 Impact of Comet Shoemaker-Levy-9 on Jupiter.

1995 First U.S. astronaut aboard *Mir*.
Nerve gas attack in Tokyo subway.
1996 China agrees to world ban on atomic testing.
1997 Russia accepts NATO expansion.
Mother Teresa dies.
IBM "Deep Blue" computer defeats human world champion, Kasparov.
1998 India conducts nuclear tests.
John Glenn returns to space.

1999 NATO air strikes against Serbia.
First nonstop balloon trip around the world.

2000 World population exceeds six billion.

About the Author

DAVID DARLING holds a Ph.D. in astronomy from the University of Manchester (England) and is the author of some forty books for both adults and children. His articles and reviews have appeared in *Astronomy, New Scientist, The New York Times,* and *Omni.* In 1998, he was a resident scholar at the Institute for Science, Engineering and Public Policy in Portland, Oregon, and he has lectured widely in the United Kingdom and United States. His books have been translated into Italian, German, Japanese, South Korean, Slovakian, and Norwegian. A native of England, he recently emigrated with his family to the United States and now lives in Minnesota.